COLLINS
COLLECTORS' CHOICE

COLLINS COLLECTORS' CHOICE

Vladimir Nabokov

Five Novels

with an introduction by
PETER QUENNELL

COLLINS
St James's Place, London
1979

William Collins Sons and Co Ltd
London · Glasgow · Sydney · Auckland
Toronto · Johannesburg

Lolita
First published in Great Britain by Weidenfeld and Nicolson 1959
The Gift
First published in Great Britain by Weidenfeld and Nicolson 1963
Invitation to a Beheading
First published in Great Britain by Weidenfeld and Nicolson 1960
King Queen Knave
First published in Great Britain by Weidenfeld and Nicolson 1968
Glory
First published in Great Britain by Weidenfeld and Nicolson 1972

First published 1979

ISBN 0 00 243562 4

Set in Linotype Baskerville
Made and Printed in Great Britain by
T. J. Press (Padstow) Ltd Padstow Cornwall

Contents

Lolita 11

The Gift 275

Invitation to a Beheading 603

King Queen Knave 737

Glory 929

Introduction

There are some personal emotions that, in an imaginative artist's life, may be either a blessing or a scourge; and nostalgia is one of them. It takes an uncommonly gifted writer to combine a romantic regret for the past with a keen appreciation of the present day; and among twentieth-century novelists only Proust and Joyce and, during our own age, Vladimir Nabokov seem to have achieved this feat, and blended memories and observations into the same harmonious literary scheme. Just as Proust could not forget Combray, or Joyce the Dublin of his youth, so Nabokov looked back again and again to his happy Russian childhood, and particularly to Vyra, his parents' country house, and the beautiful surrounding landscape, from which he drew so many of the images that haunt his novels and his stories.

Nabokov's autobiographical excursion *Speak, Memory* was the first book of his I ever read. I reviewed it, I see, for a London daily paper on November 3rd, 1951, and chose it as that paper's 'Book of the Month'; which may or may not have increased its sales. The next I opened was *Lolita,* the extraordinary *tour de force,* still, I believe, the novelist's masterpiece, that appeared in 1955 under a rather dubious imprint, the more respectable American edition being delayed until 1958, when it aroused a violent storm of praise and blame. While I read it, I rapidly became a Nabokovian enthusiast, fascinated both by his use of language and by the vision of the world his style expresses. Every distinguished novelist creates a separate world; and, having crossed the frontier, we find that the world we know has undergone a subtle change, that new arresting features have mysteriously begun to emerge, and that we now regard our fellow men and women, and the social background against which they play their parts, from a somewhat different point of view. Such is the test, I think, we should at once apply to all imaginative writers. Can we honestly pretend that, as the result of reading their books, we have enlarged our vision of existence, and see Man and Nature through freshly appreciative eyes? Were these questions applied to Vladimir Nabokov's oeuvre, I have no doubt how I myself would answer.

Especially remarkable are the generous breadth and the immense diversity of the ground he covers in his books. An exile, who had lost his true home and given up any hope of revisiting it, except, like Proust, upon the plane of memory, he remained a life-long wanderer, never so completely at ease on either side of the Atlantic Ocean that he could forget his Russian past, yet always keenly alive to alien places and people, 'the cities and the minds of men', and to the unending beauty and variety he discovered in the natural universe. As a well-educated Russia child, he had quickly learned English; but *The Real Life of Sebastian Knight,* published a year after he reached America, was the earliest novel for which he used his second language. His association with English, he tells us, was a lengthy love-affair, though his marriage with his beloved native tongue remained a strong and fertile union.

His last Russian novel, *The Gift,* written before he left Europe, between 1935 and 1937, is included in the present volume; and there, besides drawing a serio-comic picture of pre-war emigré society – Berlin was his uncongenial refuge from 1922 to 1940; and his novels and stories, written under the pseudonym 'Sirin', made a strong, if sometimes disturbing, impression upon other exiled men of letters – he evokes a house and park that closely resemble the surroundings of his childhood, and a loved and respected parent, who shares both the elder Nabokov's dignity and his passionate interest in Nature. Godunov-Cherdyntsev, too, is an expert lepidopterist, and, if I were asked to select a passage or series of passages that show the novelist at his most lyrical, I should cite the long paragraph that, half way through Chapter II, he devotes to butterflies, their marvellous migrations over seas and continents, and the strange disguises they assume.

Far from impairing his talent, the novelist's American adventures considerably strengthened and enriched it. The words 'NABOKOV, Vladimir; American author and lepidopterist' head his final entry in *Who's Who*; but, if he felt warmly grateful to his kind American hosts, and wished to commemorate his gratitude, he preserved his European sensibility, and never lost sight, so long as he lived, of the romantic *temps perdu.* The hero-villain of *Lolita* is himself a European exile, who, through the little American girl he seduces but cannot really capture, is still endeavouring to regain the past, and seeking a realm of lost happiness he has forever left behind. Hence a common feature of all Nabokov's books – a tone of poetic sympathy and ironic detachment blended, that gives his prose-style its peculiarly effective edge. The author stood alone; as creator and literary critic alike he was a stubborn individualist; and, to counterbalance the list of writers he admired, he drew up a lengthy catalogue of the fakes and bores whom he refused to countenance – Dostoevski, Stendhal, Balzac, Sainte-Beuve ('that arch-vulgarian'), Joseph Conrad, Theodore Dreiser and, of course, 'the Viennese quack' Sigmund Freud. Nor would he subscribe to the currently popular doctrine that a work of art should have a social message. 'My books', he wrote in his preface to *The Eye,* 'are blessed by a total lack of social significance . . .' The value of a book depended first and foremost on its imaginative content, on its heady 'extract of personal reality', rather than on its factual basis or its social origins. A book is not 'about something', but itself invents the subject.

He would have revolted against any suggestion, however, that writing a book was a mere aesthetic exercise; into his works he put his whole experience of life, and paid tribute, albeit an indirect tribute, to the moral qualities he most valued. 'I believe', he announced in *Strong Opinions,* 'that one day a reappraiser will come and declare that, far from having been a frivolous firebird, I was a rigid moralist kicking sin, cuffing stupidity, ridiculing the vulgar and cruel – and assigning sovereign power to tenderness, talent, and pride.' Although this self-portrait should perhaps be regarded as a playful Nabokovian quirk – he had a splendid sense of fun – Nabokov, a writer who both enjoyed life and loved and respected mankind, was certainly a benevolent humanist in the great European tradition of Rabelais and Montaigne.

PETER QUENNELL

LOLITA

PART ONE

1

Lolita, light of my life, fire of my loins. My sin, my soul. Lo-lee-ta: the tip of the tongue taking a trip of three steps down the palate to tap, at three, on the teeth. Lo. Lee. Ta.

She was Lo, plain Lo, in the morning, standing four feet ten in one sock. She was Lola in slacks. She was Dolly at school. She was Dolores on the dotted line. But in my arms she was always Lolita.

Did she have a precursor? She did, indeed she did. In point of fact, there might have been no Lolita at all had I not loved, one summer, a certain initial girl-child. In a princedom by the sea. Oh when? About as many years before Lolita was born as my age was that summer. You can always count on a murderer for a fancy prose style.

Ladies and gentlemen of the jury, exhibit number one is what the seraphs, the misinformed, simple, noble-winged seraphs, envied. Look at this tangle of thorns.

2

I was born in 1910, in Paris. My father was a gentle, easy-going person, a salad of racial genes: a Swiss citizen, of mixed French and Austrian descent, with a dash of the Danube in his veins. I am going to pass around in a minute some lovely, glossy-blue picture-postcards. He owned a luxurious hotel on the Riviera. His father and two grandfathers had sold wine, jewels and silk, respectively. At thirty he married an English girl, daughter of Jerome Dunn, the alpinist, and grand-daughter of two Dorset parsons, experts in obscure subjects – palaeopedology and Aeolian harps, respectively. My very photogenic mother died in a freak accident (picnic, lightning) when I was three, and, save for a pocket of warmth in the darkest past, nothing of her subsists within the hollows and dells of memory, over which, if you can still stand my style (I am writing under observation), the sun of my infancy had set: surely, you all know those redolent remnants of day suspended, with the midges, about some hedge in bloom or suddenly entered and traversed by the rambler, at the bottom of a hill, in the summer dusk; a furry warmth, golden midges.

My mother's elder sister, Sybil, whom a cousin of my father's had married and then neglected, served in my immediate family as a kind of unpaid governess and housekeeper. Somebody told me later that she had been in love with my father, and that he had lightheartedly taken advantage of it one rainy day and forgotten it by the time the weather cleared. I was extremely fond of her, despite the rigidity – the fatal rigidity – of some of her rules. Perhaps she wanted to make of me, in the fullness of time, a better widower than my father. Aunt Sybil had pink-rimmed azure eyes and a waxen complexion. She wrote poetry. She was poetically superstitious. She said she knew she would die soon after my sixteenth birthday, and did. Her husband, a great traveller in perfumes, spent most of his time in America, where eventually he founded a firm and acquired a bit of real estate.

I grew, a happy, healthy child in a bright world of illustrated books, clean sand, orange trees, friendly dogs, sea vistas and smiling faces. Around me the splendid Hotel Mirana revolved as a kind of private universe, a whitewashed cosmos within the blue greater one that blazed outside. From the aproned pot-scrubber to the flannelled potentate, everybody liked me, everybody petted me. Elderly American ladies leaning on their canes listed toward me like towers of Pisa. Ruined Russian princesses who could not pay my father bought me expensive bonbons. He, *mon cher petit papa*, took me out boating and biking, taught me to swim and dive and water-ski, read to me *Don Quixote* and *Les Misérables*, and I adored and respected him and felt glad for him whenever I overheard the servants discuss his various lady-friends, beautiful and kind beings who made much of me and cooed and shed precious tears over my cheerful motherlessness.

I attended an English day school a few miles from home, and there I played rackets and fives, and got excellent marks, and was on perfect terms with schoolmates and teachers alike. The only definite sexual events that I can remember as having occurred before my thirteenth birthday (that is, before I first saw my little Annabel) were: a solemn, decorous and purely theoretical talk about pubertal surprises in the rose garden of the school with an American kid, the son of a then celebrated motion-picture actress whom he seldom saw in the three-dimensional world; and some interesting reactions on the part of my organism to certain photographs, pearl and umbra, with infinitely soft partings, in Pichon's sumptuous *La Beauté Humaine* that I had filched from under a mountain of marble-bound *Graphics* in the hotel library. Later, in his delightful debonair manner, my father gave me all the information he thought I needed about sex; this was just before sending me, in the autumn of 1923, to a *lycée* in Lyon (where we were to spend three winters); but alas, in the summer of that year, he was touring Italy with Mme de R. and her daughter, and I had nobody to complain to, nobody to consult.

3

Annabel was, like the writer, of mixed parentage: half English, half-Dutch, in her case. I remember her features far less distinctly today than I did a few years ago, before I knew Lolita. There are two kinds of visual memory: one when you skilfully recreate an image in the laboratory of your mind, with your eyes open (and then I see Annabel in such general terms as: 'honey-coloured skin', 'thin arms', 'brown bobbed hair', 'long lashes', 'big bright mouth'); and the other when you instantly evoke, with shut eyes, on the dark innerside of your eyelids, the objective, absolutely optical replica of a beloved face, a little ghost in natural colours (and this is how I see Lolita).

Let me therefore primly limit myself, in describing Annabel, to saying she was a lovely child a few months my junior. Her parents were old friends of my aunt's, and as stuffy as she. They had rented a villa not far from Hotel Mirana. Bald brown Mr Leigh and fat, powdered Mrs Leigh (born Vanessa van Ness). How I loathed them! At first, Annabel and I talked of peripheral affairs. She kept lifting handfuls of fine sand and letting it pour through her fingers. Our brains were tuned the way those of intelligent European pre-adolescents were in our day and set, and I doubt if much individual genius should be assigned to our interest in the plurality of inhabited worlds, competitive tennis, infinity, solipsism and so on. The softness and fragility of baby animals caused us the same intense pain. She wanted to be a nurse in some famished Asiatic country; I wanted to be a famous spy.

All at once we were madly, clumsily, shamelessly, agonizingly in love with each other; hopelessly, I should add, because that frenzy of mutual possession might have been assuaged only by our actually imbibing and assimilating every particle of each other's soul and flesh; but there we were, unable even to mate as slum children would have so easily found an opportunity to do. After one wild attempt we made to meet at night in her garden (of which more later), the only privacy we were allowed was to be out of earshot but not out of sight of the populous part of the *plage*. There, on the soft sand, a few feet away from our elders, we would sprawl all morning, in a petrified paroxysm of desire, and take advantage of every blessed quirk in space and time to touch each other: her hand, half-hidden in the sand, would creep toward me, its slender brown fingers sleepwalking nearer and nearer; then, her opalescent knee would start on a long cautious journey; sometimes a chance rampart built by younger children granted us sufficient concealment to graze each other's salty lips; these incomplete contacts drove our healthy and inexperienced young bodies to such a state of exasperation that not even the cool blue water, under which we still clawed at each other, could bring relief.

Among some treasures I lost during the wanderings of my adult years, there was a snapshot taken by my aunt which showed Annabel, her parents and the staid, elderly, lame gentleman, a Dr Cooper, who that same summer courted my aunt, grouped around a table in a sidewalk café. Annabel did not come out well, caught as she was in the act of bending over her *chocolat glacé*, and her thin bare shoulders and the parting in her hair were about all that could be identified (as I remember that picture) amid the sunny blur into which her lost loveliness graded; but I, sitting somewhat apart from the rest, came out with a kind of dramatic conspicuousness: a moody, beetle-browed boy in a dark sport shirt and well-tailored white shorts, his legs crossed, sitting in profile, looking away. That photograph was taken on the last day of our fatal summer and just a few minutes before we made our second and final attempt to thwart fate. Under the flimsiest of pretexts (this was our very last chance, and nothing really mattered) we escaped from the café to the beach, and found a desolate stretch of sand, and there, in the violet shadow of some red rocks forming a kind of cave, had a brief session of avid caresses, with somebody's lost pair of sunglasses for only witness. I was on my knees, and on the point of possessing my darling, when two bearded bathers, the old man of the sea and his brother, came out of the sea with exclamations of ribald encouragement, and four months later she died of typhus in Corfu.

4

I leaf again and again through these miserable memories, and keep asking myself, was it then, in the glitter of that remote summer, that the rift in my life began; or was my excessive desire for that child only the first evidence of an inherent singularity? When I try to analyse my own cravings, motives, actions and so forth, I surrender to a sort of retrospective imagination which feeds the analytic faculty with boundless alternatives and which causes each visualized route to fork and re-fork without end in the maddeningly complex prospect of my past. I am convinced, however, that in a certain magic and fateful way Lolita began with Annabel.

I also know that the shock of Annabel's death consolidated the frustration of that nightmare summer, made of it a permanent obstacle to any further romance throughout the cold years of my youth. The spiritual and the physical had been blended in us with a perfection that must remain incomprehensible to the matter-of-fact, crude, standard-brained youngsters of today. Long after her death I felt her thoughts floating through mine. Long before we met we had had the same dreams. We compared notes. We found strange affinities. The same June of the same year (1919) a stray canary had fluttered into her house and mine, in two widely separated countries. Oh, Lolita, had *you* loved me thus!

I have reserved for the conclusion of my 'Annabel' phase the account of our unsuccessful first tryst. One night, she managed to deceive the vicious vigilance of her family. In a nervous and slender-leaved mimosa grove at the back of their villa we found a perch on the ruins of a low stone wall. Through the darkness and the tender trees we could see the arabesques of lighted windows which, touched up by the coloured inks of sensitive memory, appear to me now like playing cards – presumably because a bridge game was keeping the enemy busy. She trembled and twitched as I kissed the corner of her parted lips and the hot lobe of her ear. A cluster of stars palely glowed above us, between the silhouettes of long thin leaves; that vibrant sky seemed as naked as she was under her light frock. I saw her face in the sky, strangely distinct, as if it emitted a faint radiance of its own. Her legs, her lovely live legs, were not too close together, and when my hand located what it sought, a dreamy and eerie expression, half-pleasure, half-pain, came over those childish features. She sat a little higher than I, and whenever in her solitary ecstasy she was led to kiss me, her head would bend with a sleepy, soft, drooping movement that was almost woeful, and her bare knees caught and compressed my wrist, and slackened again; and her quivering mouth, distorted by the acridity of some mysterious potion, with a sibilant intake of breath came near to my face. She would try to relieve the pain of love by first roughly rubbing her dry lips against mine; then my darling would draw away with a nervous toss of her hair, and then again come darkly near and let me feed on her open mouth, while with a generosity that was ready to offer her everything, my heart, my throat, my entrails, I gave her to hold in her awkward fist the sceptre of my passion.

I recall the scent of some kind of toilet powder – I believe she stole it from her mother's Spanish maid – a sweetish, lowly, musky perfume. It mingled with her own biscuity odour, and my senses were suddenly filled to the brim; a sudden commotion in a nearby bush prevented them from overflowing – and as we drew away from each other, and with aching veins attended to what was probably a prowling cat, there came from the house her mother's voice calling her, with a rising frantic note – and Dr Cooper ponderously limped out into the garden. But that mimosa grove – the haze of stars, the tingle, the flame, the honeydew, and the ache remained with me, and that little girl with her seaside limbs and ardent tongue haunted me ever since – until at last, twenty-four years later, I broke her spell by incarnating her in another.

5

The days of my youth, as I look back on them, seem to fly away from me in a flurry of pale repetitive scraps like those morning snowstorms of used tissue paper that a train passenger sees whirling in the wake of the observation car. In my sanitary relations with women I was practical, ironical and brisk. While a college student, in London and Paris, paid ladies sufficed me. My studies were meticulous and intense, although not particularly fruitful. At first, I planned to take a degree in psychiatry as many *manqué* talents do; but I was even more *manqué* than that; a peculiar exhaustion, I am so oppressed, doctor, set in; and I switched to English literature, where so many frustrated poets end as pipe-smoking teachers in tweeds. Paris suited me. I discussed Soviet movies with expatriates. I sat with uranists in the Deux Magots. I published tortuous essays in obscure journals. I composed pastiches:

> . . . Fräulein von Kulp
> may turn, her hand upon the door;
> I will not follow her. Nor Fresca. Nor
> that Gull.

A paper of mine entitled 'The Proustian theme in a letter from Keats to Benjamin Bailey' was chuckled over by the six or seven scholars who read it. I launched upon an '*Histoire abrégée de la poésie anglaise*' for a prominent publishing firm, and then started to compile that manual of French literature for English-speaking students (with comparisons drawn from English writers) which was to occupy me throughout the 'forties – and the last volume of which was almost ready for press by the time of my arrest.

I found a job – teaching English to a group of adults in Auteuil. Then a school for boys employed me for a couple of winters. Now and then I took advantage of the acquaintances I had formed among social workers and psychotherapists to visit in their company various institutions, such as orphanages and reform schools, where pale pubescent girls with matted eyelashes could be stared at in perfect impunity remindful of that granted one in dreams.

Now I wish to introduce the following idea. Between the age limits of nine and fourteen there occur maidens who, to certain bewitched travellers, twice or many times older than they, reveal their true nature which is not human, but nymphic (that is, demoniac); and these chosen creatures I propose to designate as 'nymphets'.

It will be marked that I substitute time terms for spatial ones. In fact, I would have the reader see 'nine' and 'fourteen' as the boundaries – the mirrory beaches and rosy rocks – of an enchanted island haunted by those nymphets of mine and surrounded by a vast, misty sea. Between those age limits, are all girl-children nymphets? Of course not. Otherwise, we who are in the know, we lone voyagers, we nympholepts, would have long gone insane. Neither are good looks any criterion; and vulgarity, or at least what a given community terms so, does not necessarily impair certain mysterious characteristics, the fey grace, the elusive, shifty, soul-shattering, insidious charm that separates the nymphet from such coevals of hers as are incomparably more dependent on the spatial world of synchronous phenomena than on that intangible island of entranced time where Lolita plays with her likes. Within the same age limits the number of true nymphets is strikingly inferior to that of provisionally plain, or just nice, or 'cute', or even 'sweet' and 'attractive', ordinary, plumpish, formless, cold-skinned, essentially human little girls, with tummies and pigtails, who may or may not turn into adults of great beauty (look at the ugly dumplings in black stockings and white hats that are metamorphosed into stunning stars of the screen). A normal man given a group photograph of school girls or Girl Scouts and asked to point out the comeliest one will not necessarily choose the nymphet among them. You have to be an artist and a madman, a creature of infinite melancholy, with a bubble of hot poison in your loins and a super-voluptuous flame permanently aglow in your subtle spine (oh, how you have to cringe and hide!), in order to discern at once, by ineffable signs – the slightly feline outline of a cheekbone, the slenderness of a downy limb, and other indices which despair and shame and tears of tenderness forbid me to tabulate – the little deadly demon among the wholesome children; *she* stands unrecognized by them and unconscious herself of her fantastic power.

Furthermore, since the idea of time plays such a magic part in the matter, the student should not be surprised to learn that there must be a gap of several years, never less than ten I should say, generally thirty or forty, and as many as ninety in a few known cases, between maiden and man to enable the latter to come under a nymphet's spell. It is a question of focal adjustment, of a certain distance that the inner eye thrills to surmount, and a certain contrast that the mind perceives with a gasp of perverse delight. When I was a child and she was a child, my little Annabel was no nymphet to me; I was her equal, a faunlet in my own right, on that same enchanted island of time; but today, in September 1952, after twenty-nine years have elapsed, I think I can distinguish in her the initial fateful elf in my life. We loved each other with a premature love, marked by a fierceness that so often destroys adult lives. I was a strong lad and survived; but the poison was in the wound, and the wound remained ever open, and soon I found myself maturing amid a civilization which allows a man of twenty-five to court a girl of sixteen but not a girl of twelve.

No wonder, then, that my adult life during the European period of my existence proved monstrously twofold. Overtly, I had so-called normal relationships with a number of terrestrial women having pumpkins or pears for breasts; inside, I was consumed by a hell furnace of localized lust for every passing nymphet whom as a law-abiding poltroon I never dared approach. The human females I was allowed to wield were but palliative agents. I am ready to believe that the sensations I derived from natural fornication were much the same as those known to normal big males consorting with their normal big mates in that routine rhythm which shakes the world. The trouble was that those gentlemen had not, and I *had*, caught glimpses of an incomparably more poignant bliss. The dimmest of my pollutive dreams was a thousand times more dazzling than all the adultery the most virile writer of genius or the most talented impotent might imagine. My world was split. I was aware of not one but two sexes, neither of which was mine; both would be termed female by the anatomist. But to me, through the prism of my senses, 'they were as different as mist and mast'. All this I rationalize now. In my twenties and early thirties, I did not understand my throes quite so clearly. While my body knew what it craved for, my mind rejected my body's every plea. One moment I was ashamed and frightened, another recklessly optimistic. Taboos strangulated me. Psycho-analysts wooed me with pseudoliberations of pseudolibidoes. The fact that to me the only objects of amorous tremor were sisters of Annabel's, her handmaids and girl-pages, appeared to me at times as a forerunner of insanity. At other times I would tell myself that it was all a question of attitude, that there was really nothing wrong in being moved to distraction by girl-children. Let me remind my reader that in England, with the passage of the Children and Young Persons Act in 1933, the term 'girl-child' is defined as 'a girl who is over eight but under fourteen years' (after that from fourteen to seventeen, the statutory definition is 'young person'). In Massachusetts, US, on the other hand, a 'wayward child' is, technically, one 'between seven and seventeen years of age' (who, moreover, habitually associates with vicious or immoral persons). Hugh Broughton, a writer of controversy in the reign of James I, has proved that Rahab was a harlot at ten years of age. This is all very interesting, and I dare say you see me already frothing at the mouth in a fit; but no, I am not; I am just winking happy thoughts into a little tiddle cup. Here are some more pictures. Here is Virgil who could the nymphet sing in single tone, but probably preferred a lad's peritoneum. Here are two of King Akhnaten's and Queen Nefertiti's prenubile Nile daughters (that royal couple had a litter of six), wearing nothing but many necklaces of bright beads, relaxed on cushions, intact after three thousand years, with their soft brown puppybodies, cropped hair and long ebony eyes. Here are some brides of ten compelled to seat themselves on the fascinum, the virile ivory in the temples of classical scholarship. Marriage and cohabitation before the age of puberty are still not uncommon in certain East Indian provinces. Lepcha old men of eighty copulate with girls of eight, and nobody minds. After all, Dante fell madly in love with his Beatrice when she was nine, a sparkling girleen, painted and lovely, and bejewelled, in a crimson frock, and this was in 1274, in Florence, at a private feast in the merry month of May. And when Petrarch fell madly in love with his Laureen, she was a fair-haired nymphet of twelve running in the wind, in the pollen and dust, a flower in flight, in the beautiful plain as descried from the hills of Vaucluse.

But let us be prim and civilized. Humbert Humbert tried hard to be good. Really and truly, he did. He had the utmost respect for ordinary children, with their purity and vulnerability, and under no circumstances would he have interfered with the innocence of a child, if there was the least risk of a row. But how his heart beat when, among the innocent throng, he espied a demon child, *'enfant charmante et fourbe'*, dim eyes, bright lips, ten years in jail if you only show her you are looking at her. So life went. Humbert was perfectly capable of intercourse with Eve, but it was Lilith he longed for. The bud-stage of breast development appears early (10·7 years) in the sequence of somatic changes accompanying pubescence. And the next maturational item available is the first appearance of pigmented pubic hair (11·2 years). My little cup brims with tiddles.

A shipwreck. An atoll. Alone with a drowned passenger's shivering child. Darling, this is only a game! How marvellous were my fancied adventures as I sat on a hard park bench pretending to be immersed in a trembling book. Around the quiet scholar, nymphets played freely, as if he were a familiar statue or part of an old tree's shadow and sheen. Once a perfect little beauty in a tartan frock, with a clatter, put her heavily armed foot near me upon the bench to dip her slim bare arms into me and tighten the strap of her roller skate, and I dissolved in the sun, with my book for fig leaf, as her auburn ringlets fell all over her skinned knee, and the shadow of leaves I shared pulsated and melted on her radiant limb next to my chameleonic cheek. Another time a red-haired school girl hung over me in the *métro,* and a revelation of axillary russet I obtained remained in my blood for weeks. I could list a great number of these one-sided diminutive romances. Some of them ended in a rich flavour of hell. It happened for instance that from my balcony I would notice a lighted window across the street and what looked like a nymphet in the act of undressing before a co-operative mirror. Thus isolated, thus removed, the vision acquired an especially keen charm that made me race with all speed toward my lone gratification. But abruptly, fiendishly, the tender pattern of nudity I had adored would be transformed into the disgusting lamp-lit bare arm of a man in his underclothes reading his paper by the open window, in the hot, damp, hopeless summer night.

Rope-skipping, hopscotch. That old woman in black who sat down next to me on my bench, on my rack of joy (a nymphet was groping under me for a lost marble), and asked if I had stomach-ache, the insolent hag. Ah, leave me alone in my pubescent park, in my mossy garden. Let them play around me for ever. Never grow up.

6

Apropos: I have often wondered what became of those nymphets later? In this wrought-iron world of criss-cross cause and effect, could it be that the hidden throb I stole from them did not affect *their* future? I had possessed her – and she never knew it. All right. But would it not tell sometime later? Had I not somehow tampered with her fate by involving her image in my voluptas? Oh, it was, and remains, a source of great and terrible wonder.

I learned, however, what they looked like, those lovely, maddening, thin-armed nymphets, when they grew up. I remember walking along an animated street on a grey spring afternoon somewhere near the Madeleine. A short slim girl passed me at a rapid, high-heeled, tripping step, we glanced back at the same moment, she stopped and I accosted her. She came hardly up to my chest hair and had the kind of dimpled round little face French girls so often have, and I liked her long lashes and tight-fitting tailored dress sheathing in pearl-grey her young body which still retained – and that was the nymphic echo, the chill of delight, the leap in my loins – a childish something mingling with the professional *frétillement* of her small agile rump. I asked her price, and she promptly replied with melodious silvery precision (a bird, a very bird!) *'Cent'*. I tried to haggle but she saw the awful lone longing in my lowered eyes, directed so far down at her round forehead and rudimentary hat (a band, a posy); and with one beat of her lashes: *'Tant pis'*, she said, and made as if to move away. Perhaps only three years earlier I might have seen her coming home from school! That evocation settled the matter. She led me up the usual steep stairs, with the usual bell clearing the way for the *monsieur* who might not care to meet another *monsieur,* on the mournful climb to the abject room, all bed and *bidet.* As usual, she asked at once for her *petit cadeau,* and as usual I asked her name (Monique) and her age (eighteen). I was pretty well acquainted with the banal way of streetwalkers. They all answer *'dix-huit'* – a trim twitter, a note of finality and wistful deceit which they emit up to ten times per day, the poor little creatures. But in Monique's case there could be no doubt she was, if anything, adding one or two years to her age. This I deduced from many details of her compact, neat, curiously immature body. Having shed her clothes with fascinating rapidity, she stood for a moment partly wrapped in the dingy gauze of the window curtain listening with infantile pleasure, as pat as pat could be, to an organ-grinder in the dusk-brimming courtyard below. When I examined her small hands and drew her attention to their grubby fingernails, she said with a naïve frown

'Oui, ce n'est pas bien', and went to the wash-basin, but I said it did not matter, did not matter at all. With her brown bobbed hair, luminous grey eyes and pale skin, she looked perfectly charming. Her hips were no bigger than those of a squatting lad; in fact, I do not hesitate to say (and indeed this is the reason why I linger gratefully in that gauze-grey room of memory with little Monique) that among the eighty or so *grues* I had had operate upon me, she was the only one that gave me a pang of genuine pleasure. *'Il était malin, celui qui a inventé ce truc-là'*, she commented amiably, and got back into her clothes with the same high-style speed.

I asked for another, more elaborate, assignment later the same evening, and she said she would meet me at the corner café at nine, and swore she had never *posé un lapin* in all her young life. We returned to the same room, and I could not help saying how very pretty she was to which she answered demurely: *'Tu es bien gentil de dire ça'*, and then, noticing what I noticed too in the mirror reflecting our small Eden – the dreadful grimace of clenched-teeth tenderness that distorted my mouth – dutiful little Monique (oh, she had been a nymphet all right!) wanted to know if she should remove the layer of red from her lips *avant qu'on se couche* in case I planned to kiss her. Of course, I planned it. I let myself go with her more completely than I had with any young lady before, and my last vision that night of long-lashed Monique is touched up with a gaiety that I find seldom associated with any event in my humiliating, sordid, taciturn love life. She looked tremendously pleased with the bonus of fifty I gave her as she trotted out into the April night drizzle with Humbert Humbert lumbering in her narrow wake. Stopping before a window display she said with great gusto: *'Je vais m'acheter des bas!'* and never may I forget the way her Parisian childish lips exploded on *'bas'*, pronouncing it with an appetite that all but changed the 'a' into a brief buoyant bursting 'o' as in *'bot'*.

I had a date with her next day at 2.15 p.m. in my own rooms, but it was less successful, she seemed to have grown less juvenile, more of a woman overnight. A cold I caught from her led me to cancel a fourth assignment, nor was I sorry to break an emotional series that threatened to burden me with heart-rending fantasies and peter out in dull disappointment. So let her remain, sleek, slender Monique, as she was for a minute or two: a delinquent nymphet shining through the matter-of-fact young whore.

My brief acquaintance with her started a train of thought that may seem pretty obvious to the reader who knows the ropes. An advertisement in a lewd magazine landed me, one brave day, in the office of a Mlle Edith who began by offering me to choose a kindred soul from a collection of rather formal photographs in a rather soiled album (*'Regardez-moi cette belle brune!'*). When I pushed the album away and somehow managed to blurt out my criminal craving, she looked as if about to show me the door; however, after asking me what price I was prepared to disburse, she condescended to put me in touch with a person *qui pourrait arranger la chose*. Next day, an asthmatic woman, coarsely painted, garrulous, garlicky, with an almost farcical Provençal accent and a black moustache above a purple lip, took me to what was apparently her own domicile, and there, after explosively kissing the bunched tips of her fat fingers to signify the delectable rosebud quality of her merchandise, she theatrically drew aside a curtain to reveal what I judged was that part of the room where a large and unfastidious family usually slept. It was now empty save for a monstrously plump, sallow, repulsively plain girl of at least fifteen with red-ribboned thick black braids who sat on a chair perfunctorily nursing a bald doll. When I shook my head and tried to shuffle out of the trap, the woman, talking fast, began removing the dingy woollen jersey from the young giantess's torso; then, seeing my determination to leave, she demanded *son argent*. A door at the end of the room was opened, and two men who had been dining in the kitchen joined in the squabble. They were misshapen, bare-necked, very swarthy and one of them wore dark glasses. A small boy and a begrimed, bowlegged toddler lurked behind them. With the insolent logic of a nightmare, the enraged procuress, indicating the man in glasses, said he had served in the police, *lui*, so that I had better do as I was told. I went up to Marie – for that was her stellar name – who by then had quietly transferred her heavy haunches to a stool at the kitchen table and resumed her interrupted soup while the toddler picked up the doll. With a surge of pity dramatizing my idiotic gesture, I thrust a banknote into her indifferent hand. She surrendered my gift to the ex-detective, whereupon I was suffered to leave.

7

I do not know if the pimp's album may not have been another link in the daisy-chain; but soon after, for my own safety, I decided to marry. It occurred to me that regular hours, home-cooked meals, all the conventions of marriage, the prophylactic routine of its bedroom activities and, who knows, the eventual flowering of certain moral values, of certain spiritual substitutes, might help me, if not to purge myself of my degrading and dangerous desires, at least to keep them under pacific control. A little money that had come my way after my father's death (nothing very grand – the Mirana had been sold long before), in addition to my striking if somewhat brutal good looks, allowed me to enter upon my quest with equanimity. After considerable deliberation, my choice fell on the daughter of a Polish doctor: the good man happened to be treating me for spells of dizziness and tachycardia. We played chess; his daughter watched me from behind her easel, and inserted eyes or knuckles borrowed from me into the cubistic trash that accomplished misses then painted instead of lilacs and lambs. Let me repeat with quiet force: I was, and still am, despite *mes malheurs*, an exceptionally handsome male; slow-moving, tall, with soft dark hair and a gloomy but all the more seductive cast of demeanour. Exceptional virility often reflects in the subject's displayable features a sullen and congested something that pertains to what he has to conceal. And this was my case. Well did I know, alas, that I could obtain at the snap of my fingers any adult female I chose; in fact, it had become quite a habit with me of not being too attentive to women lest they come toppling, bloodripe, into my cold lap. Had I been a *français moyen* with a taste for flashy ladies, I might have easily found, among the many crazed beauties that lashed my grim rock, creatures far more fascinating than Valeria. My choice, however, was prompted by considerations whose essence was, as I realized too late, a piteous compromise. All of which goes to show how dreadfully stupid poor Humbert always was in matters of sex.

8

Although I told myself I was looking merely for a soothing presence, a glorified *pot-au-feu,* an animated merkin, what really attracted me to Valeria was the imitation she gave of a little girl. She gave it not because she had divined something about me; it was just her style – and I fell for it. Actually, she was at least in her late twenties (I never established her exact age for even her passport lied) and had mislaid her virginity under circumstances that changed with her reminiscent moods. I, on my part, was as naïve as only a pervert can be. She looked fluffy and frolicsome, dressed *à la gamine,* showed a generous amount of smooth leg, knew how to stress the white of a bare instep by the black of a velvet slipper, and pouted, and dimpled, and romped, and dirndled, and shook her short curly blonde hair in the cutest and tritest fashion imaginable.

After a brief ceremony at the *mairie,* I took her to the new apartment I had rented and, somewhat to her surprise, had her wear, before I touched her, a girl's plain nightshirt that I had managed to filch from the linen closet of an orphanage. I derived some fun from that nuptial night and had the idiot in hysterics by sunrise. But reality soon asserted itself. The bleached curl revealed its melanic root; the down turned to prickles on a shaved shin; the mobile moist mouth, no matter how I stuffed it with love, disclosed ignominiously its resemblance to the corresponding part in a treasured portrait of her toadlike dead mama; and presently, instead of a pale little gutter girl, Humbert Humbert had on his hands a large, puffy, short-legged, big-breasted and practically brainless *baba.*

This state of affairs lasted from 1935 to 1939. Her only asset was a muted nature which did help to produce an odd sense of comfort in our small squalid flat: two rooms, a hazy view in one window, a brick wall in the other, a tiny kitchen, a shoe-shaped bath tub, within which I felt like Marat but with no white-necked maiden to stab me. We had quite a few cosy evenings together, she deep in her *Paris-Soir,* I working at a rickety table. We went to movies, bicycle races and boxing matches. I appealed to her stale flesh very seldom, only in cases of great urgency and despair. The grocer had a little daughter whose shadow drove me mad; but with Valeria's help I did find after all some legal outlets to my fantastic predicament. As to cooking, we tacitly dismissed the *pot-au-feu* and had most of our meals at a crowded place in rue Bonaparte where there were wine stains on the tablecloth and a good deal of foreign babble. And next door, an art dealer displayed in his cluttered window a splendid, flamboyant, green, red, golden and inky blue, ancient American estampe – a locomotive with a gigantic smoke-stack, great baroque lamps and a tremendous cowcatcher, haulings its mauve coaches through the stormy prairie night and mixing a lot of spark-studded black smoke with the furry thunder clouds.

These burst. In the summer of 1939 *mon oncle d'Amérique* died bequeathing me an annual income of a few thousand dollars on condition I came to live in the States and showed some interest in his business. This prospect was most welcome to me. I felt my life needed a shake-up. There was another thing, too: moth holes had appeared in the plush of matrimonial comfort. During the last weeks I had kept noticing that my fat Valeria was not her usual self; had acquired a queer restlessness; even showed something like irritation at times, which was quite out of keeping with the stock character she was supposed to impersonate. When I informed her we were shortly to sail for New York, she looked distressed and bewildered. There were some tedious difficulties with her papers. She had a Nansen, or better say Nonsense, passport which for some reason a share in her husband's solid Swiss citizenship could not easily transcend; and I decided it was the necessity of queuing in the *préfecture*, and other formalities, that had made her so listless, despite my patiently describing to her America, the country of rosy children and great trees, where life would be such an improvement on dull dingy Paris.

We were coming out of some office building one morning, with her papers almost in order, when Valeria, as she waddled by my side, began to shake her poodle head vigorously without saying a word. I let her go on for a while and then asked if she thought she had something inside. She answered (I translate from her French which was, I imagine, a translation in its turn of some Slavic platitude): 'There is another man in my life.'

Now, these are ugly words for a husband to hear. They dazed me, I confess. To beat her up in the street, there and then, as an honest vulgarian might have done, was not feasible. Years of secret sufferings had taught me superhuman self-control. So I ushered her into a taxi which had been invitingly creeping along the curb for some time, and in this comparative privacy I quietly suggested she comment her wild talk. A mounting fury was suffocating me – not because I had any particular fondness for that figure of fun, *Mme Humbert,* but because matters of legal and illegal conjunction were for me alone to decide, and here she was, Valeria, the comedy wife, brazenly preparing to dispose in her own way of my comfort and fate. I demanded her lover's name. I repeated my question; but she kept up a burlesque babble, discoursing on her unhappiness with me and announcing plans for an immediate divorce. *'Mais qui est-ce?'* I shouted at last, striking her on the knee with my fist; and she, without even wincing, stared at me as if the answer were too simple for words, then gave a quick shrug and pointed at the thick neck of the taxi driver. He pulled up at a small café and introduced himself. I do not remember his ridiculous name but after all those years I still see him quite clearly – a stocky White Russian ex-colonel with a bushy moustache and a crew cut; there were thousands of them plying that fool's trade in Paris. We sat down at a table; the Tsarist ordered wine; and Valeria, after applying a wet napkin to her knee, went on talking – *into* me rather than to me; she poured words into this dignified receptacle with a volubility I had never suspected she had in her. And every now and then she would volley a burst of Slavic at her stolid lover. The situation was preposterous and became even more so when the taxi-colonel, stopping Valeria with a possessive smile, began to unfold *his* views and plans. With an atrocious accent to his careful French, he delineated the world of love and work into which he proposed to enter hand in hand with his child-wife Valeria. She by now was preening herself, between him and me, rouging her pursed lips, tripling her chin to pick at her blouse-bosom and so forth, and he spoke of her as if she were absent, and also as if she were a kind of little ward that was in the act of being transferred, for her own good, from one wise guardian to another even wiser one; and although my helpless wrath may have exaggerated and disfigured certain impressions, I can swear that he actually consulted me on such things as her diet, her periods, her wardrobe and the books she had read or should read. 'I think,' he said, 'she will like *Jean Christophe*?' Oh, he was quite a scholar, Mr Taxovich.

I put an end to this gibberish by suggesting Valeria pack up her few belongings immediately, upon which the platitudinous colonel gallantly offered to carry them into the car. Reverting to his professional state, he drove the Humberts to their residence and all the way Valeria talked, and Humbert the Terrible deliberated with Humbert the Small whether Humbert Humbert should kill her or her lover, or both, or neither. I remember once handling an automatic belonging to a fellow student, in the days (I have not spoken of them, I think, but never mind) when I toyed with the idea of enjoying his little sister, a most diaphanous nymphet with a black hair bow, and then shooting myself. I now wondered if Valechka (as the colonel called her) was really worth shooting, or strangling, or drowning. She had very vulnerable legs, and I decided I would limit myself to hurting her very horribly as soon as we were alone.

But we never were. Valechka – by now shedding torrents of tears tinged with the mess of her rainbow make-up – started to fill anyhow a trunk, and two suitcases, and a bursting carton, and visions of putting on my mountain boots and taking a running kick at her rump were of course impossible to put into execution with the cursed colonel hovering around all the time. I cannot say he behaved insolently or anything like that; on the contrary, he displayed, as a small sideshow in the theatricals I had been inveigled in, a discreet old-world civility, punctuating his movements with all sorts of mispronounced apologies (*j'ai demannde pardonne* – excuse me – *est-ce que j'ai puis* – may I – and so forth), and turning away tactfully when Valechka took down with a flourish her pink panties from the clothesline above the tub; but he seemed to be all over the place at once, *le gredin*, agreeing his frame with the anatomy of the flat, reading in my chair my newspaper, untying a knotted string, rolling a cigarette, counting the teaspoons, visiting the bathroom, helping his moll to wrap up the electric fan her father had given her, and carrying streetward her luggage. I sat with arms folded, one hip on the window sill, dying of hate and boredom. At last both were out of the quivering apartment – the vibration of the door I had slammed after them still rang in my every nerve, a poor substitute for the backhand slap with which I ought to have hit her across the cheekbone according to the rules of the movies. Clumsily playing my part, I stomped to the bathroom to check if they had taken my English toilet water; they had not; but I noticed with a spasm of fierce disgust that the former Counsellor of the Tsar, after thoroughly easing his bladder, had not flushed the toilet. That solemn pool of alien urine with a soggy, tawny cigarette butt disintegrating in it struck me as a crowning insult, and I wildly looked around for a weapon. Actually I dare say it was nothing but middle-class Russian courtesy (with an Oriental tang, perhaps) that had prompted the good colonel (Maximovich! his name suddenly taxies back to me), a very formal person as they all are, to muffle his private need in decorous silence so as not to underscore the small size of his host's domicile with the rush of a gross cascade on top of his own hushed trickle. But this did not enter my mind at the moment, as groaning with rage I ransacked the kitchen for something better than a broom. Then, cancelling my search, I dashed out of the house with the heroic decision of attacking him barefisted: despite my natural vigour, I am no pugilist, while the short but broad-shouldered Maximovich seemed made of pig iron. The void of the street, revealing nothing of my wife's departure except a rhinestone button that she had dropped in the mud after preserving it for three unnecessary years in a broken box, may have spared me a bloody nose. But no matter. I had my little revenge in due time. A man from Pasadena told me one day that Mrs Maximovich *née* Zborovski had died in childbirth around 1945; the couple had somehow got over to California and had been used there, for an excellent salary, in a year-long experiment conducted by a distinguished American ethnologist. The experiment dealt with human and racial reactions to a diet of bananas and dates in a constant position on all fours. My informant, a doctor, swore he had seen with his own eyes obese Valechka and her colonel, by then grey-haired and also quite corpulent, diligently crawling about the well-swept floors of a brightly lit set of rooms (fruit in one, water in another, mats in a third and so on) in the company of several other hired quadrupeds, selected from indigent and helpless groups. I tried to find the results of these tests in the *Review of Anthropology;* but they appear not to have been published yet. These scientific products take of course some time to fructuate. I hope they will be illustrated with good photographs when they do get printed, although it is not very likely that a prison library will harbour such erudite works. The one to which I am restricted these days, despite my lawyer's favours, is a good example of the inane eclecticism governing the selection of books in prison libraries. They have the Bible, of course, and Dickens (an ancient set, NY, G. W. Dillingham, Publisher, MDCCCLXXXVII); and the *Children's Encyclopaedia* (with some nice photographs of sunshine-haired Girl Scouts in shorts), and *A Murder is Announced* by Agatha Christie; but they also have such coruscating trifles as *A Vaga-*

bond in Italy by Percy Elphinstone, author of *Venice Revisited,* Boston, 1868, and a comparatively recent (1946) *Who's Who in the Limelight* – actors, producers, playwrights, and shots of static scenes. In looking through the latter volume, I was treated last night to one of those dazzling coincidences that logicians loathe and poets love. I transcribe most of the page:

> Pym, Roland. Born in Lundy, Mass, 1922. Received stage training at Elsinore Playhouse, Derby, NY. Made debut in *Sunburst*. Among his many appearances are *Two Blocks from Here, The Girl in Green, Scrambled Husbands, The Strange Mushroom, Touch and Go, John Lovely, I was Dreaming of You.*
>
> Quilty, Clare, American dramatist. Born in Ocean City, NJ, 1911. Educated at Columbia University. Started on a commercial career but turned to playwriting. Author of *The Little Nymph, The Lady who Loved Lightning* (in collaboration with Vivian Darkbloom), *Dark Age, The Strange Mushroom, Fatherly Love,* and others. His many plays for children are notable. *Little Nymph* (1940) travelled 14,000 miles and played 280 performances on the road during the winter before ending in New York. Hobbies: fast cars, photography, pets.
>
> Quine, Dolores. Born in 1882, in Dayton, Ohio. Studied for stage at American Academy. First played in Ottawa in 1900. Made New York debut in 1904 in *Never Talk to Strangers*. Has disappeared since in [a list of some thirty plays follows].

How the look of my dear love's name, even affixed to some old hag of an actress, still makes me rock with helpless pain! Perhaps, she might have been an actress too. Born 1935. Appeared (I notice the slip of my pen in the preceding paragraph, but please do not correct it, Clarence) in *The Murdered Playwright*. Quine the Swine. Guilty of killing Quilty. Oh, my Lolita, I have only words to play with!

9

Divorce proceedings delayed my voyage, and the gloom of yet another World War had settled upon the globe when, after a winter of ennui and pneumonia in Portugal, I at last reached the States. In New York I eagerly accepted the soft job fate offered me: it consisted mainly of thinking up and editing perfume ads. I welcomed its desultory character and pseudo-literary aspects, attending to it whenever I had nothing better to do. On the other hand, I was urged by a wartime university in New York to complete my comparative history of French literature for English-speaking students. The first volume took me a couple of years during which I put in seldom less than fifteen hours of work daily. As I look back on those days, I see them divided tidily into ample light and narrow shade: the light pertaining to the solace of research in palatial libraries, the shade to my excruciating desires and insomnias of which enough has been said. Knowing me by now, the reader can easily imagine how dusty and hot I got, trying to catch a glimpse of nymphets (alas, always remote) playing in Central Park, and how repulsed I was by the glitter of deodorized career girls that a gay dog in one of the offices kept unloading upon me. Let us skip all that. A dreadful breakdown sent me to a sanatorium for more than a year; I went back to my work – only to be hospitalized again.

Robust outdoor life seemed to promise me some relief. One of my favourite doctors, a charming cynical chap with a little brown beard, had a brother, and this brother was about to lead an expedition into arctic Canada. I was attached to it as a 'recorder of psychic reactions'. With two young botanists and an old carpenter I shared now and then (never very successfully) the favours of one of our nutritionists, a Dr Anita Johnson – who was soon flown back, I am glad to say. I had little notion of what object the expedition was pursuing. Judging by the number of meteorologists upon it, we may have been tracking to its lair (somewhere on Prince of Wales' Island, I understand) the wandering and wobbly north magnetic pole. One group, jointly with the Canadians, established a weather station on Pierre Point in Melville Sound. Another group, equally misguided, collected plankton. A third studied tuberculosis in the tundra. Bert, a film photographer – an insecure fellow with whom at one time I was made to partake in a good deal of menial work (he, too, had some psychic troubles) – maintained that the big men on our team, the real leaders we never saw, were mainly engaged in checking the influence of climatic amelioration on the coats of the arctic fox.

We lived in prefabricated timber cabins amid a Pre-Cambrian world of granite. We had heaps of supplies – the *Reader's Digest,* an ice-cream mixer, chemical toilets, paper hats for Christmas. My health improved wonderfully in spite or because of all the fantastic blankness and boredom. Surrounded by such dejected vegetation as willow scrub and lichens; permeated, and, I suppose, cleansed by a whistling gale; seated on a boulder under a completely translucent sky (through which, however, nothing of importance showed), I felt curiously aloof from my own self. No temptations maddened me. The plump, glossy little Eskimo girls with their fish smell, hideous raven hair and guinea pig faces, evoked even less desire in me than Dr Johnson had. Nymphets do not occur in polar regions.

I left my betters the task of analysing glacial drifts, drumlins, and gremlins, and kremlins, and for a time tried to jot down what I fondly thought were 'reactions' (I noticed, for instance, that dreams under the midnight sun tended to be highly coloured, and this my friend the photographer confirmed). I was also supposed to quiz my various companions on a number of important matters, such as nostalgia, fear of unknown animals, food-fantasies, nocturnal emissions, hobbies, choice of radio programmes, changes in outlook and so forth. Everybody got so fed up with this that I soon dropped the project completely, and only toward the end of my twenty months of cold labour (as one of the botanists jocosely put it) concocted a perfectly spurious and very racy report that the reader will find published in the *Annals of Adult Psychophysics* for 1945 or 1946, as well as in the issue of *Arctic Explorations* devoted to that particular expedition; which, in conclusion, was not really concerned with Victoria Island copper or anything like that, as I learned later from my genial doctor; for the nature of its real purpose was what is termed 'hush-hush', and so let me add merely that, whatever it was, that purpose was admirably achieved.

The reader will regret to learn that soon after my return to civilization I had another bout with insanity (if to melancholia and a sense of insufferable oppression that cruel term must be applied). I owe my complete restoration to a discovery I made while being treated at that particular very expensive sanatorium. I discovered there was an endless source of robust enjoyment in trifling with psychiatrists: cunningly leading them on; never letting them see that you know all the tricks of the trade; inventing for them elaborate dreams, pure classics in style (which make *them,* the dream-extortionists, dream and wake up shrieking); teasing them with fake 'primal scenes'; and never allowing them the slightest glimpse of one's real sexual predicament. By bribing a nurse I won access to some files and discovered, with glee, cards calling me 'potentially homosexual' and 'totally impotent'. The sport was so excellent, its results – in *my* case – so ruddy that I stayed on for a whole month after I was quite well (sleeping admirably and eating like a schoolgirl). And then I added another week just for the pleasure of taking on a powerful newcomer, a displaced (and, surely, deranged) celebrity, known for his knack of making patients believe they had witnessed their own conception.

10

Upon signing out, I cast around for some place in the New England countryside or sleepy small town (elms, white church) where I could spend a studious summer subsisting on a compact boxful of notes I had accumulated and bathing in some nearby lake. My work had begun to interest me again – I mean my scholarly exertions; the other thing, my active participation in my uncle's posthumous perfumes, had by then been cut down to a minimum.

One of his former employees, the scion of a distinguished family, suggested I spend a few months in the residence of his impoverished cousins, a Mr McCoo, retired, and his wife, who wanted to let their upper story where a late aunt had delicately dwelt. He said they had two little daughters, one a baby, the other a girl of twelve, and a beautiful garden, not far from a beautiful lake, and I said it sounded perfectly perfect.

I exchanged letters with these people, satisfying them I was housebroken, and spent a fantastic night on the train, imagining in all possible detail the enigmatic nymphet I would coach in French and fondle in Humbertish. Nobody met me at the toy station where I alighted with my new expensive bag, and nobody answered the telephone; eventually, however, a distraught McCoo in wet clothes turned up at the only hotel of green-and-pink Ramsdale with the news that his house had just burned down – possibly, owing to the synchronous conflagration that had been raging all night in my veins. His family, he said, had fled to a farm he owned, and had taken the car, but a friend of his wife's, a grand person, Mrs Haze, of 342 Lawn Street, offered to accommodate me. A lady who lived opposite Mrs Haze's had lent McCoo her limousine, a marvellously old-fashioned, square-topped affair, manned by a cheerful Negro. Now, since the only reason for my coming at all had vanished, the aforesaid arrangement seemed preposterous. All right, his house would have to be completely rebuilt, so what? Had he not insured it sufficiently? I was angry, disappointed and bored, but, being a polite European, could not refuse to be sent off to Lawn Street in that funeral car, feeling that otherwise McCoo would devise an even more elaborate means of getting rid of me. I saw him scamper away and my chauffeur shook his head with a soft chuckle. *En route,* I swore to myself I would not dream of staying in Ramsdale under any circumstances but would fly that very day to the Bermudas or the Bahamas or the Blazes. Possibilities of sweetness on technicolor beaches had been trickling through my spine for some time before, and McCoo's cousin had, in fact, sharply diverted that train of thought with his well-meaning but as it transpired now absolutely inane suggestion.

Speaking of sharp turns: we almost ran over a meddlesome suburban dog (one of those who lie in wait for cars) as we swerved into Lawn Street. A little further, the Haze house, a white-frame horror, appeared, looking dingy and old, more grey than white – the kind of place you know will have a rubber tube affixable to the tub faucet in lieu of shower. I tipped the chauffeur and hoped he would immediately drive away so that I might double back unnoticed to my hotel and bag; but the man merely crossed to the other side of the street where an old lady was calling to him from her porch. What could I do? I pressed the bell button.

A coloured maid let me in – and left me standing on the mat while she rushed back to the kitchen where something was burning that ought not to burn.

The front hall was graced with door chimes, a white-eyed wooden thingamabob of commercial Mexican origin, and that banal darling of the arty middle class, van Gogh's 'Arlésienne'. A door ajar to the right afforded a glimpse of a living room, with some more Mexican trash in a corner cabinet and a striped sofa along the wall. There was a staircase at the end of the hallway, and as I stood mopping my brow (only now did I realize how hot it had been out of doors) and staring, to stare at something, at an old grey tennis ball that lay on an oak chest, there came from the upper landing the contralto voice of Mrs Haze, who leaning over the banisters inquired melodiously, 'Is that Monsieur Humbert?' A bit of cigarette ash dropped from there in addition. Presently, the lady herself – sandals, maroon slacks, yellow silk blouse, squarish face, in that order – came down the steps, her index finger still tapping upon her cigarette.

I think I had better describe her right away, to get it over with. The poor lady was in her middle thirties, she had a shiny forehead, plucked eyebrows and quite simple but not unattractive features of a type that may be defined as a weak solution of Marlene Dietrich. Patting her bronze-brown bun, she led me into the parlour and we talked for a minute about the McCoo fire and the privilege of living in Ramsdale. Her very wide-set sea-green eyes had a funny way of travelling all over you, carefully avoiding your own eyes. Her smile was but a quizzical jerk of one eyebrow; and uncoiling herself from the sofa as she talked, she kept making spasmodic dashes at three ashtrays and the near fender (where lay the brown core of an apple); whereupon she would sink back again, one leg folded under her. She was, obviously, one of those women whose polished words may reflect a book club or bridge club, or any other deadly conventionality, but never her soul; women who are completely devoid of humour; women utterly indifferent at heart to the dozen or so possible subjects of a parlour conversation, but very particular about the rules of such conversations, through the sunny cellophane of which not very appetizing frustrations can be readily distinguished. I was perfectly aware that if by any wild chance I became her lodger, she would methodically proceed to do in regard to me what taking a lodger probably meant to her all along, and I would again be enmeshed in one of those tedious affairs I knew so well.

But there was no question of my settling there. I could not be happy in that type of household with bedraggled magazines on every chair and a kind of horrible hybridization between the comedy of so-called 'functional modern furniture' and the tragedy of decrepit rockers and rickety lamp tables with dead lamps. I was led upstairs, and to the left – into 'my' room. I inspected it through the mist of my utter rejection of it; but I did discern above 'my' bed René Prinet's 'Kreutzer Sonata'. And she called that servant maid's room a 'semi-studio'! Let's get out of here at once, I firmly said to myself as I pretended to deliberate over the absurdly, and ominously, low price that my wistful hostess was asking for board and bed.

Old-world politeness, however, obliged me to go on with the ordeal. We crossed the landing to the right side of the house (where 'I and Lo have our rooms' – Lo being presumably the maid), and the lodger-lover could hardly conceal a shudder when he, a very fastidious male, was granted a preview of the only bathroom, a tiny oblong between the landing and 'Lo's' room, with limp wet things overhanging the dubious tub (the question mark of a hair inside); and there were the expected coils of the rubber snake, and its complement – a pinkish cosy, coyly covering the toilet lid.

'I see you are not too favourably impressed,' said the lady letting her hand rest for a moment upon my sleeve: she combined a cool forwardness – the overflow of what I think is called 'poise' – with a shyness and sadness that caused her detached way of selecting her words to seem as unnatural as the intonation of a professor of 'speech'. 'This is not a neat household, I confess,' the doomed dear continued, 'but I assure you [she looked at my lips], you will be very comfortable, very comfortable, indeed. Let me show you the garden' (the last more brightly, with a kind of winsome toss of the voice).

Reluctantly I followed her downstairs again; then through the kitchen at the end of the hall, on the right side of the house – the side where also the dining room and the parlour were (under 'my' room, on the left, there was nothing but a garage). In the kitchen, the Negro maid, a plump youngish woman, said, as she took her large glossy black purse from the knob of the door leading to the back porch: 'I'll go now, Mrs Haze.' 'Yes, Louise,' answered Mrs Haze with a sigh. 'I'll settle with you Friday.' We passed on to a small pantry and entered the dining room, parallel to the parlour we had already admired. I noticed a white sock on the floor. With a deprecatory grunt, Mrs Haze stooped without stopping and threw it into a closet next to the pantry. We cursorily inspected a mahogany table with a fruit vase in the middle, containing nothing but the still glistening stone of one plum. I groped for the timetable I had in my pocket and surreptitiously fished it out to look as soon as possible for a train. I was still walking behind Mrs Haze through the dining room when, beyond it, there came a sudden burst of greenery – 'the piazza', sang out my leader, and then, without the least warning, a blue sea-wave swelled under my heart and, from a mat in a pool of sun, half-naked, kneeling, turning about on her knees, there was my Riviera love peering at me over dark glasses.

It was the same child – the same frail, honey-hued shoulders, the same silky supple bare back, the same chestnut head of hair. A polka-dotted black kerchief tied around her chest hid from my aging ape eyes, but not from the gaze of young memory, the juvenile breasts I had fondled one immortal day. And, as if I were the fairy-tale nurse of some little princess (lost, kidnapped, discovered in gypsy rags through which her nakedness smiled at the king and his hounds), I recognized the tiny dark-brown mole on her side. With awe and delight (the king crying for joy, the trumpets blaring, the nurse drunk) I saw again her lovely indrawn abdomen where my southbound mouth had briefly paused; and those puerile hips on which I had kissed the crenulated imprint left by the band of her shorts – that last mad immortal day behind the 'Roches Roses'. The twenty-five years I had lived since then, tapered to a palpitating point, and vanished.

I find it most difficult to express with adequate force that flash, that shiver, that impact of passionate recognition. In the course of the sun-shot moment that my glance slithered over the kneeling child (her eyes blinking over those stern dark spectacles – the little Herr Doktor who was to cure me of all my aches) while I passed by her in my adult disguise (a great big handsome hunk of movieland manhood), the vacuum of my soul managed to suck in every detail of her bright beauty, and these I checked against the features of my dead bride. A little later, of course, she, this *nouvelle*, this Lolita, *my* Lolita, was to eclipse completely her prototype. All I want to stress is that my discovery of her was a fatal consequence of that 'princedom by the sea' in my tortured past. Everything between the two events was but a series of gropings and blunders, and false rudiments of joy. Everything they shared made one of them.

I have no illusions, however. My judges will regard all this as a piece of mummery on the part of a madman with a gross liking for the *fruit vert. Au fond, ça m'est bien égal.* All I know is that while the Haze woman and I went down the steps into the breathless garden, my knees were like reflections of knees in rippling water, and my lips were like sand, and—

'That was my Lo,' she said, 'and these are my lilies.'

'Yes,' I said, 'yes. They are beautiful, beautiful, beautiful!'

II

Exhibit number two is a pocket diary bound in black imitation leather, with a golden year, 1947, *en escalier*, in its upper left-hand corner. I speak of this neat product of the Blank Blank Co., Blankton, Mass, as if it were really before me. Actually, it was destroyed five years ago and what we examine now (by courtesy of a photographic memory) is but its brief materialization, a puny unfledged phoenix.

I remember the thing so exactly because I wrote it really twice. First I jotted down each entry in pencil (with many erasures and corrections) on the leaves of what is commercially known as a 'typewriter tablet'; then, I copied it out with obvious abbreviations in my smallest, most satanic, hand in the little black book just mentioned.

May 30 is a Fast Day by Proclamation in New Hampshire but not in the Carolinas. That day an epidemic of 'abdominal flu' (whatever that is) forced Ramsdale to close its schools for the summer. The reader may check the weather data in the Ramsdale *Journal* for 1947. A few days before that I moved into the Haze house, and the little diary which I now propose to reel off (much as a spy delivers by heart the contents of the note he swallowed) covers most of June.

Thursday. Very warm day. From a vantage point (bathroom window) saw Dolores taking things off a clothes line in the apple-green light behind the house. Strolled out. She wore a plaid shirt, blue jeans and sneakers. Every movement she made in the dappled sun plucked at the most secret and sensitive chord of my abject body. After a while she sat down next to me on the lower step of the back porch and began to pick up the pebbles between her feet – pebbles, my God, then a curled bit of milk-bottle glass resembling a snarling lip – and chuck them at a can. *Ping*. You can't a second time – you can't hit it – this is agony – a second time. *Ping*. Marvellous skin – oh, marvellous: tender and tanned, not the least blemish. Sundaes cause acne. The excess of the oily substance called sebum which nourishes the hair follicles of the skin creates, when too profuse, an irritation that opens the way to infection. But nymphets do not have acne although they gorge themselves on rich food. God, what agony, that silky shimmer above her temple grading into bright brown hair. And the little bone twitching at the side of her dust-powdered ankle. 'The McCoo girl? Ginny McCoo? Oh, she's a fright. And mean. And lame. Nearly died of polio.' Ping. The glistening tracery of down on her forearm. When she got up to take in the wash, I had a chance of adoring from afar the faded seat of her rolled-up jeans. Out of the lawn, bland Mrs Haze, complete with camera, grew up like a fakir's fake tree and after some heliotropic fussing – sad eyes up, glad eyes down – had the cheek of taking my picture as I sat blinking on the steps, Humbert le Bel.

Friday. Saw her going somewhere with a dark girl called Rose. Why does the way she walks – a child, mind you, a mere child! – excite me so abominably? Analyse it. A faint suggestion of turned-in toes. A kind of wiggly looseness below the knee prolonged to the end of each footfall. The ghost of a drag. Very infantile, infinitely meretricious. Humbert Humbert is also infinitely moved by the little one's slangy speech, by her harsh high voice. Later heard her volley crude nonsense at Rose across the fence. Twanging through me in a rising rhythm. Pause. 'I must go now, kiddo.'

Saturday. (Beginning perhaps amended.) I know it is madness to keep this journal but it gives me a strange thrill to do so; and only a loving wife could decipher my microscopic script. Let me state with a sob that today my L. was sun-bathing on the so-called 'piazza', but her mother and some other women were around all the time. Of course, I might have sat there in the rocker and pretended to read. Playing safe, I kept away, for I was afraid that the horrible, insane, ridiculous and pitiful tremor that palsied me might prevent me from making my *entrée* with any semblance of casualness.

Sunday. Heat ripple still with us; a most favonian week. This time I took up a strategic position, with obese newspaper and new pipe, in the piazza rocker *before* L. arrived. To my intense disappointment she came with her mother, both in two-piece bathing suits, black, as new as my pipe. My darling, my sweetheart stood for a moment near me – wanted the funnies – and she smelt almost exactly like the other one, the Riviera one, but more intensely so, with rougher overtones – a torrid odour that at once set my manhood astir – but she had already yanked out of me the coveted section and retreated to her mat near her phocine mamma. There my beauty lay down on her stomach, showing me, showing the thousand eyes wide open in my eyed blood, her slightly raised shoulder blades, and the bloom along the incurvation of her spine, and the swellings of her tense narrow nates clothed in black, and the seaside of her schoolgirl thighs. Silently, the seventh-grader enjoyed her green-red-blue comics. She was the loveliest nymphet green-red-blue Priap himself could think up. As I looked on, through prismatic layers of light, dry-lipped, focusing my lust and rocking slightly under my newspaper, I felt that my perception of her, if properly concentrated upon, might be sufficient to have me attain a beggar's bliss immediately; but, like some predator that prefers a moving prey to a motionless one, I planned to have this pitiful attainment coincide with one of the various girlish movements she made now and then as she read, such as trying to scratch the middle of her back and revealing a stippled armpit – but fat Haze suddenly spoiled everything by turning to me and asking me for a light, and starting a make-believe conversation about a fake book by some popular fraud.

Monday. Delectatio morosa. I spend my doleful days in dumps and dolours. We (mother Haze, Dolores and I) were to go to Our Glass Lake this afternoon, and bathe, and bask; but a nacreous morn degenerated at noon into rain, and Lo made a scene.

The median age of pubescence for girls has been found to be thirteen years and nine months in New York and Chicago. The age varies for individuals from ten, or earlier, to seventeen. Virginia was not quite fourteen when Harry Edgar possessed her. He gave her lessons in algebra. *Je m'imagine cela.* They spent their honeymoon at Petersburg, Fla. 'Monsieur Poe-poe', as that boy in one of Monsieur Humbert Humbert's classes in Paris called the poet-poet.

I have all the characteristics which, according to writers on the sex interests of children, start the responses stirring in a little girl: clean-cut jaw, muscular hand, deep sonorous voice, broad shoulder. Moreover, I am said to resemble some crooner or actor chap on whom Lo has a crush.

Tuesday. Rain. Lake of the Rains. Mamma out shopping. L., I knew, was somewhere quite near. In result of some stealthy manoeuvring, I came across her in her mother's bedroom. Prying her left eye open to get rid of a speck of something. Checked frock. Although I do love that intoxicating brown fragrance of hers, I really think she should wash her hair once in a while. For a moment, we were both in the same warm green bath of the mirror that reflected the top of a poplar with us in the sky. Held her roughly by the shoulders, then tenderly by the temples, and turned her about. 'It's right there,' she said, 'I can feel it.' 'Swiss peasant would use the tip of her tongue.' 'Lick it out?' 'Yeth. Shly try?' 'Sure,' she said. Gently I pressed my quivering sting along her rolling salty eyeball. 'Goody-goody,' she said nictating. 'It *is* gone.' 'Now the other?' 'You dope,' she began, 'there is noth—' but here she noticed the pucker of my approaching lips. 'Okay,' she said co-operatively, and bending toward her warm upturned russet face sombre Humbert pressed his mouth to her fluttering eyelid. She laughed, and brushed past me out of the room. My heart seemed everywhere at once. Never in my life – not even when fondling my child-love in France – never—

Night. Never have I experienced such agony. I would like to describe her face, her ways – and I cannot, because my own desire for her blinds me when she is near, I am not used to being with nymphets, damn it. If I close my eyes I see but an immobilized fraction of her, a cinematographic still, a sudden smooth nether loveliness, as with one knee up under her tartan skirt she sits tying her shoe. 'Dolores Haze, *ne montrez pas vos zhambes*' (this is her mother who thinks she knows French).

A poet *à mes heures*, I composed a madrigal to the soot-black lashes of her pale-grey vacant eyes, to the five asymmetrical freckles of her bobbed nose, to the blonde down of her brown limbs; but I tore it up and cannot recall it today. Only in the tritest of terms (diary resumed) can I describe Lo's features: I might say her hair is auburn, and her lips as red as licked red candy, the lower one prettily plump – oh, that I were a lady writer who could have her pose naked in a naked light! But instead I am lanky, big-boned, woolly-chested Humbert Humbert, with thick black eyebrows and a queer accent, and a cesspoolful of rotting monsters behind his slow boyish smile. And neither is she the fragile child of a feminine novel. What drives me insane is the twofold nature of this nymphet – of every nymphet, perhaps; this mixture in my Lolita of tender dreamy childishness and a kind of eerie vulgarity, stemming from the snub-nosed cuteness of ads and magazine pictures, from the blurry pinkness of adolescent maidservants in the Old Country (smelling of crushed daisies and sweat); and from very young harlots disguised as children in provincial brothels; and then again, all this gets mixed up with the exquisite stainless tenderness seeping through the musk and the mud, through the dirt and the death, oh God, oh God. And what is most singular is that she, *this* Lolita, *my* Lolita, has individualized the writer's ancient lust, so that above and over everything there is – Lolita.

Wednesday. 'Look, make Mother take you and me to Our Glass Lake tomorrow.' These were the textual words said to me by my twelve-year-old flame in a voluptuous whisper, as we happened to bump into one another on the front porch, I out, she in. The reflection of the afternoon sun, a dazzling white diamond with innumerable iridescent spikes quivered on the round back of a parked car. The leafage of a voluminous elm played its mellow shadows upon the clapboard wall of the house. Two poplars shivered and shook. You could make out the formless sound of remote traffic; a child calling 'Nancy, Nan-cy!' In the house, Lolita had put on her favourite 'Little Carmen' record which I used to call 'Dwarf Conductors', making her snort with mock derision at my mock wit.

Thursday. Last night we sat on the piazza, the Haze woman, Lolita and I. Warm dusk had deepened into amorous darkness. The old girl had finished relating in great detail the plot of a movie she and L. had seen sometime in the winter. The boxer had fallen extremely low when he met the good old priest (who had been a boxer himself in his robust youth and could still slug a sinner). We sat on cushions heaped on the floor, and L. was between the woman and me (she had squeezed herself in, the pet). In my turn, I launched upon a hilarious account of my arctic adventures. The muse of invention handed me a rifle and I shot a white bear who sat down and said: Ah! All the while I was acutely aware of L.'s nearness and as I spoke I gestured in the merciful dark and took advantage of those invisible gestures of mine to touch her hand, her shoulder and a ballerina of wool and gauze which she played with and kept sticking into my lap; and finally, when I had completely enmeshed my glowing darling in this weave of ethereal caresses, I dared stroke her bare leg along the gooseberry fuzz of her shin, and I chuckled at my own jokes, and trembled, and concealed my tremors, and once or twice felt with my rapid lips the warmth of her hair as I treated her to a quick nuzzling, humorous aside and caressed her plaything. She, too, fidgeted a good deal so that finally her mother told her sharply to quit it and sent the doll flying into the dark and I laughed and addressed myself to Haze across Lo's legs to let my hand creep up my nymphet's thin back and feel her skin through her boy's shirt.

But I knew it was all hopeless, and was sick with longing, and my clothes felt miserably tight, and I was almost glad when her mother's quiet voice announced in the dark: 'And now we all think that Lo should go to bed.' 'I think you stink,' said Lo. 'Which means there will be no picnic tomorrow,' said Haze. 'This is a free country,' said Lo. When angry Lo with a Bronx cheer had gone, I stayed on from sheer inertia, while Haze smoked her tenth cigarette of the evening and complained of Lo.

She had been spiteful, if you please, at the age of one, when she used to throw her toys out of her crib so that her poor mother should keep picking them up, the villainous infant! Now, at twelve, she was a regular pest, said Haze. All she wanted from life was to be one day a strutting and prancing baton twirler or a jitterbug. Her grades were poor, but she was better adjusted in her new school than in Pisky (Pisky was the Haze home town in the Middle West. The Ramsdale house was her late mother-in-law's. They had moved to Ramsdale less than two years ago). 'Why was she unhappy there?' 'Oh,' said Haze, 'poor me should know, I went through that when *I* was a kid: boys twisting one's arm, banging into one with loads of books, pulling one's hair, hurting one's breasts, flipping one's skirt. Of course, moodiness is a common concomitant of growing up, but Lo exaggerates. Sullen and evasive. Rude and defiant. Stuck Viola, an Italian schoolmate, in the seat with a fountain pen. Know what I would like? If you, monsieur, happened to be still here in the fall, I'd ask you to help her with her homework – you seem to know everything, geography, mathematics, French.' 'Oh, everything,' answered monsieur. 'That means,' said Haze quickly, 'you'll *be* here!' I wanted to shout that I would stay on eternally if only I could hope to caress now and then my incipient pupil. But I was wary of Haze. So I just grunted and stretched my limbs non-concomitantly (*le mot juste*) and presently went up to my room. The woman, however, was evidently not prepared to call it a day. I was already lying upon my cold bed, both hands pressing to my face Lolita's fragrant ghost, when I heard my indefatigable landlady creeping stealthily up to my door to whisper through it – just to make sure, she said, I was through with the Glance and Gulp magazine I had borrowed the other day. From her room Lo yelled *she* had it. We are quite a lending library in this house, thunder of God.

Friday. I wonder what my academic publishers would say if I were to quote in my textbook Ronsard's '*la vermeillette fente*' or Remy Belleau's '*un petit mont feutré de mousse délicate, tracé sur le milieu d'un fillet escarlatte*' and so forth. I shall probably have another breakdown if I stay any longer in this house, under the strain of this intolerable temptation, by the side of my darling – my darling – my life and my bride. Has she already been initiated by mother nature to the Mystery of the Menarche? Bloated feeling. The Curse of the Irish. Falling from the roof. Grandma is visiting. 'Mr Uterus [I quote from a girls' magazine] starts to build a thick soft wall on the chance a possible baby may have to be bedded down there.' The tiny madman in his padded cell.

Incidentally: if I ever commit a serious murder. . . . Mark the 'if'. The urge should be something more than the kind of thing that happened to me with Valeria. Carefully mark that *then* I was rather inept. If and when you wish to sizzle me to death, remember that only a spell of insanity could ever give me the simple energy to be a brute (all this amended, perhaps). Sometimes I attempted to kill in my dreams. But do you know what happens? For instance I hold a gun. For instance I aim at a bland, quietly interested enemy. Oh, I press the trigger all right, but one bullet after another feebly drops on the floor from the sheepish muzzle. In those dreams, my only thought is to conceal the fiasco from my foe, who is slowly growing annoyed.

At dinner tonight the old cat said to me with a sidelong gleam of motherly mockery directed at Lo (I had just been describing, in a flippant vein, the delightful little toothbrush moustache I had not quite decided to grow): 'Better don't, if somebody is not to go absolutely dotty.' Instantly Lo pushed her plate of boiled fish away, all but knocking her milk over, and bounced out of the dining room. 'Would it bore you very much,' quoth Haze, 'to come with us tomorrow for a swim in Our Glass Lake if Lo apologizes for her manners?'

Later, I heard a great banging of doors and other sounds coming from quaking caverns where the two rivals were having a ripping row.

She has not apologized. The lake is out. It might have been fun.

Saturday. For some days already I had been leaving the door ajar, while I wrote in my room; but only today did the trap work. With a good deal of additional fidgeting, shuffling, scraping – to disguise her embarrassment at visiting me without having been called – Lo came in and after pottering around, became interested in the nightmare curlicues I had penned on a sheet of paper. Oh no: they were not the outcome of a bellelettrist's inspired pause between two paragraphs; they were the hideous hieroglyphics (which she could not decipher) of my fatal lust. As she bent her brown curls over the desk at which I was sitting, Humbert the Hoarse put his arm around her in a miserable imitation of blood-relationship; and still studying, somewhat shortsightedly, the piece of paper she held, my innocent little visitor slowly sank to a half-sitting position upon my knee. Her adorable profile, parted lips, warm hair were some three inches from my bared eyetooth; and I felt the heat of her limbs through her rough tomboy clothes. All at once I knew I could kiss her throat or the wick of her mouth with perfect impunity. I knew she would let me do so, and even close her eyes as Hollywood teaches. A double vanilla with hot fudge – hardly more unusual than that. I cannot tell my learned reader (whose eyebrows, I suspect, have by now travelled all the way to the back of his bald head), I cannot tell him how the knowledge came to me; perhaps my ape-ear had unconsciously caught some slight change in the rhythm of her respiration – for now she was not really looking at my scribble, but waiting with curiosity and composure – oh, my limpid nymphet! – for the glamorous lodger to do what he was dying to do. A modern child, an avid reader of movie magazines, an expert in dream-slow close-ups, might not think it too strange, I guessed, if a handsome, intensely virile grownup friend – too late. The house was suddenly vibrating with voluble Louise's voice telling Mrs Haze who had just come home about a dead something she and Leslie Tomson had found in the basement, and little Lolita was not one to miss such a tale.

Sunday. Changeful, bad-tempered, cheerful, awkward, graceful with the tart grace of her coltish subteens, excruciatingly desirable from head to foot (all New England for a lady-writer's pen!), from the black ready-made bow and bobby pins holding her hair in place to the little scar on the lower part of her neat calf (where a roller-skater kicked her in Pisky), a couple of inches above her rough white sock. Gone with her mother to the Hamiltons – a birthday party or something. Full-skirted gingham frock. Her little doves seem well formed already. Precocious pet!

Monday. Rainy morning. '*Ces matins gris si doux. . . .*' My white pyjamas have a lilac design on the back. I am like one of those inflated pale spiders you see in old gardens. Sitting in the middle of a luminous web and giving little jerks to this or that strand. *My* web is spread all over the house as I listen from my chair where I sit like a wily wizard. Is Lo in her room? Gently I tug on the silk. She is not. Just heard the toilet paper cylinder make its staccato sound as it is turned; and no footfalls has my outflung filament traced from the bathroom back to her room. Is she still brushing her teeth (the only sanitary act Lo performs with real zest)? No. The bathroom door has just slammed, so one has to feel elsewhere about the house for the beautiful warm-coloured prey. Let us have a strand of silk descend the stairs. I satisfy myself by this means that she is not in the kitchen – not banging the refrigerator door or screeching at her detested mamma (who, I suppose, is enjoying her third, cooing and subduedly mirthful, telephone conversation of the morning). Well, let us grope and hope. Ray-like, I glide in through to the parlour and find the radio silent (and mamma still talking to Mrs Chatfield or Mrs Hamilton, very softly, flushed, smiling, cupping the telephone with her free hand, denying by implication that she denies those amusing rumours, rumour, roomer, whispering intimately, as she never does, the clear-cut lady, in face to face talk). So my nymphet is not in the house at all! Gone! What I thought was a prismatic weave turns out to be but an old grey cobweb, the house is empty, is dead. And then comes Lolita's soft sweet chuckle through my half-open door, 'Don't tell Mother but I've eaten *all* your bacon.' Gone when I scuttle out of my room. Lolita, where are you? My breakfast tray, lovingly prepared by my landlady, leers at me toothlessly, ready to be taken in. Lola, Lolita!

Tuesday. Clouds again interfered with that picnic on that unattainable lake. Is it Fate scheming. Yesterday I tried on before the mirror a new pair of bathing trunks.

Wednesday. In the afternoon, Haze (common-sensical shoes, tailor-made dress), said she was driving downtown to buy a present for a friend of a friend of hers, and would I please come too because I have such a wonderful taste in textures and perfumes. 'Choose your favourite seduction,' she purred. What could Humbert, being in the perfume business, do? She had me cornered between the front porch and her car. 'Hurry up,' she said as I laboriously doubled up my large body in order to crawl in (still desperately devising a means of escape). She had started the engine, and was genteelly swearing at a backing and turning truck in front that had just brought old invalid Miss Opposite a brand new wheel chair, when my Lolita's sharp voice came from the parlour window: 'You! Where are you going? I'm coming too! Wait!' 'Ignore her,' yelped Haze (killing the motor); alas for my fair driver; Lo was already pulling at the door on my side. 'This is intolerable,' began Haze; but Lo had scrambled in, shivering with glee. 'Move your bottom, you,' said Lo. 'Lo!' cried Haze (sideglancing at me, hoping I would throw rude Lo out). 'And behold,' said Lo (not for the first time), as she jerked back, as the car leapt forward. 'It is intolerable,' said Haze, violently getting into second, 'that a child should be so ill-mannered. And so very persevering. When she knows she is unwanted. And needs a bath.'

My knuckles lay against the child's blue jeans. She was barefooted; her toenails showed remnants of cherry-red polish and there was a bit of adhesive tape across her big toe; and, God, what would I not have given to kiss then and there those delicate-boned, long-toed, monkeyish feet! Suddenly her hand slipped into mine and without our chaperon's seeing, I held, and stroked, and squeezed that little hot paw, all the way to the store. The wings of the driver's Marlenesque nose shone, having shed or burned up their ration of powder, and she kept up an elegant monologue anent the local traffic, and smiled in profile, and pouted in profile, and beat her painted lashes in profile, while I prayed we would never get to that store, but we did.

I have nothing else to report, save, *primo*: that big Haze had little Haze sit behind on our way home, and *secundo*: that the lady decided to keep Humbert's Choice for the backs of her own shapely ears.

Thursday. We are paying with hail and gale for the tropical beginning of the month. In a volume of the *Young People's Encyclopaedia*, I found a map of the States that a child's pencil had started copying out on a sheet of lightweight paper, upon the other side of which, counter to the unfinished outline of Florida and the Gulf, there was a mimeographed list of names referring, evidently, to her class at the Ramsdale School. It is a poem I know already by heart.

Angel, Grace
Austin, Floyd
Beale, Jack
Beale, Mary
Buck, Daniel
Byron, Marguerite
Campbell, Alice
Carmine, Rose
Chatfield, Phyllis

Clarke, Gordon
Cowan, John
Cowan, Marion
Duncan, Walter
Falter, Ted
Fantazia, Stella
Flashman, Irving
Fox, George
Glave, Mabel
Goodale, Donald
Green, Lucinda
Hamilton, Mary Rose
Haze, Dolores
Honeck, Rosaline
Knight, Kenneth
McCoo, Virginia
McCrystal, Vivian
McFate, Aubrey
Miranda, Anthony
Miranda, Viola
Rosato, Emil
Schlenker, Lena
Scott, Donald
Sheridan, Agnes
Sherva, Oleg
Smith, Hazel
Talbot, Edgar
Talbot, Edwin
Wain, Lull
Williams, Ralph
Windmuller, Louise

A poem, a poem, forsooth! So strange and sweet was it to discover this 'Haze, Dolores' (she!) in its special bower of names, with its bodyguard of roses – a fairy princess between her two maids of honour. I am trying to analyse the spine-thrill of delight it gives me, this name among all those others. What is it that excites me almost to tears (hot, opalescent, thick tears that poets and lovers shed)? What is it? The tender anonymity of this name with its formal veil ('Dolores') and that abstract transposition of first name and surname, which is like a pair of new pale gloves or a mask? Is 'mask' the keyword? Is it because there is always delight in the semi-translucent mystery, the flowing charshaf, through which the flesh and the eye you alone are elected to know smile in passing at you alone? Or is it because I can imagine so well the rest of the colourful classroom around my dolorous and hazy darling: Grace and her ripe pimples; Ginny and her lagging leg; Gordon, the haggard masturbator; Duncan, the foul-smelling clown; nail-biting Agnes; Viola, of the blackheads and the bouncing bust; pretty Rosaline; dark Mary Rose; adorable Stella, who has let strangers touch her; Ralph, who bullies and steals; Irving, for whom I am sorry. And there she is there, lost in the middle, gnawing a pencil, detested by teachers, all the boys' eyes on her hair and neck, *my* Lolita.

Friday. I long for some terrific disaster. Earthquake. Spectacular explosion. Her mother is messily but instantly and permanently eliminated, along with everybody else for miles around. Lolita whimpers in my arms. A free man, I enjoy her among the ruins. Her surprise, my explanations, demonstrations, ullulations. Idle and idiotic fancies! A brave Humbert would have played with her most disgustingly (yesterday, for instance, when she was again in my room to show me her drawings, school-artware); he might have bribed her – and got away with it. A simpler and more practical fellow would have soberly stuck to various commercial substitutes – if you know where to go, I don't. Despite my manly looks, I am horribly timid. My romantic soul gets all clammy and shivery at the thought of running into some awful indecent unpleasantness. Those ribald sea monsters. '*Mais allez-y, allez-y!*' Annabel skipping on one foot to get into her shorts, I seasick with rage, trying to screen her.

Same date, later, quite late. I have turned on the light to take down a dream. It had an evident antecedent. Haze at dinner had benevolently proclaimed that since the weather bureau promised a sunny weekend we would go to the lake Sunday after church. As I lay in bed, erotically musing before trying to go to sleep, I thought of a final scheme how to profit by the picnic to come. I was aware that mother Haze hated my darling for her being sweet on me. So I planned my lake day with a view to satisfying the mother. To her alone would I talk; but at some appropriate moment I would say I had left my wrist watch or my sunglasses in that glade yonder – and plunge with my nymphet into the wood. Reality at this juncture withdrew, and the Quest for the Glasses turned into a quiet little orgy with a singularly knowing, cheerful, corrupt and compliant Lolita behaving as reason knew she could not possibly behave. At 3 a.m. I swallowed a sleeping pill, and presently, a dream that was not a sequel but a parody revealed to me, with a kind of meaningful clarity, the lake I had never yet visited: it was glazed over with a sheet of emerald ice, and a pockmarked Eskimo was trying in vain to break it with a pickaxe, although imported mimosas and oleanders flowered on its gravelly banks. I am sure Dr Blanche Schwar mann would have paid me a sack of schillings for adding such a libidream to her files. Unfortunately, the rest of it was frankly eclectic. Big Haze and little Haze rode on horseback around the lake, and I rode too, dutifully bobbing up and down, bowlegs astraddle although there was no horse between them, only elastic air – one of those little omissions due to the absent-mindedness of the dream agent.

Saturday. My heart is still thumping. I still squirm and emit low moans of remembered embarrassment.

Dorsal view. Glimpse of shiny skin between T-shirt and white gym shorts. Bending, over a window sill, in the act of tearing off leaves from a poplar outside while engrossed in torrential talk with a newspaper boy below (Kenneth Knight, I suspect) who had just propelled the Ramsdale *Journal* with a very precise thud on to the porch. I began creeping up to her – 'crippling' up to her, as pantomimists say. My arms and legs were convex surfaces between which – rather than upon which – I slowly progressed by some neutral means of locomotion: Humbert the Wounded Spider. I must have taken hours to reach her: I seemed to see her through the wrong end of a telescope, and toward her taut little rear I moved like some paralytic, on soft distorted limbs, in terrible concentration. At last I was right behind her when I had the unfortunate idea of blustering a trifle – shaking her by the scruff of the neck and that sort of thing to cover my real *manège,* and she said in a shrill brief whine: 'Cut it out!' – most coarsely, the little wench, and with a ghastly grin Humbert the Humble beat a gloomy retreat while she went on wisecracking street-ward.

But now listen to what happened next. After lunch I was reclining in a low chair trying to read. Suddenly two deft little hands were over my eyes: she had crept up behind as if re-enacting, in a ballet sequence, my morning manoeuvre. Her fingers were a luminous crimson as they tried to blot out the sun, and she uttered hiccups of laughter and jerked this way and that as I stretched my arm sideways and backwards without otherwise changing my recumbent position. My hand swept over her agile giggling legs, and the book like a sleigh left my lap, and Mrs Haze strolled up and said indulgently: 'Just slap her hard if she interferes with your scholarly meditations. How I love this garden [no exclamation mark in her tone]. Isn't it divine in the sun [no question mark either].' And with a sigh of feigned content, the obnoxious lady sank down on the grass and looked up at the sky as she leaned back on her splayed-out hands, and presently an old grey tennis ball bounced over her, and L.'s voice came from the house haughtily: '*Pardonnez*, Mother. I was not aiming at *you*.' Of course not, my hot downy darling.

12

This proved to be the last of twenty entries or so. It will be seen from them that for all the devil's inventiveness, the scheme remained daily the same. First he would tempt me – and then thwart me, leaving me with a dull pain in the very root of my being. I knew exactly what I wanted to do, and how to do it, without impinging on a child's chastity; after all, I had had *some* experience in my life of pederosis; had visually possessed dappled nymphets in parks; had wedged my wary and bestial way into the hottest, most crowded corner of a city bus full of strap- hanging schoolchildren. But for almost three weeks I had been interrupted in all my pathetic machinations. The agent of these interruptions was usually the Haze woman (who, as the reader will mark, was more afraid of Lo's deriving some pleasure from me than of my enjoying Lo). The passion I had developed for that nymphet – for the first nymphet in my life that could be reached at last by my awkward, aching, timid claws – would have certainly landed me again in a sanatorium, had not the devil realized that I was to be granted some relief if he wanted to have me as a plaything for some time longer.

The reader has also marked the curious Mirage of the Lake. It would have been logical on the part of Aubrey McFate (as I would like to dub that devil of mine) to arrange a small treat for me on the promised beach, in the presumed forest. Actually, the promise Mrs Haze had made was a fraudulent one: she had not told me that Mary Rose Hamilton (a dark little beauty in her own right) was to come too, and that the two nymphets would be whispering apart, and playing apart, and having a good time all by themselves, while Mrs Haze and her handsome lodger conversed sedately in the semi-nude, far from prying eyes. Incidentally, eyes did pry and tongues did wag. How queer life is! We hasten to alienate the very fates we intended to woo. Before my actual arrival, my landlady had planned to have an old spinster, a Miss Phalen, whose mother had been cook in Mrs Haze's family, come to stay in the house with Lolita and me, while Mrs Haze, a career girl at heart, sought some suitable job in the nearest city. Mrs Haze had seen the whole situation very clearly: the bespectacled, round-backed Herr Humbert coming with his Central-European trunks to gather dust in his corner behind a heap of old books; the unloved ugly little daughter firmly supervised by Miss Phalen who had already once had my Lo under her buzzard wing (Lo recalled that 1944 summer with an indignant shudder); and Mrs Haze herself engaged as a receptionist in a great elegant city. But a not too complicated event interfered with that programme. Miss Phalen broke her hip in Savannah, Ga., on the very day I arrived in Ramsdale.

13

The Sunday after the Saturday already described proved to be as bright as the weatherman had predicted. When putting the breakfast things back on the chair outside my room for my good landlady to remove at her convenience, I gleaned the following situation by listening from the landing across which I had softly crept to the banisters in my old bedroom slippers – the only old thing about me.

There had been another row. Mrs Hamilton had telephoned that her daughter 'was running a temperature'. Mrs Haze informed *her* daughter that the picnic would have to be postponed. Hot little Haze informed big cold Haze that, if so, she would not go with her to church. Mother said 'very well' and left.

I had come out on the landing straight after shaving, soapy-earlobed, still in my white pyjamas with the cornflower blue (not the lilac) design on the back; I now wiped off the soap, perfumed my hair and armpits, slipped on a purple silk dressing gown, and, humming nervously, went down the stairs in quest of Lo.

I want my learned readers to participate in the scene I am

about to replay; I want them to examine its every detail and see for themselves how careful, how chaste, the whole wine-sweet event is if viewed with what my lawyer has called, in a private talk we have had, 'impartial sympathy'. So let us get started. I have a difficult job before me.

Main character: Humbert the Hummer. Time: Sunday morning in June. Place: sunlit living room. Props: old, candy-striped davenport, magazines, phonograph, Mexican knick-knacks (the late Mr Harold E. Haze – God bless the good man – had engendered my darling at the siesta hour in a blue-washed room, on a honeymoon trip to Vera Cruz, and mementoes, among these Dolores, were all over the place). She wore that day a pretty print dress that I had seen on her once before, ample in the skirt, tight in the bodice, short-sleeved, pink, checkered with darker pink, and, to complete the colour scheme, she had painted her lips and was holding in her hollowed hands a beautiful, banal, Eden-red apple. She was not shod, however, for church. And her white Sunday purse lay discarded near the phonograph.

My heart beat like a drum as she sat down, cool skirt ballooning, subsiding, on the sofa next to me, and played with her glossy fruit. She tossed it up into the sun-dusted air, and caught it – it made a cupped polished *plop*.

Humbert Humbert intercepted the apple.

'Give it back,' she pleaded, showing the marbled flush of her palms. I produced Delicious. She grasped it and bit into it, and my heart was like snow under thin crimson skin, and with the monkeyish nimbleness that was so typical of that American nymphet, she snatched out of my abstract grip the magazine I had opened (pity no film has recorded the curious pattern, the monogrammic linkage of our simultaneous or overlapping moves). Rapidly, hardly hampered by the disfigured apple she held, Lo flipped violently through the pages in search of something she wished Humbert to see. Found it at last. I faked interest by bringing my head so close that her hair touched my temple and her arm brushed my cheek as she wiped her lips with her wrist. Because of the burnished mist through which I peered at the picture, I was slow in reacting to it, and her bare knees rubbed and knocked impatiently against each other. Dimly there came into view: a surrealist painter relaxing, supine, on a beach, and near him, likewise supine, a plaster replica of the Venus di Milo, half-buried in sand. Picture of the Week, said the legend. I whisked the whole obscene thing away. Next moment, in a sham effort to retrieve it, she was all over me. Caught her by her thin knobby wrist. The magazine escaped to the floor like a flustered fowl. She twisted herself free, recoiled, and lay back in the righthand corner of the davenport. Then, with perfect simplicity, the impudent child extended her legs across my lap.

By this time I was in a state of excitement bordering on insanity; but I also had the cunning of the insane. Sitting there, on the sofa, I managed to attune, by a series of stealthy movements, my masked lust to her guileless limbs. It was no easy matter to divert the little maiden's attention while I performed the obscure adjustments necessary for the success of the trick. Talking fast, lagging behind my own breath, catching up with it, mimicking a sudden toothache to explain the breaks in my patter – and all the while keeping a maniac's inner eye on my distant golden goal, I cautiously increased the magic friction that was doing away, in an illusional, if not factual, sense, with the physically irremovable, but psychologically very friable texture of the material divide (pyjamas and robe) between the weight of two sunburnt legs, resting athwart my lap, and the hidden tumour of an unspeakable passion. Having, in the course of my patter, hit upon something nicely mechanical, I recited, garbling them slightly, the words of a foolish song that was then popular – O my Carmen, my little Carmen, something, something, those something nights, and the stars, and the cars, and the bars, and the barmen; I kept repeating this automatic stuff and holding her under its spell (special because of the garbling), and all the while I was mortally afraid that some act of God might interrupt me, might remove the golden load in the sensation of which all my being seemed concentrated, and this anxiety forced me to work, for the first minute or so, more hastily than was consensual with deliberately modulated enjoyment. The stars that sparkled, and the cars that parkled, and the bars, and the barmen, were presently taken over by her; her voice stole and corrected the tune I had been mutilating. She was musical and apple-sweet. Her legs twitched a little as they lay across my live lap; I stroked them; there she lolled in the right-hand corner, almost asprawl, Lola the bobbysoxer, devouring her immemorial fruit, singing through its juice, losing her slipper, rubbing the heel of her slipperless foot in its sloppy anklet, against the pile of old magazines heaped on my left on the sofa – and every movement she made, every shuffle and ripple, helped me to conceal and to improve the secret system of tactile correspondence between beast and beauty – between my gagged, bursting beast and the beauty of her dimpled body in its innocent cotton frock.

Under my glancing fingertips I felt the minute hairs bristle ever so slightly along her shins. I lost myself in the pungent but healthy heat which like summer haze hung about little Haze. Let her stay, let her stay. . . . As she strained to chuck the core of her abolished apple into the fender, her young weight, her shameless innocent shanks and round bottom, shifted in my tense, tortured, surreptitiously labouring lap; and all of a sudden a mysterious change came over my senses. I entered a plane of being where nothing mattered, save the infusion of joy brewed within my body. What had begun as a delicious distension of my innermost roots became a glowing tingle which *now* had reached that state of absolute security, confidence and reliance not found elsewhere in conscious life. With the deep hot sweetness thus established and well on its way to the ultimate convulsion, I felt I could slow down in order to prolong the glow. Lolita had been safely solipsized. The implied sun pulsated in the supplied poplars; we were fantastically and divinely alone; I watched her, rosy, gold-dusted, beyond the veil of my controlled delight, unaware of it, alien to it, and the sun was on her lips, and her lips were apparently still forming the words of the Carmen-barmen ditty that no longer reached my consciousness. Everything was now ready. The nerves of pleasure had been laid bare. The corpuscles of Krauze were entering the phase of frenzy. The least pressure would suffice to set all paradise loose. I had ceased to be Humbert the Hound, the sad-eyed degenerate cur clasping the boot that would presently kick him away. I was above the tribulations of ridicule, beyond the possibilities of retribution. In my self-made seraglio, I was a radiant and robust Turk, deliberately, in the full consciousness of his freedom, postponing the moment of actually enjoying the youngest and frailest of his slaves. Suspended on the brink of that voluptuous abyss (a nicety of physiological equipoise comparable to certain techniques in the arts) I kept repeating chance words after her – barmen, alarmin', my charmin', my carmen, ahmen, ahahamen – as one talking and laughing in his sleep while my happy hand crept up her sunny leg as far as the shadow of decency allowed. The day before she had collided with the heavy chest in the hall and – 'Look, look!' – I gasped – 'look what you've done, what you've done to yourself, ah, look'; for there was, I swear, a yellowish-violet bruise on her lovely nymphet thigh which my huge hairy hand massaged and slowly enveloped – and because of her very perfunctory underthings, there seemed to be nothing to prevent my muscular thumb from reaching the hot hollow of her groin – just as you might tickle and caress a giggling child – just that – and: 'Oh, it's nothing at all,' she cried with a sudden shrill note in her voice, and she wriggled, and squirmed, and threw her head back, and her teeth rested on her glistening underlip as she half-turned away, and my moaning mouth, gentlemen of the jury, almost reached her bare neck, while I crushed out against her left buttock the last throb of the longest ecstasy man or monster had ever known.

Immediately afterward (as if we had been struggling and now my grip had eased) she rolled off the sofa and jumped to her feet – to her foot, rather – in order to attend to the formidably loud telephone that may have been ringing for ages as far as I was concerned. There she stood and blinked, cheeks aflame, hair awry, her eyes passing over me as lightly as they did over the furniture, and as she listened or spoke (to her mother who was telling her to come to lunch with her at the Chatfields – neither Lo nor Hum knew yet what busybody Haze was plotting), she kept tapping the edge of the table with the slipper she held in her hand. Blessed be the Lord, she had noticed nothing!

With a handkerchief of multicoloured silk, on which her listening eyes rested in passing, I wiped the sweat off my forehead, and, immersed in an euphoria of release, rearranged my royal robes. She was still at the telephone, haggling with her mother (wanted to be fetched by car, my little Carmen) when, singing louder and louder, I swept up the stairs and set a deluge of steaming water roaring into the tub.

At this point I may as well give the words of that song-hit in full – to the best of my recollection at least – I don't think I ever had it right. Here goes.

O my Carmen, my little Carmen!
Something, something those something nights,
And the stars, and the cars, and the bars, and the barmen –
And, O my charmin', our dreadful fights.
And the something town where so gaily, arm in
Arm, we went, and our final row,
And the gun I killed you with, O my Carmen,
The gun I am holding now.

(Drew his ·32 automatic, I guess, and put a bullet through his moll's eye.)

14

I had lunch in town – had not been so hungry for years. The house was still Lo-less when I strolled back. I spent the afternoon musing, scheming, blissfully digesting my experience of the morning.

I felt proud of myself. I had stolen the honey of a spasm without impairing the morals of a minor. Absolutely no harm done. The conjurer had poured milk, molasses, foaming champagne into a young lady's new white purse; and lo, the purse was intact. Thus had I delicately constructed my ignoble, ardent, sinful dream; and still Lolita was safe – and I was safe. What I had madly possessed was not she, but my own creation, another, fanciful Lolita – perhaps, more real than Lolita; overlapping, encasing her; floating between me and her, and having no will, no consciousness – indeed, no life of her own.

The child knew nothing. I had done nothing to her. And nothing prevented me from repeating a performance that affected her as little as if she were a photographic image rippling upon a screen and I a humble hunchback abusing myself in the dark. The afternoon drifted on and on, in ripe silence, and the sappy tall trees seemed to be in the know; and desire, even stronger than before, began to afflict me again. Let her come soon, I prayed, addressing a lone God, and while mamma is in the kitchen, let a repetition of the davenport scene be staged, please, I adore her so horribly.

No: 'horribly' is the wrong word. The elation with which the vision of new delights filled me was not horrible but pathetic. I qualify it as pathetic. Pathetic – because despite the insatiable fire of my venereal appetite, I intended, with the most fervent force and foresight, to protest the purity of that twelve-year-old child.

And now see how I was repaid for my pains. No Lolita came home – she had gone with the Chatfields to a movie. The table was laid with more elegance than usual: candlelight, if you please. In this mawkish aura, Mrs Haze gently touched the silver on both sides of her plate as if touching piano keys, and smiled down on her empty plate (was on a diet), and said she hoped I liked the salad (recipe lifted from a woman's magazine). She hoped I liked the cold cuts, too. It had been a perfect day. Mrs Chatfield was a lovely person. Phyllis, her daughter, was going to a summer camp tomorrow. For three weeks. Lolita, it was decided, would go Thursday. Instead of waiting till July, as had been initially planned. And stay there after Phyllis had left. Till school began. A pretty prospect, my heart.

Oh, how I was taken aback – for did it not mean I was losing my darling, just when I had secretly made her mine? To explain my grim mood, I had to use the same toothache I had already simulated in the morning. Must have been an enormous molar, with an abscess as big as a maraschino cherry.

'We have,' said Haze, 'an excellent dentist. Our neighbour, in fact. Dr Quilty. Uncle or cousin, I think, of the playwright. Think it will pass? Well, just as you wish. In the fall I shall have him "brace" her, as my mother used to say. It may curb Lo a little. I am afraid she has been bothering you frightfully all these days. And we are in for a couple of stormy ones before she goes. She has flatly refused to go, and I confess I left her with the Chatfields because I dreaded to face her alone just yet. The movie may mollify her. Phyllis is a very sweet girl, and there is no earthly reason for Lo to dislike her. Really, monsieur, I am very sorry about that tooth of yours. It would be so much more reasonable to let me contact Ivor Quilty first thing tomorrow morning if it still hurts. And, you know, I think a summer camp is so much healthier, and – well, it is all so much more *reasonable* as I say than to mope on a suburban lawn and use mamma's lipstick, and pursue shy studious gentlemen, and go into tantrums at the least provocation.'

'Are you sure,' I said at last, 'that she will be happy there?' (lame, lamentably lame!).

'She'd better,' said Haze. 'And it won't be all play either. The camp is run by Shirley Holmes – you know, the woman who wrote *Campfire Girl*. Camp will teach Dolores Haze to grow in many things – health, knowledge, temper. And particularly in a sense of responsibility toward other people. Shall we take these candles with us and sit for a while on the piazza, or do you want to go to bed and nurse that tooth?'

Nurse that tooth.

15

Next day they drove downtown to buy things needed for the camp: any wearable purchase worked wonders with Lo. She seemed her usual sarcastic self at dinner. Immediately afterwards, she went up to her room to plunge into the comic books acquired for rainy days at Camp Q. (they were so thoroughly sampled by Thursday that she left them behind). I too retired to my lair, and wrote letters. My plan now was to leave for the seaside and then, when school began, resume my existence in the Haze household; for I knew already that I could not live without the child. On Tuesday they went shopping again, and I was asked to answer the phone if the camp mistress rang up during their absence. She did; and a month or so later we had occasion to recall our pleasant chat. That Tuesday, Lo had her dinner in her room. She had been crying after a routine row with her mother and, as had happened on former occasions, had not wished me to see her swollen eyes: she had one of those tender complexions that after a good cry get all blurred and inflamed, and morbidly alluring. I regretted keenly her mistake about my private aesthetics, for I simply love that tinge of Botticellian pink, that raw rose about the lips, those wet, matted eyelashes; and, naturally, her bashful whim deprived me of many opportunities of specious consolation. There was, however, more to it than I thought. As we sat in the darkness of the veranda (a rude wind had put out her red candles), Haze, with a dreary laugh, said she had told Lo that her beloved Humbert thoroughly approved of the whole camp idea 'and now', added Haze, 'the child throws a fit; pretext: you and I want to get rid of her; actual reason: I told her we would exchange tomorrow for plainer stuff some much too cute night things that she bullied me into buying for her. You see, *she* sees herself as a starlet; *I* see her as a sturdy, healthy, but decidedly homely kid. This, I guess, is at the root of our troubles.'

On Wednesday I managed to waylay Lo for a few seconds: she was on the landing, in sweatshirt and green-stained white shorts, rummaging in a trunk. I said something meant to be friendly and funny but she only emitted a snort without looking at me. Desperate, dying Humbert patted her clumsily on her coccyx, and she struck him, quite painfully, with one of the late Mr Haze's shoetrees. 'Doublecrosser', she said as I crawled downstairs rubbing my arm with a great show of rue. She did not condescend to have dinner with Hum and mum: washed her hair and went to bed with her ridiculous books. And on Thursday quiet Mrs Haze drove her to Camp Q.

As greater authors than I have put it: 'Let readers imagine', etc. On second thought, I may as well give those imaginations a kick in the pants. I knew I had fallen in love with Lolita for ever; but I also knew she would not be for ever Lolita. She would be thirteen on January 1. In two years or so she would cease being a nymphet and would turn into a 'young girl', and then, into a 'college girl' – that horror of horrors. The words 'for ever' referred only to my own passion, to the eternal Lolita as reflected in my blood. The Lolita whose iliac crests had not yet flared, the Lolita that today I could touch and smell and hear and see, the Lolita of the strident voice and the rich brown hair – of the bangs and the swirls at the sides and the curls at the back, and the sticky hot neck, and the vulgar vocabulary – 'revolting', 'super', 'luscious', 'goon', 'drip' – *that* Lolita, *my* Lolita, poor Catullus would lose for ever. So how could I afford not to see her for two months of summer insomnias? Two whole months out of the two years of her remaining nymphage! Should I disguise myself as a sombre old-fashioned girl, gawky Mlle Humbert, and put up my tent on the outskirts of Camp Q. in the hope that its russet nymphets would clamour: 'Let us adopt that deep-voiced D.P.', and drag the sad, shyly smiling Berthe *au Grand Pied* to their rustic hearth. Berthe will sleep with Dolores Haze!

Idle dry dreams. Two months of beauty, two months of tenderness, would be squandered for ever, and I could do nothing about it, but nothing, *mais rien*.

One drop of rare honey, however, that Thursday did hold in its acorn cup. Haze was to drive her to the camp in the early morning. Upon sundry sounds of departure reaching me, I rolled out of bed and leaned out of the window. Under the poplars, the car was already athrob. On the sidewalk, Louise stood shading her eyes with her hand, as if the little traveller were already riding into the low morning sun. The gesture proved to be premature. 'Hurry up!' shouted Haze. My Lolita, who was half in and about to slam the car door, wind down the glass, wave to Louise and the poplars (whom and which she was never to see again), interrupted the motion of fate: she looked up – and dashed back into the house (Haze furiously calling after her). A moment later I heard my sweetheart running up the stairs. My heart expanded with such force that it almost blotted me out. I hitched up the pants of my pyjamas, flung the door open: and simultaneously Lolita arrived, in her Sunday frock, stamping, panting, and then she was in my arms, her innocent mouth melting under the ferocious pressure of dark male jaws, my palpitating darling! The next instant I heard her – alive, unraped – clatter downstairs. The motion of fate was resumed. The blonde leg was pulled in, the car door was slammed – was re-slammed – and driver Haze at the violent wheel, rubber-red lips writhing in angry, inaudible speech, swung my darling away, while unnoticed by them or Louise, old Miss Opposite, an invalid, feebly but rhythmically waved from her vined veranda.

16

The hollow of my hand was still ivory-full of Lolita – full of the feel of her pre-adolescently incurved back, that ivory-smooth, sliding sensation of her skin through the thin frock that I had worked up and down while I held her. I marched into her tumbled room, threw open the door of the closet and plunged into a heap of crumpled things that had touched her. There was particularly one pink texture, sleazy, torn, with a faintly acrid odour in the seam. I wrapped in it Humbert's huge engorged heart. A poignant chaos was welling within me – but I had to drop those things and hurriedly regain my composure, as I became aware of the maid's velvety voice calling me softly from the stairs. She had a message for me, she said; and, topping my automatic thanks with a kindly 'you're welcome', good Louise left an unstamped, curiously clean-looking letter in my shaking hand.

> This is a confession: I love you [so the letter began; and for a distorted moment I mistook its hysterical scrawl for a schoolgirl's scribble]. Last Sunday in church – bad you, who refused to come to see our beautiful new windows! – only last Sunday, my dear one, when I asked the Lord what to do about it, I was told to act as I am acting now. You see, there is no alternative. I have loved you from the minute I saw you. I am a passionate and lonely woman and you are the love of my life.

Now, my dearest, dearest, *mon cher, cher monsieur,* you have read this; now you know. So, will you please, *at once,* pack and leave. This is a landlady's order. I am dismissing a lodger. I am kicking you out. Go! Scram! *Departez!* I shall be back by dinner-time, if I do eighty both ways and don't have an accident (but what would it matter?), and I do not wish to find you in the house. Please, please, leave at once, *now,* do not even read this absurd note to the end. Go. Adieu.

The situation, *chéri,* is quite simple. Of course, I know with *absolute certainty* that I am nothing to you, nothing at all. Oh yes, you enjoy talking to me (and kidding poor me), you have grown fond of our friendly house, of the books I like, of my lovely garden, even of Lo's noisy ways – but I am nothing to you. Right? Right. Nothing to you whatever. *But* if, after reading my 'confession', you decided, in your dark romantic European way, that I am attractive enough for you to take advantage of my letter and make a pass at me, then you would be a criminal – worse than a kidnapper who rapes a child. You see, *chéri.* If you decided to stay, *if* I found you at home (which I know I won't – and that's why I am able to go on like this), the *fact* of your remaining would only mean one thing: that you want me as much as I do you: as a life-long mate; and that you are ready to link up your life with mine for ever and ever and be a father to my little girl.

Let me rave and ramble on for a teeny while more, my dearest, since I know this letter has been by now torn by you, and its pieces (illegible) in the vortex of the toilet. My dearest, *mon très, très cher,* what a world of love I have built up for you during this miraculous June! I know how reserved you are, how 'British'. Your old-world reticence, your sense of decorum may be shocked by the boldness of an American girl! You who conceal your strongest feelings must think me a shameless little idiot for throwing open my poor bruised heart like this. In years gone by, many disappointments came my way. Mr Haze was a splendid person, a sterling soul, but he happened to be twenty years my senior, and – well, let us not gossip about the past. My dearest, your curiosity must be well satisfied if you have ignored my request and read this letter to the bitter end. Never mind. Destroy it and go. Do not forget to leave the key on the desk in your room. And some scrap of address so that I could refund the twelve dollars I owe you till the end of the month. Goodbye, dear one. Pray for me – if you ever pray.

C. H.

What I present here is what I remember of the letter, and what I remember of the letter I remember verbatim (including that awful French). It was at least twice longer. I have left out a lyrical passage which I more or less skipped at the time, concerning Lolita's brother who died at two when she was four, and how much I would have liked him. Let me see what else can I say? Yes. There is just a chance that 'the vortex of the toilet' (where the letter did go) is my own matter-of-fact contribution. She probably begged me to make a special fire to consume it.

My first movement was one of repulsion and retreat. My second was like a friend's calm hand falling upon my shoulder and bidding me take my time. I did. I came out of my daze and found myself still in Lo's room. A full-page ad ripped out of a slick magazine was affixed to the wall above the bed, between a crooner's mug and the lashes of a movie actress. It represented a dark-haired young husband with a kind of drained look in his Irish eyes. He was modelling a robe by So-and-So and holding a bridge-like tray by So-and-So, with breakfast for two. The legend, by the Rev. Thomas Morell, called him a 'conquering hero'. The thoroughly conquered lady (not shown) was presumably propping herself up to receive her half of the tray. How her bed-fellow was to get under the bridge without some messy mishap was not clear. Lo had drawn a jocose arrow to the haggard lover's face and had put, in block letters: H.H. And indeed, despite a difference of a few years, the resemblance was striking. Under this was another picture, also a coloured ad. A distinguished playwright was solemnly smoking a Drome. He always smoked Dromes. The resemblance was slight. Under this was Lo's chaste bed, littered with 'comics'. The enamel had come off the bedstead, leaving black, more or less rounded, marks on the white. Having convinced myself that Louise had left, I got into Lo's bed and re-read the letter.

17

Gentlemen of the jury! I cannot swear that certain emotions pertaining to the business in hand – if I may coin an expression – had not drifted across my mind before. My mind had not retained them in any logical form or in any relation to definitely recollected occasions; but I cannot swear – let me repeat – that I had not toyed with them (to rig up yet another expression), in my dimness of thought, in my darkness of passion. There may have been times – there must have been times, if I know my Humbert – when I had brought up for detached inspection the idea of marrying a mature widow (say, Charlotte Haze) with not one relative left in the wide grey world, merely in order to have my way with her child (Lo, Lola, Lolita). I am even prepared to tell my tormentors that perhaps once or twice I had cast an appraiser's cold eye at Charlotte's coral lips and bronze hair and dangerously low neckline, and had vaguely tried to fit her into a plausible daydream. This I confess under torture. Imaginary torture, perhaps, but all the more horrible. I wish I might digress and tell you more of the *pavor nocturnus* that would rack me at night hideously after a chance term had struck me in the random readings of my boyhood, such as *peine forte et dure* (what a Genius of Pain must have invented that!) or the dreadful, mysterious, insidious words 'trauma', 'traumatic event', and 'transom'. But my tale is sufficiently incondite already.

After a while I destroyed the letter and went to my room, and ruminated and rumpled my hair, and modelled my purple robe, and moaned through clenched teeth and suddenly— Suddenly, gentlemen of the jury, I felt a Dostoevskian grin dawning (through the very grimace that twisted my lips) like a distant and terrible sun. I imagined (under conditions of new and perfect visibility) all the casual caresses her mother's husband would be able to lavish on his Lolita. I would hold her against me three times a day, every day. All my troubles would be expelled, I would be a healthy man. 'To hold thee lightly on a gentle knee and print on thy soft cheek a parent's kiss. . . .' Well-read Humbert!

Then, with all possible caution, on mental tiptoe so to speak, I conjured up Charlotte as a possible mate. By God, I could make myself bring her that economically halved grapefruit, that sugarless breakfast.

Humbert Humbert sweating in the fierce white light, and howled at, and trodden upon by sweating policemen, is now ready to make a further 'statement' (*quel mot!*) as he turns his conscience inside out and rips off its innermost lining. I did not plan to marry poor Charlotte in order to eliminate her in some vulgar, gruesome and dangerous manner such as killing her by placing five bichloride-of-mercury tablets in her preprandial sherry or anything like that; but a delicately allied, pharmacopoeial thought did tinkle in my sonorous and clouded brain. Why limit myself to the modest masked caress I had tried already? Other visions of venery presented themselves to me swaying and smiling. I saw myself administering a powerful sleeping potion to both mother and daughter so as to fondle the latter through the night with perfect impunity. The house was full of Charlotte's snore, while Lolita hardly breathed in her sleep, as still as a painted girl-child. 'Mother, I swear Kenny never even *touched* me.' 'You either lie, Dolores Haze, or it was an incubus.' No, I would not go that far.

So Humbert the Cubus schemed and dreamed – and the red sun of desire and decision (the two things that create a live world) rose higher and higher, while upon a succession of balconies a succession of libertines, sparkling glass in hand, toasted the bliss of past and future nights. Then, figuratively speaking, I shattered the glass, and boldly imagined (for I was drunk on those visions by then and underrated the gentleness of my nature) how eventually I might blackmail – no, that is too strong a word – mauvemail big Haze into letting me consort with little Haze by gently threatening the poor doting Big Dove with desertion if she tried to bar me from playing with my legal stepdaughter. In a word, before such an Amazing Offer, before such a vastness and variety of vistas, I was as helpless as Adam at the preview of early oriental history, miraged in his apple orchard.

And now take down the following important remark: the artist in me has been given the upper hand over the gentleman. It is with a great effort of will that in this memoir I have managed to tune my style to the tone of the journal that I kept when Mrs Haze was to me but an obstacle. That journal of mine is no more; but I have considered it my artistic duty to preserve its intonations no matter how false and brutal they may seem to me now. Fortunately, my story has reached a point where I can cease insulting poor Charlotte for the sake of retrospective verisimilitude.

Wishing to spare poor Charlotte two or three hours of suspense on a winding road (and avoid, perhaps, a head-on collision that would shatter our different dreams), I made a thoughtful but abortive attempt to reach her at the camp by telephone. She had left half an hour before, and getting Lo instead, I told her – trembling and brimming with my mastery over fate – that I was going to marry her mother. I had to repeat it twice because something was preventing her from giving me her attention.

'Gee, that's swell,' she said laughing. 'When is the wedding? Hold on a sec, the pup— That pup here has got hold of my sock. Listen—' and she added she guessed she was going to have loads of fun . . . and I realized as I hung up that a couple of hours at that camp had been sufficient to blot out with new impressions the image of handsome Humbert Humbert from little Lolita's mind. But what did it matter now? I would get her back as soon as a decent amount of time after the wedding had elapsed. 'The orange blossom would have scarcely withered on the grave', as a poet might have said. But I am no poet. I am only a very conscientious recorder.

After Louise had gone, I inspected the icebox and, finding it much too puritanic, walked to town and bought the richest foods available. I also bought some good liquor and two or three kinds of vitamins. I was pretty sure that with the aid of these stimulants and my natural resources, I would avert any embarrassment that my indifference might incur when called upon to display a strong and impatient flame. Again and again resourceful Humbert evoked Charlotte as seen in the raree-show of a manly imagination. She was well groomed and shapely, this I could say for her, and she was my Lolita's big sister – this notion, perhaps, I could keep up if only I did not visualize too realistically her heavy hips, round knees, ripe bust, the coarse pink skin of her neck ('coarse' by comparison with silk and honey) and all the rest of that sorry and dull thing: a handsome woman.

The sun made its usual round of the house as the afternoon ripened into evening. I had a drink. And another. And yet another. Gin and pineapple juice, my favourite mixture, always double my energy. I decided to busy myself with our unkempt lawn. *Une petite attention.* It was crowded with dandelions, and a cursed dog – I loathe dogs – had defiled the flat stones where a sundial had once stood. Most of the dandelions had changed from suns to moons. The gin and Lolita were dancing in me, and I almost fell over the folding chairs that I attempted to dislodge. Incarnadine zebras! There are some eructations that sound like cheers – at least, mine did. An old fence at the back of the garden separated us from the neighbour's garbage receptacles and lilacs; but there was nothing between the front end of our lawn (where it sloped along one side of the house) and the street. Therefore I was able to watch (with the smirk of one about to perform a good action) for the return of Charlotte: that tooth should be extracted at once. As I lurched and lunged with the hand mower, bits of grass optically twittering in the low sun, I kept an eye on that section of suburban street. It curved in from under an archway of huge shade trees, then sped towards us down, down, quite sharply, past old Miss Opposite's ivied brick house and high-sloping lawn (much trimmer than ours) and disappeared behind our own front porch which I could not see from where I happily belched and laboured. The dandelions perished. A reek of sap mingled with the pineapple. Two little girls, Marion and Mabel, whose comings and goings I had mechanically followed of late (but who could replace my Lolita?) went toward the avenue (from which our Lawn Street cascaded), one pushing a bicycle, the other feeding from a paper bag, both talking at the top of their sunny voices. Leslie, old Miss Opposite's gardener and chauffeur, a very amiable and athletic Negro, grinned at me from afar and shouted, re-shouted, commented by gesture, that I was mighty energetic today. The fool dog of the prosperous junk dealer next door ran after a blue car – not Charlotte's. The prettier of the two little girls (Mabel, I think), shorts, halter with little to halt, bright hair – a nymphet, by Pan! – ran back down the street crumpling her paper bag and was hidden from this Green Goat by the frontage of Mr and Mrs Humbert's residence. A station wagon popped out of the leafy shade of the avenue, dragging some of it on its roof before the shadows snapped, and swung by at an idiotic pace, the sweatshirted driver roof-holding with his left hand and the junkman's dog tearing alongside. There was a smiling pause – and then, with a flutter in my breast, I witnessed the return of the Blue Sedan. I saw it glide downhill and disappear behind the corner of the house. I had a glimpse of her calm pale profile. It occurred to me that until she went upstairs she would not know whether I had gone or not. A minute later, with an expression of great anguish on her face, she looked down at me from the window of Lo's room. By sprinting upstairs, I managed to reach that room before she left it.

18

When the bride is a widow and the groom is a widower; when the former has lived in Our Great Little Town for hardly two years, and the latter for hardly a month; when Monsieur wants to get the whole damned thing over with as quickly as possible, and Madame gives in with a tolerant smile; then, my reader, the wedding is generally a 'quiet' affair. The bride may dispense with a tiara or orange blossoms securing her finger-tip veil, nor does she carry a white orchid in a prayer book. The bride's little daughter might have added to the ceremonies uniting H. and H. a touch of vivid vermeil; but I knew I would not dare be too tender with cornered Lolita yet, and therefore agreed it was not worth while tearing the child away from her beloved Camp Q.

My *soi-disant* passionate and lonely Charlotte was in everyday life matter-of-fact and gregarious. Moreover, I discovered that although she could not control her heart or her cries, she was a woman of principle. Immediately after she had become more or less my mistress (despite the stimulants, her 'nervous, eager *chéri*' – a heroic *chéri!* – had some initial trouble, for which, however, he amply compensated her by a fantastic display of old-world endearments), good Charlotte interviewed me about my relations with God. I could have answered that on that score my mind was open; I said, instead – paying my tribute to a pious platitude – that I believed in a cosmic spirit. Looking down at her fingernails, she also asked me had I not in my family a certain strange strain. I countered by inquiring whether she would still want to marry me if my father's maternal grandfather had been, say, a Turk. She said it did not matter a bit; but that, if she ever found out I did not believe in Our Christian God, she would commit suicide. She said it so solemnly that it gave me the creeps. It was then I knew she was a woman of principle.

Oh, she was very genteel: she said 'excuse me' whenever a slight burp interrupted her flowing speech, called an envelope an ahnvelope, and when talking to her lady-friends referred to me as Mr Humbert. I thought it would please her if I entered the community trailing some glamour after me. On the day of our wedding a little interview with me appeared in the Society Column of the Ramsdale *Journal,* with a photograph of Charlotte, one eyebrow up and a misprint in her name ('Hazer'). Despite this contretemps, the publicity warmed the porcelain cockles of her heart – and made my rattles shake with awful glee. By engaging in church work as well as by getting to know the better mothers of Lo's schoolmates, Charlotte in the course of twenty months or so had managed to become if not a prominent, at least an acceptable citizen, but never before had she come under that thrilling *rubrique,* and it was I who put her there,

Mr Edgar H. Humbert (I threw in the 'Edgar' just for the heck of it), 'writer and explorer'. McCoo's brother, when taking it down, asked me what I had written. Whatever I told him came out as 'several books on Peacock, Rainbow and other poets'. It was also noted that Charlotte and I had known each other for several years and that I was a distant relation of her first husband. I hinted I had had an affair with her thirteen years ago but this was not mentioned in print. To Charlotte I said that society columns *should* contain a shimmer of errors.

Let us go on with this curious tale. When called upon to enjoy my promotion from lodger to lover, did I experience only bitterness and distaste? No. Mr Humbert confessed to a certain titillation of his vanity, to some faint tenderness, even to a pattern of remorse daintily running along the steel of his conspiratorial dagger. Never had I thought that the rather ridiculous, though rather handsome Mrs Haze, with her blind faith in the wisdom of her church and book club, her mannerisms of elocution, her harsh, cold, contemptuous attitude towards an adorable, downy-armed child of twelve, could turn into such a touching, helpless creature as soon as I laid my hands upon her which happened on the threshold of Lolita's room whither she tremulously backed repeating 'no, no, please no'.

The transformation improved her looks. Her smile that had been such a contrived thing, thenceforth became the radiance of utter adoration – a radiance having something soft and moist about it, in which, with wonder, I recognized a resemblance to the lovely, inane, lost look that Lo had when gloating over a new kind of concoction at the soda fountain or mutely admiring my expensive, always tailor-fresh clothes. Deeply fascinated, I would watch Charlotte while she swapped parental woes with some other lady and made that national grimace of feminine resignation (eyes rolling up, mouth drooping sideways) which, in an infantile form I had seen Lo making herself. We had highballs before turning in, and with their help, I would manage to evoke the child while caressing the mother. This was the white stomach within which my nymphet had been a little curved fish in 1934. This carefully dyed hair, so sterile to my sense of smell and touch, acquired at certain lamplit moments in the poster bed the tinge, if not the texture, of Lolita's curls. I kept telling myself, as I wielded my brand-new large-as-life wife, that biologically this was the nearest I could get to Lolita; that at Lolita's age, Lotte had been as desirable a schoolgirl as her daughter was, and as Lolita's daughter would be some day. I had my wife unearth from under a collection of shoes (Mr Haze had a passion for them, it appears) a thirty-year-old album, so that I might see how Lotte had looked as a child; and even though the light was wrong and the dresses graceless, I was able to make out a dim first version of Lolita's outline, legs, cheekbones, bobbed nose. Lottelita, Lolitchen.

So I tom-peeped across the hedges of years, into wan little windows. And when, by means of pitifully ardent, naïvely lascivious caresses, she of the noble nipple and massive thigh prepared me for the performance of my nightly duty, it was still a nymphet's scent that in despair I tried to pick up, as I bayed through the undergrowth of dark decaying forests.

I simply can't tell you how gentle, how touching my poor wife was. At breakfast, in the depressingly bright kitchen, with its chrome glitter and Hardware and Co Calendar and cute breakfast nook (simulating that Coffee Shoppe where in their college days Charlotte and Humbert used to coo together), she would sit, robed in red, her elbow on the plastic topped table, her cheek propped on her fist, and stare at me with intolerable tenderness as I consumed my ham and eggs. Humbert's face might twitch with neuralgia, but in her eyes it vied in beauty and animation with the sun and shadows of leaves rippling on the white refrigerator. My solemn exasperation was to her the silence of love. My small income added to her even smaller one impressed her as a brilliant fortune; not because the resulting sum now sufficed for most middle class needs, but because even my money shone in her eyes with the magic of my manliness, and she saw our joint account as one of those southern boulevards at midday that have solid shade on one side and smooth sunshine on the other, all the way to the end of a prospect, where pink mountains loom.

Into the fifty days of our cohabitation Charlotte crammed the activities of as many years. The poor woman busied herself with a number of things she had foregone long before or had never been much interested in, as if (to prolong these Proustian intonations) by my marrying the mother of the child I loved I had enabled my wife to regain an abundance of youth by proxy. With the zest of a banal young bride, she started to 'glorify the home'. Knowing as I did its every cranny by heart – since those days when from my chair I mentally mapped out Lolita's course through the house – I had long entered into a sort of emotional relationship with it, with its very ugliness and dirt, and now I could almost feel the wretched thing cower in its reluctance to endure the bath of ecru and ochre and putty-buff-and-snuff that Charlotte planned to give it. She never got as far as that, thank God, but she did use up a tremendous amount of energy in washing window shades, waxing the slats of Venetian blinds, purchasing new shades and new blinds, returning them to the store, replacing them by others, and so on, in a constant chiaroscuro of smiles and frowns, doubts and pouts. She dabbled in cretonnes and chintzes; she changed the colours of the sofa – the sacred sofa where a bubble of paradise had once burst in slow motion within me. She arranged the furniture – and was pleased when she found, in a household treatise, that 'it is permissible to separate a pair of sofa commodes and their companion lamps'. With the authoress of *Your Home Is You,* she developed a hatred for little lean chairs and spindle tables. She believed that a room having a generous expanse of glass, and lots of rich wood panelling was an example of the masculine type of room, whereas the feminine type was characterized by lighter-looking windows and frailer woodwork. The novels I had found her reading when I moved in were now replaced by illustrated catalogues and homemaking guides. From a firm located at 4640 Roosevelt Blvd., Philadelphia, she ordered for our double bed a 'damask covered 312 coil mattress' – although the old one seemed to me resilient and durable enough for whatever it had to support.

A Midwesterner, as her late husband had also been, she had lived in coy Ramsdale, the gem of an eastern state, not long enough to know all the nice people. She knew slightly the jovial dentist who lived in a kind of ramshackle wooden château behind our lawn. She had met at a church tea the 'snooty' wife of the local junk dealer who owned the 'colonial' white horror at the corner of the avenue. Now and then she 'visited with' old Miss Opposite; but the more patrician matrons among those she called upon, or met at lawn functions, or had telephone chats with – such dainty ladies as Mrs Glave, Mrs Sheridan, Mrs McCrystal, Mrs Knight and others – seldom seemed to call on my neglected Charlotte. Indeed, the only couple with whom she had relations of real cordiality, devoid of any *arrière-pensée* or practical foresight, were the Farlows who had just come back from a business trip to Chile in time to attend our wedding, with the Chatfields, McCoos and a few others (but not Mrs Junk or the even prouder Mrs Talbot). John Farlow was a middle-aged, quiet, quietly athletic, quietly successful dealer in sporting goods, who had an office at Parkington, forty miles away: it was he who got me the cartridges for that Colt and showed me how to use it, during a walk in the woods one Sunday; he was also what he called with a smile a part-time lawyer and had handled some of Charlotte's affairs. Jean, his youngish wife (and first cousin), was a long-limbed girl in harlequin glasses with two boxer dogs, two pointed breasts and a big red mouth. She painted – landscapes and portraits – and vividly do I remember praising, over cocktails, the picture she had made of a niece of hers, little Rosaline Honeck, a rosy honey in a Girl Scout uniform, beret of green worsted, belt of green webbing, charming shoulder-long curls – and John removed his pipe and said it was a pity Dolly (my Dolita) and Rosaline were so critical of each other at school, but he hoped, and we all hoped, they would get on better when they returned from their respective camps. We talked of the school. It had its drawbacks, and it had its virtues. 'Of course, too many of the tradespeople here are Italians,' said John, 'but on the other hand we are still spared—' 'I wish,' interrupted Jean with a laugh, 'Dolly and Rosaline were spending the summer together.' Suddenly I imagined Lo returning from camp – brown, warm, drowsy, drugged – and was ready to weep with passion and impatience.

19

A few words more about Mrs Humbert while the going is good (a bad accident is to happen quite soon). I had been always aware of the possessive streak in her, but I never thought she would be so crazily jealous of anything in my life that had not been she. She showed a fierce insatiable curiosity for my past. She desired me to resuscitate all my loves so that she might make me insult them, and trample upon them, and revoke them apostately and totally, thus destroying my past. She made me tell her about my marriage to Valeria, who was of course a scream; but I also had to invent, or to pad atrociously, a long series of mistresses for Charlotte's morbid delectation. To keep her happy, I had to present her with an illustrated catalogue of them, all nicely differentiated, according to the rules of those American ads where schoolchildren are pictured in a subtle ratio of races, with one – only one, but as cute as they make them – chocolate-coloured round-eyed little lad, almost in the very middle of the front row. So I presented my women, and had them smile and sway – the languorous blonde, the fiery brunette, the sensual copperhead – as if on parade in a bordello. The more popular and platitudinous I made them, the more Mrs Humbert was pleased with the show.

Never in my life had I confessed so much or received so many confessions. The sincerity and artlessness with which she discussed what she called her 'love-life', from first necking to connubial catch-as-catch-can, were, ethically, in striking contrast with my glib compositions, but technically the two sets were congeneric since both were affected by the same stuff (soap operas, psychoanalysis and cheap novelettes) upon which I drew for my characters and she for her mode of expression. I was considerably amused by certain remarkable sexual habits that the good Harold Haze had had according to Charlotte who thought my mirth improper; but otherwise her autobiography was as devoid of interest as her autopsy would have been. I never saw a healthier woman than she, despite thinning diets.

Of my Lolita she seldom spoke – more seldom, in fact, than she did of the blurred, blond male baby whose photograph to the exclusion of all others adorned our bleak bedroom. In one of her tasteless reveries, she predicted that the dead infant's soul would return to earth in the form of the child she would bear in her present wedlock. And although I felt no special urge to supply the Humbert line with a replica of Harold's production (Lolita, with an incestuous thrill, I had grown to regard as *my* child), it occurred to me that a prolonged confinement, with a nice Caesarean operation and other complications in a safe maternity ward sometime next spring, would give me a chance to be alone with my Lolita for weeks, perhaps – and gorge the limp nymphet with sleeping pills.

Oh, she simply hated her daughter! What I thought especially vicious was that she had gone out of her way to answer with great diligence the questionnaires in a fool's book she had (*A Guide to Your Child's Development*), published in Chicago. The rigmarole went year by year, and Mom was supposed to fill out a kind of inventory at each of her child's birthdays. On Lo's twelfth, January 1, 1947, Charlotte Haze, *née* Becker, had underlined the following epithets, ten out of forty, under 'Your Child's Personality': aggressive, boisterous, critical, distrustful, impatient, irritable, inquisitive, listless, negativistic (underlined twice) and obstinate. She had ignored the thirty remaining adjectives, among which were cheerful, co-operative, energetic and so forth. It was really maddening. With a brutality that otherwise never appeared in my loving wife's mild nature, she attacked and routed such of Lo's little belongings that had wandered to various parts of the house to freeze there like so many hypnotized bunnies. Little did the good lady dream that one morning when an upset stomach (the result of my trying to improve on her sauces) had prevented me from accompanying her to church, I deceived her with one of Lolita's anklets. And then, her attitude towards my saporous darling's letters!

Dear Mummy and Hummy,

Hope you are fine. Thank you very much for the candy. I [crossed out and rewritten again] I lost my new sweater in the woods. It has been cold here for the last few days. I'm having a time. Love.

Dolly

'The dumb child,' said Mrs Humbert, 'has left out a word before "time". That sweater was all-wool, and I wish you would not send her candy without consulting me.'

20

There was a woodlake (Hourglass Lake – not as I had thought it was spelled) a few miles from Ramsdale, and there was one week of great heat at the end of July when we drove there daily. I am now obliged to describe in some tedious detail our last swim there together, one tropical Tuesday morning.

We had left the car in a parking area not far from the road and were making our way down a path cut through the pine forest to the lake, when Charlotte remarked that Jean Farlow, in quest of rare light effects (Jean belonged to the old school of painting), had seen Leslie taking a dip 'in the ebony' (as John had quipped) at five o'clock in the morning last Sunday.

'The water,' I said, 'must have been quite cold.'

'That is not the point,' said the logical doomed dear. 'He is subnormal, you see. And,' she continued (in that carefully phrased way of hers that was beginning to tell on my health),

'I have a very definite feeling our Louise is in love with that moron.'

Feeling. 'We feel Dolly is not doing as well', etc. (from an old school report).

The Humberts walked on, sandalled and robed.

'Do you know, Hum: I have one most ambitious dream,' pronounced Lady Hum, lowering her head – shy of that dream – and communing with the tawny ground. 'I would love to get hold of a real trained servant maid like that German girl the Talbots spoke of; and have her live in the house.'

'No room,' I said.

'Come,' she said with her quizzical smile, 'surely, *chéri,* you underestimate the possibilities of the Humbert home. We would put her in Lo's room. I intended to make a guestroom of that hole anyway. It's the coldest and meanest in the whole house.'

'What are you talking about?' I asked, the skin of my cheek-bones tensing up (this I take the trouble to note only because my daughter's skin did the same when she felt that way: dis-belief, disgust, irritation).

'Are you bothered by Romantic Associations?' queried my wife – in allusion to her first surrender.

'Hell no,' said I. 'I just wonder where will you put your daughter when you get your guest or your maid.'

'Ah,' said Mrs Humbert, dreaming, smiling, drawing out the 'Ah' simultaneously with the raise of one eyebrow and a soft exhalation of breath. 'Little Lo, I'm afraid, does not enter the picture at all, at all. Little Lo goes straight from camp to a good boarding school with strict discipline and some sound religious training. And then – Beardsley College. I have it all mapped out, you need not worry.'

She went on to say that she, Mrs Humbert, would have to overcome her habitual sloth and write to Miss Phalen's sister who taught at St Algebra. The dazzling lake emerged. I said I had forgotten my sunglasses in the car and would catch up with her.

I had always thought that wringing one's hands was a fictional gesture – the obscure outcome, perhaps, of some medieval ritual; but as I took to the woods, for a spell of despair and desperate meditation, this was the gesture ('look, Lord, at these chains!') that would have come nearest to the mute expression of my mood.

Had Charlotte been Valeria, I would have known how to handle the situation; and 'handle' is the word I want. In the good old days, by merely twisting fat Valechka's brittle wrist (the one she had fallen upon from a bicycle) I could make her change her mind instantly; but anything of the sort in regard to Charlotte was unthinkable. Bland American Charlotte frightened me. My lighthearted dream of controlling her through her passion for me was all wrong. I dared not do anything to spoil the image of me she had set up to adore. I had toadied to her when she was the awesome duenna of my darling, and a grovelling something still persisted in my attitude toward her. The only ace I held was her ignorance of my monstrous love for her Lo. She had been annoyed by Lo's liking me; but *my* feelings she could not divine. To Valeria I might have said: 'Look here, you fat fool, *c'est moi qui décide* what is good for Dolores Humbert.' To Charlotte, I could not even say (with ingratiating calm): 'Excuse me, my dear, I disagree. Let us give the child one more chance. Let me be her private tutor for a year or so. You once told me yourself—' In fact, I could not say anything at all to Charlotte about the child without giving myself away. Oh, you cannot imagine (as I had never imagined) what these women of principle are! Charlotte, who did not notice the falsity of all the everyday conventions and rules of behaviour, and foods, and books, and people she doted upon, would distinguish at once a false intonation in anything I might say with a view to keeping Lo near me. She was like a musician who may be an odious vulgarian in ordinary life, devoid of tact and taste; but who will hear a false note in music with diabolical accuracy of judgment. To break Charlotte's will, I would have to break her heart. If I broke her heart, her image of me would break too. If I said: 'Either I have my way with Lolita, and you help me to keep the matter quiet, or we part at once', she would have turned as pale as a woman of clouded glass and slowly replied: 'All right, whatever you add or retract, this is the end.' And the end it would be.

Such, then, was the mess. I remember reaching the parking area and pumping a handful of rust-tasting water, and drinking it as avidly as if it could give me magic wisdom, youth, freedom, a tiny concubine. For a while, purple-robed, heel-dangling, I sat on the edge of one of the rude tables, under the wooshing pines. In the middle distance, two little maidens in shorts and halters came out of a sun-dappled privy marked 'Women'. Gum-chewing Mabel (or Mabel's understudy) laboriously, absent-mindedly, straddled a bicycle, and Marion, shaking her hair because of the flies, settled behind, legs wide apart; and, wobbling, they slowly, absently, merged with the light and shade. Lolita! Father and daughter melting into these woods! The natural solution was to destroy Mrs Humbert. But how?

No man can bring about the perfect murder; chance, however, can do it. There was the famous dispatch of a Mme Lacour in Arles, southern France, at the close of last century. An unidentified bearded six-footer, who, it was later conjectured, had been the lady's secret lover, walked up to her in a crowded street, soon after her marriage to Colonel Lacour, and mortally stabbed her in the back, three times, while the Colonel, a small bulldog of a man, hung on to the murderer's arm. By a miraculous and beautiful coincidence, right at the moment when the operator was in the act of loosening the angry little husband's jaws (while several onlookers were closing in upon the group), a cranky Italian in the house nearest to the scene set off by sheer accident some kind of explosive he was tinkering with, and immediately the street was turned into a pandemonium of smoke, falling bricks and running people. The explosion hurt no one (except that it knocked out game Colonel Lacour); but the lady's vengeful lover ran when the others ran – and lived happily ever after.

Now look what happens when the operator himself plans a perfect removal.

I walked down to Hourglass Lake. The spot from which we and a few other 'nice' couples (the Farlows, the Chatfields) bathed was a kind of small cove; my Charlotte liked it because it was almost 'a private beach'. The main bathing facilities (or 'drowning facilities' as the Ramsdale *Journal* had had occasion to say) were in the left (eastern) part of the hourglass, and could not be seen from our covelet. To our right, the pines soon gave way to a curve of marshland which turned again into forest on the opposite side.

I sat down beside my wife so noiselessly that she started.

'Shall we go in?' she asked.

'We shall in a minute. Let me follow a train of thought.'

I thought. More than a minute passed.

'All right. Come on.'

'Was I on that train?'

'You certainly were.'

'I hope so,' said Charlotte entering the water. It soon reached the gooseflesh of her thick thighs; and then, joining her outstretched hands, shutting her mouth tight, very plain-faced in her black rubber headgear, Charlotte flung herself forward with a great splash.

Slowly we swam out into the shimmer of the lake.

On the opposite bank, at least a thousand paces away (if one could walk across water), I could make out the tiny figures of two men working like beavers on their stretch of shore. I knew exactly who they were: a retired policeman of Polish descent and the retired plumber who owned most of the timber on that side of the lake. And I also knew they were engaged in building, just for the dismal fun of the thing, a wharf. The knocks that reached us seemed so much bigger than what could be distinguished of those dwarfs' arms and tools; indeed, one suspected the director of those acrosonic effects to have been at odds with the puppet-master, especially since the hefty crack of each diminutive blow lagged behind its visual version.

The short white-sand strip of 'our' beach – from which by now we had gone a little way to reach deep water – was empty on weekday mornings. There was nobody around except those two tiny very busy figures on the opposite side, and a dark-red private plane that droned overhead, and then disappeared in the blue. The setting was really perfect for a brisk bubbling murder, and here was the subtle point: the man of law and the man of water were just near enough to witness an accident and just far enough not to observe a crime. They were near enough to hear a distracted bather thrashing about and bellowing for somebody to come and help him save his drowning wife; and they were too far to distinguish (if they happened to look too soon) that the anything but distracted swimmer was finishing to tread his wife underfoot. I was not yet at that stage; I merely want to convey the ease of the fact, the nicety of the setting! So there was Charlotte swimming on with dutiful awkwardness (she was a very mediocre mermaid), but not without a certain solemn pleasure (for was not her merman by her side?); and as I watched, with the stark lucidity of a future recollection (you know – trying to see things as you will remember having seen them), the glossy whiteness of her wet face so little tanned despite all her endeavours, and her pale lips, and her naked convex forehead, and the tight black cap, and the plump wet neck, I knew that all I had to do was to drop back, take a deep breath, then grab her by the ankle and rapidly dive with my captive corpse. I say corpse because surprise, panic and inexperience would cause her to inhale at once a lethal gallon of lake, while I would be able to hold on for at least a full minute, open-eyed under water. The fatal gesture passed like the tail of a falling star across the blackness of the contemplated crime. It was like some dreadful silent ballet, the male dancer holding the ballerina by her foot and streaking down through watery twilight. I might come up for a mouthful of air while still holding her down, and then would dive again as many times as would be necessary, and only when the curtain came down on her for good, would I permit myself to yell for help. And when some twenty minutes later the two puppets steadily growing arrived in a rowboat, one half newly painted, poor Mrs Humbert Humbert, the victim of cramp or coronary occlusion, or both, would be standing on her head in the inky ooze some thirty feet below the smiling surface of Hourglass Lake.

Simple, was it not? But what d'ye know, folks – I just could not make myself do it!

She swam beside me, a trustful and clumsy seal, and all the logic of passion screamed in my ear: Now is the time! And, folks, I just couldn't! In silence I turned shoreward and gravely, dutifully, she also turned, and still hell screamed its counsel, and still I could not make myself drown the poor, slippery, big-bodied creature. The scream grew more and more remote as I realized the melancholy fact that neither tomorrow, nor Friday, nor any other day or night, could I make myself put her to death. Oh, I could visualize myself slapping Valeria's breasts out of alignment, or otherwise hurting her – and I could see myself, no less clearly, shooting her lover in the underbelly and making him say 'akh!' and sit down. But I could not kill Charlotte – especially when things were on the whole not quite as hopeless, perhaps, as they seemed at first wince on that miserable morning. Were I to catch her by her strong kicking foot; were I to see her amazed look, hear her awful voice; were I still to go through with the ordeal, her ghost would haunt me all my life. Perhaps if the year were 1447 instead of 1947 I might have hoodwinked my gentle nature by administering her some classical poison from a hollow agate, some tender philtre of death. But in our middle-class nosy era it would not have come off the way it used to in the brocaded palaces of the past. Nowadays you have to be a scientist if you want to be a killer. No, no, I was neither. Ladies and gentlemen of the jury, the majority of sex offenders that hanker for some throbbing, sweet-moaning, physical but not necessarily coital, relation with a girl-child, are innocuous, inadequate, passive, timid strangers who merely ask the community to allow them to pursue their practically harmless, so-called aberrant behaviour, their little hot wet private acts of sexual deviation without the police and society cracking down upon them. We are not sex fiends! We do not rape as good soldiers do. We are unhappy, mild, dog-eyed gentlemen, sufficiently well integrated to control our urge in the presence of adults, but ready to give years and years of life for one chance to touch a nymphet. Emphatically, no killers are we. Poets never kill. Oh, my poor Charlotte, do not hate me in your eternal heaven among an eternal alchemy of asphalt and rubber and metal and stone – but thank God, not water, not water!

Nonetheless it was a very close shave, speaking quite objectively. And now comes the point of my perfect-crime parable.

We sat down on our towels in the thirsty sun. She looked around, loosened her bra, and turned over on her stomach to give her back a chance to be feasted upon. She said she loved me. She sighed deeply. She extended one arm and groped in the pocket of her robe for her cigarettes. She sat up and smoked. She examined her right shoulder. She kissed me heavily with open smoky mouth. Suddenly, down the sand bank behind us, from under the bushes and pines, a stone rolled, then another.

'Those disgusting prying kids,' said Charlotte, holding up her big bra to her breast and turning prone again. 'I shall have to speak about that to Peter Krestovski.'

From the debouchment of the trail came a rustle, a footfall, and Jean Farlow marched down with her easel and things.

'You scared us,' said Charlotte.

Jean said she had been up there, in a place of green concealment, spying on nature (spies are generally shot), trying to finish a lakescape, but it was no good, she had no talent whatever (which was quite true) – 'And have *you* ever tried painting, Humbert?' Charlotte, who was a little jealous of Jean, wanted to know if John was coming.

He was. He was coming home for lunch today. He had dropped her on the way to Parkington and should be picking her up any time now. It was a grand morning. She always felt a traitor to Cavall and Melampus for leaving them roped on such gorgeous days. She sat down on the white sand between Charlotte and me. She wore shorts. Her long brown legs were about as attractive to me as those of a chestnut mare. She showed her gums when she smiled.

'I almost put both of you into my lake,' she said. 'I even noticed something you overlooked. You [addressing Humbert] had your wrist watch on in, yes, sir, you had.'

'Waterproof,' said Charlotte softly, making a fish mouth.

Jean took my wrist upon her knee and examined Charlotte's gift, then put back Humbert's hand on the sand, palm up.

'You could see anything that way,' remarked Charlotte coquettishly.

Jean sighed. 'I once saw,' she said, 'two children, male and female, at sunset, right here, making love. Their shadows were giants. And I told you about Mr Tomson at daybreak. Next time I expect to see fat old Ivor in the ivory. He is really a freak, that man. Last time he told me a completely indecent story about his nephew. It appears—'

'Hullo there,' said John's voice.

21

My habit of being silent when displeased, or, more exactly, the cold and scaly quality of my displeased silence, used to frighten Valeria out of her wits. She used to whimper and wail, saying, '*Ce qui me rend folle, c'est que je ne sais à quoi tu penses quand tu es comme ça.*' I tried being silent with Charlotte – and she just chirped on, or chucked my silence under the chin. An astonishing woman! I would retire to my former room, now a regular 'studio', mumbling I had after all a learned opus to write, and cheerfully Charlotte went on beautifying the home, warbling on the telephone and writing letters. From my window, through the lacquered shiver of poplar leaves, I could see her crossing the street and contentedly mailing her letter to Miss Phalen's sister.

The week of scattered showers and shadows which elapsed after our last visit to the motionless sands of Hourglass Lake was one of the gloomiest I can recall. Then came two or three dim rays of hope – before the ultimate sunburst.

It occurred to me that I had a fine brain in beautiful working order and that I might as well use it. If I dared not meddle with my wife's plans for her daughter (getting warmer and browner every day in the fair weather of hopeless distance), I could surely devise some general means to assert myself in a general way that might be later directed toward a particular occasion. One evening, Charlotte herself provided me with an opening.

'I have a surprise for you,' she said looking at me with fond eyes over a spoonful of soup. 'In the fall we two are going to England.'

I swallowed *my* spoonful, wiped my lips with pink paper (Oh, the cool rich linens of Mirana Hotel!) and said:

'I have also a surprise for you, my dear. We two are not going to England.'

'Why, what's the matter?' she said, looking – with more surprise than I had counted upon – at my hands (I was involuntarily folding and tearing and crushing and tearing again the innocent pink napkin). My smiling face set her somewhat at ease, however.

'The matter is quite simple,' I replied. 'Even in the most harmonious of households, as ours is, not all decisions are taken by the female partner. There are certain things that the husband is there to decide. I can well imagine the thrill that you, a healthy American gal, must experience at crossing the Atlantic on the same ocean liner with Lady Bumble – or Sam Bumble, the Frozen Meat King, or a Holywood harlot. And I doubt not that you and I would make a pretty ad for the Travelling Agency when portrayed looking – you, frankly starry-eyed, I, controlling my envious admiration – at the Palace Sentries, or Scarlet Guards, or Beaver Eaters, or whatever they are called. But I happen to be allergic to Europe, including merry old England. As you well know, I have nothing but very sad associations with the Old and rotting World. No coloured ads in your magazines will change the situation.'

'My darling,' said Charlotte. 'I really—'

'No, wait a minute. The present matter is only incidental. I am concerned with a general trend. When you wanted me to spend my afternoons sunbathing on the Lake instead of doing my work, I gladly gave in and became a bronzed glamour boy for your sake, instead of remaining a scholar and, well, an educator. When you lead me to bridge and bourbon with the charming Farlows, I meekly follow. No, please, wait. When you decorate your home, I do not interfere with your schemes. When you decide – when you decide all kinds of matters, I may be in complete, or in partial, let us say, disagreement – but I say nothing. I ignore the particular. I cannot ignore the general. I love being bossed by you, but every game has its rules. I am not cross. I am not cross at all. Don't do that. But I am one half of this household, and have a small but distinct voice.'

She had come to my side and had fallen on her knees and was slowly, but very vehemently, shaking her head and clawing at my trousers. She said she had never realized. She said I was her ruler and her god. She said Louise had gone, and let us make love right away. She said I must forgive her or she would die.

This little incident filled me with considerable elation. I told her quietly that it was a matter not of asking forgiveness, but of changing one's ways; and I resolved to press my advantage and spend a good deal of time, aloof and moody, working at my book – or at least pretending to work.

The 'studio bed' in my former room had long been converted into the sofa it had always been at heart, and Charlotte had warned me since the very beginning of our cohabitation that gradually the room would be turned into a regular 'writer's den'. A couple of days after the British Incident, I was sitting in a new and very comfortable easy chair, with a large volume in my lap, when Charlotte rapped with her ring finger and sauntered in. How different were her movements from those of my Lolita, when *she* used to visit me in her dear dirty blue jeans, smelling of orchards in nymphetland; awkward and fey, and dimly depraved, the lower buttons of her shirt unfastened. Let me tell you, however, something. Behind the brashness of little Haze, and the poise of big Haze, a trickle of shy life ran that tasted the same, that murmured the same. A great French doctor once told my father that in near relatives the faintest gastric gurgle has the same 'voice'.

So Charlotte sauntered in. She felt all was not well between us. I had pretended to fall asleep the night before, and the night before that, as soon as we had gone to bed, and risen at dawn.

Tenderly, she inquired if she were not 'interrupting'.

'Not at the moment,' I said, turning volume C of the *Girls' Encyclopaedia* around to examine a picture printed 'bottom-edge' as printers say.

Charlotte went up to a little table of imitation mahogany with a drawer. She put her hand upon it. The little table was ugly, no doubt, but it had done nothing to her.

'I have always wanted to ask you,' she said (business-like, not coquettish), 'why is this thing locked up? Do you want it in this room? It's so abominably uncouth.'

'Leave it alone,' I said. I was camping in Scandinavia.

'Is there a key?'

'Hidden.'

'Oh, Hum . . .'

'Locked up love letters.'

She gave me one of those wounded-doe looks that irritated me so much, and then, not quite knowing if I was serious, or how to keep up the conversation, stood for several slow pages (Campus, Canada, Candid Camera, Candy) peering at the windowpane rather than through it, drumming upon it with sharp almond-and-rose fingernails.

Presently (at Canoeing or Canvasback) she strolled up to my chair and sank down, tweedily, weightily, on its arm, inundating me with the perfume my first wife had used. 'Would his lordship like to spend the fall *here*?' she asked, pointing with her little finger at an autumn view in a conservative Eastern State. 'Why?' (very distinctly and slowly). She shrugged. (Probably Harold used to take a vacation at that time. Open season. Conditional reflex on her part.)

'I think I know where that is,' she said, still pointing. 'There is a hotel I remember, Enchanted Hunters, quaint, isn't it? And the food is a dream. And nobody bothers anybody.'

She rubbed her cheek against my temple. Valeria soon got over that.

'Is there anything special you would like for dinner, dear? John and Jean will drop in later.'

I answered with a grunt. She kissed me on my underlip, and, brightly saying she would bake a cake (a tradition subsisted from my lodging days that I adored her cakes), left me to my idleness.

Carefully putting down the open book where she had sat (it attempted to send forth a rotation of waves, but an inserted pencil stopped the pages), I checked the hiding place of the key: rather self-consciously it lay under the old expensive safety razor I had used before she bought me a much better and cheaper one. Was it the perfect hiding place – there, under that razor, in the groove of its velvet-lined case? The case lay in a small trunk where I kept various business papers. Could I improve upon this? Remarkable how difficult it is to conceal things – especially when one's wife keeps monkeying with the furniture.

22

I think it was exactly a week after our last swim that the noon mail brought a reply from the second Miss Phalen. The lady wrote she had just returned to St Algebra from her sister's funeral. 'Euphemia had never been the same after breaking that hip.' As to the matter of Mrs Humbert's daughter, she wished to report that it was too late to enrol her this year; but that she, the surviving Phalen, was practically certain that if Mr and Mrs Humbert brought Dolores over in January, her admittance might be arranged.

Next day, after lunch, I went to see 'our' doctor, a friendly fellow whose perfect bedside manner and complete reliance on a few patented drugs adequately masked his ignorance of, and indifference to, medical science. The fact that Lo would have to come back to Ramsdale was a treasure of anticipation. For this event I wanted to be fully prepared. I had in fact begun my campaign earlier, before Charlotte made that cruel decision of hers. I had to be sure when my lovely child arrived, that very night, and then night after night, until St Algebra took her away from me, I would possess the means of putting two creatures to sleep so thoroughly that neither sound nor touch should rouse them. Throughout most of July I had been experimenting with various sleeping powders, trying them out on Charlotte, a great taker of pills. The last dose I had given her (she thought it was a tablet of mild bromides – to anoint her nerves) had knocked her out for four solid hours. I had put the radio at full blast. I had blazed in her face an olisbos-like flashlight. I had pushed her, pinched her, prodded her – and nothing had disturbed the rhythm of her calm and powerful breathing. However, when I had done such a simple thing as kiss her, she had awakened at once, as fresh and strong as an octopus (I barely escaped). This would not do, I thought; had to get something still safer. At first, Dr Byron did not seem to believe me when I said his last prescription was no match for my insomnia. He suggested I try again, and for a moment diverted my attention by showing me photographs of his family. He had a fascinating child of Dolly's age; but I saw through his tricks and insisted he prescribe the mightiest pill extant. He suggested I play golf, but finally agreed to give me something that, he said, 'would really work'; and going to a cabinet, he produced a vial of violet-blue capsules banded with dark purple at one end, which, he said, had just been placed on the market and were intended not for neurotics whom a draught of water could calm if properly administered, but only for great sleepless artists who had to die for a few hours in order to live for centuries. I love to fool doctors, and though inwardly rejoicing, pocketed the pills with a sceptical shrug. Incidentally, I had had to be careful with him. Once, in another connection, a stupid lapse on my part made me mention my last sanatorium, and I thought I saw the tips of his ears twitch. Being not at all keen for Charlotte or anybody else to know that period of my past, I had hastily explained that I had once done some research among the insane for a novel. But no matter; the old rogue certainly had a sweet girleen.

I left in great spirits. Steering my wife's car with one finger, I contentedly rolled homeward. Ramsdale had, after all, lots of charm. The cicadas whirred; the avenue had been freshly watered. Smoothly, almost silkily, I turned down into our steep little street. Everything was somehow so right that day. So blue and green. I knew the sun shone because my ignition key was reflected in the windshield; and I knew it was exactly half-past three because the nurse who came to massage Miss Opposite every afternoon was tripping down the narrow sidewalk in her white stockings and shoes. As usual, Junk's hysterical setter attacked me as I rolled downhill, and as usual, the local paper was lying on the porch where it had just been hurled by Kenny.

The day before I had ended the régime of aloofness I had imposed upon myself, and now uttered a cheerful homecoming call as I opened the door of the living room. With her cream-white nape and bronze bun to me, wearing the yellow blouse and maroon slacks she had on when I first met her, Charlotte sat at the corner bureau writing a letter. My hand still on the doorknob, I repeated my hearty cry. Her writing hand stopped. She sat still for a moment; then she slowly turned in her chair and rested her elbow on its curved back. Her face, disfigured by her emotion, was not a pretty sight as she stared at my legs and said:

'The Haze woman, the big bitch, the old cat, the obnoxious mamma, the – the old stupid Haze is no longer your dupe. She has – she has . . .'

My fair accuser stopped, swallowing her venom and her tears. Whatever Humbert Humbert said – or attempted to say – is inessential. She went on:

'You're a monster. You're a detestable, abominable, criminal fraud. If you come near – I'll scream out the window. Get back!'

Again, whatever H.H. murmured may be omitted, I think.

'I am leaving tonight. This is all yours. Only you'll never, never see that miserable brat again. Get out of this room.'

Reader, I did. I went up to the ex-semi-studio. Arms akimbo,

I stood for a moment quite still and self-composed, surveying from the threshold the raped little table with its open drawer, a key hanging from the lock, four other household keys on the table top. I walked across the landing into the Humberts' bedroom, and calmly removed my diary from under her pillow into my pocket. Then I started to walk downstairs, but stopped halfway: she was talking on the telephone which happened to be plugged just outside the door of the living room. I wanted to hear what she was saying: she cancelled an order for something or other, and returned to the parlour. I rearranged my respiration and went through the hallway to the kitchen. There, I opened a bottle of Scotch. She could never resist Scotch. Then I walked into the dining room and from there, through the half-open door, contemplated Charlotte's broad back.

'You are ruining my life and yours,' I said quietly. 'Let us be civilized people. It is all your hallucination. You are crazy, Charlotte. The notes you found were fragments of a novel. Your name and hers were put in by mere chance. Just because they came handy. Think it over. I shall bring you a drink.'

She neither answered nor turned, but went on writing in a scorching scrawl whatever she was writing. A third letter, presumably (two in stamped envelopes were already laid out on the desk). I went back to the kitchen.

I set out two glasses (to St Algebra? to Lo?) and opened the refrigerator. It roared at me viciously while I removed the ice from its heart. Rewrite. Let her read it again. She will not recall details. Change, forge. Write a fragment and show it to her or leave it lying around. Why do faucets sometimes whine so horribly? A horrible situation, really. The little pillow-shaped blocks of ice – pillows for polar teddy bear, Lo – emitted rasping, crackling, tortured sounds as the warm water loosened them in their cells. I bumped down the glasses side by side. I poured in the whisky and a dram of soda. She had tabooed my pin. Bark and bang went the icebox. Carrying the glasses, I walked through the dining room and spoke through the parlour door which was a fraction ajar, not quite space enough for my elbow.

'I have made you a drink,' I said.

She did not answer, the mad bitch, and I placed the glasses on the sideboard near the telephone, which had started to ring.

'Leslie speaking. Leslie Tomson,' said Leslie Tomson who favoured a dip at dawn. 'Mrs Humbert, sir, has been run over and you'd better come quick.'

I answered, perhaps a bit testily, that my wife was safe and sound, and still holding the receiver, I pushed open the door and said:

'There's this man saying you've been killed, Charlotte.'

But there was no Charlotte in the living room.

23

I rushed out. The far side of our steep little street presented a peculiar sight. A big black glossy Packard had climbed Miss Opposite's sloping lawn at an angle from the sidewalk (where a tartan laprobe had dropped in a heap), and stood there, shining in the sun, its doors open like wings, its front wheels deep in evergreen shrubbery. To the anatomical right of this car, on the trim turf of the lawn-slope, an old gentleman with a white moustache, well-dressed – double-breasted grey suit, polka-dotted bow-tie – lay supine, his long legs together, like a death-size wax figure. I have to put the impact of an instantaneous vision into a sequence of words; their physical accumulation in the page impairs the actual flash, the sharp unity of impression: Rug-heap, car, old-man doll, Miss O.'s nurse running with a rustle, a half-empty tumbler in her hand, back to the screened porch – where the propped-up, imprisoned, decrepit lady herself may be imagined screeching, but not loud enough to drown the rhythmical yaps of the Junk setter walking from group to group – from a bunch of neighbours already collected on the sidewalk, near the bit of checked stuff, and back to the car which he had finally run to earth, and then to another group on the lawn, consisting of Leslie, two policemen and a sturdy man with tortoise-shell glasses. At this point, I should explain that the prompt appearance of the patrolmen, hardly more than a minute after the accident, was due to their having been ticketing the illegally parked cars in a cross lane two blocks down the grade; that the fellow with the glasses was Frederick Beale, Jr, driver of the Packard; that his 79-year-old father, whom the nurse had just watered on the green bank where he lay – a banked banker so to speak – was not in a dead faint, but was comfortably and methodically recovering from a mild heart attack or its possibility; and, finally, that the laprobe on the sidewalk (where she had so often pointed out to me with disapproval the crooked green cracks) concealed the mangled remains of Charlotte Humbert who had been knocked down and dragged several feet by the Beale car as she was hurrying across the street to drop three letters in the mailbox, at the corner of Miss Opposite's lawn. These were picked up and handed to me by a pretty child in a dirty pink frock, and I got rid of them by clawing them to fragments in my trouser pocket.

Three doctors and the Farlows presently arrived on the scene and took over. The widower, a man of exceptional self-control, neither wept nor raved. He staggered a bit, that he did; but he opened his mouth only to impart such information or issue such directions as were strictly necessary in connection with the identification, examination and disposal of a dead woman, the top of her head a porridge of bone, brains, bronze hair and blood. The sun was still a blinding red when he was put to bed in Dolly's room by his two friends, gentle John and dewy-eyed Jean; who, to be near, retired to the Humberts' bedroom for the night; which, for all I know, they may not have spent as innocently as the solemnity of the occasion required.

I have no reason to dwell, in this very special memoir, on the pre-funeral formalities that had to be attended to, or on the funeral itself, which was as quiet as the marriage had been. But a few incidents pertaining to those four or five days after Charlotte's simple death have to be noted.

My first night of widowhood I was so drunk that I slept as soundly as the child who had slept in that bed. Next morning I hastened to inspect the fragments of letters in my pocket. They had got too thoroughly mixed up to be sorted into three complete sets. I assumed that '. . . and you had better find it because I cannot buy . . .' came from a letter to Lo; and other fragments seemed to point to Charlotte's intention of fleeing with Lo to Parkington, or even back to Pisky, lest the vulture snatch her precious lamb. Other tatters and shreds (never had I thought I had such strong talons) obviously referred to an application not to St A. but to another boarding school which was said to be so harsh and grey and gaunt in its methods (although supplying croquet under the elms) as to have earned the nickname of 'Reformatory for Young Ladies'. Finally, the third epistle was obviously addressed to me. I made out such items as '. . . after a year of separation we may . . .' '. . . oh, my dearest, oh my . . .' '. . . worse than if it had been a woman you kept . . .' '. . . or, maybe, I shall die . . .'. But on the whole my gleanings made little sense; the various fragments of these three hasty missives were as jumbled in the palms of my hands as their elements had been in poor Charlotte's head.

That day John had to see a customer, and Jean had to feed her dogs, and so I was to be deprived temporarily of my friends' company. The dear people were afraid I might commit suicide if left alone, and since no other friends were available (Miss Opposite was incommunicado, the McCoos were busy building a new house miles away, and the Chatfields had been recently called to Maine by some family trouble of their own), Leslie and Louise were commissioned to keep me company under the pretence of helping me to sort out and pack a multitude of orphaned things. In a moment of superb inspiration I showed the kind and credulous Farlows (we were waiting for Leslie to come for his paid tryst with Louise) a little photograph of Charlotte I had found among her affairs. From a boulder she smiled through blown hair. It had been taken in April 1934, a memorable spring. While on a business visit to the States, I had had occasion to spend several months in Pisky. We met – and had a mad love affair. I was married, alas, and she was engaged to Haze, but after I returned to Europe, we corresponded through a friend, now dead. Jean whispered she had heard some rumours and looked at the snapshot, and, still looking, handed it to John, and John removed his pipe and looked at lovely and fast Charlotte Becker, and handed it back to me. Then they left for a few hours. Happy Louise was gurgling and scolding her swain in the basement.

Hardly had the Farlows gone than a blue-chinned cleric called – and I tried to make the interview as brief as was consistent with neither hurting his feelings nor arousing his doubts. Yes, I would devote all my life to the child's welfare. Here, incidentally, was a little cross that Charlotte Becker had given me when we were both young. I had a female cousin, a respectable spinster in New York. There we would find a good private school for Dolly. Oh, what a crafty Humbert!

For the benefit of Leslie and Louise who might (and did) report it to John and Jean I made a tremendously loud and beautiful enacted long-distance call and simulated a conversation with Shirley Holmes. When John and Jean returned, I completely took them in by telling them, in a deliberately wild and confused mutter, that Lo had gone with the intermediate group on a five-day hike and could not be reached.

'Good Lord,' said Jean, 'what shall we do?'

John said it was perfectly simple – he would get the Climax

police to find the hikers – it would not take them an hour. In fact, he knew the country and—

'Look,' he continued, 'why don't I drive there right now, and you may sleep with Jean' – (he did not really add that but Jean supported his offer so passionately that it might be implied).

I broke down. I pleaded with John to let things remain the way they were. I said I could not bear to have the child all around me, sobbing, clinging to me, she was so high-strung, the experience might react on her future, psychiatrists have analysed such cases. There was a sudden pause.

'Well, you are the doctor,' said John a little bluntly. 'But after all I was Charlotte's friend and adviser. One would like to know what you are going to do about the child anyway.'

'John,' cried Jean, 'she is his child, not Harold Haze's. Don't you understand? Humbert is Dolly's real father.'

'I see,' said John. 'I am sorry. Yes, I see. I did not realize that. It simplifies matters, of course. And whatever you feel is right.'

The distraught father went on to say he would go and fetch his delicate daughter immediately after the funeral, and would do his best to give her a good time in totally different surroundings, perhaps a trip to New Mexico or California – granted, of course, he lived.

So artistically did I impersonate the calm of ultimate despair, the hush before some crazy outburst, that the perfect Farlows removed me to their house. They had a good cellar, as cellars go in this country; and that was helpful, for I feared insomnia and a ghost.

Now I must explain *my* reasons for keeping Dolores away. Naturally, at first, when Charlotte had just been eliminated and I re-entered the house a free father, and gulped down the two whisky-and-sodas I had prepared, and topped them with a pint or two of my 'pin', and went to the bathroom to get away from neighbours and friends, there was but one thing in my mind and pulse – namely, the awareness that a few hours hence, warm, brown-haired, and mine, mine, mine, Lolita would be in my arms, shedding tears that I would kiss away faster than they could well. But as I stood wide-eyed and flushed before the mirror, John Farlow tenderly tapped to inquire if I was okay – and I immediately realized it would be madness on my part to have her in the house with all those busybodies milling around and scheming to take her away from me. Indeed, unpredictable Lo herself might – who knows? – show some foolish distrust of me, a sudden repugnance, vague fear and the like – and gone would be the magic prize at the very instant of triumph.

Speaking of busybodies, I had another visitor – friend Beale, the fellow who eliminated my wife. Stodgy and solemn, looking like a kind of assistant executioner, with his bulldog jowls, small black eyes, thickly rimmed glasses and conspicuous nostrils, he was ushered in by John who then left us, closing the door upon us, with the utmost tact. Suavely saying he had twins in my stepdaughter's class, my grotesque visitor unrolled a large diagram he had made of the accident. It was, as my stepdaughter would have put it, 'a beaut', with all kinds of impressive arrows and dotted lines in varicoloured inks. Mrs H. H.'s trajectory was illustrated at several points by a series of those little outline figures – doll-like wee career girl or WAC – used in statistics as visual aids. Very clearly and conclusively, this route came into contact with a boldly traced sinuous line representing two consecutive swerves – one which the Beale car made to avoid the Junk dog (dog not shown), and the second, a kind of exaggerated continuation of the first, meant to avert the tragedy. A very black cross indicated the spot where the trim little outline figure had at last come to rest on the sidewalk. I looked for some similar mark to denote the place on the embankment where my visitor's huge wax father had reclined, but there was none. That gentleman, however, had signed the document as a witness underneath the name of Leslie Tomson, Miss Opposite and a few other people.

With his hummingbird pencil deftly and delicately flying from one point to another, Frederick demonstrated his absolute innocence and the recklessness of my wife: while he was in the act of avoiding the dog, *she* had slipped on the freshly watered asphalt and plunged forward whereas she should have flung herself not forward but backward (Fred showed how by a jerk of his padded shoulder). I said it was certainly not his fault, and the inquest upheld my view.

Breathing violently through jet-black tense nostrils, he shook his head and my hand; then, with an air of perfect *savoir vivre* and gentlemanly generosity, he offered to pay the funeral-home expenses. He expected me to refuse his offer. With a drunken sob of gratitude I accepted it. This took him aback. Slowly, incredulously, he repeated what he had said. I thanked him again, even more profusely than before.

In result of that weird interview, the numbness of my soul was for a moment resolved. And no wonder! I had actually seen the agent of fate. I had palpated the very flesh of fate – and its padded shoulder. A brilliant and monstrous mutation had suddenly taken place, and here was the instrument. Within the intricacies of the pattern (hurrying housewife, slippery pavement, a pest of a dog, steep grade, big car, baboon at its wheel), I could dimly distinguish my own vile contribution. Had I not been such a fool – or such an intuitive genius – to preserve that journal, fluids produced by vindictive anger and hot shame would not have blinded Charlotte in her dash to the mailbox. But even had they blinded her, still nothing might have happened, had not precise fate, that synchronizing phantom, mixed within its alembic the car and the dog and the sun and the shade and the wet and the weak and the strong and the stone. Adieu, Marlene! Fat fate's formal handshake (as reproduced by Beale before leaving the room) brought me out of my torpor; and I wept. Ladies and gentlemen of the jury – I wept.

24

The elms and the poplars were turning their ruffled backs to a sudden onslaught of wind, and a black thunderhead loomed above Ramsdale's white church tower when I looked around me for the last time. For unknown adventures I was leaving the livid house where I had rented a room only ten weeks before. The shades – thrifty, practical bamboo shades – were already down. On porches or in the house their rich textures lend modern drama. The house of heaven must seem pretty bare after that. A raindrop fell on my knuckles. I went back into the house for something or other while John was putting my bags into the car, and then a funny thing happened. I do not know if in these tragic notes I have sufficiently stressed the peculiar 'sending' effect that the writer's good looks – pseudo-Celtic, attractively simian, boyishly manly – had on women of every age and environment. Of course, such announcements made in the first person may sound ridiculous. But every once in a while I have to remind the reader of my appearance much as a professional novelist, who has given a character of his some mannerism or a dog, has to go on producing that dog or that mannerism every time the character crops up in the course of the book. There may be more to it in the present case. My gloomy good looks should be kept in the mind's eye if my story is to be properly understood. Pubescent Lo swooned to Humbert's charm as she did to hiccuppy music; adult Lotte loved me with a mature, possessive passion that I now deplore and respect more than I care to say. Jean Farlow, who was thirty-one and absolutely neurotic, had also apparently developed a strong liking for me. She was handsome in a carved-Indian sort of way, with a burnt sienna complexion. Her lips were like large crimson polyps, and when she emitted her special barking laugh, she showed large dull teeth and pale gums.

She was very tall, wore either slacks with sandals or billowing skirts with ballet slippers, drank any strong liquor in any amount, had had two miscarriages, wrote stories about animals, painted, as the reader knows, lakescapes, was already nursing the cancer that was to kill her at thirty-three, and was hopelessly unattractive to me. Judge then of my alarm when a few seconds before I left (she and I stood in the hallway) Jean, with her always trembling fingers, took me by the temples, and, tears in her bright blue eyes, attempted, unsuccessfully, to glue herself to my lips.

'Take care of yourself,' she said, 'kiss your daughter for me.'

A clap of thunder reverberated throughout the house, and she added:

'Perhaps, somewhere, some day, at a less miserable time, we may see each other again' (Jean, whatever, wherever you are, in minus time-space or plus soul-time, forgive me all this, parenthesis included).

And presently I was shaking hands with both of them in the street, the sloping street, and everything was whirling and flying before the approaching white deluge, and a truck with a mattress from Philadelphia was confidently rolling down to an empty house, and dust was running and writhing over the exact slab of stone where Charlotte, when they lifted the laprobe for me, had been revealed, curled up, her eyes intact, their black lashes still wet, matted, like yours, Lolita.

25

One might suppose that with all blocks removed and a prospect of delirious and unlimited delights before me, I would have mentally sunk back, heaving a sigh of delicious relief. *Eh bien, pas du tout!* Instead of basking in the beams of smiling Chance, I was obsessed by all sorts of purely ethical doubts and fears. For instance: might it not surprise people that Lo was so consistently debarred from attending festive and funeral functions in her immediate family? You remember – we had not had her at our wedding. Or another thing: granted it was the long hairy arm of Coincidence that had reached out to remove an innocent woman, might Coincidence not ignore in a heathen moment what its twin limb had done and hand Lo a premature note of commiseration? True, the accident had been reported only by the Ramsdale *Journal* – not by the Parkington *Recorder* or the Climax *Herald*, Camp Q. being in another state, and local deaths having no federal news interest; but I could not help fancying that somehow Dolly Haze had been informed already, and that at the very time I was on my way to fetch her, she was being driven to Ramsdale by friends unknown to me. Still more disquieting than all these conjectures and worries, was the fact that Humbert Humbert, a brand-new American citizen of obscure European origin, had taken no steps toward becoming the legal guardian of his dead wife's daughter (twelve years and seven months old). Would I ever dare take those steps? I could not repress a shiver whenever I imagined my nudity hemmed in by mysterious statutes in the merciless glare of the Common Law.

My scheme was a marvel of primitive art: I would whizz over to Camp Q., tell Lolita her mother was about to undergo a major operation at an invented hospital, and then keep moving with my sleepy nymphet from inn to inn while her mother got better and better and finally died. But as I travelled campward my anxiety grew. I could not bear to think I might not find Lolita there – or find, instead, another, scared, Lolita clamouring for some family friend: not the Farlows, thank God – she hardly knew them – but might there not be other people I had not reckoned with? Finally, I decided to make the long-distance call I had simulated so well a few days before. It was raining hard when I pulled up in a muddy suburb of Parkington, just before the Fork, one prong of which by-passed the city and led to the highway which crossed the hills to Lake Climax and Camp Q. I flipped off the ignition and for quite a minute sat in the car bracing myself for that telephone call, and staring at the rain, at the inundated sidewalk, at a hydrant: a hideous thing, really, painted a thick silver and red, extending the red stumps of its arms to be varnished by the rain which like stylized blood dripped upon its argent chains. No wonder that stopping beside those nightmare cripples is taboo. I drove up to a gasoline station. A surprise awaited me when at last the coins had satisfactorily clanked down and a voice was allowed to answer mine.

Holmes, the camp mistress, informed me that Dolly had gone Monday (this was Wednesday) on a hike in the hills with her group and was expected to return rather late today. Would I care to come tomorrow, and what was exactly— Without going into details, I said that her mother was hospitalized, that the situation was grave, that the child should not be told it was grave and that she should be ready to leave with me tomorrow afternoon. The two voices parted in an explosion of warmth and good will, and through some freak mechanical flaw all my coins came tumbling back to me with a hitting-the-jackpot clatter that almost made me laugh despite the disappointment at having to postpone bliss. One wonders if this sudden discharge, this spasmodic refund, was not correlated somehow, in the mind of McFate, with my having invented that little expedition before ever learning of it as I did now.

What next? I proceeded to the business centre of Parkington and devoted the whole afternoon (the weather had cleared, the wet town was like silver-and-glass) to buying beautiful things for Lo. Goodness, what crazy purchases were prompted by the poignant predilection Humbert had in those days for check weaves, bright cottons, frills, puffed-out short sleeves, soft pleats, snug-fitting bodices and generously full skirts! Oh Lolita, you are my girl, as Vee was Poe's and Bea Dante's, and what little girl would not like to whirl in a circular skirt and scanties? Did I have something special in mind? coaxing voices asked me. Swimming suits? We have them in all shades. Dream pink, frosted aqua, glans mauve, tulip red, oolala black. What about playsuits? Slips? No slips. Lo and I loathed slips.

One of my guides in these matters was an anthropometric entry made by her mother on L.'s twelfth birthday (the reader remembers that Know-Your-Child book). I had the feeling that Charlotte, moved by obscure motives of envy and dislike, had added an inch here, a pound there; but since the nymphet had no doubt grown somewhat in the last seven months, I thought I could safely accept most of those January measurements: hip girth, twenty-nine inches; thigh girth (just below the gluteal sulcus), seventeen; calf girth and neck circumference, eleven; chest circumference, twenty-seven; upper arm girth, eight; waist, twenty-three; stature, fifty-seven inches; weight, seventy-eight pounds; figure, linear; intelligence quotient, 121; vermiform appendix present, thank God.

Apart from measurements, I could of course visualize Lolita with hallucinational lucidity; and nursing as I did a tingle on my breastbone at the exact spot her silky top had come level once or twice with my heart; and feeling as I did her warm weight in my lap (so that, in a sense, I was always 'with Lolita' as a woman is 'with child'), I was not surprised to discover later that my computation had been more or less correct. Having moreover studied a midsummer sale book, it was with a very knowing air that I examined various pretty articles, sport shoes, sneakers, pumps of crushed kid for crushed kids. The painted girl in black who attended to all these poignant needs of mine turned parental scholarship and precise description into commercial euphemisms, such as '*petite*'. Another, much older woman, in a white dress, with a pancake make-up, seemed to be oddly impressed by my knowledge of junior fashions; perhaps I had a midget for mistress; so, when shown a skirt with two 'cute' pockets in front, I intentionally put a naïve male question and was rewarded by a smiling demonstration of the way the zipper worked in the back of the skirt. I had next great fun with all kinds of shorts and briefs – phantom little Lolitas dancing, falling, daisying all over the counter. We rounded up the deal with some prim cotton pyjamas in popular butcher-boy style. Humbert, the popular butcher.

There is a touch of the mythological and the enchanted in those large stores where according to ads a career girl can get a complete desk-to-date wardrobe, and where little sister can dream of the day when her wool jersey will make the boys in the back row of the classroom drool. Lifesize plastic figures of snubbed-nosed children with dun-coloured, greenish, brown-dotted, faunish faces floated around me. I realized I was the only shopper in that rather eerie place where I moved about fish-like, in a glaucous aquarium. I sensed strange thoughts form in the minds of the languid ladies that escorted me from counter to counter, from rock ledge to seaweed, and the belts and the bracelets I chose seemed to fall from siren hands into transparent water. I bought an elegant valise, had my purchases put into it, and repaired to the nearest hotel, well pleased with my day.

Somehow, in connection with that quiet poetical afternoon of fastidious shopping, I recalled the hotel or inn with the seductive name of The Enchanted Hunters which Charlotte had happened to mention shortly before my liberation. With the help of a guidebook I located it in the secluded town of Briceland, a four-hour drive from Lo's camp. I could have telephoned but fearing my voice might go out of control and lapse into coy croaks of broken English, I decided to send a wire ordering a room with twin beds for the next night. What a comic, clumsy, wavering Prince Charming I was! How some of my readers will laugh at me when I tell them the trouble I had with the wording of my telegram! What should I put: Humbert and daughter? Humberg and small daughter? Homberg and immature girl? Homburg and child? The droll mistake – the 'g' at the end – which eventually came through may have been a telepathic echo of these hesitations of mine.

And then, in the velvet of a summer night, my broodings over the philtre I had with me! Oh miserly Hamburg! Was he not a very Enchanted Hunter as he deliberated with himself over his boxful of magic ammunition? To rout the monsters of insomnia should he try himself one of those amethyst capsules? There were forty of them, all told – forty nights with a frail little sleeper at my throbbing side; could I rob myself of one such night in order to sleep? Certainly not: much too precious was each tiny plum, each microscopic planetarium with its live stardust. Oh, let me be mawkish for the nonce! I am so tired of being cynical.

26

This daily headache in the opaque air of this tombal jail is disturbing, but I must persevere. Have written more than a hundred pages and not got anywhere yet. My calendar is getting confused. That must have been around August 15, 1947. Don't think I can go on. Heart, head – everything. Lolita, Lolita, Lolita, Lolita, Lolita, Lolita, Lolita, Lolita, Lolita. Repeat till the page is full, printer.

27

Still in Parkington. Finally, I did achieve an hour's slumber – from which I was aroused by gratuitous and horribly exhausting congress with a small hairy hermaphrodite, a total stranger. By then it was six in the morning, and it suddenly occurred to me it might be a good thing to arrive at the camp earlier than I had said. From Parkington I had still a hundred miles to go, and there would be more than that to the Hazy Hills and Briceland. If I had said I would come for Dolly in the afternoon, it was only because my fancy insisted on merciful night falling as soon as possible upon my impatience. But now I foresaw all kinds of misunderstandings and was all a-jitter lest delay might give her the opportunity of some idle telephone call to Ramsdale. However, when at 9.30 a.m. I attempted to start, I was confronted by a dead battery, and noon was nigh when at last I left Parkington.

I reached my destination around half-past two; parked my car in a pine grove where a green-shirted, redheaded impish lad stood throwing horseshoes in sullen solitude; was laconically directed by him to an office in a stucco cottage; in a dying state, had to endure for several minutes the inquisitive commiseration of the camp mistress, a sluttish worn-out female with rusty hair. Dolly she said was all packed and ready to go. She knew her mother was sick but not critically. Would Mr Haze, I mean Mr Humbert, care to meet the camp counsellors? Or look at the cabins where the girls live? Each dedicated to a Disney creature? Or visit the Lodge? Or should Charlie be sent over to fetch her? The girls were just finishing fixing the Dining Room for a dance. (And perhaps afterwards she would say to somebody or other: 'The poor guy looked like his own ghost.')

Let me retain for a moment that scene in all its trivial and fateful detail: hag Holmes writing out a receipt, scratching her head, pulling a drawer out of her desk, pouring change into my impatient palm, then neatly spreading a banknote over it with a bright '. . . and five!'; photographs of girl-children; some gaudy moth or butterfly, still alive, safely pinned to the wall ('nature study'); the framed diploma of the camp's dietitian; my trembling hands; a card produced by efficient Holmes with a report of Dolly Haze's behaviour for July ('fair to good; keen on swimming and boating'); a sound of trees and birds, and my pounding heart. . . . I was standing with my back to the open door, and then I felt the blood rush to my head as I heard her respiration and voice behind me. She arrived dragging and bumping her heavy suitcase. 'Hi!' she said, and stood still, looking at me with sly, glad eyes, her soft lips parted in a slightly foolish but wonderfully endearing smile.

She was thinner and taller, and for a second it seemed to me her face was less pretty than the mental imprint I had cherished for more than a month: her cheeks looked hollowed and too much lentigo camouflaged her rosy rustic features; and that first impression (a very narrow human interval between two tiger heartbeats) carried the clear implication that all widower Humbert had to do, wanted to do, or would do, was to give this wan-looking though sun-coloured little orphan *aux yeux battus* (and even those plumbaceous umbrae under her eyes bore freckles) a sound education, a healthy and happy girlhood, a clean home, nice girl-friends of her age among whom (if the fates deigned to repay me) I might find, perhaps, a pretty little *mägdlein* for Herr Doktor Humbert alone. But 'in a wink', as the Germans say, the angelic line of conduct was erased, and I overtook my prey (time moves ahead of our fancies!), and she was my Lolita again – in fact, more of my Lolita than ever. I let my hand rest on her warm auburn head and took up her bag. She was all rose and honey, dressed in her brightest gingham, with a pattern of little red apples, and her arms and legs were of a deep golden brown, with scratches like tiny dotted lines of coagulated rubies, and the rubbed cuffs of her white socks were turned down at the remembered level, and because of her childish gait, or because I had memorized her as always wearing heelless shoes, her saddle oxfords looked somehow too large and too high-heeled for her. Goodbye, Camp Q., merry Camp Q. Goodbye, plain unwholesome food, goodbye Charlie boy. In the hot car she settled down beside me, slapped a prompt fly on her lovely knee; then, her mouth working violently on a piece of chewing gum, she rapidly cranked down the window on her side and settled back again. We sped through the striped and speckled forest.

'How's Mother?' she asked dutifully.

I said the doctors did not quite know yet what the trouble was. Anyway, something abdominal. Abominable? No, abdominal. We would have to hang around for a while. The hospital was in the country, near the gay town of Lepingville, where a great poet had resided in the early nineteenth century and where we would take in all the shows. She thought it a peachy idea and wondered if we could make Lepingville before 9 p.m.

'We should be at Briceland by dinner time,' I said, 'and tomorrow we'll visit Lepingville. How was the hike? Did you have a marvellous time at the camp?'

'Uh-huh.'

'Sorry to leave?'

'Un-un.'

'Talk, Lo – don't grunt. Tell me something.'

'What thing, Dad?' (she let the word expand with ironic deliberation).

'Any old thing.'

'Okay, if I call you that?' (eyes slit at the road).

'Quite.'

'It's a sketch, you know. When did you fall for my mummy?'

'Some day, Lo, you will understand many emotions and situations, such as for example the harmony, the beauty of spiritual relationship.'

'Bah!' said the cynical nymphet.

Shallow lull in the dialogue, filled with some landscape.

'Look Lo, at all those cows on that hillside.'

'I think I'll vomit if I look at a cow again.'

'You know, I missed you terribly, Lo.'

'*I* did not. Fact I've been revoltingly unfaithful to you, but it does not matter one bit, because you've stopped caring for me, anyway. You drive much faster than my mummy, mister.'

I slowed down from a blind seventy to a purblind fifty.

'Why do you think I have ceased caring for you, Lo?'

'Well, you haven't kissed me yet, have you?'

Inly dying, inly moaning, I glimpsed a reasonably wide shoulder of road ahead, and bumped and wobbled into the weeds. Remember she is only a child, remember she is only—

Hardly had the car come to a standstill than Lolita positively flowed into my arms. Not daring, not daring let myself go – not even daring let myself realize that *this* (sweet wetness and trembling fire) was the beginning of the ineffable life which, ably assisted by fate, I had finally willed into being – not daring really kiss her, I touched her hot, opening lips with the utmost piety, tiny sips, nothing salacious; but she, with an impatient wriggle, pressed her mouth to mine so hard that I felt her big front teeth and shared in the peppermint taste of her saliva. I knew, of course, it was but an innocent game on her part, a bit of backfisch foolery in imitation of some simulacrum of fake romance, and since (as the psychotherapist, as well as the rapist, will tell you) the limits and rules of such girlish games are fluid, or at least too childishly subtle for the senior partner to grasp – I was dreadfully afraid I might go too far and cause her to start back in revulsion and terror. And, as above all I was agonizingly anxious to smuggle her into the hermetic seclusion of The Enchanted Hunters, and we had still eighty miles to go, blessed intuition broke our embrace – a split second before a highway patrol car drew up alongside.

Florid and beetlebrowed, its driver stared at me:

'Happen to see a blue sedan, same make as yours, pass you before the junction?'

'Why, no.'

'We didn't,' said Lo, eagerly leaning across me, her innocent hand on my legs, 'but are you sure it was blue, because—'

The cop (what shadow of us was he after?) gave the little colleen his best smile and went into a U-turn.

We drove on.

'The fruithead!' remarked Lo. 'He should have nabbed *you*.'

'Why me for heaven's sake?'

'Well, the speed in this bum state is fifty, and – No, don't slow down, you dull bulb. He's gone now.'

'We have still quite a stretch,' I said, 'and I want to get there before dark. So be a good girl.'

'Bad, bad girl,' said Lo comfortably. 'Juvenile delickwent, but frank and fetching. That light was red. I've never seen such driving.'

We rolled silently through a silent townlet.

'Say, wouldn't Mother be absolutely mad if she found out we were lovers?'

'Good Lord, Lo, let us not talk that way.'

'But we *are* lovers, aren't we?'

'Not that I know of. I think we are going to have some more rain. Don't you want to tell me of those little pranks of yours in camp?'

'You talk like a book, *Dad*.'

'What have you been up to? I insist you tell me.'

'Are you easily shocked?'

'No. Go on.'

'Let us turn into a secluded lane and I'll tell you.'

'Lo, I must seriously ask you not to play the fool. Well?'

'Well – I joined in all the activities that were offered.'

'Ensuite?'

'Ansooit, I was taught to live happily and richly with others and to develop a wholesome personality. Be a cake, in fact.'

'Yes. I saw something of the sort in the booklet.'

'We loved the sings around the fire in the big stone fireplace or under the darned stars, where every girl merged her own spirit of happiness with the voice of the group.'

'Your memory is excellent, Lo, but I must trouble you to leave out the swear words. Anything else?'

'The Girl Scout's motto,' said Lo rhapsodically, 'is also mine. I fill my life with worth-while deeds such as – well, never mind what. My duty is – to be useful. I am a friend to male animals. I obey orders. I am cheerful. That was another police car. I am thrifty and I am absolutely filthy in thought, word and deed.'

'Now I do hope that's all, you witty child.'

'Yep. That's all. No – wait a sec. We baked in a reflector oven. Isn't that terrific?'

'Well, that's better.'

'We washed zillions of dishes. "Zillions" you know is schoolmarm's slang for many-many-many-many. Oh yes, last but not least, as Mother says – Now let me see – what was it? I know: We made shadowgraphs. Gee, what fun.'

'C'est bien tout?'

'C'est. Except for one little thing, something I simply can't tell you without blushing all over.'

'Will you tell me later?'

'If we sit in the dark and you let me whisper, I will. Do you sleep in your old room or in a heap with Mother?'

'Old room. Your mother may have to undergo a very serious operation, Lo.'

'Stop at that candy bar, will you,' said Lo.

Sitting on a high stool, a band of sunlight crossing her bare brown forearm, Lolita was served an elaborate ice-cream concoction topped with synthetic syrup. It was erected and brought her by a pimply brute of a boy in a greasy bow-tie who eyed my fragile child in her thin cotton frock with carnal deliberation. My impatience to reach Briceland and The Enchanted Hunters was becoming more than I could endure. Fortunately she dispatched the stuff with her usual alacrity.

'How much cash do you have?' I asked.

'Not a cent,' she said sadly, lifting her eyebrows, showing me the empty inside of her money purse.

'This is a matter that will be mended in due time,' I rejoined archly. 'Are you coming?'

'Say, I wonder if they have a washroom.'

'You are not going there,' I said firmly. 'It is sure to be a vile place. Do come on.'

She was on the whole an obedient little girl and I kissed her on the neck when we got back into the car.

'*Don't* do that,' she said looking at me with unfeigned surprise. 'Don't drool on me. You dirty man.'

She rubbed the spot against her raised shoulder.

'Sorry,' I murmured. 'I'm rather fond of you, that's all.'

We drove under a gloomy sky, up a winding road, then down again.

'Well, I'm also sort of fond of you,' said Lolita in a delayed soft voice, with a sort of sigh, and sort of settled closer to me.

(Oh, my Lolita, we shall never get there!)

Dusk was beginning to saturate pretty little Briceland, its phony colonial architecture, curiosity shops and imported shade trees, when we drove through the weakly lighted streets in search of the Enchanted Hunters. The air, despite a steady drizzle beading it, was warm and green, and a queue of people, mainly children and old men, had already formed before the box office of a movie house, dripping with jewel-fires.

'Oh, I want to see that picture. Let's go right after dinner. Oh, lets!'

'We might,' chanted Humbert – knowing perfectly well, the sly tumescent devil, that by nine, when *his* show began, she would be dead in his arms.

'Easy!' cried Lo, lurching forward, as an accursed truck in front of us, its backside carbuncles pulsating, stopped at a crossing.

If we did not get to the hotel soon, immediately, miraculously, in the very next block, I felt I would lose all control over the Haze jalopy with its ineffectual wipers and whimsical brakes; but the passers-by I applied to for directions were either strangers themselves or asked with a frown 'Enchanted what?' as if I were a madman; or else they went into such complicated explanations, with geometrical gestures, geographical generalities and strictly local clues (. . . then bear south after you hit the courthouse . . .) that I could not help losing my way in the maze of their well-meaning gibberish. Lo, whose lovely prismatic entrails had already digested the sweetmeat, was looking forward to a big meal and had begun to fidget. As to me, although I had long become used to a kind of secondary fate (McFate's inept secretary, so to speak) pettily interfering with the boss's generous magnificent plan – to grind and grope through the avenues of

Briceland was perhaps the most exasperating ordeal I had yet faced. In later months I could laugh at my inexperience when recalling the obstinate boyish way in which I had concentrated upon that particular inn with its fancy name; for all along our route countless motor courts proclaimed their vacancy in neon lights, ready to accommodate salesmen, escaped convicts, impotents, family groups, as well as the most corrupt and vigorous couples. Ah, gentle drivers gliding through summer's black nights, what frolics, what twists of lust, you might see from your impeccable highways if Kumfy Kabins were suddenly drained of their pigments and became as transparent as boxes of glass!

The miracle I hankered for did happen after all. A man and a girl, more or less conjoined in a dark car under dripping trees, told us we were in the heart of The Park, but had only to turn left at the next traffic light and there we would be. We did not see any next traffic light – in fact, The Park was as black as the sins it concealed – but soon after falling under the smooth spell of a nicely graded curve, the travellers became aware of a diamond glow through the mist, then a gleam of lakewater appeared – and there it was, marvellously and inexorably, under spectral trees, at the top of a gravelled drive – the pale palace of The Enchanted Hunters.

A row of parked cars, like pigs at a trough, seemed at first sight to forbid access; but then, by magic, a formidable convertible, resplendent, rubous in the lighted rain, came into motion – was energetically backed out by a broad-shouldered driver – and we gratefully slipped into the gap it had left. I immediately regretted my haste for I noticed that my predecessor had now taken advantage of a garage-like shelter nearby where there was ample space for another car; but I was too impatient to follow his example.

'Wow! Looks swank,' remarked my vulgar darling squinting at the stucco as she crept out into the audible drizzle and with a childish hand tweaked loose the frock-fold that had stuck in the peach-cleft – to quote Robert Browning. Under the arclights enlarged replicas of chestnut leaves plunged and played on white pillars. I unlocked the trunk compartment. A hunchbacked and hoary Negro in a uniform of sorts took our bags and wheeled them slowly into the lobby. It was full of old ladies and clergymen. Lolita sank down on her haunches to caress a pale-faced blue-freckled, black-eared cocker spaniel swooning on the floral carpet under her hand – as who would not, my heart – while I cleared my throat through the throng to the desk. There a bald porcine old man – everybody was old in that old hotel – examined my features with a polite smile, then leisurely produced my (garbled) telegram, wrestled with some dark doubts, turned his head to look at the clock, and finally said he was very sorry, he had held the room with the twin beds till half-past six, and now it was gone. A religious convention, he said, had clashed with a flower show in Briceland, and 'The name,' I said coldly, 'is not Humberg and not Humbug, but Herbert, I mean Humbert, and any room will do, just put in a cot for my little daughter. She is ten and very tired.'

The pink old fellow peered good-naturedly at Lo – still squatting, listening in profile, lips parted, to what the dog's mistress, an ancient lady swathed in violet veils, was telling her from the depths of a cretonne easy chair.

Whatever doubts the obscene fellow had, they were dispelled by that blossom-like vision. He said, he might still have a room, had one, in fact – with a double bed. As to the cot—

'Mr Potts, do we have any cots left?' Potts, also pink and bald, with white hairs growing out of his ears and other holes, would see what could be done. He came and spoke while I unscrewed my fountain pen. Impatient Humbert!

'Our double beds are really triple,' Potts cosily said tucking me and my kid in. 'One crowded night we had three ladies and a child like yours sleep together. I believe one of the ladies was a disguised man [*my* static]. However – would there be a spare cot in 49, Mr Swine?'

'I think it went to the Swoons,' said Swine, the initial old clown.

'We'll manage somehow,' I said. 'My wife may join us later – but even then, I suppose, we'll manage.'

The two pink pigs were now among my best friends. In the slow clear hand of crime I wrote: Dr Edgar H. Humbert and daughter, 342 Lawn Street, Ramsdale. A key (342!) was half-shown to me (magician showing object he is about to palm) – and handed over to Uncle Tom. Lo, leaving the dog as she would leave me some day, rose from her haunches; a raindrop fell on Charlotte's grave; a handsome young Negress slipped open the elevator door, and the doomed child went in followed by her throat-clearing father and crayfish Tom with the bags.

Parody of a hotel corridor. Parody of silence and death.

'Say, it's our house number,' said cheerful Lo.

There was a double bed, a mirror, a double bed in the mirror, a closet door with mirror, a bathroom door ditto, a blue-dark window, a reflected bed there, the same in the closet mirror, two chairs, a glass-topped table, two bedtables, a double bed: a big panel bed, to be exact, with a Tuscan rose chenille spread, and two frilled, pink-shaded nightlamps, left and right.

I was tempted to place a five-dollar bill in that sepia palm, but thought the largesse might be misconstrued, so I placed a quarter. Added another. He withdrew. Click. *Enfin seuls.*

'Are we to sleep in *one* room?' said Lo, her features working in that dynamic way they did – not cross or disgusted (though plain on the brink of it) but just dynamic – when she wanted to load a question with violent significance.

'I've asked them to put in a cot. Which I'll use if you like.'

'You are crazy,' said Lo.

'Why, my darling?'

'Because, my dahrling, when dahrling Mother finds out she'll divorce you and strangle me.'

Just dynamic. Not really taking the matter too seriously.

'Now look here,' I said, sitting down, while she stood, a few feet from me, and stared at herself contentedly, not unpleasantly surprised at her own appearance, filling with her own rosy sunshine the surprised and pleased closet-door mirror.

'Look here, Lo. Let's settle this once for all. For all practical purposes I am your father. I have a feeling of great tenderness for you. In your mother's absence I am responsible for your welfare. We are not rich, and while we travel, we shall be obliged – we shall be thrown a good deal together. Two people sharing one room, inevitably enter into a kind – how shall I say – a kind—'

'The word is incest,' said Lo – and walked into the closet, walked out again with a young golden giggle, opened the adjoining door, and after carefully peering inside with her strange smoky eyes lest she make another mistake, retired to the bathroom.

I opened the window, tore off my sweat-drenched shirt, changed, checked the pill vial in my coat pocket, unlocked the—

She drifted out. I tried to embrace her: casually, a bit of controlled tenderness before dinner.

She said: 'Look, let's cut out the kissing game and get something to eat.'

It was then that I sprang my surprise.

Oh, what a dreamy pet! She walked up to the open suitcase as if stalking it from afar, at a kind of slow-motion walk, peering at that distant treasure box on the luggage support. (Was there something wrong, I wondered, with those great grey eyes of hers, or were we both plunged in the same enchanted mist?) She stepped up to it, lifting her rather high-heeled feet rather high, and bending her beautiful boy-knees while she walked through dilating space with the lentor of one walking under water or in a flight dream. Then she raised by the armlets a copper-coloured, charming and quite expensive vest, very slowly stretching it between her silent hands as if she were a bemused bird-hunter holding his breath over the incredible bird he spread out by the tips of its flaming wings. Then (while I stood waiting for her) she pulled out the slow snake of a brilliant belt and tried it on.

Then she crept into my waiting arms, radiant, relaxed, caressing me with her tender, mysterious, impure, indifferent, twilight eyes – for all the world, like the cheapest of cheap cuties. For that is what nymphets imitate – while we moan and die.

'What's the katter with misses?' I muttered (word-control gone) into her hair.

'If you must know,' she said, 'you do it the wrong way.'

'Show, wight ray.'

'All in good time,' responded the spoonerette.

Seva ascendes, pulsata, brulans, kitzelans, dementissima. Elevator clatterans, pausa, clatterans, populus in corridoro. Hanc nisi mors mihi adimet nemo! Juncea puellula, jo pensavo fondissime, nobserva nihil quidquam; but, of course, in another moment I might have committed some dreadful blunder; fortunately, she returned to the treasure box.

From the bathroom, where it took me quite a time to shift back into normal gear for a humdrum purpose, I heard, standing, drumming, retaining my breath, my Lolita's 'oo's' and 'gee's' of girlish delight.

She had used the soap only because it was sample soap.

'Well, come on, my dear, if you are as hungry as I am.'

And so to the elevator, daughter swinging her old white purse, father walking in front (notabene: never behind, she is not a lady). As we stood (now side by side) waiting to be taken down, she threw back her head, yawned without restraint and shook her curls.

'When did they make you get up at that camp?'

'Half-past—' she stifled another yawn – 'six' – yawn in full with a shiver of all her frame. 'Half-past,' she repeated, her throat filling up again.

The dining room met us with a smell of fried fat and a faded smile. It was a spacious and pretentious place with maudlin murals depicting enchanted hunters in various postures and states of enchantment amid a medley of pallid animals, dryads and trees. A few scattered old ladies, two clergymen, and a man in a sports coat were finishing their meals in silence. The dining room closed at nine, and the green-clad, poker-faced serving girls were, happily, in a desperate hurry to get rid of us.

'Does not he look exactly, but exactly, like Quilty?' said Lo in a soft voice, her sharp brown elbow not pointing, but visibly burning to point, at the lone diner in the loud checks, in the far corner of the room.

'Like our fat Ramsdale dentist?'

Lo arrested the mouthful of water she had just taken, and put down her dancing glass.

'Course not,' she said with a splutter of mirth. 'I meant the writer fellow in the Droms ad.'

Oh, Fame! Oh, Femina!

When the dessert was plunked down – a huge wedge of cherry pie for the young lady and vanilla ice-cream for her protector, most of which she expeditiously added to her pie – I produced a small vial containing Papa's Purple Pills. As I look back at those seasick murals, at that strange and monstrous moment, I can only explain my behaviour then by the mechanism of that dream vacuum wherein revolves a deranged mind; but at the time, it all seemed quite simple and inevitable to me. I glanced around, satisfied myself that the last diner had left, removed the stopper, and with the utmost deliberation tipped the philtre into my palm. I had carefully rehearsed before a mirror the gesture of clapping my empty hand to my open mouth and swallowing a (fictitious) pill. As I expected, she pounced upon the vial with its plump, beautifully coloured capsules loaded with Beauty's Sleep.

'Blue!' she exclaimed. 'Violet blue. What are they made of?'

'Summer skies,' I said, 'and plums and figs, and the grape-blood of emperors.'

'No, seriously – please.'

'Oh, just Purpills. Vitamin X. Makes one strong as an ox or an ax. Want to try one?'

Lolita stretched out her hand, nodding vigorously.

I had hoped the drug would work fast. It certainly did. She had had a long long day, she had gone rowing in the morning with Barbara whose sister was Waterfront Director, as the adorable accessible nymphet now started to tell me in between suppressed palate-humping yawns, growing in volume – oh, how fast the magic potion worked! – and had been active in other ways too. The movie that had vaguely loomed in her mind was, of course, by the time we watertreaded out of the dining room, forgotten. As we stood in the elevator, she leaned against me, faintly smiling wouldn't you like me to tell you? – half-closing her dark-lidded eyes. 'Sleepy, huh?' said Uncle Tom who was bringing up the quiet Franco-Irish gentleman and his daughter as well as two withered women, experts in roses. They looked with sympathy at my frail, tanned, tottering, dazed rose darling. I had almost to carry her into our room. There, she sat down on the edge of the bed, swaying a little, speaking in dove-dull, long-drawn tones.

'If I tell you – if I tell you, will you promise [sleepy, so sleepy – head lolling, eyes going out], promise you won't make complaints?'

'Later, Lo. Now go to bed. I'll leave you here, and you go to bed. Give you ten minutes.'

'Oh, I've been such a disgusting girl,' she went on, shaking her hair, removing with slow fingers a velvet hair ribbon. 'Lemme tell you—'

'Tomorrow, Lo. Go to bed, go to bed – for goodness sake, to bed.'

I pocketed the key and walked downstairs.

28

Gentlewoman of the jury! Bear with me! Allow me to take just a tiny bit of your precious time! So this was *le grand moment*. I had left my Lolita still sitting on the edge of the abysmal bed, drowsily raising her foot, fumbling at the shoelaces and showing as she did so the nether side of her thigh up to the crotch of her panties – she had always been singularly absent-minded, or shameless, or both, in matters of legshow. This, then, was the hermetic vision of her which I had locked in – after satisfying myself that the door carried no inside bolt. The key, with its numbered dangler of carved wood, became forthwith the weighty sesame to a rapturous and formidable future. It was mine, it was part of my hot hairy fist. In a few minutes – say, twenty, say half an hour, *sicher ist sicher* as my uncle Gustave used to say –

I would let myself into that '342' and find my nymphet, my beauty and bride, imprisoned in her crystal sleep. Jurors! If my happiness could have talked, it would have filled that genteel hotel with a deafening roar. And my only regret today is that I did not quietly deposit key '342' at the office, and leave the town, the country, the continent, the hemisphere – indeed, the globe – that very same night.

Let me explain. I was not unduly disturbed by her self-accusatory innuendoes. I was still firmly resolved to pursue my policy of sparing her purity by operating only in the stealth of night, only upon a completely anaesthetized little nude. Restraint and reverence were still my motto – even if that 'purity' (incidentally, thoroughly debunked by modern science) had been slightly damaged through some juvenile erotic experience, no doubt homosexual, at that accursed camp of hers. Of course, in my old-fashioned, old-world way, I, Jean-Jacques Humbert, had taken for granted, when I first met her, that she was as unravished as the stereotypical notion of 'normal child' had been since the lamented end of the Ancient World BC and its fascinating practices. We are not surrounded in our enlightened era by little slave flowers that can be casually plucked between business and bath as they used to be in the days of the Romans; and we do not, as dignified Orientals did in still more luxurious times, use tiny entertainers fore and aft between the mutton and the rose sherbet. The whole point is that the old link between the adult world and the child world has been completely severed nowadays by new customs and new laws. Despite my having dabbled in psychiatry and social work, I really knew very little about children. After all, Lolita was only twelve, and no matter what concessions I made to time and place – even bearing in mind the crude behaviour of American schoolchildren – I still was under the impression that whatever went on among those brash brats, went on at a later age, and in a different environment. Therefore (to retrieve the thread of this explanation) the moralist in me by-passed the issue by clinging to conventional notions of what twelve-year-old girls should be. The child therapist in me (a fake, as most of them are – but on matter) regurgitated neo-Freudian hash and conjured up a dreaming and exaggerating Dolly in the 'latency' period of girlhood. Finally, the sensualist in me (a great and insane monster) had no objection to some depravity in his prey. But somewhere behind the raging bliss, bewildered shadows conferred – and not to have heeded them, this is what I regret! Human beings, attend! I should have understood that Lolita had *already* proved to be something quite different from innocent Annabel, and that the nymphean evil breathing through every pore of the fey child that I had prepared for my secret delectation, would make the secrecy impossible, and the delectation lethal. I should have known (by the signs made to me by something in Lolita – the real child Lolita or some haggard angel behind her back) that nothing but pain and horror would result from the expected rapture. Oh, winged gentlemen of the jury!

And she was mine, she was mine, the key was in my fist, my fist was in my pocket, she was mine. In the course of the evocations and schemes to which I had dedicated so many insomnias, I had gradually eliminated all the superfluous blur, and by stacking level upon level of translucent vision, had evolved a final picture. Naked, except for one sock and her charm bracelet, spread-eagled on the bed where my philtre had felled her – so I foreglimpsed her; a velvet hair ribbon was still clutched in her hand; her honey-brown body, with the white negative image of a rudimentary swimsuit patterned against her tan, presented to me its pale breastbuds; in the rosy lamplight, a little pubic floss glistened on its plump hillock. The cold key with its warm wooden addendum was in my pocket.

I wandered through various public rooms, glory below, gloom above: for the look of lust always is gloomy; lust is never quite sure – even when the velvety victim is locked up in one's dungeon – that some rival devil or influential god may still not abolish one's prepared triumph. In common parlance, I needed a drink; but there was no bar-room in that venerable place full of perspiring philistines and period objects.

I drifted to the Men's Room. There, a person in clerical black – a 'hearty party' *comme on dit* – checking with the assistance of Vienna, if it was still there, inquired of me how I had liked Dr Boyd's talk, and looked puzzled when I (King Sigmund the Second) said Boyd was quite a boy. Upon which, I neatly chucked the tissue paper I had been wiping my sensitive fingertips with into the receptacle provided for it, and sallied lobbyward. Comfortably resting my elbows on the counter, I asked Mr Potts was he quite sure my wife had not telephoned, and what about that cot? He answered she had not (she was dead, of course) and the cot would be installed tomorrow if we decided to stay on. From a big crowded place called The Hunters' Hall came a sound of many voices discussing horticulture or eternity. Another room, called The Raspberry Room, all bathed in light, with bright little tables and a large one with 'refreshments', was still empty except for a hostess (that type of worn woman with a glassy smile and Charlotte's manner of speaking); she floated up to me to ask if I was Mr Braddock, because if so, Miss Beard had been looking for me. 'What a name for a woman,' I said and strolled away.

In and out of my heart flowed my rainbow blood. I would give her till half-past nine. Going back to the lobby, I found there a change: a number of people in floral dresses or black cloth had formed little groups here and there, and some elfish chance offered me the sight of a delightful child of Lolita's age, in Lolita's type of frock, but pure white, and there was a white ribbon in her black hair. She was not pretty, but she was a nymphet, and her ivory pale legs and lily neck formed for one memorable moment a most pleasurable antiphony (in terms of spinal music) to my desire for Lolita, brown and pink, flushed and fouled. The pale child noticed my gaze (which was really quite casual and debonair) and, being ridiculously self-conscious, lost countenance completely, rolling her eyes and putting the back of her hand to her cheek, and pulling at the hem of her skirt, and finally turning her thin mobile shoulder blades to me in specious chat with her cow-like mother.

I left the loud lobby and stood outside, on the white steps, looking at the hundreds of powdered bugs wheeling around the lamps in the soggy black night, full of ripple and stir. All I would do – all I would dare to do – would amount to such a trifle. . . .

Suddenly I was aware that in the darkness next to me there was somebody sitting in a chair on the pillared porch, I could not really see him but what gave him away was the rasp of a screwing off, then a discreet gurgle, then the final note of a placid screwing on. I was about to move away when his voice addressed me:

'Where the devil did you get her?'

'I beg your pardon?'

'I said: the weather is getting better.'

'Seems so.'

'Who's the lassie?'

'My daughter.'

'You lie – she's not.'

'I beg your pardon?'

'I said: July was hot. Where's her mother?'

'Dead.'

'I see. Sorry. By the way, why don't you two lunch with me tomorrow. That dreadful crowd will be gone by then.'

'We'll be gone too. Good night.'

'Sorry. I'm pretty drunk. Good night. That child of yours needs a lot of sleep. Sleep is a rose, as the Persians say. Smoke?'

'Not now.'

He struck a light, but because he was drunk, or because the wind was, the flame illumined not him but another person, a very old man, one of those permanent guests of old hotels – and his white rocker. Nobody said anything and the darkness returned to its initial place. Then I heard the old-timer cough and deliver himself of some sepulchral mucus.

I left the porch. At least half an hour in all had elapsed. I ought to have asked for a sip. The strain was beginning to tell. If a violin string can ache, then I was that string. But it would have been unseemly to display any hurry. As I made my way through a constellation of fixed people in one corner of the lobby, there came a blinding flash – and beaming Dr Braddock, two orchid-ornamentalized matrons, the small girl in white, and presumably the bared teeth of Humbert Humbert sidling between the bride-like lassie and the enchanted cleric, were immortalized – in so far as the texture and print of small-town newspapers can be deemed immortal. A twittering group had gathered near the elevator. I again chose the stairs, 342 was near the fire escape. One could still – but the key was already in the lock, and then I was in the room.

29

The door of the lighted bathroom stood ajar; in addition to that, a skeleton glow came through the Venetian blind from the outside arclights; those intercrossed rays penetrated the darkness of the bedroom and revealed the following situation.

Clothed in one of her old nightgowns, my Lolita lay on her side with her back to me, in the middle of the bed. Her lightly veiled body and bare limbs formed a Z. She had put both pillows under her dark tousled head; a band of pale light crossed her top vertebrae.

I seemed to have shed my clothes and slipped into pyjamas with the kind of fantastic instantaneousness which is implied when in a cinematographic scene the process of changing is cut;

and I had already placed my knee on the edge of the bed when Lolita turned her head and stared at me through the striped shadows.

Now this was something the intruder had not expected. The whole pill-spiel (a rather sordid affair, *entre nous soit dit*) had had for object a fastness of sleep that a whole regiment would not have disturbed, and here she was staring at me, and thickly calling me 'Barbara'. Barbara, wearing my pyjamas which were much too tight for her, remained poised motionless over the little sleep-talker. Softly, with a hopeless sigh, Dolly turned away, resuming her initial position. For at least two minutes I waited and strained on the brink, like that tailor with his home-made parachute forty years ago when about to jump from the Eiffel Tower. Her faint breathing had the rhythm of sleep. Finally I heaved myself on to my narrow margin of bed, stealthily pulled at the odds and ends of sheets piled up to the south of my stone-cold heels – and Lolita lifted her head and gaped at me.

As I learned later from a helpful pharmaceutist, the purple pill did not even belong to the big and noble family of barbiturates, and though it might have induced sleep in a neurotic who believed it to be a potent drug, it was too mild a sedative to affect for any length of time a wary, albeit weary, nymphet. Whether the Ramsdale doctor was a charlatan or a shrewd old rogue, does not, and did not, really matter. What mattered, was that I had been deceived. When Lolita opened her eyes again, I realized that whether or not the drug might work later in the night, the security I had relied upon was a sham one. Slowly her head turned away and dropped on to her unfair amount of pillow. I lay quite still on my brink, peering at her rumpled hair, at the glimmer of nymphet flesh, where half a haunch and half a shoulder dimly showed, and trying to gauge the depth of her sleep by the rate of her respiration. Some time passed, nothing changed, and I decided I might risk getting a little closer to that lovely and maddening glimmer; but hardly had I moved into its warm purlieus than her breathing was suspended, and I had the odious feeling that little Dolores was wide awake and would explode in screams if I touched her with any part of my wretchedness. Please, reader: no matter your exasperation with the tender-hearted, morbidly sensitive, infinitely circumspect hero of my book, do not skip these essential pages! Imagine me; I shall not exist if you do not imagine me; try to discern the doe in me, trembling in the forest of my own iniquity; let's even smile a little. After all, there is no harm in smiling. For instance (I almost wrote 'frinstance'), I had no place to rest my head, and a fit of heartburn (they call those fries 'French', *grand Dieu!*) was added to my discomfort.

She was again fast asleep, my nymphet, but still I did not dare to launch upon my enchanted voyage. *La Petite Dormeuse ou l'Amant Ridicule.* Tomorrow I would stuff her with those earlier pills that had so thoroughly numbed her mummy. In the glove compartment – or in the Gladstone bag? Should I wait a solid hour and then creep up again? The science of nympholepsy is a precise science. Actual contact would do it in one second flat. An interspace of a millimetre would do it in ten. Let us wait.

There is nothing louder than an American hotel; and, mind you, this was supposed to be a quiet, cosy, old-fashioned, homey place – 'gracious living' and all that stuff. The clatter of the elevator's gate – some twenty yards north-east of my head but as clearly perceived as if it were inside my left temple – alternated with the banging and booming of the machine's various evolutions and lasted well beyond midnight. Every now and then, immediately east of my left ear (always assuming I lay on my back, not daring to direct my viler side toward the nebulous haunch of my bed-mate), the corridor would brim with cheerful, resonant and inept exclamations ending in a volley of good-nights. When *that* stopped, a toilet immediately north of my cerebellum took over. It was a manly, energetic, deep-throated toilet, and it was used many times. Its gurgle and gush and a long afterflow shook the wall behind me. Then someone in a southern direction was extravagantly sick, almost coughing out his life with his liquor, and his toilet descended like a veritable Niagara, immediately beyond our bathroom. And when finally all the waterfalls had stopped, and the enchanted hunters were sound asleep, the avenue under the window of my insomnia, to the west of my wake – a staid, eminently residential, dignified alley of huge trees – degenerated into the despicable haunt of gigantic trucks roaring through the wet and windy night.

And less than six inches from me and my burning life, was nebulous Lolita! After a long stirless vigil, my tentacles moved towards her again, and this time the creak of the mattress did not awake her. I managed to bring my ravenous bulk so close to her that I felt the aura of her bare shoulder like a warm breath upon my cheek. And then, she sat up, gasped, muttered with insane rapidity something about boats, tugged at the sheets and lapsed back into her rich, dark, young unconsciousness. As she tossed, within that abundant flow of sleep, recently auburn, at present lunar, her arm struck me across the face. For a second I held her. She freed herself from the shadow of my embrace – doing this not consciously, not violently, not with any personal distaste, but with the neutral plaintive murmur of a child demanding its natural rest. And again the situation remained the same: Lolita with her curved spine to Humbert, Humbert resting his head on his hand and burning with desire and dyspepsia.

The latter necessitated a trip to the bathroom for a draught of water which is the best medicine I know in my case, except perhaps milk with radishes; and when I re-entered the strange pale-striped fastness where Lolita's old and new clothes reclined in various attitudes of enchantment on pieces of furniture that seemed vaguely afloat, my impossible daughter sat up and in clear tones demanded a drink, too. She took the resilient and cold paper cup in her shadowy hand and gulped down its contents gratefully, her long eyelashes pointing cupward, and then, with an infantile gesture that carried more charm than any carnal caress, little Lolita wiped her lips against my shoulder. She fell back on her pillow (I had subtracted mine while she drank) and was instantly asleep again.

I had not dared offer her a second helping of the drug, and had not abandoned hope that the first might still consolidate her sleep. I started to move toward her, ready for any disappointment, knowing I had better wait but incapable of waiting. My pillow smelled of her hair. I moved toward my glimmering darling, stopping or retreating every time I thought she stirred or was about to stir. A breeze from wonderland had begun to affect my thoughts, and now they seemed couched in italics, as if the surface reflecting them were wrinkled by the phantasm of that breeze. Time and again my consciousness folded the wrong way, my shuffling body entered the sphere of sleep, shuffled out again, and once or twice I caught myself drifting into a melancholy snore. Mists of tenderness enfolded mountains of longing. Now and then it seemed to me that the enchanted prey was about to meet half-way the enchanted hunter, that her haunch was working its way toward me under the soft sand of a remote and fabulous beach; and then her dimpled dimness would stir, and I would know she was farther away from me than ever.

If I dwell at some length on the tremors and gropings of that distant night, it is because I insist upon proving that I am not, and never was, and never could have been, a brutal scoundrel. The gentle and dreamy regions through which I crept were the patrimonies of poets – *not* crime's prowling ground. Had I reached my goal, my ecstasy would have been all softness, a case of internal combustion of which she would hardly have felt the heat, even if she were wide awake. But I still hoped she might gradually be engulfed in a completeness of stupor that would allow me to taste more than a glimmer of her. And so, in between tentative approximations, with a confusion of perception metamorphosing her into eyespots of moonlight or a fluffy flowering bush, I would dream I regained consciousness, dream I lay in wait.

In the first antemeridian hours there was a lull in the restless hotel night. Then around four the corridor toilet cascaded and its door banged. A little after five a reverberating monologue began to arrive, in several instalments, from some courtyard or parking place. It was not really a monologue, since the speaker stopped every few seconds to listen (presumably) to another fellow, but that other voice did not reach me, and so no real meaning could be derived from the part heard. Its matter-of-fact intonations, however, helped to bring in the dawn, and the room was already suffused with lilac grey, when several industrious toilets went to work, one after the other, and the clattering and whining elevator began to rise and take down early risers and downers, and for some minutes I miserably dozed, and Charlotte was a mermaid in a greenish tank, and somewhere in the passage Dr Boyd said 'Good morning to you' in a fruity voice, and birds were busy in the trees, and then Lolita yawned.

Frigid gentlewomen of the jury! I had thought that months, perhaps years, would elapse before I dared to reveal myself to Dolores Haze; but by 6 she was wide awake, and by 6.15 we were technically lovers. I am going to tell you something very strange: it was she who seduced me.

Upon hearing her first morning yawn, I feigned handsome profiled sleep. I just did not know what to do. Would she be shocked at finding me by her side, and not in some spare bed? Would she collect her clothes and lock herself up in the bathroom? Would she demand to be taken at once to Ramsdale – to her mother's bedside – back to camp? But my Lo was a sportive lassie. I felt her eyes on me, and when she uttered at last that beloved chortling note of hers, I knew her eyes had been laughing. She rolled over to my side, and her warm brown hair came against my collarbone. I gave a mediocre imitation of waking up. We lay quietly. I gently caressed her hair, and we gently kissed. Her kiss, to my delirious embarrassment, had some rather comical refinements of flutter and probe which made me conclude she had been coached at an early age by a little Lesbian. No Charlie boy could have taught her *that.* As if to see whether I had my fill and learned the lesson, she drew away and surveyed me. Her cheekbones were flushed, her full underlip glistened, my dissolution was near. All at once, with a burst of rough glee (the sign of the nymphet!), she put her mouth to my ear – but for quite a while my mind could not separate into words the hot thunder of her whisper, and she laughed, and brushed the hair off her face, and tried again, and gradually the odd sense of living in a brand new, mad new dream world, where everything was permissible, came over me as I realized what she was suggesting. I answered I did not know what game she and Charlie had played. 'You mean you have never—?' – her features twisted into a stare of disgusted incredulity. 'You have never—' she started again. I took time out by nuzzling her a little. 'Lay off, will you,' she said with a twangy whine, hastily removing her brown shoulder from my lips. (It was very curious the way she considered – and kept doing so for a long time – all caresses except kisses on the mouth or the stark act of love either 'romantic slosh' or 'abnormal'.)

'You mean,' she persisted, now kneeling above me, 'you never did it when you were a kid?'

'Never,' I said quite truthfully.

'Okay,' said Lolita, 'here is where we start.'

However, I shall not bore my learned readers with a detailed account of Lolita's presumption. Suffice it to say that not a trace of modesty did I perceive in this beautiful hardly formed young girl whom modern co-education, juvenile mores, the campfire racket and so forth had utterly and hopelessly depraved. She saw the stark act merely as part of a youngster's furtive world, unknown to adults. What adults did for purposes of procreation was no business of hers. My life was handled by little Lo in an energetic, matter-of-fact manner as if it were an insensate gadget unconnected with me. While eager to impress me with the world of tough kids, she was not quite prepared for certain discrepancies between a kid's life and mine. Pride alone prevented her from giving up; for, in my strange predicament, I feigned supreme stupidity and had her have her way – at least while I could still bear it. But really these are irrelevant matters; I am not concerned with so-called 'sex' at all. Anybody can imagine those elements of animality. A greater endeavour lures me on: to fix once for all the perilous magic of nymphets.

30

I have to tread carefully. I have to speak in a whisper. Oh you, veteran crime reporter, you grave old usher, you once popular policeman, now in solitary confinement after gracing that school crossing for years, you wretched emeritus read to by a boy! It would never do, would it, to have you fellows fall madly in love with my Lolita! Had I been a painter, had the management of The Enchanted Hunters lost its mind one summer day and commissioned me to redecorate their dining room with murals of my own making, this is what I might have thought up, let me list some fragments:

There would have been a lake. There would have been an arbour in flame-flower. There would have been nature studies – a tiger pursuing a bird of paradise, a choking snake sheathing whole the flayed trunk of a shoat. There would have been a sultan, his face expressing great agony (belied, as it were, by his moulding caress), helping a callypygean slave child to climb a column of onyx. There would have been those luminous globules of gonadal glow that travel up the opalescent sides of juke boxes. There would have been all kinds of camp activities on the part of the intermediate group, Canoeing, Coranting, Combing Curls in the lakeside sun. There would have been poplars, apples, a suburban Sunday. There would have been a fire opal dissolving within a ripple-ringed pool, a last throb, a last dab of colour, stinging red, smarting pink, a sigh, a wincing child.

31

I am trying to describe these things not to re-live them in my present boundless misery, but to sort out the portion of hell and the portion of heaven in that strange, awful, maddening world – nymphet love. The beastly and beautiful merged at one point, and it is that borderline I would like to fix, and I feel I fail to do so utterly. Why?

The stipulation of the Roman law, according to which a girl may marry at twelve, was adopted by the Church, and is still preserved, rather tacitly, in some of the United States. And fifteen is lawful everywhere. There is nothing wrong, say both hemispheres, when a brute of forty, blessed by the local priest and bloated with drink, sheds his sweat-drenched finery and thrusts himself up to the hilt into his youthful bride. 'In such stimulating temperate climates [says an old magazine in this prison library] as St Louis, Chicago and Cincinnati, girls mature about the end of their twelfth year.' Dolores Haze was born less than three hundred miles from stimulating Cincinnati. I have but followed nature. I am nature's faithful hound. Why then this horror that I cannot shake off? Did I deprive her of her flower? Sensitive gentlewomen of the jury, I was not even her first lover.

32

She told me the way she had been debauched. We ate flavourless mealy bananas, bruised peaches and very palatable potato chips, and *die Kleine* told me everything. Her voluble but disjointed account was accompanied by many a droll *moue*. As I think I have already observed, I especially remember one wry face on an 'ugh!' basis: jelly-mouth distended sideways and eyes rolled up in a routine blend of comic disgust, resignation and tolerance for young frailty.

Her astounding tale started with an introductory mention of her tent-mate of the previous summer, at another camp, a 'very select' one as she put it. That tent-mate ('quite a derelict character', 'half-crazy', but a 'swell kid') instructed her in various manipulations. At first, loyal Lo refused to tell me her name.

'Was it Grace Angel?' I asked.

She shook her head. No, it wasn't, it was the daughter of a big shot. He—

'Was it perhaps Rose Carmine?'

'No of course not. Her father—'

'Was it, then, Agnes Sheridan perchance?'

She swallowed and shook her head – and then did a double take.

'Say, how come you know all those kids?'

I explained.

'Well,' she said. 'They are pretty bad, some of that school bunch, but not that bad. If you have to know, her name was Elizabeth Talbot, she goes now to a swanky private school, her father is an executive.'

I recalled with a funny pang the frequency with which poor Charlotte used to introduce into party chat such elegant titbits as 'when my daughter was out hiking last year with the Talbot girl'.

I wanted to know if either mother learned of those sapphic diversions?

'Gosh, no,' exhaled limp Lo mimicking dread and relief, pressing a falsely fluttering hand to her chest.

I was more interested, however, in heterosexual experience. She had entered the sixth grade at eleven, soon after moving to Ramsdale from the Middle West. What did she mean by 'pretty bad'?

Well, the Miranda twins had shared the same bed for years, and Donald Scott, who was the dumbest boy in the school, had done it with Hazel Smith in his uncle's garage, and Kenneth Knight – who was the brightest – used to exhibit himself wherever and whenever he had a chance, and—

'Let us switch to Camp Q.,' I said. And presently I got the whole story.

Barbara Burke, a sturdy blonde, two years older than Lo and by far the camp's best swimmer, had a very special canoe which she shared with Lo 'because I was the only other girl who could make Willow Island' (some swimming test, I imagine). Through July, every morning – mark, reader, every blessed morning – Barbara and Lo would be helped to carry the boat to Onyx or Eryx (two small lakes in the wood) by Charlie Holmes, the camp mistress's son, aged thirteen – and the only human male for a couple of miles around (excepting an old meek stone-deaf handyman, and a farmer in an old Ford who sometimes sold the campers eggs as farmers will); every morning, oh my reader, the three children would take a short cut through the beautiful innocent forest brimming with all the emblems of youth, dew, bird-songs, and at one point, among the luxuriant undergrowth, Lo would be left as sentinel, while Barbara and the boy copulated behind a bush.

At first, Lo had refused 'to try what it was like', but curiosity and camaraderie prevailed, and soon she and Barbara were doing it by turns with the silent, coarse and surly but indefatigable Charlie, who had as much sex appeal as a raw carrot but sported a fascinating collection of contraceptives which he used to fish out of a third nearby lake, a considerably larger and more populous one, called Lake Climax, after the booming young factory town of that name. Although conceding it was 'sort of fun' and 'fine for the complexion', Lolita, I am glad to say, held Charlie's mind and manners in the greatest contempt. Nor had her temperament been roused by that filthy fiend. In fact, I think he had rather stunned it, despite the 'fun'.

By that time it was close to ten. With the ebb of lust, an ashen sense of awfulness, abetted by the realistic drabness of a grey neuralgic day, crept over me and hummed within my temples. Brown, naked, frail Lo, her narrow white buttocks to me, her sulky face to a door mirror, stood, arms akimbo, feet (in new slippers with pussy-fur tops) wide apart, and through a fore-hanging lock tritely mugged at herself in the glass. From the corridor came the cooing voices of coloured maids at work, and presently there was a mild attempt to open the door of our room. I had Lo go to the bathroom and take a much-needed soap shower. The bed was a frightful mess with overtones of potato chips. She tried on a two-piece navy wool, then a sleeveless blouse with a swirly clathrate skirt, but the first was too tight and the second too ample, and when I begged her to hurry up (the situation was beginning to frighten me), Lo viciously sent those nice presents of mine hurtling into a corner, and put on yesterday's dress. When she was ready at last, I gave her a lovely new purse of simulated calf (in which I had slipped quite a few pennies and two mint-bright dimes) and told her to buy herself a magazine in the lobby.

'I'll be down in a minute,' I said, 'And if I were you, my dear, I would not talk to strangers.'

Except for my poor little gifts, there was not much to pack; but I was forced to devote a dangerous amount of time (was she up to something downstairs?) to arranging the bed in such a way as to suggest the abandoned nest of a restless father and his tom-boy daughter, instead of an ex-convict's saturnalia with a couple of fat old whores. Then I finished dressing and had the hoary bellboy come up for the bags.

Everything was fine. There, in the lobby, she sat, deep in an overstuffed blood-red armchair, deep in a lurid movie magazine. A fellow of my age in tweeds (the genre of the place had changed overnight to a spurious country-squire atmosphere) was staring at my Lolita over his dead cigar and stale newspaper. She wore her professional white socks and saddle oxfords, and that bright print frock with the square throat; a splash of jaded lamplight brought out the golden down on her warm brown limbs. There she sat, her legs carelessly highcrossed, and her pale eyes skimming along the lines with every now and then a blink. Bill's wife had worshipped him from afar long before they ever met: in fact, she used to secretly admire the famous young actor as he ate sundaes in Schwob's drugstore. Nothing could have been more childish than her snubbed nose, freckled face or the purplish spot on her naked neck where a fairytale vampire had feasted, or the unconscious movement of her tongue exploring a touch of rosy rash around her swollen lips; nothing could be more harmless than to read about Jill, an energetic starlet who made her own clothes and was a student of serious literature; nothing could be more innocent than the part in that glossy brown hair with that silky sheen on the temple; nothing could be more naïve— But what sickening envy the lecherous fellow whoever he was – come to think of it, he resembled a little my Swiss uncle Gustave, also a great admirer of *le découvert* – would have experienced had he known that every nerve in me was still anointed and ringed with the feel of her body – the body of some immortal daemon disguised as a female child.

Was pink pig Mr Swoon absolutely sure my wife had not telephoned? He was. If she did, would he tell her we had gone on to Aunt Clare's place? He would, indeedie. I settled the bill and roused Lo from her chair. She read to the car. Still reading, she was driven to a so-called coffee shop a few blocks south. Oh, she ate all right. She even laid aside her magazine to eat, but a queer dullness had replaced her usual cheerfulness. I knew little Lo could be very nasty, so I braced myself and grinned, and waited for a squall. I was unbathed, unshaven, and had had no bowel movement. My nerves were a-jangle. I did not like the way my little mistress shrugged her shoulders and distended her nostrils when I attempted casual small talk. Had Phyllis been in the know before she joined her parents in Maine? I asked with a smile. 'Look,' said Lo making a weeping grimace, 'let us get off the subject.' I then tried – also unsuccessfully, no matter how I smacked my lips – to interest her in the road map. Our destination was, let me remind my patient reader whose meek temper Lo ought to have copied, the gay town of Lepingville, somewhere near a hypothetical hospital. That destination was in itself a perfectly arbitrary one (as, alas, so many were to be), and I shook in my shoes as I wondered how to keep the whole arrangement plausible, and what other plausible objectives to invent after we had taken in all the movies in Lepingville. More and more uncomfortable did Humbert feel. It was something quite special, that feeling: an oppressive, hideous constraint as if I were sitting with the small ghost of somebody I had just killed.

As she was in the act of getting back into the car, an expression of pain flitted across Lo's face. It flitted again, more meaningfully, as she settled down beside me. No doubt, she reproduced it that second time for my benefit. Foolishly, I asked her what was the matter. 'Nothing, you brute,' she replied. 'You what?' I asked. She was silent. Leaving Briceland. Loquacious Lo was silent. Cold spiders of panic crawled down my back. This was an orphan. This was a lone child, an absolute waif, with whom a heavy-limbed, foul-smelling adult had had strenuous intercourse three times that very morning. Whether or not the realization of a life-long dream had surpassed all expectation, it had, in a sense, overshot its mark – and plunged into a nightmare. I had been careless, stupid and ignoble. And let me be quite frank: somewhere at the bottom of that dark turmoil I felt the writhing of desire again, so monstrous was my appetite for that miserable nymphet. Mingled with the pangs of guilt was the agonizing thought that her mood might prevent me from making love to her again as soon as I found a nice country road where to park in peace. In other words, poor Humbert Humbert was dreadfully unhappy, and while steadily and inanely driving toward Lepingville, he kept racking his brains for some quip, under the bright wing of which he might dare turn to his seat-mate. It was she, however, who broke the silence:

'Oh, a squashed squirrel,' she said. 'What a shame.'

'Yes, isn't it?' (eager, hopeful Hum).

'Let us stop at the next gas station,' Lo continued. 'I want to go to the washroom.'

'We shall stop wherever you want,' I said. And then as a lovely, lonely, supercilious grove (oaks, I thought; American trees at that stage were beyond me) started to echo greenly the rush of our car, a red and ferny road on our right turned its head before slanting into the woodland, and I suggested we might perhaps—

'Drive on,' my Lo cried shrilly.

'Righto. Take it easy.' (Down, poor beast, down.)

I glanced at her. Thank God, the child was smiling.

'You chump,' she said, sweetly smiling at me. 'You revolting creature. I was a daisy-fresh girl, and look what you've done to me. I ought to call the police and tell them you raped me. Oh you, dirty, dirty old man.'

Was she just joking? An ominous hysterical note rang through her silly words. Presently, making a sizzling sound with her lips she started complaining of pains, said she could not sit, said I had torn something inside her. The sweat rolled down my neck, and we almost ran over some little animal or other that was crossing the road with tail erect, and again my vile-tempered companion called me an ugly name. When we stopped at the filling station, she scrambled out without a word and was a long time away. Slowly, lovingly, an elderly friend with a broken nose, wiped my windshield – they do it differently at every place, from chamois cloth to soapy brush, this fellow used a pink sponge.

She appeared at last. 'Look,' she said in that neutral voice that hurt me so, 'give me some dimes and nickels. I want to call mother in that hospital. What's the number?'

'Get in,' I said. 'You can't call that number.'

'Why?'

'Get in and slam the door.'

She got in and slammed the door. The old garage man beamed at her. I swung on to the highway.

'Why can't I call my mother if I want to?'

'Because,' I answered, 'your mother is dead.'

33

In the gay town of Lepingville I bought her four books of comics, a box of candy, a box of sanitary pads, two cokes, a manicure set, a travel clock with a luminous dial, a ring with a real topaz, a tennis racket, roller skates with white high shoes, field glasses, a portable radio set, chewing gum, a transparent raincoat, sunglasses, some more garments – swooners, shorts, all kinds of summer frocks. At the hotel we had separate rooms, but in the middle of the night she came sobbing into mine, and we made it up very gently. You see, she had absolutely nowhere else to go.

PART TWO

I

It was then that began our extensive travels all over the States. To any other type of tourist accommodation I soon grew to prefer the Functional Motel – clean, neat, safe nooks, ideal places for sleep, argument, reconciliation, insatiable illicit love. At first, in my dread of arousing suspicion, I would eagerly pay for both sections of one double unit, each containing a double bed. I wondered what type of foursome this arrangement was ever intended for, since only a pharisaic parody of privacy could be attained by means of the incomplete partition dividing the cabin or room into two communicating love nests. By and by, the very possibilities that such honest promiscuity suggested (two young couples merrily swapping mates or a child shamming sleep to ear-witness primal sonorities) made me bolder, and every now and then I would take a bed-and-cot or twin-bed cabin, a prison cell of paradise, with yellow window shades pulled down to create a morning illusion of Venice and sunshine when actually it was Pennsylvania and rain.

We came to know – *nous connûmes,* to use a Flaubertian intonation – the stone cottages under enormous Chateaubriandesque trees, the brick unit, the adobe unit, the stucco court, on what the Tour Book of the Automobile Association describes as 'shaded' or 'spacious' or 'landscaped' grounds. The log kind, finished in knotty pine, reminded Lo, by its golden-brown glaze, of fried-chicken bones. We held in contempt the plain white-washed clapboard Kabins, with their faint sewerish smell or some other gloomy self-conscious stench and nothing to boast of (except 'good beds'), and an unsmiling landlady always prepared to have her gift ('. . . well, I could give you . . .') turned down.

Nous connûmes (this is royal fun) the would-be enticements of their repetitious names – all those Sunset Motels, U-Beam Cottages, Hillcrest Courts, Pine View Courts, Mountain View Courts, Skyline Courts, Park Plaza Courts, Green Acres, Mac's

Courts. There was sometimes a special line in the write-up, such as 'Children welcome, pets allowed' (*You* are welcome, *you* are allowed). The baths were mostly tiled showers, with an endless variety of spouting mechanisms, but with one definitely non-Laodicean characteristic in common, a propensity, while in use, to turn instantly beastly hot or blindingly cold upon you, depending on whether your neighbour turned on his cold or his hot to deprive you of a necessary complement in the shower you had so carefully blended. Some motels had instructions pasted above the toilet (on whose tank the towels were unhygienically heaped) asking guests not to throw into its bowl garbage, beer cans, cartons, stillborn babies; others had special notices under glass, such as Things to Do (Riding: *You will often see riders coming down Main Street on their way back from a romantic moonlight ride*. 'Often at 3 a.m.,' sneered unromantic Lo).

Nous connûmes the various types of motor court operators, the reformed criminal, the retired teacher and the business flop, among the males; and the motherly, pseudo-ladylike and madamic variants among the females. And sometimes trains would cry in the monstrously hot and humid night with heartrending and ominous plangency, mingling power and hysteria in one desperate scream.

We avoided Tourist Homes, country cousins of Funeral ones, old-fashioned, genteel and showerless, with elaborate dressing tables in depressingly white-and-pink little bedrooms, and photographs of the landlady's children in all their instars. But I did surrender, now and then, to Lo's predilection for 'real' hotels. She would pick out in the book, while I petted her in the parked car in the silence of a dusk-mellowed, mysterious side-road, some highly recommended lake lodge which offered all sorts of things magnified by the flashlight she moved over them, such as congenial company, between-meals snacks, outdoor barbecues – but which in my mind conjured up odious visions of stinking high school boys in sweatshirts and an ember-red cheek pressing against hers, while poor Dr Humbert, embracing nothing but two masculine knees, would cold-humour his piles on the damp turf. Most tempting to her, too, were those 'Colonial' Inns, which apart from 'gracious atmosphere' and picture windows, promised 'unlimited quantities of M-m-m food'. Treasured recollections of my father's palatial hotel sometimes led me to seek for its like in the strange country we travelled through. I was soon discouraged; but Lo kept following the scent of rich food ads, while I derived a not exclusively economic kick from such roadside signs as TIMBER HOTEL, *Children under 14 Free*. On the other hand, I shudder when recalling that *soi-disant* 'high-class' resort in a Midwestern state, which advertised 'raid-the-icebox' midnight snacks and, intrigued by my accent, wanted to know my dead wife's and dead mother's maiden names. A two-days' stay there cost me a hundred and twenty-five dollars! And do you remember, Miranda, that other 'ultrasmart' robbers' den with complimentary morning coffee and circulating ice water, and no children under sixteen (no Lolitas, of course)?

Immediately upon arrival at one of the plainer motor courts which became our habitual haunts, she would set the electric fan a-whirr, or induce me to drop a quarter into the radio, or she would read all the signs and inquire with a whine why she could not go riding up some advertised trail or swimming in that local pool of warm mineral water. Most often, in the slouching, bored way she cultivated, Lo would fall prostrate and abominably desirable into a red springchair or a green chaise longue, or a steamer chair of striped canvas with footrest and canopy, or a sling chair, or any other lawn chair under a garden umbrella on the patio, and it would take hours of blandishments, threats and promises to make her lend me for a few seconds her brown limbs in the seclusion of the five-dollar room before undertaking anything she might prefer to my poor joy.

A combination of naïvety and deception, of charm and vulgarity, of blue sulks and rosy mirth, Lolita, when she chose, could be a most exasperating brat. I was not really quite prepared for her fits of disorganized boredom, intense and vehement griping, her sprawling, droopy, dopey-eyed style, and what is called goofing off – a kind of diffused clowning which she thought was tough in a boyish hoodlum way. Mentally, I found her to be a disgustingly conventional little girl. Sweet hot jazz, square dancing, gooey fudge sundaes, musicals, movie magazines and so forth – these were the obvious items in her list of beloved things. The Lord knows how many nickles I fed to the gorgeous music boxes that came with every meal we had! I still hear the nasal voices of those invisibles serenading her, people with names like Sammy and Jo and Eddy and Tony and Peggy and Guy and Patty and Rex, and sentimental song hits, all of them as similar to my ear as her various candies were to my palate. She believed, with a kind of celestial trust, any advertisement or advice that appeared in *Movie Love* or *Screen Land* – Starasil Starves Pimples, or 'You better watch out if you're wearing your shirt-tails outside your jeans, gals, because Jill says you shouldn't'. If a roadside sign said: VISIT OUR GIFT SHOP – we *had* to visit it, *had* to buy its Indian curios, dolls, copper jewellery, cactus candy. The words 'novelties and souvenirs' simply entranced her by their trochaic lilt. If some café sign proclaimed Icecold Drinks, she was automatically stirred, although all drinks everywhere were ice-cold. She it was to whom ads were dedicated: the ideal consumer, the subject and object of every foul poster. And she attempted – unsuccessfully – to patronize only those restaurants where the holy spirit of Huncan Dines had descended upon the cute paper napkins and cottage-cheese-crested salads.

In those days, neither she nor I had thought up yet the system of monetary bribes which was to work such havoc with my nerves and her morals somewhat later. I relied on three other methods to keep my pubescent concubine in submission and passable temper. A few years before, she had spent a rainy summer under Miss Phalen's bleary eye in a dilapidated Appalachian farmhouse that had belonged to some gnarled Haze or other in the dead past. It still stood among its rank acres of golden rod on the edge of a flowerless forest, at the end of a permanently muddy road, twenty miles from the nearest hamlet. Lo recalled that scarecrow of a house, the solitude, the soggy old pastures, the wind, the bloated wilderness, with an energy of disgust that distorted her mouth and fattened her half-revealed tongue. And it was there that I warned her she would dwell with me in exile for months and years if need be, studying under me French and Latin, unless her 'present attitude' changed. Charlotte, I began to understand you!

A simple child, Lo would scream no! and frantically clutch at my driving hand whenever I put a stop to her tornadoes of temper by turning in the middle of a highway with the implication that I was about to take her straight to that dark and dismal abode. The farther, however, we travelled away from it west, the less tangible that menace became, and I had to adopt other methods of persuasion.

Among these, the reformatory threat is the one I recall with the deepest moan of shame. From the very beginning of our concourse, I was clever enough to realize that I must secure her complete co-operation in keeping our relations secret, that it should become a second nature with her, no matter what grudge she might bear me, no matter what other pleasures she might seek.

'Come and kiss your old man,' I would say, 'and drop that moody nonsense. In former times, when I was still your dream male [the reader will notice what pains I took to speak Lo's tongue], you swooned to records of the number one throb-and-sob idol of your coevals [Lo: 'Of my what? Speak English']. That idol of your pals sounded, you thought, like friend Humbert. But now, I am just your *old man*, a dream dad protecting his dream daughter.

'My *chère Dolorès*! I want to protect you, dear, from all the horrors that happen to little girls in coal sheds and alley ways, and, alas, *comme vous le savez trop bien, ma gentille*, in the blueberry woods during the bluest of summers. Through thick and thin I will still stay your guardian, and if you are good, I hope a court may legalize that guardianship before long. Let us, however, forget, Dolores Haze, so-called legal terminology, terminology that accepts as rational the term "lewd and lascivious cohabitation". I am not a criminal sexual psychopath taking indecent liberties with a child. The rapist was Charlie Holmes; I am the therapist – a matter of nice spacing in the way of distinction. I am your daddum, Lo. Look, I've a learned book here about young girls. Look, darling, what it says. I quote: the normal girl – normal, mark you – the normal girl is usually extremely anxious to please her father. She feels in him the forerunner of the desired elusive male ("elusive" is good, by Polonius!). The wise mother (and your poor mother would have been wise, had she lived) will encourage a companionship between father and daughter, realizing – excuse the corny style – that the girl forms her ideals of romance and of men from her association with her father. Now, what association does this cheery book mean – and recommend? I quote again: Among Sicilians sexual relations between a father and his daughter are accepted as a matter of course, and the girl who participates in such relationship is not looked upon with disapproval by the society of which she is part. I'm a great admirer of Sicilians, fine athletes, fine musicians, fine upright people, Lo, and great lovers. But let's not digress. Only the other day we read in the newspapers some bunkum about a middle-aged morals offender who pleaded guilty to the violation of the Mann Act and to transporting a nine-year-old girl across state lines for immoral purposes, whatever these are. Dolores, darling! You are not nine but almost thirteen, and I would not advise you to consider yourself my cross-country slave, and I deplore the Mann Act as lending itself to a dreadful pun, the revenge that the Gods of Semantics take against tight-zippered Philistines. I am your father, and I *am* speaking English, and I love you.

'Finally, let us see what happens if you, a minor, accused of having impaired the morals of an adult in a respectable inn, what happens if you complain to the police of my having kidnapped and raped you? Let us suppose they believe you. A minor female, who allows a person over twenty-one to know her carnally, involves her victim into statutory rape, or second-degree sodomy, depending on the technique; and the maximum penalty is ten years. So I go to jail. Okay. I go to jail. But what happens to you, my orphan? Well, you are luckier. You become the ward of the Department of Public Welfare – which I am afraid sounds a little bleak. A nice grim matron of the Miss Phalen type, but more rigid and not a drinking woman, will take away your lipstick and fancy clothes. No more gadding about! I don't know if you have ever heard of the laws relating to dependent, neglected, incorrigible and delinquent children. While I stand gripping the bars, you, happy neglected child, will be given a choice of various dwelling places, all more or less the same, the correctional school, the reformatory, the juvenile detention home, or one of those admirable girls' protectories where you knit things, and sing hymns, and have rancid pancakes on Sundays. You will go there, Lolita – *my* Lolita, *this* Lolita will leave her Catullus and go there, as the wayward girl you are. In plainer words, if we two are found out, you will be analysed and institutionalized, my pet, *c'est tout*. You will dwell, my Lolita will dwell (come here, my brown flower) with thirty-nine other dopes in a dirty dormitory (no, allow me, please) under the supervision of hideous matrons. This is the situation, this is the choice. Don't you think that under the circumstances Dolores Haze had better stick to her old man?'

By rubbing all this in, I succeeded in terrorizing Lo, who despite a certain brash alertness of manner and spurts of wit was not as intelligent a child as her IQ might suggest. But if I managed to establish that background of shared secrecy and shared guilt, I was much less successful in keeping her in good humour. Every morning during our yearlong travels I had to devise some expectation, some special point in space and time for her to look forward to, for her to survive till bedtime. Otherwise, deprived of a shaping and sustaining purpose, the skeleton of her day sagged and collapsed. The object in view might be anything – a lighthouse in Virginia, a natural cave in Arkansas converted to a café, a collection of guns and violins somewhere in Oklahoma, a replica of the Grotto of Lourdes in Louisiana, shabby photographs of the bonanza mining period in the local museum of a Rocky Mountains resort, anything whatsoever – but it had to be there, in front of us, like a fixed star, although as likely as not Lo would feign gagging as soon as we got to it.

By putting the geography of the United States into motion, I did my best for hours on end to give her the impression of 'going places', of rolling on to some definite destination, to some unusual delight. I have never seen such smooth amiable roads as those that now radiated before us, across the crazy quilt of forty-eight states. Voraciously we consumed those long highways, in rapt silence we glided over their glossy black dance floors. Not only had Lo no eye for scenery but she furiously resented my calling her attention to this or that enchanting detail of landscape; which I myself learned to discern only after being exposed for quite a time to the delicate beauty ever present in the margin of our undeserving journey. By a paradox of pictorial thought, the average lowland North-American countryside had at first seemed to me something I accepted with a shock of amused recognition because of those painted oilcloths which were imported from America in the old days to be hung above wash-stands in Central European nurseries, and which fascinated a drowsy child at bedtime with the rustic green views they depicted – opaque curly trees, a barn, cattle, a brook, the dull white of vague orchards in bloom, and perhaps a stone fence or hills of greenish gouache. But gradually the models of those elementary rusticities became stranger and stranger to the eye, the nearer I came to know them. Beyond the tilled plain, beyond the toy roofs, there would be a slow suffusion of inutile loveliness, a low sun in a platinum haze with a warm, peeled-peach tinge pervading the upper edge of a two-dimensional, dove-grey cloud fusing with the distant amorous mist. There might be a line of spaced trees silhouetted against the horizon, and hot still noons above a wilderness of clover, and Claude Lorrain clouds inscribed remotely into misty azure with only their cumulus part conspicuous against the neutral swoon of the background. Or again, it might be a stern El Greco horizon, pregnant with inky rain, and a passing glimpse of some mummy-necked farmer, and all around alternating strips of quicksilverish water and harsh green corn, the whole arrangement opening like a fan, somewhere in Kansas.

Now and then, in the vastness of those plains, huge trees would advance towards us to cluster self-consciously by the roadside and provide a bit of humanitarian shade above a picnic table, with sun flecks, flattened paper cups, samaras and discarded ice-cream sticks littering the brown ground. A great user of roadside facilities, my unfastidious Lo would be charmed by toilet signs – Guys-Gals, John-Jane, Jack-Jill and even Buck's-Doe's; while lost in an artist's dream, I would stare at the honest brightness of the gasoline paraphernalia against the splendid green of oaks, or at a distant hill scrambling out – scarred but still untamed – from the wilderness of agriculture that was trying to swallow it.

At night, tall trucks studded with coloured lights, like dreadful giant Christmas trees, loomed in the darkness and thundered by the belated little sedan. And again next day a thinly populated sky, losing its blue to the heat, would melt overhead, and Lo would clamour for a drink, and her cheeks would hollow vigorously over the straw, and the car inside would be a furnace when we got in again, and the road shimmered ahead, with a remote car changing its shape mirage-like in the surface glare, and seeming to hang for a moment, old-fashionedly square and high, in the hot haze. And as we pushed westward, patches of what the garageman called 'sage brush' appeared, and then the mysterious outlines of table-like hills, and then red bluffs ink-blotted with junipers, and then a mountain range, dun grading into blue, and blue into dream, and the desert would meet us with a steady gale, dust, grey thorn bushes, and hideous bits of tissue paper mimicking pale flowers among the prickles of wind-tortured withered stalks all along the highway; in the middle of which there sometimes stood simple cows, immobilized in a position (tail left, white eyelashes right) cutting across all human rules of traffic.

My lawyer has suggested I give a clear, frank account of the itinerary we followed, and I suppose I have reached here a point where I cannot avoid that chore. Roughly, during that mad year August 1947 to August 1948), our route began with a series of wiggles and whorls in New England, then meandered south, up and down, east and west; dipped deep into *ce qu'on appelle* Dixieland, avoided Florida because the Farlows were there, veered west, zigzagged through corn belts and cotton belts (this is not *too* clear I am afraid, Clarence, but I did not keep any notes, and have at my disposal only an atrociously crippled tour book in three volumes, almost a symbol of my torn and tattered past, in which to check these recollections); crossed and recrossed the Rockies, straggled through southern deserts where we wintered; reached the Pacific, turned north through the pale lilac fluff of flowering shrubs along forest roads; almost reached the Canadian border; and proceeded east, across good lands and bad lands, back to agriculture on a grand scale, avoiding, despite little Lo's strident remonstrations, little Lo's birthplace, in a corn, coal and hog producing area; and finally returned to the fold of the East, petering out in the college town of Beardsley.

2

Now, in perusing what follows, the reader should bear in mind not only the general circuit as adumbrated above, with its many side-trips and tourist traps, secondary circles and skittish deviactions, but also the fact that far from being an indolent *partie de plaisir*, our tour was a hard, twisted, teleological growth, whose sole *raison d'être* (these French clichés are symptomatic) was to keep my companion in passable humour from kiss to kiss.

Thumbing through that battered tour book, I dimly evoke that Magnolia Garden in a southern state which cost me four bucks and which, according to the ad in the book, you must visit for three reasons: because John Galsworthy (a stone-dead writer of sorts) acclaimed it as the world's fairest garden; because in 1900 Baedeker's Guide had marked it with a star; and finally, because . . . O, Reader, My Reader, guess! . . . because children (and by Jingo was not my Lolita a child!) will 'walk starry-eyed and reverently through this foretaste of Heaven, drinking in beauty that can influence a life'. 'Not mine,' said grim Lo, and settled down on a bench with the fillings of two Sunday papers in her lovely lap.

We passed and re-passed through the whole gamut of American roadside restaurants, from the lowly Eat with its deer head (dark trace of long tear at inner canthus), 'humorous' picture post cards of the posterior 'Kurort' type, impaled guest checks, life savers, sunglasses, adman visions of celestial sundaes, one-half of a chocolate cake under glass, and several horribly experienced flies zigzagging over the sticky sugar-pour on the ignoble counter; and all the way to the expensive place with the subdued lights, preposterously poor table linen, inept waiters (ex-convicts or college boys), the roan back of a screen actress, the sable eyebrows of her male of the moment, and an orchestra of zoot-suiters with trumpets.

We inspected the world's largest stalagmite in a cave where three south-eastern states have a family reunion; admission by age; adults one dollar, pubescents sixty cents. A granite obelisk commemorating the Battle of Blue Licks, with old bones and Indian pottery in the museum nearby, Lo a dime, very reasonable. The present log cabin boldly simulating the past log cabin where Lincoln was born. A boulder, with a plaque, in memory of the author of *Trees* (by now we are in Poplar Cove, NC, reached by what my kind, tolerant, usually so restrained tour book angrily calls 'a very narrow road, poorly maintained', to which, though no Kilmerite, I subscribe). From a hired motorboat operated by an elderly, but still repulsively handsome White Russian, a baron they said (Lo's palms were damp, the little fool), who had known in California good old Maximovich and Valeria, we could distinguish the inaccessible 'millionaires' colony' on an island, somewhere off the Georgia coast. We inspected further: a collection of European hotel picture post cards in a museum devoted to hobbies at a Mississippi resort, where with a hot wave of pride I discovered a coloured photo of my father's Mirana, its striped awnings, its flag flying above the retouched palm trees. 'So what?' said Lo, squinting at the bronzed owner of an expensive car who had followed us into the Hobby House. Relics of the cotton era. A forest in Arkansas and, on her brown shoulder, a raised purple-pink swelling (the work of some gnat) which I eased of its beautiful transparent poison between my long thumbnails and then sucked till I was gorged on her spicy blood. Bourbon Street (in a town named New Orleans) whose sidewalks, said the tour book, 'may [I liked the 'may'] feature entertainment by pickaninnies who will [I liked the 'will' even better] tap-dance for pennies' (what fun), while 'its numerous small and intimate night clubs are thronged with visitors' (naughty). Collections of frontier lore. Ante-bellum homes with iron-trellis balconies and hand-worked stairs, the kind down which movie ladies with sun-kissed shoulders run in rich Technicolor, holding up the fronts of their flounced skirts with both little hands in that special way, and the devoted Negress shaking her head on the upper landing. The Menninger Foundation, a psychiatric clinic, just for the heck of it. A patch of beautifully eroded clay; and yucca blossoms, so pure, so waxy, but lousy with creeping white flies. Independence, Missouri, the starting point of the Old Oregon Trail; and Abilene, Kansas, the home of the Wild Bill Something Rodeo. Distant mountains. Near mountains. More mountains; bluish beauties never attainable, or ever turning into inhabited hill after hill; south-eastern ranges, altitudinal failures as alps go; heart and sky-piercing snow-veined grey colossi of stone, relentless peaks appearing from nowhere at a turn of the highway; timbered enormities, with a system of neatly overlapping dark firs, interrupted in places by pale puffs of aspen; pink and lilac formations, Pharaonic, phallic, 'too prehistoric for words' (blasé Lo); buttes of black lava; early spring mountains with young-elephant lanugo along their spines; end-of-the-summer mountains, all hunched up, their heavy Egyptian limbs folded under folds of tawny moth-eaten plush; oatmeal hills, flecked with green round oaks; a last rufous mountain with a rich rug of lucerne at its foot.

Moreover, we inspected: Little Iceberg Lake, somewhere in Colorado, and the snow banks and the cushionets of tiny alpine flowers and more snow; down which Lo in red-peaked cap tried to slide, and squealed, and was snowballed by some youngsters, and retaliated in kind *comme on dit*. Skeletons of burned aspens, patches of spired blue flowers. The various items of a scenic drive. Hundreds of scenic drives, thousands of Bear Creeks, Soda Springs, Painted Canyons. Texas, a drought-struck plain. Crystal Chamber in the longest cave in the world, children under twelve free, Lo a young captive. A collection of a local lady's home-made sculptures, closed on a miserable Monday morning, dust, wind, witherland. Conception Park, in a town on the Mexican border which I dared not cross. There and elsewhere, hundreds of grey hummingbirds in the dusk, probing the throats of dim flowers. Shakespeare, a ghost town in New Mexico, where bad man Russian Bill was colourfully hanged seventy years ago. Fish hatcheries. Cliff dwellings. The mummy of a child (Florentine Bea's Indian contemporary). Our twentieth Hell's Canyon. Our fiftieth Gateway to something or other *vide* that tour book, the cover of which had been lost by that time. A tick in my groin. Always the same three old men, in hats and suspenders, idling away the summer afternoon under the trees near the public fountain. A hazy blue view beyond railings on a mountain pass, and the backs of a family enjoying it (with Lo, in a hot, happy, wild, intense, hopeful, hopeless whisper – 'Look, the McCrystals, please, let's talk to them, please' – let's talk to them, reader! – 'please! I'll do anything you want, oh, please . . .'). Indian ceremonial dances, strictly commercial. ART: American Refrigerator Transit Company. Obvious Arizona, pueblo dwellings, aboriginal pictographs, a dinosaur track in a desert canyon, printed there thirty million years ago, when I was a child. A lanky, six-foot, pale boy with an active Adam's apple, ogling Lo and her orange-brown bare midriff, which I kissed five minutes later, Jack. Winter in the desert, spring in the foothills, almonds in bloom. Reno, a dreary town in Nevada, with a nightlife said to be 'cosmopolitan and mature'. A winery in California, with a church built in the shape of a wine barrel. Death Valley. Scotty's Castle. Works of Art collected by one Rogers over a period of years. The ugly villas of handsome actresses. R. L. Stevenson's footprint on an extinct volcano. Mission Dolores: good title for book. Surf-carved sandstone festoons. A man having a lavish epileptic fit on the ground in Russian Gulch State Park. Blue, blue Crater Lake. A fish hatchery in Idaho and the State Penitentiary. Sombre Yellowstone Park and its coloured hot springs, baby geysers, rainbows of bubbling mud – symbols of my passion. A herd of antelopes in a wildlife refuge. Our hundredth cavern, adults one dollar, Lolita fifty cents. A château built by a French marquess in ND. The Corn Palace in SD; and the huge heads of presidents carved in towering granite. The Bearded Woman read our jingle and now she is no longer single. A zoo in Indiana where a large troop of monkeys lived on concrete replica of Christopher Columbus' flagship. Billions of dead, or half-dead, fish-smelling May flies in every window of every eating place all along a dreary sand shore. Fat gulls on big stones as seen from the ferry *City of Cheboygan*, whose brown woolly smoke arched and dipped over the green shadow it cast on the aquamarine lake. A motel whose ventilator pipe passed under the city sewer. Lincoln's home, largely spurious, with parlour books and period furniture that most visitors reverently accepted as personal belongings.

We had rows, minor and major. The biggest ones we had took place: at Lacework Cabins, Virginia; on Park Avenue, Little Rock, near a school; on Milner Pass, 10,759 feet high, in Colorado; at the corner of Seventh Street and Central Avenue in Phoenix, Arizona; on Third Street, Los Angeles, because the tickets to some studio or other were sold out; at a motel called Poplar Shade in Utah, where six pubescent trees were scarcely taller than my Lolita, and where she asked, *à propos de rien*, how long did I think we were going to live in stuffy cabins, doing filthy things together and never behaving like ordinary people? On N. Broadway, Burns, Oregon, corner of W. Washington, facing Safeway, a grocery. In some little town in the Sun Valley of Idaho, before a brick hotel, pale and flushed bricks nicely mixed, with, opposite, a poplar playing its liquid shadows all over the local Honour Roll. In a sage brush wilderness, between Pinedale and Farson. Somewhere in Nebraska, on Main Street, near the First National Bank, established 1889, with a view of a railway crossing in the vista of the street, and beyond that the white organ pipes of a multiple silo. And on McEwen Street, corner of Wheaton Avenue, in a Michigan town bearing his first name.

We came to know the curious roadside species, Hitchhiking Man, *Homo pollex* of science, with all its many sub-species and forms: the modest soldier, spic and span, quietly waiting, quietly conscious of khaki's viatic appeal; the schoolboy wishing to go two blocks; the killer wishing to go two thousand miles; the mysterious, nervous, elderly gent, with brand-new suitcase and clipped moustache; a trio of optimistic Mexicans; the college student displaying the grime of vacational outdoor work as proudly as the name of the famous college arching across the front of his sweatshirt; the desperate lady whose battery has just died on her; the clean-cut, glossy-haired, shifty-eyed, white-faced young beasts in loud shirts and coats, vigorously, almost priapically thrusting out tense thumbs to tempt lone women or sad-sack salesmen with fancy cravings.

'Let's take him,' Lo would often plead, rubbing her knees together in a way she had, as some particularly disgusting *pollex*, some man of my age and shoulder breadth, with the *face à claques* of an unemployed actor, walked backwards, practically in the path of our car.

Oh, I had to keep a very sharp eye on Lo, little limp Lo! Owing perhaps to constant amorous exercise, she radiated, despite her very childish appearance, some special languorous glow which threw garage fellows, hotel pages, vacationists, goons in luxurious cars, maroon morons near blued pools, into fits of concupiscence which might have tickled my pride, had it not incensed my jealousy. For little Lo was aware of that glow of hers, and I would often catch her *coulant un regard* in the direction of some amiable male, some grease monkey, with a sinewy golden-brown forearm and watch-braceleted wrist, and hardly had I turned my back to go and buy this very Lo a lollipop, than I would hear her and the fair mechanic burst into a perfect love song of wisecracks.

When, during our longer stops, I would relax after a particularly violent morning in bed, and out of the goodness of my lulled heart allow her – indulgent Hum! – to visit the rose garden or children's library across the street with a motor court neighbour's plain little Mary and Mary's eight-year-old brother, Lo would come back an hour late, with barefoot Mary trailing far behind, and the little boy metamorphosed into two gangling, golden-haired high school uglies, all muscles and gonorrhoea. The reader may well imagine what I answered my pet when – rather uncertainly, I admit – she would ask me if she could go with Carl and Al here to the roller-skating rink.

I remember the first time, a dusty windy afternoon, I did let her go to one such rink. Cruelly she said it would be no fun if I accompanied her, since that time of day was reserved for teenagers. We wrangled out a compromise: I remained in the car, among other (empty) cars with their noses to the canvas-topped open-air rink, where some fifty young people, many in pairs, were endlessly rolling round and round to mechanical music, and the wind silvered the trees. Dolly wore blue jeans and white high shoes, as most of the other girls did. I kept counting the revolutions of the rolling crowd – and suddenly she was missing. When she rolled past again, she was together with three hoodlums whom I had heard analyse a moment before the girl skaters from the outside – and jeer at a lovely leggy young thing who had arrived clad in red shorts instead of those jeans or slacks.

At inspection stations on highways entering Arizona or California, a policeman's cousin would peer with such intensity at us that my poor heart wobbled. 'Any honey?' he would inquire, and every time my sweet fool giggled. I still have, vibrating all along my optic nerve, visions of Lo on horseback, a link in the chain of a guided trip along a bridle trail: Lo bobbing at a walking pace, with an old woman rider in front and a lecherous red-necked dude-rancher behind; and I behind him, hating his fat flowery-shirted back even more fervently than a motorist does a slow truck on a mountain road. Or else, at a ski lodge, I would see her floating away from me, celestial and solitary, in an ethereal chairlift, up and up, to a glittering summit when laughing athletes stripped to the waist were waiting for her, for her.

In whatever town we stopped I would inquire, in my polite European way, anent the whereabouts of natatoriums, museums, local schools, the number of children in the nearest school and so forth; and at school bus time, smiling and twitching a little (I discovered this *tic nerveux* because cruel Lo was the first to mimic it), I would park at a strategic point, with my vagrant schoolgirl beside me in the car, to watch the children leave school – always a pretty sight. This sort of thing soon began to bore my so easily bored Lolita, and, having a childish lack of sympathy for other people's whims, she would insult me and my desire to have her caress me while blue-eyed little brunettes in blue shorts, copper-heads in green boleros, and blurred boyish blondes in faded slacks passed by in the sun.

As a sort of compromise, I freely advocated whenever and wherever possible the use of swimming pools with other girl children. She adored brilliant water and was a remarkably smart diver. Comfortably robed, I would settle down in the rich post-meridian shade after my own demure dip, and there I would sit, with a dummy book or a bag of bonbons, or both, or nothing but my tingling glands, and watch her gambol, rubber-capped, bepearled, smoothly tanned, as glad as an ad, in her trim-fitted satin pants and shirred bra. Pubescent sweetheart! How smugly would I marvel that she was mine, mine, mine, and revise the recent matitudinal swoon to the moan of the mourning doves, and devise the late afternoon one, and slitting my sun-speared eyes, compare Lolita to whatever other nymphets parsimonious chance collected around her for my anthological delectation and judgment; and today, putting my hand on my ailing heart, I really do not think that any of them ever surpassed her in desirability, or if they did, it was so two or three times at the most, in a certain light, with certain perfumes blended in the air – once in the hopeless case of a pale Spanish child, the daughter of a heavy-jawed nobleman, and another time – *mais je divague.*

Naturally, I had to be always wary, fully realizing, in my lucid jealousy, the danger of those dazzling romps. I had only to turn away for a moment – to walk, say, a few steps in order to see if our cabin was at last ready after the morning change of linen – and lo and behold, upon returning, I would find the former *les yeux perdus*, dipping and kicking her long-toed feet in the water on the stone edge of which she lolled, while, on either side of her, there crouched a *brun adolescent* whom her russet beauty and the quicksilver in the baby folds of her stomach were sure to cause to *se tordre* – oh Baudelaire! – in recurrent dreams for months to come.

I tried to teach her to play tennis so we might have more amusements in common; but although I had been a good player in my prime, I proved to be hopeless as a teacher; and so, in California, I got her to take a number of very expensive lessons with a famous coach, a husky, wrinkled old-timer, with a harem of ball boys; he looked an awful wreck off the court, but now and then, when, in the course of a lesson, to keep up the exchange, he would put out as it were an exquisite spring blossom of a stroke and twang the ball back to his pupil, that divine delicacy of absolute power made me recall that, thirty years before, I had seen *him* in Cannes demolish the great Gobert! Until she began taking those lessons, I thought she would never learn the game. On this or that hotel court I would drill Lo, and try to relive the days when in a hot gale, a daze of dust, and queer lassitude, I fed ball after ball to gay, innocent, elegant Annabel (gleam of bracelet, pleated white skirt, black velvet hair band). With every word of persistent advice I would only augment Lo's sullen fury. To our games, oddly enough, she preferred – at least, before we reached California – formless pat ball approximations – more ball hunting than actual play – with a wispy, weak, wonderfully pretty in an *ange gauche* way coeval. A helpful spectator, I would go up to that other child, and inhale her faint musky fragrance as I touched her forearm and held her knobby wrist, and push this way or that her cool thigh to show her the back-hand stance. In the meantime, Lo, bending forward, would let her sunny-brown curls hang forward as she stuck her racket, like a cripple's stick, into the ground and emitted a tremendous ugh of disgust at my intrusion. I would leave them to their game and look on, comparing their bodies in motion, a silk scarf round my throat; this was in south Arizona, I think – and the days had a lazy lining of warmth, and awkward Lo would slash at the ball and miss it, and curse, and send a simulacrum of a serve into the net, and show the wet glistening young down of her armpit as she brandished her racket in despair, and her even more insipid partner would dutifully rush out after every ball, and retrieve none; but both were enjoying themselves beautifully, and in clear ringing tones kept the exact score of their ineptitudes all the time.

One day, I remember, I offered to bring them cold drinks from the hotel, and went up the gravel path, and came back with two tall glasses of pineapple juice, soda and ice; and then a sudden void within my chest made me stop as I saw that the tennis court was deserted. I stooped to set down the glasses on a bench and for some reason, with a kind of icy vividness, saw Charlotte's face in death, and I glanced around, and noticed Lo in white shorts receding through the speckled shadow of a garden path in the company of a tall man who carried two tennis rackets. I sprang after them, but as I was crashing through the shrubbery, I saw, in an alternate vision, as if life's course constantly branched, Lo, in slacks, and her companion, in shorts, trudging up and down a small weedy area, and beating bushes with their rackets in listless search for their last lost ball.

I itemize these sunny nothings mainly to prove to my judges that I did everything in my power to give my Lolita a really good time. How charming it was to see her, a child herself, showing another child some of her few accomplishments, such as for example a special way of jumping rope. With her right hand holding her left arm behind her untanned back, the lesser nymphet, a diaphanous darling, would be all eyes, as the pavonine sun was all eyes on the gravel under the flowering trees, while in the midst of that oculate paradise, my freckled and raffish lass skipped, repeating the movements of so many others I had gloated over on the sun-shot, watered, damp-smelling sidewalks and ramparts of ancient Europe. Presently, she would hand the rope back to her little Spanish friend, and watch in her turn the repeated lesson, and brush away the hair from her brow, and fold her arms, and step on one toe with the other, or drop her hands loosely upon her still unflared hips, and I would satisfy myself that the damned staff had at last finished cleaning up our cottage; whereupon, flashing a smile to the shy, dark-haired page girl of my princess and thrusting my fatherly fingers deep into Lo's hair from behind, and then gently but firmly clasping them around the nape of her neck, I would lead my reluctant pet to our small home for a quick connection before dinner.

'Whose cat has scratched poor you?' A full-blown fleshy handsome woman of the repulsive type to which I was particularly attractive might ask me at the 'lodge', during a table d'hôte dinner followed by dancing promised to Lo. This was one of the reasons why I tried to keep as far away from people as possible, while Lo, on the other hand, would do her utmost to draw as many potential witnesses into her orbit as she could.

She would be, figuratively speaking, wagging her tiny tail, her whole behind in fact as little bitches do – while some grinning stranger accosted us and began a bright conversation with a comparative study of licence plates. 'Long way from home!' Inquisitive parents, in order to pump Lo about me, would suggest her going to a movie with their children. We had some close shaves. The waterfall nuisance pursued me of course in all our caravansaries. But I never realized how wafery their wall substance was until one evening, after I had loved too loudly, a neighbour's masculine cough filled the pause as clearly as mine would have done; and next morning as I was having breakfast at the milk bar (Lo was a late sleeper, and I liked to bring her a pot of hot coffee in bed), my neighbour of the eve, an elderly fool wearing plain glasses on his long virtuous nose and a convention badge on his lapel, somehow managed to rig up a conversation with me, in the course of which he inquired, if my missus was like his missus a rather reluctant get-upper when not on the farm; and had not the hideous danger I was skirting almost suffocated me, I might have enjoyed the odd look of surprise on his thin-lipped weather-beaten face when I drily answered, as I slithered off my stool, that I was 'thank God' a widower.

How sweet it was to bring that coffee to her, and then deny it until she had done her morning duty. And I was such a thoughtful friend, such a passionate father, such a good paediatrician, attending to all the wants of my little auburn brunette's body! My only grudge against nature was that I could not turn my Lolita inside out and apply voracious lips to her young matrix, her unknown heart, her nacreous liver, the sea-grapes of her lungs, her comely twin kidneys. On especially tropical afternoons, in the sticky closeness of the siesta, I liked the cool feel of armchair leather against my massive nakedness as I held her in my lap. There she would be, a typical kid picking her nose while engrossed in the lighter sections of a newspaper, as indifferent to my ecstasy as if it were something she had sat upon, a shoe, a doll, the handle of a tennis racket, and was too indolent to remove. Her eyes would follow the adventures of her favourite strip characters: there was one well-drawn sloppy bobby-soxer, with high cheekbones and angular gestures, that I was not above enjoying myself; she studied the photographic results of head-on collisions; she never doubted the reality of place, time and circumstance alleged to match the publicity pictures of naked-thighed beauties; and she was curiously fascinated by the photographs of local brides, some in full wedding apparel, holding bouquets and wearing glasses.

A fly would settle and walk in the vicinity of her navel or explore her tender pale areolas. She tried to catch it in her fist (Charlotte's method) and then would turn to the column 'Let's Explore Your Mind'.

'Let's explore your mind. Would sex crimes be reduced if children obeyed a few don'ts? Don't play around public toilets. Don't take candy or rides from strangers. If picked up, mark down the licence of the car.'

'. . . and the brand of the candy,' I volunteered.

She went on, her cheek (recedent) against mine (pursuant); and this was a good day, mark, O reader!

'If you don't have a pencil, but are old enough to read—'

'We,' I quip-quoted, 'medieval mariners, have placed in this bottle—'

'If,' she repeated, 'you don't have a pencil, but are old enough to read and write – this is what the guy means, isn't it, you dope – scratch the number somehow on the roadside.'

'With your little claws, Lolita.'

3

She had entered my world, umber and black Humberland, with rash curiosity; she surveyed it with a shrug of amused distaste; and it seemed to me now that she was ready to turn away from it with something akin to plain repulsion. Never did she vibrate under my touch, and a strident 'what d'you think you are doing?' was all I got for my pains. To the wonderland I had to offer, my fool preferred the corniest movies, the most cloying fudge. To think that between a Hamburger and a Humburger, she would invariably, with icy precision – plump for the former. Did I mention the name of that milk bar I visited a moment ago? It was, of all things, The Frigid Queen. Smiling a little sadly, I dubbed her My Frigid Princess. She did not see the wistful joke.

Oh, do not scowl at me, reader, I do not intend to convey the impression that I did not manage to be happy. Reader must understand that in the possession and thraldom of a nymphet the enchanted traveller stands, as it were, *beyond happiness*. For there is no other bliss on earth comparable to that of fondling a nymphet. It is *hors concours*, that bliss, it belongs to another class, another plane of sensitivity. Despite our tiffs, despite her nastiness, despite all the fuss and faces she made, and the vulgarity, and the danger, and the horrible hopelessness of it all, I still dwelled deep in my elected paradise – a paradise whose skies were the colour of hell-flames – but still a paradise.

The able psychiatrist who studies my case – and whom by now Dr Humbert has plunged, I trust, into a state of leporine fascination – is no doubt anxious to have me take my Lolita to the seaside and have me find there, at last, the 'gratification' of a lifetime urge, and release from the 'subconscious' obsession of an incomplete childhood romance with the initial little Miss Lee.

Well, comrade, let me tell you that I *did* look for a beach, though I also have to confess that by the time we reached its mirage of grey water, so many delights had already been granted me by my travelling companion that the search for a Kingdom by the Sea, a Sublimated Riviera, or whatnot, far from being the impulse of the subconscious, had become the rational pursuit of a purely theoretical thrill. The angels knew it, and arranged things accordingly. A visit to a plausible cove on the Atlantic side was completely messed up by foul weather. A thick damp sky, muddy waves, a sense of boundless but somehow matter-of-fact mist – what could be further removed from the crisp charm, the sapphire occasion and rosy contingency of my Riviera romance? A couple of semi-tropical beaches on the Gulf, though bright enough, were starred and spattered by venomous beasties and swept by hurricane winds. Finally, on a Californian beach, facing the phantom of the Pacific, I hit upon some rather perverse privacy in a kind of cave whence you could hear the shrieks of a lot of girl scouts taking their first surf bath on a separate part of the beach, behind rotting trees; but the fog was like a wet blanket, and the sand was gritty and clammy, and Lo was all gooseflesh and grit, and for the first time in my life I had as little desire for her as for a manatee. Perhaps, my learned readers may perk up if I tell them that even had we discovered a piece of sympathetic seaside somewhere, it would have come too late, since my real liberation had occurred much earlier: at the moment, in point of fact, when Annabel Haze, alias Dolores Lee, alias Loleeta, had appeared to me, golden and brown, kneeling, looking up, on that shoddy veranda, in a kind of fictitious, dishonest, but eminently satisfactory seaside arrangement (although there was nothing but a second-rate lake in the neighbourhood).

So much for those special sensations, influenced, if not actually brought about, by the tenets of modern psychiatry. Consequently, I turned away – I headed my Lolita away – from beaches which were either too bleak when lone, or too populous when ablaze. However, in recollection, I suppose, of my hopeless hauntings of public parks in Europe, I was still keenly interested in outdoor activities and desirous of finding suitable playgrounds in the open where I had suffered such shameful privations. Here, too, I was to be thwarted. The disappointment I must now register (as I gently grade my story into an expression of the continuous risk and dread that ran through my bliss) should in no wise reflect on the lyrical, epic, tragic but never Arcadian American wilds. They are beautiful, heart-rendingly beautiful, those wilds, with a quality of wide-eyed, unsung, innocent surrender that my lacquered, toy-bright Swiss villages and exhaustively lauded Alps no longer possess. Innumerable lovers have clipped and kissed on the trim of old-world mountainsides, on the innerspring moss, by a handy, hygienic rill, on rustic benches under the initialled oaks, and in so many *cabanes* in so many beech forests. But in the Wilds of America the open-air lover will not find it easy to indulge in the most ancient of all crimes and pastimes. Poisonous plants burn his sweetheart's buttocks, nameless insects sting his; sharp items of the forest floor prick his knees, insects hers; and all around there abides a sustained rustle of potential snakes – *que dis-je*, of semi-extinct dragons! – while the crab-like seeds of ferocious flowers cling, in a hideous green crust, to gartered black sock and sloppy white sock alike.

I am exaggerating a little. One summer noon, just below timberline, where heavenly-hued blossoms that I would fain call larkspur crowded all along a purly mountain brook, we did find, Lolita and I, a secluded romantic spot, a hundred feet or so above the pass where we had left our car. The slope seemed untrodden. A last panting pine was taking a well-earned breather on the rock it had reached. A marmot whistled at us and withdrew. Beneath the lap-robe I had spread for Lo, dry flowers crepitated softly. Venus came and went. The jagged cliff crowning the upper talus and a tangle of shrubs growing below us seemed to offer us protection from sun and man alike. Alas, I had not reckoned with a faint side trail that curled up in cagey fashion among the shrubs and rocks a few feet from us.

It was then that we came closer to detection than ever before, and no wonder the experience curbed for ever my yearning for rural amours.

I remember the operation was over, all over, and she was weeping in my arms – a salutory storm of sobs after one of the fits of moodiness that had become so frequent with her in the course of that otherwise admirable year! I had just retracted some silly promise she had forced me to make in a moment of blind impatient passion, and there she was sprawling and sobbing, and pinching my caressing hand, and I was laughing happily, and the atrocious, unbelievable, unbearable, and, I suspect, eternal horror that I know *now* was still but a dot of blackness in the blue of my bliss; and so we lay, when with one of those jolts that have ended by knocking my poor heart out of its groove, I met the unblinking dark eyes of two strange and beautiful children, faunlet and nymphet, whom their identical flat dark hair and bloodless cheeks proclaimed siblings if not twins. They stood crouching and gaping at us, both in blue playsuits, blending with the mountain blossoms. I plucked at the lap-robe for desperate concealment – and within the same instant, something that looked like a polka-dotted pushball among the undergrowth a few paces away, went into a turning motion which was transformed into the gradually rising figure of a stout lady with a raven-black bob, who automatically added a wild lily to her bouquet, while staring over her shoulder at us from behind her lovely carved bluestone children.

Now that I have an altogether different mess on my conscience, I know that I am a courageous man, but in those days I was not aware of it, and I remember being surprised by my own coolness. With the quiet murmured order one gives a sweat-stained distracted cringing trained animal even in the worst of plights (what mad hope or hate makes the young beast's flanks pulsate, what black stars pierce the heart of the tamer!), I made Lo get up, and we decorously walked, and then indecorously scuttled down to the car. Behind it a nifty station wagon was parked, and a handsome Assyrian with a little blue-black beard, *un monsieur très bien,* in silk shirt and magenta slacks, presumably the corpulent botanist's husband, was gravely taking the picture of a signboard giving the altitude of the pass. It was well over 10,000 feet and I was quite out of breath; and with a scrunch and a skid we drove off, Lo still struggling with her clothes and swearing at me in language that I never dreamed little girls could know, let alone use.

There were other unpleasant incidents. There was the movie theatre once, for example. Lo at the time still had for the cinema a veritable passion (it was to decline into tepid condescension during her second high school year). We took in, voluptuously and indiscriminately, oh, I don't know, one hundred and fifty or two hundred programmes during that one year, and during some of the denser periods of movie-going we saw many of the newsreels up to half-a-dozen times since the same weekly one went with different main pictures and pursued us from town to town. Her favourite kinds were, in this order: musicals, underworlders, westerners. In the first, real singers and dancers had unreal stage careers in an essentially grief-proof sphere of existence wherefrom death and truth were banned, and where, at the end, white-haired, dewy-eyed, technically deathless, the initially reluctant father of a show-crazy girl always finished by applauding her apotheosis on fabulous Broadway. The underworld was a world apart: there, heroic newspapermen were tortured, telephone bills ran to billions, and, in a robust atmosphere of incompetent marksmanship, villains were chased through sewers and storehouses by pathologically fearless cops (I was to give them less exercise). Finally, there was the mahogany landscape, the florid-faced, blue-eyed roughriders, the prim pretty schoolteacher arriving in Roaring Gulch, the rearing horse, the spectacular stampede, the pistol thrust through the shivered windowpane, the stupendous fist fight, the crashing mountain of dusty old-fashioned furniture, the table used as a weapon, the timely somersault, the pinned hand still groping for the dropped bowie knife, the grunt, the sweet crash of fist against chin, the kick in the belly, the flying tackle; and immediately after a plethora of pain that would have hospitalized a Hercules (I should know by now), nothing to show but the rather becoming bruise on the bronzed cheek of the warmed-up hero embracing his gorgeous frontier bride. I remember one matinee in a small airless theatre crammed with children and reeking with the hot breath of popcorn. The moon was yellow above the neckerchiefed crooner, and his finger was on his strumstring, and his foot was on a pine log, and I had innocently encircled Lo's shoulder and approached my jawbone to her temple, when two harpies behind us started muttering the queerest things – I do not know if I understood aright, but what I thought I did, made me withdraw my gentle hand, and of course the rest of the show was fog to me.

Another jolt I remember is connected with a little burg we were traversing at night, during our return journey. Some twenty miles earlier I had happened to tell her that the day school she would attend at Beardsley was a rather high-class non-coeducational one, with no modern nonsense, whereupon Lo treated me to one of those furious harangues of hers where entreaty and insult, self-assertion and double talk, vicious vulgarity and childish despair, were interwoven in an exasperating semblance of logic which prompted a semblance of explanation from me. Enmeshed in her wild words (swell chance . . . I'd be a sap if I took your opinion seriously. . . . Stinker. . . . You can't boss me. . . . I despise you . . . and so forth), I drove through the slumbering town at a fifty-mile-per-hour pace in continuance of my smooth highway swoosh, and a twosome of patrolmen put their spotlight on the car, and told me to pull over. I shushed Lo who was automatically raving on. The men peered at her and me with malevolent curiosity. Suddenly all dimples, she beamed sweetly at them, as she never did at my orchideous masculinity; for, in a sense, my Lo was even more scared of the law than I – and when the kind officers pardoned us and servilely we crawled on, her eyelids closed and fluttered as she mimicked limp prostration.

At this point I have a curious confession to make. You will laugh – but really and truly I somehow never managed to find out quite exactly what the legal situation was. I do not know it yet. Oh, I have learned a few odds and ends. Alabama prohibits a guardian from changing the ward's residence without an order of the court; Minnesota, to whom I take off my hat, provides that when a relative assumes permanent care and custody of any child under fourteen, the authority of a court does not come into play. Query: is the stepfather of a gaspingly adorable pubescent pet, a stepfather of only one month's standing, a neurotic widower of mature years and small but independent means, with the parapets of Europe, a divorce and a few madhouses behind him, is he to be considered a relative, and thus a natural guardian? And if not, must I, and could I reasonably dare notify some Welfare Board and file a petition (how do you file a petition?), and have a court's agent investigate meek, fishy me and dangerous Dolores Haze? The many books on marriage, rape, adoption and so on, that I guiltily consulted at the public libraries of big and small towns, told me nothing beyond darkly insinuating that the state is the super-guardian of minor children. Pilvin and Zapel, if I remember their names right, in an impressive volume on the legal side of marriage, completely ignored stepfathers with motherless girls on their hands and knees. My best friend, a social service monograph (Chicago, 1936), which was dug out for me at great pains from a dusty storage recess by an innocent old spinster, said, 'There is no principle that every minor must have a guardian; the court is passive and enters the fray only when the child's situation becomes conspicuously perilous.' A guardian, I concluded, was appointed only when he expressed his solemn and formal desire; but months might elapse before he was given notice to appear at a hearing and grow his pair of grey wings, and in the meantime the fair daemon child was legally left to her own devices which, after all, was the case of Dolores Haze. Then came the hearing. A few questions from the bench, a few reassuring answers from the attorney, a smile, a nod, a light drizzle outside, and the appointment was made. And still I dared not. Keep away, be a mouse, curl up in your hole. Courts became extravagantly active only when there was some monetary question involved: two greedy guardians, a robbed orphan, a third, still greedier, party. But here all was in perfect order, an inventory had been made, and her mother's small property was waiting untouched for Dolores Haze to grow up. The best policy seemed to be to refrain from any application. Or would some busybody, some Humane Society, butt in if I kept *too* quiet?

Friend Farlow, who was a lawyer of sorts and ought to have been able to give me some solid advice, was too much occupied with Jean's cancer to do anything more than what he had promised – namely, to look after Charlotte's meagre estate while I recovered very gradually from the shock of her death. I had conditioned him into believing Dolores was my natural child, and so could not expect him to bother his head about the situation. I am, as the reader must have gathered by now, a poor businessman; but neither ignorance nor indolence should have prevented me from seeking professional advice elsewhere. What stopped me was the awful feeling that if I meddled with fate in any way and tried to rationalize her fantastic gift, that gift would be snatched away like that palace on a mountain top in the Oriental tale which vanished whenever a prospective owner asked its custodian how come a strip of sunset sky was clearly visible from afar between black rock and foundation.

I decided that at Beardsley (the site of Beardsley College for Women) I would have access to works of reference that I had not yet been able to study, such as Woerner's Treatise 'On the American Law of Guardianship' and certain United States Children's Bureau Publications. I also decided that anything was better for Lo than the demoralizing idleness in which she lived. I could persuade her to do so many things – their list might stupefy a professional educator; but no matter how I pleaded or stormed, I could never make her read any other books than the so-called comic books or stories in magazines for American females. Any literature a peg higher smacked to her of school, and though theoretically willing to enjoy *A Girl of the Limberlost* or the *Arabian Nights*, or *Little Women*, she was quite sure she would not fritter away her 'vacation' on such highbrow reading matter.

I now think it was a great mistake to move east again and have her go to that private school in Beardsley, instead of somehow scrambling across the Mexican border while the scrambling was good so as to lie low for a couple of years in subtropical bliss until I could safely marry my little Creole; for I must confess that depending on the condition of my glands and ganglia, I could switch in the course of the same day from one pole of insanity to the other – from the thought that around 1950 I would have to get rid somehow of a difficult adolescent whose magic nymphage had evaporated – to the thought that with patience and luck I might have her produce eventually a nymphet with my blood in her exquisite veins, a Lolita the Second, who would be eight or nine around 1960, when I would still be *dans la force de l'âge*; indeed, the telescopy of my mind, or un-mind, was strong enough to distinguish in the remoteness of time a *vieillard encore vert* – or was it green rot? – bizarre, tender, salivating Dr Humbert, practising on supremely lovely Lolita the Third the art of being a granddad.

In the days of that wild journey of ours, I doubted not that as father of Lolita the First I was a ridiculous failure. I did my best; I read and reread a book with the unintentionally biblical title *Know Your Own Daughter*, which I got at the same store where I bought Lo, for her thirteenth birthday, a de luxe volume with commercially 'beautiful' illustrations, of Andersen's *The Little Mermaid*. But even at our very best moments, when we sat reading on a rainy day (Lo's glance skipped from the window to her wrist watch and back again), or had a quiet hearty meal in a crowded diner, or played a childish game of cards, or went shopping, or silently stared, with other motorists and their children, at some smashed, blood-bespattered car with a young woman's shoe in the ditch (Lo, as we drove on: 'That was the exact type of moccasin I was trying to describe to that jerk in the store'); on all those random occasions, I seemed to myself as implausible a father as she seemed to be a daughter. Was, perhaps, guilty locomotion instrumental in vitiating our powers of impersonation? Would improvement be forthcoming with a fixed domicile and a routine schoolgirl's day?

In my choice of Beardsley I was guided not only by the fact of there being a comparatively sedate school for girls located there, but also by the presence of the women's college. In my desire to get myself *casé*, to attach myself somehow to some patterned surface which my stripes would blend with, I thought of a man I knew in the department of French at Beardsley College; he was good enough to use my textbook in his classes and had attempted to get me over once to deliver a lecture. I had no intention of doing so, since, as I have once remarked in the course of these confessions, there are few physiques I loathe more than the heavy low-slung pelvis, thick calves and deplorable complexion of the average co-ed (in whom I see, maybe, the coffin of coarse female flesh within which my nymphets are buried alive); but I did crave for a label, a background, and a simulacrum, and, as presently will become clear, there was a reason, a rather zany reason, why old Gaston Godin's company would be particularly safe.

Finally, there was the money question. My income was cracking under the strain of our joy-ride. True, I clung to the cheaper motor courts; but every now and then, there would be a loud hotel de luxe, or a pretentious dude ranch, to mutilate our budget; staggering sums, moreover, were expended on sightseeing and Lo's clothes, and the old Haze bus, although a still vigorous and very devoted machine, necessitated numerous minor and major repairs. In one of our strip maps that has happened to survive among the papers which the authorities have so kindly allowed me to use for the purpose of writing my statement, I find some jottings that help me compute the following. During that extravagant year 1947–8, August to August, lodgings and food cost us around 5500 dollars; gas, oil and repairs, 1234, and various extras almost as much; so that during about 150 days of actual motion (we covered about 27,000 miles!) plus some 200 days of interpolated standstills, this modest *rentier* spent around 8000 dollars, or better say 10,000 because, unpractical as I am, I have surely forgotten a number of items.

And so we rolled East, I more devastated than braced with the satisfaction of my passion, and she glowing with health, her bi-iliac garland still as brief as a lad's, although she had added two inches to her stature and eight pounds to her weight. We had been everywhere. We had really seen nothing. And I catch myself thinking today that our long journey had only defiled with a sinuous trail of slime the lovely, trustful, dreamy, enormous country that by then, in retrospect, was no more to us than a collection of dog-eared maps, ruined tour books, old tyres, and her sobs in the night – every night, every night – the moment I feigned sleep.

4

When, through decorations of light and shade, we drove up to 14 Thayer Street, a grave little lad met us with the keys and a note from Gaston who had rented the house for us. My Lo, without granting her new surroundings one glance, unseeingly turned on the radio to which instinct led her and lay down on the living-room sofa with a batch of old magazines which in the same precise and blind manner she landed by dipping her hand into the nether anatomy of a lamp table.

I really did not mind where to dwell provided I could lock my Lolita up somewhere; but I had, I suppose, in the course of my correspondence with vague Gaston, vaguely visualized a house of ivied brick. Actually the place bore a dejected resemblance to the Haze home (a mere 400 miles distant): it was the same sort of dull grey frame affair with a shingled roof and dull green drill awnings; and the rooms, though smaller and furnished in a more consistent plush-and-plate style, were arranged in much the same order. My study turned out to be, however, a much larger room, lined from floor to ceiling with some two thousand books on chemistry which my landlord (on sabbatical leave for the time being) taught at Beardsley College.

I had hoped Beardsley School for girls, an expensive day school, with lunch thrown in and a glamorous gymnasium, would, while cultivating all those young bodies, provide some formal education for their minds as well. Gaston Godin, who was seldom right in his judgment of American habitus, had warned me that the institution might turn out to be one of those where girls are taught, as he put it with a foreigner's love for such things: 'not to spell very well, but to smell very well'. I don't think they achieved even that.

At my first interview with headmistress Pratt, she approved of my child's 'nice blue eyes' (blue! Lolita!) and of my own friendship with that 'French genius' (a genius! Gaston!) – and then, having turned Dolly over to a Miss Cormorant, she winkled her brow in a kind of *recueillement* and said:

'We are not so much concerned, Mr Humbird, with having our students become bookworms or be able to reel off all the capitals of Europe which nobody knows anyway, or learn by heart the dates of forgotten battles. What we are concerned with is the adjustment of the child to group life. This is why we stress the four D's: Dramatics, Dance, Debating and Dating. We are confronted by certain facts. Your delightful Dolly will presently enter an age group where dates, dating, date dress, date book, date etiquette, means as much to her as, say, business, business connections, business success, mean to you, or as much as [smiling] the happiness of my girls means to me. Dorothy Humbird is already involved in a whole system of social life which consists, whether we like it or not, of hot-dog stands, corner drugstores, malts and cokes, movies, square-dancing, blanket parties on beaches, and even hair-fixing parties! Naturally at Beardsley School we disapprove of some of these activities; and we rechannel others into more constructive directions. But we do try to turn our backs on the fog and squarely face the sunshine. To put it briefly, while adopting certain teaching techniques, we are more interested in communication than in composition. That is, with due respect to Shakespeare and others, we want our girls to *communicate* freely with the live world around them rather than plunge into musty old books. We are still groping perhaps, but we grope intelligently, like a gynecologist feeling a tumour. We think, Dr Humburg, in organismal and organizational terms. We have done away with the mass of irrelevant topics that have traditionally been presented to young girls, leaving no place, in former days, for the knowledges and the skills, and the attitudes they will need in managing their lives and – as the cynic might add – the lives of their husbands. Mr Humberson, let us put it this way: the position of a star is important, but the most practical spot for an icebox in the kitchen may be even more important to the budding housewife. You say that all you expect a child to obtain from school is a sound education. But what do we mean by education? In the old days it was in the main a verbal phenomenon; I mean, you could have a child learn by heart a good encyclopaedia and he or she would know as much as or more than a school could offer. Dr Hummer, do you realize that for the modern pre-adolescent child, medieval dates are of less vital value than weekend ones [twinkle]? – to repeat a pun that I heard the Beardsley college psycho-analyst permit herself the other day. We live not only in a world of thoughts, but also in a world of things. Words without experience are meaningless. What on earth can Dorothy Hummerson care for Greece and the Orient with their harems and slaves?'

This programme rather appalled me, but I spoke to two intelligent ladies who had been connected with the school, and they affirmed that the girls did quite a bit of sound reading and that the 'communication' line was more or less ballyhoo aimed at giving old-fashioned Beardsley School a financially remunerative modern touch, though actually it remained as prim as a prawn.

Another reason attracting me to that particular school may seem funny to some readers, but it was very important to me, for that is the way I am made. Across our street, exactly in front of our house, there was, I noticed, a gap of weedy wasteland, with some colourful bushes and a pile of bricks and a few scattered planks, and the foam of shabby mauve and chrome autumn roadside flowers; and through that gap you could see a shimmery section of School Road, running parallel to our Thayer Street, and immediately beyond that, the playground of the school. Apart from the psychological comfort this general arrangement should afford me by keeping Dolly's day adjacent to mine, I immediately foresaw the pleasure I would have in distinguishing from my study-bedroom, by means of powerful binoculars, the statistically inevitable percentage of nymphets among the other girl children playing around Dolly during recess; unfortunately, on the very first day of school, workmen arrived and put up a fence some way down the gap, and in no time a construction of tawny wood maliciously arose beyond that fence utterly blocking my magic vista; and as soon as they had erected a sufficient amount of material to spoil everything, those absurd builders suspended their work and never appeared again.

5

In a street called Thayer Street, in the residential green, fawn, and golden of a mellow academic townlet, one was bound to have a few amiable fine-dayers yelping at you. I prided myself on the exact temperature of my relations with them: never rude, always aloof. My west-door neighbour, who might have been a businessman or a college teacher, or both, would speak to me once in a while as he barbered some late garden blooms or watered his car, or, at a later date, defrosted his driveway (I don't mind if these verbs are all wrong), but my brief grunts, just sufficiently articulate to sound like conventional assents or interrogative pause-fillers, precluded any evolution toward chumminess. Of the two houses flanking the bit of scrubby waste opposite, one was closed, and the other contained two professors of English, tweedy and short-haired Miss Lester and fadedly feminine Miss Fabian, whose only subject of brief sidewalk conversation with me was (God bless their tact!) the young loveliness of my daughter and the naïve charm of Gaston Godin. My east-door neighbour was by far the most dangerous one, a sharp-nosed stock character whose late brother had been attached to the College as Superintendent of Buildings and Grounds. I remember her waylaying Dolly, while I stood at the living-room window, feverishly awaiting my darling's return from school. The odious spinster, trying to conceal her morbid inquisitiveness under a mask of dulcet goodwill, stood leaning on her slim umbrella (the sleet had just stopped, a cold wet sun had sidled out), and Dolly, her brown coat open despite the raw weather, her structural heap of books pressed against her stomach, her knees showing pink above her clumsy wellingtons, a sheepish frightened little smile flitting over and off her snub-nosed face, which – owing perhaps to the pale wintry light – looked almost plain, in a rustic, German, *mägdlein*-like way, as she stood there and dealt with Miss East's questions 'And where is your mother, my dear? And what is your poor father's occupation? And where did you live before?' Another time the loathsome creature accosted me with a welcoming whine – but I evaded her; and a few days later there came from her a note in a blue-margined envelope, a nice mixture of poison and treacle, suggesting Dolly come over on a Sunday and curl up in a chair to look through the 'loads of beautiful books my dear mother gave me when I was a child, instead of having the radio on at full blast till all hours of the night'.

I had also to be careful in regard to a Mrs Holigan, a charwoman and cook of sorts whom I had inherited with the vacuum cleaner from the previous tenants. Dolly got lunch at school, so that this was no trouble, and I had become adept at providing her with a big breakfast and warming up the dinner that Mrs Holigan prepared before leaving. That kindly and harmless woman had, thank God, a rather bleary eye that missed details, and I had become a great expert in bedmaking; but still I was continuously obsessed by the feeling that some fatal stain had been left somewhere, or that, on the rare occasions where Holigan's presence happened to coincide with Lo's, simple Lo might succumb to buxom sympathy in the course of a cosy kitchen chat. I often felt we lived in a lighted house of glass, and that any moment some thin-lipped parchment face would peer through a carelessly unshaded window to obtain a free glimpse of things that the most jaded *voyeur* would have paid a small fortune to watch.

6

A word about Gaston Godin. The main reason why I enjoyed – or at least tolerated with relief – his company was the spell of absolute security that his ample person cast on my secret. Not that he knew it; I had no special reason to confide in him, and he was much too self-centred and abstract to notice or suspect anything that might lead to a frank question on his part and a frank answer on mine. He spoke well of me to Beardsleyans, he was my good herald. Had he discovered *mes goûts* and Lolita's status, it would have interested him only in so far as throwing some light on the simplicity of my attitude toward *him,* which attitude was as free of polite strain as it was of ribald allusions; for despite his colourless mind and dim memory, he was perhaps aware that I knew more about him than the burghers of Beardsley did. He was a flabby, dough-faced, melancholy bachelor tapering upward to a pair of narrow, not quite level shoulders and a conical pear-head which had sleek black hair on one side and only a few plastered wisps on the other. But the lower part of his body was enormous, and he ambulated with a curious elephantine stealth by means of phenomenally stout legs. He always wore black, even his tie was black; he seldom bathed; his English was a burlesque. And, nonetheless, everybody considered him to be a supremely lovable, lovably freakish fellow! Neighbours pampered him; he knew by name all the small boys in our vicinity (he lived a few blocks away from me) and had some of them clean his sidewalk and burn leaves in his backyard, and bring wood from his shed, and even perform simple chores about the house, and he would feed them fancy chocolates, with *real* liqueurs inside – in the privacy of an orientally furnished den in his basement, with amusing daggers and pistols arrayed on the mouldy, rug-adorned walls among the camouflaged hot-water pipes. Upstairs he had a studio – he painted a little, the old fraud. He had decorated its sloping wall (it was really not more than a garret) with large photographs of pensive André Gide, Tchaikovsky, Norman Douglas, two other well-known English writers, Nijinsky (all thighs and fig-leaves), Harold D. Doublename (a misty-eyed left-wing professor at a Midwestern university) and Marcel Proust. All these poor people seemed about to fall on you from their inclined plane. He had also an album with snapshots of all the Jackies and Dickies of the neighbourhood, and when I happened to thumb through it and make some casual remark, Gaston would purse his fat lips and murmur with a wistful pout '*Oui, ils sont gentils*'. His brown eyes would roam around the various sentimental and artistic bric-a-brac present, and his own banal *toiles* (the conventionally primitive eyes, sliced guitars, blue nipples and geometrical designs of the day), and with a vague gesture toward a painted wooden bowl or veined vase, he would say '*Prenez donc une de ces poires. La bonne dame d'en face m'en offre plus que je n'en peux savourer*'. Or: '*Mississe Taille Lore vient de me donner ces dahlias, belles fleurs que j'exècre*'. (Sombre, sad, full of world-weariness.)

For obvious reasons, I preferred my house to his for the games of chess we had two or three times weekly. He looked like some old battered idol as he sat with his pudgy hands in his lap and stared at the board as if it were a corpse. Wheezing, he would meditate for ten minutes – then make a losing move. Or the good man, after even more thought, might utter: *Au roi!* with a slow old-dog woof that had a gargling sound at the back of it which made his jowls wabble; and then he would lift his circumflex eyebrows with a deep sigh as I pointed out to him that he was in check himself.

Sometimes, from where we sat in my cold study I could hear Lo's bare feet practising dance techniques in the living room downstairs; but Gaston's outgoing senses were comfortably dulled, and he remained unaware of those naked rhythms – and-one, and-two, and-one, and-two, weight transferred on a straight right leg, leg up and out to the side, and-one, and-two, and only when she started jumping, opening her legs at the height of the jump, and flexing one leg, and extending the other, and flying, and landing on her toes – only then did my pale, pompous, morose opponent rub his head or cheek as if confusing those distant thuds with the awful stabs of my formidable Queen.

Sometimes Lola would slouch in while we pondered the board – and it was every time a treat to see Gaston, his elephant eye still fixed on his pieces, ceremoniously rise to shake hands with her, and forthwith release her limp fingers, and without looking once at her, descend again into his chair to topple into the trap I had laid for him. One day around Christmas, after I had not seen him for a fortnight or so, he asked me *'Et toutes vos fillettes, elles vont bien?'* from which it became evident to me that he had multiplied my unique Lolita by the number of sartorial categories his downcast moody eye had glimpsed during a whole series of her appearances: blue jeans, a skirt, shorts, a quilted robe.

I am loath to dwell so long on the poor fellow (sadly enough, a year later, during a voyage to Europe, from which he did not return, he got involved in a *sale histoire,* in Naples of all places!). I would have hardly alluded to him at all had not his Beardsley existence had such a queer bearing on my case. I need him for my defence. There he was devoid of any talent whatsoever, a mediocre teacher, a worthless scholar, a glum repulsive fat old invert, highly contemptuous of the American way of life, triumphantly ignorant of the English language – there he was in priggish New England, crooned over by the old and caressed by the young – oh, having a grand time and fooling everybody; and here was I.

7

I am now faced with the distasteful task of recording a definite drop in Lolita's morals. If her share in the ardours she kindled had never amounted to much, neither had pure lucre ever come to the fore. But I was weak, I was not wise, my schoolgirl nymphet had me in thrall. With the human element dwindling, the passion, the tenderness, and the torture only increased; and of this she took advantage.

Her weekly allowance, paid to her under condition she fulfil her basic obligations, was twenty-one cents at the start of the Beardsley era – and went up to one dollar five before its end. This was a more than generous arrangement seeing she constantly received from me all kinds of small presents and had for the asking any sweetmeat or movie under the moon – although, of course, I might fondly demand an additional kiss, or even a whole collection of assorted caresses, when I knew she coveted very badly some item of juvenile amusement. She was, however, not easy to deal with. Only very listlessly did she earn her three pennies – or three nickels – per day; and she proved to be a cruel negotiator whenever it was in her power to deny me certain life-wrecking, strange, slow paradisal philtres without which I could not live more than a few days in a row, and which, because of the very nature of love's languor, I could not obtain by force. Knowing the magic and might of her own soft mouth, she managed – during one school year! – to raise the bonus of a fancy embrace to three, and even four bucks, O Reader! Laugh not, as you imagine me, on the very rack of joy noisily emitting dimes and quarters, and great big silver dollars like some sonorous, jingly and wholly demented machine vomiting riches; and in the margin of that leaping epilepsy she would firmly clutch a handful of coins in her little fist, which, anyway, I used to pry open afterwards unless she gave me the slip, scrambling away to hide her loot. And just as every other day I would cruise all around the school area and on comatose feet visit drugstores, and peer into foggy lanes, and listen to receding girl laughter in between my heart throbs and the falling leaves, so every now and then I would burgle her room and scrutinize torn papers in the wastebasket with the painted roses, and look under the pillow of the virginal bed I had just made myself. Once I found eight one-dollar notes in one of her books (fittingly – *Treasure Island*), and once a hole in the wall behind Whistler's 'Mother' yielded as much as twenty-four dollars and some change – say, twenty-four sixty – which I quietly removed, upon which, next day, she accused, to my face, honest Mrs Holigan of being a filthy thief. Eventually, she lived up to her IQ by finding a safer hoarding place which I never discovered; but by that time I had brought prices down drastically by having her earn the hard and nauseous way permission to participate in the school's theatrical programme; because what I feared most was not that she might ruin me, but that she might accumulate sufficient cash to run away. I believe the poor fierce-eyed child figured out that with a mere fifty dollars in her purse she might somehow reach Broadway or Hollywood – or the foul kitchen of a diner (Help wanted) in a dismal ex-prairie state, with the wind blowing, and the stars blinking, and the cars, and the bars, and the barmen, and everything soiled, torn, dead.

8

I did my best, your Honour, to tackle the problems of boys. Oh, I used even to read in the *Beardsley Star* a so-called Column for Teens, to find out how to behave!

> A word to fathers. Don't frighten away daughter's friend. Maybe it is a bit hard for you to realize that now the boys are finding her attractive. To you she is still a little girl. To the boys she's charming and fun, lovely and gay. They like her. Today you clinch big deals in an executive's office, but yesterday you were just highschool Jim carrying Jane's school books. Remember? Don't you want your daughter, now that her turn has come, to be happy in the admiration and company of boys she likes? Don't you want them to have wholesome fun together?

Wholesome fun? Good Lord!

> Why not treat the young fellows as guests in your house? Why not make conversation with them? Draw them out, make them laugh and feel at ease?

Welcome, fellow, to this bordello.

> If she breaks the rules don't explode out loud in front of her partner in crime. Let her take the brunt of your displeasure in private. And stop making the boys feel she's the daughter of an old ogre.

First of all, the old ogre drew up a list under 'absolutely forbidden' and another under 'reluctantly allowed'. Absolutely forbidden were dates, single or double or triple – the next step being, of course, mass orgy. She might visit a candy bar with her girl friends, and there giggle-chat with occasional young males, while I waited in the car at a discreet distance; and I promised her that if her group were invited by a socially acceptable group in Butler's Academy for Boys for their annual ball (heavily chaperoned, of course), I might consider the question whether a girl of fourteen can don her first 'formal' (a kind of gown that makes thin-armed teenagers look like flamingoes). Moreover, I promised her to throw a party at our house to which she would be allowed to invite her prettier girl friends and the nicer boys she would have met by that time at the Butler dance. But I was quite positive that as long as my régime lasted she would never, never be permitted to go with a youngster in rut to a movie, or neck in a car, or go to boy-girl parties at the houses of schoolmates, or indulge out of my earshot in boy-girl telephone conversations, even if 'only discussing his relations with a friend of mine.'

Lo was enraged by all this – called me a lousy crook and worse – and I would probably have lost my temper had I not soon discovered, to my sweetest relief, that what really angered her was my depriving her not of a specific satisfaction but of a general right. I was impinging, you see, on the conventional programme, the stock pastimes, the 'things that are done', the routine of youth for there is nothing more conservative than a child, especially a girl-child, be she the most auburn and russet, the most mythopoeic nymphet in October's orchard-haze.

Do not misunderstand me. I cannot be absolutely certain that in the course of the winter she did not manage to have, in a casual way, improper contact with unknown young fellows; of course, no matter how closely I controlled her leisure, there would constantly occur unaccounted-for time leaks with over-elaborate explanations to stop them up in retrospect; of course, my jealousy would constantly catch its jagged claw in the fine fabrics of nymphet falsity; but I did definitely feel – and can now vouchsafe for the accuracy of my feeling – that there was no reason for serious alarm. I felt that way not because I never once discovered any palpable hard young throat to crush among the masculine mutes that flickered somewhere in the background; but because it was to me 'overwhelmingly obvious' (a favourite expression with my Aunt Sybil) that all varieties of high school boys – from the perspiring nincompoop whom 'holding hands' thrills, to the self-sufficient rapist with pustules and a souped-up car – equally bored my sophisticated young mistress. 'All this noise about boys gags me', she had scrawled on the inside of a schoolbook, and underneath, in Mona's hand (Mona is due any minute now), there was the sly quip: 'What about Rigger?' (due too).

Faceless, then, are the chappies I happened to see in her company. There was, for instance Red Sweater who one day, the day we had the first snow – saw her home; from the parlour window I observed them talking near our porch. She wore her first cloth coat with a fur collar; there was a small brown cap on my favourite hair-do – the fringe in front and the swirl at the side and the natural curls at the back – and her damp-dark moccasins and white socks were more sloppy than ever. She pressed as usual her books to her chest while speaking or listening, and her feet gestured all the time: she would stand on her left instep with her right toe, remove it backward, cross her feet, rock slightly, sketch a few steps, and then start the series all over again. There was Windbreaker who talked to her in front of a restaurant one Sunday afternoon while his mother and sister attempted to walk me away for a chat; I dragged along and looked back at my only love. She had developed more than one conventional mannerism, such as the polite adolescent way of showing one is literally 'doubled up' with laughter by inclining one's head, and so (as she sensed my call), still feigning helpless merriment, she walked backwards a couple of steps, and then faced about, and walked toward me with a fading smile. On the other hand, I greatly liked – perhaps because it reminded me of her first unforgettable confession – her trick of sighing 'oh dear!' in humorous wistful submission to fate, or emitting a long 'no-o' in a deep almost growling undertone when the blow of fate had actually fallen. Above all – since we are speaking of movement and youth – I liked to see her spinning up and down Thayer Street on her beautiful young bicycle: rising on the pedals to work on them lustily, then sinking back in a languid posture while the speed wore itself off; and then she would stop at our mailbox and, still astride, would flip through a magazine she found there, and put it back, and press her tongue to one side of her upperlip and push off with her foot, and again sprint through pale shade and sun.

On the whole she seemed to me better adapted to her surroundings than I had hoped she would be when considering my spoiled slave-child and the bangles of demeanour she naïvely affected the winter before in California. Although I could never get used to the constant state of anxiety in which the guilty, the great, the tenderhearted live, I felt I was doing my best in the way of mimicry. As I lay on my narrow studio bed after a session of adoration and despair in Lolita's cold bedroom, I used to review the concluded day by checking my own image as it prowled rather than passed before the mind's red eye. I watched dark-and-handsome, not un-Celtic, probably high-church, possibly very high-church, Dr Humbert see his daughter off to school. I watched him greet with his slow smile and pleasantly arched thick black ad-eyebrows good Mrs Holigan, who smelled of the plague (and would head, I knew, for master's gin at the first opportunity). With Mr West, retired executioner or writer of religious tracts – who cared? – I saw neighbour what's his name, I think they are French or Swiss, meditate in his frank-windowed study over a typewriter, rather gaunt-profiled, an almost Hitlerian cowlick on his pale brow. Weekends, wearing well-tailored overcoat and brown gloves, Professor H. might be seen with his daughter strolling to Walton Inn (famous for its violet-ribboned china bunnies and chocolate boxes among which you sit and wait for a 'table for two' still filthy with your predecessor's crumbs). Seen on weekdays, around 1 p.m., saluting with dignity Argus-eyed East while manoeuvring the car out of the garage and around the damned evergreens, and down on to the slippery road. Raising a cold eye from book to clock in the positively sultry Beardsley College library, among bulky young women caught and petrified in the overflow of human knowledge. Walking across the campus with the college clergyman, the Rev. Rigger (who also taught Bible at Beardsley School). 'Somebody told me her mother was a celebrated actress killed in an aeroplane accident. Oh? My mistake, I presume. Is that so? I see. How sad.' (Sublimating her mother, eh?) Slowly pushing my little pram through the labyrinth of the supermarket, in the wake of Professor W., also a slow-moving and gentle widower with the eyes of a goat. Shovelling the snow in my shirt-sleeves, a voluminous black and white muffler around my neck. Following with no show of rapacious haste (even taking time to wipe my feet on the mat) my schoolgirl daughter into the house. Taking Dolly to the dentist – pretty nurse beaming at her – old magazines *ne montrez pas vos zhambes*. At dinner with Dolly in town, Mr Edgar H. Humbert was seen eating his steak in the continental knife-and-fork manner. Enjoying, in duplicate, a concert: two marble-faced, becalmed Frenchmen sitting side by side, with Monsieur H. H.'s musical little girl on her father's right, and the musical little boy of Professor W. (father spending a hygienic evening in Providence) on Monsieur G. G.'s left. Opening the garage, a square of light that engulfs the car and is extinguished. Brightly pyjamaed, jerking down the window shade in Dolly's bedroom. Saturday morning, unseen, solemnly weighing the winter-bleached lassie in the bathroom. Seen and heard Sunday morning, no churchgoer after all, saying don't be too late, to Dolly who is bound for the covered court. Letting in a queerly observant schoolmate of Dolly's: 'First time I've seen a man wearing a smoking jacket, sir – except in movies, of course.'

9

Her girl friends, whom I had looked forward to meet, proved on the whole disappointing. There was Opal Something, and Linda Hall, and Avis Chapman, and Eva Rosen, and Mona Dahl (save one, all these names are approximations, of course). Opal was a bashful, formless, bespectacled, bepimpled creature who doted on Dolly, who bullied her. With Linda Hall the school tennis champion, Dolly played singles at least twice a week: I suspect Linda was a true nymphet, but for some unknown reason she did not come – was perhaps not allowed to come – to our house; so I recall her only as a flash of natural sunshine on an indoor court. Of the rest, none had any claims to nymphetry except Eva Rosen. Avis was a plump lateral child with hairy legs, while Mona, though handsome in a coarse sensual way and only a year older than my aging mistress, had obviously long ceased to be a nymphet, if she ever had been one. Eva Rosen, a displaced little person from France, was on the other hand a good example of a not strikingly beautiful child revealing to the perspicacious amateur some of the basic elements of nymphet charm, such as a perfect pubescent figure and lingering eyes and high cheek-bones. Her glossy copper hair had Lolita's silkiness, and the features of her delicate milky-white face with pink lips and silverfish eye-lashes were less foxy than those of her likes – the great clan of intra-racial redheads; nor did she sport their green uniform but wore, as I remember her, a lot of black or cherry dark – a very smart black pullover, for instance, and high-heeled black shoes, and garnet-red fingernail polish. I spoke French to her (much to Lo's disgust). The child's tonalities were still admirably pure, but for school words and play words she resorted to current American and then a slight Brooklyn accent would crop up in her speech, which was amusing in a little Parisian who went to a select New England school with phoney British aspirations. Unfortunately, despite 'that French kid's uncle' being 'a millionaire', Lo dropped Eva for some reason before I had had time to enjoy in my modest way her fragrant presence in the Humbert open house. The reader knows what importance I attached to having a bevy of page girls, consolation prize nymphets, around my Lolita. For a while, I endeavoured to interest my senses in Mona Dahl who was a good deal around, especially during the spring term when Lo and she got so enthusiastic about dramatics. I have often wondered what secrets outrageously treacherous Dolores Haze had imparted to Mona while blurting out to me by urgent and well-paid request various really incredible details concerning an affair that Mona had had with a marine at the seaside. It was characteristic of Lo that she chose for her closest chum that elegant, cold, lascivious, experienced young female whom I once heard (misheard, Lo swore) cheerfully say in the hallway to Lo – who had remarked that her (Lo's) sweater was of virgin wool: 'The only thing about you that is, kiddo. . . .' She had a curiously husky voice, artificially waved dull dark hair, earrings, amber-brown prominent eyes and luscious lips. Lo said teachers had remonstrated with her on her loading herself with so much costume jewellery. Her hands trembled. She was burdened with a 150 IQ. And I also knew she had a tremendous chocolate-brown mole on her womanish back which I inspected the night Lo and she had worn low-cut pastel-coloured, vaporous dresses for a dance at the Butler Academy.

I am anticipating a little, but I cannot help running my memory all over the keyboard of that school year. In meeting my attempts to find out what kind of boys Lo knew, Miss Dahl was elegantly evasive. Lo who had gone to play tennis at Linda's country club had telephoned she might be a full half hour late, and so, would I entertain Mona who was coming to practise with her a scene from *The Taming of the Shrew*. Using all the modulations, all the allure of manner and voice she was capable of and staring at me with perhaps – could I be mistaken? – a faint gleam of crystalline irony, beautiful Mona replied: 'Well, sir, the fact is Dolly is not much concerned with mere boys. Fact is, we are rivals. She and I have a crush on the Reverend Rigger.' (This was a joke – I have already mentioned that gloomy giant of a man, with the jaw of a horse: he was to bore me to near murder with his impressions of Switzerland at a tea party for parents that I am unable to place correctly in terms of time.)

How had the ball been? Oh, it had been a riot. A what? A panic. Terrific, in a word. Had Lo danced a lot? Oh, not a frightful lot, just as much as she could stand. What did she, languorous Mona, think of Lo? Sir? Did she think Lo was doing well at school? Gosh, she certainly was quite a kid. But her general behaviour was—? Oh, she was a swell kid. But still? 'Oh, she's a doll,' concluded Mona, and sighed abruptly, and picked up a book that happened to lie at hand, and with a change of expression, falsely furrowing her brow, inquired: 'Do tell me about Ball Zack, sir. Is he really that good?' She moved up so close to my chair that I made out through lotions and creams her uninteresting skin scent. A sudden odd thought stabbed me: was my Lo playing the pimp? If so, she had found the wrong substitute. Avoiding Mona's cool gaze, I talked literature for a minute. Then Dolly arrived – and slit her pale eyes at us. I left the two friends to their own devices. One of the latticed squares in a small cob-webby casement window at the turn of the staircase was glazed with ruby, and that raw wound among the unstained rectangles and its asymmetrical position – a knight's move from the top – always strangely disturbed me.

10

Sometimes. . . . come on, how often exactly, Bert? Can you recall four, five, more such occasions? Or would no human heart have survived two or three? Sometimes (I have nothing to say in reply to your question), while Lolita would be haphazardly preparing her homework, sucking a pencil, lolling sideways in an easy chair with both legs over its arm, I would shed all my pedagogic restraint, dismiss all our quarrels, forget all my masculine pride – and literally crawl on my knees to your chair, my Lolita! You would give me one look – a grey furry question mark of a look: 'Oh no, not again' (incredulity, exasperation); for you never deigned to believe that I could, without any specific designs, ever crave to bury my face in your plaid skirt, my darling! The fragility of those bare arms of yours – how I longed to enfold them, all your four limpid lovely limbs, a folded colt, and take your head between my unworthy hands, and pull the temple-skin back on both sides, and kiss your chinesed eyes, and – 'Pulease, leave me alone, will you', you would say, 'for Christ's sake leave me alone'. And I would get up from the floor while you looked on, your face deliberately twitching in imitation of my *tic nerveux*. But never mind, never mind, I am only a brute, never mind, let us go on with my miserable story.

11

One Monday forenoon, in December I think, Pratt asked me to come over for a talk. Dolly's last report had been poor, I knew. But instead of contenting myself with some such plausible explanation of this summons, I imagined all sorts of horrors, and had to fortify myself with a pint of my 'pin' before I could face the interview. Slowly, all Adam's apple and heart, I went up the steps of the scaffold.

A huge woman, grey-haired, frowsy, with a broad flat nose and small eyes behind black-rimmed glasses – 'Sit down,' she said, pointing to an informal and humiliating hassock, while she perched with ponderous spryness on the arm of an oak chair. For a moment or two, she peered at me with smiling curiosity. She had done it at our first meeting. I recalled, but I could afford then to scowl back. Her eye left me. She lapsed into thought – probably assumed. Making up her mind she rubbed, fold on fold, her dark grey flannel skirt at the knee, dispelling a trace of chalk or something. Then she said, still rubbing, not looking up:

'Let me ask a blunt question, Mr Haze. You are an old-fashioned Continental father, aren't you?'

'Why, no,' I said, 'conservative, perhaps, but not what you would call old-fashioned.'

She sighed, frowned, then clapped her big plump hands together in a let's-get-down-to-business manner, and again fixed her beady eyes upon me.

'Dolly Haze,' she said, 'is a lovely child, but the onset of sexual maturing seems to give her trouble.'

I bowed slightly. What else could I do?

'She is still shuttling,' said Miss Pratt, showing how with her liver-spotted hands, 'between the anal and genital zones of development. Basically she is a lovely—'

'I beg your pardon,' I said 'what zones?'

'That's the old-fashioned European in you!' cried Pratt delivering a slight tap on my wrist watch and suddenly disclosing her dentures. 'All I mean is that biologic and psychologic drives – do you smoke? – are not fused in Dolly, do not fall so to speak into a – into a rounded pattern.' Her hands held for a moment an invisible melon.

'She is attractive, bright though careless' (breathing heavily, without leaving her perch, the woman took time out to look at the lovely child's report sheet on the desk at her right). 'Her marks are getting worse and worse. Now I wonder, Mr Haze—' Again the false meditation.

'Well,' she went on with zest, 'as for me, I do smoke, and, as dear Dr Pierce used to say: I'm not proud of it but I jeest love it.' She lit up and the smoke she exhaled from her nostrils was like a pair of tusks.

'Let me give you a few details, it won't take a moment. Now let me see [rummaging among her papers]. She is defiant toward Miss Redcock and impossibly rude to Miss Cormorant. Now here is one of our special research reports: Enjoys singing with group in class though mind seems to wander. Crosses her knees and wags left leg to rhythm. Type of by-words: a two-hundred-forty-two word area of the commonest pubescent slang fenced in by a number of obviously European polysyllabics. Sighs a good deal in class. Let me see. Yes. Now comes the last week in November. Sighs a good deal in class. Chews gum vehemently. Does not bite her nails though, if she did, this would conform better to her general pattern – scientifically speaking, of course. Menstruation, according to the subject, well established. Belongs at present to no church organization. By the way, Mr Haze, her mother was—? Oh, I see. And you are—? Nobody's business is, I suppose, God's business. Something else we wanted to know. She has no regular home duties, I understand. Making a princess of your Dolly, Mr Haze, eh? Well, what else have we got here? Handles books gracefully. Voice pleasant. Giggles rather often. A little dreamy. Has private jokes of her own, transposing for instance the first letters of some of her teachers' names. Hair light and dark brown, lustrous – well [laughing] you are aware of *that,* I suppose. Nose unobstructed, feet high-arched, eyes – let me see, I had here somewhere a still more recent report. Aha, here we are. Miss Gold says Dolly's tennis form is excellent to superb, even better than Linda Hall's, but concentration and point-accumulation are just 'poor to fair'. Miss Cormorant cannot decide whether Dolly has exceptional emotional control or none at all. Miss Horn reports she – I mean, Dolly – cannot, verbalize her emotions, while according to Miss Cole, Dolly's metabolic efficiency is superfine. Miss Molar thinks Dolly is myopic and should see a good ophthalmologist, but Miss Redcock insists that the girl simulates eye-strain to get away with scholastic incompetence. And to conclude, Mr Haze, our researchers are wondering about something really crucial. Now I want to ask you something. I want to know if your poor wife, or yourself, or anyone else in the family – I understand she has several aunts and a maternal grandfather in California? – oh, *had*! – I'm sorry – well, we all wonder if anybody in the family has instructed Dolly in the process of mammalian reproduction. The general impression is that fifteen-year-old Dolly remains morbidly uninterested in sexual matters, or, to be exact, represses her curiosity in order to save her ignorance and self-dignity. All right – fourteen. You see, Mr Haze, Beardsley School does not believe in bees and blossoms, and storks and love birds, but it does believe very strongly in preparing its students for mutually satisfactory mating and successful child rearing. We feel Dolly could make excellent progress if only she would put her mind to her work. Miss Cormorant's report is significant in that respect. Dolly is inclined to be, mildly speaking, impudent. But all feel that, *primo*, you should have your family doctor tell her the facts of life and, *secundo*, that you allow her to enjoy the company of her schoolmates' brothers at the Junior Club or in Dr Rigger's organization, or in the lovely homes of our parents.'

'She may meet boys at her own lovely home,' I said.

'I hope she will,' said Pratt buoyantly. 'When we questioned her about her troubles, Dolly refused to discuss the home situation, but we have spoken to some of her friends and really – well, for example, we insist you un-veto her non-participation in the dramatic group. You just must allow her to take part in *The Enchanted Hunters*. She was such a perfect little nymph in the tryout, and sometime in spring the author will stay for a few days at Beardsley College and may attend a rehearsal or two in our new auditorium. I mean it is all part of the fun of being young and alive and beautiful. You must understand—'

'I always thought of myself,' I said, 'as a very understanding father.'

'Oh no doubt, no doubt, but Miss Cormorant thinks, and I am inclined to agree with her, that Dolly is obsessed by sexual thoughts for which she finds no outlet, and will tease and martyrize other girls, or even our younger instructors because *they* do have innocent dates with boys.'

Shrugged my shoulders. A shabby *émigré*.

'Let us put our two heads together, Mr Haze. What on earth is wrong with that child?'

'She seems quite normal and happy to me,' I said (disaster coming at last? was I found out? had they got some hypnotist?).

'What worries me,' said Miss Pratt looking at her watch and

starting to go over the whole subject again, 'is that both teachers and schoolmates find Dolly antagonistic, dissatisfied, cagey – and everybody wonders why you are so firmly opposed to all the natural recreations of a normal child.'

'Do you mean sex play?' I asked jauntily, in despair, a cornered old rat.

'Well, I certainly welcome this civilized terminology,' said Pratt with a grin. 'But this is not quite the point. Under the auspices of Beardsley School, dramatics, dances and other natural activities are not technically sex play, though girls do meet boys, if that is what you object to.'

'All right,' I said, my hassock exhaling a weary sigh. 'You win. She can take part in that play. Provided male parts are taken by female parts.'

'I am always fascinated,' said Pratt, 'by the admirable way foreigners – or at least naturalized Americans – use our rich language. I'm sure Miss Gold, who conducts the play group, will be overjoyed. I notice she is one of the few teachers that seem to like – I mean who seem to find Dolly manageable. This takes care of general topics, I guess; now comes a special matter. We are in trouble again.'

Pratt paused truculently, then rubbed her index finger under her nostrils with such vigour that her nose performed a kind of war dance.

'I'm a frank person,' she said, 'but conventions are conventions, and I find it difficult . . . Let me put it this way . . . The Walkers, who live in what we call around here the Duke's Manor, you know the great grey house on the hill – they send their two girls to our school, and we have the niece of President Moore with us, a really gracious child, not to speak of a number of other prominent children. Well, under the circumstances, it is rather a jolt when Dolly, who looks like a little lady, uses words which you as a foreigner probably simply do not know or do not understand. Perhaps it might be better – Would you like me to have Dolly come up here right away to discuss things? No? You see – oh well, let's have it out. Dolly has written a most obscene four-letter word which our Dr Cutler tells me is low-Mexican for urinal with her lipstick on some health pamphlets which Miss Redcock, who is getting married in June, distributed among the girls, and we thought she should stay after hours – another half hour at least. But if you like—'

'No,' I said, 'I don't want to interfere with rules. I shall talk to her later. I shall thrash it out.'

'Do,' said the woman rising from her chair arm. 'And perhaps we can get together again soon, and if things do not improve we might have Dr Cutler analyse her.'

Should I marry Pratt and strangle her?

'. . . and perhaps your family doctor might like to examine her physically – just a routine check-up. She is in Mushroom – the last classroom along that passage.'

Beardsley School, it may be explained, copied a famous girls' school in England by having 'traditional' nicknames for its various classrooms: Mushroom, Room-In 8, B-room, Room-BA and so on. Mushroom was smelly, with a sepia print of Reynolds' 'Age of Innocence' above the chalkboard, and several rows of clumsy-looking pupil desks. At one of these, my Lolita was reading the chapter on 'Dialogue' in Baker's *Dramatic Technique*, and all was very quiet, and there was another girl with a very naked, porcelain-white neck and wonderful platinum hair, who sat in front reading too, absolutely lost to the world and interminably winding a soft curl around one finger, and I sat beside Dolly just behind that neck and that hair, and unbuttoned my overcoat and for sixty-five cents plus the permission to participate in the school play, had Dolly put her inky, chalky, red-knuckled hand under the desk. Oh, stupid and reckless of me, no doubt, but after the torture I had been subjected to, I simply had to take advantage of a combination that I knew would never occur again.

12

Around Christmas she caught a bad chill and was examined by a friend of Miss Lester, a Dr Ilse Tristramson (hi, Ilse, you were a dear, uninquisitive soul, and you touched my dove very gently). She diagnosed bronchitis, patted Lo on the back (all its bloom erect because of the fever) and put her to bed for a week or longer. At first she 'ran a temperature' in American parlance, and I could not resist the exquisite caloricity of unexpected delights – Venus febriculosa – though it was a very languid Lolita that moaned and coughed and shivered in my embrace. And as soon as she was well again, I threw a Party with Boys.

Perhaps I had drunk a little too much in preparation for the ordeal. Perhaps I made a fool of myself. The girls had decorated and plugged in a small fir tree – German custom, except that coloured bulbs had superseded wax candles. Records were chosen and fed into my landlord's phonograph. Chic Dolly wore a nice grey dress with fitted bodice and flared skirt. Humming, I retired to my study upstairs – and then every ten or twenty minutes I would come down like an idiot just for a few seconds; to pick up ostensibly my pipe from the mantlepiece or hunt for the newspaper; and with every new visit these simple actions became harder to perform, and I was reminded of the dreadfully distant days when I used to brace myself to casually enter a room in the Ramsdale house where Little Carmen was on.

The party was not a success. Of the three girls invited, one did not come at all, and one of the boys brought his cousin Roy, so there was a superfluity of two boys, and the cousins knew all the steps, and the other fellows could hardly dance at all, and most of the evening was spent in messing up the kitchen, and then endlessly jabbering about what card game to play, and sometime later, two girls and four boys sat on the floor of the living room, with all windows open, and played a word game which Opal could not be made to understand, while Mona and Roy, a lean handsome lad, drank ginger ale in the kitchen, sitting on the table and dangling their legs, and hotly discussing Predestination and the Law of Averages. After they had all gone my Lo said ugh, closed her eyes, and dropped into a chair with all four limbs starfished to express the utmost disgust and exhaustion and swore it was the most revolting bunch of boys she had ever seen. I bought her a new tennis racket for that remark.

January was humid and warm, and February fooled the forsythia: none of the townspeople had ever *seen* such weather. Other presents came tumbling in. For her birthday I bought her a bicycle, the doe-like and altogether charming machine already mentioned – and added to this a *History of Modern American Painting*: her bicycle manner, I mean her approach to it, the hip movement in mounting, the grace and so on, afforded me supreme pleasure; but my attempt to refine her pictorial taste was a failure; she wanted to know if the guy noon-napping on Doris Lee's hay was the father of the pseudo-voluptuous hoyden in the foreground, and could not understand why I said Grant Wood or Peter Hurd was good, and Reginald Marsh or Frederick Waugh awful.

13

By the time spring had touched up Thayer Street with yellow and green and pink, Lolita was irrevocably stage-struck. Pratt, whom I chanced to notice one Sunday lunching with some people at Walton Inn, caught my eye from afar and went through the motion of sympathetically and discreetly clapping her hands while Lo was not looking. I detest the theatre as being a primitive and putrid form, historically speaking; a form that smacks of stone-age rites and communal nonsense despite those individual injections of genius, such as, say, Elizabethan poetry which a closeted reader automatically pumps out of the stuff. Being much occupied at the time with my own literary labours, I did not bother to read the complete text of *The Enchanted Hunters*, the playlet in which Dolores Haze was assigned the part of a farmer's daughter who imagines herself to be a woodland witch, or Diana, or something, and who, having got hold of a book on hypnotism, plunges a number of lost hunters into various entertaining trances before falling in her turn under the spell of a vagabond poet (Mona Dahl). That much I gleaned from bits of crumpled and poorly typed script that Lo sowed all over the house. The coincidence of the title with the name of an unforgettable inn was pleasant in a sad little way: I wearily thought I had better not bring it to my own enchantress's notice, lest a brazen accusation of mawkishness hurt me even more than her failure to notice it for herself had done. I assumed the playlet was just another, practically anonymous, version of some banal legend. Nothing prevented one, of course, from supposing that in quest of an attractive name the founder of the hotel had been immediately and solely influenced by the chance fantasy of the second-rate muralist he had hired, and that subsequently the hotel's name had suggested the play's title. But in my credulous, simple, benevolent mind I happened to twist it the other way round, and, without giving the whole matter much thought really, supposed that mural, name and title had all been derived from a common source, from some local tradition, which I, an alien unversed in New England lore, would not be supposed to know. In consequence I was under the impression (all this quite casually, you understand, quite outside any orbit of importance) that the accursed playlet belonged to the type of whimsy for juvenile consumption, arranged and rearranged many times, such as *Hansel and Gretel* by Richard Roe, or *The Sleeping Beauty* by Dorothy Doe, or *The Emperor's New Clothes* by Maurice Vermont and Marion Rumpelmeyer – all this to be found in any *Plays for School Actors* or *Let's Have a Play!* In other words, I did not know – and would not have cared, if I did – that actually *The Enchanted Hunters* was a quite recent and technically original composition which had been produced for the first time only three or four months ago by a highbrow group in New York. To me – in as much as I could judge from my charmer's part – it seemed to be a pretty dismal kind of fancy work, with echoes from Lenormand and Maeterlinck and various quite British dreamers. The redcapped, uniformly attired hunters, of which one was a banker, another a plumber, a third a policeman, a fourth an undertaker, a fifth an underwriter, a sixth an escaped convict (you see the possibilities!), went through a complete change of mind in Dolly's Dell, and remembered their real lives only as dreams or nightmares from which little Diana had aroused them; but a seventh Hunter (in a *green* cap, the fool) was a Young Poet, and he insisted, much to Diana's annoyance, that she and the entertainment provided (dancing nymphs, and elves, and monsters) were his, the Poet's, invention. I understand that finally, in utter disgust at this cocksureness, barefooted Dolores was to lead check-trousered Mona to the paternal farm behind the Perilous Forest to prove to the braggart she was not a poet's fancy, but a rustic, down-to-earth lass – and a last-minute kiss was to enforce the play's profound message, namely, that mirage and reality merge in love. I considered it wiser not to criticize the thing in front of Lo: she was so healthily engrossed in 'problems of expression', and so charmingly did she put her narrow Florentine hands together, batting her eyelashes and pleading with me not to come to rehearsals as some ridiculous parents did because she wanted to dazzle me with a perfect First Night – and because I was, anyway, always butting in and saying the wrong thing, and cramping her style in the presence of other people.

There was one very special rehearsal . . . my heart, my heart . . . there was one day in May marked by a lot of gay flurry – it all rolled past, beyond my ken, immune to my memory, and when I saw Lo next, in the late afternoon, balancing on her bike, pressing the palm of her hand to the damp bark of a young birch tree on the edge of our lawn, I was so struck by the radiant tenderness of her smile that for an instant I believed all our troubles gone. 'Can you remember,' she said, 'what was the name of that hotel, *you* know [nose puckered], come on, you know – with those white columns and the marble swan in the lobby? Oh, you know [noisy exhalation of breath] – the hotel where you raped me. Okay, skip it. I mean, was it [almost in a whisper] The Enchanted Hunters? Oh, it was? [musingly] Was it?' – and with a yelp of amorous vernal laughter she slapped the glossy bole and tore uphill, to the end of the street, and then rode back, feet at rest on stopped pedals, posture relaxed, one hand dreaming in her print-flowered lap.

14

Because it supposedly tied up with her interest in dance and dramatics, I had permitted Lo to take piano lessons with a Miss Emperor (as we French scholars may conveniently call her) to whose blue-shuttered little white house a mile or so beyond Beardsley Lo would spin off twice a week. One Friday night toward the end of May (and a week or so after the very special rehearsal Lo had not had me attend) the telephone in my study, where I was in the act of mopping up Gustave's – I mean Gaston's – king's side, rang and Miss Emperor asked if Lo was coming next Tuesday because she had missed last Tuesday's and today's lessons. I said she would by all means – and went on with the game. As the reader may well imagine, my faculties were now impaired, and a move or two later, with Gaston to play, I noticed through the film of my general distress that he could collect my queen; he noticed it too, but demurred for quite a minute, and puffed and wheezed, and shook his jowls, and even shot furtive glances at me, and made hesitating half-thrusts with his pudgily bunched fingers – dying to take that juicy queen and not daring – and all of a sudden he swooped upon it (who knows if it did not teach him certain later audacities?), and I spent a dreary hour in achieving a draw. He finished his brandy and presently lumbered away, quite satisfied with this result (*mon pauvre ami, je ne vous ai jamais revu et quoiqu'il y ait bien peu de chance que vous voyiez mon livre, permettez-moi de vous dire que je vous serre la main bien cordialement, et que toutes mes fillettes vous saluent*). I found Dolores Haze at the kitchen table, consuming a wedge of pie, with her eyes fixed on her script.

They rose to meet mine with a kind of celestial vapidity. She remained singularly unruffled when confronted with my discovery, and said *d'un petit air faussement contrit* that she knew she was a very wicked kid, but simply had not been able to resist the enchantment, and had used up those music hours – O Reader, My Reader! – in a nearby public park rehearsing the magic forest scene with Mona. I said 'fine' – and stalked to the telephone. Mona's mother answered: 'Oh yes, she's in' and retreated with a mother's neutral laugh of polite pleasure to shout off stage 'Roy calling!' and the very next moment Mona rustled up, and forthwith, in a low monotonous not untender voice started berating Roy for something he had said or done and I interrupted her, and presently Mona was saying in her humblest, sexiest contralto, 'yes, sir', 'surely, sir', 'I am alone to blame, sir, in this unfortunate business' (what elocution! what poise!), 'honest, I feel very bad about it' – and so on and so forth as those little harlots say.

So downstairs I went clearing my throat and holding my heart. Lo was now in the living room, in her favourite overstuffed chair. As she sprawled there, biting at a hangnail and mocking me with her heartless vaporous eyes, and all the time rocking a stool upon which she had placed the heel of an outstretched shoeless foot, I perceived all at once with a sickening qualm how much she had changed since I first met her two years ago. Or had this happened during those last two weeks? *Tendresse?* Surely that was an exploded myth. She sat right in the focus of my incandescent anger. The fog of all lust had been swept away leaving nothing but this dreadful lucidity. Oh, she had changed! Her complexion was now that of any vulgar untidy high-school girl who applies shared cosmetics with grubby fingers to an unwashed face and does not mind what soiled texture, what pustulate epidermis comes in contact with her skin. Its smooth tender bloom had been so lovely in former days, so bright with tears, when I used to roll, in play, her tousled head on my knee. A coarse flush had now replaced that innocent fluorescence. What was locally known as a 'rabbit cold' had painted with flaming pink the edges of her contemptuous nostrils. As in terror I lowered my gaze, it mechanically slid along the underside of her tensely stretched bare thigh – how polished and muscular her legs had grown! She kept her wideset eyes, clouded-glass grey and slightly bloodshot, fixed upon me, and I saw the stealthy thought showing through them that perhaps after all Mona was right, and she, orphan Lo, could expose me without getting penalized herself. How wrong I was. How mad I was! Everything about her was of the same exasperating impenetrable order – the strength of her shapely legs, the dirty sole of her white sock, the thick sweater she wore despite the closeness of the room, her wenchy smell, and especially the dead end of her face with its strange flush and freshly made-up lips. Some of the red had left stains on her front teeth, and I was struck by a ghastly recollection – the evoked image not of Monique, but of another young prostitute in a bell-house, ages ago, who had been snapped up by somebody else before I had time to decide whether her mere youth warranted my risking some appalling disease, and who had just such flushed prominent pommettes and a dead *maman,* and big front teeth, and a bit of dingy red ribbon in her country-brown hair.

'Well, speak,' said Lo. 'Was the corroboration satisfactory?'

'Oh, yes,' I said. 'Perfect. Yes. And I do not doubt you two made it up. As a matter of fact, I do not doubt you have told her everything about us.'

'Oh, yah?'

I controlled my breath and said: 'Dolores, this must stop right away. I am ready to yank you out of Beardsley and lock you up you know where, but this must stop. I am ready to take you away the time it takes to pack a suitcase. This must stop or else anything may happen.'

'Anything may happen, huh?'

I snatched away the stool she was rocking with her heel and her foot fell with a thud on the floor.

'Hey,' she cried, 'take it easy.'

'First of all you go upstairs,' I cried in my turn and simultaneously grabbed at her and pulled her up. From that moment, I stopped restraining my voice, and we continued yelling at each other, and she said unprintable things. She said she loathed me. She made monstrous faces at me, inflating her cheeks and producing a diabolical plopping sound. She said I had attempted to violate her several times when I was her mother's roomer. She said she was sure I had murdered her mother. She said she would sleep with the very first fellow who asked her and I could do nothing about it. I said she was to go upstairs and show me all her hiding places. It was a strident and hateful scene. I held her by her knobby wrist and she kept turning and twisting it this way and that, surreptitously trying to find a weak point so as to wrench herself free at a favourable moment, but I held her quite hard and in fact hurt her rather badly for which I hope my heart may rot, and once or twice she jerked her arm so violently that I feared her wrist might snap, and all the while she stared at me with those unforgettable eyes where cold anger and hot tears struggled, and our voices were drowning the telephone, and when I grew aware of its ringing she instantly escaped.

With people in movies I seem to share the services of the machina telephonica and its sudden god. This time it was an irate neighbour. The east window happened to be agape in the living room, with the blind mercifully down, however; and behind it the damp black night of a sour New England spring had been breathlessly listening to us. I had always thought that type of haddocky spinster with the obscene mind was the result of considerable literary inbreeding in modern fiction; but now I am convinced that prude and prurient Miss East – or to explode her incognito, Miss Fenton Lebone – had been probably protruding three-quarter-way from her bedroom window as she strove to catch the gist of our quarrel.

'. . . This racket . . . lacks all sense of . . .' quacked the receiver, 'we do not live in a tenement here. I must emphatically . . .'

I apologized for my daughter's friends being so loud. Young people, you know – and cradled the next quack and a half.

Downstairs the screen door banged. Lo? Escaped?

Through the casement on the stairs I saw a small impetuous ghost slip through the shrubs; a silvery dot in the dark – hub of bicycle wheel – moved, shivered, and she was gone.

It so happened that the car was spending the night in a repair shop downtown. I had no other alternative than to pursue on foot the winged fugitive. Even now, after more than three years have heaved and elapsed, I cannot visualize that spring-night street, that already so leafy street, without a gasp of panic. Before their lighted porch Miss Lester was promenading Miss Fabian's dropsical dackel. Mr Hyde almost knocked it over. Walk three steps and run three. A tepid rain started to drum on the chestnut leaves. At the next corner, pressing Lolita against an iron railing, a blurred youth held and kissed – no, not her, mistake. My talons still tingling, I flew on.

Half a mile or so east of number fourteen, Thayer Street tangles with a private lane and a cross street; the latter leads to the town proper; in front of the first drugstore, I saw – with what melody of relief! – Lolita's fair bicycle waiting for her. I pushed instead of pulling, pulled, pushed, pulled, and entered. Look out! Some ten paces away Lolita, through the glass of a telephone booth (membraneous god still with us), cupping the tube, confidentially hunched over it, slit her eyes at me, turned away with her treasure, hurriedly hung up, and walked out with a flourish.

'Tried to reach you at home,' she said brightly. 'A great decision has been made. But first buy me a drink, dad.'

She watched the listless pale fountain girl put in the ice, pour in the coke, add the cherry syrup – and my heart was bursting with love-ache. That childish wrist. My lovely child. You have a lovely child, Mr Humbert. We always admire her as she passes by. Mr Pim watched Pippa suck in the concoction.

J'ai toujours admiré l'oeuvre ormonde du sublime Dublinois. And in the meantime the rain had become a voluptuous shower.

'Look,' she said as she rode the bike beside me, one foot scraping the darkly glistening sidewalk, 'look, I've decided something. I want to leave school. I hate that school. I hate the play, I really do! Never go back. Find another. Leave at once. Go for a long trip again. But *this* time we'll go wherever *I* want, won't we?'

I nodded. My Lolita.

'I choose? *C'est entendu?*' she asked wobbling a little beside me. Used French only when she was a very good little girl.

'Okay. *Entendu.* Now hop-hop-hop, Lenore, or you'll get soaked.' (A storm of sobs was filling my chest.)

She bared her teeth and after her adorable schoolgirl fashion, leaned forward, and away she sped, my bird.

Miss Lester's finely groomed hand held a porch-door open for a waddling old dog *qui prenait son temps.*

Lo was waiting for me near the ghostly birch-tree.

'I am drenched,' she declared at the top of her voice. 'Are you glad? To hell with the play! See what I mean?'

An invisible hag's claw slammed down an upper-floor window.

In our hallway, ablaze with welcoming lights, my Lolita peeled off her sweater, shook her gemmed hair, stretched towards me two bare arms, raised one knee:

'Carry me upstairs, please. I feel sort of romantic tonight.'

It may interest physiologists to learn, at this point, that I have the ability – a most singular case, I presume – of shedding torrents of tears throughout the other tempest.

15

The brakes were relined, the waterpipes unclogged, the valves ground, and a number of other repairs and improvements were paid for by not very mechanically-minded but prudent papa Humbert, so that the late Mrs Humbert's car was in respectable shape when ready to undertake a new journey.

We had promised Beardsley School, good old Beardsley School, that we would be back as soon as my Hollywood engagement came to an end (inventive Humbert was to be, I hinted, chief consultant in the production of a film dealing with 'existentialism', still a hot thing at the time). Actually I was toying with the idea of gently trickling across the Mexican border – I was braver now than last year – and there deciding what to do with my little concubine who was now sixty inches tall and weighed ninety pounds. We had dug out our tour books and maps. She had traced our route with immense zest. Was it thanks to those theatricals that she had now outgrown her juvenile jaded airs and was so adorably keen to explore rich reality? I experienced the queer lightness of dreams that pale but warm Sunday morning when we abandoned Professor Chem's puzzled house and sped along Main Street toward the four-lane highway. My Love's striped, black-and-white, cotton frock, jaunty blue cap, white socks and brown moccasins were not quite in keeping with the large beautifully cut aquamarine on a silver chainlet, which gemmed her throat: a spring rain gift from me. We passed the New Hotel, and she laughed. 'A penny for your thoughts,' I said and she stretched out her palm at once, but at that moment I had to apply the brakes rather abruptly at a red light. As we pulled up, another car came to a gliding stop alongside, and a very striking looking, athletically lean young woman (where had I seen her?) with a high complexion and shoulder-length brilliant bronze hair, greeted Lo with a ringing 'Hi!' – and then, addressing me, effusively, edusively (placed!), stressing certain words, said: 'What a *shame* it was to *tear* Dolly away from the play – you should have *heard* the author *raving* about her after that rehearsal—' 'Green light, you dope,' said Lo under her breath, and simultaneously, waving in bright adieu a bangled arm, Joan of Arc (in a performance we saw at the local theatre) violently outdistanced us to swerve into Campus Avenue.

'Who was it exactly? Vermont or Rumpelmeyer?'

'No – Edusa Gold – the gal who coaches us.'

'I was not referring to her. Who exactly concocted that play?'

'Oh! Yes, of course. Some old woman, Clare Something, I guess. There was quite a crowd of them there.'

'So she complimented you?'

'Complimented my eye – she kissed me on my pure brow' – and my darling emitted that new yelp of merriment which – perhaps in connection with her theatrical mannerisms – she had lately begun to affect.

'You are a funny creature, Lolita,' I said – or some such words. 'Naturally, I am overjoyed you gave up that absurd stage business. But what is curious is that you dropped the whole thing only a week before its natural climax. Oh, Lolita, you should be careful of those surrenders of yours. I remember you gave up Ramsdale for camp, and camp for a joy ride, and I could list other abrupt changes in your disposition. You must be careful. There are things that should never be given up. You must persevere. You should try to be a little nicer to me, Lolita. You should also watch your diet. The tour of your thigh, you know, should not exceed seventeen and a half inches. More might be fatal (I was kidding, of course). We are now setting out on a long happy journey. I remember—'

16

I remember as a child in Europe gloating over a map of North America that had 'Appalachian Mountains' boldly running from Alabama up to New Brunswick, so that the whole region they spanned – Tennessee, the Virginias, Pennsylvania, New York, Vermont, New Hampshire and Maine – appeared to my imagination as a gigantic Switzerland or even Tibet, all mountain, glorious diamond peak upon peak, giant conifers, *le montagnard émigré* in his bear-skin glory, and *Melis tigris goldsmithi*, and Red Indians under the catalpas. That it all boiled down to a measly suburban lawn and a smoking garbage incinerator, was appalling. Farewell, Appalachia! Leaving it, we crossed Ohio, the three states beginning with 'I', and Nebraska – ah, that first whiff of the West! We travelled very leisurely, having more than a week to reach Wace, Continental Divide, where she passionately desired to see the Ceremonial Dances marking the seasonal opening of Magic Cave, and at least three weeks to reach Elphinstone, gem of a western State where she yearned to climb Red Rock from which a mature screen star had recently jumped to her death after a drunken row with her gigolo.

Again we were welcomed to wary motels by means of inscriptions that read:

'We wish you to feel at home while here. *All* equipment was carefully checked upon your arrival. Your licence number is on record here. Use hot water sparingly. We reserve the right to eject without notice any objectionable person. Do not throw waste material of *any* kind in the toilet bowl. Thank you. Call again. The Management. PS. We consider our guests the Finest People of the World.'

In these frightening places we paid ten for twins, flies queued outside at the screenless door and successfully scrambled in, the ashes of our predecessors still lingered in the ashtrays, a woman's hair lay on the pillow, one heard one's neighbour hanging his coat in his closet, the hangers were ingeniously fixed to their bars by coils of wire so as to thwart theft, and, in crowning insult, the pictures above the twin beds were identical twins. I also noticed that commercial fashion was changing. There was a tendency for cabins to fuse and gradually form the caravansary, and, lo (she was not interested but the reader may be), a second story was added, and a lobby grew in, and cars were removed to a communal garage, and the motel reverted to the good old hotel.

I now warn the reader not to mock me and my mental daze. It is easy for him and me to decipher *now* a past destiny; but a destiny in the making is, believe me, not one of those honest mystery stories where all you have to do is keep an eye on the clues. In my youth I once read a French detective tale where the clues were actually in italics; but that is not McFate's way – even if one does learn to recognize certain obscure indications.

For instance: I would not swear that there was not at least one occasion, prior to, or at the very beginning of, the Midwest lap of our journey, when she managed to convey some information to, or otherwise get into contact with, a person or persons unknown. We had stopped at a gas station, under the sign of Pegasus, and she had slipped out of her seat and escaped to the rear of the premises while the raised hood, under which I had bent to watch the mechanic's manipulations, hid her for a moment from my sight. Being inclined to be lenient, I only shook my benign head though strictly speaking such visits were taboo, since I felt instinctively that toilets – as also telephones – happened to be for reasons unfathomable, the points where my destiny was liable to catch. We all have such fateful objects – it may be a recurrent landscape in one case, a number in another – carefully chosen by the gods to attract events of special significance for us: here shall John always stumble; there shall Jane's heart always break.

Well – my car had been attended to, and I had moved it away from the pumps to let a pickup truck be serviced – when the growing volume of her absence began to weigh upon me in the windy greyness. Not for the first time, and not for the last, had I stared in such dull discomfort of mind at those stationary trivialities that look almost surprised, like staring rustics, to find themselves in the stranded traveller's field of vision: that green garbage can, those very black, very whitewalled tyres for sale, those bright cans of motor oil, that red icebox with assorted drinks, the four, five, seven discarded bottles within the incompleted crossword puzzle of their wooden cells, that bug patiently walking up the inside window of the office. Radio music was coming from its open door, and because the rhythm was not synchronized with the heave and flutter and other gestures of wind-animated vegetation, one had the impression of an old scenic film living its own life while piano or fiddle followed a line of music quite outside the shivering flower, the swaying branch. The sound of Charlotte's last sob incongruously vibrated through me as, with her dress fluttering athwart the rhythm, Lolita veered from a totally unexpected direction. She had found the toilet occupied and had crossed over to the sign of the Conche in the next block. They said there they were proud of their home-clean rest rooms. These prepaid postcards, they said, had been provided for your comments. No postcards. No soap. Nothing. No comments.

That day or the next, after a tedious drive through a land of food crops, we reached a pleasant little burg and put up at Chestnut Court – nice cabins, damp green grounds, apple trees, an old swing – and a tremendous sunset which the tired child ignored. She had wanted to go through Kasbeam because it was only thirty miles north from her home town but on the following morning I found her quite listless, with no desire to see again the sidewalk where she had played hopscotch some five years before. For obvious reasons I had rather dreaded that side trip, even though we had agreed not to make ourselves conspicuous in any way – to remain in the car and not look up old friends. My relief at her abandoning the project was spoiled by the thought that had she felt I were totally against the nostalgic possibilities of Pisky, as I had been last year, she would not have given up so easily. On my mentioning this with a sigh, she sighed too and complained of being out of sorts. She wanted to remain in bed till teatime at least, with lots of magazines, and then if she felt better she suggested we just continue westward. I must say she was very sweet and languid, and craved for fresh fruits, and I decided to go and fetch a toothsome picnic lunch in Kasbeam. Our cabin stood on the timbered crest of a hill, and from our window you could see the road winding down, and then running as straight as a hair parting between two rows of chestnut trees, towards the pretty town, which looked singularly distinct and toy-like in the pure morning distance. One could make out an elf-like girl on an insect-like bicycle, and a dog, a bit too large proportionately, all as clear as those pilgrims and mules winding up wax-pale roads in old paintings with blue hills and red little people. I have the European urge to use my feet when a drive can be dispensed with, so I leisurely walked down, eventually meeting the cyclist – a plain plump girl with pigtails, followed by a huge St Bernard dog with orbits like pansies. In Kasbeam a very old barber gave me a very mediocre haircut: he babbled of a baseball-playing son of his, and, at every explodent, spat into my neck, and every now and then wiped his glasses on my sheet-wrap, or interrupted his tremulous scissor work to produce faded newspaper clippings, and so inattentive was I that it came as a shock to realize as he pointed to an easeled photograph among the ancient grey lotions, that the moustached young ball player had been dead for the last thirty years.

I had a cup of hot flavourless coffee, bought a bunch of bananas for my monkey, and spent another ten minutes or so in a delicatessen store. At least an hour and a half must have elasped when this homeward-bound little pilgrim appeared on the winding road leading to Chestnut Castle.

The girl I had seen on my way to town was now loaded with linen and engaged in helping a misshaped man whose big head and coarse features reminded me of the 'Bertoldo' character in low Italian comedy. They were cleaning the cabins of which there were a dozen or so on Chestnut Crest, all pleasantly spaced amid the copious verdure. It was noon, and most of them, with a final bang of their screen doors, had already got rid of their occupants. A very elderly, almost mummy-like couple in a very new model were in the act of creeping out of one of the contiguous garages; from another a red hood protruded in somewhat cod-piece fashion; and nearer to our cabin, a strong and handsome young man with a shock of black hair and blue eyes was putting a portable refrigerator into a station wagon. For some reason he gave me a sheepish grin as I passed. On the grass expanse opposite, in the many-limbed shade of luxuriant trees, the familiar St Bernard dog was guarding his mistress's bicycle, and nearby a young woman, far gone in the family way, had seated a rapt baby on a swing and was rocking it gently, while a jealous boy of two or three was making a nuisance of himself by trying to push or pull the swing board; he finally succeeded in getting himself knocked down by it, and bawled loudly as he lay supine on the grass while his mother continued to smile gently at neither of her present children. I recall so clearly these minutiae probably because I was to check my impressions so thoroughly only a few minutes later; and besides, something in me had been on guard ever since that awful night in Beardsley. I now refused to be diverted by the feeling of well-being that my walk had engendered – by the young summer breeze that enveloped the nape of my neck, the giving crunch of the damp gravel, and juicy titbit I had sucked out at last from a hollow tooth, and even the comfortable weight of my provisions which the general condition of my heart should not have allowed me to carry; but even that miserable pump of mine seemed to be working sweetly, and I felt *adolori d'amoureuse langueur,* to quote dear old Ronsard, as I reached the cottage where I had left my Dolores.

To my surprise I found her dressed. She was sitting on the edge of the bed in slacks and T-shirt, and was looking at me as if she could not quite place me. The frank soft shape of her small breasts was brought out rather than blurred by the limpness of her thin shirt, and this frankness irritated me. She had not washed; yet her mouth was freshly though smudgily painted, and her broad teeth glistened like wine-tinged ivory, or pinkish poker chips. And there she sat, hands clasped in her lap, and dreamily brimmed with a diabolical glow that had no relation to me whatever.

I plumped down my heavy paper bag and stood staring at the bare ankles of her sandalled feet, then at her silly face, then again at her sinful feet. 'You've been out,' I said (the sandals were filthy with gravel).

'I just got up,' she replied, and added upon intercepting my downward glance: 'Went out for a sec. Wanted to see if you were coming back.'

She became aware of the bananas and uncoiled herself tableward.

What special suspicion could I have? None indeed – but those muddy, moony eyes of hers, that singular warmth emanating from her! I said nothing. I looked at the road meandering so distinctly within the frame of the window. . . . Anybody wishing to betray my trust would have found it a splendid lookout. With rising appetite, Lo applied herself to the fruit. All at once I remembered the ingratiating grin of the Johnny next door. I stepped out quickly. All cars had disappeared except his station wagon; his pregnant wife was now getting into it with her baby and the other, more or less cancelled, child.

'What's the matter, where are you going?' cried Lo from the porch.

I said nothing. I pushed her softness back into the room and went in after her. I ripped her shirt off. I unzipped the rest of her. I tore off her sandals. Wildly, I pursued the shadow of her infidelity; but the scent I travelled upon was so slight as to be practically indistinguishable from a madman's fancy.

17

Gros Gaston, in his prissy way, had liked to make presents – presents just a prissy wee bit out of the ordinary, or so he prissily thought. Noticing one night that my box of chessmen was broken, he sent me next morning, with a little lad of his, a copper case: it had an elaborate Oriental design over the lid and could be securely locked. One glance sufficed to assure me that it was one of those cheap money boxes called for some reason 'luizettas' that you buy in Algiers and elsewhere, and wonder what to do with afterwards. It turned out to be much too flat for holding my bulky chessmen, but I kept it – using it for a totally different purpose.

In order to break some pattern of fate in which I obscurely felt myself being enmeshed, I had decided – despite Lo's visible annoyance – to spend another night at Chestnut Court; definitely waking up at four in the morning, I ascertained that Lo was still sound asleep (mouth open, in a kind of dull amazement at the curiously inane life we all had rigged up for her) and satisfied myself that the precious contents of the 'luizetta' were safe. There, snugly wrapped in a white woollen scarf, lay a pocket automatic: calibre ·32, capacity of magazine eight cartridges, length a little under one-ninth of Lolita's length, stock checked walnut, finish full blued. I had inherited it from the late Harold Haze, with a 1938 catalogue which cheerily said in part: 'Particularly well adapted for use in the home and car as well as on the person.' There it lay, ready for instant service on the person or persons, loaded and fully cocked with the slide lock in safety position, thus precluding any accidental discharge. We must remember that a pistol is the Freudian symbol of the Ur-father's central forelimb.

I was now glad I had it with me – and even more glad that I had learned to use it two years before, in the pine forest around my and Charlotte's glass lake. Farlow, with whom I had roamed those remote woods, was an admirable marksman, and with his ·38 actually managed to hit a humming bird, though I must say not much of it could be retrieved for proof – only a little iridescent fluff. A burly ex-policeman called Krestovski, who in the 'twenties had shot and killed two escaped convicts, joined us and bagged a tiny woodpecker – completely out of season, incidentally. Between these two sportsmen I of course was a novice and kept missing everything, though I did wound a squirrel on a later occasion when I went out alone. 'You lie here,' I whispered to my light-weight compact little chum, and then toasted it with a dram of gin.

18

The reader must now forget Chestnuts and Colts, and accompany us further west. The following days were marked by a number of great thunderstorms – or perhaps, there was but one single storm which progressed across country in ponderous frog-leaps and which we could not shake off just as we could not shake off detective Trapp: for it was during those days that the problem of the Aztec Red Convertible presented itself to me, and quite overshadowed the theme of Lo's lovers.

Queer! I who was jealous of every male we met – queer, how I misinterpreted the designations of doom. Perhaps I had been lulled by Lo's modest behaviour in winter, and anyway it would have been too foolish even for a lunatic to suppose another Humbert was avidly following Humbert and Humbert's nymphet with Jovian fireworks, over the great and ugly plains. I surmised, *donc,* that the Red Yak keeping behind us at a discreet distance mile after mile was operated by a detective whom some busybody had hired to see what exactly Humbert Humbert was doing with that minor stepdaughter of his. As happens with me at periods of electrical disturbance and crepitating lightnings, I had hallucinations. Maybe they were more than hallucinations. I do not know what she or he or both had put into my liquor but one night I felt sure somebody was tapping on the door of our cabin, and I flung it open, and noticed two things – that I was stark naked and that, white-glistening in the rain-dripping darkness, there stood a man holding before his face the mask of Jutting Chin, a grotesque sleuth in the funnies. He emitted a muffled guffaw and scurried away, and I reeled back into the room, and fell asleep again, and am not sure even to this day that the visit was not a drug-provoked dream: I have thoroughly studied Trapp's type of humour, and this might have been a plausible sample. Oh, crude and absolutely ruthless! Somebody, I imagined, was making money on those masks of popular monsters and morons. Did I see next morning two urchins rummaging in a garbage can and trying on Jutting Chin? I wonder. It may all have been a coincidence – due to atmospheric conditions, I suppose.

Being a murderer with a sensational but incomplete and unorthodox memory, I cannot tell you, ladies and gentlemen, the exact day when I first knew with utter certainty that the red convertible was following us. I do remember, however, the first time I saw its driver quite clearly. I was proceeding slowly one afternoon through torrents of rain and kept seeing that red ghost swimming and shivering with lust in my mirror, when presently the deluge dwindled to a patter, and then was suspended altogether. With a swishing sound a sunburst swept the highway, and, needing a pair of new sunglasses, I pulled up at a filling station. What was happening was a sickness, a cancer, that could not be helped, so I simply ignored the fact that our quiet pursuer, in his converted state, stopped a little behind us at a café or bar bearing the idiotic sign: 'The Bustle: A Deceitful Seatful'. Having seen to the needs of my car, I walked into the office to get those glasses and pay for the gas. As I was in the act of signing a travellers' cheque and wondered about my exact whereabouts, I happened to glance through a side window, and saw a terrible thing. A broad-backed man, baldish, in an oatmeal coat and dark-brown trousers, was listening to Lo who was leaning out of the car and talking to him very rapidly, her hand with outspread fingers going up and down as it did when she was very serious and emphatic. What struck me with sickening force was – how should I put it? – the voluble familiarity of her way, as if they had known each other – oh, for week and weeks. I saw him scratch his cheek and nod, and turn, and walk back to his convertible, a broad and thickish man of my age, somewhat resembling Gustave Trapp, a cousin of my father's in Switzerland – same smoothly tanned face, fuller than mine, with a small dark moustache and a rosebud degenerate mouth. Lolita was studying a road map when I got back into the car.

'What did that man ask you, Lo?'

'Man? Oh, that man. Oh, yes. Oh, I don't know. He wondered if I had a map. Lost his way, I guess.'

We drove on, and I said:

'Now listen, Lo. I do not know whether you are lying or not, and I do not know whether you are insane or not, and I do not care for the moment; but that person has been following us all day, and his car was at the motel yesterday, and I think he is a cop. You know perfectly well what will happen and where you will go if the police find out about things. Now I want to know exactly what he said to you and what you told him.'

She laughed.

'If he's really a cop,' she said shrilly but not illogically, 'the worst thing we could do, would be to show him we are scared. Ignore him, *Dad*.'

'Did he ask where we were going?'

'Oh, he knows *that*' (mocking me).

'Anyway,' I said, giving up, 'I have seen his face now. He is not pretty. He looks exactly like a relative of mine called Trapp.'

'Perhaps he is Trapp. If I were you – Oh, look, all the nines are changing into the next thousand. When I was a little kid,' she continued unexpectedly, 'I used to think they'd stop and go back to nines, if only my mother agreed to put the car in reverse.'

It was the first time, I think, she spoke spontaneously of her pre-Humbertian childhood; perhaps, the theatre had taught her that trick; and silently we travelled on, unpursued.

But next day, like pain in a fatal disease that comes back as the drug and hope wear off, there it was again behind us, that glossy red beast. The traffic on the highway was light that day; nobody passed anybody; and nobody attempted to get in between our humble blue car and its imperious red shadow – as if there were some spell cast on that interspace, a zone of evil mirth and magic, a zone whose very precision and stability had a glass-like virtue that was almost artistic. The driver behind me, with his stuffed shoulders and Trappish moustache, looked like a display dummy, and his convertible seemed to move only because an invisible rope of silent silk connected it with our shabby vehicle. We were many times weaker than his splendid, lacquered machine, so that I did not even attempt to outspeed him. *O lente currite noctis equi!* O softly run, nightmares! We climbed long grades and rolled downhill again, and heeded speed limits, and spared slow children, and reproduced in sweeping terms the black wiggles of curves on their yellow shields, and no matter how and where we drove, the enchanted interspace slid on intact, mathematical, mirage-like, the viatic counterpart of a magic carpet. And all the time I was aware of a private blaze on my right: her joyful eye, her flaming cheek.

A traffic policeman, deep in the nightmare of crisscross streets – at 4.30 p.m. in a factory town – was the hand of chance that interrupted the spell. He beckoned me on, and then with the same hand cut off my shadow. A score of cars launched in between us, and I sped on, and deftly turned into a narrow lane. A sparrow alighted with a jumbo breadcrumb, was tackled by another, and lost the crumb.

When after a few grim stoppages and a bit of deliberate meandering, I returned to the highway, our shadow had disappeared.

Lola snorted and said: 'If he is what you think he is, how silly to give him the slip.'

'I have other notions by now,' I said.

'You should – ah – check them by – ah – keeping in touch with him, fahther deah,' said Lo, writhing in the coils of her own sarcasm. 'Gee, you *are* mean,' she added in her ordinary voice.

We spent a grim night in a very foul cabin, under a sonorous amplitude of rain, and with a kind of prehistorically loud thunder incessantly rolling above us.

'I am not a lady and do not like lightning,' said Lo, whose dread of electric storms gave me some pathetic solace.

We had breakfast in the township of Soda, population 1,001.

'Judging by the terminal figure,' I remarked, 'Fatface is already here.'

'Your humour,' said Lo, 'is sidesplitting, deah fahther.'

We were in sage-brush country by that time, and there was a day or two of lovely release (I had been a fool, all was well, that discomfort was merely a trapped flatus), and presently the mesas gave way to real mountains, and, on time, we drove into Wace.

Oh, disaster. Some confusion had occurred, she had misread a date in the Tour Book, and the Magic Cave ceremonies were over! She took it bravely, I must admit – and, when we discovered there was in kurortish Wace a summer theatre in full swing, we naturally drifted toward it one fair mid-June evening. I really could not tell you the plot of the play we saw. A trivial affair, no doubt, with self-conscious light effects and a mediocre leading lady. The only detail that pleased me was a garland of seven little graces, more or less immobile, prettily painted, barelimbed – seven bemused pubescent girls in coloured gauze that had been recruited locally (judging by the partisan flurry here and there among the audience) and were supposed to represent a living rainbow, which lingered throughout the last act, and rather teasingly faded behind a series of multiplied veils. I remember thinking that this idea of children-colours had been lifted by authors Clare Quilty and Vivian Darkbloom from a passage in James Joyce, and that two of the colours were quite exasperatingly lovely – Orange who kept fidgeting all the time, and Emerald who, when her eyes got used to the pitch-black pit where we all heavily sat, suddenly smiled at her mother or her protector.

As soon as the thing was over, and manual applause – a sound my nerves cannot stand – began to crash all around me, I started to pull and push Lo toward the exit, in my so natural amorous impatience to get her back to our neon-blue cottage in the stunned, starry night: I always say nature is stunned by the sights she sees. Dolly-Lo, however, lagged behind, in a rosy daze, her pleased eyes narrowed, her sense of vision swamping the rest of her senses to such an extent that her limp hands hardly came together at all in the mechanical action of clapping they still went through. I had seen that kind of thing in children before but, by God, this was a special child, myopically beaming at the already remote stage where I glimpsed something of the joint authors – a man's tuxedo and the bare shoulders of a hawk-like, black-haired, strikingly tall woman.

'You've again hurt my wrist, you brute,' said Lolita in a small voice as she slipped into her car seat.

'I am dreadfully sorry, my darling, my own ultraviolet darling,' I said, unsuccessfully trying to catch her elbow, and I added, to change the conversation – to change the direction of fate, oh God, oh God: 'Vivian is quite a woman. I am sure we saw her yesterday in that restaurant, in Soda pop.'

'Sometimes,' said Lo, 'you are quite revoltingly dumb. First, Vivian is the male author, the gal author is Clare; and second, she is forty, married and has Negro blood.'

'I thought,' I said kidding her, 'Quilty was an ancient flame of yours, in the days when you loved me, in sweet old Ramsdale.'

'What?' countered Lo, her features working. 'That fat dentist? You must be confusing me with some other fast little article.'

And I thought to myself how those fast little articles forget everything, everything, while we, old lovers, treasure every inch of their nymphancy.

19

With Lo's knowledge and assent, the two post offices given to the Beardsley postmaster as forwarding addresses were PO Wace and PO Elphinstone. Next morning we visited the former and had to wait in a short but slow queue. Serene Lo studied the rogue's gallery. Handsome Bryan Bryanski, alias Anthony Bryan, alias Tony Brown, eyes hazel, complexion fair, was wanted for kidnapping. A sad-eyed old gentleman's *faux pas* was mail fraud, and, as if that were not enough, he was cursed with deformed arches. Sullen Sullivan came with a caution: Is believed armed, and should be considered extremely dangerous. If you want to make a movie out of my book, have one of these faces gently melt into my own, while I look. And moreover there was a smudgy snapshot of a Missing Girl, age fourteen, wearing brown shoes when last seen, rhymes. Please notify Sheriff Buller.

I forget my letters; as to Dolly's, there was her report and a very special-looking envelope. This I deliberately opened and perused its contents. I concluded I was doing the foreseen since she did not seem to mind and drifted toward the news-stand near the exit.

'Dolly-Lo: Well, the play was a grand success. All three hounds lay quiet having been slightly drugged by Cutler, I suspect, and Linda knew all your lines. She was fine, she had alertness and control, but lacked somehow the *responsiveness,* the *relaxed vitality,* the charm of *my* – and the author's – Diana; but there was no author to applaud us as last time, and the terrific electric storm outside interfered with our own modest off-stage thunder. Oh dear, life does fly. Now that everything is over, school, play, the Roy mess, mother's confinement (our baby, alas, did not live!), it all seems such a long time ago, though practically I still bear traces of the paint.

'We are going to New York after tomorrow, and I guess I can't manage to wriggle out of accompanying my parents to Europe. I have even worse news for you. Dolly-Lo! I may not be back at Beardsley if and when you return. With one thing and another, one being you know who, and the other not being who you think you know, Dad wants me to go to school in Paris for one year while he and Fulbright are around.

'As expected, poor Poet stumbled in Scene III when arriving at the bit of French nonsense. Remember? *Ne manque pas de dire à ton amant, Chimène, comme le lac est beau car il faut qu'il t'y mène.* Lucky beau! *Qu'il t'y* – What a tongue-twister! Well, be good, Lollikins. Best love from your Poet, and best regards to the Governor. Your Mona. PS. Because of one thing and another, my correspondence happens to be rigidly controlled. So better wait till I write you from Europe.' (She never did as far as I know. The letter contained an element of mysterious nastiness that I am too tired today to analyse. I found it later preserved in one of the Tour Books, and gave it here *à titre documentaire.* I read it twice.)

I looked up from the letter and was about to— There was no Lo to behold. While I was engrossed in Mona's witchery, Lo had shrugged her shoulders and vanished. 'Did you happen to see—' I asked of a hunchback sweeping the floor near the entrance. He had, the old lecherer. He guessed she had seen a friend and had hurried out. I hurried out too. I stopped – she had not. I hurried on. I stopped again. It had happened at last. She had gone for ever.

In later years I have often wondered why she did *not* go for ever that day. Was it the retentive quality of her new summer clothes in my locked car? Was it some unripe particle in some general plan? Was it simply because, all things considered, I might as well be used to convey her to Elphinstone – the secret terminus, anyway? I only know I was quite certain she had left me for ever. The non-committal mauve mountains half encircling the town seemed to me to swarm with painting, scrambling, laughing, panting Lolitas who dissolved in their haze. A big W made of white stones on a steep talus in the far vista of a cross street seemed the very initial of woe.

The new and beautiful post office I had just emerged from stood between a dormant movie house and a conspiracy of poplars. The time was 9 a.m. mountain time. The street was Main Street. I paced its blue side peering at the opposite one: charmit into beauty, was one of those fragile young summer mornings with flashes of glass here and there and a general air of faltering and almost fainting at the prospect of an intolerably torrid noon. Crossing over, I loafed and leafed, as it were, through one long block: Drugs, Real Estate, Fashions, Auto Parts, Café, Sporting Goods, Real Estate, Furniture Appliances Western Union, Cleaners, Grocery. Officer, officer, my daughter has run away. In collusion with a detective; in love with a blackmailer. Took advantage of my utter helplessness. I peered into all the stores. I deliberated inly if I should talk to any of the sparse foot-passengers. I did not. I sat for a while in the parked car. I inspected the public garden on the east side. I went back to Fashions and Auto Parts. I told myself with a burst of furious sarcasm – *un ricanement* – that I was crazy to suspect her, that she would turn up in a minute.

She did.

I wheeled around and shook off the hand she had placed on my sleeve with a timid and imbecile smile.

'Get into the car,' I said.

She obeyed, and I went on pacing up and down, struggling with nameless thoughts, trying to plan some way of tackling her duplicity.

Presently she left the car and was at my side again. My sense of hearing gradually got tuned in to station Lo again, and I became aware she was telling me that she had met a former girl friend.

'Yes? Whom?'

'A Beardsley girl.'

'Good. I know every name in your group. Alice Adams?'

'This girl was not in my group.'

'Good. I have a complete student list with me. Her name please.'

'She was not in my school. She is just a town girl in Beardsley.'

'Good. I have the Beardsley directory with me too. We'll look up all the Browns.'

'I only know her first name.'

'Mary or Jane?'

'No – Dolly, like me.'

'So that's the dead end' (the mirror you break your nose against). 'Good. Let us try another angle. You have been absent twenty-eight minutes. What did the two Dollys do?'

'We went to a drugstore.'

'And you had there—?'

'Oh, just a couple of cokes.'

'Careful, Dolly. We can check that, you know.'

'At least, she had. I had a glass of water.'

'Good. Was it that place there?'

'Sure.'

'Good, come on, we'll grill the soda jerk.'

'Wait a sec. Come to think it might have been further down – just around the corner.'

'Come on all the same. Go in, please. Well, let's see.' (Opening a chained telephone book.) 'Dignified Funeral Service. No, not yet. Here we are: Druggists-Retail. Hill Drug Store. Larkin's Pharmacy. And two more. That's all Wace seems to have in the way of soda fountains – at least in the business section. Well, we will check them all.'

'Go to hell,' she said.

'Lo, rudeness will get you nowhere.'

'Okay,' she said. 'But you're not going to trap me. Okay, so we did not have a pop. We just talked and looked at dresses in show windows.'

'Which? That window there for example?'

'Yes, that one there, for example.'

'Oh, Lo! Let's look closer at it.'

It was indeed a pretty sight. A dapper young fellow was vacuum-cleaning a carpet of sorts upon which stood two figures that looked as if some blast had just worked havoc with them. One figure was stark naked, wigless and armless. Its comparatively small stature and smirking pose suggested that when clothed it had represented, and would represent when clothed again, a girl child of Lolita's size. But in its present state it was sexless. Next to it, stood a much taller veiled bride, quite perfect and *intacta* except for the lack of one arm. On the floor, at the feet of these damsels, where the man crawled about laboriously with his cleaner, there lay a cluster of three slender arms, and a blonde wig. Two of the arms happened to be twisted and seemed to suggest a clasping gesture of horror and supplication.

'Look, Lo,' I said quietly. 'Look well. Is not that a rather good symbol of something or other? However' – I went on as we got back into the car – 'I have taken certain precautions. Here (delicately opening the glove compartment), on this pad, I have our boy friend's car number.'

As the ass I was I had not memorized it. What remained of it in my mind were the initial letter and the closing figure as if the whole amphitheatre of six signs receded concavely behind a tinted glass too opaque to allow the central series to be deciphered, but just translucent enough to make out its extreme edges – a capital P and a 6. I have to go into those details (which in themselves can interest only a professional psychologue) because otherwise the reader (ah, if I could visualize him as a blonde-bearded scholar with rosy lips sucking *la pomme de sa canne* as he quaffs my manuscript!) might not understand the quality of the shock I experienced upon noticing that the P had acquired the bustle of a B and that the 6 had been deleted altogether. The rest, with erasures revealing the hurried shuttle smear of a pencil's rubber end, and with parts of numbers obliterated or reconstructed in a child's hand, presented a tangle of barbed wire to any logical interpretation. All I knew was the state – one adjacent to the state Beardsley was in.

I said nothing. I put the pad back, closed the compartment, and drove out of Wace. Lo had grabbed some comics from the back seat and, mobile-white-bloused, one brown elbow out of the window, was deep in the current adventure of some clout or clown. Three or four miles out of Wace, I turned into the shadow of a picnic ground where the morning had dumped its litter of light on an empty table; Lo looked up with a semi-smile of surprise and without a word I delivered a tremendous backhand cut that caught her smack on her hot hard little cheekbone.

And then the remorse, the poignant sweetness of sobbing atonement, grovelling love, the hopelessness of sensual reconciliation. In the velvet night, at Mirana Motel (Mirana!) I kissed the yellowish soles of her long-toed feet, I immolated myself . . . But it was all of no avail. Both doomed were we. And soon I was to enter a new cycle of persecution.

In a street of Wace, on its outskirts . . . Oh, I am quite sure it was not a delusion. In a street of Wace, I had glimpsed the Aztec Red convertible, or its identical twin. Instead of Trapp, it contained four or five loud young people of several sexes – but I said nothing. After Wace a totally new situation arose. For a day or two, I enjoyed the mental emphasis with which I told myself that we were not, and never had been followed; and then I became sickeningly conscious that Trapp had changed his tactics and was still with us, in this or that rented car.

A veritable Proteus of the highway, with bewildering ease he switched from one vehicle to another. This technique implied the existence of garages specializing in 'stage-automobile' operations, but I never could discover the remises he used. He seemed to patronize at first the Chevrolet genus, beginning with a Campus Cream convertible, then going on to a small Horizon Blue sedan, and thenceforth fading into Surf Grey and Driftwood Grey. Then he turned to other makes and passed through a pale dull rainbow of paint shades, and one day I found myself attempting to cope with the subtle distinction between our own Dream Blue Melmoth and the Crest Blue Oldsmobile he had rented; greys, however, remained his favourite cryptochromism, and, in agonizing nightmares, I tried in vain to sort out properly such ghosts as Chrysler's Shell Grey, Chevrolet's Thistle Grey, Dodge's French Grey . . .

The necessity of being constantly on the lookout for his little moustache and open shirt – or for his baldish pate and broad shoulders – led me to a profound study of all cars on the road – behind, before, alongside, coming, going, every vehicle under the dancing sun: the quiet vacationist's automobile with the box of Tender-Touch tissues in the back window; the recklessly speeding jalopy full of pale children with a shaggy dog's head protruding, and a crumpled mudguard; the bachelor's tudor sedan crowded with suits on hangers; the huge fat house trailer weaving in front, immune to the Indian file of fury boiling behind it; the car with the young female passenger politely perched in the middle of the front seat to be closer to the young male driver; the car carrying on its roof a red boat, bottom up . . . The grey car slowing up before us, the grey car catching up with us.

We were in mountain country, somewhere between Snow and Champion, and rolling down an almost imperceptible grade, when I had my next distinct view of Detective Paramour Trapp. The grey mist behind us had deepened and concentrated into the compactness of a Dominion Blue sedan. All of a sudden, as if the car I drove responded to my poor heart's pangs, we were slithering from side to side, with something making a helpless plap-plap-plap under us.

'You got a flat, mister,' said cheerful Lo.

I pulled up – near a precipice. She folded her arms and put her foot on the dashboard. I got out and examined the right rear wheel. The base of its tyre was sheepishly and hideously square. Trapp had stopped some fifty yards behind us. His distant face formed a grease spot of mirth. This was my chance. I started to walk towards him – with the brilliant idea of asking him for a jack though I had one. He backed a little. I stubbed my toe against a stone – and there was a sense of general laughter. Then a tremendous truck loomed from behind Trapp and thundered by me – and immediately after, I heard it utter a convulsive honk. Instinctively I looked back – and saw my own car gently creeping away. I could make out Lo ludicrously at the wheel, and the engine was certainly running – though I remembered I had cut it but had not applied the emergency brake; and during the brief space of throb-time that it took me to reach the croaking machine which came to a standstill at last, it dawned upon me that during the last two years little Lo had had ample time to pick up the rudiments of driving. As I wrenched the door open, I was goddam sure she had started the car to prevent me from walking up to Trapp. Her trick proved useless, however, for even while I was pursuing her he had made an energetic U-turn and was gone. I rested for a while. Lo asked wasn't I going to thank her – the car had started to move by itself and – Getting no answer, she immersed herself in a study of the map. I got out again and commenced the 'ordeal of the orb', as Charlotte used to say. Perhaps I was losing my mind.

We continued our grotesque journey. After a forlorn and useless dip, we went up and up. On a steep grade I found myself behind the gigantic truck that had overtaken us. It was now groaning up a winding road and was impossible to pass. Out of its front part a small oblong of smooth silver – the inner wrapping of chewing gum – escaped and flew back into our windshield. It occurred to me that if I were really losing my mind, I might end by murdering somebody. In fact – said high-and-dry Humbert to floundering Humbert – it might be quite clever to prepare things – to transfer the weapon from box to pocket – so as to be ready to take advantage of the spell of insanity when it does come.

20

By permitting Lolita to study acting I had, fond fool, suffered her to cultivate deceit. It now appeared that it had not been merely a matter of learning the answers to such questions as what is the basic conflict in 'Hedda Gabler'?, or where are the climaxes in 'Love Under the Lindens'?, or analyse the prevailing mood of 'Cherry Orchard'; it was really a matter of learning to betray me. How I deplored now the exercises in sensual simulation that I had so often seen her go through in our Beardsley parlour when I would observe her from some strategic point while she, like a hypnotic subject or a performer in a mystic rite, produced sophisticated versions of infantile make-believe by going through the mimetic actions of hearing a moan in the dark, seeing for the first time a brand new young stepmother, tasting something she hated, such as buttermilk, smelling crushed grass in a lush orchard, or touching mirages of objects with her sly, slender, girl-child hands. Among my papers I still have a mimeographed sheet suggesting:

> 'Tactile drill. Imagine yourself picking up and holding: a pingpong ball, an apple, a sticky date, a new flannel-fluffed tennis ball, a hot potato, an ice cube, a kitten, a puppy, a horseshoe, a feather, a torchlight.
>
> Knead with your fingers the following imaginary things: a piece of bread, india rubber, a friend's aching temple, a sample of velvet, a rose petal.
>
> You are a blind girl. Palpate the face of: a Greek youth, Cyrano, Santa Claus, a baby, a laughing faun, a sleeping stranger, your father.'

But she had been so pretty in the weaving of those delicate spells, in the dreamy performance of her enchantments and duties! On certain adventurous evenings, in Beardsley, I also had her dance for me with the promise of some treat or gift, and although these routine leg-parted leaps of hers were more like those of a football cheer-leader than like the languorous and jerky motions of a Parisian *petit rat*, the rhythms of her not quite nubile limbs had given me pleasure. But all that was nothing, absolutely nothing, to the indescribable itch of rapture that her tennis game produced in me – the teasing delirious feeling of teetering on the very brink of unearthly order and splendour.

Despite her advanced age, she was more of a nymphet than ever, with her apricot-coloured limbs, in her sub-teen tennis togs! Winged gentlemen! No hereafter is acceptable if it does not produce her as she was then, in that Colorado resort between Snow and Elphinstone, with everything right: the white wide little-boy shorts, the slender waist, the apricot midriff, the white breastkerchief whose ribbons went up and encircled her neck to end behind in a dangling knot leaving bare her gaspingly young and adorable apricot shoulder blades with that pubescence and those lovely gentle bones, and the smooth, downward-tapering back. Her cap had a white peak. Her racket had cost me a small fortune. Idiot, triple idiot! I could have filmed her! I would have had her now with me, before my eyes, in the projection room of my pain and despair!

She would wait and relax for a bar or two of white-lined time before going into the act of serving, and often bounced the ball once or twice, or pawed the ground a little, always at ease, always rather vague about the score, always cheerful as she so seldom was in the dark life she led at home. Her tennis was the highest point to which I can imagine a young creature bringing the art of make-believe, although I dare say, for her it was the very geometry of basic reality.

The exquisite clarity of all her movements had its auditory counterpart in the pure ringing sound of her every stroke. The ball when it entered her aura of control became somehow whiter, its resilience somehow richer, and the instrument of precision she used upon it seemed inordinately prehensile and deliberate at the moment of clinging contact. Her form was, indeed, an absolutely perfect imitation of absolutely top-notch tennis – without any utilitarian results. As Edusa's sister, Electra Gold, a marvellous young coach, said to me once while I sat on a pulsating hard bench watching Dolores Haze toying with Linda Hall (and being beaten by her): 'Dolly has a magnet in the centre of her racket guts, but why the heck is she so polite?' Ah, Electra, what did it matter, with such grace! I remember at the very first game I watched being drenched with an almost painful convulsion of beauty assimilation. My Lolita had a way of raising her bent left knee at the ample and springy start of the service cycle when there would develop and hang in the sun for a second a vital web of balance between toed foot, pristine armpit, burnished arm and far back-flung racket, as she smiled up with gleaming teeth at the small globe suspended so high in the zenith of the powerful and graceful cosmos she had created for the express purpose of falling upon it with a clean resounding crack of her golden whip.

It had, that serve of hers, beauty, directness, youth, a classical purity of trajectory, and was, despite its spanking pace, fairly easy to return, having as it did no twist or sting to its long elegant hop.

That I could have had all her strokes, all her enchantments, immortalized in segments of celluloid, makes me moan today with frustration. They would have been so much more than the snap-shots I burned! Her overhead volley was related to her service as the envoy is to the ballade; for she had been trained, my pet, to patter up at once to the net on her nimble, vivid, white-shod feet. There was nothing to choose between her forehand and backhand drives: they were mirror images of one another – my very loins still tingle with those pistol reports repeated by crisp echoes and Electra's cries. One of the pearls of Dolly's game was a short half-volley that Ned Litam had taught her in California.

She preferred acting to swimming, and swimming to tennis; yet I insist that had not something within her been broken by me – not that I realized it then! – she would have had on the top of her perfect form the will to win, and would have become a real girl champion. Dolores, with two rackets under her arm, in Wimbledon. Dolores endorsing a Dromedary. Dolores turning professional. Dolores acting a girl champion in a movie. Dolores and her grey, humble, hushed husband-coach, old Humbert.

There was nothing wrong or deceitful in the spirit of her game – unless one considered her cheerful indifference toward its outcome as the feint of a nymphet. She who was so cruel and crafty in everyday life, revealed an innocence, a frankness, a kindness of ball-placing, that permitted a second-rate but determined player, no matter how uncouth and incompetent, to poke and cut his way to victory. Despite her small stature, she covered the one thousand and fifty-three square feet of her half of the court with wonderful ease, once she had entered into the rhythm of a rally and as long as she could direct that rhythm; but any abrupt attack, or sudden change of tactics on her adversary's part, left her helpless. At match point, her second serve, which – rather typically – was even stronger and more stylish than her first (for she had none of the inhibitions that cautious winners have), would strike vibrantly the harp-cord of the net – and ricochet out of court. The polished gem of her dropshot was snapped up and put away by an opponent who seemed four-legged and wielded a crooked paddle. Her dramatic drives and lovely volleys would candidly fall at his feet. Over and over again she would land an easy one into the net – and merrily mimic dismay by drooping in a ballet attitude, with her forelocks hanging. So sterile were her grace and whipper that she could not even win from panting me and my old-fashioned lifting drive.

I suppose I am especially susceptible to the magic of games. In my chess sessions with Gaston I saw the board as a square pool of limpid water with rare shells and stratagems rosily visible upon the smooth tesselated bottom, which to my confused adversary was all ooze and squid-cloud. Similarly, the initial tennis coaching I had inflicted on Lolita – prior to the revelations that came to her through the great Californian's lessons – remained in my mind as oppressive and distressful memories – not only because she had been so hopelessly and irritatingly irritated by every suggestion of mine – but because the precious symmetry of the court instead of reflecting the harmonies latent in her was utterly jumbled by the clumsiness and lassitude of the resentful child I mistaught. Now things were different, and on that particular day, in the pure air of Champion, Colorado, on that admirable court at the foot of steep stone stairs leading up to Champion Hotel where we had spent the night, I felt I could rest from the nightmare of unknown betrayals within the innocence of her style, of her soul, of her essential grace.

She was hitting hard and flat, with her usual effortless sweep, feeding me deep skimming balls – all so rhythmically coordinated and overt as to reduce my footwork to, practically, a swinging stroll – crack players will understand what I mean. My rather heavily cut serve that I had been taught by my father who had learned it from Decugis or Borman, old friends of his and great champions, would have seriously troubled my Lo, had I really tried to trouble her. But who would upset such a lucid dear? Did I ever mention that her bare arm bore the 8 of vaccination? That I loved her hopelessly? That she was only fourteen?

An inquisitive butterfly passed, dipping, between us.

Two people in tennis shorts, a red-haired fellow only about eight years my junior, with sunburnt bright pink shins, and an indolent dark girl with a moody mouth and hard eyes, about two years Lolita's senior, appeared from nowhere. As is common with dutiful tyros, their rackets were sheathed and framed, and they carried them not as if they were the natural and comfortable extensions of certain specialized muscles, but hammers or blunderbusses or wimbles, or my own dreadful cumbersome sins. Rather unceremoniously seating themselves near my precious coat, on a bench adjacent to the court, they fell to admiring very vocally a rally of some fifty exchanges that Lo innocently helped me to foster and uphold – until there occurred a syncope in the series causing her to gasp as her overhead smash went out of court, whereupon she melted into winsome merriment, my golden pet.

I felt thirsty by then, and walked to the drinking fountain; there Red approached me and in all humility suggested a mixed double. 'I am Bill Mead,' he said. 'And that's Fay Page, actress. Maffy On Say' – he added (pointing with his ridiculously hooded racket at polished Fay who was already talking to Dolly). I was about to reply 'Sorry, but—' (for I hate to have my filly involved in the chops and jabs of cheap bunglers), when a remarkably melodious cry diverted my attention: a bellboy was tripping down the steps from the hotel to our court and making me signs. I was wanted, if you please, on an urgent long distance call – so urgent in fact that the line was being held for me. Certainly. I got into my coat (inside pocket heavy with pistol) and told Lo I would be back in a minute. She was picking up a ball – in the continental foot-racket way which was one of the few nice things I had taught her – and smiled – she smiled at me!

An awful calm kept my heart afloat as I followed the boy up to the hotel. This, to use an American term, in which discovery, retribution, torture, death, eternity appear in the shape of a singularly repulsive nutshell, was *it*. I had left her in mediocre hands, but it hardly mattered now. I would fight, of course. Oh, I would fight. Better destroy everything than surrender her. Yes, quite a climb.

At the desk, a dignified, Roman-nosed man, with, I suggest, a very obscure past that might reward investigation, handed me a message in his own hand. The line had not been held after all. The note said:

'Mr Humbert. The head of Birdsley [*sic*] School called. Summer residence – Birdsley 2-8282. Please call back immediately. Highly important.'

I folded myself into a booth, took a little pill, and for about twenty minutes tussled with space-spooks. A quartet of propositions gradually became audible: soprano, there was no such number in Beardsley; alto, Miss Pratt was on her way to England; tenor, Beardsley School had not telephoned; bass, they could not have done so, since nobody knew I was, that particular day, in Champion, Colorado. Upon my stinging him, the Roman took the trouble to find out if there had been a long distance call. There had been none. A fake call from some local dial was not excluded. I thanked him. He said: You bet. After a visit to the purling men's room and a stiff drink at the bar, I started on my return march. From the very terrace I saw, far below, on the tennis court which seemed the size of a school child's ill-wiped slate, golden Lolita playing in a double. She moved like a fair angel among three horrible Boschian cripples. One of these, her partner, while changing sides, jocosely slapped her on her behind with his racket. He had a remarkably round head and wore incongruous brown trousers. There was a momentary flurry – he saw me, and throwing his racket – mine! – scuttled up the slope. He waved his wrists and elbows in would-be comical imitation of rudimentary wings, as he climbed, bow-legged, to the street, where his grey car awaited him. Next moment he and the greyness were gone. When I came down, the remaining trio were collecting and sorting out the balls.

'Mr Mead, who was that person?'

Bill and Fay, both looking very solemn, shook their heads.

That absurd intruder had butted in to make up a double, hadn't he, Dolly?

Dolly. The handle of my racket was still disgustingly warm. Before returning to the hotel, I ushered her into a little alley half-smothered in fragrant shrubs, with flowers like smoke, and was about to burst into ripe sobs and plead with her imperturbed dream in the most abject manner for clarification, no matter how meretricious, of the slow awfulness enveloping me, when we found ourselves behind the convulsed Mead twosome – assorted people, you know, meeting among idyllic settings in old comedies. Bill and Fay were both weak with laughter – we had come at the end of their private joke. It did not really matter.

Speaking as if it really did not really matter, and assuming, apparently, that life was automatically rolling on with all its routine pleasures, Lolita said she would like to change into her bathing things, and spend the rest of the afternoon at the swimming pool. It was a gorgeous day. Lolita!

21

'Lo! Lola! Lolita!' I hear myself crying from a doorway into the sun, with the acoustics of time, domed time, endowing my call and its tell-tale hoarseness with such a wealth of anxiety, passion and pain that really it would have been instrumental in wrenching open the zipper of her nylon shroud had she been dead. Lolita! In the middle of a trim turfed terrace I found her at last – she had run out before I was ready. Oh, Lolita! There she was playing with a damned dog, not me. The animal, a terrier of sorts, was losing and snapping up again and adjusting between his jaws a wet little red ball; he took rapid chords with his front paws on the resilient turf, and then would bounce away. I had only wanted to see where she was, I could not swim with my heart in that state, but who cared – and there she was, and there was I, in my robe – and so I stopped calling; but suddenly something in the pattern of her motions, as she dashed this way and that in her Aztec Red bathing briefs and bra, struck me . . . there was an ecstasy, a madness about her frolics that was too much of a glad thing. Even the dog seemed puzzled by the extravagance of her reactions. I put a gentle hand to my chest as I surveyed the situation. The turquoise blue swimming pool some distance behind the lawn was no longer behind that lawn, but within my thorax, and my organs swam in it like excrements in the blue sea water in Nice. One of the bathers had left the pool and, half-concealed by the peacocked shade of trees, stood quite still, holding the ends of the towel around his neck and following Lolita with his amber eyes. There he stood, in the camouflage of sun and shade, disfigured by them and masked by his own nakedness, his damp black hair or what was left of it, glued to his round head, his little moustache a humid smear, the wool on his chest spread like a symmetrical trophy, his navel pulsating, his hirsute thighs dripping with bright droplets, his tight wet black bathing trunks bloated and bursting with vigour where his great fat bullybag was pulled up and back like a padded shield over his reversed beasthood. And as I looked at his oval nut-brown face, it dawned upon me that what I had recognized him by was the reflection of my daughter's countenance – the same beatitude and grimace but made hideous by his maleness. And I also knew that the child, my child, knew he was looking, enjoyed the lechery of his look and was putting on a show of gambol and glee, the vile and beloved slut. As she made for the ball and missed it, she fell on her back, with her obscene young legs madly pedalling in the air; I could sense the musk of her excitement from where I stood, and then I saw (petrified with a kind of sacred disgust) the man close his eyes and bare his small, horribly small and even, teeth as he leaned against a tree in which a multitude of dappled Priaps shivered. Immediately afterwards a marvellous transformation took place. He was no longer the satyr but a very good-natured and foolish Swiss cousin, the Gustave Trapp I have mentioned more than once, who used to counteract his 'sprees' (he drank beer with milk, the good swine) by feats of weightlifting – tottering and grunting on a lake beach with his otherwise very complete bathing suit jauntily stripped from one shoulder. *This* Trapp noticed me from afar and working the towel on his nape walked back with false insouciance to the pool. And as if the sun had gone out of the game, Lo slackened and slowly got up ignoring the ball that the terrier placed before her. Who can say what heartbreaks are caused in a dog by our discontinuing a romp? I started to say something, and then sat down on the grass with a quite monstrous pain in my chest and vomited a torrent of browns and greens that I had never remembered eating.

I saw Lolita's eyes, and they seemed to be more calculating than frightened. I heard her saying to a kind lady that her father was having a fit. Then for a long time I lay in a lounge chair swallowing pony upon pony of gin. And next morning I felt strong enough to drive on (which in later years no doctor believed).

22

The two-room cabin we had ordered at Silver Spur Court, Elphinstone, turned out to belong to the glossily browned pine-log kind that Lolita used to be so fond of in the days of our carefree first journey; oh, how different things were now! I am not referring to Trapp or Trapps. After all – well, really. . . . After all, gentlemen, it was becoming abundantly clear that all those identical detectives in prismatically changing cars were figments of my persecution mania, recurrent images based on coincidence and chance resemblance. *Soyons logiques,* crowed the cocky Gallic part of my brain – and proceeded to rout the notion of a Lolita-maddened salesman or comedy gangster, with stooges, persecuting me, and hoaxing me, and otherwise taking riotous advantage of my strange relations with the law. I remember humming my panic away. I remember evolving even an explanation of the 'Birdsley' telephone call. . . . But if I could dismiss Trapp, as I had dismissed my convulsions on the lawn at Champion, I could do nothing with the anguish of knowing Lolita to be so tantalizingly, so miserably unattainable and beloved on the very eve of a new era, when my alembics told me she should stop being a nymphet, stop torturing me.

An additional, abominable and perfectly gratuitous worry was lovingly prepared for me in Elphinstone. Lo had been dull and silent during the last lap – two hundred mountainous miles uncontaminated by smoke-grey sleuths or zigzagging zanies. She hardly glanced at the famous, oddly shaped, splendidly flushed rock which jutted above the mountains and had been the take-off for nirvana on the part of a temperamental show girl. The town was newly built, or rebuilt, on the flat floor of a seven-thousand foot high valley; it would soon bore Lo, I hoped, and we would spin on to California, to the Mexican border, to mythical bays, saguaro deserts, fatamorganas. José Lizzarrabengoa, as you remember, planned to take his Carmen to the *Etats Unis.* I conjured up a Central American tennis competition in which Dolores Haze and various Californian schoolgirl champions would dazzingly participate. Good-will tours on that smiling level eliminate the distinction between passport and sport. Why did I hope we would be happy abroad? A change of environment is the traditional fallacy upon which doomed loves, and lungs, rely.

Mrs Haze, the brisk, brickly rouged, blue-eyed widow who ran the motor court, asked me if I were Swiss perchance, because her sister had married a Swiss ski instructor. I was, whereas my daughter happened to be half Irish. I registered, Haze gave me the key and a twinkling smile, and, still twinkling, showed me where to park the car; Lo crawled out and shivered a little: the luminous evening air was decidedly crisp. Upon entering the cabin, she sat down on a chair at a card table, buried her face in the crook of her arm and said she felt awful. Shamming, I thought, shamming, no doubt, to evade my caresses; I was passionately parched; but she began to whimper in an unusually dreary way when I attempted to fondle her. Lolita ill. Lolita dying. Her skin was scalding hot! I took her temperature, orally, then looked up a scribbled formula I fortunately had in a jotter and after laboriously reducing the, meaningless to me, degrees Fahrenheit to the intimate centigrade of my childhood, found she had 40.4, which at least made sense. Hysterical little nymphs might, I knew, run up all kinds of temperature – even exceeding a fatal count. And I would have given her a sip of hot spiced wine, and two aspirins, and kissed the fever away, if, upon an examination of her lovely uvula, one of the gems of her body, I had not seen that it was a burning red. I undressed her. Her breath was bittersweet. Her brown rose tasted of blood. She was shaking from head to toe. She complained of a painful stiffness in the upper vertebrae – and I thought of poliomyelitis as any American parent would. Giving up all hope of intercourse, I wrapped her up in a lap-robe and carried her into the car. Kind Mrs Haze in the meantime had alerted the local doctor. 'You are lucky it happened here,' she said; for not only was Blue the best man in the district, but the Elphinstone hospital was as modern as modern could be, despite its limited capacity. With a heterosexual Erlkönig in pursuit, thither I drove, half-blinded by a royal sunset on the lowland side and guided by a little old woman, a portable witch, perhaps his daughter, whom Mrs Haze had lent me, and whom I was never to see again. Dr Blue, whose learning, no doubt, was infinitely inferior to his reputation, assured me it was a virus infection, and when I alluded to her comparatively recent flu, curtly said this was another bug, he had forty such cases on his hands; all of which sounded like the 'ague' of the ancients. I wondered if I should mention, with a casual chuckle, that my fifteen-year-old daughter had had a minor accident while climbing an awkward fence with her boy friend, but knowing I was drunk, I decided to withhold the information till later if necessary. To an unsmiling blonde bitch of a secretary I gave my daughter's age as 'practically sixteen'. While I was not looking, my child was taken away from me! In vain I insisted I be allowed to spend the night on a 'welcome' mat in a corner of their damned hospital. I ran up constructivistic flights of stairs, I tried to trace my darling so as to tell her she had better not babble, especially if she felt as lightheaded as we all did. At one point, I was rather dreadfully rude to a very young and very cheeky nurse with overdeveloped gluteal parts and blazing black eyes – of Basque descent, as I learned. Her father was an imported shepherd, a trainer of sheep dogs. Finally, I returned to the car and remained in it for I do not know how many hours, hunched up in the dark, stunned by my new solitude, looking out open-mouthed now at the dimly illuminated, very square and low hospital building squatting in the middle of its lawny block, now up at the wash of stars and the jagged silvery ramparts of the *haute montagne* where at the moment Mary's father, lonely Joseph Lore, was dreaming of Oloron, Lagore, Rolas – *que sais-je!* – or seducing a ewe. Such-like fragrant vagabond thoughts have been always a solace to me in times of unusual stress, and only when, despite liberal libations, I felt fairly numbed by the endless night, did I think of driving back to the motel. The old woman had disappeared, and I was not quite sure of my way. Wide gravel roads criss-crossed drowsy rectangular shadows. I made out what looked like the silhouette of gallows on what was probably a school playground; and in another waste-like block there rose in domed silence the pale temple of some local sect. I found the highway at last, and then the motel, where millions of so-called 'millers', a kind of insect, were swarming around the neon contours of 'No Vacancy'; and, when, at 3 a.m., after one of those untimely hot showers which like some mordant only help to fix a man's despair and weariness, I lay on her bed that smelled of chestnuts and roses, and peppermint, and the very delicate, very special French perfume I latterly allowed her to use, I found myself unable to assimilate the simple fact that for the first time in two years I was separated from my Lolita. All at once it occurred to me that her illness was somehow the development of a theme – that it had the same taste and tone as the series of linked impressions which had puzzled and tormented me during our journey; I imagined that secret agent, or secret lover, or prankster, or hallucination, or whatever he was, prowling around the hospital – and Aurora had hardly 'warmed her hands', as the pickers of lavender say in the country of my birth, when I found myself trying to get into that dungeon again, knocking upon its green doors, breakfastless, stool-less, in despair.

This was Tuesday, and Wednesday or Thursday, splendidly reacting like the darling she was to some 'serum' (sparrow's sperm or dugong's dung), she was much better, and the doctor said that in a couple of days she would be 'skipping' again.

Of the eight times I visited her, the last one alone remains sharply engraved on my mind. It had been a great feat to come for I felt all hollowed out by the infection that by then was at work on me too. None will know the strain it was to carry that bouquet, that load of love, those books that I had travelled sixty miles to buy: Browning's *Dramatic Works, The History of Dancing, Clowns and Columbines, The Russian Ballet, Flowers of the Rockies, The Theatre Guild Anthology, Tennis* by Helen Wills, who had won the National Junior Girl Singles at the age of fifteen. As I was staggering up to the door of my daughter's thirteen-dollar-a-day private room, Mary Lore, the beastly young part-time nurse who had taken an unconcealed dislike to me, emerged with a finished breakfast tray, placed it with a quick crash on a chair in the corridor, and, fundament jigging, shot back into the room – probably to warn her poor little Dolores that the tyrannic old father was creeping up on crepe soles, with books and bouquet: the latter I had composed of wild flowers and beautiful leaves gathered with my own gloved hands on a mountain pass at sunrise (I hardly slept at all that fateful week).

Feeding my Carmencita well? Idly I glanced at the tray. On a yolk-stained plate there was a crumpled envelope. It had contained something, since one edge was torn, but there was no address on it – nothing at all, save a phony armorial design with 'Ponderosa Lodge' in green letters; thereupon I performed a *chassé-croisé* with Mary, who was in the act of bustling out again – wonderful how fast they move and how little they do, those rumpy young nurses. She glowered at the envelope I had put back, uncrumpled.

'You better not touch,' she said, nodding directionally: 'Could burn your fingers.'

Below my dignity to rejoin. All I said was:

'Je croyais que c'était un bill – not a *billet doux.'* Then entering the sunny room, to Lolita: *'Bonjour mon petit.'*

'Dolores,' said Mary Lore, entering with me, past me, through me, the plump whore, and blinking, and starting to fold very rapidly a white flannel blanket as she blinked: 'Dolores, your pappy thinks you are getting letters from my boy friend. It's me (smugly tapping herself on the small gilt cross she wore) gets them. And my pappy can parlay-voo as well as yours.'

She left the room. Dolores, so rosy and russet, lips freshly painted, hair brilliantly brushed, bare arms straightened out on neat coverlet, lay innocently beaming at me or nothing. On the bed table, next to a paper napkin and a pencil, her topaz ring burned in the sun.

'What gruesome funeral flowers,' she said. 'Thanks all the same. But do you mind very much cutting out the French? It annoys everybody.'

Back at the usual rush came the ripe young hussy, reeking of urine and garlic, with the *Desert News*, which her fair patient eagerly accepted, ignoring the sumptuously illustrated volumes I had brought.

'My sister Ann,' said Mary (topping information with afterthought), 'works at the Ponderosa place.'

Poor Bluebeard. Those brutal brothers. *Est-ce que tu ne m'aimes plus, ma Carmen?* She never had. At the moment I knew my love was as hopeless as ever – and I also knew the two girls were conspirators, plotting in Basque, or Zemfirian, against my hopeless love. I shall go further and say that Lo was playing a double game since she was also fooling sentimental Mary whom she had told, I suppose, that she wanted to dwell with her fun-loving young uncle and not with cruel melancholy me. And another nurse whom I never identified, and the village idiot who carted cots and coffins into the elevator, and the idiotic green love birds in a cage in the waiting room – all were in the plot, the sordid plot. I suppose Mary thought comedy father Professor Humbertoldi was interfering with the romance between Dolores and her father-substitute, roly-poly Romeo (for you *were* rather lardy, you know, Rom, despite all that 'snow' and 'joy juice').

My throat hurt. I stood, swallowing, at the window and stared at the mountains, at the romantic rock high up in the smiling plotting sky.

'My Carmen,' I said (I used to call her that sometimes), 'we shall leave this raw sore town as soon as you get out of bed.'

'Incidentally, I want all my clothes,' said the gitanilla, humping up her knees and turning to another page.

'. . . Because, really,' I continued, 'there is no point in staying here.'

'There is no point in staying anywhere,' said Lolita.

I lowered myself into a cretonne chair and, opening the attractive botanical work, attempted, in the fever-humming hush of the room, to identify my flowers. This proved impossible. Presently a musical bell softly sounded somewhere in the passage.

I do not think they had more than a dozen patients (three or four were lunatics, as Lo had cheerfully informed me earlier) in that show place of a hospital, and the staff had too much leisure. However – likewise for reasons of show – regulations were rigid. It is also true that I kept coming at the wrong hours. Not without a secret flow of dreamy *malice*, visionary Mary (next time it will be *une belle dame toute en bleu* floating through Roaring Gulch) plucked me by the sleeve to lead me out. I looked at her hand; it dropped. As I was leaving, leaving voluntarily, Dolores Haze reminded me to bring her next morning. . . . She did not remember where the various things she wanted were. . . . 'Bring me,' she cried (out of sight already, door on the move, closing, closed), 'the new grey suitcase and Mother's trunk'; but by next morning I was shivering, and boozing, and dying in the motel bed she had used for just a few minutes, and the best I could do under the circular and dilating circumstances was to send the two bags over with the widow's beau, a robust and kindly trucker. I imagined Lo displaying her treasures to Mary. . . . No doubt, I was a little delirious – and on the following day I was still a vibration rather than a solid, for when I looked out of the bathroom window at the adjacent lawn, I saw Dolly's beautiful young bicycle propped up there on its support, the graceful front wheel looking away from me, as it always did, and a sparrow perched on the saddle – but it was the landlady's bike, and smiling a little, and shaking my poor head over my fond fancies, I tottered back to my bed, and lay as quiet as a saint –

Saint, forsooth! While brown Dolores,
On a patch of sunny green
With Sanchicha reading stories
In a movie magazine –

– which was represented by numerous specimens wherever Dolores landed, and there was some great national celebration in town judging by the firecrackers, veritable bombs, that exploded all the time, and at 1.55 p.m. I heard the sound of whistling lips nearing the half-opened door of my cabin, and then a thump upon it.

It was big Frank. He remained framed in the opened door, one hand on its jamb, leaning forward a little.

Howdy. Nurse Lore was on the telephone. She wanted to know was I better and would I come today?

At twenty paces Frank used to look a mountain of health; at five, as now, he was a ruddy mosaic of scars – had been blown through a wall overseas; but despite nameless injuries he was able to man a tremendous truck, fish, hunt, drink and buoyantly dally with roadside ladies. That day, either because it was such a great holiday, or simply because he wanted to divert a sick man, he had taken off the glove he usually wore on his left hand (the one pressing against the side of the door) and revealed to the fascinated sufferer not only an entire lack of fourth and fifth fingers, but also a naked girl, with cinnabar nipples and indigo delta, charmingly tattooed on the back of his crippled hand, its index and middle digit making her legs while his wrist bore her flower-crowned head. Oh, delicious . . . reclining against the woodwork, like some sly fairy.

I asked him to tell Mary Lore I would stay in bed all day and would get into touch with my daughter sometime tomorrow if I felt probably Polynesian.

He noticed the direction of my gaze and made her right hip twitch amorously.

'Okey-dokey,' big Frank sang out, slapped the jamb, and, whistling, carried my message away, and I went on drinking, and by morning the fever was gone, and although I was as limp as a toad, I put on the purple dressing gown over my maize yellow pyjamas, and walked over to the office telephone. Everything was fine. A bright voice informed me that yes, everything was fine, my daughter had checked out the day before, around two, her uncle, Mr Gustave, had called for her with a cocker spaniel pup and a smile for everyone, and a black Caddy Lack, and had paid Dolly's bill in cash, and told them to tell me I should not worry, and keep warm, they were at Grandpa's ranch as agreed.

Elphinstone was, and I hope still is, a very cute little town. It was spread like a maquette, you know, with its neat green-wool trees and red-roofed houses over the valley floor, and I think I have alluded earlier to its model school and temple and spacious rectangular blocks, some of which were, curiously enough, just unconventional pastures with a mule or a unicorn grazing in the young July morning mist. Very amusing: at one gravel-groaning sharp turn I sideswiped a parked car but said to myself telestically – and, telepathically (I hoped), to its gesticulating owner – that I would return later, address Bird School, Bird, New Bird, the gin kept my heart alive but bemazed my brain, and after some lapses and losses common to dream sequences, I found myself in the reception room, trying to beat up the doctor, and roaring at people under chairs, and clamouring for Mary who luckily for her was not there; rough hands plucked at my dressing gown, ripping off a pocket, and somehow I seem to have been sitting on a bald brown-headed patient, whom I had mistaken for Dr Blue, and who eventually stood up, remarking with a preposterous accent: 'Now, who is neurotic, I ask?' – and then a gaunt unsmiling nurse presented me with seven beautiful, *beautiful* books and the exquisitely folded tartan lap robe, and demanded a receipt; and in the sudden silence I became aware of a policeman in the hallway, to whom my fellow motorist was pointing me out, and meekly I signed the very symbolic receipt, thus surrendering my Lolita to all those apes. But what else could I do? One simple and stark thought stood out and this was: 'Freedom for the moment is everything'. One false move – and I might have been made to explain a life of crime. So I simulated a coming out of a daze. To my fellow motorist I paid what he thought was fair. To Dr Blue, who by then was stroking my hand, I spoke in tears of the liquor I bolstered too freely a tricky but not necessarily diseased heart with. To the hospital in general I apologized with a flourish that almost bowled me over, adding however that I was not on particularly good terms with the rest of the Humbert clan. To myself I whispered that I still had my gun, and was still a free man – free to trace the fugitive, free to destroy my brother.

23

A thousand-mile stretch of silk-smooth road separated Kasbeam, where, to the best of my belief, the red fiend had been scheduled to appear for the first time, and fateful Elphinstone which we had reached about a week before Independence Day. The journey had taken up most of June for we had seldom made more than a hundred and fifty miles per travelling day, spending the rest of the time, up to five days in one case, at various stopping places, all of them also pre-arranged, no doubt. It was that stretch, then, along which the fiend's spoor should be sought; and to this I devoted myself, after several unmentionable days of dashing up and down the relentlessly radiating roads in the vicinity of Elphinstone.

Imagine me, reader, with my shyness, my distaste for any ostentation, my inherent sense of the *comme il faut*, imagine me masking the frenzy of my grief with a trembling ingratiating smile while devising some casual pretext to flip through the hotel register: 'Oh,' I would say, 'I am almost positive that I stayed here once – let me look up the entries for mid-June – no, I see I'm wrong after all – what a very quaint name for a home town, Kawtagain. Thanks very much.' Or: 'I had a customer staying here – I mislaid his address – may I . . . ?' And every once in a while, especially if the operator of the place happened to be a certain type of gloomy male, personal inspection of the books was denied me.

I have a memo here: between July 5 and November 18, when I returned to Beardsley for a few days, I registered, if not actually stayed, at 342 hotels, motels and tourist homes. This figure includes a few registrations between Chestnut and Beardsley, one of which yielded a shadow of the fiend ('N. Petit, Larousse, Ill.'); I had to space and time my inquiries carefully so as not to attract undue attention; and there must have been at least fifty places where I merely inquired at the desk – but that was a futile quest, and I preferred building up a foundation of verisimilitude and goodwill by first paying for an unneeded room. My survey showed that of the 300 or so books inspected, at least twenty provided me with a clue: the loitering fiend had stopped even more often than we, or else – he was quite capable of that – he had thrown in additional registrations in order to keep me well furnished with derisive hints. Only in one case had he actually stayed at the same motor court as we, a few paces from Lolita's pillow. In some instances he had taken up quarters in the same or in a neighbouring block; not infrequently he had lain in wait at an intermediate spot between two bespoked points. How vividly I recalled Lolita, just before our departure from Beardsley, prone on the parlour rug, studying tour books and maps, and marking laps and stops with her lipstick!

I discovered at once that he had foreseen my investigations and had planted insulting pseudonyms for my special benefit. At the very first motel office I visited, Ponderosa Lodge, his entry, among a dozen obviously human ones, read: Dr Gratiano Forbeson, Mirandola, NY. Its Italian Comedy connotations could not fail to strike me, of course. The landlady deigned to inform me that the gentleman had been laid up for five days with a bad cold, that he had left his car for repairs in some garage or other and that he had checked out on July 4. Yes, a girl called Ann Lore had worked formerly at the Lodge, but was now married to a grocer in Cedar City. One moonlit night I waylaid white-shoed Mary on a solitary street; an automaton, she was about to shriek, but I managed to humanize her by the simple act of falling on my knees and with pious yelps imploring her to help. She did not know a thing, she swore. Who was this Gratiano Forbeson? She seemed to waver. I whipped out a hundred-dollar bill. She lifted it to the light of the moon. 'He is your brother,' she whispered at last. I plucked the bill out of her moon-cold hand, and spitting out a French curse turned and ran away. This taught me to rely on myself alone. No detective could discover the clues Trapp had tuned to my mind and manner. I could not hope, of course, he would ever leave his correct name and address; but I did hope he might slip on the glaze of his own subtlety, by daring, say, to introduce a richer and more personal shot of colour than was strictly necessary, or by revealing too much through a qualitative sum of quantitative parts which revealed too little. In one thing he succeeded: he succeeded in thoroughly enmeshing me and my thrashing anguish in his demoniacal game. With infinite skill, he swayed and staggered, and regained an impossible balance, always leaving me with the sportive hope – if I may use such a term in speaking of betrayal, fury, desolation, horror and hate – that he might give himself away next time. He never did – though coming damn close to it. We all admire the spangled acrobat with classical grace meticulously walking his tightrope in the talcum light; but how much rarer art there is in the sagging rope expert wearing scarecrow clothes and impersonating a grotesque drunk! *I* should know.

The clues he left did not establish his identity but they reflected his personality, or at least a certain homogeneous and striking personality; his genre, his type of humour – at its best at least – the tone of his brain, had affinities with my own. He mimed and mocked me. His allusions were definitely highbrow. He was well-read. He knew French. He was versed in logodaedaly and logomancy. He was an amateur of sex lore. He had a feminine handwriting. He could change his name but he could not disguise, no matter how he slanted them, his very peculiar t's, w's and l's. Quelquepart Island was one of his favourite residences. He did not use a fountain pen which fact, as any psycho-analyst will tell you, meant that the patient was a repressed undinist. One mercifully hopes there are water nymphs in the Styx.

His main trait was his passion for tantalization. Goodness, what a tease the poor fellow was! He challenged my scholarship. I am sufficiently proud of my knowing something to be modest about my not knowing all; and I dare say I missed some elements in that cryptogrammic paper chase. What a shiver of triumph and loathing shook my frail frame when, among the plain innocent names in the hotel recorder, his fiendish conundrum would ejaculate in my face! I noticed that whenever he felt his enigmas were becoming too recondite, even for such a solver as I, he would lure me back with an easy one. 'Arsène Lupin' was obvious to a Frenchman who remembered the detective stories of his youth; and one hardly had to be a Coleridgian to appreciate the trite poke of 'A. Person, Porlock, England'. In horrible taste but basically suggestive of a cultured man – not a policeman, not a common goon, not a lewd salesman – were such assumed names as 'Arthur Rainbow' – plainly the travestied author of *Le Bateau Blue* – let me laugh a little too, gentlemen – and 'Morris Schmetterling', of *L'Oiseau Ivre* fame (*touché*, reader!). The silly but funny 'D. Orgon, Elmira, NY', was from Molière, of course, and because I had quite recently tried to interest Lolita in a famous eighteenth-century play, I welcomed as an old friend 'Harry Bumper, Sheridan, Wyo'. An ordinary encyclopedia informed me who the peculiar looking 'Phineas Quimby, Lebanon, N.H' was; and any good Freudian, with a German name and some interest in religious prostitution, should recognize at a glance the implication of 'Dr Kitzler, Eryx, Miss'. So far so good. That sort of fun was shoddy but on the whole impersonal and thus innocuous. Among entries that arrested my attention as undoubtable clues *per se* but baffled me in respect to their finer points I do not care to mention many since I feel I am groping in a border-land mist with verbal phantoms turning, perhaps, into living vacationists. Who was 'Johnny Randall, Ramble, Ohio'? Or was he a real person who just happened to write a hand similar to 'N. S. Aristoff, Catagela, NY'? What was the sting in 'Catagela'? And what about 'James Manor Morell, Hoaxton, England'? 'Aristophanes', 'hoax' – fine, but what was I missing?

There was one strain running through all that pseudonymity which caused me especially painful palpitations when I came across it. Such things as 'G. Trapp, Geneva, NY' was the sign of treachery on Lolita's part. 'Aubrey Beardsley, Quelquepart Island' suggested more lucidly than the garbled telephone message had that the starting-point of the affair should be looked for in the East. 'Lucas Picador, Merrymay, Pa.' insinuated that my Carmen had betrayed my pathetic endearments to the imposter. Horribly cruel, forsooth, was 'Will Brown, Dolores, Colo.' The gruesome 'Harold Haze, Tombstone, Arizona' (which at another time would have appealed to my sense of humour) implied a familiarity with the girl's past that in nightmare fashion suggested for a moment that my quarry was an old friend of the family, maybe an old flame of Charlotte's, maybe a redresser of wrongs ('Donald Quix, Sierra, Nev.'). But the most penetrating bodkin was the anagram-tailed entry in the register of Chestnut Lodge 'Ted Hunter, Cane, NH'.

The garbled licence numbers left by all these Persons and Orgons and Morells and Trapps only told me that motel keepers omit to check if guests' cars are accurately listed. References – incompletely or incorrectly indicated – to the cars the fiend had hired for short laps between Wace and Elphinstone were of course useless; the licence of the initial Aztec was a shimmer of shifting numerals, some transposed, others altered or omitted, but somehow forming interrelated combinations (such as 'WS 1564' and 'SH 1616', and 'Q 32888' or 'CU 88322') which however were so cunningly contrived as never to reveal a common denominator.

It occurred to me that after he had turned that convertible over to accomplices at Wace and switched to the stage-motor car system, his successors might have been less careful and might have inscribed at some hotel office the archetype of those interrelated figures. But if looking for the fiend along a road I knew he had taken was such a complicated, vague and unprofitable business, what could I expect from any attempt to trace unknown motorists travelling along unknown routes?

24

By the time I reached Beardsley, in the course of the harrowing recapitulation I have now discussed at sufficient length, a complete image had formed in my mind; and through the – always risky – process of elimination I had reduced this image to the only concrete source that morbid cerebration and torpid memory could give it.

Except for the Rev. Rigor Mortis (as the girls called him), and an old gentleman who taught non-obligatory German and Latin, there were no regular male teachers at Beardsley School. But on two occasions an art instructor on the Beardsley College faculty had come over to show the schoolgirls magic lantern pictures of French castles and nineteenth-century paintings. I had wanted to attend those projections and talks, but Dolly, as was her wont, had asked me not to, period. I also remembered that Gaston had referred to that particular lecturer as a brilliant *garçon*; but that was all; memory refused to supply me with the name of the château-lover.

On the day fixed for the execution, I walked through the sleet across the campus to the information desk in Maker Hall, Beardsley College. There I learned that the fellow's name was Riggs (rather like that of the minister), that he was a bachelor, and that in ten minutes he would issue from the 'Museum' where he was having a class. In the passage leading to the auditorium I sat on a marble bench of sorts donated by Cecilia Dalrymple Ramble. As I waited there, in prostatic discomfort, drunk, sleep-starved, with my gun in my fist in my raincoat pocket, it suddenly occurred to me that I was demented and was about to do something stupid. There was not one chance in a million that Albert Riggs, Ass. Prof., was hiding my Lolita in his Beardsley home, 24 Pritchard Road. He could not be the villain. It was absolutely preposterous. I was losing my time and my wits. He and she were in California and not here at all.

Presently, I noticed a vague commotion behind some white statues; a door – not the one I had been staring at – opened briskly, and amid a bevy of women students a baldish head and two bright brown eyes bobbed, advanced.

He was a total stranger to me but insisted we had met at a lawn party at Beardsley School. How was my delightful tennis-playing daughter? He had another class. He would be seeing me.

Another attempt at identification was less speedily resolved: through an advertisement in one of Lo's magazines I darted to get in touch with a private detective, an ex-pugilist, and merely to give him some idea of the *method* adopted by the fiend, I acquainted him with the kind of names and addresses I had collected. He demanded a goodish deposit and for two years – two years, reader! – that imbecile busied himself with checking those nonsense data. I had long severed all monetary relations with him when he turned up one day with the triumphant information that an eighty-year-old Indian by the name of Bill Brown lived near Dolores, Colo.

25

This book is about Lolita; and now that I have reached the part which (had I not been forestalled by another internal combustion martyr) might be called '*Dolorès Disparue*', there would be little sense in analysing the three empty years that followed. While a few pertinent points have to be marked, the general impression I desire to convey is of a side door crashing open in life's full flight, and a rush of roaring black time drowning with its whipping wind the cry of lone disaster.

Singularly enough, I seldom if ever dreamed of Lolita as I remembered her – as I saw her constantly and obsessively in my conscious mind during my daymares and insomnias. More precisely: she did haunt my sleep but she appeared there in strange and ludicrous disguises as Valeria or Charlotte, or a cross between them. That complex ghost would come to me, shedding shift after shift, in an atmosphere of great melancholy and disgust, and would recline in dull invitation on some narrow board or hard settee, with flesh ajar like the rubber valve of a soccer ball's bladder. I would find myself, dentures fractured or hopelessly mislaid, in horrible *chambres garnies* where I would be entertained at tedious vivisecting parties that generally ended with Charlotte or Valeria weeping in my bleeding arms and being tenderly kissed by my brotherly lips in a dream disorder of auctioneered Viennese bric-à-brac, pity, impotence and the brown wigs of tragic old women who had just been gassed.

One day I removed from the car and destroyed an accumulation of teen-magazines. You know the sort. Stone age at heart; up to date, or at least Mycenaean, as to hygiene. A handsome, very ripe actress with huge lashes and a pulpy red underlip, endorsing a shampoo. Ads and fads. Young scholars dote on plenty of pleats – *que c'était loin, tout cela!* It is your hostess's duty to provide robes. Unattached details take all the sparkle out of your conversation. All of us have known 'pickers' – one who picks her cuticle at the office party. Unless he is very elderly or very important, a man should remove his gloves before shaking hands with a woman. Invite Romance by wearing the Exciting New Tummy Flattener. Trims tums, nips hips. Tristram in Movielove. Yessir! The Joe-Roe marital enigma is making yaps flap. Glamorize yourself quickly and inexpensively. Cosmics. Bad girl dark hair fat father cigar; good girl red hair handsome daddums clipped moustache. Or that repulsive strip with the big gagoon and his wife, a kiddoid gnomide. *Et moi qui t'offrais mon génie* . . . I recalled the rather charming nonsense verse I used to write her when she was a child: 'nonsense', she used to say mockingly, 'is correct'.

The Squirl and his Squirrel, the Rabs and their Rabbits
Have certain obscure and peculiar habits.
Male humming birds make the most exquisite rockets.
The snake when he walks holds his hands in his pockets . . .

Other things of hers were harder to relinquish. Up to the end of 1949, I cherished and adored, and stained with my kisses and merman tears, a pair of old sneakers, a boy's shirt she had worn, some ancient blue jeans I found in the trunk compartment, a crumpled school cap, such-like wanton treasures. Then, when I understood my mind was cracking, I collected these sundry belongings, added to them what had been stored in Beardsley – a box of books, her bicycle, old coats, galoshes – and on her fifteenth birthday mailed everything as an anonymous gift to a home for orphaned girls on a windy lake, on the Canadian border.

It is just possible that had I gone to a strong hypnotist he might have extracted from me and arrayed in a logical pattern certain chance memories that I have threaded through my book with considerably more ostentation than they present themselves with to my mind even now when I know what to seek in the past. At the time I felt I was merely losing contact with reality; and after spending the rest of the winter and most of the following spring in a Quebec sanatorium where I had stayed before, I resolved first to settle some affairs of mine in New York and then to proceed to California for a thorough search there.

Here is something I composed in my retreat:

Wanted, wanted: Dolores Haze.
Hair: brown. Lips: scarlet.
Age: five thousand three hundred days.
Profession: none, or 'starlet'.

Where are you hiding, Dolores Haze?
Why are you hiding, darling?
(I talk in a daze, I walk in a maze,
I cannot get out, said the starling.)

Where are you riding, Dolores Haze?
What make is the magic carpet?

Is a Cream Cougar the present craze?
And where are you parked, my car pet?

Who is your hero, Dolores Haze?
Still one of those blue-caped star-men?
Oh the balmy days and the palmy bays,
And the cars, and the bars, my Carmen!

Oh Dolores, that juke-box hurts!
Are you still dancin', darlin'?
(Both in worn levis, both in torn T-shirts,
And I, in my corner, snarlin').

Happy, happy is gnarled McFate
Touring the States with a child wife,
Ploughing his Dolly in every State
Among the protected wild life.

My Dolly, my folly! Her eyes were *vair*,
And never closed when I kissed her.
Know an old perfume called *Soleil Vert*?
Are you from Paris, mister?

L'autre soir un air froid d'opéra m'alita:
Son félé – bien fol est qui s'y fie!
Il neige, le décor s'écroule, Lolita!
Lolita, qu'ai-je fait de ta vie?

Dying, dying, Lolita Haze,
Of hate and remorse, I'm dying.
And again my hairy fist I raise,
And again I hear you crying.

Officer, officer, there they go –
In the rain, where that lighted store is!
And her socks are white, and I love her so,
And her name is Haze, Dolores.

Officer, officer, there they are –
Dolores Haze and her lover!
Whip out your gun and follow that car.
Now tumble out, and take cover.

Wanted, wanted: Dolores Haze.
Her dream-grey gaze never flinches.
Ninety pounds is all she weighs
With a height of sixty inches.

My car is limping, Dolores Haze,
And the last long lap is the hardest,
And I shall be dumped where the weed decays,
And the rest is rust and stardust.

By psycho-analysing this poem, I noticed it is really a maniac's masterpiece. The stark, stiff, lurid rhymes correspond very exactly to certain perspectiveless and terrible landscapes and figures, and magnified parts of landscapes and figures, as drawn by psychopaths in tests devised by their astute trainers. I wrote many more poems. I immersed myself in the poetry of others. But not for a second did I forget the load of revenge.

I would be a knave to say, and the reader a fool to believe, that the shock of losing Lolita cured me of pederosis. My accursed nature could not change, no matter how my love for her did. On playgrounds and beaches, my sullen and stealthy eye, against my will, still sought out the flash of a nymphet's limbs, the sly tokens of Lolita's handmaids and rose-girls. But one essential vision in me had withered: never did I dwell now on possibilities of bliss with a little maiden, specific or synthetic, in some out-of-the-way place; never did my fancy sink its fangs into Lolita's sisters, far far away, in the coves of evoked islands. *That* was all over, for the time being at least. On the other hand, alas, two years of monstrous indulgence had left me with certain habits of lust: I feared lest the void I lived in might drive me to plunge into the freedom of sudden insanity when confronted with a chance temptation in some lane between school and supper. Solitude was corrupting me. I needed company and care. My heart was a hysterical unreliable organ. This is how Rita enters the picture.

26

She was twice Lolita's age and three-quarters of mine: a very slight, dark-haired, pale-skinned adult, weighing a hundred and five pounds, with charmingly asymmetrical eyes, an angular, rapidly sketched profile, and a most appealing *ensellure* to her supple back – I think she had some Spanish or Babylonian blood. I picked her up one depraved May evening somewhere between

Montreal and New York, or more narrowly, between Toylestown and Blake, at a darkishly burning bar under the sign of the Tigermoth, where she was amiably drunk: she insisted we had gone to school together, and she placed her trembling little hand on my ape paw. My senses were very slightly stirred but I decided to give her a try; I did – and adopted her as a constant companion. She was so kind, was Rita, such a good sport, that I dare say she would have given herself to any pathetic creature or fallacy, an old broken tree or a bereaved porcupine, out of sheer chumminess and compassion.

When I first met her she had but recently divorced her third husband – and a little more recently had been abandoned by her seventh *cavalier servant* – the others, the mutables, were too numerous and mobile to tabulate. Her brother was – and no doubt still is – a prominent, pasty-faced, suspenders-and-painted-tie-wearing politician, mayor and booster of his ball-playing, Bible-reading, grain-handling home town. For the last eight years he had been paying his great little sister several hundred dollars per month under the stringent condition that she would never never enter great little Grainball City. She told me, with wails of wonder, that for some God-damn reason every new boy friend of hers would first of all take her Grainball-ward: it was a fatal attraction; and before she knew what was what, she would find herself sucked into the lunar orbit of the town, and would be following the flood-lit drive that encircled it – 'going round and round', as she phrased it, 'like a God-damn mulberry moth'.

She had a natty little coupé; and in it we travelled to California so as to give my venerable vehicle a rest. Her natural speed was ninety. Dear Rita! We cruised together for two dim years, from summer 1950 to summer 1952, and she was the sweetest, simplest, gentlest, dumbest Rita imaginable. In comparison to her, Valechka was a Schlegel, and Charlotte a Hegel. There is no earthly reason why I should dally with her in the margin of this sinister memoir, but let me say (hi, Rita – wherever you are, drunk or hangoverish, Rita, hi!) that she was the most soothing, the most comprehending companion that I ever had, and certainly saved me from the madhouse. I told her I was trying to trace a girl and plug that girl's bully. Rita solemnly approved of the plan – and in the course of some investigation she undertook on her own (without really knowing a thing), around San Humbertino, got entangled with a pretty awful crook herself; I had the devil of a time retrieving her – used and bruised but still cocky. Then one day she proposed playing Russian roulette with my sacred automatic; I said you couldn't, it was not a revolver, and we struggled for it, until at last it went off, touching off a very thin and very comical spurt of hot water from the hole it made in the wall of the cabin room; I remember her shrieks of laughter.

The oddly prepubescent curve of her back, her ricey skin, her slow languorous columbine kisses kept me from mischief. It is not the artistic aptitudes that are secondary sexual characters as some shams and shamans have said; it is the other way around: sex is but the ancilla of art. One rather mysterious spree that had interesting repercussions I must notice. I had abandoned the search: the fiend was either in Tartary or burning away in my cerebellum (the flames fanned by my fancy and grief) but certainly not having Dolores Haze play champion tennis on the Pacific Coast. One afternoon, on our way back East, in a hideous hotel, the kind where they hold conventions and where labelled, fat, pink men stagger around, all first names and business and booze – dear Rita and I awoke to find a third in our room, a blonde, almost albino, young fellow with white eyelashes and large transparent ears, whom neither Rita nor I recalled having ever seen in our sad lives. Sweating in thick dirty underwear, and with old army boots on, he lay snoring on the double bed beyond my chaste Rita. One of his front teeth was gone, amber pustules grew on his forehead. Ritochka enveloped her sinuous nudity in my raincoat – the first thing at hand; I slipped on a pair of candy-striped drawers; and we took stock of the situation. Five glasses had been used, which, in the way of clues, was an embarrassment of riches. The door was not properly closed. A sweater and a pair of shapeless tan pants lay on the floor. We shook their owner into miserable consciousness. He was completely amnesic. In an accent that Rita recognized as pure Brooklynese, he peevishly insinuated that somehow we had purloined his (worthless) identity. We rushed him into his clothes and left him at the nearest hospital, realizing on the way that, somehow or other after forgotten gyrations, we were in Grainball. Half a year later Rita wrote the doctor for news. Jack Humbertson as he had been tastelessly dubbed was still isolated from his personal past. Oh Mnemosyne, sweetest and most mischievous of muses!

I would not have mentioned this incident had it not started a chain of ideas that resulted in my publishing in the *Cantrip Review* an essay on 'Mimic and Memory', in which I suggested among other things that seemed original and important to that splendid review's benevolent readers, a theory of perceptual time based on the circulation of the blood and conceptually depending (to fill up this nutshell) on the mind's being conscious not only of matter but also of its own self, thus creating a continuous spanning of two points (the storable future and the stored past). In result of this venture – and in culmination of the impression made by my previous *travaux* – I was called from New York, where Rita and I were living in a little flat with a view of gleaming children taking shower baths far below in a fountainous arbour of Central Park, to Cantrip College, four hundred miles away, for one year. I lodged there, in special apartments for poets and philosophers, from September 1951 to June 1952, while Rita whom I preferred not to display vegetated – somewhat indecorously, I am afraid – in a roadside inn where I visited her twice a week. Then she vanished – more humanly than her predecessor had done: a month later I found her in the local jail. She was *très digne,* had had her appendix removed, and managed to convince me that the beautiful bluish furs she had been accused of stealing from a Mrs Roland MacCrum had really been a spontaneous, if somewhat alcoholic, gift from Roland himself. I succeeded in getting her out without appealing to her touchy brother, and soon afterwards we drove back to Central Park West, by way of Briceland, where we had stopped for a few hours the year before.

A curious urge to relive my stay there with Lolita had got hold of me. I was entering a phase of existence where I had given up all hope of tracing her kidnapper and her. I now attempted to fall back on old settings in order to save what still could be saved in the way of *souvenir, souvenir que me veux-tu*? Autumn was ringing in the air. To a postcard requesting twin beds Professor Hamburg got a prompt expression of regret in reply. They were full up. They had one bathless basement room with four beds which they thought I would not want. Their note paper was headed:

THE ENCHANTED HUNTERS

NEAR CHURCHES NO DOGS

All legal beverages

I wondered if the last statement was true. All? Did they have for instance sidewalk grenadine? I also wondered if a hunter, enchanted or otherwise, would not need a pointer more than a pew, and with a spasm of pain I recalled a scene worthy of a great artist: *petite nymphe accroupie*; but that silky cocker spaniel had perhaps been a baptized one. No – I felt I could not endure the throes of revisiting that lobby. There was a much better possibility of retrievable time elsewhere in soft, rich-coloured, autumnal Briceland. Leaving Rita in a bar, I made for the town library. A twittering spinster was only too glad to help me disinter mid-August 1947 from the bound *Briceland Gazette*, and presently, in a secluded nook under a naked light, I was turning the enormous and fragile pages of a coffin-black volume almost as big as Lolita.

Reader! *Bruder!* What a foolish Hamburg that Hamburg was! Since his supersensitive system was loath to face the actual scene, he thought he could at least enjoy a secret part of it – which reminds one of the tenth or twentieth soldier in the queue who throws the girl's black shawl over her white face so as not to see those impossible eyes while taking his military pleasure in the sad, sacked village. What *I* lusted to get was the printed picture that had chanced to absorb my trespassing image while the *Gazette's* photographer was concentrating on Dr Braddock and his group. Passionately I hoped to find preserved the portrait of the artist as a younger brute. An innocent camera catching me on my dark way to Lolita's bed – what a magnet for Mnemosyne! I cannot well explain the true nature of that urge of mine. It was allied, I suppose, to that swooning curiosity which impels one to examine with a magnifying glass bleak little figures – still life practically, and everybody about to throw up – at an early morning execution, and the patient's expression impossible to make out in the print. Anyway, I was literally gasping for breath, and one corner of the book of doom kept stabbing me in the stomach while I scanned and skimmed. . . . *Brute Force* and *Possessed* were coming on Sunday, the 24th, to both theatres. Mr Purdom, independent tobacco auctioneer, said that ever since 1925 he had been an Omen Faustum smoker. Husky Hank and his petite bride were to be the guests of Mr and Mrs Reginald G. Gore, 58 Inchkeith Avenue. The size of certain parasites is one-sixth of the host. Dunkerque was fortified in the tenth century. Misses' socks, 39 c. Saddle Oxfords, 3·98. Wine, wine, wine, quipped the author of Dark Age who refused to be photographed, may suit a Persian bubble bird, but I say give me rain, rain, rain on the shingle roof for roses and inspiration every time. Dimples are caused by the adherence of the skin to the deeper tissues. Greeks repulse a heavy guerilla assault – and, ah, at last, a little figure in white, and Dr Braddock in black, but whatever spectral shoulder was brushing against his ample form – nothing of myself could I make out.

I went to find Rita who introduced me with her *vin triste* smile to a pocket-sized wizened truculently tight old man saying this was – what was that name again, son? – a former schoolmate of hers. He tried to retain her, and in the slight scuffle that followed I hurt my thumb against his hard head. In the silent painted park where I walked her and aired her a little, she sobbed and said I would soon, soon leave her as everybody had, and I sang her a wistful French ballad, and strung together some fugitive rhymes to amuse her:

> The place was called *Enchanted Hunters*. Query:
> What Indian dyes, Diana, did thy dell
> endorse to make of Picture Lake a very
> blood bath of trees before the blue hotel?

She said: 'Why blue when it is white, why blue for heaven's sake?' and started to cry again, and I marched her to the car, and we drove on to New York, and soon she was reasonably happy again high up in the haze on the little terrace of our flat. I notice I have somehow mixed up two events, my visit with Rita to Briceland on our way to Cantrip, and our passing through Briceland again on our way back to New York, but such suffusions of swimming colours are not to be disdained by the artist in recollection.

27

My letterbox in the entrance hall belonged to the type that allows one to glimpse something of its contents through a glassed slit. Several times already, a trick of harlequin light that fell through the glass upon an alien handwriting had twisted it into a semblance of Lolita's script causing me almost to collapse as I leant against an adjacent urn, almost my own. Whenever that happened – whenever her lovely, loopy, childish scrawl was horribly transformed into the dull hand of one of my few correspondents – I used to recollect, with anguished amusement, the times in my trustful, pre-dolorian past when I would be misled by a jewel-bright window opposite wherein my lurking eye, the ever alert periscope of my shameful vice, would make out from afar a half-naked nymphet stilled in the act of combing her Alice-in-Wonderland hair. There was in the fiery phantasm a perfection which made my wild delight also perfect, just because the vision was out of reach, with no possibility of attainment to spoil it by the awareness of an appended taboo; indeed, it may well be that the very attraction immaturity has for me lies not so much in the limpidity of pure young forbidden fairy child beauty as in the security of a situation where infinite perfections fill the gap between the little given and the great promised – the great rose-grey never-to-be-had. *Mes fenêtres!* Hanging above blotched sunset and welling night, grinding my teeth, I would crowd all the demons of my desire against the railing of a throbbing balcony: it would be ready to take off in the apricot and black humid evening; did take off – whereupon the lighted image would move and Eve would revert to a rib, and there would be nothing in the window but an obese partly clad man reading the paper.

Since I sometimes won the race between my fancy and nature's reality, the deception was bearable. Unbearable pain began when chance entered the fray and deprived me of the smile meant for me. '*Savez-vous qu'à dix ans ma petite était folle de vous?*' said a woman I talked to at a tea in Paris, and the *petite* had just married, miles away, and I could not even remember if I had ever noticed her in that garden, next to those tennis courts, a dozen years before. And now likewise, the radiant foreglimpse, the promise of reality, a promise not only to be simulated seductively but also to be nobly held – all this, chance denied me – chance and a change to smaller characters on the pale beloved writer's part. My fancy was both Proustianized and Procrusteanized; for that particular morning, early in September 1952, as I had come down to grope for my mail, the dapper and bilious janitor with whom I was on execrable terms started to complain that a man who had seen Rita home recently had been 'sick like a dog' on the front steps. In the process of listening to him and tipping him, and then listening to a revised and politer version of the incident, I had the impression that one of the two letters which that blessed mail brought was from Rita's mother, a crazy little woman, whom we had once visited on Cape Cod and who kept writing me to my various addresses, saying how wonderfully well matched her daughter and I were, and how wonderful it would be if we married; the other letter which I opened and scanned rapidly in the elevator was from John Farlow.

I have often noticed that we are inclined to endow our friends with the stability of type that literary characters acquire in the reader's mind. No matter how many times we reopen 'King Lear', never shall we find the good king banging his tankard in high revelry, all woes forgotten, at a jolly reunion with all three daughters and their lapdogs. Never will Emma rally, revived by the sympathetic salts in Flaubert's father's timely tear. Whatever evolution this or that popular character has gone through between the book covers, his fate is fixed in our minds, and, similarly, we expect our friends to follow this or that logical and conventional pattern we have fixed for them. Thus X will never compose the immortal music that would clash with the second-rate symphonies he has accustomed us to. Y will never commit murder. Under no circumstances can Z ever betray us. We have it all arranged in our minds, and the less often we see a particular person the more satisfying it is to check how obediently he conforms to our notion of him every time we hear of him. Any deviation in the fates we have ordained would strike us as not only anomalous but unethical. We would prefer not to have known at all our neighbour, the retired hot-dog stand operator, if it turns out he has just produced the greatest book of poetry his age has seen.

I am saying all this in order to explain how bewildered I was by Farlow's hysterical letter. I knew his wife had died but I certainly expected him to remain, throughout a devout widowhood, the dull, sedate and reliable person he had always been. Now he wrote that after a brief visit to the US he had returned to South America and had decided that whatever affairs he had controlled at Ramsdale he would hand over to Jack Windmuller of that town, a lawyer whom we both knew. He seemed particularly relieved to get rid of the Haze 'complications'. He had married a Spanish girl. He had stopped smoking and had gained thirty pounds. She was very young and a ski champion. They were going to India for their honeymonsoon. Since he was 'building a family' as he put it, he would have no time henceforth for my affairs which he termed 'very strange and very aggravating'. Busybodies – a whole committee of them, it appeared – had informed him that the whereabout of little Dolly Haze was unknown, and that I was living with a notorious divorcee in California. His father-in-law was a count, and exceedingly wealthy. The people who had been renting the Haze house for some years now wished to buy it. He suggested that I better produce Dolly quick. He had broken his leg. He enclosed a snapshot of himself and a brunette in white wool beaming at each other among the snows of Chile.

I remember letting myself into my flat and starting to say: Well, at least we shall now track them down – when the other letter began talking to me in a small matter-of-fact voice:

DEAR DAD:

How's everything? I'm married. I'm going to have a baby. I guess he's going to be a big one. I guess he'll come right for Christmas. This is a hard letter to write. I'm going nuts because we don't have enough to pay our debts and get out of here. Dick is promised a big job in Alaska in his very specialized corner of the mechanical field, that's all I know about it but it's really grand. Pardon me for withholding our home address but you may still be mad at me, and Dick must not know. This town is something. You can't see the morons for the smog. Please do send us a cheque, Dad. We could manage with three or four hundred or even less, anything is welcome, you might sell my old things, because once we get there the dough will just start rolling in. Write, please. I have gone through much sadness and hardship.

Yours expecting,

DOLLY (MRS RICHARD F. SCHILLER)

28

I was again on the road, again at the wheel of the old blue sedan, again alone. Rita had still been dead to the world when I read that letter and fought the mountains of agony it raised within me. I had glanced at her as she smiled in her sleep and had kissed her on her moist brow, and had left her for ever, with a note of tender adieu which I taped to her navel – otherwise she might not have found it.

'Alone' did I say? *Pas tout à fait.* I had my little black chum with me, and as soon as I reached a secluded spot, I rehearsed Mr Richard F. Schiller's violent death. I had found a very old and very dirty grey sweater of mine in the back of the car, and this I hung up on a branch, in a speechless glade, which I had reached by a wood road from the now remote highway. The carrying out of the sentence was a little marred by what seemed to me a certain stiffness in the play of the trigger, and I wondered if I should get some oil for the mysterious thing but decided I had no time to spare. Back into the car went the old dead sweater, now with additional perforations, and having reloaded warm Chum, I continued my journey.

The letter was dated September 18, 1952 (this was September 22), and the address she gave was 'General Delivery, Coalmont' (not 'Va.', not 'Pa.', not 'Tenn.' – and not Coalmont, anyway – I have camouflaged everything, my love). Inquiries showed this to be a small industrial community some eight hundred miles from New York City. At first I planned to drive all day and all night, but then thought better of it and rested for a couple of hours around dawn in a motor court room, a few miles before reaching the town. I had made up my mind that the fiend, this Schiller, had been a car salesman who had perhaps got to know my Lolita by giving her a ride in Beardsley – the day her bike blew a tyre on the way to Miss Emperor – and that he had got into some trouble since then. The corpse of the executed sweater, no matter how I changed its contours as it lay on the back seat of the car, had kept revealing various outlines pertaining to Trapp-Schiller – the grossness and obscene bonhomie of his body, and to counteract his taste of coarse corruption I resolved to make myself especially handsome and smart as I pressed home the nipple of my alarm clock before it exploded at the set hour of 6 a.m. Then, with the stern and romantic care of a gentleman about to fight a duel, I checked the arrangement of my papers, bathed and perfumed my delicate body, shaved my face and chest, selected a silk shirt and clean drawers, pulled on transparent taupe socks, and congratulated myself for having with me in my trunk some very exquisite clothes – a waistcoat with nacreous buttons, for instance, a pale cashmere tie and so on.

I was not able, alas, to hold my breakfast, but dismissed that physicality as a trivial contretemps, wiped my mouth with a gossamer handkerchief produced from my sleeve, and, with a blue block of ice for heart, a pill on my tongue and solid death in my hip pocket, I stepped neatly into a telephone booth in Coalmont (Ah-ah-ah, said its little door) and rang up the only Schiller – Paul, Furniture – to be found in the battered book. Hoarse Paul told me he did not know a Richard, the son of a cousin of his, and his address was, let me see, 10 Killer Street (I am not going very far for my pseudonyms). Ah-ah-ah, said the little door.

At 10 Killer Street, a tenement house, I interviewed a number of dejected old people and two long-haired strawberry-blonde incredibly grubby nymphets (rather abstractly, just for the heck of it, the ancient beast in me was casting about for some lightly clad child I might hold against me for a minute, after the killing was over and nothing mattered any more, and everything was allowed). Yes, Dick Skiller had lived there, but had moved when he married. Nobody knew his address. 'They might know at the store', said a bass voice from an open manhole near which I happened to be standing with the two thin-armed, barefoot little girls and their dim grandmothers. I entered the wrong store and a wary old Negro shook his head even before I could ask anything. I crossed over to a bleak grocery and there, summoned by a customer at my request, a woman's voice from some wooden abyss in the floor, the manhole's counterpart, cried out: Hunter Road, last house.

Hunter Road was miles away, in an even more dismal district, all dump and ditch, and wormy vegetable garden, and shack, and grey drizzle, and red mud, and several smoking stacks in the distance. I stopped at the last 'house' – a clapboard shack, with two or three similar ones farther away from the road and a waste of withered weeds all around. Sounds of hammering came from behind the house, and for several minutes I sat quite still in my old car, old and frail, at the end of my journey, at my grey goal, *finis,* my friends, *finis,* my fiends. The time was around two. My pulse was 40 one minute and 100 the next. The drizzle crepitated against the hood of the car. My gun had migrated to my right trouser pocket. A nondescript cur came out from behind the house, stopped in surprise, and started good-naturedly woof-woofing at me, his eyes slit, his shaggy belly all muddy, and then walked about a little and woofed once more.

29

I got out of the car and slammed its door. How matter-of-fact, how square that slam sounded in the void of the sunless day! *Woof*, commented the dog perfunctorily. I pressed the bell button, it vibrated through my whole system. *Personne. Je resonne. Repersonne.* From what depth this re-nonsense? Woof, said the dog. A rush and a shuffle, and woosh-woof went the door.

Couple of inches taller. Pink-rimmed glasses. New, heaped-up hairdo, new ears. How simple! The moment, the death I had kept conjuring up for three years was as simple as a bit of dry wood. She was frankly and hugely pregnant. Her head looked smaller (only two seconds had passed really, but let me give them as much wooden duration as life can stand), and her pale-freckled cheeks were hollowed, and her bare shins and arms had lost all their tan, so that the little hairs showed. She wore a brown, sleeveless cotton dress and sloppy felt slippers.

'We – e – ell!' she exhaled after a pause with all the emphasis of wonder and welcome.

'Husband at home?' I croaked, fist in pocket.

I could not kill *her*, of course, as some have thought. You see I loved her. It was love at first sight, at last sight, at ever and ever sight.

'Come in,' she said with a vehement cheerful note. Against the splintery deadwood of the door, Dolly Schiller flattened herself as best she could (even rising on tiptoe a little) to let me pass, and was crucified for a moment, looking down, smiling down at the threshold, hollow-cheeked with round *pommettes,* her watered-milk-white arms outspread on the wood. I passed without touching her bulging babe. Dolly-smell, with a faint fried addition. My teeth chattered like an idiot's. 'No, you stay out' (to the dog). She closed the door and followed me and her belly into the doll-house parlour.

'Dick's down there,' she said pointing with an invisible tennis racket, inviting my gaze to travel from the drab parlour-bedroom where we stood, right across the kitchen, and through the back-doorway where, in a rather primitive vista, a dark-haired young stranger in overalls, instantaneously reprieved, was perched with his back to me on a ladder fixing something near or upon the shack of his neighbour, a plumper fellow with only one arm, who stood looking up.

This pattern she explained from afar, apologetically ('Men will be men'); should she call him in?

No.

Standing in the middle of the slanting room and emitting questioning 'hm's', she made familiar Javanese gestures with her wrists and hands, offering me, in a brief display of humorous courtesy, to choose between a rocker and the divan (their bed after 10 p.m.). I say 'familiar' because one day she had welcomed me with the same wrist dance to her party in Beardsley. We both sat down on the divan. Curious: although actually her looks had faded, I definitely realized, so hopelessly late in the day, how much she looked – had always looked – like Botticelli's russet Venus – the same soft nose, the same blurred beauty. In my pocket my fingers gently let go and repacked a little at the tip, within the handkerchief it was nested in, my unused weapon.

'That's not the fellow I want,' I said.

The diffuse look of welcome left her eyes. Her forehead puckered as in the old bitter days:

'Not *who*?'

'Where is he? Quick!'

'Look,' she said, inclining her head to one side and shaking it in that position. 'Look, you are not going to bring that up.'

'I certainly am,' I said, and for a moment – strangely enough the only merciful, endurable one in the whole interview – we were bristling at each other as if she were still mine.

A wise girl, she controlled herself.

Dick did not know a thing of the whole mess. He thought I was her father. He thought she had run away from an upper-class home just to wash dishes in a diner. He believed anything. Why should I want to make things harder than they were by raking up all that muck?

But, I said, she must be sensible, she must be a sensible girl (with her bare drum under that thin brown stuff), she must understand that if she expected the help I had come to give, I must have at least a clear comprehension of the situation.

'Come, his name!'

She thought I had guessed long ago. It was (with a mischievous and melancholy smile) such a sensational name. I would never believe it. She could hardly believe it herself.

His name, my fall nymph.

It was so unimportant, she said. She suggested I skip it. Would I like a cigarette?

No. His name.

She shook her head with great resolution. She guessed it was too late to raise hell and I would never believe the unbelievably unbelievable—

I said I had better go, regards, nice to have seen her.

She said really it was useless, she would never tell, but on the other hand, after all – 'Do you really want to know who it was? Well, it was—'

And softly, confidentially, arching her thing eyebrows and puckering her parched lips, she emitted, a little mockingly, somewhat fastidiously, not untenderly, in a kind of muted whistle, the name that the astute reader has guessed long ago.

Waterproof. Why did a flash from Hourglass Lake cross my consciousness? I, too, had known it, without knowing it, all along. There was no shock, no surprise. Quietly the fusion took place, and everything fell into order, into the pattern of branches that I have woven throughout this memoir with the express purpose of having the ripe fruit fall at the right moment; yes, with the express and perverse purpose of rendering – she was talking but I sat melting in my golden peace – of rendering that golden and monstrous peace through the satisfaction of logical recognition, which my most inimical reader should experience now.

She was, as I say, talking. It now came in a relaxed flow. He was the only man she had ever been crazy about. What about Dick? Oh, Dick was a lamb, they were quite happy together, but she meant something different. And *I* had never counted, of course?

She considered me as if grasping all at once the incredible – and somehow tedious, confusing and unnecessary – fact that the distant, elegant, slender, forty-year-old valetudinarian in velvet coat sitting beside her had known and adored every pore and follicle of her pubescent body. In her washed-out grey eyes, strangely spectacled, our poor romance was for a moment reflected, pondered upon, and dismissed like a dull party, like a rainy picnic to which only the dullest bores had come, like a humdrum exercise, like a bit of dry mud caking her childhood.

I just managed to jerk my knee out of the range of a sketchy tap – one of her acquired gestures.

She asked me not to be dense. The past was the past. I had

been a good father, she guessed – granting me *that*. Proceed, Dolly Schiller.

Well, did I know that he had known her mother? That he was practically an old friend? That he had visited with his uncle in Ramsdale? – oh, years ago – and spoken at Mother's club, and had tugged and pulled her, Dolly, by her bare arm on to his lap in front of everybody, and kissed her face, she was ten and furious with him? Did I know he had seen me and her at the inn where he was writing the very play she was to rehearse in Beardsley, two years later? Did I know – it had been horrid of her to side-track me into believing that Clare was an old female, maybe a relative of his or a sometime lifemate – and oh, what a close shave it had been when the Wace *Journal* carried his picture.

The *Briceland Gazette* had not. Yes, very amusing.

Yes, she said, this world was just one gag after another, if somebody wrote up her life nobody would ever believe it.

At this point, there came brisk homey sounds from the kitchen into which Dick and Bill had lumbered in quest of beer. Through the doorway they noticed the visitor, and Dick entered the parlour.

'Dick, this is my Dad!' cried Dolly in a resounding violent voice that struck me as totally strange, and new, and cheerful, and old, and sad, because the young fellow, veteran of a remote war, was hard of hearing.

Arctic blue eyes, black hair, ruddy cheeks, unshaven chin. We shook hands. Discreet Bill, who evidently took pride in working wonders with one hand, brought in the beer cans he had opened. Wanted to withdraw. The exquisite courtesy of simple folks. Was made to stay. A beer ad. In point of fact, I preferred it that way, and so did the Schillers. I switched to the jittery rocker. Avidly munching, Dolly plied me with marshmallows and potato chips. The men looked at her fragile, *frileux*, diminutive, old-world, youngish but sickly, father in velvet coat and beige vest, maybe a viscount.

They were under the impression I had come to stay, and Dick with a great wrinkling of brows that denoted difficult thought, suggested Dolly and he might sleep in the kitchen on a spare mattress. I waved a light hand and told Dolly who transmitted it by means of a special shout to Dick that I had merely dropped in on my way to Readsburg where I was to be entertained by some friends and admirers. It was then noticed that one of the few thumbs remaining to Bill was bleeding (not such a wonder-worker after all). How womanish and somehow never seen that way before was the shadowy division between her pale breasts when she bent down over the man's hand! She took him for repairs to the kitchen. For a few minutes, three or four little eternities which positively welled with artificial warmth, Dick and I remained alone. He sat on a hard chair rubbing his fore-limbs and frowning. I had an idle urge to squeeze out the blackheads on the wings of his perspiring nose with my long agate claws. He had nice sad eyes with beautiful lashes, and very white teeth. His Adam's apple was large and hairy. Why don't they shave better, those young brawny chaps? He and his Dolly had had unrestrained intercourse on that couch there, at least a hundred and eighty times, probably much more; and before that – how long had she known him? No grudge. Funny – no grudge at all, nothing except grief and nausea. He was now rubbing his nose. I was sure that when finally he would open his mouth, he would say (slightly shaking his head): 'Aw, she's a swell kid, Mr Haze. She sure is. And she's going to make a swell mother.' He opened his mouth – and took a sip of beer. This gave him countenance – and he went on sipping till he frothed at the mouth. He was a lamb. He had cupped her Florentine breasts. His fingernails were black and broken, but the phalanges, the whole carpus, the strong shapely wrist were far, far finer than mine: I have hurt too much too many bodies with my twisted poor hands to be proud of them. French epithets, a Dorset yokel's knuckles, an Austrian tailor's flat finger-tips – that's Humbert Humbert.

Good. If he was silent I could be silent too. Indeed, I could very well do with a little rest in this subdued, frightened-to-death rocking chair, before I drove to wherever the beast's lair was – and then pulled the pistol's foreskin back, and then enjoyed the orgasm of the crushed trigger: I was always a good little follower of the Viennese medicine man. But presently I became sorry for poor Dick whom, in some hypnotoid way, I was horribly preventing from making the only remark he could think up ('She's a swell kid . . .').

'And so,' I said, 'you are going to Canada?'

In the kitchen, Dolly was laughing at something Bill had said or done.

'And so,' I shouted, 'you are going to Canada? Not Canada' – I re-shouted – 'I mean Alaska, of course.'

He nursed his glass and, nodding sagely, replied: 'Well, he cut it on a jagger, I guess. Lost his right arm in Italy.'

Lovely mauve almond trees in bloom. A blown-off surrealistic arm hanging up there in the pointillistic mauve. A flowergirl tattoo on the hand. Dolly and band-aided Bill reappeared. It occurred to me that her ambiguous, brown and pale beauty excited the cripple. Dick, with a grin of relief stood up. He guessed Bill and he would be going back to fix those wires. He guessed Mr Haze and Dolly had loads of things to say to each other. He guessed he would be seeing me before I left. Why do those people guess so much and shave so little, and are so disdainful of hearing aids?

'Sit down,' she said, audibly striking her flanks with her palms. I relapsed into the black rocker.

'So you betrayed me? Where did you go? Where is he now?'

She took from the mantelpiece a concave glossy snapshot. Old woman in white, stout, beaming, bowlegged, very short dress; old man in his shirtsleeves, drooping moustache, watch chain. Her in-laws. Living with Dick's brother's family in Juneau.

'Sure you don't want to smoke?'

She was smoking herself. First time I saw her doing it. *Streng verboten* under Humbert the Terrible. Gracefully, in a blue mist, Charlotte Haze rose from her grave. I would find him through Uncle Ivory if she refused.

'Betrayed you? No.' She directed the dart of her cigarette, index rapidly tapping upon it, toward the hearth exactly as her mother used to do, and then, like her mother, oh my God, with her fingernail scratched and removed a fragment of cigarette paper from her underlip. No. She had not betrayed me. I was among friends. Edusa had warned her that Cue liked little girls, had been almost jailed once, in fact (nice fact), and he knew she knew. Yes. . . . Elbow in palm, puff, smile, exhaled smoke, darting gesture. Waxing reminiscent. He saw – smiling – through everything and everybody, because he was not like me and her but a genius. A great guy. Full of fun. Had rocked with laughter when she confessed about me and her, and said he had thought so. It was quite safe, under the circumstances, to tell him. . . .

Well, Cue – they all called him Cue.

Her camp five years ago. Curious coincidence . . . took her to a dude ranch about a day's drive from Elephant (Elphinstone). Named? Oh, some silly name – Duk Duk Ranch – *you* know just plain silly – but it did not matter now, anyway, because the place had vanished and disintegrated. Really, she meant, I could not imagine how utterly lush that ranch was, she meant it had everything but everything, even an indoor waterfall. Did I remember the red-haired guy we ('we' was good) had once had some tennis with? Well, the place really belonged to Red's brother, but he had turned it over to Cue for the summer. When Cue and she came, the others had them actually go through a coronation ceremony and then – a terrific ducking, as when you cross the Equator. *You* know.

Her eyes rolled in synthetic resignation.

'Go on, please.'

Well. The idea was he would take her in September to Hollywood and arrange a tryout for her, a bit part in the tennis-match scene of a movie picture based on a play of his – *Golden Guts* – and perhaps even have her double one of its sensational starlets on the Klieg-struck tennis court. Alas, it never came to that.

'Where is the hog now?'

He was not a hog. He was a great guy in many respects. But it was all drink and drugs. And, of course, he was a complete freak in sex matters, and his friends were his slaves. I just could not imagine (I, Humbert could not imagine!) what they all did at Duk Duk Ranch. She refused to take part because she loved him, and he threw her out.

'What things?'

'Oh, weird, filthy, fancy things. I mean, he had two girls and two boys, and three or four men, and the idea was for all of us to tangle in the nude while an old woman took movie pictures.' (Sade's Justine was twelve at the start.)

'What things exactly?'

'Oh, things. . . . Oh, I – really I' – she uttered the 'I' as a subdued cry while she listened to the source of the ache, and for lack of words spread the five fingers of her angularly up-and-down-moving hand. No, she gave it up, she refused to go into particulars with that baby inside her.

That made sense.

'It is of no importance now,' she said pounding a grey cushion with her fist and then lying back, belly up, on the divan. 'Crazy things, filthy things. I said no, I'm just not going to [she used, in all insouciance really, a disgusting slang term which, in a literal French translation, would be *souffler*] your beastly boys, because I want only you. Well, he kicked me out.'

There was not much else to tell. That winter 1949, Fay and she had found jobs. For almost two years she had – oh, just drifted, oh, doing some restaurant work in small places, and then she had met Dick. No, she did not know where the other was. In New York, she guessed. Of course, he was so famous she would have found him at once if she had wanted. Fay had tried to get back to the Ranch – and it just was not there any more – it had burned to the ground, *nothing* remained, just a charred heap of rubbish. It was so *strange,* so *strange*.

She closed her eyes and opened her mouth, leaning back on the cushion, one felted foot on the floor. The wooden floor slanted, a little steel ball would have rolled into the kitchen. I knew all I wanted to know. I had no intention of torturing my darling. Somewhere beyond Bill's shack an afterwork radio had begun singing of folly and fate, and there she was with her ruined looks and her adult, rope-veined narrow hands and her goose-flesh white arms, and her shallow ears, and her unkempt armpits, there she was (my Lolita!), hopelessly worn at seventeen, with that baby, dreaming already in her of becoming a big shot and retiring around 2020 A.D. – and I looked and looked at her, and knew as clearly as I know I am to die, that I loved her more than anything I had ever seen or imagined on earth, or hoped for anywhere else. She was only the faint violet whiff and dead leaf echo of the nymphet I had rolled myself upon with such cries in the past; an echo on the brink of a russet ravine, with a far wood under a white sky, and brown leaves choking the brook, and one last cricket in the crisp weeds . . . but thank God it was not that echo alone that I worshipped. What I used to pamper among the tangled vines of my heart, *mon grand pêché radieux*, had dwindled to its essence: sterile and selfish vice, all *that* I cancelled and cursed. You may jeer at me, and threaten to clear the court, but until I am gagged and half-throttled, I will shout my poor truth. I insist the world know how much I loved my Lolita, *this* Lolita, pale and polluted, and big with another's child, but still grey-eyed, still sooty-lashed, still aburn and almond. still Carmencita, still mine; *Changeons de vi, ma Carmen, allons vivre quelque part où nous ne serons jamais séparés*; Ohio? The wilds of Massachusetts? No matter, even if those eyes of hers would fade to myopic fish, and her nipples swell and crack, and her lovely young velvety delicate delta be tainted and torn – even then I would go mad with tenderness at the mere sight of your dear wan face, at the mere sound of your raucous young voice, my Lolita.

'Lolita,' I said, 'this may be neither here nor there but I have to say it. Life is very short. From here to that old car you know so well there is a stretch of twenty, twenty-five paces. It is a very short walk. Make those twenty-five steps. Now. Right now. Come just as you are. And we shall live happily ever after.'

Carmen, voulez-vous venir avec moi?

'You mean,' she said, opening her eyes and raising herself slightly, the snake that may strike, 'you mean you will give us [us] that money only if I go with you to a motel. Is *that* what you mean?'

'No,' I said, 'you got it all wrong. I want you to leave your incidental Dick, and this awful hole, and come to live with me, and die with me, and everything with me' (words to that effect).

'You're crazy,' she said, her features working.

'Think it over, Lolita. There are no strings attached. Except, perhaps – well, no matter.' (A reprieve, I wanted to say but did not.) 'Anyway, if you refuse you will still get your . . . *trousseau*.'

'No kidding?' asked Dolly.

I handed her an envelope with four hundred dollars in cash and a cheque for three thousand six hundred more.

Gingerly, uncertainly, she received *mon petit cadeau*; and then her forehead became a beautiful pink. 'You mean,' she said, with agonized emphasis, 'you are giving us *four thousand bucks*?' I covered my face with my hand and broke into the hottest tears I had ever shed. I felt them winding through my fingers and down my chin, and burning me, and my nose got clogged, and I could not stop, and then she touched my wrist.

'I'll die if you touch me,' I said. 'You are sure you are not coming with me? Is there no hope of your coming? Tell me only this.'

'No,' she said. 'No, honey, no.'

She had never called me honey before.

'No,' she said, 'it is quite out of the question. I would sooner go back to Cue. I mean—'

She groped for words. I supplied them mentally ('*He* broke my heart. *You* merely broke my life').

'I think,' she went on – 'oops' – the envelope skidded to the floor – she picked it up – 'I think it's oh utterly *grand* of you to give us all that dough. It settles everything, we can start next week. Stop crying, please. You should understand. Let me get you some more beer. Oh, don't cry, I'm so sorry I cheated so much, but that's the way things are.'

I wiped my face and my fingers. She smiled at the *cadeau*. She exulted. She wanted to call Dick. I said I would have to leave in a moment, did not want to see him at all, at all. We tried to think of some subject of conversation. For some reason, I kept seeing – it trembled and silkily glowed on my damp retina – a radiant child of twelve, sitting on a threshold, 'pinging' pebbles at an empty can. I almost said – trying to find some casual remark – 'I wonder sometimes what has become of the little McCoo girl, did she ever get better?' – but stopped in time lest she rejoin: 'I wonder sometimes what has become of the little Haze girl. . . .' Finally, I reverted to money matters. That sum, I said, represented more or less the net rent from her mother's house; she said: 'Had it not been sold years ago?' No (I admit I *had* told her this in order to sever all connections with R.); a lawyer would send a full account of the financial situation later; it was rosy; some of the small securities her mother had owned had gone up and up. Yes, I was quite sure I had to go. I had to go, and find him, and destroy him.

Since I would not have survived the touch of her lips, I kept retreating in a mincing dance, at every step she and her belly made toward me.

She and the dog saw me off. I was surprised (this a rhetorical figure, I was not) that the sight of the old car in which she had ridden as a child and a nymphet left her so very indifferent. All she remarked was it was getting sort of purplish about the gills. I said it was hers, I could go by bus. She said don't be silly, they would fly to Jupiter and buy a car there. I said I would buy this one from her for five hundred dollars.

'At this rate we'll be millionnaires next,' she said to the ecstatic dog.

Carmencita, lui demandais-je. . . . 'One last word,' I said in my horrible careful English, 'are you quite, quite sure that – well, not tomorrow, of course, and not after tomorrow, but – well – some day, any day, you will not come to live with me? I will create a brand new God and thank him with piercing cries, if you give me that microscopic hope' (to that effect).

'No,' she said smiling, 'no.'

'It would have made all the difference,' said Humbert Humbert.

Then I pulled out my automatic – I mean, this is the kind of fool thing a reader might suppose I did. It never even occurred to me to do it.

'Good by-aye!' she chanted, my American sweet immortal dead love; for she is dead and immortal if you are reading this. I mean, such is the formal agreement with the so-called authorities.

Then, as I drove away, I heard her shout in a vibrant voice to her Dick; and the dog started to lope alongside my car like a fat dolphin, but he was too heavy and old, and very soon gave up.

And presently I was driving through the drizzle of the dying day, with the windshield wipers in full action but unable to cope with my tears.

30

Leaving as I did Coalmont around four in the afternoon (by Route X – I do not remember the number), I might have made Ramsdale by dawn had not a short-cut tempted me. I had to get on to Highway Y. My map showed quite blandly that just beyond Woodbine, which I reached at nightfall, I could leave paved X and reach paved Y by means of a transverse dirt road. It was only some forty miles long according to my map. Otherwise I would have to follow X for another hundred miles and then use leisurely looping Z to get to Y and my destination. However, the short cut in question got worse and worse, bumpier and bumpier, muddier and muddier, and when I attempted to turn back after some ten miles of purblind, tortuous and tortoise-slow progress, my old and weak Melmoth got stuck in deep clay. All was dark and muggy, and hopeless. My headlights hung over a broad ditch full of water. The surrounding country, if any, was a black wilderness. I sought to extricate myself but my rear wheels only whined in slosh and anguish. Cursing my plight, I took off my fancy clothes, changed into slacks, pulled on the bullet-riddled sweater, and waded four miles back to a roadside farm. It started to rain on the way but I had not the strength to go back for a mackintosh. Such incidents have convinced me that my heart is basically sound despite recent diagnoses. Around midnight, a wrecker dragged my car out. I navigated back to Highway X and travelled on. Utter weariness overtook me an hour later, in an anonymous little town. I pulled up at the curb and in darkness drank deep from a friendly flask.

The rain had been cancelled miles before. It was a black warm night, somewhere in Appalachia. Now and then cars passed me, red tail-lights receding, white headlights advancing, but the town was dead. Nobody strolled and laughed on the sidewalks as relaxing burghers would in sweet, mellow, rotting Europe. I was alone to enjoy the innocent night and my terrible thoughts. A wire receptacle on the curb was very particular about acceptable contents: Sweepings. Paper. No Garbage. Sherry-red letters of light marked a Camera Shop. A large thermometer with the name of a laxative quietly dwelt on the front of a drugstore. Rubinov's Jewellery Company had a display of artificial diamonds reflected in a red mirror. A lighted green clock swam in the linenish depths of Jiffy Jeff Laundry. On the other side of the street a garage said in its sleep – genuflexion lubricity; and corrected itself to Gulflex Lubrication. An aeroplane, also gemmed by Rubinov, passed, droning, in the velvet heavens. How many small dead-of-night towns I had seen! This was not yet the last.

Let me dally a little, he is as good as destroyed. Some way further across the street, neon lights flickered twice slower than my heart: the outline of a restaurant sign, a large coffee-pot, kept bursting, every full second or so, into emerald life, and every time it went out, pink letters saying Fine Foods relayed it, but the pot could still be made out as a latent shadow teasing the eye before its next emerald resurrection. We made shadowgraphs. This furtive burg was not far from The Enchanted Hunters. I was weeping again, drunk on the impossible past.

31

At this solitary stop for refreshments between Coalmont and Ramsdale (between innocent Dolly Schiller and jovial Uncle Ivor), I reviewed my case. With the utmost simplicity and clarity I now saw myself and my love. Previous attempts seemed out of focus in comparison. A couple of years before, under the guidance of an intelligent French-speaking confessor, to whom, in a moment of metaphysical curiosity, I had turned over a Protestant's drab atheism for an old-fashioned popish cure, I had hoped to deduce from my sense of sin the existence of a Supreme Being. On those frosty mornings in rime-laced Quebec, the good priest worked on me with the finest tenderness and understanding. I am infinitely obliged to him and the great Institution he represented. Alas, I was unable to transcend the simple human fact that whatever spiritual solace I might find, whatever lithophanic eternities might be provided for me, nothing could make my Lolita forget the foul lust I had inflicted upon her. Unless it can be proved to me – to me as I am now, today, with my heart and my beard, and my putrefaction – that in the infinite run it does not matter a jot that a North American girl-child named Dolores Haze had been deprived of her childhood by a maniac, unless this can be proven (and if it can, then life is a joke), I see nothing for the treatment of my misery but the melancholy and very local palliative of articulate art. To quote an old poet:

> The moral sense in mortals is the duty
> We have to pay on mortal sense of beauty.

32

There was the day, during our first trip – our first circle of paradise – when in order to enjoy my phantasms in peace I firmly decided to ignore what I could not help perceiving, the fact that I was to her not a boy friend, not a glamour man, not a pal, not even a person at all, but just two eyes and a foot of engorged brawn – to mention only mentionable matters. There was the day when having withdrawn the functional promise I had made her on the eve (whatever she had set her funny little heart on – a roller rink with some special plastic floor or a movie matinee to which she wanted to go alone), I happened to glimpse from the bathroom, through a chance combination of mirror aslant and door ajar, a look on her face . . . that look I cannot exactly describe . . . an expression of helplessness so perfect that it seemed to grade into one of rather comfortable inanity just because this was the very limit of injustice and frustration – and every limit presupposes something beyond it – hence the neutral illumination. And when you bear in mind that these were the raised eyebrows and parted lips of a child, you may better appreciate what depths of calculated carnality, what reflected despair, restrained me from falling at her dear feet and dissolving in human tears, and sacrificing my jealousy to whatever pleasure Lolita might hope to derive from mixing with dirty and dangerous children in an outside world that was real to her.

And I have still other smothered memories, now unfolding themselves into limbless monsters of pain. Once, in a sunset-ending street of Beardsley, she turned to little Eva Rosen (I was taking both nymphets to a concert and walking behind them so close as almost to touch them with my person), she turned to Eva, and so very serenely and seriously, in answer to something the other had said about its being better to die than hear Milton Pinski, some local schoolboy she knew, talk about music, my Lolita remarked:

'You know, what's so dreadful about dying is that you are completely on your own'; and it struck me, as my automaton knees went up and down, that I simply did not know a thing about my darling's mind and that quite possibly, behind the awful juvenile clichés, there was in her a garden and a twilight, and a palace gate – dim and adorable regions which happened to be lucidly and absolutely forbidden to me, in my polluted rags and miserable convulsions; for I often noticed that living as we did, she and I, in a world of total evil, we would become strangely embarrassed whenever I tried to discuss something she and an older friend, she and a parent, she and a real healthy sweetheart, I and Annabel, Lolita and a sublime, purified, analysed, defied Harold Haze, might have discussed – an abstract idea, a painting, stippled Hopkins or shorn Baudelaire, God or Shakespeare, anything of a genuine kind. Goodwill! She would mail her vulnerability in trite brashness and boredom, whereas I, using for my desperately detached comments an artificial tone of voice that set my own last teeth on edge, provoked my audience to such outbursts of rudeness as made any further conversation impossible, oh my poor, bruised child.

I loved you. I was a pentapod monster, but I loved you. I was despicable and brutal, and turpid, and everything, *mais je t'aimais, je t'aimais!* And there were times when I knew how you felt, and it was hell to know it, my little one. Lolita girl, brave Dolly Schiller.

I recall certain moments, let us call them icebergs in paradise, when after having had my fill of her – after fabulous, insane exertions that left me limp and azure-barred – I would gather her in my arms with, at last, a mute moan of human tenderness (her skin glistening in the neon light coming from the paved court through the slits in the blind, her soot-black lashes matted, her grave grey eyes more vacant than ever – for all the world a litle patient still in the confusion of a drug after a major operation) – and the tenderness would deepen to shame and despair, and I would lull and rock my lone light Lolita in my marble arms, and moan in her warm hair, and caress her at random and mutely ask her blessing, and at the peak of this human agonized selfless tenderness (with my soul actually hanging around her naked body and ready to repent), all at once, ironically, horribly, lust would swell again – and 'oh, *no*', Lolita would say with a sigh to heaven, and the next moment the tenderness and the azure – all would be shattered.

Mid-twentieth century ideas concerning child-parent relationship have been considerably tainted by the scholastic rigmarole and standardized symbols of the psycho-analytic racket, but I hope I am addressing myself to unbiased readers. Once when Avis's father had honked outside to signal papa had come to take his pet home, I felt obliged to invite him into the parlour, and he sat down for a minute, and while we conversed, Avis, a heavy, unattractive, affectionate child, drew up to him and eventually perched plumply on his knee. Now, I do not remember if I have mentioned that Lolita always had an absolutely enchanting smile for strangers, a tender furry slitting of the eyes, a dreamy sweet radiance of all her features which did not mean a thing of course but was so beautiful, so endearing that one found it hard to reduce such sweetness to but a magic gene automatically lighting up her face in atavistic token of some ancient rite of welcome – hospitable prostitution, the coarse reader may say. Well, there she stood while Mr Byrd twirled his hat and talked, and – yes, look how stupid of me, I have left out the main characteristic of the famous Lolita smile, namely: while the tender, nectared, dimpled brightness played, it was never directed at the stranger in the room but hung in its own remote flowered void, so to speak, or wandered with myopic softness over chance objects – and this is what was happening now: while fat Avis sidled up to her papa, Lolita gently beamed at a fruit knife that she fingered on the edge of the table, whereon she leaned, many miles away from me. Suddenly, as Avis clung to her father's neck and ear while, with a casual arm, the man enveloped his lumpy and large offspring, I saw Lolita's smile lose all its light and become a frozen little shadow of itself, and the fruit knife slipped off the table and struck her with its silver handle a freak blow on the ankle which made her gasp, and crouch head forward, and then, jumping on one leg, her face awful with the preparatory grimace which children hold till the tears gush, she was gone – to be followed at once and consoled in the kitchen by Avis who had such a wonderful fat pink dad and a small chubby brother, and a brand-new baby sister, and a home, and two grinning dogs, and Lolita had nothing. And I have a neat pendant to that little scene – also in a Beardsley setting. Lolita, who had been reading near the fire, stretched herself, and then inquired, her elbow up, with a grunt: 'Where is she buried anyway?' 'Who?' 'Oh, you know, my murdered mummy.' 'And *you* know where her grave is,' I said controlling myself, whereupon I named the cemetery – just outside Ramsdale, between the railway tracks and Lakeview Hill. 'Moreover,' I added, 'the tragedy of such an accident is somewhat cheapened by the epithet you saw fit to apply to it. If you really wish to triumph in your mind over the idea of death—' 'Ray', said Lo for hurray, and languidly left the room, and for a long while I stared with smarting eyes into the fire. Then I picked up her book. It was some trash for young people. There was a gloomy girl Marion, and there was her stepmother who turned out to be, against all expectations, a young, gay, understanding redhead who explained to Marion that Marion's dead mother had really been a heroic woman since she had deliberately dissimulated her great love for Marion because she was dying, and did not want her child to miss her. I did not rush up to her room with cries. I always preferred the mental hygiene of non-interference. Now, squirming and pleading with my own memory, I recall that on this and similar occasions, it was always my habit and method to ignore Lolita's states of mind while comforting my own base self. When my mother, in a livid wet dress, under the tumbling mist (so I vividly imagined her), had run panting up that ridge above Moulinet to be felled there by a thunderbolt, I was but an infant, and in retrospect no yearnings of the accepted kind could I ever graft upon any moment of my youth, no matter how savagely psychotherapists heckled me in my later periods of depression. But I admit that a man of my power of imagination cannot plead personal ignorance of universal emotions. I may also have relied too much on the abnormally chill relations between Charlotte and her daughter. But the awful point of the whole argument is this. It had become gradually clear to my conventional Lolita during our singular and bestial cohabitation that even the most miserable of family lives was better than the parody of incest, which, in the long run, was the best I could offer the waif.

33

Ramsdale revisited. I approached it from the side of the lake. The sunny noon was all eyes. As I rode by in my mud-flecked car, I could distinguish scintillas of diamond water between the far pines. I turned into the cemetery and walked among the long and short stone monuments. *Bonzhur,* Charlotte. On some of the graves there were pale, transparent little national flags slumped in the windless air under the evergreens. Gee, Ed, that was bad luck – referring to G. Edward Grammar, a thirty-five-year-old New York office manager who had just been arraigned on a charge of murdering his thirty-three-year-old wife, Dorothy. Bidding for the perfect crime, Ed had bludgeoned his wife and put her into a car. The case came to light when two county policemen on patrol saw Mrs Grammar's new big blue Chrysler, an anniversary present from her husband, speeding crazily down a hill, just inside their jurisdiction (God bless our good cops!). The car sideswiped a pole, ran up an embankment covered with beard grass, wild strawberry and cinquefoil, and overturned. The wheels were still gently spinning in the mellow sunlight when the officers removed Mrs G's body. It appeared to be a routine highway accident at first. Alas, the woman's battered body did not match up with only minor damage suffered by the car. I did better.

I rolled on. It was funny to see again the slender white church and the enormous elms. Forgetting that in an American suburban street a lone pedestrian is more conspicuous than a lone motorist, I left the car in the avenue to walk unobtrusively past 342 Lawn Street. Before the great bloodshed, I was entitled to a little relief, to a cathartic spasm of mental regurgitation. Closed were the white shutters of the Junk mansion, and somebody had attached a found black velvet hair ribbon to the white FOR SALE sign which was leaning toward the sidewalk. No dog barked. No gardener telephoned. No Miss Opposite sat on the vined porch – where to the lone pedestrian's annoyance two pony-tailed young woman in identical polka-dotted pinafores stopped doing whatever they were doing to stare at him: she was long dead, no doubt, these might be her twin nieces from Philadelphia.

Should I enter my old house? As in a Turgenev story, a torrent of Italian music came from an open window – that of the living room: what romantic soul was playing the piano where no piano had plunged and plashed on that bewitched Sunday with the sun on her beloved legs? All at once I noticed that from the lawn I had mown a golden-skinned, brown-haired nymphet of nine or ten, in white shorts, was looking at me with wild fascination in her large blue-black eyes. I said something pleasant to her, meaning no harm, an old-world compliment, what nice eyes you have, but she retreated in haste and the music stopped abruptly, and a violent-looking dark man, glistening with sweat, came out and glared at me. I was on the point of identifying myself when, with a pang of dream-embarrassment, I became aware of my mud-caked dungarees, my filthy and torn sweater, my bristly chin, my bum's bloodshot eyes. Without saying a word, I turned and plodded back the way I had come. An aster-like anaemic flower grew out of a remembered chink in the sidewalk. Quietly resurrected, Miss Opposite was being wheeled out by her nieces, on to her porch, as if it were a stage and I the star performer. Praying she would not call to me, I hurried to my car. What a steep little street. What a profound avenue. A red ticket showed between wiper and windshield; I carefully tore it into two, four, eight pieces.

Feeling I was losing my time, I drove energetically to the downtown hotel where I had arrived with a new bag more than five years before. I took a room, made two appointments by telephone, shaved, bathed, put on black clothes and went down for a drink in the bar. Nothing had changed. The bar-room was suffused with the same dim, impossible garnet-red light that in Europe years ago went with low haunts, but here meant a bit of atmosphere in a family hotel. I sat at the same little table where at the very start of my stay, immediately after becoming Charlotte's lodger, I had thought fit to celebrate the occasion by suavely sharing with her half a bottle of champagne, which had fatally conquered her poor brimming heart. As then, a moon-faced waiter was arranging with stellar care fifty sherries on a round tray for a wedding party. Murphy-Fantasia, this time. It was eight minutes to three. As I walked through the lobby, I had to skirt a group of ladies who with *mille grâces* were taking leave of each other after a luncheon party. With a harsh cry of recognition, one pounced upon me. She was a stout, short woman in pearl-grey, with a long, grey, slim plume to her small hat. It was Mrs Chatfield. She attacked me with a fake smile, all aglow with evil curiosity. (Had I done to Dolly, perhaps, what Frank Lasalle, a fifty-year-old mechanic, had done to eleven-year-old Sally Horner in 1948?) Very soon I had that avid glee well under control. She thought I was in California. How was—? With exquisite pleasure I informed her that my stepdaughter had just married a brilliant young mining engineer with a hush-hush job in the north-west. She said she disapproved of such early marriages, she would never let her Phyllis, who was now eighteen—

'Oh yes, of course,' I said quietly. 'I remember Phyllis. Phyllis and Camp Q. Yes, of course. By the way, did she ever tell you how Charlie Holmes debauched there his mother's little charges?'

Mrs Chatfield's already broken smile now disintegrated completely.

'For shame,' she cried, 'for shame, Mr Humbert! The poor boy has just been killed in Korea.'

I said didn't she think *'vient de'*, with the infinitive, expressed recent events so much more neatly than the English 'just', with the past? But I had to be trotting off, I said.

There were only two blocks to Windmuller's office. He greeted me with a very slow, very enveloping, strong, searching grip. He thought I was in California. Had I not lived at one time at Beardsley? His daughter had just entered Beardsley College. And how was—? I gave all necessary information about Mrs Schiller. We had a pleasant business conference. I walked out into the hot September sunshine a contented pauper.

Now that everything had been put out of the way, I could dedicate myself freely to the main object of my visit to Ramsdale. In the methodical manner on which I have always prided myself, I had been keeping Clare Quilty's face masked in my dark dungeon, where he was waiting for me to come with barber and priest: *'Réveillez-vous, Laqueue, il est temps de mourir!'* I have no time right now to discuss the mnemonics of physiognomization – I am on my way to his uncle and walking fast – but let me jot down this: I had preserved in the alcohol of a clouded memory the toad of a face. In the course of a few glimpses, I had noticed its slight resemblance to a cheery and rather repulsive wine dealer, a relative of mine in Switzerland. With his dumbbells and stinking tricot, and fat hairy arms, and bald patch, and pig-faced servant-concubine, he was on the whole a harmless old rascal. Too harmless, in fact, to be confused with my prey. In the state of mind I now found myself, I had lost contact with Trapp's image. It had become completely engulfed by the face of Clare Quilty – as represented, with artistic precision, by an easled photograph of him that stood on his uncle's desk.

In Beardsley, at the hands of charming Dr Molnar, I had

undergone a rather serious dental operation, retaining only a few upper and lower front teeth. The substitutes were dependent on a system of plates with an inconspicuous wire affair running along my upper gums. The whole arrangement was a masterpiece of comfort, and my canines were in perfect health. However, to garnish my secret purpose with a plausible pretext, I told Dr Quilty that, in hope of alleviating facial neuralgia, I had decided to have all my teeth removed. What would a complete set of dentures cost? How long would the process take, assuming we fixed our first appointment for some time in November? Where was his famous nephew now? Would it be possible to have them all out in one dramatic session?

A white-smocked, grey-haired man, with a crew cut and the big flat cheeks of a politician, Dr Quilty perched on the corner of his desk, one foot dreamily and seductively rocking as he launched on a glorious long-range plan. He would first provide me with provisional plates until the gums settled. Then he would make me a permanent set. He would like to have a look at that mouth of mine. He wore perforated pied shoes. He had not visited with the rascal since 1946, but supposed he could be found at his ancestral home, Grimm Road, not far from Parkington. It was a noble dream. His foot rocked, his gaze was inspired. It would cost me around six hundred. He suggested he take measurements right away, and make the first set before starting operations. My mouth was to him a splendid cave full of priceless treasures, but I denied him entrance.

'No,' I said. 'On second thoughts, I shall have it all done by Dr Molnar. His price is higher, but he is of course a much better dentist than you.'

I do not know if any of my readers will ever have a chance to say that. It is a delicious dream feeling. Clare's uncle remained sitting on the desk, still looking dreamy, but his foot had stopped push-rocking the cradle of rosy anticipation. On the other hand, his nurse, a skeleton thin, faded girl, with the tragic eyes of unsuccessful blondes, rushed after me so as to be able to slam the door in my wake.

Push the magazine into the butt. Press home until you hear or feel the magazine catch engage. Delightfully snug. Capacity: eight cartridges. Full Blued. Aching to be discharged.

34

A gas station attendant in Parkington explained to me very clearly how to get to Grimm Road. Wishing to be sure Quilty would be at home, I attempted to ring him up but learned that his private telephone had recently been disconnected. Did that mean he was gone? I started to drive to Grimm Road, twelve miles north of the town. By that time night had eliminated most of the landscape and as I followed the narrow winding highway, a series of short posts, ghostly white, with reflectors, borrowed my own lights to indicate this or that curve. I could make out a dark valley on one side of the road and wooded slopes on the other, and in front of me, like derelict snowflakes, moths drifted out of the blackness into my probing aura. At the twelfth mile, as foretold, a curiously hooded bridge sheathed me for a moment and, beyond it, a white-washed rock loomed on the right, and a few car lengths further, on the same side, I turned off the highway up gravelly Grimm Road. For a couple of minutes all was dank, dark, dense forest. Then, Pavor Manor, a wooden house with a turret, arose in a circular clearing. Its windows glowed yellow and red; its drive was cluttered with half a dozen cars. I stopped in the shelter of the trees and abolished my lights to ponder the next move quietly. He would be surrounded by his henchmen and whores. I could not help seeing the inside of that festive and ramshackle castle in terms of 'Troubled Teens', a story in one of her magazines, vague 'orgies', a sinister adult with penele cigar, drugs, bodyguards. At least, he was there. I would return in the torpid morning.

Gently I rolled back to town, in that old faithful car of mine which was serenely, almost cheerfully working for me. My Lolita! There was still a three-year-old bobby pin of hers in the depths of the glove compartment. There was still that stream of pale moths siphoned out of the night by my headlights. Dark barns still propped themselves up here and there by the roadside. People were still going to the movies. While searching for night lodgings, I passed a drive-in. In a selenian glow, truly mystical in its contrast with the moonless and massive night, on a gigantic screen slanting away among dark drowsy fields, a thin phantom raised a gun, both he and his arm reduced to tremulous dishwater by the oblique angle of that receding world – and the next moment a row of trees shut off the gesticulation.

35

I left Insomnia Lodge next morning around eight and spent some time in Parkington. Visions of bungling the execution kept obsessing me. Thinking that perhaps the cartridges in the automatic had gone stale during a week of inactivity, I removed them and inserted a fresh batch. Such a thorough oil bath did I give Chum that now I could not get rid of the stuff. I bandaged him up with a rag, like a maimed limb, and used another rag to wrap up a handful of spare bullets.

A thunderstorm accompanied me most of the way back to Grimm Road, but when I reached Pavor Manor, the sun was visible again, burning like a man, and the birds screamed in the drenched and steaming trees. The elaborate and decrepit house seemed to stand in a kind of daze, reflecting as it were my own state, for I could not help realizing, as my feet touched the springy and insecure ground, that I had overdone the alcoholic stimulation business.

A guardedly ironic silence answered my bell. The garage, however, was loaded with his car, a black convertible for the nonce. I tried the knocker. Re-nobody. With a petulant snarl, I pushed the front door – and, how nice, it swung open as in a medieval fairy tale. Having softly closed it behind me, I made my way across a spacious and very ugly hall; peered into an adjacent drawing room; noticed a number of used glasses growing out of the carpet; decided that master was still asleep in the master bedroom.

So I trudged upstairs. My right hand clutched muffled Chum in my pocket, my left patted the sticky banisters. Of the three bedrooms I inspected, one had obviously been slept in that night. There was a library full of flowers. There was a rather bare room with ample and deep mirrors and a polar bear skin on the slippery floor. There were still other rooms. A happy thought struck me. If and when master returned from his constitutional in the woods, or emerged from some secret lair, it might be wise for an unsteady gunman with a long job before him to prevent his playmate from locking himself up in a room. Consequently, for at least five minutes I went about – lucidly insane, crazily calm, an enchanted and very tight hunter – turning whatever keys in whatever locks there were and pocketing them with my free left hand. The house, being an old one, had more planned privacy than have modern glamour-boxes, where the bathroom, the only lockable locus, has to be used for the furtive needs of planned parenthood.

Speaking of bathrooms – I was about to visit a third one when master came out of it, leaving a brief waterfall behind him. The corner of a passage did not quite conceal me. Grey-faced, baggy-eyed, fluffily dishevelled in a scanty balding way, but still perfectly recognizable, he swept by me in a purple bathrobe, very like one I had. He either did not notice me, or else dismissed me as some familiar and innocuous hallucination – and, showing me his hairy calves, he proceeded, sleepwalker-wise, downstairs. I pocketed my last key and followed him into the entrance hall. He had half opened his mouth and the front door, to peer out through a sunny chink as one who thinks he has heard a half-hearted visitor ring and recede. Then, still ignoring the rain-coated phantasm that had stopped in midstairs, master walked into a cosy boudoir across the hall from the drawing room, through which – taking it easy, knowing he was safe – I now went away from him, and in a bar-adorned kitchen gingerly unwrapped dirty Chum, taking care not to leave any oil stains on the chrome – I think I got the wrong product, it was black and awfully messy. In my usual meticulous way, I transferred naked Chum to a clean recess about me and made for the little boudoir. My step, as I say, was springy – too springy perhaps for success. But my heart pounded with tiger joy, and I crunched a cocktail glass underfoot.

Master met me in the Oriental parlour.

'Now who are you?' he asked in a high hoarse voice, his hands thrust into his dressing-gown pockets, his eyes fixing a point to the north-east of my head. 'Are you by any chance Brewster?'

By now it was evident to everybody that he was in a fog and completely at my so-called mercy. I could enjoy myself.

'That's right,' I answered suavely. *'Je suis Monsieur Brustère.* Let us chat for a moment before we start.'

He looked pleased. His smudgy moustache twitched. I removed my raincoat. I was wearing a black suit, a black shirt, no tie. We sat down in two easy chairs.

'You know,' he said, scratching loudly his fleshy and gritty grey cheek and showing his small pearly teeth in a crooked grin, 'you don't *look* like Jack Brewster. I mean, the resemblance is not particularly striking. Somebody told me he had a brother with the same telephone company.'

To have him trapped, after those years of repentance and rage.

. . . To look at the black hairs on the back of his pudgy hands. . . . To wander with a hundred eyes over his purple silks and hirsute chest foreglimpsing the punctures, and mess, and music of pain. . . . To know that this semi-animated, subhuman trickster who had sodomized my darling – oh, my darling, this was intolerable bliss!

'No, I am afraid I am neither of the Brewsters.'

He cocked his head, looking more pleased than ever.

'Guess again, Punch.'

'Ah,' said Punch, 'so you have not come to bother me about those long-distance calls?'

'You do make them once in a while, don't you?'

'Excuse me?'

I said I had said I thought he had said he had never—

'People,' he said, 'people in general, I'm not accusing you, Brewster, but you know it's absurd the way people invade this damned house without even knocking. They use the *vaterre*, they use the kitchen, they use the telephone. Phil calls Philadelphia. Pat calls Patagonia. I refuse to pay. You have a funny accent, Captain.'

'Quilty,' I said, 'do you recall a little girl called Dolores Haze, Dolly Haze? Dolly called Dolores, Colo?'

'Sure, she may have made those calls, sure. Any place. Paradise, Wash., Hell Canyon. Who cares?'

'I do, Quilty. You see, I am her father.'

'Nonsense,' he said. 'You are not. You are some foreign literary agent. A Frenchman once translated my *Proud Flesh* as *La Fierté de la Chair*. Absurd.'

'She was my child, Quilty.'

In the state he was in he could not really be taken aback by anything, but his blustering manner was not quite convincing. A sort of wary inkling kindled his eyes into a semblance of life. They were immediately dulled again.

'I'm very fond of children myself,' he said, 'and fathers are among my best friends.'

He turned his head away, looking for something. He beat his pockets. He attempted to rise from his seat.

'Down!' I said – apparently much louder than I intended.

'You need not roar at me,' he complained in his strange feminine manner. 'I just wanted a smoke. I'm dying for a smoke.'

'You're dying anyway.'

'Oh, shucks,' he said. 'You begin to bore me. What do you

want? Are you French, mister? Woolly-woo-boo-are? Let's go to the barroomette and have a stiff—'

He saw the little dark weapon lying in my palm as if I were offering it to him.

'Say!' he drawled (now imitating the underworld numbskull of movies), 'that's a swell little gun you've got there. What d'you want for her?'

I slapped down his outstretched hand and he managed to knock over a box on a low table near him. It ejected a handful of cigarettes.

'Here they are,' he said cheerfully. 'You recall Kipling: *une femme est une femme, mais un Caporal est une cigarette*? Now we need matches.'

'Quilty,' I said. 'I want you to concentrate. You are going to die in a moment. The hereafter for all we know may be an eternal state of excruciating insanity. You smoked your last cigarette yesterday. Concentrate. Try to understand what is happening to you.'

He kept taking the Drome cigarette apart and munching bits of it.

'I am willing to try,' he said. 'You are either Australian, or a German refugee. Must you talk to me? This is a Gentile's house, you know. Maybe, you'd better run along. And do stop demonstrating that gun. I've an old Stern-Luger in the music room.'

I pointed Chum at his slippered foot and crushed the trigger. It clicked. He looked at his foot, at the pistol, again at his foot. I made another awful effort, and, with a ridiculously feeble and juvenile sound, it went off. The bullet entered the thick pink rug, and I had the paralysing impression that it had merely trickled in and might come out again.

'See what I mean?' said Quilty. 'You should be a little more careful. Give me that thing for Christ's sake.'

He reached for it. I pushed him back into the chair. The rich joy was waning. It was high time I destroyed him, but he must understand why he was being destroyed. His condition infected me, the weapon felt limp and clumsy in my hand.

'Concentrate,' I said, 'on the thought of Dolly Haze whom you kidnapped—'

'I did not!' he cried. 'You're all wet. I saved her from a beastly pervert. Show me your badge instead of shooting at my foot, you ape, you. Where is that badge? I'm not responsible for the rapes of others. Absurd! That joy ride, I grant you, was a silly stunt but you got her back, didn't you? Come, let's have a drink.'

I asked him whether he wanted to be executed sitting or standing.

'Ah, let me think,' he said. 'It is not an easy question. Incidentally – I made a mistake. Which I sincerely regret. You see, I had no fun with your Dolly. I am practically impotent, to tell the melancholy truth. And I gave her a splendid vacation. She met some remarkable people. Do you happen to know—'

And with a tremendous lurch he fell all over me, sending the pistol hurtling under a chest of drawers. Fortunately he was more impetuous than vigorous, and I had little difficulty in shoving him back into his chair.

He puffed a little and folded his arms on his chest.

'Now you've done it,' he said. '*Vous voilà dans de beaux draps, mon vieux.*'

His French was improving.

I looked around. Perhaps, if – perhaps I could – on my hands and knees? Risk it?

'*Alors, que fait-on?*' he asked watching me closely.

I stopped. He did not move. I stooped lower.

'My dear sir,' he said, 'stop trifling with life and death. I am a playwright. I have written tragedies, comedies, fantasies. I have made private movies out of *Justine* and other eighteenth-century sexcapades. I'm the author of fifty-two successful scenarios. I know all the ropes. Let me handle this. There should be a poker somewhere, why don't I fetch it, and then we'll fish out your property.'

Fussily, busybodily, cunningly, he had risen again while he talked. I groped under the chest trying at the same time to keep an eye on him. All of a sudden I noticed that he had noticed that I did not seem to have noticed Chum protruding from beneath the other corner of the chest. We fell to wrestling again. We rolled all over the floor, in each other's arms, like two huge helpless children. He was naked and goatish under his robe, and I felt suffocated as he rolled over me. I rolled over him. We rolled over me. They rolled over him. We rolled over us.

In its published form, this book is being read, I assume, in the first years of 2000 AD (1935 plus eighty or ninety, live long, my love); and elderly readers will surely recall at this point the obligatory scene in the Westerns of their childhood. Our tussle, however, lacked the ox-stunning fisticuffs, the flying furniture.

He and I were two large dummies, stuffed with dirty cotton and rags. It was a silent, soft, formless tussle on the part of two literati, one of whom was utterly disorganized by a drug while the other was handicapped by a heart condition and too much gin. When at last I had possessed myself of my precious weapon, and the scenario writer had been reinstalled in his low chair, both of us were panting as the cowman and the sheepman never do after their battle.

I decided to inspect the pistol – our sweat might have spoiled something – and regain my wind before proceeding to the main item in the programme. To fill in the pause, I proposed he read his own sentence – in the poetical form I had given it. The term 'poetical justice' is one that may be most happily used in this respect. I handed him a neat typescript.

'Yes,' he said, 'splendid idea. Let me fetch my reading glasses' (he attempted to rise).

'No.'

'Just as you say. Shall I read out loud?'

'Yes.'

'Here goes. I see it's in verse.'

> Because you took advantage of a sinner
> because you took advantage
> because you took
> because you took advantage of my disadvantage . . .

'That's good, you know. That's damned good.'

> . . . when I stood Adam-naked
> before a federal law and all its stinging stars

'Oh, grand stuff!'

> . . . Because you took advantage of a sin
> when I was helpless moulting moist and tender
> hoping for the best
> dreaming of marriage in a mountain state
> aye of a litter of Lolitas . . .

'Didn't get that.'

> Because you took advantage of my inner
> essential innocence
> because you cheated me –

'A little repetitious, what? Where was I?'

Because you cheated me of my redemption
because you took
her at the age when lads
play with erector sets

'Getting smutty, eh?'

a little downy girl still wearing poppies
still eating popcorn in the coloured gloam
where tawny Indians took paid croppers
because you stole her
from her wax-browed and dignified protector
spitting into his heavy-lidded eye
ripping his flavid toga and at dawn
leaving the hog to roll upon his new discomfort
the awfulness of love and violets
remorse despair while you
took a dull doll to pieces
and threw its head away
because of all you did
because of all I did not
you have to die

'Well, sir, this is certainly a fine poem. Your best as far as I am concerned.'

He folded and handed it back to me.

I asked him if he had anything serious to say before dying. The automatic was again ready for use on the person. He looked at it and heaved a big sigh.

'Now look here, Mac,' he said. 'You are drunk and I am a sick man. Let us postpone the matter. I need quiet. I have to nurse my impotence. Friends are coming in the afternoon to take me to a game. This pistol-packing farce is becoming a frightful nuisance. We are men of the world, in everything – sex, free verse, markmanship. If you bear me a grudge, I am ready to make unusual amends. Even an old-fashioned *rencontre*, sword or pistol, in Rio or elsewhere – is not excluded. My memory and my eloquence are not at their best today but really, my dear Mr Humbert, you were not an ideal stepfather, and I did not force your little protégée to join me. It was she made me remove her to a happier home. This house is not as modern as that ranch we shared with dear friends. But it is roomy, cool in summer and winter, and in a word comfortable, so, since I intend retiring to England or Florence for ever, I suggest you move in.

It is yours, gratis. Under the condition you stop pointing at me that [he swore disgustingly] gun. By the way, I do not know if you care for the bizarre, but if you do, I can offer you, also gratis, as house pet, a rather exciting little freak, a young lady with three breasts, one a dandy, this is a rare and delightful marvel of nature. Now, *soyons raisonnables*. You will only wound me hideously and then rot in jail while I recuperate in a tropical setting. I promise you, Brewster, you will be happy here, with a magnificent cellar, and all the royalties from my next play – I have not much at the bank right now but I propose to borrow – you know, as the Bard said, with that cold in his head, to borrow and to borrow and to borrow. There are other advantages. We have here a most reliable and bribable charwoman, a Miss Vibrissa – curious name – who comes from the village twice a week, alas not today, she has daughters, granddaughters, a thing or two I know about the chief of police makes him my slave. I am a playwright. I have been called the American Maeterlinck. Maeterlinck-Schmetterling, says I. Come on! All this is very humiliating, and I am not sure I am doing the right thing. Never use herculanita with rum. Now drop that pistol like a good fellow. I knew your dear wife slightly. You may use my wardrobe. Oh, another thing – you are going to like this. I have an absolutely unique collection of erotica upstairs. Just to mention one item: the folio de-luxe *Bagration Island* by the explorer and psycho-analyst Melanie Weiss, a remarkable lady, a remarkable work – drop that gun – with photographs of eight hundred and something male organs she examined and measured in 1932 on Bagration, in the Barda Sea, very illuminating graphs, plotted with love under pleasant skies – drop that gun – and moreover I can arrange for you to attend executions, not everybody knows that the chair is painted yellow—'

Feu. This time I hit something hard. I hit the back of a black rocking chair, not unlike Dolly Schiller's – my bullet hit the inside surface of its back whereupon it immediately went into a rocking act, so fast and with such zest that anyone coming into the room might have been flabbergasted by the double miracle: that chair rocking in a panic all by itself, and the armchair, where my purple target had just been, now void of all live content. Wiggling his fingers in the air, with a rapid heave of his rump, he flashed into the music room and the next second we were tugging and gasping on both sides of the door which had a key I had overlooked. I won again, and with another abrupt movement Clare the Impredictable sat down before the piano and played several atrociously vigorous, fundamentally hysterical, plangent chords, his jowls quivering, his spread hands tensely plunging, and his nostrils emitting the soundtrack snorts which had been absent from our fight. Still singing those impossible sonorities, he made a futile attempt to open with his foot a kind of seaman's chest near the piano. My next bullet caught him somewhere in the side, and he rose from his chair higher and higher, like old, grey, mad Nijinski, like Old Faithful, like some old nightmare of mine, to a phenomenal altitude, or so it seemed, as he rent the air – still shaking with the rich black music – head thrown back in a howl, hand pressed to his brow, and with his other hand clutching his armpit as if stung by a hornet, down he came on his heels and, again a normal robed man, scurried out into the hall.

I see myself following him through the hall, with a kind of double, triple, kangaroo jump, remaining quite straight on straight legs while bouncing up twice in his wake, and then bouncing between him and the front door in a ballet-like stiff bounce, with the purpose of heading him off, since the door was not properly closed.

Suddenly dignified, and somewhat morose, he started to walk up the broad stairs, and, shifting my position, but not actually following him up the steps, I fired three or four times in quick succession, wounding him at every blaze; and every time I did it to him, that horrible thing to him, his face would twitch in an absurd clownish manner, as if he were exaggerating the pain; he slowed down, rolled his eyes half closing them and made a feminine 'ah!' and he shivered every time a bullet hit him as if I were tickling him, and every time I got him with those slow, clumsy, blind bullets of mine, he would say under his breath, with a phoney British accent – all the while dreadfully twitching, shivering, smirking, but withal talking in a curiously detached and even amiable manner: 'Ah, that hurts, sir, enough! Ah, that hurts atrociously, my dear fellow. I pray you, desist. Ah – very painful, very painful, indeed. . . . God! Hah! This is abominable, you should really not—' His voice trailed off as he reached the landing, but he steadily walked on despite all the lead I had lodged in his bloated body – and in distress, in dismay, I understood that far from killing him I was injecting spurts of energy into the poor fellow, as if the bullets had been capsules wherein a heady elixir danced.

I reloaded the thing with hands that were black and bloody – I had touched something he had anointed with his thick gore.

Then I rejoined him upstairs, the keys jangling in my pockets like gold.

He was trudging from room to room, bleeding majestically, trying to find an open window, shaking his head, and still trying to talk me out of murder. I took aim at his head, and he retired to the master bedroom with a burst of royal purple where his ear had been.

'Get out, get out of here,' he said coughing and spitting; and in a nightmare of wonder, I saw this blood-spattered but still buoyant person get into his bed and wrap himself up in the chaotic bedclothes. I hit him at very close range through the blankets, and then he lay back, and a big pink bubble with juvenile connotations formed on his lips, grew to the size of a toy balloon, and vanished.

I may have lost contact with reality for a second or two – oh, nothing of the I-just-blacked-out sort that your common criminal enacts; on the contrary, I want to stress the fact that I was responsible for every shed drop of his bubbleblood; but a kind of momentary shift occurred as if I were in the connubial bedroom, and Charlotte were sick in bed. Quilty was a very sick man. I held one of his slippers instead of the pistol – I was sitting on the pistol. Then I made myself a little more comfortable in the chair near the bed, and consulted my wrist watch. The crystal was gone but it ticked. The whole sad business had taken more than an hour. He was quiet at last. Far from feeling any relief, a burden even weightier than the one I had hoped to get rid of was with me, upon me, over me. I could not bring myself to touch him in order to make sure he was really dead. He looked it: a quarter of his face gone, and two flies beside themselves with a dawning sense of unbelievable luck. My hands were hardly in better condition than his. I washed up as best I could in the adjacent bathroom. Now I could leave. As I emerged on the landing, I was amazed to discover that a vivacious buzz I had just been dismissing as a mere singing in my ear was really a medley of voices and radio music coming from the downstairs drawing room.

I found there a number of people who apparently had just arrived and were cheerfully drinking Quilty's liquor. There was a fat man in an easy chair; and two dark-haired pale young beauties, sisters no doubt, big one and small one (almost a child), demurely sat side by side on a davenport. A florid-faced fellow with sapphire-blue eyes was in the act of bringing two glasses out of the bar-like kitchen, where two or three women were chatting and chinking ice. I stopped in the doorway and said: 'I have just killed Clare Quilty.' 'Good for you,' said the florid fellow as he offered one of the drinks to the elder girl. 'Somebody ought to have done it long ago,' remarked the fat man. 'What does he say, Tony?' asked a faded blonde from the bar. 'He says,' answered the florid fellow, 'he has killed Cue.' 'Well,' said another unidentified man rising in a corner where he had been crouching to inspect some records, 'I guess we all should do it to him some day.' 'Anyway,' said Tony, 'he'd better come down. We can't wait for him much longer if we want to go to that game.' 'Give this man a drink somebody,' said the fat person. 'Want a beer?' said a woman in slacks, showing it to me from afar.

Only the two girls on the davenport, both wearing black, the younger fingering a bright something about her white neck, only they said nothing, but just smiled on, so young, so lewd. As the music paused for a moment, there was a sudden noise on the stairs. Tony and I stepped out into the hall. Quilty of all people had managed to crawl out on to the landing, and there we could see him, flapping and heavy, and then subsiding, for ever this time, in a purple heap.

'Hurry up, Cue,' said Tony with a laugh. 'I believe, he's still—' He returned to the drawing room, music drowned the rest of the sentence.

This, I said to myself, was the end of the ingenious play staged for me by Quilty. With a heavy heart I left the house and walked through the spotted blaze of the sun to my car. Two other cars were parked on both sides of it, and I had some trouble squeezing out.

36

The rest is a little flattish and faded. Slowly I drove downhill, and presently found myself going at the same lazy pace in a direction opposite to Parkington. I had left my raincoat in the boudoir and Chum in the bathroom. No, it was not a house I would have liked to live in. I wondered idly if some surgeon of genius might not alter his own career, and perhaps the whole destiny of mankind, by reviving quilted Quilty, Clare Obscure.

Not that I cared; on the whole I wished to forget the whole mess – and when I did learn he was dead, the only satisfaction it gave me was the relief of knowing I need not mentally accompany for months a painful and disgusting convalescence interrupted by all kinds of unmentionable operations and relapses, and perhaps an actual visit from him, with trouble on my part to rationalize him as not being a ghost. Thomas had something. It is strange that the tactile sense, which is so infinitely less precious to men than sight, becomes at critical moments our main, if not only, handle to reality. I was all covered with Quilty – with the feel of that tumble before the bleeding.

The road now stretched across open country, and it occurred to me – not by way of protest, not as a symbol, or anything like that, but merely as a novel experience – that since I had disregarded all laws of humanity, I might as well disregard the rules of traffic. So I crossed to the left side of the highway and checked the feeling, and the feeling was good. It was a pleasant diaphragmal melting, with elements of diffused tactility, all this enhanced by the thought that nothing could be nearer to the elimination of basic physical laws than deliberately driving on the wrong side of the road. In a way, it was a very spiritual itch. Gently, dreamily, not exceeding twenty miles an hour, I drove on that queer mirror side. Traffic was light. Cars that now and then passed me on the side I had abandoned to them, honked at me brutally. Cars coming towards me wobbled, swerved, and cried out in fear. Presently I found myself approaching populated places. Passing through a red light was like a sip of forbidden Burgundy when I was a child. Meanwhile complications were arising. I was being followed and escorted. Then in front of me I saw two cars placing themselves in such a manner as to completely block my way. With a graceful movement I turned off the road, and after two or three big bounces, rode up a grassy slope, among surprised cows, and there I came to a gentle rocking stop. A kind of thoughtful Hegelian synthesis linking up two dead women.

I was soon to be taken out of the car (Hi, Melmoth, thanks a lot, old fellow) – and was, indeed, looking forward to surrender myself to many hands, without doing anything to co-operate, while they moved and carried me, relaxed, comfortable, surrendering myself lazily, like a patient, and deriving an eerie enjoyment from my limpness and the absolutely reliable support given me by the police and the ambulance people. And while I was waiting for them to run up to me on the high slope, I evoked a last mirage of wonder and hopelessness. One day, soon after her disappearance, an attack of abominable nausea forced me to pull up on the ghost of an old mountain road that now accompanied, now traversed a brand new highway, with its population of asters bathing in the detached warmth of a pale-blue afternoon in late summer. After coughing myself inside out, I rested a while on a boulder, and then, thinking the sweet air might do me good, walked a little way toward a low stone parapet on the precipice side of the highway. Small grasshoppers spurted out of the withered roadside weeds. A very light cloud was opening its arms and moving toward a slightly more substantial one belonging to another, more sluggish, heavenlogged system. As I approached the friendly abyss, I grew aware of a melodious unity of sounds rising like vapour from a small mining town that lay at my feet, in a fold of the valley. One could make out the geometry of the streets between blocks of red and grey roofs, and green puffs of trees, and a serpentine stream, and the rich, ore-like glitter of the city dump, and beyond the town, roads criss-crossing the crazy quilt of dark and pale fields, and behind it all, great timbered mountains. But even brighter than those quietly rejoicing colours – for there are colours and shades that seem to enjoy themselves in good company – both brighter and dreamier to the ear than they were to the eye, was that vapoury vibration of accumulated sounds that never ceased for a moment, as it rose to the lip of granite where I stood wiping my foul mouth. And soon I realized that all these sounds were of one nature, that no other sounds but these came from the streets of the transparent town, with the women at home and the men away. Reader! What I heard was but the melody of children at play, nothing but that, and so limpid was the air that within this vapour of blended voices, majestic and minute, remote and magically near, frank and divinely enigmatic – one could hear now and then, as if released, an almost articulate spurt of vivid laughter, or the crack of a bat, or the clatter of a toy wagon, but it was all really too far for the eye to distinguish any movement in the lightly etched streets. I stood listening to that musical vibration from my lofty slope, to those flashes of separate cries with a kind of demure murmur for background, and then I knew that the hopelessly poignant thing was not Lolita's absence from my side, but the absence of her voice from that concord.

This then is my story. I have re-read it. It has bits of marrow sticking to it, and blood, and beautiful bright-green flies. At this or that twist of it I feel my slippery self eluding me, gliding into deeper and darker waters than I care to probe. I have camouflaged what I could so as not to hurt people. And I have toyed with many pseudonyms for myself before I hit on a particularly apt one. There are in my notes 'Otto Otto' and 'Mesmer Mesmer' and 'Lambert Lambert', but for some reason I think my choice expresses the nastiness best.

When I started, fifty-six days ago, to write *Lolita*, first in the psychopathic ward for observation, and then in this well-heated, albeit tombal, seclusion, I thought I would use these notes *in toto* at my trial, to save not my head, of course, but my soul. In mid-composition, however, I realized that I could not parade living Lolita. I still may use parts of this memoir in hermetic sessions, but publication is to be deferred.

For reasons that may appear more obvious than they really are, I am opposed to capital punishment; this attitude will be, I trust, shared by the sentencing judge. Had I come before myself, I would have given Humbert at least thirty-five years for rape, and dismissed the rest of the charges. But even so, Dolly Schiller will probably survive me by many years. The following decision I make with all the legal impact and support of a signed testament: I wish this memoir to be published only when Lolita is no longer alive.

Thus, neither of us is alive when the reader opens this book. But while the blood still throbs through my writing hand, you are still as much part of blessed matter as I am, and I can still talk to you from here to Alaska. Be true to your Dick. Do not let other fellows touch you. Do not talk to strangers. I hope you will love your baby. I hope it will be a boy. That husband of yours, I hope, will always treat you well, because otherwise my spectre shall come at him, like black smoke, like a demented giant, and pull him apart nerve by nerve. And do not pity C. Q. One had to choose between him and H. H., and one wanted H. H. to exist at least a couple of months longer, so as to have him make you live in the minds of later generations. I am thinking of aurochs and angels, the secret of durable pigments, prophetic sonnets, the refuge of art. And this is the only immortality you and I may share, my Lolita.

THE GIFT

An oak is a tree. A rose is a flower. A deer is an animal. A sparrow is a bird. Russia is our fatherland. Death is inevitable.

P. SMIRNOVSKY,
A Textbook of Russian Grammar.

I

One cloudy but luminous day, towards four in the afternoon on April the first, 192- (a foreign critic once remarked that while many novels, most German ones for example, begin with a date, it is only Russian authors who, in keeping with the honesty peculiar to our literature, omit the final digit) a moving van, very long and very yellow, hitched to a tractor that was also yellow, with hypertrophied rear wheels and a shamelessly exposed anatomy, pulled up in front of Number Seven Tannenberg Street, in the west part of Berlin. The van's forehead bore a star-shaped ventilator. Running along its entire side was the name of the moving company in yard-high blue letters, each of which (including a square dot) was shaded laterally with black paint: a dishonest attempt to climb into the next dimension. On the sidewalk, before the house (in which I too shall dwell), stood two people who had obviously come out to meet their furniture (in *my* suitcase there are more manuscripts than shirts). The man, arrayed in a rough greenish-brown overcoat to which the wind imparted a ripple of life, was tall, beetle-browed and old, with the grey of his whiskers turning to russet in the area of the mouth, in which he insensitively held a cold, half-defoliated cigar butt. The woman, thickset and no longer young, with bowlegs and a rather attractive pseudo-Chinese face, wore an astrakhan jacket; the wind, having rounded her, brought a whiff of rather good but slightly stale perfume. They both stood motionless and watched fixedly, with such attentiveness that one might think they were about to be short-changed, as three red-necked husky fellows in blue aprons wrestled with their furniture.

Some day, he thought, I must use such a scene to start a good thick old-fashioned novel. The fleeting thought was touched with a careless irony; an irony, however, that was quite unnecessary, because somebody within him, on his behalf, independently from him, had absorbed all this, recorded it, and filed it away. He himself had only moved in today, and now, for the first time, in the still unaccustomed state of local resident, he had run out to buy a few things. He knew the street and indeed the whole neighbourhood: the boardinghouse from which he had moved was not far; until now, however, the street had revolved and glided this way and that, without any connection with him; today it had suddenly stopped; henceforth it would settle down as an extension of his new domicile.

Lined with lindens of medium size, with hanging droplets of rain distributed among their intricate black twigs according to the future arrangement of leaves (tomorrow each drop would contain a green pupil); complete with a smooth tarred surface some thirty feet across and variegated sidewalks (hand-built, and flattering to the feet), it rose at a barely perceptible angle, beginning with a post office and ending with a church, like an epistolary novel. With a practised eye he searched it for something that would become a daily sore spot, a daily torture for his senses, but there seemed to be nothing of that sort in the offing, and the diffuse light of the grey spring day was not only above suspicion but even promised to mollify any trifle that in more brilliant weather would not fail to crop up; this could be anything: the colour of a building, for instance, that immediately provoked an unpleasant taste in the mouth, a smack of oatmeal, or even halvah; an architectural detail that effusively caught one's attention every time one passed by; the irritating sham of a caryatid, a hanger-on and not a support, which, even under a lighter burden, would crumble into plaster dust; or, on a tree trunk, fastened to it by a rusty thumbtack, a pointless but perpetually preserved corner of a notice in longhand (runny ink, blue runaway dog) that had outlived its usefulness but had not been fully torn off; or else an object in a shop window, or a smell that refused at the last moment to yield a memory it had seemed ready to shout, and remained instead on its street corner, a mystery withdrawn into itself. No, there was nothing like that (not yet in any case); it would be a good idea, he thought, some time at leisure to study the sequence of three or four kinds of shops and see if he were right in conjecturing that such a sequence followed its own law of composition, so that, having found the most frequent arrangement, one could deduce the average cycle for the streets of a given city, for example: tobacco shop, pharmacy, greengrocery. On Tannenberg Street these three were dissociated, occurring on different corners; perhaps, however, the rhythmic swarming had not yet established itself, and in the future, yielding to that counterpoint (as the proprietors either went broke or moved) they would gradually begin to gather according to the proper pattern: the greengrocery, with a glance over its shoulder, would cross the street, so as to be at first seven and then three doors away from the pharmacy – in somewhat the same way as the jumbled letters find their places in a film commercial; and at the end there is always one that does a kind of flip, and then hastily assumes its position (a comic character, the inevitable Jack the Sack among the new recruits); and thus they will wait until an adjacent place becomes vacant, whereupon they will both wink across at the tobacco shop, as if to say: 'Quick, over here'; and before you know it they are all in a row, forming a typical line. God, how I hate all this – the things in the shop windows, the obtuse face of merchandise, and, above all, the ceremonial of transaction, the exchange of cloying compliments before and after! And those lowered lashes of modest price . . . the nobility of the discount . . . the altruism of advertisements . . . all of this nasty imitation of good, which has a strange way of drawing in good people: Alexandra Yakovlevna, for example, confessed to me that when she goes shopping in familiar stores she is morally transplanted to a special world where she grows intoxicated from the wine of honesty, from the sweetness of mutual favours, and replies to the salesman's incarnadine smile with a smile of radiant rapture.

The type of Berlin store that he entered can adequately be determined by the presence in a corner of a small table holding a telephone, a directory, narcissi in a vase, and a large ashtray. This shop did not carry the Russian tipped cigarettes that he preferred, and he would have left empty-handed if it had not been for the tobacconist's speckled vest with mother-of-pearl buttons and his pumpkin-coloured bald spot. Yes, all my life I shall be getting that extra little payment in kind to compensate my regular overpayment for merchandise foisted on me.

As he crossed toward the pharmacy at the corner he involuntarily turned his head because of a burst of light that had ricocheted from his temple, and saw, with that quick smile with which we greet a rainbow or a rose, a blindingly white parallelogram of sky being unloaded from the van – a dresser with mirror across which, as across a cinema screen, passed a flawlessly clear reflection of boughs sliding and swaying not arboreally, but with a human vacillation, produced by the nature of those who were carrying this sky, these boughs, this gliding façade.

He walked on toward the shop, but what he had just seen – whether because it had given him a kindred pleasure or because it had taken him unawares and jolted him (as children in the hayloft fall into the resilient darkness) – released in him that pleasant something which for several days now had been at the murky bottom of his every thought, taking possession of him at the slightest provocation: my collection of poems has been published; and when, as now, his mind tumbled like this, that is, when he recalled the fifty-odd poems that had just come out, he would skim in an instant the entire book, so that in the instantaneous mist of its madly accelerated music one could not make any readable sense of the flicking lines – the familiar words would rush past, swirling amid violent foam (whose seething was transformed into a mighty flowing motion if one fixed one's eyes on it, as we used to do long ago, looking down at it from a vibrating mill bridge until the bridge turned into a ship's stern: farewell!) – and this foam, and this flickering, and a separate verse that rushed past all alone, shouting in wild ecstasy from afar, probably calling him home, all of this, together with the creamy white of the cover, was merged in a blissful feeling of exceptional purity. . . . What am I doing! he thought, abruptly, coming to his senses and realizing that the first thing he had done upon entering the next shop was to dump the change he had received at the tobacconist's onto the rubber islet in the middle of the glass counter, through which he glimpsed the submerged treasure of flasked perfumes, while the salesgirl's gaze, condescending toward his odd behaviour, followed with curiosity this absent-minded hand paying for a purchase that had not yet been named.

'A cake of almond soap, please,' he said with dignity.

Thereupon he returned with the same springy step to the house. The sidewalk before it was now empty save for three blue chairs that looked as if they had been placed together by children. Within the van a small brown piano lay supine, tied up so that it could not rise, and with its two little metal soles up in the air. On the stairs he met the movers pounding down, knees turned out, and, as he was ringing the doorbell of his new abode, he heard voices and hammering upstairs. His landlady let him in and said that she had left his keys in his room. This large, predatory German woman had a funny name: Klara Stoboy –

which to a Russian's ear sounded with sentimental firmness as 'Klara is with thee (*s toboy*).'

And here is the oblong room, and the patiently waiting suitcase . . . and at this point his carefree mood changed to revulsion: God forbid that anyone know the awful, degrading boredom, the recurrent refusal to accept the vile yoke of recurrent new quarters, the impossibility of living face-to-face with totally strange objects, the inevitability of insomnia on that daybed!

For some time he stood by the window. In the curds-and-whey sky opaline pits now and then formed where the blind sun circulated, and, in response, on the grey convex roof of the van, the slender shadows of linden branches hastened headlong toward substantiation, but dissolved without having materialized. The house directly across the way was half enclosed in scaffolding, while the sound part of its brick façade was overgrown with window-invading ivy. At the far end of the path that cut through its front yard he could make out the black sign of a coal cellar.

Taken by itself, all this was a view, just as the room was itself a separate entity; but now a middleman had appeared, and now that view became the view from this room and no other. The gift of sight which it now had received did not improve it. It would be hard, he mused, to transform the wallpaper (pale yellow, with bluish tulips) into a distant steppe. The desert of the desk would have to be tilled for a long time before it could sprout its first rhymes. And much cigarette ash would have to fall under the armchair and into its folds before it would become suitable for travelling.

The landlady came to call him to the telephone, and he, politely stooping his shoulders, followed her into the dining-room. 'In the first place, my dear sir,' said Alexander Yakovlevich Chernyshevski, 'why are they so reluctant at your old boarding-house to divulge your new number? Left there with a bang, didn't you? In the second place, I want to congratulate you. . . . What, you haven't heard yet? Honestly?' ('He hasn't heard anything about it yet,' said Alexander Yakovlevich, turning the other side of his voice toward someone out of the range of the telephone). 'Well, in that case get a firm grip on yourself and listen to this – I'm going to read it to you: "The newly published collection of poems by the hitherto unknown author Fyodor Godunov-Cherdyntsev strikes one as such a brilliant phenomenon, and the poetic talent of the author is so indisputable. . . ." You know what, I shan't go on, but you come over to our place tonight. Then you will get the whole article. No, Fyodor Konstantinovich, my good friend, I won't tell you anything now, neither who wrote this review, nor in what émigré Russian-language paper it appeared, but if you want my personal opinion, then don't be offended, but I think the fellow is treating you much too kindly. So you'll come? Excellent. We'll be expecting you.'

As he hung up the receiver Fyodor nearly knocked the stand with flexible steel rod and attached pencil off the table; he tried to catch it, and it was then that he did knock if off; then he bumped his hip against the corner of the sideboard; then he dropped a cigarette that he was pulling out of the pack as he walked; and finally he miscalculated the swing of the door which flew open so resonantly that Frau Stoboy, just then passing along the corridor with a saucer of milk in her hand, uttered an icy 'Oops!' He wanted to tell her that her pale yellow dress with bluish tulips was beautiful, that the parting in her frizzled hair and the quivering bags of her cheeks endowed her with a George-Sandesque regality; that her dining-room was the height of perfection; but he limited himself to a beaming smile and nearly tripped over the tiger stripes which had not kept up with the cat as it jumped aside; after all, though, he had never doubted that it would be this way, that the world, in the person of a few hundred lovers of literature who had left St Petersburg, Moscow and Kiev, would immediately appreciate his gift.

We have before us a thin volume entitled *Poems* (a plain swallow-taled livery, which in recent years has become just as much *de rigueur* as the braiding of not long ago – from 'Lunar Reveries' to symbolic Latin), containing about fifty twelve-line poems all devoted to a single theme: childhood. In fervently composing them, the author sought on the one hand to generalize reminiscences by selecting elements typical of any successful childhood – hence their seeming obviousness; and on the other hand he has allowed only his genuine quiddity to penetrate into his poems – hence their seeming fastidiousness. At the same time he had to take great pains not to lose either his control of the game, or the viewpoint of the plaything. The strategy of inspiration and the tactics of the mind, the flesh of poetry and the spectre of translucent prose – these are the epithets that seem to us to characterize with sufficient accuracy the art of this young poet. . . . And, having locked his door, he took out his book and threw himself on the couch – he had to re-read it right away, before the excitement had time to cool, in order to check the superior quality of the poems and fore-fancy all the details of the high approbation given them by the intelligent, delightful, as yet unnamed reviewer. And now, as he sampled and tested them, he was doing the exact opposite of what he had done a short time ago, when he had skimmed over the book in one instantaneous thought. Now he read in three dimensions, as it were, carefully exploring each poem, lifted out like a cube from among the rest and bathed from all sides in that wonderful, fluffy country air after which one is always so tired in the evening. In other words, as he read, he again made use of all the materials already once gathered by his memory for the extraction of the present poems, and reconstructed everything, absolutely everything, as a returning traveller sees in an orphan's eyes not only the smile of its mother, whom he had known in his youth, but also an avenue ending in a burst of yellow light and that auburn leaf on the bench, and everything, everything. The collection opened with the poem 'The Lost Ball', and one felt it was beginning to rain. One of those evenings, heavy with clouds, that go well with our northern firs, had condensed around the house. The avenue had returned from the park for the night, and its entrance was shrouded in dusk. Now the unfolding white shutters separate the room from the exterior darkness, whither the brighter portions of various household objects have already crossed to take up tentative positions on different levels of the helplessly black garden. Bedtime is now at hand.

Games grow halfhearted and somewhat callous. She is old and she groans painfully as she kneels in three laborious stages.

> My ball has rolled under Nurse's commode.
> On the floor a candle
> Tugs at the ends of the shadows
> This way and that, but the ball is gone.
> Then comes the crooked poker.
> It potters and clatters in vain,
> Knocks out a button
> And then half a zwieback.
> Suddenly out darts the ball
> Into the quivering darkness,
> Crosses the whole room and promptly goes under
> The impregnable sofa.

Why doesn't the epithet 'quivering' quite satisfy me? Or does the puppeteer's colossal hand appear here for an instant among the creatures whose size the eye had come to accept (so that the spectator's first reaction at the end of the show is 'How big I have grown!')? After all the room really *was* quivering, and that flickering, carousel-like movement of shadows across the wall when the light is being carried away, or the shadowy camel on the ceiling with its monstrous humps heaving when Nurse wrestles with the bulky and unstable reed screen (whose expansion is inversely proportional to its degree of equilibrium) – these are all my very earliest memories, the ones closest to the original source. My probing thought often turns toward that original source, toward that reverse nothingness. Thus the nebulous state of the infant always seems to me to be a slow convalescence after a dreadful illness, and the receding from primal nonexistence becomes an approach to it when I strain my memory to the very limit so as to taste of that darkness and use its lessons to prepare myself for the darkness to come; but, as I turn my life upside down so that birth becomes death, I fail to see at the verge of this dying-in-reverse anything that would correspond to the boundless terror that even a centenarian is said to experience when he faces the positive end; nothing, except perhaps the aforementioned shadows, which, rising from somewhere below when the candle takes off to leave the room (while the shadow of the left brass knob at the foot of my bed sweeps past like a black head swelling as it moves), assume their accustomed places above my nursery cot,

> And in their corners grow brazen
> Bearing only a casual likeness
> To their natural models.

In a whole set of poems, disarming by their sincerity . . . no, that's nonsense – Why must one 'disarm' the reader? Is he dangerous? In a whole set of excellent . . . or, to put it even more strongly, remarkable poems the author sings not only of these frightening shadows, but of brighter moments as well. Nonsense, I say! He does not write like that, my nameless, unknown eulogist, and it was only for his sake that I poetized the memory of two precious, and, I think, ancient toys. The first was an ample painted flowerpot containing an artificial plant from a sunny land, on which was perched a stuffed tropical songbird, so astonishingly lifelike that it seemed about to take wing, with black plumage and an amethyst breast; and, when the big key had been wheedled from the housekeeper Ivonna Ivanovna, inserted in the side of the pot and given several tight, vivifying turns, the little Malayan nightingale would open its beak . . . no, it would not even open its beak, for something odd had happened to the clockworn mechanism to some spring or other, which, however, stored up its action for later: the bird would not sing them, but if one forgot about it and a week later happened to walk past its lofty wardrobe-top perch, then some mysterious tremor would suddenly make it emit its magical warbling – and how marvellously, how long it would trill, puffing out its ruffled little breast; it would finish; then, on your way out, you would tread on another floorboard and in special response it would utter a final whistle, and grow silent halfway through the note. The other of the poetized toys, which was in another room, also on a high shelf, behaved in similar fashion, but with a zany suggestion of imitation – as the spirit of parody always goes along with genuine poetry. This was a clown in satin plus-fours who was propping himself on two whitewashed parallel bars and who would be set in motion by an accidental jolt,

> To the sound of a miniature music
> With a comical pronunciation

tinkling somewhere beneath his little platform, as he lifted his legs in white stockings and with pompons on the shoes, higher and higher with barely perceptible jerks – and abruptly everything stopped and he froze in an angular attitude. And perhaps it is the same with my poems? But the truthfulness of juxtapositions and deductions is sometimes better preserved on the near side of the verbal fence.

From the accumulating poetical pieces in the book we gradually obtain the image of an extremely receptive boy, living in extremely favourable surroundings. Our poet was born on July 12, 1900, in the Leshino manor, which for generations had been the country estate of the Godunov-Cherdyntsevs. Even before he reached school age the boy read through a considerable number of books from his father's library. In his interesting reminiscences so-and-so recalls how enthusiastically little Fedya and his sister Tanya, who was two years his elder, engaged in amateur theatricals, and how they would even write plays themselves for their performances. . . . That, my good man, may be true of other poets but in my case it is a lie. I have always been indifferent to the theatre; although I remember that we did have a puppet theatre with cardboard trees and a crenellated castle with celluloid windows the colour of raspberry jelly through which painted flames like those on Vereshchagin's picture of the Moscow Fire flickered when a candle was lighted inside – and it was this candle which, not without our participation, eventually caused the conflagration of the entire building. Oh, but Tanya and I were fastidious when it came to toys! From indifferent givers on the outside we would often receive quite wretched things. Anything that came in a flat carton with an illustrated cover boded ill. To one such cover I tried to devote my stipulated twelve lines, but somehow the poem did not rise. A family, seated around a circular table illuminated by a lamp: the boy is dressed in an impossible sailor suit with a red tie, the girl wears laced boots, also red; both, with expression of sensuous delectation, are stringing beads of various colours on straw-like rods, making little baskets, birdcages and boxes; and, with similar enthusiasm, their half-witted parents take part in the same pastime – the father with a prize growth on his pleased face, the mother with her imposing bosom; the dog is also looking at the table, and envious Grandma can be seen ensconced in the background. Those same children have now grown up and I often run across them in advertisements: he, with his glossy, sleekly tanned cheeks, is puffing voluptuously on a cigarette or holding in his brawny hand, with a carnivorous grin, a sandwich containing something red ('eat more meat!'); she is smiling at a stocking she herself is wearing, or, with depraved delight, pouring artificial cream on canned fruit; and in time they will become sprightly, rosy, gormandizing oldsters – and still have ahead of them the infernal black beauty of oaken caskets in a palm-decked display window. . . . Thus a world of handsome demons develops side by side with us, in a cheerfully sinister relationship to our everyday existence; but in the handsome demon there is always some secret flaw, a shameful wart on the behind of this semblance of perfection: the glamorous glutton of the advertisement, gorging himself on gelatin, can never know the quiet joys of the gourmet, and his fashions (lingering on the billboard while we move onward) are always just a little behind those of real life. Some day I shall come back to a discussion of this nemesis, which finds a soft spot for its blow exactly where the whole sense and power of the creature it strikes seem to lie.

In general Tanya and I preferred sweaty games to quiet ones – running, hide-and-seek, battles. How remarkably the word 'battle' (*srazhenie*) suggests the sound of springy compression when one rammed into the toy gun its projectile – a six-inch stick of coloured wood, deprived of its rubber suction cup in order to increase the impact with which it struck the gilt tin of a breastplate (worn by a cross between a cuirassier and a redskin), making in it a respectable little dent.

> ... You reload to the bottom the barrel,
> With a creaking of springs
> Resiliently pressing it down on the floor,
> And you see, half concealed by the door,
> That your double has stopped in the mirror,
> Rainbow feathers in head band
> Standing on end.

The author had occasion to hide (we are now in the Godunov-Cherdyntsevs' mansion on the English Quay of the Neva, where it stands even today) among draperies, under tables, behind the upright cushions of silk divans, in a wardrobe, where moth crystals crunched under one's feet (and whence one could observe unseen a slowly passing manservant, who would seem strangely different, alive, ethereal, smelling of apples and tea) and also

> Under a helical staircase,
> Or behind a lonely buffet
> Forgotten in a bare room

on whose dusty shelves vegetated such objects as: a necklace made of wolf's teeth; a small bare-bellied idol of almatolite; another, of porcelain, its black tongue stuck out in national greeting; a chess set with camels instead of bishops; an articulated wooden dragon; a Soyot snuffbox of clouded glass; ditto, of agate; a shaman's tambourine and the rabbit's foot going with it; a boot of wapiti leather with an innersole made from the bark of the blue honeysuckle; an ensiform Tibetan coin; a cup of Kara jade; a silver brooch with turquoises; a lama's lampad; and a lot of similar junk which – like dust, like the postcard from a German spa with its mother-of-pearl 'Gruss' – my father, who could not stomach ethnography, somehow happened to bring back from his fabulous travels. The real treasures – his butterfly collection, his museum – were preserved in three locked halls; but the present book of poems contains nothing about that: a special intuition forewarned the young author that some day he would want to speak in quite another way, not in miniature verse with charms and chimes but in very, very different, manly words about his famous father.

Again something has gone wrong, and one hears the flippantly flat little voice of the reviewer (perhaps even of the female sex). With warm affection the poet recalls the rooms of the family house where it (his childhood) was spent. He has been able to imbue with much lyricism the poetic descriptions of objects among which it was spent. When you listen closely . . . We all, attentively and piously . . . The strains of the past . . . Thus, for instance, he depicts lampshades, lithographs on the walls, his schoolroom desk, the weekly visit of the floor-polishers (who leave behind an odour compounded of 'frost, sweat, and mastic'), and the checking of the clocks:

On Thursdays there comes from the clock shop
A courteous old man who proceeds
To wind with a leisurely hand
All the clocks in the house.
He steals at his own watch a glance
And sets the clock on the wall.
He stands on a chair, and he waits
For the clock to discharge its noon
Completely. Then, having done well
His agreeable task,
He soundlessly puts back the chair,
And with a slight whirr the clock ticks.

Giving an occasional tongue clack with its pendulum and making a strange pause, as if to gather its strength, before striking. Its ticking, like an unrolled tape divided by strips into inches, served as an endless measure of my insomnias. It was just as hard for me to fall asleep as to sneeze without having tickled with something the inside of a nostril, or to commit suicide by resorting to means at the body's disposal (swallowing my tongue, or something like that). At the beginning of the agonizing night I could still play for time by subsisting on conversations with Tanya, whose bed stood in the next room; despite rules, we would open the door slightly, and then, when we heard our governess going to her own room, which was adjacent to Tanya's, one of us would gently shut it: a lightning barefoot sprint and then a dive into bed. While the door was ajar we would exchange conundrums from room to room, every now and then lapsing into silence (I can still hear the tone of this twin silence in the dark), she to guess mine, I to think of another. Mine were always on the fantastic and silly side, while Tanya adhered to classical models:

mon premier est un métal précieux,
mon second est un habitant des cieux,
et mon tout est un fruit délicieux.

Sometimes she would fall asleep while I waited patiently,

thinking that she was struggling with my riddle, and neither my pleading nor my imprecations would succeed in reviving her. After this I would voyage for more than an hour through the dark of my bed, arching the bedclothes over myself, so as to form a cavern, at whose distant exit I glimpsed a bit of oblique bluish light that had nothing in common with my bedroom, with the Neva night, with the rich, darkly translucent flounces of the window curtains. The cave I was exploring held in its folds and fissures such a dreamy reality, brimmed with such oppressive mystery, that a throbbing, as of a muted drum, would begin in my chest and in my ears; in there, in its depths, where my father had discovered a new species of bat, I could make out the high cheekbones of an idol hewn from the rock; and, when I finally dozed off, a dozen strong hands would overturn me and, with an awful silk-ripping sound, someone would unstitch me from top to bottom, after which an agile hand would slip inside me and powerfully squeeze my heart. Or else I would be turned into a horse, screaming in a Mongolian voice: shamans yanked at its hocks with lassos, so that its legs would break with a crunch and collapse at right angles to the body – my body – which lay with its chest pressed against the yellow ground, and, as a sign of extreme agony, the horse's tail would rise fountain-like; it dropped back, and I awoke.

Time to get up. The stove-heater pats
The glistening facings
Of the stove to determine
If the fire has grown to the top.
It has. And to its hot hum
The morning responds with the silence of snow,
Pink-shaded azure,
And immaculate whiteness.

It is strange how a memory will grow into a wax figure, how the cherub grows suspiciously prettier as its frame darkens with age – strange, strange are the mishaps of memory. I emigrated seven years ago; this foreign land has by now lost its aura of abroadness just as my own ceased to be a geographic habit. The Year Seven. The wandering ghost of an empire immediately adopted this system of reckoning, akin to the one formerly introduced by the ardent French citizen in honour of newborn liberty. But the years roll on, and honour is no consolation; recollections either melt away, or else acquire a deathly gloss, so that instead of marvellous apparitions we are left with a fan of picture postcards. Nothing can help here, no poetry, no stereoscope – that gadget which in ominous bug-eyed silence used to endow a cupola with such convexity and surround mug-carrying Karlsbad promenaders with such a diabolical semblance of space that I was tormented by nightmares after this optical diversion far more than after tales of Mongolian tortures. The particular stereo camera I remember adorned the waiting room of our dentist, an American named Lawson, whose French mistress Mme Ducamp, a grey-haired harpy, seated at her desk among vials of blood-red Lawson mouthwash, pursed her lips and nervously scratched her scalp as she tried to find an appointment for Tanya and me, and finally, with an effort and a screech, managed to push her spitting pen between la Princess Toumanoff, with a blot at the end, and Monsieur Danzas, with a blot at the beginning. Here is the description of a drive to this dentist, who had warned the day before that 'This one will have to come out'. . . .

What will it be like to be sitting
Half an hour from now in this brougham?
With what eyes shall I look at these snowflakes
And black branches of trees?
How shall I follow again with my gaze
That conical curbstone
In its cottonwool cap? How recall
On my way back my way there?
(While with revulsion and tenderness
Constantly feeling the handkerchief
Wherein carefully folded is something
Like an ivory watch charm.)

That 'cottonwool cap' is not only ambiguous but does not even begin to express what I meant – namely, the snow piled caplike on granite cones joined by a chain somewhere in the vicinity of the statue of Peter the Great. Somewhere! Alas, it is already difficult for me to gather all the parts of the past; already I am beginning to forget relationships and connections between objects that still thrive in my memory, objects I thereby condemn to extinction. If so, what insulting mockery to affirm smugly that

Thus a former impression keeps living
Within harmony's ice.

What, then, compels me to compose poems about my childhood if in spite of everything, my words go wide of the mark, or else slay both the pard and the hart with the exploding bullet of an 'accurate' epithet? But let us not despair. The man says I am a real poet – which means that the hunt was not in vain.

Here is another twelve-line poem about boyhood torments. It deals with the ordeals of winter in town when, for example, ribbed stockings chafe behind the knees, or when the shopgirl pulls an impossibly flat kid glove onto your hand, laid on the counter as if on an executioner's block. There is more: the hook's double pinch (the first time it slipped off) while you stand with outspread arms to have your fur collar fastened; but in compensation for this, what an amusing change in acoustics, how rounded all sounds become when the collar is raised; and since we have touched upon ears, how unforgettable the silky, taut, buzzing music while the strings of your cap's earflaps are being tied (raise your chin).

Merrily, to coin a phrase, youngsters romp on a frosty day. At the entrance to the public park we have the balloon vendor; look, children, how they billow and rub against each other, all full of God's sunshine, in red, blue and green shades. A beautiful sight! Please, Uncle, I want the biggest (the white one with the rooster painted on it and the red embryo floating inside, which, when its mother is destroyed, will escape up to the ceiling and a day later will come down, all wrinkled and quite tame). Now the happy children have bought their rouble balloon and the kindly hawker has pulled it out of the jostling bunch. Just a minute, my lad, don't grab, let me cut the string. After which he puts on his mittens again, checks the string around his waist, from which his scissors dangle, and pushing off with his heel, slowly begins to rise in an upright position, higher and higher into the blue sky: look, his cluster is no larger now than a bunch of grapes, while beneath him lies hazy, gilded, berimed St Petersburg, a little restored here and there, alas, according to the best pictures of our national painters.

But joking aside, it really was all very beautiful, very quiet. The trees in the park mimed their own ghosts and the whole effect revealed immense talent. Tanya and I would make fun of the sleds of our coevals, especially if they were covered with fringed, carpet-like stuff and had a high seat (equipped even with a back) and reins that the rider held as he braked with his felt boots. This kind never made it all the way to the final snow-drift, but instead went off course almost immediately and began to spin helplessly while continuing to descend, carrying a pallid, intent child who was obliged, when the sled's momentum was spent, to work with his feet in order to reach the end of the icy run. Tanya and I had weighty belly sleds from Sangalli's: such a sled consisted simply of a rectangular velvet cushion on iron runners curved at each end. You did not have to pull it on the way to the slide – it glided with so little effort and so impatiently along the snow, sanded in vain, that it bumped against your heels. Here we are at the hill.

One climbed up a sparkled-splashed platform. . . . (Water carried up in buckets to pour on the slide had *splashed* over the wooden steps so that they were coated with *sparkling* ice, but the well-meaning alliteration had not been able to get all this in.)

> One climbed a sparkle-splashed platform,
> One dashingly fell belly first
> On the sled, and it rattled
> Down the blueness; and then
> When the scene underwent a grim change
> And there sombrely burned in the nursery
> Scarlet fever on Christmas,
> Or, on Easter, diphtheria,
> One rocketed down the bright, brittle,
> Exaggerated ice hill
> In a kind of half-tropical,
> Half-Tavricheski park

where, by the power of delirium, General Nikolai Mihailovich Przhevalski was transferred, together with his stone camel, from the Alexandrovski park near us, and where he immediately turned into a statue of my father who was at that moment somewhere between Kokand and Ashkhabad, for example, or else on a slope of the Tsinin Range. What illnesses Tanya and I went through; Now together, now by turns; and how I would suffer when I heard, between the slam of a distant door and the restrained quiet sound of another one, her footfall and laughter bursting through, sounding celestially indifferent to me, unaware of me, infinitely distant from my fat compress with its tawny oilcloth filling, my aching legs, my bodily heaviness and constriction; but if it was she who was sick, how earthly and real, how like a crisp soccer ball I felt when I saw her lying in bed with an air of remoteness about her as if she had turned toward the other world, with only the limp lining of her being toward me! Let us describe the last stand before the capitulation when, not yet having stepped out of the normal course of the day, concealing from your own self the fever, the ache in your joints, and wrapping yourself up Mexican fashion, you disguise the claims of fever's chill as the demands of the game; and when, a half hour later, you have surrendered and ended up in bed, your body no longer believes that just a short time ago it was playing, crawling on all fours along the floor of the hall, along the parquet, along the quarpet. Let us describe Mother's questioning smile of alarm when she has just put the thermometer in my armpit (a task she would not entrust either to the valet or to the governess). 'Well, you've got yourself into a nice fix, haven't you?' says she, still trying to joke about it. Then a minute later: 'I knew it yesterday, I knew you had a fever, you can't fool me.' And after another minute: 'How much do you think you have?' And finally: 'I think we can take it out now' She brings the incandescent glass tube close to the light and, drawing together her lovely sealskin eyebrows – which Tanya has inherited – she looks for a long time . . . and then without saying anything she unhurriedly shakes the thermometer and slips it back into its case, looking at me as if not quite recognizing me, while my father rides his horse at a walk cross a vernal plain all blue with irises; let us describe also the delirious state in which one feels huge numbers grow, inflating one's brain, accompanied by someone's incessant patter quite unrelated to you, as if in the dark garden adjoining the madhouse of the book-of-sums several of its characters, half out (or more precisely, fifty-seven on-hundred-and-elevenths out) of their terrible world of increasing interests, appeared in their stock parts of apple-woman, four ditchdiggers and a Certain Person who had bequeathed his children a caravan of fractions, and chatted, to the accompaniment of the nocturnal sough of trees, about something extremely domestic and silly, but therefore all the more awful, all the more doomed to turn into those very numbers, into that mathematical universe expanding endlessly (an expansion which for me sheds an odd light on the macrocosmic theories of today's physicists). Let us describe finally the recovery, when there is no longer any point in shaking the mercury down, and the thermometer is carelessly left lying on the bedtable, where an assembly of books that has come to congratulate you and a few playthings (idle onlookers) are crowding out the half-empty bottles of turbid potions.

A writing case with my note paper
Is what I most vividly see:
The leaves are adorned with a horseshoe
And my monogram. I had become
Quite an expert in twisted initials,

Intaglio seals, dry flattened flowers
(Which a little girl sent me from Nice)
And sealing wax, red and bronze-gleaming.

None of the poems in the book alludes to a certain extraordinary thing that happened to me as I was recovering from a particularly severe case of pneumonia. When everyone had moved into the drawing-room (to use a Victorian cliché), one of the guests who (to go on with it) had been silent all evening. . . . The fever had ebbed away during the night and I had finally scrambled ashore. I was, let me tell you, weak, capricious and transparent – as transparent as a cut-glass egg. Mother had gone to buy me – I did not know what exactly – one of those freakish things that from time to time I coveted with the greed of a pregnant woman, afterwards forgetting them completely; but my mother made lists of these desiderata. As I lay flat in bed among bluish layers of indoor twilight I felt myself evolving an incredible lucidity, as when a distant stripe of radiantly pale sky stretched between long vesperal clouds and you can make out the cape and shallows of God knows what far-off islands – and it seems that if you release your volatile glance just a little farther you will discern a shining boat drawn up on the damp sand and receding footsteps filled with bright water. In that minute, I think, I attained the highest limit of human health: my mind had been dipped and rinsed only recently in a dangerous, supernaturally clean blackness; and now, lying still and not even shutting my eyes, I mentally saw my mother, in chinchilla coat and black-dotted veil, getting into the sleigh (which always seemed in old Russia so small compared to the tremendous stuffed bottom of the coachman) and holding her dove-grey fluffy muff to her face as she sped behind a pair of black horses covered with a blue net. Street after street unfolded without any effort on my part; lumps of coffee-coloured snow pounded against the sleigh's front. Now it had stopped. Vasiliy the footman steps down from his footboard, in the same motion unfastening the bearskin lap robe, and my mother walks briskly toward a shop whose name and display I do not have time to identify, since just at that instant my uncle, her brother, passes by and hails her (but she has already disappeared), and for several steps I involuntarily accompany him, trying to make out the face of the gentleman with whom he is chatting as they both walk away, but catching myself, I turn back and hastily flow, as it were, into the store, where my mother is already paying ten roubles for a perfectly ordinary green Faber pencil, which is then lovingly wrapped in brown paper by two clerks and handed to Vasiliy, who is already carrying it behind my mother to the sleigh, which now speeds along anonymous streets back to our house, now advancing to meet it; but here the crystalline course of my clairvoyance was interrupted by Yvonna Ivanovna's arrival with broth and toast. I needed her help to sit up in bed. She gave the pillow a swat and placed the bed tray (with its midget feet and a perpetually sticky area near its southwestern corner) across the animated blanket before me. Suddenly the door opened and Mother came in, smiling and holding a long, brown paper package like a halberd. From it emerged a Faber pencil a yard long and of corresponding thickness: a display giant that had hung horizontally in the window as an advertisement and had once happened to arouse my whimsical greed. I must still have been in that blissful state when any oddity descends among us like a demigod to mingle unrecognized with the Sunday crowd, since at that moment I felt no amazement at what had happened to me, but only remarked to myself in passing how I had been mistaken in regard to the object's size; but later, when I had grown stronger and plugged up certain chinks with bread, I would ponder with superstitious pangs about my clairvoyant spell (the only one I ever experienced), of which I was so ashamed that I concealed it even from Tanya; and I nearly burst into tears from embarrassment when we happened to meet, on my very first trip outdoors, a distant relative of Mother's, one Gaydukov, who said to her: 'Your brother and I saw you the other day near Treumann's.'

Meanwhile the air in the poems has grown warmer and we are preparing to return to the country, where we might move as early as April in the years before I began school (I began it only at the age of twelve).

The snow, gone from the slopes, lurks in ravines,
And the Petersburg spring
Is full of excitement and of anemones
And of the first butterflies.
But I don't need last year's Vanessas,
Those bleached hibernators
Or those utterly battered Brimstones,
Through transparent woods flying.
I shall not fail, though, to detect
The four lovely gauze wings
Of the softest Geometrid moth in the world
Spread flat on a mottled pale birchtrunk.

This poem is the author's own favourite, but he did not include it in the collection because, once again, the theme is connected with that of his father and economy of art advised him not to touch that theme before the right time came. Instead he reproduced such spring impressions as the first sensation immediately upon walking out of the station: the softness of the ground, its kindred proximity to your foot, and around your head the totally unrestrained flow of air. Vying with each other, furiously lavishing invitations, standing up on their boxes, flourishing their free hand and mingling their uproar with exaggerated 'whoas', the droshky drivers called to the early arrivals. A little way off an open motorcar, crimson both inside and out, awaited us: the idea of speed had already given a slant to the steering wheel (seacliff trees will understand what I mean), while its general appearance still retained – out of a false sense of propriety, I suppose – a servile link with the shape of a victoria; but if this was indeed an attempt at mimicry then it was totally destroyed by the roar of the motor with the muffler bypass opened, a roar so ferocious that long before we came in sight a peasant on a hay wagon coming the other way would jump off and try to hood his horse with a sack – after which he and his cart would often end up in the ditch or even in the field; where, a minute later, having already forgotten us and our dust, the rural stillness would collect again, cool and tender, with only the tiniest aperture left for the song of a skylark.

Perhaps one day, on foreign-made soles with heels long since worn down, feeling myself a ghost despite the idiotic substantiality of the insulators, I shall again come out of that station and without visible companions walk along the footpath that accompanies the highway the ten or so versts to Leshino. One after another the telegraph poles will hum at my approach. A crow will settle on a boulder – settle and straighten a wing that has folded wrong. The day will probably be on the greyish side. Changes in the appearance of the surrounding landscape that I cannot imagine, as well as some of the oldest landmarks that somehow I have forgotten, will greet me alternately, even mingling from time to time. I think that as I walk I shall utter something like a moan, in tune with the poles. When I reach the sites where I grew up and see this and that – or else, because of fires, rebuilding, lumbering operations or the negligence of nature, see neither this nor that (but still make out something infinitely and unwaveringly faithful to me, if only because my eyes are, in the long run, made of the same stuff as the greyness, the clarity, the dampness of those sites), then after all the excitement, I shall experience a certain satiation of suffering – perhaps on the mountain pass to a kind of happiness which it is too early for me to know (I know only that when I reach it, it will be with pen in hand). But there is one thing I shall definitely not find there awaiting me – the thing which, indeed, made the whole business of exile worth cultivating: my childhood and the fruits of my childhood. Its fruits – here they are, today, already ripe; while my childhood itself has disappeared into a distance even more remote than that of our Russian North.

The author has found effective words to describe sensations experienced upon making the transition to the countryside. How much fun it is, says he, when

> No longer one needs to put on
> A cap, or change one's light shoes,
> In order to run out again in the spring
> On the brick-coloured sand of the garden.

At the age of ten a new diversion was added. We were still in the city when the marvel rolled in. For quite a time I led it around by its ram horns from room to room; with what bashful grace it moved along the parquet floor until it impaled itself on a thumb-tack! Compared to my old, rattling and pitiful little tricycle, whose wheels were so thin that it would get stuck even in the sand of the garden terrace, the newcomer possessed a heavenly lightness of movement. This is well expressed by the poet in the following lines:

> Oh that first bicycle!
> Its splendour, its height,
> 'Dux' or '*Pobéda*' inscribed on its frame,
> The quietness of its tight tyre!
> The wavers and weavers in the green avenue
> Where sun macules glide up one's wrists
> And where molehills loom black
> And threaten one's downfall!
> But next day one skims over them,
> And support as in dreamland is lacking
> And trusting in this dream simplicity,
> The bicycle does not collapse.

And the day after that there inevitably come thoughts of 'freewheeling' – a word which to this day I cannot hear without seeing a strip of smooth, sloping, sticky ground glide past, accompanied by a barely audible murmur of rubber and an ever-so-gentle lisp of steel. Bicycling and riding, boating and bathing, tennis and croquet; picnicking under the pines; the lure of the water mill and the hayloft – this is a general list of the themes that move our author. What about his poems from the point of view of form? These, of course, are miniatures, but they are executed with a phenomenally delicate mastery that brings out clearly every hair, not because everything is delineated with an excessively selective touch, but because the presence of the smallest features is involuntarily conveyed to the reader by the integrity and reliability of a talent that assures the author's observance of all the articles of the artistic covenant. One can argue whether it is worth while to revive album-type poetry, but one certainly cannot deny that within the limits he has set himself Gudunov-Cherdyntsev has solved his prosodic problem correctly. Each of his poems iridesces with harlequin colours. Whoever is fond of the picturesque genre will appreciate this little volume. To the blind man at the church door it would have nothing to say. What vision the author has! Awaking early in the morning he knew what kind of a day it would be by looking at a chink in the shutter, which

Showed a blue that was bluer than blue
And was hardly inferior in blueness
To my present remembrance of it.

And in the evening he gazes with the same screwed-up eyes at the field, one side of which is already in shadow, while the other, farther one

Is illumed, from its central big boulder
To the edge of the forest beyond it
And is bright as by day.

It would seem to us that perhaps it was really not literature but painting for which he was destined from childhood, and while we know nothing of the author's present condition, we can nevertheless clearly picture a straw-hatted boy, sitting very uncomfortably on a garden bench with his watercolour paraphernalia and painting the world bequeathed him by his forebears:

Cells of white porcelain
Contain blue, green, red honey.
First, out of pencil lines,
On rough paper a garden is formed.

The birches, the balcony of the outbuilding,
All is spotted with sunlight. I soak
And twirl tight the tip of my paintbrush
In rich orange yellow;
And, meantime, within the full goblet,
In the radiance of its cut glass,
What colours have blazed,
What rapture has bloomed!

This, then, is Godunov-Cherdyntsev's little volume. In conclusion let us add . . . What else? What else? Imagination, do prompt me! Can it be true that all the enchantingly throbbing things of which I have dreamt and still dream through my poems have not been lost in them and have been noticed by the reader whose review I shall see before the day is over? Can it really be that he has understood everything in them, understood that besides the good old 'picturesqueness' they also contain special poetic meaning (when one's mind, after going around itself in the subliminal labyrinth, returns with newfound music that alone makes poems what they should be)? As he read them, did he read them not only as words but as chinks between words, as one should do when reading poetry? Or did he simply skim over them, like them and praise them, calling attention to the significance of their sequence, a feature fashionable in our time, when time is in fashion: if a collection opens with a poem about 'A Lost Ball', it must close with 'The Found Ball'.

Only pictures and ikons remained
In their places that year
When childhood was ended, and something
Happened to the old house: in a hurry
All the rooms with each other
Were exchanging their furniture,
Cupboards and screens, and a host
Of unwieldy big things:
And it was then that from under a sofa,
On the suddenly unmasked parquet,
Alive, and incredibly dear,
It was revealed in a corner.

The book's exterior appearance is pleasing.

Having squeezed the final drop of sweetness from it, Fyodor stretched and got up from his couch. He felt very hungry. The hands of his watch had lately begun to misbehave, now and then starting to move counterclockwise, so that he could not depend on them; to judge by the light, however, the day, about to leave on a journey, had sat down with its family for a pensive pause. When Fyodor went outside he felt immersed in a damp chill (it's a good thing I put that on), while he had been musing over his poems, rain had lacquered the street from end to end. The van had gone and in the spot where its tractor had recently stood, there remained next to the sidewalk a rainbow of oil, with the purple predominant and a plumelike twist. Asphalt's parakeet. And what had been the name of the moving company? Max Lux. Mac's luck.

Did I take the keys? Fyodor suddenly thought, stopping and thrusting his hand into his raincoat pocket. There he located a clinking handful, weighty and reassuring. When, three years ago, still during his existence here as a student, his mother had moved to Paris to live with Tanya, she had written that she just could not get used to being liberated from the perpetual fetters that chain a Berliner to the door lock. He imagined her joy upon reading the article about him and for an instant he felt maternal pride towards himself; not that but a maternal tear burned the edge of his eyelids.

But what do I care whether or not I receive attention during my lifetime, if I am not certain that the world will remember me until its last darkest winter, marvelling like Ronsard's old woman? And yet . . . I am still a long way from thirty, and here today I am already noticed. Noticed! Thank you, my land, for this remotest . . . A lyric possibility flitted past, singing quite close to his ear. Thank you, my land, for your most precious . . . I no longer need the sound 'oticed': the rhyme has kindled life, but the rhyme itself is abandoned. And maddest gift my thanks are due . . . I suppose 'meshes' waits in the wings. Did not have time to make out my third line in that burst of light. Pity. All gone now, missed my cue.

He bought some piroshki (one with meat, another with cabbage, a third with tapioca, a fourth with rice, a fifth . . . could not afford a fifth) in a Russian foodshop, which was a kind of wax museum of the old country's cuisine, and quickly finished them off on a damp bench in a small public garden.

The rain began coming down faster: someone had suddenly tilted the sky. He had to take cover in the circular shelter at the streetcar stop. There on the bench two Germans with briefcases were discussing a deal and endowing it with such dialectic details that the nature of the merchandise was lost, as when you are looking through an article in Brockhaus' Encyclopedia and lose its subject, indicated in the text only by its initial letter. Shaking her bobbed hair a girl entered the shelter with a small, wheezing, toadlike bulldog. Now this is odd: 'remotest' and 'noticed' are together again and a certain combination is ringing persistently. I will not be tempted.

The shower ended. With perfect simplicity – no dramatics, no tricks – all the streetlamps came on. He decided he could already set off for the Chernyshevskis' so as to be there towards nine, Rhine, fine, cline. As happens with drunks, something preserved him when he crossed streets in this state. Illuminated by a streetlamp's humid ray, a car stood at the curb with its motor running: every single drop on its hood was trembling. Who could have written it? Fyodor could not make a final choice among several émigré critics. This one was scrupulous but untalented; that one, dishonest but gifted; a third wrote only about prose; a fourth only about his friends; a fifth . . . and Fyodor's imagination conjured up this fifth one: a man the same age as he or even, he thought, a year younger, who had published during those same years in those same émigré papers and magazines, no more than he (a poem here, an article there), but who in some incomprehensible manner, which seemed as physically natural as some kind of emanation, had unobtrusively clothed himself in an aura of indefinable fame, so that his name was uttered not necessarily especially often, but quite differently from all the other young names; a man whose every new searing line he, Fyodor, despising himself, quickly and avidly devoured in a corner, trying by the very act of reading to destroy the marvel of it – after which for two days or so he could not rid himself either of what he had read or of his own feeling of debility or of a secret ache, as if while wrestling with another he had injured his own innermost, sacrosanct particle; a lonely, unpleasant, myopic man, with some kind of unpleasant defect in the reciprocal position of his shoulder blades. But I shall forgive everything if it is you.

He thought he was keeping his pace to a dawdle, yet the clocks that he came across on the way (the emergent giants of watchmakers' shops) advanced even more slowly and when, almost at his destination, he overtook in one stride Lyubov Markovna, who was going to the same place, he understood that he had been borne along throughout his journey by his impatience, as by an escalator that transforms even a motionless man into a runner. Why did this flabby, unloved, elderly woman still make up her eyes when she already wore a pince-nez? The lenses exaggerated the unsteadiness and crudity of the amateurish ornamentation and as a result, her perfectly innocent gaze became so ambiguous that one could not break away from it: the hypnosis of error. In fact nearly everything about her seemed based on an unfortunate misunderstanding – and one wondered if it was not even a form of insanity when she thought that she spoke German like a native, that Galsworthy was a great writer, or that Georgiy Ivanovich Vasiliev was pathologically attracted to her. She was one of the most faithful frequenters of the literary parties that the Chernyshevskis, together with Vasiliev, a fat old journalist, organized every other Saturday; today was only Tuesday; and Lyubov Markovna was still living on her impressions from the previous Saturday, sharing them generously. Men fatally became absentminded boors in her company. Fyodor himself felt he was slipping too, but fortunately they were coming to the front door and there the Chernyshevskis' maid already stood waiting, keys in hand; actually, she had been sent to meet Vasiliev, who suffered from an extremely rare disease of the heart valves – he had, in fact, made a hobby of it and sometimes arrived at the home of friends with an anatomical model of the heart and demonstrated everything very clearly and lovingly. '*We* don't need the elevator,' said Lyubov Markovna and started up the stairs with a strong plodding gait which turned to a curiously smooth and silent swing on the landings; Fyodor had a zizzag behind her at a reduced pace, as you sometimes see a dog do, weaving and shoving its nose past its master's heel now on the right, now on the left.

They were admitted by Alexandra Yakorevna herself. Fyodor had scarcely time to notice her unusual expression (as if she disapproved of something or wanted to avert something quickly), when her husband darted into the hallway on his short plump legs, waving a newspaper as he ran.

'Here it is,' he shouted, the corner of his mouth violently jerking downward (a tic acquired since the death of his son). 'Look, here it is!'

'When I married him,' observed Mme Chernyshevski, 'I expected his humour to be more subtle.'

Fyodor saw with surprise that the paper he uncertainly took from his host was a German one.

'The date!' shouted Chernyshevski. 'Go ahead, look at the date, young man!'

'April 1,' said Fyodor with a sigh, and unconsciously he folded up the paper. 'Yes, of course, I should have remembered.'

Chernyshevski began to guffaw ferociously.

'Don't be cross with him, please,' said his wife in an indolently sorrowful tone, slightly rolling her hips and gently taking the young man by the wrist.

Lyubov Markovna clicked her purse shut and sailed off toward the parlour.

It was a smallish, rather tastelessly furnished, badly lighted room with a shadow lingering in one corner and a pseudo-Tanagra vase standing on an unattainable shelf, and when at last the final guest had arrived and Mme Chernyshevski, becoming for a moment – as usually happens – remarkably similar to her own (blue, gleaming) teapot, began to pour tea, the cramped quarters assumed the guise of a certain touching, provincial cosiness. On the sofa, among cushions of various blue – all of them unappetizing and blurry – a silk doll with an angel's limp legs and a Persian's almond-shaped eyes was being squeezed alternately by two comfortably settled persons: Vasiliev, huge, bearded, wearing prewar socks arrowed above the ankle; and a fragile, charmingly debilitated girl with pink eyelids, in general appearance rather like a white mouse; her first name was Tamara (which would have better suited the doll), and her last was reminiscent of one of those German mountain landscapes that hang in picture-framing shops. Fyodor sat by the bookshelf and tried to simulate good spirits, despite the lump in his throat. Kern, a civil engineer, who prided himself on having been a close acquaintance of the late Alexander Blok (the celebrated poet), was producing a gluey sound as he extracted a date from an oblong carton. Lyubov Markovna carefully examined the pastries on a large plate with a poorly pictured bumblebee and, suddenly botching her investigation, contented herself with a bun – the sugar-powdered kind that always bears an anonymous fingerprint. The host was telling an ancient story about a medical student's April Fool's prank in Kiev. . . . But the most interesting person in the room sat a little distance apart, by the writing desk, and did not take part in the general conversation – which, however, he followed with quiet attention. He was a youth somewhat resembling Fyodor – not so much in facial features (which at that moment were difficult to distinguish) but in the tonality of his general appearance: the dunnish auburn shade of the round head which was closely cropped (a style which, according to the rules of latter-day St Petersburg romanticism, was more becoming to a poet than shaggy locks); the transparency of the large, tender, slightly protruding ears; the slenderness of the neck with the shadow of a hollow at its nape. He sat in the same pose Fyodor sometimes assumed – head slightly lowered, legs crossed, arms not so much crossed as hugging each other, as if he felt chilled, so that the repose of the body was expressed more by angular projections (knee, elbow, thin shoulder) and the contraction of all the members rather than by the general softening of the frame when a person is relaxing and listening. The shadows of two volumes standing on the desk mimicked a cuff and the corner of a lapel, while the shadow of a third volume, which was leaning against the others, might have passed for a necktie. He was about five years younger than Fyodor and, as far as the face itself was concerned, if one judged by the photographs on the walls of the room and in the adjacent bedroom (on the little table between twin beds that wept at night), here was perhaps no resemblance at all, if you discounted a certain elongation of outline combined with prominent frontal bones and the dark depth of the eye sockets – Pascal-like, according to the physiognomists – and also there might have been something in common in the breadth of the eyebrows . . . but no, it was not a matter of ordinary resemblance, but of generic spiritual similarity between two angular and sensitive boys, each odd in his own way. This youth sat with downcast eyes and a trace of mockery on his lips, in a modest, not very comfortable position, on a chair along whose seat copper tacks glinted, to the left of the dictionary-cluttered desk; and Alexander Yakovlevich Chernyshevski, with a convulsive effort, as if regaining lost balance, would tear his gaze away from that shadowy youth, as he went on with the jaunty banter behind which he tried to conceal his mental sickness.

'Don't worry, there'll be reviews,' he said to Fyodor, winking involuntarily. 'You can be sure the critics will squeeze out your blackheads.'

'By the way,' asked his wife, 'what do those "weavers and wavers" mean exactly – in the poem about the bicycle?'

Fyodor explained, relying more on gestures than on words: 'You know, when you are learning to ride a bike and you sort of swerve from side to side.'

'My favourite is the one about children's diseases, yes,' said Alexandra Yakovlevna, nodding to herself, 'that's good: Christmastime scarlet fever and Eastertime diphtheria.'

'Why not the other way around?' inquired Tamara.

Oh, how the boy had loved poetry! The glass-doored bookcase in the bedroom was full of his books: Gumilyouv and Hérédia. Blok and Rilke – and how much he knew by heart! And the notebooks. . . . One day she and I will have to sit down and go through it all. She has the strength to do it, I don't. Strange how one keeps postponing things. One would think it would be a pleasure – the only, the bitter pleasure – to go through the belongings of the dead, yet his stuff goes on lying there, untouched (the provident laziness of one's soul?); it is unthinkable that a stranger should touch it, but what a relief it would be if an accidental fire were to destroy that precious little cabinet. Chernyshevski abruptly got up and, as if by chance, moved the chair by the desk in such a way that neither it nor the shadows of the books could serve as a theme for the phantom.

By then the talk had shifted to some unlamented Soviet politician who had fallen from power after Lenin's death. 'Oh, in the years I knew him he was at the "height of glory and good deeds",' the journalist Vasiliev was saying, professionally misquoting Pushkin (who has 'hope', not 'height').

The boy who looked like Fyodor (to whom the Chernyshevskis had become so attached for this very reason) was now by the door, where he paused before leaving the room, half turning towards his father – and, despite his purely imaginary nature, how much more substantial he was than all those sitting in the room! The sofa could be seen through Vasiliev and the pale girl! Kern, the engineer, was represented only the glint of his pincenez; so was Lyubov Markovna; and Fyodor himself existed only because of a vague congruity with the deceased – while Yasha was perfectly real and live, and only the instinct of self-preservation prevented one from taking a good look at his features.

But perhaps, thought Fyodor, perhaps, this is all wrong, perhaps he [Alexander Yakovlevich Chernyshevski] is not imagining his dead son at all right now as I imagine him doing. He may be really occupied with the conversation and if his eyes are wandering it may be only because he has always been fidgety, poor soul. I am unhappy, I am bored, nothing rings true here and I don't know why I keep sitting here, listening to nonsense.

However he still continued to sit there and smoke and gently swing the toe of his foot – and while the others talked on and he talked on himself, he tried as he did everywhere and always to imagine the inner, transparent motion of this or that other person. He would carefully seat himself inside the interlocutor as in an armchair, so that the other's elbows would serve as armrests for him, and his soul would fit snugly into the other's soul – and then the lighting of the world would suddenly change and for a minute he would actually become Alexander Chernyshevski, or Lyubov Markovna, or Vasiliev. Sometimes a sporting excitement would be added to the seltzerlike effervescence of the transformation, and he felt flattered when a chance word aptly confirmed the train of thought he was divining in the other. He to whom so-called politics (that ridiculous sequence of pacts, conflicts, aggravations, frictions, discords, collapses, and the transformation of perfectly innocent little towns into the names of international treaties) meant nothing, would sometimes immerse himself with a thrill of curiosity and revulsion into the vast bowels of Vasiliev and live for an instant actuated by his, Vasiliev's, inner mechanism, where next to the 'Locarno' button there was one for 'Lockout' and where a pseudo-clever, pseudo-entertaining game was conducted by such ill-matched symbols as 'The Five Kremlin Rulers', or 'The Kurd Rebellion', or individual surnames that had lost all human connotations: Hindenburg, Marx, Painlevé, Herriot (whose macrocephalic initial in Russian, the reverse E, had become so autonomous in the columns of Vasiliev's *Gazeta* as to threaten a complete rift with the original Frenchman); this was a world of prophetic utterances, presentiments, mysterious combinations; a world that was in fact a hundredfold more spectral than the most abstract dream. And when Fyodor moved over into Mme Chernyshevski he found himself within a soul where not everything was alien to him, but where he marvelled at many things, as a prim traveller might marvel at the customs in a distant land: the bazaar at sunrise, the naked children, the din, the monstrous size of fruit. This forty-five-year-old, plain, indolent woman, who two years ago had lost her only son, had suddenly come alive: mourning had given her wings and tears had rejuvenated her – or at any rate so said those who had known her before. The memory of her son, which in her husband had become an illness, burned in her with a quickening fervour. It would be incorrect to say that this fervour filled her completely; no, it far exceeded the confines of her soul, seeming even to ennoble the absurdity of these two rented rooms into which, after the tragedy, she and her husband had moved from the large In den Zelten apartment (where her brother had lived with his family back in the years before the war). Now she regarded all her friends only in the light of their receptivity towards her loss, and also, for greater precision, recalled or imagined Yasha's opinion of this or that individual with whom she had to keep up acquaintance. She was seized with the fever of activity, with the thirst for an abundant response; her child grew within her and struggled to issue forth; the literary circle newly founded by her husband jointly with Vasiliev, in order to give himself and her something to do, seemed to her the best possible posthumous honour for her poet son. It was just at that time that I first saw her and was more than a little perplexed when suddenly this plump, terribly animated little woman with dazzling blue eyes burst into tears in the midst of her first conversation with me, as if a brimful crystal vessel had broken for no apparent reason, and, without taking her dancing gaze off me, laughing and sobbing, started saying over and over 'Goodness, how you remind me of him!' The frankness with which, during our subsequent meetings, she spoke about her son, about all the details of his death and about the way she now dreamed of him (as if big with him and as translucent as a bubble) seemed to me vulgar and shameless; it irked me even more when I learned indirectly that she was 'a little hurt' that I did not answer her with corresponding vibrations but instead only changed the subject the moment she mentioned my own grief, my own loss. Very soon, however, I noticed that this rapture of sorrow in which she managed to live without dying of a ruptured aorta was beginning somehow to draw me in and make demands on me. You know that characteristic movement when someone hands you a treasured photograph and watches you in anticipation . . . and you, having lengthily and piously gazed at the face in the snapshot, which smiles innocently and without a thought of death, feign to delay its return, feign to retard your own hand, while with a lingering glance you give back the picture, as if it would have been impolite to part with it sooner. This sequence of movements she and I repeated endlessly. Her husband would sit at his brightly lit desk in the corner, working and occasionally clearing his throat: he was compiling his dictionary of Russian technical terms, commissioned by a German publisher. All was quiet and wrong. The remains of cherry jam mingled with cigarette ash in my saucer. The more she continued to tell about Yasha, the less attractive he grew: oh no, he and I bore little resemblance to each other (far less than she supposed, projecting inward the coincidental similarity of external features, of which, moreover, she found additional ones that did not exist – in reality, the little there was within us corresponded to the little there was without), and I doubt we would have become friends if he and I had ever met. His sombreness, interrupted by the sudden shrill gaiety characteristic of humourless people; the sentimentality of his intellectual enthusiasms; his purity, which would have strongly suggested timidity of the senses were it not for the morbid over-refinement of their interpretation; his feeling for Germany; his tasteless spiritual throes ('For a whole week,' he said, 'I was in a daze' – after reading Spengler!); and finally his poetry . . . in short, everything that to his mother was filled with enchantment only repelled me. As a poet he was, in my opinion, very feeble; he did not create, he merely dabbled in poetry, just as thousands of intelligent youths of his type did; but if they did not meet with some kind of more or less heroic death – having nothing to do with Russian letters, which, however, they knew meticulously (oh, those notebooks of Yasha's, filled with prosodic diagrams expressing modulations of rhythm in the tetrameter!) – they subsequently abandoned literature altogether; and if they exhibited talent in some field, it would be in science or administration, or else simply in a well-ordered life. His poems, replete with fashionable clichés, exalted his 'grievous' love of Russia – autumn scenes à la Esenin, the smoky blue of Blok-ish bogs, the powder snow upon the wooden paving blocks of Mandelshtam's neoclassicism, and the Neva's granite parapet on which one can scarcely discern today the imprint of Pushkin's elbow. His mother would read them to me, stumbling in her agitation, with an awkward schoolgirl intonation which did not at all suit those tragically scudded iambics; Yasha himself must have recited them in an oblivious singsong, dilating his nostrils and swaying in the bizarre blaze of a kind of lyric pride, after which he would immediately sink back, again becoming humble, limp and withdrawn. The sonorous epithets that lived in his throat – *neveroyatnyy* (incredible), *hladnyy* (cold), *prekrasnyy* (beautiful) – epithets avidly employed by the young poets of his generation under the delusion that archaisms, prosaisms, or simply destitute words, having completed their life cycle, now, when used in poems, gained a kind of unexpected freshness, returning from the opposite direction – these words in Mme Chernyshevski's stumbling diction made, as it were, another half cycle, faded away again, and again revealed their decrepit poverty – thus exposing the deception of style. Besides patriotic elegies, Yasha had poems about the low haunts of adventurous sailors, about gin and jazz (which he pronounced, in the German way, as 'yatz'), and poems about Berlin, in which he attempted to endow German proper names with a lyric voice in the same way, for instance, as Italian street names resound in Russian poetry with a suspiciously apostrophes to a male he also had poems dedicated to friendship, without rhyme and without metre, full of muddled, hazy and timid emotions, of some internal spiritual bickerings, and apostrophes to a male friend in the polite form (the Russian '*vy*'), as a sick Frenchman addresses God, or a young Russian poetess her favourite gentleman. And all this was expressed in a pale, haphazard manner, with many vulgarisms and incorrect word accents peculiar to his provincial middle-class set. Misled by its augmentative suffix, he assumed that '*pozharishche*' (the site of a recent fire) meant a 'big fire', and I also remember a rather pathetic reference to 'Vrublyov's frescoes' – an amusing cross between two Russian painters (Rublyov and Vrubel) that only served to prove our dissimilarity: no, he could not have loved painting as I do. My true opinion of his poetry I concealed from his mother, while the forced sounds of inarticulate approbation that I politely made were construed by her as signs of incoherent rapture. For my birthday she gave me, beaming through her tears, Yasha's best necktie, an old-fashioned affair of watered silk, freshly ironed, with, still discernible, the label of a well-known but not elegant shop: I hardly think Yasha himself ever wore it; and in exchange for everything which she had shared with me, for her giving me a complete and detailed image of her late son, with his poetry, his neurasthenia, his enthusiasms, his death, Mme Chernyshevski imperiously demanded from me a certain amount of creative collaboration. Her husband, who was proud of his century-old name and spent hours entertaining guests with its history (his grandfather had been baptized in the reign of Nicholas I – in Volsk, I believe – by the father of the famous political writer Chernyshevski, a stout, energetic Greek Orthodox priest who liked to do missionary work among the Jews, and who, on top of the spiritual benison, would bestow upon converts the added bonus of his last name), said to me on numerous occasions, 'Look, you ought to write a little book in the form of a *biographic romancée* about our great man of the sixties – Now, now, stop frowning, I can foresee all your objections, but believe me, there are, after all, cases where the fascinating beauty of a good man's dedicated life fully redeems the falsity of his literary views, and Nikolay Chernyshevski was indeed a heroic soul. If you should decide to describe his life, there are many curious things I could tell you.' I had no desire at all to write about the great man of the sixties and even less to write about Yasha, as his mother persistently counselled for her part (so that, taken together, here was an order for a complete history of their family). But, while I was both amused and irritated by these efforts of theirs to channel my muse, I nevertheless felt that before long Mme Chernyshevski would have me cornered and, just as I was compelled to put on Yasha's necktie on my visits to her (until it occurred to me to say I was saving it for special occasions), I would have to undertake writing a long short story depicting Yasha's fate. At one time I was even weak enough (or bold enough, perhaps) to ponder how I might tackle the subject, if by any chance . . . Any corny man of ideas, any 'serious' novelist in horn-rimmed glasses – the family doctor of Europe and the seismographer of its social tremors – would no doubt have found in this story something highly characteristic of the 'frame of mind of young people in the postwar years' – a combination of words which in itself (even apart from the 'general idea' it conveyed) made me speechless with scorn. I used to feel a cloying nausea when I heard or read the latest drivel, vulgar and humourless drivel, about the 'symptoms of the age' and the 'tragedy of youth'. And, since I could not be kindled by Yasha's tragedy (though his mother did think I was affire), I would have become enmired involuntarily in a 'deep' social-interest novel with a disgusting Freudian reek. My heart stood still as I exercised my imagination, probing with my toe, as it were, the mica-thin ice over the puddle; I would go so far as to picture myself making a fair copy of my work and bringing it to Mme Chernyshevski, seating myself in such a way that the lamp would illuminate my fatal road from the left (thank you, I can see fine this way), and after a brief foreword about how difficult it had been, about the sense of responsibility I felt . . . but here everything would be obscured by the crimson mist of shame. Fortunately I did not fulfil the order – I am not sure exactly what saved me: for one thing, I kept putting it off too long; for another, certain blessed intervals occurred between our meetings; and then perhaps Mme Chernyshevski herself grew a little bored with me as a listener; be that as it may, the story remained unused by the writer – a story that was in fact very simple and sad.

Yasha and I had entered Berlin University at almost exactly

the same time, but I did not know him although we must have passed each other many times. Diversity of subjects – he took philosophy, I studied infusoria – diminished the possibility of our association. If I were to return now into that past, enriched in but one respect – awareness of the present day – and retrace exactly all my interlooping steps, then I would certainly notice his face, now so familiar to me through snapshots. It is a funny thing, when you imagine yourself returning into the past with the contraband of the present, how weird it would be to encounter there, in unexpected places, the prototypes of today's acquaintances, so young and fresh, who in a kind of lucid lunacy do not recognize you; thus a woman, for instance, whom one loves since yesterday, appears as a young girl, standing practically next to one in a crowded train, while the chance passerby who fifteen years ago asked you the way in the street now works in the same office as you. Among this throng of the past only a dozen or so faces would acquire this anachronistic importance: low cards transfigured by the radiance of the trump. And then how confidently one could . . . But alas, even when you do happen, in a dream, to make such a return journey, then, at the border of the past your present intellect is completely invalidated, and amid the surroundings of a classroom hastily assembled by the nightmare's clumsy property man, you again do not know your lesson – with all the forgotten shades of those school throes of old.

At the university Yasha made close friends with two fellow students, Rudolf Baumann, a German, and Olya G., a compatriot – the Russian-language papers did not print her name in full. She was a girl of his age and set, even, I think, from the same town as he. Their families, however, were not acquainted. Only once did I have a chance to see her, at a literary soirée about two years after Yasha's death – I remember her remarkably broad and clear forehead, her aquamarine eyes and her large red mouth with black fuzz over the upper lip and a plump mole at the wick; she stood with her arms folded across her soft bosom, at once arousing in me all the proper literary associations, such as the dust of a fair summer evening and the threshold of a highway tavern, and a bored girl's observant gaze. As for Rudolf, I never saw him myself and can conclude only from the words of others that he had pale blond hair brushed back, was swift in his movements and handsome – in a hard, sinewy way, remindful of a gundog. Thus I use a different method to study each of the three individuals, which affects both their substance and their coloration, until, at the last minute, the rays of a sun that is my own and yet is incomprehensible to me, strikes them and equalizes them in the same burst of light.

Yasha kept a diary and in those notes he neatly defined the mutual relationship between him, Rudolf and Olya as 'a triangle inscribed in a circle'. The circle represented the normal, simple, 'Euclidian' (as he put it) friendship that united all three, so that if it alone had existed their union would have remained happy, carefree and unbroken. But the triangle inscribed within it was a different system of relationships, complex, agonizing and slow in forming, which had an existence of its own, quite independent of its common enclosure of uniform friendship. This was the banal triangle of tragedy, formed within an idyllic circle, and the mere presence of such a suspiciously neat structure, to say nothing of the fashionable counterpoint of its development, would never have permitted me to make it into a short story or novel.

'I am fiercely in love with the soul of Rudolf,' wrote Yasha in his agitated, neoromantic style. 'I love its harmonious proportions, its health, the joy it has in living. I am fiercely in love with this naked, suntanned, lithe soul, which has an answer to everything and proceeds through life as a self-confident woman does across a ballroom floor. I can imagine only in the most complex, abstract manner, next to which Kant and Hegel are child's play, the fierce ecstasy I would experience if only . . . If only what? What can I do with his soul? This is what kills me – this yearning for some most mysterious tool (thus Albrecht Koch yearned for 'golden logic' in the world of madmen). My blood throbs, my hands grow icy like a schoolgirl's when I remain alone with him, and he knows this and I become repulsive to him and he does not conceal his disgust. I am fiercely in love with his soul – and this is just as fruitless as falling in love with the moon.'

Rudolf's squeamishness is understandable, but if one looks at the matter more closely, one suspects that Yasha's passion was perhaps not so abnormal after all, that his excitement was after all very much akin to that of many a Russian youth in the middle of last century, trembling with happiness when, raising his silky eyelashes, his pale-browed teacher, a future leader, a future martyr, would turn to him; and I would have refused to see in Yasha's case an incorrigible deviation had Rudolf been to the least degree a teacher, a martyr, or a leader;

and not what he really was, a so-called 'Bursch', a German 'regular guy', notwithstanding a certain propensity for obscure poetry, lame music, lopsided art – which did not affect in him that fundamental soundness by which Yasha was captivated, or thought he was.

The son of a respectable fool of a professor and a civil servant's daughter, he had grown up in wonderful bourgeois surroundings, between a cathedral-like sideboard and the backs of dormant books. He was good-natured although not good; sociable, and yet a little skittish; impulsive, and at the same time calculating. He fell in love with Olya conclusively after a bicycle ride with her and Yasha in the Black Forest, a tour which, as he later testified at the inquest, 'was an eye-opener for all three of us'; he fell in love with her on the lowest level, primitively and impatiently, but from her he received a sharp rebuff, made all the stronger by the fact that Olya, an indolent, grasping, morosely freakish girl, had in her turn (in those same fir woods, by the same round, black lake) 'realized she had fallen for' Yasha, who was just as oppressed by this as Rudolf was by Yasha's ardour, and as she herself was by the ardour of Rudolf, so that the geometric relationship of their inscribed feelings was complete, reminding one of the traditional and somewhat mysterious interconnections in the *dramatis personae* of eighteenth-century French playwrights where X is the *amante* of Y ('the one in love with Y') and Y is the *amant* of Z ('the one in love with Z').

By winter, the second winter of their friendship, they had become clearly aware of the situation; the winter was spent studying its hopelessness. On the surface everything seemed to be fine: Yasha read incessantly; Rudolf played hockey, masterfully speeding the puck across the ice; Olya studied the history of art (which, in the context of the epoch, sounds – as does the tone of the entire drama in question – like an unbearably typical, and therefore false, note); within, however, a hidden agonizing torment was growing, which became formidably destructive the moment that these unfortunate young people began to find some pleasure in their threefold torture.

For a long time they abided by a tacit agreement (each knowing, shamelessly and hopelessly, everything about the others) never to mention their feelings when the three of them were together; but whenever one of them was absent, the other two would inevitably set to discussing his passion and his suffering. For some reason they celebrated New Year's Eve in the restaurant of one of the Berlin railroad stations – perhaps because at railroad stations the armament of time is particularly impressive – and then they went slouching through the vari-coloured slush of grim festive streets, and Rudolf ironically proposed a toast to the exposure of their friendship – and since that time, at first discreetly, but soon with all the rapture of frankness, they would jointly discuss their feelings with all three present. It was then that the triangle began to erode its circumference.

The elder Chernyshevskis, as well as Rudolf's parents and Olya's mother (a sculptress, obese, black-eyed, and still handsome, with a low voice, who had buried two husbands and used to wear long necklaces that looked like bronze chains), not only did not sense that something doomful was growing, but would have confidently replied (should an aimless questioner have turned up among the angels already converging, already swarming and fussing professionally around the cradle where lay a dark little newborn revolver) that everything was all right, that everybody was happy. Afterwards, though, when everything had happened, their cheated memories made every effort to find in the routine past course of identically tinted days, traces and evidence of what was to come – and, surprisingly, they would find them. Thus Mme G., paying a call of condolence on Mme Chernyshevski, fully believed what she was saying when she insisted she had had presentiments of the tragedy for a long time – since the very day when she had come into the half-dark drawing room where, in motionless poses on a couch, in the various sorrowful inclinations of allegories on tombstone bas-reliefs, Olya and her two friends were sitting in silence; this was but a fleeting momentary harmony of shadows, but Mme G. professed to have noticed that moment, or, more likely, she had set it aside in order to return to it a few months later.

By spring the revolver had grown. It belonged to Rudolf, but for a long time passed inconspicuously from one to the other, like a warm ring sliding on a string in a parlour game, or a playing card with Black Mary. Strange as it may seen, the idea of disappearing, all three together, in order that – already in a different world – an ideal and flawless circle might be restored, was being developed most actively by Olya, although now it is hard to determine who first proposed it and when. The role of poet in this enterprise was taken by Yasha – his position seemed the most hopeless since, after all, it was the most abstract; there are, however, sorrows that one does not cure by death, since they can be treated much more simply by life and its changing yearnings: a material bullet is powerless against them, while on the other hand, it copes perfectly well with the coarser passions of hearts like Rudolf's and Olya's.

A solution had now been found and discussions of it became especially fascinating. In mid-April, at the flat the Chernyshevskis then had, something happened that apparently served as the final impulse for the *dénouement*. Yasha's parents had peacefully left for the cinema across the street. Rudolf unexpectedly got drunk and let himself go. Yasha dragged him away from Olya and all this happened in the bathroom, and presently Rudolf, in tears, was picking up the money that had somehow fallen out of his trouser pockets, and what oppression all three felt, what shame, and how tempting was the relief offered by the finale scheduled for the next day.

After dinner on Thursday the eighteenth, which was also the eighteenth anniversary of the death of Olya's father, they equipped themselves with the revolver, which had become by now quite burly and independent, and in light, flimsy weather (with a damp west wind and the violet rust of pansies in every garden) set off on streetcar fifty-seven for the Grunewald where they planned to find a lonely spot and shoot themselves one after the other. They stood on the rear platform of the tram, all three wearing raincoats, with pale puffy faces – and Yasha's big-peaked cap, which he had not worn for about four years and had for some reason put on today, gave him an oddly plebeian look; Rudolf was hatless and the wind ruffled his blond hair, thrown back from the temples; Olya stood leaning against the rear railing, gripping the black stang with a white, firm hand that had a prominent ring on its index finger – and gazed with narrowed eyes at the streets flicking by, and all the time kept stepping by mistake, on the treadle of the gentle little bell in the floor (intended for the huge, stonelike foot of the motorman when the rear of the car became the front). This group was noticed from inside the car, through the door, by Yuliy Filippovich Posner, former tutor of a cousin of Yasha's. Leaning out quickly – he was an alert, self-confident person – he beckoned to Yasha, who, recognizing him, went inside.

'Good thing I ran across you,' said Posner, and after he had explained in detail that he was going with his five-year-old daughter (sitting separately by a window with her rubber-soft nose pressed against the glass) to visit his wife in a maternity ward, he produced his wallet and from the wallet his calling card, and then, taking advantage of an accidental stop made by the car (the trolley had come off the wire on a curve), crossed out his old address with a fountain pen and wrote the new one above it. 'Here,' he said, 'give this to your cousin as soon as he comes back from Basel and remind him, please, that he still has several of my books which I need, which I need very much.'

The tramcar was speeding along the Hohenzollerndamm and on its rear platform Olya and Rudolf continued to stand just as sternly as before in the wind, but a certain mysterious change had occurred: by the act of leaving them alone, although only for a minute (Posner and his daughter got off very soon), Yasha had, as it were, broken the alliance and had initiated his separation from them, so that when he rejoined them on the platform he was, though as much unaware of it as they were, already on his own and the invisible crack, in keeping with the law governing all cracks, continued irresistibly to creep and widen.

In the solitude of the spring forest where the wet, dun birches, particularly the smaller ones, stood around blankly with all their attention turned inside themselves; not far from the dove-grey lake (on whose vast shore there was not a soul except for a little man who was tossing a stick into the water at the request of his dog) they easily found a convenient lonely spot and right away got down to business; to be more exact, Yasha got down to business: he had that honesty of spirit that imparts to the most reckless act an almost everyday simplicity. He said he would shoot himself first by right of seniority (he was a year older than Rudolf and a month older than Olya) and this simple remark rendered unnecessary the stroke of drawn lots, which, in its coarse blindness, would probably have fallen on him anyway; and throwing off his raincoat and without bidding his friends farewell (which was only natural in view of their identical destination), silently, with clumsy haste, he walked down the slippery, pine-covered slope into a ravine heavily overgrown with scrub oak and bramble bushes, which, despite April's limpidity, completely concealed him from the others.

These two stood for a long time waiting for the shot. They had no cigarettes with them, but Rudolf was clever enough to feel in the pocket of Yasha's raincoat where he found an unopened pack. The sky had grown overcast, the pines were rustling cautiously and it seemed from below that their blind branches were groping for something. High above and fabulously fast, their long necks extended, two wild ducks flew past, one slightly behind the other. Afterwards Yasha's mother used to show the visiting card, DIPL. ING. JULIUS POSNER, on the reverse of which Yasha had written in pencil, *Mummy, Daddy, I am still alive, I am very scared, forgive me.* Finally Rudolf could stand it no longer and climbed down to see what was the matter with him. Yasha was sitting on a log among last year's still unanswered leaves, but he did not turn; he only said: 'I'll be ready in a minute.' There was something tense about his back, as if he were controlling an acute pain. Rudolf rejoined Olya, but no sooner had he reached her than both of them heard the dull pop of the shot, while in Yasha's room life went on for a few more hours as if nothing had happened – the cast-off banana skin on a plate, the volume of Annenski's poems *The Cypress Chest* and that of Khodasevich's *The Heavy Lyre* on the chair by the bed, the ping-pong bat on the couch; he was killed outright; to revive him, however, Rudolf and Olya dragged him through the bushes to the reeds and there desperately sprinkled him and rubbed him, so that he was all smudged with earth, blood and silt when the police later found the body. Then the two began calling for help, but nobody came: architect Ferdinand Stockschmeisser had long since left with his wet setter.

They returned to the place where they had waited for the shot and here dusk begins to fall on the story. The one clear thing is that Rudolf, whether because a certain terrestrial vacancy had opened for him or because he was simply a coward, lost all desire to shoot himself, and Olya, even if she had persisted in her intention, could do nothing since he had immediately hidden the revolver. In the woods, where it had grown cold and dark, with a blind drizzle crepitating around, they remained for a long time until a stupidly late hour. Rumour has it that it was then that they became lovers, but this would be really too flat. At about midnight, at the corner of a street poetically named Lilac Lane, a police sergeant listened sceptically to their horrible, voluble tale. There is a kind of hysterical state that assumes the semblance of childish swaggering.

If Mme Chernyshevski had met Olya immediately after the event then perhaps some kind of sentimental sense would have come of it for them both. Unfortunately the meeting occurred only several months later, because, in the first place, Olya went away and in the second, Mme Chernyshevski's grief did not immediately take on that industrious, and even enraptured, form that Fyodor found when he came on the scene. Olya was in a certain sense unlucky: it so happened that Olya had come back for her step-brother's engagement party and the house was full of guests; and when Mme Chernyshevski arrived without warning, beneath a heavy mourning veil, with a choice selection from her sorrowful archives (photographs, letters) in her handbag, all prepared for the rapture of shared tears, she was met by a morosely polite, morosely impatient young woman in a semitransparent dress, with blood-red lips and a fat white-powdered nose, and one could hear from the little side room where she took her guest the wailing of a phonograph, and of course no communion of souls came of it. 'All I did was to take a long look at her,' recounted Mme Chernyshevski – after which she carefully snipped off, on many little snapshots, both Olya and Rudolf; the latter, however, had visited her at once and had rolled at her feet and pounded his head on the soft corner of the divan, and then he walked off with his wonderful bouncy stride down the Kurfürstendamm, which glistened after a spring shower.

Yasha's death had its most painful effect on his father. He had to spend the whole summer in a sanatorium and he never really recovered: the partition dividing the room temperature of reason from the infinitely ugly, cold, ghostly world into which Yasha had passed suddenly crumbled, and to restore it was impossible, so that the gap had to be draped in makeshift fashion and one tried not to look at the stirring folds. Ever since that day the other world began to seep into his life; but there was no way of resolving this constant intercourse with Yasha's spirit and he finally told his wife about it, in the vain hope that he might thus render harmless a phantom that secrecy had nurtured: the secrecy must have grown back, for soon he again had to seek the tedious, essentially mortal, glass-and-rubber help of doctors. Thus he lived only half in our world, at which he grasped the more greedily and desperately, and when one listened to his sprightly speech and looked at his regular features, it was difficult to imagine the unearthly experiences of this healthy-looking, plump little man, with his bald spot and the thin hair on either side, but then all the more strange was the convulsion that suddenly disfigured him; also the fact that sometimes for weeks on end he wore a grey cloth glove on his right hand (he suffered from eczema) hinted eerily at a mystery, as if, repelled by life's unclean touch, or burned by another life, he was reserving his bare handclasp for inhuman, hardly imaginable meetings. Meanwhile nothing stopped with Yasha's death and many interesting things were happening: in Russia one observed the spread of abortions and the revival of summer houses; in England there were strikes of some kind or other; Lenin met a sloppy end; Duse, Puccini and Anatole France died; Mallory and Irvine perished near the summit of Everest; and old Prince Dolgorukiy, in shoes of plaited leather thong, secretly visited Russia to see again the buckwheat in bloom; while in Berlin three-wheeled taxis appeared, only to disappear again shortly afterwards, and the first dirigible slowly stepped across the ocean and papers spoke a great deal about Coué, Chang Tso-lin and Tutankhamen, and one Sunday a young Berlin merchant with his locksmith friend set out on a trip to the country in a large, four-wheel cart with only the slightest smell of blood, rented from his neighbour, a butcher: two fat servant maids and the merchant's two small children sat in plush chairs set on the wagon, the children cried, the merchant and his pal guzzled beer and drove the horses hard, the weather was beautiful so that, in their high spirits, they deliberately hit a cleverly cornered cyclist, beat him up violently in the ditch, tore his portfolio to bits (he was an artist) and rolled on, very happy, and when he had come to his senses, the artist overtook them in a tavern garden, but the policeman who tried to establish their identities was also beaten up, after which they very happily rolled on along the highway, and when they saw that police motor-cycles were gaining on them, they opened fire with revolvers and in the ensuing gunplay a bullet killed the merry merchant's three-year-old son.

'Listen, we ought to change the subject,' Mme Chernyshevski said softly. 'I am afraid to have my husband listen to things like that. You do have a new poem, don't you? Fyodor Konstantinovich is going to read us a poem,' she proclaimed loudly, but Vasiliev, half reclining, having in one hand a monumental cigarette holder with a nicotineless cigarette, and with the other absentmindedly tousling the doll, which was executing all kinds of emotional evolutions in his lap, nevertheless went on for a good half minute about how that gay incident had been investigated in court the previous day.

'I haven't got anything with me, and I don't know anything by heart,' Fyodor repeated several times.

Chernyshevski quickly turned to him and put his small hairy hand on his sleeve. 'I have a feeling you are still cross with me.

You're not? Word of honour? I realized afterwards what a cruel joke it was. You don't look well. How are things going? You never really did explain to me why you changed your lodgings.'

He explained: at the boardinghouse where he had lived for a year and a half people he knew had suddenly moved in, very kind, innocently intrusive bores who kept 'dropping in for a chat'. Their room was near his and before long Fyodor had the feeling that the wall between them had crumbled and he was defenceless. Of course, in the case of Yasha's father no change of residence could possibly have helped.

Vasiliev had got up. Whistling softly, his huge back bent slightly, he was examining the books on the shelves; he pulled one out, opened it, stopped whistling and, wheezing instead, began reading the first page to himself. His place on the couch was taken by Lyubov Markovna and her large purse: now that her tired eyes were naked, her expression grew softer, as with a seldom humoured hand she stroked the golden back of Tamara's head.

'Yes!' Vasiliev said abruptly, slamming the book shut and cramming it into the first available opening. 'All things in the world must end, comrades. As for me, I must get up at seven tomorrow.'

Engineer Kern took a look at his wrist.

'Oh, stay a while longer,' said Mme Chernyshevski, her blue eyes beaming imploringly, and turning to the engineer, who had risen and stood behind his empty chair which he slightly moved to one side (thus a Russian merchant who has drunk his fill of tea might turn his glass upside down on its saucer), she started talking about the lecture he had agreed to deliver at the next Saturday meeting – its title was 'Alexander Blok in the War'.

'I put "Blok and War" on the announcements by mistake,' she said, 'but it doesn't make any difference, does it?'

'On the contrary, it certainly does make a difference,' replied Kern with a smile on his thin lips, but with murder behind his thick eyeglasses, without unclasping his hands which were joined on his abdomen. ' "Blok in the War" conveys the proper meaning – the personal nature of the speaker's own observations, while "Blok and War", if you will excuse me, is philosophy.'

And now they all began gradually to grow less distinct, to ripple with the random agitation of a fog, and then to vanish altogether; their outlines, weaving in figure-eight patterns, were evaporating, though here and there a bright point still glowed

– the cordial glint in an eye, the gleam of a bracelet; there was also a momentary reappearance of the intently furrowed forehead of Vasiliev, who was shaking somebody's already dissolving hand, and at the very last there was a floating glimpse of pistachio-coloured straw, decorated with silk roses (Lyubov Markovna's hat), and now everything was gone, and into the smoky parlour, without a sound, in his bedroom slippers, came Yasha, thinking that his father had already retired, and with a magic tinkling, by the light of crimson lanterns, dim beings were repairing the pavement at the corner of the square, and Fyodor, who did not have money for the streetcar, was walking home. He had forgotten to borrow from the Chernyshevskis those two or three marks that would have tided him over until he got paid for a lesson or translation: this thought alone would not have disturbed him had he not been possessed by a general feeling of wretchedness consisting of that rotten disappointment (he had imagined so vividly the success of his book), and a chill leak in his left shoe, and fear of the imminent night in a new place. He was tired, he was dissatisfied with himself for wasting the tender beginning of the night, and he was tormented by the feeling that there was some line of thought he had not pursued to its conclusion that day and now could never finish.

He was walking along streets that had already long since insinuated themselves into his acquaintance – and as if that were not enough, they expected affection; they had even purchased in advance, in his future memories, space next to St Petersburg, an adjacent grave; he walked along these dark, glossy streets and the blind houses retreated, backing or sidling into the brown sky of the Berlin night, which, nevertheless, had its soft spots here and there, spots that would melt under one's gaze, allowing it to obtain a few stars. Here at last is the square where we dined and the tall brick church and the still quite transparent poplar, resembling the nervous system of a giant; here, also, is the public toilet, reminiscent of Baba Yaga's gingerbread cottage. In the gloom of the small public garden crossed obliquely by the faint light of a streetlamp, the beautiful girl who for the last eight years had kept refusing to be incarnated (so vivid was the memory of his first love), was sitting on a cinder-grey bench, but when he got closer he saw that only the bent shadow of the poplar trunk was sitting there. He turned into his street, plunging in it as in cold water – he was so loath to go back, such melancholy was promised him by that room, that malevolent wardrobe, that daybed. He located his front door (disguised by darkness) and pulled out his keys. None of them would open the door.

'What's this . . .' he muttered crossly, looking at the key bit, and then furiously began jamming it in again. 'What the hell!' he exclaimed and retreated one step in order to throw back his head and make out the house number. Yes, it was the right house. He was just about to bend over the lock once more when a sudden truth dawned upon him: these were, of course, the boardinghouse keys, which he had carried away in his raincoat pocket by mistake when he moved today, and the new ones must have remained in the room that he now wanted to get into much more than a moment ago.

In those days Berlin janitors were for the most part opulent bullies who had corpulent wives and belonged, out of petty bourgeois considerations, to the Communist Party. White Russian tenants quailed before them: accustomed to subjection, we everywhere appoint over ourselves the shadow of supervision. Fyodor understood perfectly well how stupid it was to be afraid of an old fool with a bobbing Adam's apple, but still he could not bring himself to wake up after midnight, to summon him up out of his giant featherbed, to perform the act of pushing the button (even though it was more than likely that no one would answer, squeeze as he might); he could not bring himself to do it, especially because he did not have that ten-pfennig coin without which it was unthinkable to walk past the palm, grimly cupped at hip level, confident of receiving its tribute.

'What a mess, what a mess' he whispered, stepping away and feeling, from behind, the weight of a sleepless night settling on him from head to heels, a leaden twin whom he must carry somewhere or other. 'How stupid, *kak glupo,*' he added, pronouncing the Russian *glupo* with a soft French 'l' as his father used to do in a mildly jocular absentminded way, when perplexed.

He wondered what to do next. Wait for somebody to come out? Try to find the black-caped night watchman who looked after door locks on residential streets? Force himself after all to blow up the house by ringing the bell? Fyodor began pacing the sidewalk to the corner and back. The street was echoic and completely empty. High above it milk-white lamps were suspended, each on its own transverse wire; beneath the closest one a ghostly circle swung with the breeze across the wet asphalt. And this swinging motion, which had no apparent relation to him, with a sonorous tambourine-like sound nevertheless nudged something off the brink of his soul where that something had been resting, and now, no longer with the former distant call but reverberating loudly and close by, rang out 'Thank you, my land, for your remotest . . .' and immediately, on a returning wave, 'most cruel mist my thanks are due. . . .' And again, flying off in search of an answer: '. . . by you unnoticed. . . .' He was somnambulistically talking to himself as he paced a nonexistent sidewalk; his feet were guided by local consciousness, while the principal Fyodor Konstantinovich, and in fact the only Fyodor Konstantinovich that mattered, was already peering into the next shadowy strophe, which was swinging some yards away and which was destined to resolve itself in a yet-unkown but specifically promised harmony. 'Thank you, my land . . .' he began again, aloud, gathering momentum afresh, but suddenly the sidewalk turned back to stone under his feet, everything around him began speaking at once, and, instantly sobered, he hurried to the door of his house, for now there was a light behind it.

A middle-aged woman with high cheekbones, a karakul jacket over her shoulders, was letting a man out and had paused together with him at the door. 'So don't forget to do it, dear,' she was saying in a drab, everyday voice, when Fyodor arrived grinning and immediately recognized her: that morning she and her husband had been meeting their furniture. But he also recognized the visitor who was being let out it was the young painter Romanov, whom he had run into a couple of times at the editorial offices of the *Free Word*. With an expression of surprise on his delicate face, whose Hellenic purity was spoiled by dull, crooked teeth, he greeted Fyodor; the latter awkwardly bowed to the lady, who was rearranging the jacket slipping from her shoulder, and then bounded up the stairs with enormous strides, tripped horribly at the bend and climbed on holding the banister. Bleary-eyed Frau Stoboy in her dressing gown was awesome, but that did not last long. In his room he groped for the light and found it with difficulty. On the table he saw the glistening keys and the white book. That's already all over, he thought. Such a short time ago he had been giving copies to friends with pretentious or platitudinous inscriptions and now he was ashamed to recall those dedications and how all these last few days he had been nurtured by the joy of his book. But after all, nothing much had happened: today's deception did not exclude a reward tomorrow or after tomorrow;

somehow, however, the dream had begun to cloy and now the book lay on the table, completely enclosed within itself, delimited and concluded, and no longer did it radiate those former powerful, glad rays.

A moment later, in bed, just as his thoughts had begun to settle down for the night and his heart to sink in the snow of slumber (he always had palpitations when falling asleep), Fyodor ventured imprudently to repeat to himself the unfinished poem – simply to enjoy it once more before the separation by sleep; but he was weak, and it was strong, twitching with avid life, so that in a moment it had conquered him, covered his skin with goose pimples, filled his head with a heavenly buzz, and so he again turned on the light, lit a cigarette, and lying supine, the sheet pulled up to his chin and his feet protruding, like Antokolski's Socrates (one toe lost to Lugano's damp), abandoned himself to all the demands of inspiration. This was a conversation with a thousand interlocutors, only one of whom was genuine, and this genuine one must be caught and kept within hearing distance. How difficult this is, and how wonderful. . . . And in these talks between tamtambles, tamtam my spirit hardly knows. . . .

After some three hours of concentration and ardour dangerous to life, he finally cleared up the whole thing, to the last word, and decided that tomorrow he would write it down. In parting with it he tried reciting softly the good, warm, farm-fresh lines:

Thank you, my land; for your remotest
Most cruel mist my thanks are due.
By you possessed, by you unnoticed,
Unto myself I speak of you.
And in these talks between somnambules
My inmost being hardly knows
If it's my demency that rambles
Or your own melody that grows.

And realizing only now that this contained a certain meaning he followed it through with interest and approved it. Exhausted, happy, with ice-cold soles (the statue lies half-naked in a gloomy park), still believing in the goodness and importance of what he had performed, he got up to turn off the light. In his torn nightshirt, with his skinny chest and long turquoise-veined, hairy legs exposed, he dawdled by the mirror, still with that same solemn curiosity examining and not quite recognizing himself, those broad eyebrows, that forehead with its projecting point of close-cropped hair. A small vessel had burst in his left eye and the crimson invading it from the canthus imparted a certain gypsy quality to the dark glimmer of the pupil. Goodness, what a growth on those hollow cheeks after a few nocturnal hours, as if the moist heat of composition had stimulated the hair as well! He turned the switch, but most of the night had dissolved and all the pale and chilled objects in the room stood like people come to meet someone on a smoky railroad platform.

For a long time he could not fall asleep: discarded word-shells obstructed and chafed his brain and prickled his temples and there was no way he could get rid of them. Meanwhile the room had grown quite light and somewhere – most likely in the ivy – crazy sparrows, all together, not listening to each other, shrilled deafeningly: big recess in a little school.

Thus began his life in his new hole. His landlady could not get used to his habits of sleeping till noon, lunching none knew how or where, and dining off greasy wrapping paper. His book of poems did not get any reviews after all (somehow he had assumed it would happen automatically and had not even taken the trouble of sending out review copies), except for a brief note in Vasiliev's *Gazeta*, signed by the financial correspondent, who expressed an optimistic view of his literary future and quoted one stanza with a deadly misprint. He came to know Tannenberg Street better and it yielded him all its fondest secrets: such as the fact that next door in the basement lived an old shoemaker by the name of Kanarienvogel and there actually was a bird cage, although minus its yellow captive, in his purblind window, among samples of repaired footwear; but as for Fyodor's shoes, the cobbler looked at him over the top of the steel-rimmed spectacles of his guild and refused to repair them; so Fyodor started thinking of buying a new pair. He also learned the name of the upstairs tenants: having zoomed one day by mistake to the top landing, he read on a brass name-plate *Carl Lorentz, Geschichtsmaler,* and one day Romanov, whom he met at a street corner and who shared a studio in another part of the city with the *Geschichtsmaler,* told Fyodor a few things about him: he was a toiler, a misanthrope and a conservative, who had spent his whole life painting parades, battles, the imperial phantom with his star and ribbon, haunting the Sans-Souci park – and who now, in the uniformless republic, was impoverished and begloomed. He had enjoyed before 1914 a distinguished reputation, had visited Russia to paint the Kaiser's meeting with the Tsar, and while wintering in St Petersburg had met his present wife, Margarita Lvovna, who was at the time a young and enchanting dilettante who dabbled in all the arts. His alliance in Berlin with the Russian émigré painter had begun by accident, as a result of a newspaper advertisement. This Romanov was of quite a different cut. Lorentz developed a sullen attachment to him, but since the day of Romanov's first exhibition (in which he showed his portrait of Countess d'X, stark naked with corset marks on her stomach, holding her own self diminished to one-third life-size) had considered him a madman and a swindler. Many, however, were captivated by the young artist's bold and original gift; extraordinary successes were predicted for him and some even saw in him the originator of a neonaturalist school: after passing through all the trials of so-called modernism, he was said to have arrived at a renovated, interesting and somewhat cold narrative art. In his early works a certain trace of the cartoonist's style was still evident – for example, in that thing of his called 'Coincidence', where, on an advertising post, among the vivid, remarkably harmonious colours of playbills, astral names of cinemas and other transparent motley, one could read a notice about a lost diamond necklace (with a reward to the finder), which necklace lay right there on the sidewalk, at the very foot of the post, its innocent fire sparkling. In his 'Autumn', though, the black tailor's dummy with its ripped side, dumped in a ditch among magnificent maple leaves, was already expressiveness of a purer quality; connoisseurs found in it an abyss of sadness. But his best work to date remained one that had been acquired by a discerning tycoon and had already been extensively reproduced, called 'Four Citizens Catching a Canary'; all four were in black, broad-shouldered, tophatted (although for some reason one of them was barefoot), and placed in odd, exultant and at the same time wary poses beneath the strikingly sunny foliage of a squarely trimmed linden tree in which hid the bird, perhaps the one that had escaped from my shoemaker's cage. I was obscurely thrilled by Romanov's strange, beautiful, yet venomous art; I perceived in it both a forestalling and a forewarning: having far outdistanced my own art, it simultaneously illuminated for it the dangers of the way. As for the man himself, I found him boring to the point of revulsion – I could not stand his extremely rapid, extremely lisping speech, accompanied by a totally irrelevant, automatic rolling of his shining eyes. 'Listen,' he said, spitting at my chin, 'why don't you let me introduce you to Margarita Lorentz – she has told me to bring you over some night – do come, we hold little soirées at the studio – you know, with music, sandwiches, red lampshades – a lot of young people come – the Polonski girl, the Shidlovski brothers, Zina Mertz....'

These names were unknown to me; I felt no desire to spend evenings in the company of Vsevolod Romanov, nor did Lorentz's pug-faced wife interest me in any way – so not only did I not accept the invitation, but since that time I began avoiding the artist.

In the morning the potato-hawker's cry 'Prima Kartoffel!' rang out in the street, in a high, disciplined singsong (but how the young vegetable's heart throbs!) or else a sepulchral bass proclaimed *'Blumenerde!'* The thump of rugs being beaten was sometimes joined by a hurdy-gurdy, which was painted brown and mounted on squalid cart wheels, with a circular design on its front depicting an idyllic brook; and cranking now with his right hand, now with his left, the sharp-eyed organ-grinder pumped out a thick 'O sole mio'. That sun was already inviting me into the square. In its garden a young chestnut tree, still unable to walk alone and therefore supported by a stake, suddenly came out with a flower bigger than itself. The lilacs, however, did not bloom for a long time; but when they finally made up their mind, then, within one night, which left a considerable number of cigarette butts under the benches, they encircled the garden with ruffled richness. In a quiet lane behind the church the locust trees shed their petals on a grey June day, and the dark asphalt next to the sidewalk looked as if cream of wheat had been spilled on it. In the rose beds around the statue of a bronze runner the Dutch Glory disengaged the corners of its red petals and was followed by General Arnold Janssen. One happy and cloudless day in July, a very successful ant flight was staged: the females would take to the air, and the sparrows, also taking to the air, would devour them; and in places where nobody bothered them they kept crawling along the gravel and shedding their feeble prop-room wings. From Denmark the papers reported that as a result of a heat wave there, numerous cases of insanity were being observed: people were tearing off their clothes and jumping into the canals. Male gypsy moths dashed about in wild zigzags. The lindens went through all their involved, aromatic, messy metamorphoses.

Fyodor, in his shirt-sleeves and with sneakers on his sockless feet, would spend the greater part of the day on an indigo bench in the public garden, a book in his long tanned fingers; and when the sun beat down too hard, he would lean his head on the hot back of the bench and shut his eyes for long periods; the ghostly wheels of the city day revolved through the interior bottomless scarlet, and the sparks of children's voices darted past, and the book, open in his lap, became ever heavier and more unbooklike; but now the scarlet darkened under a passing cloud, and lifting his sweaty neck, he would open his eyes and once again see the park, the lawn with its marguerites, the freshly watered gravel, the little girl playing hopscotch with herself, the pram with the baby consisting of two eyes and a pink rattle, and the journey of the blinded, breathing, radiant disc through the cloud – then everything would blaze once again and along the dappled street, lined with restless trees, a coal truck would thunder by with the grimy driver on his high, bumpy seat, clenching the stalk of an emerald-bright leaf in his teeth.

In the late afternoon he would go to give a lesson – to a businessman with sandy eyelashes, who looked at him with a dull gaze of malevolent perplexity as Fyodor unconcernedly read him Shakespeare; or to a schoolgirl in a black jumper, whom he sometimes felt like kissing on her bent yellowish nape; or to a jolly thickset fellow who had served in the imperial navy, who said *est'* (aye-aye) and *obmozgovat'* (to dope it out), and was preparing *dat' drapu* (to blow) to Mexico, escaping secretly from his mistress, a two-hundred-pound, passionate and doleful old woman who had happened to flee to Finland in the same sleigh as he and since then, in perpetual jealous despair, had been feeding him meat pies, cream pudding, pickled mushrooms. . . . Besides these English lessons here were lucrative commercial translations – reports on the low sound conductivity of the tile floor or treatises about ball bearings; and finally, a modest but particularly precious income came from his lyrical poems, which he composed in a kind of drunken trance, and always with that same nostalgic, patriotic fervour; some of them did not materialize in final form, dissolving instead, fertilizing the innermost depths, while others, completely polished and equipped with all their commas, were taken to the newspaper office – first via a subway train with glinting reflections rapidly ascending its vertical stangs of brass, then in the strange emptiness of an enormous elevator to the ninth floor, where at the end of a corridor the colour of grey modelling clay, in a narrow little room smelling of 'the decaying corpse of actuality' (as the number one office comic used to crack), sat the secretary, a moon-like, phlegmatic person, ageless and virtually sexless, who had more than once saved the day when, angered by some item in Vasiliev's liberal paper, menacing rowdies would come, German Trotskyists hired locally, or some robust Russian Fascist, a rogue and a mystic.

The telephone jangled; ripply proofs breezed past; the theatre critic kept on reading a stray Russian newspaper from Vilna. 'Why, do we owe you money? Nothing of the kind,' the secretary would say. When the door to the room on the right opened, one could hear the juicily dictating voice of Getz, or Stupishin clearing his throat, and among the clatter of several typewriters one could make out the swift rat-tat-tat of Tamara.

At the left was Vasiliev's office; his lustrine jacket grew tight across his plump shoulders as, standing before the lectern he used as a writing table and puffing like some powerful machine, he wrote the leading article in his untidy handwriting with its schoolroom blots headed: 'No Improvement in Sight', or 'The Situation in China'. Suddenly stopping, lost in thought, he made a noise like a metal scraper as he scratched his large bearded cheek with one finger and narrowed his eye, overhung by a raffish black brow without a single grey hair in it – remembered in Russia to this day. By the window (outside which there was a similar multi-office building, with repairs going on so high in the sky that it seemed as though they might as well do something about the ragged rent in the grey cloud bank) stood a bowl with an orange and a half and an appetizing jar of yoghurt, and in the bookcase, in its locked bottom compartment, forbidden cigars and a large blue-and-red heart were preserved. A table was cluttered with the old trash of Soviet newspapers, cheap books with lurid covers, letters – requesting, reminding, rebuking – the squeezed-out half of an orange, a newspaper page with a window cut out and a portrait photograph of Vasiliev's daughter, who lived in Paris, a young woman with a charming bare shoulder and smoky hair: she was an unsuccessful actress and there was frequent mention of her in the cinema column of the *Gazeta*: ' . . . our talented compatriot Silvina Lee . . .' – although no one had ever heard of the compatriot.

Vasiliev would good-humouredly accept Fyodor's poems and print them, not because he liked them (generally he did not even read them) but because it was absolutely immaterial to him what adorned the nonpolitical part of his paper. Having ascertained once for all the level of literacy below which a given contributor by nature could not fall, Vasiliev gave him a free hand, even if the given level barely rose above zero. And poems, since they were mere trifles, passed almost entirely without control, trickling through openings where rubbish of greater weight and volume would have got stuck. But what joyful, exciting squealing arose in all the peacock coops of our émigré poetry from Latvia to the Riviera! They've printed mine! And mine! Fyodor himself, who felt he had only one rival – Koncheyev (who, by the way, was not a contributor to the *Gazeta*) – did not concern himself with his neighbours in print and rejoiced over his poems no less than the others. There were times when he could not wait for the evening mail that brought his copy and instead would buy one half an hour earlier in the street, and shamelessly, scarcely having left the news-stand, catching the reddish light near the fruitstands where mountains of oranges glowed in the blue of early twilight, would unfold the paper – and sometimes find nothing: something else had squeezed it out; but if he found it, he would gather the pages more conveniently and, resuming his progress along the sidewalk, read his poem over several times, varying the inner intonations; that is, imagining one by one the various mental ways the poem would be read, perhaps was now being read, by those whose opinion he considered important – and with each of these different incarnations he would almost physically feel a change in the colour of his eyes, and also in the colour behind his eyes, and in the taste in his mouth, and the more he liked the chef-d'oeuvre du jour, the more perfectly and succulently he could read it through the eyes of others.

Having thus dawdled away the summer, having given birth to, raised, and stopped loving for ever some two dozen poems, he went out one clear and cool day, a Saturday (tonight is the meeting), to make an important purchase. The fallen leaves lay not flat on the sidewalk but warped and stiffly crumpled so that from under each protruded a blue corner of shadow. Carrying a broom, the little old woman in a clean apron, with a small sharp face and disproportionately large feet, came out of her gingerbread cottage with its candy windows. Yes, it was autumn! He walked happily; everything was fine: morning had brought a letter from his mother, who was planning to come and visit him at Christmas, and through his deteriorating summer footwear he felt the ground with extraordinary sensitivity when he walked across an unpaved section, next to deserted vegetable-garden plots with their faint burnt odour, between houses which turned the sliced-off blackness of their outer walls towards them, and there, in front of lacy bowers, grew cabbages beaded with large bright drops, and the bluish stalks of withered carnations, and sunflowers, their heavy bulldog faces bowed. For a long time he had wanted to express somehow that it was in his feet that he had the feeling of Russia, that he could touch and recognize all of her with his soles, as a blind man feels with his palms. And it was a pity when he reached the end of that stretch of rich brown earth and once again had to step along the resonant sidewalk.

A young woman in a black dress, with a shiny forehead and quick, wandering eyes, sat down at his feet for the eighth time, sideways on a stool, nimbly extracted a narrow shoe from the rustling interior of its box, spread her elbows apart as she slackened the edges, glanced abstractedly aside as she loosened the laces, and then, producing a shoehorn from her bosom, addressed Fyodor's large, shy, poorly darned foot. Miraculously the foot entered, but having done so, went completely blind: the wiggling of toes inside had no effect on the exterior smoothness of the taut black leather. With phenomenal speed the salesgirl tied the lace ends and touched the tip of the shoe with two fingers. 'Just right,' she said. 'New shoes are always a little . . .' she went on rapidly, raising her brown eyes. 'Of course if you wish, we can make some adjustments. But they fit perfectly, see for yourself!' And she led him to the X-ray gadget and showed him where to place his foot. Looking down in the glass aperture he saw, against a luminous background, his own dark, neatly separated phalanges. With this, with this I'll step ashore. From Charon's ferry. Putting on the other shoe as well, he walked along the carpet the length of the store and back, glancing sideways at the ankle-high mirror which reflected his beautified step and his trouser leg, now looking twice its age. 'Yes, they're fine,' he said cravenly. When he was a child they used to scrape the glossy black sole with a buttonhook so it would not be slippery. He carried them off to his lesson under his arm, came home, ate, put them on, admiring them apprehensively, and left for the meeting.

They do seem all right after all – for an agonizing beginning.

The meeting was at the smallish, pathetically ornate flat of some relatives of Lyubov Markovna's. A red-haired girl in a green dress that ended above her knees was helping the Estonian maid (who was conversing with her in a loud whisper) to serve the tea. Among the familiar crowd, which contained few new faces, Fyodor at once descried Koncheyev, who was attending for the first time. He looked at the round-shouldered, almost humpbacked figure of this unpleasantly quiet man whose mysteriously growing talent could have been checked only by a ringful of poison in a glass of wine – this all-comprehending man with whom he had never yet had a chance to have the good talk he dreamt of having some day and in whose presence he, writhing, burning and hopelessly summoning his own poems to come to his aid, felt himself a mere contemporary. That young face was of the Central-Russian type and seemed a little common, common in a kind of oddly old-fashioned way; it was bounded above by wavy hair and below by starched collar wings, and at first in the presence of this man, Fyodor experienced a glum discomfort. . . . But three ladies were smiling at him from the sofa, Chernyshevski was salaaming to him from afar, Getz was raising like a banner a magazine he had brought for him, which contained Koncheyev's 'Beginning of a Long Poem' and an article by Christopher Mortus entitled 'The Voice of Pushkin's Mary in Contemporary Poetry'. Behind him somebody pronounced with the intonation of an explanatory response, 'Godunov-Cherdyntsev'. Never mind, never mind. Fyodor thought rapidly, smiling to himself, looking around and tapping the end of a cigarette against his eagle-emblazoned cigarette case, never mind, we'll still clink eggs some day, he and I, and we'll see whose will crack.

Tamara was indicating a vacant chair to him, and as he made his way to it he again thought he heard the sonorous ring of his name. When young people of his age, lovers of poetry, followed him on occasion with that special gaze that glides like a swallow across a poet's mirrory heart, he would feel inside him the chill of a quickening, bracing pride; it was the forerunner of his future fame; but there was also another, earthly fame – the faithful echo of the past: he was proud of the attention of his young coevals, but no less proud of the curiosity of older people, who saw in him the son of a great explorer, a courageous eccentric who had discovered new animals in Tibet, the Pamirs and other blue lands.

'Here,' said Mme Chernyshevski with her dewy smile, 'I want you to meet . . .' She introduced him to one Skvortsov, who had recently escaped from Moscow; he was a friendly fellow, had raylike lines around his eyes, a pear-shaped nose, a thin beard and a dapper, youthful, melodiously talkative little wife in a silk shawl – in short, a couple of that more or less academic type that was so familiar to Fyodor through his memory of the people who used to flicker around his father. Skvortsov in courteous and correct terms began by expressing his amazement at the total lack of information abroad about the circumstances surrounding the death of Konstantin Kirillovich: 'We'd thought,' his wife put in, 'that if nobody knew anything back home, that was to be expected.' 'Yes,' Skvortsov continued, 'I recall terribly clearly how one day I happened to be present at a dinner in honour of your father, and how Kozlov – Pyotr Kuzmich – the explorer, remarked wittily that Godunov-Cherdyntsev looked upon Central Asia as his private game reserve. Yes . . . That was quite a time ago, I don't think you were born then.'

At this point Fyodor suddenly noticed that Mme Chernyshevski was directing a sorrowful, meaningful, sympathy-laden gaze at him. Curtly interrupting Skvortsov, he began questioning him, without much interest, about Russia. 'How shall I put it . . .' replied the latter. 'You see it's like this . . .'

'Hello, hello, dear Fyodor Konstantinovich!' A fat lawyer who resembled an overfed turtle shouted this over Fyodor's head although already shaking his hand while pushing through the crowd, and by now he was already greeting someone else. Then Vasiliev rose from his seat and leaning lightly on the table for a moment with splayed fingers, in a position peculiar to shopkeepers and orators, announced that the meeting was opened. 'Mr Busch,' he added, 'will now read us his new, philosophical tragedy.'

Herman Ivanovitch Busch, an elderly, shy, solidly built, likeable gentleman from Riga, with a head that looked like Beethoven's, seated himself at the little Empire table, emitted a throaty rumble and unfolded his manuscript, his hands trembled perceptibly and continued to tremble throughout the reading.

From the very beginning it was apparent that the road led to disaster. The Rigan's farcical accent and bizarre solecisms were incompatible with the obscurity of his meaning. When, already in the Prologue, there appeared a 'Lone Companion' (*odinokiy sputnik* instead of *odinokiy putnik,* lone wayfarer) walking along that road, Fyodor still hoped against hope that this was a metaphysical paradox and not a traitorous *lapsus.* The Chief of the Town Guard, not admitting the traveller, repeated several times that he 'would not pass definitely' (rhyming with 'nightly'). The town was a coastal one (the lone companion was coming from the Hinterland) and the crew of a Greek vessel was carousing there. This conversation went on in the Street of Sin:

FIRST PROSTITUTE

All is water. That is what my client Thales says.

SECOND PROSTITUTE

All is air, young Anaximenes told me.

THIRD PROSTITUTE

All is number. My bald Pythagoras cannot be wrong.

FOURTH PROSTITUTE

Heraclitus caresses me whispering 'All is fire'.

LONE COMPANION (*enters*)

All is fate.

There were also two choruses, one of which somehow managed to represent the de Broglie's waves and the logic of history, while the other chorus, the good one, argued with it. 'First Sailor, Second Sailor, Third Sailor,' continued Busch, enumerating the conversing characters in his nervous bass voice edged with moisture. There also appeared three flower vendors: a 'Lilies' Woman,' a 'Violets' Woman' and a 'Woman of Different Flowers'. Suddenly something gave: little landslides began among the audience.

Before long, certain power lines formed in various directions all across the room – a network of exchanged glances between three or four, then five or six, then ten people, which represented a third of the gathering. Koncheyev slowly and carefully took a large volume from the bookshelf near which he was sitting (Fyodor noticed that it was an album of persian miniatures), and just as slowly turning it this way and that in his lap, he began to glance through it with myopic eyes. Mme Chernyshevski wore a surprised and hurt expression, but in keeping with her secret ethics, somehow tied up with the memory of her son, she was forcing herself to listen. Busch was reading rapidly, his glossy jowls gyrated, the horseshoe in his black tie sparkled, while beneath the table his feet stood pigeon-toed – and as the idiotic symbolism of the tragedy became ever deeper, more involved and less comprehensible, the painfully repressed, subterraneously raging hilarity more and more desperately needed an outlet, and many were already bending over, afraid to look, and when the Dance of the Maskers began in the square, someone – Getz it was – coughed, and together with the cough there issued a certain additional whoop, whereupon Getz covered his face with his hands and after a while emerged again with a senselessly bright countenance and humid, bald head, while on the couch Tamara had simply lain down and was rocking as if in the throes of labour, while Fyodor, who was deprived of protection, shed floods of tears, tortured by the forced noiselessness of what was going on inside him. Unexpectedly Vasiliev turned in his chair so ponderously that a leg collapsed with a crack and Vasiliev lurched forward with a changed expression, but did not fall, and this even, not funny in itself, served as a pretext for an elemental, orgiastic explosion to interrupt the reading, and while Vasiliev was transferring his bulk to another chair, Herman Ivanovich Busch, knitting his magnificent but quite unfruitful brow, jotted something on the manuscript with a pencil stub, and in the relieved calm an unidentified woman uttered something in a separate final moan, but Busch was already going on:

LILIES' WOMAN

You're all upset about something today, sister.

WOMAN OF DIFFERENT FLOWERS

Yes, the fortuneteller told me that my daughter would marry yesterday's passerby.

DAUGHTER

Oh, I did not even notice him.

LILIES' WOMAN

And he did not notice her.

'Hear, hear!' chimed in the Chorus, as in the British Parliament. Again there was a slight commotion: an empty cigarette box, on which the fat lawyer had written something, began a journey across the whole room, and everybody followed the stages of its trip; something extremely funny must have been written on it, but no one read it and it was passed dutifully from hand to hand, destined for Fyodor, and when it finally reached him, he read on it: *Later I want to discuss a certain little affair with you.*

The last act was nearing its conclusion. The god of laughter imperceptibly forsook Fyodor and he gazed meditatively at the shine of his shoe. Onto the cold shore from the ferry. The right one pinched more than the left. Koncheyev, his mouth half open, was leafing through the final pages of the album. '*Zanaves* [curtain],' exclaimed Busch, accenting the last syllable instead of the first.

Vasiliev announced that there would be an intermission. Most of the audience had a rumpled and wilted look, as after a night in a third-class coach. Busch had rolled his tragedy into a thick tube and was standing in a far corner, and it seemed to him that in the din of voices there formed and spread constant ripples of admiration; Lyubov Markovna offered him some tea and then his powerful face suddenly assumed a defenceless, gentle expression, and blissfully licking his lips, he bent towards the glass that had been handed him. Fyodor observed this from afar with a certain feeling of awe, while behind him he heard the following:

'Please give me some explanation!' (The angry voice of Mme Chernyshevski.)

'Well, you know, such things do happen . . .' (guiltily debonair Vasiliev).

'I ask for an explanation.'

'But my dear lady, what can I do now?'

'Well, didn't you read it beforehand? Didn't he bring it to you at the office? I thought you said it was a serious, interesting work. A significant work.'

'Yes, that's true, a first impression you know, when I skimmed it – I did not take into consideration how it would sound – I was fooled! It's really baffling. But go over to him, Alexandra Yakovlevna, say something to him.'

The lawyer grasped Fyodor above the elbow. 'You're just the person I'm looking for. It suddenly occurred to me that there is something for you here. A client of mine came to me – he requires a German translation of some papers of his, for a divorce case, don't you see? The Germans who are handling the affair for him have a Russian girl in their office but apparently she will be able to do only part of it, and they need someone to help her out with the rest. Would you undertake this? Here, let me take your telephone number. *Gemacht*.'

'Ladies and gentlemen, be seated please,' rang out Vasiliev's voice. 'Now we shall have a discussion of the work that has been read. Those who wish to participate please sign up.'

Just then Fyodor saw that Koncheyev, stooping and with his hand behind his lapel, was making a serpentine course towards the exit. Fyodor followed, nearly forgetting his magazine in the process. In the anteroom they were joined by old Stupishin; he frequently moved from one rented room to another but lived always so far from the centre of the city that these changes, important and complicated for him, seemed to others to happen in an ethereal world, beyond the horizon of human worries. Draping a skimpy, grey-striped scarf around his neck, he held it in place with his chin in the Russian manner while, also in the Russian manner, he got into his overcoat by means of several dorsal jerks.

'Well, he certainly gave us a treat,' he said as they descended, accompanied by the maid with the front door key.

'I confess I didn't listen very carefully,' commented Koncheyev.

Stupishin went to wait for a rare, almost legendary streetcar, while Godunov-Cherdyntsev and Koncheyev set out in the opposite direction, to walk as far as the corner.

'What nasty weather,' said Godunov-Cherdyntsev.

'Yes, it's quite cold,' agreed Koncheyev.

'Rotten – And in what part do you live?'

'Charlottenburg.'

'Well, well, that's quite a way. You're walking?'

'Oh yes, walking. I think that here I must . . .'

'Yes, you turn right, I go straight.'

They said goodbye. 'Brr, what a wind!'

'Wait, wait a minute though – I'll see you home. Surely you're a night owl like me and I don't have to expound to you on the black enchantment of stone promenades. So you didn't listen to our poor lecturer?'

'Only at the beginning, and then only with half an ear. However, I don't think it was quite as bad as that.'

'You were examining Persian miniatures in a book. Did you not notice one – an amazing resemblance! – from the collection of the St Petersburg Public Library – done, I think, by Riza Abbasi, say about three hundred years ago: that man kneeling, struggling with baby dragons, big-nosed, moustachioed – Stalin!'

'Yes, I think *that* one is the strongest of the lot. By the way, I've read your very remarkable collection of poems. Actually, of course, they are but the models of your future novels.'

'Yes, some day I'm going to produce prose in which "thought and music are conjoined as are the folds of life in sleep".'

'Thanks for the courteous quotation. You have a genuine love of literature, don't you?'

'I believe so. You see, the way I look at it, there are only two kinds of books: bedside and wastebasket. Either I love a writer fervently, or throw him out entirely.'

'A bit severe, isn't it? And a bit dangerous. Don't forget that the whole of Russian literature is the literature of one century and, after the most lenient eliminations, takes up no more than three to three and a half thousand printed sheets, and scarcely one-half of this is worthy of the bookshelf, to say nothing of the bedside table. With such quantitative scantiness we must resign ourselves to the fact that our Pegasus is piebald, that not everything about a bad writer is bad, and not all about a good one good.'

'Perhaps you will give me some examples so that I can refute them.'

'Certainly: if you open Goncharov or—'

'Stop right there! Don't tell me you have a kind word for Oblomov – that first "Ilyich" who was the ruin of Russia – and the joy of social critics? Or you want to discuss the miserable hygienic conditions of Victorian seductions? Crinoline and damp garden bench? Or perhaps the style? What about his "Precipice" where Rayski at moments of pensiveness is shown with "rosy moisture shimmering between his lips"? – which reminds me somehow of Pisemski's protagonists, each of whom under the stress of violent emotion "massages his chest with his hand"!'

'Here I shall trap you. Aren't there some good things in the same Pisemski? For example, those footmen in the vestibule, during a ball, who play catch with a lady's velveteen boot, horribly muddy and worn. Aha! And since we are speaking of second-rank authors, what do you think of Leskov?'

'Well, let me see. . . . Amusing Anglicisms crop up in his style, such as "*eto byla durnaya veshch*" [this was a bad thing] instead of simply "*plokho delo*". As to his contrived punning distortions – No, spare me, I don't find them funny. And his verbosity – Good God! His "Soboryane" could easily be condensed to two newspaper *feuilletons*. And I don't know which is worse – his virtuous Britishers or his virtuous clerics.'

'And yet . . . how about his image of Jesus "the ghostly Galilean, cool and gentle, in a robe the colour of ripening plum"? Or his description of a yawning dog's mouth with "its bluish palate as if smeared with pomade"? Or that lightning of his that at night illumines the room in detail, even to the magnesium oxide left on a silver spoon?'

'Yes, I grant you he has a Latin feeling for blueness: *lividus.* Lyov Tolstoy, on the other hand, preferred violet shades and the bliss of stepping barefoot with the rooks upon the rich dark soil of ploughed fields! Of course, I should never have bought them.'

'You're right, they pinch unbearably. But we have moved up to the first rank. Don't tell me you can't find weak spots there too? In such stories as "The Blizzard"—'

'Leave Pushkin alone: he is the gold reserve of our literature. And over there is Chekhov's hamper, which contains enough food for years to come, and a whimpering puppy, and a bottle of Crimean wine.'

'Wait, let's go back to the forebears. Gogol? I think we can accept his "entire organism". Turgenev? Dostoevski?'

'Bedlam turned back into Bethlehem – that's Dostoevski for you. "With one reservation", as our friend Mortus says. In the "Karamazovs" there is somewhere a circular mark left by a wet wine glass on an outdoor table. That's worth saving if one uses your approach.'

'But don't tell me all is well with Turgenev? Remember those inept tête-à-têtes in acacia arbours? The growling and quivering of Bazarov? His highly unconvincing fussing with those frogs? And in general, I don't know if you can stand the particular intonation of the Turgenevian row of dots at the close of a "fading phrase" and the maudlin endings of his chapters. Or should we forgive all his sins because of the grey sheen of Mme Odintsev's black silks and the outstretched hind legs of some of his graceful sentences, those rabbitlike postures assumed by his resting hounds?'

'My father used to find all kinds of howlers in Turgenev's and Tolstoy's hunting scenes and descriptions of nature, and as for the wretched Aksakov, let's not even discuss his disgraceful blunders in that field.'

'Now that the dead bodies have been removed we might, perhaps, proceed to the poets? All right. By the way, speaking of dead bodies, has it ever occurred to you that in Lermontov's most famous short poem the "familiar corpse" at the end is extremely funny? What he really wanted to say was "corpse of the man she once knew". The posthumous acquaintance is unjustified and meaningless.'

'Of late it's Tyutchev who shares my night lodgings most often.'

'A worthy house guest. And how do you feel about Nekrasov's iambic – or don't you have a taste for him?'

'Oh, I do. There is, in his best verse, a certain guitar twang, a sob and a gasp, which for instance Fet, a more refined artist, somehow lacks.'

'I have a feeling that Fet's secret weakness is his rationality and stress on antitheses – This hasn't escaped you, has it?'

'Our oafish school-of-social-intent writers criticized him for the wrong reasons. No, I can forgive him everything for "rang out in the darkening meadow", for "dew-tears of rapture shed the night", for the wing-fanning, "breathing" butterfly.'

'And so we move on to the next century: mind the step. You and I began to rave about poetry in our boyhood, didn't we? Refresh my memory – how did it go? – "how the rims of the clouds palpitate" . . . Poor old Balmont!'

'Or, illuminated from Blok's side, "Clouds of chimerical solace". Oh, but it would have been a crime to be choosy here. My mind in those days accepted ecstatically, gratefully, completely, without critical carpings, all of the five poets whose names began with "B" – the five senses of the new Russian poetry.'

'I'd be interested to know which of the five represents taste. Yes, yes, I know – there are aphorisms that, like airplanes, stay up only while they are in motion. But we were talking about the dawn. How did it begin with you?'

'When my eyes opened to the alphabet. Sorry, that sounds pretentious, but the fact is, since childhood I have been afflicted with the most intense and elaborate *audition colorée.*'

'So that you too, like Rimbaud, could have—'

'Written not a mere sonnet but a fat opus, with auditive hues he never dreamt of. For instance, the various numerous "*a*'s" of the four languages which I speak differ for me in tinge, going from lacquered-black to splintery-grey – like different sorts of wood. I recommend to you my pink flannel "*m*". I don't know if you remember the insulating cotton wool which was removed with the storm windows in spring? Well, that is my Russian "*y*" or rather "ugh", so grubby and dull that words are ashamed to begin with it. If I had some paints handy I would mix burnt-sienna and sepia for you so as to match the colour of a gutta-percha "*ch*" sound; and you would appreciate my radiant "*s*" if I could pour into your cupped hands some of those luminous sapphires that I touched as a child, trembling and not understanding when my mother, dressed for a ball, uncontrollably sobbing, allowed her perfectly celestial treasures to flow out of their abyss into her palm, out of their cases onto black velvet, and then suddenly locked everything up and did not go anywhere after all, in spite of the impassioned persuasions of her brother, who kept pacing up and down the rooms giving fillips to the furniture and shrugging his epaulets, and if one turned the curtain slightly on the side window of the oriel, one could see, along the receding riverfront, façades in the blue-blackness of the night, the motionless magic of an imperial illumination, the ominous blaze of diamond monograms, coloured bulbs in coronal designs . . .'

'*Buchstaben von Feuer,* in short . . . Yes, I know what is coming. Shall I finish this banal and soul-rending tale for you? How you delighted in any poem that happened along. How at ten you were writing dramas, and at fifteen elegies – and all about sunsets, sunsets . . . Blok's "Incognita" who "passed slowly in between the drunkards". By the way, who was she?'

'A young married woman. It lasted a little less than two years, until my escape from Russia. She was lovely and sweet – you know, with large eyes and slightly bony hands – and somehow I have remained faithful to her even to this day. Her taste in poetry was limited to fashionable gypsy lyrics, she adored poker and she died of typhus – God knows where, God knows how.'

'And what comes now? Would you say it's worth going on writing verse?'

'Oh, decidedly! To the very end. Even at this moment I am happy, in spite of the degrading pain in my pinched toes. To tell the truth, I again feel that turbulence, that excitement. . . . Once again I shall spend the whole night . . .'

'Show me. Let's see how it works: It is with *this,* that from the slow black ferry . . . No, try again: Through snow that falls on water never freezing . . . Keep trying: Under the vertical slow snow in grey-enjambment-Lethean weather, in the usual season, with *this* I'll step upon the shore some day. That's better but be careful not to squander the excitement.'

'Oh that's all right. My point is that one cannot help being happy with this tingling sensation in the skin of your brow. . . .'

'. . . as from an excess of vinegar in chopped beet. Do you know what has just occurred to me? That river is not the Lethe but rather the Styx. Never mind. Let's proceed: And now a crooked bough looms near the ferry, and Charon with his boathook, in the dark, reaches for it, and catches it, and very . . .'

'. . . slowly the bark revolves, the silent bark. Homeward,

homeward! I feel tonight like composing with pen in hand. What a moon! What a black smell of leaves and earth from behind those railings.'

'And what a pity no one has overheard the brilliant colloquy that I would have liked so much to hold with you.'

Never mind, it won't be wasted. In fact, I'm glad it turned out this way. Whose business is it that actually we parted at the very first corner, and that I have been reciting a fictitious dialogue with myself as supplied by a self-teaching handbook of literary inspiration?

2

The rain fell lightly, but with the elusive suddenness of an angel, a rainbow had already appeared. In languorous self-wonder, pinkish-green with a purplish suffusion along its inner edge (it hung suspended over the heaped field, above and before a distant wood, one tremulous portion of which showed through it. Stray arrows of rain that had lost both rhythm and weight and the ability to make any sound, flashed at random, this way and that, in the sun. Up the rain-washed sky, from behind a raven cloud, a cloud of ravishing whiteness was extricating itself and shining with all the detail of a monstrously complicated moulding.

'Well, well, it's over,' he said in a low voice and emerged from under the shelter of aspens that crowded where the greasy, clayey *zemskaya* (rural district) road – and what a bump in this designation! – descended into a hollow, gathering there all its ruts into an oblong pit, full to the brim with thick café crème.

My darling! Pattern of Elysian hues! Once in Ordos my father, climbing a hill after a storm, inadvertently entered the base of a rainbow – the rarest occurrence! – and found himself in coloured air, in a play of light as if in paradise. He took one more step – and left paradise.

The rainbow was already fading. The rain had quite stopped, it was scorching hot, a horsefly with satiny eyes settled on his sleeve. A cuckoo began to call in a copse, listlessly, almost questioningly: the sound swelled like a cupule, and again, like a cupule, unable to find a solution. The poor, fat bird probably flew farther away, for everything was repeated from the beginning in the manner of a reduced reflection (it sought, who knows, a place for the best, the saddest effect). A huge butterfly, flat in flight, bluish-black with a white band, described a supernaturally smooth arc, settled on the damp earth, closed its wings and with that disappeared. This is the kind that now and then a panting peasant lad brings one, cramming it with both hands into his cap. This is the kind that soars up from under the mincing hooves of the doctor's well-behaved little pony, when the doctor, holding the almost superfluous reins in his lap or else simply tying them to the front board, pensively drives along the shady road to the hospital. But on occasion you find four black-and-white wings with brick-coloured undersides scattered like playing cards over a forest footpath: the rest, eaten by an unknown bird.

He jumped a puddle where two dung-beetles had fastened onto a straw, getting in each other's way, and printed his sole on the edge of the road: a highly significant footprint, ever looking upward and ever seeing him who has vanished. Walking through a field, alone, beneath the magnificently rushing clouds, he remembered how, with his first cigarettes in his first cigarette case, he had approached an old reaper here and asked for a light; the peasant had taken out a box from his gaunt breast and given it to him unsmilingly, but the wind was blowing, match after match went out before it had hardly flared and after every one he grew more ashamed, while the man watched with a kind of detached curiosity the impatient fingers of the wasteful young squire.

He went deeper into the wood; planks had been laid along the path, black and slimy, with reddish-brown aments and leaves that had stuck to them. Who was this had propped a russula, breaking open its white fan? In reply came the sound of hallooing: girls were gathering mushrooms and bilberries, the latter seeming so much darker in the basket than on their stalks! Among the birches there was an old acquaintance, with a double trunk, a birch-lyre, and beside it an old post with a board on it; nothing could be made out on it except bullet marks; a Browning had once been fired at it by his English tutor – also Browning – and then Father had taken the pistol, swiftly and dexterously ramming bullets into the clip, and knocked out a smooth *K* with seven shots.

Farther on, a bog orchis bloomed unceremoniously in a patch of marshy ground, behind which he had to cross a back road, and off to the right a white wicket gate gleamed: the entrance to the park. Trimmed with ferns outside, luxuriantly lined with jasmine and honeysuckle inside, in places darkened by fir needles, in others lightened by birch leaves, this huge, dense and multi-pathed park stood poised in an equilibrium of sun and shadow, which formed from night to night a variable, but in its variability a uniquely characteristic harmony. If circles of warm light palpitated underfoot in the avenue, then a thick velvet stripe was sure to stretch across in the distance, behind it again came that tawny sieve, while farther, at the bottom, there deepened a rich blackness that, transferred to paper, would satisfy the water colourist only as long as the paint remained wet, so that he would have to put on layer after layer to retain its beauty – which would immediately fade. All paths led to the house, but geometry notwithstanding, it seemed the quickest way was not by the straight avenue, slim and sleek with a sensitive shadow (rising like a blind woman to meet you and touch your face) and with a burst of emerald sunlight at the very end, but by any of its tortuous and unweeded neighbours. He walked along his favourite one toward the still invisible house, past the bench on which according to established tradition his parents used to sit on the eve of his father's regular departures on his travels. Father, knees apart, twirling his spectacles or a carnation in his hands, had his head lowered, with a boater tipped onto the back of it and with a taciturn almost mocking smile around his puckered eyes and in the soft corners of his mouth, somewhere in the very roots of his trimmed beard; and Mother was telling him something, from the side, from below, from beneath her large, trembling white hat; or was pressing out crunchy little holes in the dumb sand with the tip of her parasol. He walked past a boulder with rowan saplings clambering onto it (one had turned to offer a hand to the younger), past a small grass-grown plat which had been a pond in Grandfather's time and past some shortish fir trees which used to become quite round in winter under their burden of snow: the snow used to fall straight and slow, it could fall like that for three days, five months, nine years – and already, ahead, in a clear space traversed by white specks, one glimpsed a dim yellow blotch approaching, which suddenly came into focus, shuddered, thickened and turned into a tramcar, and the wet snow drifted slantingly, plastering over the left face of a pillar of glass, the tram stop, while the asphalt remained black and bare, as if incapable by nature of accepting anything white, and among the signs over chemists' shops, stationers' and grocers', which swam before the eyes and, at first, were even incomprehensible, only one would still appear to be written in Russian: Kakao. Meanwhile, around him everything that had just been imagined with such pictorial clarity (which in itself was suspicious, like the vividness of dreams at the wrong time of day or after a soporific) paled, corroded, disintegrated, and if one looked around, then (as in a fairy tale the stairs disappear behind the back of whoever is mounting them) everything collapsed and disappeared, a farewell configuration of trees, standing like people come to see someone off and already swept away, a scrap of rainbow faded in the wash, the path, of which there remained only the gesture of a turn, a butterfly on a pin with only three wings and no abdomen, a carnation in the sand, by the shade of the bench, the very last most persistent odds and ends, and in another moment all this yielded Fyodor without a struggle to his present, and straight out of his reminiscence (swift and senseless, visiting him like an attack of a fatal illness at any hour, in any place), straight from the hothouse paradise of the past, he stepped onto a Berlin tramcar.

He was going to a lesson, was late as usual, and as usual there grew in him a vague, evil, heavy hatred for the clumsy sluggishness of this least gifted of all methods of transport, for the hopelessly familiar, hopelessly ugly streets going by the wet window, and most of all for the feet, sides and necks of the native passengers. His reason knew that they could also include genuine, completely human individuals with unselfish passions, pure sorrows, even with memories shining through life, but for some reason he got the impression that all these cold, slippery eyes, looking at him as if he were carrying an illegal treasure (which his gift was, essentially), belonged only to malicious hags and crooked hucksters. The Russian conviction that the German is in small numbers vulgar and in large numbers – unbearably vulgar was, he knew, a conviction unworthy of an artist; but nonetheless he was seized with a trembling, and only the gloomy conductor with hunted eyes and a plaster on his finger, eternally and painfully seeking equilibrium and room to pass amidst the convulsive jolts of the car and the cattle-like crowding of standing passengers, seemed outwardly, if not a human being, then at least a poor relation to a human being. At the second stop a lean man in a short coat with a fox-fur collar, wearing a green hat and frayed spats, sat down in front of Fyodor In settling down he bumped him with his knee and with the corner of a fat briefcase with a leather handle, and this trivial thing turned his irritation into a kind of pure fury, so that, staring fixedly at the sitter, reading his features, he instantly concentrated on him all his sinful hatred (for this poor, pitiful, expiring nation) and knew precisely why he hated him: for that low forehead, for those pale eyes; for *Vollmilch* and *Extrastark,* implying the lawful existence of the diluted and the artificial; for the Punchinello-like system of gestures (threatening children not as we do – with an upright finger, a standing reminder of Divine Judgment – but with a horizontal digit imitating a waving stick); for a love of fences, rows, mediocrity; for the cult of the office; for the fact that if you listen to his inner voice (or to any conversation on the street) you will inevitably hear figures, money; for the lavatory humour and crude laughter; for the fatness of the backsides of both sexes, even if the rest of the subject is not fat; for the lack of fastidiousness; for the visibility of cleanliness – the gleam of saucepan bottoms in the kitchen and the barbaric filth of the bathrooms; for the weakness for dirty little tricks, for taking pains with dirty tricks, for the abominable object stuck carefully on the railings of the public gardens; for someone else's live cat, pierced through with wire as revenge on a neighbour, and the wire cleverly twisted at one end; for cruelty in everything, self-satisfied, taken for granted; for the unexpected, rapturous helpfulness with which five passersby help you to pick up some dropped farthings; for. . . . Thus he threaded the points of his biased indictment, looking at the man who sat opposite him – until the latter took a copy of Vasiliev's newspaper from his pocket and coughed unconcernedly with a Russian intonation.

That's wonderful, thought Fyodor, almost smiling with delight. How clever, how gracefully sly and how essentially good life is! Now he made out in the newspaper reader's features such a compatriotic softness – in the corners of the eyes, large nostrils, a Russian-cut moustache – that it became at once both funny and incomprehensible how anyone could have been deceived. His thoughts were cheered by this unexpected respite and had already taken a different turn. The pupil he was visiting was a scantily educated but inquisitive old Jew who the previous year had conceived a sudden desire to learn how to 'chat in French', which seemed to the old man both more attainable and more becoming to his years, character, and experience of life than the dry study of the grammar of a language. Invariably at the beginning of the lesson, groaning and mixing a multitude of Russian and German words with a pinch of French, he described his exhaustion after the day's work (he was manager of a sizeable paper factory), and went from these lengthy complaints to a discussion – in French! – landing immediately up to the ears in hopeless darkness, of international politics, and with this demanded miracles: that all this wild, viscous and ponderous stuff, comparable to the transportation of stones over a washed-out road, should turn suddenly into filigreed speech. Entirely lacking in the ability to remember words (and liking to talk of this not as a shortcoming but as an interesting characteristic of his nature), he not only made no progress but even managed in a year of studying to forget those few French phrases with which Fyodor had found him, and on the basis of which the old man had thought to construct in three or four evenings his own animated, light, portable Paris. Alas, the time passed fruitlessly, proving the futility of the effort and the impossibility of the dream – and then the instructor turned out to be inexperienced, completely lost when the unfortunate factory manager suddenly needed exact information (what's 'dandy roll' in French?) which, out of delicacy, the questioner immediately renounced, and both were momentarily embarrassed, like an innocent youth and maiden in some old idyll who inadvertently touch one another. It gradually became unendurable. Since the pupil referred more and more despondently to the tiredness of his brain and more and more often postponed the lessons (his secretary's heavenly voice on the telephone was the melody of happiness!), it seemed to Fyodor that the latter had finally become convinced of his teacher's ineptitude, but that he was prolonging the mutual torment out of pity for his worn trousers, and would continue to do so to the grave.

And now, sitting in the tramcar, he saw with ineffable vividness how in seven or eight minutes he would enter the familiar study, furnished in Berliner animal luxury, would settle in the deep leather armchair beside the low, metal table with its glass cigarette box opened for him, and its lamp fashioner like a terrestrial globe, would light a cigarette, cross his legs with cheap gaiety and come face to face with the agonized, submissive gaze of his hopeless pupil, would hear so clearly his sigh and the ineradicable '*Nu, voui*' with which he interlarded his answers; but suddenly the unpleasant feeling of lateness was replaced in Fyodor's soul by a distinct and somehow outrageously joyful decision not to appear at all for the lesson – to get off at the next stop and return home to his half-read book, to his unworldly cares, to the blissful mist in which his real life floated, to the complex, happy, devout work which had occupied him for about a year already. He knew that today he would receive payment for several lessons, knew that otherwise he would have to smoke and eat again on credit, but he was quite reconciled to this for the sake of that energetic idleness (everything is here, in this combination), for the sake of the lofty truancy he was allowing himself. And he was allowing it not for the first time. Shy and exacting, living always uphill, spending all his strength in pursuit of the innumerable beings that flashed inside him, as if at dawn in a mythological grove, he could no longer force himself to mix with people either for money or for pleasure, and therefore he was poor and solitary. And, as if to spite common fate, it was pleasant to recall how once in the summer he had not gone to a party in a 'suburban villa' solely because the Chernyshevskis had warned him that a man would be there who 'perhaps could help him'; or how the previous autumn he had not found time to communicate with a divorce bureau which needed a translator – because he was composing a verse drama, because the lawyer promising him this income was importunate and stupid, because, finally, he put it off too long and then was unable to make up his mind.

He worked his way out onto the car's platform. Just then the wind searched him cruelly after which Fyodor drew the belt of his mackintosh tighter and adjusted his scarf, but the small amount of tram warmth had already been taken away from him. The snow had ceased falling, but where it went no one knew; here remained only a ubiquitous dampness which was evidenced both in the swishing sound of motor tyres and in the piglike sharpness of the ear-torturing, ragged squeal of car horns, and in the darkness of the day, shivering with cold, with sadness, with loathing for itself, and in the particular shade of yellow of the already lighted shop windows, in the reflections and refractions, in the liquid lights, in all this sick irretention of electric light. The tram came out on the square and, braking excruciatingly, stopped, but it was only a preliminary stop, because in front, by the stone island crowded with people standing by to board, two other trams had got stuck, both with cars coupled on, and this inert agglomeration was also evidence somehow of the disastrous imperfection of the world in which Fyodor still continued to reside. He could stand it no longer, he jumped out and strode across the slippery square to another tramline on which, by cheating, he could return to his own district on the same ticket – good for one transfer but not at all for a return journey; but the honest, official calculation that a passenger would travel in one direction only was undermined in certain cases by the fact that, knowing the routes, one could turn a straight journey imperceptibly into an arc, bending back to the point of departure. This clever system (pleasant evidence of a certain purely German flaw in the planning of tram routes) was willingly followed by Fyodor; from absentmindedness however, from an incapacity to cherish a material advantage for any length of time, and already thinking of something else, he paid automatically for the new ticket he had intended to save on. And even then the cheat prospered, even then not he but the city transport department proved to be out of pocket, and furthermore for a much, much greater sum (the price of a Nord Express ticket!) than could have been expected: crossing the square and turning into a side street, he walked towards the tram stop through a small, at first glance, thicket of fir trees, gathered here for sale on account of the approach of Christmas; they formed between them a kind of small avenue; swinging his arms as he walked he brushed his fingertips against the wet needles; but soon the tiny avenue broadened out, the sun burst forth and he emerged onto a garden terrace where on the soft red sand one could make out the sigla of a summer day: the imprints of a dog's paws, the beaded tracks of a wagtail, the Dunlop stripe left by Tanya's bicycle, dividing into two waves at the turn, and a heel dent where with a light, mute movement containing perhaps a quarter of a pirouette she had slid off it to one side and started walking, keeping hold of the handlebars. An old wooden house in the so-called 'abietineous' style, painted a pale green, with like-coloured drainpipes, carved designs under the roof and a high stone foundation (where in the grey putty one could fancy one saw the round pink cruppers of walled-up horses), a large, sturdy and extraordinarily expressive house, with balconies on a level with the lime branches, and verandas decorated with precious glass, sailed forward to meet him in a cloud of swallows, with a full spread of awnings, its lightning conductor cleaving through the blue sky and the bright white clouds extending an endless embrace. Sitting on the stone steps of the foremost veranda, illuminated squarely by the sun, are: Father, obviously just back from a swim, turbaned in a shaggy towel so that one cannot see – and how one would like to! – his dark crop, streaked with grey and tapering to a peak on his forehead; Mother, all in white, staring straight in front of her and somehow so youthfully hugging her knees; next to her – Tanya, in an ample blouse, the end of her black braid lying on her collarbone, her smooth parting lowered, holding in her arms a fox terrier whose mouth is creased in a wide smile from the heat; higher up – Yvonna Ivanovna, who for some reason has not come out, her features blurred but her slim waist, her belt and her watch chain clearly visible; to one side, lower down, reclining and resting his head in the lap of the round-faced girl (velvet neck-ribbon, silk bows) who gave Tanya music lessons, his father's brother, a stout army doctor, a joker and a very handsome man; lower still, two sour little glowering schoolboys. Fyodor's cousins: one in a school cap, the other without – the one without to be killed seven years later in the battle of Melitopol; at the very bottom, on the sand, in exactly the same pose as his mother – Fyodor himself, as he was then, though he had changed little since that time, white teeth, black brows, short hair, wearing an open shirt. One forgot who had taken it, but this transient, faded and generally insignificant (how many others and better were there) photograph, unsuitable even for copying, had alone been saved by a miracle and had become priceless, reaching Paris among his mother's belongings and brought by her to Berlin last Christmas; for now, choosing her son a present, she was guided not by what was most costly to get but by what was most difficult to part with.

She had come to him for two weeks, after a three-year separation, and in the first moment when, powdered to a deathly pallor, wearing black gloves and black stockings and an old seal-skin coat thrown open, she had descended the iron steps of the coach, glancing with equal quickness first at him and then at what was underfoot, and the next moment, her face twisted with the pain of happiness, was clinging to him, blissfully moaning, kissing him anywhere – ear, neck – it had seemed to him that the beauty of which he had been so proud had faded, but as his vision adjusted itself to the twilight of the present, so different at first from the distantly receding light of memory, he again recognized in her everything that he had loved: the pure outline of her face, narrowing down to the chin, the changeful play of those green, brown, yellow, entrancing eyes under their velvet brows, the long, light stance, the avidity with which she lit a cigarette in the taxi, the attention with which she suddenly looked – unblinded, therefore, by the excitement of the meeting, as any other would have been – at the grotesque scene noticed by both of them: an imperturbable motorcyclist carrying a bust of Wagner in his sidecar; and already by the time they were coming up to the house the light of the past had overtaken the present, had soaked it to saturation point, and everything became the same as it had been in this very Berlin three years previously, as it had once been in Russia, as it had been, and would be, forever.

A spare room was found at Frau Stoboy's place and there, on the first evening (an opened dressing case, rings taken off and laid on the marble washstand), lying on the sofa and ever so quickly eating raisins, without which she could not pass a single day, she spoke of what she had constantly returned to for almost nine years now, repeating over again – incoherently, gloomily, ashamedly, turning her eyes away, as if confessing to something secret and terrible – that she believed more and more that Fyodor's father was alive, that her mourning was ridiculous, that the vague news of his death had never been confirmed by anyone, that he was somewhere in Tibet, in China, in captivity, in prison, in some desperate quagmire of troubles and privations, that he was convalescing after some long, long illness – and suddenly, flinging open the door noisily, stamping on the step, he would enter. And to an even greater degree than before these words made Fyodor feel both happier and more frightened. Accustomed willy nilly to consider his father dead all these years, he sensed something grotesque in the possibility of his return. Was it admissible that life could perform not only miracle, but miracles necessarily deprived (otherwise they would be unbearable) of even the tiniest hint of the supernatural? The miracle of this return would consist in its earthly nature, in its compatibility with reason, in the swift introduction of an incredible event into the accepted and comprehensible linkage of ordinary days; but the more the necessity for such naturalness grew with the years, the more difficult it became for life to meet it, and now what frightened him was not simply the imagining of a ghost, but the imagining of one that would not be frightening. There were days when it seemed to Fyodor that suddenly on the street (in Berlin there are littl cul-de-sacs where at dusk the soul seems to dissolve) he would be approached by an old man of seventy, in fairy-tale rags, shrouded to the eyes in beard, who would wink and say, as he had once been wont to: Hello, Son!' His father often appeared to him in dreams, as if just returned from some monstrous penal servitude, having experienced physical tortures which it was forbidden to mention, now changed into clean linen – it was impossible to think of the body underneath – and with a completely uncharacteristic expression of unpleasant, momentous sullenness, with a sweaty brow and slightly bared teeth, sitting at table in the circle of his hushed family. But when, overcoming his sensation of the spuriousness of the very style foisted on fate, he nevertheless forced himself to imagine the arrival of a live father, aged but undoubtedly his, and the most complete, most convincing possible explanation of his silent absence, he was seized, not by happiness, but by a sickening terror – which, however, immediately disappeared and yielded to a feeling of satisfied harmony when he removed this meeting beyond the boundary of earthly life.

But on the other hand. . . . It happens that over a long period you are promised a great success, in which from the very start you do not believe, so dissimilar is it from the rest of fate's offerings, and if from time to time you do think of it, then you do so as it were to indulge your fantasy – but when, at last, on a very ordinary day with a west wind blowing, the news comes – simply, instantaneously and decisively destroying any hope in it – then you are suddenly amazed to find that although you did not believe in it, you had been living with it all this time, not realizing the constant, close presence of the dream, which had long since grown fat and independent, so that now you cannot get it out of your life without making a hole in that life. Thus had Fyodor, in spite of all logic and not daring to envision its realization, lived with the familiar dream of his father's return, a dream which had mysteriously embellished his life and somehow lifted it above the level of surrounding lives, so that he could see all sorts of distant and interesting things, just as, when a little boy, his father used to lift him by his elbows thus enabling him to see what was interesting over a fence.

After the first evening, when she had renewed her hope and become convinced that the same hope was alive in her son, Elizaveta Pavlovna no longer referred to it in words, but as usual, it was taken for granted in all their conversations, especially since they did not converse much aloud: frequently, after several minutes of animated silence, Fyodor would suddenly notice that the whole time they both knew very well what it was about, this double, almost subgramineal speech which emerged as a single stream, as a word understood to both of them. And someimes they would play like this: sitting side by side and silently imagining to themselves that each was taking the same Leshino walk, they went out of the park, took the path along the field (there was a river to the left behind the alders), across the shady graveyard where sun-flecked crosses were measuring something terribly large with their arms and where it was somehow awkward to pick the raspberries, across the river, upwards again, through the wood, to another bend of the river, to the Pont des Vaches and father, through the pines and along the Chemin du Pendu – familiar nicknames, not grating to their Russian ears but thought up when their grandfathers had been children. And suddenly, in the middle of this silent walk being performed by two minds, using according to the rules of the game the rate of a human footstep (although they could have flown over their whole domains in a single instant), both stopped and said where they had got to, and when it turned out, as it often did, that neither one had outpaced the other, having halted in the same coppice, the same smile flashed upon mother and son and shone through their common tear.

Very soon they again got into their inner rhythm of intercourse, for there was little new that they did not know already from letters. She told him in great detail about the recent wedding of Tanya, who had now gone off to Belgium until January with a husband still unknown to Fyodor, an agreeable, quiet, very polite and completely unremarkable gentleman 'working in the field of radio'; and that when they returned she would move into a new flat with them in an enormous house near one of the Paris gates: she was glad to be leaving the small hotel with the steep dark staircase, where she had been living with Tanya in a tiny but many-cornered room completely swallowed up by a mirror and visited by bedbugs of various calibre – from transparent pink baby ones to leathery brown fatties – which congregated first behind the wall calendar with a Russian landscape by Levitan on it and then closer to the field of action, in the inside pocket of the torn wallpaper, directly above the double bed; but the pleasant prospect of a new home was not unmixed with dread: she had an antipathy to her son-in-law and there was something forced in Tanya's brisk, showy happiness – 'You see, he's not quite our set,' she confessed, stressing this with a certain tightening of the jaws and a downward look; but that was not all, and anyway Fyodor had already heard about that other man whom Tanya loved but who did not love her.

They went out quite often; as always Elizaveta Pavlovna seemed to be looking for something, rapidly spanning the world with a skimming glance of her shimmery eyes. The German holiday proved wet, puddles made the sidewalks seem full of holes, the Christmas tree lights burned dully in the windows, and here and there at street corners a commercial Santa Claus in a red stormcoat and with hungry eyes was distributing handbills. In the windows of a department store some villain had had the idea of setting up dummy skiers on artificial snow beneath the Star of Bethlehem. Once, they saw a modest Communist procession walking through the slush – with wet flags – most of the marchers battered by life, some crookbacked, others lame or sickly, a lot of plain-looking women and several sedate petty-bourgeois. Fyodor and his mother went to have a look at the apartment house where the three of them had lived for two years, but the janitor had already changed, the former proprietor had died, strange curtains hung in the familiar windows, and somehow there was nothing their hearts could recognize. They visited a cinema where a Russian film was being shown which conveyed with particular *brio* the globules of sweat rolling down the glistening faces of the factory workers – while the factory owner smoked a cigar all the time. And of course he took her to see Mme Chernyshevski.

The introduction was not altogether a success. Mme Chernyshevski met her guest with a doleful tenderness meant to show that the experience of grief had linked them long and closely; but Elizaveta Pavlovna was most of all interested in what the other woman thought of Fyodor's verses and in why no one was writing about them. 'May I embrace you before you go?' asked Mme Chernyshevski, preparatorily rising on tiptoe – she was a head shorter than Elizaveta Pavlovna, who bent down toward her with an innocent and radiant smile which quite destroyed the meaning of the embrace. 'It's all right, one must be brave,' said the lady, letting them out onto the stairs and covering her chin with the end of the downy shawl in which she was wrapped. 'One must be brave; I've learned to be so brave that I could give lessons in endurance, but I think you've also come well through this school.'

'You know,' said Elizaveta Pavlovna, stepping lightly but cautiously down the stairs and not turning her lowered head toward her son, 'I think I'll just buy cigarette papers and tobacco, otherwise it comes out so dear,' and immediately she added in the same voice: 'Goodness, how sorry I am for her.' And indeed, it was impossible not to pity Mme Chernyshevski. Her husband had been kept over three months already in an institute for the mentally ailing, in 'the semi-loony bin' as he himself playfully expressed it in moments of lucidity. As long ago as October Fyodor had once visited him there. In the sensibly furnished ward sat a fatter, rosier, beautifully shaven and completely insane Chernyshevski, in rubber slippers and a waterproof cloak with a hood. 'Why, are you dead?' was the first thing he asked, more discontent than surprised. In his capacity as 'Chairman of the Society for Struggle With the Other World' he was continually devising methods to prevent permeation by ghosts (his doctor, employing a new system of 'logical connivance', did not oppose this) and now, probably on the basis of its nonconductive quality in another sphere, he was trying out rubber, but evidently the results achieved so far were mainly negative since, when Fyodor was about to take a chair for himself which was standing to one side, Chernyshevski said irritably: 'Leave it alone, you see very well there are two sitting on it already', and this 'two', and the rustling cloak which plashed up with every movement, and the wordless presence of the attendant, as if this had been a meeting in prison, and the whole of the patient's conversation seemed to Fyodor an unbearable, caricatured vulgarization of that complex, transparent and still noble though half-insane state of mind in which Chernyshevski had so recently communicated with his lost son. With the broad-comedy inflections he had formerly reserved for jokes – but which he now used in earnest – he launched into extensive lamentations, all for some reason in German, over the fact that people were wasting money to invent anti aircraft guns and poison gases and not caring at all about the conduct of another, million times more important, struggle. Fyodor had a healed-over scrape on the side of his temple – that morning he had knocked it against one of the ribs of a radiator in hastily recovering the top of a toothpaste tube which had rolled underneath it. Suddenly breaking off his speech, Chernyshevski pointed squeamishly and anxiously at his temple. '*Was haben Sie da?*' he asked, with a grimace of pain, and then smiled unpleasantly, and growing more and more angry and agitated, began to say that you could not get by him – he had recognized right away, he said, a recent suicide. The attendant came up to Fyodor and asked him to leave. And walking through the funereally luxuriant garden, past unctuous beds in which bass-toned, dark crimson dahlias were blooming in blessed sleep and eternal repose, toward the bench where he was awaited by Mme Chernyshevski (who never went in to her husband but spent whole days in the immediate vicinity of his quarters, preoccupied, brisk, always with packages) – walking over the variegated gravel between myrtle shrubs resembling furniture and taking the visitors he passed for paranoiacs, troubled Fyodor kept pondering over the fact that the misfortune of the Chernyshevskis appeared to be a kind of mocking variation on the theme of his own hope-suffused grief, and only much later did he understand the full refinement of the corollary and all the irreproachable compositional balance with which these collateral sounds had been included in his own life.

Three days before his mother's departure, in a large hall which was well known to Berlin Russians and which belonged to a society of dentists, judging by the portraits of venerable tooth doctors that looked down from the walls, an open literary evening was held in which Fyodor Konstantinovich also took part. Few people had turned up and it was cold; by the doors the same a thousand times seen representatives of the local Russian intelligentsia stood around smoking, and as usual, catching sight of some familiar, friendly face, Fyodor hurried toward it with sincere pleasure, only to have it replaced by boredom after the first burst of conversation. Elizaveta Pavlovna was joined in the first row by Mme Chernyshevski; and from the fact that his mother occasionally turned her head this way and that while adjusting her hairdo from behind, Fyodor, hovering about the hall, concluded that she was little interested in the society of her neighbour. At last the programme began. First to read was a name writer who in his time had appeared in all the Russian reviews, a grey-haired, clean-shaven old man rather resembling a hoopoe, with eyes which were too good-natured for literature; in a sensibly everyday kind of voice he read a tale of Petersburg life on the eve of the revolution, with an ether-sniffing vamp, chic spies, champagne, Rasputin and apocalyptically apoplectic sunsets over the Neva. After him a certain Kron, writing under the pseudonym of Rostislav Strannyy (Rostislav the Strange) gladdened us with a long story about a romantic adventurer in the town of a hundred eyes, beneath skies unknown; for the sake of beauty his epithets were placed after the nouns, his verbs had also flown off somewhere or other and for some reason the word *storozhko*, 'warily' was repeated about a dozen times. ('She warily let fall a smile'; 'The chestnuts broke warily into blossom'.) After the interval poets came thick and fast: a tall youth with a buttonlike face, another, shortish but with a large nose, an elderly lady wearing pince-nez, another, younger, one – and finally Koncheyev, who, in contrast to the triumphant precision and polish of the others, muttered his verses in a low tired voice; but there dwelt independently in them such music, in the seemingly dark verse such a chasm of meaning yawned at one's feet, so convincing were the sounds and so unexpectedly, out of the very same words every poet was stringing together, there sprang up, played, and slipped away without ever quenching one's thirst a unique perfection, bearing no resemblance to words and in no need of words, that for the first time that evening the applause was not feigned. Last to appear was Godunov-Cherdyntsev. From the poems written during the summer he read those which Elizaveta Pavlovna liked so much – on Russia:

> The yellow birches, mute in the blue sky . . .

and on Berlin, beginning with the stanza:

> Things here are in a sorry state;
> Even the moon is much too rough
> Though it is rumoured to come straight
> From Hamburg where they make the stuff . . .

and the one which moved her most of all, although she did not think to connect it with the memory of a young woman, long dead, whom Fyodor had loved when sixteen:

> One night between sunset and river
> On the old bridge we stood, you and I.
> Will you ever forget it, I queried,
> —That particular swift that went by?
> And you answered, so earnestly: Never!
>
> And what sobs made us suddenly shiver,
> What a cry life emitted in flight!
> Till we die, till tomorrow, for ever,
> You and I on the old bridge one night.

But it was getting late, many people were moving toward the exit, one lady was putting on her coat with her back to the platform, the applause was sparse. . . . The damp night gleamed black on the street, with raging wind: never, never will we reach home. But nonetheless a tram came, and hanging on a strap in the gangway over his mother sitting by the window. Fyodor thought with heavy revulsion of the verses he had writen that day, of word-fissures, of the leakage of poetry, and at the same time, with proud, joyous energy, with passionate impatience, he was already looking for the creation of something new, something still unknown, genuine, corresponding fully to the gift which he felt like a burden inside himself.

On the eve of her departure they both sat up late in his room, she, in the armchair, easily and skilfully (whereas formerly she could not sew a button on) darning and mending his pitiful things while he, on the sofa, biting his nails, was reading a thick battered book; earlier, in his youth, he had skipped some of the pages – 'Angelo', 'Journey to Arzrum' – but lately it was precisely in these that he had found particular pleasure. He had only just got to the words: 'The frontier held something mysterious for me; to travel had been my favourite dream since childhood', when suddenly he felt a sweet, strong stab from somewhere. Still not understanding, he put the book to one side and slipped blind fingers into a boxful of homemade cigarettes. At that moment his mother said without raising her head: 'What did I just remember! Those funny rhymes about butterflies and moths which you and he composed together when we were out walking, you remember. "Your blue stripe, Catocalid, shows from under its grey lid".' 'Yes,' replied Fyodor, 'some were downright epics: "A dead leaf is not hoarier than a newborn *arborea*".' (What a surprise it had been! Father had only just brought back the very first specimen from his travels, having found it during the initial trek through Siberia – he had not even had time to describe it yet – and on the first day after his return, in the Leshino park, two paces from the house, with no thought of lepidoptera, while strolling with his wife and children, throwing a tennis ball for the fox terriers, basking in his return, in the balmy weather and the health and gaiety of his family, but unconsciously noting with the experienced eye of a hunter every insect along his path, he had suddenly pointed out to Fyodor with the tip of his cane a plump reddish-grey *Epicnaptera* moth, with sinuate margins, of the leaf-mimicking kind, hanging asleep from a stalk under a bush; he had been about to walk on (the members of this genus look very much alike) but then squatted down, wrinkled his forehead, inspected his find and suddenly said in a bright voice: *'Well, I'm damned!* I need not have gone so far!' 'I always said so,' interposed his wife with a laugh. The furry little monster in his hand belonged to the new species he had just brought back – and now it had cropped up here, in the Province of St Petersburg, whose fauna had been so well investigated! But, as often happens, the momentum of mighty coincidence did not stop there, it was good for one more stage: only a few days later his father learned that this new moth had just been described from St Petersburg specimens by a fellow scientist, and Fyodor cried all night long: they had beaten Father to it!)

And now Elizaveta Pavlovna was about to return to Paris. They stood for a long time on the narrow platform waiting for the train, next to the luggage elevator, while on the other lines the sad city trains stopped for a moment, hastily banging their doors. The Paris express rushed in. His mother boarded and immediately thrust her head through the window, smiling. By the neighbouring opulent sleeping car, seeing off an unpretentious old lady, stood a couple: a pale, red-lipper beauty in a black silk coat with a high fur collar, and a famous stunt flyer; everyone was staring at him, at his muffler, at his back, as if expecting to find wings on it.

'I have a suggestion to make,' said his mother gaily as they parted. 'I have about seventy marks left which are quite useless to me, and you must eat better. I can't look at you, you're so thin. Here, take them.' *'Avec joie,'* he replied, instantly envisioning a year's pass to the state library, milk chocolate and some mercenary young German girl whom, in his baser moments, he kept planning to get for himself.

Pensive, abstracted, vaguely tormented by the thought that somehow in his talks with his mother he had left the main thing untold, Fyodor returned home, took off his shoes, broke off the corner of a chocolate bar together with its silver paper, moved the book left open on the sofa closer. . . . 'The harvest rippled, awaiting the sickle.' Again that divine stab! And how it called, how it *prompted* him, the sentence about the Terek ('In faith, the river was awesome!') or – even more fitly, more intimately – about the Tartar women: 'They were sitting on horseback, swathed in yashmaks: all one could see were their eyes and the heels of their shoes.'

Thus did he hearken to the purest sound from Pushkin's tuning fork – and he already knew exactly what this sound required of him. Two weeks after his mother's departure he wrote her about what he had conceived, what he had been helped to conceive by the transperent rhythm of 'Arzrum', and she replied as if she had already known about it:

> It is a long time since I have been as happy as I was with you in Berlin, but watch out, this is no easy undertaking. I feel in my heart that you will accomplish it wonderfully, but remember that you need a great deal of exact information and very little family sentimentality. If you need anything I'll tell you all I can, but

take care of the special research where you are, and this is most important, take all his books and those of Grigoriy Efimovich, and those of the Grand Duke, and lots more; of course you know how to obtain all this, and be sure to get into touch with Vasiliy Germanovich Krüger, search him out if he's still in Berlin, they once travelled together, I remember, and approach other people, you know whom better than I, write to Avinov, to Verity, write to that German who used to visit us before the war, Benhaas? Banhaas? Write to Stuttgart, to London, to Tring, in Oxford, everywhere, *débrouille-toi* because I know nothing of these matters and all these names merely sing in my ears, but how certain I am that you will manage, my darling.

He continued, however, to wait – the planned work was a wafture of bliss, and he was afraid to spoil that bliss by haste and moreover the complex responsibility of the work frightened him, he was not ready for it yet. Continuing his training programme during the whole of spring, he fed on Pushkin, inhaled Pushkin (the reader of Pushkin has the capacity of his lungs enlarged). He studied the accuracy of the words and the absolute purity of their conjunction; he carried the transparency of prose to the limits of blank verse and then mastered it: in this he was served by a living example in the prose of Pushkin's *History of the Pugachyov Rebellion*:

God help us not to see a Russian riot
Senseless and merciless . . .

To strengthen the muscles of his muse he took on his rambles whole pages of *Pugachyov* learned by heart as a man using an iron bar instead of a walking stick. Toward him out of a Pushkin tale came Karolina Schmidt, 'a girl heavily rouged, of meek and modest appearance', who acquired the bed in which Schoning died. Beyond Grunewald forest a postmaster who resembled Simeon Vyrin (from another tale) was lighting his pipe by the window, and there also stood pots with balsam flowers. The sky-blue *sarafan* of the Damsel turned Peasant could be glimpsed among the alder bushes. He was in that state of feeling and mind 'when reality, giving way to fancies, blends with them in the nebulous visions of first sleep'.

Pushkin entered his blood. With Pushkin's voice merged the voice of his father. He kissed Pushkin's hot little hand, taking it for another, large hand smelling of the breakfast *kalach* (a blond roll). He remembered that his and Tanya's nurse hailed from the same place that Pushkin's Arina came from – namely Suyda, just beyond Gatchina: this had been within an hour's ride of their area – and she had also spoken 'singsong like'. He heard his father on a fresh summer morning as they walked down to the river bath-house, on whose plank wall shimmered the golden reflection of the water, repeating with classic fervour what he considered to be the most beautiful not only of Pushkin's lines but of all the verses ever written in the world: '*Tut Apollon-ideal, tam Niobeya-pechal'* ' (Here is Apollo-ideal, there is Niobe-grief) and the russet wing and mother-of-pearl of a Niobe fritillary flashed over the scabiosas of the riverside meadow, where, during the first days of June, there occurred sparsely the small Black Apollo.

Indefatigably, in ecstasy, he was really preparing his work now (in Berlin with an adjustment of thirteen days it was also the first days of June), collected material, read until dawn, studied maps, wrote letters and met with the necessary people. From Pushkin's prose he had passed to his life, so that in the beginning the rhythm of Pushkin's era commingled with the rhythm of his father's life. Scientific books (with the Berlin Library's stamp always on the ninety-ninth page), such as the familiar volumes of *The Travels of a Naturalist* in unfamiliar black and green bindings, lay side by side with the old Russian journals in which he sought Pushkin's reflected light. There, one day, he stumbled over the remarkable *Memoirs of the Past* of A. N. Suhoshchokov, in which there were among other things two or three pages concerning his grandfather, Kirill Ilyich (his father had once referred to them with displeasure), and the fact that the writer of these memoirs mentioned him incidentally in connection with his thoughts on Pushkin now seemed somehow to have particular significance, even though he portrayed Kirill Ilyich as a gay dog and a good-for-nothing.

Suhoshchokov wrote:

> They say that a man whose leg is cut off at the hip can feel it for a long time, moving non-existent toes and flexing non-existent muscles. Thus will Russia long continue to feel the living presence of Pushkin. There is something seductive, like an abyss, in his fatal destiny, and indeed, he himself felt that he had had, and would have, a special reckoning with fate. In addition to the poet's extracting poetry out of his past, he also found it in tragic thoughts about the future. The triple formula of human existence: irrevocability, unrealizability, inevitability – was well known to him. But how he wanted to live! In the above-mentioned album of my 'academic' aunt he personally wrote a poem which I can remember to this day, both mentally and visually, so that I can even see its position on the page:

Oh no, my life has not grown tedious,
I want it still, I love it still.
My soul, although its youth has vanished,
Has not become completely chill.
Fate will yet comfort me; a novel
Of genius I shall yet enjoy,
I'll see yet a mature Mickiéwicz,
With something I myself may toy.

I do not think one could find any other poet who peered so often – now in jest, now superstitiously, or with inspired seriousness – into the future. Right to this day there lives in the Province of Kursk, topping the hundred mark, an old man whom I remember as being already elderly, stupid and malicious – but Pushkin is no longer with us. Meeting in the course of my long life with remarkable talents and living through remarkable events, I have often meditated on how he would have reacted to this and that: why, he could have seen the emancipation of the serfs and could have read *Anna Karenin*! . . . Returning now to these reveries of mine I recall that once in my youth I had something in the nature of a vision. This psychological episode is closely linked with the recollection of a personage still thriving to this very day, whom I shall call Ch. – I trust he will not blame me for this revival of a distant past. We were acquanited through our families – my grandfather had once been friendly with his father. In 1836, while abroad, this Ch. who was then quite young – barely seventeen – quarrelled with his family (and in so doing hastened, so they say, the decease of his sire, a hero of the Napoleonic War), and in the company of some Hamburg merchants sailed nonchalantly off to Boston, from there landing in Texas where he successfully took up cattle breeding. In that manner twenty years passed. The fortune he had made he lost playing écarté on a Mississippi keel-boat, won it back in the gaming houses of New Orleans, blued it all over again, and after one of those scandalously prolonged, noisy smoky duels on closed premises which were then fashionable in Louisiana – and after many other adventures – he became homesick for Russia where, conveniently, a demesne was awaiting him, and with the same carefree easiness with which he had left it, he returned to Europe. Once, on a winter's day in 1858, he visited us unexpectedly at our house on the Moyka, in St Petersburg; Father was away and the guest was received by us youngsters. As we looked at this outlandish fop in his soft black hat and black clothes, the romantic gloom of which caused his silk shirt with its sumptuous pleats, and his blue, lilac and pink waistcoat with diamond buttons to stand out particularly dazzlingly, my brother and I could hardly contain our laughter and decided there and then to take advantage of the fact that during all these years he had heard absolutely nothing of his homeland, as if it had fallen through some trap door, so that now, like a forty-year-old Rip van Winkle waking up in a transformed St Petersburg, Ch. was hungry for any news, the which we undertook to give him plenty of, mixed with our outrageous fabrications. To the question, for instance, was Pushkin alive and what was he writing, I blasphemously replied, 'Why he came out with a new poem the other day.' That night we took our guest to the theatre. It did not turn out too well, however. Instead of treating him to a new Russian comedy we showed him *Othello* with the famous black tragedian Aldridge. At first our American planter seemed to be highly amused by the appearance of a genuine Negro on the stage. But he remained indifferent to the marvellous power of his acting and was more taken up with examining the audience, especially our St Petersburg ladies (one of whom he soon afterwards married), who were devoured at that moment with envy for Desdemona.

'Look who's sitting next to us,' my brother suddenly said to Ch. in a low voice. 'There to our right.'

In the neighbouring box there sat an old man . . . Of shortish stature, in a worn tailcoat, with a sallow and swarthy complexion, dishevelled ashen side-whiskers, and sparse, grey-streaked tousled hair, he was taking a most eccentric delight in the acting of the African: his thick lips twitched, his nostrils were dilated, and at certain bits he even jumped up and down in his seat and banged with delight on the para, his rings flashing.

'Who's that?' asked Ch.

'What, don't you recognize him? Look closer.'

'I don't recognize him.'

Then my brother made big eyes and whispered, 'Why, that's Pushkin!' Ch. looked again . . . and after a minute became interested by something else. It seems funny now to recall what a strange mood came upon me then: the prank as happens from time to time, rebounded, and this frivolously summoned ghost did not want to disappear: I was quite incapable of tearing myself away from the neighbouring box; I looked at those harsh wrinkles, that broad nose, those large ears . . . shivers ran down my back, and not all of Othello's jealousy was able to drag me away. What if this is indeed Pushkin, I mused, Pushkin at sixty, Pushkin spared two decades ago by the bullet of the fatal coxcomb, Pushkin in the rich autumn of his genius. . . . This is he; this yellow hand grasping those lady's opera glasses wrote *Anchar, Graf Nulin, The Egyptian Nights*. . . . The act finished; applause thundered. Grey-haired Pushkin stood up abruptly, and still smiling, with a bright sparkle in his youthful eyes, quickly left his box.

Suboshchokov errs in depicting my grandfather as an empty-headed rake. It was simply that the latter's interests were situated on a different plane from the intellectual habitus of a young dilettante member of the St Petersburg literary set which our memoirist was then. Even if Kirill Ilyich had been pretty wild in his youth, once married he not only settled down but also entered government service, simultaneously doubling his inherited fortune by successful operations and later retiring to his country place, where he manifested extraordinary skill in farming, produced a new sort of apple on the side, left a curious 'Discours' (the fruit of winter leisure) on the 'Equality Before the Law in the Animal Kingdom' plus a proposal for a clever reform under the kind of intricate title that was fashionable then, 'Visions of an Egyptian Bureaucrat', and as an old man accepted an important consular post, in London. He was kind, brave and truthful, and had his quirks and passions – what more could be needed? A tradition has subsisted in the family that, having sworn not to game, he was physically incapable of remaining in a room where there was a pack of cards. An ancient Colt revolver that had served him well and a medallion with the portrait of a mysterious lady attracted indescribably my boyhood dreams. His life, which had retained to the end the freshness of its stormy beginning, ended peacefully. He returned to Russia in 1883, no longer a Louisiana duellist but a Russian dignitary, and on a July day, on the leather sofa in the little blue corner room where I later kept my collection of butterflies, he expired without suffering, talking all the while in his deathbed delirium about a big river and the music and lights.

My father was born in 1860. A love of lepidoptera was inculcated into him by his German tutor. (By the way: what has happened to those originals who used to teach natural history to Russian children – green net, tin box on a sling, hat stuck with pinned butterflies, long, learned nose, candid eyes behind spectacles – where are they all, where are their frail skeletons – or was this a special breed of Germans, for export to Russia, or am I not looking properly?) After completing early (in 1876) his schooling in St Petersburg, he received his university education in England, at Cambridge, where he studied biology under Professor Bright. His first journey, around the world, he made while my grandfather was still alive, and from then until 1918 his whole life consisted of travelling and the writing of scientific works. The main ones among them are: *Lepidoptera Asiatica* (8 volumes published in parts from 1890 to 1917), *The*

Butterflies and Moths of the Russian Empire (the first four out of six proposed volumes came out 1912-1916) and, best known to the general public, *The Travels of a Naturalist* (7 volumes 1892-1912). These works were unanimously recognized as classics and he was still a young man when his name occupied one of the first places in the study of the Russo-Asiatic fauna, side by side with the names of its pioneers, Fischer von Waldheim, Menetriés, Eversmann.

He worked in close touch with his remarkable Russian contemporaries. Kholodkovski calls him 'the conquistador of Russian entomology'. He collaborated with Charles Oberthur, Grand Duke Nikolai Mihailovich, Leech and Seitz. Scattered throughout entomological journals are hundreds of his papers, of which the first – 'On the peculiarities of the occurrence of certain butterflies in the Province of St Petersburg' (Horae Soc. Ent. Ross.) – is dated 1877, and the last – '*Austautia simonoides* n. sp., a Geometrid Moth Mimiking a Small Parnassius' (Trans. Ent. Soc. London) – is dated 1916. He conducted a weighty and acrimonious polemic with Staudinger, author of the notorious *Katalog*. He was vice-president of the Russian Entomological Society, Full Member of the Moscow Soc. of Investigators of Nature, Member of the Imperial Russian Geographical Soc., and Honorary Member of a multiude of learned societies abroad.

Between 1885 and 1918 he covered an incredible amount of territory, making surveys of his route on a three-mile scale for a distance of many thousands of miles and forming astounding collections. During these years he completed eight major expeditions which in all lasted eighteen years; but between them there was also a multitude of minor journeys, 'diversions', as he called them, considering as part of these minutae not only his trips to the less-well-investigated countries of Europe but also the journey around the world he had made in his youth. Tackling Asia in earnest he investigated Eastern Siberia, Altai, Fergana, the Pamirs, Western China, 'the islands of the Gobi Sea and its coasts', Mongolia, and the 'incorrigible continent of Tibet' and described his travels in precise, weighty words.

Such is the general scheme of my father's life, copied out of an encyclopedia. It still does not sting, but I can already hear a living voice within it. It remains to be said that in 1898, at thirty-eight years of age, he married Elizaveta Pavlovna Vezhin, the twenty-year-old daughter of a well-known statesman; that he had two children by her; that in the intervals between his journeys. . . .

An agonizing, somehow sacrilegious question, hardly expressible in words: was her life with him happy, together and apart? Shall we disturb this inner world or shall we limit ourselves to a mere description of routes – *arida quaedam viarum descripto?* 'Dear Mamma, I now have a great favour to ask of you. Today is the 8th of July, his birthday. On any other day I could never bring myself to ask you. Tell me something about you and him. Not the sort of thing I can find in our shared memories but the sort of thing you alone have gone through and preserved.' And here is part of the reply:

> . . . imagine – a honeymoon trip, the Pyrenees, the divine bliss of everything, of the sun, the brooks, the flowers, the snowy summits, even the flies in the hotels – and of being every moment together. And then, one morning, I had a headache or something, or the heat was too much for me. He said he would go for a half hour's stroll before lunch. With odd clearness I remember sitting on a hotel balcony (around me peace, the mountains, the wonderful cliffs of Gavarnie) and reading for the first time a book not intended for young girls, *Une Vie* by Maupassant, I remember I liked it very much at the time. I look at my little watch and I see that it is already lunchtime, more than an hour has passed since he left. I wait. At first I am a little cross, then I begin to worry. Lunch is served on the terrace and I am unable to eat. I go out onto the lawn in front of the hotel, I return to my room, I go outside again. In another hour I was in an indescribable state of terror, agitation, God knows what. I was travelling for the first time, I was inexperienced and easily frightened, and then there was *Une Vie* . . . I decided that he had abandoned me, the most stupid and terrible thoughts kept getting into my head, the day was passing, it seemed to me that the servants were gloating at me – oh, I cannot convey to you what it was like! I had even begun to thrust some dresses into a suitcase in order to return immediately to Russia, and then I suddenly decided he was dead, I ran out and began to babble something crazy and to send for the police. Suddenly I saw him walking across the lawn, his face more cheerful than I had ever seen it before, although he had been cheerful the whole time; there he came, waving his hand to me as if nothing had happened, and his light trousers had wet green spots on them, his panama had gone, his jacket was torn on one side. . . . I expect you have already guessed what had happened. Thank God at least that he finally caught it after all – in his handkerchief, on a sheer cliff – if not he would have spent the night in the mountains, as he coolly explained to me. . . .

But now I want to tell you about something else, from a slightly later period, when I already knew what a really good separation could be. You were quite small then, coming up to three, you can't remember. That spring he went off to Tashkent. From there he was due to set off on a journey on the first of June and to be away for not less than two years. That was already the second big absence during our time together. I often think now that if all the years he spent without me from the day of our wedding were added together they would amount in all to no more than his present absence. And I also think of the fact that it sometimes seemed to me then that I was unhappy, but now I know that I was always happy, that that unhappiness was one of the colours of happiness. In short, I don't know what came over me that spring, I had always been sort of batty when he went away, but that time I was quite disgracefully so. I suddenly decided that I would catch up with him and travel with him at least till autumn. Secretly I gathered a thousand things together; I had absolutely no idea what was needed, but it seemed to me that I was stocking up everything well and properly. I remember binoculars, and an alpenstock, and a camp-bed, and a sun helmet, and a hareskin coat straight out of *The Captain's Daughter,* and a little mother-of-pearl revolver, and some great tarpaulin affair that I was afraid of, and a complicated water bottle that I couldn't unscrew. In short, think of the equipment of Tartarin de Tarascon: How I managed to leave you little ones, how I said good-bye to you – that's in a kind of mist, and I don't remember any more how I slipped out from Uncle Oleg's surveillance, how I got to the station. But I was both frightened and cheerful, I felt myself a heroine, and on the stations everyone looked at my English travelling costume with its short (*entendons-nous*: to the ankle) checked skirt, with the binoculars over one shoulder and a kind of purse over the other. That's how I looked when I jumped out of the tarantass in a settlement just outside of Tashkent, when in the brilliant sunlight, I shall never forget it, I caught sight of your father within a hundred yards of the road: he was standing with one foot resting on a white stone, one elbow on a fence, and talking to two Cossacks. I ran across the gravel, shouting and laughing; he turned slowly, and when I suddenly stopped in front of him like a fool, he looked me all over, slit his eyes, and in a horribly unexpected voice spoke three words: 'You go home.' And I immediately turned, and went back to my carriage, and got in it, and saw he had put his foot in exactly the same place and had again propped his elbow, continuing his conversation with the Cossacks. And now I was driving back, in a trance, petrified, and only somewhere deep within me preparations had started for a storm of tears. But then after a couple of miles [and here a smile broke through the written line] he overtook me, in a cloud of dust, on a white horse, and we parted this time quite differently, so that I resumed my way to St Petersburg almost as cheerfully as I had left it, only that I kept worrying about you two, wondering how you were, but no matter, you were in good health.

No – somehow it seems to me that I do remember all this, perhaps because it was subsequently often mentioned. In general our whole daily life was permeated with stories about Father, with worry about him, expectations of his return, the hidden sorrow of farewells and the wild joy of welcomings. His passion was reflected in all of us, coloured in different ways, apprehended in different ways, but permanent and habitual. His home museum, in which stood rows of oak cabinets with glassed drawers, full of crucified butterflies (the rest – the plants, beetles, birds, rodents and reptiles – he gave to his colleagues to study), where it smelled as it probably smells in Paradise, and where the laboratory assistants worked at tables along the one-piece windows, was a kind of mysterious central hearth, illuminating from inside the whole of our St Petersburg house – and only the noonday roar of the Petropavlovsk cannon could invade its quiet. Our relatives, non-entomological friends, the servants and the meekly touchy Yvonna Ivanovna talked of butterflies not as of something really existing but as of a certain attribute of my father, which existed only insofar as he existed, or as of an ailment with which everybody had long since got used to coping, so that with us entomology turned into some sort of routinary hallucination, like a harmless domestic ghost that sits down, no longer surprising anyone, every evening by the fireside. At the same time, none of our countless uncles and aunts took any interest in his science and had hardly even read his popular work, read and re-read by dozens of thousands of cultured Russians. Of course Tanya and I had learned to appreciate Father from earliest childhood and he seemed even more enchanting to us than, say, that Harold about whom he told stories to us, Harold who fought with the lions in the Byzantine arena, who pursued brigands in Syria, bathed in the Jordan, took eighty fortresses by storm in Africa, 'the Blue Land', saved the Icelanders from starvation – and was famed from Norway to Sicily, from Yorkshire to Novgorod. Then, when I fell under the spell of butterflies, something unfolded in my soul and I relived all my father's journeys, as if I myself had made them: in my dreams I saw the winding road, the caravan, the many-hued mountains, and envied my father madly, agonizingly, to the point of tears – hot and violent tears that would suddenly gush out of me at table as we discussed his letters from the road or even at the simple mention of a far, far place. Every year, with the approach of spring, before moving to the country, I would feel within me a pitiful fraction of what I would have felt before departing for Tibet. On the Nevski Avenue, during the last days of March, when the wooden blocks of the spacious street pavements gleamed dark blue from the damp and the sun, one might see, flying high over the carriages, along the façades of the houses, past the city hall, past the lindens in the square, past the statue of Catherine, the first yellow butterfly. In the classroom the large window was open, sparrows perched on the windowsill and teachers let lessons go by, leaving in their stead squares of blue sky, with footballs falling down out of the blueness. For some reason I always had bad marks in geography and what an expression our geography teacher would have when he used to mention my father's name, how the inquisitive eyes of my comrades turned on me at this point and how within me the blood rose and fell from suppressed rapture and from fear of expressing that rapture – and now I think of how little I know, how easy it is for me to make some idiotic blunder in describing my father's researches.

At the beginning of April, to open the season, the members of the Russian Entomological Society used to make a traditional trip to the other side of Black River, in a suburb of St Petersburg, where in a birch grove which was still naked and wet, still showing patches of holey snow, there occurred on the trunks, its feeble transparent wings pressed flat agaist the papery bark, our favourite rarity, a speciality of the province. Once or twice they took me with them too. Among these elderly family men cautiously, tensely practising sorcery in an April wood, there was an old theatre critic, a gynaecologist, a professor of international law and a general – for some reason I can recall especially clearly the figure of this general (X. B. Lambovski – there was something Paschal about him), his fat back bending low, with one arm placed behind it, next to the figure of my father, who had sunk on his haunches with a kind of Oriental ease – both were carefully examining in search of pupae a handful of reddish earth dug up with a trowel – and even to this day I am wondering what the coachmen waiting on the road made of all this.

Sometimes, in the country, Grandmother would sail into our schoolroom, Olga Ivanovna Vezhin, plump, fresh-complexioned, in mittens and lace: '*Bonjour les enfants*' she would sing out sonorously and then, heavily accenting the prepositions, she informed us: '*Je viens de voir* DANS *le jardin,* PRES *du cèdre,* SUR *une rose un papillon de toute beauté: il était bleu, vert, pourpre, doré – et grand comme ça.*' 'Quickly take your net,' she continued, turning to me, 'and go into the garden. Perhaps you can still catch it.' And she sailed out, completely oblivious to the fact that if such a fabulous insect were to come my way (it was not even worth a guess as to what banal garden visitor her imagination had so adorned), I would have died of heartbreak. Sometimes, to give me special pleasure, our French governess would choose a certain fable of Florian's for me to learn by heart, about another impossibly gaudy *petit-maître* butterfly. Sometimes some aunt or other would give me a book by Fabre, whose popular works, full of chitchat, inaccurate observations and downright mistakes, my father treated with scorn. I also remember this: one day, upon missing my net I went out to look for it on the veranda and met my uncle's orderly returning from somewhere with it on his shoulder, all flushed and with a kindly and shy smile on his rosy lips: 'Just see what I've caught for you,' he proclaimed in a satisfied voice, dumping the net on the floor; the mesh was secured near the frame by a bit of string, so that a bag was formed in which a variety of live matter swarmed and rustled – and good heavens, what rubbish there was in it: thirty-odd grasshoppers, the head of a daisy, a couple of dragonflies, ears of wheat, some sand, a cabbage butterfly crushed out of all recognition, and finally, an edible toadstool noticed on the way and added just in case. The Russian common people know and love their country's nature. How many jeers, how many conjectures and questions have I had occasion to hear when, overcoming my embarrassment, I walked through the village with my net! 'Well, that's nothing,' said my father, 'you should have seen the faces of the Chinese when I was collecting once on some holy mountain, or the look the progressive schoolmistress in a Volga town gave me when I explained to her what I was doing in that ravine.'

How to describe the bliss of our walks with Father through the woods, the fields and the peat bogs, or the constant summer thought of him if he was away, the eternal dream of making some discovery and of meeting him with this discovery – How to describe the feeling I experienced when he showed me all the spots where in his own childhood he had caught this and that – the beam of a half-rotted little bridge where he had caught his first peacock butterfly in '71, the slope of the road down to the river where he had once fallen on his knees, weeping and praying (he had bungled his stroke, it had flown for ever!). And what fascination there was in his words, in the kind of special fluency and grace of his style when he spoke about his subject, what affectionate precision in the movements of his fingers turning the screw of a spreading board or a microscope, what a truly enchanting world was unfolded in his lessons! Yes, I know this is not the way to write – these exclamations won't take me very deep – but my pen is not yet accustomed to following the outlines of his image, and I myself abominate these accessory curlicues. Oh, don't look at me, my childhood, with such big, frightened eyes.

The sweetness of the lessons! On a warm evening he would take me to a certain small pond to watch the aspen hawk moth swing over the very water, dipping in it the tip of its body. He showed me how to prepare genital armatures to determine species which were externally indistinguishable. With a special smile he brought to my attention the black Ringlet butterflies in our park which with mysterious and elegant unexpectedness appeared only in even years. He mixed beer with treacle for me on a dreadfully cold, dreadfully rainy autumn night in order to catch at the smeared tree trunks that glistened in the light of a kerosene lamp a multitude of large, banded moths, silently diving and hurrying towards the bait. He variously warmed and cooled the golden chrysalids of my tortoiseshells so that I was able to get from them Corsican, arctic and entirely unusual forms looking as if they had been dipped in tar and had silky fuzz sticking to them. He taught me how to take apart an ant-hill and find the caterpillar of a Blue which had concluded a barbaric pact with its inhabitants, and I saw how an ant, greedily tickling a hind segment of that caterpillar's clumsy, sluglike little body, forced it to excrete a drop of intoxicant juice, which it swallowed immediately. In compensation it offered its own larvae as food; it was as if cows gave us Chartreuse and we gave them our infants to eat. But the strong caterpillar of one exotic species of Blue will not stoop to his exchange, brazenly devouring the infant ants and then turning into an impenetrable chrysalis which finally, at the time of hatching, is surrounded by ants (those failures in the school of experience) awaiting the emergence of the helplessly crumpled butterfly in order to attack it; they attack – and nevertheless she does not perish: 'I have never laughed so much,' said my father, 'as when I realized that nature had supplied her with a sticky substance which caused the feelers and feet of those zealous ants to get stuck together, so that they rolled and writhed all around her while she herself, calm and invulnerable, let her wings strengthen and dry.'

He told me about the odours of butterflies – musk and vanilla; about the voices of butterflies; about the piercing sound given out by the monstrous caterpillar of a Malayan hawkmoth, an improvement on the mouselike squeak of our Death's Head moth; about the small resonant tympanum of certain tiger moths; about the cunning butterfly in the Brazilian forest which imitates the whirr of a local bird. He told me about the incredible artistic wit of mimetic disguise, which was not explainable by the struggle for existence (the rough haste of evolution's unskilled forces), was too refined for the mere deceiving of accidental predators, feathered, scaled and otherwise (not very fastidious, but then not too fond of butterflies), and seemed to have been invented by some waggish artist precisely for the intelligent eyes of man (a hypothesis that may lead far an evolutionist who observes apes feeding on butterflies); he told me about these magic masks of mimicry; about the enormous moth which in a state of repose assumes the image of a snake looking at you; of a tropical geometrid coloured in perfect imitation of a species of butterfly infinitely removed from it in nature's system, the illusion of the orange abdomen possessed by one being humorously reproduced in the other by the orange-coloured inner margins of the secondaries; and about the curious harem of that famous African swallowtail, whose variously disguised females copy in colour, shape and even flight half a dozen different species (apparently inedible), which are also the models of numerous other mimics. He told me about migrations, about the long cloud consisting of myriads of white pierids that moves through the sky, indifferent to the direction of the wind, always at the same level above the ground, rising softly and smoothly over hills and sinking again into valleys, meeting perhaps another cloud of butterflies, yellow, filtering through it without stopping and without soiling its own whiteness – and floating farther, to settle on trees toward night-time which stand until morning as if bestrewn with snow – and then taking off again to continue their journey – whither? Why? A tale not yet finished by nature or else forgotten. 'Our thistle butterfly,' he said, 'the "painted lady" of the English, the "*belle dame*" of the French, does not hibernate in Europe as related species do; it is born on the African plains; there, at dawn, the lucky traveller may hear the whole steppe, glistening in the first rays, crackle with an incalculable number of hatching chrysalids.' From there, without delay it begins its journey north, reaching the shores of Europe in early spring, suddenly enlivening the gardens of the Crimea and the terraces of the Riviera; without lingering, but leaving individuals everywhere for summer breeding, it proceeds farther north and by the end of May, by now in single specimens, it reaches Scotland, Heligoland, our parts and even the extreme north of the earth; it has been caught in Iceland! With a strange crazy flight unlike anything else the bleached, hardly recognizable butterfly, choosing a dry glade, 'wheels' in and out of the leshino firs, and by the end of the summer, on thistleheads, on asters, its lovely pink-flushed offspring is already revelling in life. 'Most moving of all,' added my father, 'is that on the first cold days a reverse phenomenon is observed, the ebb: the butterfly hastens southward, for the winter, but of course it perishes before it reaches the warmth.'

Simultaneously with the Englishman Tutt, who observed the same thing in the Swiss Alps as he in the Pamirs, my father discovered the true nature of the corneal formation appearing beneath the abdomen in the impregnated females of Parnassians, and explained how her mate, working with a pair of spatulate appendages, places and moulds on her a chastity belt of his own manufacture, shaped differently in every species of this genus, being sometimes a little boat, sometimes a hellical shell, sometimes – as in the case of the exceptionally rare dark-cinder grey *orpheus* Godunov – a replica of a tiny lyre. And as a frontispiece to my present work I think I would like to display precisely this butterfly – for I can hear him talk about it, can see the way he took the six specimens he had brought back out of their six thick triangular envelopes, the way he lowered his eyes with the field magnifier close to the abdomen of the only female – and how reverently his laboratory assistant relaxed in a damp jar the dry, glossy, tightly folded wings in order later to drive a pin smoothly through the insect's thorax, stick it in the cork groove of the spreading board, hold down flat upon it by means of broad strips of semitransparent paper its open, defenceless, gracefully expanded beauty, then slip a bit of cotton wool under its abdomen and straighten its black antennae – so that it dried that way forever. Forever? In the Berlin museum there are many of my father's captures and these are as fresh today as they were in the eighties and nineties. Butterflies from Linnaeus' collection now in London have subsisted since the eighteenth century. In the Prague museum one can see that same example of the showy Atlas moth that Catherine the Great admired. Why then do I feel so sad?

His captures, his observations, the sound of his voice in scientific words, all this, I think, I will preserve. But that is still so little. With the same relative permanence I would like to retain what it was, perhaps, that I loved most of all about him: his live masculinity, inflexibility and independence, the chill and the warmth of his personality, his power over everything that he undertook. As if playing a game, as if wishing in passing to imprint his force on everything, he would pick out here and there something from a field outside entomology and thus he left his mark upon almost all branches of natural science: there is only one plant described by him out of all those he collected, but that one is a spectacular species of birch; one bird – a most fabulous pheasant; one bat – but the biggest one in the world. And in all parts of nature our name echoes a countless number of times, for other naturalists gave his name either to a spider, or to a rhododendron, or to a mountain ridge – the latter, by the way, made him angry: 'To ascertain and preserve the ancient native name of a pass,' he wrote, 'is always both more scientific and more noble than to saddle it with the name of a good acquaintance.'

I liked – only now understood how much I liked it – that special easy knack he showed in dealing with a horse, a dog, a gun, a bird or a peasant boy with a two-inch splinter in his back – he was constantly being brought people who were wounded, maimed, even infirm, even pregnant women, who probably took his mysterious occupation for voodoo practice. I liked the fact that, in contradistinction to the majority of non-Russian travellers, Sven Hedin for example, he never changed his clothes for Chinese ones on his wanderings; in general he kept aloof, was severe and resolute in the extreme in his relations with the natives, showing no indulgence to mandarins and lamas; and in camp he practised shooting, which served as an excellent precaution against any importuning. He was entirely uninterested in ethnography, a fact that for some reason greatly irritated certain geographers, and his great friend, the Orientalist Krivtsov, almost wept when reproaching him: 'If only you had brought back one wedding song, Konstantin Kirillovich, had described one local dress!' There was one professor at Kazan who attacked him especially; proceeding from some sort of humanitarian-liberal premises he convicted him of scientific aristocratism, of a haughty contempt for Man, of disregard for the reader's interests, of dangerous eccentricity – and of much more. And once at an international banquet in London (and this episode pleases me most of all), Sven Hedin, sitting next to my father, asked him how it had happened that, travelling with unprecedented freedom over the forbidden parts of Tibet, in the immediate vicinity of Lhasa, he had not gone to look at it, to which my father replied that he had not wanted to sacrifice even one hour's collecting for the sake of visiting 'one more filthy little town' – and I can see so clearly how his eyes must have narrowed as he spoke.

He was endowed with an even temper, self-control, strong will-power and a vivid sense of humour; but when he became angry his wrath was like a sudden stroke of frost (Grandmother said behind his back: 'All the clocks in the house stopped'), and I can well remember those sudden silences at table and the kind of absentminded look that immediately appeared on Mother's face (ill-wishers among our female kin maintained that she 'trembled before Kostya'), and how one of the governesses at the end of the table would hastily place her palm on a glass which was on the point of tinkling. The cause of his wrath could be a blunder by someone, a miscomputation by the steward (Father was well versed in the estate affairs), a flippant remark made about an intimate of his, trite political sentiments in the spirit of soapbox patriotism brought out by some ill-starred guest, or finally some misdemeanour or other of mine. He who in his time had slaughtered countless multitudes of birds, he who had once brought the newly wed botanist Berg the *complete* vegetable covering of a motley little mountain meadow in one piece, the size of a room in area (I imagined it rolled up in a case like a Persian carpet), which he had found somewhere at some fantastic height among bare cliffs and snow – he could not forgive me a Leshino sparrow wantonly shot down with a Montecristo rifle or the young pondside aspen I had slashed with a sword. He could not stand procrastination, hesitation, the blinking eyes of a lie, could not stand hypocrisy or syrupiness – and I am sure that had he caught me out in physical cowardice he would have laid a curse on me.

I have not said everything yet; I am coming up to what is perhaps most important. In and around my father, around this clear and direct strength, there was something difficult to convey in words, a haze, a mystery, an enigmatic reserve which made itself felt sometimes more, sometimes less. It was as if this genuine, very genuine man possessed an aura of something still unknown but which was perhaps the most genuine of all. It had no direct connection either with us, or with my mother, or with the externals of life, or even with butterflies (the closest of all to him, I daresay); it was neither pensiveness nor melancholy – and I have no means of explaining the impression his face made on me when I looked through his study window from outside and saw how, having suddenly forgotten his work (I could feel inside me how he had forgotten it – as if something had fallen through or trailed off), his large wise head turned slightly away from the desk and resting on his fist, so that a wide crease was raised from his cheek to his temple, he sat for a minute without moving. It sometimes seems to me nowadays that – who knows – he might go off on his journeys not so much to seek something as to flee something, and that on returning, he would realize that it was still with him, inside him, unriddable, inexhaustible. I cannot track down a name for his secret, but I only know that that was the source of that special – neither glad nor morose, having indeed no connection with the outward appearance of human emotions – solitude to which neither my mother nor all the entomologists of the world had any admittance. And strange: perhaps the estate watchman, a crooked old man who had twice been singed by night lightning, the sole person among our rural retainers who had learned without my father's help (who had taught it to a whole regiment of Asian hunters) to catch and kill a butterfly without mangling it (which, of course, did not stop him advising me with a businesslike air not to be in a hurry to catch small butterflies, 'tiddlers' as he expressed it, in spring, but to wait till summer when they would have grown up), namely he, who frankly and with no fear or surprise considered that my father knew a thing or two that nobody else knew, was in his own way right.

However that may have been, I am convinced now that our life then really was imbued with a magic unknown in other families. From conversations with my father, from daydreams in his absence, from the neighbourhood of thousands of books full of drawings of animals, from the precious shimmer of the collections, from the maps, from all the heraldry of nature and the cabbalism of Latin names, life took on a kind of bewitching lightness that made me feel as if my own travels were about to begin. Thence, I borrow my wings today. Among the old, tranquil, velvet-framed family photographs in my father's study there hung a copy of the picture: Marco Polo leaving Venice. She was rosy, this Venice, and the water of her lagoon was azure, with swans twice the size of the boats, into one of which tiny violet men were descending by way of a plank, in order to board a ship which was waiting a little way off with sails furled – and I cannot tear myself away from this mysterious beauty, these ancient colours which swim before the eyes as if seeking new shapes, when I now imagine the outfitting of my father's caravan in Przhevalsk, where he used to go with post-horses from Tashkent, having dispatched in advance by slow convoy a store of supplies for three years. His Cossacks went round the neighbouring villages buying horses, mules and camels; they prepared the pack boxes and pouches (what was there not in these Sartish yagtans and leather bags tried by centuries, from cognac to pulverized peas, from ingots of silver to nails for horseshoes); and after a requiem on the shore of the lake by the burial rock of the explorer Przhevalski, crowned with a bronze eagle – around which the intrepid local pheasants were wont to roost – the caravan took the road.

After that I see the caravan, before it gets drawn into the mountains, winding among hills of a paradisean green shade, depending both on their grassy raiment and on the apple-bright epidotic rock, of which they are composed. The compact, sturdy Kalmuk ponies walk in single file forming echelons: the paired packloads of equal weight are seized twice with lariats so that nothing can shift and a Cossack leads every echelon by the bridle. In front of the caravan, a Berdan rifle over his shoulder and a butterfly net at the ready, wearing spectacles and a nankin blouse, Father rides on his white trotter accompanied by a native horseman. Closing the detachment comes the geodesist Kunitsyn (this is the way I see it), a majestic old man who has spent half a lifetime in imperturbable wanderings, with his instruments in cases – chronometers, surveying compasses, an artificial horizon – and when he stops to take a bearing or to note down azimuths in his journal, his horse is held by an assistant, a small anaemic German, Ivan Ivanovich Viskott, formerly chemist at Gatchina, whom my father had once taught to prepare bird skins and who took part from then on in all the expeditions, until he died of gangrene in the summer of 1903 in Dyn-Kou.

Farther I see the mountains: the Tyan-Shan range. In search of passes (marked on the map according to oral data but first explored by my father) the caravan ascended over steep slopes and narrow ledges, slipped down to the north, to the steppe teeming with saigas, ascended again to the south, here fording torrents, there trying to get across high water – and up, up, along almost impassable trails. How the sunlight played! The dryness of the air produced an amazing contrast between light and shadow: in the light there were such flashes, such a wealth of brilliance, that at times it became impossible to look at a rock, at a stream; and in the shadow a darkness which absorbed all detail, so that every colour lived a magically multiplied life and the coats of the horses changed as they entered the cool of the poplars.

The boom of water in the gorge was enough to stun a man; head and breast filled with an electric agitation; the water rushed with awesome force – as smooth, however, as molten lead – then suddenly swelled out monstrously as it reached the rapids, its varicoloured waves piling up and falling over the lustrous brows of the stones with a furious roar; and then, crashing from a height of twenty feet, out of a rainbow and into darkness, it ran farther, now changed: seething, smoke-blue and snowlike from the foam, it struck first one side and then the other of the conglomeratic canyon in such a way that it seemed the reverberating mountain fastness could never withstand it; on its banks, meanwhile, in blissful quiet, the irises were in bloom – and suddenly a herd of marals dashed out of a black firewood onto a dazzling Alpine meadow and halted, quivering. No, it was only the air quivering . . . they had already vanished.

I can conjure up with particular clarity – in this transparent and changeable setting – my father's principal and constant occupation, the occupation for whose only sake he undertook these tremendous journeys. I see him leaning down from the saddle amid a clatter of sliding stones to sweep in with a swing of his net on the end of its long handle (a twist of the wrist causing the end of the muslin bag, full of rustling and throbbing, to flip across the ring, thus preventing escape) some royal relative of our Apollos, which had been skimming with a ranging flight over the dangerous screes; and not only he but also the other riders (the Cossack corporal Semyon Zharkoy, for example, or the Buryat Buyantuyev, or else that representative of mine whom I sent in the wake of my father throughout my boyhood) work their way fearlessly up the rocks, in pursuit of the white, richly ocellated butterfly which they catch at last; and here it is in my father's fingers, dead, its hairy yellowish incurved body resembling a willow catkin, and the glazy underside of its crisp folded wings showing the blood-red maculation at their roots.

He avoided dawdling in Chinese roadhouses, especially overnight, because he disliked them for their 'bustle devoid of feeling' that consisted solely of shouting without the slightest hint of laughter; but strangely enough, in his memory later the smell of these inns, that special air belonging to any place where Chinese dwell – a rancid mixture of kitchen fumes, smoke from burned manure, opium and the stable – spoke more to him of his beloved hunting than the recollected fragrancy of mountain meadows.

Moving across the Tyan-Shan with the caravan I can now see evening approaching, drawing a shadow over the mountain slopes. Postponing until the morning a difficult crossing (a ramshackle bridge has been thrown across the turbulent river, consisting of stone slabs on top of brushwood, but the way up on the other side is steepish, and, moreover, as smooth as glass), the caravan settles down for the night. While the colours of sunset still linger in the aerial tiers of the sky, and supper is being prepared, the Cossacks, having first taken off the animals' sweatcloths and felt under-blankets, wash the wounds made by the packs. In the darkling air the clear ring of shoeing resounds above the ample noise of water. It has grown quite dark. Father has climbed a rock looking for a place to suit his calcium lamp for catching moths. Thence one can see in Chinese perspective (from above), in a deep gully, the redness, transparent in the darkness, of the campfire; through the edges of its breathing flame seem to float the broad-shouldered shadows of men, endlessly changing their outlines, and a red reflection trembles, without moving from the spot, on the seething water of the river. But above, all is quiet and dark, only rarely does a bell tinkle: the horses, who have already stood to receive their portion of dry fodder, are now roaming among the granite debris. Overhead, frighteningly and entrancingly close, the stars have come out, each conspicuous, each a live orbicle, clearly revealing its globular essence. Moths begin to come to the lure of the lamp: they describe crazy circles around it, hitting the reflector with a ping; they fall, they crawl over the spread sheet into the circle of light, grey, with eyes like burning coals, vibrating, flying up and falling again – and a large, brightly illuminated, unhurriedly skilful hand, with almond-shaped fingernails, rakes noctuid after noctuid into the killing jar.

Sometimes he was quite alone, without even this nearness of

men sleeping in camp tents, on felt mattresses, around the camel bedded down on the campfire ashes. Taking advantage of lengthy halts in places with abundant food for the caravan animals, Father would go away for several days on reconnaissance, and in doing so, carried away by some new pierid, more than once ignored the rule of mountain hunting: never to follow a path of no return. And now I continually ask myself what did he use to think about in the solitary night: I try fervently in the darkness to divine the current of his thoughts, and I have much less success with this than with my mental visits to places which I have never seen. What did he think about? About a recent catch? About my mother, about us? About the innate strangeness of human life, a sense of which he mysteriously transmitted to me? Or perhaps I am wrong in retrospectively forcing upon him the secret which he carries now, when newly gloomy and preoccupied, concealing the pain of an unknown wound, concealing death as something shameful, he appears in my dreams, but which then he did not have – but simply was happy in that incompletely named world in which at every step he named the nameless.

After spending the whole summer in the mountains (not one summer but several, in different years, which are superimposed one on another in translucent layers) our caravan moved east through a gulch ino a stony desert. We saw gradually disappear both the bed of the stream as it split and fanned out, and those plants that to the last remain faithful to travellers: stunted ammodendrons, lasiagrostis, and ephedras. Having loaded the camels with water we plunged into spectral wilds where here and there big pebbles covered completely the yielding, reddish-brown clay of the desert, in places mottled with crusts of dirty snow and outcrops of salt, which we took in the distance for the walls of the town we sought. The way was dangerous as a result of the terrible storms, during which at midday everything was blanketed in a salty brown fog; the wind roared, granules of gravel lashed one's face, the camels lay down and our tarpaulin tent was torn to shreds. Because of these storms the surface of the land has changed unbelievably, presenting the fantastic outlines of castles, colonnades and staircases; or else the hurricane would scour out a hollow – as if here in this desert the elemental forces that had fashioned the world were still furiously in action. But there were also days of a wonderful lull, when horned larks (Father aptly called them 'gigglers') poured forth their mimetic trills and flocks of ordinary sparrows accompanied our emaciated animals. On occasion we would pass the day in isolated settlements consisting of two or three homesteads and a ruined temple. At other times we would be attacked by Tanguts in sheepskin coats and red-and-blue woollen boots: a brief colourful episode on the way. And then there were the mirages – the mirages where nature, that exquisite cheat, achieved absolute miracles: visions of water were so clear that they reflected the *real* rocks nearby!

Farther came the quiet sands of the Gobi, dune after dune went by like waves revealing short ochre horizons, and all that was audible in the velvet air was the laboured, quickened breathing of the camels and the scrape of their broad feet. The caravan went onward, now ascending to the crest of a dune now plunging downwards, and by the evening its shadow had attained gigantic proportions. The five-carat diamond of Venus disappeared in the west together with the glow of the sunset, which distorted everything in its blanched, orange and violet light. And Father loved to recall how once at such a sunset, in 1893, in the dead heart of the Gobi desert he had met with – taking them at first for phantoms projected by the prismatic rays – two cyclists in Chinese sandals and round felt hats, who turned out to be the Americans Sachtleben and Allen, riding all across Asia to Peking for fun.

Spring awaited us in the mountains of Nan-Shan. Everything foretold it: the babbling of the water in the brooks, the distant thunder of the rivers, the whistle of the creepers which lived in holes on the slippery wet hillsides, the delightful singing of the local larks, and 'a mass of noises whose origins are hard to explain' (a phrase from the notes of a friend of my father's, Grigoriy Efimovich Grum-Grzhimaylo, which is fixed in my mind forever and full of the amazing music of truth because written not by an ignorant poet but by a naturalist of genius). On the southern slopes we had already met our first interesting butterfly – Potanin's subspecies of Butler's pierid – and in the valley to which we descended by way of a torrent bed we found real summer. All the slopes were studded with anemones and primulae. Przhevalski's gazelle and Strauch's pheasant tempted the hunters. And what sunrises there were! Only in China is the early mist so enchanting, causing everything to vibrate, the fantastic outlines of hovels, the dawning crags. As into an abyss, the river runs into the murk of the prematutinal twilight that still hangs in the gorges, while higher up, along flowing waters, all glimmers and scintillates, and quite a company of blue magpies has already awakened in the willows by the mill.

Escorted by fifteen Chinese foot soldiers armed with halberds and carrying enormous, absurdly bright banners, we crossed passes through the ridge a number of times. In spite of it being the middle of summer, night frosts were so bad there that in the morning the flowers were filmed with rime and had become so brittle that they snapped underfoot with a surprising, gentle tinkle; but two hours later, just as soon as the sun began to be warm, the wonderful Alpine flora again resplended, again scented the air with resin and honey. Clinging to steep banks we made our way under the hot blue sky; grasshoppers shot from under our feet, the dogs ran with their tongues hanging out, seeking refuge from the heat in the short shadows thrown by the horses. The water in the wells smelled of gunpowder. The trees seemed to be a botanist's delirium: a white rowan with alabaster berries or a birch with red bark!

Placing one foot on a fragment of rock and leaning slightly on the handle of his net, my father looks down from a high spur, from the glacier boulders of Tanegma, at the lake Kuka-Nor – a huge spread of dark blue water. There down below on the golden steppes a herd of kiangs rushes past, and the shadow of an eagle flicks across the cliffs; overhead there is perfect peace, silence, transparency . . . and again I ask myself what Father is thinking about when he is not busy collecting and stands there like that, quite still . . . appearing as it were on the crest of my recollection, torturing me, enrapturing me – to the point of pain, to an insanity of tenderness, envy and love, tormenting my soul with his inscrutable solitariness.

There were the times when going up the Yellow River and its tributaries, on some splendid September morning, in the lily thickets and hollows on the banks, he and I would take Elwes' Swallowtail – a black wonder with tails in the shape of hooves. On inclement evenings, before sleeping, he would read Horace, Montaigne, and Pushkin – the three books he had brought with him. One winter when crossing the ice of a river I noticed in the distance a line of dark objects strung across it, the large horns of twenty wild yaks which had been caught in crossing by the suddenly forming ice; through its thick crystal the immobilization of their bodies in a swimming attitude was clearly visible; the beautiful heads lifted above the ice would have seemed alive if the birds had not already pecked out their eyes; and for some reason I recalled the tyrant Shiusin, who used to cut open pregnant women out of curiosity and who, one cold morning, seeing some porters fording a stream, ordered their legs to be amputated at the shin in order to inspect the condition of the marrow in their bones.

In Chang during a fire (some wood prepared for the construction of a Catholic mission was burning) I saw an elderly Chinese at a safe distance from the fire throwing water assiduously, determinedly and without tiring over the *reflection* of the flames on the walls of his dwelling; convinced of the impossibility of proving to him that his house was not burning we abandoned him to his fruitless occupation.

Frequently we had to push our way through, ignoring Chinese intimidation and interdictions: good marksmanship is the best passport. In Tatsien-Lu shaven-headed lamas roamed about the crooked, narrow street spreading the rumour that I was catching children in order to brew their eyes into a potion for the belly of my Kodak. There on the slopes of a snowy range, which were drowned in the rich, rosy foam of great rhododendrons (we used their branches at night for our campfires), I looked in May for the slate-grey, orange-spotted larvae of the Imperatorial Apollo and for its chrysalis, fastened by means of a silk thread to the underside of a stone. That same day, I remember, we glimpsed a white Tibetan bear and discovered a new snake: it fed on mice, and the mouse I extracted from its stomach also turned out to be an undescribed species. From the rhododendrons and from the pines draped in lacy lichen came a heady smell of resin. In my vicinity some witch doctors with the wary and crafty look of competitors were collecting for their mercenary needs Chinese rhubarb, whose root bears an extraordinary resemblance to a caterpillar, right down to its prolegs and spiracles – while I, in the meantime, found under a stone the caterpillar of an unknown moth, which represented not in a general way but with absolute concreteness a copy of that root, so that it was not quite clear which was impersonating which – or why.

Everyone tells lies in Tibet: it was devilishly hard to obtain the exact names of places or directions for the right roads; involuntarily I too deceived them: since they were unable to distinguish a light-haired European from a white-haired one they took me, a young chap with hair bleached in the sun, for an ancient old man. Everywhere on the masses of granite one could read the 'mystic formula,' a shamanic jumble of words which certain poetic travellers 'translate' prettily as: oh, jewel in the lotus, oh! Some kind of officials were sent out to me from

Lhasa who conjured me not to do something and threatened to do something to me – I paid little attention to them; however, I remember one idiot, particlarly tiresome, in yellow silk under a red umbrella; he was sitting astride a mule whose natural dolefulness was doubled by the presence under its eyes of thick icicles formed from frozen tears.

From a great height I saw a dark marshy depression all trembling from the play of innumerable springs, which recalled the night sky with stars scattered over it – and that is what it was called: the Starry Steppe. The passes ascended beyond the clouds, marches were tough. We rubbed the pack animals' wounds with a mixture of iodoform and vaseline. On occasion, having camped in a completely deserted spot, I would suddenly see in the morning that around us during the night a wide circle of brigands' tents had grown up like black toadstools – which, however, very quickly disappeared.

Having explored the uplands of Tibet I headed for Lob-Nor in order to return from there to Russia. The Tarym, overcome by the desert, exhausted, forms with its last waters an extensive reedy swamp, the present-day Kara-Koshuk-Kul, Przhevalski's Lob-Nor – and Lob-Nor at the time of the Khans, whatever Ritthofen might say. It is fringed with salt marshes but the water is salt only at the edges – for those rushes would not grow around a salt lake. One spring I was five days going round it. There in twenty-foot-high reeds I had the luck to discover a remarkable semi-aquatic moth with a rudimentary system of veins. The bunchy salt marsh was strewn with the shells of molluscs. In the evenings the harmonious, melodic sounds of swan flights reverberated through the silence; the yellow of the rushes distinctly brought out the lustreless white of the birds. In 1862, sixty Russian Old-Believers with their wives and children lived for half a year in these parts, after which they went to Turfan, and where they went thence nobody knows.

Farther on comes the desert of Lob: a stony plain, tiers of clay precipices, glassy salt ponds; that pale fleck in the grey air is a lone individual of Roborovski's White, carried away by the wind. In this desert are preserved traces of an ancient road along which Marco Polo passed six centuries before I did: its markers are piles of stones. Just as I had heard in a Tibetan gorge the interesting drum-like roar which had frightened our first pilgrims, so in the desert during the sandstorms I also saw and heard the same as Marco Polo: 'the whisper of spirits calling you aside' and the queer flicker of the air, an endless progression of whirlwinds, caravans and armies of phantoms coming to meet you, thousands of spectral faces in their incorporeal way pressing upon you, through you, and suddenly dispersing. In the twenties of the fourteenth century when the great explorer was dying, his friends gathered by his bedside and implored him to reject what in his book had seemed incredible to them – to water down its miracles by means of judicious deletions; but he responded that he had not recounted even a half of what he had in fact seen.

All this lingered bewitchingly, full of colour and air, with lively movement in the foreground and a convincing backdrop; then, like smoke from a breeze, it shifted and dispersed – and Fyodor saw again the dead and impossible tulips of his wallpaper, the crumbling mound of cigarette butts in the ashtray, and the lamp's reflection in the black windowpane. He threw open the window. The written-up sheets of paper on his desk started; one folded over, another glided onto the floor. The room immediately turned damp and cold. Down below, an automobile went slowly along the dark empty street – and, strangely enough, this very slowness reminded Fyodor of a host of petty, unpleasant things -- the day just past, the missed lesson – and when he thought that next morning he would have to phone the deceived old man, his heart was oppressed by an abominable despondency. But once the window was closed again, already feeling the void between his bunched fingers, he turned to the patiently waiting lamp, to the scattered first drafts, to the still-warm pen which now quietly slipped back into his fingers (explaining the void and filling it) and returned at once to that world which was as natural to him as snow to the white hare or water to Ophelia.

He remembered with incredible vividness, as if he had preserved that sunny day in a velvet case, his father's last return, in July 1912. Elizaveta Pavlovna had already gone the six miles to the station to meet her husband: she always met him alone and it always happened that no one knew with any clearness which side they would return on, to the right or left of the house, since there were two roads, one longer and smoother – along the highway and through the village; the other shorter and bumpier – through Peshchanka. Fyodor put on his riding breeches just in case and ordered his horse saddled, but nonetheless he could not make up his mind to ride out and meet his father because he was afraid of missing him. He tried vainly to come to terms with inflated, exaggerated time. A rare butterfly taken a day or two before among the blueberries of a peat bog had not yet dried on the spreading board: he kept touching its abdomen with the end of a pin – alas it was still soft, and this meant it was impossible to take off the paper strips completely covering the wings which he was so keen to show his father in all their beauty. He loafed about the manor, feeling the weight and pain of his agitation, and envying the way the others got through these big, empty minutes. From the river came the desperately ecstatic shrieks of the village boys bathing, and this hubbub, playing constantly in the depths of the summer day, sounded like distant ovations. Tanya was swinging enthusiastically and powerfully on the swing in the garden, standing on the seat; the violet shadow of the foliage swept over her flying white skirt in variegations that made one blink, and her blouse now lagged behind, now clung to her back, designating the hollow between the drawn-back shoulders; beneath her, one fox terrier was barking at her, another was chasing a wagtail; the ropes creaked joyfully and it seemed that Tanya was soaring up like that in order to see over the trees into the road. Our French governess, under her moiré parasol, with rare politeness was sharing her misgivings ('the train was two hours late or else would not come at all') with Mr Browning, whom she hated, while the latter stood slapping his gaiters with a riding stick – he was no polyglot. Yvonna Ivanovna kept visiting first one and then the other veranda with that discontented expression on her small face with which she greeted all joyful events. Around the outbuildings there was especial animation: servants pumped water, hacked firewood, and the gardener came bringing two oblong, red-stained baskets of strawberries. Zhaksybay, an elderly Kirghiz, thickset, fat-faced, with intricate wrinkles around his eyes, who had saved Konstantin Kirillovich's life in '92 (he had shot a she-bear that was mauling him) and who now lived in peace, nursing his hernia, in their Leshino house, had put on his blue *beshmet* with halfmoon pockets, polished boots, red skullcap with spangles and silk, tasselled sash, and settled down on a bench near the kitchen porch, where by now he had been sitting for quite a time sunning himself, a silver watch chain gleaming on his chest, in quiet and festive expectation.

Suddenly, running heavily up the curved path which led down to the river, there appeared out of deep shadow, with a wild glint in his eyes and with a mouth that was already shaped for a shout though still silent, the old, grey, side-whiskered footman Kazimir: he was running with the news that beyond the nearest bend, the sound of hooves had been heard on the bridge (a swift wooden drumming which was immediately cut off) – a guarantee that the victoria was about to come bowling next minute along the dirt road parallel to the park. Fyodor rushed in that direction – between the tree trunks, over the moss and bilberries – and there beyond the marginal path one could see, as they skimmed above the level of the young firs, the driver's head and indigo sleeves sweeping by with the impetuosity of a vision. He dashed back – and the abandoned swing was still quivering in the garden, while by the porch stood the empty victoria with its crumpled travelling rug; his mother was walking up the steps, trailing behind her a smoke-coloured scarf – and Tanya was hanging on the neck of her father, who had taken a watch from his pocket with his free hand and was looking at it, for he always liked to know how fast he had got home from the station.

The following year, busy with scientific work, he did not go anywhere, but by the spring of 1914 he had already begun to prepare for a new expedition to Tibet together with the ornithologist Petrov and the English botanist Ross. War with Germany suddenly cancelled all this.

He looked upon the war as a tiresome obstacle which became more and more tiresome as time went on. His kinsfolk were for some reason certain that Konstantin Kirillovich would volunteer and set off right away at the head of a detachment: they considered him an eccentric, but a manly eccentric. Actually, Konstantin Kirillovich, who was now over fifty but had retained untapped reserves of health, agility, freshness and strength – and perhaps was even more ready than before to overcome mountains, Tanguts, bad weather and a thousand other dangers undreamt of by stay-at-homes – now not only stayed at home but tried not to notice the war, and if he ever spoke about it, he did so only with angry contempt. 'My father,' wrote Fyodor, recalling that time, 'not only taught me a great deal but also trained my very thoughts, as a voice or hand is trained, according to the rules of his school. Thus I was rather indifferent to the cruelty of war; I even conceded that one could take a certain delight in the accuracy of a shot, in the danger of a reconnaissance or in the delicacy of a manoeuvre; but these little pleasures (which are better represented moreover in other special branches of sport, such as: tiger hunting, noughts and crosses, professional boxing) in no way compensated for that touch of dismal idiocy which is inherent in any war.'

However, in spite of 'Kostya's unpatriotic position' as Aunt Ksenia expressed it (solidly and skilfully using 'high connections' to hide her officer-husband away in the shadows of the rear) the house was penetrated by the cares of war. Elizaveta Pavlovna was drawn into Red Cross work, which had people comment that her energy 'was making up for her husband's idleness', he being 'more concerned with Asian bugs than with the glory of Russian arms' as was actually pointed out, by the way, in one jaunty newspaper. Phonograph records revolved with the words of the love song 'The Sea Gull' reclad in khaki (. . . here a young ensign with an infantry section . . .); coy nurses appeared in the house with little curls peeping out from under their regulation head-dress and a deft way of tapping cigarettes on their cigarette cases before lighting up; the doorkeeper's son ran away to the front and Konstantin Kirillovich was asked to assist his return; Tanya began visiting her mother's military hospital to give Russian grammar lessons to a placid, bearded Oriental whose leg was being cut off ever higher in an attempt to overtake the gangrene; Yvonna Ivanovna knit woollen wrist-warmers; on holidays the variety artist Feona entertained the soldiers with vaudeville songs; the hospital staff staged *Vova Makes the Best of It,* a play on draft dodgers; and the newspapers printed versicles dedicated to the war:

> Today thou art Fate's scourge o'er our dear land,
> But with bright joy the Russian's gaze will shine
> When he sees Time dispassionately brand
> The German Attila with Shame's own sign!

In the spring of 1915, instead of getting ready to move from St Petersburg to Leshino, which always seemed as natural and unshakable as the succession of months in the calendar, we went for the summer to our Crimean estate – on the coast between Yalta and Alupka. On the sloping lawns of the heavenly-green garden, his face distorted with anguish, his hands trembling with happiness, Fyodor boxed southern butterflies; but the genuine Crimean rarities were to be found not here among the myrtles, wax shrubs, and magnolias but much higher, in the mountains, among the rocks of Ai-Petri and on the grassy plateau of the Yayla; more than once that summer his father accompanied him up a trail through the pinewoods in order to show him, with a smile of condescension for this European trifle, the Satyrid recently described by Kuznetsov, which was flitting from stone to stone in the very place where some vulgar daredevil had carved his name in the sheer rock. These walks were Konstantin Kirillovich's only distraction. It was not that he was gloomy or irritable (these limited epithets did not tally with his spiritual style) but that, putting it simply, he was fretting – and Elizaveta Pavlovna and the children were perfectly aware of what it was he wanted. Suddenly in August he went away for a short time; where he went no one except those closest to him knew; he covered up his journey so thoroughly as to excite the envy of any travelling terrorist; it was funny and frighening to imagine how Russian public opinion would have wrung its little hands had it learned that at the height of the war Godunov-Cherdyntsev had travelled to Geneva to meet a fat, bald, extraordinarily jovial German professor (a third conspirator was also present, an old Englishman wearing thin-rimmed spectacles and a roomy grey suit), that they had come together there in a small room in a modest hotel for a scientific consultation, and that having discussed what was necessary (the subject was a work of many volumes, stubbornly continuing publication in Stuttgart with longstanding co-operation of foreign specialists on separate groups of butterflies) they peaceably parted – each in his own direction. But this trip did not cheer him up; on the contrary, the constant dream weighing on him even increased its secret pressure. In the autumn they returned to St Petersburg; he worked strenuously on the fifth volume of *Butterflies and Moths of the Russian Empire*, went out rarely and – fuming more at his opponent's blunders than at his own – played chess with the recently widowed botanist Berg. He would look through the daily papers with an ironical smile; he would take Tanya on his knees, then lapse into pensiveness, and his hand on Tanya's round shoulder would grow pensive too. Once in November he was given a telegram at table; he unsealed it, read it to himself, read it again to judge by the second movement of his eyes, laid it aside, took a sip of port wine from a ladle-shaped goblet of gold, and imperturbably continued his conversation with a poor relative of ours, a little old man with freckles all over his skull who came to dinner twice a month and invariably brought Tanya soft, sticky toffees – *tyanushki*. When the guests had departed he sank into an armchair, took off his glasses, passed his palm from top to bottom over his face and announced in an even voice that Uncle Oleg had been dangerously wounded in the stomach by a grenade fragment (while working at a first-aid post under fire) – and immediately there stood out in Fyodor's soul, tearing it with its sharp edges, one of those numberless deliberately grotesque dialogues that the brothers had still so recently indulged in at table:

UNCLE OLEG (*in a bantering tone*)

Well, tell me, Kostya, did you ever happen to see on the Wie reservation the little bird So-was?

FATHER (*curtly*)

I'm afraid I did not.

UNCLE OLEG (*warming up*)

And Kostya, did you never see Popovski's horse stung by Popov's fly?

FATHER (*even more curtly*)

Never.

UNCLE OLEG (*completely ecstatic*)

And have you never had occasion, for example, to observe the diagonal motion of entoptic swarms?

FATHER (*looking him straight in the eye*)

I have.

That same night he set out for Galicia to get him, brought him back extremely quickly and comfortably, obtained the best of the best doctors, Gershenzon, Yezhov, Miller-Melnitski, and himself attended two protracted operations. By Christmas his brother was well. And then something suddenly changed in Konstantin Kirillovich's mood: his eyes came to life and softened, one again heard that musical humming which he used to emit on the move when he was particularly pleased about something, he went off somewhere, certain boxes arrived and departed and in the house, around all this mysterious gaiety of the master's, one could sense a growing feeling of indefinite, expectant perplexity – and once when Fyodor happened to be passing through the gilt reception hall, bathed in spring sunshine, he suddenly noticed the brass handle of the white door leading into Father's study jiggle but not turn, as if someone was limply fingering it without opening the door; but then it quietly opened and Mother came out with a vague meek smile on her tear-stained face, making an odd gesture of helplessness as she went past Fyodor. He knocked on his father's door and entered the study. 'What do you want?' asked Konstantin Kirillovich without looking up or stopping writing. 'Take me with you,' said Fyodor.

The fact that at the most alarming time, when Russia's borders were crumbling and her inner flesh was being eaten away, Konstantin Kirillovich suddenly planned to abandon his family for two years for the sake of a scientific expedition into a remote country, struck most people as a wild caprice, a monstrous frivolity. There was even talk that the government 'would not permit purchase of provision', that 'the madman' would get neither travelling companions nor pack animals. But no farther away than in Turkestan the peculiar smell of the epoch was hardly perceptible; practically the only reminder of it was a reception organized by some district administrators to which the guests brought gifts to aid the war (a little later a rebellion broke out among the Kirghiz and the Cossacks in connection with the summons to do war work). Just before his departure in June 1916, Godunov-Cherdyntsev came from town to Leshino to bid his family farewell. Until the very last minute Fyodor dreamed that his father would take him with him – once he had said he would do so as soon as his son was fifteen – 'At any other time I would take you,' he said now, as if forgetting that for him time was always *another* one.

In itself this last farewell was in no way different from preceding ones. After the orderly succession of embraces worked out by family custom, both parents, donning identical amber goggles with suede blinkers, settled themselves in a red touring car; all around stood the servants; leaning on his stick, the old watchman remained at a distance by the lightning split poplar; the driver, a short, fat, round little man in velveteen livery and orange gaiters – with a carroty nape and a topaz on his pudgy hand – straining horribly, jerked, jerked again, started the engine (Mother and Father began to vibrate in their seats), got quickly behind the steering wheel, shifted a lever on it, pulled on his gauntlets, and turned his head. Konstantin Kirillovich gave him a pensive nod and the car moved off; the fox terrier choked with barking as it squirmed wildly in Tanya's arms, turning over onto its back and twisting its head over her shoulder; the red back of the car disappeared round the bend and then, from behind the fir trees, on top of a rising whine there sounded the sharp change of gears, followed by a comfortably receding murmur; all was still, but a few moments later, from the village beyond the river came again the triumphant roar of the engine, which gradually faded away forever. Yvonna Ivanovna, weeping profusely, went for some milk for the cat. Tanya, affecting to sing, returned to the cool, resonant, empty house. The shade of Zhaksybay, who had died the preceding autumn, slipped off the porch bench and went back to its quiet, handsome paradise, rich in roses and sheep.

Fyodor walked across the park, opened the tuneful wicket gate and cut across the road where the thick tyres had just imprinted their tracks. A familiar black-and-white beauty rose smoothly off the ground and described a wide circle, also taking part in the seeing-off. He turned into the trees and came by way of a shady path, where golden flies hung aquiver in transversal sunbeams, to his favourite clearing, boggy, blooming, moistly glistening in the hot sun. The divine meaning of this wood meadow was expressed in its butterflies. Everyone might have found something here. The holidaymaker might have rested on a stump. The artist might have screwed up his eyes. But its truth would have been probed somewhat deeper by knowledge-amplified love: by its 'wide-open orbs' – to paraphrase Pushkin.

Freshly emerged and because of their fresh, almost orange coloration, merry-looking Selene Fritillaries floated with a kind of enchanting demureness on outstretched wings, flashing ever so rarely, like the fins of a goldfish. An already rather bedraggled but still powerful Swallowtail, minus one spur and flapping its panoply, descended on a camomile, took off as if backing from it, and the flower it left straightened up and started to sway. A few Black-veined Whites flew about lazily; one or two were spattered with bloodlike pupal discharge (spots of which on the white walls of cities predicted to our ancestors the fall of Troy, plagues, earthquakes). The first chocolate *Aphantopus* Ringlets were already fluttering, with a bouncy, unsteady motion over the grass, and pale micros rose from it, immediately falling again. A blue-and-red Burnet moth with blue antennae, resembling a beetle in fancy dress, was settled on a scabiosa in company with a midge. Hastily abandoning the meadow to alight on an alder leaf, a female cabbage butterfly by means of an odd upturn of her abdomen and the flat spread of her wings (somewhat reminiscent of flattened-back ears), informed her badly rubbed pursuer that she was already impregnated. Two violet-tinged Coppers (*their* females were not yet out) tangled in lightning-swift flight in mid-air, zoomed, spinning one around the other, scrapping furiously, ascending ever higher and higher – and suddenly shot apart, returning to the flowers. An Amandus Blue in passing annoyed a bee. A dusky Freya Fritillary flicked by among the Selenas. A small humming-bird moth with a bumblebee's body and glasslike wings, beating invisibly, tried from the air a flower with its long proboscis, darted to another and then to a third. All this fascinating life, by whose present blend one could infallibly tell both the age of the summer (with an accuracy almost to within one day), the geographical location of the area, and the vegetal composition of the clearing – all this that was living, genuine and eternally dear to him, Fyodor perceived in a flash, with one penetrating and experienced glance. Suddenly he placed a fist against the trunk of a birch tree and leaning on it, burst into tears.

Although his father had no liking for folklore, he used to cite one remarkable Kirghiz fairy tale. The only son of a great khan, having lost his way during a hunt (thus begin the best fairy tales and thus end the best lives), caught sight among the trees of something sparkling. Coming closer he saw it was a girl gathering brushwood, in a dress made of fish-scales; however, he could not decide what precisely was sparkling so much, the girl's face or her clothing. Going with her to her old mother, the young prince offered to give her as bride-money a nugget of gold the size of a horse's head. 'No,' said the girl, 'but here, take this tiny bag – it's little bigger than a thimble as you can see – go and fill it.' The prince, laughing ('Not even one,' he said, 'will go in'), threw in a coin, threw in another, a third, and then all that he had with him. Extremely puzzled, he went off to consult his father.

All his treasures gathering,
public funds and everything,
in the bag the good khan threw;
shook, and listened, shook anew;
threw in twice as much again:
just a dingle in the drain!

They summoned the old woman. 'That,' she said, 'is a human eye – it wants to encompass everything in the world'; then she took a pinch of earth and filled up the bag immediately.

The last reliable evidence concerning my father (not counting his own letters) I found in some notes by the French missionary (and learned botanist) Barraud, who in the summer of 1917 chanced to meet him in the mountains of Tibet, near the village of Chetu. 'I was amazed to see,' writes Barraud (*Exploration catholique* for 1923), 'a saddled white horse grazing in a mountain meadow. Presently a man in European dress appeared, descending from the rocks; he greeted me in French and turned out to be the famous Russian traveller Godunov. I had not seen a European for over eight years. We passed several delightful minutes on the sward in the shade of a rock, discussing a fine nomenclatorial point in connection with the scientific name of a tiny, light blue iris which grew in the vicinity, and then, exchanging an amicable farewell, we parted, he to his companions calling him from a ravine and I to Father Martin, dying in a remote hostelry.'

Beyond this there is a fog. Judging by my father's last letter, brief as usual but unusually alarmed, which was delivered to us by a miracle at the beginning of 1918, he was preparing soon after he met Barraud to make the return journey. Having heard of the revolution he asked us in it to move to Finland, where our aunt had a country house, and he wrote that according to his calculations he would be home 'with the maximum haste' by the summer. We waited two summers for him, until the winter of 1919. We lived some of the time in Finland and some in St Petersburg. Our house had long since been plundered but Father's museum, the heart of the house, as if retaining the invulnerability inherent in sacred objects, survived whole (later coming under the jurisdiction of the Academy of Sciences), and this joy completely compensated for the demise of chairs and tables familiar since childhood. We lived in St Petersburg in two rooms in Grandmother's flat. For some reason or other she was twice taken off for questioning. She caught cold and died. A few days after that, on one of those terrible winter evenings, hungry and hopeless, which played such an ominously close part in the civil disorder, an unknown youth visited me, in pincenez, unprepossessing and uncommunicative, and asked me to call immediately on his uncle, the geographer Berezovski. He did not know or did not want to say what for, but suddenly everything somehow crumbled inside me and I began to live mechanically. Nowadays, several years later, I sometimes meet this Misha in the Russian bookshop in Berlin where he works – and every time I see him, although we talk little, I feel a hot shiver run down the whole of my spinal column and my whole being relives our brief road together. My mother was not there when this Misha came (this name I shall also remember forever) but we met her on our way downstairs; not knowing my companion she anxiously asked where I was going. I replied I was going for some hair clippers of which we had happened to be speaking a few days beforehand. Later I often dreamed about them, those non-existent clippers, which took the most unexpected forms – mountains, landing stages, coffins, hand organs – but I always knew with a dreamer's instinct that it was clippers. 'Wait,' cried Mother, but we were already downstairs. We walked along the street quickly and silently, he slightly ahead of me. I looked at the masks of the houses, at the humps of the snowdrifts, and I tried to outwit fate by imagining to myself (and thus destroying its possibility in advance) the still uncomprehended, black, fresh grief which I would carry back home. We entered a room which I recall as being completely yellow, and there an old man with a pointed beard, wearing a field jacket and jackboots, informed me without preamble that according to still unverified information my father was no longer living. Mother was waiting for me below, on the street.

During the next six months (until Uncle Oleg almost forcibly took us abroad) we tried to find out how, and where, he had perished – and indeed whether he had perished at all. Apart from the fact that it happened in Siberia (Siberia is a big place!) on the return journey from Central Asia, we found out nothing at all. Can it be that they hid from us the place and circumstances of his mysterious death and have continued to hide them to this day? (His biography in the Soviet Encyclopaedia ends simply with the words: *He died in 1919.*) Or did the contradictoriness of the vague evidence truly rule out any explicitness in their answers? Once in Berlin we learned one or two supplementary things from various sources and from various people, but these supplements turned out to be nothing but new layers of uncertainty rather than glimpses through it. Two shaky versions, both more or less of a deductive nature (and telling us nothing, moreover, about the most important point: how exactly did he die – if he died), were entangled in one another and mutually contradictory. According to one of them, news of his death was brought to Semipalatinsk by a Kirghiz; according to the other, it was brought by a Cossack to Ak-Bulat. What was my father's route? Was he going from Semirechie to Omsk (by way of the feather-grass steppe, with the guide on a piebald pony) or from the Pamirs to Orenburg through the Turgay region (by way of the sandy steppe, with the guide on a camel, he himself on a horse, birchbark-stirrupped, from well to well, avoiding villages and railway lines)? How did he pass through the storm of the peasant war, how did he steer clear of the Reds? I cannot make anything out. And then, what kind of *shapka-nevidimka,* 'invisible-making cap', could have fitted him, who would have worn even that at a rakish angle? Did he hide in fishermen's huts (as Krüger supposes) at the post 'Aralskoye more' among the stolid Urals Old-Believers? And if he died, how did he die? 'What is your profession?' Pugachyov asked the astronomer Lowitz. 'Counting the stars.' Whereupon they hanged him so he could be nearer the stars. Oh, how did he die? From illness? From exposure? From thirst? By the hand of man? And if – by somebody's hand, can that hand be still living, taking bread, raising a glass, chasing flies, stirring, pointing, beckoning, lying motionless, shaking other hands? Did he return their fire for a long time? Did he save a last bullet for himself? Was he taken alive? Did they bring him to the parlour car at the railway headquarters of some punitive detachment (I can see its hideous locomotive stoked with dried fish), having suspected him of being a White spy (and not without reason: he knew well the White general, Lavr Kornilov, with whom once in his youth he had travelled over the Steppe of Despair and whom in later years he had seen in China)? Did they shoot him in the ladies' room of some godforsaken station (broken looking glass, tattered plush), or did they lead him out into some kitchen garden one dark night and wait for the moon to peep out? How did he wait with them in the dark? With a smile of disdain? And if a whitish moth had hovered among the shadowy burdocks he would, even at that moment, I *know,* have followed it with that same glance of encouragement with which, on occasion, after evening tea, smoking his pipe in our Leshino garden, he used to greet the pink hawks sampling our lilacs.

But sometimes I get the impression that all this is a rubbishy rumour, a tired legend, that it has been created out of those same suspicious granules of approximate knowledge that I use myself when my dreams muddle through regions known to me only by hearsay or out of books, so that the first knowledgeable person who has really seen at the time the places referred to will refuse to recognize them, will make fun of the exoticism of my thoughts, the hills of my sorrow, the precipices of my imagination, and will find in my conjectures just as many topographical errors as he will anachronisms. So much the better. Once the rumour of my father's death is a fiction, must it not then be conceded that his very journey out of Asia is merely attached in the shape of a tail to this fiction (like that kite which in Pushkin's story young Grinyov fashioned out of a map), and that perhaps, if my father even did set out on this return journey (and was not dashed to pieces in an abyss, not held in captivity by Buddhist monks) he chose a completely different road? I have even had occasion to hear surmises (sounding like belated advice) that he could well have proceeded west to Ladakh in order to go south into India, or why could he not have pushed on to China and from there, on any ship to any port in the world?

'Whether it was this way or that, Mother, all material connected with his life is now collected at my place. Out of swarms of drafts, long manuscript extracts from books, indecipherable jottings on miscellaneous sheets of paper, pencilled remarks straggling over the margins of other writings of mine; out of half-crossed-out sentences, unfinished words, and improvidently abbreviated already forgotten names, hiding from full view among my papers; out of the fragile staticism of irredeemable information, already destroyed in places by a too swift movement of thought, which in turn dissolved into nothingness; out of all this I must now make a lucid, orderly book. At times I feel that somewhere it has already been written by me, that it is here, hiding in this inky jungle, that I have only to free it part by part from the darkness and the parts will fall together of themselves. . . . But what is the use of that to me when this labour of liberation now seems to me so difficult and complicated and when I am so much afraid I might dirty it with a flashy phrase, or wear it out in the course of transfer onto paper, that I already doubt whether the book will be written at all. You yourself wrote to me of the demands which in such a task should be presupposed. But now I am of the opinion that I would fulfil them badly. Do not scold me for weakness and cowardice. Sometime I shall read you at random disjointed and inchoate extracts from what I have written: how little it resembles my statuesque dream! All these months while I was making my research, taking notes, recollecting and thinking, I was blissfully happy: I was certain that something unprecedentedly beautiful was being created, that my notes were merely small props for the work, trail-marks, pegs, and that the most important thing was developing and being created of itself, but now I see, like waking up on the floor, that besides these pitiful notes there is nothing. What shall I do? You know, when I read his or Grum's books and I hear their entrancing rhythm, when I study the position of the words that can neither be replaced nor rearranged, it seems to me a sacrilege to take all this and dilute it with myself. If you like I'll admit it: I myself am a mere seeker of verbal adventures, and forgive me if I refuse to hunt down my fancies on my father's own collecting ground. I have realized, you see, the impossibility of having the imagery of his travels germinate without contaminating them with a kind of secondary poetization, which keeps departing farther and farther from that real poetry with which the live experience of these receptive, knowledgeable and chaste naturalists endowed their research.'

'Of course I understand and sympathize,' answered his mother. 'It is a pity you cannot manage it, but of course you must not force yourself. On the other hand I am convinced that you are exaggerating a little. I am convinced that, if you thought less about style, about difficulties, about the poetaster's cliché that "with a kiss starts the death of romance", etc., you would produce something very good, very true and very interesting. Only if you imagine him reading your book and you feel it grates upon him, and makes you ashamed, then, of course, give it up, give it up. But I know this cannot be, I know he would tell you: well done. Even more: I am convinced that some day you shall yet write this book.'

The external stimulus to the cancel of his work was provided for Fyodor by his removal to another lodging. To his landlady's credit it must be said that she had put up with him for a very long time, for two years. But when she was offered the chance of obtaining an ideal roomer in April – an elderly spinster rising at seven thirty, working in an office till six, dining at her sister's and retiring at ten – Frau Stoboy requested Fyodor to find himself another roof within the month. He continually postponed his inquiries, not only out of laziness and an optimistic tendency to endow a stretch of granted time with the rounded shape of eternity, but also because he found it unbearably nasty to invade alien worlds for the purpose of discovering a place for himself. Mme Chernyshevski, however, promised him her assistance. March was drawing to an end when, one evening, she said to him:

'I think I have something for you. You once saw here Tamara Grigorievna, the Armenian lady. She has had a room in the flat of a Russian family but now wants to turn it over to somebody.'

'Which means it's a bad room if she wants to get rid of it,' remarked Fyodor carelessly.

'No, it's simply that she's going back to her husband. However, if you don't like it in advance then I won't do anything about it.'

'I didn't mean to offend you,' said Fyodor. 'I like the idea very much, really I do.'

'Naturally, there's no guarantee the room is not already disposed of, but still I would advise you to give her a ring.'

'Oh, of course,' said Fyodor.

'Since I know you,' continued Mme Chernyshevski, already leafing through a black notebook, 'and since I know you'll never ring yourself . . .'

'I'll do it first thing tomorrow,' said Fyodor.

'. . . since you will never do it – Uhland forty-eight thirty-one – I'll do it myself. I'll get her right now and you can ask her everything.'

'Stop, wait a minute,' said Fyodor anxiously. 'I have no idea what I have to ask.'

'Don't worry, she'll tell you herself.' And Mme Chernyshevski, rapidly repeating the number under her breath, stretched her hand toward the little table with the telephone.

As soon as she put the receiver to her ear her body assumed its usual telephone posture on the sofa; from a sitting attitude she slipped into a reclining one, adjusted her skirt without looking, and her blue eyes wandered here and there as she waited to be connected. 'It would be nice—' she began, but then the girl answered and Mme Chernyshevski said the number with a kind of abstract exhortation in her tone and a special rhythm in her pronunciation of the figures – as if 48 was the thesis and 31 the antithesis adding in the shape of a synthesis: *ja wohl.*

'It would be nice,' she re-addressed Fyodor, 'if she went there with you. I'm sure you've never in your life . . .' Suddenly, with a smile, dropping her eyes, moving a plump shoulder and slightly crossing her outstretched legs: 'Tamara Grigorievna?' she asked in a new voice, suave and inviting. She laughed softly as she listened, pinching a fold in her skirt. 'Yes, it's me, you're right. I thought that as always you wouldn't recognize me. All right – let's say often.' Settling her tone even more comfortably: 'Well, what's new?' She listened to what was new, blinking; as if in parenthesis she pushed a box of fruit-paste bonbons in Fyodor's direction; then the toes of her small feet in their shabby velvet slippers began to rub gently against one another; they stopped. 'Yes, so I've heard, but I thought he had a permanent practice.' She continued to listen. One could make out in the silence the infinitely small drumming of the voice from another world. 'Well, that's ridiculous,' said Alexandra Yakovlevna, 'oh, that's ridiculous.' . . . 'So that's how things are with you,' she drawled after a moment, and then, to a quick question which sounded to Fyodor like a microscopic bark, she replied with a sigh: 'Yes, more or less, nothing new. Alexander Yakovlevich is well, keeps himself busy, he's at a concert now, and I have nothing to report, nothing special. Right now I have here . . . Well, of course, it amuses him, but you can't imagine how I sometimes dream of going away somewhere with him, even if only for a month. What's that? Oh, anywhere. Generally speaking, things get a little depressing at times, but otherwise there's nothing new.' She slowly inspected her palm and remained like that with her hand before her. 'Tamara Grigorievna, I have Godunov-Cherdyntsev here. By the way, he's looking for a room. Do those people of yours. . . . Oh, that's wonderful. Wait a minute, I'm passing him the receiver.'

'How do you do?' said Fyodor, bowing to the telephone. 'I've been told by Alexandra Yakovlevna—'

Loudly, so that it even tickled his middle ear, an extraordinarily nimble and distinct voice took over the conversation. 'The room's not yet rented,' began the almost unknown Tamara Grigorievna, 'and as it happens they would very much like to have a Russian boarder. I'll tell you right away who they are. The name is Shchyogolev, that tells you nothing, but in Russia he was public prosecutor, a very, very cultured and pleasant gentleman. . . . Then there is his wife, who is also extremely nice, and a daughter from the first marriage. Now listen: they live at 15 Agamemnonstrasse, a wonderful district, in a small flat but *hoch-modern*, central heating, bath – in short, everything you could wish for. The room you'll live in is delightful, but [with a retractive intonation] it looks out onto the yard, that of course is a small minus. I'll tell you how much I paid for it, I paid thirty-five marks a month. It is quiet and has a fine day bed. Well, there we are. What else can I tell you? I had my meals there and I must confess the food was excellent, excellent, but you must ask them the price yourself. I was on a diet. Here's what we'll do now. I have to be there in any case tomorrow morning, about half past eleven. I'm very punctual, so you come there too.'

'Wait a second,' said Fyodor (for whom to rise at ten was the equivalent of rising at five for anyone else). 'Wait a second. I'm afraid that tomorrow . . . Perhaps it might be better if I. . . .'

He wanted to say: 'give you a ring,' but Mme Chernyshevski, who was sitting nearby, made such eyes that with a gulp he instantly corrected himself: 'Yes, I think on the whole I can,' he said without animation, 'thank you, I'll come.'

'Well then [in a narrative tone], it's 15, Agamemnonstrasse, third floor, with an elevator. So that's what we'll do. Until tomorrow then, I shall be very glad to see you.'

'Good-bye,' said Fyodor Konstantinovich.

'Wait,' cried Alexandra Yakovlevna, 'please don't ring off.'

The next morning when he arrived at the stipulated address – in an irritable mood, with a woolly brain and with only half of him functioning (as if the other half of him had still not opened on account of the earliness of the hour) – it turned out that Tamara Grigorievna not only was not there but had rung to say she could not come. He was received by Shchyogolev himself (no one else was at home), who turned out to be a bulky, chubby man whose outline reminded one of a carp, about fifty years old, with one of those open Russian faces whose openness is almost indecent. It was a fairly full face of oval cut, with a tiny black tuft just under the lower lip. He had a remarkable hair style that was also somehow indecent: thin black hair evenly smoothed down and divided by a parting which was not quite in the middle of the head and yet not quite to one side either. Big ears, simple male eyes, a thick yellowish nose and a moist smile completed the general pleasant impression. 'Godunov-Cherdyntsev,' he repeated, 'of course, of course, an extremely well-known name. I once knew . . . let me see – isn't your father Oleg Kirillovich? Aha, uncle. Where's he living now? In Philadelphia? Hm, that's quite a way. Just look where we émigrés get to! Amazing. And are you in touch with him? I see, I see. Well, never put off to tomorrow what you have already done – ha-ha! come. I'll show you your quarters.'

To the right of the hallway there was a short passage immediately turning right again at a right-angle to become another embryo corridor that terminated in the half-open door of the kitchen. The left wall had two doors, the first of which, with an energetic intake of breath, Shchyogolev threw back. Turning its head, there froze before us a small oblong room with ochred walls, a table by the window, a couch along one wall and a wardrobe by the other. To Fyodor, it seemed repellent, hostile, completely 'unhandy' in regard to his life, as if positioned several fateful degrees out of true (with a dusty sunbeam representing the dotted line that marks the bias of a geometric figure when it is revolved) in relation to that imaginary rectangle within whose limits he might be able to sleep, read and think; but even if by a miracle he had been able to adjust his life to fit the angle of this deviant box, nevertheless its furniture, colour, view onto the asphalt yard – everything about it was unendurable, and he decided at once that he would not take it.

'Well, here it is,' said Shchyogolev jauntily, 'and here's the bathroom next door. It needs a little cleaning up in here. Now, if you don't mind . . .' He bumped violently into Fyodor in turning around in the narrow corridor and uttering an apologetic 'Och!' grasped him by the shoulder. They returned to the entrance hall. 'Here is my daughter's room, here is ours,' he said, pointing to two doors on the left and right. 'And here's the dining room,' and opening a door in the depths, he held it in that position for several seconds, as if taking a time exposure. Fyodor passed his eyes over the table, a bowl of nuts, a sideboard. . . . By the far window, near a small bamboo table, stood a high-backed armchair: across its arms there lay in airy repose a gauze dress, pale bluish and very short (as was worn then at dances), and on the little table gleamed a silvery flower and a pair of scissors.

'That's all,' said Shchyogolev, carefully closing the door, 'you see – cosy, homely; everything we have is small, but we do have everything. If you wish to have your grub with us you're very welcome, we'll talk to my missus about that; between you and me she's not a bad cook. Since you're Mrs Abramov's friend, we'll charge you the same as her, we won't ill-treat you, you'll live snug as a thug in the jug,' and Shchyogolev laughed fruitily.

'Yes, I think the room will suit me,' said Fyodor, trying not to look at him. 'In fact, I would like to move in on Wednesday.'

'Please yourself,' said Shchyogolev.

Have you ever happened, reader, to feel that subtle sorrow of parting with an unloved abode? The heart does not break, as it does in parting with dear objects. The humid gaze does not wander around holding back a tear, as if it wished to carry away in it a trembling reflection of the abandoned spot; but in the best corner of our hearts we feel pity for the things which we did not bring to life with our breath, which we hardly noticed and are now leaving forever. This already dead inventory will not be resurrected later in one's memory: the bed will not follow us, shouldering its own self; the reflection in the dresser will not rise from its coffin; only the view from the window will abide for a while, like the faded photograph, fitted into a cemetery cross, of a trim-haired, steady-eyed gentleman in a starched collar. I would like to wish you good-bye, but you would not even hear my greeting. Nevertheless, good-bye. I lived here exactly two years, thought here about many things, the shadows of my caravan passed over this wallpaper, lilies grew out of the cigarette ash on the carpet – but now the journey is over. The torrents of books have gone back to the ocean of the library. I do not know if I shall ever read the drafts and extracts rammed under the linen in my suitcase, but I do know that I will never look in here again.

Fyodor sat on his suitcase and locked it; went around the room gave a final check to the drawers, and found nothing: corpses do not steal. A fly climbed up the windowpane, impatiently slipped, half fell and half flew downwards, as if shaking something, and started to crawl again. The house opposite, which he had found in scaffolding the April before last, was evidently in need of repairs again now: prepared boards were stacked by the sidewalk. He carried his things out, went to say good-bye to the landlady, for the first and last time shaking her hand, which turned out to be dry, strong and cold, gave her back the keys and left. The distance from the old residence to the new was about the same as, somewhere in Russia, that from Pushkin Avenue to Gogol Street.

3

Every morning just after eight he was guided out of his slumber by the same sound behind the thin wall, two feet from his temple. It was the clean, round-bottomed ring of a tumbler being replaced on a glass shelf; after which the landlord's daughter cleared her throat. Then came the spasmodic *trk-trk* of a revolving cylinder, then the sound of flushed water, choking, groaning and abruptly ceasing, then the bizarre internal whine of a bath tap that finally turned into the rustle of a shower. A slip-bolt clacked and footsteps receded past his door. From an opposite direction came other footsteps, dark and heavy, with a slight shuffle: that was Marianna Nikolavna hurrying to the kitchen to get some coffee for her daughter. One could hear the gas at first refusing with noisy bursts to catch light; subdued, it flared and hissed steadily. The first footsteps returned, now heeled; in the kitchen a fast angrily agitated conversation started up. Just as some people speak with a southern or Moscow pronunciation so did mother and daughter invariably speak to one another in the accents of a quarrel. Their voices were similar, both swarthy and smooth, but one more coarse and somehow cramped, the other freer and purer. In the rumble of the mother's there was a pleading even a guilty pleading; in the daughter's increasingly short replies there rang hostility. To the accompaniment of this indistinct morning storm Fyodor Konstantinovich would again fall peacefully asleep.

Through his patchily thinning slumber he made out the sounds of cleaning; the wall would suddenly collapse on him: that meant a mop handle that had been insecurely leaning against his door. Once a week the janitor's wife, fat, heavily breathing, reeking of stale sweat, came with a vacuum cleaner, and then all hell broke loose, the world was shattered to bits, a hellish grinding pervaded one's very soul, destroying it, and drove Fyodor out of his bed, out of his room and out of the house. But usually, around ten o'clock, Marianna Nikolavna took her turn in the bathroom and after her came, hawking up phlegm as he went, Ivan Borisovich. He flushed the toilet as many as five times but did not use the bath, contenting himself with the murmur of the little washbasin. By half past ten everything in the house was quiet: Marianna Nikolavna had gone away to do her shopping, Shchyogolev on his shady affairs. Fyodor Konstantinovich descended into a blissful abyss where the warm remnants of his slumber mingled with a feeling of happiness, both from the previous day and still to come.

Quite often now he began the day with a poem. Lying supine with the first satisfying tasty, large and long-lasting cigarette between his parched lips, he again after a break of almost ten years was composing that particular kind of poem of which a gift is made in the evening so as to be reflected in the wave that has carried it out. He compared the structure of these verses with that of the others. The words of the others had been forgotten. Only here and there among the erased letters had rhymes been preserved, rich ones interspersed with poor ones: kiss-bliss, wind in – linden – leaves – grieves. During that sixteenth summer of his life he had first taken up the serious writing of poetry; before that, except for entomological doggerel, there had been nothing. But a certain atmosphere of composition had been long known and familiar to him: at home, everyone did some scribbling – Tanya wrote in a little album with a little key to it; Mother wrote touchingly unpretentionus prose-poems about the beauty of the native weald; Father and Uncle Oleg made up occasional verses – and these occasions were not infrequent; and

Aunt Ksenya – she wrote poems only in French, temperamental and 'musical' ones, with a complete disregard for the subtleties of syllabic verse; her outpourings were very popular in St Petersburg society, particularly the long poem 'La Femme et la Panthère,' and also a translation of Apukhtin's 'A Pair of Boys' – one stanza of which went:

> Le gros grec d'Odessa, le juif de Varsovie,
> Le jeune lieutenant, le général âgé,
> Tous ils cherchaient en elle un peu de folle vie,
> Et sur son sein rêvait leur amour passager.

Finally there had been one 'real' poet, Mother's cousin, Prince Volkhovskoy, who had published on velvety paper an exquisitely printed, thick, expensive volume of languorous poems *Auroras and Stars,* all in Italian viny vignettes, with a portrait photograph of the author in the front and a monstrous list of misprints at the back. The verses were broken up into departments: Nocturnes, Autumn Motifs, The Chords of Love. Most of them were emblazoned with a motto and under all there was the exact date and place: *Sorrento, Ai-Todor,* or *In the Train.* I do not remember anything of these pieces except the oft-repeated word 'transport': which even then sounded to me like a means of moving from one place to another.

My father took little interest in poetry, making an exception only for Pushkin. He knew him as some people know the liturgy, and liked to declaim him while out walking. I sometimes think that an echo of Pushkin's 'The Prophet', still vibrates to this day in some resonantly receptive Asian gully. He also quoted, I remember, the incomparable 'Butterfly' by Fet, and Tyutchev's 'Now the dim-blue shadows mingle'; but that which our kinsfolk liked, the watery, easily memorized poesy of the end of the last century, avidly waiting to be set to music as a cure for verbal anaemia, he ignored utterly. As to *avant-garde* verse, he considered it rubbish – and in his rubbish – and in his presence I did not publicize my own enthusiasms in this sphere. Once when with a smile of irony already prepared he leafed through the books of poets scattered on my desk and as luck would have it happened on the worst item by the best of them (that famous poem by Blok where there appears an impossible, unbearable *dzhentelmen* representing Edgar Poe, and where *Kovyor,* carpet, is made to rhyme with the English 'Sir' transliterated as *syor*), I was so annoyed that I quickly pushed Severyanin's *The Thunder-Bubbling Cup* into his hand so that he could better unburden his soul upon it. In general I considered that if he would forget for the nonce the kind of poetry I was silly enough to call 'classicism' and tried without prejudice to grasp what it was I loved so much, he would have understood the new charm that had appeared in the features of Russian poetry, a charm that I sensed even in its most absurd manifestations. But when today I tote up what has remained to me of this new poetry I see that very little has survived, and what has is precisely a natural continuation of Pushkin, while the motley husk, the wretched sham, the masks of mediocrity and the stilts of talent – everything that my love once forgave or saw in a special light (and that seemed to my father to be the true face of innovation – 'the mug of modernism' as he expressed it), is now so old-fashioned, so forgotten as even Karamzin's verses are not forgotten; and, when on someone else's shelf I came across this or that collection of poems which had once lived with me as brother, I feel in them only what my father then felt without actually knowing them. His mistake was not that he ran down all 'modern poetry' indiscriminately, but that he refused to detect in it the long, life-giving ray of his favourite poet.

I met her in June 1916. She was twenty-three. Her husband, a distant relative of ours, was at the front. She lived in a small villa inside the boundaries of our estate and often used to visit us. Because of her I almost forgot butterflies and completely overlooked the revolution. In the winter of 1917 she went away to Novorossisk – and it was only in Berlin that I accidentally heard about her terrible death. She was a thin little thing, with chestnut hair combed high, a gay look in her big black eyes, dimples on her pale cheeks, and tender mouth which she made up out of a flacon of fragrant ruby-red liquid by putting the glass stopper to her lips. In all her ways there was something I found lovable to the point of tears, something indefinable at the time, but now appearing to me as a kind of pathetic insouciance. She was not intelligent, she was poorly educated and banal, that is, your exact opposite . . . no, no, I do not mean at all that I loved her more than you, or that those assignations were happier than my evening meetings with you . . . but all her shortcomings were concealed in such a tide of fascination, tenderness and grace, such enchantment flowed from her most fleeting, irresponsible word, that I was prepared to look at her and listen to her eternally – but what would happen now if she were resurrected – I don't know, you should not ask stupid questions. In the evenings I used to see her home. Those walks will come in handy sometime. In her bedroom there was a little picture of the Tsar's family and a Turgenevian odour of heliotrope. I used to return long after midnight (my tutor, fortunately, had gone back to England), and I shall never forget that feeling of lightness, pride, rapture and wild night hunger (I particularly yearned for curds-and-whey with black bread) as I walked along our faithfully and even fawningly soughing avenue toward the dark house (only Mother had a light on) and heard the barking of the watchdogs. It was then also that my versificatory illness began.

At times I would be sitting at lunch, seeing nothing, my lips moving – and to my neighbour who had asked for the sugar bowl I would pass my glass or a napkin ring. Despite my inexperienced desire to transpose into verse the murmur of love filling me (well do I remember Uncle Oleg saying that if he were to publish a volume of poetry he would certainly call it *Heart Murmur*), I had already rigged up my own, albeit poor and primitive, wordsmithy; thus, in selecting adjectives, I was already aware that ones like 'innumerable' or 'intangible' would simply and conveniently fill the yawning gap, which was longing to sing, from the caesura to the word closing the line ('for we shall dream innumerable dreams'); and again that for this last word one could take an additional adjective, of only two syllables, so as to combine it with the long centre piece ('Of loveliness intangible and tender'), a melodic formula which, by the way, has had a quite disastrous effect on Russian, as well as on French poetry. I knew that handy adjectives of the amphibrachic type (a trisyllable that one visualizes in the shape of a sofa with three cushions – the middle one dented) were legion in Russian – and how many such 'dejécted', 'enchánted' and 'rebéllious' I wasted; that we had also plenty of trochees ('ténder'), but far fewer dactyls ('sórrowful'), and these somehow all stood in profile; that finally anapaestic and iambic adjectives were on the rare side, and in addition always rather dull and inflexible, like 'incompléte' or 'forlórn'. I knew further that great long ones like 'incomprehénsible' and 'infinitésimal' would come into the tetrameter bringing with them their own orchestras, and that the combination 'unwanted and misunderstood' gave a certain moiré quality to the line; look at it this way – it is an amphibrach, and that way – an iamb. A little later Andrey Bely's monumental research on 'half stresses' (the 'comp' and the 'ble' in the line 'Incomprehensible desires') hypnotized me with its system of graphically marking off and calculating these scuds, so that I immediately re-read all my old tetrameters from this new point of view and was terribly pained by the paucity of modulations. When plotted, their diagrams proved to be plain and gappy, showing none of those rectangles and trapeziums that Bely had found for the tetrameters of great poets; whereupon for the space of almost a whole year – an evil and sinful year – I tried to write with the aim of producing the most complicated and rich scud-scheme possible:

> In miserable meditations,
> And aromatically dark,
> Full of interconverted patience,
> Sighs the semidenuded park.

and so on for half-a-dozen strophes: the tongue stumbled but one's honour was saved. When graphically expressed by joining the 'half-stresses' ('ra', 'med', 'ar', 'cal', etc.), in the verses and from one verse to another, this monster's rhythmic structure gave rise to something in the nature of that wobbly tower of coffeepots, baskets, trays and vases which a circus clown balances on a stick, until he runs into the barrier of the arena when everything slowly leans over the nearest spectators (screaming horribly) but on falling turns out to be safely strung on a chord.

As a result, probably, of the weak motive power of my little lyrical rollers, verbs and other parts of speech interested me less. Not so with questions of metre and rhythm. Overcoming a natural preference for iambics, I dangled after ternary metres; later on departures from metre fascinated me. That was the time when Balmont in his poem beginning 'I will be reckless, I will be daring' launched that artificial iambic tetrameter with the bump of an extra syllable after the second foot, in which, as far as I know, not a single good poem was ever written. I would give this prancing hunchback a sunset to carry or a boat and was amazed that the former faded and the latter sank. Things went easier with the dreamy stutter of Blok's rhythms, but as soon as I began to use them my verse was imperceptibly infiltrated by stylized medievalizing – blue page-boys, monks, princesses – similar to the way that in a German tale the shadow of Bonaparte visits the antiquary Stolz at night to look for the ghost of its tricorn.

As my hunt for them progressed, rhymes settled down into a practical system somewhat on the order of a card index. They were distributed in little families – rhyme-clusters, rhymescapes.

Letuchiy (flying) immediately grouped *tuchi* (clouds) over the *kruchi* (steeps) of the *zhguchey* (burning) desert and of *neminuchey* (inevitable) fate. *Nebosklon* (sky) let the muse onto the *balkon* (balcony) and showed her a *klyon* (maple). *Tsvety* (flowers) and *ty* (thou) summoned *mechty* (fancies) in the midst of *temnoty* (darkness), *Svechi, plechi, vstrechi,* and *rechi* (tapers, shoulders, meetings, and speeches) created the old-world atmosphere of a ball at the Congress of Vienna or on the town governor's birthday. *Glaza* (eyes) shone blue in the company of *biryuza* (turquoise), *groza* (thunderstorm), and *strekoza* (dragonfly), and it was better not to get involved in the series. *Derevya* (trees) found themselves dully paired with *kochevya* (nomad encampments) as happens in the game in which one has to collect cards with the names of cities, with only two representing Sweden (but a dozen in the case of France!). *Veter* (wind) had no mate, except for a not very attractive setter running about in the distance, but by shifting into the genitive, one could get words ending in 'meter' to perform (*vetra-geometra*). There were also certain treasured freaks, rhymes to which, like rare stamps in an album, were represented by blanks. Thus it took me a long time to discover that *ametistovyy* (amethystine) could be rhymed with *perelistyvay* (turn the pages), with *neistovyy* (furioso), and with the genitive case of an utterly unsuitable *pristav* (police constable). In short, it was a beautifully labelled collection that I had always close to hand.

I do not doubt that even then, at the time of that ugly, crippling school (which I would hardly have bothered with at all were I a typical poet who never fell for the blandishments of harmonious prose) I nevertheless knew true inspiration. The agitation which seized me, swiftly covered me with an icy sheet, squeezed my joints and jerked at my fingers. The lunatic wandering of my thought which by unknown means found the door in a thousand leading into the noisy night of the garden, the expansion and contraction of the heart, now as vast as the starry sky and then as small as a droplet of mercury, the opening arms of a kind of inner embracement, classicism's sacred thrill, mutterings, tears – all this was genuine. But at that moment, in a hasty and clumsy attempt to resolve the agitation, I clutched at the first hackneyed words available, at their ready-made linkages, so that as soon as I had embarked on what I thought to be creation, on what should have been the expression, the living connection between my divine excitement and my human world, everything expired in a fatal gust of words, whereas I continued to rotate epithets and adjust rhymes without noticing the split, the debasement and the betrayal – like a man relating his dream (like any dream infinitely free and complex, but clotting like blood upon waking up), who unnoticed by himself and his listeners rounds it out, cleans it up and dresses it in the fashion of hackneyed reality, and if he begins thus: 'I dreamt that I was sitting in my room,' monstrously vulgarizes the dream's devices by taking it for granted that the room had been furnished exactly the same as his room in real life.

Farewell forever: on a winter day, with large snowflakes falling since morning, drifting anyhow – vertically, slantwise, even upwards. Her big arctics and tiny muff. She was taking away with her absolutely everything – including the park where they used to meet in summer. There remained only his rhymed inventory plus the briefcase under his arm, the shabby briefcase of an upper-former who had skipped school. An odd constraint, the desire to say something important, silence, vague insignificant words. Love, to put it simply, repeats at the last parting the musical theme of shyness that precedes its first avowal. The reticulate touch of her salty lips through the veil. At the station there was vile animal bustle: this was the time when the black and white seeds of the flower of happiness, sunshine and freedom were being liberally sown. Now it has grown up. Russia is populated with sunflowers. This is the largest, most fat-faced and stupidest of flowers.

Poems: about parting, about death, about the past. It is impossible to define (but it seems this happened abroad) the exact period of change in my attitude to writing poetry, when I became sick of the workshop, the classification of words and the collection of rhymes. But how excruciatingly difficult it was to break, scatter and forget all that: Faulty habits clung firmly, words accustomed to go together did not want to be uncoupled. In themselves they were neither bad nor good, but their combination in groups, the mutual guarantee of rhymes, the rank-grown rhythms – all this made them foul, hideous and dead. To consider himself a mediocrity was hardly any better than believing he was a genius: Fyodor doubted the first and conceded the second, but more important, strove not to surrender to the fiendish despair of a blank sheet. Since there were things he wanted to express just as naturally and unrestrainedly as the lungs want to expand, hence words suitable for breathing ought to exist. The oft repeated complaints of poets that, alas, no words are available, that words are pale corpses, that words are incapable of expressing our thingummy-bob feelings (and to prove it a torrent of trochaic hexameters is set loose) seemed to him just as senseless as the staid conviction of the eldest inhabitant of a mountain hamlet that yonder mountain has never been climbed by anyone and never will be; one fine, cold morning a long lean Englishman appears – and cheerfully scrambles up to the top.

The first feeling of liberation stirred in him when he was working on the little volume *Poems*, published two years ago now. It had remained in his consciousness as a pleasant exercise. One or two out of those fifty octaves, it was true, he was now ashamed of – for example that one about the bicycle, or the dentist – but on the other hand, there were some vivid and genuine bits: the lost and found ball, for instance, had come out very nicely, and the rhythm of its last two lines still continued to sing in his ear with the same inspired expressiveness as before. He had published the book at his own expense (having sold an accidental survivor of his former wealth, a flat, gold cigarette case with the date of a distant summer night scratched on it – oh that creak of her wicket gate wet with dew!) and out of the total of five hundred copies printed, four hundred and twenty-nine still lay, dusty and uncut, forming a neat mesa in the distributor's warehouse. Nineteen had been presented to different people, and one he had kept himself. Sometimes he wondered about the exact identity of the fifty-one who had bought his book. He imagined a roomful of these people (like a meeting of stockholders – 'readers of Godunov-Cherdyntsev') and they were all alike, with thoughtful eyes and a small white volume in their affectionate hands. He learned for sure the fate of only one copy: it had been bought two years ago by Zina Mertz.

He lay and smoked, and gently composed, revelling in the womblike warmth of the bed, the quietness of the flat and the lazy passage of time: Marianna Nikolavna would not be returning for a while and dinner was not earlier than one fifteen. During the past three months the room had been completely domesticated and its movement in space now coincided exactly with that of his life. The ring of a hammer, the hiss of a pump, the roar of an engine being checked, German bursts of German voices – all this humdrum complex of noises coming every morning from left of the yard, where there were garages and car workshops, had long since become familiar and harmless – a barely noticeable pattern in the stillness and not a violation of it. He could touch the little table by the window with his toe, if he stretched it from under the army blanket, and with a sideways projection of his arm he could reach the wardrobe by the left wall (which, by the way, sometimes for no reason, suddenly opened with the officious look of some fool of an actor who has come onto the stage at the wrong time). On the table stood the Leshino photograph, a bottle of ink, a lamp beneath cloudy glass and a saucer with traces of jam on it; reviews were lying around, the Soviet *Krasnaya Nov'*, and the émigré *Sovremennye Zapiski,* and a little volume of verse by Koncheyev, *Communication,* which had only just come out. Collapsed on the rug by his couch were yesterday's paper and an émigré edition of *Dead Souls.* None of this did he see for the moment, but it was all there: a small society of objects schooled to become invisible and in this finding their purpose, which they could only fulfil through the constancy of their miscellaneousness. His euphoria was all-pervading – a pulsating mist that suddenly began to speak with a human voice. Nothing in the world could be better than these moments. Love only what is fanciful and rare; what from the distance of a dream steals through; what knaves condemn to death and fools can't bear. To fiction be as to your country true. Now is our time. Stray dogs and cripples are alone awake. Mild is the summer night. A car speeds by: Forever that last car has taken the last banker out of sight. Near that streetlight veined time-leaves masquerade in chrysoprase with a translucent gleam. Beyond that gate lies Baghdad's crooked shade, and yon star sheds on Pulkovo its beam. Oh, swear to me—

From the hall came the jangling peal of the telephone. By tacit consent Fyodor attended to it when the others were out. And what if I don't get up now? The ringing went on and on, with brief pauses to catch its breath. It did not wish to die; it had to be killed. Unable to hold out, with a curse Fyodor gained the hall phantom-fast. A Russian voice asked irritably who was speaking. Fyodor recognized it instantly: it was an unknown person – by the whim of chance a fellow countryman – who already the day before had got the wrong number and now again, because of the similarity of the numbers, had blundered into the wrong connection. 'For Christ's sake go away,' said Fyodor and hung up with disgusted haste. He visited the bathroom for a moment, drank a cup of cold coffee in the kitchen, and dashed back into bed. What shall I call you? Half-Mnemo*syne*? There's a half-shim*mer* in your surname too. In dark Berlin, it is so strange to roam, oh, my half-fantasy, with you. A bench stands under the translucent tree. Shivers and sobs re-animate you there, and all life's wonder in your gaze I see, and see the pale fair radiance of your hair. In honour of your lips when they kiss mine I might devise a metaphor some time: Tibetan mountain-snows, their glancing shine, and a hot spring near flowers touched with rime. Our poor nocturnal property – that wet asphaltic gloss, that fence and that street-light – upon the ace of fancy let us set to win a world of beauty from the night. Those are not clouds – but star-high mountain spurs; not lamplit blinds but camplight on a tent! O swear to me that while the heartblood stirs, you will be true to what we shall invent.

At midday the peck of a key (now we switch to the prose-rhythm of Bely) was heard, and the lock reacted in character, clacking: that was Marianna (stopgap) Nikolavna home from the market; with a ponderous step and a sickening swish of her mackintosh she carried a thirty-pound netful of shopping past his door and into the kitchen. Muse of Russian prose-rhythm! Say farewell forever to the cabbage dactylics of the author of *Moscow*. All feeling of comfort was now gone. Of the morning capaciousness of time nothing remained. The bed had turned into a parody of a bed. In the sounds of dinner being prepared in the kitchen there was an unpleasant reproach, and the perspective of washing and shaving seemed as flat and impossible as the perspective of the early Italians. And with this, too, you will have to part some day.

A quarter past twelve, twenty past twelve, half past . . . He allowed himself one last cigarette in the tenacious although already tedious warmth of the bed. The anachronism of his pillow became more and more obvious. Without finishing his cigarette he got up and passed immediately from a world of many interesting dimensions into one that was cramped and demanding, with a different pressure, which instantly caused his body to tire and his head to ache; into a world of cold water: the hot was not running today.

A poetic hangover, dejection, the 'sad animal' . . . The day before he had forgotten to rinse his safety razor, between its teeth there was stony foam, the blade had rusted – and he had no other. A pale self-portrait looked out of the mirror with the serious eyes of all self-portraits. On a tenderly itchy spot to one side of his chin, among the hairs which had grown up overnight (how many yards of them shall I cut off in my life?), there had appeared a yellow-headed pimple which instantly became the hub of Fyodor's existence, a rallying point for all the unpleasant feelings now trekking in from different parts of his being. He squeezed it out – although he knew it would later swell up three times as big. How awful all this was. Through the cold shaving-soap foam pierced the little red eye: *L'oeil regardait Caïn.* Meanwhile the blade had no effect on the hairs, and the feet of the bristles when he checked them with his fingers produced a sense of hellish hopelessness. Drop of blood dew appeared in the vicinity of his Adam's apple but the hairs were still there. The Steppe of Despair. On top of everything else the bathroom was on the darkish side and even if he had put on the light the immortelle-like yellowness of daytime electricity would have been no help at all. Finishing his shave anyhow, he squeamishly climbed into the bath and groaned under the icy impact of the shower; then he made a mistake with the towels and thought miserably that he would be smelling all day of Marianna Nikolavna. The skin of his face smarted, revoltingly chafish, with one particularly hot little ember on the side of his chin. Suddenly the door handle of the bathroom was jerked vigorously (that was Shchyogolev returning). Fyodor Konstantinovich waited for the footfalls to recede and then popped back into his room.

Soon afterwards he entered the dining-room. Marianna Nikolavna was ladling out the soup. He kissed her rough hand. Her daughter, who was just back from work, came to the table with slow steps, worn out and seemingly dazed by her office; she sat down with graceful languor – a cigarette in her long fingers, powder on her lashes, a turquoise silk jumper, short-cut fair hair brushed back from the temple, sullenness, silence, ash. Shchyogolev gulped down a dram of vodka, tucked his napkin into his collar and began to slop up his soup, looking over his spoon affably but cautiously at his stepdaughter. She was slowly mixing a white exclamation mark of sour cream into her borshch, but then, shrugging her shoulders, she pushed her plate away. Marianna Nikolavna, who had been gloomily watching her, threw her napkin on the table and left the dining-room.

'Come on, eat, Aida,' said Shchyogolev, thrusting out his wet lips. Without a word of reply, as if he was not there – only the nostrils of her narrow nose quivered – she turned in her chair, easily and naturally twisted her long body, obtained an ashtray from the sideboard behind her, placed it by her plate and flicked some ash into it. Marianna Nikolavna, with a hurt look beglooming her ample crudely made-up face, returned from the kitchen. The daughter placed her left elbow on the table and slightly leaning on it slowly began her soup.

'Well, Fyodor Konstantinovich,' began Shchyogolev, having satisfied his first hunger, 'it seems matters are coming to a head! A complete break with England, and Hinchuk walloped! You know it's already beginning to smell of something serious. You remember, only the other day I said Koverda's shot was the first signal! War! You have to be very, very naïve to deny it's inevitable. Judge for yourself, in the Far East, Japan cannot put up with . . .'

And Shchyogolev launched on a discussion of politics. Like many unpaid windbags he thought that he could combine the reports he read in the papers by paid windbags into an orderly scheme, upon following which a logical and sober mind (in this case his mind) could with no effort explain and foresee a multitude of world events. The names of countries and of their leading representatives became in his hands something in the nature of labels for more or less full but essentially identical vessels, whose contents he poured this way and that. France was AFRAID of something or other and therefore would never ALLOW it. England was AIMING at something. This statesman CRAVED a rapprochement, while that one wanted to increase his PRESTIGE. Someone was PLOTTING and someone was STRIVING for something. In short, the world Shchyogolev created came out as some kind of collection of limited, humourless, faceless and abstract bullies, and the more brains, cunning and circumspection he found in their mutual activities the more stupid, vulgar and simple his world became. It used to be quite awesome when he came across another similar lover of political prognoses. For example, there was a Colonel Kasatkin, who used to come sometimes to dinner, and then Shchyogolev's England clashed not with another Shchyogolev country but with Kasatkin's England, equally non-existent, so that in a certain sense international wars turned into civil wars, although the warring sides existed on different levels which could never come into contact with one another. At present, while listening to his landlord, Fyodor was amazed by the family likeness between the countries mentioned by Shchyogolev and the various parts of Shchyogolev's own body: thus 'France' corresponded to his warningly raised eyebrows; some kind of 'limitrophes' to the hairs in his nostrils, some 'Polish corridor' or other went along his oesophagus; 'Danzig' was the click of his teeth; and Russia was Shchyogolev's bottom.

He talked all through the next two courses (goulash, kissel) and after that, picking his teeth with a broken match, went to take a nap. Marianna Nikolavna busied herself with the dishes before doing the same. Her daughter, having not uttered a single word, went back to her office.

Fyodor had only just managed to clear the bedclothes from the couch before a pupil arrived, the son of an émigré dentist, a fat, pale youth in horn-rimmed spectacles, with a fountain pen in his breast pocket. Attending, as he did, a Berlin high school, the poor boy was so steeped in the local habitus that even in English he made the same ineradicable mistakes as any skittle-headed German would have made. There was no force on earth, for example, which could have stopped him using the past continuous instead of the simple past, and this endowed every of his accidental activities of the day before with a kind of idiotic permanence. Equally stubbornly he handled the English 'also' like the German '*also*', and in overcoming the thorny ending of the word 'clothes' he invariably added a superfluous sibilant syllable ('clothes-zes'), as if skidding after having cleared an obstacle. At the same time he expressed himself fairly freely in English and had only sought the aid of a coach because he wanted to get the highest mark in the final examination. He was self-satisfied, discursive, obtuse and germanically ignorant; i.e., he treated everything he did not know with scepticism. Firmly believing that the humorous side of things had long since been worked out in the proper place for it (the back page of a Berlin illustrated weekly), he never laughed, or limited himself to a condescending snicker. The only thing that could just barely amuse him was a story about some ingenious financial operation. His whole philosophy of life had been reduced to the simplest proposition: the poor man is unhappy, the rich man is happy. This legalized happiness was playfully put together to the accompaniment of first-class dance music, out of various items of technical luxury. For the lesson he always did his best to come a little before the hour and tried to leave a little after it.

Hurrying to his next trial, Fyodor left together with him, and the latter, accompanying him as far as the corner, endeavoured to collect a few more English expressions gratis, but Fyodor, with dry glee, lapsed into Russian. They parted at the crossroads. It was a windy and shabby crossroads, not quite grown to the rank of a square although there was a church, and a public garden, and a corner pharmacy, and a public convenience with thujas around it, and even a triangular island with a kiosk, at which tram conductors regaled themselves with milk. A multitude of streets diverging in all directions, jumping out from behind corners and skirting the above-mentioned places of prayer and refreshment, turned it all into one of those schematic little pictures on which are depicted for the edification of beginning motorists all the elements of the city, all the possibilities for them to collide. To the right one saw the gates of a tram depot with three beautiful birches standing out against its cement background, and if, say, some absent-minded tramdriver forgot to pause by the kiosk three yards before the lawful tram stop (a woman with parcels invariably making fussily to get off and being held back by everybody) in order to throw the switch with the point of his iron rod (alas, such absent-mindedness almost never occurred), the tram would have solemnly turned in under the glass dome where it spent the night and was serviced. The church which loomed to the left was encircled with a low belt of ivy; in the parterre surrounding it grew several dark bushes of rhododendron with purple flowers, and at night one used to see a mysterious man here with a mysterious lantern looking for earthworms on the turf – for his birds? for fishing? Opposite the church across the street, beneath the radiance of a lawn-sprinkler that waltzed on one spot with the ghost of a rainbow in its dewy arms, was the green oblong lawn of the public garden, with young trees along either side (a silver fir among them) and a pi-shaped walk, in whose shadiest corner there was a sandpit for children; but *we* touch this kind of rich sand only when we are burying someone we know. Behind the garden there was an abandoned soccer field, along which Fyodor walked towards the Kurfürstendamm. The green of the lindens, the black of the asphalt, the truck tyres leaning against the railings by the shop for motorcar accessories, the beaming young bride on a poster displaying a packet of margarine, the blue of a tavern sign, the grey of house fronts getting older as they got closer to the avenue – all this flickered by him for the hundredth time. As always, when a few steps from the Kurfürstendamm, he saw his bus sweep across the vista in front of him: the stop was immediately around the corner, but Fyodor did not get there in time and was forced to wait for the next one. Over the entrance to a cinema a black giant cut out of cardboard had been erected, with turned-out feet, the blotch of a moustache on his white face beneath a bowler hat, and a bent cane in his hand. In wicker armchairs on the terrace of a neighbouring café businessmen sprawled in identical poses with their hands identically gabled in front of them, all very similar to one another as regards snouts and ties but probably varied in the extent of their solvency; and by the curb stood a small car with a heavily damaged wing, broken windows and a bloody handkerchief on the running board; a half-a-dozen people still loafed around, gaping at it. Everything was sun mottled; a puny old man with a dyed little beard and wearing cloth spats sat sunning himself on a green bench, with his back to the traffic, while opposite him across the sidewalk, an elderly, rosy-faced beggar woman with legs cut off at the pelvis was set down like a bust at the foot of a wall and was selling paradoxical shoelaces. Between the houses could be seen a vacant lot and on it something was modestly and mysteriously blooming; beyond it the continuous slaty-black backs of houses that seemed to have turned to leave, carried strange, attractive and seemingly completely autonomous whitish designs, reminding one not quite of the canals on Mars and not quite of something very distant and half-forgotten, like an accidental expression from a once-heard fairy tale or old scenery for some unknown play.

Down the helical stairs of the bus that drew up came a pair of charming silk legs: we know of course that this has been worn threadbare by the efforts of a thousand male writers, but nevertheless down they came, these legs – and deceived: the face was revolting. Fyodor climbed aboard, and the conductor, on the open top deck, smote its plated side with his palm to tell the driver he could move on. Along this side and along the toothpaste advertisement upon it swished the tips of soft maple twigs – and it would have been pleasant to look down from above on the gliding street ennobled by perspective, if it were not for the everlasting, chilly thought: there he is, a special, rare and as yet undescribed and unnamed variant of man, and he is occupied with God knows what, rushing from lesson to lesson, wasting his youth on a boring and empty task, on the mediocre teaching of foreign languages – when he has his own language, out of which he can make anything he likes – a midge, a mammoth, a thousand different clouds. What he should be really teaching was that mysterious and refined thing which he alone – out of ten thousand, a hundred thousand, perhaps even a million men – knew how to teach. For example – multi-level thinking: you look at a person and you see him as clearly as if he were fashioned of glass and you were the glass blower, while at the same time without in the least impinging upon that clarity you notice some trifle on the side – such as the similarity of the telephone receiver's shadow to a huge, slightly crushed ant, and (all this simultaneously) the convergence is joined by a third thought – the memory of a sunny evening at a Russian small railway station; i.e., images having no rational connection with the conversation you are carrying on while your mind runs around the outside of your own words and along the inside of those of your interlocutor. Or: a piercing pity – for the tin box in a waste patch, for the cigarette card from the series *National Costumes* trampled in the mud, for the poor, stray word repeated by the kindhearted, weak, loving creature who has just been scolded for nothing – for all the trash of life which by means of a momentary alchemic distillation – the 'royal experiment' – is turned into something valuable and eternal. Or else: the constant feeling that our days here are only pocket money, farthings clinking in the dark, and that somewhere is stocked the real wealth, from which life should know how to get dividends in the shape of dreams, tears of happiness, distant mountains. All this and much more (beginning with the very rare and painful so-called 'sense of the starry sky', mentioned it seems in only one treatise [Parker's *Travels of the Spirit*], and ending with professional subtleties in the sphere of serious literature), he would have been able to teach, and teach well, to anyone who wanted it, but no one wanted it – and no one could, but it was a pity, he would have charged a hundred marks an hour, the same as certain professors of music. And at the same time he found it amusing to refute himself: all this was nonsense, the shadows of nonsense, presumptuous dreams. I am simply a poor young Russian selling the surplus from a gentleman's upbringing, while scribbling verses in my spare time, that's the total of my little immortality. But even this shade of multifaceted thought, this play of the mind with its own self, had no prospective pupils.

The bus rolled on – and presently he arrived at his destination – the place of a lone and lonesome young woman, very attractive in spite of her freckles, always wearing a black dress opened at the neck and with lips like sealing-wax on a letter in which there was nothing. She continually looked at Fyodor with pensive curiosity, not only taking no interest in the remarkable novel by Stevenson which he had been reading with her for the past three months (and before that they had read Kipling at the same rate), but also not understanding a single sentence, and noting down words as you would note down the address of someone you knew you would never visit. Even now – or more exactly, precisely now and with greater agitation than before, Fyodor (although in love with another who was incomparable in fascination and intelligence) wondered what would happen if he placed his palm on this slightly trembling little hand with the sharp fingernails, lying so invitingly close – and because he knew what would happen then his heart suddenly began to thump and his lips immediately went dry; at this point, however, he was involuntarily sobered by a certain intonation of hers, her little laugh, the smell of that certain scent which somehow was always used by the very women who liked him, although to him this dullish, sweetish-brown smell was unbearable. She was a worthless, cunning woman with a sluggish soul; but even now, when the lesson was over and he had gone out into the street, he was seized by a vague feeling of annoyance; he could imagine much better than he had just been able to, in her presence, how gaily and yieldingly her compact little body would probably have responded to everything, and with painful vividness he saw in an imaginary mirror his hand on her back and her smooth auburn head thrown back, and then the mirror significantly emptied and he experienced that most trivial of all feelings on earth: the stab of a missed opportunity.

No, that was not so – he had missed nothing. The sole joy of these unrealizable embraces was their ease of evocation. During the past ten years of lonely and restrained youth, living on a cliff where there was always a bit of snow and from where it was a long way down to the little brewery town at the foot of the mountain, he had become accustomed to the thought that between the deceit of casual love and the sweetness of its temptation there was a void, a gap in life, an absence of any real action on his part, so that on occasion, when he looked at a passing girl, he imagined simultaneously both the stupendous possibility of happiness and repugnance for its inevitable imperfection – charging this one instant with a romantic image, but diminishing its triptych by the middle section. He knew therefore that their reading of Stevenson would never be interrupted by a Dantean pause, knew that if such a break should take place he would not experience a thing, except a devastating chill because the demands of the imagination were unfulfillable, and because the vacuousness of a gaze, forgiven for the sake of beautiful, moist eyes, inevitably corresponded to a defect as yet concealed – the vacuous expression of breasts, which it was impossible to forgive. But sometimes he envied the simple love life of other men and the way they probably had of whistling while taking off their shoes.

Crossing Wittenberg Square where, as in a colour film, roses were quivering in the breeze around an antique flight of stairs which led down to an underground station, he walked towards the Russian bookshop: between lessons there was a chink of spare time. As always happened when he came to this street (beginning under the auspices of a huge department store that sold all forms of local bad taste, and ending after several cross-roads in burgherish calm, with poplar shadows on the asphalt, all chalked over by hopscotchers, he met an elderly, morbidly embittered St Petersburg writer who wore an overcoat in summer to hide the shabbiness of his suit, a dreadfully skinny man with bulging dark brown eyes, wrinkles of fastidious distaste around his apish mouth, and one long, curved hair growing out of a big black pore on his broad nose – a detail which attracted Fyodor Konstantinovich's attention much more than the conversation of this clever schemer, who embarked immediately he met anyone upon something in the nature of a fable, a long far-fetched anecdote of yore, which turned out to be merely a prelude to some amusing gossip about a mutual acquaintance. Fyodor had barely got rid of him when he caught sight of two more writers, a good-naturedly gloomy Muscovite whose carriage and aspect were somewhat reminiscent of the Napoleon of the island period, and a satirical poet from the Berlin Russian-émigré paper, a frail little man with a kindly wit and a quiet, hoarse voice. These two, like their predecessor, invariably turned up in this region, which they used for leisurely walks, rich in encounters, so that it seemed as if on this German street there had encroached the vagabond phantom of a Russian boulevard, or as if on the contrary a street in Russia, with several natives taking the air, swarmed with the pale ghosts of innumerable foreigners flickering among those natives like a familiar and barely noticeable hallucination. They chatted about the writer just encountered, and Fyodor sailed on. After a few steps he noticed Koncheyev reading on the stroll the feuilleton at the bottom of the Paris Russian-émigré paper, with a marvellous angelic smile on his round face. The engineer Kern came out of a Russian food shop, cautiously thrusting a small parcel into the briefcase pressed against his chest, and on a cross street (like the confluence of people in a dream or in the last chapter of Turgenev's *Smoke*) he caught a glimpse of Marianna Nikolavna Shchyogolev with some other lady, moustachioed and very stout, who perhaps was Mme Abramov. Immediately after that Alexander Yakovlevich Chernyshevski cut across the street – no, a mistake – a stranger not even very like him.

Fyodor Konstantinovich reached the bookshop. In the window he could see, among the zigzags, cogs and numerals of Soviet cover designs (this was the time when the fashion there was to have titles like *Third Love, The Sixth Sense* and *Point Seventeen*), several new émigré publications: a corpulent new romance by General Kachurin, *The Red Princess*, Koncheyev's *Communication*, the pure white paperbacks of two venerable novelists, an anthology of recitable poetry published in Riga, the minute, palm-sized volume of a young poetess, a handbook *What a Driver Should Know*, and the last work of Dr Utin, *The Foundations of a Happy Marriage*. There were also several old St Petersburg engravings – in one of which a mirror-like transposition had put the rostral column on the wrong side of the neighbouring buildings.

The owner of the shop was not there: he had gone to the dentist's and his place was being taken by a rather accidental young lady reading a Russian translation of Kellerman's *The Tunnel* in a fairly uncomfortable pose in the corner. Fyodor Konstantinovich approached the table where the émigré periodicals were displayed. He unfolded the literary number of the Paris Russian *News* and with a chill of sudden excitement he saw that the feuilleton by Christopher Mortus was devoted to *Communication*. 'What if he demolishes it?' Fyodor managed to think with a mad hope, already, however, hearing in his ears not the melody of detraction but the sweeping roar of deafening praise. He greedily began to read.

'I do not remember who said – perhaps Rozanov said it somewhere,' began Mortus stealthily; and citing first this unauthentic quotation and then some thought expressed by somebody in a Paris café after someone's lecture, he began to narrow these artificial circles around Koncheyev's *Communication;* but even so, to the very end he never touched the centre, but only directed now and then a mesmeric gesture toward it from the circumference – and again revolved. The result was something in the nature of those black spirals on cardboard circles which are everlasting spinning in the windows of Berlin ice-cream parlours in a crazy effort to turn into bull's-eyes.

It was a venomously disdainful 'dressing down' without a

single remark to the point, without a single example – and not so much the critic's words as his whole manner made a pitiful and dubious phantom out of a book which Mortus could not fail to have read with delight and from which he avoided quoting in order not to damage himself with the disparity between what he wrote and what he was writing about; the whole review seemed to be a séance for the summoning of a spirit which is announced in advance to be, if not a fraud, at least a delusion of the senses. 'These poems,' ended Mortus, 'induce in the reader an indefinite but insuperable repulsion. People friendly to Koncheyev's talent will probably think them enchanting. We shall not quarrel – perhaps this is really so. But in our difficult times with their new responsibilities, when the very air is imbued with a subtle moral *angoisse* (an awareness of which is the infallible mark of "genuineness" in a contemporary poet), abstract and melodious little pieces about dreamy visions are incapable of seducing anyone. And in truth it is with a kind of joyous relief that one passes from them to any kind of "human document", to what one can read "between the words" in certain Soviet writers (granted even without talent), to an artless and sorrowful confession, to a private letter dictated by emotion and despair.'

At first Fyodor Konstantinovich felt an acute almost physical pleasure from this article, but it immediately dispersed and was replaced by a queer sensation, as if he had been taking part in a sly, evil business. He recalled Koncheyev's smile of a moment ago – over these very lines, of course – and it occurred to him that a similar smile might apply to him, Godunov-Cherdyntsev, whom envy had leagued with the critic. Here he recalled that Koncheyev himself in his critical reviews had more than once – from the heights and in fact just as unscrupulously – stung Mortus (who was, by the way, in private life, a woman of middle age, the mother of a family, who in her youth had published excellent poems in the St Petersburg review *Apollo* and who now lived modestly two steps from the grave of Marie Bashkirtsev, suffering from an incurable eye illness which endowed Mortus' every line with a kind of magic value). And when Fyodor realized the infinitely flattering hostility of this article he felt disappointed that no one wrote about *him* like that.

He also looked through a little illustrated weekly published by Russian émigrés in Warsaw and found a review on the same subject, but of a completely different cut. It was a *critique-bouffe*. The local Valentin Linyov, who from issue to issue used to pour out his formless, reckless, and not altogether grammatical literary impressions, was famous not only for not being able to make sense of the book he reviewed but also for not having, apparently, read it to the end. Jauntily using the author as a springboard, carried away by his own paraphrase, extracting isolated phrases in support of his incorrect conclusions, misunderstanding the initial pages and thereafter energetically pursuing a false trail, he would make his way to the penultimate chapter in the blissful state of a passenger who still does not know (and in his case never finds out) that he has boarded the wrong train. It invariably happened that having leafed blindly through a long novel or a short story (size played no part in it) he would provide the book with his own ending – usually exactly opposite to the author's intention. In other words, if, say, Gogol had been a contemporary and Linyov were writing about him, Linyov would remain firmly of the innocent conviction that Hlestakov was indeed the inspector-general. But when, as now, he wrote about poetry, he artlessly employed the device of so-called 'inter-quotational footbridges'. His discussion of Koncheyev's book boiled down to his answering for the author a kind of implied album questionnaire (Your favourite flower? Favourite hero? Which virtue do you prize most?): 'The poet,' Linyov wrote of Koncheyev, 'likes [there followed a string of quotations, forcibly distorted by their combination and the demands of the accusative case]. He dreads [more bleeding stumps of verse]. He finds solace in – [*même jeu*]; but on the other hand [three-quarters of a line turned by means of quotes into a flat statement]; at times it seems to him that' and here Linyov inadvertently extricated something more or less whole:

> Days of ripening vines! In the avenues, blue-shaded statues.
> The fair heavens that lean on the motherland's shoulders of snow.

– and it was as if the voice of a violin had suddenly drowned the hum of a patriarchial cretin.

On another table, a little farther, Soviet editions were laid out, and one could bend over the morass of Moscow magazines, over a hell of boredom, and even try to make out the agonizing constriction of capitalized abbreviations, carried like doomed cattle all over Russia and horribly recalling the lettering on freight cars (the banging of their buffers, the clanking, the hunchbacked greaser with a lantern, the piercing melancholy of godforsaken stations, the shudder of Russian rails, infinitely long-distance trains). Between *The Star* and *The Red Lamp* (trembling in railway smoke) lay an edition of the Soviet chess magazine *8 × 8*. As Fyodor leafed through it, rejoicing over the human language of the problem diagrams, he noticed a small article with the picture of a thin-bearded old man, glowering over his spectacles, the article was headed 'Chernyshevski and Chess'. He thought that this might amuse Alexander Yakovlevich and partly for this reason and partly because in general he liked chess problems he took the magazine; the girl, tearing herself away from Kellerman, 'couldn't say' how much it cost, but knowing that Fyodor was anyway in debt to the shop she indifferently let him go. He went away with the pleasant feeling that he would have some fun at home. Being not only an excellent solver of problems but also being gifted to the highest degree with the ability to compose them, he found therein not only a rest from his literary labours but certain mysterious lessons. As a writer he derived something from the very sterility of these exercises.

A chess composer does not necessarily have to play well. Fyodor was a very indifferent player and played unwillingly. He was fatigued and infuriated by the disharmony between the lack of stamina of his chess thought in the process of the contest and that exclamation-mark-rating brilliance for which it strove. For him the construction of a problem differed from playing in about the same way as a verified sonnet does from the polemics of publicists. The making of such a problem began far from the board (as the making of verse began far from paper) with the body in a horizontal position on the sofa (i.e., when the body becomes a distant, dark blue line: its own horizon) when suddenly, from an inner impulse which was indistinguishable from poetic inspiration, he envisioned a bizarre method of embodying this or that refined idea for a problem (say, the combination of two themes, the Indian and the Bristol – or something completely new). For some time he delighted with closed eyes in the abstract purity of a plan realized only in his mind's eye; then he hastily opened his Morocco board and the box of weighty pieces, set them out roughly, on the run, and it immediately became clear that the idea so purely embodied in his brain would demand, here on the board – in order to free it of its thick, carved shell – inconceivable labours, a maximum of mental strain, endless trials and worries, and most of all – that consistent resourcefulness out of which, in the chess sense, truth is constructed. Pondering the alternatives, thus and thus excluding cumbrous constructions, the blots and blanks of support pawns, struggling with duals, he achieved the utmost accuracy of expression, the utmost economy of harmonious forces. If he had not been certain (as he also was in the case of literary creation) that the realization of the scheme already existed in some other world, from which he transferred it into this one, then the complex and prolonged work on the board would have been an intolerable burden to the mind, since it would have to concede, together with the possibility of realization, the possibility of its impossibility. Little by little the pieces and squares began to come to life and exchange impressions. The crude might of the queen was transformed into refined power, restrained and directed by a system of sparkling levers; the pawns grew cleverer; the knights stepped forth with a Spanish caracole. Everything had acquired sense and at the same time everything was concealed. Every creator is a plotter; and all the pieces impersonating his ideas on the board were here as conspirators and sorcerers. Only in the final instant was their secret spectacularly exposed.

One or two more refining touches, one more verification – and the problem was ready. The key to it, White's first move, was masked by its apparent absurdity – but it was precisely by the distance between this and the dazzling denouement that one of the problem's chief merits was measured; and in the way that one piece, as if greased with oil, went smoothly behind another after slipping across the whole field and creeping up under its arm, constituted an almost physical pleasure, the titillating sensation of an ideal fit. Now on the board there shone, like a constellation, a ravishing work of art, a planetarium of thought. Everything here cheered the chess player's eye: the wit of the threats and defences, the grace of their interlocked movement, the purity of the mates (so many bullets for exactly so many hearts); every polished piece seemed to be made especially for its square; but perhaps the most fascinating of all was the fine fabric of deceit, the abundance of insidious tries (the refutation of which had its own accessory beauty), and of false trails carefully prepared for the reader.

The third lesson that Friday was with Vasiliev. The editor of the Berlin émigré daily had established relations with an obscure English periodical and now contributed a weekly article to it on the situation in Soviet Russia. Having a smattering of the language, he wrote his article out in rough, with gaps and Russian phrases interspersed, and demanded from Fyodor a literal translation of the usual phrases found in leaders: you're only young once, wonders never cease, this is a lion and not a dog (Krïlov), troubles never come singly, Peter's been paid without robbing Paul, jack of all trades, master of none, you can't make a silk purse out of a sow's ear, necessity is the mother of invention, it's only a lovers' tiff, hark at the pot calling the kettle black, birds of a feather flock together, the poor man always gets the blame, it's no use crying over spilt milk, we need Reform, not reforms. And very often there occurred the expression 'it produced the impression of an exploding bomb'. Fyodor's task consisted in dictating from Vasiliev's rough copy Vasiliev's article in its corrected form direct into the typewriter – this seemed extraordinarily practical to Vasiliev, but actually the dictation was monstrously dragged out as a result of the agonizing pauses. But oddly enough, the method of using old saws and fables turned out to be a condensed way of conveying something of the '*moralités*' characteristic of all conscious manifestations of the Soviet authorities: reading through the finished article which had seemed rubbish as he dictated it, Fyodor detected under the clumsy translation and the author's journalistic effects the movement of a logical and forceful idea, which progressed steadily towards its goal – and calmly produced a mate in the corner.

Accompanying him afterwards to the door, Vasiliev with a sudden fierce knitting of his bristly brows said quickly:

'Well, did you see what they have done to Koncheyev? I can imagine how it affected him, what a blow, what a flop.'

'He couldn't care less, I know that,' replied Fyodor, and an expression of momentary disappointment appeared on Vasiliev's face.

'Oh, he's just putting it on,' he retorted resourcefully, cheering up again. 'In reality he's sure to be stunned.'

'I don't think so,' said Fyodor.

'In any case I'm sincerely grieved for him,' ended Vasiliev, with the look of one who had no wish at all to part with his grief.

Somewhat weary but glad of the fact that his working day was over, Fyodor Konstantinovich boarded a tram and opened his magazine (again that glimpse of Chernyshevski's inclined face – all I know about him is that he was 'a syringe of sulphuric acid', as Rozanov, I think, says somewhere, and that he wrote the novel *What to Do?*, which blends in my mind with another social writer's *Whose Fault?*). He became absorbed in an examination of the problems and soon satisfied himself that if it had not been for two end-games of genius by an old Russian master plus several interesting reprints from foreign publications, this *8 × 8* would not have been worth buying. The conscientious student exercises of the young Soviet composers were not so much 'problems' as 'tasks': cumbrously they treated of this or that mechanical theme (some kind of 'pinning' and 'unpinning') without a hint of poetry; these were chess comic strips, nothing more, and the shoving and jostling pieces did their clumsy work with proletarian seriousness, reconciling themselves to the presence of double solutions in the flat variants and to the agglomeration of police pawns.

Having missed his stop he still managed to jump off at the public garden, turning at once on his heels as a man usually does after abruptly leaving a tram, and went by the church along Agamemnonstrasse. It was early evening, the sky was cloudless and the motionless and quiet sunshine endowed every object with a peaceful, lyrical air of festivity. A bicycle, leaned against a yellow-lit wall, was slightly bent outwards, like one of the side horses of a troika, but even more perfect in shape was its transparent shadow on the wall. An elderly, stoutish gentleman, waggling his rear, was hurrying to tennis, wearing a fancy shirt and city trousers and carrying three grey balls in a net, and beside him walking swiftly on rubber soles was a German girl of the sporting sort, with an orange face and golden hair. Behind the brightly painted pumps a radio was singing in a gas station, while above its pavilion vertical yellow letters stood against the light blue of the sky – the name of a car firm – and on the second letter, on the '*E*' (a pity that it was not on the first, on the '*B*' – would have made an alphabetic vignette) sat a live blackbird, with a yellow – for economy's sake – beak, singing louder than the radio. The house in which Fyodor lived was a corner one and stuck out like a huge red ship, carrying a complex and glassy turreted structure on its bow, as if a dull, sedate architect had suddenly gone mad and made a sally into the sky. On all the little balconies which girdled the house in tier after tier there was something green blossoming, and only the Shchyogolevs' was untidily empty, with an orphaned pot on the parapet and a corpse hung out in moth-eaten furs to air.

Right at the very beginning of his stay in this flat Fyodor, supposing that he would need complete peace in the evenings, had reserved himself the right to have supper in his room. On the table among his books there now awaited him two grey sandwiches with a glossy mosaic of sausage, a cup of stale tea and a plate of pink kissel (from the morning). Chewing and sipping, he again opened *8 × 8* (he was again glared at by a butting N. G. Ch.) and began to enjoy thoroughly a study in which the few white pieces seemed to be hanging over an abyss and yet won the day. Then he found a charming four-mover by an American master, the beauty of which consisted not only of the cleverly hidden mating device but also of the fact that in reply to a tempting but incorrect attack, Black, by drawing in and blocking his own pieces, managed to construct just in time a hermetic stalemate. Then in one of the Soviet productions (P. Mitrofanov, Tver) a beautiful example turned up of how to come a cropper: Black had NINE pawns – the ninth having evidently been added at the last minute, in order to cure a cook, as if a writer had hastily changed 'he will surely be told' in the proofs to the more correct 'he will doubtless be told' without noticing that this was immediately followed by: 'of her doubtful reputation'.

Suddenly he felt a bitter pang – why had everything in Russia become so shoddy, so crabbed and grey, how could she have been so befooled and befuddled? Or had the old urge 'toward the light' concealed a fatal flaw, which in the course of progress toward the objective had grown more and more evident, until it was revealed that this 'light' was burning in the window of a prison overseer, and that was all? When had this strange dependence sprung up between the sharpening of thirst and the muddying of the source? In the forties? in the sixties? and 'what to do' now? Ought one not to reject any longing for one's homeland, for any homeland besides that which is with me, within me, which is stuck like the silver sand of the sea to the skin of my soles, lives in my eyes, my blood, gives depth and distance to the background of life's every hope? Some day, interrupting my writing, I will look through the window and see a Russian autumn.

Some friends of the Shchyogolevs, gone to Denmark for the summer, had recently left Boris Ivanovich a radio. One could hear him diddling with it, strangling squeakers and creakers, moving ghostly furniture. An odd pastime!

The room meanwhile had grown dark; above the blackened outlines of the houses beyond the yard, where the windows were already alight, the sky had an ultramarine shade and in the black wires between black chimneys there shone a star – which, like any star, could only properly be seen by switching one's vision, so that all the rest moved away out of focus. He propped his cheek on his fist and sat there at the table, looking through the window. In the distance a large clock (whose position he was always promising himself to define, but always forgot, the more so since it was never audible under the layer of daytime sounds) slowly chimed nine o'clock. It was time to go and meet Zina.

They usually met on the other side of the railway bridge, on a quiet street in the vicinity of Grunewald, where the massifs of the houses (dark crossword puzzles, in which not everything was yet filled in by yellow light) were interrupted by waste plots, kitchen gardens and coal-houses ('the ciphers and sighs of the darkness' – a line of Koncheyev's), where there was, by the way, a remarkable fence made out of another one which had been dismantled somewhere else (perhaps in another town) and which had previously surrounded the camp of a wandering circus, but the boards had now been placed in senseless order, as if nailed together by a blind man, so that the circus beasts once painted on them, and reshuffled during transit, had disintegrated into their component parts – here there was the leg of a zebra, there a tiger's back, and some animal's haunch appeared next to another creature's reversed paw: life's promise of a life to come had been kept with respect to the fence, but the rupture of the earthly images on it destroyed the earthly value of immortality; at night, however, little could be made out of it, while the exaggerated shadows of the leaves (nearby there was a streetlight) lay on the boards quite logically, in perfect order – this served as a kind of compensation, the more so since it was impossible to transfer them to another place, with the boards, having broken up and mixed the pattern: they could only be transferred *in toto*, together with the whole night.

Waiting for her arrival. She was always late – and always came by another road than he. Thus it transpired that even Berlin could be mysterious. Within the linden's bloom the streetlight winks. A dark and honeyed hush envelopes us. Across the curb one's passing shadow slinks: across a stump a sable ripples thus. The night sky melts to peach beyond that gate. There water gleams, there Venice vaguely shows. Look at that street – it runs to China straight, and yonder star above the Volga glows. Oh, swear to me to put in dreams your trust, and to believe in fantasy alone, and never let your soul in prison rust, nor stretch your arm and say: a wall of stone.

She always unexpectedly appeared out of the darkness, like a shadow leaving its kindred element. At first her ankles would catch the light: she moved them close together as if she walked along a slender rope. Her summer dress was short, of night's own colour, the colour of the streetlights and the shadows, of tree trunks and of shining pavement – paler than her bare arms and darker than her face. This kind of blank verse Blok dedicated to Georgi Chulkov. Fyodor kissed her on her soft lips, she leaned her head for a moment on his collarbone and then, quickly freeing herself, walked beside him, at first with such sorrow on her face as if during their twenty hours of separation an unheard-of disaster had taken place, but then little by little she came to herself and now smiled – smiled as she never did during the day. What was it about her that fascinated him most of all? Her perfect understanding, the absolute pitch of her instinct for everything that he himself loved? In talking to her one could get along without any bridges, and he would barely have time to notice some amusing feature of the night before she would point it out. And not only was Zina cleverly and elegantly made to measure for him by a very painstaking fate, but both of them, forming a single shadow, were made to the measure of something not quite comprehensible, but wonderful and benevolent and continuously surrounding them.

When he had first moved in with the Shchyogolevs and seen her for the first time he had had the feeling that he already knew a great deal about her, that even her name had been long familiar to him, and certain characteristics of her life, but until he spoke to her he was unable to make out whence and how he knew it. At first he saw her only at dinner and he watched her carefully, studying her every movement. She hardly spoke to him, although by certain signs – not so much by the pupils of her eyes as by their lustre that seemed slanted at him – he felt that she was noticing every glance of his and that all her movements were restricted by the lightest shrouds of that very impression she was producing on him; and because it seemed completely impossible to him that he should have any part in her life, he suffered when he detected something particularly enchanting in her and was glad and relieved when he glimpsed some flaw in her beauty. Her pale hair which radiantly and imperceptibly merged into the sunny air around her head, the light blue vein on her temple, another on her long, tender neck, her delicate hand, her sharp elbow, the narrowness of her hips, the weakness of her shoulders and the peculiar forward slant of her graceful body, as if the floor over which, gathering speed like a skater, she hastened, was always gently sloping away towards the haven of the chair or table on which lay the object she sought – all this was perceived by him with agonizing distinctness and then, during the day, was repeated an infinity of times in his memory, returning ever more lazily, pallidly and jerkily, losing life and dwindling as a result of the automatic repetitions of the disintegrating image to a mere sketch broken and blurred, in which nothing of the original life subsisted; but as soon as he saw her again, all this subconscious work directed at the destruction of her image, whose power he feared more and more, went by the board, and beauty again flared forth – her nearness, her frightening accessibility to his gaze, the reconstituted union of all the details. If, during those days, he had had to answer before some pretersensuous court (remember how Goethe said, pointing with his cane at the starry sky: 'There is my conscience!') he would scarcely have decided to say that he loved her – for he had long since realized that he was incapable of giving his entire soul to anyone or anything: its working capital was too necessary to him for his own private affairs; but on the other hand, when he looked at her he immediately reached (in order to fall off again a minute later) such heights of tenderness, passion and pity as are reached by few loves. And at night, especially after long periods of mental work, half coming out of sleep not by the way of reason as it were, but through the back door of delirium, with a mad, long-drawn-out rapture, he felt her presence in the room on a camp-bed hastily and carelessly prepared by a property man, two paces away from him, but while he nursed his excitement and revelled in the temptation, in the shortness of the distance, in the heavenly possibilities, which, incidentally, had nothing of the flesh (or rather, had some blissful replacement for the flesh, expressed in semi-dreamlike terms), he was enticed back into the oblivion of sleep whence he hopelessly retreated, thinking he still continued to hold his prize. Actually she never appeared in his dreams, remaining content to delegate various representatives of hers and confidantes, who bore no resemblance to her but who produced sensations that made a fool of him – to which the bluish dawn was a witness.

And then, waking completely to the sounds of the morning, he immediately landed in the very thick of the happiness sucking at his heart, and it was good to be alive, and there glimmered in the mist some exquisite event which was just about to happen. But on trying to imagine Zina all he saw was a faint sketch which her voice behind the wall was incapable of igniting with life.

And an hour or two later he met her at table and everything was renewed, and he again understood that without her there would not be any morning mist of happiness.

One evening, a fortnight after he had moved in, she knocked on his door and with a haughtily resolute step, and an almost contemptuous expression on her face, entered, holding in her hand a small volume hidden in a pink cover. 'I have a request,' she said briskly and curtly. 'Will you sign this for me?' Fyodor took the book – and recognized in it a pleasantly worn, pleasantly softened up by two years of use (this was something quite new to him) copy of his collection of poems. He began very slowly to unstopper his bottle of ink – although at other times, when he wanted to write, the cork would pop out as that in a bottle of champagne; meanwhile, Zina, watching his fingers fumbling the cork, added hastily: 'Only your name, please, only your name.' F. Godunov-Cherdyntsev signed his name and was about to put the date, but thought better of it, fearing she might detect in this some vulgar emphasis. 'That's fine, thank you,' she said and went out, blowing on the page.

The next day but one was Sunday, and around four it suddenly became clear that she was alone at home; he was reading in his room; she was in the dining-room and kept making short expeditions from time to time into her own room across the hall, whistling as she went, and in her light crisp footfalls there was a topographical enigma since a door from the dining-room led straight into her room. But we are reading and we will keep on reading. 'Longer, longer, and for as long as possible, shall I be in a strange country. And although my thoughts, my name, my works will belong to Russia, I myself, my mortal organism, will be removed from it' (and at the same time, on his walks in Switzerland, the man who could write *thus,* used to strike dead with his cane the lizards running across his path – 'the devil's brood' – as he said with the squeamishness of a Ukrainian and the hatred of a fanatic). An unimaginable return! The régime; what do I care! Under a monarchy – flags and drums, under a republic – flags and elections. . . . Again she went by. No, reading was out – too excited, too full of the feeling that another in his place would have sauntered out and addressed her with casual savoir-faire; but when he imagined himself sailing out and butting into the dining-room and not knowing what to say, he began to wish that she would soon go out or that the Shchyogolevs would come home. And at the very moment when he decided to stop listening and give his undivided attention to Gogol, Fyodor quickly got up and went into the dining-room.

She was sitting by the door to the balcony and with her gleaming lips half parted was aiming a thread at a needle. Through the open door one could see the little sterile balcony and hear the tinny ringing and clinking of leaping raindrops – it was a heavy, warm, April shower.

'Sorry, I didn't know you were here,' said mendacious Fyodor. 'I only wanted to say something about that book of mine: it's not the real thing, the poems are bad, I mean, they're not all bad, but generally speaking. Those I've been publishing these last two years in the *Gazeta* are much better.'

'I liked very much the one you recited at that evening of poetry,' she said. 'The one about the swallow that cried out.'

'Oh, were you there? Yes. But I have even better ones, I assure you.'

She suddenly jumped up from her chair, threw her darning on the seat, and with her arms dangling, leaned forward, taking quick small gliding steps, she sped into her room and returned with some newspaper clippings – his and Koncheyev's poems.

'But I don't think I have everything here,' she remarked.

'I didn't know that such things happened,' said Fyodor and added awkwardly: 'Now I'll ask them to make little holes around them with a perforator – you know, like coupons, so that you can tear them out more easily.'

She continued to busy herself with a stocking stretched over a wooden mushroom and without lifting her eyes, but smiling quickly and slyly, she said:

'I also know that you used to live at seven Tannenberg Street, I often went there.'

'You did?' said Fyodor, amazed.

'I used to know Lorentz's wife in St Petersburg – she gave me drawing lessons.'

'How queer,' said Fyodor.

'Romanov is now in Munich,' she continued. 'A most objectionable character, but I always liked his things.'

They talked about Romanov and about his pictures. He had reached full maturity. Museums were buying his stuff. Having passed through everything, loaded with rich experience, he had returned to an expressive harmony of line. You know his 'Footballer'? There's a reproduction in this magazine, here it is. The pale, sweaty, tensely distorted face of a player depicted from top to toe preparing at full speed to shoot with terrible force at the goal. Tousled red hair, a burst of mud on his temple, the taut muscles of his bare neck. A wrinkled, soaking wet, violet singlet, clinging in spots to his body, comes down low over his spattered shorts, and is crossed with the wonderful diagonal of a mighty crease. He is in the act of hooking the ball sideways; one raised hand with wide-splayed fingers is a participant in the general tension and surge. But most important, of course, are the legs: a glistening white thigh, an enormous scarred knee, boots swollen with dark mud, thick and shapeless, but nevertheless marked by an extraordinarily precise and powerful grace. The stocking has slipped down one vigorously twisted calf, one foot is buried in rich mud, the other is about to kick – and how! – the hideous, tar-black ball – and all this against a dark grey background saturated with rain and snow. Looking at this picture one could *already* hear the whiz of the leather missile, *already* see the goalkeeper's desperate dive.

'And I know something else,' said Zina. 'You were supposed to help me with a translation, Charski told you about it, but for some reason you didn't turn up.'

'How queer,' repeated Fyodor.

There was a bang in the hall – that was Marianna Nikolavna returning – and Zina deliberately got up, gathered the cuttings together and went to her room – only later did Fyodor understand why she considered it necessary to act that way, but at the moment it seemed to him like discourtesy – and when Mrs Shchyogolev came into the dining-room the result was as if he had been stealing sugar out of the sideboard.

One evening a few days later he overheard an angry conversation from his room – the gist of which was that guests were due to arrive and that it was time for Zina to go downstairs with the key. He heard her go, and after a brief inner struggle, he thought himself up a walk – say to the slot machine by the public garden for a postage stamp. To complete the illusion, he put on a hat, although he practically never wore one. The minute light went out while he was on his way down but immediately there was a click and it went on again: that was she downstairs who had pressed the button. He found her standing by the glass door, playing with the key looped on her finger, the whole of her brightly illuminated, everything glistened – the turquoise knit of her jumper, her fingernails and the even little hairs on her forearm.

'It's unlocked,' she said, but he stopped, and both of them

began to look through the glass at the dark, mobile night, at the gas lamp, at the shadow of the railings.

'It doesn't look as if they're coming,' she muttered, softly clinking the keys.

'Have you been waiting long?' he asked. 'If you like I'll take a turn,' and at that moment the light went out. 'If you like I'll stay here all night,' he added in the darkness.

She laughed, and then sighed abruptly, as if fed up with waiting. Through the glass the ashen light from the street fell on both of them and the shadow of the iron design on the door undulated over her and continued obliquely over him, like a shoulder-belt, while a prismatic rainbow lay on the wall. And, as often happened with him – though it was deeper this time than ever before – Fyodor suddenly felt – in this glassy darkness – the strangeness of life, the strangeness of its magic, as if a corner of it had been turned back for an instant and he had glimpsed its unusual lining. Close to his face there was her soft cinereous cheek cut across by a shadow, and when Zina suddenly, with mysterious bewilderment and a mercurial sparkle in her eyes, turned towards him and the shadow lay across her lips, oddly changing her, he took advantage of the absolute freedom in this world of shadows to take her by her ghostly elbows; but she slipped out of the pattern and with a quick jab of her finger restored the light.

'Why?' he asked.

'I'll explain it some other time,' replied Zina, not taking her eyes off him.

'Tomorrow,' said Fyodor.

'All right, tomorrow. Only I want to warn you that there is not going to be any conversation between you and me at home. That's final and for good.'

'Then let's . . .' he began, but at this point stocky Colonel Kasatkin and his tall, faded wife loomed on the other side of the door.

'A very good evening to you, my pretty,' said the colonel, cleaving the night at a single stroke. Fyodor went out into the street.

The next day he contrived to catch her on the corner as she returned from work. They arranged to meet after supper by a bench which he had spied out the night before.

'Well, why?' he asked when they had sat down.

'For five reasons,' she said. 'In the first place because I'm not a German girl, in the second place because only last Wednesday I broke up with my fiancé, in the third place because it would be – well, pointless, in the fourth place because you don't know me at all, and in the fifth place . . .' She fell silent, and Fyodor cautiously kissed her burning, melting, sorrowing lips. 'That's why,' she said, her fingers running over his and strongly compressing them.

Thenceforth they met every evening. Marianna Nikolavna, who never dared to ask her about anything (the very hint of a question would draw forth the familiar storm), guessed that her daughter was meeting someone, the more so since she knew of the mysterious fiancé. He was a strange, sickly, unbalanced person (that, at least, is how Fyodor imagined him from Zina's description – and, of course, those *described* people are usually endowed with one basic characteristic: they never smile) whom she had met when she was sixteen, three years before, he being twelve years older than she, and in this seniority there was also something dark, unpleasant and embittered. Then again, according to her account, their meetings had taken place without any sentiments of love being expressed, and because she never made reference to even a single kiss, the impression was given that this had been simply an endless succession of tedious conversations. She resolutely refused to reveal his name or even his type of work (although she gave him to understand that he had been, in a sense, a man of genius) and Fyodor was secretly grateful to her for this, realizing that a ghost with neither name nor environment would fade out more easily – but nevertheless he experienced pangs of disgusting jealousy which he strove not to probe, but this jealousy was always present just around the corner, and the thought that somewhere, somewhen, for all he knew, he might meet the anxious, mournful eyes of this gentleman, caused everything around him to assume nocturnal habits of life, like nature during an eclipse. Zina swore that she had never loved him, that from lack of willpower she had been dragging out a tired romance with him and would have continued to do so had it not been for Fyodor coming along; but he was unable to discern any particular lack of willpower in her, rather he noticed a mixture of feminine shyness and unfeminine resoluteness in everything. Despite the complexity of her mind, a most convincing simplicity was natural to her, so that she could permit herself much that others would be unable to get away with, and the very speed of their coming together seemed to Fyodor completely natural in the sharp light of her directness.

At home she behaved in such a way that it was monstrous to

imagine an evening rendezvous with this alien, sullen young lady; but it was not pretence, rather it was also an idiosyncratic form of directness. When he once jokingly stopped her in the little corridor she paled with anger and did not come to meet him that evening, and later she forced him to swear on oath that he would never do that again. Very soon he understood why this was so: the domestic situation was of such a low-grade variety that with it as a background the fugitive touching of hands between a boarder and the landlord's daughter would have been turned simply into 'goings on'.

Zina's father, Oscar Grigorievich Mertz, had died of angina pectoris in Berlin four years ago, and immediately after his death Marianna Nikolavna had married a man whom Mertz would not have allowed over his threshold, one of those cocky and corny Russians who, when the occasion presented itself, savour the word 'Yid' as if it were a fat fig. But whenever good Shchyogolev was away, there quite simply appeared in the house one of his fishy business friends, a skinny Baltic baron with whom Marianna Nikolavna deceived him – and Fyodor, who had happened to see the baron once or twice, could not help wondering with a shudder of disgust what they could find in one another, and, if they found anything, what procedure did they adopt, this elderly, fleshy woman with a toad's face and this old skeleton with decaying teeth.

If it was sometimes agonizing to know that Zina was alone in the flat and that their agreement prevented him talking to her, it was agonizing in a totally different way when Shchyogolev remained alone at home. No lover of solitude, Boris Ivanovich would soon begin to get bored, and from his room Fyodor would hear the rustling growth of this boredom, as if the flat were slowly being overgrown with burdocks – which had now grown up to his door. He would pray to fate that something might distract Shchyogolev, but (until he got the radio) salvation was not forthcoming. Inevitably came the ominous, tactful knock and Boris Ivanovich, horribly smiling, squeezed sideways into the room. 'Were you asleep? Did I disturb you?' he would ask, seeing Fyodor flat on his back on the sofa, and then, ingressing entirely, he would shut the door tightly behind him and sit by Fyodor's feet, sighing. 'It's deadly dull, deadly dull,' he would say, and would launch upon some pet subject. In the realm of literature he had a high opinion of *L'homme qui assassina* by Claude Farrère, and in the realm of philosophy he had studied the *Protocols of the Sages of Zion*. He could discuss these two books for hours and it seemed that he had read nothing else in his life. He was generous with stories of judicial practice in the provinces and with Jewish anecdotes. Instead of 'we had some champagne and set out' he expressed him as follows: 'We cracked a bottle of fizz – and hup.' As with most babblers, his reminiscences always contained some extraordinary conversationalist who told him endless things of interest. 'I've never met another as clever as he in all my life,' (he would remark somewhat uncivilly) – and since it was impossible to imagine Boris Ivanovich in the role of a silent listener, one had to allow that this was a special form of split personality.

Once, when he had noticed some written-up sheets of paper on Fyodor's desk, he said, adopting a new heartfelt tone of voice: 'Ah, if only I had a tick or two, what a novel I'd whip off! From real life. Imagine this kind of thing: an old dog – but still in his prime, fiery, thirsting for happiness – gets to know a widow, and she has a daughter, still quite a little girl – you know what I mean – when nothing is formed yet but already she has a way of walking that drives you out of your mind – A slip of a girl, very fair, pale, with blue under the eyes – and of course she doesn't even look at the old goat. What to do? Well, not long thinking, he ups and marries the widow. Okay. They settle down the three of them. Here you can go on indefinitely – the temptation, the eternal torment, the itch, the mad hopes. And the upshot – a miscalculation. Time flies, he gets older, she blossoms out – and not a sausage. Just walks by and scorches you with a look of contempt. Eh? D'you feel here a kind of Dostoevskian tragedy? That story, you see, happened to a great friend of mine, once upon a time in fairyland when Old King Cole was a merry old soul,' and Boris Ivanovich, turning his dark eyes away, pursed his lips and emitted a melancholy, bursting sound.

'My better half,' he said on another occasion, 'was for twenty years the wife of a kike and got mixed up with a whole rabble of Jew in-laws. I had to expend quite a bit of effort to get rid of that stink. Zina [he alternately called his stepdaughter either this or Aïda, depending on his mood], thank God, doesn't have anything specific – you should see her cousin, one of these fat little brunettes, you know, with a fuzzy upperlip. In fact, it has occurred to me that my Marianna, when she was Madam Mertz, might have had other interests – one can't help being drawn to one's own people, you know. Let her tell you herself how she suffocated in that atmosphere, what relatives she acquired – oh, my Gott – all gabbling at table and she pouring out the tea. And to think that her mother was a lady-in-waiting of the Empress and that she herself had gone to the Smolny School for young ladies – and then she went and married a yid – to this very day she can't explain how it happened: he was rich, she says, and she was stupid, they met in Nice, she eloped to Rome with him – in the open air, you know, it all looked different – well, but when afterwards the little clan closed upon her, she saw she was stuck.'

Zina told it quite differently. In her version the image of her father took on something of Proust's Swann. His marriage to her mother and their subsequent life were tinted with a romantic haze. Judging by her words and judging also by the photographs of him, he had been a refined, noble, intelligent and kindly man – even in these stiff St Petersburg cabinet pictures with a gold stamped signature on the thick cardboard, which she showed Fyodor at night under a streetlamp, the old-fashioned luxuriance of his blond moustache and the height of his collars did nothing to spoil his delicate features and direct, laughing gaze. She told him about his scented handkerchief, and his passion for trotting races and music, and that time in his youth when he had routed a visiting grand master of chess, and the way he recited Homer by heart: in talking of him she selected things that might touch Fyodor's imagination, since it seemed to her she detected something sluggish and bored in his reaction to her reminiscences of her father, that is to the most precious thing she had to show him. He himself noticed this strangely delayed responsiveness of him. Zina had one quality which embarrassed him: her home life had developed in her a morbidly acute pride, so that even when talking to Fyodor she referred to her race with challenging emphasis, as if stressing the fact that she took for granted (a fact which its stressing denied) that he regarded Jews, not only without hostility present to a greater or lesser degree in the majority of Russians, but did so without the chilly smile of forced goodwill. In the beginning she drew these strings so taut that he, who in general did not give a damn about the classification of people according to race, or racial interrelations, began to feel a bit awkward for her, and on the other hand, under the influence of her burning, watchful pride he became aware of a kind of personal shame for listening silently to Shchyogolev's loathsome rot and to his trick of garbling Russian, in imitation of a farcical Jewish accent as when he said, for instance, to a wet guest who had left traces on the carpet: 'Oy, vat a mudnik!'

For a certain time after her father's death their former friends and relatives from his side had automatically continued to visit her mother and her; but little by little they thinned out and fell away, and only one old couple for a long time continued to come, feeling sorry for Marianna Nikolavna, feeling sorry for the past and trying to ignore Shchyogolev's retreating to his bedroom with a cup of tea and a newspaper. But Zina had continued to preserve her connection with the world her mother had betrayed, and on visits to these former family friends she changed extraordinarily, grew softer and kinder (she herself remarked upon this), as she sat at the tea table among the quiet conversations of old people about illnesses, weddings and Russian literature.

At home she was unhappy and this unhappiness she despised. She also despised her work, even though her boss was a Jew – however, a German Jew, i.e., first of all a German, so that she had no qualms about abusing him in Fyodor's presence. So vividly, so bitterly and with such revulsion did she tell him about that lawyer's office, where she had already been working for two years, that he saw and smelled everything as if he himself were there every day. The atmosphere of her office reminded him somehow of Dickens (in a German paraphrase, it is true) – a semi-insane world of gloomy lean men and repulsive chubby ones, subterfuge, black shadows, nightmare snouts, dust, stench and women's tears. It began with a dark, steep, incredibly dilapidated staircase which was fully matched by the sinister decrepitude of the office premises, a state of affairs not true only of the chief barrister's office with its overstuffed armchairs and giant glass-topped-table furnishings. The main office, large, plain, with bare, shuddering windows, was choked with an accumulation of dirty, dusty furniture – especially dreadful was the sofa, of a dull purple colour with protruding springs, a horrible, obscene object dumped here after gradually passing through the offices of all three directors – Traum, Baum and Käsebier. The innumerable shelves blocking every inch of wall were crammed with grim blue folders that stuck out their long labels, along which from time to time crawled a hungry, litigious bedbug. By the windows worked four typists: one was a hunchback who spent her salary on clothes; the second was a slender, flighty little thing whose father, a butcher had been killed with a meat hook by his hot-tempered son; the third was a defenceless young girl who was slowly collecting a trousseau, and the fourth was a married woman, a buxom blonde, whose soul was little more than a replica of her apartment and who recounted movingly how after a day of SPIRITUAL LABOUR she felt such a thirst for the relaxation of physical work that upon coming home she would throw open all the windows and joyously set about the washing. The office manager, Hamekke (a fat, coarse animal with smelly feet and a perpetually oozing furuncle on the nape, who liked to recall how in his sergeant days he had made clumsy recruits clean the barrack-room floor with toothbrushes), used to persecute the latter two with particular pleasure – one because the loss of her job for her would have meant not getting married, the other because she forthwith began to cry – those abundant, noisy tears which were so easy to provoke afforded him wholesome pleasure. Hardly literate, but gifted with an iron grip, immediately able to grasp the most unsavoury aspect of any case, he was highly prized by his employers, Traum, Baum and Käsebier (a complete German idyll, with little tables amid the greenery and a wonderful view). Baum was rarely to be seen; the office maidens found that he dressed marvellously, and in truth his suit was as rigid as on a marble statue, with everlastingly creased pants and a white collar attached to a coloured shirt. Käsebier cringed before his prosperous clients (for that matter all three of them cringed), but when he grew angry with Zina he accused her of putting on airs. The boss, Traum, was a shortish man with hair distributed in such a way as to conceal his bald spot, with a profile like the outside of a half-moon, tiny hands and a shapeless body, more wide than it was fat. He loved himself with a passionate and completely reciprocated love, was married to a rich, elderly widow, and having something of the actor in his nature, strove to do everything in style, spending thousands for show and haggling with his secretary over a nickel; he demanded of his employees that they refer to his wife as *'die gnädige Frau'* ('the missus telephoned', 'the missus left a message') and plumed himself on a sublime ignorance of what went on at the office, although in fact he knew everything through Hamekke, right down to the last blot. In his capacity as one of the legal consultants to the French Embassy he often travelled to Paris, and since his outstanding characteristic was a tremendously smooth effrontery in the pursual of advantages, he energetically struck up useful acquaintances while there, shamelessly asking for recommendations, badgering, foisting himself upon people without feeling the snubs – his skin was like the armour on a peba. In order to gain popularity in France he wrote little books in German on

French themes (*Three Portraits* for example – the Empress Eugénie, Briand and Sarah Bernhardt), and in the course of their preparation, the collecting of materials turned into the collecting of connections. These hastily compiled works, in the terrible *style moderne* of the German republic (and essentially yielding little to the works of Ludwig and the Zweigs), were dictated by him to his secretary between business, when he suddenly feigned a flow of inspiration, which flow, incidentally, always coincided with a stretch of leisure time. Some French professor into whose friendship he had insinuated himself once answered a most tender epistle of his with (for a Frenchman) extremely blunt criticism: 'You write the name Deschanel at times with an *accent aigu* and at others without it. Since a certain uniformity is necessary here it would be good if you were to take a firm decision as to which system you wish to adhere to, and then stick to it. If for any reason you should desire to write this name correctly, then write it without an *accent*.' Traum at once responded with a rapturously grateful letter, continuing at the same time to ask for favours. Oh, how well he could round out and sweeten his letters, what Teutonic warblings and whistlings there were in the endless modulation of his openings and conclusions, what courtesies: '*Vous avez bien voulu bien vouloir....*'

His secretary, Dora Wittgenstein, who had worked for him for fourteen years, shared a small musty office with Zina. This ageing woman with bags under her eyes, smelling of carrion through her cheap eau de cologne, who worked for any number of hours and who had dried up in the service of Traum, resembled an unfortunate, worn-out horse whose whole muscular system had been displaced, leaving only a few iron tendons. She was little educated, organized her life according to two or three generally accepted concepts and in her dealings with French was guided by certain private rules of her own. When Traum was writing his periodic 'book' he would call her to his house on Sundays, haggle over her payment and keep her for extra time; and sometimes she would proudly inform Zina that his chauffeur had driven her home – or at least as far as the tram stop.

Zina had to work not only at translations but also, as did all the other typists, at copying out the long applications presented at court. Frequently she also had to take down in shorthand, in the presence of a client, the circumstances of his case, very often dealing with divorce. These cases were all fairly sordid – lumps of all sorts of muck and stupidity stuck together. A person from

Kottbus, divorcing a wife who, according to him, was abnormal, accused her of consorting with a great Dane; the chief witness was the janitress, who through the door had allegedly heard the wife talking to the hound and expressing delight concerning certain details of its organism.

'To you it's only funny,' said Zina crossly, 'but honestly I can't go on, I can't, and I would abandon all this scum right away if I didn't know that another office would have the same scum, or worse. This worn-out feeling in the evening is something phenomenal, it baffles any description. What am I good for now? My spine aches so much from that typewriter that I feel like howling. And the main thing is that this will never end, because if it came to an end there'd be nothing to eat – Mother can't do anything, she can't even work as a cook because she'd only sob in her employer's kitchen and break the dishes, and her filthy husband only knows how to go bankrupt – in my opinion he was already bankrupt when he was born. You've no idea how I hate him, he's a swine, a swine, a swine. . . .'

'One could make ham out of him,' said Fyodor. 'I also had a fairly hard day. I wanted to write a poem for you, but somehow it hasn't quite cleared up yet.'

'My darling, my joy,' she exclaimed, 'can all this be true – this fence and that blurry star? When I was little I didn't like drawing anything that didn't finish, so I didn't draw fences because they don't finish on paper; you can't imagine a fence that finishes, but I always did something complete, a pyramid, or a house on a hill.'

'And I liked horizons most of all, and diminishing dashes beneath it – to represent the wake of the sun setting beyond the sea. And the greatest childhood torment of all was an unsharpened or broken crayon pencil.'

'But then the sharpened ones . . . Do you remember the white one? Always the longest – not like the red and blue ones – because it didn't do much work, do you remember?'

'But how much it wanted to please! The drama of the albino. *L'inutile beauté*. Anyhow, later I let it have its fill. Precisely because it drew the invisible and one could imagine lots of things. In general there await us unlimited possibilites. Only no angels, or if there must be an angel, then with a huge chest cavity, and wings like a hybrid between a bird of paradise and a condor, and talons to carry the young soul away – not "embraced" as Lermontov has it.'

'Yes, I also think that we can't end here. I can't imagine that we could cease to exist. In any case I wouldn't like to turn into anything.'

'Into diffused light? What do you think of that? Not too good, I'd say. I am convinced that extraordinary surprises await us. It's a pity one can't imagine what one can't compare to anything. Genius is an African who dreams up snow. Do you know what it was that most amazed the very first Russian pilgrims when they were crossing Europe?'

'The music?'

'No, the fountains in the cities, the wet statues.'

'It sometimes annoys me that you have no feeling for music. My father had such an ear that sometimes he would lie on the sofa and hum a whole opera, from beginning to end. Once he was lying like that and someone came into the next room and began talking to Mother – and he said to me: "That voice belongs to so-and-so, I saw him twenty years ago in Carlsbad and he promised to come and see me one day." That's what his ear was like.'

'And I met Lishnevski today and he mentioned a friend of his who complained that Carlsbad was no longer what it used to be. Those were the days! he said: "you stand with your mug of water and there next to you is King Edward . . .handsome, imposing man . . . suit of real English cloth". . . . Now why are you offended? What's the matter?'

'Never mind. There are some things you'll never understand.'

'Don't say that. Why is your skin hot here and cold there? You are not cold? Better take a look at that moth by the lamp.'

'I saw it long ago.'

'Do you want me to tell you why moths fly toward the light? No one knows that.'

'And you know?'

'It always seems to me that in a minute I'll guess if I just think hard enough. My father used to say that it resembled most of all a loss of equilibrium, as when learning to ride a bike you are lured by a ditch. Light in comparison with darkness is a void. Look at it circling! But there's something deeper here – in a minute I'll get it.'

'I'm sorry that you didn't write your book after all. Oh, I have a thousand plans for you. I have such a clear feeling that one day you'll really lash out. Write something huge to make everyone gasp.'

'I'll write,' said Fyodor Konstantinovich jokingly, 'a biography of Chernyshevski.'

'Anything you like. But it must be quite, quite genuine. I don't need to tell you how much I like your poems, but they are never quite up to your measure, all the words are one size smaller than your real words.'

'Or a novel. It's queer, I seem to remember my future works, although I don't even know what they will be about. I'll recall them completely and write them. Tell me, by the way, how do you tend to see it: are we going to meet all our lives like this, side by side on a bench?'

'Oh no,' she replied in a musically dreamy voice. 'In the winter we'll go to a dance, and this summer, when I have my holiday, I'll go to the sea for two weeks and send you a postcard of the breakers.'

'I'll also go to the sea for two weeks.'

'I don't think so. And then don't forget that we must meet sometime in the Tiergarten in the rosarium, where the statue of the princess is with the stone fan.'

'Pleasant prospects,' said Fyodor.

Bue a few days later he happened to come across that same copy of *8 × 8*; he leafed through it, looking for unfinished bits, and when all the problems turned out to be solved, he ran his eyes over the two-column extract from Chernyshevski's youthful diary; he glanced through it, smiled, and began to read it over with interest. The drolly circumstantial style, the meticulously inserted adverbs, the passion for semicolours, the bogging down of thought in midsentence and the clumsy attempts to extricate it (whereupon it got stuck at once elsewhere, and the author had to start worrying it out all over again), the drubbing-in, rubbing-in tone of each word, the knight-moves of sense in the trivial commentary on his minutest actions, the viscid ineptitude of these actions (as if some workshop glue had got onto the man's hands, and both were left), the seriousness, the limpness, the honesty, the poverty – all this pleased Fyodor so much, he was so amazed and tickled by the fact that an author with such a mental and verbal style was considered to have influenced the literary destiny of Russia, that on the very next morning he signed out the complete works of Chernyshevski from the state library. And as he read, his astonishment grew, and this feeling contained a peculiar kind of bliss.

When, a week later, he accepted a telephone invitation from Alexandra Yakovlevna ('Why does one never see you? Tell me, are you free tonight?'), he did not take *8 × 8* with him to show to his friends: this little magazine now had a sentimental value for him, the memory of an encounter. Among the guests there he found the engineer Kern and a capacious, very smooth-cheeked and taciturn gentleman with a fat, old-fashioned face, by the name of Goryainov, who was well known for the fact that being able to imitate beautifully (by stretching his mouth wide, making moist ruminant sounds, and speaking in falsetto) a certain unfortunate, cranky journalist with a poor reputation, he had grown so accustomed to this image (which thus had its revenge on him) that not only did he also pull down the corners of his mouth when imitating other of his acquaintances, but even began to look like it himself in normal conversation. Alexander Chernyshevski, grown thinner and quieter after his illness – this being the price of redeeming his health for a while – seemed that evening quite lively again, and even his familiar tic had returned; but Yasha's ghost no longer sat in the corner, leaning on his elbow among disarrayed books.

'Are you still pleased with your lodgings?' asked Alexandra Yakovlevna. 'Well, I'm very glad. You don't flirt with the daughter? No? Apropos, I remember the other day that at one time Mertz and I had some common acquaintances – he was a wonderful man, a gentleman in all senses of the word – but I don't think she cares very much to admit her origins. She does admit them? Well, I don't know. I suspect you don't quite understand these matters.'

'In any case she's a girl with character,' said the engineer Kern. 'I once saw her at a meeting of the dance committee. She looked down her nose at everything.'

'And what's her nose like?' asked Alexandra Yakovlevna.

'You know, to tell you the truth I didn't look at it very carefully, and in the final analysis all girls aspire to be beauties. Let's not be catty.'

Goryainov, who sat with his hands clasped on his stomach, was silent except that occasionally he lifted his fleshy chin with a bizarre jerk and shrilly cleared his throat, as if calling to someone. 'Yes, thank you, I would indeed,' he said with a bow whenever he was offered jam or a glass of tea, and if he wished to impart something to his neighbour he did not turn toward him but moved his head closer, still looking ahead, and having imparted it or asked a question, slowly moved away again. In a conversation with him there were strange gaps because he did not back your speeches in any way and did not look at you, but would let the brown gaze of his small, elephant eyes stray around the room, and would convulsively clear his throat. When he spoke of himself it was always in a gloomily humorous vein. His whole appearance evoked for some reason such obsolete associations as, for example: department of the interior, cold vegetable soup, glossy rubbers, stylized snow falling outside the window, stolidity, Stolypin, statist.

'Well, my friend,' said Chernyshevski vaguely, moving to a seat by Fyodor, 'what have you got to say for yourself? You don't look too well.'

'You remember,' said Fyodor, 'once about three years ago you gave me the happy advice to describe the life of your renowned namesake?'

'Absolutely not,' said Alexander Yakovlevich.

'A pity – because now I'm thinking of getting down to it.'

'Oh, really? Are you serious?'

'Quite serious,' said Fyodor.

'But how did such a wild thought get into your head?' chimed in Mme Chernyshevski. 'Why, you ought to write – I don't know – say, the life of Batyushkov or Delvig, something in the orbit of Pushkin – but what's the point of Chernyshevski?'

'Firing practice,' said Fyodor.

'An answer which is, to say the least, enigmatic,' remarked the engineer Kern, and the rimless glass of his pince-nez gleamed as he attempted to crack a nut with his palms. Dragging them by one leg, Goryainov passed him the crackers.

'Why not,' said Alexander Yakovlevich, coming out of a brief spell of musing. 'I begin to like the idea. In our terrible times when individualism is trampled underfoot and thought is stifled it must be a great joy for a writer to immerse himself in the bright era of the sixties. I welcome it.'

'Yes, but it's so distant from him!' said Mme Chernyshevski. 'There's no continuity, no tradition. Frankly speaking, I myself wouldn't be very interested in resuscitating everything that I felt in this connection when I was a college student in Russia.'

'My uncle,' said Kern, cracking a nut, 'was thrown out of school for reading *What to Do?*'

'And what is your opinion?' said Alexandra Yakovlevna addressing Goryainov.

Goryainov spread his hands. 'I don't have any particular one,' he said in a thin voice, as if mimicking someone. 'I've never read Chernyshevski, but when I come to think of it. . . . A most boring, Lord forgive me, figure!'

Alexander Yakovlevich leaned back slightly in his armchair,

blinking, twitching, his face alternately lighting up in a smile and then fading again, and said:

'Nevertheless I welcome Fyodor Konstantinovich's idea. Of course a lot strikes us today as both comic and boring. But in that era there is something sacred, something eternal. Utilitarianism, the negation of art and so on – all this is merely an accidental wrapping, under which it is impossible not to distinguish its basic features: reverence for the whole human race, the cult of freedom, ideas of equality – equality of rights. It was an era of great emancipations, the peasants from the landowners, the citizen from the state, women from domestic bondage. And don't forget that not only were the best principles of the Russian liberation movement born then – a thirst for knowledge, steadfastness of spirit, heroic self-sacrifice – but also it was precisely in this era, fed by it in one way or another, that such giants as Turgenev, Nekrasov, Tolstoy and Dostoevsky were developing. Moreover it goes without saying that Nikolai Gavrilovich Chernyshevski himself was a man with a vast, versatile mind, with enormous, creative willpower, and the fact that he endured dreadful sufferings for the sake of his ideology, for the sake of humanity, for the sake of Russia, more than redeems a certain harshness and rigidity in his critical views. Moreover I maintain that he was a superb critic – penetrating, honest, brave. . . . No, no, it's wonderful, you must certainly write it!'

The engineer Kern had already been on his feet for some time, walking about the room, shaking his head and bursting to say something.

'What are we talking about?' he suddenly exclaimed, taking hold of the back of a chair. 'Who cares what Chernyshevski thought of Pushkin? Rousseau was a lousy botanist, and I wouldn't have been treated by Dr Chekhov for anything in the world. Chernyshevski was first of all a learned economist and that's how he should be regarded – and with all my respect for Fyodor Konstantinovich's poetic talents, I am somewhat doubtful that he is capable of appreciating the merits and demerits of his man's *Commentaries on John Stuart Mill.*'

'Your comparison is absolutely wrong,' said Alexandra Yakovlevna. 'It's ridiculous! Chekhov didn't leave the slightest trace in medicine, Rousseau's musical compositions are mere curiosities, but in this case no history of Russian literature can omit Chernyshevski. But there's something else I don't understand,' she continued swiftly. 'What interest does Fyodor Konstantinovich have in writing about people and times to which his whole mentality is completely alien? Of course I don't know what his approach will be. But if he, let's speak plainly, wants to show up the progressive critics then it's worth the effort: Volynski and Eichenwald did this long ago.'

'Oh, come, come,' said Alexander Yakovlevich, '*das kommt nicht in Frage*. A young writer has become interested in one of the most important epochs in Russian history and is about to write a literary biography of one of its major figures. I don't see anything strange in that. It's not very difficult to get to know the subject, he'll find more than enough books, and the rest all depends on talent. You say approach, approach. But granted a talented approach to a given subject, sarcasm is *a priori* excluded, is irrelevant. That's how it seems to me at least.'

'Did you see how Koncheyev was attacked last week?' asked the engineer Kern, and the conversation took another turn.

Out on the street when Fyodor was saying good-bye to Goryainov the latter retained his hand in his own large, soft hand and said puckering up his eyes: 'Let me tell you, my lad, you're quite a joker. Recently there died the social-democrat Belenki – a kind of perpetual émigré, so to speak: he was exiled by both the Tsar and the proletariat, so that whenever he indulged in his reminiscences he would begin: '*U nas v Zheneve*, chez nous à Genève. . . . Perhaps you'll write about him as well?'

'I don't understand?' said Fyodor half-questioningly.

'No, but on the other hand I understood perfectly. You are as much preparing to write about Chernyshevski as I am about Belenki, but then you made a fool of your audience and stirred up an interesting argument. All the best, good night,' and he left with his slow, heavy gait, leaning on a cane and holding one shoulder slightly higher than the other.

The way of life to which he had become addicted while studying his father's activities was now renewed for Fyodor. It was one of those repetitions, one of those thematic voices with which, according to all the rules of harmony, destiny enriches the life of observant men. But now, taught by experience, he did not allow himself his former slovenliness in the use of sources and provided even the smallest note with an exact label of its origin. In front of the national library, near a stone pool, pigeons strolled cooing among the daisies on the lawn. The books to be taken out arrived in a little wagon along sloping rails at the bottom of the apparently small premises, where they awaited distribution, and where there seemed to be only a few books lying around on the shelves when in fact there was an accumulation of thousands.

Fyodor would embrace his portion, struggling with its disintegrating weight, and walk to the bus stop. From the very beginning the image of his planned book had appeared to him extraordinarily distinctly in tone and outline, he had the feeling that for every detail he ran to earth there was already a place prepared and that even the work of hunting up material was already bathed in the light of the forthcoming book, just as the sea throws a blue light on a fishing boat, and the boat itself together with this light is reflected in the water. 'You see,' he explained to Zina, 'I want to keep everything as it were on the very brink of parody. You know those idiotic "*biographies romancées*" where Byron is coolly slipped a dream extracted from one of his own poems? And there must be on the other hand an abyss of seriousness, and I must make my way along this narrow ridge between my own truth and a caricature of it. And most essentially, there must be a single uninterrupted progression of thought. I must peel my apple in a single strip, without removing the knife.'

As he studied his subject he saw that in order to completely soak himself in it he would have to extend his field of activity two decades in either direction. Thus an amusing feature of the age was revealed to him – essentially trifling, but proving to be a valuable guideline: during fifty years of utilitarian criticism, from Belinski to Mihailovski, there was not a single moulder of opinion who did not take the opportunity to jeer at the poems of Fet. And into what metaphysical monsters turned sometimes the most sober judgments of these materialists on this or that subject, as if the Word, Logos, were avenging itself on them for being slighted! Belinski, that likeable ignoramus, who loved lilies and oleanders, who decorated his window with cacti (as did Emma Bovary), who kept five kopecks, a cork and a button in the empty box discarded by Hegel and who died of consumption with a speech to the Russian people on his bloodstained lips, startled Fyodor's imagination with such pearls of realistic thought as, for example: 'In nature everything is beautiful, excepting only those ugly phenomena which nature herself has left unfinished and hidden in the darkness of the earth or water (molluscs, worms, infusoria, and so on).' Similarly, in Mihailovski it was easy to discover a metaphor floating belly upwards as for example: '[Dostoevski] struggled like a fish against the ice, ending up at times in the most humiliating positions'; this *humiliated fish* rewarded one for working through all the writings of the 'reporter on contemporary issues'. From here there was a direct transition to the fighting lexicon of the present day, to the style of Steklov speaking of Chernyshevski's times ('The plebeian writer who nestled in the pores of Russian life . . . branded routine opinions with the battering ram of his ideas'), or to the idiom of Lenin who in his polemical heat attained the heights of absurdity: ('Here there is no fig leaf . . . and the idealistic stretches out his hand directly to the agnostic'). Russian prose, what crimes are committed in thy name! A contemporary critic wrote about Gogol: 'His people are deformed grotesques, his characters, Chinese-lantern shadows, the events he depicts, impossible and ridiculous,' and this fully corresponded to the opinions held by Skabichevski and Mihailovski about Chekhov – opinions that, like a fuse lit at the time, have now blown these critics to bits.

He read Pomyalovski (honesty in the role of tragic passion) and found there this lexical fruit salad: 'little raspberry-red lips like cherries.' He read Nekrasov, and sensing a certain urban-journalist defect in his (frequently enchanting) poetry, he found an apparent explanation for the vulgarisms in his pedestrian *Russian Women* ('How jolly, furthermore, To share your every thought in common With someone you adore') in the discovery that despite his walks in the country he confused gadflies with bumblebees and wasps ([over the flock] 'a restless swarm of bumblebees' and ten lines lower down: the horses under the smoke of a bonfire 'seek shelter from the wasps'). He read Herzen and was again better able to understand the flaw (a false glib glitter) in his generalizations when he noticed that this author, having a poor knowledge of English (witnessed by his surviving autobiographical reference, which begins with the amusing Gallicism 'I am born'), had confused the sounds of two English words 'beggar' and 'bugger' and from this had made a brilliant deduction concerning the English respect for wealth.

Such a method of evaluation, taken to its extreme, would be even sillier than approaching writers and critics as exponents of general ideas. What is the significance of Suhoshchokov's Pushkin's not liking Baudelaire, and is it fair to condemn Lermontov's prose because he twice refers to some impossible 'crocodile' (once in a serious and once in a joking comparison)? Fyodor stopped in time, thus preventing the pleasant feeling that he had discovered an easily applicable criterion from being impaired by its abuse.

He read a great deal – more than he had ever read. Studying the short stories and novels of the men of the sixties he was surprised by their insistence on the various ways their characters saluted one another. Meditating over the thraldom of Russian thought, that eternal tributary to this or that Golden Horde, he was carried away by weird comparisons. Thus, in paragraph 146 of the censorship code for 1826, in which authors were enjoined to 'uphold chaste morals and not to replace them solely by beauty of the imagination', one had only to replace 'chaste' by 'civic' or some such word in order to get the private censorship code of the radical critics; and similarly, when the reactionary Bulgarin informed the government in a confidential letter of his readiness to colour the characters in the novel he was writing to suit the censor, one could not help thinking of the later fawning that even such authors as Turgenev indulged in before the Court of Progressive Public Opinion; and the radical Shchedrin, using a cart shaft to fight with and ridiculing Dostoevski's sickness, or Antonovich, who called that author 'a whipped and expiring animal', were little different from right-winger Burenin, who persecuted the unfortunate poet Nadson. In the writings of another radical critic, Zaytsev, it was comical to find, forty years before Freud, the theory that 'all these aesthetic feelings and similar illusions "elevating us" are only modifications of the sexual instinct . . .'; this was the same Zaytsev who called Lermontov a 'disillusioned idiot', bred silkworms in leisured exile at Locarno (they never cocooned), and often crashed down the stairs from shortsightedness.

Fyodor tried to sort out the mishmash of philosophical ideas of the time, and it seemed to him that in the very roll call of names, in their burlesque consonance, there was manifested a kind of sin against thought, a mockery of it, a blemish of the age, when some extravagantly praised Kant, others *Kont* (Comte), others again Hegel or Schlegel. And on the other hand he began to comprehend by degrees that such uncompromising radicals as Chernyshevski, with all their ludicrous and ghastly blunders, were, no matter how you looked at it, real heroes in their struggle with the governmental order of things (which was even more noxious and more vulgar than was their own fatuity in the realm of literary criticism), and that other oppositionists, the liberals or the Slavophiles, who risked less, were by the same token worth less than these iron squabblers.

He sincerely admired the way Chernyshevski, an enemy of capital punishment, made deadly fun of the poet Zhukovski's infamously benign and meanly sublime proposal to surround executions with a mystic secrecy (since, in public, he said, the condemned man brazenly puts on a bold face, thus bringing the law into disrepute) so that those attending the hanging would not see but would only hear solemn church hymns from behind a curtain, for an execution should be moving. And while reading this Fyodor recalled his father saying that innate in every man is the feeling of something insuperably abnormal about the death penalty, something like the uncanny reversal of action in a looking glass that makes everyone left-handed: not for nothing is everything reversed for the executioner: the horse-collar is put on upside down when the robber Razin is taken to the scaffold; wine is poured for the headsman not with a natural turn of the wrist but backhandedly; and if, according to the Swabian code, an insulted actor was permitted to seek satisfaction by striking the *shadow* of the offender, in China, it was precisely an actor – a shadow – who fulfilled the duties of the executioner, all responsibility being as it were lifted from the world of men and transformed into the inside-out one of mirrors.

He clearly sensed a deception on a governmental scale in the actions of the 'Tsar-Liberator', who very soon got bored with all his business of granting freedoms; for it was the Tsar's boredom that gave the chief hue to reaction. After the manifesto the police fired into the people at the station of Bezdna – and Fyodor's epigrammatic vein was tickled by the tastless temptation to regard the further fate of Russia's rulers as the run between the stations Bezdna (Bottomless) and Dno (Bottom).

Gradually, as a result of all these raids on the past of Russian thought, he developed a new yearning for Russia that was less physical than before, a dangerous desire (with which he successfully struggled) to confess something to her and to convince her of something. And while piling up knowledge, while extracting his finished creation out of this mountain, he remembered something else: a pile of stones on an Asian pass; warriors going on campaign each placed a stone there; on the way back each took a stone from the pile; that which was left represented forever the number of those fallen in battle. Thus in a pile of stones Tamerlane foresaw a monument.

By winter he had already got into the writing of it, having passed imperceptibly from accumulation to creation. Winter, like most memorable winters and likc all winters introduced for the sake of a narrational phrase, turned out (they always 'turn out' in such cases) to be cold. At his evening trysts with

Zina in an empty little café where the counter was painted an indigo colour and where dark blue gnomelike lamps, miserably posing as vessels of cosiness, glowed on six or seven little tables, he read her what he had written during the day and she listened, her painted lashes lowered, leaning on one elbow, playing with a glove or a cigarette case. Sometimes the proprietor's dog would come up, a fat mongrel bitch with low-hanging bubs, and would place its head on Zina's knee, and beneath the stroking and smiling hand that smoothed back the skin on its silky round forehead, the dog's eyes would take a Chinese slant, and when she was given a lump of sugar, she would take it, waddle in a leisurely manner into a corner, roll up there and very loudly start crunching. 'Wonderful, but I'm not sure you can say it like that in Russian,' said Zina sometimes, and after an argument he would correct the expression she had questioned. Chernyshevski she called Chernysh for short and got so used to considering him as belonging to Fyodor, and partly to her, that his actual life in the past appeared to her as something of a plagiarism. Fyodor's idea of composing his biography in the shape of a ring, closed with the clasp of an apocryphal sonnet (so that the result would be not the form of a book, which by its finiteness is opposed to the circular nature of everything in existence, but a continuously curving, and thus infinite sentence), seemed at first to her to be incapable of embodiment on flat, rectangular paper – and so much the more was she overjoyed when she noticed that nevertheless a circle was being formed. She was completely unconcerned whether or not the author clung assiduously to historical truth – she took that on trust, for if it were not thus it would simply not have been worth writing the book. A deeper truth, on the other hand, for which he alone was responsible and which he alone could find, was for her so important that the least clumsiness or fogginess in his words seemed to be the germ of a falsehood, which had to be immediately exterminated. Gifted with a most flexible memory, which twined like ivy around what she perceived, Zina by repeating such word-combinations as she particularly liked ennobled them with her own secret convolution, and whenever Fyodor for any reason changed a turn of phrase which she had remembered, the ruins of the portico stood for a long time on the golden horizon, reluctant to disappear. There was an extraordinary grace in her responsiveness which imperceptibly served him as a regulator, if not as a guide. And sometimes when at least three customers had gathered, an old lady pianist in pince-nez would sit at the upright piano in the corner and play Offenbach's Barcarolle as a march.

He was already approaching the end of his work (the hero's birth, to be precise) when Zina said it would not hurt him to relax and therefore on Saturday they would go together to a fancy-dress ball at the house of an artist friend of hers. Fyodor was a bad dancer, could not stand German bohemians and moreover refused point-blank to *put fantasy in a uniform,* which is what in effect masked balls do. They compromised on his wearing a half mask and a dinner jacket that had been made about four years previously and not worn more than four times in the interim. 'And I'll go as a—' she began dreamily, but cut herself short. 'Only not as a boyar maiden and not as Columbine, I beg you,' said Fyodor. 'That would be just like me,' said she, scornfully. 'Oh, I assure you it's terribly gay,' she added tenderly, to dissipate his gloom. 'Why, after all we'll be all alone in the crowd. I so want to go! We'll be the whole night together and no one will know who you are, and I've thought myself up a costume specially for you.' He conscientiously imagined her with a naked tender back and pale bluish arms – but here all kinds of excited bestial faces slipped through illegally, the coarse trash of noisy German revels; bad liquor inflamed his gullet, he belched from the chopped-egg sandwiches; but he again concentrated his thoughts, revolving to the music, on Zina's transparent temple vein. 'Of course it'll be gay, of course we'll go,' he said with conviction.

It was decided that she should set off at nine and he would follow an hour later. Cramped by the time limit, he did not sit down to work after supper but fiddled around with a new émigré magazine where Koncheyev was twice mentioned fleetingly, and these casual references, which implied the poet's general recognition, were more valuable than even the most favourable review: only six months ago this would have provoked in him what Pushkin's envious Salieri felt, but now he himself was amazed by his own indifference to another's fame. He looked at his watch and slowly began to change. He unearthed his drowsy-looking dinner jacket, and lapsed into thought. Still meditating, he took out a starched shirt, put his evasive collar studs in, climbed into it, shivering from its rigid chill. Again was motionless for a moment, then automatically pulled on his black trousers with a stripe, and remembering that he had made up his mind only that morning to cross out the last of the sentences he had written the previous day, he bent over the already heavily corrected page. As he read the sentence over, he wondered – should he leave it intact after all; made an insertion mark, wrote in an additional adjective, froze over it – and swiftly crossed out the whole sentence. But to leave the paragraph in that condition, i.e., its construction hanging over a precipice with a boarded window and a crumbling porch, was a physical impossibility. He examined his notes for this part and suddenly – his pen stirred and started to fly. When he looked again at his watch it was three in the morning, he had the chills, and everything in the room was dim from tobacco smoke. Simultaneously he heard the click of the American lock. His door was ajar, and as she passed by it through the hall, Zina caught sight of him, pale, with mouth wide open, in an unbuttoned starched shirt with suspenders trailing on the floor, pen in hand and the half-mask on his desk showing black against the whiteness of paper. She locked herself in her room with a bang and everything again grew quiet. 'That's a fine mess,' said Fyodor in a low voice. 'What have I done?' Thus he never found out what dress Zina had gone in; but the book was finished.

A month later, on a Monday, he took the fair copy to Vasiliev, who as early as last autumn, knowing of his investigations, had half offered to have the *Life of Chernyshevski* published by the house attached to the *Gazeta*. The following Wednesday Fyodor was again there, chatting quietly with old Stupishin, who used to wear bedroom slippers at the office. Suddenly the study door opened and filled with the bulk of Vasiliev, who looked blackly at Fyodor for a moment, and then said impassively: 'Be so good as to come in,' and moved to one side for him to slip through.

'Well, have you read it?' asked Fyodor as he took a seat across the table.

'I have,' replied Vasiliev in a gloomy bass.

'Personally,' said Fyodor briskly, ' I would like it to come out this spring.'

'Here's your manuscript,' said Vasiliev suddenly, knitting his brows and handing him the folder. 'Take it. There can be no question of my being party to its publication. I assumed that this was a serious work, and it turns out to be a reckless, anti-social, mischievous improvisation. I am amazed at you.'

'Well, that's nonsense, you know,' said Fyodor.

'No, my dear sir, it's not nonsense,' roared Vasiliev, irately fingering the objects on his desk, rolling a rubber stamp, changing the positions of meek books 'for review', conjoined accidentally, with no hopes for permanent happiness. 'No, my dear sir! There are certain traditions of Russian public life which the honourable writer does not dare to subject to ridicule. I am absolutely indifferent to whether you have talent or not, I only know that to lampoon a man whose works and sufferings have given sustenance to millions of Russian intellectuals is unworthy of any talent. I know that you won't listen to me, but nevertheless [and Vasiliev, grimacing with pain, clutched at his heart] I beg you as a friend not to try to publish this thing, you will wreck your literary career, mark my words, everyone will turn away from you.'

'I prefer the backs of their heads,' said Fyodor.

That night he was invited to the Chernyshevskis, but Alexandra Yakovlevna put him off at the last minute: her husband was 'down with flu' and 'ran a high temperature'. Zina had gone to the cinema with someone so that he only met her the next evening. ' "Kaput on the first try," as your stepfather would put it,' he said in reply to her question about the manuscript and (as they used to write in the old days) briefly recounted his conversation at the editorial office. Indignation, tenderness toward him, the urge to help him immediately, found expression with her in a burst of enterprising energy. 'Oh, *that's* how it is!' she exclaimed. 'All right. I'll get the money for publication, that's what I'll do.'

'For the baby a meal, for the father a coffin,' he said (transposing the words in a line of Nekrasov's poem about the heroic wife who sells her body to get her husband his supper), and another time she would have taken offence at this bold joke.

She borrowed somewhere a hundred and fifty marks and added seventy of her own which she had put away for winter – but this sum was insufficient, and Fyodor decided to write to Uncle Oleg in America, who regularly helped his mother and who also used occasionally to send a few dollars to him. The composition of this letter was put off from day to day, however, just as he put off, in spite of Zina's exhortations, an attempt to get his book printed serially by an émigré literary magazine in Paris, or to interest the publishing house there which had brought out Koncheyev's verses. In her free time she undertook to type the manuscript in the offices of a relation of hers and from him she collected another fifty marks. She was angered by Fyodor's inertia – a consequence of his hatred for any practical affairs. He in the meantime occupied himself lightheartedly with composing chess problems, dreamily went about his lessons, and rang up Mme Chernyshevski daily: Alexander Yakovlevich's flu had changed into an acute inflammation of the kidneys. One day in the Russian bookshop he noticed a tall, portly gentleman with a large-featured face, wearing a black felt hat (a strand of chestnut hair falling from under it) who glanced at him affably and even with a kind of encouragement. Where have I met him? thought Fyodor quickly, trying not to look. The other approached and offered his hand, generously, naïvely, defencelessly spreading it wide, spoke . . . and Fyodor remembered: it was Busch, who two and a half years ago had read his play at that literary circle. Recently he had published it and now, pushing Fyodor with his hip, nudging him with his elbow, an infantine smile trembling on his noble, always slightly sweaty face, he produced a wallet, from the wallet an envelope and from the envelope a clipping – a pitiful little review which had appeared in the Rigan émigré newspaper.

'Now,' he said with awesome weightiness, 'this Thing is also coming out in German. Moreover I am now working on a Novel.'

Fyodor tried to get away from him, but the latter left the shop with him and suggested they should go together, and since Fyodor was on his way to a lesson, and thus was tied to a definite route, all he could do to try and save himself from Busch was to quicken his step, but this so speeded up his companion's speech that he slowed down again in horror.

'My Novel,' said Busch, looking into the distance and stretching aside his hand, with a rattling cuff protruding from the sleeve of his black overcoat, in order to stop Fyodor Konstantinovich (the overcoat, the black hat and the strand of hair gave him the appearance of a hypnotist, a chess maestro or a musician), 'my Novel is the tragedy of a philosopher who has discovered the absolute formula. He starts speaking and speaks thus [Busch, like a conjurer, plucked a notebook out of the air and began to read on the move]: "One has to be a complete ass not to deduct from the fact of the atom the fact that the universe itself is merely an atom, or, it would be truer to say, some kind of trillionth of an atom. This was realized with his intuition already by that genius Blaise Pascal. But let us proceed, Louisa! [At the sound of this name Fyodor started and clearly heard the sounds of the German grenadier march: 'Fa-are-well, Louisa! wipe your eyes and don't cry; not every bullet kills a good guy,' and this subsequently continued to sound as if passing under the window of Busch's subsequent words.] Exert, my dear, your attention. First, let me give a fanciful example. Let us assume that a certain physicist has managed to track down, out of the absolute-unthinkable sum of atoms out of which the All is composited, that fatal atom with which our reasoning is concerned. We are supposing that he has brought his splitting down to the least essence of that very atom, at which moment the Shadow of a Hand [the physicist's hand!] falls on our universe with catastrophic results, because the universe is but the final fraction of one, I think, central atom, of those it consists of. It's not easy to understand, but if you understand this you will understand everything. Out of the prison of mathematics! The whole is equal to the smallest part of the whole, the sum of the parts is equal to one part of the sum. This is the secret of the world, the formula of absolute-infinity, but having made such a discovery, the human personality can no longer go on walking and talking. Shut your mouth, Louisa!" That's him talking to a cutie, his lady friend,' added Busch with good-natured indulgence, shrugging one mighty shoulder.

'If you're interested, I can read it to you from the beginning sometime,' he continued. 'The theme is colossal. And you, may I ask, what are you doing?'

'I?' said Fyodor with a slight smile. 'I have also written a book, a book about the critic Chernyshevski, only I can't find a publisher for it.'

'Ah! The popularizator of German materialism – of Hegel's traducers, the grobianistic philosophers! Very honourable. I am more and more convinced that my publisher will take your work with pleasure. He's a comic personality and for him literature is a closed book. But I have the position of adviser to him and he will hear me out. Give me your telephone number. I'll be seeing him tomorrow – and if he agrees in principle, then I'll skim through your manuscript, and I dare to hope that I'll recommend it in the most flattering manner.'

What rot, thought Fyodor and therefore was extremly surprised when the next day the kind soul did in fact ring. The publisher turned out to be a plumpish man with a sad nose, reminding him somewhat of Alexander Yakovlevich, with the same red ears and a stipple of black hairs along each side of his polished baldpate. His list of published books was small, but remarkably eclectic: translations of some German psychoanalytic novels done by an uncle of Busch's; *The Poisoner* by Adelaida Sventozarov; a collection of funny stories; an anonymous poem entitled 'I'; but among this trash there were two or three genuine books, such as, for example, the wonderful *Stairway to the Clouds* by Hermann Lande and also his *Metamorphoses of Thought*. Busch reacted to the *Life of Chernyshevski* as to a good slap at Marxism (to the delivery of which Fyodor had not given the least thought when writing his work) and at the second meeting the publisher, evidently the nicest of men, promised to publish the book by Easter; i.e., in a month's time. He gave no advance and offered five per cent on the first thousand copies, but on the other hand he raised the author's percentage to thirty on the second thousand, which seemed to Fyodor both just and generous. However, he was completely indifferent to this side of the business (and to the fact that the sales of émigré writers seldom reached five hundred copies). Other emotions overwhelmed him. Having shaken the moist hand of radiant Busch he emerged onto the street like a ballerina flying out onto the fluorescent stage. The drizzle seemed a dazzling dew, happiness stood in his throat, rainbow nimbi trembled around the street-lamps, and the book he had written talked to him at the top of its voice, accompanying him the whole time like a torrent on the other side of a wall. He headed for the office where Zina worked; opposite that black building, with benevolent-looking windows inclined toward him, he found the pub where they were to meet.

'Well, what news?' she asked, entering quickly.

'No, he won't take it,' said Fyodor watching, with delighted attention, her face cloud as he toyed with his power over it and anticipated the exquisite light he was about to summon.

4

Alas! In vain historians pry and probe:
The same wind blows, and in the same live robe
Truth bends her head to fingers curved cupwise;

And with a woman's smile and a child's care
Examines something she is holding there
Concealed by her own shoulder from our eyes.

A sonnet, apparently barring the way, but perhaps, on the contrary, providing a secret link which would explain everything – if only man's mind could withstand that explanation. The soul sinks into a momentary dream – and now, with the peculiar theatrical vividness of those risen from the dead they come out to meet us: Father Gavriil, a long staff in his hand, wearing a silk, garnet-red chasuble, with an embroidered sash across his big stomach; and with him, already illuminated by the sun, an extremely attractive little boy – pink, awkward, delicate. They draw near. Take off your hat, Nikolay. Hair with a russet glint, freckles on his little forehead, and in his eyes the angelic clarity characteristic of nearsighted children. Afterwards (in the quiet of their poor distant parishes) priests with names derived from Cypress, Paradise, and Golden Fleece recalled his bashful beauty with some surprise: the cherub, alas, proved to be pasted on tough gingerbread which was too hard for many to bite into.

Having greeted us, Nikolay again dons his hat, a grey, downy top hat, and quietly withdraws, very sweet in his homemade little coat and nankeen breeches, while his father, a kindly cleric who dabbles in horticulture, entertains us with talk of Saratov cherries, plums and pears. A whirl of torrid dust veils the picture.

As is invariably noted at the beginning of positively all literary biographies, the little boy was a glutton for books. He excelled in his studies. For his first writing exercise he painstakingly reproduced: 'Obey your sovereign, honour him and submit to his laws,' and the compressed ball of his index finger thus remained ink-stained forever. Now the thirties are over and the forties have begun.

At the age of sixteen he had a sufficient grasp of languages to read Byron, Eugène Sue and Goethe (being ashamed to the end of his days of his barbarous pronunciation) and already had a command of seminary Latin, owing to his father's being an educated man. Besides this he took Polish with a certain Sokolovski, while a local orange merchant taught him Persian – and also tempted him with the use of tobacco.

Upon entering the Saratov seminary, he showed himself there to be a meek pupil and was never once flogged. He was nicknamed 'the little toff', although in fact he was not averse to general fun and games. In the summer he played dibs and took pleasure in bathing; never did he learn to swim, however, nor to fashion sparrows out of clay, nor to make nets for catching tiddlers: the holes came out uneven and the threads got tangled – fish are harder to catch than human souls (but even the souls later escaped through the rents). In winter, in the snowy darkness, a rowdy gang used to tear downhill in a huge, horse-drawn, flat sled while roaring out dactylic hexameters – and the chief of police, in his nightcap, would pull aside his curtain and grin encouragingly, happy that the seminarists' frolics would frighten off any night burglars.

He would have been a priest, like his father, and would have reached, very likely, a high rank – but for the regrettable incident with Major Protopopov. This was a local landowner, a bon vivant, a wencher, a dog lover: it was his son that Father Gavriil too hastily recorded in the parish register as illegitimate; meanwhile, it transpired that the wedding had been celebrated – without fuss, true, but honourably – forty days before the child's birth. Dismissed from his post as member of the consistory, Father Gavriil fell into such a depression that his hair turned grey. 'That's how they reward the labours of poor priests,' repeated his wife wrathfully – and it was decided to give Nikolay a secular education. What later became of the young Protopopov – did he find out one day that because of him . . . ? Was he seized with a sacred thrill. . . . ? Or tiring rapidly of the pleasures of ebullient youth . . . withdrawing. . . . ?

Incidentally: the landscape which not long before had with wondrous languor unfolded along the passage of the immortal *brichka*; all that Russian viatic lore, so untrammelled as to bring tears to the eyes; all the humbleness that gazes from the field, from a hillock, from between oblong clouds; that suppliant, expectant beauty which is ready to rush toward you at the slightest sigh and share your tears; in short, the landscape hymned by Gogol passed unnoticed before the eyes of the eighteen-year-old Nikolay Gavrilovich, who with his mother was travelling in a carriage drawn by their own horses from Saratov to St Petersburg. The whole way he kept reading a book. It goes without saying that he preferred his 'war of words' to the 'corn ears bowing in the dust'.

Here the author remarked that in some of the lines he had already composed there continued without his knowledge a fermentation, a growth, a swelling of the pea, or, more precisely: at one or another point the further development of a given theme became manifest – the theme of the 'writing exercises' for example: already during his student days Nikolay Gavrilovich was copying out for his own benefit Feuerbach's 'Man is what he eats' (it comes out smoother in German and even better with the help of the spelling now accepted in Russian: *chelovek est' to chto est*). We remark also that the theme of 'nearsightedness' develops, too, beginning with the fact that as a child he knew only those faces which he kissed and could see only four out of the seven stars of the Great Bear. His first – copper – spectacles donned at the age of twenty. A teacher's silver spectacles bought for six roubles so as to distinguish his students in the Cadet School. The gold spectacles of a moulder of public opinion put on in the days when *The Contemporary* was penetrating to the most fabulous depths of the Russian countryside. Again copper spectacles, bought at a little trading post beyond Lake Baikal, where they also sold felt boots and vodka. The yearning for spectacles in a letter to his sons from Yakutsk territory – requesting lenses for such and such vision (with a line marking the distance at which he could make out writing). Here the theme of spectacles dims for a time. . . . Let us follow another theme – that of 'angelic clarity'. This is how it develops subsequently: Christ died for mankind because he loved mankind, which I also love, for which I shall also die. 'Be a second Saviour,' his best friend advises him – and how he glows – oh, timid! Oh, weak! (an almost Gogolian exclamation mark appears fleetingly in his student diary). But the 'Holy Ghost' must be replaced by 'Common Sense'. Is not poverty the mother of vice? Christ should first have shod everybody and crowned them with flowers and only then have preached morality. Christ the Second would begin by putting an end to material want (aided here by the machine which we have invented). And strange to say, but . . . something came true – yes, it was as if something came true. His biographers mark his thorny path with evangelical signposts (it is well known that the more leftist the Russian commentator the greater is his weakness for expressions like 'the Golgotha of the revolution'). Chernyshevski's passions began when he reached Christ's age. Here the role of Judas was filled by Vsevolod Kostomarov; the role of Peter by the famous poet Nekrasov, who declined to visit the gaoled man. Corpulent Herzen, ensconced in London, called Chernyshevski's pillory column 'The companion piece of the Cross'. And in a famous Nekrasov iambic there was more about the Crucifixion, about the fact that Chernyshevski had been 'sent to remind the earthly kings of Christ'. Finally, when he was completely dead and they were washing his body, that thinness, that steepness of the ribs, that *dark pallor* of the skin and those long toes vaguely reminded one of his intimates of 'The Removal from the Cross' – by Rembrandt, is it? But even this isn't the end of the theme: there is still the posthumous outrage, without which no holy life is complete. Thus the silver wreath with the inscription on its ribbon TO THE APOSTLE OF TRUTH FROM THE INSTITUTE OF HIGHER EDUCATION OF THE CITY OF KHARKOV was stolen five years later from the ironworked chapel; moreover the cheerful sacrilegist broke the dark-red glass and scratched his name and the date on the frame with a splinter of it. And then a third theme is ready to unfold – and to unfold quite fantastically if we don't keep an eye on it: the theme of 'travelling', which can lead to God knows what – to a tarantass with a gendarme in azure uniform, and even more – to a Yakutsk sled harnessed to half a dozen dogs. Goodness, that Vilyuisk captain of the police is also called Protopopov! But for the time being all is very pacific. The comfortable travelling carriage rolls on, Nikolay's mother Eugenia Egorovna dozes with a handkerchief spread over her face, while her son reclines beside her reading a book – and a hole in the road loses its meaning of hole, becoming merely a typographical unevenness, a jump in the line – and now again the words pass evenly by, the trees pass by and their shadow passes over the pages. And here at last is St Petersburg.

He liked the blueness and transparency of the Neva – what an abundance of water in the capital, how pure that water was (he quickly ruined his stomach on it); but he particularly liked the orderly distribution of the water, the sensible canals: how nice when you can join this with that and that with this; and derive the idea of good from that of conjunction. In the mornings he would open his window and with a reverence still heightened by the general cultural side of the spectacle, would cross himself facing the shimmering glitter of the cupolas; St Isaac's, in the process of construction, was all in scaffolding – we'll write a letter to Father about the 'fired gold leaf' of the domes, and one to Grandmother about the locomotive. . . . Yes, he had actually seen a train – to which poor Belinski (our hero's predecessor) had so recently looked forward when, with wasted lungs, ghastly, shivering, he had been wont to contemplate for hours through tears of civic joy the construction of the first railway station – that same station, again, on whose platform a few years later the half-demented Pisarev (our hero's successor), wearing a black mask and green gloves, was to slash a handsome rival over the face with a riding crop.

In my work (said the author), ideas and themes continue to grow without my knowledge or consent – some of them fairly crookedly – and I know what is wrong: 'the machine' is getting in the way; I must fish this awkward spillikin out of an already composed sentence. A great relief. The subject is perpetual motion.

The pottering with perpetual motion lasted about five years, until 1853, when – already a schoolteacher and a betrothed man – he burned the letter with diagrams that he had once prepared when he feared he would die (from that fashionable disease, aneurysm) before endowing the world with the blessing of eternal and extremely cheap motion. In the descriptions of his absurd experiments and in his commentaries on them, in this mixture of ignorance and ratiocination, one can already detect that barely perceptible but fatal flaw which gave his later utterances something like a hint of quackery; an imaginary hint, for we must keep in mind that the man was as straight and firm as the trunk of an oak, 'the most honest of the honest' (his wife's expression); but such was the fate of Chernyshevski that everything turned against him: no matter what subject he touched there would come to light – insidiously, and with the most taunting inevitability – something that was completely opposed to his conception of it. He, for instance, was for synthesis, for the force of attraction, for the living link (reading a novel he would kiss the page where the author appealed to the reader) and what was the answer he got? Disintegration, solitude, estrangement. He preached soundness and commonsense in everything – and as if in response to someone's mocking summons, his destiny was cluttered with blockheads, crackbrains and madmen. For everything he was returned 'a negative hundredfold', in Strannolyubski's happy phrase, for everything he was back-kicked by his own dialectic, for everything the gods had their revenge on him; for his sober views on the unreal roses of poets, for doing good by means of novel writing, for his belief in knowledge – and what unexpected, what cunning forms this revenge assumed! What if, he muses in 1848, one attached a pencil to a mercury thermometer, so that it moved according to the changes in temperature? Starting with the premise that temperature is something eternal – But excuse me, who is this, who is this making laborious notes in cipher of his laborious speculations? A young inventor, no doubt, with an infallible eye, with an innate ability to fasten, to attach, to solder inert parts together, having them give birth in result to the miracle of movement – and lo! a loom is already humming, or an engine with a tall smokestack and a top-hatted driver is overtaking a thoroughbred trotter. Right here is the chink with the nidus of revenge, since this sensible young man, who – let us not forget – is only concerned with the good of all mankind, has eyes like a mole, while his blind, white hands move on a different plane from his faulty but obstinate and muscular mind. Everything that he touches falls to pieces. It is sad to read in his diary about the appliances of which he tries to make use – scale-arms, bobs, corks, basins – and nothing revolves, or if it does, then according to unwelcome laws, in the reverse direction to what he wants: an eternal motor going in reverse – why, this is an absolute nightmare, the abstraction to end all abstractions, infinity with a minus sign, plus a broken jug into the bargain.

We – consciously – have flown ahead; let us return to that jog-trot, to that rhythm of Nikolay's life to which our ear had already become attuned.

He chose the philogical faculty. His mother went to pay her respects to the professors in order to cajole them: her voice would acquire flattering overtones and gradually she would begin to wax tearful and blow her nose. Out of all the St Petersburg products she was most struck by articles made of crystal. Finally 'they' (the respectful pronoun he used in speaking of his mother – that wonderful Russian plural which, as later his own aesthetics, 'attempts to express quality by quantity') returned to Saratov. For the road she bought herself an enormous turnip.

At first Nikolay Gavrilovich went to live with a friend, but subsequently he shared an apartment with a cousin and her husband. The plans of these apartments, as of all his other abodes, were drawn by him in his letters. The exact definition of the relations between objects always fascinated him and therefore he loved plans, columns of figures and visual representations of things, the more so since his agonizingly circumstantial style could in no way compensate for the art of literary portrayal, which for him was unattainable. His letters to his relatives are the letters of a model youth: instead of imagination he was prompted by his obliging good nature as to what another would relish. The reverend liked all sorts of events – humorous or horrible incidents – and his son carefully fed him with them over a period of several years. We find mentioned therein Izler's entertainments, his replicas of Carlsbad – *minerashki* (miniature spas) at which venturesome St Petersburg ladies used to ascend in captive balloons; the tragic case of the rowboat overturned by a steamer on the Neva, one of the victims being a colonel with a large family; the arsenic intended for mice, which got into some flour and poisoned over a hundred people; and of course, of course the new fad, table-turning – all gullibility and fraud in the opinion of both correspondents.

Just as in the sombre Siberian years one of his principal epistolary chords was the assurance addressed to his wife and children – always on the same high, but not quite correct note – that he had plenty of money, please don't send money, so in his youth he begs his parents not to worry about him and contrives to live on twenty roubles a month; of this, about two and a half roubles went on white bread and on pastries (he could not bear tea alone, just as he could not bear reading alone; i.e., he invariably used to chew something with a book: over gingerbread biscuits he read *The Pickwick Papers,* over zwiebacks, the *Journal des Débats*), while candles and pens, boot polish and soap came to a rouble: he was, let us note, unclean in his habits, untidy, and at the same time had matured grossly; add to this a bad diet, perpetual colic plus an uneven struggle with the desires of the flesh, ending in a secret compromise – and the result was that he looked sickly, his eyes had dimmed, and of his youthful beauty nothing remained except perhaps that expression of a kind of wonderful helplessness which fugitively lit up his face when a man he respected had treated him well ('he was kind to me – a youth timorous and submissive,' he later wrote of the scholar Irinarch Vvedenski, with a pathetic Latin intonation: *animula vagula, blandula . . .*); he himself never doubted his unattractiveness, accepting the thought of it but fighting shy of mirrors: even so, when preparing to make a visit sometimes, especially to his best friends, the Lobodovskis, or wishing to ascertain the cause of a rude stare, he would peer gloomily at his reflection, would see the russety fuzz which looked as if stuck onto his cheeks, count the ripe pimples – and then begin to squeeze them, and at that so brutally that afterwards he did not dare to show himself.

The Lobodovskis! His friend's wedding had produced on our twenty-year-old hero one of those extraordinary impressions, which in the middle of the night cause a youth to sit down in nothing but his underwear to write his diary. This exciting wedding was celebrated on May 19, 1848; that same day sixteen years later, Chernyshevski's civil execution was carried out. A coincidence of anniversaries, a card index of dates. That is how fate sorts them in anticipation of the researcher's needs; a laudable economy of effort.

He felt joyful at this wedding. What is more, he derived a secondary joy from his basic one ('That means I am able to nourish a pure attachment to a woman') – yes, he was always doing his utmost to turn his heart so that one side was reflected in the glass of reason, or, as his best biographer, Strannolyubski, puts it: 'He distilled his feelings in the alembics of logic.' But who could have said that he was occupied at that moment with thoughts of love? Many years later in his flowery *Sketches from Life* this same Vasiliy Lobodovski made a careless error when he said that his best man at the wedding, the student 'Krush-edolin', looked as serious 'as if he were subjecting in his mind to an exhaustive analysis certain learned works from England that he had just read'.

French romanticism gave us the poetry of love, German romanticism the poetry of friendship. The young Chernyshevski's sentimentality was a concession to an epoch when friendship was magnanimous and moist. Chernyshevski cried willingly and often. 'Three tears rolled down,' he notes with characteristic accuracy in his diary – and the reader is tormented momentarily with the involuntary thought, can one have an odd number of tears, or is it only the dual nature of the source which makes us demand an even number? ' "Remind me not of foolish tears that many times I shed, alas, when my repose oppressive was," ' writes Nikolay Gavrilovich in his diary, addressing his wretched youth, and to the sound of Nekrasov's plebeian fhymery he really does shed a tear: 'At this spot in the manuscript there is the trace of a spilled tear,' comments his son Mihail in a footnote. The trace of another tear, far hotter, bitterer and more precious, has been preserved on his celebrated letter from the fortress; but Steklov's description of this second tear contains, according to Strannolyubski, certain inaccuracies – which will be discussed later. Then, in the days of his exile and especially in the Vilyuisk dungeon – But hold! the theme of tears is expanding beyond all reason . . . let us return to its point of departure. Now, for example, a funeral is being conducted for a student. In the light blue coffin lies a waxen youth. Another student, Tatarinov (who looked after him when he was ill but who had hardly known him before) bids him farewell: 'He looks long at him, kisses him, and looks again, endlessly . . .' The student Chernyshevski, jotting this down, is himself faint with tenderness; and Strannolyubski, commenting on these lines, suggests a parallel between them and the sorrowful fragment by Gogol, 'Nights at a Villa'.

But to tell the truth . . . young Chernyshevski's dreams in connection with love and friendship are not distinguished for their refinement – and the more he yields to them the more clearly comes out their fault – their rationality; he was able to bend the silliest daydream into a logical horseshoe. Musing in detail over the fact that Lobodvski, whom he sincerely admires, is developing tuberculosis, and that in consequence Nadezhda Yegorovna will remain a young widow, helpless and destitute, he pursues a particular aim. He needs a dummy image in order to justify his falling in love with her, so he substitutes for it the urge to assist a poor woman, or in other words sets his love upon a utilitarian foundation. For otherwise the palpitations of a fond heart are not to be explained by the limited means of that rough-hewn materialism, to whose blandishments he had already hopelessly succumbed. And then, only yesterday, when Nadezhda Yegorovna 'was sitting without a shawl, and of course her "missionary" [a plain dress] was slit a little at the front and one could see a certain part just below her neck' (a turn of phrase bearing an unusual resemblance to the idiom of literary characters in Zoshchenko's impersonations of Soviet-bred Philistine simpletons), he had asked himself with honest anxiety whether he would have looked at 'that part' in the early days after his friend's wedding. And so, gradually burying his friend in his dreams, with a sigh, with an air of unwillingness and as if submitting to a duty, he sees himself deciding to marry the young widow – a melancholy union, a chaste union (and all these dummy images are repeated even more fully in his diary when he subsequently obtains the hand of Olga Sokratovna). The actual beauty of the poor woman was still in doubt, and the method which Chernyshevski selected in order to verify her charms predetermined the whole of his later attitude to the concept of beauty.

At first he established the best specimen of grace in Nadezhda Yegorovna: chance provided him with a living picture in an idyllic vein, albeit somewhat cumbersome. 'Vasiliy Petrovich knelt on a chair facing its back, she approached and began to tilt the chair; she tilted it a little and then laid her little face against his chest . . . A candle stood on the tea table . . . and the light fell well enough on her; i.e., a half-light, because she was in her husband's shadow, but clear.' Nikolay Gavrilovich looked closely, trying to find something that would not be quite

right; he did not find any coarse features, but he still hesitated.
What should one do next? He was constantly comparing her features with the features of other women, but the defectiveness of his eyesight prevented the accumulation of the live specimens essential to a comparison. Willy-nilly he was forced to have recourse to the beauty apprehended and registered by others; i.e., to women's portraits. Thus from the very beginning the concept of art became for him – a myopic materialist (which in itself is an absurd combination) – something subsidiary and applied, and he was now able by experimental means to test something which love had suggested to him: the superiority of Nadezhda Yegorovna's beauty (her husband called her 'dearie' and 'dolly'), that is Life, to the beauty of all other 'female heads', that is Art ('Art'!).

On the Nevski Avenue poetic pictures were exhibited in the windows of Junker's and Daziaro's. Having studied them thoroughly he returned home and noted down his observations. Oh, what a miracle! The comparative method always provided the necessary result. The Calabrian charmer's nose in the engraving was so-so: 'Particularly unsuccessful was the glabella as well as the parts lying near the nose, on both sides of its bridge.' A week later, still uncertain whether the truth had been sufficiently tested, or else wishing to revel once again in the already familiar compliancy of the experiment, he went once more to the Nevski to see if there were not some new beauty in a shop window. On her knees in a cave, Mary Magdalene was praying before a skull and cross, and of course her face in the light of the lampad was very sweet, but how much better was Nadezhda Yegorovna's semi-illumined face! On a white terrace over the sea were two girls: a graceful blonde was sitting on a stone bench with a young man; they were kissing, while a graceful brunette kept a lookout, holding aside a crimson curtain 'which separated the terrace from the remaining parts of the house', as we remark in our diary, for we always like to establish what relation a given detail bears to its speculative environment. Naturally Nadezhda Yegorovna's little neck is far more pleasing. Hence comes an important conclusion: life is more pleasing (and therefore better) than painting, for what is painting, poetry, indeed all art, in its purest form? It is 'a crimson sun sinking into an azure sea'; it is picturesque folds in a dress; it is the 'rosy nuances which the shallow writer wastes on illuminating his glossy chapters'; it is garlands of flowers, fays, fauns, Phrynae . . . The farther it goes the cloudier it gets: the rubbishy idea grows. The luxury of feminine forms now implies luxury in the economic sense. The concept of 'fantasy' appears to Nikolay Gavrilovich in the shape of a transparent but ample-breasted Sylphide, corsetless and practically naked, who, playing with a light veil, flies down to the poetically poeticizing poet. A couple of columns, a couple of trees – not quite cypresses and not quite poplars – some kind of urn that holds little attraction for Nikolay Gavrilovich – and the supporter of pure art is sure to applaud. Contemptible fellow! Idle fellow! And indeed, rather than all this trash, how could one not prefer an honest description of contemporary manners, civic indignation, heart-to-heart jingles?

One can safely assume that during those minutes when he was glued to the shop windows his disingenuous master's dissertion, 'The Aesthetic Relations of Art to Reality', was composed in its entirety (it is no wonder that he subsequently wrote it right down, straight from the shoulder, in three nights; but it is more of a wonder how, even after a wait of six years, he nonetheless received a master's degree for it).

There were languorous and dim evenings when he lay supine on his dreadful leathern couch – a thing of lumps and rents with an inexhaustible (just pull) supply of horsehair – and 'my heart beat somehow wonderously from Michelet's first page, from Guizot's views, from thoughts of Nadezhda Yegorovna, and all this together', and then he would begin to sing off-key, in a ululant voice – he sang 'the song of Marguerite', simultaneously thinking of the Lobodvskis' relations with one another – and 'gently tears rolled from my eyes'. Suddenly he would rise from his couch with the decision to see her immediately; it was, we imagine, an October evening, clouds flew overhead, a sour stench came from the saddlers' and carriage-makers' workshops on the ground floors of houses painted a dreary yellow, and merchants in smocks and sheepskin coats, keys in hand, were already locking up their stores. One bumped into him but he passed quickly by. A ragged lamplighter, his hand-cart rumbling over the cobbles, was bringing lamp oil to a bleary lamp on a wooden post; he wiped the glass with an oily rag and moved on creakily to the next – a long way off. It was beginning to drizzle. Nikolay Gavrilovich flew along with the swift gait of a poor Gogolian character.

At night he was unable to sleep for a long time, tormented by the questions: would Vasiliy Petrovich Lobodovski manage to educate his wife sufficiently so that she might be a helper to him; and in order to stimulate his friend's feelings, should he not send, for example, an anonymous letter which would inflame her husband with jealousy? This already foretells the methods used by the heroes of Chernyshevski's novels. Similar, very carefully calculated but boyishly absurd schemes were thought up by exiled Chernyshevski, old man Chernyshevski, for attaining the most touching objectives. Look how this theme takes advantage of a momentary lack of attention and blossoms out. Halt, roll up again. There is, in fact, no need to go so far ahead. In the student diary one can find the following example of calculation: to print a false manifesto (proclaiming the abolition of conscription) in order to stir up the peasants by a trick; but then he himself abjured it, knowing as a dialectician and a Christian that an inner rot must eat away the whole of a created structure, and that a good end, justifying bad means, will only reveal its fatal kinship with them. Thus politics, literature, painting, even vocal art, were pleasantly entwined with Nikolay Gavrilovich's amorous emotions (we have returned to the point of departure).

How poor he was, how dirty and sloppy, how far removed from the lure of luxury . . . Attention! This was not so much proletarian chastity as the natural disregard with which an ascetic treats the prickle of a permanent hair shirt or the bite of sedentary fleas. Even a hair shirt, however, has at times to be repaired. We are present when the inventive Nikolay Gavrilovich contemplates darning his old trousers; he turned out to have no black thread, so what there was he undertook to soak in ink, an anthology of German verse was lying nearby, open at the beginning of William Tell. As a result of his waving the thread about (in order to dry it), several drops of ink fell on the page; the book did not belong to him. He found a lemon in a paper bag behind the window and attempted to get the blots out, but he only succeeded in dirtying the lemon, plus the windowsill where he had left the pernicious thread. Then he sought the aid of a knife and began to scrape (this book with the punctured poems is now in the Leipzig University library; unfortunately it has not been possible to ascertain how it got there). Ink, indeed, was the natural element of Chernyshevski (he literally bathed in it), who used to smear with it the cracks in his shoes when he was out of shoe polish; or else, in order to disguise a hole in his shoe, he would wrap his foot in a black tie. He broke crockery, soiled and spoiled everything. His love for materiality was not reciprocated. Subsequently, during penal servitude, he turned out to be not only incapable of doing any of a convict's special tasks but also was famous for his inability to do anything at all with his hands (at the same time he was constantly butting in to help his fellow man: 'Keep out of what does not concern you, you pillar of virtue,' the other convicts used to say gruffly). We have already glimpsed the confusedly hurrying youth being shoved on the street. He rarely grew angry; once, however, not without pride, he noted how he had revenged himself upon a young cabdriver who had caught him a blow with his shaft: wordlessly diving across the sled between the legs of two startled merchants, he tore out a tuft of his hair. In general, however, he was mild and open to insults, but secretly he felt himself capable of 'the most desperate, the most crazy' actions. On the side he began dabbling in propaganda by conversing with mujiks, with an occasional Neva ferryman or an alert pastry cook.

Enter the theme of pastry shops. They have seen a good deal in their time. It was there that Pushkin gulped down a glass of lemonade before his duel; there that Sophia Perovski and her companions each took a portion (of what? history did not quite manage to . . .) before proceeding to the Canal Quay to assassinate Alexander II. Our hero's youth had been bewitched by pastry shops, so that later, while on hunger strike in the fortress, he – in *What to Do?* – filled this or that speech with an involuntary howl of gastric lyricism: 'Do you have a pastry shop in the vicinity? I wonder if they have ready-made walnut tarts – to my taste they're the best of the tarts, Maria Alexeyevna.' But in contradiction to his future recollection, pastry shops and cafés seduced him not at all with their victuals – not with puff pastry made with rancid butter and not even with cherry-jam doughnuts; newspapers, gentlemen, newspapers, that is what they seduced him with! He tried various cafés – choosing such as had the most newspapers, or places where it was simpler and freer. Thus at Wolf's 'both last times, instead of his [read: Wolf's] white bread I had coffee with a [read: my] five-kopeck-twist, the last time not hiding' – i.e., the first of these last two times (the punctilious detail of his diary causes an itching in the cerebellum) he did, not knowing how they would accept pastry brought from outside. The place was warm and quiet and only now and then did a southwest little wind blowing from the newspaper pages cause the candle flames to vacillate ('disturbances have already touched the Russian entrusted to us' as the Tsar put it). 'May I have the *Indépendance belge?* Thank you.' The candle flames straighten up, it is quiet (but shots ring out on the Boulevard des Capucines, the *révolution* is nearing the Tuileries – and now Louis Philippe takes to flight: along the Avenue de Neuilly, in a fiacre).

And afterwards he was plagued by heartburn. In general he fed on all sorts of odds and ends, being indigent and impractical. Nekrasov's ditty is appropriate here:

> Since delicacies tougher
> Than tinware I would eat,
> Such bellyaches I'd suffer
> That death itself seemed sweet.
> I'd walk *miles* with that feeling,
> I'd read until day broke.
> My room had a low ceiling
> And goodness how I'd smoke!

Nikolay Gavrilovich, incidentally, did not smoke without reason – it was precisely Zhukov cigarettes that he used for relieving indigestion (and also toothache). His diary, particularly for the summer and autumn of 1849, contains a multitude of most exact references as to how and where he vomited. Besides smoking, he treated himself with rum and water, hot oil, English salts, centaury with bitter-orange leaves, and constantly, conscientiously, with a kind of gusto, employed the Roman method and probably he would ultimately have died of exhaustion if he (graduated as a candidate and retained at the university for advanced work) had not gone to Saratov.

And then in Saratov . . . But no matter how much we should like to lose no time in getting out of this back alley, to which talk of *patisseries* has led us, and cross to the sunny side of Nikolay Gavrilovich's life, still (for the sake of a certain hidden continuity) we must hang around here a little longer. Once, in great need, he rushed into a tenement house on the Gorohovaya (there follows a wordy description – with afterthoughts – of the house's location) and was already adjusting his dress when 'a girl in red' opened the door. Catching sight of his hand – he had wanted to hold the door – she let out a cry, 'as is usually the case'. The heavy creak of the door, its loose, rusty hook, the stink, the icy cold – all this is dreadful . . . and yet the queer fellow is quite prepared to debate with himself about true purity, noting with satisfaction that 'I didn't even try to discover whether she was good-looking'. When dreaming, on the other hand, he looked with a keener eye, and the contingency of sleep was kinder to him than his public destiny – but even her, how delighted he is that when in his dream he thrice kisses the gloved hand of 'an extremely fair-haired' lady (the mother of a presupposed pupil sheltering him in his dream, all this in the style of Jean-Jacques), he is unable to reproach himself for a single carnal thought. His memory, too, turned out to be keen-eyed when he recalled that circuitous young yearning for beauty. At the age of fifty in a letter from Siberia he evokes the angelic image of a girl he had once noticed in his youth at an exhibition of Industry and Agriculture; 'Now there was a certain aristocratic family walking along,' he narrates in his later, Biblically slow style. 'She appealed to me, this girl, verily she appealed to me . . . I walked alongside about three paces away and admired her . . . They belonged obviously to the highest society. Everyone saw this from their extraordinarily nice manners [there is a little Dickensian fly in this treacly pathos, as Strannolyubski would remark, but still we must not forget that this is being written by an old man half-crushed by penal servitude, as Steklov would justly put it]. The crowd gave way before them . . . I was quite free to walk at about three paces distance without taking my gaze off that girl [poor satellite!]. And this lasted for an hour or more.' (Oddly enough, exhibitions in general, for instance the London one of 1862 and the Paris one of 1889, had a strong effect on his fate; thus Bouvard and Pécuchet, when undertaking a description of the life of the Duke of Angoulême, were amazed by the role played in it . . . by bridges.)

It follows from all this that upon arriving in Saratov he could not help but fall in love with the twenty-year-old daughter of Doctor Sokrat Vasiliev, a gypsyish young lady with ear-rings hanging from the long lobes of her ears, which were half-concealed by folds of dark hair. A teasing, affected creature, 'the cynosure and ornament of provincial balls' (in the words of a nameless contemporary), she seduced and stupefied our clumsy virgin with the rustle of her sky-blue *Choux* and the melodiousness of her speech. 'Look, what a charming little arm,' she would say, stretching it out toward his misted glasses – a bare, dusky arm with a glistening bloom along it. He rubbed himself with attar of rosses and shaved bloodily. And what serious compliments he thought up! 'You should be living in Paris,' he said earnestly, having learned elsewhere that she was a 'democrat'; Paris for her, however, meant not the heart of science but the kingdom of strumpets, so that she was offended.

Before us is 'The Diary of my Relations with Her Who now Constitutes my Happiness'. The easily carried-away Steklov refers to this unique production (reminding one most of all of an extremely conscientious business report) as 'an exultant hymn of love'. The maker of the report draws up a project for declaring his love (which is accurately put into effect in February, 1853, and approved without delay) with points for and against marriage (he feared, for example, lest his restive spouse should take it into her head to wear male dress – in the manner of George Sand) and with an estimate of expenses when married, which contains absolutely everything – two stearine candles for the winter evenings, ten kopecks' worth of milk, the theatre; and at the same time he notifies his bride that in view of his way of thinking ('I am frightened neither by dirt not by [setting loose] drunken peasants with clubs, nor by slaughter') sooner or later he is 'sure to get caught', and for greater honesty he tells her about the wife of Iskander (Herzen), who being pregnant ('excuse me for going into such details'), upon hearing the news that her husband had been arrested in Italy and sent to Russia, 'fell dead'. Olga Sokratovna, as Aldanov might have added at this point, would not have fallen dead.

'If some day,' he wrote further, 'your name is stained by rumour, so that you cannot hope to have any husband . . . I will always be ready at one word from you to become your husband.' A chivalrous position, but based on far from chivalrous premises, and this characteristic turn leads us back at once to the familiar path of those earlier quasi fantasies of love, with his detailed thirst for self-sacrifice and the protective coloration of his compassion; which did not prevent him from having his pride smart when his bride warned him that she was not in love with him. His betrothal period had a German touch about it, with Schillerian songs, with a countinghouse of caresses: 'I undid at first two and then three buttons on her mantilla . . .' He urgently wanted her to place her foot (in its blunt-toed, grey bottekin stitched with coloured silk) on top of his head: his voluptuousness fed on symbols. Sometimes he read to her from Lermontov or Koltsov; he read poetry in the monotone of a Psalter lector.

But that which occupies the place of honour in the diary and which is particularly important for an understanding of much of Nikolay Gavrilovich's fate is his detailed account of the joke ceremonies with which the Saratov evenings were richly adorned. He could not polka nimbly and was a bad dancer of the *Grossvater*, but on the other hand he loved clowning, for even the penguin is not above a certain playfulness when he surrounds the female he courts with a ring of pebbles. Young people, as the phrase goes, would get together, and setting in motion a device of coquetry fashionable in those days and among that set, Olga Sokratovna would feed one or another of the guests at table from a saucer, like a child, while Nikolay Gavrilovich, miming jealously, would press a napkin to his heart and threaten to pierce his breast with a fork. In her turn she would pretend to be cross with him. He would then beg forgiveness (all this is horribly unfunny) and kiss the exposed parts of her arms, which she tried to hide, saying: 'How dare you!' The penguin assumed 'a serious, mournful look, because indeed it was possible that I had said something which would have given offence to another (i.e., a less bold girl) in her place'. On holidays he played tricks in the Temple of God, amusing his bride-to-be – but the Marxist commentator (i.e., Steklov) errs in seeing in this 'a healthy blasphemousness'. As the son of a priest Nikolay felt quite at home in church (thus the young prince who crowns a cat with his father's crown is decidedly not expressing any sympathy with popular government). Even less can one reproach him with mocking the Crusaders because he chalked a cross upon the back of everyone in turn: the mark of Olga Sokratovna's lovesick admirers. And after some more horseplay of the same sort there takes place – let us remember this – a mock duel with sticks.

Now a few years later when he was arrested, the police confiscated this old diary, which was written in an even hand with little striggles and was in a home-made code, with such abbreviations as *weakns! sillns!* (weakness, silliness), *lbrty, =ty* (liberty, equality) and *ch-k* (*chelovek,* man, —not Cheka, Lenin's police).

It was deciphered by people who were evidently incompetent, since they made a number of mistakes: for example, they read *dzrya* as *druzya* (friends) instead of *podozreniya* (suspicions), which twisted the sentence 'I shall arouse strong suspicions' into 'I have strong friends'. Chernyshevski grasped at this and began to maintain that the whole diary was the draft of a novel, a writer's invention, since he, he said, 'did not then have any influential friends, whereas this was obviously a character with powerful friends in the government'. It is not important (although the question is interesting in itself) whether he remembered the actual words in his diary exactly; what is important is that subsequently these words are given a curious alibi in *What to Do?* where their inner 'draft' rhythm is fully worked out (for instance in the song of one of the girls at the picnic: 'Oh maid, I dwell in gloomy woods, I am an evil friend, and perilous will be my life, and sad will be my end'). Lying in prison and knowing that the dangerous diary was being deciphered, he hastened to send the Senate 'examples of my manuscript drafts'; i.e., things which he had written exclusively in order to justify his diary, turning it ex post facto also into some draft for some novel. (Strannolyubski makes the direct supposition that it was this that impelled him to write in jail *What to Do?* – dedicated, by the way, to his wife, and begun on St Olga's day.) Therefore he could express his indignation over the fact that a judicial meaning was being given to scenes he had invented. 'I place myself and others in various positions and develop them quite fancifully . . . One "I" speaks of the possibility of arrest, another "I" is beaten with a stick in front of his fiancée.' He hoped, recalling this part of his old diary, that the detailed account of all sorts of parlour games would be regarded in itself as 'fanciful', since a sedate person would hardly . . . The sad thing was that in official circles he was considered not a sedate person, but precisely a buffoon, and it was in the very buffoonery of his journalistic devices in the *Contemporary* that they detected a fiendish infiltration of harmful ideas. And for a complete conclusion of the theme of the Saratov *petits-jeux* let us move on still farther, as far as the penal servitude, where their echo still lives in the playlets he composes for his comrades and especially in the novel *The Prologue* (written at the Alexandrov works in 1866), where there are both a student who unfunnily plays the fool, and a young beauty feeding her admirers. If we add to this that the protagonist (Volgin), when talking to his wife of the danger threatening him, refers to a warning he has given her before marriage, then it is impossible not to conclude that here finally we have a late piece of truth inserted by Chernyshevski to prop up his ancient assertion that his diary was merely an author's draft . . . for the very flesh of *The Prologue*, through all the dross of the feeble invention, now seems indeed to be a novelistic continuation of the Saratov jottings.

He was engaged to teach grammar and literature in the gymnasium there and proved to be an extremely popular teacher: in the unwritten classification which the boys applied swiftly and exactly to all the instructors, he was assigned to the type of nervous, absentminded, good-natured fellow who would easily lose his temper but who was also easily led off the subject – to fall at once into the soft paws of the class virtuoso (Fioletov junior in this case): at the critical moment when disaster already seemed inevitable for those who did not know the lesson, and there was only a short time until the caretaker rang his bell, he would ask a saving, delaying question: 'Nikolay Gavrilovich, there is something here about the Convention . . .' and forthwith Nikolay Gavrilovich would kindle, would go to the board and crushing the chalk would draw a plan of the hall where the National Convention of 1792-95 held its meetings (he was, as we know, a great expert at plans), and then, becoming more and more animated, he would also point out the places where the members of every party had sat.

During those years in the provinces he evidently behaved rather imprudently, frightening moderate people and God-fearing youths with the harshness of his views and the brashness of his ways. A slightly touched-up story has been preserved to the effect that the coffin had hardly been lowered at his mother's funeral before he lit up a cigarette and went off arm-in-arm with Olga Sokratovna, whom he married ten days later. But the upper-formers were swept away by him; some of them subsequently became attached to him with that rapturous ardour with which the young people of this didactic era clung to the teacher who was on the brink of becoming a leader; as far as 'grammar' was concerned, it must be said in all conscience that his charges never learned to handle commas. Were many of their number there forty years later at his funeral? According to some sources there were two, according to others, none at all. And when the funeral procession was about to stop by the Saratov school building in order to chant a litany, the director sent to inform the priest that this, you know, was undesirable, and accompanied by a stumbling, long-skirted October wind, the procession went by.

Much less successful than his career in Saratov was his teaching after his transfer to St Petersburg, where for several months during 1854 he taught in the Second Cadet Corps. The cadets behaved rowdily at his lessons. Shouting shrilly at the recreants only served to augment the confusion. You couldn't get very warmed up about Montagnards there! Once during an interval there was some noise in one of the classrooms. The officer on guard went in, barked, and left relative order behind him; in the meantime noise broke out in another classroom which (the interval was now over) Cherynshevski had just entered with his briefcase under his arm. Turning to the officer, he stopped him with a touch of his hand and said with restrained irritation, looking over his glasses: 'No, sir, you can't come here now.'

The officer felt insulted; the teacher refused to apologize and left. Thus began the theme of 'officers'.

The preoccupation with enlightenment, however, had now been formed in him for the rest of his life, and from 1853 to 1862 his journalistic activities were thoroughly imbued with an aspiration to feed the lean Russian reader with a diet of the most variegated information: the portions were huge, the bread supply inexhaustible, and nuts were provided on Sundays; for while stressing how important were the meat dishes of politics and philosophy, Nikolay Gavrilovich never forgot the sweet either. From his review of Amarantov's *Indoor Magic* it is clear that he had tried out this entertaining physics at home, and to one of the best tricks, namely 'carrying water in a sieve', he added his own amendment: like all popularizers, he had a weakness for such *Kunststücke;* nor must we forget that hardly a year had passed since by agreement with his father he had finally abandoned his idea for perpetual motion.

He loved to read almanacs, noting for the general information of the *contemporary* subscribers (1855): 'A guinea is six roubles and forty-seven and a half kopecks; the North American dollar is one silver rouble and thirty-one kopecks;' or else he would inform them that 'telegraph towers between Odessa and Ochakov have been built from donations'. A genuine encyclopedist, a kind of Voltaire – with the stress, true, on the first syllable – he unstintingly copied out thousands of pages (he was always ready to embrace the rolled-up carpet of any chance subject and unfold the whole of it before the reader), translated a whole library, cultivated all genres right down to poetry, and dreamed to the end of his life of composing 'a critical dictionary of ideas and facts' (which recalls Flaubert's caricature, that '*Dictionnaire des idées recues*' whose ironic epigraph – 'the majority is always right' – Chernyshevski would have adopted in all seriousness). On this subject he writes to his wife from the fortress, telling her with passion, sorrow, bitterness, about all the titanic works which he will still complete. Later, during all the twenty years of his Siberian isolation, he sought solace in this dream; but then, one year before his death, when he learned of Brockhaus's dictionary, he saw in it its realization. Then he yearned to translate it (otherwise 'they would stuff it with all sorts of rubbish, such as minor German artists'), deeming that such a work would be the crown of his entire life; it turned out that this, too, had been already undertaken.

In the beginning of his journalistic pursuits, writing on

Lessing (who had been born exactly a hundred years before him, and a resemblance to whom he himself admitted), he said: 'For such natures there exists a sweeter service than service to one's favourite science – and that is service to the development of one's people.' Like Lessing, he was accustomed to develop general ideas on the basis of particular cases. And remembering that Lessing's wife had died in childbirth, he feared for Olga Sokratovna, about whose first pregnancy he wrote to his father in Latin, just as, a hundred years before, Lessing had done.

Let us shed a little light here: on the twenty-first of December, 1853, Nikolay Gavrilovich intimated that according to knowledgeable women his wife had conceived. Her labour was difficult. It was a boy. 'My sweety-tweety,' cooed Olga Sokratovna over her first-born – very soon, however, becoming disenchanted with little Sasha. The doctors warned them that a second child would kill her. Still, she became pregnant anew – 'somehow in expiation of our sins, against my will,' he wrote plaintively, in dull anguish, to Nekrasov. . . . No, it was something else, stronger than fear for his wife, that oppressed him. According to some sources, Chernyshevski contemplated suicide during the fifties; he even seems to have drunk – what an awe-inspiring vision: a drunken Chernyshevski! There was no use hiding it – the marriage had turned out unhappy, thrice unhappy, and even in later years, when he had managed with the aid of his reminiscences to 'freeze his past into a state of static happiness' (Strannolyubski), nevertheless he still bore the marks of that fateful, deadly heartache – made of pity, jealousy and wounded pride – which a husband of quite a different stamp had experienced and had dealt with in quite a different way: Pushkin.

Both his wife and the infant Victor survived; and in December, 1858, she again almost died, giving birth to a third son, Misha. Amazing times –heroic, prolific, wearing a crinoline – that symbol of fertility.

'They are intelligent, educated, kind, I know it – while I am stupid, uneducated, bad,' Olga Sokratovna would say (not without that spasm of the soul termed *nadryv*) in reference to her husband's relatives, the Pypin sisters, who with all their kindness did not spare 'this hysteric, this unbalanced wench with her insufferable temper'. How she used to fling the plates around! What biographer can stick the pieces together? And that passion for moving . . . Those weird indispositions . . . In her old age, she loved to recall how on a dusty, sunny evening at Pavlosk, in a phaeton with trotter, she had overtaken Grand

Duke Konstantin, suddenly throwing off her blue veil and smiting him with a fiery glance, or how she had deceived her husband with the Polish émigré, Ivan Fyodorovich Savitski, a man renowned for the length of his moustaches: 'Raffy [*Kanashka,* a vulgar nickname] knew about it . . . Ivan Fyodorovich and I would be in the alcove, while he went on writing at his desk by the window.' One feels very sorry for Raffy; he must have been sorely tormented by the young men who surrounded his wife and were in different stages of amorous intimacy with her. Mme Chernyshevski's parties were particularly enlivened by a gang of Caucasian students. Nikolay Gavrilovich hardly ever came out to join them in the parlour. Once, on a New Year's Eve, the Georgians, led by the guffawing Gogoberidze, burst into his study, dragged him out, and Olga Sokratovna threw a mantilla over him and forced him to dance.

Yes, one pities him – and nevertheless . . . Well, he could have given her a good thrashing with a strap, sent her to the devil, or even portrayed her with all her sins, wails, wanderings and innumerable betrayals in one of those novels with which he occupied his prison leisure. But no! In *The Prologue* (and partly in *What to Do?*) we are touched by his attempts to rehabilitate his wife. There are no lovers around, only reverential admirers; nor is there that cheap coquetry which led men whom she called *mushchinki,* (an awful diminutive) to think her even more accessible than she really was, and all one finds is the vitality of a witty, beautiful woman. Dissipation becomes emancipation, and respect for her battling husband (some respect she did feel for him, but to no purpose) is made to dominate all her other feelings. In *The Prologue* the student Mironov, in order to mystify a friend, tells him that Volgin's wife is a widow. This so upsets Mme Volgin that she bursts into tears – and likewise the heroine of *What to Do?,* representing the same woman, pines among giddy clichés for her arrested husband. Volgin leaves the printing office and hurries to the opera house where he carefully scans through a pair of binoculars one side of the auditorium, then the other; whereupon tears of tenderness gush from under the lenses. He came to verify that his wife, sitting in her box, was more attractive and more elegant than anyone else – in exactly the same way as Chernyshevski himself in his youth had compared Nadezhda Lobodovski with 'women's heads'.

And here we find ourselves again surrounded by the voices of his aesthetics – for the motifs of Chernyshevski's life are now obedient to me – I have tamed its themes, they have become accustomed to my pen; with a smile I let them go: in the course of development they merely describe a circle, like a boomerang or a falcon, in order to end by returning to my hand; and even if any should fly far away, beyond the horizon of my page, I am not perturbed; it will fly back, just as this one has done.

And so: on May 10, 1855, Chernyshevski was defending at the University of St Petersburg the dissertation with which we are already familiar, 'The Relations of Art to Reality', written in three August nights in 1853; i.e., precisely at that time when 'the vague, lyrical emotions of his youth that had suggested to him considering art in terms of a pretty girl's portrait, had finally ripened and now produced this pulpy fruit in natural correlation with the apotheosis of his marital passion' (Strannolyubski). It was at this public debate that 'the intellectual trend of the sixties' was first proclaimed, as old Shelgunov later recalled, noting with discouraging naïveté that the president of the University, Pletnyov, was not moved by the speech of the young scholar whose genius he failed to perceive. . . . The audience, on the other hand, was in ectasy. So many people had piled in that some had to stand in the windows. 'They descended like flies on carrion,' snorted Turgenev, who must have felt wounded in his capacity of professed aesthete, although he himself was not averse to pleasing the flies.

As often happens with unsound ideas which have not freed themselves of the flesh or have been overgrown by it, one can detect in the 'young scholar's' aesthetic notions his own physical style, the very sound of his shrill, didactic voice. 'Beauty is life. That which pleases us is beautiful; life pleases us in its good manifestations. . . . Speak of life, and only of life [thus continues this sound, so willingly accepted by the acoustics of the century], and if humans do not live humanely – why, teach them to live, portray for them the lives of exemplary men and well-organized societies.' Art is thus a substitute or a verdict, but in no wise the equal of life, just as 'an etching is artistically far inferior to the picture' from which it has been taken (a particularly charming thought). 'The only thing, however,' pronounced the discourser clearly, 'in which poetry can stand higher than reality is in the embellishment of events by the addition of accessory effects and by making the character of the personages described correspond with the events in which they take part.'

Thus in denouncing 'pure art' the men of the sixties, and

good Russian people after them right up to the nineties, were denouncing – in result of misinformation – their own false conception of it, for just as twenty years later the social writer Garshin saw 'pure art' in the paintings of Semiradski (a rank academician) – or as an ascetic may dream of a feast that would make an epicurean sick – so Chernyshevski, having not the slightest notion of the true nature of art, saw its crown in conventional, slick art (i.e., anti-art), which he combated – lunging at nothing. At the same time one must not forget that the other camp, the camp of the 'aesthetes' – the critic Druzhinin with his pedantry and tasteless lambency, or Turgenev with his much too elegant 'visions' and misuse of Italy – often provided the enemy with exactly that cloying stuff which it was so easy to condemn.

Nikolay Gavrilovich castigated 'pure poetry' wherever he found it – in the most unexpected byways. Criticizing a reference book in the pages of *The Contemporary* (1854), he quoted a list of entries which in his opinion were too long: Labyrinth, Laurel, Lenclos (Ninon de) – and a list of entries which were too short: Laboratory, Lafayette, Linen, Lessing. An eloquent cavil! A motto that fits the whole of his intellectual life! The oleographic billows of 'poetry' gave birth (as we have seen) to full-bosomed 'luxury'; the 'fantastic' took a grim economic turn. 'Illuminations . . . Confetti fluttering down to the streets from balloons,' he enumerates (the subject is the festivities and gifts occasioned by the christening of Louis Napoleon's son), 'colossal bonbonnières descending on parachutes. . . .' And what things the rich have: 'Beds of rosewood . . . wardrobes with hinges and sliding mirrors . . . damask hangings . . . And over there the poor toiler. . . .' The link has been found, the antithesis obtained; with tremendous accusatory force and an abundance of articles of furniture, Nikolay Gavrilovich exposes all their immorality. 'Is it surprising that the seamstress endowed with good looks little by little slackens her moral principles . . . Is it surprising that, having changed her cheap muslin dress, washed a hundred times, for Alençon lace, and her sleepless nights of work by a bit of gutting candle for other sleepless nights at a public masquerade or at a suburban orgy she . . . whirling . . .' etc. (and, having thought it over, he demolished the poet Nikitin, not because the latter versified badly, but because being an inhabitant of the Voronezh backwoods he had no right whatever to be talking about marble colonnades and sails).

The German pedagogue Kampe, folding his little hands on

his stomach, once said: 'To spin a pound of wool is more useful than to write a folume off ferses.' We too, with equally stolid seriousness, are annoyed at poets, at healthy fellows who would be better doing nothing, but who busy themselves with cutting trifles 'out of very nice coloured paper'. Get it clear, trickster, get it clear, arabesquer, 'the power of art is the power of its commonplaces' and nothing more. What should interest a critic most is the conviction expresse in a writer's work. Volynski and Strannolyubski both note a certain odd inconsistency here (one of those fatal inner contradictions that are revealed all along our hero's path): the dualism of the monist Chernyshevski's aesthetics – where 'form' and 'content' are distinct, with 'content' pre-eminent – or, more exactly, with 'form' playing the role of the soul and 'content' the role of the body; and the muddle is augmented by the fact that this 'soul' consists of mechanical components, since Chernyshevski believed that the value of a work was not a qualitative but a quantitative concept, and that 'if someone were to take some miserable, forgotten novel and carefully cull all its flashes of observation, he would collect a fair number of sentences that would not differ in worth from those constituting the pages of works we admire'. Even more: 'It is sufficient to take a look at the trinkets fabricated in Paris, at those elegant articles of bronze, porcelain and wood, in order to understand how important it is nowadays to draw a line between an artistic and an unartistic product' (this elegant bronze explains a lot).

Like words, things also have their cases, Chernyshevski saw everything in the nominative. Actually, of course, any genuinely new trend is a knight's move, a change of shadows, a shift that displaces the mirror. A serious màn, moderate, respecting education, arts and crafts, a man who has accumulated a profusion of values in the sphere of thought – who perhaps has shown a fully progressive discrimination during the period of their accumulation but now has no desire whatsoever for them to be suddenly subjected to a reconsideration – such a man is much more angered by irrational innovation than by the darkness of antiquated ignorance. Thus Chernyshevski, who like the majority of revolutionaries was a complete bourgeoise in his artistic and scientific tastes, was enraged by 'the squaring of boots' or 'the extraction of cubic roots from boot tops'. 'All Kazan knew Lobachevski,' he writes to his sons from Siberia in the seventies, 'all Kazan was of the unanimous opinion that the man was a complete fool. . . . What on earth is "the curvature of a ray" or "curved space"? What is "geometry without the axiom of parallel lines"? Is it possible to write Russian without verbs? Yes, it is – for a joke. Whispers, timid respiration, trills of nightingale. Written by a certain Fet, a well-known poet in his time. An idiot with few peers. He wrote this seriously, and people laughed at him till their sides ached.' (Fet he detested as he also did Tolstoy; in 1856, while buttering up Turgenev – whom he wanted in *The Contemporary* – he wrote him 'that no "Youth's" [Tolstoy's *Childhood and Adolescence*] nor even Fet's poetry . . . can sufficiently vulgarize the public for its not being able to . . .' – there follows a vulgar compliment.)

Once in 1855, when expatiating on Pushkin and wishing to give an example of 'a senseless combination of words,' he hastily cited a 'blue sound' of his own invention – prophetically calling down upon his own head Blok's 'blue-ringing hour' that was to chime half a century later. 'A scientific analysis shows the absurdity of such combinations,' he wrote, unaware of the physiological fact of 'coloured hearing'. 'Isn't it all the same,' he asked (of the reader in Bakhmuchansk or Novomirgorod, who joyfully agreed with him), 'whether we have a blue-finned pike or [as in a Derzhavin poem] a pike with a blue fin [of course the second, *we* would have cried – that way it stands out better, in profile!], for the genuine thinker has no time to worry about such matters, especially if he spends more time in the public square than he does in his study?' The 'general outline' is another matter. It was a love of generalities (encyclopedias) and a contemptuous hatred of particularities (monographs) which led him to reproach Darwin for being puerile and Wallace for being inept ('. . . all these learned specialities, from the study of butterfly wings to the study of Kaffir dialects'). Chernyshevski had on the contrary a dangerously wide range, a kind of reckless and self-confident 'anything-will-do' attitude which casts a doubtful shadow over his own specialized work. 'The general interest,' however, was given his own interpretation: his premise was that the reader was most of all interested in the 'productive' side of things. Reviewing a magazine (in 1855), he praises such items as 'the Thermometric Condition of the Earth' and 'Russian Coalfields', while decisively rejecting as too special the only article one would want to read, 'The Geographical Distribution of the Camel'.

Extraordinarily indicative in respect of all this is Chernyshevski's attempt to prove (*The Contemporary* for 1856) that the ternary metre (anapaest, dactyl) is more natural to Russian than the binary one (iamb, trochee). The first (except when it is used in the making of the noble, 'sacred' – and therefore hateful – dactylic hexameter) seems more natural to Chernyshevski, 'more wholesome', in the way that a bad rider thinks a gallop is 'simpler' than trotting. The point, however, was not so much in this as in that 'general rule' to which he subjected everything and everyone. Confused by the rhythmic emancipation of Nekrasov's broad-rolling verse and by Koltsov's elementary anapaests ('Why asleep, *muzhicohyók*?') Chernyshevski scented something democratic in the ternary metre, something which charmed the heart, something 'free' but also didactic, as opposed to the aristocratic air of the iamb: he believed that poets who wished to convince should use the anapaest. However, this was not all: in Nekrasov's ternary verse it happens especially often that one-syllable or two-syllable words occur in the unstressed parts of the feet and lose their accentual individuality, while their collective rhythm on the other hand is heightened: the parts are sacrificed to the whole (as for instance in the anapaestic line 'Volga, Vólga, in spríng overflówing' where the first 'Volga' occupies the two depressions of the first foot: Volga Vól). All I have just said is nowhere, of course, examined by Chernyshevski himself, but it is curious that in his own verses, produced by him during the Siberian nights, in that terrible ternary metre whose very shoddiness has a tang of madness about it, Chernyshevski unwittingly parodies Nekrasov's device and carries it to absurdity by cramming into the depressions two-syllable words normally accented not on the first syllable (as 'Volga') but on the second, and doing it thrice in one line – surely a record: 'Remote hílls, remote pálmas, surprised girl of the nórth' (verses to his wife, 1875). Let us repeat: all this leaning toward a line created in the image and likeness of definite socio-economic gods was unconscious on Chernyshevski's part, but it is only by making this tendency clear that one can understand the true background of his strange theory. With all this he had no understanding of the real, violinic essence of the anapaest; neither did he understand the iamb, the most flexible of all measures when it comes to transforming stresses into scuds, into those rhythmical deviations from the metre which according to his memories from the seminary seemed to Chernyshevski unlawful; finally he did not understand the rhythm of Russian prose; it is only natural, therefore, that the very method he applied to prove his theory had its revenge on him: in the passages of prose he quoted he divided the number of syllables by the number of stresses and got the result of three, not the two he would have got, he said, had the binary metre been more becoming to the Russian language; but he did not take into account the main thing: the paeons! For in the very passages he quotes, whole pieces of sentences follow the scudded rhythm of blank verse, the most blue-blooded of all metres; i.e., precisely the iamb!

I am afraid that the cobbler who visited Apelles' studio and criticized what he did not understand was a mediocre cobbler. Is all really well from the mathematical point of view in those learned economic works of his, whose analysis demands an almost superhuman curiosity on the part of the investigator? Are they really deep, those commentaries of his on Mill (in which he strove to reconstruct certain theories 'in keeping with the new plebeian element in thought and life')? Do all the boots he made really fit? Or is it merely an old man's coquetry which prompts him twenty years later to recall complacently the errors in his logarithmic calculations concerning the effect of certain agricultural improvements on the grain harvest? Sad, all of this, very sad. Our overall impression is that materialists of this type fell into a fatal error: neglecting the nature of the thing itself, they kept applying their most materialist method merely to the relations between objects, to the void between objects and not to the objects themselves; i.e., they were the naïvest of metaphysicians precisely at that point where they most wanted to be standing on the ground.

Once in his youth there had been an unfortunate morning: he was called on by a book pedlar he knew, old, long-nosed Vasiliy Trofimovich, bent like a babajaga beneath the weight of a huge canvas sack full of prohibited and semi-prohibited books. Not knowing foreign languages, hardly able to spell our Roman letters and weirdly pronouncing the titles in a thick peasant way, he guessed instinctively the degree of seditiousness of this or that German. That morning he sold Nikolay Gavrilovich (both of them squatting on their haunches beside a pile of books) a still uncut volume of Feuerbach.

In those days Andrey Ivanovich Feuerbach was preferred to Egor Fyodorovich Hegel. *Homo feuerbachi* is a cogitating muscle. Andrey Ivanovich found that man differs from the ape only in his point of view; he could hardly, however, have studied the apes. A half-century after him Lenin refuted the theory that 'the earth is the sum of human sensations' with 'the earth existed before man did'; and to his trade announcement: We now turn Kant's unknowable "thing in itself", into a "thing for us", by means of organic chemistry,' he added quite seriously that 'since alizarin has existed in coal without our knowledge, then things must exist independently of our cognition'. Similarly, Chernyshevski explained: 'We see a tree; another man looks at the same object. We see by the reflection in his eyes that his image of the tree looks exactly the same as our tree. Thus we all see objects as they really exist.' All this wild rubbish has its own private hilarious twist: the 'materialists'' constant appeal to trees is especially amusing because they are so badly acquainted with nature, particularly with trees. That tangible object which according to Chernyshevski 'acts much more strongly than the abstract concept of it' (the Anthropological Principle in Philosophy) is simply beyond their ken. Look what a terrible abstraction resulted, in the final analysis, from 'materialism'! Chernyshevski did not know the difference between a plough and the wooden *soha*; he confused beer with Madeira; he was unable to name a single wild flower except the wild rose; and it is characteristic that this deficiency of botanical knowledge was immediately made up by a 'generalization' when he maintained with the conviction of an ignoramus that 'they [the flowers of the Siberian taiga] are all just the same as those which bloom all over Russia!' There lurks a secret retribution in the fact that he who had constructed his philosophy on a basis of knowing the world was now placed, naked and alone, amidst the bewitched, strangely luxuriant, and still incompletely described nature of northeast Siberia: an elemental, mythological punishment which had not been taken into account by his human judges.

Only a few years earlier the smell of Gogol's Petrushka had been explained away by the fact that everything existing was rational. But the time for hearty Russian Hegelianism was now past. The moulders of opinion were incapable of understanding Hegel's vital truth: a truth that was not stagnant, like shallow water, but flowed like blood, through the very process of cognition. The simpleton Feuerbach was much more to Chernyshevski's taste. There is always a danger, however, that one letter will fall out of the cosmic, and this danger was not evaded by Chernyshevski in his article 'Communal Ownership', when he began to operate with Hegel's tempting triad, giving such examples as: the gasiformity of the world is the thesis, while the softness of the brain is the synthesis; or, even stupider: a cudgel turning into a carbine. 'There lies concealed in the triad,' says Strannolyubski, 'a vague image of the circumference controlling all life of the mind, and the mind is confined inescapably within it. This is truth's merry-go-round, for truth is always round; consequently, in the development of life's forms a certain pardonable curvature is possible: the hump of truth; but no more.'

Chernyshevski's 'philosophy' goes back through Feuerbach, to the Encyclopedists. On the other hand, applied Hegelianism, working gradually left, went through that same Feuerbach to join Marx, who in his *Holy Family* expresses himself thus:

> . . . . no great intelligence
> Is needed to distinguish a connection
> Between the teaching of materialism
> Regarding inborn tendency to good;
> Equality of man's capacities—
> Capacities that generally are
> Termed mental; the great influence
> Exterior circumstances have on man;
> Omnipotent experience; sway of habit
> And of upbringing; the extreme importance
> Of industry; the moral right to pleasure,
> And communism.

I have put it into blank verse so it would be less boring.

Steklov is of the opinion that with all his genius, Chernyshevski cannot rank with Marx, in relation to whom he stands as the Barnaul craftsman Polzunov stands to Watt. Marx himself ('that petty bourgeois to the marrow of his bones' according to the testimony of Bakunin, who could not stand Germans) referred once or twice to the 'remarkable' writings of Chernyshevski, but he left more than one contemptuous note in the margins of the chief work on economics '*des grossen russichen Gelehrten*' (Marx in general disliked Russians). Chernyshevski repaid him in like coin. Already in the seventies he was treating everything new with negligence, with malevolence. He was particularly fed up with economics, which had ceased to be a weapon for him and by this token took on in his mind the aspect of an empty toy, of 'pure science'. Lyatski is quite wrong when – with a passion for navigational analogies common to many – he compares the exiled Chernyshevski to a man 'watching from a deserted shore the passage of a gigantic ship (Marx's ship) on its way to discover new lands'; the expression is especially unfortunate in view of the fact that Chernyshevski himself, as if anticipating the analogy and wishing to refute it in advance, said of *Das Kapital* (sent to him in 1872): 'I glanced through but didn't read it; I tore off the pages one by one and made them into little *ships* [my italics], and launched them on the Vilyui.'

Lenin considered Chernyshevski to be 'the one true great writer who managed to remain on a level of unbroken philosophical materialism from the fifties right up until 1888' (he knocked one year off). Once, on a windy day, Krupskaya turned to Lunacharski and said to him with soft sorrow: 'There was hardly anyone Vladimir Ilyich liked so much . . . I think he had a great deal in common with Chernyshevski.' 'Yes, they undoubtedly had much in common,' adds Lunacharski, who had tended at first to treat this remark with scepticism. 'They had in common both clarity of style and mobility of speech . . . breadth and depth of judgment, revolutionary fire . . . that combination of enormous content with a modest exterior, and finally their joint moral make-up.' Steklov calls Chernyshevski's article, 'The Anthropological Principle in Philosophy', the 'first philosophical manifesto of Russian communism'; it is significant that this first manifesto was a schoolboy's rendering, an infantile assessment of the most difficult moral questions. 'The European theory of materialism,' says Strannolyubski, rephrasing Volynski somewhat, 'took on with Chernyshevski a simplified, muddled, and grotesque form. Passing scornful and impertinent judgment on Schopenhauer, under whose critical fingernail his own saltatory thinking would not have survived for a second, he recognized out of all former thinkers, by a strange association of ideas and according to his mistaken memories, only Spinoza and Aristotle, whom he imagined himself to be continuing.'

Chernyshevski hammered unsound syllogisms together; the moment he had gone the syllogisms collapsed and the nails were left sticking out. In eliminating metaphysical dualism he fell into gnoseological dualism, and having lightheartedly taken matter as the first principle, he got hopelessly lost among concepts presupposing something that creates our perception of the external world itself. The professional philosopher Yurkevich had no trouble at all in pulling him to pieces. Yurkevich kept wondering how does Chernyshevski account for the spatial motion of the nerves being transformed into nonspatial sensation? Instead of replying to the poor professor's detailed article, Chernyshevski reprinted exactly a third of it in *The Contemporary* (i.e., as much as was allowed by law) and broke it off in the middle of a word, with no comment. He most definitely did not give a hoot for the opinions of specialists, and he saw no harm in not knowing the details of the subject under examination: details were for him merely the aristocratic element in the nation of our general ideas.

'His head thinks about the problems of humanity . . . while his hand carries out unskilled labour,' he wrote of his 'socially conscious workman' (and we cannot help recalling those woodcuts in ancient anatomical atlases, where a pleasant-faced youth is depicted nonchalantly leaning against a column and showing the educated world all his viscera). But the political régime that was supposed to appear as the synthesis in the syllogism, where the thesis was the commune, resembled not so much Soviet Russia as the utopias of his day. The world of Fourier, the harmony of the twelve passions, the bliss of collective living, the rose-garlanded workmen – all this could not fail to please Chernyshevski, who was always looking for 'coherency'. Let us dream of the phalanstery living in a palace: 1,800 souls – and all happy! Music, flags, cakes. The world is run by mathematics and well run at that; the correspondence which Fourier established between our desires and Newton's gravity was particularly captivating; it defined Chernyshevski's attitude to Newton for all his life, and it is pleasant to compare the latter's apple with Fourier's apple costing the commercial traveller a whole fourteen sous in a Paris restaurant, a fact that led Fourier to ponder the basic disorder of the industrial mechanism, just as Marx was led to acquaint himself with economic problems by the question of the wine-making gnomes ('small peasants') in the Moselle Valley: a graceful origination of grandiose ideas.

While defending communal ownership of the land because of its simplifying the organization of associations in Russia, Chernyshevski was prepared to agree to the emancipation of the peasants without land, the ownership of which would have led in the long run to new encumbrances. At this point sparks flash from our pen. The liberation of the serfs! The era of great reforms! No wonder that in a burst of vivid prescience the young Chernyshevski noted in his diary in 1848 (the year somebody dubbed 'the vent of the century'): 'What if we are indeed living in the times of Cicero and Caesar, when *seculorum novus nascitur ordo,* and there comes a new Messiah, and a new religion, and a new world? . . .'

The fifties are now in full fan. It is permitted to smoke on the streets. One may wear a beard. The overture to *William Tell* is thundered out on every musical occasion. Rumours spread that the capital is being moved to Moscow; that the old calendar is going to be replaced by the new. Under this cover Russia is busily gathering material for Saltikov's primitive but juicy satire. 'What is this talk of a new spirit in the air, I'd like to know,' said General Zubatov, 'only the flunkeys have grown rude, otherwise everything has stayed the way it was.' Landowners and notably their wives began to dream terrible dreams not listed in dream books. A new heresy appeared: Nihilism. 'A scandalous and immoral doctrine rejecting everything that cannot be palpated,' says Dahl with a shudder, in his definition of this strange word (in which 'nihil', nothing, corresponds as it were to 'material'). Persons in holy orders had a vision: an enormous Chernyshevski strides along the Nevsky Prospect wearing a wide-brimmed hat and carrying a cudgel.

And that first rescript in the name of the Vilno governor, Nazimov! And the Tsar's signature, so handsome, so robust, with two full-blooded, mighty flourishes, which were to be later torn off by a bomb! And the ecstasy of Nikolay Gavrilovich: 'The blessing promised to the meek and the peacemakers crowns Alexander the Second with a happiness which no other of Europe's sovereigns has yet known. . . .'

But soon after the provincial committees were formed, Chernyshevski's ardour cooled: he was incensed by the self-seeking of the nobles in most of them. His final disillusionment came in the second half of 1858. The size of the compensation! The smallness of the allotments! The tone of *The Contemporary* became sharp and frank; the expressions 'infamous' and 'infamy' began pleasantly to enliven the pages of this dullish magazine.

Its director's life was not rich in events. For a long time the public did not know his face. Nowhere was he seen. Already famous, he remained as it were in the wings of his busy, talkative thought.

Always, as was the custom then, in a dressing gown (spotted even behind with candle grease) he sat all day long in his little study with its blue wallpaper – good for the eyes – and its window overlooking the yard (a view of the log-pile covered with snow), at a large desk heaped with books, printer's proofs and cuttings. He worked so feverishly, smoked so much and slept so little that the impression he produced was almost frightening: skinny, nervy, his gaze at once blear and piercing, his hands shaky, his speech jerky and distracted (on the other hand he never suffered from headache and naïvely boasted of this as a mark of a healthy mind). His capacity for work was monstrous, as was, for that matter, that of most Russian critics of the last century. To his secretary Studentski, a former seminarist from Saratov, he dictated a translation of Schlosser's history and in between, while the latter was taking it down, he himself would go on writing an article for *The Contemporary* or would read something, making notes in the margins. He was pestered by callers. Not knowing how to escape from an importunate guest, he would, to his own chagrin, get more and more involved in a conversation. Leaning his elbow on the mantelpiece and fiddling with something, he would talk in a shrill, squeaky voice, but whenever his thoughts wandered, he would drawl and chew monotonously, with an abundance of 'well's'. He had a peculiar quiet chuckle (causing Leo Tolstoy to break into a sweat), but when he laughed out loud he went off into fits and roared deafeningly (at which Turgenev, hearing these roulades from afar, would take to his heels).

Such methods of knowledge as dialectical materialism curiously resemble the unscrupulous advertisements for patent medicines, which cure all illnesses at once. Still, such an expedient can occasionally help with a cold. There was quite definitely a smack of class arrogance about the attitudes of contemporary well-born writers toward plebian Chernyshevski. Turgenev, Grigorovich and Tolstoy called him 'the bedbug-stinking gentleman' and among themselves jeered at him in all kinds of ways. Once at Turgenev's country place, the first two, together with Botkin and Druzhinin, composed and acted a domestic farce. In a scene where a couch was supposed to catch fire, Turgenev had to come out running with the cry . . . here the common efforts of his friends had persuaded him to utter the unfortunate words which in his youth he had allegedly addressed to a sailor during a fire on board ship: 'Save me, save me, I am my mother's only son.' Out of this farce the utterly talentless Grigorovich subsequently concocted his completely mediocre *School of Hospitality*, where he endowed one of the characters, the splenetic writer Chernushin, with the features of Nikolay Gavrilovich: mole's eyes looking oddly askance, thin lips, a flattened, crumpled face, gingery hair fluffed up on the left temple and a euphemistic stench of burnt rum. It is curious that the notorious wail ('Save me,' etc.) is attributed here to Chernushin, which gives colour to Strannolyubski's idea that there was a kind of mystic link between Turgenev and Chernyshevski. 'I have read his disgusting book [the dissertation]' writes the former in a letter to his fellow mockers. 'Raca! Raca! Raca!

you know that there is nothing in the world more terrible than this Jewish curse.'

'This "raca" or "raka",' remarks the biographer superstitiously, 'resulted seven years later in Rakeev (the police colonel who arrested the anathematized man), and the letter itself had been written by Turgenev on precisely the 12th of July, Chernyshevski's *birthday* . . .' (it seems to us that Strannolyubski is stretching it a bit).

That same year Turgenev's *Rudin* appeared, but Chernyshevski attacked it (for its caricature of Bakunin) only in 1860, when Turgenev was no longer necessary to *The Contemporary*, which he had left as a result of Dobrolyubov's directing a snake hiss at his 'On the Eve'. Tolstoy could not tolerate our hero: 'One keeps hearing him,' he wrote, 'hearing that thin, nasty little voice of his saying obtuse, nasty things . . . as he keeps waxing indignant in his corner until someone says "shut up" and looks him in the eye.' 'The aristocrats turned into coarse ruffians,' remarks Steklov in this connection, 'when they talked with inferiors, or about people who were inferior to them socially.' 'The inferior', however, did not remain in debt; knowing how much Turgenev prized every word spoken against Tolstoy, Chernyshevski, in the fifties, freely enlarged upon Tolstoy's *poshlost* (vulgarity) and *hvastovstvo* (bragging) – 'the bragging of a thickheaded peacock about a tail which doesn't even cover his vulgar bottom,' etc. 'You are not some Ostrovski or some Tolstoy,' added Nikolay Gavrilovich, 'you are an honour to us' (and *Rudin* was already out – had been out for two years).

The other literary reviews picked at him as much as they could. The critic Dudyshkin (in *The National Commentator*) huffily aimed his dudeen at him: 'Poetry for you is merely chapters of political economy transposed into verse.' His ill-wishers in the mystical camp spoke about Chernyshevski's 'evil lure', about his physical resemblance to the Devil (for instance, Prof. Kostomarov). Other journalists, of a plainer cast, like Blagosvetlov (who considered himself a dandy and despite his radicalism had as footboy a real, undyed blackamoor) talked about Chernyshevski's dirty rubbers and German-cum-sexton's style of dress. Nekrasov stood up for the 'sensible fellow' (whom he had got for *The Contemporary*) with a limp smile, admitting that he had managed to lay the stamp of monotony on the magazine by stuffing it with mediocre tales denouncing bribe-taking and policemen; but he praised his colleague for his fruitful labours: thanks to him the magazine had 4,700 subscribers in

1858 and three years later – 7,000. Nikolay Gavrilovich's relations with Nekrasov were friendly but no more; there is a hint concerning some financial arrangements which displeased him. In 1883, in order to divert the old man, his cousin Pypin suggested that he should write some 'portraits of the past'. Chernyshevski depicted his first meeting with Nekrasov with the meticulousness and laboriousness already familiar to us (giving a complex plan of all their mutual movements about the room including practically the number of footsteps), a detailism sounding like an insult inflicted on Father Time and his honest work, if one remembers that thirty years had elapsed since these manoeuvres took place. He placed Nekrasov the poet above all others (above Pushkin, above Lermontov and Koltsov). *La Traviata* made Lenin weep; similarly, Chernyshevski, who confessed that poetry of the heart was even dearer to him than poetry of ideas, used to burst into tears over those of Nekrasov's verses (even iambic ones!) which expressed everything he himself had experienced, all the torments of his youth, all the phases of his love for his wife. And no wonder: Nekrasov's iambic pentameter enchants us particularly by its hortatory, supplicatory and prophetic force and by a very individual caesura after the second foot, a caesura which in Pushkin, say, is a rudimentary organ insofar as it controls the melody of the line, but which in Nekrasov becomes a genuine organ of breathing, as if it had turned from a partition into a pit, or as if the two foot part of the line and the three foot part had moved asunder, leaving after the second foot an interval full of music. As he listened to these hollow-chested verses, to this guttural, sobbing articulation—

> Oh, do not say the life you lead is dismal,
> And do not call a jailer one half-dead!
> Before me Night yawns chilly and abysmal.
> The arms of Love before you are outspread.
>
> I know, to you another is now dearer,
> It irks you now to spare me and to wait.
> Oh, bear with me! My end is drawing nearer,
> Let Fate complete what was begun by Fate!

—Chernyshevski could not help thinking that his wife should not hasten to deceive him; could not help identifying the nearness of the end with the shadow of the prison already stretching out toward him. And that was not all: evidently this connection was felt – not in the rational but in the Orphic sense – also by the poet who wrote these lines, for it is precisely their rhythm ('Oh, do not say') that was echoed with a bizarre haunting quality in the poem he subsequently wrote about Chernyshevski:

> Oh, do not say he has forgotten caution,
> For his own Fate himself he'll be to blame . . .

Thus Nekrasov's sounds were *pleasing* to Chernyshevski; i.e., they happened to satisfy that elementary aesthetic for which he mistook all along his own circumstantial sentimentality. Having described a large circle, having taken in many matters concerning Chernyshevski's attitude to various branches of knowledge, and yet not having impaired for a moment our smooth curve, we have now returned with new forces to his philosophy of art. Now it is time to sum it up.

Like all the rest of our radical critics having a weakness for easy gain, he eschewed courtly compliments to lady writers, and energetically demolished Evdokia Rastopchin or Avdotia Glinka. 'An incorrect and careless patter' (as Pushkin puts it) left him unmoved. Both he and Dobrolyubov flayed literary coquettes with gusto – but in real life . . . Well, look what was done to them, look how they were twisted and tortured with peals of laughter (water nymphs laugh thus along streams flowing close to hermitages and other places of salvation) by the daughters of Doctor Vasiliev.

His tastes were eminently solid. He was *épaté* by Hugo. He was impressed by Swinburne (which is not at all strange, come to think of it). In the list of books which he read in the fortress the name of Flaubert is spelled with an '*o*' –and, indeed, he placed him below Zacher-Masoch and Spielhagen. He loved Béranger the way average Frenchmen loved him. 'For goodness' sake,' exclaims Steklov, 'you say that this man was not poetic? Why, do you not know that he would declaim Béranger and Ryleyev with tears of rapture?!' His tastes only congealed in Siberia – and by a strange delicacy of historical fate, Russia did not produce during the twenty years of his banishment a single genuine writer (until Chekhov) whose beginning he had not seen for himself during the active period of his life. From conversations with him in the eighties in Astrakhan it becomes apparent that: 'Yes, sir, it is the title of count that made one consider Tolstoy "a great writer of the Russian land" '; and when bothersome visitors asked him whom he thought the best living writer he named a complete nonentity: Maxim Belinski.

In his youth he noted in his diary: 'Political literature is the highest literature.' In the fifties when discussing at length Belinski (Vissarion, of course), something the government disapproved of, he followed him in saying that 'literature cannot fail to be the handmaiden of one or another ideological trend', and that writers 'incapable of being animated by sympathy toward what is being accomplished around us by the force of historical movement . . . will never in any circumstances produce anything great', for 'history does not know of any works of art that were created exclusively from the idea of beauty'. In the forties Belinski maintained that 'George Sand can unconditionally be included in the roll of European poets (in the German sense of *Dichter*), while the juxtaposition of Gogol's name with those of Homer and Shakespeare offends both decency and common sense' and that 'not only Cervantes, Walter Scott and Cooper, as artists pre-eminently, but also Swift, Sterne, Voltaire and Rousseau have an incomparably and immeasurably greater significance in the whole history of literature than Gogol'. Belinski was seconded three decades later by Chernyshevski (when, it is true, George Sand had already ascended to the attic, and Cooper had descended to the nursery), who said that 'Gogol is a very minor figure in comparison, for example, with Dickens or Fielding or Sterne'.

Poor Gogol! His exclamation (like Pushkin's) 'Rus!' is willingly repeated by the men of the sixties, but now the troika needs paved highways, for even Russia's *toska* ('yearning') has become utilitarian. Poor Gogol! Esteeming the seminarist in the critic Nadezhdin (who used to write 'literature' with three '*t*'s), Chernyshevski found that his influence on Gogol would have been more beneficial than Pushkin's, and regretted that Gogol was not aware of such a thing as a principle. Poor Gogol! Why, that gloomy buffoon Father Matvey had also adjured him to renounce Pushkin. . . .

Lermontov came off luckier. His prose jerked from Belinski (who had a weakness for the conquests of technology) the surprising and most charming comparison of Pechorin to a steam engine, shattering all who were careless enough to get under its wheels. In his poetry the middle-class intellectuals felt something of the sociolyrical strain that later came to be called 'Nadsonism'. In this sense Lermontov was the first Nadson of Russian literature. The rhythm, the tone, the pale, tear-diluted idiom of 'civic' verse up to and including 'as victims you fell in the fateful contest' (the famous revolutionary song of the first years of our century), all of this goes back to such Lermontov lines as:

> Farewell, our dear comrade! Alas, upon earth
> Not long did you dwell, blue-eyed singer!
> A plain cross of wood you have earned, and with us
> Your memory always shall linger . . .

Lermontov's real magic, the melting vistas in his poetry, its paradisial picturesqueness and the transparent tang of the celestial in his moist verse – these, of course, were completely inaccessible to the understanding of men of Chernyshevski's camp.

Now we are approaching his most vulnerable spot; for it has long become customary to measure the degree of flair, intelligence and talent of a Russian critic by his attitude to Pushkin. And this is how it will remain until Russian literary criticism discards its sociological, religious, philosophical and other textbooks, which only help mediocrity to admire itself. Only then will you be free to say what you please: You may then criticize Pushkin for any betrayals of his exigent muse and at the same time preserve both your talent and your honour. Upbraid him for letting one hexameter creep into the pentameters of *Boris Godunov* (ninth scene), for a metrical error in the twenty-first line of 'The Feast During the Plague', for repeating the phrase 'every minute' (*pominutno*) five times within sixteen lines in 'The Blizzard', but for God's sake stop that irrelevant chitchat.

Strannolyubski sagaciously compares the critical utterances of the sixties concerning Pushkin with the attitude to him, three decades earlier, of the chief of police Count Benckendorff or that of the director of the third section, Von Fock. In truth, Chernyshevski's highest praise for a writer, like that of the ruler Nicholas I or the radical Belinski, was: sensible. When Chernyshevski or Pisarev called Pushkin's poetry 'rubbish and luxury', they were only repeating Tolmachyov, author of *Military Eloquence*, who in the thirties had termed the same subject: 'trifles and baubles'. When Chernyshevski said that Pushkin was 'only a poor imitator of Byron', he reproduced with monstrous accuracy the definition given by Count Vorontsov (Pushkin's boss in Odessa): 'A poor imitator of Lord Byron.' Dobrolyubov's favourite idea that 'Pushkin lacked a solid, deep education' is in friendly chime with Vorontsov's remark: 'One cannot be a genuine poet without constantly working to broaden one's knowledge, and his is insufficient.' 'To be a genius it is not enough to have manufactured *Eugene Onegin*' wrote the progressive Nadezhdin, comparing Pushkin to a tailor, an inventor of waistcoat patterns, and thus concluding an intellectual pact with the reactionary Count Uvarov, Minister of Education, who remarked on the occasion of Pushkin's death. 'To write jingles does not mean yet to achieve a great career.'

Chernyshevski equated genius with commonsense. If Pushkin was a genius, he argued perplexedly, then how should one interpret the profusion of corrections in his drafts? One can understand some 'polishing' in a fair copy but this was the rough work itself. It should have flowed effortless since common sense speaks its mind immediately, for it *knows* what it wants to say. Moreover, as a person ridiculously alien to artistic creation, he supposed that 'polishing' took place on paper while the 'real work' – i.e., 'the task of forming the general plan' – occurred 'in the mind' – another sign of that dangerous dualism, that crack in his 'materialism', whence more than one snake was to slither and bite him during his life. Pushkin's originality filled him with fears. 'Poetic works are good when *everyone* [my italics] says after reading them: yes, this is not only verisimilar, but also it could not be otherwise, for that's how it always is.'

Pushkin does not figure in the list of books sent to Chernyshevski at the fortress, and no wonder: despite Pushkin's services ('he invented Russian poetry and taught society to read it' – two statements completely untrue), he was nevertheless above all a writer of witty little verses about women's little feet – and 'little feet' in the intonation of the sixties – when the whole of nature had been Philistinized into *travka* (diminutive of 'grass') and *pichuzhki* (diminutive of 'birds') – already meant something quite different from Pushkin's *'petits pieds'*, something that had now become closer to the mawkish *'Füsschen'*. It seemed particularly astonishing to him (as it did also to Belinski) that Pushkin became so 'aloof' toward the end of his life. 'An end was put to those friendly relations whose monument has remained the poem "Arion",' explains Chernyshevski in passing, but how full of sacred meaning was this casual reference to the forbidden subject of Decembrism for the reader of *The Contemporary* (whom we suddenly imagine as absentmindedly and hungrily biting into an apple – transferring the hunger of his reading to the apple, and again eating the words with his eyes). Therefore Nikolay Gavrilovich must have been more than a little irritated by a stage direction in the penultimate scene of *Boris Godunov*, a stage direction resembling a sly hint and an encroachment upon civic laurels hardly deserved by the author of 'vulgar drivel' (see Chernyshevski's remarks on the poem 'Stamboul is by the giaours now lauded'): 'Pushkin comes surrounded by the people.'

'Reading over the most abusive critics,' wrote Pushkin during an autumn at Boldino, 'I find them so amusing that I don't understand how I could have been angry at them; meseems, if I wanted to laugh at them, I could think of nothing better than just to reprint them with no comment at all.' Curiously enough, that is exactly what Chernyshevski did with Professor Yurkevich's article: a grotesque repetition! And now 'a revolving speck of dust has got caught in a ray of Pushkin's light, which has penetrated between the blinds of Russian critical thought', to use Strannolyubski's caustic metaphor. We have in mind the following magic gamut of fate: in his Saratov diary Chernyshevski applied two lines from Pushkin's 'The Egyptian Nights' to his courtship, completely misquoting the second one, with a characteristic (for him who had no ear) distortion: 'I [he] met the challenge of delight / As warfare's challenge met I'd have (instead of 'As he would meet in days of war / The challenge of a savage battle'). For this 'I'd have', fate – the ally of the muses (and herself an expert in conditional forms), took revenge on him – and with what refined stealth in the evolution of the punishment!

What connection, it seems, could there be between this ill-starred misquotation and Chernyshevski's remark ten years later (in 1862): 'If people were able to announce all their ideas concerning public affairs at . . . meetings there would be no need to make magazine articles out of them'? However, at this point Nemesis is already awakening. 'Instead of writing, one would speak,' continues Chernyshevski, 'and if these ideas had to reach everyone who had not taken part in the meeting they could be noted down by a stenographer.' And vengeance unfolds: in Siberia, where his only listeners were the larches and the Yakuts, he was haunted by the image of a 'platform' and a 'lecture hall', in which it was *so* convenient for the public to gather and where the latter would ripple *so* responsively, for, in the final analysis, he, as Pushkin's Improvvisatore (he of the 'Egyptian Nights') but a poorer versificator, had chosen for his profession – and later as an unrealizable ideal – variations on a given theme; in the very twilight of life he composes a work in which he embodies his dream: from Astrakhan, not long before his death, he sends Lavrov his 'Evenings at the Princess Starobelski's' for the literary review *Russian Thought* (which did not find it possible to print them), and follows this up with 'An Insertion' – addressed straight to the printer:

> In that part where it says that the people have gone from the salon dining-room into the salon proper, which has been prepared for them to listen to Vyazovski's fairy tale, and there is a description of the arrangement of the auditorium . . . the distribution of the male and female stenographers into two sections at two tables either is not indicated or else is indicated unsatisfactorily. In my draft this part reads as follows: 'Along the sides of the platform stood two tables for the stenographers . . . Vyazovski went up to the stenographers, shook hands with them, and stood chatting with them while the company took their places.' The lines in the fair copy whose sense corresponds to the passage quoted from my draft should be replaced now by the following lines: 'The men, forming a constricted frame, stood near the stage and along the walls behind the last chairs; the musicians with their stands occupied both sides of the stage, . . . The improvvisatore, greeted by deafening applause rising from all sides. . .'

Sorry, sorry, we've mixed everything up – got hold of an extract from Pushkin's 'The Egyptian Nights'. Let us restore the situation: 'Between the platform and foremost hemicycle of the auditorium [writes Chernyshevski to a nonexistent printer], a little to the right and left of the platform, stood two tables: at the one which was on the left in front of the platform, if you looked from the middle of the hemicycles toward the platform . . .' etc., etc. – with many more words of the same sort, none of them really expressing anything.

'Here is a theme for you,' said Charski to the improvvisatore. 'The poet himself chooses the subjects for his poems; the multitude has no right to direct his inspiration.'

We have been led a long way by the impetus and revolution of the Pushkin theme in Chernyshevski's life; meanwhile a new character – whose name once or twice has already burst impatiently into our discourse – is awaiting his entrance. Now it is just time for him to appear – and here he comes in the tightly buttoned, blue-collared regulation coat of a university student, fairly reeking of *chestnost'* ('progressive principle'), ungainly, with tiny, shortsighted eyes and a scanty Newport Frill (that *barbe en collier* which seemed so symptomatic to Flaubert); he offers his hand jabwise; i.e., thrusting it oddly forward with the thumb turned out, and introduces himself in a catarrhally confidential little bass: Dobrolyubov.

Their first meeting (summer 1856) was recalled almost thirty years later by Chernyshevski (when he also wrote about Nekrasov) with his familiar wealth of detail, essentially sickly and impotent, but supposed to set off the irreproachability of thought in its transactions with time. Friendship joined these two men in a monogrammatic union which a hundred centuries are incompetent to untie (on the contrary: it becomes even faster in the consciousness of posterity). This is not the place to enlarge upon the literary activities of the younger man. Let us merely say he was uncouthly crude and uncouthly naïve; that in the satirical review *The Whistle* he poked fun at the distinguished Dr Pirogov while parodying Lermontov (the use of some of Lermontov's lyrical poems as a canvas for journalistic jokes about people and events was in general so widespread that in the long run it turned into a caricature of the very art of parody); let us say also, in Strannolyubski's words, that 'from the push given it by Dobrolyubov, literature rolled down an inclined plane, with the inevitable result, once it had rolled to zero, that it was put into inverted commas: the student brought some "literature"' (meaning propaganda leaflets). What else can one add? Dobrolyubov's humour? Oh, those blessed times when 'mosquito' was *in itself* funny, a mosquito settling on someone's nose twice as funny, and a mosquito flying into a governmental office and biting a civil servant caused the listeners to groan and double up with laughter!

Much more engaging than Dobrolyubov's obtuse and ponderous critique (all this pleiade of radical critics in fact wrote with their *feet*) is the frivolous side of his life, that feverish, romantic sportiveness which subsequently supplied Chernyshevski with material for the 'love intrigues' of Levitski (in *The Prologue*). Dobrolyubov was extraordinarily prone to falling in love (here we catch a glimpse of him playing assiduously *durachki*, a simple card game, with a much-decorated general whose daughter he courts). He had a German girl in Staraya Russa, a strong, onerous tie. From immoral visits to her, Chernyshevski held him back in the full sense of the word: for a long time they would wrestle, both of them limp, scrawny and sweaty – toppling all over the floor, colliding with the furniture – all the time silent, all you could hear was their wheezing; then, stumbling into one another, they would both search for their spectacles beneath the upturned chairs. At the beginning of 1859, gossip reached Chernyshevski that Dobrolyubov (just like d'Anthès), in order to cover his 'intrigue' with Olga Sokratovna, wanted to marry her sister (who already had a fiancé). Both the young women played outrageous tricks on Dobrolyubov; they took him to masked balls dressed as a Capuchin or an ice-cream vendor and confided all their secrets in him. Walks with Olga Sokratovna 'completely bemused' him. 'I know there is nothing to be gained here,' he wrote to a friend, 'because not a single conversation goes by without her mentioning that although I am a good man, nevertheless I am too clumsy and almost repulsive. I understand that I should not try to gain anything anyway, since in any case I am fonder of Nikolay Gavrilovich than of her. But at the same time I am powerless to leave her alone.' When he heard the gossip, Nikolay Gavrilovich, who entertained no illusions concerning his wife's morals, still felt some resentment: the betrayal was a double one; he and Dobrolyubov had a frank explanation and soon afterwards he sailed to London to 'maul Herzen' (as he subsequently expressed it); i.e., to give him a good scolding for his attacks on that same Dobrolyubov in the *Kolokol* (*The Bell*), a liberal periodical published abroad, but of less radical views than the endemic *Contemporary*.

Perhaps, however, the object of this meeting was not only to intercede for his friend: Dobrolyubov's name (especially later, in connection with his death), Chernyshevski very skilfully handled 'as a matter of revolutionary tactics'. According to certain reports from the past his main object in visiting Herzen was to discuss the publishing of *The Contemporary* abroad: everyone had a premonition that soon it would be closed down. But in general this trip is surrounded with such a haze and has left so few traces in Chernyshevski's writings that one would almost prefer, in spite of the facts, to consider it apocryphal. He who had always been interested in England, he who had nourished his soul on Dickens and his mind on *the Times* – how avidly he should have gulped it down, how many impressions he should have garnered, how insistently he should later have kept turning back to it in memory! Actually, Chernyshevski never spoke of his journey and whenever anyone really pressed him, he would reply briefly: 'Well, what's there to talk about – there was fog, the ship rocked, what else could there be?' Thus, life itself (how many times now) refuted his axiom: 'The tangible object acts much more strongly than the abstract concept of it.'

However that may have been, on the 26th June (New Style?), 1859, Chernyshevski arrived in London (everyone thought that he was in Saratov) and stayed there until the 30th. An oblique ray pierces the fog of these four days: Mme Tuchkov-Ogaryov walks through a drawing-room and into a sunny garden, carrying in her arms her year-old baby girl dressed in a little lace pelerine. In the drawing-room (the action takes place in Putney, at Herzen's house) Alexander Ivanovich is walking back and forth (these indoor walks were very much the thing in those days) with a gentleman of medium height whose face is unattractive 'but illumined by a wonderful expression of self-abnegation and submissiveness to fate' (which most likely was merely a trick of the memoirist's memory, recalling that face through the prism of a fate which had already been accomplished). Herzen introduced his companion to her. Chernyshevski stroked the infant's hair and said in his quiet voice: 'I also have some like this, but I hardly ever see them.' (He used to confuse the names of his children: little Victor was in Saratov, where he soon died, for the fate of children does not forgive such slips of the pen – but he sent a kiss to 'little Sasha' who had already been back to St Petersburg.) 'Say how do you do, give us your hand,' said Herzen rapidly, and then immediately began to reply to something that had been said by Chernyshevski: 'Yes, exactly – that's why they sent them to the Siberian mines'; while Mme Tuchkov floated into the garden and the oblique ray was extinguished forever.

Diabetes and nephritis added to tuberculosis soon put an end to Dobrolyubov. He was dying in the late autumn of 1861; Chernyshevski paid him a daily call and from there went about his conspiratorial affairs, which were amazingly well concealed from police spies. It is generally considered that he was the author of the proclamation 'To the Serfs of Landowners'. 'There was not much talk,' recalls Shelgunov (who wrote the one 'To the Soldiers'); and evidently not even Vladislav Kostomarov, who printed these appeals, knew with any certainty about Chernyshevski's authorship. Their style is very reminiscent of Count Rastopchin's corny little placards against Napoleon's invasion: 'So this is what it comes to, this thorough-true freedom. . . . And let courts be just and let all be alike before justice. . . . And what's the sense of kicking up a ruction in one village only?' If this was written by Chernyshevski (incidentally, '*bulga*', 'ruction', is a Volga word), it was in any case touched up by someone else.

According to information stemming from the People's Freedom organization, Chernyshevski suggested to Sleptsov and his friends in July, 1861, that they form a basic cell of five – the nucleus of an 'underground' society. The system consisted in every member forming, moreover, his own cell, and thus knowing only eight people. Only the centre knew all the members. All the members were known only to Chernyshevski. This account does not seem free from some stylization.

But let us repeat: he was ideally cautious. After the student disorders of October, 1861, he was put under permanent surveillance, but the agents' work was not distinguished for its subtlety: Nikolay Gavrilovich had as a cook the wife of the house janitor, a tall red-cheeked old woman with a somewhat unexpected name: Musa. She was bribed with no trouble – five roubles for coffee, to which she was much addicted. In return Musa used to supply the police with the contents of her employer's wastebasket.

Meanwhile, on November 17, 1861, at twenty-five years of age, Dobrolyubov died. He was buried in the Volkov cemetery 'in a simple oak coffin' (the coffin in such cases is always simple) next to Belinski. 'Suddenly there stepped forth an energetic, clean-shaven gentleman,' recalls a witness (Chernyshevski's appearance was still unfamiliar), and since few people had gathered, and this irritated him, he started to speak of it with detailed irony. While he was speaking, Olga Sokratovna shook with tears, leaning upon the arm of one of those devoted students who were always with her: another, besides his own regulation cap, held the raccoon cap of the 'boss', who with his fur coat unbuttoned – in spite of the frost – took out an exercise book and began in an angry, didactic voice to read from it Dobrolyubov's lumpy grey poems about honest principles and approaching death; hoarfrost shone on the birches; and a little to one side, next to the doddering mother of one of the gravediggers, in new felt boots and full of humility, stood an agent of the Secret Police. 'Yes,' concluded Chernyshevski, 'we are not concerned here with the fact that the censorship, by cutting his articles to bits, brought Dobrolyubov to a disease of the kidneys. For his own glory he did enough. For his own sake he had no reason to live longer. For men of such a cast and with such aspirations life has nothing but burning grief to offer. Honest principles – that was his fatal illness,' and pointing with his rolled-up notebook to an adjacent, empty place on the other side, Chernyshevski exclaimed: 'There is not a man in Russia worthy of occupying that grave!' (There was: it was occupied soon afterwards by Pisarev.)

It is difficult to escape the impression that Chernyshevski, who in his youth had dreamed of being the leader of a national uprising, was now revelling in the rarefied air of danger surrounding him. This significance in the secret life of his country he acquired inevitably, by agreement with his epoch, a family likeness with which he himself realized. Now, it seemed, he needed only a day, only an hour's run of luck in the game of history, one moment of passionate union between chance and destiny, in order to soar. A revolution was expected in 1863, and in the cabinet of the future constitutional government he was listed as prime minister. How he nursed that precious ardour within him! That mysterious 'something' which Steklov talks about in spite of his Marxism, and which was extinguished in Siberia (although 'learning' and 'logic' and even 'implacability' remained), undoubtedly existed in Chernyshevski and manifested itself with unusual strength just before his banishment to Siberia. Magnetic and dangerous, it was this that frightened the government far more than any proclamations. 'This demented gang is thirsting for blood, for outrages,' excitedly said the reports. 'Deliver us from Chernyshevski. . . .'

'Desolation . . . Lone mountain ranges . . . A myriad lakes and marshes . . . A shortage of the most essential things . . . Inefficient postmasters . . . [All this] exhausts even the patience of genius.' (This is what he had copied into *The Contemporary* from the geographer Selski's book on the Yakutsk province – thinking of certain things, supposing certain things – perhaps having a presentiment.)

In Russia the censorship department arose before literature; its fateful seniority has been always in evidence: and what an urge to give it a tweak! Chernyshevski's activities on *The Contemporary* turned into a voluptuous mockery of the censorship, which unquestionably was one of our country's most remarkable institutions. And right then, at a time when the authorities were fearful, for example, lest 'musical notes should conceal anti-governmental writings in code' (and so commissioned well-paid experts to decode them), Chernyshevski, in his magazine, under the cover of elaborate clowning, was frenziedly promulgating Feuerbach. Whenever, in articles about Garibaldi or Cavour (one shrinks from computing the miles of small print this indefatigable man translated from *the Times*), in his commentaries on Italian events, he kept adding in brackets with drilling insistence after practically every other sentence: 'Italy', 'in Italy', 'I am talking about Italy' – the already corrupted reader knew that he meant he was talking about Russia and the present question. Or else: Chernyshevski would pretend he was chattering about anything that came to mind, just for the sake of incoherent and vacant prattle – but suddenly, striped and spotted with words, dressed in verbal camouflage, the important idea he wished to convey would slip through. Subsequently the whole gamut of this 'buffoonery' was carefully put together by Vladislav Kostomarov for the information of the secret police; the work was mean, but it gave essentially a true picture of 'Chernyshevski's special devices'.

Another Kostomarov, a professor, says somewhere that Chernyshevski was a first-rate chess player. Actually neither Kostomarov nor Chernyshevski knew much about chess. In his youth, it is true, Nikolay Gavrilovich once bought a set, attempted even to master a handbook, managed more or less to learn the moves, and messed about with it for quite a time (noting this messing about in detail); finally, tiring of this empty pastime, he turned over everything to a friend. Fifteen years later (remembering that Lessing had got to know Mendelssohn over a chessboard) he founded the St Petersburg Chess Club, which was opened in January, 1882, existed through spring, gradually declining, and would have failed of itself had it not been closed down in connection with the 'St Petersburg fires'. It was simply a literary and political circle situated in the so-called Ruadze House. Chernyshevski would come and sit at a table, tapping upon it with a rook (which he called a 'castle'), and relate innocuous anecdotes. The radical Serno-Solovievich would arrive – (this is a Turgenevian dash) and strike up a conversation with someone in a secluded corner. It was fairly empty. The drinking fraternity – the minor writers Pomyalovski, Kurochkin, Krol – would vociferate in the bar. The first, by the way, did a little preaching of his own, promoting the idea of communal literary work – 'Let's organize,' he said, 'a society of writer-labourers for investigating various aspects of our social life, such as: beggars, haberdashers, lamplighters, firemen – and pool in a special magazine all the material we get.' Chernyshevski derided him and a silly rumour went around to the effect that Pomyalovski had 'bashed his mug in'. 'It's all lies, I respect you too much for that,' wrote Pomyalovski to him.

In a large auditorium situated in that same Ruadze House there took place on March 2, 1862, Chernyshevski's first (if you do not count his dissertation defence and the graveside speech in the frost) public address. Officially the proceeds of the evening were to go to needy students; but in actual fact it was in aid of the political prisoners Mihailov and Obruchev, who had recently been arrested. Rubinstein brilliantly performed an extremely stirring march, Professor Pavlov spoke of Russia's millennium – and added ambiguously that if the government stopped at the first step (the emancipation of the peasants) 'it would stop on the brink of an abyss – let those with ears to hear, hear'. (They heard him; he was immediately expulsed.) Nekrasov read some poor but 'powerful' verses dedicated to the memory of Dobrolyubov, and Kurochkin read a translation of Béranger's 'The Little Bird' (the captive's languishment and the rapture of sudden freedom); Chernyshevski's speech was also on Dobrolyubov.

Greeted with massive applause (the youth of those days had a way of keeping their palms hollowed while they clapped, so that the result resembled a cannon salvo), he stood for a while, blinking and smiling. Alas, his appearance did not please the ladies eagerly awaiting the *tribune* – whose portrait was unobtainable. An uninteresting, they said, face, haircut *à la moujik*, and for some reason wearing not tails but a short coat with braid and a horrible tie – 'a colour catastrophe' (Olga Ryzhkov, *A Woman of the Sixties: Memoirs*). Besides that he came somehow unprepared, oratory was new to him, and trying to conceal his agitation he adopted a conversational tone which seemed too modest to his friends and too familiar to his ill-wishers. He began by talking about his briefcase (from which he took a notebook), explaining that the most remarkable part of it was the lock with a small cogwheel: 'Look, you give it a turn and the briefcase is locked, and if you want to lock it even more positively, it turns a different way and then comes off and goes in your pocket, and on the spot where it was, here on this plaque, there are carved arabesques: very, very nice.' Then in a high, edifying voice he started to read an article by Dobrolyubov that everybody knew, but suddenly broke off and (as in the authorial digressions in *What to Do?*) chummily taking the audience into his confidence, began to explain in great detail that he had not been Dobrolyubov's guide; while speaking, he played ceaselessly with his watch chain – something that stuck in the minds of all the memoirists and was to provide a theme for scoffing journalists; but, when you come to think of it, he might have been fiddling with his watch because there was indeed very little free time left to him (four months in all!) His tone of voice, 'négligé with spirit' as they used to say in the seminary, and the complete absence of revolutionary insinuations annoyed his audience; he had no success whatsoever, while Pavlov was almost chaired. The memoirist Nikoladze remarks that as soon as Pavlov had been banished from St Petersburg, people understood and appreciated Chernyshevski's caution; he himself – subsequently, in his Siberian wilderness, where a live and avid auditorium appeared to him sometimes only in febrile dreams – keenly regretted that lame speech, that fiasco, repining at himself for not having seized that unique opportunity (since he was in any case doomed to ruin!) and not delivering from that lectern in the Ruadze hall a speech of iron and fire, that very speech which the hero of his novel was about to give, very likely, when upon returning to freedom he took a droshky and cried to the driver: 'The Galleries!'

Events went very fast that windy spring. Fires broke out here and there. And suddenly – against this orange-and-black background – a vision. Running and holding on to his hat, Dostoevski sweeps by: where to?

Whit Monday (May 28, 1862), a strong wind is blowing; a conflagration has begun on the Ligovka and then the desperadoes set fire to the Apraxin Palace. Dostoevski is running, firemen are galloping 'and in pharmacy windows, in gaudy glass globes, upside down are in passing reflected' (as seen by Nekrasov). And over there, thick smoke billows over the Fontanka canal in the direction of Chernyshyov Street, where presently a new, black column arises. . . . Meanwhile Dostoevski has arrived. He has arrived at the heart of the *blackness,* at Chernyshevski's place, and starts to beg him hysterically to *put a stop* to all this. Two aspects are interesting here: the belief in Nikolay Gavrilovich's satanic powers, and the rumours that the arson was being carried out according to the same plan which the Petrashevskians had drawn up as early at 1849.

Secret agents, in tones also not void of mystic horror, reported that during the night at the height of the disaster 'laughter was heard coming from Chernyshevski's window'. The police endowed him with a devilish resourcefulness and smelled a trick in his every move. Nikolay Gavrilovich's family went to spend the summer at Pavlovsk, a few miles from St Petersburg, and there, a few days after the fires, on June 10th to be precise (dusk, mosquitoes, music), a certain Lyubetski, adjutant major of the Uhlan regiment of the Guards, a dashing fellow, with a name like a kiss, noticed as he was leaving the 'vauxhall' two ladies capering about like mad things, and in the simpleness of his heart taking them for young Camelias (loose women), he 'made an attempt to grasp them both by the waist'. The four students who were with them surrounded him and threatened him with retribution, announcing that one of the ladies was the wife of the writer Chernyshevski and the other her sister. What, in the opinion of the police, is the husband's design? He tries to get the case to be submitted to the court of the officers' association – not out of considerations of honour but merely for the clandestine purpose of bringing military men and university students together. On July 5th he had to visit the Secret Police Department in connection with his complaint. Potapov, its chief, refused his petition, saying that according to his information the Uhlan was prepared to apologize. Chernyshevski curtly renounced any claims and changing the subject asked: 'Tell me, the other day I sent my family off to Saratov and am preparing myself to go there for a rest [*The Contemporary* had already been closed]; but if I should need to take my wife abroad, to a spa – you see she suffers from nervous pains – could I leave without hindrance?' 'Of course you could,' replied Potapov good-naturedly; and two days later the arrest took place.

All this was preceded by the following event: a 'universal exhibition' has just opened in London (the nineteenth century was unusually fond of exhibiting its wealth – a plentiful and tasteless dowry, which the present one has squandered); gathered there were tourists and merchants, correspondents and spies; one day at an enormous banquet Herzen, in a fit of carelessness, in view of everyone handed a certain Vetoshnikov, who was preparing to leave for Russia, a letter to the radical journalist Serno-Solovievich, who was asked to direct Chernyshevski's attention to the announcement made in *The Bell* concerning its willingness to publish *The Contemporary* abroad. The nimble foot of the messenger had hardly had time to touch Russia's sands when he was seized.

Chernyshevski was then living near the church of St Vladimir (later his Astrakhan addresses were also defined by their proximity to this or that holy building) in a house where, before him, had lived Muravyov (later a cabinet minister), whom he was to depict with such helpless loathing in *The Prologue*. On July 7th two friends had come to see him: Doctor Bokov (who subsequently used to send medical advice to the exile) and

Antonovich (a member of 'Land and Freedom', who in spite of his close friendship with Chernyshevski did not suspect that the latter was connected with that society). They were sitting in the drawing-room, where they were presently joined by Colonel Rakeev, a thickset black-uniformed police officer with an unpleasant, wolfish profile. He sat down with the air of a guest; actually, he had come to arrest Chernyshevski. Again historical patterns come into that odd contact 'which thrills the gamester in a historian' (Strannolyubski): this was the same Rakeev who as an embodiment of the government's contemptible scurry had whisked Pushkin's coffin out of the capital into posthumous exile. Having chatted a few minutes for the sake of decorum, Rakeev informed Chernyshevski with a polite smile (which caused Doctor Bokov to 'turn chill inside') that he would like to have a word with him alone. 'Then let's go to my study,' replied the latter and headed for it so precipitately that Rakeev, though not exactly disconcerted – he was too experienced for that – did not consider it possible in his role of guest to follow him with equal speed. But Chernyshevski immediately returned, his Adam's apple convulsively bobbing as he washed something down with cold tea (*swallowed papers* according to Antonovich's sinister guess), and looking over his spectacles, he let his guest enter first. His friends, having nothing better to do (waiting in the drawing-room where most of the furniture was shrouded in dust-covers seemed uncommonly bleak), went out for a stroll ('It can't be . . . I can't believe it,' Boskov kept repeating), and when they returned to the house, the fourth in Bolshoy Moskovski street, they were alarmed to see that there now stood at the door – in a kind of meek and thus all the more loathsome expectation – a prison carriage. First Bokov went in to say good-bye to Chernyshevski, then – Antonovich. Nikolay Gavrilovich was sitting at his desk, playing with a pair of scissors, while the colonel sat next to it, one leg folded over the other; they were chatting – still for the sake of decorum – about the advantages of Pavlovsk over other holiday areas. 'And then the company there is so excellent,' the colonel was saying with a slight cough.

'What, you too are going without waiting for me?' said Chernyshevski, turning to his apostle. 'Unfortunately I have to . . .' replied Antonovich, in deep confusion. 'Well, good-bye then,' said Nikolay Gavrilovich in a joking tone of voice, and lifting his hand high, he lowered it with a swoop into Antonovich's: a type of comradely farewell which subsequently became very widespread among Russian revolutionaries.

'And so,' exclaims Strannolyubski at the beginning of the greatest chapter in his incomparable monograph, 'Chernyshevski has been seized!' That night the news of the arrest flies around the whole city. Many a breast is swelled with resonant indignation. Many a hand is clenched. . . . But there were not a few gloating sneers: Aha, they've put the ruffian away, removed the 'impudent, yowling yokel', as it was expressed by the (slightly cracked, anyway) lady novelist Kokhanovski. Next, Strannolyubski gives a striking description of the complex work which the authorities had to carry out in order to create the evidence 'which should have been there but was not', for a very curious situation had arisen: judicially speaking there was nothing to fasten on to and they had to build a scaffolding for the law to climb up and work. So they worked with 'dummy quantities', calculating to remove carefully all the dummies only when the emptiness enclosed by the law was filled up by something actual. The case built up against Chernyshevski was a phantom; but it was the phantom of genuine guilt; and then – from outside, artificially, by a roundabout route – they managed to find a certain solution to the problem which almost coincided with the true one.

We have three points. C, K, P. A cathetus is drawn, CK. To offset Chernyshevski, the authorities picked out a retired Uhlan cornet, Vladislav Dmitrievich Kostomarov, who the previous August in Moscow had been reduced to the ranks for printing seditious publications – a man with a touch of madness and a pinch of Pechorinism about him, and also a verse-maker: he left a scolopendrine trace in literature as the translator of foreign poets. Another cathetus is drawn, KP. The critic Pisarev in the periodical *The Russian Word* writes about these translations, scolding the author for 'The magnificent tiara's Coruscation like a pharos' [from Hugo], praising his 'simple and heartfelt' rendering of some lines by Burns (which came out as 'And first of all, and first of all / Let all men honest be / Let's pray that man be to each man / A brother first of all . . .' etc.), and in connection with Kostomarov's report to his readers that Heine died an unrepentant sinner, the critic roguishly advises the 'grim denouncer' to 'take a good look at his own public activities'. Kostomarov's derangement was evidenced in his florid graphomania, in the senseless somnambulistic (even though made-to-order) composition of counterfeit letters studded with

French phrases; and finally in his macabre playfulness: he signed his reports to Putilin (a detective): *Feofan Otchenashenko* (Theophanus Ourfatherson) or *Ventseslav Lyutyy* (Wenceslaus the Fiend). And, indeed, he was fiendish in his taciturnity, funest and false, boastful and cringing. Endowed with curious abilities, he could write in a feminine hand – explaining this himself by the fact that he was 'visited at the full moon by the spirit of Queen Tamara'. The plurality of hands he could imitate in addition to the circumstance (yet one more of destiny's jokes) that his normal handwriting recalled that of Chernyshevski considerably heightened the value of this hypnotic betrayer. For indirect evidence that the appeal proclamation 'To the Serfs of Landowners' had been written by Chernyshevski, Kostomarov was given, first, the task of fabricating a note, allegedly from Chernyshevski, containing a request to alter one word in the appeal; and, secondly, of preparing a letter (to 'Aleksey Nikolaevich') that would furnish proof of Chernyshevski's active participation in the revolutionary movement. Both the one and the other were then and there concocted by Kostomarov. The forgery of the handwriting is quite evident: at the beginning the forger still took pains but then he seems to have grown bored by the work and to be in a hurry to get it over: to take but the word 'I', *ya* (formed in Russian script somewhat like a proof-reader's dele). In Chernyshevski's genuine manuscripts it ends with an outgoing stroke which is straight and strong – and even curves a little to the right – while here, in the forgery, this stroke curves with a kind of queer jauntiness to the left, toward the head, as if the *ya* were saluting.

While these preparations went on, Nikolay Gavrilovich was held in the Alekseevski Ravelin of the Peter-and-Paul Fortress, in close proximity to the twenty-two-year-old Pisarev, who had been imprisoned there four days before him: the hypotenuse is drawn, CP, and the fateful triangle CPK is consolidated. At first, life in prison did not oppress Chernyshevski: the absence of importunate visitors even seemed refreshing . . . but the hush of the unknown soon began to chafe him. A 'deep' matting swallowed without a trace the steps of the sentries pacing along the corridors. . . . The only sound that came from the outside was a clock's classic striking which vibrated long in one's ears. . . . It was a life whose portrayal demands from a writer an abundance of dots. . . . It was that unkind Russian isolation from which sprang the Russian dream of a kind multitude. By lifting a corner of the green baize curtain the sentry could look through the peephole in the door at the prisoner sitting on his green wooden bed or on a green chair, wearing a dressing gown of frieze and a peaked cap – one was permitted to keep one's own headgear as long as it was not a top hat – which does credit to the government's sense of harmony but creates by the law of negatives a rather tenacious image (as for Pisarev, he sported a fez). He was allowed a goose-quill pen, and one could write on a small green table with a sliding drawer, 'whose bottom, like Achilles' heel, had remained unpainted' (Strannolyubski).

Autumn passed. A small rowan tree grew in the prison yard. Prisoner number nine was not fond of walking; at the beginning, however, he went out every day, reasoning (a quirk of thought extremely characteristic for him) that during this time the cell was searched – consequently a refusal to go out for a walk would cause the administration to suspect he was hiding something there; but when he had become convinced that this was not so (by leaving threads here and there as marks), he sat down to write with a light heart: by winter he had finished his translation of Schlosser and had begun to translate Gervinus and T. B. Macaulay. He also wrote one or two things of his own. Let us recall the 'Diary' – and from one of our much earlier paragraphs let us pick up the loose ends of some sentences dealing in advance with his writings in the fortress . . . or no – let us go, if you please, even farther back, to the 'lachrymatory theme', which began to rotate on the initial pages of our mysteriously revolving story.

Before us is Chernyshevski's famous letter to his wife dated December 5th, 1862: a yellow diamond among the dust of his numerous works. We examine this harsh-looking and ugly but amazingly legible handwriting, with its resolute strokes at the tails of the words, with loopy *R*'s and *P*'s and the broad, fervent crosses of the 'hard signs' – and our lugs dilate with a pure emotion such as we have not experienced for a long time. Strannolyubski justly designates this letter as the beginning of Chernyshevski's brief flowering. All the fire, all the power of will and mind allotted him, everything that was supposed to burst forth at the hour of a national uprising, to burst forth and clutch in its hold, even if only for a short time, the supreme power . . . to jerk violently the bridle and perhaps to crimson the lip of Russia, the rearing steed, with blood – all this now found a sick outlet in his correspondence. One can say, in fact, that here was the aim and crown of all his life's dialectic which had long been accumulating in muffled depths – these iron, fury-driven epistles to the commission examining his case, which he included in letters to his wife, the exultant rage of his arguments and this chain-rattling megalomania. 'Men will remember us with gratitude,' he wrote to Olga Sokratovna, and he turned out to be right: it was precisely *this* sound which echoed and spread through all the remaining space of the century, making the hearts of millions of intellectual provincials beat with sincere and noble tenderness. We have already referred to that part of the letter where he talks of his plans for compiling dictionaries. After the words 'as was Aristotle' come the words: 'I have begun speaking, however, of my thoughts: they are a secret; you must not tell anyone about what I say to you alone.' 'Here,' comments Steklov, 'on these two lines a teardrop has fallen and Chernyshevski had to repeat the blurred letters.' This is not quite right. The teardrop fell (near the fold of the sheet) *before* the writing of these two lines; Chernyshevski had to rewrite two words, 'secret' and 'about' (one at the beginning of the first line, the other at the beginning of the second), words which he had started to trace each time on the wet place and which remained therefore unfinished.

Two days afterwards, getting more and more angry and more and more believing in his invulnerability, he began to 'maul' his judges. This second letter to his wife can be divided up into points: (1) I told you in connection with the rumour about my possible arrest that I was not mixed up in any affair and that the government would be forced to apologize if it arrested me. (2) I assumed this because I knew they were following me – they boasted that they were doing it very well, and I relied on their boast, for my calculation was that, knowing how I lived and what I did, they would know that their suspicions were groundless. (3) It was a stupid calculation. For I also knew that in our country, people are incapable of doing anything properly. (4) Thus by my arrest they have compromised the government. (5) What can 'we' do? Apologize? But what if 'he' doesn't accept the apology, but says: You have compromised the government, it is my duty to explain this to the government. (6) Therefore 'we' shall postpone the unpleasantness. (7) But the government asks from time to time whether Chernyshevski is guilty – and finally the government will obtain an answer. (8) It is that answer I am waiting for.

'The copy of a rather curious letter from Chernyshevski,'

added Potapov in pencil. 'But he is mistaken: no one will have to apologize.'

A few days after that he began to write his novel, *What to Do?* – and by January 15th he had sent the first portion to Pypin; a week later he sent a second, and Pypin handed both to Nekrasov for *The Contemporary*, which had again been permitted (beginning with February). At the same time *The Russian Word* was allowed after a similar eight-month suspension; and in the impatient expectation of journalistic profit, the dangerous fezzed neighbour had already dipped his pen.

It is gratifying to be able to state that at this juncture some mysterious force resolved to try to save Chernyshevski at least from *this* mess. He was having a particularly hard time – how could one fail to have compassion? On the 28th, because the government, exasperated by his attacks, had refused him permission to see his wife, he began a hunger strike: hunger strikes were then a novelty in Russia and the exponent they found was clumsy. The guards noticed that he was wasting, but the food seemed to be getting eaten. . . . When, however, four days later, struck by the putrid smell in the cell, the warders searched it, they established that the solid food had been hidden among the books while the cabbage soup had been poured into cracks. On Sunday, February 3rd, at about 1 p.m., the military doctor attached to the fortress examined the prisoner and found that he was pale, his tongue fairly clear, his pulse a little weak – and on that same day at that same hour Nekrasov, on his way home (corner of Liteynaya and Basseynaya streets) in a hackney sleigh, lost the pink-paper package containing two manuscripts, each threaded through at the corners and entitled *What to Do?* While remembering with the lucidity of despair the whole of his route, he did not recall the fact that when nearing his house he had laid the package beside him in order to take out his purse – and just then the sleigh had turned . . . a crunch as it skidded . . . and *What to Do?* rolled off unnoticed: this was the attempt of the mysterious force – in this case centrifugal – to confiscate the book whose success was destined to have such a disastrous effect upon the fate of its author. But the attempt failed: on the snow near the Maryinski Hospital the pink package was picked up by a poor clerk burdened with a large family. Having plodded home, he donned his spectacles and examined his find . . . he saw that it was the beginning of some kind of literary work and without a tremor, and not burning his sluggish fingers, he put it aside. 'Destroy it!' begged a hopeless voice: in vain. A notice of its loss was printed in the Saint Petersburg *Police Gazette*. The clerk carried the package to the indicated address, for which he received the promised reward: fifty silver roubles.

In the meantime his jailers had begun to give Nikolay Gavrilovich appetite-stimulating drops; twice he took them and then, suffering greatly, he announced that he would take no more, for he was refusing to eat not from absence of appetite but from caprice. On the morning of the 6th, 'owing to lack of experience in discerning the symptoms of suffering', he ended his hunger strike and had breakfast. On the 12th, Potapov informed the commandant that the commission could not permit Chernyshevski to see his wife until he had completely recovered. The following day the commandant reported that Chernyshevski was well and writing at full blast. Olga Sokratovna came with loud complaints – about her health, about the Pypins, about the shortage of money, and then through her tears began to laugh at the little beard her husband had grown, finally getting even more upset and commencing to embrace him.

'That will do, my dear, that will do,' he kept saying quite calmly – using the tepid tone he invariably maintained in his relations with her: actually he loved her passionately, hopelessly. 'Neither I nor anyone else can have any grounds for thinking I shall not be set free,' he told her in parting, with particular emphasis.

Another month passed. On March 23rd there was the confrontation with Kostomarov. Vladislav Dmitrievich glowered and obviously got tangled up in his own lies. Chernyshevski, with a slight smile of disgust, replied abruptly and contemptuously. His superiority was striking. 'And to think,' exclaims Steklov, 'that at this time he was writing the buoyant *What to Do?*'

Alas! To write *What to Do?* in the fortress was not so much surprising as reckless – even for the very reason that the authorities attached it to his case. In general the history of this novel's appearance is extremely interesting. The censorship permitted it to be published in *The Contemporary,* reckoning on the fact that a novel which was 'something in the highest degree anti-artistic' would be certain to overthrow Chernyshevski's authority, that he would simply be laughed at for it. And indeed, what worth, for example, are the 'light' scenes in the novel? 'Verochka was supposed to drink half a glass for her wedding, half a glass for her shop and half a glass for the health of Julie [a redeemed Parisian prostitute who is now the girl friend of one of the characters!] She and Julie started a romp, with screams and clamour. . . . They began to wrestle and both fell on the sofa . . . and they no longer wanted to get up, but only continued screaming and laughing and both fell asleep.' Sometimes the turn of phrase smacks of folksy barrack lore and sometimes of . . . Zoshchenko: 'After tea . . . she went to her room and lay down. So there she is, reading in her comfy bed, but the book sinks away from her eyes and now Vera Pavlovna is thinking, Why is it that somehow I feel lately somewhat dull sometimes?' There are also many charming solecisms – here is a specimen: when one of the characters, a doctor, has pneumonia and calls in a colleague: 'For a long time they palpated the sides of one of them.'

But nobody laughed. Not even the great Russian writers laughed. Even Herzen, who found it 'vilely written', immediately qualified this with: 'On the other hand there is much that is good and healthy.' Still, he could not resist remarking that the novel ends not simply with a phalanstery but with 'a phalanstery in a brothel'. For of course the inevitable happened: the eminently pure Chernyshevski (who had never been to a brothel, in his artless aspiration to equip communal love with especially beautiful trappings, involuntarily and unconsciously, out of the simplicity of his imagination, had worked his way through to those very ideals that had been evolved by tradition and routine in houses of ill repute; his gay 'evening ball', based on freedom and equality in relations between the sexes (first one and then another couple disappears and returns again), is extremely reminiscent of the concluding dances in *Mme Tellier's Establishment*.

And nevertheless it is impossible to handle this old magazine (March, 1863), containing the first instalment of the novel, without a certain thrill; here also is Nekrasov's poem 'Green Noise' ('Endure while you can still endure . . .'), and the derisive dressing down of Aleksey Tolstoy's romance *Prince Serebryanyy*. . . . Instead of the expected sneers, an atmosphere of general, pious worship was created around *What to Do?* It was read the way liturgical books are read – not a single work by Turgenev or Tolstoy produced such a mighty impression. The inspired Russian reader understood the good that the talentless novelist had vainly tried to express. It would seem that, having realized its miscalculation, the government should have interrupted the serialization of *What to Do?* It behaved much more cleverly.

Chernyshevski's neighbour had now also done some writing. He had been receiving *The Contemporary* and on October 8th, he sent *The Russian Word* an article from the fortress, 'Thoughts about Russian Novels', at which the Senate informed the Governor-General that this was nothing else but an analysis of Chernyshevski's novel, with praise for his work and a detailed exposition of the materialistic ideas in it. In order to characterize Pisarev it was indicated that he was subject to 'dementia melancholica', for which he had been treated: in 1859 he had spent four months in a lunatic asylum.

Just as, in his boyhood, he had arrayed all his notebooks in rainbow covers, so, as a grown man, Pisarev would suddenly abandon some urgent work in order to painstakingly colour wood-cuts in books, or when going off to the country, would order a red-and-blue summer suit of sarafan calico from his tailor. This professed utilitarian's mental illness was distinguished by a kind of perverted aestheticism. Once at a student gathering he suddenly stood up, gracefully raised his curved arm, as if requesting permission to speak, and in this sculpturesque pose fell down unconscious. Another time, to the alarm of his hostess and fellow guests, he began to undress, throwing off with gay alacrity his velvet jacket, motley vest, checkered trousers – At this point they overpowered him. Amusingly enough there are commentators who call Pisarev an 'epicure', referring, for example, to his letters to his mother – unbearable, bilious, teeth-clenching phrases about life being beautiful; or else, to illustrate his 'sober realism' they quote his outwardly sensible and clear – but actually completely insane – letter from the fortress to an unknown maiden, with a proposal of marriage: 'The woman who agrees to lighten and warm my life will receive from me all the love which was spurned by Raissa when she threw herself at the neck of her handsome eagle.'

Now, condemned to a four-year imprisonment for his small part in the general disturbances of the time (which were based in a way on a blind belief in the printed word, especially the secretly printed word), Pisarev wrote about *What to Do?*, reviewing it bit by bit for *The Russian Word* as the instalments appeared in *The Contemporary*. Although in the beginning the Senate was puzzled by the novel's being praised for its ideas instead of being ridiculed because of its style, and expressed the fear that the praises might have a deleterious effect on the younger generation, the authorities soon realized how important it was in the present case to obtain by this method a complete picture of Chernyshevski's perniciousness, which Kostomarov had only outlined in the list of his 'special devices'. 'The government,' says Strannolyubski 'on the one hand permitting Chernyshevski to produce a novel in the fortress and on the other permitting Pisarev, his fellow captive, to produce articles explaining the intentions of this novel, acted with complete awareness, waiting curiously for Chernyshevski to babble himself out and watching what would come of it – in connection with the abundant discharges of his incubator neighbour.'

The business went smoothly and promised a great deal, but it was necessary to put pressure on Kostomarov since one or two definite proofs of guilt were needed, while Chernyshevski continued to boil and jeer in great detail, branding the commission as 'clowns' and 'an incoherent quagmire which is completely stupid'. Therefore Kostomarov was taken to Moscow and there the citizen Yakolev, his former copyist, a drunkard and a rowdy, gave important testimony (for this he received an overcoat which he drank away so noisily in Tver that he was put in a strait-jacket): while doing his copying 'on account of the summer weather in a garden pavilion', he allegedly heard Nikolay Gavrilovich and Vladislav Dmitrievich as they were strolling arm-in-arm (a not implausible detail), talking about greetings from well-wishers to the serfs (it is difficult to find one's way in this mixture of truth and promptings). At a second interrogation in the presence of a replenished Kostomarov, Chernyshevski said somewhat unfortunately that he had visited him only once and not found him in; then he added forcefully: 'I'll go grey, I'll die, but I will not change my testimony.' The testimony of his not being the author of the proclamation is written by him in a trembling hand – trembling with rage rather than fright.

However that may have been, the case was coming to an end. There followed the Senate's 'definition': very nobly it found Chernyshevski's unlawful dealings with Herzen unproved (for Herzen's 'definition' of the Senate see below, at the end of this paragraph). As for the appeal 'To the Serfs of Landowners' . . here the fruit had already ripened on the espaliers of forgery and bribes: the absolute moral conviction of the senators that Chernyshevski was the author thereof was transformed into judicial proof by the letter to 'Aleksey Nikolaevich' (meaning, apparently, A. N. Pleshcheev, a peaceful poet, dubbed by Dostoevski 'an all-round blond' – but for some reason no one insisted too much on Plescheev's part, if any, in the matter).

Thus in Chernyshevski's person they condemned a phantasm closely resembling him; an invented guilt was wonderfully rigged up to look like the real one. The sentence was comparatively light – compared with what one is generally able to devise in this line: he was to be exiled for fourteen years of penal servitude and then to live in Siberia forever. The 'definition' went from the 'savage ignoramuses' of the Senate to the 'grey villains' of the State Council, who completely subscribed to it, and then went on to the sovereign, who confirmed it but reduced the term of penal servitude by half. On May 4th, 1864, the sentence was announced to Chernyshevski, and on the 19th, at 8 o'clock in the morning, on Mytninski Square, he was executed.

It was drizzling, umbrellas undulated, the square was beslushed, and everything was wet; gendarmes' uniforms, the darkened wood of the scaffold, the smooth, black pillar with chains, glossy from the rain. Suddenly the prison carriage appeared. From it emerged, with extraordinary celerity, as if they had rolled out, Chernyshevski in an overcoat and two peasant-like executioners; all three walked with swift steps along a line of soldiers to the scaffold. The crowd lurched forward and the gendarmes pressed back the front ranks; restrained cries sounded here and there: 'Close the umbrellas!' While an official read the sentence, Chernyshevski, who already knew it, sulkily looked around him; he fingered his beard, adjusted his spectacles and spat several times. When the reader stumbled and barely got out 'soshulistic ideas' Chernyshevski smiled and then, recognizing someone in the crowd, nodded, coughed, shifted his stance: from beneath the overcoat his black trousers concertinaed over his rubbers. People standing near could see on his chest an oblong plaque with an inscription in white: STATE CRIMIN (the last syllable had not gone in). At the conclusion of the reading the executioners lowered him to his knees; the elder one, with a backhander, knocked the cap off his long, combed-back, light auburn hair. The face, tapering chinward, its large forehead shining, was now bent down, and with a resounding crack they managed to break an insufficiently incised sword over him. Then they took his hands, which seemed unusually white and weak, and put them in black irons secured to the pillar: he had to stand that way for a quarter of an hour. The rain increased: the younger executioner picked up Chernyshevski's cap and jammed it on his inclined head – and slowly, with difficulty, the chains got in his way – Chernyshevski straightened it. Behind a fence to the left one could see the scaffolding of a house under construction; workmen climbed onto the fence from the other side, one could hear the scrape of their boots; they climbed up, hung there, and abused the criminal from afar. The rain fell; the elder executioner consulted his silver watch. Chernyshevski kept turning his wrists slightly without looking up. Suddenly, out of the better-off part of the crowd, bouquets began to fly. The gendarmes, jumping, tried to intercept them in mid-air. Roses exploded in the air; fleetingly one was able to see a rare combination: a policeman, wreathed. Bobbed-haired ladies in black burnouses threw racemes of lilac. Meanwhile Chernyshevski was hastily released from his chains and his dead body borne away. No – a slip of the pen; alas, he was alive, he was even cheerful! Students ran beside the carriage with cries of 'Farewell, Chernyshevski! *Au revoir!*' He thrust his head out of the window, laughed and shook his finger at the most zealous runners.

'Alas, alive,' we exclaimed, for how could one not prefer the death penalty, the convulsions of the hanged man in his hideous cocoon, to that funeral which twenty-five insipid years later fell to Chernyshevski's lot. The paw of oblivion began slowly to gather in his living image as soon as he had been removed to Siberia. Oh yes, oh yes, no doubt students for years sang the song: 'Let us drink to him who wrote *What to Do?* . . .' But it was to the past they drank, to past glamour and scandal, to a great shade . . . but who would drink to a tremulous little old man with a tic, making clumsy paper boats for Yakut children somewhere in those fabulous backwoods? We affirm that his book drew out and gathered within itself all the heat of his personality – a heat which is not to be found in its helplessly rational structures but which is concealed as it were between the words (as only bread is hot) and it was inevitably doomed to be dispersed with time (as only bread knows how to go stale, and hard). Today, it seems, only Marxists are still capable of being interested by the ghostly ethics contained in this dead little book. To follow easily and freely the categorical imperative of the general good, here is the 'rational egoism' which researchers have found in *What to Do?* Let us recall for comic relief Kautski's conjecture that the idea of egoism is connected with the development of commodity production, and Plekhanov's conclusion that Chernyshevski was nevertheless an 'idealist', since it comes out in his book that the masses must catch up with the intelligentsia out of calculation – and calculation is an opinion. But the matter is simpler than that: the idea that calculation is the foundation of every action (or heroic accomplishment) leads to absurdity: in itself calculation can be heroic! Anything which comes into the focus of human thinking is spiritualized. Thus the 'calculation' of the materialists was ennobled; thus, for those in the know, matter turns into an incorporeal play of mysterious forces. Chernyshevski's ethical structures are in their own way an attempt to construct the same old 'perpetual motion' machine, where matter moves other matter. We would very much like this to revolve: egoism-altruism-egoism-altruism . . . but the wheel stops from friction. What to do? Live, read, think. What to do? Work at one's own development in order to achieve the aim of life, which is happiness. What to do? (But Chernyshevski's own fate changed the business-like question to an ironic exclamation.)

Chernyshevski would have been transferred to a private domicile much sooner if it had not been for the affair of the Karakozovites (adherents of Karakozov, who attempted to assassinate Alexander the Second in 1866): it was made clear at their trial that they had wanted to give Chernyshevski the opportunity of escaping from Siberia and heading a revolutionary movement – or at least publishing a political review in Geneva; and checking the dates, the judges found in *What to Do?* a forecast of the date of the attempt on the Tsar's life. The protagonist Rakhmetov, on his way abroad, 'said among other things that three years later he would return to Russia, it seemed, not then, but three years later [a highly significant repetition typical of our author], he would be needed in Russia'. Meanwhile the last part of the novel was signed on April 4, 1863, and exactly three years later to the day the attempt took place. Thus even figures, Chernyshevski's goldfish, let him down.

Rakhmetov is forgotten today; but in those years he created a whole school of life. With what piety its readers imbibed the sporty, revolutionary element in the novel: Rakhemtov, who 'adopted a boxer's diet', followed also a dialectical régime: 'Therefore if fruit was served he absolutely ate apples and absolutely did not eat apricots (since the poor did not); oranges he ate in St Petersburg, but did not eat in the provinces, because you see in St Petersburg the common people eat them, while in the provinces they do not.'

Where did that young, round little face suddenly flit from,

with its large, childishly prominent forehead and cheeks like two cups?

Who is this girl resembling a hospital nurse, wearing a black dress with a white turn-down collar and a little watch on a cord? It is Sophia Perovski, who is to hang for the assassination of the Tsar in 1881. Coming to Sebastopol in 1872, she toured the surrounding villages on foot in order to become acquainted with the life of the peasants: she was in her period of Rakhmetovism – sleeping on straw, living on milk and gruels. And returning to our initial position we repeat: Sophia Perovski's instantaneous fate is a hundred times more to be envied than the fading glory of a reformer! For as copies of *The Contemporary* with the novel, passing from hand to hand, became more and more tattered, so did Chernyshevski's enchantments fade; and the esteem for him, which had long since turned into a sentimental convention, was no longer able to make hearts glow when he died in 1889. The funeral passed quietly. There were few comments in the newspapers. At the requiem held for him in St Petersburg the workmen in town clothes, whom the dead man's friends had brought for the sake of atmosphere, were taken by a group of students for plainclothesmen and insulted – which restored a certain equilibrium: was it not the fathers of these workmen who had abused the kneeling Chernyshevski from over the fence?

On the day following that mock execution, at dusk, 'with shackles on my feet and a head full of thoughts', Chernyshevski left St Petersburg forever. He travelled in a tarantass, and since 'to read books on the way' was permitted only beyond Irkutsk, he was extremely bored for the first month and a half of the journey. On July 23rd they brought him at last to the mines of the Nerchin mountain district at Kadaya: ten miles from China, four thousand six hundred from St Petersburg. He was not made to work much. He lived in a badly caulked cottage and suffered from rheumatism. Two years passed. Suddenly a miracle happened: Olga Sokratovna prepared to join him in Siberia.

During most of his imprisonment in the fortress she, it is said, had been coursing about in the provinces and caring so little about her husband's fate that her relatives even wondered whether she was not deranged. On the eve of the public disgrace she had sped back to St Petersburg, and on the morning of the 20th had sped off again. We would never have believed her capable of making the trip to Kadaya if we had not known her ability to move easily and hectically from one place to another. How he awaited her! Starting at the beginning of summer in 1866, together with seven-year-old Misha and a Dr Pavlinov (Dr Peacock – we are again entering the sphere of beautiful names), she got as far as Irkutsk, where she was held up for two months; there they stayed in a hotel with the enchantingly idiotic name (possibly distorted by biographers but most probably selected with particular care by sly fate) of Hotel de Amour et Co. Dr Pavlinov was not permitted to go any farther: he was replaced by a captain in the gendarmes, Hmelevski (a perfected edition of the dashing Pavlovsk hero), passionate, drunken, and brazen. They arrived on August 23rd. In order to celebrate the meeting of man and wife, one of the exiled Poles, a former cook of Count di Cavour, the Italian statesman of whom Chernyshevski had once written so much and so caustically, baked one of those pastries on which his late master had been wont to stuff himself. But the meeting was not a success: it is amazing how everything bitter and heroic which life manufactured for Chernyshevski was invariably accomplished by a flavouring of vile farce. Hmelevski hovered about and would not leave Olga Sokratovna alone; in her gypsy eyes there lurked something hunted but also enticing – against her will, perhaps. In return for her favours he is even alleged to have offered to arrange her husband's escape, but the latter resolutely refused. In short, the constant presence of this shameless man made things so difficult (and what plans we had made!) that Chernyshevski himself persuaded his wife to set out on the return journey, and this she did on August 27th, having stayed thus, after a three-month journey, only four days – four days, reader! – with the husband whom she was now leaving for seventeen odd years. Nekrasov dedicated *Peasant Children* to her. It is a pity he did not dedicate to her his *Russian Women*.

During the last days of September, Chernyshevski was transferred to Aleksandrovski Zavod, a settlement twenty miles from Kadaya. He spent the winter there in prison, together with some Karakozovites and rebellious Poles. The dungeon was equipped with a Mongolian speciality – 'stakes': posts dug vertically into the ground and surrounding the prison in a solid ring. In June of the following year, having completed his probationary term, Chernyshevski was released on parole and took a room in the house of a sexton, a man who looked very much like him: grey purblind eyes, a sparse beard, long, tangled hair. . . . Always a little drunk, always sighing, he would sorrowfully answer the questions of the curious with 'The dear fellow keeps writing and writing!' But Chernyshevski stayed there no more than two months. His name was taken in vain at political trials. The half-witted artisan Rozanov testified that the revolutionaries wanted to catch and cage 'a bird with royal blood in order to ransom Chernyshevski'. Count Shuvalov sent the Irkutsk Governor-General a telegram: THE AIM OF THE EMIGRES IS TO FREE CHERNYSHEVSKI (STOP) PLEASE TAKE ALL POSSIBLE MEASURES IN REGARD TO HIM. Meanwhile the exile Krasovski, who had been transferred at the same time as he, had fled (and perished in the taiga, after having been robbed), so that there was every reason to jail dangerous Chernyshevski once again and to deprive him for a month of the right to correspondence.

Suffering intolerably from draughts, he never removed either his fur-lined dressing gown or his lambskin shapka. He moved about like a leaf blown by the wind, with a nervous stumbling gait, and his shrill voice could be heard now here and now there. His trick of logical reasoning was intensified – 'in the manner of his father-in-law's namesake', as Strannolyubski so whimsically puts it. He lived in the 'office': a spacious room divided by a partition; along the entire wall in the larger part there ran a low 'sleeping shelf', in the nature of a platform; there, as if on a stage (or the way in zoos they exhibit a melancholy beast of prey among its native rocks) stood a bed and a table, which were essentially the natural furnishing of his whole life. He used to get up after midday, would drink tea all day and lie reading the whole time; he would sit down to do some real writing only at midnight, since during the day his immediate neighbours, some nationalist Poles who were completely indifferent to him, would indulge in fiddling and torture him with their unlubricated music: by profession they were wheelwrights. To the other exiles he used to read on winter evenings. They noticed once that although he was calmly and smoothly reading a tangled tale, with lots of 'scientific' digressions, he was looking at a blank notebook. A gruesome symbol!

It was then that he wrote a new novel. Still full of the success of *What to Do?* he expected much from it – most of all he expected the money which, printed abroad, the novel was supposed one way or another to bring in for his family. *The Prologue* is extremely autobiographical. When referring to it once, we spoke of its peculiar attempt to rehabilitate Olga Sokratovna; it conceals a similar attempt, in Strannolyubski's opinion, to rehabilitate the author's own person, for, underlining on the one hand Volgin's influence, which reaches the point where 'high dignitaries sought his favours through his wife' (because they supposed he had 'connections with London'; i.e., with Herzen, of whom the newly fledged liberals were mortally afraid), the author on the other hand insists obstinately on Volgin's suspiciousness, timidity and inactivity: 'To wait and wait as long as possible, to wait as quietly as possible.' One gets the impression that the stubborn Chernyshevski wants to have the last word in the quarrel, putting firmly on record what he had repeatedly said to his judges: 'I must be considered on the basis of my actions and there were no actions and could not have been any.'

Concerning the 'light' scenes in *The Prologue* we had better keep silent. Through their morbidly circumstantial eroticism one can make out such a throbbing tenderness for his wife that the least quotation from them might appear to be exaggerated derision. Instead let us listen to this pure sound – in his letters to her during those years: 'My dearest darling, I thank you for being the light of my life.' . . . 'I would be even here one of the happiest men in the world if it did not occur to me that this fate, which is very much to my personal advantage, is too hard in its effects on your life, my dear friend.' . . . 'Will you forgive me the grief to which I have subjected you?'

Chernyshevski's hopes for literary profits were not realized: the émigrés not only misused his name but also pirated his works. And entirely fatal for him were the attempts made to free him, attempts which were in themselves courageous but which seem senseless to us, who can see from the hilltop of time the disparity between the image of a 'fettered giant' and the real Chernyshevski whom these efforts by his would-be saviours only enraged: 'These gentlemen,' he said later, 'didn't even know that I can't ride a horse.' This inner contradiction resulted in nonsense (a particular shade of nonsense already long known to us). It is said that Ippolit Myshkin, disguised as a gendarme officer, went to Vilyuisk where he demanded of the district police chief that the prisoner be handed over to him, but spoiled the whole business by putting his shoulder knot on the left side instead of the right. Before this, namely in 1871, there was Lopatin's attempt in which everything was absurd: the way he suddenly abandoned the Russian translation of *Das Kapital* that he was making in London, in order to get for Marx, who had learned to read Russian, '*den grossen russischen Gelehrten*'; his journey to Irkutsk in the guise of a member of the Geographical Society (with the Siberian residents taking him for a government inspector incognito); his arrest following a tip-off from Switzerland; his flight and capture; and his letter to the Governor-General of Eastern Siberia in which he told him all about his project with inexplicable frankness. All this only worsened Chernyshevski's situation. Legally his settlement was supposed to begin on August 10, 1870. But only on December 2nd was he moved to another place, to a place which turned out to be far worse than penal servitude – to Vilyuisk.

'Forsaken by God in a dead end of Asia,' says Strannolyubski, 'in the depths of the Yakutsk region, far to the northeast, Vilyuisk was nothing but a hamlet standing on a huge pile of sand heaped up by the river, and surrounded by a boundless bog overgrown by taiga scrub.' The inhabitants (500 people) were: Cossacks, half-wild Yakuts, and a small number of low middle-class citizens (whom Steklov describes very picturesquely: 'The local society consisted of a pair of officials, a pair of clerics and a pair of merchants' – as if he were talking about the Ark). There Chernyshevski was lodged in the best house, and the best house turned out to be the jail. The door of his damp cell was lined with black oilcloth; the two windows which anyway were right up against the palisade were barred up. In the absence of any other exiles, he found himself in complete solitude. Despair, helplessness, the consciousness of having been deceived, a dizzy feeling of injustice, the ugly shortcomings of arctic life, all this almost drove him out of his mind. On the morning of July 10, 1872, he suddenly began to break the door lock with a pair of tongs, shaking all over, and mumbling, and crying out: 'Has the sovereign or a minister come that the police sergeant dares to lock the door at night?' By winter he had calmed down a bit, but from time to time there were certain reports . . . and here we are granted one of those rare correlations that constitute the researcher's pride.

Once (in 1853), his father had written him (regarding his *A Tentative Lexicon of the Hypatian Chronicle*): 'You would do better to write some tale or other . . . tales are still in fashion in good society.' Many years afterwards Chernyshevski informs his wife that he has thought up in his prison and wants to set down in writing 'an ingenious little tale' wherein he will portray her in the form of two girls: 'It will be quite a good little tale [repeating his father's rhythm]. If only you knew how much I have laughed to myself when depicting the various noisy frolics of the younger one, how much I cried with tenderness when depicting the pathetic meditations of the elder!' 'At night

Chernyshevski,' reported his jailers, 'sometimes sings, sometimes dances and sometimes weeps and sobs.'

The mail went out of Yakutsk once a month. The January number of a St Petersburg magazine was received only in May. He tried to cure the illness he had developed (goitre) with the aid of a textbook. The exhausting catarrh of the stomach that he had known as a student now returned with new peculiarities. 'I am nauseated by the subject of "peasants" and "peasant ownership of the land," ' he wrote to his son, who had thought to interest him by sending him some books on economics. The food was repulsive. He ate almost nothing but cooked cereals: straight from the pot – with a silver tablespoon, of which almost a quarter was worn away on the pot's earthenware sides during the twenty years that he himself was wearing away. On warm summer days he would stand for hours with his trousers rolled up in a shallow stream (which could hardly have been beneficial); or, with his head wrapped in a towel against the mosquitoes, which made him look like a Russian peasant woman, he would stroll along forest paths with his plaited mushroom basket, never plunging into the denser wildwood. He would forget his cigarette case under a larch, which he was some time in learning to distinguish from a pine. The flowers which he gathered (whose names he did not know) he wrapped in cigarette paper and sent to his son Misha, who acquired that way 'a small herbarium of the Vilyuisk flora': thus did Princess Volèonski in Nekrasov's poem about the Decembrists' wives bequeath her grandchildren 'a collection of butterflies, plants of Chita'. Once an eagle appeared in his yard . . . 'it had come to peck at his liver,' remarks Strannolyubski, 'but did not recognize Prometheus in him'.

The pleasure which he had experienced in his youth from the orderly disposition of the St Petersburg waters now received a late echo: from nothing to do he dug out canals – and almost flooded one of the Vilyuisk residents' favourite roads. He quenched his thirst for spreading culture by teaching manners to Yakuts, but just before, the native would remove his cap at a distance of twenty paces and in that position would meekly freeze. The practicality and good sense he used to advocate now dwindled to his advising the water-carrier to substitute a regular yoke of wood for the crook made of hair, which cut his palms; but the Yakut did not change his routine. In the little town where all they did was play cards and have passionate discussions about the price of Chinese cotton, his yearning for activity in public affairs led him to the Old-Believers, about whose plight Chernyshevski wrote an extraordinarily long and detailed memoir (including even Vilyuisk gossip) and coolly sent it off addressed to the Tsar, with the friendly suggestion he pardon them because they 'esteem him as a saint'.

He wrote a lot but burned almost everything. He informed his relatives that the results of his 'learned work' would undoubtedly be accepted sympathetically; this work was ashes and a mirage. Out of the whole heap of writings which he produced in Siberia, besides *The Prologue*, only two or three stories and a 'cycle' of unfinished 'novellas' have been preserved. . . . He also wrote poems. In texture they are no different from those versificatory tasks which he had once been given in the seminary, when he had reset a psalm of David in the following manner:

Upon me lay one duty only—
To mind my father's flock of sheep,
And hymns I early started singing
For to extol the Lord withal.

In 1875 (to Pypin) and again in 1888 (to Lavroy) he sends 'an ancient Persian poem': a ghastly thing! In one of the strophes the pronoun 'their' is repeated *seven* times ('Their country is barren, Their bodies are fleshless, And through their torn garments their ribs one can tell. Their faces are broad, and their features are flattened; Upon their flat features the soul does not dwell') while in the monstrous chains of the genitive case ('Of howls of the ache of their craving for blood') now, at the parting with literature, under a very low sun, there is evidence of the author's familiar leaning toward congruity, toward links. To Pypin he writes heartrending letters expressing his stubborn desire to thwart the administration and occupy himself with literature: 'This thing [*The Academy of Azure Mountains*, signed Denzil Elliot – purporting to be from the English] is of high literary merit. . . . I am patient, but – I hope no one intends to prevent me from working for my family. . . . I am famous in Russian literature for the carelessness of my style. . . . When I want to I can also write in all sorts of good styles.'

Weep ye, O! for Lilybaeum;
We with you together weep.
Weep ye, O! for Agrigentum;
Reinforcements we await.

'What is [this] hymn to the Maid of the Skies? An episode from the prose story of Empedocles' grandson . . . And what is the story of Empedocles' grandson? One of the innumerable stories in *The Academy of Azure Mountains.* The Duchess of Cantershire has set off with a company of fashionable friends on a yacht through the Suez Canal to the East Indies in order to visit her tiny kingdom at the foot of the Azure Mountains, near Golconda. There they do what intelligent and good people of fashion do: They tell stories – stories that will follow in the next packages from Denzil Elliot to the editor of *The Messenger of Europe*' (Stasyulevich – who did not print any of this).

One feels dizzy, the letters swim and fade in one's eyes – and here we again pick up the theme of Chernyshevski's spectacles. He asked his relatives to send him new ones, but in spite of his efforts to explain it particularly graphically, he nonetheless made a mess of it, and six months later he received from them number 'four and a half instead of five or five and a quarter'.

He gave an outlet to his passion for instruction by writing to Sasha about the mathematician Fermat, to Misha about the struggle between Popes and Emperors, and to his wife about medicine, Carlsbad, and Italy. . . . It ended the way it was bound to end: the authorities requested him to stop writing 'learned letters'. This so offended and shook him that for over six months he did not write any letters at all (the authorities never saw the day when they would get from him those humble petitions which, for instance, Dostoevski used to dispatch from Semipalatinsk to the strong of this world). 'There is no news from Papa,' wrote Olga Sokratovna to her son in 1879. 'I wonder if he, my dear one, is still alive,' and she can be forgiven much for this intonation.

Yet one more jackanapes with a name ending in 'ski' suddenly pops up as an extra: on March 15, 1881, 'your unknown pupil Vitevski', as he recommends himself, but according to police information a tippling doctor at the Stavropol district hospital, sends him a wire to Vilyuisk protesting with completely superflous heat against an anonymous opinion that Chernyshevski was responsible for the assassination of the Tsar: 'Your works are filled with peace and love. You never desired this (i.e., the assassination).' Whether because of these artless words or because of something else, the government softened and in the middle of June it showed its jail tenant a bit of thoughtful kindness: it had the walls of his domicile papered in '*gris perle* with a border', and the ceiling covered with calico, which in toto cost the exchequer 40 roubles and 88 kopecks, i.e., somewhat more than Yakovlev's overcoat and Musa's coffee. And already the following year the haggling over Chernyshevski's ghost was concluded, after negotiations between the Volunteer Security Guards (the secret police) and the executive committee of the underground People's Freedom concerning the preservation of law and order during Alexander the Third's coronation, with the decision that if the latter went off smoothly, Chernyshevski would be freed: thus he was bartered in exchange for tsars – and vice versa (a process that subsequently found its material expression when the Soviet authorities substituted in Saratov his statue for that of Alexander the Second). A year later, in May, a petition was submitted in his sons' names (he, of course, knew nothing of this), in the most florid and tear-jerking style imaginable. The Minister of Justice, Nabokov, made the appropriate report and 'His Majesty deigned to permit the transfer of Chernyshevski to Astrakhan'.

At the end of February, 1883 (overburdened time was already having difficulty in dragging his destiny), the gendarmes, without a word of the resolution, suddenly took him to Irkutsk. No matter – leaving Vilyuisk was in itself a happy event, and more than once during the summer voyage up the long Lena (revealing such kinship with the Volga in its meanders) the old man broke into a dance, chanting dactylic hexameters. But in September the voyage ended and with it the sensation of freedom. On the very first night Irkutsk appeared as the same kind of casemate in the deepest of provincial backwoods. In the morning he was visited by the chief of the gendarmerie, Keller. Nikolay Gavrilovich sat leaning his elbow on the table and did not respond at once. 'The Emperor has pardoned you,' said Keller, and repeated it even louder, seeing that the other was apparently half-asleep or beclouded. 'Me?' said the old man suddenly, then stood up, placed his hands on the herald's shoulders and, shaking his head, burst into tears. In the evening, feeling as if convalescent after a long illness, but still weak, with a delicious mist permeating his being, he had tea at the Kellers', talking incessantly and telling the latters' children 'more or less Persian fairy tales – about asses, roses, robbers . . .' as one of his hearers recalled. Five days later he was taken to Krasnoyarsk, from there to Orenburg – and in the late autumn at between six and seven in the evening he drove with post-horses through Saratov; there, in the yard of an inn by the gendarmerie, in the mobile darkness, a wretched little lamp swayed so much in the wind that one simply could not distinguish properly Olga Sokratovna's changeable, young, old, young face wrapped in a woollen kerchief – she had rushed headlong to this unhoped-for meeting; and that same night Chernyshevski (who could tell his thoughts?) was dispatched farther.

With great mastery and with the utmost vividness of exposition (it might almost be taken for compassion) Strannolyubski describes his installation in his Astrakhan residence. No one met him with open arms, he was invited by no one, and very soon he understood that all the grandiose plans which had been his only support in exile must now melt away in an inanely lucid and quite imperturbable stillness.

To his Siberian illness Astrakhan added yellow fever. He frequently caught cold. He suffered acute palpitations of the heart. He smoked heavily and untidily. But worst of all, he was extremely nervous. He had an odd way of jumping up in the middle of a conversation – an abrupt movement stemming as it were from the day of his arrest, when he had dashed into his study, forestalling the funest Rakeyev. On the street he could be mistaken for a little old artisan: stoop-shouldered, wearing a cheap summer suit and a crumpled cap. 'But tell me . . .' 'But don't you think . . .' 'But . . .': casual busybodies used to bother him with absurd questions. The actor Syroboyarski kept on asking him 'Shall I marry or no?' There were two or three last little denunciations which fizzed like damp fireworks. The company he kept consisted of some local Armenians – grocers and haberdashers. Educated people were surprised by the fact that somehow he did not take much interest in public affairs. 'Well, what do you want,' he would reply cheerlessly, 'what can I make of it all? Why, I haven't even once attended a trial by jury, not once been to a meeting of the zemstvo . . .'

Hair smoothly parted, with uncovered ears too big for her, and with a 'bird's nest' just below the crown of her head – here she is again with us (she has brought candy and kittens from Saratov); there is on her long lips that same mocking half-smile, the martyred line of her brows is still sharper, and the sleeves of her dress are now puffed out above the shoulders. She is already past fifty (1833–1918) but her character is still the same, neurotically naughty; her hysterical fits culminate sometimes into convulsions.

During these last six years of his life, poor, old, unwanted Nikolay Gavrilovich translates with machine-like steadiness volume after volume of Georg Weber's *Universal History* for the publisher Soldatenkov – and at the same time, moved by his ancient, irrepressible need to air his opinions, he tries gradually to smuggle through Weber some of his own ideas. He signs his translation 'Andreyev', and in his review of the first volume (in *The Examiner*, February 1884) a critic remarks that this 'is a kind of pseudonym, since in Russia there are as many Andreyevs as there are Ivanovs, and Petrovs'; this is followed by stinging allusions to the heaviness of the style and by a small reprimand: 'There was no need for Mr Andreyev to dilate in his Foreword on the merits and demerits of Weber, who has long been known to the Russian reader. His textbook came out as early as the fifties and simultaneously three volumes of his *Course of Universal History* in the translation of E. and V. Korsh. . . . He would be well advised not to ignore the works of his predecessors.'

E. Korsh, a lover of arch-Russian terminology instead of that accepted by German philosophers, was by now an eighty-year-old man, an assistant of Soldatenkov's, and in this capacity he proof-read the 'Astrakhan translator,' introducing corrections which enraged Chernyshevski, who in letters to the publisher set about 'mauling' Evgeniy Fyodorovich according to his old system, at first demanding furiously that the proof-reading be given to somebody else 'who understands better that there is not another man in Russia who knows the Russian literary language as well as I do', and then, when he had got his own way, employing another device: 'Can I really be interested in such trifles? However, if Korsh wants to continue to read the proofs, ask him not to make corrections, they are indeed ridiculous.' With no less bitter pleasure he also mauled Zaharyin, who out of the goodness of his heart had spoken to Soldatenkov regarding a monthly payment (of 200 roubles) to Chernyshevski in view of Olga Sokratovna's extravagance. 'You were fooled by the effrontery of a man whose mind has been befuddled by drunkenness,' wrote Chernyshevski to Soldatenkov, and setting in motion the whole apparatus of his logic – rusty, creaky but still as wriggly as ever, he at first justified his ire by the fact that he was being taken for a thief who wished to acquire capital, and then explained that his anger was actually only a sham for Olga Sokratovna's sake: 'Thanks to the fact that she learned of her extravagance from my letter to you, and I didn't give in to her when she asked me to soften my expression, there were no convulsions.' At this point (the end of 1888) another brief review happened along – by now on Weber's tenth volume. The terrible state of his mind, wounded pride, an old man's crotchetiness and the last, hopeless attempts to shout down the silence (a feat even more difficult than Lear's attempt to shout down the storm), all this must be remembered when you read through his spectacles the review on the inside of the pale-pink cover of *The Messenger of Europe*:

> . . . Unfortunately it appears from the Foreword that the Russian translator has remained true to his simple duties as a translator only in the first six volumes, but beginning with the seventh volume he has laid upon himself a new duty . . . 'to clean up' Weber. It is hardly possible to be grateful to him for the kind of translation where the author is 'refurbished', and such an authoritative author, at that, as Weber.

'It would seem,' remarks Strannolyubski here (somewhat mixing his metaphors), 'that with this careless kick destiny had given the last suitable touch to the chain of retribution it had forged for him.' But that is not so. There remains for our inspection one more – most terrible, most complete, ultimate punishment.

Of all the madmen who tore Chernyshevski's life into shreds, the worst was his son; not the youngest, of course, Mihail (Misha), who lived a quiet life, lovingly working away at tariff questions (he was employed in the railroads department): he had been evolved from his father's 'positive number' and was a good son, for at the time (1896–98) when his prodigal brother (which makes a moralistic picture) was publishing his *Fantastic Tales* and a collection of futile poems, he was piously beginning his monumental edition of his late father's works, which he had practically brought to conclusion when he died, in 1924, surrounded by general esteem – ten years after Alexander (Sasha) had died suddenly in sinful Rome, in a small room with a stone floor, declaring his superhuman love for Italian art and crying in the heat of wild inspiration that if people would only listen to him life would be different! Created apparently out of everything his father could not stand, Sasha, hardly out of his boyhood, developed a passion for everything that was weird, chimerical, and incomprehensible to his contemporaries – he lost himself in E.T.A. Hoffmann and Edgar Poe, was fascinated by pure mathematics, and a little later he was one of the first in Russia to appreciate the French *'poètes maudits'*. The father, vegetating in Siberia, was unable to look after the development of his son (who was brought up by the Pypins) and what he learned he interpreted in his own way, the more so since they concealed Sasha's mental disease from him. Gradually, however, the purity of this mathematics began to irritate Chernyshevski – and one can easily imagine with what feelings the youth used to read those long letters from his father, beginning with a deliberately debonair joke and then (like the conversations of that Chekhov character who used to begin so well – 'an old alumnus, you know, an incurable idealist . . .') concluding with irate abuse; this passion for mathematics enraged him not only as a manifestation of something non-utilitarian: by jeering at everything modern, Chernyshevski whom life had outdistanced would unburden himself concerning all the innovators, eccentrics and failures of this world.

His kindhearted cousin, Pypin, in January 1875, sends him to Vilyuisk an embellished description of his student son, informing him of what might please the creator of Rakhmetov (Sasha, he wrote, had ordered an eighteen-pound metal ball for gymnastics) and what must be flattering to any father: with restrained tenderness, Pypin, recalling his youthful friendship with Nikolay Gavrilovich (to whom he was much indebted), relates that Sasha is just as clumsy, just as angular as his father was, and also laughs as loud in the same treble tones. . . . Suddenly, in the autumn of 1877, Sasha joined the Nevski infantry regiment, but before he reached the active army (the Russo-Turkish war was in progress) he fell ill with typhus (in his constant misfortunes one is aware of a legacy from his father, who also used to break everything and drop everything). Returning to St Petersburg he lived alone, giving lessons and publishing articles on the theory of probability. After 1882 his mental ailment was aggravated, and more than once he had to be placed in a nursing-home. He was afraid of space, or more exactly, he was afraid of slipping into a different dimension – and in order to avoid perishing he clung continuously to the safe, solid – with Euclidean pleats – skirt of Pelageya Nikolaevna Fanderflit (née Pypin).

From Chernyshevski, who had now moved to Astrakhan, they continued to hide this. With a kind of sadistic obstinacy, with pedantic callousness matching that of any prosperous bourgeois in Dickens or Balzac, he called his son in his letters 'a big ludicrous freak' and an 'eccentric pauper' and accused him of a desire 'to remain a beggar'. Finally Pypin could stand it no longer and explained to his cousin with a certain warmth that although Sasha may not have become 'a cold and calculating businessman' he had in compensation 'acquired a pure and honourable soul'.

And then Sasha came to Astrakhan. Nikolay Gavrilovich saw those radiant, bulging eyes, heard that strange, evasive speech . . . Having entered the service of the oilman Nobel, and being entrusted to accompany a barge-load along the Volga, Sasha, en route, one sultry, oil-soaked, satanic noon, knocked the bookkeeper's cap off, threw the keys into the rainbow water, and went home to Astrakhan. That same summer four of his poems appeared in *The Messenger of Europe*; they show a gleam of talent:

> If life's hours appear to you bitter,
> Do not rail against life, for it's best
> To admit it's your fault you've been born with
> An affectionate heart in your breast.
> And if you do not wish to acknowledge
> Even such a self-evident fault . . .

(Incidentally, let us note the ghost of an additional syllable in 'life's hou-urs' matching *zhiz-en'*, instead of *zhizn'* which is extremely characteristic of unbalanced Russian poets of the woebegone sort: a flaw corresponding, it would seem, to something lacking in their lives, something that might have turned life into song. The last line quoted has however an authentic poetic ring.)

The joint domicile of father and son was a joint hell. Chernyshevski drove Sasha to agonizing insomnia with his endless admonitions (as a 'materialist' he had the fanatic effrontery to suppose that the main cause of Sasha's disorder was his 'pitiful material condition'), and he himself suffered in a way that he had not done even in Siberia. They both breathed easier when that winter Sasha went away – at first to Heidelberg with the family in which he was tutor and then to St Petersburg 'because of the need to get medical advice'. Petty, falsely funny misfortunes continued to spatter him. Thus we learn from a letter of his mother's (1888) that while 'Sasha was pleased to go out for a stroll, the house in which he was living burned down', and everything that he possessed burned with it; and, by now utterly destitute, he moved to the country house of Strannolyubski (the critic's father?).

In 1889, Chernyshevski received permission to go to Saratov. Whatever emotions this might have awakened in him, these were in any case poisoned by an intolerable family worry:

Sasha, who had always had a pathological passion for exhibitions, suddenly undertook a most extravagant and happy trip to the notorious *Exposition universelle* in Paris – having at first got stuck in Berlin, where it was necessary to send him money in the consul's name with a request to dispatch him back; but no: when he received the money Sasha made his way to Paris, had his fill 'of the wonderful wheel, of the gigantic, filigree tower' – and again was penniless.

Chernyshevski's feverish work on huge masses of Weber (which turned his brain into a forced labour factory and represented in fact the greatest mockery of human thought) did not cover unlooked-for expenditures – and day after day dictating, dictating, dictating, he felt that he could not go on, could not go on turning world history into roubles – and in the meantime he was also tormented by the panicky fear that from Paris, Sasha would come crashing into Saratov. On October 11th, he wrote Sasha that his mother was sending him the money for his return to St Petersburg, and – for the millionth time – advised him to take any job and do everything that his superiors might tell him to do: 'Your ignorant, ridiculous sermons to your superiors cannot be tolerated by any superiors' (thus ends the 'theme of writing exercises'). Continuing to twitch and mutter, he sealed the envelope and himself went to the station to mail the letter. Through the town whirled a cruel wind, which on the very first corner chilled the hurrying, angry little old man in his light coat. The following day, despite a fever, he translated *eighteen* pages of close print; on the 13th he wanted to continue, but he was persuaded to desist; on the 14th delirium set in: *'Inga, inc* [nonsense words, then a sigh] I'm quite unsettled . . . Paragraph . . . If some thirty thousand Swedish troops could be sent to Schleswig-Holstein they would easily rout all the Danes' forces and overrun . . . all the islands, except, perhaps Copenhagen, which will resist stubbornly, but in November, in parentheses put the ninth, Copenhagen also surrendered, semicolon; the Swedes turned the whole population of the Danish capital into shining silver, banished the energetic men of the patriotic parties to Egypt . . . Yes, yes, where was I . . . New paragraph . . .' Thus he rambled on for a long time, jumping from an imaginary Weber to some imaginary memoirs of his own, laboriously discoursing about the fact that 'the smallest fate of this man has been decided, there is no salvation for him . . . Although microscopic, a tiny particle of pus has been found in his blood, his fate has been decided . . .' Was he talking about himself, was it in himself that he felt this tiny particle that had kept mysteriously impairing all he did and experienced in life? A thinker, a toiler, a lucid mind, populating his utopias with an army of stenographers – he had now lived to see his *delirium* taken down by a secretary. On the night of the 16th he had a stroke – he felt the tongue in his mouth to be somehow thick; after which he soon died. His last words (at 3 A.M. on the 17th) were: 'A strange business: in this book there is not a single mention of God.' It is a pity that we do not know precisely *which* book he was reading to himself.

Now he lay surrounded by the dead tomes of Weber; a pair of spectacles in their case kept getting into everybody's way.

Sixty-one years had passed since that year of 1828 when the first omnibuses had appeared in Paris and when a Saratov priest had noted down in his prayer book: 'July 12th, in the third hour of morning, a son born, Nikolay . . . Christened the morning of the 13th before mass. Godfather: Archpriest Fyod. Stef. Vyazovski . . .' This name was subsequently given by Chernyshevski to the protagonist and narrator of his Siberian novellas – and by a strange coincidence it was thus, or nearly thus (F.V. . . . ski) that an unknown poet signed, in the magazine *Century* (1909, November), fourteen lines dedicated, according to information which we possess, to the memory of N. G. Chernyshevski – a mediocre but curious sonnet which we here give in full:

What will it say, your far descendant's voice—
Lauding your life or blasting it outright:
That it was dreadful? That another might
Have been less bitter? That it was your choice?

That your high deed prevailed, and did ignite
Your dry work with the poetry of Good,
And crowned the white brow of chained martyrhood
With a closed circle of ethereal light?

5

About a fortnight after *The Life of Chernyshevski* appeared it was greeted by the first, artless echo. Valentin Linyov (in a Russian émigré paper published in Warsaw) wrote as follows:

'Boris Cherdyntsev's new book opens with six lines of verse which the author for some reason calls a sonnet (?) and this is followed by a pretentiously capricious description of the well-known Chernyshevski's life.

'Chernyshevski, says the author, was the son of "a kindly cleric" (but does not mention when and where he was born); he finished the seminary and when his father, having lived a holy life which inspired even Nekrasov, died, his mother sent the young man to study in St Petersburg, where he immediately, practically on the station, because intimate with the then "moulders of opinion", as they were called, Pisarev and Belinski. The youth entered the university and devoted himself to technical inventions, working very hard and having his first romantic adventure with Lyubov' Yegorovna Lobachevski, who infected him with a love for art. After a clash on romantic grounds with some officer or other in Pavlovsk, however, he was forced to return to Saratov, where he proposed to his future bride and soon afterwards married her.

'He returned to Moscow, devoted himself to philosophy, wrote a great deal (the novel *What Are We to Do?*) and became friends with the outstanding writers of his time. Gradually he was drawn into revolutionary work and after one turbulent meeting, where he spoke together with Dobrolyubov and the well-known Professor Pavlov, who was still quite a young man at the time, Chernyshevski was forced to go abroad. For a while he lived in London collaborating with Herzen, but then he returned to Russia and was immediately arrested. Accused of planning the assassination of Alexander the Second, Chernyshevski was sentenced to death and publicly executed.

'This in brief is the story of Chernyshevski's life, and everything would have been all right if the author had not found it necessary to equip his account of it with a host of unnecessary details which obscure the sense, and with all sorts of long digressions on the most diverstified themes. And worst of all, having described the scene of the hanging and put an end to his hero, he is not satisfied with this and for the space of still many more unreadable pages he ruminates on what would have happened "if" – if Chernyshevski, for example, had not been executed but had been exiled to Siberia, like Dostoevski.

'The author writes in a language having little in common with Russian. He loves to invent words. He loves long, tangled sentences, as for example: "Fate sorts (?) them in anticipation (?) of the researcher's needs (?)"! or else he places solemn but not quite grammatical maxims in the mouths of his characters, like, "The poet himself chooses the subjects for his poems, the multitude has no right to direct his inspiration".'

Almost simultaneously with this entertaining review appeared that of Christopher Mortus (Paris) – which so aroused Zina's indignation that from that time her eyes glared and her nostrils dilated at the very least mention of this name.

'When speaking of a new young author [wrote Mortus quietly] one usually experiences the feeling of a certain awkwardness: will one not rattle him, will one not injure him by a too "glancing" remark? It seems to me that in the present instance there are no grounds for such fears. Godunov-Cherdyntsev is a novice, true, but a novice endowed with extreme self-confidence, and to rattle him is probably no easy matter. I do not know whether his book presages any future "achievements" or not, but if this is a beginning it cannot be called a particularly reassuring one.

'Let me qualify this. Strictly speaking, it is completely unimportant whether Godunov-Cherdyntsev's effort is creditable or not. One man writes well, another badly, and everyone is awaited at the end of the road by the Theme "which none can evade". It is a question, I think, of something quite different. That golden time has passed irretrievably when the critic or reader could be interested above all by the "artistic" quality or exact degree of talent of a book. Our émigré literature – I am speaking of genuine, "undoubted" literature people of faultless taste will understand me – has become plainer, more serious, drier – at the expense of art, perhaps, but in compensation producing (in certain poems by Tsypovich and Boris Barski and in the prose of Koridonov . . .) sounds of such sorrow, such music and such "hopeless", heavenly charm that in truth it is not worth regretting what Lermontov called "the dull songs of the earth".

'In itself the idea of writing a book about an outstanding public figure of the sixties contains nothing reprehensible. One sits down and writes it – fine; it comes out – fine; worse books than that have come out. But the author's general mood, the "atmosphere" of his thinking fills one with queer and unpleasant misgivings. I will refrain from discussing the question: how appropriate is the appearance of such a book at the present time? After all, no one can forbid a person to write what he pleases! But it seems to me – and I am not alone in feeling this – that at the bottom of Godunov-Cherdyntsev's book there lies something which is in essence profoundly tactless, something jarring and offensive. . . . It is his right, of course (although even this could be questioned), to take this or that attitude toward the "men of the sixties", but in "debunking" them he cannot but awake in any sensitive reader surprise and disgust. How irrelevant all this is! How inopportune! Let me define my meaning. The fact that it is precisely now, precisely today, that this tasteless operation is being performed is in itself an affront to that significant, bitter, palpitating something which is ripening in the catacombs of our era. Oh, of course, the "men of the sixties", and in particular Chernyshevski, expressed in their literary judgments much that was mistaken and perhaps ridiculous. Who is not guilty of this sin? And is it such a big sin, after all? But in the general "intonation" of their criticism there transpired a certain kind of truth – a truth which, no matter how paradoxical it seems, has become close and comprehensible to us precisely today, precisely now. I am talking not of their attacks on bribe-takers nor of the emancipation of women. . . . That, of course, is not the point! I think I shall be properly understood (insofar as another can be understood) if I say that in some final and infallible sense their and our needs coincide. Oh, I know, we are more sensitive, more spiritual, more "musical" than they were, and our final aim – beneath that resplendent black sky under which life streams on – is not simply "the commune" or "the overthrow of the despot". But to us, as to them, Nekrasov and Lermontov, especially the latter, are closer than Pushkin. I shall take just this simplest of examples because it immediately clarifies our affinity – if not kinship – with them. That chilliness, that foppishness, that "irresponsible" quality they sensed in a certain part of Pushkin's poetry is perceptible to us, too. One may object that we are more intelligent, more receptive. . . . All right, I agree; but essentially it is not a question of Chernyshevski's "rationalism" (or Belinski's or Dobrolyubov's, names and dates do not matter), but of the fact that then, as now, spiritually progressive people understood that mere "art" and the "lyre" were not a sufficient pabulum. We, their refined and weary grandchildren, also want something that is above all human; we demand the values which are essential to the soul. This "utilitarianism" is more elevated, perhaps, than theirs, but in some respects it is more urgent even than the one they preached.

'I have digressed from the immediate theme of my article. But then, sometimes, one can express one's opinion with much more exactitude and authenticity by wandering "around the theme" – in its fertile environs. . . . As a matter of fact, the analysis of *any* book is awkward and pointless, and, moreover, we are interested not in the way an author executed his "task" nor even in the "task" itself, but only in the author's attitude toward it.

'And let me add this: are they really so necessary, these excursions into the realm of the past, with their stylized squabbles and artificially vivified way of life? Who wants to know about Chernyshevski's relations with women? In our bitter, tender, ascetic times there is no place for this kind of mischievous research, for this idle literature – which, anyway, is not devoid of a certain arrogant audacity that is bound to repel even the most well-disposed of readers.'

After this, reviews poured. Professor Anuchin of Prague University (a well-known public figure, a man of shining moral purity and of great personal courage – the same Professor Anuchin who in 1922, not long before his deportation from Russia, when some revolvered leatherjackets had come to arrest him but became interested in his collection of ancient coins and were slow in taking him away, had calmly said, pointing to his watch: 'Gentlemen, history does not wait.') printed a detailed analysis of *The Life of Chernyshevski* in an émigré magazine appearing in Paris.

'Last year [he wrote], a remarkable book came out by Professor Otto Lederer of Bonn University, *Three Despots* (Alexander the Misty, Nicholas the Chill, and Nicholas the Dull). Motivated by a passionate love for the freedom of the human spirit and a burning hatred for its suppressors, Dr Lederer in certain of his appraisals was unjust – taking no account at all, for instance, of that national Russian fervour which so powerfully gave body to the symbol of the throne; but excessive zeal, and even blindness, in the process of exposing evil is always more understandable and forgivable than the least mockery – no matter how witty it may be – of that which public opinion feels to be objectively good. However, it is precisely this second road, the road of eclectic mordancy, that has been chosen by Mr Godunov-Cherdyntsev in his interpretation of the life and works of N. G. Chernyshevski.

'The author has undoubtedly acquainted himself thoroughly and in his own way conscientiously with his subject; undoubtedly, also, he has a talented pen – certain ideas he puts forward, and juxtapositions of ideas, are undoubtedly shrewd; but with all this his book is repellent. Let us try to examine calmly this impression.

'A certain epoch has been taken and one of its representatives chosen. But has the author assimilated the concept of "epoch"? No. First of all one senses in him absolutely no consciousness of that *classification of time*, without which history turns into an arbitrary gyration of multicoloured spots, into some kind of impressionistic picture with a walking figure upside down against a green sky that does not exist in nature. But this device (which destroys, by the way, any scholarly value of the work in question, in spite of its swaggering erudition) does not, nevertheless, constitute the author's chief fault. His chief fault is in the manner in which he portrays Chernyshevski.

'It is completely unimportant that Chernyshevski understood less about questions of poetry than a young aesthete of today. It is completely unimportant that in his philosophical conceptions Chernyshevski kept aloof from those transcendental subtleties which please Mr Godunov-Cherdyntsev. What is important is that, whatever Chernyshevski's views may have been on art and science, they represented the *Weltanschauung* of the most progressive men of his era, and were moreover indissolubly linked with the development of social ideas, with their ardent, beneficial, activating force. It is in this aspect, in this sole true light, that Chernyshevski's system of thought acquires a significance which far transcends the sense of those groundless arguments – unconnected in any way with the epoch of the sixties – which Mr Godunov-Cherdyntsev uses in venomously ridiculing his hero.

'But he makes fun, not only of his hero: he also makes fun of his reader. How else can one qualify the fact that among the well-known authorities on Chernyshevski a non-existent authority is cited, to whom the author pretends to appeal? In a certain sense it would be possible if not to forgive then at least to understand scientificially the scoffing at Chernyshevski, if Mr Godunov-Cherdyntsev were a heated supporter of those whom Chernyshevski attacked. It would at least be a point of view, and reading the book the reader would make a constant adjustment for the author's partisan approach, in that way arriving at the truth. But the pity is that with Mr Godunov-Cherdyntsev there is nothing to adjust to and the point of view is "everywhere and nowhere"; not only that, but as soon as the reader, as he descends the course of a sentence, thinks he has at last sailed into a quiet backwater, into a realm of ideas which may be contrary to those of Chernyshevski but are apparently shared by the author – and therefore can serve as a basis for the reader's judgment and guidance – the author gives him an unexpected fillip and knocks the imaginary prop from under him, so that he is once more unaware as to whose side Mr Godunov-Cherdyntsev is on in his campaign against Chernyshevski – whether he is on the side of the advocates of art for art's sake, or of the government, or of some other of Chernyshevski's enemies whom the reader does not know. As far as jeering at the hero himself is concerned, here the author passes all bounds. There is no detail too repulsive for him to disdain. He will probably reply that all these details are to be found in the "Diary" of the young Chernyshevski; but there they are in their place, in their proper environment, in the correct order and perspective, among many other thoughts and feelings which are much more valuable. But the author has fished out and put together precisely these, as if someone had tried to restore the image of a person by making an elaborate collection of his combings, fingernail parings, and bodily excretions.

'In other words the author is sneering throughout the whole of his book at the personality of one of the purest and most valorous sons of liberal Russia – not to speak of the passing kicks with which he rewards other progressive Russian thinkers, a respect for whom is in our consciousness an immanent part of their historical essence. In his book, which lies absolutely outside the humanitarian tradition of Russian literature and therefore outside literature in general, there are no factual untruths (if one does not count the fictitious "Strannolyubski" already mentioned, two or three doubtful details, and a few slips of the pen), but that "truth" which it contains is worse than the most prejudiced lie, for such a truth goes in direct contradiction to that noble and chaste truth (an absence of which deprives history of what the great Greek called "*tropotos*") which is one of the inalienable treasures of Russian social thought. In our day, thank God, books are not burned by bonfire, but I must confess that if such a custom were still in existence, Mr Godunov-Cherdyntsev's books could justifiably be considered the first candidate for fuelling a public square.'

After that Koncheyev had his say in the literary annual *The Tower*. He began by drawing a picture of flight during an invasion or an earthquake, when the escapers carry away with them everything that they can lay hands on, someone being sure to burden himself with a large, framed portrait of some long-forgotten relative. 'Just such a portrait [wrote Koncheyev] is for the Russian intelligentsia the image of Chernyshevski, which was spontaneously but accidentally carried away abroad by the émigrés, together with other, more useful things,' and this is how Koncheyev explained the stupefaction occasioned by the appearance of Fyodor Konstantinovich's book: 'Somebody suddenly confiscated the portrait.' Farther on, having finished once and for all with considerations of an ideological nature and embarked upon an examination of the book as a work of art, Koncheyev began to praise it in such a way that as he read the review Fyodor felt a burning radiance forming around his face and quicksilver racing through his veins. The article ended with the following: 'Alas! Among the emigration one will hardly scrape up a dozen people capable of appreciating the fire and fascination of this fabulously witty composition; and I would maintain that in today's Russia you could not find even one to appreciate it, if I had not happened to know of the existence of two such people, one living on the north bank of the Neva and the other – somewhere in distant Siberia exile.'

The monarchist organ *The Throne* devoted to *The Life of Chernyshevski* a few lines in which it pointed out that any sense or value in the unmasking of 'one of the ideological mentors of Bolshevism' was completely undermined by 'the cheap liberalizing of the author, who goes wholly over to the side of his sorry, but pernicious hero as soon as the long-suffering Russian Tsar finally has him safely tucked away. . . . And in general,' added the reviewer, Pyotr Levchenko, 'it is high time one ceased writing about so-called cruelties of "the tsarist régime" with regard to "pure souls" who are of no interest to anybody. The Red Freemasonry will only rejoice over Count Godunov-Cherdyntsev's work. It is lamentable that the bearer of such a name should engage in hymning "social ideals" which have long since turned into cheap idols.'

The pro-Communist Russian-language daily in Berlin, *Up!* (this was the one which Vasiliev's *Gazeta* invariably termed 'the reptile'), had an article devoted to the celebration of the centenary of Chernyshevski's birth, and concluded thus: 'They have also bestirred themselves in our blessed emigration: a certain Godunov-Cherdyntsev with swashbuckling brashness has hurried to concoct a booklet – for which he has dragged in material from all over the place – and has given out his vile slander as *The Life of Chernyshevski*. Some Prague professor or other has hastened to find this work "talented and conscientious" and everyone chummily joined in. It is dashingly written and in no way differs in its internal style from Vasilev's leaders about "The imminent end of Bolshevism".'

The last dig was particularly amusing in view of the fact that in his *Gazeta* Vasiliev resolutely opposed the slightest reference to Fyodor's book, telling him honestly (although the other had not asked) that had he not been on such friendly terms with him he would have printed a devastating review – 'not even a damp spot would have remained' of the author of *The Life of Chernyshevski*. In short, the book found itself surrounded by a good, thundery atmosphere of scandal which helped sales; and at the same time, in spite of the attacks, the name of Godunov-Cherdyntsev immediately came to the fore, rising over the motley storm of critical opinion, in full view of everyone, vividly and firmly. But there was one man whose opinion Fyodor was no longer able to ascertain. Alexander Yakovlevich Chernyshevski had died not long before the book appeared.

When the French thinker Delalande was asked at somebody's funeral why he did not uncover himself (*ne se découvre pas*), he replied: 'I am waiting for death to do it first (*qu'elle se découvre la première*). There is a lack of metaphysical gallantry in this, but death deserves no more. Fear gives birth to sacred awe, sacred awe erects a sacrificial altar, its smoke ascends to the sky, there assumes the shape of wings, and bowing fear addresses a prayer to it. Religion has the same relation to man's heavenly condition that mathematics has to his earthly one: both the one and the other are merely the rules of the game. Belief in God and belief in numbers: local truth and truth of location. I know that death in itself is in no way connected with the topography of the hereafter, for a door is merely the exit from the house and not a part of its surroundings, like a tree or a hill. One has to get out somehow, 'but I refuse to see in a door more than a hole, and a carpenter's job' (*Delalande, Discours sur les ombres*, p. 45). And then again: the unfortunate image of a 'road' to which the human mind has become accustomed (life as a kind of journey) is a stupid illusion: we are not going anywhere, we are sitting at home. The other world surrounds us always and is not at all the end of some pilgrimage. In our earthly house, windows are replaced by mirrors; the door, until a given time, is closed; but air comes in through the cracks. 'For our stay-at-home senses the most accessible image of our future comprehension of those surroundings which are due to be revealed to us with the disintegration of the body is the liberation of the soul from the eyesockets of the flesh and our transformation into one complete and free eye, which can simultaneously see in all directions, or to put it differently: a supersensory insight into the world accompanied by our inner participation.' (Ibid. p. 64). But all this is only symbols – symbols which become a burden to the mind as soon as it takes a close look at them. . . .

Is it not possible to understand more simply, in a way more satisfying to the spirit without the aid of this elegant atheist and equally without the aid of popular faiths? For religion subsumes a suspicious facility of general access that destroys the value of its revelations. If the poor in spirit enter the heavenly kingdom I can imagine how gay it is there. I have seen enough of them on earth. Who else makes up the population of heaven? Swarms of screaming revivalists, grubby monks, lots of rosy, shortsighted souls of more or less Protestant manufacture – what deathly boredom! I am running a high temperature for the fourth day now, and can no longer read. Strange – I used to think before that Yasha was always near me, that I had learned to communicate with ghosts, but now, when I am perhaps dying, this belief in ghosts seems to me something earthly, linked with the very lowest earthly sensations and not at all the discovery of a heavenly America.

Somehow simpler. Somehow simpler. Somehow at once! One effort – and I'll understand all. The search for God: the longing of any hound for a master; give me a boss and I shall kneel at his enormous feet. All this is earthly. Father, headmaster, rector, president of the board, tsar, God. Numbers, numbers – and one wants so much to find the biggest number, so that all the rest may mean something and climb somewhere. No, that way you end up in padded dead ends – and everything ceases to be interesting.

Of course I am dying. These pinchers behind and this steely pain are quite comprehensible. Death steals up from behind and grasps you by the sides. Funny that I have thought of death all my life, and if I have lived, have lived only in the margin of a book I have never been able to read. Now who was it? Oh, years ago in Kiev . . . Goodness, what was his name? Would take out a library book in a language he didn't know, make notes in it and leave it lying about so visitors would think: He knows Portuguese, Aramaic. *Ich habe dasselbe getan*. Happiness, sorrow – exclamation marks *en marge*, while the context is absolutely unknown. A fine affair.

It is terribly painful to leave life's womb. The deathly horror of birth. *L'enfant qui naît ressent les affres de sa mère.* My poor little Yasha! It is very queer that in dying I get farther away from him, when the opposite should have been true – ever nearer and nearer. . . . His first word was *muha,* a fly. And immediately afterwards there was a telephone call from the police: to come and identify the body. How will I leave him now? In these rooms . . . He will have nobody to haunt . . . Because *she* would not notice . . . Poor girl. How much? Five thousand eight hundred . . . plus that other money . . . which makes, let me see . . . And afterwards? David might help – but then he might not.

. . . In general, there has been nothing in life except getting ready for an examination – which all the same nobody can get ready for. 'Dreadful is death to man and mite alike.' Will all my friends go through it? Incredible! *Eine alte Geschichte:* the name of a film Sandra and I went to see the day before his death.

Oh, no. Under no circumstances. She can keep talking about it as much as she pleases. Was it yesterday that she talked about it? Or ages ago? No, they won't be taking me to any hospital. I'll lie here. I've had enough of hospitals. It would mean to go mad again just before the end. No, I'll stay here. How difficult it is to turn one's thoughts over: like logs. I feel much too ill to die.

'What did he write his book about, Sandra? Well, tell me, you should remember! We talked about it once. About some priest – no? Oh, you never . . . anything . . . Bad, difficult . . .'

After this he hardly spoke, having fallen into a twilight condition; Fyodor was admitted to him and forever remembered the white bristle on his sunken cheeks, the dull shade of his bald head, and the hand crusted with grey eczema, stirring like a crawfish on the sheet. The following day he died, but before that he had a moment of lucidity, complaining of pains and then saying (it was darkish in the room because of the lowered blinds): 'What nonsense. Of course there is nothing afterwards.' He sighed, listened to the trickling and drumming outside the window and repeated with extreme distinctness: 'There is nothing. It is as clear as the fact that it is raining.'

And meanwhile outside the spring sun was playing on the roof tiles, the sky was dreamy and cloudless, the tenant upstairs was watering the flowers on the edge of her balcony, and the water trickled down with a drumming sound.

In the window of the mortician's on the corner of Kaiserallee there was exhibited as an enticement (just as Cook's exhibits a Pullman model) a miniature crematorium interior: rows of little chairs before a little pulpit, little dolls sitting on them the size of a bent auricular finger, and in front, and somewhat apart, one could recognize the little widow by the square inch of handkerchief she had raised to her face. The German seductivity of this model had always amused Fyodor, so that now it was somewhat disgusting to enter a real crematorium, where from beneath laurels in tubs a real coffin with a real body was lowered to the sounds of heavyweight organ music into exemplary nether regions, right into the incinerator. Mme Chernyshevski did not hold a handkerchief but sat motionless and straight, her eyes shimmering through the black crepe veil. The faces of friends and acquaintances bore the guarded expressions usual in such cases: a mobility of the pupils accompanied by a certain tension in the muscles of the neck. The lawyer Charski sincerely blew his nose; Vasiliev, who as a public figure had had a great deal of funeral experience, carefully followed the parson's pauses (Alexander Yakovlevich had turned out at the last minute to be a Protestant). Engineer Kern flashed the lenses of his pince-nez impassively. Goryainov repeatedly freed his fat neck from its collar but did not go so far as to clear his throat; the ladies who had used to visit the Chernyshevskis all sat together; the writers also sat together – Lishnevski, Shahmatov and Shirin; there were many people whom Fyodor did not know – for instance, a prim gentleman with a blond little beard and unusually red lips (a cousin, it seemed, of the dead man), and also some Germans with top hats on their knees, who tactfully sat in the back row.

Upon the conclusion of the service the mourners, according to the scheme of the crematorium's master of ceremonies, were supposed to go up to the widow one at a time and offer words of condolence, but Fyodor resolved to avoid this and went out onto the street. Everything was wet, sunny and somehow nudely bright; on a black football field trimmed with young grass, schoolgirls in shorts were doing calisthenics. Behind the crematorium's shiny, gutta-percha grey dome one could see the turquoise turrets of a mosque, and on the other side of the square gleamed the green cupolas of a white Pskovan-type church, which had recently grown up out of the corner house and thanks to architectural camouflage seemed almost detached. On a terrace by the entrance to the park two badly wrought bronze boxers, also recently erected, had frozen in attitudes that completely disagreed with the reciprocal harmony of pugilism: instead of its collected, crouched, round-muscled grace there were two naked soldiers scrapping in a bathhouse. A kite being flown from an open space behind some trees made a red little rhombus high in the blue sky. With surprise and vexation Fyodor noticed that he was unable to keep his thoughts on the image of the man who had just been reduced to ashes and gone up in smoke; he tried to concentrate, to imagine to himself the recent warmth of their live relationship, but his soul refused to budge and lay there, sleepy eyes shut, content with its cage. The braked line from *King Lear,* consisting entirely of five 'nerves' – that was all he could think of. 'And so I'll never see him again,' he told himself, unoriginally, but this thin goad snapped without displacing his soul. He tried to think about death, but reflected instead that the soft sky, edged on one side with a long cloud like a pale and tender border of fat, would have resembled a slice of ham had the blue been pink. He tried to imagine some kind of extension of Alexander Yakovlevich beyond the corner of life – but at the same time could not help noticing through the window of a cleaning and pressing shop near the Orthodox church, a worker with devilish energy and an excess of steam, as if in hell, torturing a pair of flat trousers. He tried to confess something to Alexander Yakovlevich, and repent at least for the cruel mischievous thoughts he had fleetingly had (concerning the unpleasant surprise he was preparing for him with his book) and suddenly he recalled a vulgar triviality: how Shchiogolev had once said in some connection or other: 'When good friends of mine die, I always think that up there they will do something to improve my destiny here, ho, ho, ho!' He was in a troubled and obscured state of mind which was incomprehensible to him, just as everything was incomprehensible, from the sky to that yellow tram rumbling along the clear track of the Hohenzollerndamm (along which Yasha had once gone to his death), but gradually his annoyance with himself passed and with a kind of relief – as if the responsibility for his soul belonged not to him but to someone who knew what it all meant – he felt that all this skein of random thoughts, like everything else as well – the seams and sleaziness of the spring day, the ruffle of the air, the coarse, variously intercrossing threads of confused sounds – was but the reverse side of a magnificent fabric, on the front of which there gradually formed and became alive images invisible to him.

He found himself by the bronze boxers; in the flower beds

around them rippled pale, black-blotched pansies (somewhat similar facially to Charlie Chaplin); he sat on a bench where once or twice at night he had sat with Zina – for of late a kind of restlessness had carried them far beyond the bounds of the dark, quiet lane where they had at first sought shelter. Nearby a woman sat knitting; next to her a small child, entirely clothed in light blue wool, ending above in the pompon of a cap and below in foot straps, was ironing the bench with a toy tank; sparrows twittered in the bushes and from time to time made concerted raids on the turf, on the statues; a sticky smell came from the poplar buds, and far beyond the square the domed crematorium now had a sated, clean-licked look. From a distance Fyodor could see tiny figures dispersing . . . he could even make out someone leading Alexandra Yakolevna to a toy automobile (tomorrow he would have to call on her), and a group of her friends gathering at the tram stop; he saw them concealed for a moment by the immobilized tram and then, with legerdemain magic, they were gone when the shutter was removed.

Fyodor was about to walk home when a lisping voice called him from behind: it belonged to Shirin, author of the novel *The Hoary Abyss* (with an Epigraph from the Book of Job) which had been received very sympathetically by the émigré critics. ('Oh Lord, our Father! Down Broadway in a feverish rustle of dollars, hetaeras and businessmen in spats, shoving, falling and out of breath, were running after the golden calf, which pushed its way, rubbing against walls between the skyscrapers, then turned its emaciated face to the electric sky and howled. In Paris, in a low-class dive, the old man Lachaise, who had once been an aviation pioneer but was now a decrepit vagabond, trampled under his boots an ancient prostitute, Boule de Suif. Oh Lord, why—? Out of a Moscow basement a killer came out, squatted by a kennel and began to coax a shaggy pup: little one, he repeated, little one . . . In London, lords and ladies danced the Jimmie and imbibed cocktails, glancing from time to time at a platform where at the end of the eighteenth ring a huge Negro had laid his fair-haired opponent on the carpet with a knockout. Amid arctic snows the explorer Ericson sat on an empty soapbox and thought gloomily: The pole or not the pole? . . . Ivan Chervyakov carefully trimmed the fringe of his only pair of pants. Oh Lord, why dost Thou permit all this?') Shirin himself was a thickset man with a reddish crew cut, always badly shaved and wearing large spectacles behind which, as in two aquariums, swam two tiny, transparent eyes – which were completely impervious to visual impressions. He was blind like Milton, deaf like Beethoven, and a blockhead to boot. A blissful incapacity for observation (and hence complete uniformedness about the surrounding world – and a complete inability to put a name to anything) is a quality quite frequently met with among the average Russian literati, as if a beneficent fate were at work refusing the blessing of sensory cognition to the untalented so that they will not wantonly mess up the material. It happens, of course, that such a benighted person has some little lamp of his own glimmering inside him – not to speak of those known instances in which, through the caprice of resourceful nature that loves startling adjustment and substitutions, such an inner light is astonishingly bright – enough to make the envy of the ruddiest talent. But even Dostoevski always brings to mind somehow a room in which a lamp burns during the day.

As he walked now across the park with Shirin, Fyodor derived disinterested pleasure from the amusing thought that he had for companion a deaf and blind man with blocked nostrils who regarded this state with complete indifference, although he was not averse at times to sighing naïvely about the intellectual's alienation from nature: recently Lishnevski had related that Shirin had arranged to meet him about some business in the Zoological Garden and when after an hour's conversation Lishnevski had casually drawn his attention to a hyena in its cage, it transpired that Shirin had hardly realized that one keeps animals in a zoological garden, and glancing briefly at the cage had remarked automatically: 'Yes, the likes of us don't know much about the animal world,' and immediately continued discussing that which particularly disturbed him in life: the activities and composition of the Committee of the Society of Russian Writers in Germany. And now he was in an extreme degree of agitation since 'a certain event had come to a head'.

Chairman of the Committe was Georgiy Ivanovich Vasiliev, and for this of course there were good reasons: his pre-Soviet reputation, his many years of editorial activity, and most important – that inexorable almost awesome honesty for which his name was famous. On the other hand, his bad temper, polemical harshness, and (despite great public experience), complete ignorance of people, not only did not harm this honesty but on the contrary imparted a certain tang to it. Shirin's dissatisfaction was directed not against him but against the five remaining members of the Committee, first because not one of them (as two-thirds, incidentally, of the whole membership of the society) was a professional writer, and secondly because three of them (including the treasurer and the vice-president) were – if not scoundrels as the partial Shirin maintained – then at least shade-lovers in their bashful but deft activities. For some time past now a rather comical (in Fyodor's opinion) and absolutely outrageous (in Shirin's terminology) affair had been going on with the Union's funds. Every time a member asked for a loan or a grant (the difference between which was about the same as that between a ninety-nine-year lease and life ownership) one had to track down these funds which at the least attempt to catch up with them became amazingly fluid and ethereal, as if they were always situated equidistantly between three points represented by the treasurer and two members of the Committee. The chase was complicated by the fact that for a long time now Vasiliev had not been on speaking terms with these three members, refusing even to communicate with them in writing, and in recent times had been dispensing loans and grants out of his own pocket, leaving others to get the money from the Union to repay him. In the end the money would be extracted in dribs and drabs, but then it usually turned out that the treasurer had borrowed it from an outsider, so that transactions never caused any change in the phantasmal state of the exchequer. Lately members of the Society who appealed particularly often for aid had begun to grow visibly nervous. A general meeting had been called for next month and Shirin had prepared for it a plan of resolute action.

'There was a time,' he said, striding down a path in the park with Fyodor and automatically following its cunningly unobtrusive convolutions, 'there was a time when all the people who went on the Committee of our Union were highly respectable, like Podtyagin, Ivan Luzhin, Zilanov, but some died and others are in Paris. Somehow Gurman oozed through into it and then gradually pulled his pals in. For this trio the passive participation of the extremely decent – I'm saying nothing – but completely inert Kern and Goryainov is a convenient cover, a kind of camouflage. And Gurman's strained relations with Georgiy Ivanovich is a guarantee of inactivity on his part also. The ones to blame for all this are us, the members of the Union. If it were not for our idleness, carelessness, lack of organization, indifferent attitude to the Union and flagrant impracticality in social work it would never have happened that Gurman and his chums from year to year elected either themselves or else people congenial to them. It is time to put an end to this. Their list as always will be circulated at the coming elections . . . But we will then put our own, one hundred per cent professional: president – Vasiliev, vice-president – Getz, members of the board: Lishnevski, Shahmatov, Vladimirov, you and I – and then we'll reconstitute the Inspection Committee, the more so since Belenki and Chernyshevski have dropped out.'

'Oh no, please,' said Fyodor (admiring in passing Shirin's definition of death), 'don't count on me. I never went and never will go on any committee.'

'Stop it!' exclaimed Shirin, frowning. 'That's not fair.'

'On the contrary, very fair. And anyway – if I am a member of the Union it's only out of absentmindedness. To tell the truth, Koncheyev is right to stand aside from all this.'

'Koncheyev!' said Shirin angrily. 'Koncheyev is an absolutely useless handicraftsman working on his own, and is completely devoid of any general interests. But you ought to be interested in the fate of the Union if only because you – excuse my directness – borrow money from it.'

'That's just it. You can see for yourself that if I go on the Committee I shan't possibly be able to give handouts to myself.'

'Bosh. Why not? It's a completely legal procedure. You will simply get up and go to the lavatory – and so become for a moment, so to speak, an ordinary member, while your colleagues discuss your request. All these are empty excuses that you've just thought up.'

'How's your new novel?' asked Fyodor. 'Is it nearly finished?'

'We're not talking about my novel now. I ask you very seriously to give your assent. We need young blood. Lishnevski and I have given much thought to this list.'

'Under no circumstances,' said Fyodor. 'I don't want to play the fool.'

'Well, if you call your public duty playing the fool . . .'

'If I go on the Committee I shall certainly be playing the fool, so I am refusing precisely out of respect for duty.'

'Very sad,' said Shirin. 'Will we really have to take Rostislav Strannyy instead of you?'

'Of course! Wonderful! I adore Rostislav.'

'Actually I had reserved him for the Inspection Committee. There's also Busch, of course . . . But do think it over, please. It's not a trifling matter. We shall have a regular battle with these gangsters. I am preparing a speech that will really make them sit up. Think it over, do, you still have a whole month.'

During that month Fyodor's book came out and two or three notices had had time to appear, so that he set off for the general meeting with the pleasant feeling that he would find more than one enemy reader there. It took place as usual in the upper premises of a large café, and when he arrived everybody was already there. A phenomenally dexterous waiter with darting eyes was serving beer and coffee. The members of the Society were seated at little tables. The creative writers formed a close-knit group, and one could already hear the energetic '*psst, psst*' of Shahmatov, who had been served the wrong order. In the back behind a long table sat the Committee: the bulky, extremely gloomy Vasiliev, with Goryainov and engineer Kern on his right, and the three others on his left. Kern, whose main interest was turbines but who had once been on friendly terms with Alexander Blok, and the former official of a former government department, Goryainov, who could recite marvellously 'Woe from Wit' as well as Ivan the Terrible's dialogue with the Lithuanian ambassador (when he used to do a splendid imitation of a Polish accent), bore themselves with quiet distinction: they had betrayed long ago their three unrighteous colleagues. Of these, Gurman was a fat man with a bald head half occupied by a coffee-coloured birth-mark, massive sloping shoulders, and a disdainfully offended expression on his thick, purplish lips. His relationship to literature was limited to a brief and entirely commercial connection with some German publisher of technical guides; the principal theme of his personality, the pith of his existence, was speculation – he was particularly keen on Soviet bills of exchange. Next to him sat a small but sturdily resilient barrister, with a jutting jaw, a rapacious gleam in his right eye (the left one was half-closed by nature), and a whole store of metal in his mouth – an alert, fiery man, something of a swashbuckler in his own way, who was always challenging people to arbitration, and he would talk of this (I called him out, he refused) with the precise severity of a hardened duellist. Gurman's other friend, loose-fleshed, grey-skinned, languid, wearing horn-rimmed spectacles, his whole aspect resembling a peaceful toad that wants only one thing – to be left in complete peace in a damp place – had somewhen somewhere written notes on economic questions, although the evil-tongued Lishnevski denied him even this, swearing that his sole printed effort was a letter in pre-Revolution days to the editor of an Odessa newspaper in which he had indignantly dissociated himself from a villainous namesake, who subsequently turned out to be his relative, then his double, and finally himself, as if there was in action here the irrevocable law of capillary attraction and fusion.

Fyodor sat between the novelists Shahmatov and Vladimirov, by a wide window behind which the night gleamed wetly black, with two-toned (the Berlin imagination did not stretch to any more) illuminated signs – ozone-blue and oporto-red – and rumbling electric trains with rapidly and distinctly lighted insides gliding above the square along a viaduct, against whose archivolts below slow, grinding trams seemed to keep butting without finding a loophole.

Meanwhile the chairman of the board had stood up and proposed the election of a chairman for the meeting. There sounded from various places: 'Kraevich, lets have Kraevich . . .' and Professor Kraevich (no relation to the author of the textbook on physics – he was a professor of international law), a mobile, angular old man in a knitted waistcoat and unbuttoned jacket, swept up to the presidium table extraordinarily fast, holding his left hand in his trouser pocket and tossing up his pince-nez on the end of its cord with his right; he sat down between Vasiliev and Gurman (who was slowly and gloomily twisting a cigarette into an amber holder), immediately stood up again, and pronounced the meeting opened.

I wonder, thought Fyodor, glancing sideways at Vladimirov, I wonder if he has read my book? Vladimirov put down his glass and looked at Fyodor, but said nothing. Beneath his jacket he was wearing an English sports sweater with a black-and-orange border along its triangular opening; the receding hair on either side of his forehead exaggerated the latter's dimensions, his large nose was strongly boned, his greyish-yellow teeth glistened unpleasantly beneath his slightly raised lip and his eyes looked out with intelligence and indifference – he had studied, it seemed, at an English university and flaunted a pseudo-British manner. At twenty-nine he was already the author of two novels – outstanding for the force and swiftness of their mirror-like style – which irritated Fyodor perhaps for the very reason that he felt a certain affinity with him. As a conversationalist Vladimirov was singularly unattractive. One blamed him for being derisive, supercilious, cold, incapable of thawing to friendly discussions – but that was also said about Koncheyev and about Fyodor himself, and about anyone whose thoughts lived in their own private house and not in a barrack-room or a pub.

When a secretary had also been elected, Professor Kraevich proposed that all should stand to honour the memory of the two deceased members of the Society; and during their five-second petrification the excommunicated waiter scanned the tables, having forgotten who had ordered the ham sandwich he had just brought in on a tray. Everyone stood as he could. Gurman, for example, his skew-bald head lowered, was holding his hand palm upwards on the table, as if he had just cast the dice and had frozen in astonishment at his loss.

'Allo! Hier!' shouted Shahmatov, who had been waiting anxiously for the moment when with a clatter of relief life would be seated again – and then the waiter quickly raised his index finger (he had remembered), glided over to him, and with a tinkle put the plate down on the imitation marble. Shahmatov immediately began to cut the sandwich, holding his knife and fork crosswise; on the edge of the plate a yellow blob of mustard projected, as is usually the case, a yellow horn. Shahmatov's complaisantly Napoleonic face with its strand of steely-blue hair slanting toward the temple appealed particularly to Fyodor at these gastronomic moments. Next to him, drinking tea with lemon, and himself very lemony, with sadly arched eyebrows, sat the satirist from the *Gazeta*, whose pseudonym, Foma Mur, contained according to his own assertion 'a complete French novel (*femme, amour*), a page of English literature (Thomas Moore), and a touch of Jewish scepticism (Thomas the Apostle)'. Shirin was sharpening a pencil over an ashtray: he was very much offended at Fyodor for refusing 'to figure' in the election list. Of the writers, there were also: Rostislav Strannyy – a rather dreadful person with a bracelet on his hairy wrist; the parchment-pale, raven-haired poetess, Anna Aptekar; a theatre critic – a skinny, singularly quiet young man with an elusive something about him recalling a daguerreo-type of the Russian forties; and, of course, kindly Busch, his eyes resting paternally on Fyodor, who, with half an ear cocked to the Society president's report, had now transferred his gaze from Busch, Lishnevski, Shirin and the other writers to the general mass of those present, among whom were several journalists, as for instance old Stupishin, whose spoon was working its way through a wedge of mocha cake, many reporters, and – sitting alone and admitted here on God knows what basis – Lyubov Markovna in her timorously gleaming pince-nez; and in general there was a large number of those whom Shirin severely termed 'the outside element': the imposing lawyer Charski, holding his fourth cigarette of the night in his white, always trembling hand; a bearded little jobber who had once published an obituary notice in a Bundist paper; a gentle, pale old man, tasting of apple paste, who enthusiastically discharged his duties as the precentor of a church choir; an enormous, enigmatic fat man who lived as a hermit in a pine wood near Berlin, some said in a cave, and had there compiled a collection of Soviet anecdotes; a separate group of rowdies, conceited failures; a pleasant young man of unknown means and position ('a Soviet agent', said Shirin simply and darkly); another lady – someone's former secretary; her husband – the brother of a well-known publisher; and all these people, from the illiterate bum with a heavy, drunken gaze, who wrote denunciatorily mystical verses which not a single newspaper had yet agreed to publish, to the repulsively small, almost portable lawyer, Poshkin, who when talking to people said 'I pot' for 'I put' and 'coshion' for 'cushion' as if establishing an alibi for his name; all of these, in Shirin's opinion, damaged the Society's dignity and were liable to immediate expulsion.

'And now,' said Vasiliev, after finishing his report, 'I bring to the notice of the meeting that I resign as Chairman of the Society and will not stand for re-election.'

He sat down. A little chill ran through the assembly. Beneath the burden of sorrow, Gurman closed his heavy lids. An electric train slid bowlike over a bass string.

'Next comes . . .' said Professor Kraevich, raising his pince-nez to his eyes, and looking at the agenda, 'the treasurer's report. If you please.'

Gurman's resilient neighbour, immediately adopting a challenging tone of voice, flashing his good eye and powerfully twisting his valuable-crammed mouth, commenced to read . . . figures were emitted like sparks, metallic words bounced . . . 'entered the current year' . . . 'debited' . . . 'audited' . . . while Shirin, in the meantime, swiftly began to note something on the reverse side of a cigarette pack, added it up, and triumphantly exchanged glances with Lishnevski.

Having read to the end, the treasurer shut his mouth with a click, while some distance off a member of the Auditorial Committee had already risen, a Georgian socialist with a pock-marked face and black hair like a shoe-brush, and briefly enumerated his favourable impressions. After this Shirin asked for the floor and at once there was a whiff of something jolly, alarming, and improper.

He began by seizing on the fact that the expenditure for the New Year's charity dance was inexplicably large; Gurman wanted to reply . . . the chairman, aiming his pencil at Shirin, asked him if he had finished. . . . 'Let him speak, no cutting short!' shouted Shahmatov from his seat – and the chairman's pencil, quivering like a serpent's tongue, was aimed at him before returning to Shirin, who, however, bowed and sat down. Gurman rose heavily, carrying his sorrowful burden with disdain and resignation, and began to speak . . . but Shirin soon interrupted him and Kraevich grasped his bell. Gurman finished, after which the treasurer instantly asked for the floor, but Shirin was already up and continuing: 'The explanation of the honourable gentleman from the stock exchange . . .' The chairman rang his bell and requested more moderation, threatening to refuse permission to speak. Shirin again bowed and said that he had only one question: in the funds, according to the treasurer's words, there were three thousand and seventy-six marks and fifteen pfennigs – could he see this money right now?

'Bravo,' shouted Shahmatov – and the least attractive member of the Union, the mystical poet, guffawed, applauded and almost fell off his chair. The treasurer, paling to a snowy shine, began to speak in a rapid patter . . . While he was speaking and being interrupted by impossible exclamations from the audience, a certain Shuf, lean, clean-shaven, looking somewhat like a Red Indian, left his corner, went up to the committee table unnoticed on his rubber soles, and suddenly slammed his red fist down on it, so that even the bell gave a jump. 'You're lying,' he bellowed and returned to his seat.

A row was breaking out on all sides when to Shirin's chagrin it transpired that there was yet another faction wishing to seize power – namely the group that was always left out, and that included both the mystic and the Red Indian, as well as the little bearded fellow and several seedy and unbalanced individuals, one of whom suddenly began to read from a piece of paper a list of candidates for election to the committee, all of whom were completely unacceptable. The battle took a new turn, sufficiently tangled, now that there were three warring sides. Such expressions flew about as 'black marketeer', 'you're not fit to duel' and 'you've already been thrashed'. Even Busch spoke, trying to drown insulting ejaculations, but because of the natural obscurity of his style no one could understand what he was talking about until, sitting down, he explained that he was fully in agreement with the preceding speaker. Gurman, his nostrils alone expressing sarcasm, busied himself with his cigarette holder. Vasiliev left his seat and retired to a corner, where he pretended to read a newspaper. Lishnevski delivered a crushing speech directed mainly against the board member resembling a peaceful toad, who merely spread his hands and directed a helpless glance at Gurman and the treasurer, both of whom tried not to look at him. Finally, when the poet-mystic stood up, shakily swaying, and with a highly promising smile on his sweaty, leathery face began to speak in verse, the chairman furiously rang his bell and announced an interval, after which the elections were due to be held. Shirin flew over to Vasiliev and commenced to talk to him persuasively, while Fyodor, feeling suddenly bored, found his mackintosh and made his way out onto the street.

He was angry with himself: fancy sacrificing for the sake of this preposterous divertissement the fixed star of his nightly meeting with Zina! The desire to see her at once tortured him with its paradoxical impossibility: if she had not slept six yards from the head of his bed, access to her would have been much easier. A train stretched over the viaduct: the yawn begun by a woman in the lighted window of the first car was completed by another woman – in the last one. Fyodor Konstantinovich strolled toward the tram stop along an oily-black, blaring street. The illuminated sign of a music hall ran up the steps of vertically placed letters, they went out all together, and the light again scrambled up: what Babylonian word would reach up to the sky? . . . a compound name for a trillion tints: diamondimlunalilithlilasafieryviolentviolet and so on – and how many more! Perhaps he should try to phone? He only had a dime in his pocket and he had to decide: to phone meant that in any case he would not be able to take the tram, but to phone for nothing, that is not to get Zina herself (to get her through her mother was not permitted by the code) and then to return on foot would be a bit too galling. I'll risk it. He went into a beerhouse, rang, and everything was over in a twinkle! he got the wrong number, that very number which the anonymous Russian was always trying to get who always got the Shchyogolevs. So what – he would have to hoof it, as Boris Ivanovich would say.

At the next corner his approach automatically triggered off

the doll-like mechanism of the prostitutes who always patrolled there. One of them even tried to look like somebody lingering by a shop window, and it was sad to think that these pink corsets on their golden dummies were known to her by heart, by heart. . . . 'Sweety,' said another with a questioning smile. The night was warm with a dusting of stars. He walked at a swift pace and his bared head felt light from the narcotic night air – and farther on when he walked along gardens there came floating to him phantoms of lilacs, the darkness of foliage, and wonderful naked odours spreading on the lawn.

He was hot, and his forehead was burning when finally, quietly clicking the door shut behind him, he found himself in the dark hall. The opaque glass in the upper part of Zina's door resembled a radiant sea: she must be reading in bed, he thought, but while he stood and looked at this mysterious glass she coughed, rustled, and the light went out. What an absurd torture. Go in there, go in . . . Who would know? People like her mother and stepfather sleep with insensible, hundred per cent sleep of peasants. Zina's punctiliousness: she would never open at the clinking tap of a fingernail. But she knows I am standing in the dark hall and suffocating. This forbidden room during recent months had become a sickness, a burden, a part of himself, but inflated and sealed off: the pneumothorax of the night.

He stood for another moment – and on tiptoe stole into his room. All in all, French emotions. Fama Mour. Sleep, sleep – the heaviness of spring is utterly untalented. Take oneself in hand: a monastic pun. What next? What exactly are we waiting for? In any case I won't find a better wife. But do I need a wife at all? 'Put that lyre away, I've no room to move . . .' No, I would never hear that from her – that's the point.

And a few days later, simply and even somewhat sillily, a solution was indicated to a problem which had seemed so complex that one could not help wondering if there was not a mistake in its construction. Boris Ivanovich, whose affairs during recent years had been getting worse and worse, was most unexpectedly offered by a Berlin firm quite a respectable representative's position in Copenhagen. In two months, by the first of July, he had to move there for at least a year, and perhaps forever if all went well. Marianna Nikolavna who for some reason loved Berlin (familiar haunts, excellent sanitary arrangements – she herself, though, was filthy) felt sad at going away, but when she thought of the improvements in life awaiting her, her grief was dispersed. Thus it was decided that from July Zina would remain alone in Berlin, continuing to work for Traum, until Shchyogolev 'had found her a 'job' in Copenhagen, where Zina would go 'at the first summons' (i.e., that is what the Shchyogolevs thought – Zina had decided quite, quite differently). It remained to regulate the question of the apartment. The Shchyogolevs did not want to sell it, so they began to seek somebody to let it to. They found such a person. A young German with a great commercial future, accompanied by his fiancée – a plain, unmade-up, domestically sturdy girl in a green coat – inspected the apartment – dining-room, bedroom, kitchen, Fyodor in bed – and was satisfied. However, he was taking the apartment only from August, so that for another month after the Shchyogolevs' departure Zina and the lodger would be able to stay there. They counted the days: fifty, forty-nine, thirty, twenty-five – every one of these numbers had its own face: a beehive, a magpie in a tree, the silhouette of a knight, a young man. Their evening meetings had since spring gone beyond the shores of their initial street (lamp, lime, fence), and now their restless wanderings carried them in ever widening circles into distant and ever new corners of the city. Now it was a bridge over a canal, then a trellised bosket in a park, behind which lights ran past, then an unpaved street between misty wastes where dark vans were standing, then some strange arcades which were impossible to find during the daytime. Change of habits before migration; excitement; a languorous pain in the shoulders.

The newspapers diagnosed the still young summer as being exceptionally hot, and indeed there was a long dotted line of beautiful days, interrupted from time to time by the interjection of a thunderstorm. In the morning, while Zina was wilting from the stinking heat in the office (the sweaty armpits of Hamekke's jacket alone were more than enough . . . and what about the typists' necks melting like wax, what about the sticky blackness of carbon paper?), Fyodor would go to spend the whole day in Grunewald, abandoning his lessons and trying not to think of the long-since-due payment for his room. Never before had he got up at seven, it would have seemed monstrous – but now in life's new light (in which blended somehow the maturing of his gift, a premonition of new labours, and the approach of complete happiness with Zina) he experienced a direct pleasure from the speed and lightness of these early risings, from that burst of motion, from the ideal simplicity of three-second dressing: shirt, trousers and sneakers on bare feet – after which he took a laprobe under his arm, with his swim-trunks wrapped in it, thrust on his way through the hall an orange and a sandwich into his pockets and was already running down the stairs.

A turned-back doormat held the door in a wide-open position while the janitor energetically beat the dust out of another mat by slapping it against the trunk of an innocent lime tree: what have I done to deserve this? The asphalt was still in the dark blue shadow of the houses. On the sidewalk gleamed the first, fresh excrements of a dog. A black hearse, which yesterday had been standing outside a repair shop, rolled cautiously out of a gate and turned down the empty street, and inside it, behind the glass and among artificial white roses, in place of a coffin, lay a bicycle: whose? why? The dairy was already open, but the lazy tobacconist was still asleep. The sun played on various objects along the right side of the street, like a magpie picking out the tiny things that glittered: and at the end of it, where it was crossed by the wide ravine of a railroad, a cloud of locomotive steam suddenly appeared from the right of the bridge, disintegrated against its iron ribs, then immediately loomed white again on the other side and wavily streamed away through the gaps in the trees. Crossing the bridge after this, Fyodor, as usual, was gladdened by the wonderful poetry of railroad banks, by their free and diversified nature: a growth of locusts and sallows, wild grass, bees, butterflies – all this lived in isolation and unconcern in the harsh vicinity of coal dust glistening below between the five streams of rails, and in blissful estrangement from the city coulisses above, from the peeled walls of old houses toasting their tattooed backs in the morning sunshine. Beyond the bridge, near the small public garden, two elderly postal workers, having completed their check of a stamp machine and grown suddenly playful, were stealing up from behind the jasmine, one behind the other, one imitating the other's gestures, toward a third – who with eyes closed was humbly and briefly relaxing on a bench before his working day – in order to tickle his nose with a flower. Where shall I put all these gifts with which the summer morning rewards me – and only me? Save them up for future books? Use them immediately for a practical handbook: *How to Be Happy?* Or getting deeper, to the bottom of things: understand what is concealed behind all this, behind the play, the sparkle, the thick, green grease-paint of the foliage? For there really is something, there is something! And one wants to offer thanks but there is no one to thank. The list of donations already made: 10,000 days – from Person Unknown.

He walked farther, past iron railings, past the deep gardens of bankers' villas with their grotto shadows, boxwood, ivy and lawns pearled with watering – and there among the elms and limes the first pines already appeared, sent out far ahead by the Grunewald pinewoods (or, on the contrary: stragglers behind the regiment?). Whistling loudly and rising (uphill) on the pedals of his three-wheeled bicycle, a baker's roundsman went by; a water-sprayer crawled slowly by with a wet hissing sound – a whale on wheels generously irrigating the asphalt. Some one with a briefcase slammed a vermilion-pointed garden gate and set off for some unknown office. Fyodor emerged on his heels onto the boulevard (still the same Hohenzollerndamn at whose beginning they burned poor Alexander Yakovlevich), and there, its lock flashing, the briefcase ran for a tram. Now it was not far to the forest and he quickened his step, already feeling the sun's hot mask on his upturned face. The pickets of a fence flicked by, speckling his vision. On yesterday's vacant lot a small villa was being built, and since the sky was looking in through the gaps of future windows, and since burdocks and sunlight had taken advantage of the slowness of the work to make themselves comfortable within the unfinished white walls, these had acquired the pensive cast of ruins, like the word 'sometime', which serves both the past and the future. Toward Fyodor came a young girl with a bottle of milk; she bore some resemblance to Zina – or, rather, contained a particle of that fascination, both special and vague, which he found in many girls, but with particular fullness in Zina, so that they all possessed some mysterious kinship with Zina, about which he alone knew, although he was completely incapable of formulating the indicia of this kinship (outside of which women evoked painful disgust in him) – and now, as he looked back at her and caught her long familiar, golden, fugitive outline that promptly vanished forever, he felt for a moment the impact of a hopeless desire, whose whole charm and richness was in its unquenchability. Oh trite demon of cheap thrills, do not tempt me with the catchword 'my type'. Not that, not that, but something beyond that. Definition is always finite, but I keep straining for the faraway; I search beyond the barricades (of words, of senses, of the world) for infinity, where all, all the lines meet.

At the end of the boulevard the green edge of the pinewood

came into sight, with the gaudy portico of a recently constructed pavilion (in whose atrium was to be found an assortment of rest-rooms – men's, women's and children's), through which – according to the scheme of the local Lenôtres – one had to go in order to enter at first a newly laid-out rock garden, with Alpine flora along geometric paths, which served – still according to that same scheme – as a pleasant threshold to the forest. But Fyodor turned to the left, avoiding the threshold: it was nearer that way. The still wild edge of the pinewood stretched endlessly along an avenue for automobiles, but the next step on the part of the city fathers was inevitable: fence the whole of this free access with endless railings, so that the portico became the entrance of *necessity* (in the most literal, elementary sense). I built this ornamental thing for you but you weren't attracted; so now if you please: it is ornamental and regimental. But (by a mental jump back again: f3–gl) it could hardly have been better when this forest – now retreated, now crowded around the lake (and like us, in our own departure from hairy ancestors, having kept only a marginal vegetation) – used to stretch to the very heart of the present city, and a noisy, princely rabble galloped among its wilds with horns and hounds and beaters.

The forest as I found it was still alive, rich, full of birds. There occurred orioles, pigeons and jays; a crow flew by, its wings panting: *kshoo, kshoo, kshoo*; a redheaded woodpecker was rapping against a pine trunk – and sometimes, I presume, imititating its own rap vocally whereupon it came out particularly loud and convincingly (for the female's benefit); for there is nothing in nature more bewitchingly divine than her ingenious deceptions cropping up in unexpected places: thus a forest grasshopper (starting his little motor but never able to get it going: *tig-tsig-tsig* – and breaks off), having jumped and landed, immediately readjusts the position of his body by turning in such a way as to make the direction of his dark stripes coincide with those of the fallen needles (or with their shadows!). But careful: I like to recall what my father wrote: 'When closely – no matter how closely – observing events in nature we must, in the very process of observation, beware of letting our reason – that garrulous dragoman who always runs ahead – prompt us with explanations which then begin imperceptibly to influence the very course of observation and distort it: thus the shadow of the instrument falls upon the truth.'

Give me your hand, dear reader, and let's go into the forest together. Look: first – at these glades with patches of thistle, nettle or willow herb, among which you will find all kinds of junk: sometimes even a ragged mattress with rusty, broken springs; don't disdain it! Here is a dark thicket of small firs where I once discovered a pit which had been carefully dug out before its death by the creature that lay therein, a young, slender-muzzled dog of wolf ancestry, folded into a wonderfully graceful curve, paws to paws. And now come bare hillocks with no undergrowth – merely a carpet of brown needles beneath simplistic pines, which have a hammock stretched between them full of someone's unexacting body – and the wire skeleton of a discarded lampshade is also here, lying on the ground. Farther we have a barren surrounded by locust trees – and there on the grey, burning, sticky sand sits a woman in underwear, her dreadful bare legs stretched out, and darns a stocking, while beside her crawls a child dark-groined from the dust. You can still see from here the thoroughfare and the sparkle of automobile radiators skimming by – but you only have to penetrate a little deeper, and the forest reasserts itself, the pines become nobler, moss creaks underfoot, and some bum is invariably asleep here, a newspaper covering his face: the philosopher prefers moss to roses. Here is the exact spot where a small airplane fell the other day: someone who was taking his girl for a morning ride in the blue got overexuberant, lost control of his joystick, and plunged with a screech and a crackle straight into the pines. I, unfortunately, came too late: they had had time to clear up the wreckage, and two mounted policemen were riding at a walk toward the road – but one could still see the imprint of a daring death beneath the pines, one of which had been shaved from top to bottom by a wing, and the architect Stockschmeisser walking with his dog was explaining to a nurse and child what had happened; but a few days later all traces had disappeared (there was only the yellow wound on the pine tree), and already in complete ignorance an old man and his old woman facing each other – she in her bodice and he in his underpants – were doing uncomplicated gymnastics on the same spot.

Farther on it became very nice: the pines had come into their own, and between their pinkish, scaly trunks the feathery foliage of low rowans and the vigorous greenery of oaks broke the stripiness of the pinewood sun into an animated dapple. In the density of an oak, when you looked from below, the overlapping of shaded and illumined leaves, dark green and bright emerald, seemed to be a jigsaw fitting together of their wavy edges, and on these leaves, now letting the sun caress its yellow-brown silk and now tightly closing its wings, there settled an Angle Wing butterfly with a white bracket on its dark mottled underside; suddenly taking off it alighted on my bare chest, attracted by human sweat. And still higher above my upturned face, the summits and trunks of the pines participated in a complex exchange of shadows, and their leafage reminded me of algae swaying in transparent water. And if I tilted my head back even farther, so that the grass behind (inexpressibly, primevally green from this point of upturned vision) seemed to be growing downward into empty, transparent light, I experienced something similar to what must strike a man who has flown to another planet (with a different gravity, different density and a different stress on the senses) – especially when a family out for a stroll went by upside down, with every step they took becoming a strange, elastic jerk, and a lobbed ball seemed to be falling – ever more slowly – into a dizzy abyss.

If one advanced even farther – not to the left where the pinewood stretched endlessly, and not to the right where it was interrupted by a coppice of young birches, freshly and childishly smelling of Russia – the forest again thinned out, lost its undergrowth and straggled down sandy inclines at the foot of which the broad lake rose in pillars of light. The sun changefully illuminated the opposite bank, and when with the onset of a cloud the very air seemed to close, like a great blue eye and then slowly open again, one shore always lagged behind the other in the process of gradually fading and lighting up. There was practically no sandy border on the other side, and the trees descended all together to the dense reeds, while higher up one could find hot, dry slopes overgrown with clover, sorrel and spurge, and fringed with the rich dark green of oaks and beeches that went trembling down to the damp hollows below, in one of which Yasha Chernyshevski had shot himself.

When in the mornings I entered this world of the forest, whose image I had raised as it were by my own efforts above the level of those artless Sunday impressions (paper trash, a crowd of picnickers) out of which the Berliners' conception of 'Grunewald' was composed; when on these hot, summer weekdays I walked over to its southern side, into its depths, to wild secret spots, I felt as much delight as if this was a primeval paradise within two miles from Agamemnonstrasse. Coming to a favourite nook of mine which magically combined a free flow of sunshine with protection by the shrubbery, I would strip to the skin and lie down supine on the rug, placing my unnecessary trunks beneath my head. Thanks to the suntan coating my entire body (so that only my heels, palms and the raylike lines around my eyes kept their natural tint), I felt myself an athlete, a Tarzan, an Adam, anything you like, only not a naked town-dweller. The awkwardness with which nakedness is usually accompanied depends upon the awareness of our defenceless whiteness, which has long since lost all connection with the colours of the surrounding world and for that reason finds itself in artificial disharmony with it. But the sun's impact restores the deficiency, makes us equal in our naked rights with nature, and the brazen body no longer experiences shame. All this sounds like a nudist brochure – but one's own truth is not to blame if it coincides with the truth some poor fellow has borrowed.

The sun bore down. The sun licked me all over with its big, smooth tongue. I gradually felt that I was becoming moltenly transparent, that I was permeated with flame and existed only insofar as it did. As a book is translated into an exotic idiom, so was I translated into sun. The scrawny, chilly, hiemal Fyodor Godunov-Cherdyntsev was now as remote from me as if I had exiled him to the Yakutsk province. He was a pallid copy of me, whereas this aestival one was his magnified bronze replica. My personal I, the one that wrote books, the one that loved words, colours, mental fireworks, Russia, chocolate and Zina – had somehow distintegrated and dissolved; after being made transparent by the strength of the light, it was now assimilated to the shimmering of the summer forest with its satiny pine needles and heavenly-green leaves, with its ants running over the transfigured, most radiant-hued wool of the laprobe, with its birds, smells, hot breath of nettles and spermy odour of sun-warmed grass, with its blue sky where droned a high-flying plane that seemed filmed over with blue dust, the blue essence of the firmament: the plane was bluish, as a fish is wet in water.

One might dissolve completely that way. Fyodor raised himself and sat up. A streamlet of sweat flowed down his clean-shaven chest and fell into the reservoir of his navel. His flat belly had a brown and mother-of-pearl sheen to it. Over the glistening black ringlets of his pubic hair a lost ant scrambled nervously. His shins shone glossily. Pine needles had got stuck between his toes. With his bathing trunks he wiped his short-cropped head, sticky nape and neck. A squirrel with an arched back loped across the turf, from tree to tree, in a wavy and almost clumsy course. The scrub oaks, elder shrubs, pine trunks – everything was dazzlingly spotted, and a small cloud, in no way defiling the face of the summer day, felt its way slowly past the sun.

He got up, took a step – and immediately the weightless paw of a leafy shadow descended upon his left shoulder; it slipped off again at the next step. Fyodor consulted the position of the sun and dragged his rug a yard or so aside to prevent the shade of the leaves from encroaching upon him. To move around naked was astonishing bliss – the freedom around his loins especially pleased him. He walked between the bushes, listening to the vibration of insects and the rustling of the birds. A wren crept like a mouse through the foilage of a small oak; a sand wasp flew by low down, carrying a benumbed caterpillar. The squirrel he had just seen climbed up the bark of a tree with a spasmodic, scrabbly sound. Somewhere in the vicinity sounded girlish voices, and he stopped in a pattern of shadow, which stayed motionless along his arm but palpitated rhythmically on his left side, between the ribs. A golden, stumpy little butterfly, equipped with two black commas, alighted on an oak leaf, half opening its slanting wings, and suddenly shot away like a golden fly. And as often happened on these woodland days, especially when he glimpsed familiar butterflies, Fyodor imagined his father's isolation in other forests – gigantic infinitely distant, in comparison with which this one was but brushwood, a tree stump, rubbish. And yet he experienced something akin to that Asiatic freedom spreading wide on the maps, to the spirit of his father's peregrinations – and here it was most difficult of all to believe that despite the freedom, despite the greenery and the happy, sun-shot dark shade, his father was nonetheless dead.

The voices sounded closer and then receded. A horsefly that had settled unnoticed on his thigh managed to jab him with its blunt proboscis. Moss, turf, sand, each in its own way communicated with the soles of his bare feet, and each in its own way the sun and the shade stroked the hot silk of his body. His senses sharpened by the unrestricted heat were tantalized by the possibility of sylvan encounters, mythical abductions. *Le sanglot dont j'étais encore ivre.* He would have given a year of his life, even a leap-year, for Zina to be here – or any of her corps de ballet.

He again lay flat, then again got up; with a beating heart he listened to sly, vague, vaguely promising noises; then, pulling on only his trunks and hiding laprobe and clothes under a bush, he went off to wander through the woods around the lake.

Here and there, thinly on weekdays, there occurred more or less orange bodies. He avoided looking closely for fear of switching from Pan to Punch. But sometimes, next to a school satchel and beside her shiny bicycle propped against a tree trunk, a lone nymph would sprawl, her legs bared to the crotch and suede-soft to the eye, and her elbows thrown back, with the hair of her armpits glistening in the sun; temptation's arrow had hardly had time to sing out and pierce him before he noticed, a short distance away at three equidistant points, forming a magic triangle (around whose prize?) and strangers to one another, three motionless hunters visible in between the tree trunks: two young fellows (one lying prone, the other on his side) and an elderly man, coatless, with armbands on his shirt-sleeves, sitting solidly on the grass, motionless and eternal, with sad but patient eyes, and it seemed that these three pairs of eyes striking the same spot would finally, with the help of the sun, burn a hole in the black bathing tights of that poor little German girl, who never raised her ointment-smeared lids.

He descended to the sandy shore of the lake and here in the roar of voices the charmed fabric which he himself had so carefully spun completely fell to pieces, and he saw with revulsion the crumpled, twisted, deformed by life's nor'easter, more or less naked or more or less clothed – the latter were the more terrible – bodies of bathers (petty bourgeois, idle workers) stirring on the dirty-grey sand. At the point where the shore road went along the lake's narrow lip, the latter was fenced off by stakes supporting tortured-looking remnants of sagging wire, and the place by these stakes was particularly valued by the beach habitués – partly because trousers could be conveniently hung by their suspenders on them (while underwear was laid on the dusty nettles) and partly because of the vague feeling of security from having a fence at one's back.

Old men's grey legs covered with growths and swollen veins; flat feet; the tawny crust of corns; pink porcine paunches; wet, shivering, pale, hoarse-voiced adolescents; the globes of breasts; voluminous posteriors; flabby thighs; bluish varices, gooseflesh; the pimply shoulder blades of bandy-legged girls; the sturdy necks and buttocks of muscular hooligans; the hopeless, godless vacancy of satisfied faces; romps, guffaws, roisterous splashing – all this formed the apotheosis of that renowned German goodnaturedness which can turn so easily at any moment into frenzied hooting. And over all this, especially on Sundays when the crowding was vilest of all, there reigned an unforgettable smell, the smell of dust, of sweat, of aquatic slime, of unclean underwear, of aired and dried poverty, the smell of dried, smoked, potted souls a penny a piece. But the lake itself, with vivid green clumps of trees on the other side and a rippling wake of sunshine in the middle, bore itself with dignity.

Having selected a private little creak among the bulrushes, Fyodor took to the water. Its warm opacity enveloped him, sparks of sunshine danced before his eyes. He swam for a long time, half an hour, five hours, twenty-four, a week, another. Finally, on the twenty-eighth of June around 3 p.m., he came out on the other shore.

Having made his way out of the lakeside spinach he at once found himself in a grove and from there he climbed onto a hot slope where he quickly dried in the sun. On the right was a ravine overgrown with oakbrush and bramble. And today, just as every time that he came here, Fyodor descended into that hollow which always attracted him, as if he had been somehow guilty of the death of the unknown youth who had shot himself here – precisely here. He reflected that Alexandra Yakovlevna used to come here as well, rummaging purposefully among the bushes with her tiny black-gloved hands. . . . He had not known her then and could not have seen it – but from her account of her multiple pilgrimages he felt it had been exactly like that: the search for something, the rustling of leaves, the prodding umbrella, the radiant eyes, the lips trembling with sobs. He recalled how he had met her this spring – for the last time – after her husband's death, and the strange sensation that overwhelmed him when looking at her lowered face with its unworldly frown, as if he had never really seen her before and was now making out on her face the resemblance to her deceased husband, whose death was expressed on it through some hitherto concealed, funereal blood relationship. A day later she went away to some relatives in Riga, and already her face, the stories about her son, the literary evenings at her house, and Alexander Yakovlevich's mental illness – all this that had served its time – now rolled up of its own accord and came to an end, like a bundle of life tied up crosswise, which will long be kept but which will never again be untied by our lazy, procrastinating, ungrateful hands. He was seized by a panicky desire not to allow it to close and get lost in a corner of his soul's lumber room, a desire to apply all this to himself, to his eternity, to his truth, so as to enable it to sprout up in a new way. There is a way – the only way.

He ascended another slope and there at the top by a path which descended again, sitting on a bench beneath an oak tree, and slowly, pensively tracing the sand with his cane, was a round-shouldered young man in a black suit. How hot he must be, thought the naked Fyodor. The sitter looked up . . . The sun turned and slightly raised his face with a photographer's delicate gesture, a bloodless face with wide-set, myopically grey eyes. Between the corners of his starched collar (the type once called in Russia 'dog's delight') a stud gleamed above the slack knot of his tie.

'How sunburned you are,' said Koncheyev, 'it can hardly be good for you. And where, pray, are your clothes?'

'Over there,' said Fyodor, 'on the other side, in the woods.'

'Someone might steal them,' remarked Koncheyev. 'It's not for nothing there's a proverb: Freehanded Russian, light-fingered Prussian.'

Fyodor sat down and said: 'There is no such proverb. By the way, do you know where we two are? Beyond those blackberry bushes, down below, is the place where the Chernyshevski boy, the poet, shot himself.'

'Oh, was it here?' said Koncheyev without especial interest. 'You know, his Olga recently married a furrier and went off to the United States. Not quite the lancer whom Pushkin's Olga married, but still . . .'

'Aren't you hot?' asked Fyodor.

'Not a bit. I have a weak chest and I always freeze. But of course when one sits next to a naked man one is physically aware that there exist men's outfitters, and one's body feels blind. On the other hand it seems to me that any mental work must be completely impossible for you in such a denuded state.'

'A good point,' grinned Fyodor. 'One seems to live more superficially – on the surface of one's own skin. . . .'

'That's it. All you're concerned with is patrolling your body and trailing the sun. But thought likes curtains and the camera obscura. Sunlight is good in the degree that it heightens the value of shade. A jail with no jailer and a garden with no gardener – that is I think the ideal arrangement. Tell me, did you read what I said about your book?'

'I did,' replied Fyodor, watching a little geometrid caterpillar that was checking the number of inches between the two writers. 'I did indeed. At first I wanted to write you a letter of thanks

– you know, with a touching reference to undeservingness and so on – but then I thought that this would have introduced an intolerable human smell into the domain of free opinion. And besides – if I produced a good book I should thank myself and not you, just as you have to thank yourself and not me for understanding what was good – isn't that true? If we start bowing to one another, then, as soon as one of us stops the other will feel hurt and depart in a huff.'

'I didn't expect truisms from you,' said Koncheyev with a smile. 'Yes, all that is so. Once in my life, only once, I thanked a critic, and he replied: "Well, as a matter of fact, I really liked your book!" and that "really" sobered me forever. By the way. I didn't say everything I could have said about you . . . You were so taken to task for non-existent defects that I no longer wanted to harp on those that were obvious to me. Furthermore, in your next work you will either get rid of them or they will develop into special virtues all your own, the way a speck on an embryo turns into an eye. You are a zoologist, aren't you?'

'In a way – as an amateur. But what are those defects? I wonder if they coincide with the ones I know.'

'First, an excessive trust in words. It sometimes happens that your words in order to introduce the necessary thought have to smuggle it in. The sentence may be excellent, but still it is smuggling, and moreover gratuitous smuggling, since the lawful road is open. But your smugglers under the cover of an obscure style, with all sorts of complicated contrivances, import goods that are duty free anyway. Secondly, there is a certain awkwardness in the reworking of the sources: You seem to be undecided whether to enforce your style upon past speeches and events or to make their own more salient. I took the trouble to confront one or two passages in your book with the context in the complete edition of Chernyshevski's works, same copy you must have used: I found your cigarette ash between the pages. Thirdly, you sometimes bring up parody to such a degree of naturalness that it actually becomes a genuine serious thought, but on *this* level it suddenly falters, lapsing into a mannerism that is yours and not a parody of a mannerism, although it is precisely the kind of thing you are ridiculing – as if somebody parodying an actor's slovenly reading of Shakespeare had been carried away, had started to thunder in earnest, but had accidentally garbled a line. Fourthly, one observes in one or two of your transitions something mechanical, if not automatic, which suggests you are pursuing *your own* advantage, and taking the course you find easier. In one passage, for example, a mere pun serves as such a transition. Fifthly and finally, you sometimes say things chiefly calculated to prick your contemporaries, but any woman will tell you that nothing gets lost so easily as a hairpin – not to speak of the fact that the least swerve of fashion may make pins obsolete: think how many sharp little objects have been dug up whose exact use not a single archaeologist can tell! The real writer should ignore all readers but one, that of the future, who in his turn is merely the author reflected in time. That, I think, is the sum of my complaints against you and generally speaking they are trivial. They are completely eclipsed by the brilliance of your achievements – about which I could still say a fair bit.'

'Oh, that is less interesting,' said Fyodor, *who during this tirade* (as Turgenev, Goncharov, Count Salias, Grigorovich and Boborykin used to write) had been nodding his head with an approving *mien*. 'You diagnosed my shortcomings very well,' he continued, 'and they correspond to my own complaints against myself, although, of course, I put them in a different order – some of the points run together while others are subdivided further. But besides the defects you have noted in my book, I am aware of at least three more – they, perhaps, are the most important of all. Only I'll never tell you them – and they won't be there in my next book. Do you want to talk about your poetry now?'

'No thank you, I'd rather not,' said Koncheyev fearfully. 'I have reasons for thinking that you like my work, but I am organically averse to discussing it. When I was small, before sleep I used to say a long and obscure prayer which my dead mother – a pious and very unhappy woman – had taught me (she, of course, would have said that these two things are incompatible, but even so it's true that happiness doesn't take the veil). I remembered this prayer and kept saying it for years, almost until adolescence, but one day I probed its sense, understood all the words – and as soon as I understood I immediately forgot it, as if I had broken an unrestorable spell. It seems to me that the same thing might happen to my poems – that if I try to rationalize them I shall instantly lose my ability to write them. You, I know, corrupted your poetry long ago with words and meaning – and you will hardly continue writing verse now. You are too rich, too greedy. The Muse's charm lies in her poverty.'

'You know, it's odd,' said Fyodor, 'once, about three years ago, I imagined most vividly a conversation with you on these subjects – and you know it came out somewhat similar! Although, of course, you shamelessly played up to me and all that. The fact that I know you so well without knowing you makes me unbelievably happy, for that means there are unions in the world which don't depend at all on massive friendships, asinine affinities or "the spirit of the age", nor on any mystical organizations or associations of poets, where a dozen tightly knit mediocrities "glow" by their common efforts.'

'At all events I want to warn you,' said Koncheyev frankly, 'not to flatter yourself as regards our similarity: you and I differ in many things, I have different tastes, different habits; your Fet, for instance, I can't stand, and on the other hand I am an ardent admirer of the author of *The Double* and *The Possessed,* whom you are disposed to slight. . . . There is much about you I don't like – your St Petersburg style, your Gallic taint, your neo-Voltaireanism and weakness for Flaubert – and I find, forgive me, your obscene sporty nudity simply offensive. But then, with these reservations, it would be true probably to say that somewhere – not here but on another plane, of whose angle, by the way, you have an even vaguer idea than I – somewhere on the outskirts of our existence, very far, very mysteriously and inexpressibly, a rather divine bond is growing between us. But perhaps you feel and say all this because I praised your book in print – that also happens, you know.'

'Yes, I know. I thought of that myself. Especially since formerly I used to envy your fame. But in all conscience—'

'Fame?' interrupted Koncheyev. 'Don't make me laugh. Who knows my poems? A thousand, a thousand five hundred, at the very outside two thousand intelligent expatriates, of whom again ninety per cent don't understand them. Two thousand out of three million refugees! That's provincial success, but not fame. In the future, perhaps, I shall recoup, but a great deal of time will have to elapse before the Tungus and the Kalmuk of Pushkin's "*Exegi monumentum*" begin to tear out of each other's hands my "Communication", with the Finn looking enviously on.'

'But there is a comforting feeling,' said Fyodor meditatively. 'One can borrow on the strength of the legacy. Doesn't it amuse you to imagine that one day, on this very spot, on this lakeside, beneath this oak tree, a visiting dreamer will come and sit and imagine in his turn that you and I once sat here?'

'And the historian will dryly tell him that we never took a walk together, that we were hardly acquainted and that if we did meet we only talked about routine trifles.'

'But nevertheless try! Try to experience that strange, future, retrospective thrill. . . . All the little hairs on the soul stand on end! It would be a good thing in general to put an end to our barbaric perception of time; I find it particularly charming when people talk about the earth freezing in a trillion years and everything disappearing unless our printing shops are moved in good time to a neighbouring star. Or the drivel about eternity: so much time has been allotted to the universe that the date of its end should *already* have come, just as it is impossible in a single segment of time to imagine *whole* an egg lying on a road along which an army is endlessly marching. How stupid! Our mistaken feeling of time as a kind of growth is a consequence of our finiteness which, being always on the level of the present, implies its constant rise between the watery abyss of the past and the aerial abyss of the future. Existence is thus an eternal transformation of the future into the past – an essentially phantom process – a mere reflection of the material metamorphoses taking place within us. In these circumstances the attempt to comprehend the world is reduced to an attempt to comprehend that which we ourselves have deliberately made incomprehensible. The absurdity at which searching thought arrives is only a natural, generic sign of its belonging to man, and striving to obtain an answer is the same as demanding of chicken broth that it begin to cluck. The theory I find most tempting – that there is no time, that everything is the present situated like a radiance outside our blindness – is just as hopeless a finite hypothesis as all the others. "You will understand when you are big," those are really the wisest words that I know. And if one adds to this that nature was seeing double when she created us (oh, this accursed pairing which is impossible to escape: horse-cow, cat-dog, rat-mouse, flea-bug), that symmetry in the structure of live bodies is a consequence of the rotation of worlds (a top that spins for sufficiently long will begin, perhaps, to live, grow and multiply), and that in our straining toward assymmetry, toward inequality, I can detect a howl for genuine freedom, an urge to break out of the circle. . . .'

'Herrliches Wetter – in der Zeitung steht es aber, dass es morgen bestimmt regnen wird,' said finally the young German who was sitting beside Fyodor on the bench and who had seemed to him to resemble Koncheyev.

Imagination again – but what a pity! I had even thought up a dead mother for him in order to trap truth. . . . Why can a conversation with him never blossom out into reality, break through to realization? Or is this a realization, and nothing better is needed . . . since a real conversation would be only disillusioning – with the stumps of stuttering, the chaff of hemming and hawing, the debris of small words?

'*Da kommen die Wolken schon*,' continued the Koncheyevoid German, pointing his finger at a full-breasted cloud rising in the west. (A student, most probably. Perhaps with a philosophical or musical vein. Where is Yasha's friend now? He would hardly be likely to come here.)

'*Halb fünf ungefähr*,' he added in response to Fyodor's question, and gathering his cane he left the bench. His dark, stooping figure receded along the shady footpath. (Perhaps a poet? After all, there must be poets in Germany. Puny ones, local ones – but all the same not butchers. Or only a garnish for the meat?)

He was too lazy to swim back to the other side; he followed leisurely the trail that skirted the lake along its northern edge. At the spot where wide sandy declivity reached the water, with the uncovered roots of apprehensive pines supporting the sliding bank, there were some more people, and down below on a strip of grass lay three naked corpses, white, pink and brown, like a triple sample of the sun's action. Farther on, along the bend of the lake, there was a marshy stretch, and the dark almost black oil of the path stuck refreshingly to his bare heels. He went upwards again over a needle-scattered slope, and walked through the speckled forest toward his lair. All was cheerful, sad, sunny, shady – he did not feel like returning home but it was time. For a moment he lay down by an old tree that had seemed to have beckoned to him – 'Show you something interesting.' A little song sounded among the trees, and presently there came into view, walking at a brisk pace, five nuns, round-faced, wearing black dresses and white coifs – and the little song, half schoolgirlish, half angelic, hovered about them the whole time, while first one and then another bent down on the move to pluck a modest flower (invisible to Fyodor, although he was lying close by) and then straightened up very nimbly, simultaneously drawing level with the others, taking up the rhythm and adding this ghost-flower to a ghostly nosegay with an idyllic gesture (the thumb and index touching for an instant, the other fingers delicately curved) – and it all looked so much like a staged scene – and how much skill there was in everything, what an infinity of grace and art, what a director lurked behind the pines, how well everything was calculated – their walking slightly out of order and then levelling out again, three in front and two behind, and the fact that one of the girls behind giggled briefly (a very cloistral sense of humour) because suddenly one of those in front had, with a touch of expansiveness, almost splashed her hands over a particularly heavenly note, and the way the song dwindled as it receded, while a shoulder continued to stoop and fingers sought a stalk of grass (but the latter, merely swaying, remained to gleam in the sun . . . where had this happened before – what had straightened up and started to sway? . . .) – and now they all departed through the trees on quick feet in button shoes, and some half-naked little boy, pretending to seek a ball in the grass, rudely and automatically repeated a snatch of their song (in what musicians call a 'clowning refrain'). How it had been mounted! How much labour had gone into this light, swift scene, into this deft traverse, what muscles there were beneath that heavy-looking, black cloth, which would be exchanged after the intermission for gossamer ballet skirts!

A cloud blocked the sun, the light in the forest drifted and gradually faded. Fyodor walked to the clearing where he had left his clothes. In the hole beneath a bush which always sheltered them so obligingly he now found only a single sneaker; his rug, his shirt and his trousers had vanished. There is a story to the effect that a passenger who inadvertently dropped his glove out of a train window promptly threw out its mate so that at least the person who found them should have a pair. In this case the thief had acted the other way: the old, badly worn sneakers were probably no good to him, but in order to make fun of his victim he had separated the pair. Furthermore, a scrap of newspaper had been left in the sneaker with a pencilled inscription: '*Vielen Dank.*'

Fyodor wandered all around finding no one and nothing. The shirt was frayed and he did not mind losing it, but he was somewhat grieved about the plaid laprobe (brought all the way from Russia) and the good flannel pants quite recently bought. Together with the trousers had gone twenty marks, obtained two days before for at least partial payment of his room. Also gone were a small pencil, a handkerchief, and a bunch of keys. The latter somehow was worst of all. If nobody happened to be at home, which might easily be the case, it would be impossible to get into the apartment.

The edge of a cloud dazzlingly caught fire, and the sun slipped out. It emitted such hot, blissful strength that forgetting his vexation Fyodor lay down on the moss and began to watch the next snowy colossus draw near, eating up the blue as it advanced: the sun slid into it smoothly, its rim of funeral fire quivering and splitting as it glided through the white cumulus – and then, finding a way out, it first threw out three rays and then expanded, filling the eyes with spotted fire, blackballing them (so that no matter where you looked domino patterns glided past) – and as the light got stronger or died away, all the shadows in the forest breathed and did push-ups.

A small incidental relief was supplied by the fact that thanks to the Shchyogolevs' going away the following day to Denmark there would be an extra set of keys – which meant he could keep quiet about the loss of his bunch. Going away, going away, going away! He imagined what he had constantly been imagining during the past two months – beginning (tomorrow night!) of his full life with Zina – the release, the slaking – and meanwhile a sun-charged cloud, filling up, growing, with swollen, turquoise veins, with a fiery itch in its thunder-root, rose in all its turgid, unwieldy magnificence and embraced him, the sky and the forest, and to resolve this tension seemed a monstrous joy incapable of being borne by man. A ripple of wind ran over his chest, his excitement slowly subsided, the air grew dark and sultry, it was necessary to hurry home. Once more he searched under the bushes, then shrugged his shoulders, pulled the elastic belt of his trunks tighter – and set out on his way back.

When he left the forest and started to cross a street, the tarry stickiness of the asphalt under his bare foot proved to be a pleasant novelty. It was also interesting to walk on the sidewalk. Dream lightness. An elderly passerby in a black felt hat stopped, looked back after him and made a coarse remark – but immediately, by way of happy compensation, a blind man, sitting with a concertina against a stone wall, mumbled his small request for alms and squeezed out a polygon of music as if there were nothing out of the way (it was odd, though – surely he must have heard that I was barefoot). Two schoolboys shouted at the naked passerby as they rode past clinging to the back of a tram, and then the sparrows returned to the turf between the rails whence they had been frightened by the clattering yellow car. Drops of rain had begun to fall, and it was as if someone were applying a silver coin to different parts of his body. A young policeman detached himself from a newspaper stand and came over to him.

'It's forbidden to walk about the city like that,' he said, looking Fyodor in the navel.

'Everything's been stolen,' explained Fyodor briefly.

'That mustn't happen,' said the policeman.

'Yes, but it happened all the same,' said Fyodor nodding (several people had already stopped by them and were following the dialogue with curiosity).

'Whether you've been robbed or not, you can't go about the streets naked,' said the policeman, growing angry.

'Quite, but I have to get somehow to the taxi stand – see?'

'You can't in that state.'

'Unfortunately I am unable to turn into smoke or grow a suit.'

'And I'm telling you you can't walk about like that,' said the policeman. ('Unheard-of shamelessness,' commented someone's thick voice from the back.)

'In that case,' said Fyodor, 'it remains for you to fetch me a taxi while I stand here.'

'Standing in the nude is also impossible,' said the policeman.

'I'll take off my trunks and imitate a statue,' suggested Fyodor.

The policeman took out his notebook and so fiercely tore the pencil out of the pencil-held that he dropped it on the sidewalk. Some workman or other servilely picked it up.

'Name and address,' said the policeman, boiling.

'Count Fyodor Godunov-Cherdyntsev,' said Fyodor.

'Stop being funny and tell me your name,' roared the policeman.

Another one came up, with a higher rank, and inquired what the matter was.

'My clothes were stolen in the forest,' said Fyodor patiently and suddenly felt that he was completely wet from the rain. One or two standers-by had run beneath the shelter of an awning and an old woman standing by his elbow put up her umbrella, nearly gouging his eye out.

'Who stole them?' asked the sergeant.

'I don't know and what's more, I don't care,' said Fyodor. 'Right now I want to go home and you are detaining me.'

The rain suddenly grew heavier and swept across the asphalt; the whole of its surface seemed to be covered with jumping little candles. The policemen (all matted and blackened by the damp) probably considered the cloudburst to be an element in which bathing trunks were, if not appropriate, then at least permissible. The younger one again tried to obtain Fyodor's address, but his senior waved his hand, and the two of them, slightly quickening their sedate pace, retreated under the awning of a grocer's shop. The glistening Fyodor Konstantinovich ran through the noisy splashing of the rain, turned a corner, and shot into an automobile.

Arriving home and telling the driver to wait, he pressed the button which until 8 p.m. automatically opened the front door and hurled himself up the stairs. He was let in by Marianna Nikolavna; the hall was full of people and things: Shchyogolev in his shirt-sleeves, two fellows struggling with a box (in which, it seems, was the radio), a comely milliner with a hatbox, a coil of wire, a pile of linen from the laundry . . .

'You're crazy!' cried Marianna Nikolavna.

'For God's sake pay the taxi,' said Fyodor, wriggling his cold body through the people and things – and finally, over a barricade of trunks, he crashed his way through to his room.

They had supper all together that evening, and later on were to come the Kasatkins, the baltic baron, another person or two. . . . At table Fyodor gave an embellished account of his misadventure, and Shchyogolev laughed heartily, while Marianna Nikolavna wanted to know (not without reason) how much cash there had been in the pants. Zina only shrugged her shoulders and with unusual frankness urged Fyodor to help himself to the vodka, obviously fearing that he had caught a chill.

'Well – our last evening!' said Boris Ivanovich, having laughed to his heart's content. 'May you prosper, signor. Someone told me the other day that you dashed off a pretty nasty paper on Petrashevski. Very laudable. Listen, Mamma, there's another bottle there, no point in taking it with us, give it to the Kasatkins.'

'. . . so you're going to remain an orphan [he continued, starting on the Italian salad and devouring it with the utmost sloppiness]. I don't think our Zinaida Oscarovna will look after you too well. Eh, princess?'

'. . . Yes, that's how it is, my dear chap, one twist of fate, and the king is mate. I never thought that fortune would smile on me – touch wood, touch wood. Why, only last winter I was wondering what to do: tighten my belt or sell Marianna Nikolavna for scrap? You and I had a year and a half of cohabitation, if you'll excuse the expression, and tomorrow we part – probably forever. Man is fate's plaything. Happy today, pappy tomorrow.'

When supper was over and Zina had gone down to let the guests in, Fyodor retreated noiselessly to his room, where everything was animated by rain and wind. He half-closed the casements of his window, but a moment later the night said: 'No,' and with a kind of wide-eyed insistence, disdaining blows, entered again. 'I was so tickled to learn that Tanya has a little girl, and I am terribly glad for her and for you. The other day I wrote Tanya a long, lyrical letter, but I have an uncomfortable feeling that I put the wrong address on it: instead of "122" I put some other number, without thinking, just as I did once before, I don't know why this happens – one writes an address heaps of times, automatically and correctly, and then all of a sudden one hesitates, one looks at it consciously, and one sees you're not sure of it, it seems unfamiliar – very queer . . . You know, like taking a simple word, say "ceiling" and seeing it as "sealing" or "sea-ling" until it becomes completely strange and feral, something like "iceling" or "inglic". I think that *some day* that will happen to the whole of life. In any case wish Tanya from me everything gay, green and Leshino-summery. Tomorrow my landlord and landlady are going away and I am beside myself with joy: *Beside myself* – a very pleasant situation, like on a rooftop at night. I'll stay at Agamemnonstrasse another month and then move. I don't know how things will work out. By the way, my Chernyshevski is selling rather well. Who exactly was it told you that Bunin praised it? They already seem ancient history to me now, my exertions over the book, and all those little storms of thought, those cares of the pen – and now I am completely empty, clean, and ready to receive new lodgers. You know, I'm black as a gypsy from the Grunewald sun. Something is beginning to take shape – I think I'll write a classical novel, with "types", love, fate, conversations . . .'

The door suddenly opened, Zina half entered and without letting go of the door handle threw something on his desk.

'Pay this to Mamma,' she said; she glanced at him through slitted eyes and disappeared.

He unfolded the banknote. Two hundred marks. The amount seemed colossal, but a moment's calculation showed that it would only just suffice for the two past months –eighty plus eighty, and thirty-five for the coming one, from now on without board. But everything grew confused when he began to consider that for the past month he had not been taking lunch, but on the other hand had been receiving bigger suppers; besides that he had contributed during that time ten (or fifteen?) marks, and on the other hand he owed for telephone conversations and for one or two other trifles, such as today's taxi. The solution to the problem was beyond him, it bored him; he thrust the money beneath a dictionary.

'. . . and with descriptions of nature. I am very glad that you're reading my thing over again, but now it's time to forget it – it was only an exercise, a tryout, an essay before the school holidays. I have missed you a great deal and perhaps (I repeat, I don't know how it will work out . . .) I'll visit you in Paris. Generally speaking I'd abandon tomorrow this country, oppressive as a headache – where everything is alien and repulsive to me, where a novel about incest or some trash, some cloyingly rhetorical, pseudo-brutal tale about war is considered the crown of literature; where in fact there is no literature, and hasn't been for a long time, where sticking out of the fog of a most monotonous democratic dampness – also pseudo – you have the same old jackboot and helmet; where our native enforced "social intent" in literature has been replaced by social opportunity – and so on, and so on . . . I could go on much longer – and it is amusing that fifty years ago every Russian thinker with a suitcase used to scribble exactly the same – an accusation so obvious as to have become even banal. Earlier, on the other hand, in the golden middle of last century, goodness, what transports! "Little gemütlich Germany" – ach, brick cottages, ach, the kiddies go to school, ach, the peasant doesn't beat his horse with a club! . . . Never mind – he has his own German way of torturing it, in a cosy nook, with red-hot iron. Yes, I would have left long ago, but there are certain personal circumstances (not to mention my wonderful solitude in this country, the wonderful, beneficent contrast between my inner habitus and the terribly cold world around me; you know, in cold countries houses are warmer than in the south, better insulated and heated), but even these personal circumstances are capable of taking such a turn that soon, perhaps, I'll leave the Fetterland and bring them with me. And when will we return to Russia? What idiotic sentimentality, what a rapacious groan must our innocent hope convey to people in Russia. But our nostalgia is not historical – only human – how can one explain this to them? It's easier for me, of course, than for another to live outside Russia because I know for certain that I shall return – first because I took away the keys to her, and secondly because, no matter when, in a hundred, two hundred years – I shall live there in my books – or at least in some researcher's footnote. There; now you have a historical hope, a literary-historical one . . . "I lust for immortality – even for its earthly shadow!" Today I am writing you non-stop nonsense (non-stop trains of thought) because I am well and happy – and besides that, all this has something to do in a roundabout way with Tanya's baby.

'The literary review you ask about is called *The Tower*. I don't have it but I think you'll find it in any Russian bookshop. Nothing came from Uncle Oleg. When did he send it? I think you've mixed something up. Well, that's it. Keep well, *je t'embrasse*. Night, rain quietly falling – it has found its nocturnal rhythm, and can now go on for infinity.'

He heard the hall fill with departing voices, heard somebody's umbrella fall and the elevator summoned by Zina rumble and come to a halt. All was still again. Fyodor went into the dining-room where Shchyogolev sat cracking the last nuts, chewing on one side, and Marianna Nikolavna was clearing the table. Her plump, dark pink face, the glossy wings of her nose, violet eyebrows, apricot hair turning to bristly blue on her fat shaven nape, her azure orb with its mascara-fouled canthus, momentarily immersing its gaze in the dreggy ooze on the bottom of the teapot, her rings, her garnet brooch, the flowery shawl on her shoulder – all this together constituted a crudely but richly daubed picture in a somewhat hackneyed genre. She put on her spectacles and took out a sheet with figures on it when Fyodor asked how much he owed her. At this Shchyogolev raised his eyebrows in surprise: he had been sure that they would not get another penny from their lodger, and being essentially a kindly man he had advised his wife only yesterday not to press Fyodor but to write him a week or two later from Copenhagen with a threat to approach his relatives. After settling up, Fyodor retained three and a half marks out of the two hundred and went off to bed. In the hallway he met Zina returning from below. 'Well?' she said, holding her finger on the switch – a half-interrogative, half-urging interjection which meant approximately: 'Are you coming this way? I'm putting out the light here, so hurry up.' The dimple on her naked arm, pale-silk-clad leg in velvet slippers, lowered face. Darkness.

He went to bed and began to fall asleep to the whisper of the rain. As always on the border between consciousness and sleep all sorts of verbal rejects, sparkling and tinkling, broke in: 'The crystal crunching of that Christian night beneath a chrysolitic star' . . . and his thought, listening for a moment, aspired to gather them and use them and began to add of its own: Extinguished, Yasnaya Polyana's light, and Pushkin dead, and Russia far . . . but since this was no good, the stipple of rhymes extended farther: 'A falling star, a cruising chrysolite, an aviator's avatar . . .' His mind sank lower and lower into a hell of alligator alliterations, into infernal co-operatives of words. Through their nonsensical accumulation a round button on the pillowcase prodded him in the cheek; he turned on his other side and against a dark backdrop naked people ran into the Grunewald lake, and a monogram of light resembling an infuorian glided diagonally to the highest corner of his subpalpebral field of vision. Behind a certain closed door in his brain, holding on to its handle but turning away from it, his mind commenced to discuss with somebody a complicated and important secret, but when the door opened for a minute it turned out that they were talking about chairs, tables, stables. Suddenly in the thickening mist, by reason's last tollgate, came the silver vibration of a telephone bell, and Fyodor rolled over prone, falling . . . The vibration stayed in his fingers, as if a nettle had stung him. In the hall, having already put back the receiver into its black box, stood Zina – she seemed frightened. 'That was for you,' she said in a low voice. 'Your former landlady, Frau Stoboy. She wants you to come over immediately. There's somebody waiting for you at her place. Hurry.' He pulled on a pair of flannel trousers and gasping for breath went along the street. At this time of year in Berlin there is something similar to the St Petersburg white nights: the air was transparently grey, and the houses swam past like a soapy mirage. Some night workers had wrecked the pavement at the corner, and one had to creep through narrow passages between planks, everyone being given at the entrance a small lamp which at the exit was to be left on a hook screwed into a post or else simply on the sidewalk next to some empty milk bottles. Leaving his bottle as well he ran farther through the lustreless streets, and the premonition of something incredible, of some impossible superhuman surprise splashed his heart with a snowy mixture of happiness and horror. In the grey murk, blind children wearing dark spectacles came out of a school building in pairs and walked past him; they studied at night (in economically dark schools which in the daytime housed seeing children), and the clergyman accompanying them resembled the Leshino village schoolmaster, Bychkov. Leaning against a lamp-post and hanging his tousled head, his scissor-like legs in striped pantaloons splayed wide and his hands stuffed in his pockets, a lean drunkard stood as if just come from the pages of an old Russian satirical rag. There was still light in the Russian bookstore – they were serving books to the night taxicab drivers and through the yellow opacity of the glass he noticed the silhouette of Misha Berezovski who was handing out Petrie's black atlas to someone. Must be hard to work nights! Excitement lashed him again as soon as he reached his former haunts. He was out of breath from running, and the rolled-up laprobe weighed heavy on his arm – he had to hurry, but he could not recall the layout of the streets, and the ashy night confused everything, changing as in a negative image the relationship between dark and light parts, and there was no one to ask, everybody was asleep. Suddenly a poplar loomed and behind it a tall church with a violet-red window divided into harlequin rhombuses of coloured light: inside a night service was in progress, and an old lady in mourning with cotton-wool under the bridge of her spectacles hastened to mount the steps. He found his street, but at the end of it a post with a gauntleted hand on it indicated that one had to enter from the other end where the post office was, since at this end a pile of flags had been prepared for tomorrow's festivities. But he was afraid of losing it in the course of a detour and moreover the post office – that would come afterwards – if Mother had not *already* been sent a telegram. He scrambled over boards, boxes and a toy grenadier in curls, and caught sight of the familiar house, and there the workmen had already stretched a red strip of carpet across the sidewalk from door to curb, as it used to be done in front of their house on the Neva Embankment on ball nights. He ran up the stairs and Frau Stoboy immediately let him in. Her cheeks glowed and she wore a white hospital overall – she had formerly practised medicine. 'Only don't get all worked up,' she said. 'Go to your room and wait there. You must be prepared for anything,' she added with a vibrant note in her voice and pushed him into the room which he had thought he would never in his life enter again. He grasped her by the elbow, losing control over himself, but she shook him off. 'Somebody has come to see you,' said Stoboy, 'he's resting . . . Wait a couple of minutes.' The door banged shut. The room was exactly as if he had been still living in it: the same swans and lilies on the wallpaper, the same painted ceiling wonderfully ornamented with Tibetan butterflies (there, for example, was *Thecla bieti*). Expectancy, awe, the frost of happiness, the surge of sobs merged into a single blinding agitation as he stood in the middle of the room incapable of movement, listening and looking at the door. He knew *who* would enter in a moment, and was amazed now that he had doubted this return: doubt now seemed to him to be the obtuse obstinacy of one half-witted, the distrust of a barbarian, the self-satisfaction of an ignoramus. His heart was bursting like that of a man before execution, but at the same time this execution was such a joy that life faded before it, and he was unable to understand the disgust he had been wont to experience when, in hastily constructed dreams, he had evoked what was now taking place in real life. Suddenly, the door shuddered (another, remote one had opened somewhere beyond it) and he heard a familiar tread, an indoor Morocco-padded step. Noiselessly but with terrible force the door flew open, and on the threshold stood his father. He was wearing a gold embroidered skullcap and a black Cheviot jacket with breast pockets for cigarette case and magnifying glass; his brown cheeks with their two sharp furrows running down from both sides of his nose were particularly smoothly shaven; hoary hairs gleamed in his dark beard like salt; warmly, shaggily, his eyes laughed out of a network of wrinkles. But Fyodor stood and was unable to take a step. His father said something, but so quietly that it was impossible to make anything out, although one somehow knew it to be connected with his return, unharmed, whole, human, and real. And even so it was terrible to come closer – so terrible that Fyodor felt he would die if the one who had entered should move toward him. Somewhere in the rear rooms sounded the warningly rapturous laughter of his mother, while his father made soft chucking sounds hardly parting his lips, as he used to do when taking a decision or seeking something on the page of a book . . . then he spoke again – and this again meant that everything was all right and simple, that this was the true resurrection, that it could not be otherwise, and also: that he was pleased – pleased with his captures, his return, his son's book about him – and then at last everything grew easy, a light broke through, and his father with confident joy spread out his arms. With a moan and a sob Fyodor stepped toward him, and in the collective sensation of woollen jacket, big hands and the tender prickle of trimmed moustaches there swelled an ecstatically happy, living, enormous, paradisal warmth in which his icy heart melted and dissolved.

At first the superposition of a thingummy on a thingabob and the pale, palpitating stripe that went upwards were utterly incomprehensible, like words in a forgotten language or the parts of a dismantled engine – and this senseless tangle sent a shiver of panic running through him: I have woken up in the grave, on the moon, in the dungeon of dingy non-being. But something in his brain turned, his thoughts settled and hastened to paint over the truth – and he realized that he was looking at the curtain of a half-open window, at a table in front of the window: such is the treaty with reason – the theatre of earthly habit, the livery of temporary substance. He lowered his head onto the pillow and tried to overtake a fugitive sense – warm, wonderful, all-explaining – but the new dream he dreamt was an uninspired compilation, stitched together out of remnants of daytime life and fitted to it.

The morning was overcast and cool, with grey-black puddles on the yard's asphalt, and one could hear the nasty flat thumping of carpet being beaten. The Shchyogolevs had finished their packing; Zina had gone off to work and at one o'clock was due to meet her mother for lunch at the Vaterland. Luckily they had not suggested that Fyodor join them – on the contrary, Marianna Nikolavna, as she warmed up some coffee for him in the kitchen where he sat in his dressing gown, disconcerted by the bivouac-like atmosphere in the apartment, warned him that a little Italian salad and some ham had been left in the larder for lunch. It turned out, incidentally, that the luckless person who was getting their number by mistake, had rung up the previous night: this time he had been tremendously agitated, something had happened – something which remained unknown.

For the tenth time Boris Ivanovich transferred from one valise to another a pair of shoes on shoe trees, all clean and shiny – he was unusually meticulous over footwear.

Then they dressed and went out, while Fyodor shaved, carried out long and successful ablutions, and cut his toenails – it was especially pleasant to get under a tight corner, and *clip!* – the parings shot all over the bathroom. The janitor knocked but was unable to enter because the Shchyogolevs had locked the hall door on the American lock, and Fyodor's keys had gone forever. Through the letter-box, clacking the shutter, the mailman threw in the Belgrade newspaper *For Tsar and Church*, to which Boris Ivanovich subscribed, and later someone thrust in (leaving it to stick out boatlike) a leaflet advertising a new hairdresser's. At exactly half past eleven there came a loud barking from the stairs and the agitated descent of the Alsatian which was taken for a walk at this time. With a comb in his hand he went out onto the balcony to see if the weather was clearing up, but although it did not rain, the sky remained hopelessly and wanly white – and one could not believe that yesterday it had been possible to lie in the forest. The Shchyogolevs' bedroom was cluttered up with paper rubbish, and one of the suitcases was open – at the top a pear-shaped object of rubber was lying on a wafer towel. An itinerant moustache came into the yard with cymbals, a drum, a saxophone – completely hung with metallic music, with bright music on his head, and with a monkey in a red jersey – and sang for a long time, tapping his foot and jangling – without managing, however, to drown out the volleying at the carpets on their trestles. Cautiously pushing the door, Fyodor visited Zina's room, where he had never been before, and with the bizarre sensation of a glad moving in he looked for a long time at the briskly ticking alarm clock, at the rose in a glass with its stem all studded with bubbles, at the divan that became a bed at night and at the stockings drying on the radiator. He had a bite to eat, sat down at his desk, dipped his pen, and froze over a blank sheet. The Shchyogolevs returned, the janitor came, Marianna Nikolavna broke a bottle of scent – and he still sat over the glowering sheet and only came to himself when the Shchyogolevs were getting ready to go to the station. There were still two hours until the train's departure, but then the station was a long way off. 'I must confess – I like to get there on the cock,' said Boris Ivanovich buoyantly as he took hold of his shirt cuff and sleeve in order to climb into his overcoat. Fyodor tried to help him (the other with a polite exclamation, still only halfway in, shied away and suddenly, in the corner, turned into a horrible hunchback), and then went to say goodbye to Marianna Nikolavna, who with an oddly altered expression (as if she were dimming and coaxing her reflection) was in the act of putting on a blue hat with a blue veil before the wardrobe mirror. All at once Fyodor felt strangely sorry for her and after a moment's thought he offered to go to the stand for a taxi. 'Yes, please,' said Marianna Nikolavna and rushed ponderously to the sofa for her gloves.

There proved to be no cabs at the stand, all had been taken, and he was forced to cross the square and look there. When he finally drove up to the house the Shchyogolevs were already standing below, having carried their suitcases down themselves (the 'heavy luggage' had been dispatched the day before).

'Well, God take care of you,' said Marianna Nikolavna, and kissed him with gutta-percha lips on the forehead.

'Sarotska, Sarotska, send us a telegramotska!' cried Boris the parodist, waving his hand, and the taxi turned and sped away.

Forever, thought Fyodor with relief and whistling went upstairs.

Only here did he realize that he was unable to enter the apartment. It was particularly galling to raise the brass postal shutter and look through at a bunch of keys lying starwise on the hall floor: Marianna Nikolavna had pushed them back in after locking the door behind her. He went down the stairs much more slowly than he had gone up. Zina, he knew, was planning to go from work to the station: considering that the train would be leaving in about two hours, and that the bus ride would take an hour, she (and the keys) would not be back in less than three hours. The streets were windy and grey: he had no one to go to, and he never went alone into pubs or cafés, he hated them fiercely. In his pocket there were three and a half marks; he bought some cigarettes, and since the gnawing need to see Zina (now, when everything was allowed) was really what was taking away all light and sense from the street, from the sky and the air, he hastened to the corner where the necessary bus stopped. The fact that he was wearing bedroom slippers and an ancient crumpled suit, spotted in front, with trousers a button short on the fly, baggy knees and a patch of his mother's making on the bottom, did not disturb him in the least. His tan and the open collar of his shirt gave him a certain pleasant immunity.

It was some kind of a national holiday. Three kinds of flags were sticking out of the house windows: black-yellow-red, black-white-red, and plain red; each one meant something, and funniest of all, this something was able to excite pride or hatred in someone. There were large flags and small flags, on short poles and on long ones, but none of this exhibitionism of civic excitement made the city any more attractive. On the Tauentzienstrasse the bus was held up by a gloomy procession; policemen in black leggings brought up the rear in a slow truck and among the banners there was one with a Russian inscription containing two mistakes: *serb* instead of *serp* (sickle) and *molt* instead of *molot* (hammer). Suddenly he imagined official festivals in Russia, soldiers in long-skirted overcoats, the cult of firm jaws, a gigantic placard with a vociferous cliché clad in Lenin's jacket and cap, and amidst the thunder of stupidities, the kettledrums of boredom, and slave-pleasing splendours – a little squeak of cheap truth. There it is, eternalized, ever more monstrous in its heartiness, a repetition of the Hodynka coronation festivities with its free candy packages – look at the size of them (now much bigger than the original ones) – and with its superbly organized removal of dead bodies . . . Oh, let everything pass and be forgotten – and again in two hundred years' time an ambitious failure will vent his frustration on the simpletons dreaming of a good life (that is if there does not come *my* kingdom, where everyone keeps to himself and there is no equality and no authorities – but if you don't want it, I don't insist and don't care).

The Potsdam square, always disfigured by city work (oh, those old postcards of it where everything is so spacious, with the droshki drivers looking so happy, and the trains of tight-belted ladies brushing the dust – but with the same fat flower-girls). The pseudo-Parisian character of Unter den Linden. The narrowness of the commercial streets beyond it. Bridge, barge, sea gulls. The dead eyes of old hotels of the second, third, hundredth class. A few more minutes of riding, and there was the station.

He caught sight of Zina in a beige georgette dress and a white little hat running up the steps. She was running with her pink elbows pressed to her sides, holding her handbag under her arm – and when he caught up with her and half embraced her, she turned round with that tender, blurry smile, with that happy sadness in her eyes with which she always greeted him when they met alone. 'Listen,' she said, in a flurried voice. 'I'm late, let's run.' But he replied that he had already said good-bye to them and would wait for her outside.

The low sun settling behind the rooftops seemed to have fallen out of the clouds that covered the rest of the sky (but they were by now quite soft and aloof, as if painted in melting undulations upon a greenish ceiling); there, in that narrow slit, the sky was on fire, and opposite, a window and some metallic letters shone like copper. A porter's long shadow, pushing the shadow of a barrow, sucked in that shadow, but at the turning it protruded again at a sharp angle.

'We'll miss you, Zina,' said Marianna Nikolavna, from the window of the carriage. 'But in any case take your vacation in August and come over – we'll see if you can't perhaps stay for good.'

'I don't think so,' said Zina. 'Ah yes, I gave you my keys today. Don't take them with you, please.'

'I left them in the hall . . . And Boris's are in the desk . . . Never mind: Godunov will let you in,' added Marianna Nikolavna appeasingly.

'Well, well. Good luck to it,' said Boris Ivanovich from behind his wife's plump shoulder and rolled his eyes. 'Ah, Zinka, Zinka, just you come over and you shall ride a bicycle and swill milk – that's the life!'

The train gave a shudder and started to move. Marianna Nikolavna kept waving for a long time. Shchyogolev drew in his head like a tortoise (and having sat down, probably emitted a Russian grunt).

She skipped down the steps – her bag now hung from her fingers, and the last rays of the sun caused a bronze gleam to dance in her eyes as she flew up to Fyodor. They kissed as ardently as if she had just arrived from far off, after a long separation.

'And now let's go and have some supper,' she said, taking his arm. 'You must be starved.'

He nodded. Now how to explain it? Why this strange embarrassment – instead of the exultant, voluble freedom I had been so eagerly looking forward to? It was as if I had grown disused from her, or else was unable to adjust myself and her, the former her, to this freedom.

'What's the matter with you – you seem out of sorts?' she asked observantly after a silence (they were walking toward the bus stop).

'It's sad to part with Boris the Brisk,' he replied, trying to see if a joke would resolve his emotional constraint.

'And I think it's yesterday's escapade,' said Zina, smiling, and he detected in her tone of voice a high-strung ring, which in its own way corresponded to his own confusion and thus both stressed and augmented it.

'Nonsense. The rain was warm. I feel wonderful.'

The bus rolled up, they boarded it. Fyodor paid for two tickets from his palm. Zina said: 'I get my wages only tomorrow, so that all I have now is two marks. How much do you have?'

'Very little. Out of your two hundred I was left only three-fifty and more than a half of that I have blowed.'

'We have enough for supper, though,' said Zina.

'Are you quite sure you like the idea of a restaurant? Because I don't too much.'

'Never mind, resign yourself. In general now it's all over with healthy home cooking. I can't even make an omelette. We must think about how to manage things. But for now I know an excellent place.'

Several minutes of silence. The streetlamps and shop windows were beginning to light up; the streets had grown pinched and grey from that immature light, but the sky was radiant and wide, and the sunset cloudlets were trimmed with flamingo down.

'Look, the photos are ready.'

He took them from her cold fingers. Zina standing in the street before her office, with legs placed tightly together and the shadow of a lime trunk crossing the sidewalk, like a boom lowered in front of her; Zina sitting sideways on a windowsill with a crown of sunshine around her head; Zina at work, badly taken, dark-faced – but to compensate this, her regal typewriter enthroned in the foreground, with a gleam on its carriage lever.

She thrust them back in her bag, took out and put back her monthly tram ticket in its cellophane holder, took out a small mirror, looked into it, baring the filling in her front tooth, replaced the mirror inside, clicked the bag shut, lowered it onto her knees, looked at her shoulder, brushed off a bit of fluff, put on her gloves, turned her head to the window – doing all this in rapid succession, with her features in motion, her eyes blinking and a kind of inner biting and sucking in of her cheeks. But now she sat motionless, looking away, the sinews in her pale neck stretched tight and her white-gloved hands lying on the glossy leather of her handbag.

The *défilé* of the Brandenburg Gate.

Beyond the Potsdam square, just as they were approaching the canal, an elderly lady with prominent cheekbones (where had I seen her?) and with a goggle-eyed, trembling little dog under her arm made a dive for the exit, swaying and struggling with phantoms, and Zina looked up at her with a fleeting heavenly glance.

'Did you recognize her?' she asked. 'That was Lorentz. I think she's mad at me because I never ring her up. Quite a superfluous woman, really.'

'There's a smut on your cheek,' said Fyodor. 'Careful, don't smear it.'

Again the handbag, handkerchief, mirror.

'We soon have to get out,' she said presently. 'What?'

'Nothing. I agree. Let's get out where you like.'

'Here,' she said two stops later, taking his elbow, sitting again from a jolt, rising finally and fishing out her bag as if from water.

The lights had already taken shape; the sky was quite faint. A truck went by with a load of young people returning from some civic orgy, waving something or other and shouting something or other. In the middle of a treeless public garden consisting of a large oblong flower-bed rimmed by a footpath, an army of roses was in bloom. The small, open enclosure of a restaurant (six little tables) opposite this garden was separated from the sidewalk by a whitewashed barrier topped with petunias.

Beside them a boar and his sow were feeding, the waiter's black fingernail dipped into the sauce, and yesterday a lip with a sore on it had been pressed to the gold border of my beer glass. . . . The mist of some sorrow had enveloped Zina – her cheeks, her narrowed eyes, her throat pit, her fragile clavicle – and this was somehow enhanced by the pale smoke from her cigarette. The scuffing of passers-by seemed to stir up the thickening darkness.

Suddenly, in the frank evening sky, very high . . .

'Look,' she said. 'What a beauty!'

A brooch with three rubies was gliding over the dark velvet – so high that not even the hum of the engine was audible.

She smiled, parting her lips and looking upwards.

'Tonight?' he said, also looking upwards.

Only now had he entered into the order of feelings he used to promise himself, when formerly he imagined how they would slip together out of a thraldom that had gradually asserted itself in the course of their meetings, and grown habitual, even though it was based on something artificial, something unworthy, in fact, of the significance it had acquired: now it seemed incomprehensible why on any of those four hundred and fifty-five days she and he had not simply moved out of the Shchyogolevs' apartment to dwell together; but at the same time he knew subrationally that this external obstacle was merely a pretext, merely an ostentatious device on the part of fate, which had hastily put up the first barrier to come to hand in order to engage meantime in the important, complicated business that secretly required the very delay in development which had seemed to depend on a natural obstruction.

Pondering now fate's methods (in this white, illuminated little enclosure, in Zina's golden presence and with the participation of the warm, concave darkness immediately behind the carved radiance of the petunias), he finally found a certain thread, a hidden spirit, a chess idea for his as yet hardly planned 'novel', to which he had glancingly referred yesterday in the letter to his mother. It was of this that he spoke now, spoke in such a way as if it were really the best and most normal expression of his happiness – which was also expressed in a more accessible edition by such thing as the velvetiness of the air, three emerald lime leaves that had got into the lamplight, the icy cold beer, the lunar volcanoes of mashed potato, vague voices, footfalls, the stars among the ruins of clouds. . . .

'Here is what I'd like to do,' he said. 'Something similar to destiny's work in regard to us. Think how fate started it three and a half odd years ago. . . . The first attempt to bring us together was crude and heavy! That moving of furniture, for example: I see something extravagant in it, "a no-holds-barred" something, for it was quite a job moving the Lorentzes and all their belongings into the house where I had just rented a room! The idea lacked subtlety: to have us meet through Lorentz's wife. Wishing to speed things up, fate brought in Romanov, who rang me up and invited me to a party at his place. But at this point fate blundered: the medium chosen was wrong, I disliked the man and a reverse result was achieved: because of him I began to avoid an acquaintance with the Lorentzes – so that all this cumbersome construction went to the devil, fate was left with a furniture van on her hands and the expenses were not recovered.'

'Watch out,' said Zena, 'she might take offence at this criticism now and revenge herself.'

'Listen further. Fate made a second attempt, simpler this time but promising better success, because I was in need of money and should have grasped at the offer of work – helping an unknown Russian girl to translate some documents; but this also failed. First because the lawyer Charski also turned out to be an unsuitable middleman, and secondly because I hate working on translations into German – so that it again miscarried. Then finally, after this failure, fate decided to take no chances, to install me directly in the place where you lived. As a go-between she chose not the first person to come along, but someone I liked who energetically took the matter in hand and did not allow me to dodge it. At the last minute, true, there occurred a hitch that almost ruined everything: in her haste – or from stinginess – destiny did not produce you at the time of my visit: of course, after talking five minutes to your stepfather – whom fate had been careless enough to let out of his cage – I decided not to take the unattractive room I had glimpsed over his shoulder. And then, at the end of her tether, unable to show me you immediately, fate showed me as a last desperate manoeuvre your bluish ball dress on the chair – and strange to say, I myself don't know why but the manoeuvre worked, and I can imagine what a sigh of relief fate must have heaved.'

'Only that wasn't my dress, it was my cousin Raissa's – she's very nice but a perfect fright – I think she left it for me to take something off or sew something on.'

'Then it was still more ingenious. What resourcefulness! The most enchanting things in nature and art are based on deception. Look, you see – it began with a reckless impetuosity and ended with the finest of finishing touches. Now isn't that the plot for a remarkable novel? What a theme! But it must be built up, curtained, surrounded by dense life – my life, my professional passions and cares.'

'Yes, but that will result in an autobiography with mass executions of good acquaintances.'

'Well, let's suppose that I so shuffle, twist, mix, rechew and rebelch everything, add such spices of my own and impregnate things so much with myself that nothing remains of the autobiography but dust – the kind of dust, of course, which makes the most orange of skies. And I shan't write it now, I'll be a long time preparing it, years perhaps . . . In any case I'll do something else first – I want to translate something in my own manner from an old French sage – in order to reach a final dictatorship over words, because in my *Chernyshevski* they are still trying to vote.'

'That's all marvellous,' said Zina. 'I like it all immensely. I think you'll be such a writer as has never been before, and Russia will simply pine for you – when she comes to her senses too late. . . . But do you love me?'

'What I am saying is in fact a kind of declaration of love,' replied Fyodor.

'A "kind of" is not enough. You know at times I shall probably be wildly unhappy with you. But on the whole it does not matter, I'm ready to face it.'

She smiled, opening her eyes wide and raising her eyebrows, and then she leaned slightly backwards in her chair and began to powder her chin and nose.

'Ah, I must tell you – this is magnificent – he has a famous passage which I think I can say by heart if I go right on, so don't interrupt me, it's an approximate translation: there was once a man . . . he lived as a true Christian; he did much good, sometimes by word, sometimes by deed, and sometimes by silence;

he observed the fasts; he drank the water of mountain valleys (that's good, isn't it?); he nurtured the spirit of contemplation and vigilance; he lived a pure, difficult, wise life; but when he sensed the approach of death, instead of thinking about it, instead of tears of repentance and sorrowful partings, instead of monks and a notary in black, he invited guests to a feast, acrobats, actors, poets, a crowd of dancing girls, three magicians, jolly Tollenburg students, a traveller from Taprobana, and in the midst of melodious verses, masks and music he drained a goblet of wine and died, with a carefree smile on his face. . . . Magnificent, isn't it? If I have to die one day that's exactly how I'd like it to be.'

'Only minus the dancing girls,' said Zina.

'Well, that's only a symbol of gay company. . . . Perhaps, now, we can go?'

'We have to pay,' said Zina. 'Call him over.'

After this they were left with eleven pfennigs, counting the blackened coin which she had picked up a day or two before from the sidewalk: it would bring luck. As they walked down the street he felt a quick tremor along his spine, and again that emotional constraint, but now in a different, languorous form. It was a twenty minutes' slow walk to the house, and the air, the darkness and the honeyed scent of blooming lindens caused a sucking ache at the base of the chest. This scent evanesced in the stretch from linden to linden, being replaced there by a black freshness, and then again, beneath the next canopy, an oppressive and heady cloud would accumulate, and Zina would say, tensing her nostrils: 'Ah, smell it,' and again the darkness would be drained of savour and again would be heavy with honey. Will it really happen tonight? Will it really happen now? The weight and the threat of bliss. When I walk with you like this, ever so slowly, and hold you by the shoulder, everything slightly sways, my head hums, and I feel like dragging my feet; my left slipper falls off my heel, we crawl, dawdle, dwindle in a mist – now we are almost all melted. . . . And one day we shall recall all this – the lindens, and the shadow on the wall, and a poodle's unclipped claws tapping over the flagstones of the night. And the star, the star. And here is the square and the dark church with the yellow light of its clock. And here, on the corner, the house.

Good-bye, my book! Like mortal eyes, imagined ones must close some day. Onegin from his knees will rise – but his creator strolls away. And yet the ear cannot right now part with the music and allow the tale to fade; the chords of fate itself continue to vibrate; and no obstruction for the sage exists where I have put The End: the shadows of my world extend beyond the skyline of the page, blue as tomorrow's morning haze – nor does this terminate the phrase.

INVITATION TO A BEHEADING

I

In accordance with the law the death sentence was announced to Cincinnatus C. in a whisper. All rose, exchanging smiles. The hoary judge put his mouth close to his ear, panted for a moment, made the announcement and slowly moved away, as though ungluing himself. Thereupon Cincinnatus was taken back to the fortress. The road wound around its rocky base and disappeared under the gate like a snake in a crevice. He was calm; however, he had to be supported during the journey through the long corridors, since he planted his feet unsteadily, like a child who has just learned to walk, or as if he were about to fall through like a man who has dreamt that he is walking on water only to have a sudden doubt: but is this possible? Rodion, the jailer, took a long time to unlock the door of Cincinnatus' cell – it was the wrong key – and there was the usual fuss. At last the door yielded. Inside, the lawyer was already waiting. He sat on the cot, shoulder-deep in thought, without his dress coat (which had been forgotten on a chair in the courtroom – it was a hot day, a day that was blue all through); he jumped up impatiently when the prisoner was brought in. But Cincinnatus was in no mood for talking. Even if the alternative was solitude in this cell, with its peephole like a leak in a boat – he did not care, and asked to be left alone; they all bowed to him and left.

So we are nearing the end. The right-hand, still untasted part of the novel, which, during our delectable reading, we would lightly feel, mechanically testing whether there were still plenty left (and our fingers were always gladdened by the placid, faithful thickness), has suddenly, for no reason at all, become quite meagre: a few minutes of quick reading, already downhill, and – O horrible! The heap of cherries, whose mass had seemed to us of such a ruddy and glossy black, had suddenly become discrete drupes: the one over there with the scar is a little rotten, and this one has shrivelled and dried up around its stone (and the very last one is inevitably hard and unripe). O horrible! Cincinnatus took off his silk jerkin, put on his dressing gown and, stamping his feet a little to stop the shivering, began walking around the cell. On the table glistened a clean sheet of paper and, distinctly outlined against this whiteness, lay a beautifully sharpened pencil, as long as the life of any man except Cincinnatus, and with an ebony gleam to each of its six facets. An enlightened descendant of the index finger. Cincinnatus wrote: 'In spite of everything I am comparatively. After all I had premonitions, had premonitions of this finale.' Rodion was standing on the other side of the door and peering with a skipper's stern attention through the peephole. Cincinnatus felt a chill on the back of his head. He crossed out what he had written and began shading gently; an embryonic embellishment appeared gradually and curled into a ram's horn. O horrible! Rodion gazed through the blue porthole at the horizon, now rising, now falling. Who was becoming seasick? Cincinnatus. He broke out in a sweat, everything grew dark, and he could feel the rootlet of every hair. A clock struck – four or five times – with the vibrations and revibrations, and reverberations proper to a prison. Feet working, a spider – official friend of the jailed – lowered itself on a thread from the ceiling. No one, however, knocked on the wall, since Cincinnatus was as yet the sole prisoner (in such an enormous fortress!).

Sometime later Rodion the jailer came in and offered to dance a waltz with him. Cincinnatus agreed. They began to whirl. The keys on Rodion's leather belt jangled; he smelled of sweat, tobacco and garlic; he hummed, puffing into his red beard; and his rusty joints creaked (he was not what he used to be, alas – now he was fat and short of breath). The dance carried them into the corridor. Cincinnatus was much smaller than his partner. Cincinnatus was light as a leaf. The wind of the waltz made the tips of his long but thin moustache flutter, and his big limpid eyes looked askance, as is always the case with timorous dancers. He was indeed very small for a full-grown man. Marthe used to say that his shoes were too tight for her. At the bend in the corridor stood another guard, nameless, with a rifle and wearing a doglike mask with a gauze mouthpiece. They described a circle near him and glided back into the cell, and now Cincinnatus regretted that the swoon's friendly embrace had been so brief.

With banal dreariness the clock struck again. Time was advancing in arithmetical progression: it was now eight. The ugly little window proved accessible to the sunset; a fiery parallelogram appeared on the side wall. The cell was filled to the ceiling with the oils of twilight, containing extraordinary pigments. Thus one would wonder, is that some reckless colourist's painting there to the right of the door, or another window, an ornate one of a kind that already no longer exists. (Actually it was a parchment sheet hanging on the wall with two columns of detailed 'rules for prisoners'; the bent corner, the red letters of the heading, the vignettes, the ancient seal of the city – namely, a furnace with wings – provided the necessary materials for the evening illumination.) The cell's quota of furniture consisted of a table, a chair and the cot. Dinner (those condemned to death were entitled to get the same meals as the wardens) had already been standing and growing cold on its zinc tray for a long time. It grew quite dark. Suddenly the place was filled with golden, highly-concentrated electric light.

Cincinnatus lowered his feet from the cot. A bowling ball rolled through his head, diagonally from nape to temple; it paused and started back. Meanwhile the door opened and the prison director entered.

He was dressed as always in a frock coat and held himself exquisitely straight, chest out, one hand in his bosom, the other behind his back. A perfect toupee, black as pitch, and with a waxy parting, smoothly covered his head. His face, selected without love, with its thick sallow cheeks and somewhat obsolete system of wrinkles, was enlivened in a sense by two, and only by two, bulging eyes. Moving his legs evenly in his columnar trousers, he strode from the wall to the table, almost to the cot – but, in spite of his majestic solidity, he calmly vanished, dissolving into the air. A minute later, however, the door opened once again, this time with the familiar grating sound, and, dressed as always in a frock coat, his chest out, in came the same person.

'Having learned from trustworthy sources that your fate has been sort of sealed,' he began in a fruity bass, 'I have deemed it my duty, dear sir . . .'

Cincinnatus said: 'Kind. You. Very.' (This still had to be arranged.)

'You are very kind,' said an additional Cincinnatus, having cleared his throat.

'Mercy,' exclaimed the director, unmindful of the tactlessness of that word. 'Mercy! Think nothing. Duty. I always. But why, may I be so bold as to ask, have you not touched your food?'

The director removed the cover and raised to his sensitive nose the bowl of coagulated stew. He took a potato with two fingers and began to chew powerfully, already picking out with an eyebrow something on another dish.

'I do not know what better food you could want,' he said with displeasure, and, shooting out his cuffs, sat down at the table so as to be more comfortable while eating the rice pudding.

Cincinnatus said: 'I should still like to know if it will be long now.'

'Excellent sabayon! Should still like to know if it will be long now. Unfortunately I myself do not know. I am always informed at the last moment; I have complained many times and can show you all the correspondence on the subject if you are interested.'

'So it may be tomorrow morning?' asked Cincinnatus.

'If you are interested,' said the director, '. . . Yes, downright delicious and most satisfying, that is what I'll tell you. And now, *pour la digestion*, allow me to offer you a cigarette. Have no fear, at most this is only the one before last,' he added wittily.

'It is not out of curiosity that I ask,' said Cincinnatus. 'It is true that cowards are always inquisitive. But I assure you . . . Even if I can't control my chills and so forth – that does not mean everything. A rider is not responsible for the shivering of his horse. I want to know why for this reason: the compensation for a death sentence is knowledge of the exact hour when one is to die. A great luxury, but one that is well earned. However, I am being left in that ignorance which is tolerable only to those living at liberty. And furthermore, I have in my head many projects that were begun and interrupted at various times . . . I simply shall not pursue them if the time remaining before my execution is not sufficient for their orderly conclusion. This is why . . .'

'Oh, will you please stop mumbling,' the director said irritably. 'In the first place, it is against the rules, and in the second – I am telling you in plain Russian and for the second time – I do not know. All I can tell you is that your fate-mate is expected to arrive any day now; and when he does arrive, and has rested, and got used to the surroundings, he will still have to test the instrument, if, of course, he has not brought his own, which is altogether likely. How's the tobacco? Not too strong?'

'No,' answered Cincinnatus, after looking absent-mindedly at his cigarette. 'Only it seems to me that according to the law . . . not you, perhaps, but the administrator of the city . . . is supposed to . . .'

'We've had our chat, and that will do,' said the director. 'Actually I came here not to listen to complaints but to . . .' Blinking, he rummaged first in one pocket, then in another; finally from an inside breast pocket he produced a sheet of ruled paper, obviously torn from a school notebook.

'There is no ash tray here,' he observed, gesturing with his cigarette; 'oh well, let us drown it in what's left of the rest of this sauce . . . So. I would say the light is a bit harsh. Maybe if we . . . Oh, never mind; it will have to do.'

He unfolded the paper and, without putting on his horn-rimmed glasses, but holding them in front of his eyes, he began to read distinctly

' "Prisoner! In this solemn hour, when all eyes" . . . I think we had better stand,' he interrupted himself with concern and and rose from his chair. Cincinnatus also rose.

' "Prisoner, in this solemn hour, when all eyes are upon thee, and thy judges are jubilant, and thou art preparing for those involuntary bodily movements that directly follow severance of the head, I address to thee a parting word. It is my lot – and this I will never forget – to provide thy sojourn in gaol with all that multitude of comforts which the law allows. I shall therefore be glad to devote all possible attention to any expression of thy gratitude, preferably, however, in written form and on one side of the sheet." '

'There,' said the director, folding his glasses. 'That will be all. I shall not keep you any longer. Let me know if you should need anything.'

He sat down at the table and began to write rapidly, thus indicating that the audience was over. Cincinnatus went out.

On the corridor wall dozed the shadow of Rodion, hunched over on the shadow of a stool, with only a fringe of beard outlined in rufous. Further on, at the bend in the wall, the other guard had taken off his uniform mask and was wiping his face with his sleeve. Cincinnatus started down the stairs. The stone steps were narrow and slippery, with the impalpable spiral of a ghostly railing. Upon reaching the bottom he again went along corridors. A door with the sign 'office' in mirrorlike inversion was wide open; moonlight glistened on an inkwell and a waste-basket rustled and rattled furiously under the table: a mouse must have fallen into it. Cincinnatus, after passing many other doors, stumbled, hopped, and found himself in a small court-yard, filled with various parts of the dismantled moon. This night the password was silence, and the soldier at the gate responded with silence to Cincinnatus' silence and let him pass; likewise at all the other gates. Leaving behind the misty mass of the fortress he began to slide down a steep, dewy bank of turf, reached a pale path between cliffs, twice, three times crossed the bends of the main road – which, having finally shaken off the last shadow of the fortress, ran more straight and free – and a filigrane bridge across a dried-up rivulet brought Cincinnatus to the city. He climbed to the top of a steep incline, turned left on Garden Street, and sped past a shrubbery in greyish bloom. A lighted window flashed somewhere; behind some fence a dog shook its chain but did not bark. The breeze was doing all it could to cool the fugitive's bare neck. Now and then a wave of fragrance would come from the Tamara Gardens. How well he knew that public park! There, where Marthe, when she was a bride, was frightened of the frogs and cockchafers . . . There, where, whenever life seemed unbearable, one could roam, with a meal of chewed lilac bloom in one's mouth and firefly tears in one's eyes . . . That green turfy tamarack park, the languor of its ponds, the tum-tum-tum of a distant band . . . He turned on Matterfact Street, past the ruins of an ancient factory, the pride of the town, past whispering lindens, past the festive-looking white bungalows of the telegraph employees, perpetually celebrating somebody's birthdate, and came out on Telegraph Street. From there a narrow lane went uphill, and again the lindens began to murmur discreetly. Two men, supposedly on a bench, were quietly conversing in the obscurity of a public garden. 'I say he's wrong,' said one. The other replied unintelligibly, and both gave a kind of sigh which blended naturally with the sough of the foliage. Cincinnatus ran out into a circular plaza where the moon stood watch over the familiar statue of a poet that looked like a snowman – a cube for a head, legs stuck together – and, after a few more pattering steps, was in his own street. On the right the moon cast dissimilar patterns of branches on the walls of similar houses, so that it was only by the expression of the shadows, by the interciliary bar between two windows, that Cincinnatus recognized his own house. Marthe's top-floor window was dark but open. The children must be sleeping on the hook-nosed balcony – there was a glimpse of something white there. Cincinnatus ran up the front steps, pushed open the door, and entered his lighted cell. He turned around, but already he was locked in. O horrible! The pencil glistened on the table. The spider sat on the yellow wall.

'Turn off the light!' shouted Cincinnatus.

His observer through the peephole turned it off. Darkness and silence began to merge but the clock interfered; it struck eleven times, thought for a moment, and struck once more, and Cincinnatus lay supine gazing into the dark, where bright dots were scattering and gradually disappearing. Darkness and silence merged completely. It was then and only then (that is, lying supine on a prison cot, after midnight, after a horrible, horrible, I simply cannot tell you what a horrible day) that Cincinnatus C. clearly evaluated his situation.

At first, against the background of that black velvet which lines at night the underside of the eyelids, Marthe's face appeared as in a locket; her doll-like rosiness; her shiny forehead with its childlike convexity; her thin eyebrows, slanting upward, high above her round hazel eyes. She began to blink, turning her head, and there was a black velvet ribbon on her soft, creamy-white neck, and the velvety quiet of her dress flared at the bottom, blending with the darkness. That is how he saw her among the audience, when they led him up to the freshly painted defendants' bench on which he did not dare sit, but stood beside it (and still he got emerald paint all over his hands, and the newspaper men greedily photographed the fingerprints he had left on the back of the bench). He could see their tense foreheads, he could see the gaudy pantaloons of the fops, and the hand-mirrors and iridescent scarves of the women of fashion; but the faces were indistinct – of all the spectators he remembered only round-eyed Marthe. The defence counsel and the prosecutor, both wearing makeup and looking very much alike (the law required that they be uterine brothers but such were not always available, and then makeup was used), spoke with virtuoso rapidity the five thousand words allotted to each. They spoke alternately and the judge, following the rapid exchanges, would move his head, right and left and all the other heads followed suit; only Marthe, half-turned, sat motionless like an astonished child, her gaze fixed on Cincinnatus, standing next to the bright green park bench. The defence counsel, an advocate of classic decapitation, won easily over the inventive prosecutor, and the judge summed up the case.

Fragments of these speeches, in which the words 'translucence' and 'opacity' rose and burst like bubbles, now sounded in Cincinnatus's ears, and the rush of blood became applause, and Marthe's locket-like face remained in his field of vision and faded only when the judge – who had moved so close that on his large swarthy nose he could see the enlarged pores, one of which, on the very extremity, had sprouted a lone but long hair – pronounced in a moist undertone, 'with the gracious consent of the audience, you will be made to don the red tophat' – a token phrase that the courts had evolved, whose true meaning was known to every schoolboy.

'And yet I have been fashioned so painstakingly,' thought Cincinnatus as he wept in the darkness. 'The curvature of my spine has been calculated so well, so mysteriously. I feel, tightly rolled up in my calves, so many miles that I could yet run in my lifetime. My head is so comfortable . . .'

The clock struck a half, pertaining to some unknown hour.

2

The morning papers, brought to him with a cup of tepid chocolate by Rodion, the local sheet *Good Morning Folks*, and the more serious daily *Voice of the Public*, teemed as always with colour photographs. In the first one he found the façade of his house: the children looking out from the balcony, his father-in-law looking out of the kitchen window, a photographer looking out of Marthe's window; in the second one there was the familiar view from this window, looking out on the garden, showing the apple tree, the open gate and the figure of the photographer shooting the façade. In addition he found two snapshots of himself, depicting him in his meek youth.

Cincinnatus was the son of an unknown transient and spent his childhood in a large institution beyond the Strop River (only in his twenties did he casually meet twittering, tiny, still so young-looking Cecilia C., who had conceived him one night at the Ponds when she was still in her teens). From his earliest years Cincinnatus, by some strange and happy chance comprehending his danger, carefully managed to conceal a certain peculiarity. He was impervious to the rays of others, and therefore produced when off his guard a bizarre impression, as of a lone dark obstacle in this world of souls transparent to one other; he learned however to feign translucence, employing a complex system of optical illusions, as it were – but he had only to forget himself, to allow a momentary lapse in self control, in the manipulation of cunningly illuminated facets and angles at which he turned his soul, and immediately there was alarm. In the midst of the excitement of a game his coevals would suddenly forsake him, as if they had sensed that his lucid gaze and the azure of his temples were but a crafty deception and that actually Cincinnatus was opaque. Sometimes, in the midst of a sudden silence, the teacher, in chagrined perplexity, would gather up all the reserves of skin around his eyes, gaze at him for a long while, and finally say: 'What is wrong with you, Cincinnatus?' Then Cincinnatus would take hold of himself, and clutching his own self to his breast, would remove that self to a safe place.

In the course of time the safe places became ever fewer: the solicitous sunshine of public concern penetrated everywhere, and the peephole in the door was placed in such a way that in the whole cell there was not a single point that the observer on the other side of the door could not pierce with his gaze. Therefore Cincinnatus did not crumple the motley newspapers, did not hurl them, as his double did (the double, the gangrel, that accompanies each of us – you, and me, and him over there – doing what we would like to do at that very moment, but cannot . . .). Cincinnatus very calmly laid the papers aside and finished his chocolate. The brown skim that had mantled the chocolate became shrivelled scum on his lips. Then Cincinnatus put on the black dressing gown (which was too long for him), the black slippers with pompons, and the black skullcap, and began walking about the cell, as he had done every morning since the first day of his confinement.

Childhood on suburban lawns. They played ball, pig, daddy-longlegs, leapfrog, rumpberry, poke. He was light and nimble, but they did not like to play with him. In winter the city slopes were covered with a smooth sheet of snow, and what fun it was to hurtle down on the so-called 'glassy' Saburov sleds. How quickly night would fall, when one was going home after sledding . . . What stars, what thought and sadness up above, and what ignorance below. In the frosty metallic dark the edible windows glowed with amber and crimson light; women in fox furs over silk dresses ran across the street from house to house; the electric 'wagonette' stirred up a momentary luminescent blizzard as it sped by over the snow-powdered track.

A small voice: 'Arkady Ilyich, take a look at Cincinnatus . . .'

He was not angry at the informers, but the latter multiplied and, as they matured, became frightening. Cincinnatus, who seemed pitch-black to them, as though he had been cut out of a cord-size block of night, opaque Cincinnatus would turn this way and that, trying to catch the rays, trying with desperate haste to stand in such a way as to seem translucent. Those around him understood each other at the first word, since they had no words that would end in an unexpected way, perhaps in some archaic letter, an upsilamba, becoming a bird or a catapult with wondrous consequences. In the dusty little museum on Second Boulevard, where they used to take him as a child, and where he himself would later take his charges, there was a collection of rare, marvellous objects, but all the townsmen except Cincinnatus found them just as limited and transparent as they did each other. *That which does not have a name does not exist.* Unfortunately everything had a name.

'Nameless existence, intangible substance,' Cincinnatus read on the wall where the door covered it when open.

'Perpetual name-day celebrants, you can just . . .' was written in another place.

Further to the left, in a strong and neat hand, without a single superfluous line: 'Note that when they address you . . .' The continuation had been erased.

Next to this, in clumsy childish letters: 'I will collect fines from writers', signed 'director of the prison'.

One could make out yet another line, an ancient and enigmatic one: 'Measure me while I live – after, it will be too late.'

'In any case I have been measured,' said Cincinnatus, resuming his journey and rapping lightly with his knuckles on the walls. 'But now I don't want to die! My soul has burrowed under the pillow. Oh, I don't want to! It will be cold getting out of my warm body. I don't want to . . . wait a while . . . let me doze some more.'

Twelve, thirteen, fourteen. At fifteen Cincinnatus went to work in the toy workshop, where he was assigned by reason of his small stature. In the evenings he would feast on ancient books to the lazy enchanting lap of wavelets in the Floating Library, in memoriam of Dr Sineokov, who had drowned at just that spot in the city river. The grinding of chains, the little gallery with its orange-coloured lamp shades, the plash, the water's smooth surface oiled by the moon, and, in the distance, lights flickering past in the black web of a lofty bridge. Later, however, the valuable volumes began to suffer from the damp, so that in the end it was necessary to drain the river, channelling all the water over to the Strop by means of a specially dug canal.

In the shop he struggled for a long time with intricate trifles and worked on rag dolls for schoolgirls; here there was little hairy Pushkin in a fur carrick, and ratlike Gogol in a flamboyant waistcoat, and old little Tolstoy with his fat nose, in a peasant's smock, and many others, as for example Dobrolyubov, in *spec*tacles without lenses and all buttoned up. Having artifically developed a fondness for this mythical Nineteenth Century, Cincinnatus was ready to become completely engrossed in the mists of that antiquity and find therein a false shelter, but something else distracted him.

There, in that little factory, worked Marthe; her moist lips half open, aiming a thread at the eye of a needle. 'Hi, Cincinnatik!' And so began those rapturous wanderings in the very, very spacious (so much so that even the hills in the distance would be hazy from the ecstasy of their remoteness) Tamara Gardens, where, for no reason, the willows weep into three brooks, and the brooks, in three cascades, each with its own small rainbow, tumble into the lake, where a swan floats arm in arm with its reflection. The level lawns, the rhododendrons, the oak groves, the merry gardeners in their green jackboots playing hide-and-seek the whole day through; some grotto, some idyllic bench, on which three jokers had left three neat little heaps (it's a trick – they are imitations made of brown painted tin), some baby deer, bounding into the avenue and before your very eyes turning into trembling mottles of sunlight – that is what those gardens were like! There, there is Marthe's lisping prattle, her white stockings and velvet slippers, her cool breast and her rosy kisses tasting of wild strawberries. If only one could see from here – at least the treetops, at least the distant range of hills . . . Cincinnatus tied the dressing gown a little tighter. Cincinnatus moved the table and began dragging it backwards as it shrieked with rage: how unwillingly, with what shudderings it moved across the stone floor! Its shudderings were transmitted to Cincinnatus's fingers and to Cincinnatus's palate as he retreated toward the window (that is, toward the wall where way, way up there was the inclined cavity of the window). A loud spoon fell, the cup began to dance, the pencil started to roll, one book began sliding upon another. Cincinnatus lifted the bucking chair on to the table. Finally he climbed up himself. But of course he could see nothing, only the hot sky with a few white hairs thinly combed back – the remnants of clouds that could not tolerate the blueness. Cincinnatus could barely stretch as far as the bars beyond which rose the window tunnel with more bars at the end, and their shadowed repetition on the peeling walls of the stone incline. There, on the side, written in the same neat, contemptuous hand as one of the half-erased sentences he had read before, was the inscription: 'You cannot see anything. I tried it too.'

Cincinnatus was standing on tiptoe, holding the iron bars with his small hands, which were all white from the strain, and half of his face was covered with a sunny grating, and the gold of his left moustache shone, and there was a tiny golden cage in each of his mirrorlike pupils, while below, from behind, his heels rose out of the too-large slippers.

'A little more and you'll have a fall,' said Rodion, who had been standing nearby for a full half minute and now firmly clenched the leg of the trembling chair. 'It's all right, it's all right. You can climb down now.'

Rodion had cornflower-blue eyes and, as always, his splendid red beard. This attractive Russian countenance was turned upwards toward Cincinnatus, who stepped on it with his naked sole – that is, his double stepped on it, while Cincinnatus himself had already descended from the chair to the table. Rodion, embracing him like a baby, carefully took him down, after which he moved the table with a violinlike sound to its previous place and sat on the edge, dangling the foot that was in the air, and bracing the other against the floor, having assumed the imitation-jaunty pose of operatic rakes in the tavern scene, while Cincinnatus picked at the sash of his dressing gown, and did his best not to cry.

Rodion was singing in his bass-baritone, rolling his eyes, brandishing the empty mug. Marthe used to sing that same dashing song once. Tears gushed from the eyes of Cincinnatus. On a climactic note Rodion sent the mug crashing against the floor and slid off the table. His song went on in chorus, even though he was alone. Suddenly he raised both arms and went out.

Sitting on the floor, Cincinnatus looked upward through his tears; the shadow of the bars had already moved. He tried – for the hundredth time – to move the table, but, alas, the legs had been bolted down for ages. He ate a pressed fig and began again to walk about the cell.

Nineteen, twenty, twenty-one. At twenty-two he was transferred to a kindergarten, as a teacher in division F, and at that time he married Marthe. Almost immediately after he had assumed his new duties (consisting of keeping busy little children who were lame, hunchbacked or crosseyed) an important personage made a second-degree complaint against him. Cautiously, in the form of a conjecture, there was expressed the suggestion of Cincinnatus's basic illegality. Together with this memorandum the city fathers also examined the old complaints that had been made from time to time by the more perceptive of his colleagues at the workshop. The chairman of the education committee and certain other official figures took turns locking themselves up with him and making on him the tests prescribed by law. For several days in a row he was not allowed to sleep, and was compelled to keep up rapid senseless small talk until it bordered on delirium, to write letters to various objects and natural phenomena, enact everyday scenes, and to imitate various animals, trades and maladies. All of this he performed, all of this he passed, because he was young, resourceful, fresh, yearning to live, to live for a while with Marthe. Reluctantly they released him, allowing him to continue working with children of the lowest category, who were expendable, in order to see what would come of it. He took them for walks, in pairs, while he turned the handle of a small portable music box that looked like a coffee grinder on holidays he would swing with them at the playground – the whole cluster would be still and breathless as it soared and would squeal as it plummeted down. Some of them he taught to read.

Meanwhile Marthe began deceiving him during the very first year of their marriage; anywhere and with anybody. Generally when Cincinnatus came home she would have a certain sated half-smile on her face as she pressed her plump chin against her neck, as if reproaching herself, and gazing up with her honest hazel eyes, would say in a soft cooing voice, 'Little Marthe did it again today.' He would look at her for a few seconds, pressing his palm to his cheek like a woman, and then, howling soundlessly, would go off through all the rooms full of her relatives and lock himself in the bathroom, where he would stamp his feet, let the water run and cough so as to cover up the sound of weeping. Sometimes, to justify herself, she would explain to him, 'You know what a kind creature I am: it's such a small thing, and it's such a relief to a man.'

Soon she became pregnant, and not by him. She bore a boy, immediately got pregnant again – again not by him – and bore a girl. The boy was lame and evil-tempered, the girl dull, obese and nearly blind. Because of their defects both children ended up in his kindergarten, and it was odd to see nimble, sleek, rosy Marthe leading home this cripple and this stocky tot. Gradually Cincinnatus stopped watching himself altogether, and one day, at some open meeting in the city park, there was a sudden wave of alarm and someone said in a loud voice, 'Citizens, there is among us a—' Here followed a strange, almost forgotten word, and the wind swished through the locust trees, and Cincinnatus found nothing better than to get up and walk away, absentmindedly picking leaves from bushes bordering the path. And ten days later he was arrested.

'Tomorrow, probably,' said Cincinnatus as he slowly walked about the cell. 'Tomorrow, probably, said Cincinnatus and sat down on the cot, kneading his forehead with the palm of his hand. A sunset ray was repeating effects that were already familiar. 'Tomorrow, probably,' said Cincinnatus with a sigh. 'It was too quiet today, so tomorrow, bright and early . . .'

For a while they were all silent – the earthenware pitcher with water at the bottom that had offered drink to all the prisoners of the world; the walls, with their arms around each other's shoulders like a foursome discussing a square secret in inaudible whispers; the velvet spider, somehow resembling Marthe; the large black books on the table . . .

'What a misunderstanding,' said Cincinnatus and suddenly burst out laughing. He stood up and took off the dressing gown, the skullcap, the slippers. He took off the linen trousers and shirt. He took off his head like a toupee, took off his collarbones like shoulder straps, took off his rib cage like a hauberk. He took off his hips and his legs, he took off his arms like gauntlets and threw them in a corner. What was left of him gradually dissolved, hardly colouring the air. At first Cincinnatus simply revelled in the coolness; then, fully immersed in his secret medium, he began freely and happily to . . .

The iron thunderclap of the bolt resounded, and Cincinnatus instantly grew all that he had cast off, the skullcap included. Rodion the jailer brought a dozen yellow plums in a round basket lined with grape leaves, a present from the director's wife.

Cincinnatus, your criminal exercise has refreshed you.

3

Cincinnatus was awakened by the doomlike din of voices mounting in the corriodor.

Even though the day before he had prepared for such an awakening, still he could not cope with his breathing and the beating of his heart. Folding the dressing gown over his heart so that it would not see – be quiet, it is nothing (as one says to a child at the moment of an incredible disaster) – covering his heart and raising himself slightly, Cincinnatus listened. There was the shuffling of many feet, at various levels of audibility; there were voices, also at various depths; one surged up, with a question; another, closer, responded. Hastening from afar, someone whizzed by and started to slide over the stone as over ice. In the midst of the hubbub the director's bass uttered several words, indistinct but definitely imperative. The most frightening thing was that all this bustle was pierced by a child's voice – the director had a small daughter. Cincinnatus distinguished both the whining tenor of his lawyer and the muttering of Rodion . . . And again somebody on the run asked a booming question, and somebody boomingly answered. A huffing, a crackling, a clattering, as if someone were probing with a stick under a bench. 'Couldn't find it?' the director inquired distinctly. Footsteps ran past. Footsteps ran past. Ran past and returned. Cincinnatus could not bear it any longer; he lowered his feet to the floor: they had not let him see Marthe after all . . . Should I begin dressing, or will they come to costume me? Oh, have done with it, come in . . .

However, they tortured him for another two minutes or so. Suddenly the door opened, and, gliding, his lawyer rushed in.

He was ruffled and sweaty. He was fiddling with his left cuff and his eyes were wandering around.

'I lost a cuff link,' he exclaimed, panting rapidly like a dog. 'Must have – rushed against some – when I was with sweet little Emmie – she's always so full of mischief – by the coat-tails – every time I drop in – and the point is that I heard something – but I didn't pay any – look, the chain must have – I was very fond of – well, it's too late now – maybe I can still – I promised all the guards – it's a pity, though—'

'A foolish, sleepy error,' said Cincinnatus quietly. 'I misinterpreted the fuss. This sort of thing is not good for the heart.'

'Oh, thanks, don't worry about it, it's nothing,' absent-mindedly muttered the lawyer. And with his eyes he literally scoured the corners of the cell. It was plain that he was upset by the loss of that precious object. It was plain. The loss of the object upset him. The object was precious. He was upset by the loss of the object.

With a soft groan Cincinnatus went back to bed. The other sat down at the foot of the cot.

'As I was coming to see you,' said the lawyer, 'I was so spry and cheerful . . . But now this trifle has distressed me – for, after all, it is a trifle, you will agree; there are more important things. Well, how are you feeling?'

'In the mood for a confidential chat,' replied Cincinnatus with eyes closed. 'I want to share with you some conclusions I have reached. I am surrounded by some sort of wretched spectres, not by people. They torment me as can torment only senseless visions, bad dreams, dregs of delirium, the drivel of nightmares and everything that passes down here for real life. In theory one would wish to wake up. But wake up I cannot without outside help, and yet I fear this help terribly, and my very soul has grown lazy and accustomed to its snug swaddling clothes. Of all the spectres that surround me, you, Roman Vissarionovich, are probably the most wretched, but on the other hand – in view of your logical position in our invented habitus – you are in a manner of speaking, an adviser, a defender . . .'

'At your service,' said the lawyer, glad that Cincinnatus had at last become talkative.

'So this is what I want to ask you: on what grounds do they refuse to tell me the exact execution date? Wait a minute, I am not finished yet. The so-called director avoids a straight answer, and refers to the fact that – wait a minute! I want to know in the first place, who has the authority to appoint the day. I want to know in the second place, how to get some sense out of that institution, or individual, or group of individuals . . .'

The lawyer, who had just been impatient to speak, now for some reason was silent. His made-up face with its dark blue eyebrows and long harelip revealed no particular mental activity.

'Leave your cuff alone,' said Cincinnatus, 'and try to concentrate.'

Roman Vissarionovich jerkily changed the position of his body and clasped his restless fingers. In a plaintive voice he said, 'It is exactly for that tone . . .'

'That I am being executed,' said Cincinnatus. 'I know that. Go on!'

'Let's change the subject, I implore you,' cried Roman Vissarionovich. 'Can't you even now remain within legitimate limits? This is really awful. It is beyond my endurance. I dropped in merely to ask if you didn't have some legitimate wishes . . . for instance' (here his face lit up), 'perhaps you should like to have printed copies of the speeches made at the trial? In case of such desire you must immediately submit the necessary petition, which you and I could prepare right now, with detailed specifications as to just how many copies of the speeches you require and for what purpose. I happen to have a free hour – Oh, please, please let's do this! I have even brought a special envelope.'

'Just out of curiosity . . .' said Cincinnatus, 'but first . . . Then, there is really no chance of getting an answer?'

'A special envelope,' repeated the lawyer to tempt him.

'All right, let's have it,' said Cincinnatus, and tore the thick, stuffed envelope into crimpy scraps.

'You shouldn't have done that,' cried the lawyer, on the verge of tears. 'You shouldn't have done that at all. You don't even realize what you have done. Perhaps there was a pardon in there. It won't be possible to get another!'

Cincinnatus picked up a handful of scraps and tried to reconstruct at least one coherent sentence, but everything was mixed up, distorted, disjointed.

'This is the sort of thing you always do,' whined the lawyer, clutching his temples and pacing across the cell. 'Perhaps your salvation was right in your very hands, and you . . . It's horrible! Well, what shall I do with you? It's lost and gone now . . . And I was so pleased! I was preparing you so carefully!'

'May I?' said the director in a distended voice as he opened the door ajar. 'I shan't disturb you?'

'Please come in, Rodrig Ivanovich, please come in,' said the lawyer. 'Please come in, dear Rodrig Ivanovich. Only it is not very cheerful in here . . .'

'Well, and how is our doomed friend today?' quipped the elegant, dignified director, compressing in his meaty purple paws the cold little hand of Cincinnatus. 'Is everything all right? No aches or pains? Still gossiping with our indefatigable Roman Vissarionovich? Oh, by the way, dear Roman Vissarionovich, I have some good news for you – my little romp just found your cuff link on the stairs, *Là voici.* This is French gold, isn't it? Very, very dainty. I usually do not make compliments, but I must say . . .'

They both walked over to a corner, pretending to examine the charming trinket, discuss its history and value, marvel at it. Cincinnatus took this opportunity to take up from under the cot, and, with a high, purling sound, which became hesitant at the end, to . . .

'Yes, indeed, in excellent taste, excellent,' the director was repeating as he walked back from the corner with the lawyer. 'So you are feeling well, young man,' he meaninglessly addressed Cincinnatus, who was climbing back into bed. 'However you must not be childish. The public, and all of us, as representatives of the public, are interested only in your welfare – that must be obvious by now. We are ready to make things easier for you by relieving your loneliness. In a few days a new prisoner will be moving in to one of our de luxe cells. You will become acquainted, and that will entertain you.'

'In a few days?' asked Cincinnatus. 'Then there *will* be a few more days?'

'Listen to him,' chuckled the director. 'He has to know everything. How do you like that, Roman Vissarionovich?'

'Oh, my friend, you are so right,' sighed the lawyer.

'Yes, sir,' continued the former, giving his keys a rattle. 'You ought to be more co-operative, mister. All the time he's haughty, angry, snide. Last night I brought him some of them plums, you know, and what do you think? His excellency did not choose to eat them, his excellency was too proud. Yes sir! I started to tell you about that there new prisoner. You will have your fill of chit-chat with him. No need to mope as you do. Isn't that right, Roman Vissarionovich?'

'That's right, Rodion, that's right,' concurred the lawyer with an involuntary smile.

Rodion stroked his beard and went on: 'I've got to feeling very sorry for the poor gentleman – I come in, I look, he's up on the table-and-chair, trying to reach the bars with his little hands and feet, like a sick monkey. And with the sky real blue, and the swallows a-flying, and cloudlets a-high – such bliss, such blessings! I take the gentleman down from the table like a baby, and myself I bawl – yes, just as I'm standing here – I bawl and bawl . . . I really went all to pieces, I was so sorry for him.'

'Well, shall we take him upstairs, what do you think?' the lawyer suggested hesitantly.

'Why, sure thing, that we can,' drawled Rodion with sedate benevolence. 'We can always do that.'

'Drape yourself in your dressing gown,' uttered Roman Vissarionovich.

Cincinnatus said, 'I obey you, spectres, werewolves, parodies. I obey you. However, I demand – yes, demand' (and the other Cincinnatus began to stamp his feet hysterically, losing his slippers) 'to be told how long I have left to live . . . and whether I shall be allowed to see my wife.'

'You probably will,' replied Roman Vissarionovich, after exchanging glances with Rodion. 'Just don't you talk so much. All right, let's go.'

'If you please,' said Rodion, giving the unlocked door a shove with his shoulder.

All three went out: first Rodion, bowlegged, in old faded breeches, baggy in the seat; behind him the lawyer, in a frock coat, with a smudge on his celluloid collar and an edging of pinkish muslin at the back of his head where the black wig ended; and finally, behind him, Cincinnatus, losing his slippers, wrapping himself more tightly in his dressing gown.

At the bend in the corridor the other, nameless, guard gave them a salute. The pale stony light alternated with regions of darkness. They walked, and walked. One bend followed another. Several times they passed the very same design of dampness on the wall, looking like some dreadful ribby horse. Here and there it was necessary to turn on light; a dusty bulb, up above or at the side, would burst into bitter yellow light. Sometimes, also, it would be burned out, and then they would shuffle on through dense darkness. At one spot, where an unexpected and inexplicable sunbeam fell from above and glowed mistily as it broke on the eroded flagstones, Emmie, the director's daughter, in a bright checkered frock and checkered socks – a mere child, but with the marble calves of a little ballerina – was bouncing a ball, rhythmically against the wall. She turned, brushing a blonde lock from her cheek with the fourth and fifth fingers of her hand, and followed the brief little procession with her eyes. Rodion gave a playful jingle with his keys as he passed; the lawyer lightly stroked her glowing hair; but she was staring at Cincinnatus, who gave her a frightened smile. Upon reaching the next bend of the passage, all three glanced back. Emmie was gazing after them, while she lightly plopped the glossy red and blue ball in her hands.

Again they walked in darkness for a long time, until they came to a dead end where a ruby bulb shone above a coiled fire hose. Rodion unlocked a low iron door; beyond it a stone staircase wound steeply upward. Here the order changed somewhat: Rodion marked time as he let first the lawyer and then Cincinnatus pass; upon which he softly fell in at the end of the procession.

It was not easy to climb the steep staircase, whose progress was accompanied by a gradual thinning of the gloom in which it grew, and they climbed for such a long time that, out of boredom, Cincinnatus began counting the steps, reaching a three-digit number, but then stumbled and lost count. It grew lighter by degrees. Exhausted, Cincinnatus was climbing like a child, beginning with the same foot each time. One more twist, and suddenly there was a solid rush of wind, a dazzling expansion of summer sky, and the air was pierced by the cry of swallows.

Our travellers found themselves on a broad terrace at the top of a tower, whence there was a breathtaking view, since not only was the tower huge, but the whole fortress towered hugely on the crest of a huge cliff, of which it seemed to be a monstrous outgrowth. Far below one could see the almost vertical vineyards, and the creamy road that wound down to the dry river bed; a tiny person in red was crossing the convex bridge; the speck running in front of him was most likely a dog.

Further away the sun-flooded town described an ample hemicycle: some of the varicoloured houses proceeded in even rows, accompanied by round trees, while others, awry, crept down slopes, stepping on their own shadows; one could distinguish the traffic moving on First Boulevard, and an amethystine shimmer at the end, where the famous fountain played; and still further, toward the hazy folds of the hills that formed the horizon, there was the dark stipple of oak groves, with, here and there, a pond gleaming like a handmirror, while other bright ovals of water gathered, glowing through the tender mist, over there to the west, where the serpentine Strop had its source.

Cincinnatus, his palm pressed to his cheek, in motionless, ineffably vague and perhaps even blissful despair, gazed at the glimmer and haze of the Tamara Gardens and at the dove-blue melting hills beyond them – oh, it was a long time before he could take his eyes away . . .

A few paces from him, the lawyer leaned his elbows on the broad stone parapet, whose top was overgrown with some kind of enterprising vegetable. His back was soiled with chalk. He peered pensively into space, his left patent-leather shoe placed upon his right, and so distending his cheeks with his fingers that his lower eyelids turned out. Rodion had found a broom somewhere and kept silent as he swept the terrace flagstones.

'How bewitching all this is,' said Cincinnatus, addressing the gardens, the hills (and for some reason it was especially pleasant to repeat the word 'bewitching' in the wind, somewhat as children cover and then expose their ears, amused at this renewal of the audible world). 'Bewitching! I have never seen those hills look exactly like that, so mysterious. Somewhere among their folds, in their mysterious valleys, couldn't I . . . No, I had better not think about it.'

He made a complete tour of the terrace. Flatlands stretched

off to the north, with cloud shadows scudding across them; meadows alternated with grainfields. Beyond a bend of the Strop one could see the weed-blurred outlines of the ancient airport and the structure where they kept the venerable, decrepit aeroplane, with motley patches on its rusty wings, which was still sometimes used on holidays, principally for the amusement of cripples. Matter was weary. Time gently dozed. There was in town a certain man, a pharmacist, whose great-grandfather, it was said, had left a memoir describing how merchants used to go to China by air.

Cincinnatus completed his trip around the terrace and returned to its south parapet. His eyes were making highly illegal excursions. Now he thought he distinguished that very bush in flower, that bird, that path disappearing under a canopy of ivy—

'That will do now,' said the director good-naturedly, tossing the broom in a corner and putting on again his frockcoat. 'Come along home.'

'Yes, it's time,' responded the lawyer, looking at his watch.

And the same little procession started back. In front was director Rodrig Ivanovich, behind him lawyer Roman Vissarionovich, and behind him prisoner Cincinnatus, who after so much fresh air was beset by spasms of yawning. The back of the director's frock-coat was soiled with chalk.

4

She came in, taking advantage of Rodion's morning visit, slipping beneath his hands, which were carrying the tray.

'Tut, tut, tut,' said he, exorcising a storm of chocolate. With his soft foot he closed the door behind him, and muttered into his moustache, 'What a naughty child . . .'

Meanwhile Emmie had hidden from him, squatting behind the table.

'Reading a book eh?' observed Rodion, beaming with kindness. 'That's a worthwhile pastime.'

Without raising his eyes from the page Cincinnatus emitted an iambic assent, but his eyes no longer grasped the text.

Rodion finished his uncomplicated duties, chased with a rag the dust dancing in a ray of sunlight, fed the spider, and left.

Emmie was still squatting, but a little less restrained, swaying a little as if on springs, her downy arms crossed, her pink mouth slightly open and her long, pale, almost white lashes nictating as she looked across the table-top at the door. An already familiar gesture: rapidly, with a haphazard selection of fingers, she brushed the flaxen hair from her temple, casting a sidelong glance at Cincinnatus, who had laid aside his book and was waiting to see what would come next.

'He is gone,' said Cincinnatus.

She left her squatting position, but was still stooping and looking at the door. She was embarrassed and did not know what to undertake. Suddenly she showed her teeth and, with a flash of ballerina calves, flew to the door – which of course proved to be locked. Her moire sash quickened the air in the cell.

Cincinnatus asked her the usual two questions. Mincingly she gave her name and answered that she was twelve.

'And are you sorry for me?' asked Cincinnatus.

To this she made no answer. She raised up to her face the clay pitcher, which was standing in a corner. It was empty, hollow-sounding. She hoo-hooted into its depths a few times, and an instant later darted away; now she was leaning against the wall, supporting herself only with her shoulder blades and elbows, sliding forward on her tensed feet in their flat shoes, and straightening up again. She smiled to herself, and then, as she continued slithering, glanced at Cincinnatus with a slight scowl, as one looks at the low sun. All indications were that this was a wild, restless child.

'Aren't you just a little bit sorry for me?' said Cincinnatus. 'It isn't possible. I cannot imagine it. Come on over here, you foolish little doe, and tell me on what day I shall die.'

Emmie, however, made no reply, but slid down to the floor. There she quietly seated herself, pressing her chin against her bent knees, over which she stretched the hem of her skirt.

'Tell me, Emmie, please . . . Surely you know all about it – I can tell that you know . . . Your father has talked at the table, your mother has talked in the kitchen . . . Everybody is talking. Yesterday there was a neat little window cut out of the newspaper – that means people are discussing it, and I am the only one . . .'

As if caught in a whirlwind she jumped up from the floor, and, flying again to the door, began pounding on it, not with her palms, but, rather, with the heels of her hands. Her loose, silky-blonde hair ended in hanging curls.

'If only you were grown up,' mused Cincinnatus, 'if your soul had a slight touch of my patina, you would, as in poetic antiquity, feed a potion to the turnkey, on a night that is murky. Emmie!' he exclaimed, 'I implore you – and I shall not desist – tell me, when shall I die?'

Gnawing on a finger, she went over to the table, where the books towered in a pile. She flung one open, leafed through the pages, making them snap and almost ripping them out, banged it shut, picked up another. A rippling something kept running across her face: first she would wrinkle her freckled nose, then her tongue would distend her cheek from within.

The door clanged. Rodion, probably having looked through the peephole, came in, rather angry.

'Shoo, young lady! I'm the one who will catch it for this.'

She broke into shrill laughter, dodged his crablike hand and rushed to the open door. There, on the threshold, she abruptly stopped with a dancer's magic precision and – perhaps blowing a kiss, or perhaps concluding a pact of silence – looked over her shoulder at Cincinnatus; whereupon, with the same rhythmic suddenness, she was off, running with long, high, springy steps, already preparing for flight.

Rodion, grumbling, jingling, trudged off after her.

'Wait a minute!' cried Cincinnatus. 'I have finished all the books. Bring me again the catalogue.'

'Books . . .' Rodion scoffed huffily and locked the door behind him with pronounced resonance.

What anguish! Cincinnatus, what anguish! What stone anguish, Cincinnatus – the merciless bong of the clock, and the obese spider, and the yellow walls, and the roughness of the black wool blanket. The skim on the chocolate. Pluck it with two fingers at the very centre and snatch it whole from the surface, no longer a flat covering, but a wrinkled brown little skirt. The liquid is tepid underneath, sweetish and stagnant. Three slices of toast with tortoise shell burns. A round pat of butter embossed with the monogram of the director. What anguish, Cincinnatus, how many crumbs in the bed!

He lamented for a while, groaned, cracked all his joints, then he got up from the cot, put on the abhorred dressing gown, and began to wander around. Once again he examined all the inscriptions on the walls in the hope of somewhere discovering a new one. Like a fledgling crow on a stump, he stood for a long while on the chair, motionlessly gazing up at the beggarly ration of sky. He walked some more. Once more he read the eight rules for inmates, which he already knew by heart:

1. Leaving the prison building is positively forbidden.
2. A prisoner's meekness is a prison's pride.
3. You are firmly requested to maintain quiet between one and three p.m. daily.
4. You are not allowed to entertain females.
5. Singing, dancing and joking with the guards is permitted only by mutual consent and on certain days.
6. It is desirable that the inmate should not have at all, or, if he does, should immediately himself suppress nocturnal dreams whose content might be incompatible with the condition and status of the prisoner, such as: resplendent landscapes, outings with friends, family dinners, as well as sexual intercourse with persons who in real life and in the waking state would not suffer said individual to come near, which individual will therefore be considered by the law to be guilty of rape.
7. Inasmuch as he enjoys the hospitality of the prison, the prisoner should in his turn not shirk participation in cleaning and other work of prison personnel in such measure as said participation is offered him.
8. The management shall in no case be responsible for the loss of property or of the inmate himself.

Anguish, anguish, Cincinnatus. Pace some more, Cincinnatus, brushing with your robe first the walls, then the chair. Anguish! The books heaped on the table have all been read. And, even though he knew that they had all been read, Cincinnatus searched, rummaged, peeked into a thick volume . . . Without sitting down, he leafed through the already familiar pages.

It was a bound magazine, published once upon a time, in a barely remembered age. The prison library, considered the second in the city for its size and the rarity of its volumes, kept several such curiosities. That was a remote world, where the simplest objects sparkled with youth and an inborn insolence, proceeding from the reverence that surrounded the labour devoted to their manufacture. Those were years of universal fluidity; well-oiled metals performed silent soundless acrobatics; the harmonious lines of men's suits were dictated by the unheard-of limberness of muscular bodies; the flowing glass of enormous windows curved around corners of buildings; a girl in a bathing suit flew like a swallow so high over a pool that it seemed no larger than a saucer; a high-jumper lay supine in the air, having already made such an extreme effort that, if it were not for the flag-like folds of his shorts, he would seem to be in lazy repose; and water ran, glided endlessly; the gracefulness of falling water, the dazzling details of bathrooms; the satiny ripples of the ocean with a two-winged shadow falling on it. Everything was lustrous and shimmering; everything gravitated passionately toward a kind of perfection whose definition was absence of friction. Revelling in all the temptations of the circle, life whirled to a state of such giddiness that the ground fell away and, stumbling, falling, weakened by nausea and languor – ought I to say it? – finding itself in a new dimension, as it were . . . Yes, matter has grown old and weary, and little survived of those legendary days – a couple of machines, two or three fountains – and no one regrets the past, and even the very concept of 'past' has changed.

'But then perhaps,' thought Cincinnatus, 'I am misinterpreting these pictures. Attributing to the epoch the characteristics of its photograph. The wealth of shadows, the torrents of light, the gloss of a tanned shoulder, the rare reflection, the fluid transitions from one element to another – perhaps all of this pertains only to the snapshot, to a particular kind of heliotypy, to special forms of that art, and the world really never was so sinuous, so humid and rapid – just as today our unsophisticated cameras record in their own way our hastily assembled and painted world.'

'But then perhaps' (Cincinnatus began to write rapidly on a sheet of ruled paper) 'I am misinterpreting . . . Attributing to the epoch . . . This wealth . . . Torrents . . . Fluid transitions . . . And the world really never was . . . Just as . . . But how can these ruminations help my anguish? Oh, my anguish – what shall I do with you, with myself? How dare they conceal from me . . . I, who must pass through an ordeal of supreme pain, I, who in order to preserve a semblance of dignity (anyway I shall not go beyond silent pallor – I am no hero anyway . . .), must during that ordeal keep control of all my faculties, I, I . . . am gradually weakening . . . the uncertainty is horrible – well, why don't you tell me, do tell me – but no, you have me die anew every morning . . . On the other hand, were I to know, I could perform . . . a short work . . . a record of verified thoughts . . . Some day someone would read it and would suddenly feel just as if he had awakened for the first time in a strange country. What I mean to say is that I would make him suddenly burst into tears of joy, his eyes would melt, and, after he experiences this, the world will seem to him cleaner, fresher. But how can I begin writing when I do not know whether I shall have time enough, and the torture comes when you say to yourself, "Yesterday there would have been enough time" – and again you think, "If only I had begun yesterday . . ." And instead of the clear and precise work that is needed, instead of a gradual preparation of the soul for that morning when it will have to get up, when – when you, soul, will be offered the executioner's pail to wash in – Instead, you involuntarily indulge in banal senseless dreams of escape – alas, of escape . . . Today, when she came running in, stamping and laughing – that is, I mean – No, I still ought to record, to leave something. I am not an ordinary – I am the one among you who is alive – Not only are my eyes different, and my hearing, and my sense of taste – not only is my sense of smell like a deer's, my sense of touch like a bat's – but, most important, I have the capacity to conjoin all of this in one point – No, the secret is not revealed yet – even this is but the flint – and I have not even begun to speak of the kindling, of the fire itself. My life. Once, when I was a child, on a distant school excursion, when I had got separated from the others – although I may have dreamt it – I found myself, under the sultry sun of midday, in a drowsy little town, so drowsy that when a man who had been dozing on a bench beneath a bright white-washed wall at last got up to help me find my way, his blue shadow on the wall did not immediately follow him. Oh, I know, I know, there must have been some oversight, on my part, and the shadow did not linger at all, but simply, shall we say, and it caught on the wall's unevenness . . . but here is what I want to express; between his movement and the movement of the laggard shadow – that second, that syncope – there is the rare kind of time in which I live – the pause, the hiatus, when the heart is like a feather . . . And I would write also about the continual tremor – and about how part of my thoughts is always crowding around the invisible umbilical cord that joins this world to something – to what I shall not say yet . . . But how can I write about this when I am afraid of not having time to finish and of stirring up all these thoughts in vain? When she came rushing in today – only a child – here is what I want to say – only a child, with certain loopholes for my thoughts – I wondered, to the rhythm of an ancient poem – could she not give the guards a drugged potion, could she not rescue me? If only she would remain the child she is, but at the same time mature and understand – and then it would be feasible: her burning cheeks, a black windy night, salvation, salvation . . . And I'm wrong when I keep repeating that there is no refuge in the world for me. There is! I'll find it! A lush ravine in the desert! A patch of snow in the shadow of an alpine crag! This is unhealthy, though – what I am doing: as it is I am weak, and here I am exciting myself, squandering the last of my strength. What anguish, oh, what anguish . . . And it is obvious to me that I have not yet removed the final film from my fear.'

He became lost in thought. Then he dropped the pencil, got up, began walking. The striking of the clock reached his ears. Using its chimes as a platform, footfalls rose to the surface; the platform floated away, but the footfalls remained and now two persons entered the cell: Rodion with the soup and the Librarian with the catalogue.

The latter was a man of tremendous size but sickly appearance, pale, with shadows under his eyes, with a bald spot encircled by a dark crown of hair, with a long torso in a blue sweater, faded in places and with indigo patches on the elbows. He had his hands in the pockets of his pants, which were narrow as death, and clutched under his arm a large book, bound in black leather. Cincinnatus had already once had the pleasure of seeing him.

'The catalogue,' said the Librarian, whose speech was distinguished by a kind of defiant laconicism.

'Fine, leave it here,' said Cincinnatus, 'I shall choose something. If you would like to wait, to sit down for a minute, please do. If, however, you should like to go . . .'

'To go,' said the Librarian.

'All right. Then I shall return the catalogue through Rodion. Here, you may take these back with you . . . These magazines of the ancients are wonderfully moving . . . With this weighty volume I went down, you know, as with a ballast, to the bottom of time. An enchanting sensation.'

'No,' said the Librarian.

'Bring me some more – I'll copy out the years I want. And some novel, a recent one. You are going already? You have everything?'

Left alone, Cincinnatus went to work on the soup, simultaneously leafing through the catalogue. Its nucleus was carefully and attractively printed; amid the printed text numerous titles were inserted in red ink, in a small but precise hand. It was difficult for someone who was not a specialist to make sense of the catalogue, since the titles were arranged not in alphabetical order, but according to the number of pages in each, with notations as to how many extra sheets (in order to avoid duplication) had been pasted into this or that book. Therefore Cincinnatus searched without any definite goal in mind, picking out whatever happened to seem attractive. The catalogue was kept in a state of exemplary cleanness; this made it all the more surprising that on the white verso of one of the first pages a child's hand had made a series of pencil drawings, whose meaning at first escaped Cincinnatus.

5

'Please accept my sincerest congratulations,' said the director in his unctuous bass as he entered Cincinnatus's cell next morning. Rodrig Ivanovich seemed even more spruce than usual: the dorsal part of his best frock coat was stuffed with cotton padding like a Russian coachman's, making his back look broad, smooth, and fat; his wig was glossy as new; the rich dough of his chin seemed to be powdered with flour, while in his buttonhole there was a pink waxy flower with a speckled mouth. From behind his stately figure – he had stopped on the threshold – the prison employees peeked curiously, also decked out in their Sunday best, also with their hair slicked down; Rodion had even put on some little medal.

'I am ready. I shall get dressed at once. I knew it would be today.'

'Congratulations,' repeated the director, paying no attention to Cincinnatus's jerky agitation. 'I have the honour to inform you that henceforth you have a neighbour – yes, yes, he has just moved in. You have grown tired of waiting, I bet? Well, don't worry – now, with a confidant, with a pal, to play and work with, you won't find it so dull. And, what is more – but this, of course, must remain strictly between ourselves – I can inform you that permission has come for you to have an interview with your spouse, *demain matin*.'

Cincinnatus lay back down on the cot and said, 'Yes, that's fine. I thank you, rag doll, coachman, painted swine . . . Excuse me, I am a little . . .'

Here the walls of the cell started to bulge and dimple, like reflections in disturbed water; the director began to ripple, the cot became a boat. Cincinnatus grabbed the side in order to keep his balance, but the oarlock came off in his hand, and, neck-deep, among a thousand speckled flowers, he began to swim, got tangled, began sinking. Sleeves rolled up, they started poking at him with punting poles and grappling hooks, in order to snare him and pull him to the shore. They fished him out.

'Nerves, nerves, a regular little woman,' said the prison doctor – alias Rodrig Ivanovich – with a smile. 'Breathe freely. You can eat everything. Do you ever have night sweats? Go on as you are, and, if you are very obedient, maybe we shall let you take a quick peek at the new boy . . . but mind you, only a quick peek . . .'

'How long . . . that interview . . . how much time shall we be given? . . . ' Cincinnatus uttered with difficulty.

'In a minute, in a minute. Do not be in such a hurry, do not get excited. We promised to show him to you, and we will. Put on your slippers, straighten your hair. I think that . . .' The director looked interrogatively at Rodion, who nodded. 'But please observe absolute silence,' he again addressed Cincinnatus, 'and don't grab at anything with your hands. Come, get up, get up. You haven't deserved this – you, my friend, are behaving badly, but still you have the permission – Now – not a word, quiet as a mouse . . .'

On tiptoe, balancing with his arms, Rodrig Ivanovich left the cell and with him went Cincinnatus in his oversize shuffling slippers. In the depths of the corridor Rodion was already stooping at the door with imposing bolts: he had pushed aside the cover of the peephole and was peering into it. Without turning, he made a motion with his hand demanding even greater silence and then imperceptibly changed the gesture into a different, beckoning one. The director rose even higher on tiptoe and turned with a threatening grimace, but Cincinnatus could not help scraping a little with his feet. Here and there, in the semi-darkness of the passageways, the shadowy figures of the prison employees gathered, stooped, shaded their eyes with their hands as if to make out something in the distance. Laboratory assistant Rodion let the boss look through the focused eyepiece. His back emitting a solid squeak, Rodrig Ivanovich bent to peer in . . . Meanwhile, in the grey shadows, indistinct figures noiselessly changed their positions, noiselessly summoned each other, formed ranks, and already their many silent feet were working in place like pistons, preparing to step out. At last the director slowly moved away and tugged Cincinnatus lightly by the sleeve, inviting him, as a professor would a layman who had dropped in, to examine the slide. Cincinnatus meekly placed his eye against the luminous circle. At first he saw only bubbles of sunlight and bands of colour, but then he distinguished a cot, identical to the one he had in his cell; piled nearby were two good suitcases with gleaming locks and a large oblong case like the kind used to carry a trombone.

'Well, do you see anything?' whispered the director, stooping close to him, and reeking of lilies in an open grave. Cincinnatus nodded, even though he did not yet see the main attraction; he shifted his gaze to the left, and then really saw something.

Seated on a chair, sideways to the table, as still as if he were made of candy, was a beardless little fat man, about thirty years old, dressed in old-fashioned but clean and freshly ironed prison pyjamas; he was all in stripes – in striped socks, and brand-new morocco slippers – and revealed a virgin sole as he sat with one stubby leg crossed over the other and clasped his shin with his plump hands; a limpid aquamarine sparkled on his auricular finger, his honey-blonde hair was parted in the middle of his remarkably round head, his long eyelashes cast shadows on his cherubic cheek, and the whiteness of his wonderful, even teeth gleamed between his crimson lips. He seemed to be all frosted with gloss, melting just a little in the shaft of sunlight falling on him from above. There was nothing on the table except an elegant travelling clock encased in leather.

'That'll do now,' whispered the director with a smile, 'me want to looky too,' and he again attached himself to the bright hole. Rodion indicated by signs to Cincinnatus that it was time to go home. The shadowy figures of the employees were respectfully approaching in single file: behind the director there was already a whole queue of people waiting to get a look; some had brought along their eldest sons.

'We certainly are spoiling you,' muttered Rodion in conclusion, and for a long time was unable to unlock the door of Cincinnatus's cell, even honouring it with a potent bit of Russian swearing, which turned the trick.

Everything became quiet. Everything was the same as always.

'No, not everything – tomorrow you will come,' Cincinnatus said aloud, still trembling from his recent swoon. 'What shall I say to you,' he continued thinking, murmuring, shuddering. 'What will you say to me? In spite of everything I loved you, and will go on loving you – on my knees, with my shoulders drawn back, showing my heels to the headsman and straining my goose neck – even then. And afterwards – perhaps most of all *afterwards* – I shall love you, and one day we shall have a real, all-embracing explanation, and then perhaps we shall somehow fit together, you and I, and turn ourselves in such a way that we form one pattern, and solve the puzzle: draw a line from point A to point B . . . without looking, or, without lifting the pencil . . . or in some other way . . . we shall connect the points, draw the line, and you and I shall form that unique design for which I yearn. If they do this kind of thing to me every morning, they will get me trained and I shall become quite wooden.'

Cincinnatus had a fit of yawning – the tears streamed down his cheeks, and still hump after hump swelled under his palate. It was nerves – he was not sleepy. He had to find something to keep him busy until tomorrow – fresh books had not yet arrived. He had not returned the catalogue yet . . . Oh yes, the little drawings! But now, in the light of tomorrow's interview . . .

A child's hand, undoubtedly Emmie's, had drawn a set of pictures, forming (as it had seemed to Cincinnatus yesterday) a coherent narrative, a promise, a sample of phantasy. First there was a horizontal line – that is, this stone floor; on it was a rudimentary chair somewhat like an insect, and above was a grating made of six squares. Then came the same picture but with the addition of a full moon, the corners of its mouth drooping sourly beyond the grating. Next, a stool composed of three strokes with an eyeless (hence, sleeping) jailer on it and, on the floor, a ring with six keys. Then the same key ring, only a little larger, with a hand, extremely pentadactyl and in a short sleeve, reaching for it. Here it begins to get interesting. The door is ajar in the next drawing, and beyond it something looking like a bird's spur – all that is visible of the fleeing prisoner. Then he himself, with commas on his head instead of hair, in a dark little robe, represented to the best of the artist's ability by an isosceles triangle; he is being led by a little girl: prong-like legs, wavy skirt, parallel lines of hair. Then the same again, only in the form of a plan: a square for the cell, an angled line for the corridor, with a dotted line indicating the route and an accordionlike staircase at the end. And finally the epilogue: the dark tower, above it a pleased moon, with the corners of its mouth curling upward.

No – this was only self-deception, nonsense. The child had doodled aimlessly . . . Let us copy out the titles and lay the catalogue aside. Yes, the child . . . With the tip of her tongue showing at the right corner of her mouth, tightly holding the stubby pencil, pressing down upon it with a finger white with effort . . . And then, after connecting a particularly successful line, leaning back, rolling her head this way and that, wriggling her shoulders, and, going back to work on the paper, shifting her tongue to the left corner . . . so painstakingly . . . Nonsense, let's not dwell on it any more . . .

Trying to think of a way to enliven the listless hours, Cincinnatus decided to tidy up for tomorrow's Marthe. Rodion agreed to haul in another tub like the one in which Cincinnatus had splashed on the eve of the trial. While waiting for the water Cincinnatus sat down at the table; today the table was a little wobbly.

'The interview,' wrote Cincinnatus, 'signifies, in all probability, that my terrible morning is already nearing. The day after tomorrow, at this very time, my cell will be empty. But I am happy that I shall see you. We used to go up to the workshops by two different staircases, the men by one, the women by the other, but would meet on the penultimate landing. No longer can I conjure Marthe as she was when I first met her, but I can recall having noticed at once that she opens her mouth a little an instant before laughing, and the round hazel eyes, and the coral earrings – oh, how I should like to reproduce her as she was, all new and still solid – and then the gradual softening – the fold between cheek and neck when she turned her head toward me, already grown warm, and almost alive. Her world. Her world consists of simple components, simply joined; I think that the simplest cookbook recipe is more complicated than the world that she bakes as she hums: every day for herself, for me, for everyone. But whence – even then, in the first days – whence the malice and obstinacy that suddenly . . . So soft, so amusing and warm, and then suddenly . . . At first I thought she was doing it deliberately, perhaps to show how another in her place might have grown shrewish and stubborn. Can you imagine my amazement when I realized that this was her real self! Because of what trifles – my foolish one, how little your head was, if one feels through all that auburn, thick mass to which she knows how to impart an innocent sleekness with a girlish gloss on the top of her head. "Your little wife looks so quiet and gentle, but she bites, I tell you," her first unforgettable lover said to me, and the base thing is that the verb was not being used figuratively . . . because it was true that at a certain moment . . . one of those memories that one should drive away, or else it will overpower and crush you. Little Marthe did it again . . . And once I saw, I saw, I saw – from the balcony I saw – and since that day I would never enter any room without first announcing my approach from afar – by a cough, or a meaningless exclamation. How awful it was to glimpse that contortion, that breathless haste – all that had been mine in the shadowed seclusion of the Tamara Gardens, and that I had afterward lost. Count how many she had . . . endless torture: to talk at dinner with one or another of her lovers, appear cheerful, crack nuts, crack jokes, and all the while to be mortally afraid to bend down, and chance to see the nether half of that monster whose upper half was quite presentable, having the appearance of a young woman and a young man visible down to the waist at table, peacefully feeding and chatting; and whose nether half was a writhing, raging quadruped. I descended into hell to retrieve a dropped napkin. Later Marthe would say to herself (in that same first person plural), "We are very much ashamed that we were seen," and pouted. And I still love you. Inescapably, fatally, incurably . . . As long as the oaks stand in those gardens, I will . . . When they gave you official proof that I was not wanted, that I was to be shunned – you were surprised that you had noticed nothing yourself – and yet it was so easy to hide it from you! I remember how you implored me to reform, with no real understanding what it was in me that ought to be reformed and how one would go about it, and even now you do not understand anything, do not for a moment stop to think whether you understand or not, and, when you wonder, your wonder is almost cozy. Still, when the bailiff began going around the courtroom with the hat, you too threw in your scrap of paper.'

As the tub rocked at the wharf, an innocent, gay, inviting steam rose above it. Impulsively, in two quick motions, Cincinnatus heaved a sigh and laid aside the filled sheets. From his modest footlocker he produced a clean towel. Cincinnatus was so small and slender that he was able to get all of himself into the washing tub. He sat there as in a canoe and floated peacefully. A reddish evening ray, mingling with the steam, aroused a motley tremor in the small world of the stone cell. Reaching shore, Cincinnatus stood up and stepped out on to land. As he dried himself he struggled with dizziness and palpitations. He was very thin, and now, as the light of the setting sun exaggerated the shadows of his ribs, the very structure of his rib cage seemed a triumph of cryptic coloration inasmuch as it expressed the barred nature of his surroundings, of his gaol. My poor little Cincinnatus. As he dried himself, trying to find some diversion in his own body, he kept examining his veins and he could not help thinking how he would soon be uncorked, and all the contents would run out. His bones were light and thin; his meek toe nails (you dear ones, you innocent ones) gazed up at him with childlike attention; and, as he sat thus on the cot – naked, his entire skinny back, from coccyx to cervical vertebrae, exposed, to the observers on the other side of the door (he could hear whispers, rustling movements, a discussion of something or other – but never mind, let them look), Cincinnatus might have passed for a sickly youth – even the back of his head, with its hollowed nape and tuft of wet hair, was boyish – and exceptionally handy. From the same valise Cincinnatus took a small mirror and a vial of depilatory water which always reminded him of that marvellously hirsute mole which Marthe had on her side. He rubbed it into his prickly cheeks, removing the prickliness and carefully avoiding the moustache.

Nice and clean now. He heaved a sigh and put on the cool nightshirt, still smelling of home washing.

It grew dark. He lay in bed and kept floating. At the customary hour Rodion turned on the light and removed the bucket and tub. The spider lowered itself to him on a thread and settled on the finger which Rodion offered to the furry beastie, chatting with it as with a canary. Meanwhile the door to the corridor remained ajar, and all at once something stirred there . . . for an instant the twining tips of pale curls drooped, and then disappeared when Rodion moved as he gazed up at the tiny black aerialist receding up under the circus dome. The door still remained a quarter of the way open. Heavy Rodion, with his leather apron and his crinky red beard, lumbered about the cell, and, when the clock (closer now because of the direct communication) began its hoarse rattle prior to striking, he produced a thick watch from a recess in his belt and checked the time. Then, supposing Cincinnatus to be asleep, he watched him for a rather long time, leaning on his broom as on a halberd. Having reached who knows what conclusions he moved again . . . Just then, silently and not very fast, a red-and-blue ball rolled in through the door, followed one leg of a right triangle straight under the cot, disappeared for an instant, thumped against the chamber pot, and rolled out along the other cathetus – that is, toward Rodion, who all without noticing it, happened to kick it as he took a step; then, following the hypotenuse, the ball departed into the same chink through which it had entered. Shouldering the broom, Rodion left the cell. The light went out.

Cincinnatus did not sleep, did not sleep, did not sleep – no, he was asleep, but with a moan scrambled out again – and now again he did not sleep, slept, did not sleep, and everything was jumbled—

Marthe, the executioner's block, her velvet – and how will it turn out . . . which will it be? A beheading or a tryst? Everything merged totally, but he did open his eyes for just one more wink when the light went on and Rodion entered on tiptoe, took the catalogue in its black binding from the table, went out, and it became dark.

6

What was it – through everything terrible, nocturnal, unwieldy –what was that thing? It had been last to move aside, reluctantly yielding to the huge, heavy wagons of sleep, and now it was first to hurry back – so pleasant, so very pleasant – swelling, growing more distinct, suffusing his heart with warmth: Marthe is coming today!

Just then Rodion brought a lilac letter on a salver as they do in plays. Cincinnatus perched on the bed and read the following: 'A million apologies! An inexcusable blunder! Upon consulting the text of the law it was discovered that an interview is granted only upon expiration of one week following the trial. Hence we shall postpone it until tomorrow. Best of health, old boy, regards. Everything the same here, one worry after another, the paint sent for the sentry boxes again turned out to be worthless, about which I had already written, but without results.'

Rodion, trying not to look at Cincinnatus, was gathering yesterday's dishes from the table. It must be a dreary day: the light penetrating from above was grey, and compassionate Rodion's dark leather clothes seemed damp and stiff.

'Oh well,' said Cincinnatus, 'as you wish, as you wish . . . I am powerless anyway.' (The other Cincinnatus . . . a little smaller, was crying, all curled up in a ball.) 'All right, let it be tomorrow. But I should like to ask you to call . . .'

'Right away,' blurted out Rodion with such alacrity that he seemed to have been longing just for this; he was about to dash off but just then the director, who had been waiting too impatiently at the door, appeared just a split second too early, so that they collided.

Rodrig Ivanovich was holding a wall calendar and did not know where to lay it down.

'A million apologies,' he cried, 'an inexcusable blunder! Upon consulting the text of the law . . .' Having repeated his message verbatim Rodrig Ivanovich seated himself at Cincinnatus's feet and added hurriedly, 'In any case you may submit a complaint, but I consider it my duty to warn you that the next congress will take place in the fall, and by then a lot of water – and not only water – will have flowed over the dam. Do I make myself clear?'

'I do not intend to complain,' said Cincinnatus, 'but wish to ask you, is there in the so-called order of so-called things of which your so-called world consists even one thing that might be considered an assurance that you will keep a promise?'

'A promise?' asked the director in surprise, ceasing to fan himself with the cardboard part of the calendar (depicting the fortress at sunset, a watercolour). 'What promise?'

'That my wife will come tomorrow. So you will not agree to guarantee it in this case – but I am phrasing my question more broadly: is there in this world, can there be, any kind of security at all, any pledge of anything, or is the very idea of guarantee unknown here?'

A pause.

'Isn't it too bad though about Roman Vissarionovich,' said the director, 'have you heard? He is in bed with a cold, and apparently quite a serious one . . .'

'I have a feeling that you will not answer me at any cost; that is logical, for even irresponsibility in the end develops its own logic. For thirty years I have lived among spectres that appear solid to the touch, concealing from them the fact that I am alive and real – but now that I have been caught, there is no reason to be constrained with you. At least I shall test for myself all the unsubstantiality of this world of yours.'

The director cleared his throat and went on as if nothing had happened: 'So serious, in fact, that I as a doctor am not certain whether he will be able to attend – that is, whether he will recover in time – *bref*, whether he will be able to make it to your show . . .'

'Go away,' said Cincinnatus through clenched teeth.

'Do not be crestfallen,' continued the director. 'Tomorrow, tomorrow the thing you dream of will become a reality . . . It's a cute calendar, though, isn't it? A work of art. No, this isn't for you.'

Cincinnatus closed his eyes. When he opened them again, the director was standing in the centre of the cell with his back toward him. The leather apron and red beard, apparently left behind by Rodion, were still cluttering the chair.

'Today we shall have to do a particularly good job of cleanup your abode,' he said without turning, 'so as to prepare it for tomorrow's interview . . . While we are washing the floor in here, I shall ask you to—'

Cincinnatus shut his eyes again, and the voice, grown smaller in volume, went on: '. . . I shall ask you to step out into the corridor. It will not take long. Let us make a real effort, so that tomorrow, in a fitting manner, neatly, smartly, festively . . .'

'Get out,' cried Cincinnatus, raising himself and shaking all over.

'Quite impossible,' Rodion announced gravely, fussing with his apron straps. 'We must do some work here. Just look at all the dust . . . You'll say thankee yourself.'

He inspected himself in a pocket mirror, fluffed up the whiskers on his cheeks and, at last approaching the cot, handed Cincinnatus his things. The slippers were providently stuffed with wadded paper, while the hem of the dressing gown was carefully folded back and pinned. Cincinnatus, a bit unsteady on his feet, got dressed and, leaning a little on the arm of Rodion, went out into the corridor. There he sat down on a stool, folding his arms into his sleeves like a sick man. Leaving the door of the ward wide open, Rodion began cleaning. The chair was placed atop the table; the sheet was stripped from the cot; the pail handle clinked; the draught riffled through the papers on the table, and one sheet glided to the floor. 'What are you mopping there?' shouted Rodion, raising his voice above the noise of the water, the sloshing and clatter, 'You ought to take a bit of a walk along the corridors there . . . Go on, don't be afraid – I'll be right here in case anything happens – all you have to do is holler.'

Cincinnatus obediently rose from the stool, but barely had he moved along the cold wall – undoubtedly related to the rock on which the fortress had risen – barely had he walked a few steps away (and what steps! – feeble, weightless, meek), barely had he consigned Rodion, the open door, and the pails to a receding perspective, when Cincinnatus felt the surge of freedom. It flowed more fully when he turned the corner. Except for the sweaty smears and the cracks, the bare walls were adorned by nothing; only in one place someone had scrawled in ochre, with a house painter's stroke, 'Testing brush, testing bru—' with an ugly run of paint under it. From the unaccustomed exertion of walking alone, Cincinnatus's muscles grew limp and there was a stitch in his side.

It was then that Cincinnatus stopped and, looking around him as if he had just entered this stony solitude, summoned up all his will, evoked the full extent of his life, and endeavoured to comprehend his situation with the utmost exactitude. Accused of the most terrible of crimes, gnostical turpitude, so rare and so unutterable that it was necessary to use circumlocutions like 'impenetrability', 'opacity', 'occulsion'; sentenced for that crime to death by beheading; emprisoned in the fortress in expectation of the unknown but near and inexorable date (which he distinctly anticipated as the wrenching, yanking and crunch of a monstrous tooth, his whole body being the inflamed gum, and his head that tooth); standing now in the prison corridor with a sinking heart – still alive, still unimpaired, still Cincinnatic – Cincinnatus C. felt a fierce longing for freedom, the most ordinary, physical, physically feasible kind of freedom, and instantly he imagined, with such sensuous clarity as though it all was a fluctuating corona emanating from him, the town beyond the shallowed river, the town, from every point of which one could see – now in this vista, now in that, now in crayon, and now in ink – the tall fortress within which he was. And so powerful and sweet was this tide of freedom that everything seemed better than it really was: his jailers, who in fact were everyone, seemed more tactable; in the confining phenomena of life his reason sought out a possible trail, some kind of vision danced before his eyes – like a thousand iridescent needles of light that surround the dazzling reflection of the sun in a nickel-plated sphere . . . Standing in the prison corridor and listening to the ample sonorities of the clock, which had just begun its leisurely enumeration, he imagined life in the city as it generally was at this fresh morning hour: Marthe, eyes lowered, is walking with an empty basket from the house along the blue sidewalk, followed at a distance of three paces by a dark-moustachioed young blade; the electric wagonets in the shape of swans or gondolas, where you sit as in a carrousel cradle, keep gliding in an endless stream along the boulevard; couches and armchairs are being carried out of furniture warehouses for airing, and passing schoolchildren sit down on them to rest, while the little orderly, his wheelbarrow loaded with all their books, mops his brow like a full-grown labourer; spring-powered, two-seat 'clocklets', as they are called here in the provinces, click along over the freshly sprinkled pavement (and to think that these are the degenerate descendants of the machines of the past, of those splendid lacquered stream-lined automobiles . . . what made me think of that? ah yes, the photos in the magazine); Marthe picks out some fruit; decrepit, dreadful horses, which have long since ceased to marvel at the sights of hell, deliver merchandise from the factories to the city distributors; street bread vendors, white-shirted, with gilded faces, shout as they juggle their baton loaves, tossing them high in the air, catching them and twirling them once again; at a window overgrown with wisteria a gay foursome of telegraph workers are clinking glasses and drinking toasts to the health of passers-by: a famed punster, a gluttonous, coxcombed old man in red silk trousers, is gorging himself on fried chuckricks at a pavilion on the Lesser Ponds; the clouds disperse, and, to the accompaniment of a brass band, dappled sunlight runs along the sloping streets, and visits the side alleys; pedestrians walk briskly; the smell of lindens, of carburine and of damp gravel is in the air; the perpetual fountain at the mausoleum of Captain Somnus profusely irrigates with its spray the stone captain, the bas-relief at his elephantine feet and the quivering roses; Marthe, her eyes lowered, is walking homeward with a full basket, followed at a distance of three paces by a fair-haired fop . . . These are the things that Cincinnatus saw and heard through the walls as the clock struck, and, even though in reality everything in this city was always quite dead and awful by comparison with the secret life of Cincinnatus and his guilty flame, even though he knew this perfectly well and knew also that there was no hope, yet at this moment he still longed to be on those bright familiar streets . . . but then the clock finished ringing, the imaginary sky grew overcast, and the jail was back in force.

Cincinnatus held his breath, moved, stopped again, listened: somewhere ahead, at an indeterminate distance, there was a tapping.

It was a rhythmic, quick, blunt sound, and Cincinnatus, all his nerves a-flutter, heard in it an invitation. He walked on, very attentive, very ethereal and lucid; he turned he knew not how many corners. The noise ceased, but then seemed to have flown nearer, like an invisible woodpecker. Tap, tap, tap. Cincinnatus quickened his pace, and once again the dark passage made a bend. Suddenly it became lighter – though still not like day –

and now the noise became definite and almost smug. Ahead, in a flood of pale light, Emmie was bouncing a ball against the wall.

At this point the passage was wide, and at first it seemed to Cincinnatus that the left wall contained a large, deep window, through which all that strange additional light was flowing. Emmie, as she bent down to retrieve her ball, and at the same time to pull up her sock, looked at him slyly and shyly. The little blonde hairs stood erect on her bare arms and shins. Her eyes shone between her whitish lashes. Now she straightened up, brushing the flaxen curls from her face with the same hand in which she was holding the ball.

'You aren't supposed to walk here,' she said – she had something in her mouth; it rolled behind her cheek and knocked against her teeth.

'What is that you are sucking?' asked Cincinnatus.

Emmie stuck out her tongue; on its independently live tip lay a piece of brilliant barberry-red hard candy.

'I have some more,' she said. 'Want one?'

Cincinnatus shook his head.

'You aren't supposed to walk here,' repeated Emmie.

'Why?' asked Cincinnatus.

She shrugged one shoulder and, grimacing, arching the hand in which she held the ball, tensing her calves, she went over to the spot where he had thought there was a niche, a window, and, fidgeting, suddenly seeming all legs, settled herself on a sill-like projection of stone.

No, it was only the semblance of a window; actually it was a glazed recess, a showcase, and it displayed in its false depth – yes, of course, how could one help but recognize it! – a view of the Tamara Gardens. This landscape, daubed in several layers of distance, executed in blurry green hues and illuminated by concealed bulbs, was reminiscent not so much of a terrarium or some model of theatrical scenery as of the backdrop in front of which a wind orchestra toils and puffs. Everything was reproduced fairly accurately as far as grouping and perspective was concerned, and, were it not for the drab colours, the stirless treetops and the torpid lighting, one could slit one's eyes and imagine oneself gazing through an embrasure, from this very prison, at those very gardens. The indulgent gaze recognized those avenues, that curly verdancy of groves, the portico at the right, the detached poplars, and, in the middle of the unconvincing blue of the lake, the pale blob that was probably a swan. Afar, in a stylized mist, the hills humped their round backs, and above them, in that kind of slate-blue firmament under which Thespians live and die, cumulus clouds stood still. And all of this was somehow not fresh, antiquated, covered with dust, and the glass through which Cincinnatus was looking bore smudges, from some of which a child's hand could be reconstructed.

'Won't you please take me out there?' whispered Cincinnatus. 'I beseech you.'

He was sitting next to Emmie on the stone projection and both of them were peering into the artificial remoteness beyond the glass; enigmatically, she kept following winding paths with her finger, and her hair smelled of vanilla.

'Pop's coming,' she suddenly said in a husky, hurried voice; then she hopped to the floor and vanished.

It was true: Rodion was approaching, keys a-jangle, from the direction opposite the one whence Cincinnatus had come (who thought for a moment it was a reflection in a mirror).

'Home you go,' he said jokingly.

The light behind the glass went out and Cincinnatus took a step, intending to return by the same route as he had come.

'Hey, hey, where are you off to?' exclaimed Rodion. 'Go straight that way.'

And only then did Cincinnatus realize that the bends in the corridor had not been leading him away anywhere, but rather formed a great polyhedro – for now, as he turned a corner, he saw his door in the distance, and, before he reached it, passed the cell where the new prisoner was kept. The door of this cell was wide open, and inside, the likable shorty whom he had seen before, dressed in his striped pyjamas, was standing on a chair and tacking the calendar to the wall: tap, tap, like a woodpecker.

'No peeking, my fair damsel,' said Rodion good-naturedly to Cincinnatus. 'Home, home. And what a cleaning job we've done on your place, eh? Now we don't have to be ashamed about bringing guests in.'

He seemed particularly proud of the fact that the spider was enthroned in a clean, impeccably correct web, which had been created, it was clear, just a moment before.

7

An enchanting morning! freely, without the former friction, it penetrated through the barred glass washed yesterday by Rodion. Nothing could look more festive than the yellow paint of the walls. The table was covered by a clean tablecloth, which did not yet cling because of the air under it. The liberally doused stone floor exhaled fontal freshness.

Cincinnatus put on the best clothes he had with him – and while he was pulling on the white silk stockings which he, as a teacher, was entitled to wear at gala performances – Rodion brought in a wet cut-glass vase with jowly peonies from the director's garden and placed it on the table, in the centre . . . no, not quite in the centre; he backed out and in a minute returned with a stool and an additional chair, and arranged the furniture not haphazardly but with judgment and taste. He came back several times, and Cincinnatus did not dare ask, 'will it be soon?' and – as happens at that particularly inactive hour when, all dressed up, you are awaiting guests – he strolled around, now perching in unaccustomed corners, now straightening the flowers in the case, so that at last Rodion took pity on him and said it would not be long now.

Punctually at ten, Rodrig Ivanovich appeared, in his best, most monumental frock coat, pompous, aloof, excited yet composed; he set down a massive ash tray and inspected everything (with the exception only of Cincinnatus), acting like a majordomo engrossed in his job, who gives his attention to the neatness of the inanimate inventory only, leaving the animate to shift for themselves. He returned carrying a green flask equipped with a rubber bulb and began spraying pine fragrance, rather unceremoniously pushing aside Cincinnatus when the latter happened to get in his way. The chairs Rodrig Ivanovich arranged differently from Rodion, and for a long time he stared, goggle-eyed, at the backs, which did not match – one was lyrate, the other square. He puffed up his cheeks and let out the air with a whistle, and at last turned to Cincinnatus.

'And how about you? Are you ready? he asked. 'Did you find everything you needed? Are your shoe buckles in order? Why is it wrinkled, or something, over here? Shame on you – Let's see your paws. *Bon*. Now try not to get all dirty. I think it won't be long now . . .'

He went out, and his succulent, authoritative bass reverberated through the corridor. Rodion opened the cell door, securing it in that position, and unrolled a caramel-striped runner on the threshold. 'Coming,' he whispered with a wink and disappeared again. Now a key made a threefold clank in a lock somewhere, confused voices were audible, and a gust stirred the hair on Cincinnatus's head.

He was very agitated, and his quivering lips continuously assumed the shape of a smile. 'Right this way. Here we are already,' he could hear the sonorous comments of the director, and in the next instant the latter appeared, gallantly leading in by the elbow the plump, striped little prisoner who, before coming in, paused on the mat, noiselessly brought together his morocco feet, and bowed gracefully.

'Allow me to present to you M'sieur Pierre,' said the director to Cincinnatus in jubilant tones. 'Come in, come in, M'sieur Pierre. You can't imagine how you have been awaited here – Get acquainted, gentlemen – The long-awaited meeting – An instructive spectacle . . . Do bear with us, M'sieur Pierre, do not find fault . . .'

He did not even know what he was saying – he was bubbling over, cutting heavy little capers, rubbing his hands, bursting with delighted embarrassment.

M'sieur Pierre, very calm and composed, walked in, bowed once again, and Cincinnatus mechanically joined him in a handshake; the other man retained Cincinnatus's escaping fingers in his small soft paw a second longer than is customary – as a gentle elderly doctor draws out a handshake, so gently, so appetizingly – and now he released it.

In a melodious, high-pitched voice coming from the throat M'sieur Pierre said, 'I too am extremely happy to make your acquaintance at last. I make bold to hope that we may get to know each other more closely.'

'Exactly, exactly,' roared the director, 'oh, please, be seated . . . Make yourself at home . . . Your colleague is so happy to see you here that he is at a loss for words.'

M'sieur Pierre seated himself, and here it became evident that his legs did not quite reach the floor; however this did not detract in the least from his dignity or that particular grace with which nature endows a few select little fat men. His crystal-bright eyes gazed politely at Cincinnatus, while Rodrig Ivanovich, who had also sat down at the table, tittering, urging, intoxicated with pleasure, looked from one to the other, greedily following the impression made on Cincinnatus by the guest's every word.

M'sieur Pierre said: 'You bear an extraordinary resemblance to your mother. I myself never had the chance of seeing her, but Rodrig Ivanovich kindly promised to show me her photograph.'

'At your service,' said the director, 'we'll obtain one for you.'

M'sieur Pierre continued: 'Anyway, apart from this, I have been a photography enthusiast ever since I was young; I am thirty now, and you?'

'He is exactly thirty,' said the director.

'You see, I guessed right. So, since this is your hobby too, let me show you—'

Briskly, he produced from the breast pocket of his pyjama top a bulging wallet, and from it a thick batch of home snapshots of the smallest size. Riffling through them as through a deck of tiny cards, he began placing them one by one on the table, and Rodrig Ivanovich would grab each with delighted exclamations, examine it for a long time, and slowly, still admiring the snapshot, or else reaching for the next, would pass it on – even though all was still and silent there. The pictures showed M'sieur Pierre, M'sieur Pierre in various poses – now in a garden, with a giant prize tomato in his hand, now perching with one buttock on some railing (profile, with pipe), now reading in a rocking chair, a glass with a straw standing near him . . .

'Excellent, marvellous,' Rodrig Ivanovich would comment, fawning, shaking his head, feasting his eyes on every shot or else holding two at a time and shifting his gaze from one to the other. 'My, my, what biceps you have in this one! Who would think – with your graceful physique. Overwhelming! Oh, how charming – talking with the little birdie!'

'A pet,' said M'sieur Pierre.

'Most entertaining! What do you know . . . And this here . . . Eating a watermelon, no less!'

'Yep,' said M'sieur Pierre. 'You have already looked through those. Here are some more.'

'Charming, let me tell you. Let's have that other batch – he hasn't seen them yet . . .'

'Here I am juggling three apples,' said M'sieur Pierre.

'Isn't that something!' said the director clucking his tongue.

'At breakfast,' said M'sieur Pierre. 'This is me, and that is my late father.'

'Yes, yes, of course I recognize him . . . That noble brow!'

'On the banks of the Strop,' said M'sieur Pierre. 'Have you been there?' he asked turning to Cincinnatus.

'I don't think he has,' replied Rodrig Ivanovich. 'And where was this taken? What an elegant little overcoat! You know something, you look older in this one. Just a second, I want to see that one again, with the watering can.'

'There . . . That is all I have with me,' said M'sieur Pierre, and again addressed Cincinnatus: 'If only I had known that you are so interested, I would have brought along more – I have a good dozen albums.'

'Wonderful, stunning,' repeated Rodrig Ivanovich, wiping with a lilac-coloured handkerchief his eyes, grown moist from all these joyous titters and ejaculations.

M'sieur Pierre reassembled the contents of his wallet. Suddenly there was a deck of cards in his hands.

'Think of a card please, any card,' he proposed, laying the cards out on the table; he pushed the ash tray aside with his elbow; he continued laying.

'We have thought of one,' said the director jauntily.

Indulging in a bit of hocus-pocus M'sieur Pierre put his index finger to his forehead; then he quickly gathered up the cards, smartly made the pack crackle and threw out a trey of spades.

'This is amazing,' exclaimed the director, 'Simply amazing!'

The deck vanished just as suddenly as it had appeared, and, making an imperturbable face, M'sieur Pierre said: 'This little old woman comes to the doctor and says, "I have a terrible malady, Mr Doctor," she says, "I've an awful fright I'll die of it . . ." "And what are the symptoms?" "My head shakes, Mr Doctor," ' and M'sieur Pierre, mumbling and shaking, imitated the little old woman.

Rodrig Ivanovich burst into riotous mirth, struck the table with his fist, nearly fell off his chair; then had a fit of coughing; moaned; and with a great effort regained control of himself.

'M'sieur Pierre, you are the life of the party,' he said, still shedding tears, 'truly the life of the party! I haven't heard such a hilarious anecdote in all my life!'

'How melancholy we are, how tender,' said M'sieur Pierre to Cincinnatus, thrusting out his lips as if he were trying to make a sulking child laugh. 'We keep so still, and our little moustache is all quivering, and the vein on our neck is throbbing, and our little eyes are misty . . .'

'It's all from joy,' quickly inserted the director. '*N'y faites pas attention.*'

'Yes, it is indeed a happy day, a red-letter day,' said M'sieur Pierre. 'I am bubbling over with excitement myself . . . I don't want to boast, but in me, my dear colleague, you will find a rare combination of outward sociability and inward delicacy, the art of the causerie and the ability to keep silent, playfulness and seriousness . . . Who will console a sobbing infant, and glue his broken toy together? M'sieur Pierre. Who will intercede for a poor widow? M'sieur Pierre. Who will provide sober advice, who will recommend a medicine, who will bring glad tidings? Who? Who? M'sieur Pierre. All will be done by M'sieur Pierre.'

'Remarkable! What talent!' exclaimed the director, as though he had been listening to poetry; yet all the time from beneath a twitching eyebrow he kept glancing at Cincinnatus.

'Therefore, it seems to me,' went on M'sieur Pierre. 'Oh yes, by the way,' he interrupted himself, 'are you satisfied with your quarters? You are not cold at night? Do they give you enough to eat?'

'He gets the same as I,' answered Rodrig Ivanovich. 'The board is excellent.'

'All aboard,' quipped M'sieur Pierre.

The director was getting ready to roar again, but just then the door opened and the gloomy, lanky librarian appeared with a stack of books under his arm. A woollen scarf was wound around his throat. Without saying hello to anyone he dumped the books on the cot, and for a moment stereometric apparitions of those same books, composed of dust, hung above them in the air, they hung, vibrated, and dispersed.

'Wait a minute,' said Rodrig Ivanovich. 'I don't think you have met.'

The librarian nodded, without looking, while polite M'sieur Pierre rose from his chair.

'Please, M'sieur Pierre,' begged the director, putting his hand to his shirt front, 'please show him your trick!'

'Oh, it's hardly worth it – it's really nothing,' M'sieur Pierre modestly began but the director would not stop:

'It's a miracle! Red magic! We all beg you! Oh, do it for us . . . Wait, wait just a minute,' he shouted to the librarian, who was already starting toward the door. 'Just a minute, M'sieur Pierre will show you something. Please, please! Don't go . . .'

'Think of one of these cards,' pronounced M'sieur Pierre with mock solemnity; he shuffled the deck; he threw out the five of spades.

'No,' said the librarian and left.

M'sieur Pierre shrugged a round little shoulder.

'I'll be right back,' muttered the director and went out also.

Cincinnatus and his guest remained alone.

Cincinnatus opened a book and buried himself in it, that is, he kept reading the first sentence over and over. M'sieur Pierre looked at him with a kind smile, with one little paw lying palm up on the table, just as if he were offering to make peace with Cincinnatus. The director returned. In his tightly clenched fist was a woollen scarf.

'Maybe you can use it, M'sieur Pierre,' he said; then he handed over the scarf, sat down, exhaled noisily like a horse, and began examining his thumb, from the end of which a half-broken nail protruded like a sickle.

'What were we talking about?' exclaimed M'sieur Pierre with charming tact, just as if nothing had happened. 'Yes, we were talking about photographs. Some time I'll bring my camera and take your picture. That will be fun. What are you reading? May I take a look?'

'You ought to put the book aside,' remarked the director with a rasp of exasperation in his voice; 'after all, you do have a guest.'

'Oh, let him be,' smiled M'sieur Pierre.

There was a pause.

'It is growing late,' said the director after consulting his watch.

'Yes, we'll be going in a minute . . . My, what a little grouch . . . Look at him, his little lips all a-tremble . . . any moment now the sun will peek out from behind the clouds . . . Grouch, grouch! . . .'

'Let's go,' said the director, rising.

'Just a moment . . . I like it so much here that I can hardly tear myself away . . . In any case, my dear neighbour, I shall take advantage of your permission to visit you often, often – that is, of course, if you grant me permission – and you will, won't you? . . . Good-bye for now, then. Good-bye! Good-bye!'

Bowing comically, in imitation of someone, M'sieur Pierre withdrew; the director once again took him by his elbow, emitting voluptuous nasal sounds. They left, but at the last minute his voice was heard to say: 'Excuse me, I forgot something, I'll catch up with you in a moment,' and the director gushed back into the cell; he approached Cincinnatus, and for an instant the smile left his purple face: 'I am ashamed,' he hissed through his teeth, 'ashamed of you. You behaved like . . . I'm coming, I'm coming,' he yelled, beaming once again, then he snatched the vase of peonies from the table, and splashing water as he went, left the cell.

Cincinnatus kept staring into the book. A drop had fallen on the page. Through the drop several letters turned from brevier to pica, having swollen as if a reading glass were lying over them.

8

There are some who sharpen a pencil toward themselves, as if they were peeling a potato, and there are other who slice away from themselves, as though whittling a stick . . . Rodion was of the latter number. He had an old penknife with several blades and a corkscrew. The corkscrew slept on the outside.)

'Today is the eighth day' (wrote Cincinnatus with the pencil, which had lost more than a third of its length) 'and not only am I still alive, that is, the sphere of my own self still limits and eclipses my being, but, like any other mortal, I do not know my mortal hour and can apply to myself a formula that holds for everyone: the probability of a future decreases in inverse proportion to its theoretical remoteness. Of course in my case discretion requires that I think in term of very small numbers – but that is all right, that is all right – I am alive. I had a strange sensation last night – and it was not the first time – I am taking off layer after layer, until at last . . . I do not know how to describe it, but I know this: through the process of gradual divestment I reach the final, indivisible, firm, radiant point, and this point says: I am! like a pearl ring embedded in a shark's gory fat – O my eternal, my eternal . . . and this point is enough for me – actually nothing more is necessary. Perhaps as a citizen of the next century, a guest who has arrived ahead of time (the hostess is not yet up), perhaps simply a carnival freak in a gaping, hopelessly festive world, I have lived an agonizing life, and I would like to describe that agony to you – but I am obsessed by the fear that there will not be time enough. As far back as I can remember myself – and I remember myself with lawless lucidity, I have been my own accomplice, who knows too much, and therefore is dangerous. I issue from such burning blackness, I spin like a top, with such propelling force, such tongues of flame, that to this day I occasionally feel (sometimes during sleep, sometimes while immersing myself in very hot water) that primordial palpitation of mine, that first branding contact, the mainspring of my "I". How I wriggled out, slippery, naked! Yes, from a realm forbidden and inaccessible to others, yes, I know something, yes . . . but even now, when it is all over anyway, even now – I am afraid that I may corrupt someone. Or will nothing come of what I am trying to tell, its only vestiges being the corpses of strangled words, like hanged men . . . evening silhouettes of gammas and gerunds, gallow crows – I think I should prefer the rope, since I know authoritatively and irrevocably that it shall be the axe; a little time gained, time, which is now so precious to me that I value every respite, every postponement . . . I mean time allotted to thinking; the furlough I allow my thoughts for a free journey from fact to fantasy and return . . . I mean much more besides, but lack of writing skill, haste, excitement, weakness . . . I know something. I know something. But expression of it comes so hard! No, I cannot . . . I would like to give up – yet I have the feeling of boiling and rising, a tickling, which may drive you mad if you do not express it somehow. On no, I do not gloat over my own person, I do not get all hot wrestling with my soul in a darkened room; I have no desires, save the desire to express myself – in defiance of all the world's muteness. How frightened I am. How sick with fright. But no one shall take me away from myself. I am frightened – and now I am losing some thread, which I held so palpably only a moment ago. Where is it? It has slipped out of my grasp! I am trembling over the paper, chewing the pencil through to the lead, hunching over to conceal myself from the door through which a piercing eye stings me in the nape, and it seems I am right on the verge of crumpling everything and tearing it up. I am here through an error – not in this prison, specifically – but in this whole terrible, striped world; a world which seems not a bad example of amateur craftsmanship, but is in reality calamity, horror, madness, error – and look, the curio slays the tourist, the gigantic carved bear brings its wooden mallet down upon me. And yet, ever since early childhood, I have had dreams . . . In my dreams the world was ennobled, spiritualized; people whom in the waking state I feared so much appeared there in a shimmering refraction, just as if they were imbued with and enveloped by that vibration of light which in sultry weather inspires the very outlines of objects with life; their voices, their step, the expressions of their eyes and even of their clothes – acquired an exciting significance; to put it more simply, in my dreams the world would come alive, becoming so captivatingly majestic, free and ethereal, that afterwards it would be oppressive to breathe the dust of this painted life. But then I have long since grown accustomed to the thought that what we call dreams is semi-reality, the promise of reality, a foreglimpse and a whiff of it; that is, they contain, in a very vague, diluted state, more genuine reality than our vaunted waking life which, in its turn, is semi-sleep, an evil drowsiness into which penetrate in grotesque disguise the sounds and sights of the real world, flowing beyond the periphery of the mind – as when you hear during sleep a dreadful insidious tale because a branch is scraping on the pane, or see yourself sinking into snow because your blanket is sliding off. But how I fear awakening! How I fear that second, or rather split second, already cut short then, when, with a lumberjack's grunt – But what is there to fear? Will it not be for me simply the shadow of an axe, and shall I not hear the downward vigorous grunt with the ear of a different world? Still I am afraid! One cannot write it off so easily. Neither is it good that my thoughts keep getting sucked into the cavity of the future – I want to think about something else, clarify other things . . . but I write obscurely and limply, like Pushkin's lyrical duelist. Soon, I think, I shall evolve a third eye on the back of my neck, between my brittle vertebrae: a mad eye, wide open, with a dilating pupil and pink venation on the glossy ball. Keep away! Even stronger, more hoarsely: hands off! I can foresee it all! And how often do my ears ring with the sob I am destined to emit and the terrible gurgling cough, uttered by the beheaded tyro. But all of this is not the point, and my discourse on dreams and waking are also not the point . . . Wait! There, I feel once again that I shall really express myself, shall bring the words to bay. Alas, no one taught me this kind of chase, and the ancient inborn art of writing is long since forgotten – forgotten are the days when it needed no schooling, but ignited and blazed like a forest fire – today it seems just as incredible as the music that once used to be extracted from a monstrous pianoforte, music that would nimbly ripple or suddenly hack the world into great, gleaming blocks – I myself picture all this so clearly, but you are not I, and therein lies the irreparable calamity. Not knowing how to write, but sensing with my criminal intuition how words are combined, what one must do for a commonplace word to come alive and to share its neighbour's sheen, heat, shadow, while reflecting itself in its neighbour and renewing the neighbouring word in the process, so that the whole line is live iridescence; while I sense the nature of this kind of word propinquity, I am nevertheless unable to achieve it, yet that is what is indispensable to me for my task, a task of not now and not here. Not here! The horrible "here", the dark dungeon, in which a relentlessly howling heart is encarcerated, this "here" holds and constricts me. But what gleams shine through at night, and what— It exists, my dream world, it must exist, since, surely there must be an original of the clumsy copy. Dreamy, round, and blue, it turns slowly toward me. It is as if you are lying supine, with eyes closed, on an overcast day, and suddenly the gloom stirs under your eyelids, and slowly becomes first a langorous smile, then a warm feeling of contentment, and you know that the sun has come out from behind the clouds. With just such a feeling my world begins; the misty air gradually clears, and it is suffused with such radiant, tremulous kindness, and my soul expands so freely in its native realm – But then what, then what? Yes, that is the line beyond which I lose control . . . Brought up into the air, the word bursts, as burst those spherical fishes that breathe and blaze only in the compressed murk of the depths when brought up in the net. However I am making one last effort – and I think I have caught my prey . . . but it is only a fleeting apparition of my prey! *There, tam, là-bas,* the gaze of men glows with inimitable understanding; *there* the freaks that are tortured here walk unmolested; *there* time takes shape according to one's pleasure, like a figured rug whose folds can be gathered in such a way that two designs will meet – and the rug is once again smoothed out, and you live on, or else superimpose the next image on the last, endlessly, endlessly, with the leisurely concentration of a woman selecting a belt to go with her dress – now she glides in my direction, rhythmically butting the velvet with her knees, comprehending everything and comprehensible to me . . . *There, there* are the originals of those gardens where we used to roam and hide in this world; *there* everything strikes one by its bewitching evidence, by the simplicity of perfect good; *there* everything pleases one's soul, everything is filled with the kind of fun that children know; *there* shines the mirror that now and then sends a chance reflection here . . . And what I say is not it, not quite it, and I am getting mixed up, getting nowhere, talking nonsense, and the more I move about and search in the water where I grope on the sandy bottom for a glimmer I have glimpsed, the muddier the water grows, and the less likely it becomes that I shall grasp it. No, I have as yet said nothing, or, rather, said only bookish words . . . and in the end the logical thing would be to give up and I would give up if I were labouring for a reader existing today, but as there is in the world not a single human who can speak my language; or, more simply, not a single human who can speak; or, even more simply, not a single human; I must think only of myself, of that force which urges me to express myself. I am cold, weakened, afraid, the back of my head blinks and cringes, and once again gazes with insane intensity, but, in spite of everything, I am chained to this table like a cup to a drinking fountain, and will not rise till I have said what I want. I repeat (gathering new momentum in the rhythm of repetitive incantations), I repeat: there is something I know, there is something I know, there is something . . . When still a child, living still in a canary-yellow, large, cold house where they were preparing me and hundreds of other children for secure nonexistence as adult dummies, into which all my coevals turned without effort or pain; already then, in those accursed days, amid rag books and brightly painted school materials and soul-chilling draughts, I knew without knowing, I knew without wonder, I knew as one knows oneself, I knew what it is impossible to know – and, I would say, I knew it even more clearly than I do now. For life has worn me down: continual uneasiness, concealment of my knowledge, pretence, fear, a painful straining of all my nerves – not to let down, not to ring out . . . and even to this day I still feel an ache in that part of my memory where the very beginning of this effort is recorded, that is, the occasion when I first understood that things which to me had seemed natural were actually forbidden, impossible, that any thought of them was criminal. Well do I remember that day! I must have just learned how to make letters, since I remember myself wearing on my fifth finger the little copper ring that was given to children who already knew how to copy the model words from the flower beds in the school garden, where petunias, phlox and marigold spelled out lengthy adages. I was sitting with my feet up on the low window sill and looking down as my schoolmates, dressed in the same kind of long pink smocks as I, held hands and circled around a beribboned pole. Why was I left out? In punishment? No. Rather, the reluctance of the other children to have me in their game and the mortal embarrassment, shame and dejection I myself felt when I joined them made me prefer that white nook of the sill, sharply marked off by the shadow of the half-open casement. I could hear the exclamations required by the game and the strident commands of the red-haired "pedagoguette"; I could see her curls and her spectacles, and with the squeamish horror that never left me I watched her give the smallest children shoves to make them whirl faster. And that teacher, and the striped pole, and the white clouds, now and then letting through the gliding sun, which would suddenly spill out passionate light, searching for something, were all repeated in the flaming glass of the open window . . . In short, I felt such fear and sadness that I tried to submerge within myself, to slow down the slip out of the senseless life that was carrying me onward. Just then, at the end of the stone gallery where I was sitting, appeared the senior educator – I do not recall his name – a fat, sweaty, shaggy-chested man, who was on his way to the bathing place. While still at a distance he shouted to me, his voice amplified by the acoustics, to go into the garden; he approached quickly and flourished his towel. In my sadness, in my abstraction, unconsciously and innocently, instead of descending into the garden by the stairs (the gallery was on the third floor), not thinking what I was doing, but really acting obediently, even submissively, I stepped straight from the window sill on to the elastic air and – feeling nothing more than a half-sensation of barefootedness (even though I had shoes on) – slowly and quite naturally strode forward, still absently sucking and examining the finger in which I had caught a splinter that morning . . . Suddenly, however, an extraordinary, deafening silence brought me out of my reverie, and I saw below me, like pale daisies, the upturned faces of the stupefied children, and the pedagoguette, who seemed to be falling backward; I saw also the globes of the trimmed shrubs, and the falling towel that had not yet reached the lawn; I saw myself, a pink-smocked boy, standing transfixed in mid-air; turning around, I saw, but three aerial paces from me, the window I had just left, and, his hairy arm extended in malevolent amazement, the—'

(Here, unfortunately, the light in the cell went out – Rodion always turned it off exactly at ten.)

9

And again the day began with a din of voices. Rodion was gloomily giving instructions, and three other attendants were assisting him. The entire family of Marthe had arrived for the interview, bringing with them all their furniture. Not thus, not thus had he imagined this long-awaited meeting . . . How they lumbered in! Marthe's aged father, with his huge bald head, and bags under his eyes, and the rubbery tap of his black cane; Marthe's brothers, identical twins except that one had a golden moustache and the other a pitch-black one; Marthe's maternal grandparents, so old that one could already see through them; three vivacious female cousins, who, however, were not admitted for some reason at the last minute; Marthe's children – lame Diomedon and obese little Pauline; at last Marthe herself, wearing her best black dress, with a velvet ribbon around her cold white neck, and holding a hand mirror; a very proper young man with a flawless profile was constantly at her side.

The father-in-law, leaning on his stick, seated himself in a leather armchair that had arrived with him, with an effort put a fat suede foot up on a stool and, angrily shaking his head, fixed his gaze, from beneath heavy eyelids, on Cincinnatus, who felt the familiar dull sensation at the sight of the frogs ornamenting the father-in-law's warm jacket, the folds around his mouth that seemed to express eternal disgust, and the purple blotch of a birthmark on his corded temple, with a swelling resembling a big raisin right on the vein.

The grandfather and grandmother (the one all shaky and shrivelled, in patched trousers, the other with her white hair bobbed, and so slim that she might have encased herself in a silk umbrella sheath) settled side by side in two identical high-backed chairs; the grandfather tightly clutched in his small hirsute hands a bulky portrait, in a gilt frame, of his mother, a misty young woman, in turn holding a portrait.

Meanwhile, furniture, household utensils, even individual sections of walls continued to arrive. There came a mirrored wardrobe, bringing with it its own private reflection (namely, a corner of the connubial bedroom with a stripe of sunlight across the floor, a dropped glove, and an open door in the distance). A cheerless little tricycle with orthopaedic attachments was rolled in. It was followed by the inlaid table which had supported a flat garnet flacon and a hairpin for the last ten years. Marthe sat down on her black couch, embroidered with roses.

'Woe, woe!' proclaimed the father-in-law, striking the floor with his cane. Frightened little smiles appeared on the faces of the oldsters. 'Don't, daddy, we've been through it a thousand times,' Marthe said quietly, and shrugged a chilly shoulder. Her young man offered her a fringed shawl but she, forming the rudiment of a tender smile with one corner of her thin lips, waved away his sensitive hand. ('The first thing I look at in a man is his hands.') He was dressed in the smart black uniform of a telegraph employee and perfumed with violet scent.

'Woe!' repeated the father-in-law forcefully and began to curse Cincinnatus in detail and with relish. Cincinnatus's gaze was drawn to Pauline's green polka-dotted dress: red-haired, cross-eyed, bespectacled, arousing not laughter but sadness with those polka dots and that plumpness, dully moving her fat legs in brown wool stockings and button shoes, she would approach those present and study each, gazing gravely and silently with her small dark eyes, which seemed to meet behind the bridge of her nose. The poor thing had a napkin tied around her neck – evidently they had forgotten to take it off after breakfast.

The father-in-law paused to regain breath, then struck another blow with his cane, whereupon Cincinnatus said, 'Yes, I am listening.'

'Silence, insolent fellow,' shouted the former, 'I am entitled to expect from you – if only today, when you stand at death's door – a little respect. How you managed to get yourself on the block . . . I want an explanation from you – how you could . . . how you dared . . .'

Marthe asked her young man something in a low voice; he was carefully rummaging around, probing all around himself and under himself on the couch; 'no, no, it's all right,' he answered just as softly, 'I must have dropped it on the way . . . Don't worry, it'll turn up . . . But tell me, are you sure you're not cold?' Shaking her head negatively, Marthe lowered her soft palm on to his wrist; and, taking her hand away immediately, she straightened her dress across the knees and in a harsh whisper called her son, who was bothering his uncles, who in turn kept pushing him away – he was preventing them from listening. Diomedon, in a grey blouse with an elastic at the hips, twisting his whole body in a rhythmic distortion, nevertheless quite rapidly covered the distance between them and his mother. His left leg was healthy and rosy; the right one resembled a rifle in its complicated harness: barrel, straps, sling. His round hazel eyes and sparse eyebrows were his mother's, but the lower half of his face, with its bulldog jowls – this, of course, was someone else's. 'Sit here,' whispered Marthe and, with a quick slap, arrested the hand mirror which was trickling off the couch.

'You tell me,' the father-in-law was continuing, 'how you dared, you, a happy family man – splendid furniture, wonderful children, a loving wife – how you dared not consider all this, you villain? It seems to me sometimes that I am no more than an old moron and understand nothing, because otherwise I must allow for such loathsomeness . . . Silence!' he roared, and again the oldsters started and smiled.

A black cat stretched, straining back one hind paw, rubbed itself against Cincinnatus's leg, then was suddenly on the sideboard, and from there noiselessly leaped on to the shoulder of the lawyer who, having just tiptoed in, was sitting in a corner on a plush hassock – he had a bad cold and, over a handkerchief held ready for use, was inspecting the assembled company and the various household items that made the cell look like the site of an auction; the cat startled him, and he threw it off with a convulsive movement.

The father-in-law was thundering on, multiplying curses and already beginning to grow hoarse. Marthe placed her hand over her eyes; her young man, tensing his jaw muscles, was watching her. On a settee with a curved back sat Marthe's brothers; the dark one, in a tawny suit and open shirt collar, was holding music paper rolled into a tube and as yet bearing no music – he was one of the city's foremost singers; his twin, in sky-blue plus-fours, a dandy and a wit, had brought a present for his brother-in-law – a bowl of bright fruit made of wax. He had also fixed a crepe arm band on his sleeve and kept indicating it with his finger as he tried to catch Cincinnatus's eye.

At the peak of his eloquence the father-in-law suddenly choked and gave his chair such a wrench that quiet little Pauline, who had been standing by him and looking at his mouth, toppled backwards behind the chair, where she lay still, hoping that nobody noticed. With a crackle the father-in-law began opening a cigarette box. Everyone was quiet.

The various trampled sounds began to straighten up. Marthe's brother, the brunette, cleared his throat and softly began to sing '*Mali é trano t'amesti . . .*' He stopped short and looked at his brother, who made terrible eyes at him. The lawyer, smiled at something, again applied himself to his handkerchief. On the couch, Marthe was talking in a whisper with her escort, who was pleading with her to throw the shawl over herself – the prison air was a little damp. When they spoke they used the formal second person plural, but with what a cargo of tenderness this second person plural was laden as it sailed along the horizon of their barely audible conversation . . . The little old man, trembling awfully, got up from his chair, handed the portrait to his old woman and, shielding the flame that was trembling like himself, went up to Cincinnatus's father-in-law, and was going to light his . . . But the flame went out, and the latter frowned angrily.

'You have really become a nuisance with your stupid lighter,' said he glumly, but already without wrath; then the atmosphere really grew animated, and everybody began talking simultaneously. *'Male é trano t'amesti!'* Marthe's brother sang full voice; 'Diomedon, leave the cat alone this instant,' said Marthe. 'You already strangled one the other day, one every day is too much. Take it way from him, please, Victor, dear.' Availing herself of the general animation, Pauline crawled out from behind the chair and quietly got up. The lawyer walked over to Cincinnatus's father-in-law and gave him a light.

'Take the word "anxiety",' Cincinnatus's brother-in-law, the wit, was saying to him. 'Now take away the word "tiny", Eh? Comes out funny, doesn't it? Yes, friend, you've really got yourself in a mess. In truth, what made you do such a thing?'

Meanwhile the door opened imperceptibly. M'sieur Pierre and the director stood on the threshold, hands clasped identically behind their backs, and quietly, delicately moving only their eyeballs, were examining the assemblage. They stood and looked like this for more than a minute before leaving.

'Listen to me,' the brother-in-law was saying, breathing hotly. 'I'm your old pal. Do as I say. Repent, my little Cincinnatus. Come on, do me this favour. You don't know, they might still let you off. Eh? Think how unpleasant it is to have your chump lopped off. What do you have to lose? Come on – don't be a blockhead.'

'Greetings, greetings, greetings,' said the lawyer, coming over to Cincinnatus. 'Don't embrace me, I still have a bad cold. What is the conversation about? How can I be of service?'

'Let me pass,' murmured Cincinnatus, 'I have to say a couple of words to my wife . . .'

'Now, my dearest, let us discuss the question of property,' said the father-in-law, refreshed, and extended his cane in such a way that Cincinnatus stumbled over it. 'Wait, wait a minute, I am speaking to you!'

Cincinatus kept going; he had to get around a large table, set for ten persons, and then squeeze between the screen and the wardrobe in order to reach Marthe, who reclined on the couch. The young man had covered her feet with the shawl. Cincinnatus almost made it, but just then there was an angry shriek from Diomedon. He turned around and saw Emmie, who had entered in some unknown way and was now teasing the boy: imitating his lameness, she was dragging one leg with various complicated contortions. Cincinnatus caught her by the arm, but she broke loose and ran off. Pauline waddled after her in a silent ecstasy of curiosity.

Martha turned to him. The young man very correctly stood up. 'Marthe, just a couple of words, I beg you,' said Cincinnatus rapidly; he tripped over the cushion on the floor and sat down awkwardly on the edge of the couch, at the same time wrapping his ash-smeared dressing gown around himself. 'A slight migraine,' said the young man. 'What can you expect? Such excitement is bad for her.' 'You are right,' said Cincinnatus. 'Yes, you are right. I should like to ask you . . . I must – in private—' 'Beg pardon, sir,' said the voice of Rodion close to him. Cincinnatus stood up; Rodion and another employee, looking each other in the eye, grasped the couch on which Marthe was reclining, grunted, picked it up and carried it toward the door. 'Good-bye, good-bye,' Marthe called childishly, swaying in time with the step of the porters, but suddenly she closed her eyes and covered her face. Her escort walked solicitously behind, carrying the black shawl he had picked up from the floor, a bouquet, his uniform cap, and a solitary glove. There was commotion all around. The brothers were packing the dishes in a trunk. Their father, breathing asthmatically, was overcoming the multisegmented screen. The lawyer was offering everyone a vast sheet of wrapping paper obtained by him from some unknown source; he was seen unsuccessfully attempting to wrap in it a bowl containing a pale-orange little fish in clouded water. Amid the commotion the ample wardrobe with its private reflection stood like a pregnant woman, carefully holding and turning aside its glass belly so no one would brush against it. It was tilted backward and, in a reeling hug, carried away. People were coming up to Cincinnatus to say good-bye. 'Well, let's let bygones be bygones,' said the father-in-law and, with cold politeness, kissed Cincinnatus's hand as custom demanded. The blond brother sat the dark one on his shoulders and in that position they took leave of Cincinnatus and departed, like a live mountain. The grandparents were shivering, bowing and holding up the hazy portrait. The employees kept carrying out the furniture. The children approached: Solemn Pauline raised up her face; Diomedon, on the contrary, gazed down at the floor. The lawyer led them away by their respective hands. The last to fly up to him was Emmie, pale, tear-stained, her nose pink and her mouth wet and quivering; she was silent, but suddenly, with a slight crackle, she rose on her toes, twined her hot arms around his neck, whispered incoherently and uttered a loud sob. Rodion seized her by the wrist – judging by his grumbling he had been calling her for a long time; now he dragged her firmly toward the exit. Arching back her body, turning toward Cincinnatus her head with its streaming hair and extending to him, palm upturned, her lovely arm (with the appearance of a ballet captive but with the shadow of genuine despair), Emmie unwillingly followed Rodion as he dragged her; her eyes kept rolling back, her shoulder strap slipped off, and now, with a swinging motion, as though he were emptying a water bucket, he splashed her out into the corridor. Then, still muttering, he returned with a dustpan to pick up the corpse of the cat that lay flat under a chair. The door slammed with a crash. It was now hard to believe that in this cell, only a moment ago—

10

'When the lone wolf cub gets better acquainted with my views he will stop shying away from me. A certain amount of progress, however, has already been achieved, and I welcome it with all my heart,' M'sieur Pierre was saying, seated sidewise to the table as was his wont, his plump calves compactly crossed, and one hand playing soundless chords on the oilcloth. Cincinnatus, his head propped on his hand, lay on the cot.

'We are alone now, and it's raining,' went on M'sieur Pierre; 'such weather is ideal for intimate chit-chat. Let us settle once for all . . . I get the impression that you are surprised, even irritated by the administration's attitude toward me; it is as if I were in a privileged position – no, no, don't argue – let us have it out. Allow me to tell you two things. You know our dear director (by the way, the wolf cub is not entirely fair to him, but we'll talk about that later), you know how impressionable he is, how enthusiastic, how he is carried away with every novelty – I think he must have been carried away with you the first few days – so the passion that now inflames him for me need not upset you. Let's not be so jealous, my friend. In the second place, strangely enough, you are evidently still unaware of why I ended up here, but when I tell you, there are many things you will understand. Excuse me, what is that you have on your neck – right here, here – yes, here.'

'Where?' Cincinnatus asked mechanically, feeling his neck vertebrae.

M'sieur Pierre went over to him and sat down on the edge of the cot. 'Right here,' he said, 'but I see now that it was only a shadow. I thought I saw . . . a little swelling of some kind. You seem uncomfortable when you move your head. Does it hurt? Did you catch a chill?'

'Oh, stop pestering me, please,' Cincinnatus said, sorrowfully.

'No, just a minute. My hands are clean – allow me to feel here. It seems, after all . . . Does it hurt here? How about here?'

With his small but muscular hand he was rapidly touching Cincinnatus's neck and examining it carefully, breathing through the nose with a slight wheeze.

'No, nothing. Everything is in order,' he said at last, Moving away and slapping the patient on the nape – 'Only you do have an awfully thin one – otherwise everything is normal, it's just that sometimes, you know . . . Let's see your tongue. The tongue is a mirror of the stomach. Cover up, cover up, it's chilly in here. What were we chatting about? Refresh my memory.'

'If you were really interested in my welfare,' said Cincinnatus, 'then you would leave me alone. Go away, please.'

'You mean you really do not want to hear what I have to say,' M'sieur Pierre objected with a smile, 'you really are so obstinately convinced that your conclusions are infallible – conclusions that are unknown to me – mark that, unknown.'

Lost in sadness, Cincinnatus said nothing.

'Allow me to tell you, though,' M'sieur Pierre went on with a certain solemnity, 'what was the nature of my crime. I was accused – justly or not, that is a different matter – I was accused . . . of what, do you suppose?'

'Well, come on out with it,' said Cincinnatus with a melancholy sigh.

'You will be amazed. I was accused of attempting to . . . Oh ungrateful, distrustful friend . . . I was accused of attempting to help you escape from here.'

'Is that true?' asked Cincinnatus.

'I never lie,' M'sieur Pierre said imposingly. 'Perhaps there are times when one ought to lie – that is another matter – and perhaps such scrupulous veracity is foolish and in the end does no good – that may all be so. But the fact remains, I never lie. I ended up here, my fine friend, because of you. I was arrested at night. Where? Let us say in Upper Elderbury. Yes, I am an Elderburian. Salt works, fruit orchards. Should you ever want to come and call on me, I shall treat you to some of our elderburies (I assume no responsibility for the pun – it appears in our city seal). There – not in the seal, but in the jail – your obedient servant spent three days. Then they transferred me here.'

'You mean you wanted to save me . . .' Cincinnatus said pensively.

'Whether I wanted to or not is my business, friend of my heart, cockroach-under-the-hearth. In any case I was accused of it – you know, informers are a young and hot-headed breed, so here I am: "here in rapture I'm standing before you . . ." – remember the song? The principal evidence against me was some sketch of this fortress that supposedly had my marks on it. You see, I was supposed to have thought out every last detail of your escape, my little cockroach.'

'You were supposed to, or . . . ?' asked Cincinnatus.

'What a naïve, delightful creature he is!' grinned M'sieur Pierre, displaying a multitude of teeth. 'He wants everything to be so simple – as, alas, it never is in real life!'

'One would still like to know,' said Cincinnatus.

'What? Whether my judges were right? Whether I really was planning to save you? Shame, shame . . .'

'Then it is true?' whispered Cincinnatus.

M'sieur Pierre got up and began to walk about the cell. 'Let us leave the matter,' he said resignedly. 'Decide for yourself, distrustful friend. One way or another, but I ended up here because of you. And I'll tell you more: we shall mount the scaffold together too.'

He kept walking about the cell with a noiseless, springy step, the soft parts of his body, enclosed in prison pyjamas, bouncing slightly, and Cincinnatus, with dejected attention, followed every step of the nimble fatty.

'For the heck of it I shall believe you,' Cincinnatus said finally,

'We'll see what will come of it. You hear me, I believe you. And, to make it more convincing, I even thank you.'

'Oh, what for – there's no need . . .' said M'sieur Pierre and sat down again by the table. 'I simply wanted you to be informed. That's fine. Now we've both got a load off our chests, haven't we? I don't know about you, but I feel like crying. And this is a good feeling. Cry, do not restrain those salutary tears.'

'How horrible it is here,' said Cincinnatus cautiously.

'There's nothing horrible about it. By the way, I've wanted to reproach you for a long time about your attitude toward the life here. No, no, don't turn away, allow me, as a friend . . . You are not fair either to our good Rodion or, even more important, to his excellency the director. All right – he is not very bright, a little pompous, something of a scatterbrain – and he is not adverse to delivering speeches – it's all true, and I myself sometimes am not in the mood for him and, of course, cannot share with him my inmost thoughts, as I do with you, especially when my soul – pardon the expression – aches. But whatever faults he might have, he is a straightforward, honest and kind man. Yes, a man of rare kindness – do not argue – I would not say it if I did not know, and I never speak idly, and I have more experience and know life and people better than you. That's why it hurts me to see with what cruel coldness, what haughty contempt you reject Rodrig Ivanovich. I can sometimes read such pain in his eyes . . . As for Rodion, how is it that you who are so intelligent are unable to perceive through his assumed gruffness all the touching benignity of this grown-up child. Oh, I realize that you are nervous, that you are sex starved – still, Cincinnatus – you'll forgive me, but it isn't right, it isn't right at all . . . And, in general, you slight people . . . You scarcely touch the marvellous dinners we get here. All right, supposing you don't care for them – believe me, I too know a little about gastronomy – but you sneer at them, and yet someone cooked them, someone worked hard . . . I know, it sometimes gets boring here, and you feel like going for a walk or having a romp – but why think only of yourself, of your desires, why haven't you smiled even once at the painstaking little jokes of dear pathetic Rodrig Ivanovich? . . . Perhaps he cries afterwards, and does not sleep nights, remembering how you reacted . . .'

'In any case your defence is clever,' said Cincinnatus, 'but I am an expert in dolls. I shall not yield.'

'It's a pity,' said M'sieur Pierre in a hurt tone. 'I ascribe it to your youth,' he added after a pause. 'No, no, you must not be so unfair . . .'

'Tell me,' asked Cincinnatus, 'do they keep you in the dark too? The fateful churl has not arrived yet? The hacking fest isn't set for tomorrow?'

'You should not use such words,' remarked M'sieur Pierre confidentially. 'Particularly with that intonation . . . There is something vulgar in it, something unworthy of a gentleman. How can you pronounce such things – I am surprised at you . . .'

'But tell me, when?' asked Cincinnatus.

'In due time,' M'sieur Pierre replied evasively. 'Why such foolish curiosity? And in general . . . No, you still have a lot to learn – this sort of thing won't do. This arrogance, these preconceptions . . .'

'But how they drag it out . . .' Cincinnatus said drowsily. 'Of course one does get accustomed to it . . . You hold your soul in readiness from one day to the next – and still they will take you by surprise. Ten days have passed like this, and I haven't gone crazy. And then, of course, there is always some hope . . . Indistinct, as if under water, but therefore all the more attractive. You speak of escape . . . I think, I surmise, that there is someone else too who is concerned with it . . . Certain hints . . . But what if this is only deception, a fold of the fabric mimicking a human face . . .'

He sighed and paused.

'This is curious,' said M'sieur Pierre. 'What are these hopes, and who is this saviour?'

'Imagination,' replied Cincinnatus. 'And you – would you like to escape?'

'What do you mean "escape"? Where to?' asked M'sieur Pierre in amazement.

Cincinnatus sighed again.

'What difference does it make where? We might, you and I . . . I don't know, though, whether, with your build, you are able to run fast. Your legs . . .'

'Come, come, what kind of nonsense is that?' said M'sieur Pierre, squirming in his chair. 'Only in fairy tales do people escape from prison. As for your remarks about my physique, kindly keep them to yourself.'

'I feel sleepy,' said Cincinnatus.

M'sieur Pierre rolled up his right sleeve. There appeared a tattoo. Under the wonderfully white skin his muscle bulged and rolled. He assumed a firm stance, grasped the chair with one hand, turned it upside down and slowly began lifting it. Swaying from the effort, he held it for a moment high above his head and slowly lowered it. This was only a preliminary.

Concealing his laboured respiration, he wiped his hands long and carefully with a red handkerchief, while the spider, as the youngest member of the circus family, performed a simple trick above his web.

Throwing him the handkerchief, M'sieur Pierre shouted a French exclamation and suddenly was standing on his hands. His spherical head gradually became suffused with beautiful rosy blood; his left trouser leg slid down, exposing his ankle; his upside-down eyes – as happens with anyone in this position – looked like the eyes of an octopus.

'How about that?' he asked, bouncing back on to his feet and readjusting his clothes. From the corridor came a tumult of applause, and then, separately, the clown began to clap, loose-jointedly, as he walked – before falling over the barrier.

'Well?' repeated M'sieur Pierre. 'How's that for strength? And will my agility do? Or haven't you seen enough yet?'

In one leap M'sieur Pierre hopped up on the table, stood on his hands, and grasped the back of the chair in his teeth. The music paused breathlessly. M'sieur Pierre was lifting the chair, clenched firmly between his teeth; his tensed muscles were quivering; his jaw was creaking.

The door softly swung open, and there entered – in jack boots, with a whip, powdered and spotlit with blinding violet light – the circus director. 'Sensational! A unique performance!' he whispered, and, taking off his top hat, he sat down by Cincinnatus.

Something gave, and M'sieur Pierre, releasing the chair from his mouth, turned a somersault and was again standing on the floor. Apparently, however, not everything was well. He at once covered his mouth with his handkerchief, glanced quickly under the table, then inspected the chair, and, suddenly seeing what he sought, attempted, with a subdued oath, to yank off the back of the chair his hinged denture, which was embedded there. Magnificently displaying all its teeth it held on with a bulldog grip. Whereupon, without losing his head, M'sieur Pierre embraced the chair and departed with it.

Rodrig Ivanovich, who had noticed nothing, was applauding wildly. The arena, however, remained empty. He cast a suspicious look at Cincinnatus, clapped some more, but without the former ardour, gave a little start and, in obvious distress, left the box.

And thus the performance ended.

II

Now newspapers were no longer brought to the cell: having noticed that everything that might have any connection with the execution was clipped out, Cincinnatus himself had declined to receive them. Breakfast had grown simpler: instead of chocloate – albeit weak chocolate – he would receive some slop with a flotilla of tea leaves; the toast was so hard he could not bite through it. Rodion made no secret of the fact that he had grown bored with serving the silent and fastidious prisoner.

He would deliberately busy himself for a longer and longer time in the cell. His flame-red beard, the imbecile azure of his eyes, his leather apron, his clawlike hands – all this accumulated through repetition to form such a depressing, tedious impression that Cincinnatus would turn away toward the wall while the cleaning was in progress.

And that is how is was this day – only the return of the chair, with the deep imprints of bulldog teeth on the top edge of its straight back, served as a distinguishing feature for the day's beginning. Together with the chair Rodion brought a note from M'sieur Pierre; a fleecily curling script, elegant punctuation marks, signature like a seven-veil dance. In jocular and kindly words his neighbour thanked him for yesterday's friendly chat and expressed hope that it would be repeated shortly. 'Let me assure you,' thus ended the note, 'that I am physically very, very strong [twice underlined with a ruler], and if you are still not convinced of this, I shall be honoured sometime to show you certain further interesting [underlined] demonstrations of agility and astounding muscular development.'

After this, for two hours, with imperceptible intervals of mournful torpor, Cincinnatus, now pinching at his moustache, now flipping the pages of a book, walked about the cell. He had by now made a completely precise study of it – he knew it much better than, for instance, the room where he had lived for many years.

This is how matters stood with the walls: their number was unalterably four; they were painted a uniform yellow; but, because of the shadow covering it, the basic hue seemed dark and smooth, claylike as it were, in comparison with that shifting spot where the bright ochre reflection of the window spent the day: here, in the light, all the small protuberances of the thick yellow paint were in evidence – even the wavy curve of the tracings left by the joint passage of brush hairs – and there was the familiar scratch which the precious parallelogram of sunlight would reach at ten in the morning.

A creeping, heel-clutching chill rose from the dusky stone floor; an underdeveloped, mean little echo inhabited some part of the slightly concave ceiling, with a light (wire-enclosed) in its centre – no, that is, not quite in the centre: a flaw that agonizingly irritated the eye –and, in this sense, no less agonizing was the unsuccessful attempt to paint over the iron door.

Of the three items of furniture – cot, table, chair – only the last was movable. The spider also moved. Up above, where the sloping window recess began, the well-nourished black beastie had found points of support for a first-rate web with the same resourcefulness as Marthe displayed when she would find, in what seemed the most unsuitable corner, a place and a method for hanging out laundry to dry. Its paws folded so that the furry elbows stuck out at the sides, it would gaze with round hazel eyes at the hand with the pencil extended toward it, and would begin to back away, without taking its eyes off it. It was most eager, however, to take a fly or a moth from the large fingers of Rodion – and now, for example, in the south-west part of the web there hung a butterfly's orphaned hind wing, cherry-red, with a silky shading, and with blue lozenges along its crenellated edge. It stirred slightly in a delicate draft.

The inscriptions on the walls had by now been wiped away. The list of rules likewise had disappeared. Also taken away – or perhaps broken – was the classic pitcher with spelaean water in its resonant depths. All was bare, redoubtable, and cold in this chamber where the prisonlike character was suppressed by the neutrality of a waiting room – whether office, hospital or some other kind – when it is already getting to be evening, and one hears only the humming in one's ears . . . and the horror of this waiting was somehow connected with the incorrectly located centre of the ceiling.

Library volumes, in black shoe-leatherlike bindings, lay on the table, which had been covered for some time already with a checkered oilcloth. The pencil, which had lost its slender length and was well chewed, rested on violently scribbled pages, stacked windmill fashion. Here also had been thrown a letter to Marthe, completed by Cincinnatus the day before, that is, the day after the interview: but he could not make up his mind to send it, and had therefore let it lie a while, as though expecting from the thing itself that fruition which his irresolute thoughts, in need of another climate, simply could not achieve.

The subject will now be the precious quality of Cincinnatus; his fleshy incompleteness; the fact that the greater part of him was in a quite different place, while only an insignificant portion of it was wandering, perplexed, here – a poor, vague Cincinnatus, a comparatively stupid Cincinnatus, trusting, feeble and foolish as people are in their sleep. But even during this sleep – still, still – his real life showed through too much.

Cincinnatus's face, grown transparently pallid, with fuzz on its sunken cheeks and a moustache with such a delicate hair texture that it seemed to be actually a bit of dishevelled sunlight on his upper lip; Cincinnatus's face, small and still young despite all the torments, with gliding eyes, eerie eyes of changeable shade, was, in regard to its expression, something absolutely inadmissible by the standards of his surroundings, especially now, when he had ceased to dissemble. The open shirt, the black dressing gown that kept flying open, the oversize slippers on his slender feet, the philosopher's skullcap on the top of his head and the ripple (there was a draft coming from somewhere after all!) running through the transparent hair on his temples completed a picture, the full indecency of which it is difficult to put into words – produced as it was of a thousand barely noticeable, overlapping trifles: of the light outline of his lips, seemingly not quite fully drawn but touched by a master of masters; of the fluttering movements of his empty, not-yet-shaded-in hands; of the dispersing and again gathering rays in his animated eyes; but even all of this, analysed and studied, still could not fully explain Cincinnatus: it was as if one side of his being slid into another dimension, as all the complexity of a tree's foliage passes from shade into radiance, so that you cannot distinguish just where begins the submergence into the shimmer of a different element. It seemed as though at any moment, in the course of his movements about the limited space of the haphazardly invented cell, Cincinnatus would step in such a way as to slip naturally and effortlessly through some chink of the air into its unknown coulisses to disappear there with the same easy smoothness with which the flashing reflection of a rotated mirror moves across every object in the room and suddenly vanishes, as if beyond the air, in some new depth of ether. At the same time, everything about him breathed with a delicate, drowsy, but in reality exceptionally strong, ardent and independent life: his veins of the bluest blue pulsated; crystal-clear saliva moistened his lips; the skin quivered on his cheeks and his forehead, which was edged with dissolved light . . . and all this so teased the observer as to make him long to tear apart, cut to shreds, destroy utterly this brazen elusive flesh, and all that it implied and expressed, all that impossible, dazzling freedom – enough, enough – do not walk any more, Cincinnatus, lie down on your cot, so you will not arouse, will not irritate . . . And in truth Cincinnatus would become aware of the predatory eye in the peephole following him and lie down or sit at the table and open a book.

The black pile of books on the table consisted of the following: first, a contemporary novel that Cincinnatus had not bothered to read during his period of existence at liberty; second, one of those anthologies, published in countless editions with condensed rehashes of and excerpts from ancient literature; third, bound issues of an old magazine; fourth, several bedraggled little volumes of a work in an unknown tongue, brought him by mistake – he had not ordered them.

The novel was the famous *Quercus*, and Cincinnatus had already read a good third of it, or about a thousand pages. Its protagonist was an oak. The novel was a biography of that oak. At the place where Cincinnatus had stopped the oak was just starting on its third century; a simple calculation suggested that by the end of the book it would reach the age of six hundred at least.

The idea of the novel was considered to be the acme of modern thought. Employing the gradual development of the tree (growing lone and mighty at the edge of a canyon at whose bottom the waters never ceased to din), the author unfolded all the historic events – or shadows of events – of which the oak could have been a witness; now it was a dialogue between two warriors dismounted from their steeds – one dappled, the other dun – so as to the rest under the cool ceil of its noble foliage; now highwaymen stopping by and the song of a wild-haired fugitive damsel; now, beneath the storm's blue zigzag, the hasty passage of a lord escaping from royal wrath; now, upon a spread cloak a corpse, still quivering with the throb of the leafy shadows; now a brief drama in the life of some villagers. There was a paragraph a page and a half long in which all the words began with 'p'.

It seemed as though the author were sitting with his camera somewhere among the topmost branches of the Quercus, spying out and catching his prey. Various images of life would come and go, pausing among the green macules of light. The normal periods of inaction were filled with scientific descriptions of the oak itself, from the viewpoints of dendrology, ornithology, coleopterology, mythology – or popular descriptions, with touches of folk humour. Among other things there was a detailed list of all the initials carved in the bark with their interpretations. And, finally, no little attention was devoted to the music of waters, the palette of sunsets, and the behaviour of the weather.

Cincinnatus read for a while and laid it aside. This work was unquestionably the best that his age had produced; yet he overcame the pages with a melancholy feeling, plodded through the pages with dull distress, and kept drowning out the tale in the stream of his own meditation: what matters to me all this, distant, deceitful and dead – I, who am preparing to die? Or else he would begin imagining how the author, still a young man, living, so they said, on an island in the North Sea – would be dying himself and it was somehow funny that eventually the author must needs die – and it was funny because the only real, genuinely unquestionable thing here was only death itself, the inevitability of the author's physical death.

The light would move along the wall. Rodion would appear with what he called frühstück. Again a butterfly wing would slide between his fingers, leaving coloured powder on them.

'Can it be that *he* has not arrived yet?' asked Cincinnatus; it was already not the first time he had asked this question, which greatly angered Rodion, and again he did not reply.

'And another interview – will they grant me that?' asked Cincinnatus.

In anticipation of the usual heartburn he lay down on the cot and, turning toward the wall, for a long, long time helped patterns form on it, from tiny blobs of the glossy paint and their round little shadows; he would discover, for example a diminutive profile with a large mouselike ear; then he would lose it and was unable to reconstruct it. This cold ochre smelled of the grave, it was pimply and horrible, yet his gaze still persisted in selecting and correlating the necessary little protuberances – so starved he was for even a vague semblance of a human face.

Finally he turned over, lay on his back and, with the same attention, began to examine the shadows and cracks on the ceiling.

'Anyway, they have succeeded in softening me,' mused Cincinnatus. 'I have grown so limp and soggy that they will be able to do it with a fruit knife.'

For some time he sat on the edge of the cot, his hands compressed between his knees, all hunched over. Letting out a shuddering sigh he began to roam. It is interesting, though, in what language this is written. The small, crowded ornate type, with dots and squiggles within the sickle-shaped letters, seemed to be oriental – it was somehow reminiscent of the inscriptions on museum daggers. Such old little volumes, with their faded pages . . . some tinged with tawny blotches.

The clock struck seven, and shortly Rodion appeared with dinner.

'You are sure *he* still has not come?' asked Cincinnatus.

Rodion was about to leave, but turned on the threshold.

'Shame on you,' he said with a sob in his voice, 'day and night you do nothing . . . a body feeds you here, tends you lovingly, wears himself out for your sake, and all you do is ask stupid questions. For shame, you thankless man . . .'

Time, humming evenly, continued to pass. The air in the cell grew dark, and when it had become quite dense and dull, the light came on in business-like fashion in the centre of the ceiling – no, not quite in the centre, that was just it – an agonizing reminder. Cincinnatus undressed and got in bed with *Quercus*. The author was already getting to the civilized ages, to judge by the conversation of three merry wayfarers, Tit, Pud, and the Wandering Jew who were taking swigs of wine from their flasks on the cool moss beneath the black vespertine oak.

'Will no one save me?' Cincinnatus suddenly asked aloud and sat up on the bed (opening his pauper's hands, showing that he had nothing).

'Can it be that no one will?' repeated Cincinnatus, gazing at the implacable yellowness of the walls and still holding up his empty palms.

The draft became a leafy breeze. From the dense shadows above there fell and bounced on the blanket a large dummy acorn, twice as large as life, splendidly painted a glossy buff, and fitting its cork cup as snugly as an egg.

12

He was awakened by a muted tapping, scratching, and the sound of something crumbling somewhere. Just as when, having fallen asleep healthy last night, you wake up past midnight in a fever. He listened to these sounds for quite a long while – trup, trup, tock-tock-tock – without any thought about their meaning, simply listening, because they had awakened him and because his hearing had nothing else to do. Trup, tap, scratch, crumble-crumble. Where? To the right? To the left? Cincinnatus raised himself up a little.

He listened – his whole head became an organ of hearing, his whole body a tense heart; he listened and already began to make sense out of certain indications: the weak distillation of darkness within the cell . . . the dark had settled to the bottom . . . Beyond the bars of the window, a grey twilight – that meant it was three or half past three . . . The guards asleep in the cold . . . The sounds were coming from somewhere below . . . no, it was, rather, from above, no, it was still below, just on the other side of the wall, at floor level, like a large mouse scratching with iron claws.

Cincinnatus was especially excited by the concentrated self-confidence of the sounds, the insistent seriousness with which they pursued, in the quiet of the fortress night, perhaps a distant, but none the less attainable goal. With baited breath, with a phantomlike lightness, like a sheet of tissue paper, he slipped off – and tiptoed along the sticky, clinging, wall – to the corner from which it seemed – it seemed to be – but coming closer, he realized that he was mistaken – the tapping was more to the right and higher up; he moved, and again got confused, fooled by the aural deception that occurs when a sound, traversing diagonally one's head, is hurriedly served by the wrong ear.

Stepping awkwardly, Cincinnatus brushed against the tray, which was standing on the floor near the wall. 'Cincinnatus!' said the tray reproachfully; and then the tapping ceased with abrupt suddenness, which conveyed to the listener a heartening rationality; and, standing motionless by the wall, pressing down with his toe the spoon on the tray and tilting his open, hollow head, Cincinnatus felt that the unknown digger was also standing and listening.

A half-minute passed and the sounds, quieter, more restrained, but more expressive and wiser, began again. Turning and slowly moving his sole off the zinc, Cincinnatus tried again to ascertain their location: to the right, if one stood facing the door . . . yes, to the right, and, in any case, still far off . . . after listening a long time that was all he was able to conclude. Finally moving back toward the cot to get his slippers – he could not stand it barefoot any longer – he startled the loud-legged chair, which never spent the night in the same spot twice, and again the sounds ceased, this time for good; that is, they might have resumed after a cautious interval, but morning was already coming into its own and Cincinnatus saw – with the eyes of habitual imagination – Rodion, all steaming from the dampness and opening in a yawn his bright-red mouth as he stretched on his stool in the hall.

All morning long Cincinnatus listened and calculated how he could make known his attitude to the sounds in case they should recur. A summer thunderstorm, simply yet tastefully staged, was performed outside: it was as dark as evening in the cell, thunder was heard, now substantial and round, now sharp and crackly, and lightning printed the shadows of the bars in unexpected places. At noon Rodrig Ivanovich arrived.

'You have company,' he said, 'but first I wanted to find out . . .'

'Who?' asked Cincinnatus, at the same time thinking: please, not now . . . (that is, please do not let the tapping resume now).

'You see, here's the way it is,' said the director, 'I am not sure that you wish . . . You see, it's your mother – *votre mére paraît-il.*'

'My mother?' asked Cincinnatus.

'Well, yes – mother, mummy, mama – in short, the woman who gave birth to you. Shall I admit her? Make up your mind quickly.'

'. . . I have only seen her once in my life,' said Cincinnatus, 'and I really have no feeling . . . no, no, it's not worth it, don't, it would be pointless.'

'As you wish,' said the director and went out.

A minute later, cooing politely, he led in diminutive Cecilia C., clad in a black raincoat. 'I shall leave you two alone,' he added benevolently, 'even though it is against our rules, sometimes there are situations . . . exceptions . . . mother and son . . . I defer . . .'

Exit, backing out like a courtier.

In her shiny black raincoat and a similar waterproof hat with lowered brim (giving it something of the appearance of a sou'wester), Cecelia C. remained standing in the centre of the cell, looking with a clear gaze at her son; she unbuttoned herself; she sniffled noisily and said in her rapid, choppy way: 'What a storm, what mud, I thought I'd never make it up here, streams and torrents coming down the road at me . . .'

'Sit down,' said Cincinnatus, 'don't stand like that.'

'Say what you will, but it's quiet here in your place,' she went on, sniffling all the while and rubbing her finger firmly as if it were a cheese grater, under her nose, so that the pink tip wrinkled and wagged. 'I'll say one thing, it's quiet and fairly clean. By the way, over at the maternity ward, we don't have private quarters as big as this. Oh, that bed – my dear, just look what a mess your bed is!'

She plopped down her midwife's bag, nimbly pulled the black cotton gloves off her small, mobile hands, and, stooping low over the cot, began making the bed afresh. Her back in the belted coat with its seal-like sheen, her mended stockings . . .

'Now, that's better,' she said, straightening up; then, standing for a moment with arms akimbo, she looked askance at the book-cluttered table.

She was youthful, and all her features were a model for those of Cincinnatus, which had emulated them in their own way; Cincinnatus himself was vaguely aware of this resemblance as he looked at her sharp-nosed little face, and protruding, luminous eyes. Her dress was opened in front, revealing a triangle of red sun-tanned freckled skin; in general, however, the integument was the same as that from which a piece had once been taken for Cincinnatus – a pale, thin skin, with sky-blue veins.

'Tsk, tsk, a little straightening up would be in order here too . . .' she prattled and, as quickly as she did everything else, busied herself with the books, arranging them in even piles. In passing, her interest was caught by an illustration in an open magazine; she fished out of her raincoat pocket a kidney-shaped case and, dropping the corners of her mouth, put on a pince-nez. 'Came out back in '26,' she said with a laugh. 'Such a long time ago, it's really hard to believe it.'

(Two photographs: in one the President of the Isles shaking with a dental smile the hand of the venerable great granddaughter of the last of the inventors at the Manchester railroad station; in the other, a two-headed calf born in a Danube village.)

She sighed causelessly, pushed the volume aside, knocked the pencil off, did not catch it in time, and said 'oops!'

'Leave as is,' said Cincinnatus, 'There can be no disorder here – only a shifting about.'

'Here, I brought you this. (She pulled a pound bag out of her coat pocket, pulling out the lining as well.) 'Here. Some candy. Suck on it to your heart's content.'

She sat down and puffed out her cheeks.

'I climbed, and climbed, and finally made it, and now I am tired,' she said, puffing deliberately; then she froze, gazing with vague longing at the cobweb up above.

'Why did you come?' asked Cincinnatus pacing about the cell. 'It doesn't do you any good, and it doesn't do me any good. Why? It is neither kind, nor interesting. For I can see perfectly well that you are just as much of a parody as everybody and everything else. And if they treat me to such a clever parody of a mother . . . But imagine, for instance, that I have pinned my hopes on some distant sound – how can I have faith in it, if even *you* are a fraud? And you speak of "candy"! Why not "goodies"? And why is your raincoat wet when your shoes are dry – see, that's careless. Tell the prop man for me.'

Hastily and guiltily, she said, 'But I wore rubbers – I left them down in the office, word of honour.'

'Oh, enough, enough. Just don't start explaining. Play your role – go heavy on the prattle and the unconcern – and you won't have to worry, it'll get by.'

'I came because I am your mother,' she said softly, and Cincinnatus burst out laughing:

'No, no, don't let it degenerate into farce. Remember, this is a drama. A little comedy is all right, but still you ought not to walk too far from the station – the drama might leave without you. You'd do better to . . . yes, I'll tell you what, why don't you tell me again the legend about my father. Can it be true that he vanished into the dark of night, and you never found out who he was or where he came from – it's strange . . .'

'Only his voice – I didn't see the face,' she answered as softly as before.

'That's it, that's it, play up to me – I think perhaps we'll make him a runaway sailor,' dejectedly continued Cincinnatus, snapping his fingers and pacing, pacing, 'or a sylvan robber making a guest appearance in a public park. Or a wayward craftsman, a carpenter . . . Come, quickly, think of something.'

'You don't understand,' she cried (in her excitement she stood up and immediately sat down again). 'It's true, I don't know who he was – a tramp, a fugitive, anything is possible . . . But why can't you understand . . . yes, it was a holiday, it was dark in the park, and I was still a child, but that's beside the point. The important thing is that it was not possible to make a mistake! A man who is being burned alive knows perfectly well that he isn't taking a dip in our Strop. Why, what I mean is, one can't be wrong . . . Oh, can't you understand?'

'Can't understand what?'

'Oh, Cincinnatus, he too was . . .'

'What do you mean, "he too"?'

'He was also like you, Cincinnatus. . . .'

She quite lowered her face, dropping her pince-nez into her cupped hand.

Pause.

'How do you know this?' Cincinnatus asked morosely. 'How can you suddenly notice . . .'

'I am not going to tell you anything more,' she said without raising her eyes.

Cincinnatus sat down on the cot and lapsed into thought. His mother blew her nose with an extraordinarily loud trumpet sound, which one would hardly expect from so small a woman, and looked up at the window recess. Evidently the weather had cleared, for one felt the close presence of blue skies, and the sun had painted its stripe on the wall – now it would pale, then brighten again.

'There are cornflowers now in the rye,' she said, speaking fast, 'and everything is so wonderful – clouds are scudding, everything is so restless and bright. I live far from here, in Doctorton, and when I come to this city of yours, when I drive across the fields in the little old gig, and see the Strop gleaming, and this hill with the fortress on it, and everything, it always seems to me that a marvellous tale is being repeated over and over again, and I either don't have the time to, or am unable to grasp it, and still somebody keeps repeating it to me, with such patience! I work all day at our ward, I take everything in my stride, I have lovers, I adore ice-cold lemonade, although I've dropped smoking, because of heart trouble – and here I am sitting with you . . . I sit here and I don't know why I sit, why I bawl, and why I tell you all this, and now I shall be hot trudging down in this coat and this wool dress, the sun will be absolutely fiendish after a storm like that . . .'

'No, you're still only a parody,' murmured Cincinnatus.

She smiled interrogatively.

'Just like this spider, just like those bars, just like the striking of that clock,' murmured Cincinnatus.

'So,' she said, and blew her nose again.

'So, that's how it is,' she repeated.

They both remained silent, not looking at each other, while the clock struck with nonsensical resonance.

'When you go out,' said Cincinnatus, 'note the clock in the corridor. The dial is blank; however, every hour the watchman washes off the old hand and daubs on a new one – and that's how we live, by tarbrush time, and the ringing is the work of the watchman, which is why he is called a "watch" man.'

'You oughtn't to joke like that,' said Cecilia C. 'There are, you know, all sorts of marvellous gimmicks. I remember, for instance when I was a child, there were objects called "*nonnons*" that were popular, and not only among children, but among adults too, and, you see, a special mirror came with them, not just crooked, but completely distorted. You couldn't make out anything of it, it was all gaps and jumble and made no sense to the eye – yet the crookedness was no ordinary one, but calculated in just such a way as to . . . Or rather, to match its crookedness they had made . . . No, wait a minute, I am explaining badly. Well, you would have a crazy mirror like that and a whole collection of different "*nonnons*", absolutely absurd objects, shapeless, mottled, pockmarked, knobbly things, like some kind of fossils – but the mirror, which completely distorted ordinary objects, now, you see, got real food, that is, when you placed one of these incomprehensible, monstrous objects so that it was reflected in the incomprehensible, monstrous mirror, a marvellous thing happened; minus by minus equalled plus, everything was restored, everything was fine, and the shapeless speckledness became in the mirror a wonderful, sensible image, flowers, a ship, a person, a landscape. You could have your own portrait custom made, that is, you received some nightmarish jumble, and this thing was you, only the key to you was held by the mirror. Oh, I remember what fun it was, and how it was a little frightening – what if suddenly nothing should come out? – to pick up a new, incomprehensible "*nonnon*" and bring it near the mirror, and see your hand get all scrambled, and at the same time see the meaningless "*nonnon*" turn into a charming picture, so very, very clear . . .'

'Why do you tell me all this?' asked Cincinnatus.

She was silent.

'What's the point of all this? Don't you know that one of these days, perhaps tomorrow . . .'

He suddenly noticed the expression in Cecilia C.'s eyes – just for an instant, an instant – but it was as if something real, unquestionable (in this world, where everything was subject to question), had passed through, as if a corner of this horrible life had curled up, and there was a glimpse of the lining. In his mother's gaze, Cincinnatus suddenly saw that ultimate, secure, all-explaining and from-all-protecting spark that he knew how to discern in himself also. What was this spark so piercingly expressing now? It does not matter what – call it horror, or pity . . . But rather let us say this; the spark proclaimed such a tumult of truth that Cincinnatus's soul could not help leaping for joy. The instant flashed and was gone. Cecilia C. got up, making an incredible little gesture, namely, holding her hands apart with index fingers extended, as if indicating size – the length, say of a babe . . . Then she immediately began fussing, picking up from the floor her plump black bag, adjusting the lining of her pocket.

'There now,' she said, in her former prattling tone, 'I've stayed a while and now I'll be going. Eat my candy. I've overstayed. I'll be going, it's time.'

'Oh yes, it's time!' thundered Rodrig Ivanovich with fierce mirth as he flung open the door.

Head bent, she slipped out. Cincinnatus, trembling, was about to step forward . . .

'Have no worry,' said the director, raising his palm. 'This little midwife presents no danger to us. Back!'

'But I would still . . .' began Cincinnatus.

'*Arrière!*' roared Rodrig Ivanovich.

Meanwhile, M'sieur Pierre's compact striped little figure appeared in the depths of the corridor. He was smiling pleasantly from afar, but restraining his pace slightly, and letting his eyes roam about furtively, as people do when they have walked in on a row, but do not want to stress their awareness of it. He was carrying a checkerboard and a box before him and had a punchinello doll and something else under his arm.

'You've had company?' he inquired politely of Cincinnatus when the director had left them alone in the cell. 'Your mama visited you? That's fine, that's fine. And now I, poor, weak little M'sieur Pierre, have come to amuse you and amuse myself for a while. Just see how my punch looks at you. Say hello to uncle. Isn't he a scream? Sit up, there, chum. Look, I've brought you lots of entertaining things. Would you like a game of chess first? Or cards? Do you play anchors? Splendid game! Come, I'll teach you!'

13

He waited and waited, and now, at last, in the stillest hour of night, the sounds got busy once again. Alone in the dark, Cincinnatus smiled. I am quite willing to admit that they are also a deception but right now I believe in them so much that I infect them with truth.

They were still more firm and precise than the previous night; they no longer were hacking away blindly; how could one doubt their approaching, advancing movement? How modest they were! How intelligent! How mysteriously calculating and insistent! Was it an ordinary pick or some outlandish implement made of some useless substance alloyed with omnipotent human will – but whatever it was, he knew that someone, somehow, was cutting a passage.

The night was cold; the grey, greasy reflection of the moon, dividing itself into squares, fell on the inner wall of the window recess; the whole fortress seemed to be filled to the brim with thick darkness on the inside, and glazed by the moonlight on the outside, with black broken shadows that slithered down rocky slopes and silently tumbled into the moats; yes, the night was impassive and stony – but within it, in its deep, dark womb, undermining its might, something was hacking its way through that was quite foreign to the night's substance and order. Or is this all but obsolete romantic rot, Cincinnatus?

He picked up the submissive chair and brought it down hard, first on the floor, then several times on the wall, trying, at least by means of rhythm, to impart meaning to his pounding. And, in fact, the one who was tunnelling through the night first paused, as if trying to decide whether the answering blows were friendly or not, and suddenly renewed his labours with such a jubilantly animated sound that Cincinnatus was certain his response had been understood.

He was now satisfied that it was he to whom that someone was coming, that it was he whom that someone wanted to rescue, and, continuing to knock on the more sensitive sections of the stone, he evoked – in a different register and key, fuller, more complex, more enchanting – repetitions of the simple rhythms that he offered.

He was already thinking of how to set up an alphabet when he noticed that not the moon but a different, uninvited light was diluting the darkness, and he had barely noticed this when the sounds ceased. For quite a while afterwards there was a crumbling sound, but gradually this also grew silent, and it was hard to imagine that such a short time ago the stillness of night was being invaded by ardent, persistent activity, by a creature, sniffing, wheezing, with flattened muzzle, and again digging in frenzy, like a hound tunnelling his way to a badger.

Through his brittle drowsiness he saw Rodion entering; and it was already past noon when he awoke fully, and thought, as always, that the end was not yet today, and it could have been today, just as easily as it might be tomorrow, but tomorrow was still far away.

All day long he harked to the humming in his ears, kneading his hands, as though silently exchanging with his own self a welcoming grip; he walked around the table, where the letter lay, still unsent; or else he would imagine the glance of yesterday's guest, momentary, breathtaking, like a hiatus in this life; or he would listen in fancy to Emmie's rustling movements. Well, why not drink this mush of hope, this thick, sweet slop . . . my hopes are still alive . . . and I thought that at least now, at least here, where solitude is held in such high esteem, it might divide into two parts only, for you and for me, instead of multiplying as it did – noisy, manifold, absurd, so that I could not even come near you, and your terrible father nearly broke my legs with his cane . . . this is why I am writing – this is my last attempt to explain to you what is happening, Marthe . . . make an exceptional effort and understand, if only through a fog, if only with a corner of your brain, but understand what is happening, Marthe, understand that they are going to kill me – can it be so difficult – I do not ask lengthy widow's lamentations from you, or mourning lilies, but implore you, I need it so badly – now, today – just grow afraid like a child that they are going to do something terrible to me, a vile thing that makes you sick, and you scream so in the middle of the night that even when you already hear nurse approaching, with her 'hush, hush,' you still keep on screaming, that is how you must be afraid, Marthe, even though you love me little, you must still understand, even if only for an instant, and then you may forget again. How can I stir you? Oh, our life together was horrible, horrible, but I cannot stir you with that, I tried hard at first, but, you know, our tempos were different, and I immediately fell behind. Tell me, how many hands have palpated the pulp that has grown so generously around your hard, bitter little soul? Yes, like a ghost I return to your first betrayals and, howling, rattling my chains, walk through them. The kisses I spied. Your and his kisses, which most resembled some sort of feeding, intent, untidy, and noisy. Or when you, with eyes closed tight, devoured a spurting peach and then, having finished, but still swallowing, with your mouth still full, you cannibal, your glazed eyes wandered, your fingers were spread, your inflamed lips were all glossy, your chin trembled, all covered with drops of the cloudy juice, which trickled down on to your bared bosom, while the Priapus who had nourished you suddenly, with a convulsive oath, turned his bent back to me, who had entered the room at the wrong moment. 'All kinds of fruit are good for Marthe,' you would say with a certain sweet-slushy moistness in your throat, all gathering into one damp, sweet, accursed little fold – and if I return to all of this, it is to get it out of my system, to purge myself – and also so that you will know, so that you will know . . . What? Probably I am mistaking you for someone else, after all, when I think that you will understand me, as an insane man mistakes his visiting kin for galaxies, logarithms, low-haunched hyenas – but there are also madmen – and they are invulnerable – who take themselves for madmen – and here the circle closes. Marthe, in some such circle you and I revolve – oh, if only you could break away for an instant! – then you can go back to it, I promise you . . . I do not ask a great deal of you, only break away for an instant and understand that they are murdering me, that we are surrounded by dummies, and that you are a dummy yourself. I do not know why I was so tormented by your betrayals, rather I myself know why, but I do not know the words I must choose to make you understand why I was so tormented. Such words do not come in the small size that fits your everyday needs. And yet I shall try again: 'they are murdering me!' – all right, all together once more: 'they are murdering me!' – and again: 'murdering!' . . . I want to write this in such a way that you will cover your ears, your membranaceous, simian ears that you hide under strands of beautiful feminine hair – but I know them, I see them, I pinch them, the cold little things, I worry them with my fingers to somehow warm them, bring them to life, render them human, force them to hear me. Marthe I want you to obtain another interview, and, of course, come alone, come alone! So-called life is finished for me, before me there is only the polished block, and my jailers have managed to drive me to such a state that my handwriting – see – is like a drunken man's – but it does not matter, I shall have strength enough, Marthe, for such a talk with you as we have never yet had, that is why it is so necessary that you come again, and do not think that this letter is a forgery – it is I, Cincinnatus, who am writing, it is I, Cincinnatus, who am weeping; and who was, in fact, walking around the table, and then, when Rodion brought his dinner, said:

'This letter. This letter I shall ask you to . . . Here is the address . . .'

'You'd do better to learn to knit like everybody else,' grumbled Rodion, 'so you could knit me a cache-knee. Writer, indeed! You just saw your missus, didn't you?'

'I shall try to ask you anyway,' said Cincinnatus; 'are there, besides me and that rather obtrusive Pierre, any other prisoners here?'

Rodion flushed but remained silent.

'And the headsman hasn't arrived yet?' asked Cincinnatus.

Rodion was about to furiously slam the already screeching door, but, as the day before, there entered, morocco slippers squeaking stickily, striped jelly-body quivering, hands carrying a chess set, cards, a cup-and-ball game—

'My humblest respects to friend Rodion,' said M'sieur Pierre, in his reedy voice, and, without breaking stride, quivering, squeaking, he walked into the cell.

'I see,' he said, seating himself, 'that the dear fellow took a letter with him. Must have been the one that was lying here on the table yesterday, eh? To your spouse? No, no, a simple deduction, I don't read other people's letters, although it's true it was lying right in plain sight, while we were going at our game of anchors. How about some chess today?'

He spread out a checkerboard made of wool and with his plump hand, cocking the little finger, he set up the pieces, which were fashioned of kneaded bread, according to an old prisoner's recipe, so solidly, that a stone might envy them.

'I'm a bachelor myself, but of course I understand . . . Forward. I shall quickly . . . Good players do not take a long time to think. Forward. I caught just a glimpse of your spouse – a juicy little piece, no two ways about it – what a neck, that's what

I like . . . Hey, wait a minute, that was an oversight, allow me to take my move back. Here, this is better. I am a great aficionado of women, and the way they love me, the rascals, you simply wouldn't believe it. You were writing to your spouse there about her pretty eyes and lips. Recently, you know, I had . . . Why can't my pawn take it? Oh, I see. Clever, clever. All right, I retreat. Recently I had sexual intercourse with an extraordinarily healthy and splendid individual. What pleasure you experience, when a large brunette . . . What is this? That's a snide move on your part. You must warn your opponent, this won't do. Here, let me change my last move. Co. Yes, a gorgeous, passionate creature – and, you know, I'm no piker myself, I've got such a spring that – wow! Generally speaking, of the numerous earthly temptations, which, in jest, but really with the utmost seriousness, I intend to submit gradually for your consideration, the temptation of sex . . . No, wait a minute, I haven't decided yet if I want to move that piece there. Yes, I will. What do you mean, checkmate? Why checkmate? I can't go here; I can't go there; I can't go anywhere. Wait a minute, what was the position? No, before that. Ah, now that's a different story. A mere oversight. All right, I'll move here. Yes, a red rose between her teeth, black net stockings up to here, and not-a-stitch besides – that's really something, that's the supreme . . . and now, instead of the raptures of love, dank stone, rusty iron, and ahead – well, you know yourself what lies ahead. Now this I overlooked. And what if I move otherwise? Yes, this is better. The game is mine, anyway – you make one mistake after another. What if she *was* unfaithful to you – didn't you also hold her in your embraces? When people ask me for advice I always tell them, "Gentlemen, be inventive. There is nothing more pleasant, for example, than to surround oneself with mirrors and watch the good work going on there – wonderful!" Hey! Now this is far from wonderful. Word of honour, I thought I had moved to this square, not to that. So therefore you were unable . . . Back, please. Simultaneously I like to smoke a cigar and talk of insignificant matters, and I like her to talk too – there's nothing to be done, I have a certain streak of perversion in me . . . Yes, how grievous, how frightening and hurtful to say farewell to all this – and to think that others, who are just as young and sappy, will continue to work and work . . . ah! I don't know about you, but when it comes to caresses I love what we French wrestlers call "*macarons*": you give her a nice slap on the neck, and, the firmer the meat . . . First of all, I can take your knight, secondly, I can simply move my king away; all right – there. No, stop, stop, I'd like to think for a minute after all. What was your last move? Put that piece back and let me think. Nonsense, there's no checkmate here. You, it seems to me – if you do not mind my saying so – are cheating: this piece stood here, or maybe here, but not there, I am absolutely certain. Come, put it back, put it back . . .'

As though accidentally, he knocked over several men, and, unable to restrain himself, with a groan, he mixed up the remainder. Cincinnatus sat leaning on one elbow; he was pensively picking at a knight which, in the neck region, seemed not loath to return to the mealy state whence it had sprung.

'Let's start some other game, you don't know how to play chess,' fussily cried M'sieur Pierre and opened up a vari-coloured board for 'goose'. He cast the dice, and immediately climbed from 3 to 27 –although then he had to come back down while Cincinnatus zoomed from 22 to 46. The game dragged on for a long time. M'sieur Pierre would grow purple, stamp his feet, fume, crawl under the table after the dice and emerge holding them in his palm and swearing that that was exactly the way they had been lying on the floor.

'Why do you smell like that?' asked Cincinnatus with a sigh. M'sieur Pierre's plump face twisted into a forced smile.

'It runs in the family,' he explained with dignity. 'Feet sweat a little. I've tried alums, but nothing works. I must say that, although I have been afflicted with this since childhood, and although any suffering is customarily regarded with respect, no one has ever yet been so tactless . . .'

'I can't breathe,' said Cincinnatus.

14

The sounds were still closer, and now they hurried so that it would have been a sin to distract them by tapping out questions. And they continued later than the night before, and Cincinnatus lay prone on the flagstones, spread-eagled as one who has been felled by a sunstroke, and indulging the mummery of the senses, clearly visualized through the tympanum the secret passage, lengthening with every scrape, and sensed – as if thus the dark.

tight pain in his chest were relieved – how the stones were being loosened, and he had already begun guessing, as he looked at the wall, where it would crack and burst open with a crash.

Crackling and rustling noises were still audible when Rodion came in. Behind him, in ballet shoes on her bare feet and a tartan dress, Emmie darted in and, as she had done once before, hid under the table, crouching there on her haunches, so that her flaxen hair, curling at the tips, covered her face and her knees, and even her ankles. Barely had Rodion gone when she sprang up and went straight to Cincinnatus, who was sitting on the cot, and, overturning him, began scrambling all over him. Her cold fingers and hot elbows dug into him, she bared her teeth, a fragment of green leaf had stuck to her front teeth.

'Sit still,' said Cincinnatus, 'I'm exhausted – I didn't weep a slink all night – sit still and tell me . . .'

Fidgeting, Emmie buried her forehead in his chest; her curls tumbling and hanging to one side, revealed the bare upper part of her back, which had a hollow that moved with her shoulder blades and was evenly covered with a blonde down, which looked as though it had been combed in a symmetrical pattern.

Cincinnatus stroked her warm head, trying to raise it. She snatched at his fingers and began pressing them to her quick lips.

'What a snuggling pet you are,' said Cincinnatus drowsily. 'That will do, enough now. Tell me . . .'

But she was seized by an outburst of childish boisterousness. The muscular child rolled Cincinnatus about like a puppy. 'Stop it!' cried Cincinnatus. 'Aren't you ashamed of yourself?'

'Tomorrow,' she said suddenly, squeezing him and gazing at him between the eyes.

'Tomorrow I'll die?' asked Cincinnatus.

'No, I'll rescue you,' Emmie said pensively (she was seated astride him).

'That's very nice indeed,' said Cincinnatus. 'Saviours from all sides! This ought to have happened sooner – I'm nearly insane. Please get off, you are heavy and hot.'

'We'll run away and you'll marry me.'

'Maybe when you are a little older; only I already have one wife.'

'A fat, old one,' said Emmie.

She hopped off the cot and ran around the room, as ballerinas run, at a fast striding pace, shaking her hair, and then she leaped, as though flying, and finally pirouetted in one spot, flinging out a multitude of arms.

'School will be starting again soon,' she said, settling the next moment on Cincinnatus's lap; suddenly, forgetting everything else in the world, she became engrossed in a new occupation – she began picking at a black lengthwise scab on her shiny shin; the scab was already half off, and one could see the tender pink scar.

Through slitted eyes, Cincinnatus gazed at her inclined profile, rimmed with a bloom of sunlight, and he felt suffused with drowsiness.

'Ah, Emmie, remember, remember what you have promised. Tomorrow! Tell me, how will you do it?'

'Give me your ear,' said Emmie.

Putting one arm around his neck, she made a hot, moist and utterly unintelligible noise in his ear. 'I can't hear anything,' said Cincinnatus.

Impatiently she brushed the hair back from her face and again nestled up to him.

'Bu . . . bu . . . bu,' she bumbled and buzzed – and then jumped away, and flew up – and now was resting on the slightly swaying trapeze, her extended toes joined in a sharp wedge.

'Still, I'm counting on this very much,' said Cincinnatus through mounting sleepiness; slowly he pressed his wet, singing ear to the pillow.

As he was falling asleep he could feel her climbing over him, and then it seemed dimly to him that she or someone else was endlessly folding some shiny fabric, taking it by the corners and folding, and stroking it with the palm, and folding it again – and for a moment he came to from Emmie's squeal as Rodion dragged her out of the cell.

Then he thought he heard the precious sounds behind the wall start cautiously again . . . how risky! After all, it was broad daylight . . . but they could not restrain themselves, and ever so quietly pushed closer and closer to him, while he, fearing lest the guards hear, began walking about, stamping his feet, coughing, humming, and when, with a violently beating heart, he sat down at the table, the sounds had already ceased.

Then, toward evening, as was now customary, M'sieur Pierre arrived, in a brocade skullcap; casually, being quite at home, he lay down on Cincinnatus's cot and, lighting a long meerschaum pipe with a carved houri, propped himself up on an elbow in a cloud of luxurious smoke. Cincinnatus sat at the table, munching the last of his supper, fishing the prunes out of their brown juice.

'I put some foot powder on them today,' M'sieur Pierre said briskly. 'So no complaints or comments, please. Let us continue our conversation of yesterday. We were talking of pleasures.

'The pleasure of love,' said M'sieur Pierre, 'is achieved by means of the most beautiful and healthful of all known physical exercises. I said "achieved" but perhaps "extracted" would be even more apt, inasmuch as we are dealing precisely with a systematic and persistent extraction of pleasure buried in the very bowels of the belaboured creature. During leisure hours the labourer of love immediately strikes the observer with the falcon-like expression of his eyes, his cheerful disposition, and his fresh complexion. Observe also my gliding gait. Thus we have before us a certain phenomenon, which we may call by the general term "love" or "erotic pleasure".'

At this point, walking on tiptoe and indicating by gestures that they should not pay him any notice, the director came in and sat down on a stool that he himself had brought.

M'sieur Pierre turned on him a gaze beaming with benevolence.

'Go on, go on,' whispered Rodrig Ivanovich, 'I've come to listen – *pardon*, just one moment – I'll just put it so I can lean against the wall. *Voilà*. I'm worn out, though. And you?'

'That's because you are not used to it,' said M'sieur Pierre. 'Allow me, then, to continue. We were discussing, Rodrig Ivanovich, the pleasures of life, and had just examined Eros in a general way.'

'I see,' said the director.

'I made the following points – excuse me, dear colleague, for repeating myself, but I would like to make it interesting for Rodrig Ivanovich also. I made the point, Rodrig Ivanovich, that a man condemned to die finds it hardest of all to forget woman, woman's delicious body.'

'And the poetry of moonlit nights,' added Rodrig Ivanovich, casting a stern glance at Cincinnatus.

'No, please don't interfere with my development of the subject; if you have something to add, you may do so afterwards. All right – let me continue. In addition to the pleasures of love there are a whole number of others, and to them we shall now pass on. More than once, probably, you have felt your chest expand on a wonderful spring day, when the buds swell and feathered songsters enliven the groves, clad in their first sticky leafage. The first modest flowers peep coquettishly out of the grass, as if they would entice the passionate lover of nature, as they whisper timidly: "Oh, don't, don't pick us, our life is short." The chest expands and breathes deep on such a day, when the birdies sing, and the first modest leaves appear on the first trees. Everything rejoices, everything is jubilant.'

'A masterful description of April,' said the director, giving his jowls a shake.

'I think that everyone has experienced this,' continued M'sieur Pierre, 'and now, when any day now we shall all be ascending the scaffold, the unforgettable memory of such a spring day makes one cry out: "O come back, come back; let me live you over once again." '

' "Live you over once again",' repeated M'sieur Pierre, rather frankly consulting a scroll-like crib, all covered with fine writing.

'Next,' said M'sieur Pierre, 'we pass on to pleasures of a spiritual order. Remember the times when, in a fabulous picture gallery, or museum, you would suddenly stop and be unable to take your eyes off some piquant torso – made, alas, of bronze or marble. This we can call the pleasure of art; it occupies an important place in life.'

'I'll say it does,' said Rodrig Ivanovich in a nasal voice, and looked at Cincinnatus.

'Gastronomic pleasures,' continued M'sieur Pierre. 'See the best varieties of fruit hanging from tree branches; see the butcher and his helpers dragging a pig, squealing as if it were being slaughtered; see, on a pretty plate, a substantial chunk of white lard; see the table wine and cherry brandy; see the fish – I don't know about the rest of you, but I am a great fancier of bream.'

'I approve,' Rodrig Ivanovich said resonantly.

'This splendid feast must be forsaken. Many other things must be forsaken as well: festive music, favourite knick-knacks, such as a camera or a pipe; friendly talks; the bliss of relieving oneself, which some hold to be on a par with the pleasure of love; sleep after dinner; smoking . . . What else? Favourite knick-knacks . . . Yes, we already had that' (again the crib notes appeared) 'pleasure . . . I've said that too. Well, various other trifles . . .'

'May I add something,' the director asked ingratiatingly, but M'sieur Pierre shook his head:

'No, that's quite enough. I think I have unfolded before the mental eye of my dear colleague such vistas of sensual realms . . .'

'I only wanted to say something on the subject of edibles,' the director remarked in a low voice. 'I think certain details could be mentioned here. For instance, *en fait de potage* . . . All right, all right, I shan't say a word,' he concluded in alarm as he met the gaze of M'sieur Pierre.

'Well,' M'sieur Pierre addressed Cincinnatus, 'what will you say to all this?'

'What am I supposed to say?' said Cincinnatus. 'Dreary, obtrusive nonsense.'

'He's incorrigible,'exclaimed Rodrig Ivanovich.

'It's just a pose on his part,' said M'sieur Pierre with an ominous porcelain smile. 'Believe me, he has feeling enough for the full beauty of the phenomena I have described.'

'. . . But fails to understand certain things,' Rodrig Ivanovich interjected smoothly. 'He does not understand that if he were now honestly to admit the error of his ways, honestly admit that he is fond of the same things as you and I – for example, turtle soup for the first course – they say it's sensationally good – that is, I only want to observe that if he were honestly to admit and repent – yes, repent – that is my point – then he could have some remote – I do not want to say hope, but nevertheless . . .'

'I left out the part about gymnastics,' muttered M'sieur Pierre checking his little scroll. 'What a pity!'

'No, no, you spoke very well, very well,' sighed Rodrig Ivanovich. 'Couldn't be better. You roused in me certain desires that had lain dormant for decades. Will you stay a while? Or are you coming with me?'

'With you. He's a regular sourpuss today. Doesn't even look at you. You offer him kingdoms, and he sulks. And I ask so little – one word, a nod. Well, nothing to be done. Let's away, Rodrigo.'

Soon after their departure the light went out and Cincinnatus transferred himself to his cot in darkness (how nasty to find somebody else's ashes, but no other place to lie down) and, liberating his melancholy in a crackling of cartileges and vertebrae, he stretched, and drew in a breath, and held it a quarter of a minute and more. Maybe it was just stonemasons. Making repairs. An aural deception: perhaps it is all going on far, far away (he exhaled). He lay on his back, wriggling his toes, which protruded from beneath the blanket and turning his face now toward impossible salvation, now toward inevitable execution. The light flashed on again.

Scratching at the red-haired chest under his shirt, Rodion

arrived to fetch the stool. Seeing the object he sought, he promptly sat down on it and with a loud grunt, kneaded his lowered face with his enormous palm, and apparently got ready to have a nap.

'He still has not arrived?' asked Cincinnatus.

Rodion immediately got up and left with the stool.

Click. Black.

Perhaps because a certain integral period of time – a fortnight – had elapsed since the trial, perhaps because the nearing of the friendly sounds promised him a change of fortune, Cincinnatus spent this night in a mental review of the hours he had passed in the fortress. Involuntarily yielding to the temptation of logical development, involuntarily (be careful, Cincinnatus!) forging into a chain all the things that were quite harmless as long as they remained unlinked, he inspired the meaningless with meaning, and the lifeless with life. With the stone darkness for background he now permitted the spotlighted figures of all his usual visitors to appear – it was the very first time that his imagination was so condescending toward them. There was the tiresome little co-prisoner, with his shiny face, resembling the wax apple which Cincinnatus's waggish brother-in-law had brought the other day; there was the fidgety, lean lawyer, disengaging his shirt cuffs from the sleeves of his frock coat; there was the sombre librarian, and, in smooth black toupee, corpulent Rodrig Ivanovich, and Emmie, and Marthe's entire family, and Rodion, and others, vague guards and soldiers – and by evoking them – not believing in them, perhaps, but still evoking them – Cincinnatus allowed them the right to exist, supported them, nourished them with himself. Added to all this was the possibility that, at any moment, the exciting knocks might resume, a possibility that had the effect of an intoxicating anticipation of music – so that Cincinnatus was in a strange, tremulous, dangerous state – and the distant clock struck with a kind of mounting exultation – and now, emerging from the darkness, the lighted figures joined hands and formed a ring – and, slightly swaying to one side, lurching, lagging, they began a circling movement, which at first was stiff and dragging, but then gradually became more even, free and rapid, and now they were whirling in earnest, and the monstrous shadow of their shoulders and heads passed and repassed ever more quickly across the stone vaults, and the inevitable joker who, when whirling in a reel, kicks his legs high, to amuse his more prim companions, cast on the walls the huge black zigzags of his hideous prance.

15

The morning passed quietly, but at about five in the afternoon there started a noise of shattering force: whoever it was he worked furiously and clattered shamelessly; actually however, he had not come much nearer since yesterday.

Suddenly an extraordinary thing happened: some inner obstruction collapsed, and now the noises sounded with such vivid intensity (having in an instant made the transition from background to foreground, right up to the footlights) that their proximity was obvious: they were right there, directly behind the wall, which was melting like ice, and would break through it any instant now.

And then the prisoner decided that it was time to act. With terrible haste, trembling, but still trying to keep control over himself, he got out and put on the rubber shoes, the linen trousers and the jacket he had been wearing when arrested; he found a handkerchief, two handkerchiefs, three handkerchiefs (a fleeting vision of sheets tied together); just in case, he put in his pocket a chance piece of string with a wooden handle for carrying packages still attached (it wouldn't go in completely – the end remained hanging out); he rushed to the bed, intending to fluff up the pillow and cover it with the blanket in such a way as to create the semblance of a sleeping man; he did not do this, but lunged instead to the table with the intention of taking along what he had written; but here also he changed direction at the halfway point, for the triumphant, mad, pounding noises were confusing his thoughts . . . He was standing straight as an arrow, his hands at his seams, when, in perfect fulfilment of his dreams, the yellow wall cracked about a yard above the floor in a lightninglike pattern, immediately bulged from the pressure within, and suddenly burst open with a great crash.

Out of the black hole, in a cloud of debris, pick in hand, all dusted with white, twisting and threshing like a fat fish among the dust, and rippling with laughter, climbed M'sieur Pierre, and right behind him, but in crab fashion, fat backside first, revealing a tear from which a tuft of white cotton protruded, coatless, and also covered with all kinds of rubble, also splitting with mirth, came Rodrig Ivanovich. Having tumbled out of the hole, they both sat down on the floor and now shook with unrestrained laughter, with all the transitions from guffaw to chuckle and back again, with piteous squeals in the intervals between outbursts, all the while nudging each other, falling over each other . . .

'It's us, it's us, it's us,' M'sieur Pierre finally managed with an effort, turning his chalk-white face to Cincinnatus, while his little yellow wig rose with a comic whistle and settled again.

'It's us,' said Rodrig Ivanovich in an unaccustomed falsetto and once again began to guffaw, flinging up his soft legs, clad in an *Auguste*'s grotesque spats.

'Ooph!' said M'sieur Pierre, who had suddenly quieted down; he got up off the floor and, striking one palm against the other, looked back at the hole: 'Quite a little job we've done, Rodrig Ivanovich! Come, get up, my fine friend, that's enough. What a job! Oh well, now we can make use of this splendid tunnel . . . Allow me to invite you, dear neighbour, to come and have a glass of tea with me.'

'If you so much as touch me . . .' murmured Cincinnatus and, as on one side, white, sweaty M'sieur Pierre stood ready to embrace him and shove him in, and, on the other, stood Rodrig Ivanovich, also with open arms, bare-shouldered, and with dickey loose and awry, both of them gathering momentum before piling on him, Cincinnatus took the only possible direction, namely the one being indicated to him. M'sieur Pierre was nudging him lightly from behind, helping him crawl into the opening. 'Join us,' he said to Rodrig Ivanovich, but the latter declined, pleading disarray.

Flattened out and with eyes shut tight, Cincinnatus crawled on all fours, M'sieur Pierre crawled behind, and the pitch darkness, full of crumbling and crackling, squeezed Cincinnatus from all sides, pressed on his spine, prickled his palms and his knees; several times Cincinnatus found himself in a cul-de-sac, and then M'sieur Pierre would tug at his calves, making him back out of the dead end, and every instant a corner, a protrusion, he knew not what, would brush painfully against his head, and all in all he was overcome by such terrible, inmitigated dejection that, had there not been a wheezing, butting companion behind, he would have lain down and died then and there. At last, however, after they had been moving for a long time through the narrow, coal-black darkness (in one place, off to the side, a red lantern imparted a dull lustre to the blackness), after the closeness, the blindness, and the stuffiness, a pale luminosity expanded in the distance: there was a bend there, and finally came the exit; awkwardly and meekly Cincinnatus fell out on to the stone floor, into M'sieur Pierre's sun-drenched cell.

'Welcome,' said his host, climbing out after him; he promptly produced a clothesbrush and began skilfully brushing off blinking Cincinnatus, considerately restraining and softening the strokes in any area that might be sensitive. As he did so he bent over, and, as if enmeshing him in something, kept walking around Cincinnatus, who stood perfectly still, astounded by a certain extraordinarily simple thought; astounded, rather, not by the thought but by the fact that it had not come to him sooner.

'With your permission I'll change,' spoke M'sieur Pierre and pulled off his dusty sweater; for an instant, with sham casualness, he flexed his arm, casting a sidelong glance at his turquoise-and-white biceps and exuding his characteristic stench. Around his left nipple there was a imaginative tattoo – two green leaves – so that the nipple itself seemed to be a rosebud (made of marchpane and candied angelica). 'Have a seat, please,' he said, putting on a robe with bright arabesques. 'It's all I have, but it's mine. My quarters, as you see, are almost exactly like yours. Only I keep them clean and decorate them . . . I decorate them as best I can.' (He gaped slightly, as if from uncontrollable excitement.)

I decorate. The wall calendar with the water colour of the fortress at sunset exhibited a crimson numeral. A crazy-quilt blanket covered the cot. Above it, attached by thumbtacks, hung salacious photographs and a formal picture of M'sieur Pierre; a gofered paper fan stuck its crimped pleats from behind the edge of the frame. On the table lay an alligator-skin album, the face of a gold travelling clock glistened, and half a dozen velvety pansies looked out in various directions over the burnished rim of a porcelain mug bearing a German landscape. In a corner of the cell stood a large case containing possibly some musical instrument.

'I am exceedingly happy to see you here in my place,' M'sieur Pierre was saying as he promenaded back and forth, passing each time through an oblique ray of sunlight in which plaster dust still danced. 'I feel that in the past week we have become such good friends, have come together so well, so warmly, as seldom happens. I see you are interested to know what is inside. Just let me [he caught his breath], let me finish and then I shall show you . . .'

'Our friendship,' continued M'sieur Pierre, pacing and gasping slightly, 'has flowered in the hothouse-like atmosphere of a prison, where it was nourished by the same alarms and the same hopes. I think I know you better now than anyone else does in the whole world, and certainly more intimately than your wife knew you. Therefore I find it particularly painful when you give in to a feeling of spite or are inconsiderate of people . . . Just now, for instance, when we came to you so joyously, you again insulted Rodrig Ivanovich with your assumed indifference to the surprise in which he had taken part so kindly, so energetically – and do not forget he is no longer young, and has many troubles of his own. No, I would rather not talk about this now . . . I only want to establish that not the slightest shade of feeling on your part escapes me, and therefore I personally feel that the well-known accusation is not quite fair . . . To me you are transparent as – excuse the sophisticated simile – a blushing bride is transparent to the gaze of an experienced bridegroom. I don't know, there's something wrong with my breathing – excuse me, it will pass in a moment. But, if I have made such a close study of you and – why keep it a secret? – have grown fond, very fond of you, then you also must needs have grown to know me, grown accustomed to me – more than that, grown attached to me, as I to you. To achieve such a friendship – that was my first task, and it seems I have performed it successfully. Successfully. Now we are going to have tea. I can't understand why they don't bring it.'

Clutching at his chest, he sat down at the table across from Cincinnatus but instantly sprang up again: from under his pillow he produced a morocco purse, from the purse a chamois sheath, and from the sheath a key; he went to the large case that was standing in the corner.

'I see that you are amazed by my neatness,' he said as he carefully inclined the propped up case, which proved to be heavy and cumbersome. 'But you see, neatness adorns the life of a lone bachelor, who thus proves to himself . . .'

He opened the case. There, upon black velvet, lay a broad, shiny axe.

'. . . proves to himself that he does have a little nest . . . A little nest,' M'sieur Pierre went on, locking the case again, leaning it against the wall, and himself leaning, 'a little nest that he has deserved, built, filled with his warmth. . . . In general, there is an important philosophical theme here, but from certain indications it seems to me that you, as I, are not in the wood for themes just now. Do you know what? Here is my advice: we'll have our cup of tea later; right now, though, go back to your place and lie down for a while – yes, go. We are both young – you must not remain here any longer. Tomorrow they will explain to you, but now please go. I too am excited, I too am not in complete control of myself, you must understand this . . .'

Cincinnatus was quietly fiddling with the locked door.

'No, no – you use our tunnel. We didn't put in all this work for nothing. Crawl in, crawl in. I drape the hole, or else it would not look well. Go . . .'

'By myself,' said Cincinnatus.

He climbed into the black opening, and hurting his knees anew, began to crawl on all fours, deeper and deeper into the narrow darkness. M'sieur Pierre yelled something after him about tea and then apparently drew the curtain, for Cincinnatus immediately felt cut off from the bright cell where he had just been.

Breathing the rough air with difficulty, running into sharp projections – and expecting, without especial fear, that the tunnel would collapse – Cincinnatus groped blindly through the winding passage, found himself in stone cul-de-sacs and, like some patient retreating animal, moved backwards; then, feeling out the tunnel's continuation, crawled on. He was impatient to lie down on something soft, even if it were only his cot, to pull the covers up over his head, and not think about anything. This return journey dragged out so that, skinning his shoulders, he began to hurry as much as the constant apprehension of a dead end would permit him. The closeness made him groggy, and he was just deciding to stop, to lie prone, to imagine that he was in bed and with this to go to sleep, when abruptly the surface along which he was crawling began to slope, and he glimpsed the gleam of a reddish chink ahead and caught a whiff of dampness and mould just as though he had passed from the bowels of the fortress wall into a natural cave, and from the low ceiling, muffled up bats, hanging like wrinkled fruit, awaited their cue, each holding on by a claw, head down; the chink opened in a blaze of light, and there was a breath of fresh evening air, and Cincinnatus crawled from a crack in the rock to freedom.

He found himself on one of the many turfy taluses which, like dark-green waves, lapped up sharply at various levels among the rocks and ramparts of the terraced fortress. At first he was so dizzy from liberty, altitude and space that he clutched at the damp turf and hardly noticed anything besides the loud evening cries of the swallows as they snipped the coloured air with their black scissors; the glow of sunset had invaded half the sky; and, right behind his head, there swept up with awful swiftness the blind stone steeps of the fortress out of which he had oozed like a drop of water; while at his feet there were fantastic precipices and clover-scented mists.

He regained his breath and got used to the brightness dazzling him, to the trembling of his body, to the impact of the freedom that reverberated afar and welled up within him. He glued his back to the rock and contemplated the hazy landscape. Far below, where twilight had already settled, he could barely discern, through wisps of mist, the ornate hump of the bridge. While yonder, on the other side, the blurred blue city, its windows like embers, was either still borrowing the sunset's blaze or else perhaps had lit up at its own expense; he could make out the gradual threading of the bright beads of street lights as they were being lit along Steep Avenue – and there was an exceptionally distinct, delicate arch at its upper end. Beyond the city everything shimmered dimly, merged, and dissolved; but, above the invisible Gardens, in the rosy depths of the sky, stood a chain of translucent and fiery cloudlets, and there stretched a long violet bank with burning rents along its lower edge – and while Cincinnatus gazed, yonder, yonder on oak-covered hill flashed with Venetian Green and slowly sank into shadow.

Intoxicated, weak, slipping on the coarse turf, and catching his balance, he set off downward, and immediately, from behind a projection of the rampart, where a black bramble bush rustled its warning. Emmie darted out to him, her face and legs painted pink by the sunset, and, firmly grasping him by the hand, dragged him after her. All her movements betrayed excitement, rapturous haste. 'Where are we going? Down?' Cincinnatus inquired haltingly, laughing from impatience. She quickly led him along the fortress wall. A small green door opened in the wall. Stairs, leading down, passed imperceptibly underfoot. Again a door creaked; beyond it was a darkish passage in which stood trunks, a wardrobe, and a ladder resting against the wall, and there was a smell of kerosene; it was now apparent that they had entered the director's apartment by the back way for, now no longer clutching his fingers quite so tightly, already absent-mindedly releasing them. Emmie led him into a dining room where they were all sitting and drinking tea at a lighted oval table. Rodrig Ivanovich's napkin amply covered his chest; his wife – thin, freckled, with white eyelashes – was passing the pretzels to M'sieur Pierre, who had dressed up in a Russian shirt embroidered with cocks; balls of coloured wool and glassy knitting needles lay in a basket by the samovar. A sharp-nosed little old crone in a mobcap and black shawl was hunched at one end of the table.

When he saw Cincinnatus the director gaped, and something drooled from one corner of his mouth.

'Pfui, you naughty child!' said the director's wife to Emmie with a slight German accent.

M'sieur Pierre, who was stirring his tea, demurely lowered his eyes.

'What's the meaning of this escapade?' Rodrig Ivanovich said through the trickling melon juice. 'To say nothing of the fact that this is against all regulations!'

'Let them be,' said M'sieur Pierre without raising his eyes. 'After all, they are both children.'

'It's the end of her vacation, so she wants to play a prank,' put in the director's wife.

Emmie sat down at the table, deliberately making her chair scrape, fidgeting and wetting her lips and, having dismissed Cincinnatus for ever, began spreading sugar (which immediately assumed an orange hue) on her shaggy slice of melon; thereupon she bit into it busily, holding it by the ends, which reached her ears, and brushing her neighbour with her elbow. Her neighbour continued to sip his tea, holding the spoon protruding from it between second and third fingers, but inconspicuously reached under the table with his left hand. 'Eek!' cried Emmie as she gave a ticklish start, without, however, taking her mouth from the melon.

'Sit down over there for the time being,' said the director, with his fruit knife indicating to Cincinnatus a green armchair with an antimacassar that stood aloof in the damask dusk near the folds of the window draperies. 'When we finish I'll take you back. I said sit down. What's the matter with you? What's wrong with him? What a slow-witted fellow!'

M'sieur Pierre leaned over to Rodrig Ivanovich and, blushing slightly, imparted to him something.

The latter's larynx emitted a regular thunderclap:

'Well, congratulations, congratulations,' he said, restraining with difficulty the gusts of his voice. 'This is good news! – It's high time you informed him – We all . . .' He glanced at Cincinnatus and was about to launch on a formal—

'No, not yet, my friend, don't embarrass me,' murmured M'sieur Pierre, touching his sleeve.

'In any case, you won't refuse another tumbler of tea,' said

Rodrig Ivanovich playfully, and then, after a moment of reflection and some champing, he addressed Cincinnatus.

'Hey, you there. You can look at the album meanwhile. Child, give him the album. For her' (gesture with the knife) 'return to school our dear guest has made her – has made her a – Pardon me, Pyotr Petrovich, I've forgotten what you called it.'

'A photohoroscope,' M'sieur Pierre replied modestly.

'Shall I leave the lemon in?' asked the director's wife.

The hanging kerosene lamp, whose light did not reach the back of the dining room (where only the gleam of a pendulum flashed as it hacked off the solid seconds), flooded the cozily spread table with a familial light, which graded into the chinking sounds of the tea ritual.

16

Let us be calm. The spider had sucked dry a small downy moth with marbled forewings, and three houseflies, but was still hungry and kept glancing at the door. Let us be calm. Cincinnatus was a mass of scrapes and bruises. Be calm; nothing had happened. Last night, when they brought him back to the cell, two employees were just finishing plastering the place where lately the hole had gaped. That place was now marked only by swirls of paint a bit rounder and thicker than elsewhere, and he had a stifling sensation whenever he glanced at the wall, which again was blind, deaf and impenetrable.

Another vestige of the previous day was the alligator album with its massive dark silver monogram that he had taken along in a fit of meek abstraction: that singular photohoroscope put together by the resourceful M'sieur Pierre, that is, a series of photographs depicting the natural progression of a given person's entire life. How was this done? Thus: extensively retouched snapshots of Emmie's present face were supplemented by shots of other people – for the sake of costume, furniture and surroundings – so as to create the entire décor and stage properties of her future life. Consecutively stuck into the polygonal little windows of the solid, gilt-edged cardboard, and supplied with finely inscribed dates, these sharp and, at first sight, genuine photographs pictured Emmie first as she was at present; then at fourteen, an attaché case in her hand; then at sixteen, in tights and tutu, with gaseous wings growing from her back, seated relaxed on a table, and lifting a goblet of wine amid rakes; then, at eighteen, in *femme-fatale* weeds, at a railing above a waterfall; then . . . oh, in many more aspects and poses, even to the very last, horizontal.

By means of retouching and other photographic tricks, what appeared to be progressive changes in Emmie's face had been achieved (incidentally, the trickster had made use of her mother's photographs); but one had only to look closer and it became repulsively obvious how trite was this parody of the work of time. The Emmie who was leaving by the stage door, in furs, with flowers pressed to her shoulder, had limbs that had never danced; while in the next shot, showing her already in her bridal veil, the groom at her side was tall and slender, but had the round little face of M'sieur Pierre. At thirty she already had what was supposed to look like wrinkles, drawn in without meaning, without life, without knowledge of their true significance, but conveying something very bizarre to the expert, as a chance stirring of a tree's branches may coincide with a sign gesture comprehensible to a deaf-mute. And at forty Emmie was dying – and here allow me to congratulate you on an inverse error: her face in death could never pass for the face of death!

Rodion bore this album away, mumbling that the young lady was just leaving, and when he next appeared he deemed it necessary to announce that the young lady had left:

(Sighing) 'Gone, gone . . .' (To the spider) 'Enough, you've had enough . . .' (Showing his palm) 'I don't have anything for you.' (To Cincinnatus again) 'It'll be dull, so dull without our little daughter . . . how she flitted about, what music she made, our spoiled darling, our golden flower.' (Pause. Then in a different tone) 'What's the matter, good sir, why don't you ask those catchy questions any more? Well? So, so,' Rodion convincingly replied to himself and withdrew with dignity.

After dinner, quite formally, no longer in prison garb but in a velvet jacket, an arty bow tie and new, high-heeled, insinuatingly squeaking boots with glossy legs (making him somehow resemble an operatic woodman), M'sieur Pierre came in, and, behind him, respectfully yielding to him first place in perambulation, speech, everything, came Rodrig Ivanovich and the lawyer with his briefcase. The three of them settled themselves at the table in wicker chairs (brought from the waiting room), while Cincinnatus walked about the cell, in single combat with shameful fear; but presently he also sat down.

Somewhat clumsily (with a clumsiness that was, however, practised and familiar) fussing with the briefcase, yanking open its black cheek, holding it partly on his knee, partly leaning it against the table – it would slip off one point, then off the other – the lawyer produced a large writing pad and locked or rather buttoned up the briefcase, which yielded too readily and therefore at first muffed the fastening nip; he was just placing it on the table, but changed his mind and, taking it by the collar, lowered it to the floor, leaning it against a leg of his chair where it assumed the drooping position of a drunk; he then produced from his lapel an enamelled pencil, on the back swing opened the pad and, paying attention to no one and nothing, began covering the detachable pages with even writing; however, this very inattention made all the more obvious the connection between the rapid movement of his pencil and the conference for which everyone had gathered here.

Rodrig Ivanovich was sitting in the easy chair, leaning back slightly, making the chair creak by the pressure of his solid back, with one purplish paw resting on the arm of his chair and the other thrust in the bosom of his frock coat; every once in a while he would jerk his flabby cheeks and his chin, powdered like a Turkish delight, as if freeing them from some viscous and absorbing element.

M'sieur Pierre, seated in the centre, poured himself water from a decanter, then ever so carefully placed his hands on the table, fingers interlaced (an artificial aquamarine flashing on his little finger) and, lowering his long eyelashes for ten seconds or so, pondered reverently how he would begin his speech.

'Kind gentlemen,' M'sieur Pierre finally said in a high voice, without raising eyes, 'first of all and before anything else, allow me to outline by means of a few deft strokes what has already been accomplished by me.'

'Proceed, we beg you,' said the director resonantly, making his chair emit a stern creak.

'You gentlemen are of course aware of the reasons for the amusing mystification that is required by the tradition of our craft. After all, how would it be if I had announced myself right at the start, and offered my friendship to Cincinnatus C.? This, gentlemen, would have certainly resulted in repelling him, frightening him, antagonizing him – in short, I would have committed a fatal blunder.'

The speaker took a sip from his glass and carefully set it aside.

He went on, batting his eyelashes: 'I need not explain how

precious to the success of our common undertaking is that atmosphere of warm camaraderie which, with the help of patience and kindness, is gradually created between the sentenced and the executor of the sentence. It is difficult or even impossible to recall without a shudder the barbarity of long-bygone days, when these two, not knowing each other at all, strangers to each other, but bound together by implacable law, met face to face only at the last instant before the sacrament itself. This has all been changed just as the ancient, barbaric wedding ceremony, more closely resembling a human sacrifice – when the submissive virgin was hurled by her parents into the tent of a stranger – has changed with the passing of time.'

(Cincinnatus found in his pocket a piece of tinfoil chocolate wrapper and began kneading it.)

'And so, gentlemen, in order to establish the friendliest possible relations with the condemned, I moved into a gloomy cell like his, in the guise of a prisoner like him, if not more so. My innocent deception could not but succeed and therefore it would be strange for me to feel any remorse; but I do not want the cup of our friendship to be poisoned by the slightest drop of bitterness. In spite of the fact that there are witnesses present, and that I know myself to be absolutely in the right, I ask' (he stretched his hand out to Cincinnatus) 'your forgiveness.'

'Yes, that's real tact for you,' said the director in a low voice, and his inflamed froglike eyes grew damp; he produced a folded handkerchief and was about to dab at his palpitating eyelid, but thought better of it, and instead fixed a severe, expectant gaze on Cincinnatus. The lawyer also glanced, but only in passing, as he silently moved his lips, which had begun to look like his handwriting, that is, without breaking his connection with the line, which had separated from the paper but was ready to resume its course upon it instantly.

'Your hand!' roared the director, and took such a whack at the table that he hurt his thumb.

'No, don't force him if he does not want to,' M'sieur Pierre said gently. 'After all, it is only a formality. Let us continue.'

'Oh, righteous one,' trilled Rodrig Ivanovich, bestowing upon M'sieur Pierre a glance as moist as a kiss.

'Let us continue,' said M'sieur Pierre. 'During this time I have succeeded in establishing a close friendship with my neighbour. We passed . . .'

Cincinnatus looked under the table. M'sieur Pierre for some reason lost countenance, began to fidget and cast a sidelong glance down. The director, lifting a corner of the oilcloth, also looked down and then glanced suspiciously at Cincinnatus. The lawyer, in his turn, made a dive, then looked around at everybody and resumed writing. Cincinnatus straightened up. (Nothing special – he had dropped his little ball of tinfoil.)

'We passed,' M'sieur Pierre went on in a hurt voice, 'long evenings together in constant talks, games and various amusements. Like children, we engaged in contests of strength; I, poor, weak little M'sieur Pierre naturally, oh, naturally was no match for my mighty cocval. We discussed everything – such as sex and other lofty subjects, and the hours flew by like minutes, the minutes like hours. Sometimes, in peaceful silence . . .'

Here Rodrig Ivanovich suddenly tittered. '*Impayable, ce* "naturally",' he whispered, getting the joke a little late.

'. . . Sometimes, in peaceful silence, we would sit side by side, almost with our arms about each other, each thinking his own twilight thoughts, and the thoughts of both of us would flow together like rivers when we opened our lips to speak. I shared with him my experience in romance, taught him the art of chess, entertained him with a timely anecdote. And so the days passed. The results are before you. We grew to love each other, and the structure of Cincinnatus's soul is as well known to me as the structure of his neck. Thus it will be not an unfamiliar, terrible somebody but a tender friend that will help him mount the crimson steps, and he will surrender himself to me without fear forever, for all death. Let the will of the public be carried out!' (He got up; the director got up also; the lawyer, engrossed in his writing, only rose slightly.)

'So. Now, Rodrig Ivanovich, I shall ask you to announce my title officially and to introduce me.'

The director hastily put on his glasses, examined a slip of paper, and in a megaphone voice addressed Cincinnatus:

'All right – This is M'sieur Pierre. *Bref* – the performer of the execution. . . . I am grateful for the honour,' he added and, with an astonished expression on his face, dropped back into his chair.

'Well, you didn't manage that too well,' said M'sieur Pierre with displeasure. 'After all, there are certain official forms of procedure and they ought to be followed. I am certainly no pedant, but at such an important moment . . . It's no use holding your hand to your chest, you botched it, friend. No, no, stay seated, enough. Now let us continue. Roman Vissarionovich, where is the programme?'

'I gave it to you,' the lawyer said glibly. 'However . . .' and he began to rummage in his briefcase.

'I found it, don't bother,' said M'sieur Pierre, 'so . . . the performance is scheduled for the day after tomorrow . . . In Thriller Square. Couldn't they have picked a better place . . . Remarkable!' (Goes on reading, muttering to himself) 'Adults will be admitted . . . Circus subscription stubs will be honoured . . . So, so, so . . . The performer of the execution, in red pantaloons . . . now this is nonsense – they've overdone it, as usual . . .' (To Cincinnatus) 'Day after Tomorrow, then. Did you understand—? And tomorrow, as our glorious custom demands, you and I must go visit the city fathers – I think you have the little list, don't you, Rodrig Ivanovich?'

Rodrig Ivanovich began to slap at various parts of his cotton-padded body, rolling his eyes and for some reason getting up. At last the list was found.

'All righty,' said M'sieur Pierre. 'Add it to your file, Roman Vissarionovich. I think that does it. Now, according to the law, the floor belongs to—'

'Oh, no, *c'est vraiment superflu* . . .' Rodrig Ivanovich interrupted hastily. 'After all, that's a very antiquated law.'

'According to the law,' M'sieur Pierre, repeated firmly, turning to Cincinnatus, 'the floor is yours.'

'Honest one!' said the director in a breaking voice, his jelly jowls shaking.

Silence ensued. The lawyer was writing so quickly that the flashing of his pencil hurt the eyes.

'I shall wait one whole minute,' said M'sieur Pierre, placing a thick watch on the table before him.

The lawyer inhaled jerkily and began gathering up the thickly covered sheets.

The minute passed.

'The conference is concluded,' said M'sieur Pierre. 'Let us go, gentlemen. Roman Vissarionovich, you will let me look over the minutes before you have them mimeographed, won't you? No, a little later – right now my eyes are tired.'

'I must admit,' said the director, 'in spite of myself I sometimes regret that we no longer use the sys . . .' He bent over to M'sieur Pierre's ear in the doorway.

'What's that you're saying, Rodrig Ivanovich?' the lawyer inquired jealously. The director whispered it to him also.

'Yes, you're right,' agreed the lawyer. 'However, the dear little law can be circumvented. For example, if we stretch the chop-chop out to several times . . .'

'Now, now,' said M'sieur Pierre, 'enough of that, you jokers, I never make notches.'

'No, we were just speaking theoretically,' the director smiled ingratiatingly; 'only in the old days, when it was legal to use—' The door slammed shut, and the voices faded in the distance.

Almost immediately, however, another guest called on Cincinnatus – the librarian, coming to fetch the books. His long, pale face with its halo of dusty-black hair around a bald spot, his long tremulous torso in the bluish sweater, his long legs in the truncated trousers – all of this together created an odd, morbid impression, as if the man had been squashed and flattened out. However, it seemed to Cincinnatus that, with the book dust, a film of something remotely human had settled on the librarian.

'You must have heard,' said Cincinnatus, 'the day after tomorrow will be my extermination. I shan't be taking any more books.'

'You will not,' said the librarian.

Cincinnatus went on: 'I should like to weed out a few noxious truths. Do you have a minute? I want to say that now, when I know exactly . . . How delightful was that very ignorance that so depressed me . . . No more books . . .'

'Would you like something about gods?' the librarian suggested.

'No, don't bother. I don't feel like reading that.'

'Some do,' said the librarian.

'Yes, I know, but really, it's not worthwhile.'

'For the last night,' the librarian finished his thought with difficulty.

'You are awfully talkative today,' said Cincinnatus with a smile. 'No, take all this away. I wasn't able to finish *Quercus*! Oh yes, by the way, this was brought me by mistake . . . these little volumes . . . Arabic, aren't they? . . . unfortunately I hadn't time to study the Oriental languages.'

'Pity,' said the librarian.

'It's all right, my soul will make up for it. Wait a minute, do not go yet. Although I know, of course, that you are only bound in human skin, as it were, yet . . . I am content with little . . . The day after tomorrow—'

But, trembling, the librarian left.

17

Tradition required that on the eve of the execution its passive and active participants together make a brief farewell visit to each of the chief officials; however, in order to shorten the ritual, it was decided that those persons would assemble at the suburban house of the deputy city manager (the manager himself, who was the deputy's nephew, was away, visiting friends in Pritomsk) and that Cincinnatus and M'sieur Pierre would drop in for an informal supper.

It was a dark night, and a strong warm wind was blowing when, dressed in identical capes, on foot, escorted by six soldiers carrying halberds and lanterns, they crossed the bridge and entered the sleeping city where, avoiding the main streets, they began to climb a flinty path between rustling gardens.

(Just before that, on the bridge Cincinnatus had turned, freeing his head from the hood of his cloak: the blue, elaborate, many-towered, huge bulk of the fortress rose into the dull sky, where a cloud had barred an apricot moon. The dark air above the bridge blinked and twitched because of the bats. 'You promised . . .' whispered M'sieur Pierre, giving him a slight squeeze on the elbow, and Cincinnatus again pulled on his cowl.)

This nocturnal promenade which had promised to be so rich with sad, carefree, singing, murmuring impressions – for what is a recollection, if not the soul of an impression? – proved in reality to be vague and insignificant and flashed by so quickly as happens only amid very familiar surroundings, in the dark, when the varicoloured fractions of day are replaced by the integers of night.

At the end of a narrow and gloomy lane, where the gravel crunched and there was a smell of juniper, there suddenly appeared a theatrically lighted carriage porch with whitewashed columns, friezes on the pediment, and potted laurels, and hardly pausing in the vestibule, where servants flitted to and fro like birds of paradise, shedding plumes on the black and white tiles, Cincinnatus and M'sieur Pierre entered a hall buzzing with a large gathering. All were assembled here.

Here the custodian of the city fountains could be at once recognized by his characteristic shock of hair; here the telegraph chief's uniform flashed with golden medals; here, with his obscene nose, was the ruddy director of supplies; and the lion-tamer with an Italian name; and the judge, deaf and venerable; and, in green patent-leather shoes, the park administrator; and a multitude of other stately, respectable, grey-haired individuals with repulsive faces. There were no ladies present, unless one counted the district superintendent of schools, a very stout, elderly woman in a grey frock coat cut like a man's, with large flat cheeks and a smooth hairdo as shiny as steel.

Someone slipped on the parquetry, to the accompaniment of general laughter. A chandelier dropped one of its candles. Someone had already placed a bouquet on a small coffin that had been set out for exhibition. Standing apart with Cincinnatus, M'sieur Pierre was calling his charge's attention to these phenomena.

Just then, however, the host, a swarthy old man with a goatee, clapped his hands. The doors were flung open, and everyone moved into the dining room. M'sieur Pierre and Cincinnatus were seated side by side at the head of a dazzling table, and everyone began to glance, with restraint at first, then with benevolent curiosity – which in some began to turn into surreptitious tenderness – at the pair, identically clad in Elsinore jackets; then, as a lambent smile gradually appeared on M'sieur Pierre's lips and he began to talk, the eyes of the guests turned more and more openly toward him and Cincinnatus who was unhurriedly, diligently and intently – as if seeking the solution to a problem – balancing his fish knife in various ways, now on the salt shaker, now on the incurvation of the fork, now leaning it against the slender crystal vase with a white rose that distinctly adorned his place.

The footman, recruited from among the town's most adroit dandies – the best representatives of its purple youth – briskly served the food (sometimes even leaping across the table with a dish), and everyone noticed the polite solicitude with which M'sieur Pierre took care of Cincinnatus, immediately switching from a conversational smile to momentary seriousness, while he carefully placed a choice morsel on Cincinnatus's plate; whereupon, with the former playful twinkle on his pink, hairless face he would resume his witty conversation, directed to the whole table – and suddenly, leaning over just a little, grabbing the gravy boat or the pepper shaker, he would glance interrogatively at Cincinnatus; the latter, however, did not touch any of the food, but continued, just as silently, attentively and diligently, to shift the knife about.

'Your remark,' M'sieur Pierre said gaily, turning to the city traffic chief, who had managed to get a word in and was now pleasurably anticipating a scintillating reply, 'your remark reminds me of the well-known anecdote about the Hippocratic oath.'

'Tell it, we don't know it, do tell it,' voices begged him from all sides.

'I comply with your wish,' said M'sieur Pierre. 'To a gynaecologist comes this—'

''Scuse the intermission,' said the lion-tamer (grey-haired and moustachioed, with a crimson ribbon across his chest), 'but is the gent convicted that the anecdotus is wholesomely for the ears of . . . ?' He emphatically indicated Cincinnatus with his eyes.

'Quite, quite,' M'sieur Pierre replied sternly, 'I would never allow myself the slightest impropriety in the presence of . . . As I was saying, to a gynaecologist comes this little old lady' (M'sieur Pierre stuck out his lower lip slightly). 'She says, "I've got quite a serious illness and I'm afraid it'll be the death of me." "What are the symptoms?" asked the doctor. "Oh doctor, my head shakes . . ." ' and M'sieur Pierre, mumbling and shaking, mimicked the old woman.

The guests roared. At the other end of the table the deaf judge, his face in agonized contortions as if constipated with laughter, was thrusting his large, humid ear in the face of his guffawing, selfish neighbour, and, tugging at his sleeve, implored him to repeat the story of M'sieur Pierre, who, meanwhile, was jealously following the fate of his anecdote across the whole length of the table, and was satisfied only when somebody had assured the sufferer's curiosity.

'Your remarkable aphorism that life is a medical secret,' said the custodian of fountains, creating such a spray of fine saliva that a rainbow formed near his mouth, 'might very well be applied to the odd thing that happened the other day in my secretary's family. Can you imagine . . .'

'Well, my little Cincinnatus, are you afraid?' one of the glittering footmen asked Cincinnatus as he poured him wine; Cincinnatus looked up, it was his waggish brother-in-law. 'Afraid, aren't you? Here, have a drink on the brink.'

'What's going on here?' M'sieur Pierre coldly said, putting the babbler in his place, and the latter promptly stepped away, and now he was bending over with his bottle at the elbow of the next guest.

'Gentlemen!' exclaimed the host, rising from his chair and

holding his glass containing an icy pale-yellow drink at the level of his starched chest. 'I propose a toast to . . .'

'Bitter, bitter, sweeten it with a kiss,' said a recent best man, and the rest of the guests joined in the chanting.

'Let us . . . a *bruderschaft* . . . I implore you—' M'sieur Pierre said to Cincinnatus in a changed voice, his face twisted in supplication, 'do not refuse me this, I implore you, this is the way it is done always, always . . .'

Cincinnatus was fiddling with the curled petal tips of the moist white rose, which he had absently pulled out of the overturned vase.

'I have the right, finally, to demand,' M'sieur Pierre whispered convulsively, and suddenly, with a gasp of forced laugh, he poured a drop of wine from his glass on top of Cincinnatus's head, and then sprinkled himself also.

Cries of 'Bravo!' were heard from all sides, and neighbour would turn to neighbour, expressing in dramatic pantomime his wonder and delight, and the unbreakable glasses clinked, and heaps of apples each as big as a child's head shone among the dusty-blue bunches of grapes on a silver ship breasting the air, and the table seemed to slope up like a diamond mountain, and the many-armed chandelier journeyed through the mists of plafond art, shedding tears, shedding beams, in vain search of a landing.

'I am touched, touched,' M'sieur Pierre was saying, as they took turns coming up to him to congratulate him. As they did so, some of them stumbled, and a few sang. The father of the city firemen was disgracefully drunk; two of the servants were trying stealthily to haul him away, but he sacrificed his coat-tails like a lizard does its tail, and remained. The respectable woman, who supervised the schools, flushing blotchily, was silently and tensely leaning away as she defended herself from the supply director, who was playfully aiming at her with his finger, which resembled a carrot, as though he were about to transfix her or tickle her, all the while repeating, 'tee-tee-tee!'

'Friends, let us go out on the terrace,' announced the host, whereupon Marthe's brother and the son of the late Dr Sineokov pulled open a drapery with a rattle of wooden rings; the swaying light of painted lanterns revealed a stone veranda, bordered further by the tenpinlike uprights of a balustrade, between which showed black the hourglasses of night.

The sated guests, their bellies gurgling, settled themselves in low armchairs. Some lounged by the columns, others near the balustrade. Near it, too, stood Cincinnatus, twirling in his fingers the mummy of a cigar, and beside him, not turning to him but incessantly touching him either with his back, or with his side, M'sieur Pierre was saying to the accompaniment of approving exclamations from his listeners:

'Photography and fishing – those are my two chief passions. It may seem odd to you, but fame and honour are nothing to me compared with rural quiet. I see you are smiling sceptically, kind sir' (he said in passing to one of the guests who at once repudiated his smile), 'but I swear to you that this is so, and I do not swear idly. The love of nature was bequeathed to me by my father, who never lied either. Many of you, of course, remember him and can confirm this, even in writing, if it should become necessary.'

Standing by the balustrade, Cincinnatus peered vaguely into the darkness, and just then, as if by request, the darkness paled enticingly, as the moon, now clear and high, glided out from behind the black fleece of cloudlets, varnished the shrubs, and let its light trill in the ponds. Suddenly, with an abrupt start of the soul, Cincinnatus realized that he was in the very thick of the Tamara Gardens which he remembered so well and which had seemed so inaccessible to him; he realized that he had walked here with Marthe many times, past this very house in which he was now and which had then appeared to him as a white villa with boarded-up windows, glimpsed through the foliage on the hillock . . . Now, exploring the surroundings with a diligent eye, he easily removed the murky film of night from the familiar lawns and also erased from them the superfluous lunar dusting, so as to make them exactly as they were in his memory. As he restored the painting smudged by the soot of night, he saw groves, paths, brooks taking shape where they used to be . . . In the distance, pressing against the metallic sky, the charmed hills stood still, glossed with blue and folded in gloom. . . .

'A porch, moon's torch, and he, and she,' recited M'sieur Pierre smiling at Cincinnatus, who noticed that everyone was looking at him with tender, expectant sympathy.

'Admiring the landscape?' said the park superintendent to him with a confidential air, hands clasped behind his back. 'You . . .' He stopped short and, as if somewhat embarrassed, turned to M'sieur Pierre: 'Excuse me . . . do I have your permission? After all I haven't been introduced . . .'

'Please, please, you don't have to ask my permission,' M'sieur

Pierre replied courteously and, touching Cincinnatus's elbow, said in a low voice. 'This gentleman would like to chat with you, my dear.'

The park superintendent cleared his throat into his fist and repeated, 'The landscape . . . Admiring the landscape? Right now you can't see very much. But just you wait, exactly at midnight – so our chief engineer has promised me . . . Nikita Lukich! Over here, Nikita Lukich!'

'Coming,' Nikita Lukich responded in a jaunty bass, and obligingly stepped forward, cheerfully turning now to one, now to the other, his youthful, fleshy face with the white brush of a moustache, and placing a hand comfortably on the shoulder of the park superintendent and on that of M'sieur Pierre.

'I was just telling him, Nikita Lukich, that you promised, exactly at midnight, in honour of . . .'

'Why of course,' the chief engineer interrupted. 'We shall have the surprise without fail. Don't you worry about that. By the way, what time is it, boys?'

He relieved the other's shoulders of the pressure of his broad hands and, with a preoccupied mien, went inside.

'Well, in eight hours or so we shall already be in the square,' said M'sieur Pierre, squeezing shut the lid of his watch. 'We shan't be getting much sleep. You aren't cold, are you, my dear? The nice man said there would be a surprise. I must say they are spoiling us. That fish we had for dinner was without equal.'

'. . . Stop it, leave me alone,' said the husky voice of the lady administrator, whose massive back and grey bun were coming straight at M'sieur Pierre as she retreated from the supply director's index finger. 'Tee-tee,' he squeaked playfully, 'tee-tee.'

'Take it easy, madam,' croaked M'sieur Pierre. 'My corns aren't state property.'

'Bewitching woman,' the supply director remarked in passing, totally without expression and, capering, headed toward a group of men standing by the columns; then his shadow was lost among their shadows, and a breeze made the Japanese lanterns sway, and in the dark there would be revealed now a hand pompously preening a moustache, now a cup raised to senile, fish lips that were trying to get the sugar from the bottom.

'Attention!' the host shouted, passing like a whirlwind among the guests.

And, first in the garden, then beyond it, then still further, along the walks, in groves, in glades and on lawns, singly and in clusters, ruby, sapphire, and topaz lamps lit up, gradually inlaying the night with gems. The guests began to 'oh!' and 'ah!' M'sieur Pierre inhaled sharply and grabbed Cincinnatus by the wrist. The lights covered an ever-increasing area: now they stretched out along a distant valley, now they were on the other side of it, in the form of an elongated brooch, now they already studied the first slopes; once there they passed on from hill to hill, nestling in the most secret folds, groping their way to the summits, crossing over them! 'Oh, how beautiful,' whispered M'sieur Pierre, for an instant pressing his cheek against the cheek of Cincinnatus.

The guests applauded. For three minutes a good million light bulbs of diverse colours burned, artfully planted in the grass, in branches, on cliffs, and all arranged in such a way as to embrace the whole nocturnal landscape with a grandiose monogram of 'P' and 'C', which, however, had not quite come off. Thereupon the lights went out all at once and solid darkness reached up to the terrace.

When engineer Nikita Lukich reappeared they surrounded him and wanted to toss him. It was time, however, to begin thinking about a well deserved rest. Before the guests left, the host offered to photograph M'sieur Pierre and Cincinnatus by the balustrade. M'sieur Pierre, even thought he was the one who was being photographed, nevertheless directed this operation. A burst of light illuminated the white profile of Cincinnatus and the eyeless face beside him. The host himself handed them their capes and went out to see them off. In the vestibule morose soldiers were clattering sleepily as they sorted out their halberds.

'I am ineffably flattered by your visit,' the host said to Cincinnatus in parting. 'Tomorrow – or rather this morning – I shall be there, of course, and not only in an official capacity but also in a personal one. My nephew tells me that a large gathering is expected.

'Well good luck to you,' said he to M'sieur Pierre in between the traditional three kisses on the cheeks.

Cincinnatus and M'sieur Pierre, with their escort of soldiers, plunged into the lane.

'On the whole you are a good fellow,' said M'sieur Pierre when they had gone a little distance, 'only why do you always. . . . Your shyness makes an extremely unfavourable impression on new people. I don't know about you,' he added, 'but although I am delighted with the illumination and so forth, I have heartburn and a suspicion that not all the cooking was done with creamery butter.'

They walked a long time. It was very dark and foggy.

A blunt knock-knock-knock came from somewhere off to the left as they were descending Steep Avenue. Knock-knock-knock.

'The scoundrels,' muttered M'sieur Pierre. 'Didn't they swear it was all done?'

At last they crossed the bridge and started uphill. The moon had already been removed and the dark towers of the fortress blended with the clouds.

At the third gate, Rodrig Ivanovich was waiting in dressing gown and nightcap.

'Well, how was it?' he asked impatiently.

'Nobody missed you,' M'sieure Pierre said dryly.

18

'Tried to sleep, could not, only got chilled all through, and now it is dawn' (Cincinnatus wrote rapidly, illegibly, leaving words unfinished, as a running man leaves an incomplete footprint), 'now the air is pale, and I am so frozen that it seems to me that the abstract concept of "cold" must have as its concrete form the shape of my body, and they are going to come for me any time now. It makes me ashamed to be afraid, but I am desperately afraid – fear, never halting, rushes through me with an ominous roar, like a torrent, and my body vibrates like a bridge over a waterfall, and one has to speak very loud to hear oneself above the roar. I am ashamed, my soul has disgraced itself – for this ought not to be, *ne dolzhno bïlo bï bït'* – only on the bark of the Russian language could such a fungus bunch of verbs have sprouted – oh, how ashamed I am that my attention is occupied, my soul blocked by such dithering details, they push through, with lips wet, to say farewell, all kinds of memories come to say farewell: I, a child, am sitting with a book in the hot sun on the bank of a dinning stream, and the water throws its wavering reflection on the lines of an old, old poem – "Love at the sloping of our years" – but I know I should not yield – "Becomes more tender and superstitious" – neither to memories, nor to fear, nor to this passionate syncope: ". . . and superstitious" – and I had hoped so much that everything would be orderly, all simple and neat. For I know that the horror of death is nothing really, a harmless convulsion – perhaps even healthful for the soul – the choking wail of a newborn child or a furious refusal to release a toy – and that there once lived, in caverns where there is the tinkle of a perpetual stillicide, and stalactites, sages who rejoiced at death and who – blunderers for the most part, it is true – yet who in their own way, mastered – and even though I know all this, and know yet another main, paramount thing that no one here knows – nevertheless, look, dummies, how afraid I am, how everything in me trembles, and dins, and rushes – and any moment now they will come for me, and I am not ready, I am ashamed . . .'

Cincinnatus got up, made a running start and smashed headlong into the wall – the real Cincinnatus, however, remained sitting at the table, staring at the wall, chewing his pencil, and presently shuffled his feet under the table and continued to write, a little less rapidly:

'Save these jottings – I do not know whom I ask, but save these jottings – I assure you that such a law exists, look it up, you will see! – let them lie around for a while – how can that hurt you? – and I ask you so earnestly – my last wish – how can you not grant it? I must have at least the theoretical possibility of having a reader, otherwise, really, I might as well tear it all up. There, that is what I needed to say. Now it is time to get ready.'

He paused again. It had already grown quite light in the cell, and Cincinnatus knew by the position of the light that half-past five was about to strike. He waited until he heard the distant ringing, and went on writing, but now quite slowly and haltingly, just as if he had spent all his strength on some initial exclamation.

'My words all mill about in one spot,' wrote Cincinnatus. 'Envious of poets. How wonderful it must be to speed along a page and, right from the page, where only a shadow continues to run, to take off into the blue. The untidiness, sloppiness of an execution, of all the manipulations, before and after. How cold the blade, how smooth the axe's grip. With emery paper. I suppose the pain of parting will be red and loud. The thought, when written down, becomes less oppressive, but some thoughts are like a cancerous tumour: you express it, you excise it, and it grows back worse than before. It is hard to imagine that this very morning, in an hour or two . . .'

But two hours passed, and more, and, just as always, Rodion brought breakfast, tidied the cell, sharpened the pencil, removed the close-stool, fed the spider. Cincinnatus did not ask him anything, but, when Rodion had left, and time dragged on at its customary trot, he realized that once again he had been duped, that he had strained his soul to no purpose, and that everything had remained just as uncertain, viscous and senseless as before.

The clock had just finished striking three or four (he had dozed off and then half awakened, and so had not counted the strokes, but had only retained an approximate impression of their sum of sound) when suddenly the door opened and Marthe came in. Her cheeks were flushed, the comb at the back of her head had worked loose, the tight bodice of her black velvet dress was heaving – and something did not fit right, and this made her appear lopsided, and she kept trying to straighten her dress, tugging at it, or very rapidly wriggling her hips, as if something underneath were wrong and uncomfortable.

'Some cornflowers for you,' she said, tossing a blue posy upon the table, and at the same time, nimbly lifting the hem of her skirt above her knee, she put on the chair a plump little leg in a white stocking, pulling it up to the place where the garter had left its imprint on the tender, quivering fat. 'My, how hard it was to get permission! Of course, I had to agree to a little concession – the usual story. Well, how are you, my poor little Cin-Cin?'

'I must confess I was not expecting you,' said Cincinnatus. 'Sit down somewhere.'

'I tried yesterday, no luck – and today I said to myself, I'll get through if it's the last thing I do. He kept me for an hour, your director. Spoke *very* highly of you, by the way. Oh, how I hurried today, how I was afraid that I would be too late. What a mob there was in Thriller Square this morning!'

'Why did they call it off?' asked Cincinnatus.

'Well, they said everybody was tired, didn't get enough sleep. You know, the crowd simply did not want to leave. You ought to be proud.'

Oblong, marvellously burnished tears crept down Marthe's cheeks and chin, closely following all their contours – one even flowed down her neck as far as the clavicular dimple . . . Her eyes, however, kept on gazing just as roundly, her short fingers with white spots on the nails kept spreading out, and her thin mobile lips kept emitting words:

'There are some who insist that now it's been postponed for a long time, but then you can't really find out from anyone. You simply cannot imagine all the rumours, the confusion . . .'

'What are you crying about?' asked Cincinnatus with a smile.

'I don't know myself – I'm just worn out . . .' (In a low chesty voice): 'I'm sick and tired of all of you. Cincinnatus, Cincinnatus, what a mess you have got yourself into! . . . The things people say about you – it's dreadful! Oh, listen,' she suddenly began in a different tempo, beaming, smacking her lips, and preening herself. 'The other day – when was it? – yes, day before yesterday, there comes to me this little dame, a lady doctor or something – a total stranger, mind you, in an awful raincoat, and begins hawing and hemming. "Of course," she says, "you understand." I says, "No, so far I don't understand a thing." She says: "Oh, I know who you are, you don't know me" . . . I says . . .' (Marthe miming her interloctress, assumed a fussy and fatuous tone, slowing soberly, however, on the drawn-out 'says', and, now that she was conveying her own words, she depicted herself as being calm as snow). 'In a word, she tried to tell me that she was your mother – though I think even her age wouldn't be right, but we'll overlook that. She said she was terribly afraid of being persecuted, since, you see, they had questioned her and subjected her to all sorts of things. I says: "What do I have to do with all this and why should you want to see me?" She says: "Oh, yes, I know you are terribly kind, you'll do all you can." I says: "What makes you think I'm kind?" She says: : "Oh, I know" – and asks if I couldn't give her a paper, a certificate, that I would sign hand and foot, stating that she had never been at our house and had never seen you . . . This, you know, seemed so funny to Marthe, so funny! I think' (in a drawling, low-pitched voice) 'that she must have been some kind of crank, a nut, don't you think so? In any case, I of course did not give her anything. Victor and the others said it might compromise me – since it would seem that I knew your every move, if I knew you weren't acquainted with her – and so she left, very crestfallen, I would say.'

'But it really *was* my mother,' said Cincinnatus.

'Maybe, maybe. After all it's not so important. But tell me, why are you so dull and glum, Cin-Cin? I imagined you would be so happy to see me, but you . . .'

She glanced at the cot, then at the door.

'I don't know what the rules are here,' she said under her breath, 'but if you need it badly, Cin-Cin, go ahead, only do it quickly.'

'Oh, don't – what nonsense,' said Cincinnatus.

'Well, as you please. I only wanted to give you a treat because it's the last interview and all that. Oh, by the way, do you know who wants to marry me? Guess who – you'll never guess. Remember that old grouch who used to live next door to us, who kept stinking with his pipe across the fence, and always used to peek when I climbed the apple tree? Can you imagine? And the thing is, he was perfectly serious! Can you see me marrying him, the old scarecrow? Ugh! Anyway I feel it's time I had a good, long rest – you know, close my eyes, stretch out, not think about anything, and relax absolutely alone of course or else with someone who would really care, and understand everything, everything . . .'

Her short, coarse eyelashes again glistened, and the tears crept down, visiting every dimple on her apple-rosy cheeks.

Cincinnatus took one of these tears and tasted it: it was neither salty nor sweet – merely a drop of luke-warm water. Cincinnatus did not do this.

Suddenly the door squealed and opened an inch; a red-haired finger beckoned to Marthe. She quickly went to the door.

'Well, what do you want, it isn't time yet, is it, I was promised a whole hour,' she whispered rapidly. Something was said in reply.

'Not on your life!' she said indignantly. 'You can tell him that. The agreement was that I should do it only with the direct—'

She was interrupted; she listened carefully to the insistent mumbling; she looked down, frowning, and scraping the floor with the toe of her slipper.

'Well, all right,' she blurted out, and with innocent vivacity turned to her husband: 'I'll be back in five minutes, Cin-Cin.'

(While she was gone he thought that not only had he not even begun his urgent talk with her, but that now he could no longer formulate those important things . . . At the same time his heart was aching, and the same old memory whimpered in a corner; but it was time, it was time to wean himself from all this anguish.)

She returned only in three quarters of an hour, snorting contemptuously. She put one foot on the chair, snapped her garter, and, angrily readjusted the pleats below her waist, sat down at the table, precisely as she had been sitting before.

'All for nothing,' she said with a sneer and began fingering the blue flowers on the table. 'Well, why don't you tell me something, my little Cin-Cin, my cockerel? . . . You know I picked them myself, I don't care for poppies, but these are lovely. Shouldn't try if you can't manage it,' she added unexpectedly in a different tone of voice, narrowing her eyes. 'No, Cin-Cin, I wasn't speaking to you.' (Sigh) 'Well, tell me something, console me.'

'My letter – did you . . .' began Cincinnatus, then cleared his throat. 'Did you read my letter carefully?'

'Please, please,' cried Marthe, clutching her temples, 'let's talk about anything but that letter!'

'No, let us talk about it,' said Cincinnatus.

She jumped up, spasmodically straightening her dress, and began speaking incoherently, lisping a little, as she did when she was angry. 'That was a horrible letter, that was some kind of delirium, I didn't understand it, anyway; one might have thought you had been sitting here alone with a bottle and writing. I didn't want to bring up that letter, but now that you . . . Listen, you know the transmitters read it – they copied it, and they said to themselves, "Oho! She must be in cahoots with him, if he writes to her like that." Can't you see, I don't want to know anything about your affairs, you have no right to send me such letters, to drag me into your criminal—'

'I did not write you anything criminal,' said Cincinnatus.

'That's what you think, but everyone was horrified by your letter, simply horrified! Me, I'm stupid maybe, and don't know anything about the laws, but still my instinct told me that every word of yours was impossible, unspeakable . . . Oh, Cincinnatus, what a position you put me in – and the children – think of the children . . . Listen – please listen to me for just a minute—' she went on with such ardour that her speech became quite unintelligible, 'renounce everything, everything. Tell them that you are innocent, that you were merely swaggering, tell them, repent, do it – even if it doesn't save your head, think of me – already they are pointing fingers at me and saying, "That's her, the widow, that's her!'

'Wait, Marthe, I don't understand. Repent of what?'

'That's right! Mix me up in it, ask me leading . . . If I knew all the answers, why, then I'd be your accomac . . . accomplice! That's quite obvious. No, enough, enough. I'm dreadfully afraid of all this . . . Tell me one last time, are you sure you don't want to repent, for my sake, for all our sakes?'

'Good-bye, Marthe,' said Cincinnatus.

She sat down and lapsed into thought, leaning on her right elbow, and sketching her world on the table with her left hand.

'How dreadful, how dull,' she said, heaving a deep, deep sigh. She frowned and drew a river with her fingernail. 'I thought we would meet quite differently. I was ready to give you everything.

And this is what I get for my pains! Well, what's done is done.' (The river flowed into a sea – off the edge of the table.) 'You know, I'm leaving with a heavy heart. Yes, but how am I going to get out?' she remembered suddenly, innocently and even cheerfully. 'They won't be coming for me for a while yet, I talked them into giving me oodles of time.'

'Don't worry,' said Cincinnatus, 'every word we say . . . They will open it in a moment.'

He was not mistaken.

'Bye, bye-bye,' chirped Marthe. 'Wait, stop pawing me, let me say good-bye to my husband. Bye-bye. If you need anything in the way of shirts or anything . . . Oh yes, the children asked me to give you a big, big kiss. There was something else . . . Oh, I nearly forgot – daddy took the wine-cup I gave you – he says you promised him—'

'Hurry, hurry, little lady,' interrupted Rodion, kneeing her in a familiar fashion toward the door.

19

Next morning they brought him the newspapers and this reminded him of the first days of his confinement. He noticed at once the colour photographs: under a blue sky, the square, packed so densely with a motley crowd that only the very edge of the red platform was visible. In the column dealing with the execution half the lines were blacked out, and out of the remainder Cincinnatus could fish only what he already knew from Marthe – that the maestro was not feeling too well, and that the performance was postponed, possibly for a long time.

'What a treat you are getting today,' said Rodion, not to Cincinnatus but to the spider.

In both hands, most carefully, but at the same time squeamishly (care prompted him to press it to his chest, distaste made him hold it away) he carried a towel gathered together in a lump in which something large stirred and rustled.

'Got it on a window pane in the tower. The monster! See how it flops and flaps – you can hardly hold it . . .'

He was going to pull up the chair, as he always did, in order to stand up on it and deliver the victim to the voracious spider on his solid web (the beast was already puffing himself up, sensing the prey) but something went wrong – his gnarled, fearful fingers happened to release the main fold of the towel, and he immediately cried out and cringed, as people cry out and cringe whom not a bat but an ordinary house mouse inspires with revulsion and terror. Something large, dark, and furnished with feelers, disengaged itself from the towel, and Rodion emitted a loud yell, tramping in one place, afraid to let the thing escape but not daring to grab it. The towel fell; and the fair captive clung to Rodion's cuff, clutching it with all six of its adhesive feet.

It was only a moth, but what a moth! It was as large as a man's hand; it had thick, dark-brown wings with a hoary lining and grey-dusted margins; each wing was adorned in the centre with an eye-spot, shining like steel.

Its segmented limbs, in fluffy muffs, now clung, now unstuck themselves, and the upraised vanes of its wings, through whose underside the same staring spots and wavy grey pattern showed, oscillated slowly, as the moth, groping its way, crawled up the sleeve, while Rodion, quite panic-stricken, rolling his eyes, throwing away, and forsaking his own arm, wailed, 'Take it off'n me! take it off'n me!'

Upon reaching his elbow, the moth began noiselessly flapping its heavy wings; they seemed to outbalance its body, and on Rodion's elbow joint, the creature turned over, wings hanging down, still tenaciously clinging to the sleeve – and now one could see its brown, white-dappled abdomen, its squirrel face, the black globules of its eyes and its feathery antennae resembling pointed ears.

'Take it away!' implored Rodion, beside himself, and his frantic gesturing caused the splendid insect to fall off; it struck the table, paused on it in mighty vibration, and suddenly took off from its edge.

But to me your daytime is dark, why did you disturb my slumbers? Its flight, swooping and lumbering, lasted only a short time. Rodion picked up the towel and, swinging wildly, attempted to knock down the blind flyer; but suddenly it disappeared as if the very air had swallowed it.

Rodion searched for a while, did not find it, and stopped in the centre of the cell, turning toward Cincinnatus, arms akimbo. 'Eh? What a rascal!' he ejaculated after an expressive silence. He spat; he shook his head and pulled out a throbbing match box with spare flies, with which the disappointed animal had to be satisfied. Cincinnatus, however, had seen perfectly well where the moth had settled.

When at last Rodion departed, crossly removing his beard together with his shaggy cap of hair, Cincinnatus walked from the cot to the table. He was sorry he had returned all the books, and sat down to write to pass the time.

'Everything has fallen into place,' he wrote, 'that is, everything has duped me – all of this theatrical, pathetic stuff – the promises of a volatile maiden, a mother's moist gaze, the knocking on the wall, a neighbour's friendliness, and, finally, those hills which broke out in a deadly rash. Everything has duped me as it fell into place, everything. This is the dead end of this life, and I should not have sought salvation within its confines. It is strange that I should have sought salvation. Just like a man grieving because he has recently lost in his dreams some thing that he had never had in reality, or hoping that tomorrow he would dream that he found it again. That is how mathematics is created; it has its fatal flaw. I have discovered it. I have discovered the little crack in life, where it broke off, where it had once been soldered to something else, something genuinely alive, important and vast – how capacious my epithets must be in order that I may pour them full of crystalline sense . . . it is best to leave some things unsaid, or else I shall get confused again. Within this irreparable little crack decay has set in – ah, I think I shall yet be able to express it all – the dreams, the coalescence, the disintegration – no, again I am off the track – all my best words are deserters and do not answer the trumpet call, and the remainder are cripples. Oh, if only I had known that I was yet to remain here for such a long time, I would have begun at the beginning and gradually, along a high road of logically connected ideas, would have attained, would have completed, my soul would have surrounded itself with a structure of words . . . Everything that I have written here so far is only the froth of my excitement, a senseless transport, for the very reason that I have been in such a hurry. But now, when I am hardened, when I am almost fearless of . . .'

Here the page ended, and Cincinnatus realized that he was out of paper. However he managed to dig up one more sheet.

'. . . death,' he wrote on it, continuing his sentence, but he immediately crossed out that word; he must say it differently, with greater precision: 'execution', perhaps, 'pain' or 'parting' – something like that; twirling the stunted pencil in his fingers, he paused in thought, and a little brown fuzz had stuck to the edge of the table where the moth had quivered only a short time ago, and Cincinnatus, remembering it, walked away from the table, leaving on it the blank sheet with only the one solitary word on it, and that one crossed out, and bent down (pretending that he was fixing the back of his slipper) by the cot, on whose iron leg, quite near the floor, it was settled, asleep, its visionary wings spread in solemn invulnerable torpor; only he was sorry for the downy back where the fuzz had rubbed off leaving a bald spot, as shiny as a chestnut – but the great dark wings, with their ashen edges and perpetually open eyes, were inviolable – the forewings, lowered slightly, lapped over the hind ones, and this drooping attitude might have been one of somnolent fragility, were it not for the monolithic straightness of the upper margins and the perfect symmetry of all the diverging lines – and this was so enchanting that Cincinnatus, unable to restrain himself, stroked with his fingertip the hoary ridge near the base of the right wing, then the ridge of the left one (what gentle firmness! what unyielding gentleness!); the moth, however, did not awaken, and he straightened up and, sighing slightly, moved away; he was about to sit down at the table again when suddenly the key scraped in the lock and the door opened, whining, rattling and groaning in keeping with all the rules of carceral counterpoint. Rosy M'sieur Pierre, in a pea-green hunting habit, first inserted his head and then came in completely, and behind him came two others, whom it was almost impossible to recognize as the director and the lawyer: haggard, pallid, both dressed in coarse grey shirts, shabbily shod – without any make-up, without padding and without wigs, with rheumy eyes, with scrawny bodies that one could glimpse through candid ribs – they turned out to resemble each other, and their identical heads moved identically on their thin necks, pale bald bumpy heads, with a bluish stipple on the sides and protruding ears.

Attractively rouged M'sieur Pierre bowed, bringing together his patent-leather boot tops, and said in a comic falsetto:

'The carriage is waiting, if you please, sir.'

'Where are we going?' asked Cincinnatus, genuinely not understanding at first, so convinced had he been that it must happen at dawn.

'Where, where . . .' M'sieur Pierre mimicked him. 'You know where. Off to do chop-chop.'

'But we don't have to go this very minute, do we?' asked Cincinnatus, and was himself surprised at what he was saying, 'I haven't quite prepared myself . . .' (Cincinnatus is that you speaking?)

'Yes, this very minute. Good heavens, my friend, you have had nearly three weeks to prepare yourself. One would think that's sufficient. These are my assistants, Rod and Rom, please be kind to them. They may be puny-looking fellows, but they are diligent.'

'We do our best,' droned the fellows.

'I almost forgot,' continued M'siur Pierre. 'According to the law you are still entitled to . . . Roman, old boy, would you hand me the list?'

Roman, exaggeratedly hurrying, produced from under the lining of his cap a black-bordered card, folded in two; while he was getting it out, Rodrig kept mechanically tapping his sides, and seemed to be searching in his breast pockets, without taking his imbecile eyes off his comrade.

'For the sake of simplicity,' said M'sieur Pierre, 'here is a prepared menu of last wishes. You may choose one and only one. I shall read it aloud. Now then: a glass of wine; or a brief trip to the toilet; or a cursory inspection of the prison collection of French postcards; or . . . what's this . . . number four – composing an address to the director expressing . . . expressing gratitude for his considerate . . . Well, I never! Rodrig, you scoundrel, you have added this yourself. I don't understand, how you dared. This is an official document! Why, this is a personal insult especially when I am so meticulous in regard to the laws, when I try so hard . . .'

In his anger M'sieur Pierre flung the card to the floor; Rodrig immediately picked it up, smoothed it out, muttering guiltily, 'Don't you worry . . . it wasn't me. Romka was the joker . . . I know the regulations. Everything is in order here . . . all the desires *du jour* . . . or else à la carte . . .'

'Outrageous! Intolerable!' M'sieur Pierre was shouting as he paced up and down the cell. 'I am not well, and in spite of that I am carrying out my duties. They serve me with spoiled fish, they offer me a disgusting whore, they treat me with unheard of disrespect, and then they expect clean work from me. No sir! Enough! The cup of long-suffering has been drained! I simply refuse – do it yourselves, chop, butcher as best you can, wreck my instrument . . .'

'The public idolizes you,' said obsequious Roman. 'We beseech you, be calm, maestro. If something was not just right, it was the result of an oversight, a foolish mistake, an overzealous, foolish mistake, and only that! So please forgive us. Won't the pet of women, the darling of everyone, put aside that wrathful expression for the smile with which he is wont to drive to distraction . . .'

'That'll do, that'll do, smooth talker,' said M'sieur Pierre, relenting a little. 'Anyway I perform my duty more conscientiously than others I could name. All right, I forgive you. But we still have to decide about that damned last wish. Well, what have you selected?' he asked Cincinnatus (who had quietly sat down on the cot). 'Come on, come on. I want to get it over with, and the squeamish don't have to look.'

'To finish writing something,' whispered Cincinnatus half questioningly but then he frowned, straining his thoughts, and suddenly understood that everything had in fact been written already.

'I don't understand what he is saying,' said M'sieur Pierre. 'Perhaps someone understands, but I don't.'

Cincinnatus raised his head. 'Here is what I would like,' he spoke clearly, 'I ask three minutes – go away for that time or at least be quiet – yes, a three-minute intermission – after that, so be it, I'll act to the end of my role in your idiotic production.'

'Let us compromise at two and a half minutes,' said M'sieur Pierre, taking out his thick watch. 'Concede half a minute, won't you, friend? You won't. Well, be a robber then – I agree to it.'

He leaned against the wall in a relaxed pose; Roman and Rodrig followed his example, but Rodrig's foot twisted under him and he nearly fell, casting a panic-stricken look at the maestro.

'Sh-sh, you son of a bitch,' M'sieur Pierre hissed. 'And anyway, why are you making yourselves so comfortable? Hands out of your pockets! Look out!' (Still rumbling he sat down on the chair.) 'Rod, I have a job for you – you can gradually begin cleaning up here; just don't make too much noise.'

A broom was handed Rodrig through the door and he set to work.

First of all, with the end of the broom, he knocked out the whole grating in the recess of the window; there came a distant, feeble 'hurrah', as if from an abyss, and a gust of fresh air entered the cell – the sheets of paper flew off the table, and Rodrig scuffed them into a corner. Then, with the broom, he pulled down the thick grey cobweb and with it the spider, which he had once nursed with such care. To while away the time Roman picked up the spider. Crudely but cleverly made, it consisted of a round plush body with twitching legs made of springs, and, there was, attached to the middle of its back, a long elastic, by the end of which Roman was holding it suspended, moving his hand up and down so that the elastic alternately contracted and extended and the spider rose and fell. M'sieur Pierre cast a sidelong cold glance at the toy and Roman, raising his eyebrows, hastily pocketed it. Rod, meanwhile, wanted to pull out the drawer of the table, tugged with all his strength, budged it, and the table split in two. At the same time the chair on which M'sieur Pierre was seated emitted a plaintive sound, something gave, and M'sieur Pierre nearly dropped his watch. Plaster began to fall from the ceiling. A crack described a tortuous course across the wall. The cell, no longer needed, was quite obviously disintegrating.

'. . . Fifty-eight, fifty-nine, sixty,' counted M'sieur Pierre. 'That's all. Up, please. It's a fine day, the ride will be most enjoyable, anyone else in your place would be in a hurry to start.'

'Just an instant more. I find it ludicrous and disgraceful that my hands should tremble so – but I can neither stop nor hide it, and, yes, they tremble and that's all. My papers you will destroy, the rubbish you will sweep out, the moth will fly away at night through the broken window, so that nothing of me will remain within these four walls, which are already about to crumble. But now dust and oblivion are nothing to me; I feel only one thing – fear, fear, shameful, futile fear . . .' Actually Cincinnatus did not say all this; he was silently changing his shoes. The vein on his forehead was swollen, the blonde locks fell on it, his shirt had a wide-opened embroidered collar, which imparted a certain extraordinary youthful quality on his neck and to his flushed face with its blond quivering moustache.

'Let's go!' shrieked M'sieur Pierre.

Cincinnatus, trying not to brush against anyone or anything, placing his feet as if he were walking on bare, sloping ice, finally made his way out of the cell, which in fact was no longer there.

20

Cincinnatus was led through stone passageways. Now ahead, now behind, a distracted echo would leap out – all its burrows were crumbling. Often there were stretches of darkness because bulbs had burned out. M'sieur Pierre demanded that they go in step.

Now they were joined by several soldiers in the regulation canine masks, and then Rodrig and Roman, with the master's permission, went on ahead, with long, pleased strides, swinging their arms in businesslike fashion, and overtaking each other. Shouting, they disappeared around a corner.

Cincinnatus, who, alas, had suddenly lost the capactiy of walking, was supported by M'sieur Pierre and a soldier with the face of a borzoi. For a very long time they clambered up and down staircases – the fortress must have suffered a mild stroke, as the descending stairs were in reality ascending and vice versa. Again there were long corridors, but of a more inhabited kind; that is, they visibly demonstrated – either by linoleum, or by wallpaper, or by a sea chest against the wall – that they adjoined living quarters. At one bend there was even a smell of cabbage soup. Further on the passed a glass door with the inscription 'ffice', and after another period of darkness they abruptly found themselves in the courtyard, vibrant with the noonday sun.

Throughout this whole journey Cincinnatus was busy trying to cope with his choking, wrenching, implacable fear. He realized that this fear was dragging him precisely into that false logic of things that had gradually developed around him, but from which he had still somehow been able to escape that morning. The very thought that this chubby, red-cheeked hunter was going to hack at him was already an inadmissable sickening weakness, drawing Cincinnatus into a system that was perilous to him. He fully understood all this, but, like a man unable to resist arguing with a hallucination, even though he knows perfectly well that the entire masquerade is staged in his own brain, Cincinnatus tried in vain to out-wrangle his fear, despite his understanding that he ought actually to rejoice at the awakening whose proximity was presaged by barely noticeable phenomena, by the peculiar effects on everyday implements, by a certain general instability, by a certain flaw in all visible matter – but the sun was still realistic, the world still held together, objects still observed an outward propriety.

Outside the third gate the carriage was waiting. The soldiers did not accompany them further, but sat down on logs piled by the wall, and began taking off their cloth masks. The prison staff and the guards' families pressed timidly and greedily around the gate – barefoot children would run out, trying to get into the picture, and immediately would dart back, and their kerchiefed mothers would shush them, and the hot light gilded the scattered straw, and there was the odour of warm nettles, while off to one side a dozen geese crowded, gobbling discreetly.

'Well, let's get going,' M'sieur Pierre said jauntily and put on his pea-green hat with a pheasant feather.

An old, scarred carriage, which listed with a groan when springy little M'sieur Pierre mounted the step, was hitched to a bay nag with bared teeth, with lesions shiny from flies on its sharply protruding haunches, all in all so lean and so ribby that its trunk seemed to be enclosed in a set of hoops. There was a red ribbon in its mane. M'sieur Pierre squeezed over to make room for Cincinnatus and asked if the bulky case that was placed at their feet were in his way. 'Please, my dear fellow, try not to step on it,' he added. Rodrig and Roman climbed on the box. Rodrig, who was playing the coachman, snapped the long whip, the horse gave a start, was unable to move the carriage immediately and sank on its haunches. A discordant cheer inopportunely rang out from the staff. Rising and leaning forward, Rodrig gave the horse's nose a lash, and, when the carriage moved spasmodically off, he nearly fell backwards on the box from the jolt, drawing the rein tight and crying 'whoa!'

'Easy, easy,' said M'sieur Pierre with a smile, touching Rodrig's back with a plump hand in a smart glove.

The pale road coiled several times, with evil picturesqueness, around the base of the fortress. In places the grade was fairly steep, and then Rodrig would hastily wind tight the scrunching brake handle. M'sieur Pierre, his hands resting on the bulldog head of his cane, gaily looked around at the cliffs, the green inclines between them, the clover and vines, and the whirling white dust, and, while he was at it, also caressed with his gaze the profile of Cincinnatus who was still engaged in his inner struggle. The scrawny, grey, bent backs of the two men sitting on the box were perfectly identical. The hoofs clipped and clopped. Horseflies circled like satellites. At times the carriage overtook hurrying pilgrims (the prison cook, for instance, with his wife), who would stop, shielding themselves from the sun and dust, and then quicken their pace. One more turn and then the road stretched out toward the bridge, having disentangled itself from the slowly revolving fortress (which already stood quite poorly, the perspective was disorganized, (something had come loose and dangled).

'I'm sorry I flared up like that,' M'sieur Pierre was saying gently. 'Don't be angry with me, duckie. You understand yourself how it hurts to see others being sloppy when you put your whole soul into your work.'

They clattered across the bridge. News of the execution had only just now begun to spread through the town. Red and blue boys ran after the carriage. A man who feigned insanity, an old fellow of Jewish origin who had for many years been fishing for non-existent fish in a waterless river, was collecting his chattels, hurrying to join the very first group of townspeople heading for Thriller Square.

'. . . but there's no point in dwelling on that,' M'sieur Pierre was saying. 'Men of my temperament are volatile but also get over it quickly. Rather let us turn our attention to the conduct of the fair sex.'

Several girls, hatless, jostling and squealing, were buying up all the flowers from a fat flower vendor with browned breasts, and the boldest among them managed to throw a bouquet into the carriage, nearly knocking the cap off Roman's head. M'sieur Pierre shook a finger.

The horse, its bleary eye looking askance at the flat spotted dogs, extending their bodies as they raced at its hoofs, strained up Garden Street, and the crowd was already catching up – another bouquet hit the carriage. Now they were turning right, past the huge ruins of the ancient factory, then along Telegraph Street, already ringing, moaning, tooting with the noise of instruments tuning up, then through an unpaved, whispering lane, past a public garden where two beared men in civilian dress got up from a bench when they saw the carriage, and, gesticulating emphatically, began indicating it to each other – both dreadfully excited, square-shouldered – and now they were running, energetically and angularly lifting their legs, toward the same place as everyone else. Beyond the public garden the corpulent white statue had been split in two – by a thunderbolt, said the papers.

'In a moment we shall be driving past your house,' said M'sieur Pierre very softly.

Roman began fidgeting on the box and twisting around to Cincinnatus, cried:

'In a moment we shall be driving past your house,' and at once he turned away again, bouncing up and down, like a pleased urchin.

Cincinnatus did not want to look, but still he looked. Marthe was sitting in the branches of the barren apple tree waving a handkerchief, while in the garden next door, among sunflowers and hollyhocks, a scarecrow in a crushed top hat was waving its sleeve. The wall of the house, especially at the spots where leafy shadows had once played, had peeled strangely, and part of the roof— But they had driven past.

'Really, there is something heartless about you,' said M'sieur Pierre with a sigh and impatiently stuck his cane into the back of the driver, who rose slightly and, with frenzied lashings of his whip, achieved a miracle: the nag broke into a gallop.

Now they were driving along the boulevard. The agitation in the city continued to mount. The motley façades of the houses swayed and flapped, as they were hastily decorated with welcoming posters. One small house was especially well decked out: its door opened quickly, a youth came out, and his entire family followed to see him off – this day he had reached execution-attending age; mother was smiling through her tears, granny was thrusting a sandwich into his knapsack, kid brother was handing him his staff. The ancient stone bridges arching above the streets (once such a boon to pedestrians, but now used only by gawkers and street supervisors) were already teeming with photographers. M'sieur Pierre kept tipping his hat. Dandies on their shiny clockwork cycles passed the carriage and craned their necks. A person in Turkish trousers came running out of a cafe with a pail of confetti, but, missing, sent his vari-coloured blizzard into the face of a cropped fellow who had just come running from the opposite sidewalk with a bien-venue platter of 'bread and salt'.

All that remained of the statue of Captain Somnus was the legs up to the hips, surrounded by roses – it too must have been struck by lightning. Somewhere ahead a brass band was scorching away at the march '*Golubchik*'. White clouds moved jerkily across the whole sky – I think the same ones pass over and over again, I think there are only three kinds, I think it is all stage-setting, with a suspicious green tinge . . .

'Now, now, come on, no foolishness,' said M'sieur Pierre. 'Don't you dare start fainting. It's unworthy of a man.'

And now they had arrived. There were as yet relatively few spectators, but they continued to flow in endlessly. In the centre of the plaza – no, not quite in the centre, that precisely was the dreadful part – rose the vermilion platform of the scaffold. The old electrically powered municipal hearse stood modestly at a slight distance. A combined brigade of telegraphers and firemen was maintaining order. The band was apparently playing with all its might, since the conductor, a one-legged cripple, was waving furiously; now, however, not a sound was audible.

M'sieur Pierre, raising his plump shoulders, climbed gracefully out of the carriage and immediately turned, wishing to assist Cincinnatus, but Cincinnatus got out from the other side. There was some booing.

Rodrig and Roman hopped off the box; all three pressed around Cincinnatus.

'By myself,' said Cincinnatus.

It was about twenty paces to the scaffold, and, in order that no one might touch him, Cincinnatus was compelled to trot. Somewhere in the crowd a dog barked. Upon reaching the crimson steps, Cincinnatus stopped. M'sieur Pierre took him by the elbow.

'By myself,' said Cincinnatus.

He mounted the platform, where the block was, that is, a smooth, sloping slab of polished oak, of sufficient size so that one could easily lie on it with outspread arms. M'sieur Pierre climbed up also. The public buzzed.

While they were fussing with the buckets and spreading the sawdust, Cincinnatus, not knowing what to do, leaned against the wooden railing, but a slight tremor was running all through it and some curious spectators below started to palpate his ankles; he moved away and, a little short of breath, wetting his lips, his arms folded somewhat awkwardly across his chest, as if he did it for the first time, he began looking around. Something had happened to the lighting, there was something wrong with the sun, and a section of the sky was shaking. Poplars had been planted around the square, but they were stiff and rickety – one of them was very slowly . . .

But again a buzzing noise passed through the crowd: Rodrig and Roman, stumbling, shoving against each other, puffing and grunting, clumsily carried the heavy case up the steps and plunked it down on the board floor. M'sieur Pierre threw off his jacket, remaining clad in a singlet. A turquoise woman was tattooed on his white biceps, while, in one of the first rows of the crowd, which was pressing around the very scaffold (regardless of the firemen's entreaties), stood the same woman in the flesh, and also her two sisters, as well as the little old man with the fishing rod, and the tanned flower woman, and the youth with his staff, and one of Cincinnatus's brothers-in-law, and the librarian, reading a newspaper, and that stout fellow Nikita Lukich the engineer – and Cincinnatus also noticed a man whom he used to meet every morning on the way to the kindergarten, but whose name he did not know. Beyond these first rows there followed other rows where eyes and mouths where not so clearly drawn; and beyond them, there were layers of very hazy, and, in their haziness, identical faces, and then – the furthest ones were really quite badly daubed on the backdrop. Another poplar fell.

Suddenly the band stopped – or rather, now that it stopped, one realized that it had been playing all this time. One of the musicians, plump and placid, taking apart his instrument, shook the saliva out of its shiny joints. Beyond the orchestra was a limp, green, allegorical prospect: a portico, cliffs, a soapy cascade.

Nimbly and energetically (so that Cincinnatus involuntarily recoiled) the deputy city director jumped up on the platform, and casually placing one high-raised foot on the block (he was a master of relaxed eloquence) proclaimed in a loud voice:

'Townspeople! One brief remark. Lately in our streets a tendency has been observed on the part of certain individuals of the younger generation to walk so fast that we oldsters must move aside and step into puddles. I would also like to say that after tomorrow a furniture exhibition will open at the corner of First Boulevard and Brigadier Street and I sincerely hope to see all of you there. I also remind you that tonight, there will be given with sensational success the new comic opera *Socrates Must Decrease*. I have also been asked to tell you that the Kifer Distributing Centre has received a large selection of ladies' belts, and the offer may not be repeated. Now I make way for other performers and hope, townspeople, that you are all in good health and lack nothing.'

Sliding with the same nimbleness between the cross-pieces of the railing, he jumped down from the platform to the accompaniment of an approbatory murmur. M'sieur Pierre, who had already put on a white apron (from under which his jack boot showed), was carefully wiping his hands on a towel, and calmly, benevolently looking around. As soon as the deputy director had finished, he tossed the towel to his assistants and stepped over to Cincinnatus.

(The square black snouts of the photographers swayed and froze still.)

'No excitement, no fuss, please,' said M'sieur Pierre. 'We shall first of all remove our little shirt.'

'By myself,' said Cincinnatus.

'That's the boy. Take the little shirt away, men. Now I shall show you how to lie down.'

M'sieur Pierre dropped on to the block. The audience buzzed.

'Is this clear?' asked M'sieur Pierre, springing up and straightening his apron (it had come apart at the back, Rodrig helped tie it). 'Good. Let's begin. The light is a bit harsh . . . Perhaps you could . . . There, that's fine. Thank you. Perhaps just a wee bit more . . . Excellent! Now I shall ask you to lie down.'

'By myself, by myself,' said Cincinnatus and lay face down as he had been shown, but at once he covered the back of his neck with his hands.

'What a silly boy,' said M'sieur Pierre from above. 'If you do that how can I . . . (yes, give it here; then, immediately after, the bucket). And anyway why all this contraction of muscles? There must be no tension at all. Perfectly at ease. Remove your hands, please . . . (give it to me now). Be quite at ease and count aloud.'

'To ten,' said Cincinnatus.

'What was that, my friend?' said M'sieur Pierre as if asking him to repeat, and softly added, already beginning to heave, 'Step back a little, gentlemen.'

'To ten,' repeated Cincinnatus, spreading out his arms.

'I am not doing anything yet,' said M'sieur Pierre with an extraneous note of gasping effort, and the shadow of his swing was already running along the boards, when Cincinnatus began counting loudly and firmly: one Cincinnatus was counting, but the other Cincinnatus had already stopped heeding the sound of the unnecessary count which was fading away in the distance; and, with a clarity he had never experienced before – at first almost painful, so suddenly did it come, but then suffusing him with joy, he reflected: why am I here? Why am I lying like this? And, having asked himself these simple questions, he answered them by getting up and looking around.

All around there was a strange confusion. Through the headsman's still swinging hips the railing showed. On the steps the pale librarian sat doubled up, vomiting. The spectators were quite transparent, and quite useless, and they all kept surging and moving away – only the back rows, being painted rows, remained in place. Cincinnatus slowly descended from the platform and walked off through the shifting debris. He was overtaken by Roman, who was now many times smaller and who was at the same time Rodrig: 'What are you doing!' he croaked, jumping up and down. 'You can't, you can't! It's dishonest toward him, toward everybody . . . Come back, lie down – after all, you were lying down, everything was ready, everything was finished!' Cincinnatus brushed him aside and, he, with a bleak cry, ran off, already thinking only of his own safety.

Little was left of the square. The platform had long since collapsed in a cloud of reddish dust. The last to rush past was a woman in a black shawl, carrying the tiny executioner like a larva in her arms. The fallen trees lay flat and reliefless, while those that were still standing, also two-dimensional, with a lateral shading of the trunk to suggest roundness, barely held on with their branches to the ripping mesh of the sky. Everything was coming apart. Everything was falling. A spinning wind was picking up and whirling: dust, rags, chips of painted wood, bits of gilded plaster, pasteboard bricks, posters; an arid gloom fleeted; and amidst the dust, and the falling things, and the flapping scenery, Cincinnatus made his way in that direction where, to judge by the voices, stood beings akin to him.

KING QUEEN KNAVE

I

The huge black clock hand is still at rest but is on the point of making its once-a-minute gesture; that resilient jolt will set a whole world in motion. The clock facc will slowly turn away, full of despair, contempt, and boredom, as one by one the iron pillars will start walking past, bearing away the vault of the station like bland atlantes; the platform will begin to move past, carrying off on an unknown journey cigarette butts, used tickets, flecks of sunlight and spittle; a luggage handcart will glide by, its wheels motionless; it will be followed by a news stall hung with seductive magazine covers – photographs of naked, pearl-gray beauties; and people, people, people on the moving platform, themselves moving their feet, yet standing still, striding forward, yet retreating as in an agonizing dream full of incredible effort, nausea, a cottony weakness in one's calves, will surge back, almost falling supine.

There were more women than men as is always the case at partings. Franz's sister, with the pallor of the early hour on her thin cheeks, and an unpleasant, empty-stomach smell, dressed in a checked cape that surely one would never see on a city girl; and his mother, small, round, all in brown like a compact little monk. See the handkerchiefs beginning to flutter.

And not only did they slip away, those two familiar smiles; not only did the station depart removing its newsstand, its luggage cart, and a sandwich-and-fruit vendor with such nice, plump, lumpy, glossy red strawberries positively crying to be bitten into, all their achenes proclaiming their affinity with one's own tongue's papillae – but alas gone now; not only did all this fall behind; the entire old burg in its rosy autumn morning mist moved as well: the great stone *Herzog* in the square, the dark cathedral, the shop signs – top hat, a fish, the copper basin of a barber. There was no stopping the world now. In grand style houses pass by, the curtains flap in the open windows of his home, its floors crackle a little, the walls creak, his mother and sister are drinking their morning coffee in the swift draft, the furniture shudders from the quickening jolts, and ever more rapidly, more mysteriously, travel the houses, the cathedral, the square, the sidestreets. And even though by now tilled fields had long been unfolding their patchwork past the railway car window, Franz still felt in his very bones the receding motion of the townlet where he had lived for twenty years. Besides Franz, the wooden-benched third-class compartment contained two old ladies in corduroy dresses; a plump inevitably red-cheeked woman with the inevitable basket of eggs in her lap; and a blond youth in tan shorts, sturdy and angular, very much like his own rucksack, which was tightly stuffed and looked as if it had been hewed of yellow stone: this he had energetically shaken off and heaved onto the shelf. The seat by the door, opposite Franz, was occupied by a magazine with the picture of a breathtaking girl; and at a window in the corridor, his back to the compartment, stood a broad-shouldered man in a black overcoat.

The train was now going fast. Franz suddenly clutched his side, transfixed by the thought that he had lost his wallet which contained so much: the solid little ticket, and a stranger's visiting card with a precious address, and an inviolate month of human life in reichsmarks. The wallet was there all right, firm and warm. The old ladies began to stir and rustle, unwrapping sandwiches. The man in the corridor turned and, with a slight lurch, retreating half a step, and then overcoming the sway of the floor, entered the compartment.

Most of the nose had gone or had never grown. To what remained of its bridge the pale parchment-like skin adhered with a sickening tightness; the nostrils had lost all sense of decency and faced the flinching spectator like two sudden holes, black and asymmetrical; the cheeks and forehead showed a geographical range of shades – yellowish, pinkish, and very glossy. Had he inherited that mask? And if not, what illness, what explosion, what acid had disfigured him? He had practically no lips; the absence of eyelashes lent his blue eyes a startled expression. And yet the man was smartly dressed, well groomed and well built. He wore a double-breasted suit under his heavy overcoat. His hair was as sleek as a wig. He pulled up the knees of his trousers as he sat down with a leisurely movement, his grey-gloved hands opened the magazine he had left on the seat.

The shudder that had passed between Franz's shoulder blades now tapered to a strange sensation in his mouth. His tongue felt repulsively alive; his palate nastily moist. His memory opened its gallery of waxworks, and he knew, he knew that there, at its far end somewhere a chamber of horrors awaited him. He remembered a dog that had vomited on the threshold of a butcher's shop. He remembered a child, a mere toddler, who, bending with the difficulty of its age, had laboriously picked up and put to its lips a filthy thing resembling a baby's pacifier. He remembered an old man with a cough in a streetcar who had fired a clot of mucus into the ticket collector's hand. These were images that Franz usually held at bay but that always kept swarming in the background of his life greeting with a hysterical spasm any new impression that was kin to them. After a shock of that sort in those still recent days he would throw himself prone on his bed and try to fight off the fit of nausea. His recollections of school seemed always to be dodging away from possible, impossible, contacts with the grubby, pimply, slippery skin of some companion or other pressing him to join in a game or eager to impart some spitterish secret.

The man was leafing through the magazine, and the combination of his face with its enticing cover was intolerably grotesque. The ruddy egg woman sat next to the monster, her sleepy shoulder touching him. The youth's rucksack rubbed against his slick sticker-mottled black valise. And worst of all, the old ladies ignoring their foul neighbour munched their sandwiches and sucked on fuzzy sections of orange, wrapping the peels in scraps of paper and popping them daintly under the eat. But when the man put down his magazine and, without taking off his gloves, himself began eating a bun with cheese, glancing around provokingly, Franz could stand it no longer. He rose quickly, he lifted like a martyr his pale face, shook loose and pulled down his humble suitcase, collected his raincoat and hat and, banging his suitcase awkwardly against the doorjamb, fled into the corridor.

This particular coach had been hooked on to the express at a recent station, and the air in it was still fresh. He immediately felt a sense of relief. But the dizziness had not quite passed. A wall of beech trees was flickering by the window in a speckled sequence of sun and shade. He began tentatively to walk along the corridor clutching at knobs and things, and peering into the compartments. Only one had a free seat; he hesitated and went on, shaking off the image of two pasty-faced children with dust-black hands, their shoulders hunched up in expectation of a blow from their mother right on the nape as they quietly kept sliding off the seat to play among greasy scraps of papers on the unmentionable floor at the passengers' feet. Franz reached the end of the car and paused, struck by an extraordinary thought. This thought was so sweet, so audacious and exciting, that he had to take off his glasses and wipe them. 'No, I can't, out of the question,' said Franz under his breath, already realizing, however, that he could not conquer the temptation. Then checking the knot of his tie with thumb and forefinger, he crossed in a burst of clangor the unsteady connecting plates, and with an exquisite sinking feeling in the pit of his stomach passed into the next car.

It was a second-class schnellzug car, and to Franz second-class was something brightly attractive, even slightly sinful, smacking of spicy extravagance like a sip of thick white liqueur or that enormous grapefruit resembling a yellow skull that he had once bought on the way to school. About first-class one could not dream at all – that was for diplomats, generals, and almost unearthly actresses! Second, though . . . second. . . . If he could only get up the courage. They said his late father (a seedy notary) had on occasion – long ago, before the war – travelled second-class. Yet, Franz could not make up his mind. He stopped at the beginning of the corridor, by the placard listing the car inventory, and now it was no longer a fence-like forest glancing by but vast meadows majestically gliding past, and, in the distance, parallel to the tracks, flowed a highway, along which sped lickety-split a lilliputian automobile.

The conductor just then making his rounds brought him out of his difficulty. Franz bought a supplement promoting his ticket to the next rank. A short tunnel deafened him with its resounding darkness. Then it was light again but the conductor had vanished.

The compartment that Franz entered with a silent unacknowledged bow was occupied by only two people – a handsome bright-eyed lady and a middle-aged man with a clipped tawny moustache. Franz hung up his raincoat and sat down carefully. The seat was soft; there was such a cosy semi-circular projection at temple level separating one seat from the next; the photographs on the wall were so romantic – a flock of sheep, a cross on a rock, a waterfall. He slowly stretched out his long feet, slowly took a folded newspaper from his pocket. But he was unable to read. Benumbed with luxury he merely held the newspaper open and from behind it examined his fellow travellers. Oh, they were charming. The lady wore a black suit and a diminutive black hat with a little diamond swallow. Her face was serious, her eyes cold, a little dark down, the sign of passion, glistened above her upper lip, and a gleam of sun brought out the creamy texture of her neck at the throat with its two delicate transverse lines as if traced with a fingernail across it, one above the other: also a token of all kinds of marvels, according to one of his schoolmates, a precocious expert. The man must be a foreigner, judging by his soft collar and tweeds. Franz, however, was mistaken.

'I'm thirsty,' said the man with a Berlin accent. 'Too bad there's no fruit. Those strawberries were positively dying to be sampled.'

'It's your own fault,' answered the lady in a displeased voice, adding a little later: 'I still cannot get over it – it was such a silly thing to do.'

Dreyer briefly cast up his eyes to a makeshift heaven and made no reply.

'It's your own fault,' she repeated and automatically pulled at her pleated skirt, automatically noticing that the awkward young man with the glasses who had appeared in the door corner seemed to be fascinated by the sheer silk of her legs.

'Anyway,' she said, 'it's not worth discussing.'

Dreyer knew that his silence irritated Martha unspeakably. There was a boyish gleam in his eye, and the soft folds about his lips were undulating because he was rolling a mint in his mouth. The incident that had irritated his wife was actually pretty silly. They had spent August and half of September in Tyrol, and now, on the way home, had stopped for a few days on business in that quaint little town, and there he had called on his cousin Lina with whom he had danced in his youth, some twenty-five years ago. His wife had flatly refused to accompany him. Lina, now a roly-poly creature with false teeth but just as talkative and amiable as ever, found that the years had left their mark on him but that it might have been worse; she served him excellent coffee, told him about her children, said she was sorry they were not at home, asked about Martha (whom she did not know) and his business (about which she was well informed); then, after a pious pause, she wondered if he could give her a piece of advice. . . .

It was warm in the room where around the aged chandelier, with gray little glass pendants like dirty icicles, flies were describing parallelograms, lighting every time on the same pendants (which for some reason amused him), and the old chairs extended their plush-covered arms with comical cordiality. An old pug dozed on an embroidered cushion. In reply to the expectant interrogatory sigh of his cousin he had suddenly said, coming to life with a laugh: 'Well, why don't you have him come to see me in Berlin? I'll give him a job.' And that was what his wife could not forgive him. She called it 'swamping the business with poor relations'; but when you come down to it, how can one poor relation swamp anything? Knowing that Lina would invite his wife, and that Martha would not go in any circumstance, he had lied, telling his cousin that they were leaving the same evening. Instead, Martha and he had visited a fair and the splendid vineyards of a business friend. A week later at the station, when they had already settled down in their compartment, he had glimpsed Lina from the window. It was a wonder they had not run into her somewhere in town. Martha wanted to avoid her seeing them at all cost, and even though the idea of buying a nest of fruit for the trip appealed to him greatly he did not put his head out of the window, did not beckon with a soft 'psst' the young vendor in the white jacket.

Comfortably dressed, in perfect health, a coloured mist of vague pleasant thoughts in his head and a peppermint in his mouth, Dreyer sat with crossed arms, and the soft folds of the fabric in the crook of his arms matched the soft folds of his cheeks, and the outline of his clipped moustache, and the wrinkles fanning templeward from his eyes. With a peculiar blandly amused gleam in his eyes he gazed from under his brows at the green landscape gliding in the window, at Martha's handsome profile rimmed with sunlight, and the cheap suitcase of the bespectacled young man who was reading a newspaper in the corner by the door. Idly he considered that passenger, palpating him from all sides. He noted the so-called 'lizard' pattern of the young fellow's green-and-garnet tie which obviously had cost ninety-five pfennigs, the stiff collar, and also the cuffs and front of his shirt – a shirt incidentally which only existed in an abstract form since all its visible parts, judging by a treacherous gloss, were pieces of starched armour of rather low quality but greatly esteemed by a frugal provincial who attaches them to an invisible undergarment made at home of unbleached cloth. As to the young man's suit, it evoked a delicate melancholy in Dreyer as he reflected not for the first time on the pathetically short life of every new cut: that kind of three-button, narrow-lapelled blue jacket with a pin stripe had disappeared from most Berlin stores at least five years ago.

Two alarmed eyes were suddenly born in the lenses, and Dreyer turned away. Martha said:

'It is all so silly. I wish you had listened to me.'

Her husband sighed and said nothing. She wanted to go on

– there were still lots of pithy rebukes she could make but she felt the young man was listening and, instead of words, leaned her elbow abruptly on the window side of the table leaf – pulling up the skin of her cheek with her knuckles. She sat that way until the flicker of woods in the window became irksome; she slowly straightened her ripe body, annoyed and bored, then leaned back and closed her eyes. The sun penetrated her eyelids with solid scarlet, across which luminous stripes moved in succession (the ghostly negative of the passing forest), and a replica of her husband's cheerful face, as if slowly rotating toward her, got mixed up in this barred redness, and she opened her eyes with a start. Her husband, however, was sitting relatively far, reading a book bound in purple morocco. He was reading attentively and with pleasure. Nothing existed beyond the sunlit page. He turned the page, looked around, and the outside world avidly, like a playful dog waiting for that moment, darted up to him with a bright bound. But pushing Tom away affectionately, Dreyer again immersed himself in his anthology of verse.

For Martha that frolicsome radiance was simply the stuffy air in a swaying railway car. It is supposed to be stuffy in a car: that is customary and therefore good. Life should proceed according to plan, straight and strict, without freakish twists and wiggles. An elegant book is all right on a drawing-room table. In a railway car, to allay boredom, one can leaf through some trashy magazine. But to imbibe and relish . . . poems, if you please . . . in an expensive binding . . . a person who calls himself a businessman cannot, must not, dare not act like that. But for that matter, perhaps, he may be doing it on purpose, to spite me. Just another of his show-off whims. Very well, my friend, keep showing off. How nice it would be to pluck that book out of his hands and lock it up in a suitcase.

At that instant the sun seemed to lay bare her face, flowing over her smooth cheeks and lending an artificial warmth to her eyes with their large elastic-looking pupils amid the dove-grey iris and adorable dark lids slightly creased like violets, radiantly lashed and rarely blinking as if she were constantly afraid of losing sight of an essential goal. She wore almost no make-up – only in the minute transverse fissures of her full lips there seemed to be drying traces of orange-red paint.

Franz, who had been hiding behind his newspaper in a state of blissful nonexistence, living on the outside of himself, in the chance motions and chance words of his travelling companions, now started to assert himself and openly, almost arrogantly, looked at the lady.

Yet only a moment ago his thoughts always tending to morbid associations had blended, in one of those falsely harmonious images that are significant within the dream but meaningless when one recalls it, two recent events. The transition from the third-class compartment, where a noseless monster reigned in silence, into this sunny plush room appeared to him like the passage from a hideous hell through the purgatory of the corridors and intervestibular clatter into a little abode of bliss. The old conductor who had punched his ticket a short while ago and promptly vanished might have been as humble and omnipotent as St Peter. Pious popular prints that had frightened him in childhood came to life again. He transformed the conductor's click into that of a key unlocking the gates of paradise. So a grease-painted gaudy-faced actor in a miracle play passes across a long stage divided into three parts, from the jaws of the devil into the shelter of angels. And Franz, in order to drive away the old obsessive fantasy, eagerly started to seek human, everyday tokens that would break the spell.

Martha helped him. While looking sideways out of the window she yawned: he glimpsed the swell of her tense tongue in the red penumbra of her mouth and the flash of her teeth before her hand shot up to her mouth to stop her soul from escaping; whereupon she blinked, dispersing a tickling tear with the beat of her eyelashes. Franz was not one to resist the example of a yawn, especially one that resembled somehow those luscious autumn strawberries for which his hometown was famous. At the moment when, unable to overcome the force prying his palate, he convulsively opened his mouth, Martha happened to glance at him, and he realized, snarling and weeping, that she realized he had been looking at her. The morbid bliss he had shortly before experienced as he looked at her dissolving face now turned into acute embarrassment. He knit his brows under her radiant and indifferent gaze and, when she turned away, mentally calculated, as though his fingers had rattled across the counters of a secret abacus, how many days of his life he would give to possess this woman.

The door slid open, and an excited waiter, the herald of some frightful disaster, thrust his head in, barked his message, and dashed on to the next compartment to cry his news.

Basically Martha was opposed to those fraudulent frivolous meals, with the railway company charging you exorbitant prices for mediocre food, and this almost physical sensation of needless expense, mixed with the feeling that someone, snug and robust, wanted to cheat her proved to be so strong that were it not for a ravenous hunger she would certainly not have gone that long vacillating way to the dining car. She vaguely envied the bespectacled young man who reached into the pocket of his raincoat hanging beside him and pulled out a sandwich. She got up and took her handbag under her arm. Dreyer found the violet ribbon in his book, marked his page with it, and after waiting a couple of seconds as if he could not immediately make the transition from one world to the other, gave his knees a light slap and stood up too. He instantly filled the whole compartment, being one of those men who despite medium height and moderate corpulence create an impression of extraordinary bulk. Franz retracted his feet. Martha and her husband lurched past him and went out.

He was left alone with his grey sandwich in the now spacious compartment. He munched and gazed out of the window. A green bank was rising there diagonally until it suffused the window to the top. Then, resolving an iron chord, a bridge banged overhead and instantly the green slope vanished and open country unfurled – fields, willows, a golden birch tree, a winding brook, beds of cabbage. Franz finished his sandwich, fidgeted cozily, and closed his eyes.

Berlin! In that very name of the still unfamiliar metropolis, in the lumber and rumble of the first syllable and in the light ring of the second there was something that excited him like the romantic names of good wines and bad women. The express seemed already to be speeding along the famous avenue lined for him with gigantic ancient lindens beneath which seethed for him a flamboyant crowd. The express sped past those lindens grown so luxuriantly out of the avenue's resonant name, and ('derlin, derlin' went the bell of the waiter summoning belated diners) shot under an enormous arch ornamented with mother-of-pearl spangles. Farther on there was an enchanting mist where another picture postcard turned on its stand showing a translucent tower against a black background. It vanished, and, in a brilliantly lit-up emporium, among gilded dummies, limpid mirrors, and glass counters, Franz strolled about in cut-away, striped trousers, and white spats, and with a smooth movement of his hand directed customers to the departments they needed. This was no longer a wholly conscious play of thought, nor was it yet a dream; and at the instant that sleep was about to trip him up, Franz regained control of himself and directed his thoughts according to his wishes. He promised himself a lone treat that very night. He bared the shoulders of the woman that had just been sitting by the window, made a quick mental test (did blind Eros react? clumsy Eros did, unsticking its folds in the dark); then, keeping the splendid shoulders, changed the head, substituting for it the face of that seventeen-year-old maid who had vanished with a silver soup ladle almost as big as she before he had had time to declare his love; but that head too he erased and, in its place, attached the face of one of those bold-eyed, humid-lipped Berlin beauties that one encounters mainly in liquor and cigarette advertisements. Only then did the image come to life: the bare-bosomed girl lifted a wine glass to her crimson lips, gently swinging her apricot-silk leg as a red backless slipper slowly slid off her foot. The slipper fell off, and Franz, bending down after it, plunged softly into dark slumber. He slept with mouth agape so that his pale face presented three apertures, two shiny ones (his glasses) and one black (his mouth). Dreyer noticed this symmetry when an hour later he returned with Martha from the dining car. In silence they stepped over a lifeless leg. Martha put her handbag on the collapsible window table, and the bag's nickel clasp with its cat's eye immediately came to life as a green reflection began dancing in it. Dreyer took out a cigar but did not light it.

The dinner, particularly that wiener schnitzel, had turned out to be pretty good, and Martha was not sorry now that she had agreed to go. Her complexion had grown warmer, her exquisite eyes were moist, her freshly painted lips glistened. She smiled, only just baring her incisors, and this contented, precious smile lingered on her face for several instants. Dreyer lazily admired her, his eyes slightly narrowed, savouring her smile as one might an unexpected gift, but nothing on earth could have made him show that pleasure. When the smile disappeared he turned away as a satisfied gawker drifts away after the bicyclist has picked himself up, and the street vendor has replaced on his cart the scattered fruit.

Franz crossed his legs like one very lame and slow but did not wake up. Harshly the train began braking. There glided past a brick wall, an enormous chimney, freight cars standing on a siding. Presently it grew dark in the compartment: they had entered a vast domed station.

'I'll go out, my love,' said Dreyer, who liked to smoke in the open air.

Left alone, Martha leaned back in the corner, and having nothing better to do looked at the bespectacled corpse in the corner, thinking indifferently that this, perhaps, was the young man's stop and he would miss it. Dreyer strode along the platform, drummed with five fingers on the windowpane as he passed, but his wife did not smile again. With a puff of smoke he moved on. He strolled leisurely, with a bouncing gait, his hands clasped behind his back, and his cigar thrust forward. He reflected that it would be nice some day to be promenading like this beneath the glazed arches of a remote station somewhere on the way to Andalusia, Bagdad or Nizhni Novgorod. Actually one could set off any time; the globe was enormous and round, and he had enough spare cash to circle it completely half-a-dozen times. Martha, though, would refuse to come, preferring a trim suburban lawn to the most luxuriant jungle. She would only sniff sarcastically were he to suggest they take a year off. 'I suppose,' he thought, 'I ought to buy a paper. I guess the stock market is also an interesting and tricky subject. And let us see if our two aviators – or is it some wonderful hoax? – have managed to duplicate in reverse direction that young American's feat of four months ago. America, Mexico, Palm Beach. Willy Wald was there, wanted us to accompany him. No, there is no breaking her down. Now then, where is the newsstand? That old sewing machine with its arthritic pedal wrapped up in brown paper is so clear right now, and yet in an hour or two I shall forget it forever; I shall forget that I looked at it; I shall forget everything. . . .' Just then a whistle blew, and the baggage car moved. Hey, that's my train!

Dreyer made for the newsstand at a smart trot, selected a coin from his palm, snatched the paper he wanted, dropped it, retrieved it, and dashed back. Not very gracefully, he hopped onto a passing step, and could not open the door immediately. In the struggle he lost his cigar but not his paper. Chuckling and panting, he walked through one car, another, a third. In the next to last corridor a big fellow in a black overcoat who was pulling a window shut moved to let him by. Glancing at him as he passed, Dreyer saw the grinning face of a grown man with the nose of a baby monkey. 'Curious,' thought Dreyer; 'ought to get such a dummy to display something funny.' In the next car he found his compartment, stepped across the lifeless leg, by now a familiar fixture, and quietly sat down. Martha was apparently asleep. He opened the paper, and then noticed that her eyes were fixed upon him.

'Crazy idiot,' she said calmly and closed her eyes again. Dreyer nodded amiably and immersed himself in his paper.

The first chapter of a journey is always detailed and slow. Its middle hours are drowsy, and the last ones swift. Presently Franz awoke and made some chewing motions with his lips. His travelling companions were sleeping. The light in the window had dimmed, but in compensation the reflection of Martha's little bright swallow had appeared in it. Franz glanced at his wrist, at the watch face sturdily protected by its metal mesh. A lot of time, however, had escaped from that prison cell. There was a most repulsive taste in his mouth. He carefully wiped with a special square of cloth his glasses, and made his way out into the corridor in search of the toilet. As he stood there holding on to an iron handle, he found it strange and dreadful to be connected to a cold hole where his stream glistened and bounced, with the dark headlong-rushing naked earth so near, so fateful.

An hour later the Dreyers also woke up. A waiter brought them café-au-lait in bulky cups, and Martha criticized each sip she took. Dusk deepened in the faded fields which seemed to run faster and faster. Then rain began to patter softly against the window: a rillet would snake down the glass, stop hesitantly, and then again resume its quick downward zigzag course. Outside the corridor's windows a narrow orange sunset smouldered beneath a black thunderhead. Presently the light went on in the compartment. Martha looked at length in a little mirror, baring her teeth and raising her upper lip.

Dreyer, still replete with the pleasant warmth of slumber, looked at the dark-blue window, at the raindrops, and thought that tomorrow was Sunday, and that in the morning he would go to play tennis (which he had recently taken up with the desperate zeal of middle age), and that it would be a shame if the weather interfered with his plans. He asked himself if he had made any progress, unconsciously tensing his right shoulder, and remembered the beautifully groomed, sun-swept court in his favourite Tyrol resort, and the fabled player who had arrived for a local match in a white flannel overcoat with an English club muffler around his neck and three rackets under his arm, and then unhurriedly with professional gestures had taken off that coat, and the long striped scarf, and the white sweater under the coat, and then with a flash of his arm bared to the elbow had ringingly offered poor Paul von Lepel the indolent and terrible present of the first practice ball.

'Autumn, rain,' said Martha slamming her handbag shut.

'Oh, just a drizzle,' Dreyer corrected her softly.

The train, as if it were already within the magnetic field of the metropolis, was now travelling with incredible speed. The windowpanes had grown completely dark – one could not even distinguish the sky. The fiery stripe of an express flashed by in the opposite direction, and was cut off with a bang forever. It had been a hoax after all – that flight to America. Franz, who had returned to the compartment, suddenly clutched convulsively at his side. Another hour passed and in the murky gloom there appeared distant clusters of light, diamond-like conflagrations.

Soon Dreyer stood up. Franz, with a chill of excitement in all his frame, stood up too. The ritual of arrival had begun. Dreyer pulled down his bags (he enjoyed handing them to porters through the window). Franz, standing on tiptoe, pulled at his suitcase too. Their backs collided elastically, and Dreyer laughed. Franz started putting on his raincoat, failed to find the armhole at the first poke, donned his bottle-green hat, and went out into the corridor with his reluctant suitcase. More lights specked the darkness now and suddenly a street with an illuminated tram was revealed seemingly under his very feet; it disappeared again behind house walls that were being rapidly shuffled and dealt out again.

'Come on, hurry!' implored Franz.

A minor station flew past, just a platform, a half-opened jewel box, and all grew dark again as if no Berlin existed within miles. At last a topaz light spread out over a thousand tracks and rows of wet railway cars. Slowly, surely, smoothly, the huge iron cavity of the station drew in the train, which at once grew sluggish, and then, with a jolt, redundant.

Franz descended into the smoky damp. As he passed by the car he had lived in, he saw his tawny-moustached travelling companion lowering a window and hailing a porter. For a moment he regretted to have parted forever with that adorable, capricious, sloe-eyed lady. Together with the hurrying crowd he walked down the tremendously long platform, surrendered his ticket to its taker with an impatient hand, and continued past innumerable posters, counters, flower shops, people burdened with unnecessary bags, to an archway and freedom.

2

Golden haze, puffy bedquilt. Another awakening, but perhaps not yet the final one. This occurs not infrequently: You come to, and see yourself, say, sitting in an elegant second-class compartment with a couple of elegant strangers; actually, though, this is a false awakening, being merely the next layer of your dream, as if you were rising up from stratum to stratum but never reaching the surface, never emerging into reality. Your spellbound thought, however, mistakes every new layer of the dream for the door of reality. You believe in it, and holding your breath leave the railway station you have been brought to in immemorial fantasies and cross the station square. You discern next to nothing, for the night is blurred by rain, your spectacles are foggy, and you want as quickly as possible to reach the ghostly hotel across the square so as to wash your face, change your shirt cuffs and then go wandering along dazzling streets. Something happens, however – an absurd mishap – and what seemed reality abruptly loses the tingle and tang of reality. Your consciousness was deceived: you are still fast asleep. Incoherent slumber dulls your mind. Then comes a new moment of specious awareness: this golden haze and your room in the hotel, whose name is 'The Montevideo.' A shopkeeper you knew at home, a nostalgic Berliner, had jotted it down on a slip of paper for you. Yet who knows? Is this reality, *the* final reality, or just a new deceptive dream?

Lying on his back Franz peered with myopic agonizingly narrowed eyes at the blue mist of a ceiling, and then sideways at a radiant blur which no doubt was a window. And in order to free himself from this gold-tinted vagueness still so strongly reminiscent of a dream, he reached toward the night table and groped for his glasses.

And only when he had touched them, or more precisely the handkerchief in which they were wrapped as in a winding sheet, only then did Franz remember that absurd mishap in a lower layer of dream. When he had first come into this room, looked around, and opened the window (only to reveal a dark backyard and a dark noisy tree) he had, first of all, torn off his soiled collar that had been oppressing his neck and had hurriedly begun washing his face. Like an imbecile, he had placed his glasses on the edge of the washstand, beside the basin. As he lifted the heavy thing in order to empty it into the pail, he not only knocked the glasses off the edge of the stand, but sidestepping in awkward rhythm with the sloshing basin he held, had heard an ominous crunch under his heel.

In the process of reconstructing this event in his mind, Franz grimaced and groaned. All the festive lights of Friedrichstrasse had been stamped out by his boot. He would have to take the glasses to be repaired: only one lens was still in place and that was cracked. He palpated rather than re-examined the cripple. Mentally he had already gone out of doors in search of the proper shop. First that, and then the important, rather frightening visit. And, remembering how his mother had insisted that he make the call on the very first morning after his arrival ('it will be just the day when you can find a businessman at home'), Franz also remembered that it was Sunday.

He clucked his tongue and lay still.

Complicated but familiar poverty (that cannot afford spare sets of expensive articles) now resulted in primitive panic. Without his glasses he was as good as blind, yet he must set out on a perilous journey across a strange city. He imagined the predatory spectres that last night had been crowding near the station, their motors running and their doors slamming, when still safely bespectacled but with his vision dimmed by the rainy night he had started to cross the dark square. Then he had gone to bed after the mishap without taking the walk he had been looking forward to, without getting his first taste of Berlin at the very hour of its voluptuous glitter and swarming. Instead, in miserable self compensation, he had succumbed again, that first night, to the solitary practice he had sworn to give up before his departure.

But to pass the entire day in that hostile hotel room amid vague hostile objects, to wait with nothing to do until Monday, when a shop with a sign (for the seeing!) in the shape of a giant blue pince-nez would open – such a prospect was unthinkable. Franz threw back the quilt and, barefoot, padded warily to the window.

A light-blue, delicate, marvellously sunny morning welcomed him. Most of the yard was taken up by the sable velvet of what seemed to be a spreading tree shadow above which he was just able to distinguish the blurry orange-red hue of what looked like rich foliage. Booming city, indeed! Out there all was as quiet as in the remote serenity of a luminous rural autumn.

Aha, it was the room that was noisy! Its hubbub comprised

the hollow hum of irksome human thoughts, the clatter of a moved chair, under which a much needed sock had long been hiding from the purblind, the plash of water, the tinkle of small coins that had foolishly fallen out of an elusive waistcoat, the scrape of his suitcase as it was dragged to a far corner where there would be no danger of one's tripping over it again; and there was an additional background noise – the room's own groan and din like the voice of a magnified seashell, in contrast with that sunny startling miraculous stillness preserved like a costly wine in the cool depths of the yard.

At last Franz overcame all the blotches and banks of fog, located his hat, recoiled from the embrace of the clowning mirror and made for the door. Only his face remained bare. Having negotiated the stairs, where an angel was singing as she polished the banisters, he showed the desk clerk the address on the priceless card and was told what bus to take and where to wait for it. He hesitated for a moment, tempted by the magic and majestic possibility of a taxi. He rejected it not only because of the cost but because his potential employer might take him for a spendthrift if he arrived in state.

Once in the street he was engulfed in streaming radiance. Outlines did not exist, colours had no substance. Like a woman's wispy dress that has slipped off its hanger, the city shimmered and fell in fantastic folds, not held up by anything, a discarnate iridescence limply suspended in the azure autumnal air. Beyond the nacrine desert of the square, across which a car sped now and then with a new metropolitan trumpeting, great pink edifices loomed, and suddenly a sunbeam, a gleam of glass, would stab him painfully in the pupil.

Franz reached a plausible street corner. After much fussing and squinting he discovered the red blur of the bus stop which rippled and wavered like the supports of a bathhouse when you dive under it. Almost directly the yellow mirage of a bus came into being. Stepping on somebody's foot, which at once dissolved under him as everything else was dissolving, Franz seized the handrail and a voice –evidently the conductor's – barked in his ear: 'Up!' It was the first time he had ascended this kind of spiral staircase (only a few old trams served his hometown), and when the bus jerked into motion he caught a frightening glimpse of the asphalt rising like a silvery wall, grabbed someone's shoulder, and carried along by the force of an inexorable curve, during which the whole bus seemed to heel over, zoomed up the last steps and found himself on top. He sat down and looked around with helpless indignation. He was floating very high above the city. On the street below people slithered like jellyfish whenever the traffic froze. Then the bus started again, and the houses, shade-blue on one side of the street, sun-hazy on the other, rode by like clouds blending imperceptibly with the tender sky. This is how Franz first saw the city – fantasmally tinted, ethereal, impregnated with swimming colours, in no way resembling his crude provincial dream.

Was he on the right bus? Yes, said the ticket dispenser.

The clean air whistled in his ears, and the horns called to each other in celestial voices. He caught a whiff of dry leaves and a branch nearly brushed against him. He asked a neighbour where he should get off. It turned out to be a long way yet. He began counting the stops so as not to have to ask again, and tried in vain to distinguish cross streets. The speed, the airiness, the odour of autumn, the dizzy mirror-like quality of the world all merged into so extraordinary a feeling of disembodiment that Franz deliberately moved his neck in order to feel the hard head of his collar stud, which seemed to him the only proof of his existence.

At last his stop came. He clambered down the steep stairs and cautiously stepped onto the sidewalk. From receding heights a faceless traveller shouted to him: 'On your right! First street on your—' Franz, vibrating responsively, reached the corner and turned right. Stillness, solitude, a sunny mist. He felt he was losing his way, melting in this mist, and most important, he could not distinguish the house numbers. He felt weak and sweaty. Finally, spying a cloudy passer-by, he accosted him and asked where number five was. The pedestrian stood very near him, and the shadow of foliage played so strangely over his face that for an instant Franz thought he recognized the man from whom he had fled the day before. One could maintain with almost complete certainty that this was a dappled whim of sun and shade; and yet it gave Franz such a shock that he averted his eyes. 'Right across the street, where you see that white fence,' the man said jauntily, and went on his way.

Franz did not see any fence but found a wicket, groped for the button and pressed it. The gate emitted an odd buzzing sound. He waited a little and pressed again. Again the wicket buzzed. No one came to open it. Beyond lay the greenish haze of a garden with a house floating there like an indistinct reflection. He tried to open the gate himself, but found it unyielding. Biting his lips he rang once more and held his finger on the button for a long time. The same monotonous buzzing. He suddenly realized what the trick was: leaned against the gate as he rang, and it opened so angrily that he nearly fell. Someone called to him: 'Whom do you want?' He turned toward the voice and distinguished a woman in a light-coloured dress standing on the gravel path that led to the house.

'My husband is not home yet,' the voice said after a little pause when Franz had replied.

Slitting his eyes he made out the flash of earrings and dark smooth hair. She was neither a fearful nor fanciful woman but in his clumsy eagerness to see better he had come up so close that for a ridiculous moment she thought this impetuous intruder was about to take her head between his hands.

'It's very important,' said Franz. 'You see, I'm a relative of his.' Stopping in front of her he produced his wallet and began to rummage in it for the famous card.

She wondered where she had seen him before. His ears were of a translucent red in the sun, and tiny drops of sweat gemmed his innocent forehead right at the roots of his short dark hair. A sudden recollection, like a conjuror, put eyeglasses on the inclined face and immediately removed them again. Martha smiled. At the same time Franz found the card and raised his head.

'Here,' he said. 'I was told to come. On a Sunday.'

She looked at the card and smiled again.

'Your uncle has gone to play tennis. He will be back for lunch. But we've already met, you know.'

'Bitte?' said Franz, straining his eyes.

Later, when he remembered this meeting, the mirage of the garden, that sun-melting dress, he marvelled at the length of time it had taken him to recognize her. At three paces he was able to make out a person's features at least as clearly as a normal human eye would through a gauze veil. Rather naively he told himself that he had never seen her hatless before, and had not expected her to wear her hair with a parting in the middle and a chignon behind (the only particular in which Martha did not follow the fashion); still it was not so simple to explain how it could have happened that, even in that dim perception of the phantom form, there had not worked again and at once the same tremor, the same magic that had fascinated him the day before. It seemed to him afterwards that on that morning he had been plunged in a vague irreproducible world existing for one brief Sunday, a world where everything was delicate and weightless, radiant and unstable. In this dream anything could happen: so it did turn out after all that Franz had not awakened in his hotel bed that morning but had merely passed into the next stratum of sleep. In the unsubstantial radiance of his myopia, Martha bore no resemblance at all to the lady in the train who had glowed like a picture and yawned like a tigress. Her madonna-like beauty that he had glimpsed and then lost now appeared in full as if this were her true essence now blooming before him without any admixture, without flaw or frame. He could not have said with certitude if he found this blurry lady attractive. Nearsightedness is chaste. And besides, she was the wife of the man on whom depended his whole future, out of whom he had been ordered to squeeze everything he possibly could, and this fact made her seem at the very moment of acquaintance more distant, more unattainable than the glamorous stranger of the preceding day. As he followed Martha up the path to the house he gesticulated, kept apologizing for his infirmity, broken glasses, closed shops, and extolling the marvels of coincidence, so intoxicating was his desire to dispose her favourably toward him as quickly as possible.

On the lawn near the porch stood a very tall beach umbrella and under it a small table and several wicker armchairs. Martha sat down, and Franz, grinning and blinking, sat down beside her. She decided that she had stunned him completely with the sight of her small but expensive garden which contained among other things five beds of dahlias, three larches, two weeping willows, and one magnolia, and did not bother to ascertain if those poor wild eyes could distinguish a beach umbrella from an ornamental tree. She enjoyed receiving him so elegantly *auf englische Weise,* dazzling him with undreamt-of wealth, and was looking forward to showing him the villa, the miniatures in the parlour, and the satinwood in the bedroom, and hearing this rather handsome boy's moans of respectful admiration. And, since generally her visitors were people from her own circle whom she had long since grown tired of dazzling, she felt tenderly grateful to this provincial with his starched collar and narrow trousers for giving her an opportunity to renew the pride she had known in her first months of marriage.

'It's so quiet here,' said Franz. 'I thought Berlin would be so noisy.'

'Oh, but we live almost in the country,' she answered, and feeling herself seven years younger, added: 'the next villa over there belongs to a count. A very nice old man, we see a lot of him.'

'Very pleasant – this quiet simple atmosphere,' said Franz, steadily developing the theme and already foreseeing a blind alley.

She looked at his pale pink-knuckled hand with a nice long index lying flat on the table. The thin fingers were trembling slightly.

'I have often tried to decide,' she said, 'whom does one know better – somebody one has been in the same room with for five hours or somebody one has seen for ten minutes every day during a whole month.'

'Bitte?' said Franz.

'I suppose,' she went on, 'the real factor here is not the amount of time but that of communication – the exchange of ideas on life and living conditions. Tell me, how are you related to my husband exactly? Second cousin, isn't it? You're going to work here, that's nice, boys like you should be made to work a lot. His business is enormous – I mean, my husband's firm. But then I'm sure you've already heard about his celebrated emporium. Perhaps emporium is too strong a word, it carries men's things only, but there is everything, everything – neckties, hats, sporting goods. Then there's his office in another part of the town and various banking operations.'

'It will be hard to begin,' said Franz, drumming with his fingers. 'I'm a little scared. But I know your husband is a wonderful man, a very kind good man. My mother worships him.'

At this moment there appeared from somewhere, as if in token of sympathy, the spectre of a dog which turned out upon closer examination to be an Alsatian. Lowering its head, the dog placed something at Franz's feet. Then it retreated a little, dissolved momentarily, and waited expectantly.

'That's Tom,' said Martha. 'Tom won a prize at the show. Didn't you, Tom' (she spoke to Tom only in the presence of guests).

Out of respect for his hostess, Franz picked up the object the dog was offering him. It proved to be a wet wooden ball covered with tangible tooth marks. As soon as he took up the ball, raising it up to his face, the spectre of the dog emerged with a bound from the sunny haze, becoming alive, warm, active, and nearly knocking him off his chair. He quickly got rid of the ball. Tom vanished.

The ball landed right among the dahlias but of course Franz did not see this.

'Fine animal,' he observed with revulsion as he wiped his wet hand against the chintzed chair arm. Martha was looking away, worried by the storm in the flowerbed which Tom was trampling in frantic search of his plaything. She clapped her hands. Franz politely clapped too, mistaking admonishment for applause. Fortunately at that moment a boy rode by on a bicycle, and Tom, instantly forgetting the ball, lunged headlong toward the garden fence and dashed along its entire length barking furiously. Then he immediately calmed down, trotted back and lay down by the porch steps under Martha's cold eye, lolling his tongue and folding back one front paw like a lion.

As Franz listened to what Martha was telling him, in the vibrant petulant tones he was getting used to, about the Tyrol, he felt that the dog had not gone too far away, and might bring back any moment that slimy object. Nostalgically he remembered a nasty old lady's nasty old pug (a relative and great enemy of his mother's pet) that he had managed to kick smartly on several occasions.

'But somehow, you know,' Martha was saying, 'one felt hemmed in. One imagined those mountains might crash down on the hotel, in the middle of the night, right on our bed, burying me under them and my husband, killing everybody. We were thinking of going on to Italy but somehow I lost the lust. He's pretty stupid, our Tom. Dogs that play with balls are always stupid. A strange gentleman arrives but for him it's a brand-new member of the family. This is your first visit, isn't it, to our great city? How do you like it here?'

Franz indicated his eyes with a polite pinkie: 'I'm quite blind,' he said. 'Until I get some new glasses, I cannot appreciate anything. All I see are just colours, which after all is not very interesting. But in general I like it. And it's so quiet here, under this yellow tree.'

For some reason the thought crossed his mind – a streak of fugitive fancy – that at that very moment his mother was returning from church with Frau Kamelspinner, the taxidermist's wife. And meanwhile – wonder of wonders – he was having a difficult but delicious conversation with this misty lady in this radiant mist. It was all very dangerous; every word she said might trip him.

Martha noticed his slight stammer and the nervous way he had of sniffing now and then. 'Dazzled and embarrassed, and so very young,' she reflected with a mixture of contempt and tenderness, 'warm, healthy young wax that one can manipulate and mould till its shape suits your pleasure. He should have shaved, though, before coming.' And she said by way of experiment, just to see how he would react:

'If you plan to work at a smart store, my good sir, you must cultivate a more confident manner and get rid of that black down on your manly jaws.'

As she had expected, Franz lost what composure he had.

'I shall get new spectables, I mean respectacles,' he expostulated, or so his flustered lisp sounded.

She allowed his confusion to spin itself out, telling herself that it was very good for him. Franz really did feel most uncomfortable for an instant but not quite in the way she imagined. What put him off was not the remonstrance but the sudden coarseness of her tone, a kind of throaty 'hep!,' as if, to set the example, she were jerking back her shoulders at the word 'confident.' This was not in keeping with his misty image of her.

The jarring interpolation passed quickly: Martha melted back into the glamorous haze of the world surrounding him and resumed her elegant conversation.

'Autumn is chillier around here than in your native orchards. I love luscious fruit but I also like a crisp cold day. There is something about the texture and temperature of my skin that simply thrills in response to a breeze or a keen frost. Alas, I have to pay for it.'

'Back home there is still bathing,' observed Franz. He was all set to tell her about the celebrated limpid lyrical river running through his native town under arched bridges, and then between cornfields and vineyards; about how nice it was to go swimming there in the buff, diving right off the little 'nicker raft' you could hire for a few coppers; but at that instant a car honked and drew up at the gate, and Martha said: 'Here is my husband.'

She fixed her eyes on Dreyer, wondering if his aspect would impress the young cousin, and forgetting that Franz had seen him before and could hardly see him now. Dreyer came at his fast bouncy walk. He wore an ample white overcoat with a white scarf. Three rackets, each in a differently coloured cloth case – maroon, blue, and mulberry – protruded from under his arm; his face with its tawny moustache glowed like an autumn leaf. She was less vexed by his exotic attire than that the conversation had been interrupted, that she was no longer alone with Franz, that it was no longer exclusively she who engrossed and amazed him. Involuntarily her manner toward Franz changed, as if there had been 'something between them,' and now came the husband, causing them to behave with greater reserve. Besides, she certainly did not want to let Dreyer see that the poor relative whom she had criticized before knowing him had not turned out too bad after all. Therefore when Dreyer joined them she wanted to convey to him by means of an inconspicuous bit of pantomime that his arrival would now liberate her at last from a boring guest. Unfortunately Dreyer as he approached did not take his eyes off Franz who, peering at the gradually condensing light part of the mottled mist, got up and was preparing to make a bow. Dreyer, who was observant in his own way and fond of trivial mnemonic tricks (he often played a game with himself, trying to recollect the pictures in a waiting room, that pathetic limbo of pictures), had immediately, from a distance, recognized their recent travelling companion and wondered if perhaps he had brought the unopened letter from a milliner that Martha had mislaid during the journey. But suddenly another, much more amusing, thought dawned upon him. Martha, accustomed to the fireworks of his face, saw his cropped moustache twitch and the rays of wrinkles on the temple side of his eyes multiply and quiver. The next instant he burst out laughing so violently that Tom, who had been jumping around him, could not help barking. Not only the coincidence tickled Dreyer but also the conjecture that Martha had probably said something nasty about his relative while the relative had been sitting right there in the compartment. Just what Martha had said, and whether Franz could have heard it, he would never be able to recall now but something there had surely been, and this itchy uncertainty intensified the humourous aspect of the coincidence. In the no-time of human thought he also recalled – while the dog drowned his cousin's greeting – how an acquaintance once had rung him up while he was taking a tumultuous shower, and Martha had shouted through the bathroom door: 'That stupid old Wasserschluss is calling' – and five paces away the telephone receiver on the table was cupping its ear like an eavesdropper in a farce.

He laughed as he shook Franz's hand, and was still laughing when he dropped into one of the wicker chairs. Tom continued to bark. Suddenly Martha lunged forward and, rings blazing, gave the dog a really hard slap with the back of her hand. It hurt, and with a whimper Tom slunk away.

'Delightful,' said Dreyer (the delight quite gone), wiping his eyes with an ample silk handkerchief. 'So you are Franz – Lina's boy. After such a coincidence we must do away with formalities – please don't call me sir but Uncle, dear Uncle.'

'Avoid vocatives,' thought Franz quickly. Nevertheless, he began to feel at ease. Dreyer, blowing his nose in the haze, was indistinct, absurd, and harmless like those total strangers who impersonate people we know in our dreams and talk to us in phony voices like intimate friends.

'I was in fine form today,' Dreyer said to his wife, 'and you know something, I'm hungry. I imagine young Franz is hungry too.'

'Lunch will be served in a minute,' said Martha. She got up and disappeared.

Franz, feeling even more at ease, said: 'I must apologize – I've broken my glasses and can hardly distinguish anything, so I get mixed up a little.'

'Where are you staying?' asked Dreyer.

'At the Video,' said Franz. 'Near the station. It was recommended to me by an experienced person.'

'Fine. Yes, you are a good dog, Tom. Now first of all you must find a nice room, not too far from us. For forty or fifty marks a month. Do you play tennis?'

'Certainly,' replied Franz, remembering a backyard, a second-hand brown racket purchased for one mark at a bric-a-brac shop from under the bust of Wagner, a black rubber ball, and an uncooperative brick wall with a fatal square hole in which grew one wallflower.

'Fine. So we can play on Sundays. Then you will need a decent suit, shirts, soft collars, ties, all kinds of things. How did you get on with my wife?'

Franz grinned, not knowing the answer.

'Fine,' said Dreyer. 'I suspect lunch is ready. We'll talk about business later. We discuss business over coffee around here.'

His wife had come out on the porch. She gave him a long cold glance, coldly nodded, and went back into the house. 'That hateful, undignified, genial tone he always must take with inferiors,' she reflected as she passed through the ivory-white front hall where the impeccable, hospitable white comb and white-backed brush lay on the doily under the pier glass. The entire villa, from whitewashed terrace to radio antenna, was that way – neat, clean-cut, and on the whole unloved and inane. The master of the house deemed it a joke. As for the lady, neither aesthetic nor emotional considerations ruled her taste; she simply thought that a reasonably wealthy German businessman in the nineteen-twenties, in Berlin-West, ought to have a house exactly of that sort, that is, belonging to the same suburban type as those of his fellows. It had all the conveniences, and the majority of those conveniences went unused. There was, for example, in the bathroom a round, face-sized swivel mirror – a grotesque magnifier, with an electric light attached. Martha had once given it to her husband for shaving but very soon he had grown to detest it: it was unbearable every morning to see one's brightly illuminated chin swollen to about three times its natural volume and studded with rusty bristles that had sprouted overnight. The chairs in the parlour resembled a display in a good store. A writing desk with an unnecessary upper stage, consisting of unnecessary little drawers, supported, in place of a lamp, a bronze knight holding a lantern. There were lots of well dusted but uncaressed porcelain animals with glossy rumps, as well as varicoloured cushions, against which no human cheek had ever nestled; and albums – huge arty things with photographs of Copenhagen porcelain and Hagenkopp furniture – which were opened only by the dullest or shyest guest. Everything in the house, including the jars labelled sugar, cloves, chicory, on the shelves of the idyllic kitchen, had been chosen by Martha, to whom, seven years previously, her husband had presented on its green-turfed tray the freshly built little villa, still empty and ready to please. She had acquired paintings and distributed them throughout the rooms under the supervision of an artist who had been very much in fashion that season, and who believed that any picture was acceptable as long as it was ugly and meaningless, with thick blobs of paint, the messier and muddier the better. Following the count's advice, Martha had also bought a few old oils at auctions. Among them was the magnificent portrait of a noble-looking gentleman, with sidewhiskers, wearing a stylish morning coat, who stood leaning on a slender cane, illuminated as if by sheet lightning against a rich brown background. Martha bought this with good reason. Right beside it, on the dining-room wall, she placed a daguerreotype of her grandfather, a long-since-deceased coal merchant who had been suspected of drowning his first wife in a tarn around 1860, but nothing was proved. He also had sidewhiskers, wore a morning coat, and leaned on a cane; and his proximity to the sumptuous oil (signed by Heinrich von Hildenbrand) neatly transformed the latter into a family portrait. 'Grandpa,' Martha would say, indicating the genuine article with a wave of her hand that indolently included in the arc it described the anonymous nobleman to whose portrait the deceived guest's gaze shifted.

Unfortunately, though, Franz was able to make out neither the pictures nor the porcelain no matter how skillfully Martha directed his attention to the room's charms. He perceived a delicate blend of colour, felt the freshness of abundant flowers, appreciated the yielding softness of the carpet underfoot, and thus perceived by a freak of fate the very quality that the furnishings of the house lacked but that, in Martha's opinion, ought to have existed, and for which she had paid good money: an aura of luxury, in which, after the second glass of pale golden wine, he began slowly to dissolve. Dreyer refilled his glass, and breakfastless Franz, who had not dared to partake of the enigmatic first course, realized that his lower extremities had by now dissolved completely. He twice mistook the bare forearm of the servant maid for that of Martha but then became aware that she sat far away like a wine-golden ghost. Dreyer, ghostly too, but warm and ruddy, was describing a flight he had made two or three years ago from Munich to Vienna in a bad storm; how the plane had tossed and shaken, and how he had felt like telling the pilot 'Do stop for a moment'; and how his chance travelling companion, an old Englishman, kept calmly solving a crossword puzzle. Meanwhile Franz was experiencing fantastic difficulties with the vol-au-vent and then with the dessert. He had the feeling that in another minute his body would melt completely leaving only his head, which, with its mouth stuffed with a cream puff, would start floating about the room like a balloon. The coffee and the curaçao all but finished him. Dreyer, slowly rotating before him like a flaming wheel with human arms for spokes, began discussing the job awaiting Franz. Noting the state in which the poor fellow was, he did not go into details. He did say, however, that very soon Franz would become an excellent salesman, that the aviator's principal enemy is not wind but fog, and that, as the salary would not be much at first, he would undertake to pay for the room and would be glad if Franz dropped in every evening if he desired, though he would not be surprised if next year air service were established between Europe and America. The merry-go-round in Franz's head never stopped; his armchair travelled around the room in gliding circles. Dreyer considered him with a kindly smile, and, in anticipation of the tongue-lashing Martha would give him for all this jollity, kept mentally pouring out upon Franz's head the contents of an enormous cornucopia, for he had to reward Franz somehow for the exhilarating fun lavished upon him by the imp of coincidence through Franz. He must reward not only him, but cousin Lina too for that wart on her cheek, for her pug, for the rocking chair with its green sausage-shaped nape rest bearing the embroidered legend 'Only one little half hour.' Later, when Franz, exhaling wine and gratitude, bade his uncle good-bye, carefully descended the steps to the garden, carefully squeezed through the gate, and, still holding his hat in his hand, disappeared round the corner, Dreyer imagined what a nice nap the poor boy would have back in his hotel room, and then himself felt the blissful weight of drowsiness and went up to the bedroom.

There, in an orange peignoir, her bare legs crossed, her velvety-white neck nicely set off by the black of her low thick chignon – Martha sat at her dressing table polishing her nails. Dreyer saw in the mirror the gloss of her smooth bandeaux, her knit brows, her girlish breasts. A robust but untimely throb dispelled sleepiness. He sighed. It was not the first time he regretted that Martha regarded afternoon lovemaking as a decadent perversion. And since she did not raise her head, he understood she was angry.

He said softly – trying to make matters worse so as to stop regretting: 'Why did you disappear after lunch? You might have waited until he left.'

Without raising her eyes Martha answered: 'You know perfectly well we've been invited today to a very important and very smart tea. It wouldn't hurt if you got cleaned up too.'

'We still have an hour or so,' said Dreyer. 'Actually I thought I'd take a nap.'

Martha remained silent as she worked rapidly with the chamois polisher. He threw off his so-called Norfolk jacket, then sat down on the edge of the couch, and began taking off his red-sand-stained tennis shoes.

Martha bent even lower and abruptly said: 'Amazing how some people have no sense of dignity.'

Dreyer grunted and leisurely got rid of his flannel trousers, then of his white silk socks.

A minute or so later Martha chucked something with a clatter onto the glass surface of her dressing table and said: 'I'd like to know what that young man thinks of you now. No formalities, call me Uncle. . . . It's unheard-of.'

Dreyer smiled, wiggling his toes. 'Enough playing on public courts,' he said. 'Next spring I'll join a club.'

Martha abruptly turned toward him and, leaning her elbow on the arm of her chair, dropped her chin on her fist. One leg crossed over the other was swinging slightly. She surveyed her husband, incensed by the look of half-mischief, half-desire in his eyes.

'You've got what you wanted,' she continued. 'You've taken care of your dear nephew. I bet you've made him heaps of promises. And will you please cover your obscene nudity.'

Draping himself in a dressing gown, Dreyer made himself comfortable on the cretonne couch. What would happen, he wondered, if he now said something like this: You too have your peculiarities, my love, and some of them are less pardonable than a husband's obscenity. You travel second-class instead of first because second is just as good and the saving is colossal, amounting to the stupendous sum of twenty-seven marks and sixty pfennigs which would otherwise have disappeared into the pockets of the swindlers who invented first-class. You hit a lovable and loving dog because a dog is not supposed to laugh aloud. All right: let's assume this is all right. But allow me to play a little too – leave me my nephew. . . .

'Evidently you do not wish to speak to me,' said Martha. 'Oh, well. . . .' She went back to work on her gem-like nails. Dreyer reflected: If only just once you let yourself go, come, come on, have some good fun and a good fit of crying. After that surely you'll feel better.

He cleared his throat, preparing the way for words, but as had happened more than once, decided at the last minute not to say anything. There is no knowing if it was from a wish to irritate her with silence or simply the result of contented laziness, or perhaps an unconscious fear of dealing a final blow to something he wanted to preserve. Leaning back against the three-cornered cushion, his hands thrust deep into his dressing-gown pockets, he remained contemplating silent Martha; presently his gaze roamed away to his wife's wide bed under its white blanket cover, batiste trimmed with lace, washable, ninety by ninety inches, and severely separated from his, also lace-covered, by a night table on which sprawled a leggy rag doll with a black face. This doll, and the bedspreads, and the pretentious furniture were both amusing and repelling.

He yawned and rubbed the bridge of his nose. Perhaps it would be wiser to change at once and then read for half an hour on the terrace. Martha threw off her orange peignoir, and as she drew back her elbows to adjust a necklace her angelically lovely bare shoulder blades came together like folding wings. He wondered wistfully how many hours must pass till she let him kiss those shoulders; hesitated, thought better of it, and went to his dressing room across the passage.

As soon as the door had noiselessly closed behind him, Martha sprang up and furiously, with a wrenching twist, locked it. This was utterly out of character: a singular impulse she would have been at a loss to explain, and all the more senseless since she would need the maid in a minute, and would have to unlock the door anyway. Much later, when many months had passed, and she was trying to reconstruct that day, it was this door and this key that she recalled most vividly, as if an ordinary door key happened to be the correct key to that not quite ordinary day. However, in wringing the neck of the lock she failed to dispell her anger. It was a confused and turbulent seething that found no release. She was angry that Franz's visit had given her a strange pleasure, and that for this pleasure she had to thank her husband. The upshot was that in their arguments about inviting or not inviting a poor relative she had been wrong, and her wayward and wacky husband right. Therefore she tried not to acknowledge the pleasure so that her husband might remain in the wrong. The pleasure, she knew, would soon be repeated, and she also knew that had she been absolutely sure her attitude would have caused her husband not to receive Franz again, she might not have said what she had said just now. For the first time in her married life she experienced something that she had never expected, something that did not fit like a legitimate square into the parquet pattern of their life after the dismal surprises of their honeymoon. Thus, out of a trifle, out of a chance stay in a ridiculous provincial town, something had started to grow, joyful and irreparable. And there was no vacuum cleaner in the world that could instantly restore all the rooms of her brain to their former immaculate condition. The vague quality of her sensations, the difficulty of figuring out logically just why she had liked that awkward, eager, provincial boy with tremulous long fingers and pimples between his eyebrows, all this vexed her so much that she was ready to curse the new green dress laid out on the armchair, the plump posterior of Frieda who was rummaging in the lower drawer of the commode, and her own morose reflection in the mirror. She looked at a jewel in which an anniversary was coldly reflected, and remembered that her thirty-fourth birthday had passed the other day, and with a strange impatience began consulting her mirror to detect the threat of a wrinkle, the hint of a sagging fold. Somewhere a door closed softly, and the stairs creaked (they were not supposed to creak!), and her husband's cheerful off-key whistle receded out of earshot. 'He is a poor dancer,' thought Martha. 'He may be good at tennis but he will always be a poor dancer. He does not like dancing. He does not understand how fashionable it is nowadays. Fashionable and indispensable.'

With muted resentment against inefficient Frieda, she thrust her head through the soft, gathered circumference of the dress. Its green shadow flew downward past her eyes. She emerged erect, smoothed her hips, and suddenly felt that her soul was temporarily circumscribed and contained by the emerald texture of that cool frock.

Below, on the square terrace, with its cement floor and the purple and pink asters on its wide balustrade, Dreyer sat in a canvas chair by a garden table, and with his open book resting in his lap gazed into the garden. Beyond the fence, the black car, the expensive Icarus, was already waiting inexorably. The new chauffeur, his elbows placed on the fence from the outside, was chatting with the gardener. A cold late-afternoon lucency penetrated the autumn air; the sharp blue shadows of the young trees stretched along the sunny lawn, all in the same direction as if anxious to see which would be first to reach the garden's white lateral wall. Far off, across the street, the pistachio facades of apartment houses were very distinct, and there, melancholically leaning on a red quilt laid on the window sill, sat a bald little man in shirt-sleeves. The gardener had already twice taken hold of his wheelbarrow but each time had turned again to the chauffeur. Then they both lit cigarettes. And the wispy smoke was clearly set off as it floated along the glossy black side of the car. The shadow seemed to have moved just a bit farther but the sun still bore down triumphantly on the right from behind the corner of the count's villa, which stood on higher ground with taller trees. Tom walked indolently along the flowerbed. From a sense of duty and without the least hope of success, he started after a low-flitting sparrow, and then lay down by the wheelbarrow with his nose on his paws. The very word terrace – how spacious, how cool! The pretty ray of a spiderweb stretched obliquely from the corner flower of the balustrade to the table standing beside it. The cloudlets in one part of the pale clean sky had funny curls, and were all alike as on a maritime horizon, all hanging together in a delicate flock. At last having heard all there was to hear and told all there was to tell, the gardener moved off with his wheelbarrow, turning with geometrical precision at the intersections of gravel paths, and Tom, rising lazily, proceeded to walk after him like a clockwork toy, turning when the gardener turned. *Die toten Seelen* by a Russian author, which had long been slipping down Dreyer's knee, slid onto the flags of the floor, and he felt too lazy to pick it up. So pleasant, so spacious. . . . The first to finish would be no doubt that apple tree over there. The chauffeur got into his seat. It would be interesting to know just what he was thinking about now. This morning his eyes had oddly twinkled. Could it be that he drinks? Wouldn't that be a scream, a tippling chauffeur. Two men in top hats, diplomats or undertakers, went by; the top hats and black coats floated by along the fence. Out of nowhere came a Red Admiral butterfly, settled on the edge of the table, opened its wings and began to fan them slowly as if breathing. The dark-brown ground was bruised here and there, the scarlet band had faded, the fringes were frayed – but the creature was still so lovely, so festive. . . .

3

On Monday Franz splurged: he purchased what the optician assured him was an American article. The rims were of tortoise shell – allowing no doubt for the well-known fact that chelonians are frequently and variously mocked. When the proper lenses had been inserted and he donned his new spectacles, Franz experienced at once a feeling of comfort and peace in his heart as well as behind his ears. The haze dissolved. The unruly colours of the universe were confined once more to their official compartments and cells.

There still remained one thing he had to do in order to establish and affirm himself in this freshly marked-out world: he had to find himself a dwelling place. Franz smiled indulgently and smugly as he recalled Dreyer's promise of the previous day to pay for many luxuries. Uncle Dreyer was a somewhat fantastic but highly useful institution. And Uncle was perfectly right: how indeed could Franz do without some decent clothes? First, however, let us find that room.

No sun today. A sober chill emanated from the low drab sky. Berlin taxis turned out to be a very dark green with a neat black-and-white checkered border across the doors. Here and there a blue mailbox had been freshly painted in celebration of autumn and looked singularly shiny and sticky. He found the streets of this quarter disappointingly quiet, as actually streets in a great city were not supposed to be. It was fun to memorize their names and the whereabouts of useful shops and offices – pharmacy, grocery, post office, police station. Why did the Dreyers insist on living so far from the centre? He was displeased that there were so many vacant lots, so many little parks and lawny squares, so many pines and birches, houses under construction, vegetable gardens. It all reminded him too much of his backwoods home. He thought he recognized Tom in a dog being walked by a plump but not uncomely housemaid. Children were playing ball or whipping their tops right on the asphalt. He too had once played like that. Only one thing really told him he was in the metropolis: some strollers wore marvellous clothes! For instance, plus-fours, very baggy below the knee, so as to make the wool-stockinged shin look handsomely slender. That particular style he had never seen before, though boys in his hometown also wore knickerbockers. Then there was the high-class fop in a double-breasted jacket, very wide in the shoulders, and ultra-tight around the hips, and with incredibly elephantine trouser legs the tremendous cuffs of which practically concealed his shoes. The hats, too, were splendid, and the flamboyant ties; and the girls, the girls. Kind Dreyer!

He walked slowly shaking his head, clucking his tongue, looking around every moment. The kissable cuties, he thought almost aloud, and inhaled with a hiss through clenched teeth. What calves! What bottoms! Enough to drive one crazy!

At home when walking along the cloyingly familiar streets, he had experienced, of course, the same aching reaction to fugitive charm many times a day. But in his morbid shyness he did not dare look too insistently in those days. Here it was a different matter. He was disguised as a stranger, and these girls were accessible, (again that hiss), they were accustomed to avid glances, they welcomed them, and it was possible to accost any one of them, and start a brilliant and brutal conversation. He would do just that but first he had to find a room in which to rip off her dress and possess her. Forty to fifty marks, Dreyer had said. That meant fifty, at least.

Franz decided to act systematically. At the door of every third or fourth house a small notice board announced rooms for rent. He consulted a newly bought map of the city, checked once again the distance from Uncle's villa and found he was close enough. A nice, new-looking house with a nice green door to which a white card was affixed attracted him, and he blithely rang the bell. Only after he had pressed it he noticed that the sign said 'fresh paint'! But it was too late. A window opened on his right. A bob-haired, bare-shouldered young girl in a black slip, clutching a white kitten to her breast, peered out at Franz. His lips went dry in the arid blast. The girl was enchanting: a simple little seamstress, no doubt, but enchanting, and let us hope not too expensive. 'Whom do you want?' she asked. Franz gulped, smiled foolishly, and said with quite unexpected impudence, by which he himself was at once embarrassed: 'Maybe you, eh?'

She looked at him with curiosity.

'Come on,' said Franz awkwardly, 'let me in.'

The girl turned away and was heard to say to someone in the room: 'I don't know what he wants. Better ask him yourself.' Over her shoulder appeared the head of a middle-aged man with a pipe between his teeth. Franz tipped his hat, turned on his heel, and walked on. He noticed that he was still grinning horribly and emitting a thin moan. 'Nonsense,' he thought with rage, 'it's nothing. Forget it.'

It took him two hours to inspect eleven rooms in four different blocks. Strictly speaking, any one of them was delightful. But each had a tiny defect. One, for example, had not been tidied up yet, and as he looked into the dull eyes of the woman in mourning who was answering his questions with a kind of listless despair, Franz decided her husband had just died in that very room which she was rather fraudulently offering him. Another room had a simpler shortcoming: it cost five marks more than the price mentioned by Dreyer; otherwise it was perfect. The third room revealed brown stains on the walls, and a mousetrap in the corner. The fourth was connected with a smelly toilet that could also be reached from the corridor and was used by a neighbour's family. The fifth. . . . But in a singularly short time these rooms with their virtues and flaws became confused in Franz's mind, and only one remained immaculate and distinct: the one that cost fifty-five marks. He had a sudden feeling there was no reason to prolong his quest, and that anyway he would not venture to decide by himself, fearing to make a bad choice and deprive himself of a million other rooms; on the other hand, it was hard to imagine anything better than the room that had caught his fancy. It gave on a pleasant by-street with a delicatessen shop. A palace-like affair that the landlord said would be a movie house was being built on the corner, and this gave life to the surroundings. A picture above the bed showed a naked girl leaning forward to wash her breasts in a misty pond.

'Good,' he reflected. 'It is now a quarter to one. Time for a meal. A brilliant idea: eat at the Dreyers'. I'll ask them what I should pay particular attention to when making my choice, and if he does not think that five extra marks. . . .'

Cleverly using his map (and promising himself incidentally that as soon as he had taken care of business he would go by subway to what was surely the gayest part of this sprawling city), Franz arrived without difficulty at the villa. It was painted a grainy grey, and had a solid, compact, one might even say appetizing, look. In the garden heavy red apples hung in clusters on the young trees. As he walked up the crunching path, he saw Martha standing on the porch step. She wore a hat and a moleskin coat, and was checking the dubious whiteness of the sky, trying to decide whether or not to open her umbrella. She did not smile when she noticed Franz.

'My husband is not at home,' she said, fixing him with her beautiful cold eyes. 'He is lunching in town today.'

Franz glanced at the handbag jutting from under her arm, at the artificial purple pansy pinned to the huge collar of her coat, at the stubby umbrella with its sparkling knob, and realized that she too was leaving.

'Pardon me for having disturbed you,' he said, inwardly cursing his fate.

'Oh, it's perfectly all right,' said Martha, and they both moved in the direction of the gate. Franz wondered what to do next – bid her goodbye? Go on walking beside her? Martha with a displeased expression kept looking straight ahead, her full warm lips half open. Then she quickly wet them and said: 'This is so unpleasant. I have to walk. We wrecked the car last night.'

There had indeed been an unpleasant accident on the way home after a tea and a dance. In an ill-timed attempt to pass a truck, the chauffeur had first hit a wooden railing where the tram tracks were being repaired, and swerving sharply had collided with the side of the truck; the Icarus had spun around and crashed into a pole. While this motorized frenzy was in progress, Martha and her husband had assumed all imaginable positions, and had finally found themselves on the floor. Dreyer had asked sympathetically if she were not hurt. The shock, the search for the beads of her necklace, the crowd of gawkers, the vulgar aspect of the smashed car, the foul-mouthed truck driver, the arrogant policeman who was not amused by Dreyer's jokes – all this brought Martha to a state of such irritation that she had had to take two sleeping pills, and had slept only two hours.

'A wonder I did not get killed,' she said sullenly. 'But even our chauffeur was not hurt, which is a pity.' And slowly stretching out her hand, she helped Franz open the wicket which he was vainly pushing and rattling.

'No question about it, cars are dangerous playthings,' he said noncommitally. Now it was definitely time to take leave.

Martha noticed and approved his hesitation.

'Which way are you going?' she asked, transferring her umbrella from right hand to left. The glasses he had got were very becoming. He looked like the actor Hess in *The Hindu Student,* a movie.

'Don't know myself,' said Franz, smirking rather freely. 'You see I was just coming to ask Uncle's advice about the room.' This first 'Uncle' came out unconvincingly, and he resolved not to repeat it for a while so as to let the word ripen on its twig.

'I can help too,' said Martha. 'Tell me what's the trouble.'

Imperceptibly they had begun to move and were now walking slowly along the wide sidewalk on which broken chestnuts and claw-like crisp leaves lay here and there. Franz blew his nose and began telling her about the room.

'Why, that's unheard of,' Martha interrupted. 'Fifty-five? I'm sure you can haggle a little.'

A forethrill of triumph went through Franz but he decided not to rush things.

'The landlord is a closefisted old codger, the devil himself would not make him budge.'

'You know what?' Martha said suddenly. 'I would not mind going there and talking to him myself.'

Franz exulted. What luck! To say nothing of how splendid it was to stroll along with this red-lipped beauty in her moleskin coat! The sharp autumn air, the susurration of tyres – this was the life! Add a new suit and a flaming tie – and his happiness would be complete.

'Where is Mr Tom today?' he inquired. 'I thought I saw him going for a walk.'

'No, he's locked up in the gardener's shed. He's a good dog but a little neurotic. As I always say, dogs are acceptable pets if they are clean.'

'Cats are cleaner,' said Franz.

'Oh, I abominate cats. Dogs understand when you scold them, but cats are hopeless – no contact with human beings, no gratitude, nothing.'

'We shot lots of stray ones back home, a school friend and I. Especially along the river in spring.'

'There's something wrong with my left heel,' said Martha. 'I need your support for a moment.' She placed two light fingers upon his shoulder as she glanced backward and downward. It was nothing. With the tip of her umbrella she scraped off the dead leaf her heel had transfixed.

They reached the square. At least two future stories of the new corner house could be discerned through the scaffolding of the present.

Martha pointed with her umbrella. 'We know,' she said, 'the man who works for the partner of the director of the cinema company who is building that house there.'

It would not be ready till sometime next year. The workmen were moving as in a dream.

Franz frantically racked his brain for some more fruitful theme. The coincidence!

'I still can't forget how strangely we met on the train. It's incredible!'

'Yes, a coincidence,' said Martha, thinking her own thoughts.

'Listen,' she said as they started to climb the steep staircase of the fifth floor, 'I'd rather my husband did not know I helped you. No, there is no mystery here. Simply, I would rather he did not.'

Franz made a bow. It was no concern of his. Yet he wondered if what she had said were flattering or insulting. Hard to decide. They had now been standing for some time before the door. No one answered the bell. Franz rang again. The door flew open. A little old man with hanging braces and no collar thrust out a rumpled face, and let them in silently.

'I'm back again,' said Franz. 'Could I see the room once more?'

The old fellow made a kind of rapid salute and shuffled ahead through a long darkish passage.

'Good heavens, what a squalid hole,' thought Martha squeamishly. Was she right in coming here? She imagined her husband's mischievous smile: You reproached me, and now you're helping him yourself.

The room, however, turned out to be reasonably bright and clean. By the left-hand wall stood a wooden, probably creaky bed, a washstand, and a stove. On the right, two chairs and a pretentious armchair of moth-eaten plush. There was a small table in the centre and a chest-of-drawers in a corner. Over the bed hung a picture. Puzzled, Franz stared at it. A bare-bosomed slave girl on sale was being leered at by three hesitant lechers. It was even more artistic than the bathing September nymph. *She* must have been in some other room – yes, of course, in the one with the stench.

Martha felt the mattress. It was firm and hard. She took off one glove, stroked the bed table, and consulted the face of her finger. A fashionable song she liked, *Black-eyed Natasha*, came from two different radios on two different levels, mingling buoyantly with the musical clanking of contruction work somewhere outside.

Franz looked hopefully at Martha. She pointed her umbrella at the barish right-hand wall and inquired in a neutral voice without looking at the old man: 'Why did you remove the couch? Obviously, you had something here before.'

'The couch was beginning to sag and is being repaired,' answered the old man and cocked his head.

'You will put it back later,' observed Martha, and raising her eyes, she switched on the light for an instant. The old man looked up too.

'All right,' said Martha and again extended her umbrella. 'You furnish sheets, don't you?'

'Sheets?' repeated the old man after her with surprise. Then, cocking his head to the other side, he pursed his lips, thought for a moment, and replied: 'Yes, we can dig up some sheets.'

'And how about service and cleaning?'

The old man poked himelf in the chest.

'I do everything,' he said. 'I *make* everything. I alone.'

Martha went over to the window, looked at a truck with planks in the street, then walked back.

'And how much was it you wanted?' she asked with indifference.

'Fifty-five,' alertly said the man.

'Including electricity and morning coffee?'

'Has the gentleman got a job?' the old man inquired, nodding in the direction of Franz.

'Yes,' promptly said Franz.

'Fifty-five for everything,' said the old man.

'That is expensive,' said Martha.

'That is not expensive,' said the old man.

'That is extremely expensive,' said Martha.

The old man smiled.

'Oh well,' shrug-sighed Martha and turned toward the door.

Franz realized that the room was about to float away forever. He squeezed and tortured his hat as he tried to catch Martha's eye.

'Fifty-five,' the old man repeated pensively.

'Fifty,' said Martha.

The old man opened his mouth, and closed it again firmly. 'Very well,' he said at last. 'But the lights have to be out by eleven.'

'Naturally,' flowed in Franz. 'Naturally – I quite understand.'

'When do you wish to move in?' asked his landlord.

'Today, right now,' said Franz. 'I just have to get my suitcase from the hotel.'

'How about a small deposit?' the old man proposed with a subtle smile.

The room itself seemed to be smiling. How strange to recall the cluttered attic of his youth! His mother at the Singer machine while he tried to sleep. How could he have endured it so long? When they emerged again onto the street, there remained in his consciousness a warm hollow formed as it were by his new room's sinking into a soft mass of minor impressions. As she bade him goodbye at the corner, Martha saw the glitter of gratitude behind his glasses. And as she headed for the photo shop with some undeveloped Tyrol snapshots, she recalled the conversation with legitimate pride.

A drizzle had set in. The doors of flower shops opened wide to catch the moisture. Now it was really raining. She could not find a taxi; raindrops were managing to get under her umbrella and wash the powder off her nose. A dull restlessness replaced elation. Both yesterday and today were novel and absurd days, and certain not quite intelligible, but significant, outlines were showing through confusedly. And, like that darkish solution in which mountain views would presently float and grow clear, this rain, this delicate pluvial damp, developed shiny images in her soul. Once again a rain-soaked, ardent, strong, blue-eyed man, a vacational acquaintance of her husband's, took advantage of a cloudburst in Zermatt to bluster her into the recess of a porch and push against her and pant out his passion, his sleepless nights, and she shook her head, and he vanished behind the corner of memory. Once again in her drawing room that fool of a painter, a languid rascal with dirty fingernails, glued his lips to her bare neck and she waited a moment to make out what she felt, and feeling nothing, struck him in the face with her elbow. Once again – and this image was a recent one – a wealthy businessman, an American with bluish-grey hair and a long upper lip, murmured as he played with her hand that certainly she would come to his hotel room, and she smiled and regretted vaguely that he was a foreigner. In the company of these chance phantoms rapidly touching her with cold hands, she reached home, shrugged her shoulders and cast them aside as casually as she did her open umbrella which she left on the porch to dry.

'I'm an idiot,' she said. 'What's the matter? What's wrong with me? Why worry? It must happen sooner or later. It is inevitable.'

Her mood changed again. With pleasure she gave Frieda a dressing down because the dog had somehow got back into the house and tracked dirt on the carpet. She devoured a pile of small sandwiches at tea. She called the garage to find out if Dreyer had rented a car as he had promised. She called the cinema to reserve two tickets for the première on Friday; then called her husband; and then old Mrs Hertwig when it turned out that Dreyer would be busy. And Dreyer was indeed very busy. He had grown so absorbed in an unexpected offer from another firm, in a series of cautious negotiations and courteous conferences that for several days he did not remember Franz; or rather he would remember him at the wrong moments – while relaxing neck-deep in warm water; while driving from office to factory; while smoking a cigarette in bed. Franz would appear gesticulating wildly at the wrong telescope end of his mind; Dreyer would mentally promise to attend to him soon, and immediately would start thinking about something else.

To Franz that was no comfort. When the first agreeable excitement of housewarming had passed, he asked himself what he should do next. Martha had taken down his landlord's telephone number but nothing happened after that. He did not dare to phone himself nor did he dare call on the Dreyers without warning, not trusting chance, which last time had so magnificently transfigured his inopportune visit. He must wait. Evidently, sooner or later, he would be summoned. But he did not relish the delay. At half past seven on the very first morning the landlord in person brought him a sticky cup of weak coffee and on a saucer two lumps of sugar, one with a brown corner, and remarked in an admonishing tone: 'Now don't be late for work. Drink this and jump into your clothes. Do not flush the toilet too hard. Take care not to be late.'

Franz decided that he had no alternative but leave the house for the whole day in order to perform the job that the old fellow had invented for him, and stay out until five or six, and then have a bite in town before returning. Thus perforce he explored the city, or rather what seemed to him its most metropolitan section. The obligatory nature of those excursions envenomed the novelty. By evening he would be much too exhausted to carry out his plan, his old glorious plan, of sauntering along seductive streets and taking a good preliminary look at genuine harlots. But how to get there? His map seemed to be curiously misleading. One cloudless day, having strayed far enough, he found himself on a broad dreary boulevard with many steamship line offices and art shops: he glanced at the street sign and realized it was the world-famous avenue that had seemed so sublime in his dreams. Its rather skimpy lindens were shedding their leaves. The winged arch at one end was sheathed in scaffolding. He traversed wildernesses of asphalt. He walked along a canal: in one place there was a rainbow-like splotch of oil on the water, and an intoxicating aroma of honey, reminding him of childhood, wafted from a barge where pink-shirted men were unloading mountains of pears and apples; from a bridge he saw two women in glistening bathing caps, intently snorting and rhythmically striking out with their arms as they swam side by side. He spent two hours in a museum of antiquities, examining with awe statues and sarcophagi, and the revolting profiles of brown men driving chariots. He took long rests in shabby pubs and on the fairly confortable benches of an immense park. He plunged into the depths of the subway and, perched on a red leather seat, looking at the shiny stangs, up which raced golden reflections, waited impatiently for the coaly clattering blackness to be replaced at last by paradises of luxury and sin that kept eluding him. He also wanted very much to find Dreyer's emporium about which they used to speak with such reverence in his hometown. The fat telephone directory, however, listed only his home and office. Evidently it must have some other name. And continuing to remain unaware that the heart of the city had moved to the west, Franz dismally wandered through the central and northern streets where he thought the smartest stores and the liveliest trade must be.

He did not dare buy anything, and this tormented him. In this short time he had already managed to spend quite a bit of money and now Dreyer had disappeared. Everything was somehow uncertain, everything filled him with uneasiness. He tried to make friends with his landlord who so insistently turned him out of the house for the whole day. But the old man was untalkative and kept lurking in the unknown depths of his little apartment. The first night, however, he met Franz in the corridor, warned him again that the water closet chain should be pulled very gently or it would be jerked off and explained to him at length the mysteries of the district police station for which he supplied him with some forms where Franz had to fill in name, marital status, and place of birth. 'And another thing,' said the old fellow, 'about that lady friend of yours. She must not visit you here. I know you are young. I was young once myself. I would be quite ready to give you my permission but there is my wife, you see – she happens to be away temporarily – but I know she would never allow such visits.'

Franz flushed and hastily nodded in assent. His landlord's assumption flattered and excited him. He imagined her fragrant, warm-looking lips, her creamy skin, but cut short the habitual swell of desire. 'She is not for me,' he thought glumly, 'she is remote and cold. She lives in a different world, with a very rich and still vigorous husband. She'd send me packing if I were to grow enterprising; my career would be ruined.' On the other hand, he thought he might find himself a sweetheart anyway. She too would be shapely, sleek, ripe-lipped and dark-haired. And with this in mind he decided to take certain measures. In the morning, when the landlord brought him his coffee. Franz cleared his throat and said: 'Listen, if I paid you a small supplement, would you. . . . Would I. . . . What I mean is, could I entertain anyone if I wished?'

'That depends,' said the old man.

'A few extra marks,' said Franz.

'I understand,' said the old man.

'Five marks more per month,' said Franz.

'That's generous,' said the old man, and as he turned to go added in a sly admonitory tone: 'But take care not to be late for work.'

Thus Martha's haggling had all been for nought. Having resolved to pay the extra sum secretly, Franz knew perfectly well he had acted rashly. His money was melting away, and still Dreyer did not telephone. For four days running he left the house in disgust punctually at eight, returning at nightfall in a fog of fatigue. He was completely fed up by now with the celebrated avenue. He sent a postcard to his mother with a view of the Brandenburg Gate, and wrote that he was well, and that Dreyer was a very kind uncle. There was no use frightening her, though perhaps she deserved it. And only on Friday night, when Franz was already lying in bed and saying to himself with a tremor of panic that they had all forgotten him, that he was completely alone in a strange city, and thinking with a certain evil joy that he would stop being faithful to the radiant Martha presiding over his nightly surrenders and ask lewd old Enricht, his landlord, to let him have a bath in the grimy tub of the flat and direct him to the nearest brothel. At that instant Enricht in a sleepy voice called him to the telephone.

With terrible haste and excitement, Franz pulled on his pants and rushed barefoot into the passage. A trunk managed to bang him on the knee as he made for the gleam of the telephone at the end of the corridor. Owing perhaps to his being unaccustomed to telephones, he could not identify at first the voice barking in his ear. 'Come to my house this minute,' the voice said clearly at last. 'Do you hear me? Please hurry, I am waiting for you.'

'Oh, how are you, how are you?' Franz babbled, but the telephone was dead. Dreyer put down the receiver with a flourish and continued rapidly jotting down the things he had to do tomorrow. Then he glanced at his watch, reflecting that his wife would be back from the cinema any moment now. He rubbed his forehead, and then with a sly smile took from a drawer a bunch of keys, and a sausage-shaped flashlight with a convex eye. He still had his coat on, for he had just come home and without shedding it had strode right to his study as he always did when he was in a hurry to write something down or telephone someone. Now he noisily pushed back his chair, and began taking off his voluminous camel-hair coat as he walked to the front hall to hang it up there. Into its capacious pocket he dropped the keys and the flashlight. Tom, who was lying by the door, got up and rubbed his soft head against Dreyer's leg. Dreyer resonantly locked himself up in the bathroom where three or four senile mosquitoes slept on the whitewashed wall.

A minute later, turning down and buttoning up his sleeves at the wrists, he proceeded with another leisurely homy gait toward the dining room.

The table was laid for two, and a dark red Westphalian ham reposed on a dish, amid a mosaic of sausage slices. Large grapes, brimming with greenish light, hung over the edge of their vase. Dreyer plucked off one and tossed it in his mouth. He cast a sidelong glance at the salami but decided to wait for Martha. The mirror reflected his broad back clothed in grey flannel and the tawny strands of his smoothly brushed hair. He turned around quickly as though feeling that someone was watching him, and moved away; all that remained in the mirror was a white corner of the table against the black background broken by a crystal glimmer on the sideboard. He heard a faint sound from the far side of that stillness: a little key was seeking a sensitive point in the stillness; it found and pierced that point, and gave one crisp turn, and then everything came to life. Dreyer's grey shoulder passed and repassed in the mirror as he paced hungrily round the table. The front door slammed and in came Martha. Her eyes glistened, she was wiping her nose firmly with a Chanel-scented handkerchief. Behind her came the fully awakened dog.

'Sit down, sit down, my love,' said Dreyer briskly, and turned on the sophisticated electric current to warm the tea water.

'Lovely film,' she said. 'Hess was wonderful, though I think I liked him better in *The Prince*.'

'In what?'

'Oh you remember, the student at Heidelberg disguised as a Hindu prince.'

Martha was smiling. In fact, she smiled fairly often of late, which gladdened Dreyer ineffably. She was in the pleasant position of a person who has been promised a mysterious treat in the near future. She was willing to wait awhile, knowing that the treat would come without fail. That day she had summoned the painters to have them brighten up the south side of the terrace wall. A banquet scene in the film had made her hungry, and now she intended to betray her diet, then roll into bed, and perhaps allow Dreyer his long-deferred due.

The front door bell tinkled. Tom barked briskly. Martha raised her thin eyebrows in surprise. Dreyer got up with a chuckle, and, chewing as he went, marched into the front hall.

She sat half-turned toward the door, holding her raised cup. When Franz, jokingly nudged on by Dreyer, stepped into the dining room, clicked his heels, and quickly walked up to her, she beamed so beautifully, her lips glistened so warmly that within Dreyer's soul a huge merry throng seemed to break out in deafening applause, and he thought that after a smile like that everything was bound to go well: Martha, as she once used to, would tell him in breathless detail the entire foolish film as the preface and price of a submissive caress; and on Sunday, instead of tennis, he would go riding with her in the rustling, sun-flecked, orange-and-red park.

'First of all, my dear Franz.' he said, drawing up a chair for his nephew, 'have a bite of something. And here is a drop of kirsch for you.'

Like an automaton, Franz stuck out his hand across the table, aiming for the proffered snifter, and knocked over a slender vase enclosing a heavy brown rose ('Which should have been removed long ago,' reflected Martha). The liberated water spread across the tablecloth.

He lost his composure, and no wonder. In the first place, he had not expected to see Martha. Secondly, he had thought Dreyer would receive him in his study and inform him about a very, very important job that had to be tackled immediately. Martha's smile had stunned him. He ascertained to himself the reason for his alarm. Like the fake seed a fakir buries in the ground only to draw out of it at once, with manic magic, a live rose tree, Martha's request that he conceal from Dreyer their innocent adventure – a request to which he had barely paid attention at the time, now, in the husband's presence had fabulously swelled, turning into a secret erotic bond. He also remembered old Enricht's words about a lady friend, and those words confirmed as it were the bliss and the shame. He tried to cast off the spell – but, meeting her unbearably intense gaze, dropped his eyes and helplessly continued to dab the wet tablecloth with his handkerchief despite Dreyer's trying to push his hand away. Moments ago he had been lying in bed and now here he sat, in this resplendent dining room, suffering as if in a dream because he could not halt the dark streamlet that had rounded the saltcellar, and under cover of the plate's rim was endeavouring to reach the edge of the table. Still smiling (the tablecloth would have to be changed tomorrow anyway), Martha shifted her gaze to his hands, to the gentle play of the knuckles under the taut skin, to the hairy wrist, to the long groping fingers, and felt oddly aware she had nothing woollen on her body that night.

Abruptly Dreyer got up and said: 'Franz, this is not very

hospitable, but it can't be helped. It's getting late, and you and I must be on our way.'

'On our way?' Franz uttered in confusion, thrusting the wet ball of his handkerchief into his pocket. Martha glanced at her husband with cold surprise.

'You'll understand presently,' said Dreyer, his eyes twinkling with an adventurous light that was all too familiar to Martha. 'What a bore,' she thought angrily, 'what is he up to?'

She stopped him for a moment in the front hall and asked him in rapid whisper: 'Where are you going, where are you going? I demand to be told where you are going.'

'On a wild spree,' replied Dreyer, hoping to provoke another marvellous smile.

She winced in disgust. He patted her on the cheek and went out.

Martha wandered back to the dining room and stood lost in thought behind the chair Franz had vacated. Then with irritation she lifted the tablecloth where the water had been spilled, and slipped a plate bottom up under it. The looking glass, which was working hard that night, reflected her green dress, her white neck under the dark weight of her chignon, and the gleam of her emerald earrings. She remained unconscious of the mirror's attention, and as she slowly went about putting the fruit knives away her reflection would reappear every now and then. Frieda joined her for a minute or two. Then the light in the dining room clicked off, and, nibbling at her necklace, Martha went upstairs to her bedroom.

'I bet he wants me to think he is kidding because he isn't. I bet it's exactly the way it will be,' she thought. 'He'll fix him up with some dirty slut. And that will be the end of it.'

As she undressed, she felt she was about to cry. Just you wait, just you wait till you get home. Especially if you were pulling my leg. And what manners, what manners! You invite the poor boy and then whisk him away. In the middle of the night! Disgraceful!

Once again, as so many times previously, she went over all her husband's transgressions in her memory. It seemed to her that she remembered them all. They were numerous. That did not prevent her, however, from assuring her married sister Hilda, when the latter would come from Hamburg, that she was happy, that her marriage was a happy one.

And Martha really did believe that her marriage was no different from any other marriage, that discord always reigned, that the wife always struggled against her husband, against his peculiarities, against his departures from the accepted rules, and all this amounted to happy marriage. An unhappy marriage was when the husband was poor, or had landed in prison for some shady business, or kept squandering his earnings on kept women. Therefore Martha never complained about her situation, since it was a natural and customary one.

Her mother had died when Martha was three – a not unusual arrangement. A first stepmother soon died too, and that also ran in some families. The second and final stepmother, who died only recently, was a lovely woman of quite gentle birth whom everybody adored. Papa, who had started his career as a saddler and ended it as the bankrupt owner of an artificial leather factory, was desperately eager she marry the 'Hussar,' as for some reason he dubbed Dreyer, whom she barely knew when he proposed in 1920, at the same time that Hilda became engaged to the fat little purser of a second-rate Atlantic liner. Dreyer was getting rich with miraculous ease; he was fairly attractive, but bizarre and unpredictable; sang off-key silly arias and made her silly presents. As a well-bred girl with long lashes and glowing cheeks, she said she would make up her mind the next time he came to Hamburg. Before leaving for Berlin he gave her a monkey which she loathed; fortunately, a handsome young cousin with whom she had gone rather far before he became one of Hilda's first lovers taught it to light matches, its little jersey caught fire, and the clumsy animal had to be destroyed. When Dreyer returned a week later, she allowed him to kiss her on the cheek. Poor old Papa got so high at the party that he beat up the fiddler, which was pardonable – seeing all the hard luck he had encountered in his long life. It was only after the wedding, when her husband cancelled an important business trip in favour of a ridiculous honeymoon in Norway –why Norway of all places? – that certain doubts began to assail her; but the villa in Grunewald soon dissipated them, and so on, not very interesting recollections.

4

In the darkness of the taxi (the unfortunate Icarus was still being repaired, and the rented substitute, a quirky Oriole, had not been a success), Dreyer remained mysteriously silent. He might have been asleep, had not his cigar glowed rhythmically. Franz was silent too, wondering uneasily where he was being taken. After the third or fourth turn he lost all sense of direction.

Up to now he had explored, besides the quiet quarter where he lived, only the avenue of lindens and its surroundings at the other end of the city. Everything that lay between those two live oases was a *terra incognita* blank. He gazed out of the window and saw the dark streets gradually acquiring a certain limpidity, then dimming again, then again welling with light, waning once more, brightening again, until having matured in the darkness they suddenly burst forth scintillating with fabulous colours, gemmed cascades, blazing advertisements. A tall steepled church glided past under the umber sky. Presently, skidding slightly on the damp asphalt, the car drew up at the curb.

Only then did Franz understand. In sapphire letters with a diamond flourish prolonging the final vowel, a glittering forty-foot sign spelled the word D*A*N*D*Y which now he remembered hearing before, the fool that he was! Dreyer took him under the arm and led him up to one of the ten radiantly lit display windows. Like tropical blossoms in a hothouse, ties and socks vied in delicate shades with the rectangle of folded shirts or drooped lazily from gilded bows, while in the depths an opal-tinted pyjama with the face of an Oriental idol stood fully erect, god of that garden. But Dreyer did not allow Franz to dally in contemplation. He led him smartly past the other windows, and there flashed by in turn an orgy of glossy footwear, a Fata Morgana of coats, a graceful flight of hats, gloves, and canes, and a sunny paradise of sports articles; then Franz found himself in a dark passageway where stood an old man in a black cape with a badge on his visored cap next to a slender-legged woman in furs. They both looked at Dreyer. The watchman recognized him and put his hand to his cap. The bright-eyed prostitute glanced at Franz and modestly moved away. As soon as he disappeared behind Dreyer in the gloom of a courtyard, she resumed her talk with the watchman about rheumatism and its cures.

The yard formed a triangular dead end between windowless walls. There was an odour of damp mingled with that of urine and beer. In one corner, either something was dumped, or else it was a cart with its shafts in the air. Dreyer produced the flashlight from his pocket, and a skimming circle of grey light outlined a grating, the moving shadows of descending steps, an iron door. Taking a childish delight in choosing the most mysterious entrance, Dreyer unlocked the door. Franz ducked and followed him into a dark stone passage where the round of flitting light now picked out a door. If any illegal attempt had been made to tamper with it, it would have emitted a wild ringing. But for this door too Dreyer had a small noiseless key, and again Franz ducked. In the murky basement through which they walked one could distinguish sacks and crates piled here and there and something like straw rustled underfoot. The mobile beam turned a corner, and yet another door appeared. Beyond it rose a bare staircase that melted into the blackness. They shuffled up the stone steps, explorers of a buried temple. With dream-like unexpectedness they emerged presently into a vast hall. The light glanced across metallic gallows, then along folds of drapery, gigantic wardrobes, swinging mirrors and broad-shouldered black figures. Dreyer stopped, put away his light and said softly in the dark 'Attention!' His hand could be heard fumbling, and a single pear-shaped bulb brightly illuminated a counter. The remainder of the hall – an endless labyrinth – remained submerged in darkness, and Franz found it a little eerie to have this one nook singled out by the strong light. 'Lesson One,' Dreyer said solemnly, and with a flourish went behind the counter.

It is doubtful if Franz benefited from this fantastic night lesson – everything was too strange, and Dreyer impersonated a salesman with too much whimsey. And yet, despite the baroque nonsense there was something about the angular reflections and the surrounding spectral abyss, where vague fabrics that had been handled and re-handled during the day reposed in weary attitudes, which long remained in Franz's memory and imparted a certain dark luxurious colouring, at least at first, to the basic background against which his everyday salesman's toil began to sketch later its plain, comprehensible, often tiresome pattern. And it was not on personal experience, not on the recollection of distant days when he actually had worked behind the counter, that Dreyer drew that night as he showed Franz how to sell neckties. Instead, he soared into the ravishing realm of inutile imagination, demonstrating not the way ties should be sold in real life, but the way they might be sold if the salesman were both artist and clairvoyant.

'I want a simple blue one,' Franz, prompted by him, would say in a wooden schoolboy voice.

'Certainly, sir,' Dreyer answered briskly and, whisking off several cardboard boxes from a shelf, nimbly opened them on the counter.

'How do you like this one?' he inquired not without a shadow of pensiveness, knotting a mottled magenta-and-black tie on his hand and holding it away a little as if admiring it himself in the capacity of an independent artist.

Franz was silent.

'An important technique,' explained Dreyer, changing his voice. 'Let's see if you got the point. Now you go behind the counter. In this box here there are some solid-coloured ties. They cost four-five marks. And here we have stylish ones on the 'orchid' side, as we say, at eight, ten, or even fourteen, the Lord forgive us. Now then, you are the salesman and I am a young man, a ninny if you'll excuse me – inexperienced, irresolute, easily tempted.'

Franz self-consciously went behind the counter. Hunching his shoulders and narrowing his eyes as if he were near-sighted, Dreyer said in a high-pitched quaver: 'I want a plain blue one. . . . And please, not too expensive.' 'Smile,' he added in a prompter's whisper.

Franz bent low over one of the boxes, fumbled awkwardly and produced a plain blue tie.

'Aha, I caught you!' Dreyer exclaimed cheerfully. 'I knew you had not understood, or else you are colour-blind, and then goodbye dear uncle and aunt. Why on earth must you give me the cheapest one? You should have done as I did – stun the ninny first with an expensive one, no matter what colour. But be sure it's gaudy and costly, or costly and elegant, and maybe squeeze out of him 'an extra throb and an extra bob,' as they say in London. Here, take this one. Now knot it on your hand. Wait, wait – don't worry it like that. Swing it around your finger. Thus! Remember the slightest delay in the rhythm costs you a moment of the customer's attention. Hypnotize him with the flip of the tie you display. You must make it *bloom* before the idiot's eyes. No, that's not a knot, that's some kind of tumour. Watch. Hold your hand straight. Let's try this expensive vampire red. Now we suppose it is I who am looking at it, and I still don't yield to temptation.'

'But I wanted a plain blue one,' said Dreyer in a high voice – and then, again in a whisper: 'Ah, no – keep pushing the vampire one in his stupid face, perhaps you'll wear him down. And watch him, watch his eyes – if he looks at the thing that's already something. Only if he does not look at all and begins to frown, and clear his damned throat – only then, you understand, only then give him what he requested – always choosing the dearest of the three plain blues, of course. But even as you yield to his coarse request, give, you know, a slight shrug, look at me now – and smile sort of disdainfully as if to say "this isn't fahionable at all, frankly, this is for peasants, for droshky coachmen . . . but if you really want it"—'

'I'll take this blue one,' said Dreyer in his comedy voice.

Franz grimly handed him the tie across the counter. Dreyer's guffaw awakened a rude echo. 'No,' he said, 'no, my friend. Not at all. First, you lay it aside to your right, then you inquire if he does not need something else, for instance, handkerchiefs, or some fancy studs, and only after he has thought a bit and shaken his calf's head, only then produce this fountain pen (which is a present) and write out and give him the price slip for the cashier. But the rest is routine. No, keep it, I said. You will be shown that part tomorrow by Mr Piffke, a very pedantic man. Now let's continue.'

Dreyer hoisted himself a little heavily to a sitting position on the counter, casting as he did so a sharp black shadow that dived head first into the darkness which seemed to have moved closer the better to hear. He started to finger the silks in the boxes, and to instruct Franz how to remember ties by touch and tint, how to develop, in other words (lost on Franz), a chromatic and tactile memory, how to eradicate from one's artistic and commercial consciousness styles and specimens that had been sold out – so as to make room for new ones in one's mind, and how to determine the price in marks immediately and then add the pfennigs from the tag. Several times he jumped off the counter, gesticulating grotesquely, impersonating a customer irritated by everything he was shown; the brute who objected to his being told the price before he had asked for it; and the saint to whom price was no object; also an old lady buying a tie for her grandson, a fireman at Potsdam; or a foreigner unable to express anything comprehensible – a Frenchman who wants a *cravate,* an Italian who demands a *cravatta,* a Russian who pleads gently for a *galstook.* Whereupon he would reply at once to himself, pressing his fingers lightly against the counter, and for each occasion inventing a particular variety of intonation and smile. Then seating himself again and slightly swinging his foot in its glossy shoe (as his shadow flapped a black wing on the floor), he discussed the tender and cheerful attitude a salesman should have toward man-made things, and he confessed that sometimes one felt absurdly sorry for outmoded ties and obsolete socks that were still so neat and fresh but completely unwanted; an odd, dreamy smile hovered under his moustache, and alternately creased and smoothed out the wrinkles at the corners of his eyes and mouth – whilst extenuated Franz, leaning against a wardrobe, listened in a torpor to him.

Dreyer paused – and as Franz realized that the lesson was over, he could not help casting a covetous glance at the iridescent wonders now scattered, in real life, on the counter. Again producing his flashlight and turning off the switch on the wall, Dreyer led Franz over a waste of dark carpeting into the shadowy depths of the hall. He flung off in passing the canvas of a small table and trained his light on cuff links sparkling like eyes on their blue velvet cushion. A little further with playful nonchalance he tipped off its stand a huge beach ball which rolled soundlessly away into the dark, far, far, all the way to the Bay of Pomerania and its soft white sands.

They walked back along the stone passages, and as he was locking the last door Dreyer recalled not without pleasure the enigmatic disorder he had left behind while neglecting to think that perhaps someone else would be held responsible for it.

As soon as they emerged from the dark courtyard into the wetly gleaming street, Dreyer hailed a passing taxi and offered Franz a lift home.

Franz hesitated, staring at the festive vista (at last!) of the animated boulevard.

'Or do you have a date with a' (Dreyer consulted his wrist watch) 'sleepy sweetheart?'

Franz licked his lips and shook his head.

'As you wish,' said Dreyer with a laugh and, thrusting his head out of the cab, he shouted in parting: 'Be at the store tomorrow, nine o'clock sharp.'

The lustre of the black asphalt was filmed by a blend of dim hues, through which here and there vivid rends and oval holes made by rain puddles revealed the authentic colours of deep reflections – a vermilion diagonal band, a cobalt wadge, a green spiral – scattered glimpses into a humid upside-down world, into a dizzy geometry of gems. The kaleidoscopic effect suggested someone's jiggling every now and then the pavement so as to change the combination of numberless coloured fragments. Meanwhile, shafts and ripples of life passed by, marking the course of every car. Shop windows, bursting with tense radiance, oozed, squirted, and splashed out into the rich blackness.

And at every corner, emblem of ineffable happiness, stood a sleek-hosed harlot whose features there was no time to study: another already beckoned in the distance, and beyond her, a third. And Franz knew without any doubt where those mysterious live beacons led. Every street lamp, its halo spreading like a spiky star, every rosy glow, every spasm of golden light, and the silhouettes of lovers pulsating against each other in every recess of porch and passage; and those half-opened painted lips that fleeted past him; and the black, moist, tender asphalt – all of it was assuming a specific significance and finding a name.

Saturated with sweat, limp with delicious languor, moving with the slow motion of a sleepwalker called back to his rumpled warm pillow, Franz went back to bed, without having noticed how he had re-entered the house and reached his room. He stretched, he passed his palms over his hairy legs, unglued and cupped himself, and almost instantly Sleep, with a bow, handed him the key of its city: he understood the meaning of all the lights, sounds, and perfumes as everything blended into a single blissful image. Now he seemed to be in a mirrored hall, which wondrously opened on a watery abyss, water glistened in the most unexpected places: he went toward a door past the perfectly credible motorcycle which his landlord was starting with his red heel, and, anticipating indescribable bliss, Franz opened the door and saw Martha standing near the bed. Eagerly he approached but Tom kept getting in the way; Martha was laughing and shooing away the dog. Now he saw quite closely her glossy lips, her neck swelling with glee, and he too began to hurry, undoing buttons, pulling a blood-stained bone out of the dog's jaws, and feeling an unbearable sweetness welling up within him; he was about to clasp her hips but suddenly could no longer contain his boiling ecstasy.

Martha sighed and opened her eyes. She thought she had been awakened by a noise in the street: one of their neighbours had a remarkably loud motorcycle. Actually, it was only her husband snoring away with particular abandon. She recalled she had gone to bed without awaiting his return, raised herself, and called to him sharply; then, reaching across the night table, she began roughly tousling his hair, the only trick that worked. His snoring ceased, his lips smacked once or twice. The light on the table flashed on showing the pink of her hand.

'The awakening of the lion,' said Dreyer, rubbing his eyes with his fist like a child.

'Where did you go?' Martha asked, glaring at him.

He stared sleepily at her ivory shoulder, at the rose of a bared breast, at the long strand of ebony hair falling on her cheek, and gave a soft chuckle as he slowly leaned back on his pillows.

'I've been showing him Dandy,' he muttered cozily. 'A night lesson. He can now knot a tie on his paw or his tail. Very entertaining and instructive.'

Ah, that was it. Martha felt so relieved, so magnanimous, that she almost offered . . . but she was also too sleepy. Sleepy and very happy. Without speaking she switched off the light.

'Let's go riding Sunday – what do you say?' a voice murmured tenderly in the dark. But she was already lost in dream. Three lecherous Arabs were haggling over her with a bronze-torsoed handsome slaver. The voice repeated its question in an even more tender, even more questioning tone. A melancholy pause. Then he turned his pillow in quest of a cooler hollow, sighed, and presently was snoring again.

In the morning, as Dreyer was hurriedly enjoying a soft-boiled egg with buttered toast (the most delicious meal known to man) before dashing off to the emporium, Frieda informed him that the repaired car was waiting at the door. Here Dreyer remembered that in the past few days, and particularly after the recent smash, he had repeatedly had a rather amusing thought which he had somehow never brought to its conclusion. But he must act cautiously, in a roundabout manner. A blunt question would lead nowhere. The rascal would leer and deny everything. Would the gardener know? If he did, he would shield him. Dreyer gulped down his coffee and, blinking, poured himself a second cup. Of course, I could be mistaken. . . .

He sipped up the last sweet drop, threw his napkin on the table and hurried out; the napkin slowly crept off the edge of the table and fell limply onto the floor.

Yes, the car had been well repaired. It gleamed with its new coat of black paint, the chrome of its headlight rims, the blazon-like emblem that crested the radiator grill: a silver boy with azure wings. A slightly embarrassed smile bared the chauffeur's ugly gums and teeth as he doffed his blue cap and opened the door. Dreyer glanced at him askance.

'Hello, hello,' he said, 'so here we are together again.' He buttoned all the buttons of his overcoat and continued: 'This must have cost a tidy sum – I haven't looked at the bill yet. But that's not the point. I'd be willing to pay even more for the sheer fun of it. A most exhilarating experience, to be sure. Unfortunately, neither my wife nor the police saw the joke.'

He tried to think of something else to add, failed, unbuttoned his coat again, and got into the car.

'I gave his physiognomy a thorough examination,' he reflected to the accompaniment of the motor's gentle purr. 'Still it is impossible to draw any conclusion yet. Of course, his eyes are sort of twinkly, of course, they have those little bags under them. But that may be normal with him. Next time I'll have to take a good sniff.'

That morning, as agreed, he visited the emporium and introduced Franz to Mr Piffke. Piffke was burly, dignified, and smartly dressed. He had blond eyelashes, baby-coloured skin, a profile that had prudently stopped halfway between man and teapot, and a second-rate diamond on his plump auricular. He felt for Franz the respect due to the boss's nephew, while Franz gazed with envy and awe at the architectonic perfection of Piffke's trouser creases and the transparent handkerchief peeping out of his breast pocket.

Dreyer did not even mention the lesson of the night before. With his complete approval Piffke assigned Franz not to the tie counter, but to the sporting-goods department. Piffke went to work on Franz with zeal, and his training methods turned out to be very different from Dreyer's, containing as they did a great deal more arithmetic than Franz had expected.

Neither had he expected his feet to ache so much, from constant standing, or his face, from the mechanical expression of affability. As usual in autumn, that part of the emporium was much quieter than the others. Various bodybuilding appliances, ping-pong paddles, striped woollen scarves, soccer boots with black cleats and white laces moved fairly well. The existence of public pools accounted for a continued small demand for bathing suits; but their real season had passed, while the time for skates and skis had not yet come. Thus no rush of customers hampered Franz's training and he had complete leisure to learn his job. His main colleagues were two girls, one red-haired and sharp-nosed, the other a stout energetic blonde inexorably accompanied by a sour smell; and an athletically built young man wearing the same kind of tortoise shell glasses as Franz. He casually informed Franz about the prizes he had won in swimming competitions, and Franz envied him, being himself an excellent swimmer. It was with Schwimmer's help that Franz selected the cloth for two suits and a supply of ties, shirts, and socks. It was he, too, who helped Franz to unravel some minor mysteries of salesmanship far more astutely than Piffke, whose true function was to promenade about the place and grandly arrange meetings between customer and salesman.

During the first few days Franz, dazed and self-conscious and trying not to shiver (his department was over-ventilated and full of its own athletic drafts), simply stood in a corner trying not to attract attention, avidly following the actions of his colleagues, memorizing their professional movements and intonations, and then abruptly, with unbearable clarity, imagining Martha – the way she had of putting her hand to the back of her chignon, or glancing at her nails and emerald ring. Very soon, however, under the approving solicitous gaze of Mr Schwimmer, Franz started selling on his own.

He remembered forever his first customer, a stout old man who asked for a ball. A ball. At once this ball went off bouncing in his imagination, multiplying and scattering, and Franz's head became the playground for all the balls in the store, small, medium, and large – yellow leather ones with stitched sections, fluffy white ones bearing the violet signature of their maker, little black ones hard as stone, extra-light orange-and-blue ones of vacational size, balls of rubber, celluloid, wood, ivory, and they all rolled off in different directions leaving behind a single sphere shining in the middle of his mind when the customer added placidly: 'I need a ball for my dog.'

'Third shelf on your right, Tooth-Proof,' came Schwimmer's prompt whisper, and Franz with a grin of relief and sweat on his brow started to open one wrong box after another but at last found what was needed.

In a month or so he had grown completely accustomed to his work; he no longer got flustered; would boldly bid the inarticulate to repeat their request; and would condescendingly counsel the puny and shy. Fairly well built, fairly broad-shouldered, slim but not skinny, he observed with pleasure his passage in a harem of mirrors and the glances of obviously infatuated shopgirls, and the flash of three silver clips over his heart: Uncle's fountain pen and two pencils, lilac and lead. He might have passed, indeed, for a perfectly respectable, perfectly ordinary salesman, were it not for a blend of details that only a detective of genius might have discerned – a predatory angularity of nostril and cheekbone, a strange weakness about the mouth as if he were always out of breath or had just sneezed, and those eyes, those eyes, poorly disguised by glasses, restless eyes, tragic eyes, ruthless and helpless, of an impure greenish shade with inflamed blood vessels around the iris. But the only detective around was an elderly woman always with the same parcel, who did not bother patrolling Sports but had quite a lot to do in the Neckties department.

Acting upon impeccable Piffke's delicately formulated suggestions, Franz acquired sybarite habits of personal hygiene. He now washed his feet at least twice a week and changed his starched collar and cuffs practically every day. Every evening he brushed his suit and shined his shoes. He used all sorts of nice lotions, smelling of spring flowers and Piffke. He hardly ever skipped his Saturday bath. He put on a clean shirt every Wednesday and Sunday. He made a point of changing his warm underwear at least once in ten days. How shocked his mother would be, he reflected, if she saw his laundry bills!

He accepted with alacrity the tedium of his job, but disliked intensely the necessity of having meals with the rest of the staff. He had hoped that in Berlin he would gradually get over his morbid juvenile squeamishness, but it kept finding mean opportunities to torture him. At table he sat between the plump blonde and the champion swimmer. Whenever she stretched toward the bread basket or the salt, her armpit flooded him with nausea reminding him of a detested spinster teacher at school. The champion on his other side had another infirmity – that of spitting whenever he spoke, and Franz found himself reverting to his schooldays' system of protecting his plate from the spray with forearm and elbow. Only once did he accompany Mr Schwimmer to the public pool. The water proved to be much too cold and far from clean, and his colleague's roommate, a sunlamp-tanned young Swede, had embarrassing manners.

Basically, though, the emporium, the glossy goods, the brisk or suave dialogue with the customer (who always seemed to be the same actor changing his voice and mask), all this routine was a superficial trickle of repetitive events and sensations which touched him as little as if he was one of those figures of fashion with waxen or wooden faces in suits pressed by the iron of perfection, arrested in a state of colourful putrefaction on their temporary pedestals and platforms, their arms half-bent and half-extended in a parody of pastoral appeal. Young female customers and fleet-footed bob-haired salesgirls from other departments hardly excited him at all. Like the coloured commercial tills advertising furniture or furs that succeed each other on the cinema screen for a long time, unaccompanied by music, before a fascinating film starts, all the details of his work were as inevitable as they were trivial. Around six it all stopped abruptly. And then the music would start playing.

Almost nightly – and what monstrous melancholy lurked in that 'almost' – he would visit the Dreyers. He dined there only on Sundays, and not every Sunday at that. On weekdays, after a bite at the same cheap restaurant where he had lunched, he took the bus or walked to their villa. A score of evenings had gone by, and everything remained the same: The welcome buzz of the wicket, the pretty lantern illuminating the path through a pattern of ivy, the damp exhalation of the lawn, the gravel's crunch, the tinkle of the doorbell winging off into the house in quest of the maid, the burst of light, Frieda's placid face, and suddenly – life, the tender reverberations of radio music.

She was generally alone; Dreyer, a fantastic but punctual person, would arrive exactly in time for what Franz called supper, and the evening tea, and would always telephone when he thought he might be late. In his presence Franz felt uncomfortable to the point of numbness, and therefore managed to evolve in those days a certain air of grim familiarity in response to Dreyer's natural joviality. But while he was alone with Martha, he had a constant sensation of languorous pressure somewhere at the top of his spine; his chest felt tight, his legs weak; his fingers retained for a long time the cool strength of her handshake. He would compute within half an inch the exact degree to which she showed her legs while walking about the room and while sitting with her legs crossed, and he perceived almost without looking the tense sheen of her stocking, the swell of her left calf over the right knee; and the fold of her skirt, sloping, soft, supple, in which one would have liked to bury one's face. Sometimes, when she got up and walked past him to the radiola, the light would fall at such an angle as to let the outline of her thighs show through the light fabric of her skirt, and once she got a ladder-like run in her stocking and, licking her finger, quickly dabbed at the silk. Occasionally, the sensation of languid weight became too much for him, and taking advantage of her looking away, he would search her beauty for some little fault on which he could prop his mind and sober his fancy, and thus allay the relentless stir of his senses. Now and then he had the impression that he had indeed found the saving flaw – a hard line near the mouth, a pockmark above the eyebrow, a top prominent pout of those full lips in profile, a dark shadow of down above them, especially noticeable when the powder came off. But one turn of her head or the slightest change of expression would restore to her face such adorable charm that he slipped back into his private abyss even deeper. By means of those rapid glances he made a complete study of her, followed and forefelt her gestures, anticipated the banal but to him unique movement of her alertly raised hand when one end of a tiny comb would slacken its grip on her heavy bun. Most of all he was tormented by the grace and power of her bare white neck, by that rich delicately grained texture of skin and the fashionable glimpses of nudity allowed by short flimsy skirts. At every new visit he added something to the collection of enchantments which he would gloat over later in his solitary bed, choosing the one his frenzied fancy would work on and spend itself. There was the evening when he saw a minute brown birthmark on her arm. There was the moment when she bent low from her seat to turn back the corner of a rug and he noticed the parting of her breasts and was relieved when the black silk of her bodice became taut again. There was also the night when she was getting ready for a dance, and he was stunned to observe that her armpits were as smooth and white as a statue's.

She questioned him about his childhood, his mother, a dull theme, his native town, an even duller one. Once Tom put his muzzle in Franz's lap and yawned, enveloping him in an unendurable odour – foul herring, carrion. 'That is how my childhood smells,' muttered Franz as he pushed the dog's head away. She did not hear or did not understand, and asked what he had said. But he did not repeat his confession. He talked about his school, about the dust and the boredom, about his mother's indigestible pies, and about the butcher next door, a dignified gentleman in a white waistcoat who at one time used to come to dinner every day, and eat mutton in a disgustingly professional manner. 'Why disgustingly?' Martha interrupted in surprise. 'God, what nonsense I'm spouting,' he thought, and with mechanical enthusiasm described for the hundredth time the river, the boating, the diving, the beer-drinking under the bridge.

She would switch the radio from song to speech, and he would reverently listen to a Spanish lesson, a lecture on the benefits of athletics, to Mr Streseman's conciliatory tones, and then – back to some bizarre nasal music. She would tell him in detail the plot of a film, the story of Dreyer's lucky speculations in the days of the inflation, and the gist of an article on the removal of fruit stains. And all the time she would be thinking: 'How much longer would he need to get started?' and simultaneously she was amused and even a little touched that he was so unsure of himself and that without her help he would probably never get started at all. Gradually, however, vexation began to predominate. November was being squandered on trifles as money is squandered on trifles when you get stranded in some dull town. With a vague resentment, she recalled that her sister had already had at least four of five lovers in succession, and that Willy Wald's young wife had had two simultaneously. And yet Martha was already past thirty-four. It was high time. In turn, she had been given a husband, a beautiful villa, antique silver, an automobile; the next gift on her list was Franz. Yet it was all not quite so simple; there intruded an alien little breeze, a special ardour, a suspicious softness. . . .

It was no use trying to sleep. Franz opened his window. At the transit from autumn to winter, quirky nights occur when suddenly, out of nowhere, there passes a breath of warm humid air, a belated sigh of summer. He stood in his new zebra pyjamas holding on to the window frame, then leaned out, morosely released a long spurt of saliva, and listened, waiting for it to splatter against the sidewalk. However, since he lived on the fifth floor, and not on the second as he had at home, Franz heard nothing. With a slow clatter he shut the window and went back to bed. That night he realized, as one becomes abruptly aware of suffering from a fatal illness, that he had already known Martha for more than two months, and was draining his passion in useless fantasies. And Franz told the pillow, in the half-obscene, half-grandiloquent idiom he affected when talking to himself: 'Never mind – better betray my career than wait till my brain cracks. Tomorrow, yes, tomorrow, I'll grab her and tumble her, on the sofa, on the floor, on the table, on broken crockery . . .' Crazy Franz!

Tomorrow came. He went home after work, changed his socks, brushed his teeth, put on his new silk scarf and marched to the bus stop with martial determination. On the way he kept persuading himself that of course she loved him, that only out of pride she concealed her feeling, and that was a pity. If only she leaned toward him as if by chance, and brushed her cheek against his temple over a blurred album, or if she did again, as she had the other night – if she pressed for a moment her back to his before the front-hall mirror and said, turning her perfumed head: 'I'm an inch taller than you,' or if – but here he pulled himself together and soundlessly told the bus conductor: 'That's weakness, and there should be no weakness.' Let her be tonight even colder than usual – no matter – now, now, now. . . . As he rang the bell there flashed through his mind a poltroon's hope that perhaps by some chance Dreyer had already come home. Dreyer had not.

As Franz passed through the first two rooms, he pictured how in an instant he would push open that door over there, enter her boudoir, see her in a low-cut black dress with emeralds around her neck, immediately embrace her, hard, make her crunch, make her faint, make her spill her jewels; he pictured it so vividly that for a split second he saw before him his own receding back, saw his hand, saw himself opening the door, and because that sensation was a foray into the future, and it is forbidden to ransack the future, he was swiftly punished. In the first place, as he caught up with himself, he tripped and sent the door flying open. In the second, the room Martha called the boudoir was empty. In the third, when she came in she was wearing a beige dress with a high neck and a long line of buttons. In the fourth place, such a familiar helpless timidity came over him that all he could hope for was to speak more or less articulately.

Martha had decided that tonight he would kiss her for the first time. Characteristically, she chose one of her monthly days lest she succumb too soon, and in the wrong spot, to a yearning that otherwise she could no longer resist. In anticipation of that prudently circumscribed embrace she did not immediately settle down on the sofa near him. As tradition demanded, she turned on the radio, brought a little silver case with Libidettes (Viennese cigarettes), re-arranged the fold of a window curtain, turned on the opal glow of a table lamp, switched off the ceiling light, and (choosing the worst subject imaginable) began telling Franz how the day before Dreyer had started on some mysterious new project – a profitable one, let us hope; she picked up and placed on the back of a chair a pink woollen shawl, and only then gently sat down next to Franz, not quite comfortably folding one leg under her and adjusting the pleats of her skirt.

For no reason at all, he began extolling Uncle, saying how frightfully grateful he was, and how fond he had grown of him. Martha nodded absently. He would alternately puff on his cigarette, or hold it next to his knee, drawing the cardboard tip across the fabric of his trouser leg. The smoke like a flow of spectral milk crept along the clingy nap. Martha extended her hand and with a smile touched his knee as if playing with this phantom larva of smoke. He felt the tender pressure of her fingers. He was hungry, sweaty, and completely impotent.

'. . . And my mother in every letter, you know, sends him her respectful love, her regards, her thanks.'

The smoke dissolved. Franz kept sniffing as he did when he was especially nervous. Martha got up and turned off the radio. He lit another cigarette. She had now thrown the pink shawl over her shoulders and, like a woman in some old-fashioned romances, gazed at him fixedly from the far corner of the settee. With a wooden laugh, he recounted an anecdote from yesterday's paper. Then, nudging the door with his paw, a very sad, very sleek, very hopeless Tom appeared, and Franz for the first time actually talked to the astonished animal. And at last, thank God, beloved Dreyer arrived.

Franz came home around eleven, and as he was proceeding along the passage on tiptoe to the foul little water closet he heard a chuckle coming from the landlord's door. The door was ajar. He peeped into the room as he passed. Old Enricht, clad only in his nightshirt, was standing on all fours with his wrinkled and hoary rear toward a brilliant cheval glass. Bending low his congested face, fringed with white hair, like the head of the professor in the 'Hindu Prince' farce, he was peering back through the archway of his bare thighs at the reflection of his bleak buttocks.

5

There was indeed an air of mystery about Dreyer's new project. It all began one Wednesday in mid-November when he received a visit from a nondescript stranger with a cosmopolitan name and no determinable origin. He might have been Czech, Jewish, Bavarian, Irish – it was entirely a matter of personal evaluation.

Dreyer was sitting in his office (a huge quiet place with huge unique windows, with a huge desk, and huge leather armchairs) when, having traversed an olive-green corridor past glass expanses full of the hurricane-like clatter of typewriters, this nondescript gentleman was ushered in. He was hatless but wore a topcoat and warm gloves.

The card that had preceded him by a couple of minutes bore the title of 'Inventor' under his name. Now Dreyer was fond, perhaps over-fond, of inventors. With a mesmeric gesture, he deposited his guest in the leathern luxury of an over-stuffed chair (with an ashtray affixed to its giant paw) and, toying with a red-and-blue pencil, sat down half-facing him. The man's thick eyebrows wiggled like furry black caterpillars, and the freshly shaven parts of his melancholy face had a dark turquoise cast.

The inventor began from afar, and this Dreyer approved. All business ought to be handled with that artful caution. Lowering his voice, the inventor passed with laudable smoothness from the preface to the substance. Dreyer laid down his pencil. Suavely and in detail the Magyar – or Frenchman, or Pole – stated his business.

'You say, then, that it has nothing to do with wax?' asked Dreyer. The inventor raised his finger. 'Absolutely nothing, though I call it "voskin," a trade name that will be in all dictionaries tomorrow. Its main component is a resilient, colourless product resembling flesh. I particularly stress its elasticity, its pliability, its rippliability, so to speak.'

'Speak by all means,' said Dreyer. 'And what about that "electric impellent" – I don't quite understand; what do you mean, for example, by "contractive transmission"?'

The inventor smiled a wise smile. 'Ah, that's the whole point. Obviously, it would be much simpler if I showed you the blueprints; but it is also obvious that I'm not yet inclined to do so. I have explained how you can apply my invention. Now it's up to you to give me the funds for the construction of the first sample.'

'How much would you need?' asked Dreyer with curiosity. The inventor replied in detail.

'Don't you think,' said Dreyer with a mischievous glint in his eye, 'that perhaps your imagination is worth much more? I highly respect and value the imagination in others. If for example a man came to me and said: "My dear *Herr Direktor,* I would like to dream a little. How much will you pay me for dreaming?" then, maybe, I would begin negotiations with him. Whereas you, my dear inventor, you offer at once something practical, factory production and so forth. Who cares about realization? I am duty-bound to believe in a dream but to believe in the embodiment of that dream – Puh!' (one of Dreyer's lipbursts).

At first the inventor did not understand; then he understood and was offended.

'In other words, you simply refuse?' he asked gloomily.

Dreyer sighed. The inventor clucked his tongue, and leaned back in his chair clasping and unclasping his hands.

'This is my life's work,' he said at last, staring into space. 'Like Hercules, I have been struggling with the tentacles of a dream for ten years, mastering this softness, this flexibility, this plexibility, this stylized animation, if I may use the expression.'

'*Of course* you may,' said Dreyer. 'I'd even say that's better than the – what was it – "ripplexibility"? Tell me,' he began, picking up the pencil again – a good sign (though his interlocutor could not know it), 'have you approached anyone else with that offer?'

'Well,' said the inventor with perfectly mimicked sincerity, 'I confess this is the first time. In fact, I have just arrived in Germany. This *is* Germany, isn't it?' he added, looking around.

'So I'm told,' said Dreyer.

There was a fruit-bearing pause.

'Your dream is enchanting,' said Dreyer pensively, 'enchanting.'

The other grimaced and flared up: 'Stop harping on dreams, sir. They have come true, they have become flesh, in more senses than one, even though I may be a pauper, and cannot build my Eden and eidolons. Have you ever read Epicritus?'

Dreyer shook his head.

'Nor have I. But do give me a chance to prove that I am no quack. They told me you were interested in such innovations. Just think what a delight this would be, what an adornment, what an astounding, and permit me to say even artistic, achievement.'

'What guarantee do you offer me?' asked Dreyer, relishing the entertainment.

'The guarantee of the human spirit,' the inventor said trenchantly.

Dreyer laughed. 'That's more like it. You revert to my original viewpoint.'

He thought for a moment, then added: 'I think I want to roll your offer around in my head. Who knows, maybe I'll see your invention in my next dream. My imagination must become steeped in it. At the moment I can say neither yes nor no. Now run along home. Where are you staying?'

'Hotel Montevideo,' said the inventor. 'An idiotically misleading name.'

'But also a familiar one, though I can't remember why. Video, video. . . .'

'I see you have my friend's Pugowitz Tapwater Filter,' said the inventor, pointing at the faucet in the corridor with the air of Rembrandt indicating a Claude Lorraine.

'Video, video,' repeated Dreyer. 'No, I don't know. Well, ponder our talk. Decide if you really want to kill a delightful fancy by selling it to the factory, and in a week or ten days I'll ring you up. And – pardon me for alluding to this – I hope you'll be a bit more communicative, a bit more trusting.'

When his visitor had left, Dreyer sat motionless, his hands thrust deep into his trouser pockets. 'No, he is not a charlatan,' he reflected. 'Or at least he is not aware of being one. Why not have a little fun? If it is all he says, the results really may be curious.' The telephone emitted a discreet buzz, and for a time he forgot about the inventor.

That evening, however, he hinted to Martha that he was about to embark on a completely new project, and when she asked if it were profitable, he narrowed his eyes and nodded: 'Oh, very, very profitable, my love.' Next morning, as he was snorting under the shower, he decided not to receive the inventor again. At lunchtime, in a restaurant, he remembered him with pleasure and decided that the invention was something unique and irresistible. Upon coming home to supper he remarked to Martha casually that the project had fallen through. She was wearing her beige dress and was wrapped in a pink shawl, though it was quite warm in the house. Franz, whom he considered an amusing simpleton, was as usual jumpy and gloomy. He soon went home, saying he had smoked too much and had a headache. As soon as he had gone, Martha went up to the bedroom. In the boudoir on the tripod table by the sofa a silver box remained open. Dreyer took a Libidette from it and burst out laughing. 'Contractive transmission! Animated flexibility! No, he can't be cheating. I think his idea is awfully attractive.'

When he in turn went up to bed, Martha seemed to be asleep. After several centuries had elapsed, the bed table lamp went out. Presently she opened her eyes and listened. He was snoring. She lay on her back, gazing into the dark. Everything irritated her – that snoring, that gleam in the dark, probably in the looking glass, and incidentally, her own self.

'That was the wrong approach,' she thought. 'Tomorrow night I'll take drastic measures. Tomorrow night.'

Franz, however, did not appear either the next evening or on Sunday. On Friday he had gone to a movie, and on Saturday, to a café with his colleague Schwimmer. At the cinema, an actress with a little black heart for lips and with eyelashes like the spokes of an umbrella was impersonating a rich heiress impersonating a poor office girl. The café turned out to be dark and dull. Schwimmer kept talking about the goings-on among boys in summer camps, and a rouged whore with a repulsive gold tooth was looking at them and swinging her leg, and half-smiling at Franz every time she shook off the ash of her cigarette.

It would have been so simple, thought Franz, to grasp her when she touched my knee. Agony. . . . Should I perhaps wait a while and not see her for a few days? But then life is not worth living. The next time I swear, yes, I swear. I swear by my mother and sister.

On Sunday his landlord brought him his coffee as usual at nine-thirty. Franz did not at once dress and shave as he did on weekdays, but merely pulled on his old dressing gown over his pyjamas, and sat down at the table to write his weekly letter: 'Dear Mama,' he wrote in his crawling hand, 'how are you? How is Emmy? Probably . . .—'

He paused, crossed out the last word and lapsed into thought, picking his nose, looking at the rainy day in the window. Probably they were on their way to church now. In the afternoon there would be coffee with whipped cream. He imagined his mother's fat florid face and dyed hair. What did she care about him? She had always loved Emmy more. She had still boxed his ears when he was seventeen, eighteen, even nineteen – last year, in fact. Once at Easter, when he was quite small but already bespectacled, she had ordered him to eat a little chocolate bunny that had been well licked by his sister. For having licked the candy meant for him Emmy received a light slap on the behind, but to him, for having refused to touch the slimy brown horror, she delivered such a backhand whack in the face that he flew off his chair, hit his head against the sideboard and lost consciousness. His love for his mother was never very deep but even so it was his first unhappy love, or rather he regarded her as a rough draft of a first love, for although he had craved for her affection because his schoolbooks of stories (*My Soldier Boy, Hanna Comes Home*) told him, as they had from immemorial time, that mothers always doted upon their sons and daughters, he actually could not stand her physical appearance, mannerisms, and emanations, the depressing, depressingly familiar odour of her skin and clothes, the bedbug-brown fat birthmark on her neck, the trick she had of scratching with a knitting needle the unappetizing parting of her chestnut hair, her enormous dropsical ankles, and all the kitchen faces she made by which he could unerringly determine what she was preparing – beer soup or bull hodes, or that dreadful local dainty *Budenzucker*.

Perhaps – in retrospection, at least – he had suffered less from her indifference, meanness, fits of temper, than from the embarrassment and detestation when she pinched his cheek in feigned fondness before a guest, usually the next-door butcher, or in the latter's presence forced him in folly and fun to kiss his sister's schoolmate Christina whom he adored from a distance, and to whom he would have apologized for those dreadful moments had she paid the least attention to him. Perhaps, in spite of everything, his mother missed him now? She never wrote anything about her feelings in her infrequent letters.

Still it was nice to feel sorry for oneself, it brought hot tears to one's eyes. And Emmy – she was a good girl. She would marry the butcher's assistant. Best butcher in town. Damn this rain. Dear Mama. What else? Maybe a description of the room?

He replaced his right slipper, which had aged more quickly than the left one and kept falling off his foot when he dangled it, and looked around.

'As I already wrote you, I have an excellent room, but I never described it to you properly. It has a mirror and a washstand. Above the bed there is the beautiful picture of a lady in an Oriental setting. The wallpaper has brownish flowers. In front of me, against the wall, there is a chest-of-drawers.'

At that moment there came a light knock, Franz turned his head, and the door opened a crack. Old Enricht thrust his head in, winked, disappeared, and said to somebody on the other side of the door: 'Yes, he is at home. Go right in.'

She was wearing her beautiful moleskin coat thrown open over a veily, vapory dress; the rain that had caught her between taxi and entrance had had time to dot with dark stains her pearl-grey helmet-like hat; she stood pressing closely together her legs in apricot silk, as if on a parade. Still standing thus, she reached behind her and closed the door. She took off her gloves. Intently, unsmilingly, she stared at Franz as if she had not expected to see him. He covered his bare Adam's apple with his hand and uttered a long sentence but noticed with surprise that seemingly no words had been produced, as if he had tapped them out on a typewriter in which he had forgotten to insert a ribbon.

'Excuse me for bursting in like this,' said Martha, 'but I was afraid you might be ill.'

Palpitating and blinking, his lower lip drooping, Franz began helping her to get rid of her coat. The silk lining was crimson, as crimson as lips and flayed animals, and smelled of heaven. He placed her coat and hat on the bed, and one last staunch little observer in the storm of his consciousness, after the rest of his thoughts had scattered, noted that this was like a train passenger marking the seat he is about to occupy.

The room was damp, and Martha, who had not much under her dress besides her gartered stockings, shivered.

'What's the matter?' she said. 'I thought you would be glad to see me, and you don't say a word.'

'Oh, I'm talking,' answered Franz, doing his best to outshout the hum around him.

Now they were standing face to face in the middle of the room, between the unfinished letter and the unmade bed.

'I don't care much for your dressing gown,' she said, 'but I love your pyjamas. What nice stuff,' she continued, rubbing it between finger and thumb near his open throat. 'Look, he sleeps with his pen in his breast pocket, the perfect little businessman.'

He began with her hands, burying his mouth in their warm palms, fondling her cold knuckles, kissing her bracelet. She gently plucked off his glasses and, as if blind herself, groped for his dressing-gown pockets, maddening him in the process. Her face was now sufficiently close to his and sufficiently removed from the invisible world for his next step. Holding her by the hips, he fed on her half-opened active mouth; she freed herself, fearing that his young impatience might resolve itself too soon; he nuzzled her in her deep soft neck.

'Please,' he murmured, 'please, I implore you.'

'Silly,' she said. 'Why, of course. But you have to lock the door first.'

He made for the door, automatically resuming his glasses and leaving in front of her, on the floor, his right slipper in token of his speedy return. Then, his desire exposed and his eyes wicked behind their strong lenses, he attempted to push her toward the bed.

'Wait, wait a moment, my sweet,' she said, holding him with one cold hand and frantically fumbling in her bag with the other, 'Look, you must put this on; I'll do it for you, you awkward brutal darling.'

'Now,' she cried when he was magnificently sheathed; and baring her thighs, and not bothering to lie down, and revelling in his ineptitude, she directed his upward thrusts until they drove home, whereupon, her face working, she threw her head back and dug her ten nails in his nates.

As soon as it was over, Martha staggered and sat down hard on the edge of the bed against which she had been standing. Everything had been so wonderful that she did not immediately become aware of her second-best bag of imitation crocodile under her.

Franz wanted to continue at once but she said that first of all she must take off her dress and stockings, and make herself comfy in bed. The coat and hat were transferred to a chair. What Martha called 'your macky' was rinsed and slipped on again. Franz and Martha admired each other. Her breasts were disappointingly small but charmingly shaped. 'I never thought you'd be so lean and hairy,' she said, stroking him. His vocabulary was even more primitive.

Presently the bed stirred into motion. It glided off on its journey creaking discreetly as does a sleeping car when the express pulls out of a dreamy station. 'You, you, you,' uttered Martha, softly squeezing him between her knees at every gasp, and following with moist eyes the shadows of angels waving their handkerchiefs on the ceiling, which was moving away faster and faster.

Now the room was empty. Objects lay, stood, sat, hung in the carefree postures man-made things adopt in man's absence. The mock crocodile lay on the floor. A blue-tinted cork, which had been recently removed from a small ink bottle when a fountain pen had to be refilled, hesitated for an instant, then rolled in a semi-circle to the edge of the oilcloth-covered table, hesitated again, and jumped off. With the help of the lashing rain the wind tried to open the window but failed. In the rickety wardrobe a blue black-spotted tie slithered off its twig like a snake. A paperback novelette on the chest-of-drawers left open at Chapter Five skipped several pages.

Suddenly the looking glass made a signal – a warning gleam. It reflected a bluish armpit and a lovely bare arm. The arm stretched – and fell back lifeless. Slowly, the bed returned to Berlin from Eden. It was greeted by a blast of music from the radio upstairs which changed immediately to excited speech which in its turn was replaced by the same music but now more remote. Martha lay with closed eyes, and her smile formed two sickle-shaped dimples at the sides of her tightly closed mouth. The once impenetrable black strands were now thrown back from her temples, and Franz as he lay beside her leaning on his elbow gazed at her tender naked ear, at her limpid forehead, and at last found again in this face that madonna-like something which, prone as he was to content himself with such comparisons, he had already noted three months ago.

'Franz,' said Martha without opening her eyes, 'Franz, it was paradise! I've never, never. . . .'

She left an hour later, promising her poor pet that next time she would take less cruel precautions. Before going she thoroughly studied every corner of the room, picked up Franz's pyjamas, took out the fountain pen from its pocket and put it on the bed table, changed the position of the chair, observed that socks were torn and buttons missing, and said that a general fixing up was in order for the room – embroidered doilies, perhaps, and definitely a couch with two or three gay cushions. About that couch she reminded the landlord, whom she found very quietly walking up and down the corridor evidently waiting for a chance to sweep the room and collect the coffee things. Smiling now at her, now at Franz, rubbing his rustling palms, he said that as soon as his wife returned the couch would also return. Since in all truthfulness he had not taken any couch to be repaired (the vacant place had been occupied by a previous tenant's upright piano), he took great pleasure in answering Martha's precise questions. He was quite content with his life in general, grey old Enricht in his felt househoes with buckles, especially since the day he discovered that he had the remarkable gift of transforming himself into all kinds of creatures – a horse, a hog, or a six-year-old girl in a sailor cap. For actually (but this of course was a secret) he was the famed illusionist and conjuror Menetek-El-Pharsin.

Martha liked his courteous ways but Franz warned her that he was a little odd. 'Oh, my darling,' she said on the way downstairs, 'this could not be better. This quiet old man is so much safer than would have been a nosy old crone. Au revoir, my treasure. You may give me a kiss – a quick one.'

His street was decidely dingy. Perhaps, when that 'Ciné-palace' was finished, it would look better. A special poster in a wooden frame facing the sidewalk at a strategic point depicted an illusory future – a soaring edifice of glittering glass which stood aloof in a spacious area of blue air, although actually ugly tenement houses snuggled up to its very slowly rising walls. The scaffolded half-finished stories above the promised cinema were to contain an exhibition hall for rent, a beauty salon, a photographic atelier, many other attractions.

In one direction the street terminated in a dead end, in the other it ran into a small square where a modest open-air market was set up on Tuesdays and Fridays. From there two streets branched out: to the left, a crooked alley which used to flaunt red flags on the days of political celebration, and on the right, a long populous street; one noticed there a large store where every article cost a quarter be it a bust of Schiller or a kitchen pan. She was cold but happy. The street abutted on a stone portico with a white U on blue glass, a subway station. Then one turned left onto a rather nice boulevard. Then the houses stopped; here and there a villa was being built, or a wasteland was partitioned into small vegetable gardens. Then came houses again, big new ones, pink and pistachio. Martha turned past the last of these and was on her street. Beyond her villa there was a large avenue serviced by two trams, number 113 and 108, and one bus.

She passed quickly along the gravel path leading to the porch. At that instant the sun swept across the soft under-belly of the white sky, found a slit, and radiantly burst through. The small trees along the path responded immediately with all their moist droplets of light. The lawn scintillated in its turn. A sparrow's crystal wing flashed as it flew by.

When Martha entered the house, pink optical mottles drifted before her eyes in the comparative darkness of the front hall. In the dining room the table was not yet laid. In the bedroom the sudden sun was already carefully folded on the carpet and on the blue couch. She proceeded to change, smiling, sighing happily, acknowledging with thanks her reflection in the mirror.

A little later, as she stood in the centre of the bedroom in a garnet-red dress, with smooth temples and just a touch of make-up, she heard Tom's idiotically lyrical bark downstairs followed by a stranger's loud voice. On her way at the turn of the staircase she met the ascending stranger who passed swiftly, whistling and tapping the banisters with his riding crop. 'Hello, my love,' he said without stopping, 'I'll be down in ten minutes.' And taking the last two or three steps in one ponderous stride, he grunted cheerfully and cast a downward glance at her retreating bandeaux. 'Hurry up,' she said, not looking back, 'and please get rid of that horsy smell.'

At lunch, in the midst of small talk and tinkle – that particular tinkle half-glass, half-metal, peculiar to the process of human feeding – Martha still did not recognize the master of the house with his mobile cropped moustache and his way of rapidly tossing into his mouth now a radish, now a bit of the roll he kept kneading on the tablecloth as he talked. Not that she experienced any special constraint. She was no Emma, and no Anna. In the course of her conjugal life she had grown accustomed to grant her favours to her wealthy protector with such skill, with such calculation, with such efficient habits of physical practice, that she who thought herself ripe for adultery had long grown ready for harlotry.

On her right sat a somewhat coarse-looking old man with a glamorous title; on her left there was plump Willy Wald with big red cheeks, and three even folds of fat over the back of his collar. Next to him sat his noisy mother, also corpulent, with the same prominent dark moist eyes. Her rasping voice kept abruptly passing into rich gurgling laughter, so different from her speech that a blind man might mistake her for two different people. Next to the old count sparkled young Mrs Wald, who was powdered to a death-like pallor and had unnaturally arching eyebrows, and could keep her three gigolos as far as we were concerned. And between them, opposite Martha, concealed now by a fleshy dahlia, now by crystal facets, there sat talking and laughing a completely superfluous Dr Dreyer. Everything except him was fine. The food, especially the goose, and the heavy profile of bald kindly Willy, and the conversation about cars, and the wit of the count, and his anecdote about the skin-lifting operation of an aging star, after which her chin was adorned with a new dimple that had been formerly her navel, which he communicated to her *sotto voce*. She did not talk much herself. But her silence was so vibrant, so responsive, with such an animated smile on her half-open glistening lips, that she seemed unusually talkative. Dreyer could not help admiring her from behind the fat pink corners of the dahlias. And the sensation that she was after all happy with him made him almost condone the unfrequency of her caresses.

'How can one love a man whose mere touch makes one feel sick,' she confessed to Franz at one of their next meetings, when he began insisting she tell him if she loved her husband.

'Then I'm the first?' he asked eagerly. 'The first?'

In answer she bared her shining teeth and slowly pinched his cheek. Franz clasped her legs and looked up at her, rolling his head as he tried to catch her fingers in his mouth. She was sitting in the armchair already dressed and ready to leave but unable to make herself go, and he huddled on his knees before her, tousled, with blinking glasses, in his new white braces. He had just put on her street shoes for her, for, while visiting him, she would wear bed slippers with crimson pompoms. This pair of slippers (his modest but considerate gift) our lovers kept in the lower drawer of the corner chest, for life not unfrequently imitates the French novelists. That drawer contained, moreover, a little arsenal of contraceptive implementa, gradually accumulated by Martha, who after a miscarriage in the first year of her marriage had developed a morbid fear of pregnancy. As he put the pretty slippers away till next time, he thought what a glamorous feminine touch all this added to the room, which had grown more attractive in other ways too. On the table three pink dahlias were on their lastlegs in a dark-blue vase with a single oblong reflection. Lacy doilies had appeared here and there, and soon the tenaciously anticipated couch was to move in weightily; Martha had already acquired two peacock cushions for it. In a container of celluloid a round cake of violet-scented beige soap adorned the washstand for Martha's use. The young man's own toiletry had been supplemented by a bottle of Anticaprine and a skin lotion with a spotted face on the label. All his things had been checked and counted; his underwear bore lovingly sewn-on monograms; one unforgettable morning she glided into the emporium, demanded to be shown the most elegant ties available, chose three of them and vanished with them, passing through his department and drowning alternately in the many mirrors, and the fact that she had not even glanced at him added a strange sparkle to that crystal tryst. They now hung in his wardrobe like trophies; and there was a slowly ripening intoxicating project: a tuxedo!

Love helped Franz to mature. This first affair resembled a diploma of which one could be proud. All day he was tormented by the desire to show this diploma to fellow salesmen but prudence restrained him from even hinting at it. Around half past five (Piffke, thinking this would please the boss, would let him go a little earlier than the others) he would come tearing breathlessly into his room. Soon Martha arrived with a couple of sandwiches from the neighbouring delicatessen. The rather droll but endearing contrast between his thin body and one cocked part of it, shortish but exceptionally thick, would cause his mistress to croon in praise of his manhood: 'Fatty is greedy! Oh, greedy! . . .' Or she might say: 'I bet (she adored bets), I bet you a new sweater that you can't do it again.' But time is no friend of lovers. At a little past seven she had to leave. She was as punctual as she was passionate. And around nine Franz would generally go and have supper at Uncle's.

Warm, warmly flowing happiness filled physical Franz to the brim, pulsated in wrist and temple, pounded in his breast, and issued from his finger in a ruby drop when he pricked himself accidentally at the store: he frequently had to deal with pins in his department (though not as much as the adjusting tailor, Kottmann, who resembled the 'cat's-whiskers' fish found in the remote river of an abolished boyhood, when with bristling mouth he circled around a chalk-marked customer). But on the whole his hands had now grown more nimble, and he no longer had trouble with the light lids and tissue paper of flat cardboard boxes as he had during the first weeks. Those rapid behind-the-counter exercises had as it were prepared his hands for other motions and contact, also rapid and nimble, causing Martha to purr with pleasure, for she particularly loved his forelimbs, and loved them most of all when with a succession of rhapsodic touches they would run all over her milk-white body. Thus a shop counter was the mute keyboard on which Franz had rehearsed his happiness.

But as soon as she had gone, as soon as supper hour approached, and he had to face Dreyer, everything changed. As happens in dreams, when a perfectly harmless object inspires us with fear and thereafter is frightening every time we dream of it (and even in real life retains disquietening overtones), so Dreyer's presence became for Franz a refined torture, an implacable menace. When for the first time after her visit, he had walked the short distance between the gate and the porch (yawning nervously and plucking at his glasses as he went); when for the first time in the capacity of clandestine lover of the lady of the house he had glanced askance at innocent Frieda and crossed the threshold rubbing his rain-wet hands, Franz was overwhelmed with such an eerie feeling that in his fright and confusion he had aimed a kick at Tom, who was welcoming him in the drawing room with an unexpected burst of affection; as Franz waited for his hosts, he superstitiously searched the bright eyes of the cushions for omens of disaster. A high-strung and abject coward in matters of feeling (and such cowards are doubly wretched since they lucidly perceive their cowardice and fear it), he could not help cringing when, with a banging of doors in a dramatic draft, Martha and Dreyer entered simultaneously from two different rooms as if on a too harshly lit stage. Then he snapped to attention and in this attitude felt himself ascending through the ceiling, through the roof, into the black-brown sky, while, in reality, drained empty, he was shaking hands with Martha, with Dreyer. He dropped back on his feet out of that dark nonexistence, from those unknown and rather silly heights, to land firmly in the middle of the room (safe, safe!) when hearty Dreyer described a circle with his index finger and jabbed him in the navel; Franz mimicked a gasp and giggled; and as usual Martha was coldly radiant. His fear did not pass but only subsided temporarily: one incautious glance, one eloquent smile, and all would be revealed, and a disaster beyond imagination would shatter his career. Thereafter whenever he entered this house, he imagined that the disaster had happened – that Martha had been found out, or had confessed everything in a fit of insanity or religious self-immolation to her husband; and the drawing room chandelier invariably met him with a sinister refulgence.

He would weigh every joke of Dreyer's, scrape at it, sniff at it, with trepidation, checking it for some crafty allusion, but there was nothing. Luckily for Franz, his observant uncle's interest in any object, animated or not, whose distinctive features he had immediately grasped, or thought he had grasped, gloated over and filed away, would wane with its every subsequent reappearance. The bright perception became the habitual abstraction. Natures like his spend enough energy in tackling with all the weapons and vessels of the mind the enforced impressions of existence to be grateful for the neutral film of familiarity that soon forms between the newness and its consumer. It was too boring to think that the object might change of its own accord and assume unforeseen characteristics. That would mean having to enjoy it again, and he was no longer young. He had appreciated the poor bloke's simplicity and vulgarity almost at their first anonymous rendezvous in the train. Thenceforth, from the first moment of actual acquaintance, he had thought of Franz as of an amusing coincidence in human form: the form was that of a timid provincial nephew with a banal mind and limited ambitions. Similarly Martha, for more than seven years now, had remained the same distant, thrifty, frigid wife whose beauty would occasionally come alive and welcome him with the paradisal smile he had first fallen in love with. Neither of these images changed basically; they simply became more compactly filled up with fitting characteristics. Thus an experienced artist sees only that which is in keeping with his initial concept.

On the other hand, Dreyer would feel a kind of humiliating itching when an object did not immediately yield to his voracious eye, did not assume obediently such a posture as to give him a chance to wrestle with it. A couple of months had passed since the car accident. He had had time to make his will as he had intended to do all along on his fiftieth birthday (which, bless her cold heart, his only inheritor had let pass without a shadow of celebration), and still he could not determine a silly little thing about his chauffeur which if true would certainly lead to another accident sooner or later. With a twitch of his nostril he would probe the man's tobacco reek for a gayer smell; observed him when he went bow-legged around the car; and, at the most perilous hours – Saturday night – would unexpectedly summon him and laboriously conduct a trivial conversation while he watched whether the other did not behave in too free a fashion. He hoped that some day he would be told that the man, alas, was not fit to come, but alas that day never came. At times it seemed to him that the Icarus was taking the turns a little faster, a little more cheerfully than usual. It was just on such a day of carefree swerves, made especially interesting by the fact that the first real snow of the year had fallen on the eve and had now melted into a slippery mush, that he noticed a hatless man through the window who looked exactly as if he had hinges for joints, crossing the street with mincing steps. That reminded him of his talk with the amiable inventor. When he reached his office, he promptly had him called at the Montevideo, and was very pleased when old Sarah Reich, his secretary, announced that the inventor would be right over. However, neither Dreyer, nor Miss Reich (who had her own dreadful troubles), nor anyone at all in the world ever found out that the lonely and homesick inventor happened to live in the very same room where Franz had spent the night of his arrival; where a great ash tree, now leafless, was visible from the window; and where one could notice, if one looked very carefully, that some minute glass dust had become imbedded in the cracks of the linoleum by the washstand. It is significant that Fate should have lodged him there of all places. It was a road that Franz had travelled – and all at once Fate remembered and sent in pursuit this practically nameless man who of course knew nothing of his important assignment, and never found out anything about it, as for that matter no one else ever did, not even old Enricht.

'Welcome,' said Dreyer, 'sit down.'

The inventor did.

'Well,' asked Dreyer, toying with his favourite pencil.

The inventor blew his nose, carefully wrapped up the results, and spent a long time tucking the handkerchief – an article that some new invention should have long replaced – into his pocket.

'I come to you with the same offer,' he said at last.

'Any additional details,' suggested Dreyer, pencilling concentric blue circles on his blotter.

The inventor nodded and started to speak. The telephone on the desk buzzed. Dreyer gave his visitor a gentle smile and energetically put the receiver to his ear. 'It's me. I forgot – did you say you would not be back for supper tonight?'

'That's right, my love.'

'And you'll be home late?'

'After midnight. Meeting of the board and festivities. Go to a restaurant with Franz or something.'

'I don't know. Maybe I shall.'

'Wonderful,' said Dreyer. ''Goody-bye. Oh, wait – if you want the car— Hullo!' But she had already hung up.

The inventor was pretending not to listen. Dreyer noticed this and said with a coy snicker: 'That was my little girl friend.'

The inventor smirked indulgently in response and resumed his explanations. Dreyer began a new set of concentric circles, Miss Reich brought a batch of letters and silently disappeared. The inventor continued to talk. Dreyer threw down the pencil, reclined limply in his armchair and surrendered to the fascination.

'What was that?' he interrupted. 'The noble slowness of a sleepwalker's progress?'

'Yes, if desired,' said the inventor. 'Or at the other extreme, the restrained agility of a convalescent.'

'Go on, go on,' Dreyer said, closing his eyes. 'This is pure witchcraft.'

6

An unprepossessing sullen little café, not far from where Franz lives. Three men engrossed in a silent game of skat. The wife of one of them, pregnant and veal-pale, sleepily following their game. A plain girl with a nervous tic, leafing through an old picture magazine and stopping at the messy death of a riddle: an indelible pencil had rapaciously filled in most of the crossword's blank squares. A lady in a moleskin coat (that impressed the proprietress of the place) and a young man in tortoise shell glasses, sipping cherry brandy and gazing into each other's eyes. A drunk in an unemployed-looking cap tapping on the thick glass behind which coins had bunched together forming a metal sausage – the losses of all those who had put a coin in the slot and had moved the handle to activate the little tin juggler while his tiny bright balls followed the winding grooves. The counter, chilled by beer foam, gives off a fish-like sheen. The proprietress has two green wool soccer balls for breasts. She yawns as she looks toward a dark nook where the waiter, half-concealed by a screen, is devouring a mountain of mashed potatoes. On the wall behind her tocks a cuckoo clock of carved wood surmounted by a pair of antlers and beside it there is an oleograph depicting the meeting of Bismarck and Napoleon III. The rustle of the card players grows softer and softer. It has now stopped altogether.

'You chose well – we can be sure nobody will see us here.'

He caressed her hand on the table: 'Yes, but it's getting late, darling, maybe it's time to go.'

'Your uncle won't be back till midnight or later. We have time.'

'Forgive me for dragging you to such a squalid place.'

'No-no, not at all. I told you, it's quite a good choice. Let's imagine you are a Heidelberg student. How nice you would look in a cerevis.'

'And you are a princess incognito? I'd like us to drink champagne, with couples dancing around us, and beautiful Hungarian music.'

She propped her elbow on the table, drawing back the skin of her cheek with her fist. Silence.

'Tell me, would you like to eat something? I'm afraid you have grown still thinner.'

'Oh, what does it matter. All my life I've been unhappy. And now you are with me.'

Motionless, the players gazed at their cards. The puffy woman leaned exhausted against her husband's shoulder. The girl had lapsed into thought and her face had ceased twitching. The picture magazine's pages drooped on their stick like a flag in the calm. Silence. Torpor.

Martha was the first to stir: Franz, too, tried to shake off that strange drowsiness; blinked, tugged at the lapels of his jacket.

'I love him but he is poor,' she said jokingly. And suddenly her expression changed. She imagined that she, too, was penniless, and that here, in this shabby little tavern, among befuddled workmen and cheap floozies, in this deafening silence with only that clock clucking, a sticky wine glass before each, the two of them were whiling away their Saturday night.

She fancied with horror that this tender pauper really was her husband, her young husband, whom she would never, never give up. Darned stockings, two modest dresses, a broken comb, one room with a bloated mirror, her hands coarse from washing and cooking, this tavern where for one reichsmark you could get really drunk. . . .

She felt so terrified that she dug her nails into his hand.

'What's happened? Dearest, I don't understand.'

'Get up,' she said, 'pay and let's go. It's so stuffy in here, I can't breathe.'

As she inhaled the matter-of-fact cold of the night, she intantly regained her wealth and, pressing against him, rapidly switched feet so as to be in step with him; he groped for and found her warm wrist among the folds of her furs.

Next morning, as she lay in bed in her pretty bright room, Martha recalled her fanciful fears with a smile. 'Let us be realistic,' she reassured herself. 'It's all quite simple. I simply have a lover. That ought to embellish, not complicate, my existence. And that's just what it is – a pleasant embellishment.

And if, by any chance—' But strange, she could find no specific direction for her thoughts; Franz's street terminated in a dead end which her mind reached invariably. She could not imagine, say, that Franz did not exist, or that some other admirer was floating out of a mist with a rose in his hand, for, as he came nearer, it was always Franz. This day like all days to come was suffused and coloured by her passion for Franz. She tried to think of the past, of those impossible years when she did not yet know him, but it was not her own past she conjured up, it was his: his little town where she had happened to stop on her way grew up in her thoughts and there, in the haze, was Franz's white green-roofed house, never seen by her in real life but described by him many times, and the brick schoolhouse around the corner, and the frail little boy with glasses. What Franz had told her about his childhood was more important than anything she had actually experienced; and she did not understand why that was so, and argued with herself in an attempt to refute what impinged on her sense of conformity and clarity.

Particularly painful was that inner discord when she had to attend to some household project or ponder an important purchase that in no way concerned Franz. For example, at odd moments the idea of acquiring a new car kept cropping up; then she would tell herself that this had nothing to do with Franz, that he was being left out, and somehow cheated; and despite her long-standing dream of substituting a certain fashionable make of limousine for the somewhat seedy Icarus, all the fun of such an acquisition was spoiled. A dress that she would wear for Franz, or a Sunday dinner that she could compose of his favourite dishes – these matters were different. And at first all these misgivings and pleasures were strange to her as if she had grown ten years younger and was learning to live in a new way, and needed time to get accustomed to it.

Another perplexity stemmed from the fact that her house, of which she had grown even fonder since Franz had become practically a member of the family, contained someone else besides him and her. There he stuck out, tawny-moustached and ruddy, eating at one table with her and sleeping in the adjacent bed, and demanding her attention in one way or another. His financial affairs interested her even more than in that already very distant year when a lot of ballast jettisoned from the balloon of inflation had come pouring into his pockets where it turned into that alchemistical dream – *valuta*. As before, he told her little. This interest of hers in Dreyer's ventures did not combine organically with the new, piercing, moaning, and throbbing meaning of her life. She felt she could not be fully happy without such a blending of bank and bed, and yet she did not know how to achieve harmony, how to eliminate the discord. He had once shown her a slip of paper on which he had totalled up for her benefit his fortune in round numbers: 'Is it enough?' he asked with a smile, 'what do you think?' There were those 700,000 untouchable dollars in a safe in Hamburg. There was another fortune in stocks. There were considerable resources of a more fluid and changeable nature that constituted the blood system of his business. There was the will he had recently made which had cost her two nights of strenuous love-making but which had completely excluded, thank goodness, a wayward young brother in South Africa who, she suspected, was very much looking forward to his share.

'So we are practically millionaires,' she said with one of those rare resplendent responses for which her husband was ready to pay considerably more than he owned: 'On the saddleback, on the saddleback, darling,' he answered.

No matter what happened, she meditated, at the exchange or in his frivolous transactions, there remained sufficient funds for many years of idle life – until, say, she was sixty, or, say, fifty-eight and Franz a still ardent forty-five. However, as long as Mr Dreyer existed, he must continue to earn. Therefore veering from enthusiasm to a show of anxious gloom, she urged him to accumulate more in Hamburg and gamble less in Berlin, and coldly gave him back the slip of paper. They were standing by the desk where Parsifal held his lighted lantern, and one could tell by the peculiar stillness muffling the villa that snow was falling, smothering the garden in dark, dark white. December turned out to be colder than usual with spectacularly low temperatures to be eagerly noted by the forgetful old-timers of the press who had gone through the same rigmarole a couple of years earlier. Dreyer gave his watch a worried glance. The three of them were going to a variety show. Like a child he was afraid to be late. Martha reached for the newspaper lying on the table and looked through the advertisements and the local news, learning that a luxurious villa was for sale for 500,000 reichsmark, and that a car had overturned killing its occupant, the famous actor Hess, on his way to his sick wife's bedside. 'Good God,' she exclaimed, 'this is unheard-of.' In the adjacent boudoir Franz was listening without much interest to the radio's rich voice giving details of the crash.

The vast theatre was crowded; its enormous stage was still curtained. They squeezed into one of those exceptionally narrow boxes in which one becomes so acutely aware what an uncomfortable, tangly and tingly thing a pair of human legs is. It was especially hard on lanky Franz. As if it were not enough that his lower extremities had grotesquely lengthened, Martha, strictly adhering to every rule of adultery, pressed the side of her silky knee against his awkwardly bent right leg while Dreyer, sitting to his left and a little behind, leaned lightly against his shoulder and kept tickling his ear with the corner of the programme he was consulting. Poor Franz was torn between the fear that the husband might notice something and the delight of feeling the silky sparks coursing through his body.

'Such a huge theatre,' he muttered, slightly shifting his shoulder so as to escape from Dreyer's repulsive golden-haired hand. 'I can imagine how much they make every night. Let me see – about two thousand seats—'

Dreyer, as he went through the programme for the second or third time, exclaimed: 'Ah, that will be good: trick cyclists.'

The lights dimmed slowly. The pressure of Martha's knee increased recklessly, but then relaxed as the orchestra began to play a potpourri from *Lucia di Lammermoor* (which in the circumstances was pretty apt, though lost on our audience).

They were shown many entertaining things. Martha found the programme very acceptable. Dreyer thought it a jolly good show, Franz loved every bit of it. A man in a top hat juggled dummy bottles to which he suddenly added his hat; four Japanese flew hither and thither on rhythmically creaking trapezes and while pausing in between stunts tossed to each other a bright handkerchief with which they fastidiously wiped their hands; a clown, constantly on the point of losing his baggy trousers, flopped all over the stage emitting a sharp whistle as he skidded before falling with a whack on his face; a horse, so white it might have been powdered, delicately played pace in time to music; a crazy family of cyclists extracted all that was humanly possible and more from the properties of the wheel; a black lustrous seal gave throaty cries like a drowning bather, and then slithered smooth and slick as if greased down a board into the green water of a pool where a half-naked girl greeted the happy beast with a kiss on the nose. Now and then Dreyer grunted with pleasure and nudged Franz. After the seal had received its ultimate reward, a live mackerel which it succulently snapped up in mid-air, and galloped off on its flappers, the curtain was drawn for the public to re-pick themselves, as the French say; when it opened again, a woman in silver shoes and a spangled evening dress stood bathed in light in the centre of the darkened stage with a luminous violin to which she applied a star-flashing bow. The spotlight diligently drenched her now in pink now in green; a diadem shimmered on her brow. Her playing was languorous and really delicious and suffused Martha with such excitement, such exquisite sadness that she half-closed her eyes and found Franz's hand in the darkness; and he experienced the same sensation – a poignant rapture in harmony with their love. The musical phantasmagoria (as that item was listed) sparkled and swooned, the violin sang and moaned, the pink and the green were joined by blue and violet – and then Dreyer could stand it no longer.

'I have my eyes and ears closed,' he said in a weepy whisper, 'let me know when this obscene abomination is over.'

Martha gave a start; Franz thought that all was lost, that he had seen them holding hands. At the same moment the stage grew black and the house thundered in an avalanche of applause.

'You understand absolutely nothing about art,' said Martha dryly. 'You only disturb other people who want to listen.'

Dreyer exhaled in noisy relief. Then, with fussy gestures, with swift jerks of his eyebrows, like a man who is in a hurry to forget, he looked up the next number on the programme.

'Ah, that's more like it,' he said. 'The Gutter-Perchers, whoever they are, and then a world-famous conjuror.'

'Close call,' Franz was thinking at that moment. 'That time it was really a close call. Phew! . . . We've got to be extremely careful. . . . Of course, it's wonderful sitting here and knowing she's mine, and he sitting next to us and not knowing. But it is all so dangerous. . . .'

The performance concluded with a motion picture, as was still customary in circuses and music halls ever since the first 'bioscope' was shown there as a fascinating curiosity. On the flickering screen, strangely flat after the live stage, a chimpanzee in degrading human clothes performed human actions degrading to an animal. Martha laughed heartily, remarking: 'Just look how smart he is!' Franz clucked his tongue in amazement, and insisted in all seriousness that it was a dwarf in disguise.

When they came out into the frosty street lighted like yet another scene by the theatre's electric signs, and the faithful Icarus rolled up with a kind of clownish zeal, Dreyer reproached himself for having neglected lately to observe his chauffeur's behaviour. Now was the perfect moment to make a little check. As the chauffeur was hurriedly pulling on his fur gauntlets, Dreyer tried to catch with his nose the steam issuing from the man's mouth. The chauffeur met his glance and, baring his bad teeth, innocently raised his eyebrows.

'Chilly, chilly, isn't it,' said Dreyer quickly.

'Not too bad,' replied the chauffeur, 'not too bad.'

'Can't smell anything,' thought Dreyer. 'And yet I'm sure that while he was waiting. . . . Flushed face, merry eyes. Well, let's see how he is going to drive.'

The chauffeur drove remarkably well. Franz, respectfully perched on the edge of one of the two folding seats of the luxurious vehicle, listened to the smooth hum of its speed, examined the artificial daisies in their little silver vase, the speaking tube hanging on its steel hook, the travelling clock which had its own concept of time, and the ashtray with one gold-tipped cigarette butt in it. A snowy night with aureoled street lights ran past the wide windows.

'I'll get out here,' he said, recognizing a square and a statue. 'It's just a short walk to my house from here.'

'Oh, I'll take you there,' replied Dreyer with a little yawn. 'What's your exact address?'

Martha caught Franz's eye and shook her head. He understood. Dreyer, accustomed as he was to seeing his nephew nearly every evening at his house, had never bothered to ask where he actually lived, and this should be left in silent and propitious obscurity. Franz nervously cleared his throat and said:

'No, really, I'd like to stretch my legs.'

'As you wish,' said Dreyer in the middle of a yawn and, leaning across Franz, knocked on the glass partition with his fist.

'Why knock?' Martha observed crossly; 'there's a tube for this purpose, isn't there?'

Franz found himself in a deserted white square. He put up the collar of his raincoat, thrust his hands into his pockets and, hunching over, walked quickly in the direction of his house. On Sundays, on the elegant street in the western section of the city, he would wear his new overcoat and walk quite differently. Now, however, was not the moment for that – the cold was intense. That big-city Sunday walk had not been easy to copy. It consisted of stretching one's arms well down and crossing one's hands (good gloves were essential) below the last button of one's overcoat as if to keep it in place as one advanced at a very slow strut, with toes pointing out at each step. Thus promenaded the Kurfürstendamm dandies, sometimes in pairs, now and then looking around at a girl without changing the position of their hands but merely giving a slight backward jerk of the shoulder.

Despite the cold, Franz felt multiplied and exaggerated as one does after a show, and he even began to whistle. 'To hell with her husband. One must be braver. Such bliss is not bestowed on everyone. What was she doing now? She must be home and undressing. That yellow-bristled pig. Pestering her, no doubt. To hell with him! Now she is sitting on the bed, peeling off her stockings. Three or four houses more, and she will be naked. I should buy her a lacy nightdress. Keep it among my pyjamas. When I reach that street lamp, she will lower her head on the pillow. I cross the street, and she turns off the light. They share the same bedroom. No, he is getting old, he will leave her alone. One more block: she has fallen asleep. That's my street. Wonderful violinist – and so beautifully staged, there was really something heavenly about it. The conjuror was good too. Simple tricks, no doubt: make good money by deceiving people. Now she is sound asleep. She sees my house in dream and hears the divine violin. Damn this key. Always starts by behaving as if it had never been in this lock before. Stair light not working again. You could really come crashing down if you happened to trip. And this key is acting up, too.'

In the dim corridor, by the slightly brighter door of his room, stood old Enricht shaking his head disapprovingly. He wore a mouse-grey dressing gown and checkered booties.

'Oh-oh-oh,' he said. 'Going to bed after midnight. Shame on you.'

Franz was about to walk on but the old man clutched at his sleeve.

'I can't be angry tonight,' he said with feeling. 'It's a joyful occasion for me: the wife is back!'

'Congratulations,' said Franz.

'But no joy is perfect,' Enricht went on without releasing Franz's sleeve. 'My little old lady arrived sick.'

Franz gave a commiserating grunt.

'There she is,' cried the landlord. 'Sitting there in the armchair. Have a look.'

He opened the door wider and over the back of the chair Franz glimpsed a grey head with something white pinned to its crown.

'See what I mean?' said the old man, staring at Franz with

shining eyes. 'And now good night,' he added and, slipping into his room, closed the door.

Franz proceeded on his way. But then stopped short and went back. 'Listen,' he said through the door. 'How about that couch?'

A hoarse, strained, old-womanish voice replied: 'The couch is already in your room. I gave you my own couch.'

'Two old crackpots,' thought Franz with a squeamish grimace. True enough, the furniture family in his room had grown. It was a hard decrepit couch of a drab grey, patterned with forget-me-nots. Still, it was a couch. When Martha came the next day she wrinkled her nose and, keeping it wrinkled, felt the stuffing, located a sick spring, and raised the shabby fringe.

'Oh well, there is nothing to be done,' she said at last. 'I have no intention of quarrelling with his old lady. A pity she has returned. One more pair of ears. Put those two cushions there. Now it looks better.' And soon they grew used to it, to its modest colouration and to the disapproving creaks it emitted in rhythm to their ebullient love-making.

It was not only a couch, however, that enriched Franz's room. Once, in a particularly benevolent moment, Dreyer gave him some extra cash from his waistcoat pocket (real green dollars!), and a fortnight later, just in time for Christmas, a new lodger appeared in Franz's wardrobe: the long-awaited tuxedo.

'That's all very well,' said Martha, 'but it's not all. You have to learn to dance. Tomorrow night after supper we'll put a nice record on the phonograph, and I'll give you your first lesson. It will be rather fun to have Uncle watch us.'

Franz arrived in his new dinner jacket. She reprimanded him for wearing it needlessly but found it very becoming. It was nine o'clock. Dreyer was expected any minute. He was very precise in this respect, always telephoning to say he would be so many minutes earlier or later, for he was extremely fond of hearing his wife's soft, smooth, formal voice over the phone – her voice in a kind of early Florentine perspective, so different from matter-of-fact reality. Martha was always surprised at his telephoning about those trifling minutes and seconds, and despite her own careful attitude toward measured time, her husband's punctuality in this respect puzzled and irritated her. Tonight he had not telephoned, and yet he was already half an hour late. Out of natural reverence toward the sacred crease of each trouser-leg, Franz avoided sitting down and walked around the room, skirting Martha's armchair but not daring to kiss her because of the maid's proximity.

'I'm hungry,' said Martha. 'I can't understand why he does not come.'

'Let's start the phonograph. You'll teach me while we're waiting.'

'I'm not in the mood. I said after supper.'

Another ten minutes passed. She got up abruptly and summoned Frieda.

A succulent omelette and a bit of liver revived her. 'Close it,' she said to Franz, indicating the door left open by Frieda, whom a bad toothache had been afflicting all day. When Franz returned to his seat, Martha enveloped him in a smile of contented adoration. It so happened that this was the first time she was having supper at home alone with Franz. Yes, the dinner jacket could not be better. She must give him some nice cuff links instead of those stud-like horrors.

'Oh, my own big sweet darling,' she said softly, stretching her arm toward him across the dinner cloth.

'Careful,' whispered Franz, looking around. He did not trust the pictures on the wall – the old baron in the frock coat and his redoubtable double staring down, ready to pounce. The glittering sideboard was all eyes. Cloaked eavesdroppers lurked in the folds of the drapery. A famous practical joker, Curtius Dreyerson, might be crouching under the table. Good thing at least that Tom had stayed in the front hall. And the maid might come back any moment. In this castle one must take no liberties. Nevertheless, powerless to oppose her smiling desire, he stroked her bare arm. She slowly caressed his nose with her fingers, beaming and wetting her lips. He had the awful sensation that at that very instant Dreyer would suddenly step from behind a curtain: the jester turned executioner.

'Eat, drink, my lord. We are *chez nous,*' said Martha, laughing.

She was wearing a black tulle dress, her lips were painted, her green earrings aflame, and her hair, divided by the mathematically pure line of its parting, glistened more than ever with the melanite lustre that was one of the jewels of her beauty. A low lamp with an orange shade cast a voluptuous light on the table. Franz, his worshipful glasses glinting at Martha, sucked on a leg of cold chicken. She leaned toward him, took the glossy-headed, half-bared bone out of his hand and, laughing with eyes alone, began gnawing at it with relish, holding it daintily, her little finger cocked, her lashes beating, her lips growing fuller and brighter. 'You are ravishing,' Franz whispered. 'I adore you.'

'If only we could sup like this every night, just you and I,' said Martha. With a toss of her head she chased a momentary frown and cried in a slightly false tone: 'Would you pour me some of that precious cognac, please, and let us drink to our union.'

'I don't think I'll have any. I'm afraid I would not learn to dance afterwards,' said Franz, carefully tipping the diminutive decanter.

But what did she care about dancing. . . . She longed to remain in this oval lake of light, basking in the certainty that it would be thus again tomorrow, and the next night, and thus to the end of their lives. My dining room, my earrings, my silver, my Franz.

Suddenly she snatched at her left wrist, to turn the tiny face of her watch, which always contrived to slip around to where a blue vein trifurcated.

'More than an hour late. Something must have happened. Ring the bell, please – there, it's hanging above you.'

It irked him that her husband's absence alarmed her. What in hell did it matter if he were late. All the better. She simply had no right to be alarmed.

'Why must I ring?' he said, thrusting his hands into his coat pockets.

Martha opened her eyes wide. 'I think I asked you to press that bell button.'

Under the long ray of her gaze he gave way as usual, and rang the bell.

'If you have had all you want, we can move to the drawing room. Have some grapes, though. Here, this bunch.'

He started upon the grapes, which were large and expensive-looking but not half as good as the vulgar 'crams' of his native town. The shadow of the electric bell swinging on its cord moved like a ghostly pendulum across the tablecloth. Frieda came in, looking pale and dazed.

Martha asked: 'My husband did not call while I was out, did he?'

Frieda froze still for an instant, then clutched at her temples. 'Goodness,' she said. '*Herr Direktor* did call about eight – said he was just leaving for home, and to go ahead with supper. I'm so sorry.'

'An abscessed tooth,' said Martha, 'should not have made you insane.'

'I'm so sorry,' repeated the maid helplessly.

'Completely insane,' said Martha.

Frieda remained silent and, blinking with suspicious frequency, started gathering up the used plates.

'Later,' snapped Martha.

The maid hurried out, no longer containing her sobs.

'Incredible female,' muttered Martha angrily, leaning her elbows on the table and propping her chin between her joined fists. 'Didn't she see us sitting down to table? Didn't she bring the omelette herself? Wait a minute – I didn't realize that she had actually *served* it.' Martha's glittering finger pointed. 'Ring once more, please.'

Franz obediently raised his hand.

'No, don't bother,' said Martha. 'I'll have a good talk with her before she goes to bed.'

An extraordinary agitation had seized Martha.

'Unless my watch and that clock are as dotty as she, it is now half past eleven. Uncle is certainly taking his time driving home.'

'Something must have delayed him,' Franz responded glumly. He was deeply hurt by her agitation.

She turned off the dining-room lights. They went into the parlour. Martha picked up the telephone receiver, listened, then slammed it down again. 'It's in order,' she said, 'I simply don't understand. Maybe, I ought to ring up—'

With his hands clasped behind his back, Franz was walking to and fro about the room. The poor fellow's eyes smarted. He wondered if he had not better leave, slamming the door after him. Martha flipped through her telephone index ('fits neatly under the phone, holds five hundred entries'), and found the home number of her husband's secretary.

Sarah Reich had just fallen asleep, and now the first pill of the night was thrown away.

'That's certainly odd,' she replied. 'I saw him leave myself. Yes. In the Icarus. It was – wait a minute – yes, about eight – and it is now only midnight. . . . I mean, almost midnight.'

'Thanks,' said Martha, and the cradle of the telephone jangled.

She went to the window and drew aside the blue curtain. The night was clear. The day before it had started to thaw, then the freeze had set in again. That morning a cripple walking in front of her had slipped on the bare ice. It was frightfully funny to see his wooden stump erect while he sprawled on his stupid back. Without opening her mouth, Martha broke into convulsive laughter. Franz thought she had uttered a sob and went to her side in confusion. She clutched his shoulder, her cheek rubbed against his face.

'Careful – my glasses,' mumbled Franz – not for the first time in the course of the last weeks.

'Start the music,' she cried, letting him go. 'We'll dance, we'll enjoy ourselves. And don't you dare be frightened – I'll speak to you as tenderly as I wish any time I feel like it – do you hear?'

Franz reverentially turned the crank of the large lacquered box that must have cost more money than all the records it would ever consume. When he looked up, Martha was sitting on the sofa gazing at him with a strange morose expression.

'I thought you'd choose a record meanwhile,' said Franz.

She turned away. 'No, I definitely don't feel like dancing.'

Franz heaved a sigh. He had seen her in difficult moods, but this was something special.

He sat down beside her on the sofa. A door shut somewhere. Frieda going to bed? Still listening intently, he kissed Martha, first on the hair, then on the lips. Her teeth were chattering. 'Give me my shawl,' she said. He picked up the pink woolly shawl from a corner hassock. She consulted her watch.

Franz got up abruptly. 'I'm going home,' he said.

'You are what?'

'Going home. I have to get up much earlier than old secretaries and fat maids.'

'You shall stay,' said Martha.

He considered her, reflecting vaguely that there was something behind all this. But what?

'You know what I have just remembered?' Martha said suddenly, as he plucked at his trouser knees and sat down. 'I remembered that rude policeman writing his report. Give me your little red book. And a pencil. There,' she continued, getting up and standing straight and stiff. 'That's how he held the notebook in front of him. Trembled with fury, and wrote in it.'

'What policeman? What are you talking about?'

'That's right. You weren't there. I've got used to including you, retroactively, if you know what I mean, in everything that ever happened.'

'Stop it,' said Franz. 'You frighten me.'

'I don't care if you're frightened. In fact I don't care if – Forgive me, darling. I'm talking nonsense. I'm just over-eager, I suppose.'

She settled down on the sofa again, with the address book in her lap. She doodled some lines on a page. Then wrote her family name, and slowly crossed it out. She looked at him askance, once more wrote Dreyer in large characters, slitted her eyes, and started blacking it out. The pencil tip broke. She tossed the book and the pencil to him, and got up.

The clock tocked rather than ticked, and tock clicked and clocked. Martha stood before him as if trying to hypnotize him, to transfer some simple thought to his young dull brain.

The front door banged in the unbearable silence, and Tom's rejoicing voice burst forth.

'My spells don't work,' said Martha, and a bizarre spasm distorted her beautiful face.

Dreyer came in not quite as jauntily as he usually did. Nor did he greet Franz with a joke.

'Why so late?' asked Martha. 'Why didn't you call?'

'Just happened that way, my love, just happened that way.' He attempted a smile but nothing came of it. He stared at his nephew's clothes. The pants were much too narrow, the lapels too shiny.

'Well, it's time for me to be going,' cried Franz hoarsely.

He was in such a silly panic that he could not remember afterwards how he said goodbye, or put on his overcoat, or reached the street.

'You're not telling the truth,' said Martha. 'Something has happened. What is it?'

'A boring story, my love. A man has been killed.'

'Jokes again, always jokes,' moaned Martha.

'Not this time,' Dreyer said quietly. 'We smashed into a streetcar, at full speed. Number seventy-three. I only lost my hat and took a healthy bump against something. In these cases it's always the driver who comes off worst. The ambulance people were angels. We took him to the hospital while he was still alive. Died there. Real angels. Better don't ask for details.'

In the dining room they sat facing each other across the table. Dreyer was finishing what remained of the cold chicken. Martha, her face pale and glossy, with drops of sweat over her lip where the tiny black hairs showed, stared with her fingers pressed to her temples at the white, white, intolerably white tablecloth.

7

When the inevitable explosion (somehow sensed as inevitable just before it occurred) was on the point of interrupting an absorbing although incoherent conversation with an unshaven Magyar or Basque about treating surgically, with buckets of blood, a seal's tail to enable the seal to walk upright, Dreyer abruptly returned to the mortality of a winter morning, and with desperate haste, as if he were dealing with an infernal machine, stopped the alarm clock that was about to ring.

Martha's bed was already empty. A bad tingle in his left arm connected like an electric buzzer the previous day with the present one. Along the corridor, sobbing loudly, shuffled soft-hearted Frieda. With a sigh he examined the huge violet bruise on his thick shoulder.

While lying in the tub, he heard Martha perform in the next room the panting, crunching, flopping exercises that were in fashion that year. He had a quick breakfast, lit a cigar, smiled with pain as he put on his overcoat, and went out.

The gardener (who was also the watchman) was standing by the fence, and Dreyer thought it might be well, even at this late date, to solve by means of a direct question the mystery that had preoccupied him for so long.

'A calamity, a real calamity,' observed the gardener gravely. 'And to think that back in his village he has left a comparatively young father and four little sisters. A skid on the ice, and *kaputt*. He had hoped so much to drive a big truck some day.'

'Yes,' nodded Dreyer. 'Cracked his skull, his rib cage—'

'A good merry chap,' said the gardener with feeling. 'And now he is dead.'

'Listen,' began Dreyer, 'you did not happen to notice— You see, I have a strong suspicion—'

He faltered. A trifle – the tense of a verb – stopped him. Instead of asking 'does he drink?' it would have to be 'did he drink?' This shift of tense caused a wobble in logic.

'. . . as I was saying, have you noticed – there is something wrong with the latch of the big parlour window. I mean, the catch does not work properly; anybody could get in from the outside.'

'*Finis*,' he mused, as he sat in a taxi with his hand in the strap. 'The end of a life, the end of a joke. I shall sell Icarus without repairing it. She does not want another car, and I think she is right. It's best to wait awhile till Fate forgets.'

The reason Martha did not want a car was less metaphysical. It might seem a bit strange and suspicious not to use one's own car to go two or three times a week in the late afternoon to lessons in rhythmic inclinations and gesticulations ('Flora, accept these lilies' or 'Let us unfold our veils in the wind'). and the reason she could not use it was that she would have to bribe her chauffeur to be silent about her real destination. Therefore she had to resort to other means of transportation, of the most varied kind, including even the subway, which brought one very conveniently from any part of the city (and a roundabout route was essential though it took only fifteen minutes to walk the distance) to a certain street corner where a rather fantastic house was being slowly built. She casually mentioned to Dreyer that she loved taking a bus or a tram whenever she had a chance because it was a shame not to take advantage of the cheap, exhilaratingly cheap, methods of transportation put at one's disposal by a generous city. He said he was a generous citizen who preferred a taxi or a private car. By taking these precautions, Martha believed that nobody would ever guess that she transposed or curtailed or missed altogether those delightful contortions and scattering of invisible flowers in the delightful company of other barefooted ladies in more or less comical tunics.

On the day that businessman Dreyer, owner of the Dandy department store, and his chauffeur briefly appeared in the city news section of her newspaper, Martha arrived a little earlier than usual. Franz was not yet back from work. She sat down on the couch, took off her hat, slowly removed her gloves. That day her face was particularly pale. She wore her high-neck beige dress with little buttons in front. When Franz's familiar footsteps sounded in the corridor and he entered (with that abrupt unceremoniousness with which we enter our own room, assuming that it is empty), she did not smile. Franz emitted an exclamation of pleased surprise and without taking off his hat began to shower Martha's neck and ear with rapid kisses.

'You know about it already?' she asked, and her eyes had the strange expression he had hoped never to see again.

'You bet,' he answered and, getting up from the couch, shed his raincoat and striped scarf. 'Everybody was discussing it at the store. They asked me all kinds of questions. I was really scared when he came in looking so grim yesterday. What a dreadful thing.'

'What's dreadful, Franz?'

He was already coatless and collarless, and was noisily washing his hands.

'Well, all that jagged glass hitting you in the face, that crunch of metal and bones, and blood, and blackness. I don't know why but I picture such things so clearly. Makes me want to vomit.'

'That is just nerves, Franz, nerves. Come here.'

He sat down close to her and, trying not to notice that she was absorbed in remote dreary thoughts of her own, softly asked:

'No pompons today?'

She did not hear the sweet euphemism, or did not seem to hear it.

'Franz,' she said, stroking and restraining his hand, 'do you realize what a miracle it was? I had a presentiment yesterday which did not work.'

'There we go again,' he thought, 'how long will she bore me with her concern for him?'

He turned away and attempted to whistle, but no sound came out and he remained brooding with puckered lips.

'What's the matter with you, Franz? Stop acting like a fool. I'm closed for repairs today' (another sweet euphemism).

She drew him to her by the neck; he would not yield but her diamond-like gaze slashed him, and he went all limp and whimpery, the way a child's balloon collapses with a pitful squeak. Tears of resentment fogged his glasses. He pressed his head to her shoulder: 'I can't go on like this,' he whined. "Already last night I wondered if your feeling for me was really serious. Worrying about that old uncle of mine! It means you care for him! Oh, it's so painful—'

Martha blinked, then understood his mistake. 'So that's what it is,' she drawled with a laugh. 'Oh, you poor dear.'

She took his head in her hands, looked intently and sternly into his eyes, and then slowly, with her mouth half open, as if she were about to give him a gentle bite, drew close to his face, and took possession of his lips.

'Shame on you,' she said, releasing him slowly, 'shame on you,' she repeated with a nod. 'I never thought you were that silly. No, just a minute – I want you to understand how silly you are. No, wait. You can't touch me but I can certainly touch you, and nibble you, and even swallow you whole if I want.'

'Listen,' she said a little while later, after that stunt, quite new to Franz, had been brought to a satisfactory close. 'Listen, Franz, how wonderful it would be if I didn't have to go today. Today, or tomorrow, or ever. Of course, we could not live in a tiny room like this.'

'We would rent a larger, brighter room,' said Franz with assurance.

'Yes. Let's dream a little. Larger and much brighter. Maybe even two rooms, what do you think? Or perhaps three? And of course a kitchen.'

'And lots of beautiful knives,' said Franz, 'meat cleavers, and cheese cutters, and a roast pork slicer, but you would not do any cooking. You have such precious nails.'

'Yes, naturally, we'd have a cook. What did we decide – three rooms?'

'No, four,' said Franz after a moment's thought. 'Bedroom, drawing room, sitting room, dining room.'

'Four. Fine. A regular four-room apartment. With kitchen. With bath. And we'll have the bedroom all done in white, won't we? And the other rooms blue. And there'll be a reception room with lots and lots of flowers. And an extra room upstairs, just in case, for guests, say. . . . For a wee little guest, maybe.'

'What do you mean – "upstairs"?'

'Why, of course – it will be a villa.'

'Ah, I see,' nodded Franz.

'Let's continue, darling. A detached villa, then. With a pretty entrance hall. We enter. Rugs, pictures, silverware, embroidered sheets. Right? And a garden, fruit trees. Magnolias. Is that so, Franz?'

He sighed. 'All this will come only in ten years, or more. It will be a long time before I earn sufficiently for you to divorce him.'

Martha fell silent as if she were not in the room. Franz turned to her with a smile, ready to play on, but the smile faded: she was looking at him with narrowed eyes, biting her lip.

'Ten years,' she said bitterly. 'You little fool! You really want to wait ten years?'

'That's how it looks to me,' Franz replied. 'I don't know. Maybe, if I'm very lucky . . . but, for instance, take Mr Piffke; he's been with the store right from the start, and that's you know how many years. But he lives very modestly. He doesn't make more than four hundred fifty a month. His wife works too. They have a tiny apartment full of boxes and things.'

'Thank God you understand,' said Martha. 'You see, sweetheart, one cannot deposit dreams at the bank. They aren't dependable securities, and the dividends they bring are nothing.'

'Then what shall we do?' said frightened Franz. 'You know I'm ready to marry you immediately. I can't exist without you. Without you I'm like an empty sleeve. But I can't even afford one of those nice new floormats we sell at the store, let alone carpets. And then, of course, I'd have to look for another job – and I don't know anything (wrinkling his face), I have no experience in anything. That means learning all over again. We'd have to live in a damp, shabby little room, saving on food and clothes.'

'Yes, there would be no longer any uncle to help,' said Martha dryly. 'No uncle at all.'

'The whole idea is unthinkable,' said Franz.

'Absolutely unthinkable,' said Martha.

'Why are you angry with me?' he asked after a moment's silence. 'As if I were responsible or something. It's really not my fault. Well, let's dream on, if you want. Only don't get angry. I have seventeen units, like Uncle— Want me to describe them for you?'

'In ten years,' she said with a laugh, 'in ten years, my dear, men's fashions will have changed substantially.'

'There – you are angry again.'

'Yes, I'm angry; not with you, though, but with Fate. You see, Franz – no, you wouldn't understand.'

'I'll understand,' said Franz.

'All right then. You see, people generally make all kinds of plans, very good plans, but completely fail to consider one possibility: death. As if no one could ever die. Oh, don't look at me as if I were saying something indecent.'

She now had exactly the same odd expression as last night when she tried to impersonate a policeman.

'It's time for me to go,' said Martha with a frown. She got up and looked at herself in the mirror.

'Christmas trees are already sold in the streets,' she said, raising her elbows as she put on her hat. 'I want to buy a tree, a huge very expensive fir tree, and lots of presents to go under it. Please, give me four hundred and twenty marks. I'm out of pocket.'

'And you're also very nasty,' sighed Franz.

He accompanied her down the dark stairs. He walked her to the square. The builders had started on the facade of the new cinema. The sidewalk was very slippery, the glare ice glistened under the street lamps.

'You know something, treasure?' she said when bidding him good-bye at the corner. 'I might have been in deep mourning today. And very becoming it would have been. It's just by chance that I'm not in mourning. Ponder that, my little nephew.'

Exactly what she wanted happened then: Franz looked at her, opened his mouth, and suddenly burst out laughing. She rocked with laughter, too. A gentleman with a fox terrier, who was waiting near by for the dog to make up its mind in regard to a lamppost, glanced at the merry couple with approval and envy. 'In mourning,' said Franz, choking with laughter. She nodded, laughing. 'In mourning,' said Franz, stifling a rich guffaw in the palm of his hand. The man with the fox terrier shook his head and moved on. 'I adore you,' uttered Franz in a weak voice, and for quite a while gazed after her with moist eyes.

However, as soon as she turned away to go home Martha's face again grew stern. Franz meanwhile wiped his glasses with his handkerchief and ambled off, continuing to chuckle to himself. 'Yes, it really was a matter of chance. If only the owner of the car had sat beside the chauffeur. Just supposing he'd gone and sat there. There she would be today – a widow. A rich widow, an adorable mistress, a wonderful wife. How drolly she put it: yours is honey; his, poison. And then again, who needs an elaborate crack-up. After all, car accidents are not necessarily fatal; much too often one gets away with bruises, a fracture, lacerations, one mustn't make too complicated demands on chance: exactly that way, please, make the brains squirt out. There are other possibilities: illnesses, for example. Perhaps he has a bad heart and does not know it. And look at all the influenza people who croak. Then we'd really start living. The store would go on doing business. The money would roll in. But then more likely he'll outlive his wife and make it all the way to the twenty-first century. Why, there was something in the papers about a Turk who was a hundred and fifty years old, and still produced children, the filthy old brute.'

Thus he mused, vaguely and crudely, unaware that his thoughts were spinning along from the push given them by Martha. The thought of marriage had also come from her. Oh, but it was a good thought. If he derived such pleasure from Martha's satisfying him twice in one hour three or four times a week, what varied ectasies would she grant him if she were available twenty-four hours a day! He employed this method of calculating happiness quite guilelessly, the way a greedy child imagines a country with chocolate-cream mud and ice-cream snow.

In those days – which as a very old and very sick man, guilty of worse sins than avunculicide, he remembered with a grin of contempt – young Franz was oblivious to the corrosive probity of his pleasant daydreams about Dreyer's dropping dead. He had plunged into a region of delirium, blithely and light-heartedly. His subsequent meetings with Martha appeared to be as natural and tender as all the previous ones but, just as that modest little room, with its unpretentious old furniture and its naively dark corridor, had for master a person, or persons, incurably though not obviously insane, there lurked in those meetings something strange – a little eerie and shameful at first, but already enthralling, already all-powerful. Whatever Martha said, however charmingly she smiled, Franz sensed an irresistible insinuation in her every word and glance. They were like heirs sitting in a dim-lit parlour while in the bedroom doomed Plutus pleads with the doctor and curses the priest; they might talk about trifles, about the approach of Christmas, about the intense activity of skis and wool at the emporium; one might talk about anything although perhaps a little more soberly than before – for one's hearing is strained, one's eyes had a changeable gleam; a secret impatience allows one no peace as one waits and waits for the grim physician to come out on tiptoe, with an eloquent sigh, and lo – through the crack of the door one glimpses the long back of the cleric, representative of a boundlessly charitable Church, in the act of bending over the white, white bed.

Theirs was a pointless vigil. Martha knew perfectly well that he never seemed to have even so much as a toothache or a cold. Therefore it was particularly irritating to her when just before the holidays she herself contracted a chill; the poor girl developed a dry cough, a tease and a wheeze in the bronchia, night sweats, and spent the day in a kind of dull trance, dazed by the so-called *Grippe*, heavy-headed and with ears abuzz. When Christmas came she felt no better. That evening, nevertheless, she put on a sheer flame-coloured dress, very low cut at the back, and deafened by aspirin, trying to dispell her illness by will power, supervised the preparation of the punch, the laying of the table, the ruddy smoky activity of the cook.

In the parlour, its silvery crown touching the ceiling, all decked out in flimsy tinselry, all studded with still unlit red and blue bulbs, a fresh luxuriant fir tree stood, indifferent to its buffoonish array. In an uncozy nook between the parlour and the entry, a bright and rather bare place, termed for some reason a reception room, where among the wicker furniture grew and bloomed potted plants – cyclamens, seven dwarf cactuses, a peperomia with painted leaves – and where the tangerine glow of an electric fireplace could not beat the draft from a plate-glass window, Dreyer in evening dress sat reading an English book while waiting for his guests. The scene was laid on the Island of Capri. He moved his lips as he read and peeked pretty often into a fat dictionary which kept shuttling between his lap and a glass-topped table. Not knowing what to do with herself during this prolonged lull before the first ring, Martha sat down at a little distance from him on a settee and lifted her foot off the floor, examining from every angle her pointed shoe. The stillness was intolerable. Dreyer accidentally dropped the dictionary and, making his generously starched shirt crackle, retrieved it without taking his eyes off his book. What could she do with that oppression, that tightness in the chest? Coughing alone could not relieve it; there was only one thing that could make the whole world well: the sudden and total disappearance of that self-satisfied bulky man with the leonine brows and freckled hands. The acuteness of her hatred reached such a pitch of perception that for a moment she had the illusion that his chair was empty. But his cuff link described a flashing arc as he shut the dictionary, and he said, smiling at her consolingly: 'Goodness, what a cold you have. I can hear a veritable orchestra of wheezes tuning up in you.'

'Spare me your metaphors and put your book away,' said Martha. 'The guests will be here any moment. And that dictionary. There's nothing more untidy than a dictionary on a chair.'

'*All right, my treasury,*' he answered in English, and walked away with his books, mentally lamenting his unsure pronunciation and meagre though exact vocabulary.

The chair by the glowing grate now stood empty, but that did not help. With her whole being she experienced his presence, there, behind the door, in the next room, and the next, and the next; the house was suffocating from him; the clocks ticked with an effort and the cold folded napkins stood stifling on the festive table with a strangled rose in each individual vase – but how to cough him up, how to breathe freely again? It now seemed to her that it had always been thus, that she had hated him hopelessly since the first days and nights of their marriage when he kept pawing and licking her like an animal, in a locked hotel room in white Salsborg. He now stood in her path, in her plain, straight path, like a solid obstacle, that ought somehow to be removed to let her resume her plain straight existence. How dared he enforce upon her the complications of adultery? How dared he stand in the queue before her? Our cruellest enemy is less hateful than the burly stranger whose placid back keeps us from squeezing through to a ticket window or to the counter of a sausage shop. She walked to and fro, she drummed on a window. She tore off a diseased cyclamen leaf, she felt she would suffocate any moment. At that instant the doorbell sounded. Martha checked her hairdo and walked quickly – not to the front door but back to the door of the drawing room in order to make an elegant entrance from afar to meet her guests.

During the next half hour the bell rang again and again. First to arrive were the inevitable Walds in their Debler limousine; then came Franz shivering from the cold; then, almost simultaneously, the count with a bouquet of mediocre pinks and a paper manufacturer with his wife; then – two loud, half-naked, ill-groomed girls whose late father had been their host's partner in happier days; then – the snub-nosed, gaunt, and taciturn director of the Fatum Insurance Company; and a rosy-cheeked civil engineer in triplicate – that is, with a sister and a son comically resembling him. All this company gradually warmed up and coalesced until it formed a single many-limbed but otherwise not over-complex creature that made mirthful noise, and drank, and whirled. Only Martha and Franz were unable to identify themselves, as they should have by all the laws of a hearty holiday, with this animated, flushed, palpitating mass. She was pleased to note how unresponsive Franz was to the practically naked charms of those two practically identical vulgar young things with revoltingly thin arms, and snaky backs, and insufficiently spanked little popos. The injustice of life – in ten years' time they would be still a little younger than I am now, all three of them as a matter of fact.

Every now and then her eyes and those of Franz would meet, but even without looking he and she always clearly sensed the changing correlation of their respective whereabouts: while he walked diagonally across the parlour with a glass of punch for

Ida or Isolda – no, for old Mrs Wald – Martha was putting a rustling paper hat on bald Willy at the other end of the room; as Franz sat down and started listening to what the engineer's sister, pink-cheeked and plain, had to say, Martha combined the oblique and the straight line by going from Willy to the door, and then to the dining-room table laden with hors-d'oeuvres. Franz lit a cigarette, Martha put a mandarin on a plate. Thus a chess player playing blind feels his trapped bishop and his opponent's versatile queen move in relentless relation to each other. There was a vaguely regular rhythm established in those coordinations. And not for an instant was it interrupted. She and especially Franz felt the existence of this invisible geometric figure; they were two points moving through it, and the interrelation between those two points could be plotted at any given moment; and though they seemed to move independently they were nonetheless securely bound by the invisible, inexorable lines of that figure.

The parquet was already littered with motley paper trash; already someone had broken a glass and stood speechless with sticky fingers outspread. Willy Wald, already high, wearing a golden hat and garlanded with paper ribbons, his innocent blue eyes opened wide, was recounting to the gruff old count his recent trip to Russia, ardently extolling the Kremlin, the caviar, the commissars. Presently Dreyer, coatless, flushed, still holding a chef's knife and wearing a chef's cap, took Willy aside and began whispering something to him, while the rosy engineer went on telling the other guests about three masked individuals who, one Christmas night, had broken in and robbed the whole company. The phonograph broke into song in the adjoining boudoir. Dreyer started to dance with one of the pretty sisters, and then caught up the other, and the girls giggled and curved their supple bare backs as he tried to dance with both together. Franz stood by the window drapery, regretting that he still had not had time to learn to dance. He saw Martha's white hand on somebody's black shoulder, then her profile, then the birthmark under her left shoulder blade and somebody's thumb upon it, then the madonna profile again, and again the raisin in the cream; and her silk-sheening legs which the hem of her short skirt revealed up to the knee moved hither and thither, and seemed (if one looked at them only) to belong to a woman who did not know what to do with herself from restlessness and anticipation: she steps, now slowly, now quickly, this way and that, turns abruptly, steps again in her excruciating impatience.

Martha danced automatically, feeling not so much the rhythm of the music as the syncopic changes between her and Franz, who was standing by the drapery with folded arms and moving eyes. She noticed Dreyer reach through the drapery; he must have opened the window a little, for it grew cooler in the room. As she danced, she kept checking Franz's position: he was there, the dear sentinel; she searched for her husband with her eyes; he had left the room and she told herself that the sudden coolness and well-being were due precisely to his absence. On gliding closer to Franz she bathed him in such a familiar meaningful look that he lost countenance and smiled at the engineer whose face was presented to him by the whim of a whirl. Again and again the phonograph was wound, and among many pairs of ordinary legs flashed those strong, graceful, ravishing legs, and Franz, dizzy from the wine and the gyrations of the dancers, became aware of a certain terpsichorean tumult in his poor head as if all his thoughts were learning to foxtrot.

Then something happened. In mid-dance Isolda cried: 'Oh, look! The drape!'

Everyone looked, and, indeed, the window curtain stirred strangely, altered its folds, and swelled slowly. Simultaneously the lights went out. In the darkness an oval light began to move about the room, the drapery parted, and in the unsteady glimmer, a masked man suddenly appeared, dressed in an old military coat and carrying a menacing flashlight in his fist. Ida gave a piercing scream. The engineer's voice calmly pronounced in the dark: 'I suspect that's our genial host.' Then, after a curious pause, filled by the phonograph which had gone on dutifully playing in the dark, there sounded Martha's tragic voice. She gave such a howl of warning that the two girls and the old count surged back toward the door (blocked by merry Willy). The masked figure emitted a hoarse sound and, training the light on Martha, moved forward. It is possible that the girls were genuinely frightened. It is also possible that one or two of the men were beginning to doubt its being a prank. Martha, who went on crying for help, noticed with cold exultation that the engineer standing beside her had reached back under his dinner jacket and had produced something from his hip pocket. She realized what her screams meant, what prompted them, and what they should cause to happen; and, secure in her performance, she screamed still louder, urging, hallooing.

Franz could not bear it any longer. He stood nearest of all to the intruder, had recognized him at once by his tailor-made tuxedo trousers, and now his nimble fingers ripped the mask off the intruder's face. Meanwhile Mr Fatum had finally overcome panting Willy and switched on the lights. In the centre of the room, dressed in a combination of apache scarf and soldier's coat, stood Dreyer roaring with laughter, now swaying, now squatting, all red and tousled, and pointing his finger at Martha. Quickly deciding how she should now resolve her feigned terror, she turned her back upon her husband, rearranged the strap on one bare shoulder, and calmly went off to the faltering phonograph. He rushed after her and, still laughing, hugged and kissed her. 'Oh, I knew it was you all along,' she said – which, of course, was quite true.

Franz had been trying for some time to fight off the welling of nausea but now he was going to be sick, and he hurriedly left the room. Behind him the hubbub continued; they were all laughing and shouting, probably crowding around Dreyer, squeezing him, squeezing him, squeezing both him and Martha, who wriggled. With his handkerchief pressed to his lips, Franz made for the front hall, and wrenched open the door of the toilet. Old Mrs Wald came flying out like a bomb and disappeared behind the bend of the wall. 'My God, my God,' he muttered, doubled over. He emitted horrible sounds, recognizing in the intermittent torrent a medley of food and drink the way a sinner in hell retastes the hash of his life. Breathing heavily, squeamishly wiping his mouth with a bit of toilet paper, he waited for a moment, and pulled the chain. On his way back he paused in the entrance hall and listened. Through an open door a mirror reflected the ominously blazing Christmas tree. The phonograph was singing again. Suddenly he saw Martha.

She went up to him quickly, looking over her shoulder like a conspirator in a play. They were alone in the brightly lit hall, and from beyond the door came noise, laughter, the squeals of a helpless pig, the quawks of a tortured turkey.

'No luck,' said Martha. 'I'm sorry, dear.'

Her piercing eyes were at once in front of him and all around him. Then she started to cough, clutched at her side and dropped in a chair.

He asked: 'What do you mean – no luck?'

'It cannot go on like this,' muttered Martha between fits of coughing. 'It simply cannot. Why, look at yourself – you're as pale as death.'

The noise in the house was swelling and drawing nearer; it

seemed as though that enormous tree were bellowing with all its lights.

'. . . as death,' said Martha.

Franz felt another onset of nausea; the voices surged forward; sweaty Dreyer rushed past, escaping from Wald and the engineer, and after them came the others guffawing and gibbering, and Tom, locked up in the garage, was barking his head off. And the noise of the hunt seemed to pursue Franz as he vomited in the deserted street and staggered home. At the corner of the square the scaffolding that cocooned the future Kino-Palazzo was adorned on the very top with a bright Christmas tree. The latter could be also seen, but only as a tiny coloured blur in the starry sky from the Dreyers' bedroom window.

'Either of the two would make a marvellous little wife for good old Franz,' said Dreyer as he undressed.

'That's what you think,' said Martha, glaring into her dressing-table mirror.

'Ida, of course, is the more beautiful,' continued drunken Dreyer, 'but Isolda with that fluffy pale hair and that way of gasping she has while one is telling her something comical—'

'Why don't you sample her? Or both together?'

'I wonder,' mused Dreyer as he took off his drawers. He laughed and added: 'My love, what about you tonight? After all, it is Christmas.'

'Not after your idiotic joke,' said Martha, 'and if you pester me with your lust I'll take my pillow to the guest room.'

'I wonder,' repeated Dreyer as he got into bed and laughed again. He had never tried them together. Might be fun! Separately he had had them only on two occasions: Ida three summers ago quite unexpectedly in the woods of Spandau during a picnic; and Isolda a little later in a Dresden hotel. Hopelessly bad stenographers, both of them.

Franz had never gone to bed yet at half past four in the morning. He woke up in the afternoon feeling hungry, healthy, and happy. He remembered with pleasure snatching that mask off. The roaring darkness that had pursued him like a nightmare had been transformed, now that he had surrendered himself to it, into a hum of euphoria.

He dined at the nearby tavern and went back home to wait for Martha. At ten minutes past seven she had not come. At twenty minutes to eight he knew she was not coming. Should he wait till tomorrow? He dared not ring her up: Martha had forbidden him and herself to telephone lest it became a sweet habit which in its turn might lead to the wrong ears' overhearing a careless caressive phrase. The urge to tell her how strong and well he felt, despite all that wine and venison, and music, and terror, was even stronger than his desire to know if her cold was better.

As he reached their street, an empty taxi overtook him and pulled up at the villa. He decided his visit was ill-timed – they were probably going out. He paused at the fence of the garden expecting them to emerge, she in her lovely furs, he in his camel-hair coat. Then, changing his mind again, Franz hurried toward the porch.

The front door was ajar. Frieda was pulling half-strangled Tom upstairs by his collar. In the entrance hall Franz saw an opulent suitcase of real leather and a splendid pair of hickory skis of a type they did not have at the store. In the parlour husband and wife stood facing each other. He was talking rapidly, and she was smiling like an angel and nodding in silence.

'Ah, Franz, there you are,' he said, turning, and caught his nephew by his stuffed shoulder. 'You've come just at the right moment. I'm off for three weeks or so.'

'What are those skis doing there?' asked Franz, and realized with surprise that Dreyer had ceased to frighten him.

'Mine. I'm going to Davos. And take this' (five dollars).

He kissed his wife on the cheek. 'Nurse your cold, dear. Have a good time over the holidays. Tell Franz to take you to the theatre. Don't be cross with me, darling, for leaving you behind. Snow is for men and single girls. You can't change that.'

'You'll be late for your train,' said Martha, slitting sweet eyes at him.

He glanced at his golden watch, mimicked panic, and grasped his valise. The taxi driver helped with the skis. Uncle, aunt and nephew crossed the garden. After all that frost a drizzle had set in! Hatless and wearing her moleskin coat, Martha strolled to the wicket with an indolent swing of the hips, her hands invisibly clasped in her joined coat-sleeves. It took quite a long time to arrange the long skis on the roof of the taxi. At last the door slammed. The taxi drove off. Franz mechanically noted its licence number: 22221. This unexpected '1' seemed odd after so many '2's. They walked slowly back toward the house along the crunching path.

'It's thawing again,' said Martha. 'Today my cough is much less harsh.'

Franz thought for a moment and said: 'Yes. But there are still some cold days ahead.'

'Possibly,' said Martha.

When they entered the empty house, Franz had the impression they had returned from a funeral.

8

She began teaching him obstinately and fervidly.

After the first embarrassments, stumblings, and perplexities, he gradually began to understand what she was communicating to him, doing so with almost no words of explanation, almost entirely through pantomime. He gave his full attention both to her and to the ululating sound which, now rising, now falling, accompanied him constantly; and already he perceived, in that sound, rhythmic demands, a compelling meaning, regular breaks and beats. What Martha wanted of him was proving to be so simple. As soon as he had assimilated something, she would nod silently, looking down the while with an intent smile, as though following the motions and growth of an already distinct shadow. His awkwardness, that feeling of having a limp and a hump, which tormented him in the beginning – all this soon disappeared; instead, the erect poise, the specious grace and pace she was teaching him enslaved him totally: now he could no longer disobey the sound whose mystery he had solved. Vertigo became a habitual and pleasurable state, an automaton's somnambulic languor, the law of his existence; now Martha would gently exult, and press her temple against his, knowing that they were at one, that he would do the proper thing. While teaching him she restrained her impatience, the impatience he had once noticed in the flash and flicker of her elegant legs. Now she stood before him and, holding up her pleated skirt between finger and thumb, she repeated the steps in slow motion so that he might see for himself the magnified turn of toe and heel. He would attempt a scooping caress but she would slap his hand away and go on with the lesson. And when, under the pressure of her strong palm, he learned how to turn and spin; when his steps had finally fallen in with hers; when a glance at the mirror told her that the clumsy lesson had become a harmonious dance; then she increased the pace, give her excitement its head, and her rapid cries expressed fierce satisfaction with his obedient piston slide.

He came to know the reeling expanse of parquetry in huge halls surrounded by loges; he leaned his elbow on the faded plush of their parapet; he wiped her powder off his shoulder; he saw himself and her in surfeited mirrors; he paid predatory waiters out of her black silk purse; his mackintosh and her beloved moleskin coat embraced for hours on end in the darkness of heavily laden hangers under the guard of sleepy cloakroom girls; and the sonorous names of all the fashionable ballrooms and dancing cafés – tropical, crystal, royal – became as familiar to him as the names of the streets of the little town where he had dwelt in a previous life. And presently they would be sitting out the next dance, still panting from amorous exertions, side by side on the drab couch in his dingy room.

'Happy New Year,' said Martha, 'our year. Write to your mother, whom I certainly would like to know, that you are having a splendid time. Think how surprised she will be later . . . afterwards . . . when I shall meet her.'

He asked: 'When? Have you fixed a deadline?'

'As soon as possible. The sooner the better.'

'Oh, we mustn't dawdle.'

She leaned back on the cushions, her hands behind her head. 'A month – perhaps two. We have to plan very carefully, my dear love.'

'I'd go mad without you,' said Franz. 'Everything upsets me – this wallpaper, the people in the street, my landlord. His wife never shows herself. It's so strange.'

'You must be calmer. Otherwise nothing will work out. Come here. . . .'

'I know it will turn out wonderfully,' he said, pressing against her. 'Only we must make sure of everything. The smallest mistake. . . .'

'Oh, how can you doubt, my strong, stout Franz!'

'No, of course not. God, no. Oh, my God, no. It's just that we have to find a sure method.'

'Fast, darling, much faster – don't you hear the rhythm? . . .'

They were no longer coupling on the couch but foxtrotting among gleaming white tables on the bright-lit floor of a café. The orchestra was playing and gasping for breath. There was among the dancers a tall American Negro who smiled tolerantly as one passionate pair bumped into him and his blonde partner.

'We'll find it, we must find it,' continued Martha in a rapid patter in time to the music; 'after all, we are within our rights.'

He saw her long sweet burning eye, and the geranium lobe of her little ear from beneath her sleek bandeau. If only he could glide thus forever, an eternal piston rod in a vacuum of delight, and never, never part from her. . . . But there still existed the store, where he bowed and turned like a jolly doll, and there still were the nights when like a dead doll he lay supine on his bed not knowing whether he was asleep or awake, and who was that, shuffling and two-stepping, and whispering in the corridor, and why was the alarm clock jazzing in his ear? But let us say we are awake, and here comes bushy-browed old Enricht bringing two cups of coffee – why two? And how depressing those torn silk socks on the floor.

One such blurry morning, a Sunday, when he and Martha in her beige dress were walking decorously about the snow-powdered garden, she wordlessly showed him a snapshot she had just received from Davos. It showed a smiling Dreyer, in a Scandinavian ski suit, clutching his poles; his skis were beautifully parallel, and all around was bright snow, and on the snow one could distinguish the photographer's narrow-shouldered shadow.

When the photographer (a fellow-skier and teacher of English, Mr Vivian Badlook) had clicked the shutter and straightened up, Dreyer, still beaming, moved his left ski forward; however, he was standing on a slight incline, the ski went further than he had intended, and with a great flourish of ski poles he tumbled heavily on his back while both girls shot past shrieking with laughter. For a while he could not get the damned skis uncrossed, and his arm kept going into the snow up to the elbow. By the time he got up, disfigured by the snow, and put on his snow-crusted mittens, and cautiously began to glide down, his face bore a solemn expression. He had dreamed of performing all kinds of Christianias and telemarks, flying downhill, turning sharply in a cloud of snow – but apparently God had not willed it. In the snapshot, though, he looked like a real skier, and he admired it before slipping it into the envelope. But that morning as he stood by the window in his yellow pyjamas and looked at the green larches and the cobalt sky he reflected that he had been there two weeks, and yet his skiing and his English were even worse than the previous winter. From the snow-blue road came the jingle of sleighbells; Isolda and Ida were giggling in the bathroom; but enough was enough. He remembered with a pang of pleasure the inventor, who must already be at work in the laboratory set up for him; he also remembered a number of other entertaining projects connected with the expansion of the Dandy store; he pondered all this, took a look at the snowy slope crisscrossed with shiny ski tracks, and decided to depart for home ahead of time leaving his girl friends to their own devices, which were not negligible; and there was another amusing thought that he deliberately kept in the back of his mind: it would be fun to come home unexpectedly, and catch Martha's soul unawares, and see whether she would let escape a radiant smile of surprise or meet him with her usual ironic morosity as she certainly would if warned of his arrival. Despite his keen sense of humour, Dreyer was too naively self-centred to realize how thoroughly those sudden returns had been exploited in ribald tales.

Franz ripped the photo into little bits which the wind carried across the wet lawn.

'Silly,' said Martha, 'why did you do that? He's sure to ask me if I pasted it in the album.'

'Some day I'll tear up the album too,' said Franz.

An eager Tom had come running toward them: he hoped Franz might have thrown a ball or a pebble but a rapid search revealed nothing.

A couple of days later Frieda was allowed to spend the week-end with the family of her brother, a fireman in Potsdam and the brightest Rembrandtesque gleam in her gloomy light. Tom was compelled to spend more time than usual in the gardener's quarters next to the carless garage. Martha and Franz, yielding to the agonizing desire to assert themselves, to be free, to enjoy their freedom, decided, if only for one evening, to live as they craved to live: it was to be a dress rehearsal of future happiness.

'Today you are master here,' she said. 'Here's your study, here's your armchair, here if you want is the paper: the market has rallied.'

He flung off his jacket and sauntered through all the rooms as if reviewing them upon returning to his own comfortable house from a long and difficult journey.

'Everything in order? Is my lord happy?'

He put his arm around her shoulder and they stood side by side before the mirror. He was poorly shaven that evening, and intead of a waistcoat had put on a rather casual dark-red sweater; there was something homey and quiet about Martha too. Her recently washed hair did not lie smoothly, and she wore a woollen jumper that was unbecoming but somehow right.

'Mr and Mrs Bubendorf. You know, once we were standing like this, and I was sure you'd kiss me for the first time, but you didn't.'

'I'm now an inch taller,' he said with a laugh. 'Look, we are almost the same height.'

He sank into the leather armchair, and she sat in his lap, and the fact that she had gained weight and was quite bottom-heavy made things all the more cozy.

'I love your ear,' he said, lifting up a strand of hair with a nose-wrinkling horse-nuzzle.

A clock began chiming gently and tunefully in the next room. Franz laughed softly.

'Imagine if he were suddenly to come in now – just like that.'

'Who?' asked Martha. 'I don't understand whom you're speaking about.'

'I mean him. If he should come home all at once. He has such a stealthy way of opening doors.'

'Oh, you are speaking of my late husband, oh, I see,' said Martha in a smoky voice. 'No, my deceased was always a man of precision. He would let me know – no, no, Franz, not now, after supper, perhaps. I think he meant to be an example to his little wife, who otherwise might visit him – I said no – without warning in that little room with the couch he has at the back of his office.'

Silence. Matrimonial well-being.

'The deceased,' chuckled Franz, 'the deceased.'

'Do you remember him well?' murmured Martha, rubbing her nose against his neck.

'Vaguely. And you?'

'The red fur on his belly and—'

In atrocious, disparaging and quite inaccurate terms she described the dead man's private parts.

'Pah,' said Franz. 'Don't make me throw up.'

'Franz,' she said, her eyes beaming, 'no one will ever find out!'

Well accustomed by now to the idea, by now quite tame and bloodthirsty, he nodded in silence. A certain numbness was invading his lower limbs.

'We did it so simply, so neatly,' said Martha, slitting her eyes as if in dim recollection, 'not the merest shadow of suspicion. Nothing. And why, sir? Because destiny is on our side. It could not have been otherwise. Remember the funeral? Piffke's tulips? Isolda's and Ida's violets bought from a street beggar?'

He mutely asquiesced again.

'It was during the final thaw. We had forsythias in the bay window. Remember? I was still coughing but it was already a soft wet delicious cough. Ah, getting rid of the last thick gob.'

Franz winced. Another pause.

'You know, my knees are getting sort of tired. No, wait, don't get up. Just move over a little. That's right.'

'My treasure, my all,' she cried, 'my darling husband. I never imagined there could be such a marriage as ours.'

He passed his lips along her warm neck and said:

'Isn't it time for us to lie down for a bit, eh?'

'What about some cold cuts and beer? No? Okay, we shall eat afterwards.'

She rose, leaning hard on him as she did so. Then she stretched herself.

'Let's go up,' she said with a contented yawn, 'to our bedroom.'

'Is that all right?' asked Franz. 'I thought we'd do it here.'

'Of course not. Oh, come on, get up. It's already past ten.'

'You know. . . . I'm still a little scared of the deceased,' said Franz, biting his lip.

'Oh, he won't be coming for a week yet. That's as sure as death. What's there to be scared of? Little fool! Or don't you want me?'

'Oh, I do,' said Franz, 'but you must cover his bed; I don't want to see it. It would put me off.'

She turned off the lights in the parlour and he followed her up an inner staircase that was short and creaky; then they passed through a baby-blue corridor.

'Why on earth are you walking on tiptoe?' exclaimed Martha with a loud laugh. 'Can't you understand – we're married, married!'

She showed him the mangle room which she used for her Hindu-kitch exercises, her dressing room, his and her bathroom, and finally their bedroom.

'The deceased used to sleep on that bed there,' she said. 'But of course the sheets have been changed. Let me put this tiger rug over it. So. Would you like to wash or something?'

'No, I'll wait for you here,' said Franz, examining a soft doll on the night table.

'All right. Undress quick and hop into my bed. I have a great need.'

She left the door ajar. Her pleated skirt and jumper were already lying on a chair. From the toilet across the corridor came the steady thick rapid sound of his sister making water. It stopped. Martha passed into the bathroom.

He suddenly felt that in this cold, inimical, unbearably white room where everything reminded him of the dead man, he was unable to undress, let alone make love. With revulsion and fear he gazed at the next bed.

Then he strained his ears. He thought he heard a door slam downstairs followed by creeping steps. He darted to the corridor. Simultaneously Martha came out of the bathroom stark naked.

'Something's happened,' he said in a spitting whisper. 'We're not alone any more. Listen to that noise.'

Martha frowned. Wrapping herself in a negligee, she went down the corridor and stopped with her head bent sidewise.

'I'm telling you! . . . I've heard.'

'I too had a bizarre feeling,' said Martha in a low voice. 'I know, darling, you are terribly disappointed, but we'd better not go on with this madness. It won't be long now. You'd better go. I'll come tomorrow as usual.'

'But if I meet somebody downstairs?'

'There's no one there, Franz. Here, take my keys. You'll return them tomorrow.'

She accompanied him as far as the main staircase, still listening. Now she was puzzled and upset as he.

Oh! Down in the hall harsh bangs resounded. Franz stopped, clutching at the banister, but she gave a laugh of relief.

'I know what it is,' she said. 'That's the downstairs toilet. It sometime bangs at night if there is a big wind, and if you don't close it well.'

'I'll admit I was a little frightened,' said Franz.

'All the same, you'd better go, darling. We mustn't take risks. Close that door in passing, will you.'

He embraced her. She let herself be kissed on the bare shoulder, drawing back herself the lace of her negligee to grant him that farewell treat. She remained standing on the landing of the theatrically illumined blue staircase until with a winky-winky he was gone.

A strong clean wind hit him in the face. The gravel path crunched pleasantly and securely beneath his feet. Franz inhaled deeply; then he cursed. She was so sinful and beautiful!

He felt a man again. Why was he such a coward? To think that a spectre, a cadaver, had turned him out of the house where he, Franz, was the real master! Muttering as he went (something that happened to him rather often of late), he walked swiftly along the dark sidewalk, and then without looking right or left began diagonally crossing the street at the place where he always crossed it on his way home.

A taxicab's horn, nasal and nasty, made him jump back. Still muttering, Franz turned the corner. Meanwhile the taxi braked and uncertainly pulled up to the curb. The driver got out and opened the door. 'What number, did you say?' he asked. No answer. The driver, reaching into the darkness, shook his fare by the shoulder. Finally the latter opened his eyes, leaned forward. 'Number five,' he replied to the driver's question. 'You're a little off.'

The bedroom window glowed. Martha was arranging her hair for the night. Suddenly she froze, still with raised elbows. Now she heard quite distinctly a loud clatter as if something had fallen. She darted toward the stairs. From the front hall came peels of laughter – familiar laughter, alas. He was laughing because, having turned awkwardly with the long skis on his shoulder, he had dropped one of them while knocking off with the other the white brush which flew up like a bird from the looking-glass shelf, after which he had tripped over his own suitcase.

'*I am the voyageur,*' he cried in his best English. '*I half returned from shee-ing!*'

The next instant he knew perfect happiness. There was a magnificent smile on Martha's face. Oh, no doubt, he was pretty to look at, tanned, trimmed by gravity, shedder of at least five pounds (as if Martha and Franz had already started to demolish him), but she was looking not at him: she was looking somewhere over his head, welcoming not him, but wise fate that had so simply and honestly averted a crude, ridiculous, dreadfully overworked disaster.

'A miracle saved us,' she later told Franz (for people talk very lightly of miracles), 'but let this be a lesson. You can see for yourself: it's impossible to wait any longer. Lucky once, lucky twice, and then – caught. And what can we expect then? Let us suppose he gives me a divorce. Let us even suppose I catch him with a stenographer. He does not have to support me, if I remarry. What next? I'm just as poor as you. My relatives in Hamburg are not going to help me.'

Franz shrugged.

'I wonder if you understand,' she said, 'that his widow inherits a fortune.'

'Why do you tell me this? We have discussed it sufficiently. I know perfectly well that there's only one solution.'

Then, as she peered through the slippery glint of his glasses deep into the mire of his greenish eyes, she knew that she had achieved her end, that he had been fully prepared, was completely ripe, and that the time had come to act. She was right. Franz no longer had a will of his own; the best he could do was to refract her will in his own way. The easy fulfillment of two merged dreams had become familiar to him, owing to a very simple interplay of sensations. By now Dreyer had already been several times murdered and buried. Not a future happiness, but a future recollection had been rehearsed on a bare stage, before a dark and empty house. With stunning unexpectedness, the corpse had returned out of nowhere, had walked in like an animated snowman, had begun talking as if he were alive. But what of it? It would be easy now and not at all frightening to cope with this sham existence, to make the corpse a corpse once more, and this time for good.

The discussion of methods of murder became with them an everyday matter. No uneasiness, no shame accompanied it; neither did they experience the dark thrill gamblers know, or the comfortable horror a family man enjoys when reading about the destruction of another family, with gory details, in a family newspaper. The words 'bullet' and 'poison' began to sound about as normal as 'bouillon' or 'pullet,' as ordinary as a doctor's bill or pill. The process of killing a man could be considered as calmly as the recipes in a cookbook, and no doubt Martha first of all thought of poison because of a woman's innate domestic bent, an instinctive knowledge of spices and herbs, of the healthful and the harmful.

From a second-rate encyclopedia they learned about all sorts of dismal Lucrezias and Locustas. A hollow-diamond ring, filled with rainbow venom, tormented Franz's imagination. He would dream at night of a treacherous handshake. Half-awake, he would recoil and not dare to move: somewhere under him, on the sheet, the prickly ring had just rolled, and he was terrified it might sting him. But in the daytime, by Martha's serene light, all was simple again. Tofana, a Sicilian girl, who dispatched 639 people, sold her 'aqua' in vials mislabelled with the innocent image of a saint. The Earl of Leicester had a mellower method: his victim would blissfully sneeze after a pinch of lethal stuff. Martha would impatiently shut the P-R volume and search in another. They learned, with complete indifference, that toxemia caused anemia and the Roman law saw in deliberate toxication a blend of murder and betrayal. 'Deep thinkers,' remarked Martha with a snarling laugh, sharply turning the page. Still she could not get to the heart of the matter. A sardonic 'See' sent her to something called 'alkaloids.' Another 'See' led to the fang of a centipede, magnified, if you please. Franz, unaccustomed to big encyclopedias, breathed heavily as he looked over her shoulder. Climbing through the barbed wire of formulae, they read for a long time about the uses of morphine, until having reached in some tortuous way a special case of pneumonia cruposa, Martha suddenly understood that the toxin in question belonged to a domesticated variety. Turning to another letter, they discovered that strychnine caused spasms in frogs and laughing fits in some islanders. Martha was beginning to fume. She kept brutally yanking out the thick tomes and squeezing them back any which way in the bookcase. There were fleeting glimpses of coloured plates: military decorations, Etruscan vases, gaudy butterflies. . . . 'Here, this is more like it,' said Martha, and she read in a low solemn voice: 'vomiting, a feeling of dejection, a singing in the ears – don't wheeze like that, please – a sensation of itching and burning over the entire surface of the skin, the pupils narrowed to the size of a pinhead, the testicles become like oranges. . . .' Franz remembered how as an adolescent he had looked up 'onanism' in a much smaller encyclopedia at school, and remained terrified and chaste for almost a week.

'Chucks,' said Martha, 'that's all medical rot. Who wants to know about cures or about traces of arsenic found in a stinking dead ass. I suppose we need some special works. There is a treatise mentioned here in parentheses, but it is a work written in the sixteenth century in Latin. Why people should use Latin is beyond me. Pull yourself together, Franz – he's here.'

She unhurriedly put the volume back and unhurriedly closed the glass doors of the cabinet. From the ancient world of the dead came Dreyer, whistling as he approached with the bouncing dog. But she did not give up the idea of poison. In the morning, alone, she again scanned the evasive articles in the encyclopedia, trying to find that plain, unhistorical, unspectacular, matter-of-fact potion or powder that she so clearly imagined. By accident at the end of one paragraph, she came upon a brief bibliography of plausible-looking modern works. She sought Franz's advice as to whether they ought to obtain one of them. He gave her a blank look but said that if it were necessary he would go and buy it. But she was afraid to let him go alone. They might tell him that the book had to be ordered or it would turn out to consist of ten volumes costing twenty-five marks each. He might get flustered, foolishly leave his address. If she were to accompany him he would of course behave splendidly – naturally and casually as if he were a student of medicine or chemistry – but it was dangerous to go together, and that was why public libraries were taboo. And once you get involved in the book racket and begin running from shop to shop, the devil knows what kind of nonsense might ensue. In her mind she now reviewed the little she had known before and the little she had dug up about poisoners' techniques. Two things she had gleaned: first, that every poison has its echo – an antidote; and, secondly, that a sudden death led to an inquisitive zestful autopsy. However, for quite some time longer, with the obedient cooperation of Franz (who once quite on his own, the dutiful darling, bought at a street stall *The True Story of the Marquise de Brinvilliers*), Martha continued to toy with the idea. The most attractive poison seemed to be cyanide. It had a brisk something about it with no romantic trimmings: an ordinary mouse that has swallowed an insignificant fraction of one gram falls dead before it can run thirty inches. She saw the stuff as a pinch of colourless powder which could be dropped unnoticed with a lump of sugar into a cup of tea. 'It says here that in certain cases cyanide cannot be traced in the cadaver. What certain cases? Tell us! Oh, it would be simple,' she said to Franz. 'We'd have tea together in the evening with those delicious little éclairs Menzel makes, and he'd swallow his sweet tea and cream – you know the quick way he does it – and suddenly – poof!'

'Well, let's get that powder,' he replied. 'I would get it if I had any idea how and where. Should I go to a pharmacy, or what?'

'I don't know either,' said Martha, 'I've read in a detective story about shady little cafés where one gets in touch with sellers of cocaine. But that's a long way to the stuff we need. Poisons are out, I'm afraid, unless of course we managed to bribe a doctor so that he would not dissect him, but that's too risky. Somehow I was absolutely certain they existed, those absolutely safe poisons. How stupid they don't. What a pity, Franz, you're not studying medicine; you could find out, you could decide then.'

'I'm ready to do anything,' he said in a strained voice, for at that moment he was bending and pulling off his shoes – they were new and pinched. 'I'm game for anything.'

'We've wasted a lot of time,' sighed Martha. 'Of course, I'm no scientist. I'm only a woman.'

She carefully folded on a chair the dress she had taken off. The February wind was rattling the windowpane, and she shivered as she stepped out of her panties. In the beginning of the winter she had started putting on warm underwear for her visits to him, but he had hated her incongruous appearance in those oatmeal tights which were almost as long and as tedious to peel off as his own and made her hips and bosom appear like those of a certain particularly offensive, dully rounded dummy in the store opposite the service lift. And after a while she stopped wearing anything but his favourite against her gooseflesh.

'One must study poisons for years and years,' she said, tidily rolling down her stockings, which she wanted to keep but did not want to tear. 'Hopeless, hopeless,' she sighed as she loosened the bedcovers (it would be warmer today between sheets, though she knew he preferred the couch). 'You will be a chemist of genius with a long white beard when at last we offer him that cup of tea!'

Meanwhile, slowly and meticulously, Franz was draping his jacket over the broad shoulders of a special hanger (filched from the store), after having removed and placed on the table a wallet containing a five-dollar bill, seven marks and six post stamps; a little notebook; a fountain pen; two pencils; his keys; and a letter to his mother he had forgotten to mail, Ruminative, naked, morose, he sniffed one armpit, and tossed his undervest under the washstand. It landed on the floor next to a rubber basin with Martha's rather depressing paraphernalia. He kicked the vest into a corner – she could wash it for him after tomorrow, with the socks, which were still comparatively clean. Well, to work, old soldier. Because he wore glasses even for lovemaking, he reminded her of a handsome, hairy young pearl diver ready to pry the live pearl out of its rosy shell as in that Russian ballet they had seen together, or that picture of conches facing the last page in volume M. He took off his wristwatch, listened to it and put it on the night table, near the alarm clock. There was less than half an hour left; they had dwelt too long on the cyanide.

'Darling, hurry up,' said Martha from under the blankets.

'God, what a corn I've developed,' he grunted, placing his bare foot on the edge of the chair and examining the hard yellow bump on his fifth toe. 'And yet it's the right size of shoes. I don't know, maybe my feet are still growing.'

'Franz, do come, dear. You can inspect it later.'

In due time he did in fact give his corn a thorough examination. Martha, after a brisk ablution, lay down again, replete with physical bliss. The callus was like stone to the touch. He pressed it with his finger, and shook his head. A kind of listless seriousness accompanied all his movements. He pouted, he scratched the crown of his head. Then, with the same listless thoroughness, he began studying the other foot, which seemed smaller and smelled differently. He just could not reconcile in his mind the fact that the size was correct and yet the shoes pinched. There they stood, the rascals, side by side. American type, knobbly-nosed, a nice reddish brown. He eyed them suspiciously – they had cost quite a lot even with a *Rabatt*. He slowly unhooked his glasses, breathed on the lenses, his mouth forming a lower-case *o*, and wiped them with a corner of the sheet. Then, just as slowly he put them on.

Martha looked at the clock. Yes, it was time to get dressed and go.

'You absolutely must come to supper tonight,' she said, pull-up her stocking and snapping her garters. 'I don't mind so much when there are guests but to sit alone with him – I can't bear it any more. . . . And put on your old shoes. Tomorrow you'll go and have these stretched for you. Free, of course. Every day is precious, oh, how precious!'

He was sitting on the bed, clasping his knees and staring at a point of light on the decanter that stood on the washstand. With his round head and prominent ears he seemed so special, so lovable to her. In his attitude, in his fixed gaze, there was the immobility of hypnosis. It crossed her mind that one word from her at this very moment could make him rise and follow her – as he was, as naked as a little boy – down the stairs, through the streets. . . . Her feeling of happiness now attained such a degree of brightness, and she imagined so vividly the regular well-planned, straightforward course of their common existence after the elimination, that she was afraid to disturb Franz's immobility, the immobile image of future happiness. She quickly finished dressing, slipped into her coat, took her hat, threw him a kiss, and was off. In the front hall, before a slightly better mirror than the one in her lover's room, she powdered her nose and put on her hat. How becomingly her cheeks were burning!

The landlord emerged from the toilet and made her a low bow.

'How is your wife feeling?' she asked, looking back as she took hold of the doorknob.

He bowed again.

She reflected that this wizard-like old codger was sure to know something about methods of poisoning people. It would be curious to know what they do, he and that invisible old woman of his. And for a few days longer she could not rid herself of the dream of magic powders instantly dissolving in death's nothingness, even though she knew already that nothing would come of it. A complicated, dangerous, outdated practice! Yes, that was it – outdated. 'Whereas in the middle of the last century an average of fifty cases of poisoning were investigated annually, statistics show that in modern time—' Yes, that was the point.

Dreyer raised the cup to his lip. Involuntarily Franz met Martha's eyes. The snow-white table described a slow circle with a crystal vase for hub. Dreyer put his half-empty cup down, and the table stopped revolving.

'. . . The light there is not particularly good,' he continued. 'And it's cold. The resonance is terrific. Every jump is echoed. I think the place used to be a riding school. But of course that's the only way to keep in training. One's serve does not fall apart during the winter. In any event (a final swallow of tea) spring, thank Heavens, is in the air, and it will soon be possible to play out of doors. My new club comes to life in April, And then I'll invite you. Eh, Franz?'

The previous day, at nine in the morning, he had created a minor sensation by appearing in Sports Goods, which he seldom visted during the winter. From behind a stucco column Franz saw him stop to chat with the respectfully bowing Piffke. The salesgirls and Mr Schwimmer stood at attention. An early customer, who wanted another ball for his dog, was ignored for an instant. 'Regards to your cockroaches,' said Dreyer to Piffke cryptically and merrily, and came up to the counter behind which in the meantime Franz had slipped and feigned to be occupied with pad and pencil.

'Work, work, my boy,' he said with the absentminded geniality with which he always addressed his nephew, whom he had filed away in his mind long ago under 'cretin' with cross references to 'milksop' and '*sympathisch.*' Then he advanced with humourously outstretched hand toward an unresponsive young man of painted wood who had been changed recently into tennis togs. The shopgirls had dubbed him Ronald.

Dreyer stood before the red-sweatered oaf for a long time looking with contempt at his posture and olive face, and thinking with a tender excitement about the task which the happy inventor was struggling with. From the way Ronald held his racket it was obvious he could not hit a single ball – even an abstract ball in his world of wood. Ronald's stomach was sucked in, his face bore an expression of inane self-satisfaction. Dreyer noticed with a shock that Ronald was wearing a tie. Encouraging people to wear ties for tennis!

He turned. Another young man (more or less alive, and even wearing glasses) dutifully listened to the boss's brief instructions.

'By the way, Franz,' added Dreyer, 'show me the very best rackets.'

Franz complied. Touched, Piffke watched with a melting gaze from afar. Dreyer selected an English racket. He gave the amber strings a couple of twangy fillips. He balanced it on the back of his finger to see which was heavier, frame or grip. He swung it in a passable imitation of a good player's backhand drive. It was a comfortable thirteen and a half.

'Keep it in a press,' he said to Franz. Emotion clouded the young man's glasses.

'Token of affection, modest gift,' said Dreyer in an explanatory patter and, casting an unfriendly last glance at vulgar Ronald, he walked away, with Piffke trotting beside him.

Although strictly speaking it was not at all part of his job, Franz embraced the wooden corpse and started undoing his tie. As he worked at it, he could not help touching the stiff cold neck. Then he undid a tight button. The shirt collar opened. The dead body was a brownish green with darker blotches and paler discolourations. Because of the open collar Ronald's fixed condescending grin became even more caddish and indecent. Ronald had a dark-brown smear under one eye as if he had been punched there. Ronald had a pied chin. Ronald's nostrils were clogged with black dust. Franz tried to recall where he had seen that horrible face before. Yes, of course – long, long ago, in the train. In the same train there had been a beautiful lady wearing a black hat with a little diamond swallow. Cold, fragrant, madonna-like. He tried to resurrect her features in his memory but failed to do so.

9

A purposeful gaiety, a dash of excitement now marked the rains. They no longer drizzled aimlessly; they breathed, they spoke. Violet crystals, like bath salts, were dissolved in rain water. Puddles consisted not of liquid mud but limpid pigments that made beautiful pictures reflecting housefronts, lampposts, fences, blue-and-white sky, a bare instep, a bicycle pedal. Two fat taxi drivers, a garbage collector in his sand-coloured apron, a housemaid with golden hair ablaze in the sun, a white baker with glistening rubbers on his bare feet, a bearded old émigré with a dinner pail in his hand, two women with two dogs, and a grey-suited man in a grey borsalino had crowded together on the sidewalk looking up at the corner turret of an apartment house across the street where, conversing shrilly, a score of swallows swarmed. Then the yellow garbage collector rolled his yellow can up to the truck, the chauffeurs returned to their vehicles, the baker hopped back on his bicycle, the pretty servant maid went into a stationery store, the women trailed off behind their dogs, which were beside themselves with new scents; the last to move off was the man in grey, and only the bearded old foreigner with his dinner pail and a Russian-language newspaper remained in a trance gazing up at a roof in remote Tula.

The man in the grey hat walked slowly, squinting because of sudden flashes of zigzag light cast by passing windshields. There was something in the air that produced an amusing feeling of dizziness, alternate waves of warm and cold flowing over his body beneath his silk shirt, a funny levity, an ethereal flutter, a loss of identity, name, profession.

He had just lunched and, theoretically, was supposed to return to his office; on this first day of spring, however, the notion of 'office' had quietly evaporated.

Toward him along the sunlit side of the street came a slender bob-haired lady in a karakul coat and a boy of four or five in a blue sailor suit rolling beside her on a tricycle.

'Erica,' exclaimed the man, and stopped with outspread arms.

The boy, pedalling energetically, rolled past, but his mother paused, blinking in the sunlight.

She was now more elegant, the features of her mobile, intelligent, bird-like face seemed even more delicate than in the past. But the aura, the flame of her former charm had gone. She was twenty-six at the time they had parted.

'I've seen you twice in eight years,' she said, in that familiar, rasping, rapid little voice. 'Once you went by in an open car, and once I saw you at the theatre – you were with a tall dark lady. That was your wife, wasn't it? I was sitting—'

'That's right, that's right,' he said, laughing with pleasure and weighing on his large palm her little hand in its tight white glove. 'But you were the last person I expected to meet today, though it is the best day to meet. I thought you went back to Vienna. The play was *King, Queen, Knave,* and now they are making a film out of it. I saw you too. And what about you – are you married?'

She was talking at the same time, so that their dialogue is hard to record. Music paper would be necessary with two clefs. As he was saying: 'You were the last person' . . . , she was already continuing: '. . . ten seats or so away from you. You haven't changed, Kurt. Only your moustache is cropped now. Yes, this is my boy. No, I'm not married. Yes, mostly in Austria. Yes, yes, *King, Queen, Knave.*'

'Seven years,' said old Kurt. 'Let's walk here a little' (guiding the pleased boy's tricycle into a small public garden). 'You know, I just saw the first— No, not quite that much—'

'. . . millions! I know you are making millions. I'm getting along all right myself' ('not quite that much,' Kurt put in, 'but tell me—') '. . . I'm very happy. I had only four lovers after you, but to make up for it, each was richer than the last, and now I'm exceptionally nicely established. He has a consumptive wife, the daughter of a general. She lives abroad. In fact, he has just left to spend a month with her at Davos.' ('Goodness, I've been there last Christmas.') 'He is elderly and very chic. And he adores me. And you, Kurt, are you happy?'

Kurt smiled and gave a little push to the boy in blue, who had come to a parting of paths: the child looked up at him with round eyes; then, making a tooting noise with his lips, pedalled on.

'. . . no, his father is a young Englishman. And look, his hair is done just like mine, but the colour is still redder. If anyone had told me then, when we stood on that stairs—'

He listened to her rapid chatter and recalled a thousand trifles, an old poem she liked to repeat ('I am the page of High Burgundy'), chocolates with liqueur inside ('No, this one is with marzipan again – always marzipan for little Erica – I want one with curaçao or at least kirsch'), the paunchy kings of moonlit stone in the Tiergarten, so dignified on a spring night with the lilacs in grey fluffy bloom under the arc lights, and moving patterns on the white stairs. Such sweet smells, oh, God . . . those two brief happy years when Erica had been his mistress he visualized as an irregular series of such trifles: the picture composed of postage stamps in her front hall; her way of jumping up and down on the sofa or of sitting on her hands, or of suddenly sprinkling his face with rapid little pats, and *La Bohème*, which she adored, the trips to the country when they had fruit wine on a terrace; the brooch she had lost there . . . All these vaporous frivolous pathetic memories came alive within him while Erica was telling him at top speed about her new apartment, her piano, her lover's business.

'Are you happy at least, Kurt?' she asked again.

'Remember—' he said, and sang offkey but with feeling: '*Mi chiamano Mimi . . .*'

'Oh, I'm not Bohemian any more,' she laughed with a little shake of her head. 'But you are still the same, Kurt: so (she shaped several consecutive words with her no longer maddening mouth, not finding the right one) – so lacking in common sense.'

'Such a nitwit,' he said, and gave the little boy, expectantly hunched over the handlebars, another push; tried to stroke his curly head, but he was already too far.

'You haven't replied; are you happy?' insisted Erica. 'Tell me, please, please.'

The poem's lilt kept coming back to him and he quoted:

'Her lips were pale, but when kissed, glowed red,
  And if the end one guesses,
Still I must not tell what I leave unsaid.
  About a queen's caresses.

Don't you remember, Erica, you would recite it with curtseys, oh, don't you remember?'

'I certainly don't. But I was asking you, Kurt. Does your wife love you?'

'Well, how should I put it. You see. . . . She is not what you'd call a passionate woman. She does not make love on a bench in the park, or on a balcony like a swallow.'

'Is she faithful to you, your queen?'

'Ihr' blasse Lippe war rot im Kuss. . . .'

'I bet she deceives you.'

'But I'm telling you she's cold and reasonable, and self-controlled. Lovers! She does not know the first letter of adultery.'

'You're not the best witness in the world,' laughed Erica. 'You never knew I deceived you until his fiancée rang you up. Oh, I can just see what you do with your wife. You love her and don't notice her. You love her – oh, ardently – and don't bother about what she's like inside. You kiss her and still don't notice her. You've always been thoughtless, Kurt, and in the long run you'll always be what you've been, the perfectly happy egotist. Oh, I have studied you carefully.'

'So have I,' he said.

'Thus speaks the page of High Burgundy
The train of a queen he bears,
Dum-dee-dee her mouth, her mouth dum-dee,
On the marble-pillared stairs.'

'You know, Kurt, to be quite frank, there were moments when you made me simply miserable. I would realize that you were merely skimming along the surface. You seat a person on a little shelf and think she'll keep sitting like that forever. But, you know, she tumbles off, and you think she still is sitting there, and even when she vanishes, you don't give a hoot.'

'On the contrary, on the contrary,' he interrupted, 'I'm very observant. The colour of your hair was blond and now it is reddish.'

As in the past, she gave him a tap of assumed exasperation.

'I've long stopped being cross with you, Kurt. Come and have coffee with me soon. He won't be back till mid-May. We'll have a chat, we'll remember old times.'

'Certainly, certainly,' he said, feeling suddenly bored, and knowing perfectly well that he would never do it.

She handed him her card (which a couple of minutes later he tore up and crammed into the ashtray of a taxi); she shook his hand many times in parting, still chattering very fast. Funny Erica. . . . That little face, the batting eyelashes, the turned-up nose, the hoarse hurried patter. . . .

The boy on the tricycle also proffered his hand and immediately wheeled away, his knees coming high and fast. Dreyer looked back as he walked and waved his hat several times; then he begged pardon of a clumsy lamppost, put on his hat, and walked on. On the whole – an unnecessary encounter. Now I shall never remember Erica as I remembered her before. Erica number two will always be in the way, so dapper and quite useless, with the useless little Vivian on his tricycle. Now was it right to let her infer that I am not quite happy? In what way am I unhappy? Why talk like that? Why should I want a hot little whore in my house? Perhaps her whole charm lies in the fact that she is so cold. After all, there should be a cold shiver in the sensation of true happiness. She's exactly that chill. Erica with her dyed hair cannot understand that the queen's coldness is the best guarantee, the best loyalty. I should not have answered like that. And besides, everything around, those sparkling puddles – why do bakers wear rubbers without socks, I don't know – but every day, every instant all this around me laughs, gleams, begs to be looked at, to be loved. The world stands like a dog pleading to be played with. Erica has forgotten a thousand little sayings and songs, and that poem and Mimi in her pink hat, and the fruit wine, and the spot of moonlight on the bench that first time. I think I'll make a date with Isida tomorrow.

Next day Dreyer was particularly cheerful. At the office he dictated to Miss Reich an absolutely impossible letter to an old respectable firm. In the evening, in the strangely lighted workshop where a miracle was slowly coming to life, he gave the inventor such slaps on the back that the latter doubled up. He telephoned he would be late for supper, and when he came home at half past ten, he kidded poor Franz, examining him on the science of salesmanship, asking him absurd questions such as: What would you do if my wife visited your department and before your very eyes stole Ronald? Franz, to whom humour, and especially Dreyer's humour, came a little hard, would open his eyes and spread his hands. This amused Dreyer, who was easily amused. Martha toyed with a teaspoon, now and then touching a glass with it and extinguishing the vibration with a cold finger.

In the course of that month she and Franz had investigated several new methods, and as before, she spoke of this or that procedure with such austere simplicity that Franz felt no fear, no discomfort, for a strange rearrangement of emotions was taking place in him. Dreyer had divided in two. There was the dangerous irksome Dreyer who walked, spoke, tormented him, guffawed; and there was a second, purely schematic, Dreyer, who had become detached from the first – a stylized playing card, a heraldic design – and it was this that had to be destroyed. Whatever method of annihilation was mentioned, it applied precisely to this schematic image. This Dreyer number two was very convenient to manipulate. He was two-dimensional and immobile. He resembled those photographs of close relatives cut out along the outline of the figure and reinforced with cardboard that people, fond of cheap effects, place on their desks. Franz was not conscious of the special substance and stylized appearance of this inanimate personage, and therefore did not pause to wonder why those sinister discussions were so easy and harmless. Actually Martha and he spoke of two different individuals: Martha's subject was deafeningly loud, intolerably vigorous and vivacious; he threatened her with a priapus that had already once inflicted upon her an almost mortal wound, smoothed his obscene moustache with a little silver brush, snored at night with triumphant reverberations; while Franz's man was lifeless and flat, and could be burned or taken apart, or simply thrown away like a torn photograph. This elusive gemination had already begun when Martha rejected poisoning as 'an attempt on human life with inadequate means' (a bit of subtle legality treated extensively in the long-suffering encyclopedia), and as something incompatible with matter-of-fact modern mores. She began talking of firearms. Her chilly rationality, combined, alas, with clumsy ignorance, produced rather weird results. Subliminally mustering recruits from the remotest regions of her memory, unknowingly recalling the details of elaborate and nonsensical shootings described in trashy novelettes, and thereby plagiarizing villainy (an act which after all had been avoided only by Cain), Martha proposed the following: first, Franz would acquire a revolver; then ('By the way, I know how to shoot,' Franz interjected) – fine, that helped ('Though you know, darling, you still ought to practise a little, somewhere in a quiet lane'). The plan was this: She would keep Dreyer downstairs until midnight ('How will you manage that?' 'Don't interrupt, Franz, a woman knows how'). At midnight, while Dreyer was celebrating her sudden submissiveness with champagne, she would go to the window in the next room, draw back the curtain, and stand there for a while with a sparkling flute glass in her raised hand. That would be the signal. From his post near the garden fence Franz would clearly see her within the fire-bright rectangle. She would leave the window open and rejoin Dreyer on the parlour divan. He would probably be sitting, his clothes in disarray, drinking champagne and eating chocolates. Franz would immediately vault the gate in the dark ('It's easy to do; of course, there are some iron spikes on it but you're such a fine athlete') and, quickly crossing the garden, on tiptoe so as not to leave any telltale foot traces, would enter through the French window she would have left ajar. The door to the parlour would be open. From its threshold he would fire half a dozen times in quick succession, as they do in American movies. For appearance's sake, before vanishing, he would take the dead saloonkeeper's wallet and perhaps the two ancient French silver candlesticks from the mantelpiece. Then he would go the way he had come. Meanwhile she would run upstairs, undress, and go to bed. And that was all.

Franz nodded.

Another way was as follows: She would go to the country alone with Dreyer. The two of them would go for a good tramp. He loved walking. She and Franz would have chosen beforehand a nice lonely spot ('In the woods,' said Franz, picturing to himself a dark grove of pines and oaks and that old dungeon on its wooded hill where cobolds had haunted his childhood). He would be waiting behind the tree with the reloaded revolver. When they had again killed him, Franz would shoot her through the hand ('Yes, that's necessary, darling, it is always done, it must look as if we had been attacked by robbers'). Franz would again take the wallet (which he could return to her later with the candlesticks).

Franz nodded.

These two projects were the basic ones. The others were merely variations on the theme. Believing, with so many novelists, that if the details were correct the plot and characters would take care of themselves, Martha carefully worked out the theme of the burglarized villa and that of the forest robbery (the two unfortunately tended rather to get mixed up). Here Franz turned out to have an unexpected and most fortunate gift: he could imagine with diagrammatic clarity his movements and those of Martha and coordinate them in advance with those concepts of time, space, and matter which had to be taken into account. In this lucid and flexible pattern only one thing remained always stationary, but this fallacy went unnoticed by Martha. The blind spot was the victim. The victim showed no signs of life before being deprived of it. If anything, the corpse which had to be moved and handled before burial seemed more active than its biological predecessor. Franz's thoughts travelled around this fixed point with acrobatic agility. All the necessary movements and their sequence were admirably calculated. The thing called Dreyer at the present time would differ from the future Dreyer only inasmuch as a vertical line differs from a horizontal. A difference of angle and perspective – nothing more. Martha unwittingly encouraged Franz in those abstractions because she always took for granted that Dreyer would be caught unawares and have no time to defend himself. For the rest, she imagined quite vividly and realistically how he would raise his eyebrows on seeing his nephew point a pistol at him, how he would begin to laugh, assuming that the weapon was a toy, and how he would finish his laughter in another world. When, in order to abolish all risk, she placed Dreyer in the position of a piece of merchandise, packaged, tied up and ready to be delivered, she did not realize how much easier this made things for Franz. 'Smart boy,' she would laugh, kissing him on the cheek, 'bright, bright darling.' Reacting to her praise, he presented a kind of estimate (which had to be burned afterwards, unfortunately): the number of paces from fence to window; the number of seconds needed to cover that distance; the distance from window to door and from door to armchair (into which Dreyer had been transferred from the couch at a certain point in their planning), and from the revolver hanging as it were in mid-air to the back of the conveniently placed head. And while Dreyer was actually sitting in that armchair and reading the Sunday papers in a shaft of April sunlight, Martha with a glowing comb in her chignon, wearing a new pink tailor-made dress, and coatless Franz, with Tom following them, a black ball in his jaws, would busily pace to and fro in the garden and along the wall of the villa up to the parlour window, and back again to the wicket, counting steps, memorizing them, rehearsing approaches and retreats, and Dreyer, arms akimbo, would come out on the terrace and presently join them in the garden and help discuss in his turn the new arrangement of flagged paths and flowerbeds that she and Franz were so diligently planning.

They continued their planning when alone in the drab beloved little room, with the still unsold big-nippled slave girl above the bed and a brand-new expensive, unwanted tennis racket in its frame. It was time to think of obtaining the weapon. As soon as they got to that stage, a ridiculous obstacle arose. They were both certain that a permit had to be obtained for the purchase of a revolver. Neither Martha nor Franz had the least idea how one obtained such a permit. They would have to make inquiries, go to the police maybe, and that might mean having to write and sign applications. It now became apparent that the acquisition of the tool was something many times vaguer than the image of its use. Martha could not tolerate such a paradox. She eliminated it by seeking out insurmountable difficulties in the execution of the project as well. There was for example the gardener – who acted also as a (bribable? druggable?) watchman – a level-headed husky old rascal who had sharp eyes for intruders and squashed caterpillars with a special juicy squeak and a special horrible twitch of iron-nailed finger and thumb which caused Franz, the first time he witnessed that green garrotte, to cry out like a girl. There was the policeman who frequently passed along the street as though strolling; miscalculations and flaws also turned up in the forest plan: after an excursion to Grunewald, Franz reported that it contained more picnickers than pines. There were lots of other woods in the suburbs, but one had to find a way to get him to go there. And when the fulfilment of these projects receded to its proper place, the question of procuring the weapon no longer seemed so insoluble: there existed probably friendly gun dealers in the northern part of the city who did not bother about permits, and once the gun was there, surely chance was on their side, and would place the target in the right position at the right moment. Thus Martha satisfied in passing her innate sense of correct relationships ('First things first' and 'If you want two noses, you should be content with one eye' were her favourite proverbs).

So now the time came to obtain a small dependable revolver. She imagined how Franz – slow, lanky, shy Franz – would make the rounds of gunshops, how the friendly salesman would suddenly start asking him tricky questions, how the idiot would remember later Franz's tortoise shell glasses and the explanatory gestures of his thin, white, innocent hands, how later, after the gun had been used and buried, some meddlesome detective would ferret all this out. . . . Now, if *she* should go and buy it. . . . Perhaps she thought Tom had the rabies and she wanted to shoot him, and actually did for practice – women can also learn to shoot well. And suddenly an extraneous image floated by, stopped, turned, and floated on like those cute objects that move by themselves in commercial cinema advertisements. She realized why the image of the revolver had in her mind such a definite form and colour, though she knew nothing about guns. Willy's face emerged from the depth of her memory; he laughed his fat laugh, and bent low examining something, and holding back Tom, who thought it was a plaything for him. She made another effort and remembered that Dreyer was sitting at his desk and showing Willy – what? a revolver! Willy had turned it in his hands, laughing, and the dog barked. She could remember nothing more, but that was sufficient. And she was amazed and gladdened to see how painstakingly and providently her mind had conserved for a couple of years that fleeting but absolutely indispensable image.

It was yet another Sunday. Dreyer and Tom went out for a little walk. All the windows in the villa were open. Sunlight made itself comfortable in unexpected corners of the rooms. On the terrace a breeze ruffled the pages of the April issue (already old) of a magazine with a photograph of the newly discovered, really lovely arms of Venus. First of all, Martha thoroughly explored the desk drawers. Among blue folders containing documents, she found several sticks of gold-tinted sealing wax, a flashlight, three guldens and one shilling, an exercise book with English words written in it, his grinning passport (who grins in official circumstances?), a pipe, broken, that she had given him a long long time ago, an old little album of faded snapshots, a recent snapshot of a girl that might have been Isolda Portz had she not worn a smart ski suit in the photo, a box of thumbtacks, pieces of string, a watch crystal, and other trivial junk the accumulation of which always infuriated Martha. Most of these articles, including the copybook and the winter sports advertisement, she deposited in the wastebasket. She thrust back the drawers violently and, leaving the deafened desk, went up to the bedroom. There she rummaged through two white chests-of-drawers, finding among other things a hard ball that bore Tom's toothmarks which God knows how had got into the drawer where her husband's ten pairs of shoes stood in two neat rows. She threw the ball out of the window. She ran downstairs. In passing by a mirror she noticed that the powder had come off her nose and her eyes were positively haggard. Should she see a lung doctor or a heart specialist? Or both? She inspected a few more drawers in various rooms, chiding herself for looking in absurd places, and finally decided that the gun was either in the safe, to which she did not have a key (the Will was there, the treasure, the future!), or else at the office. She tried the accursed desk again. It cringed and stood holding its breath at her menacing approach. The drawers began clacking like slaps on the face. Not here! Not here! Not here! She noticed a brown briefcase in one. She lifted it angrily. Beneath it she saw deep in the drawer a small revolver with a mother-of-pearl handle. Simultaneously her husband's voice came from nearby, and pushing the briefcase back, she quickly closed the drawer.

'Heavenly day,' Dreyer was saying in a singsong voice. 'Almost like summer.'

Morosely, without turning, she said:

'I'm looking for some pills. You had pyramidon in your desk. My head is splitting.'

'I don't know. Nobody's head should split on such a lovely day.'

He seated himself on the leather arm of a chair and wiped his brow with a handkerchief.

'You know what, my love,' he said. 'I've got an idea. Listen – what's Franz's telephone number? – I'll call him up, and we'll all drive to the tennis club. Good idea? Charming idea?'

'When do you want to lunch? He is coming for lunch. Why don't you ring somebody else and play after lunch?'

'It's only ten now. We can lunch at half past one. It's a shame to waste such weather. You come too. Okay, okay, okay?'

She consented to come only because she knew how unbearable it would be for Franz to be with him alone. 'I'll call him,' she said.

The landlord asked who she was, and why she wanted to talk to his lodger. But Martha told him to mind his own business. Franz, taken by surprise, arrived in an ordinary suit, having simply changed to sneakers. Dreyer, puffing with impatience and afraid that at any moment a thunderhead might form in the sky, rushed him upstairs and issued him a pair of white flannel pants which he had bought in London a couple of years ago, and which were too tight for him. Standing there, arms akimbo, eyes bulging, head cocked, he watched as Franz changed. The poor boy stank like a goat. And those long drawers on a day like this! Whoever sewed on that monogram was not a professional – at least not a professional seamstress. Franz, numbed with embarrassment, well aware that his underwear was not what it should be, and grotesquely fearful that something about the whole situation might give away the messy secrets of adultery, had trouble with the changing of trousers, as he stepped from foot to foot, hopping and extending one leg, and trying to persuade himself that it was only a bad dream.

Dreyer too began stepping from one foot to the other. The awfulness dragged on. The trousers seemed too long and too voluminous, and in the course of that sack race a spasmodic movement landed Franz on the top of a broken luggage rack which had no business to be in the dressing room. Dreyer made vague motions as if he wanted to help. No less nightmarish was the business of buttoning the dummy's fly, which he was told to do himself. After which the fitter with two fingers delicately pulled up the waist, adjusted the side straps, expertly slipped a belt around the wooden waist, and sank on one knee to measure the leg with a tape which he wore as one does a dancing serpent. Finally he gave a chuckle of relief and approval, and dealt Franz a robust slap on the buttocks. The blow kept vibrating for quite a long time in the poor fellow's system whereas his double squeamishly advanced on bent legs, tucking in his bottom. The tingle endured even in the taxi. When they got out Dreyer gave him another exuberant slap, this time with Franz's racket, which he was about to forget in the cab. *'Aber lass doch,'* said Martha to her vulgar husband.

On the terra-cotta red courts white figures darted to and fro, while hired children picked up the balls at top speed. All around, a tall wire fencing was hung with green tarpaulin. White tables and wicker armchairs stood in front of the clubhouse. Everything was very clean and sharply defined. Martha fell into conversation with a blond-legged beautiful pale-eyed woman in a white skirt no bigger than a paper lampshade. They ordered drinks – an ice-cold American coffee-dark concoction. Dreyer went inside to change. Dark Martha and the platinum lady spoke loudly but Franz did not catch a single word. A stray ball bounced past him onto a table, onto a chair, onto the turf. He picked it up and examined it: it was quite new and signed in violet by a firm well represented at the Dandy. Franz put the ball on the table. Two other young women went by with bare arms and legs, putting the red soles of their silk-laced white shoes (Mercury – no, Loveset) down on the lawn quite flat as if walking barefoot. Their eyes were happy, their mouths red. All that was in the past, dreams and desires of a boyhood long gone. They blinded him with a blended smile, mistaking him for somebody. Beside one of the further courts a kind of judge, or guardian of games, sat on a stepladder chair watching the ball cross the net, and like an automaton shaking his head in rhythm – denying, denying, denying, they are not for you. In the black aperture of the door appeared a dazzling white Dreyer.

'Let's go,' he cried, and with a bouncing step, a fluffy towel around his neck, two rackets under his arm, and a box of new balls in his hand, headed for court number six. Martha said au revoir to the lady and moved to another chair to watch the two players. On the court, with the thoroughness of an executioner preparing the block, Dreyer was already measuring the height of the net with his racket. Franz stood on the side of the court near his mistress, looking up at a passing airplane. With stern tenderness she took note of his dear boyish neck, his shining glasses, his elegant tennis trousers which were a bit too roomy around the hips but otherwise very becoming. Having completed his sinister manipulations, Dreyer jogged heavily to his base line. Franz remained standing in the centre of his own rectangle. A scrawny little girl with a blank expression on her freckled face bounced toward him one of the balls from the box. As the ball jumped, it struck him in the groin, he tried to pat it down with his racket but it passed between his legs and she threw him another which eluded him too. This time, however, he ran after it, and finally picked it up from under the feet of a player on the adjacent court, who muffed his shot and glared at him. Zestful Franz ran back with the pocketed ball and assumed his former position. With a tolerant grin Dreyer waved at him to stand further back and ladled out a warm-up underhand serve in tolerably correct style copied from that of the club coach Count Zubov. Franz swung at it and with a beginner's luck returned it by means of a tremendous, though unorthodox, whack that propelled the ball well beyond Dreyer's reach. Martha could not refrain from applauding. Dreyer dealt out another underhand serve. Franz's weapon swished mightily but the ball flew by unscathed and was neatly fielded by the little girl behind him. Then, taking his time, Franz held the ball found in his pocket at arm's length, gauged the altitude, dropped the ball, and attempted to hit it on the rebound. Again nothing happened except that he stepped on the ball and nearly fell. He trotted to the net, where the ball had finally got entangled. Dreyer told him to go well back and continued to send him ball after ball. Franz lunged and whirled but his main stroke remained a swing in a void. The little girl, who was beginning to enjoy herself, kept flitting this way and that, cupping every ball in her tiny hands, and with nonchalant precision rolling it or tossing it back to Dreyer.

'Stop getting in the way,' cried Martha to the impudent little catcher, but the child did not hear or did not understand. She had a brass ring on her finger. Might be a dirty little gypsy or something.

The ordeal continued. Finally Franz in the ecstasy of despair did get a crack at the ball, and it soared over the roof of the pavilion.

Dreyer slowly walked up to the net and beckoned to Franz.

'Have I won?' asked Franz, panting.

'No,' said Dreyer, 'I just want to explain something. We are not playing American baseball or English cricket. This is a game called "lawn tennis" because it was first played on grass.' He invariably mispronounced 'lawn' as if rhymed with 'down.'

Then, slowly and sadly, Dreyer returned to his base line, and the same thing began all over again. Martha could bear it no longer. She shouted from where she sat:

'Enough, enough! You see perfectly well he can't—'

She had wanted to shout 'can't play' but a gust of spring wind cut off the ultimate word. Franz intently examined the strings of his racket. A young fellow, also lanky and also wearing glasses, who had been watching the play with predatory irony, stepped forward and bowed, and Dreyer, indicating with his racket to Franz that he could go, joyfully greeted the newcomer, whom he knew to be a strong player.

Franz walked over to Martha and sat down beside her. His face was pale and drawn, and glistened with sweat. She was smiling at him but he wiped his glasses and did not look her way. 'Dear,' she whispered, trying to catch his eye; she caught it, but he shook his head gloomily, his teeth clenched.

'Everything is all right,' she said softly. 'It won't happen again. I'll tell you something,' she added still more softly. 'Listen, I found it.'

His gaze slipped away but she firmly recaptured it. '. . . I found it in the desk. You'll simply take it the day before. Understand?'

He blinked. 'You'll catch cold like that,' she said. 'There's a bad wind blowing. Put on your sweater and coat, darling.'

'Not so loud,' whispered Franz. 'Please.'

She smiled, looked around, shrugged.

'I must explain to you. . . . No, listen, Franz – I have a completely new plan.'

Dreyer had just made a good shot, gently slicing the ball close to the net, and glanced from under his brows at his wife, pleased that she was looking at him.

'You know what,' whispered Martha. 'Let's go. I must explain everything to you.'

Dreyer missed a volley and returned to his base line, shaking his head. Martha called him over. She told him that her headache was worse, and that she should not be late for lunch. Dreyer nodded and went on with the game.

They could not find a taxi but anyway it was only a few minutes of fast walking. They cut across a park where happy lovers were melting in each other's arms on yesteryear's dry leaves. She began explaining on the way.

The plan was delightfully innocent: it was based on his study of English. Occasionally he would ask her to dictate something to him. She knew fewer words than he but her pronunciation was perhaps a little better than his or at least different from his: her 'lawn' for example rhymed with 'own' and not 'down,' which was ridiculous, as she had told him many times, the obstinate fool. He used to take down her dictation in an exercise book. Then he would compare what he had written with the text. And it was on such a dictation that everlasting happiness in a private park would depend. They would take a Tauchnitz novel and find a suitable sentence in it, such as 'I could not have acted otherwise' or 'I am shooting myself because I am tired of life.' The rest was clear. 'In your presence,' she said, 'I shall dictate to him the chosen sentence. Of course, he must write it not in a copybook but on a clean sheet of letter paper. In fact I have already destroyed that copybook. As soon as he has written that down but just before he has lifted his head you'll come up to him very close and a little behind him, as if you wanted to look over his shoulder, and then very carefully—'

10

Almost three months had already elapsed since that unforgettable day when the Inventor (by now capitalized in Dreyer's mind) had produced the first samples of his automannequins, as he called them. Because of the strong naked lighting, his workshop resembled a medical laboratory, and indeed it had been exactly that in the past. Demonstrations were conducted in a large bare room that had been once a repository for dead bodies and parts of such bodies, which ribald students (some of them, though not all, respectable old surgeons today) frequently used to place in various attitudes and reciprocal positions suggestive of strange orgies. The Inventor and Dreyer stood in a corner of the room and watched in silence.

In the centre of the brightly illuminated floor, a plump little figure about a foot and a half tall, tightly bundled in brown sackcloth that left exposed only a pair of short blood-red legs made of some substance resembling rubber and shod in baby boots with buttons, walked back and forth with a very natural human-like motion, swaggering a wee bit and turning at every tenth step with a built-in little cry between 'hep' and 'help' meant to disguise the slight creak of its mechanism. Dreyer, hands clasped on his stomach, watched with soft emotion, as a sentimental visitor watches a child – perhaps his own little bastard – to whose first toddle he is being treated by a proud mother. The Inventor, who had let his beard grow and now looked like an Oriental priest in mufti, kept tapping his foot lightly in time to the movements of the little figure. 'Goodness,' said Dreyer suddenly in a high-pitched voice, as if he were ready to burst into tears of tenderness. The hooded gnome did in fact walk about very catchingly. That brown cloth was there only for decency's sake. Afterwards, when the mechanism had died, the Inventor unwrapped his prototypical automannequin and laid bare its works: a delicate system of joints and muscles, and three small but remarkably heavy batteries. One thing about this invention could be discerned even in this first crude model; what impressed one was not so much those electrical ganglia and the rhythmic transmission of current as the springy, somewhat stylized, but wonderfully lifelike gait of the mechanical infant. Paradoxically, it paced the floor more like a meditating mathematician than a babe in the wood. The secret of this motion lay in the flexibility of voskin – the very special stuff with which the Inventor had replaced live bones and live flesh. The two pseudopodia of this original voskiddy seemed alive not because it moved them (a mechanized 'strollie' or *zhivulya* are after all no rarity, they breed like rabbits on sidewalks around Easter or Christmas) but rather because the material itself, animated by a so-called galvanobiotic current, remained active all the time – rippling, tensing, slackening as if organically alive or even conscious, a double ripple grading into triple dapple with the smoothness of reflections in water. It walked without jerking – this was the wonder of it. And it was this that Dreyer appreciated most while reacting rather indifferently to the technical mystery, imparted to him first in code, then in coded explanation of the code, by the cagy Inventor.

'What is its sex? Can you tell me?' asked Dreyer as the brown little figure stopped before him.

'Not differentiated yet,' answered the Inventor. 'But in a month or two there will be two males and one female over five feet high.'

In other words, the infant had to grow up. It was necessary to create not only a semblance of human legs, but also the semblance of a graceful human body and expressive face. The Inventor, however, was neither an artist nor an anatomist. Dreyer therefore found him two helpers: an old sculptor whose work was so lifelike that he managed to convey the impression of acute chorea, for example, or, say, the beginning of a sneeze; and a professor of physiology who, in trying to explain the well-known capacity of waking up at a self-imposed hour, had written a long treatise which explained nothing but contained the first description of the 'self-awareness' of muscles with beautiful illustrations in colour. The workshop soon began to look as if those medical students had again been horsing about with dismembered cadavers. The professor of anatomy and the fantastic sculptor assisted the Inventor very successfully. One was lean, pale, nervous, with long hair combed back and a huge Adam's apple; the other was sedate and bald, and wore a high starched collar. Their appearance afforded Dreyer a source of endless delight, since the first was the professor, and the second, the artist.

He could now clearly imagine the full-grown, perfect, elegantly dressed automannequins walking back and forth in a huge bay window of the emporium, among potted plants, discreetly disappearing to change their clothes behind the scenes, and stalking in again to the delight of the populace. It was a poetical vision and no doubt a lucrative enterprise. In mid-May he bought the patent rights from the Inventor at a comparatively low price and now he was debating – what would be better – to create a sensation on the Kurfürstendamm by putting those figures literally into circulation or to sell the invention to a foreign syndicate: the former was richer fun, the latter, safer profit.

As happens in the lives of many businessmen, he began to feel in that spring of 1928 that his affairs somehow or other were assuming a certain independent existence. The part of his funds that was in a state of constant fruitful gyration moved by momentum, and moved too rapidly; he seemed to be losing control over his wealth, seemed no longer able to stop this great golden wheel at will. Half of his fortune was reasonably safe; but the other, which he had created in a year of freakish luck – at a time when luck, a light touch, and his special kind of imagination were needed – had now become too lively, too mobile. An optimist by nature, he hoped that this was but a temporary loss of control and did not for an instant suppose that the increased spin might transform the wheel of fortune into the shimmer of its gyration, and that if he stopped the wheel with his hand, it would prove to have been nothing but its own golden ghost. But Martha, who now more than ever loathed her husband's whimsical levity (even though it had once helped him to become rich), could not help feeling that he might dance his way into some financial disaster before she was able to remove him and halt the light-hearted spin herself.

The store was doing good business but the profits did not accumulate as solidly as they should have. The stock market had recently given a sudden shiver; he had gambled on it and lost, and now was gambling again. In all this Martha saw a doomful admonition. She might have been willing to grant him a reprieve for some solid deal, for she admitted that she 'trusted his scent'; but that juggling with shares was too risky. Why procrastinate when every passing month might mean a further dwindling of wealth?

On that sunny and terrible morning, as soon as she and Franz returned from the tennis club, she led him to the study to show him the revolver. From the threshold she indicated with a rapid glance and a barely perceptible motion of the shoulder the desk at the far end of the room. There, in a drawer, lay the instrument of their happiness.

'In a moment you'll see it,' whispered Martha and glided toward the desk. But at that instant Tom entered the room with a bold buoyant step. 'Get that dog out of here,' said Franz. 'I can't do anything with the dog here.' 'Out!' cried Martha. Tom laid back his ears, extended his gentle grey muzzle, and slunk behind a chair. 'Oh, get him out,' said Franz through clenched teeth with a convulsive shudder. Martha clapped her hands. Tom slipped beneath the chair and emerged on the other side. She gestured threateningly. Tom jumped back in time and, licking his chops with a hurt expression, trotted toward the door. On the threshold he looked back, one front paw raised. Martha, however, was coming at him. He submitted to the inevitable. She slammed the door shut. An obliging draft promptly banged the windowpane. 'All right now, let's hurry,' she said crossly. 'Why are you sulking there? Come here.'

She quickly yanked open the drawer. She lifted the brown briefcase. Under it, a gleaming object showed. Franz mechanically extended his hand and took it. He turned it this way and that.

'Are you sure—' he began apathetically.

He heard Martha snort, and looked up. She uttered a dry laugh and walked away.

'Put it back,' she said, standing at the window and drumming on the pane. No wonder Willy had laughed.

'I said put it back. You see perfectly well it's a cigar lighter.'

'Yes, of course. But really quite like a little revolver. Very fancy, isn't it? I think I saw a couple of them at the store.' Noiselessly, he shut the drawer.

That day Martha realized a saddening thing. Until then she had acted or wanted to act all her life. Now she saw that some kind of atrocious dreamland was encroaching upon her charts. A beginner's self-confidence might be pardonable – but that pardonable phase had come and gone. All right – she should never have accepted to marry that clown with the foul-smelling monkey in his arms; all right – she should not have been impressed by his money, she should not have hoped in her youthful naivete to make an ordinary, dignified, obedient husband out of that joker. But at least she had arranged her life the way she wished. Almost eight years of grim struggle. He wanted to take her to Ceylon or Florida, if you please, instead of buying this elegant villa. She needed a sedentary husband. A subdued and grave husband. She needed a dead husband.

There were several days when she retired as it were into the remotest deserts of her spirit to review her blunders and collect her forces so as to return purified to the task, and thenceforth commit none of the former errors. Elaborate combinations, complicated details, phony weapons – all this was to be abandoned. From now on the motto would be: simplicity and routine. The sought-for method must be absolutely natural, absolutely pure. Intermediaries please abstain. Poison was a procuress; the pistol, a pimp. Each might betray her. One must stop buying novelettes about the Borgias. One cannot kill a man with a cigar lighter as some had apparently thought she had thought.

Franz shook his head or nodded it, according to this or that turn of her earnest speech. The little room was brimming with sunlight. He was sitting on the window ledge. The panes were thrown open and secured with wedges of wood. In spite of its being a holiday, the builders were stubbornly at work, clinking and knocking higher and higher. A girl's voice cried something from a window below, and another girl's voice, still more angelic, responded from a balcony on the opposite side of the street. This was the season of guitar music on the river at home, of rafts gently singing in the shadow of the willows.

His back began to feel hot. He slid off the window ledge onto the floor. With her legs tightly crossed, showing a strip of fat thigh under her skirt, Martha sat sideways at the table. In the inexorable light her skin looked coarser and her face seemed broader, perhaps because her chin was propped on her fist. The corners of her damp lips were lowered, her eyes looked upward. A complete stranger within Franz's consciousness observed in passing that she rather resembled a toad. Martha moved her head. Reality returned. And once again everything became oppressive, dark, and relentless.

'. . . strangle him,' she muttered. 'If we could simply strangle him. With our bare hands.'

The great Dr Hertz had told her a couple of years before that her cardiogram showed a remarkable, not necessarily dangerous, but certainly incurable abnormality which he had seen only in one other woman, a Hohenzollern, who was still alive at almost forty, and now it seemed to Martha that her heart would burst, unable to withstand the feeling of hatred that Dreyer's every move and sound aroused in her. Sometimes at night, when he approached her with a tender little laugh, she felt an urge to dig her hands into his neck and squeeze, squeeze with all her might. And vice versa, when on a recent occasion she had made him promise not to sell the best of his three apartment houses for the ridiculous price he was offered by Willy, and in generous compensation had offered him of her own accord a brief caress, his unexpected lack of manly response had revolted her as much as his advances. She realized how difficult it was in these circumstances to reason logically, to develop simple, smooth, elegant plans, when everything within her was screaming and raging. Yet if she must survive something had to be done. Dreyer was spreading out monstrously before her, like a conflagration in a cinema picture. Human life, like fire, was dangerous and difficult to extinguish; but, as in the case of fire, there must be, there simply must be, some universally accepted, natural method of quenching a man's fierce life. Enormous, tawny-haired tanned from tennis; wearing bright yellow pyjamas, redly yawning; radiating heat and health, and making the various grunting noises that a man who cannot control his gross physicality makes when waking up and stretching, Dreyer filled the whole bedroom, the whole house, the whole world.

More and more often, and with a recklessness she no longer noticed, Martha escaped from that triumphant presence to her lover's room, arriving even at hours when he was still at the store and the vibrant sounds of construction in the sky were not yet replaced by nearby radios, and would darn a sock, her black brows sternly drawn together as she awaited his return with confident and legitimate tenderness. Without his obedient lips and young body she could not live more than a single day. At that instant in their meeting when still feeling the receding ripples of pleasure she would open her eyes, it seemed strange to her that Dreyer had not been destroyed by her lover's thrusts. She would soon try to entice sluggish Franz anew, and having succeeded not without trouble (that job at the store exhausted the poor pet!), she would feel again that Dreyer was perishing, that each frantic stroke wounded him more deeply, and finally, that he collapsed in terrible pain, howling, discharging his intestinal fluids, and dissolving in the unbearable splendour of her joy.

Yet, as if nothing had happened, he would revive, walk noisily through all the rooms and, cheerful and hungry, sit opposite her at meals, folding a slice of ham, spearing it with an energetic fork, and making a circular motion with his moustache as he chewed.

'Help me, Franz, oh, help me,' she would murmur sometimes, shaking him by the shoulders.

His eyes were totally submissive behind their well-wiped lenses. However, he could not think of anything. His imagination was at her command; it was ready to work for her, but it was she who had to give his fancy its impulse and food. Outwardly he had changed a great deal during these last months: he had lost weight, his protruding cheekbones made him look more than ever like a hungry Hindu, a curious debility blurred his movements as if he were existing only because existing was the proper thing to do; but one did it unwillingly and would have been glad to return at any moment to a state of animal stupor. His day ran its course automatically but his nights were formless and full of terror. He took sleeping pills. The morning jolt of his alarm clock was like a coin dropped into a vending machine. He would rise; shuffle to the smelly toilet (a little dark hell in its own right), shuffle back, wash his hands, brush his teeth, shave, wipe the soap from his ears, dress, walk to the subway station, get on a non-smoking car, read the same old advertisement ditty overhead, and to the rhythm of its crude trochee reach his destination, climb the stone staircase, squint at the mottled pansies in the bright sun on a large flowerbed in front of the exit, cross the street, and do everything in the store that he was supposed to do. Returning home in the same way, he would do once again all that was expected of him. After her departure, he would read the newspaper for a quarter of an hour or so because it was customary to read newspapers. Then he would walk over to his uncle's villa. At supper he would sometimes repeat what he had read in the paper, reproducing every other sentence verbatim but strangely jumbling the facts in between, so that Dreyer had fun egging him on and then correcting him. Around eleven he would leave. He would make his way home always along the same sidewalk. A quarter of an hour later he would be undressing. The light would go out.

His thoughts were characterized by the same monotony as his actions, and their order corresponded to the order of his day. Why has he stopped the coffee? Can't flush if the chain comes off every time. Dull blade. Piffke shaves with his collar on in the public washroom. These white shorts are not practical. Today is the ninth – no, the tenth – no, the eleventh of June. She's again on the balcony. Bare arms, parched geraniums. Train more crowded every morning. Clean your teeth with Dentophile, every minute you will smile. They are fools who offer their seats to big strong women. Clean your teeth with Dentophile, clean your minute with your smile. Out we file.

And behind these regular everyday thoughts, as behind words written on glass, lay darkness, a darkness into which one ought not to peer. One was treated, however, to strange glimpses. Once it seemed to him that a police official, smelling strongly of cheese, with a briefcase under his arm, kept looking at him with suspicion from the opposite seat. His mother's letters contained terrifying insinuations: she maintained for example that he misspelled words or left them unfinished. At the store, the face of a rubber sea lion, intended for the amusement of bathers, began to resemble the face of Dreyer, and Franz was glad when a Mrs Steller, Robbe Avenue 1, had him pack it and send it to her. Catching a whiff of blooming lindens, he would remember nostalgically the schoolyard in his hometown where they touched the bark of a lime in a game of tag. Once a young girl with bouncing breasts, in a short red frock, almost ran into him; she carried a bunch of keys in her hand, and he fancied he recognized in her a janitor's daughter he had longed for, many ages ago. These were mere ephemeral glints of consciousness; he would instantly revert to semi-existence.

Then at night, in his drugged sleep, something more significant would burst through. Together with naked Martha, he would be sawing off the head of Piffke in a public toilet, even though in the first place he was undistinguishable from the Dreyers' dead chauffeur, and in the second, was called Dreyer in the language of dreams. Horror and helpless revulsion merged in those nightmares with a certain nonterrestrial sensation, known to those who have just died, or have suddenly gone insane after deciphering the meaning of everything. Thus, in one dream, Dreyer stood on a ladder slowly winding a red phonograph, and Franz knew that in a moment the phonograph would bark the word that solved the universe after which the act of existing would become a futile, childish game like putting one's foot on every flag edge at every step. The phonograph would croon a familiar song about a sad Negro and the Negro's love, but by Dreyer's expression and shifty eyes Franz would understand that it was all a ruse, that he was being cleverly fooled, that within the song lurked the very word that must not be heard, and he would wake up screaming, and could not identify a pale square in the distance until it became a pale window in the dark, and then he would drop his head on the pillow again. All at once Martha, her face dreadful – waxy, glossy, heavy-jowled, with the wrinkles of age and grey hair – would run in, grab him by the wrist, and drag him onto a balcony suspended high above the street, and on the pavement below stood a policeman holding something in front of him, and slowly growing until his face reached the balcony and, holding a newspaper, in a loud voice he read Franz's death sentence to him.

His colleagues in the sports department, athletic Schwimmer and his effeminate Swedish friend (who now sold bathing suits), happened one day to notice his pallor and advised him to sunbathe on the banks of the Grunewald lake on Sundays. But an icy indolence hung upon Franz, and besides, an hour of leisure meant an hour with Martha. As for her, she mistook his moodiness for the malady from which she herself suffered, the white-hot fever of incessant murderous thought. It gladdened her when, in Dreyer's presence, upon meeting her gaze, Franz would sometimes start clenching and unclenching his hands, breaking matches, or fiddling with the saltcellar. She believed that her death rays ran clear through him, and that she had only to stab him with that beam of light, and then a tense particle of his soul where the imprisoned image of death lay hidden would explode and make a gigantic Franz stamp on the crawling hornet. Conversely, she was irritated when Franz complained. She would shrug her shoulders as she listened to his muttering.

'Don't you understand – he is insane,' Franz would repeat. 'I know he's insane.'

'Nonsense, not insane, a little peculiar. This is even an advantage. Stop twitching, please.'

'But it's horrible,' Franz insisted. 'He has stopped bringing me coffee, I don't know when, and then he suddenly appeared with a bowl of red beef tea.'

'Oh, stop. Who cares? He is quite harmless. He has a sick wife.'

Franz kept shaking his head. 'One never sees her. I've rattled the door thousands of times to get him out of the toilet but it's always he, not she. I don't like it.'

'Silly. Why, I tell you, that's an advantage. Nobody snoops on us. It's my impression that we are very lucky in this respect.'

'God knows what goes on in that room of theirs,' sighed Franz. 'Such strange noises come from there sometimes. Not laughter, rather the clucking of a hen.'

'That will do,' said Martha quietly.

He stopped speaking, sitting naked on the edge of the bed and staring at the floor.

'Oh, darling, darling,' she said cheerlessly and impetuously. 'Does this matter? Don't you feel the days are going by while we keep aimlessly discussing things, not knowing where to begin? Don't you see, this way we'll drive ourselves to the point where one fine day we'll simply pounce on him, tear him apart? . . . We can't go on like that. We've got to think of something. And you know lately he's been so terribly alive. Is he stronger than we? Is he more alive than this, and this, and *this?*'

But she was right, oh, she was right! The old boy was aflame with rich life. He was young, his backhand was now as good as his forehand, his digestion was a dream, he would go to Brazil or Zanzibar next winter. Isolda was expensive and unfaithful but every once in a while he purged himself erotically with her in the pretty little flat he had rented for both of the sisters (Ida however had soon been whisked away to Dresden by a jealous lover); at a party given by the Commercial Consul of Luxembourg, tall Martha with her black silks, lovely shoulders and emerald ear pendants, had eclipsed all the other ladies. He had decided to conceal from her, until the proper moment, his special project, although it was true that on three or four occasions he had hinted at a new extraordinary undertaking. But then again how would he go about explaining to her what absorbed him. It was impossible. She would dismiss it as an inane whim. Mechanical mannequins indeed! What next, Pygmalion? You, Galatea. No, that was a hopeless line. She would say: 'You're spending your time on rubbish.' Yes, but what marvellous rubbish. He smiled at the thought that she too had her eccentricities. The iced rose water applied to her face at bed time. Those Hindukitsch gymnastics nearly every day. He ran his cane clatteringly along the pales of a fence. They were walking along the sunlit side of the street. His companion, the black-bearded Inventor, kept hinting that it might not be a bad idea to cross over to the other, shady, sidewalk. But Dreyer did not listen. If he enjoyed the sun, others were bound to enjoy it too. 'It's still quite a long way,' sighed his companion. 'Are you quite sure you want to walk?' 'With your permission,' said Dreyer absentmindedly, and quickened his pace. What fun it was to be alive. At that moment, for example, this black-bearded genius was taking him to see something most amusing. If he were to stop a passer-by and ask him, 'Try to guess, friend, what I'm on my way to see, and *why* I must see it?' The passer-by would never be able to answer. And, as if that were not enough, all those people in the street scurrying by, waiting at streetcar stops: what a bunch of secrets, astonishing professions, incredible recollections. That fellow, for instance, with the cane and the very English yellow moustache: who knows, perhaps during the war he had been assigned the dreary and preposterous task of transmuting for national use sundry elements of captured enemy uniforms; but after two years of it, the material had begun to dwindle, and he was sent to the front where he enjoyed the exhilaration of at least one good battle among the ruins of a village, once renowned for its hops and hogs, and then hostilities were suspended, and a last soldier was killed by a sack of declaration-of-peace leaflets dropped from an airplain. But why assign one's own memories to strangers? That old man there on the bench had been in his youth – oh, I don't know – perhaps, a celebrated acrobat; or that black-bearded foreigner, rather a dull companion between us be it said, had perhaps made a spectacular invention. Nothing was known, and anything was possible.

'To the right,' said the dull companion, breathing heavily. 'That building over there with the statues.'

In an annex to the courthouse, the police had staged an exhibition of crime. One respectable burgher, who suddenly, for no good reason, had dismembered a neighbour's child, was found to have in his apartment an artificial woman. She could walk, wring her hands, and make water, and was now in that police museum. Impelled by professional anxiety, the Inventor wanted to take a look at her. They were led to her by a retired gendarme whom Dreyer bribed to make the mechanism work. The poor woman turned out to be rather crudely made, and the mysterious substance of which the papers had spoken was, thank God, only gutta-percha. Her power to move was also exaggerated. A clockwork device permitted her to close her glass eye and spread her legs. They could be filled up with hot water. Her body hair was real, and so were the brown locks falling over her shoulders. All things considered, there was nothing new about her – merely a vulgar doll. The scornful and happy Inventor left at once but Dreyer, always afraid of missing something entertaining, strolled through all the rooms. He examined the faces of criminals, enlarged photographs of ears, messy fingerprints, kitchen knives, ropes, faded shreds of clothing, dusty jars, dirty test tubes – a thousand trivial articles that had been wronged – and again rows of photographs, the pasty faces of unwashed, bady dressed murderers, and the puffy faces of their victims who in death came to resemble them; and it was all so shabby, so stupid, that Dreyer could not help smiling. He was thinking what a talentless person one must be, what a poor thinker or hysterical fool, to murder one's neighbour. The deathly grey of the exhibits, the banality of crime, pieces of bourgeois furniture, a frightened little console on which a bloody imprint had been found, hazel nuts injected with strychnine, buttons, a tin basin, again photographs – all this trash expressed the very essence of crime. How much those simpletons were missing! Missing not only the wonders of everyday life, the simple pleasure of existence, but even such instants as this, the ability to look with curiosity upon what was essentially boring. And then the final Bore: at dawn, breakfastless, pale, top-hatted city fathers driving to the execution. The weather is cold and foggy. What an ass one must feel in a top hat at five in the morning! The condemned man is led into the prison yard. The executioner's assistants plead with him to behave decently, and not to struggle. Ah, here's the axe. Presto – the audience is shown the severed head. What should a frock-coated burgher do when looking at it – give it a nod of commiseration, a frown of reproach, a smile of encouragement as if to say: 'See, how simple and quick it all was'? Dreyer caught himself thinking that it might be interesting to wake up at the crack of dawn and, after a thorough shave and a hearty meal, go out in striped prison pyjamas into the yard, touch the plump executioner's muscles with some appropriate joke, give the whole assembly a friendly wave of the hand, take a good last stare at the white official faces. . . . Yes, all those faces are uncommonly pale. Here, for example, is a young chap who chopped his parents to death: how big-eared and pimply he is. Here is a sullen gentleman who left a trunk at the station with his fiancée's corpse. And here's Dr Guillotin's invention – oh, no, that's a medieval Swiss contraption of exactly the same type – board, wooden collar, two uprights, the blade between them. Monsieur Guillotin, you are an impostor! Ah, the American dentist's chair. The dentist is masked. The patient also has a mask with holes for the eyes. They slit his trouserleg at the calf to attach the electrode. Aha. The current is turned on. Hop-hop, as over a bumpy road. What dreary fools! A collection of idiotic faces and tormented objects.

It was lovely outside, a lush wind was blowing. The soles of passers-by left silver traces on the sun-glorified asphalt. How lovely, blue and fragrant, our Berlin is in the summer. It wouldn't be bad by the sea either. Those clouds are radiant – vacation clouds. Workmen lazily repairing the pavement. How good it all is. How amusing it would be, he thought, to search the faces of those workmen, of those passers-by, for the facial expressions he had just seen in countless photographs. And to his surprise, in everyone he met Dreyer recognized a criminal, past, present, or future; soon he was so carried away with this game that he began inventing a special crime for each. He watched a round-shouldered man with a suspicious suitcase; he went up to him and asked for a light. The man shook the ashes off his cigarette and made the commonplace little connection but Dreyer noticed how that hand trembled, and felt sorry that he could not reveal a detective's badge. Face after face slipped by, eyes avoided his, and even in plump, motherly housewives he distinguished the skeletons of murder. Thus he walked, spinning his cane like a propeller, having an exceptionally good time, grinning involuntarily at strangers, and noting with pleasure their momentary embarrassment. Then he grew tired of the game, felt hungry and thirsty, and quickened his step. As he drew near the gate, he noticed his wife and nephew in the garden. They were standing motionless side by side, watching him approach. And he felt a pleasant relief at seeing at last two familiar, two perfectly human faces.

II

'Please, my dear,' said Willy Wald, 'don't. You have already taken two stealthy looks at your wrist and then at your husband. Really, it's not late.'

'And have some more strawberries,' said Willy's wife.

Dreyer said: 'We'll have to stay a while, my love. Because I can't remember my story.'

'Please try to recall it,' said Willy from the depths of his armchair.

'. . . or some liqueur, perhaps,' said Mrs Wald in her tired, melodious, affected voice.

Dreyer pounded his forehead with his fist. 'I've got the beginning and the middle. My emporium for the end!'

'Don't worry, it will come,' said Willy. 'If you go on worrying your wife will get even more bored. She's a strict lady. I'm afraid of her.'

'. . . at this time tomorrow we shall be on our way to Pris,' said Mrs Wald, gathering momentum, but her husband interrupted.

'She's taking me to Paris! I know it's a fizzy city, but it always gives me heartburn. Still I'm going, I'm going. By the way, you haven't told me of your own summer plans. I've heard of a fellow who could not remember a funny story and burst a blood vessel.'

'It's not the fact that I can't remember it that hurts,' Dreyer said plaintively. 'What hurts is that I'll remember it the minute we part. No, we haven't decided yet. Isn't that so, my love? We haven't decided yet? In fact' (turning to Willy), 'we haven't discussed it at all. I know she hates the Alps. Venice means nothing to her. It's all very difficult. There was a twist at the end, such an amusing one. . . .'

'Drop it, drop it,' puffed Willy. 'How come you haven't decided yet? It's the end of June. High time.'

'Perhaps,' said Dreyer with a quizzical glance at his wife, 'perhaps we might go to the seaside.'

'Water,' nodded Willy. 'Lots of blue water. That's good. So would I, with delight. But I'm being dragged off to Paris. I am a remarkably good diver, though you wouldn't believe it.'

'I can't even swim,' glumly answered Dreyer. 'I'm no good at some sports. Same thing with skiing. I seem always to stay at the same point: the swing, the knack, the equipoise, just aren't there. I'm not sure those new skis were the right ones for me. My love, I know you hate the seaside but let's go there once more. We'll take Franz and Tom with us. We'll splash and puddle. And you'll go boating with Franz, and get as brown as milk chocolate.'

And Martha smiled. Not that she realized whence came that breath of moist freshness. The magic lantern of fancy slipped a coloured slide in – a long sandy beach on the Baltic where they had once been in 1924, a white pier, bright flags, striped booths, a thousand striped booths – and now they were thinning, they broke off, and beyond for many miles westward stretched the empty whiteness of the sands between heather and water. Water. What do you do to extinguish a fire? An infant could tell you that.

'We'll go to Gravitz,' she said, turning to Willy.

She grew unusually animated. Her glossy lips parted. Her elongated eyes flashed like jewels. Two sickle-shaped dimples appeared on her flaming cheeks. Excitedly she began telling Elsa Wald about a little dressmaker (they are always 'little') whom she had discovered. And ecstatically she praised Elsa's perfume. Dreyer, eating strawberries, watched her and rejoiced. She had simply never beamed and babbled so prettily when visiting the Walds ('they are your friends, not mine').

'We'll have to have a serious talk,' she said on the way home. 'Sometimes you do get good ideas. Look, tomorrow morning you write and reserve two adjacent rooms and a single one at the Seaview Hotel. But the dog we'll leave – it would only be a bother. You'd better make haste or there'll be no rooms left.'

Being a little drunk, he glued himself to her warm nape. She pushed him away quite good-naturedly and said:

'I see you're not only a lecher but also a liar.'

He suddenly looked worried. 'What do you mean?'

'I thought,' she said, 'you told me – when was that? A year ago? – that you were taking lessons at the Freibad, and that you now swam like a fish.'

'An inexcusable exaggeration,' he answered, much relieved. 'A very poor fish, really. I keep afloat for three meters, and then I sink like a log.'

'Except that logs don't sink,' said Martha merrily.

Make haste! But now haste was lighthearted. With waves and sunlight all around, how easy to breathe, to kill, to love. The single word 'water' had resolved everything. Although Martha knew nothing about mathematical problems and the pleasure of elegant proof, she recognized the solution of her problem at once by its simplicity and limpidity. This harmonious obviousness, this elementary grace made her ashamed – as well she might be – of her gropings and clumsy fancies. She felt an inordinate desire to see Franz that very minute, or at least to do something – to cable him the code word at once, but for the time being the message ran MIDNIGHT TAXI STOP RAIN GATE FRONT HALL STAIRS BEDROOM PLEASE STOP ALL RIGHT HURRY UP GOOD NIGHT. And tomorrow was Sunday – how do you like that! She had warned Franz that if the weather did not improve she would not go to see him because Dreyer would not be playing tennis. But even this delay, which once would have driven her into a rage, now seemed trifling in the light of her newfound confidence.

She woke up a little later than usual, and her first sensation was that the night before something exquisite had happened. On the terrace Dreyer had finished his coffee and was reading the newspaper. When she came down, radiant, wearing pale-green crepe, he rose and kissed her cool hand as he always did at their Sunday morning meetings, but this time he added to it a good-natured twinkle of gratitude. The silver sugar bowl blazed blindingly in the sun, dimmed slowly, and flamed forth again.

'Can the courts still be wet?' said Martha.

'I've telephoned,' he answered, and went back to his paper. 'They are soaked. An archeologist has found a tomb in Egypt with toys and blue thistles three thousand years old.'

'Thistles are not blue,' said Martha, reaching for the coffee pot. 'Have you written about the rooms?'

He nodded without raising his eyes and went on nodding even more gently as he read his paper, cheerfully reminding himself between the nods and the lines to dictate it tomorrow at the office.

Oh, keep nodding . . . keep playing the fool . . . it does not matter now. He's a first-rate swimmer – that's not tennis for you! She, too, was born on the banks of a big river, and could stay afloat for hours, for days, forever.

She used to lie on her back, and the water would lap and rock her, so delicious, so cool. And the bracing breeze penetrating you as you sat naked with a naked boy of your age among the forget-me-nots. These thoughts came without effort. She need not invent, she had only to develop what was already there in outline. How happy her darling would be! Should she ring him up and say only one word: *Wasser?*

Dreyer noisily folded his paper as if wrapping a bird in it and said: 'Let's go and have a walk, eh? What do you say?'

'You go,' she replied. 'I have to write some letters. We must head off Hilda, you know.'

He thought: what if I ask her, tenderly, tenderly. It's a free morning. We are lovers again.

But emotional energy had never been his forte, and he said nothing.

A minute later, Martha, from the terrace, saw him walk to the gate with his raincoat over his arm, open the wicket, let Tom pass first like a lady, and saunter off, lighting up a cigar as he went.

She sat motionless. The sugar bowl alternately blazed and dimmed. All at once a grey little spot appeared on the tablecloth; then another beside it. A drop fell on her hand. She rose, looking up. Frieda began hurriedly clearing away the dishes and the tablecloth, also glancing now and then at the sky. Thunder rumbled, and an astonished sparrow landed on the balustrade – and darted away. Martha went into the house. The door of the hallway toilet was banging. Frieda, already half-drenched, with the tablecloth in her embrace, laughing and muttering to herself, rushed from the terrace kitchenward. Martha stood at the centre of the oddly dark parlour. Now everything outside was gurgling, murmuring, breathing. She wondered if she should first ring him up, but her impatience was too strong – the fuss with the telephone would be a waste of time. She put on her mackintosh with a rustling sound and snatched up an umbrella. Frieda brought her hat and handbag from the bedroom. 'You ought to wait it out,' said Frieda. 'It's a regular deluge.' Martha laughed and said she had quite forgotten an appointment at a café with Mrs Bayader and another lady, an expert in rhythmic respiration ('Mixed respiration,' Frieda, who knew more than she ought to have known, kept snorting every now and then the whole morning.) The rain began drumming on the taut silk of her umbrella. The wicket swung shut, splashing her hand. She walked quickly along the mirrory sidewalk, hurrying toward the taxi stand. The sun struck the long streams of rain causing them to slant, as it were, and presently they turned golden and mute. Again and again the sun struck, and the shattered rain now flew in single fiery drops, and the asphalt cast reflections of iridescent violet, and everything grew so bright and hot that wet-haired Dreyer shed his raincoat as he walked, and Tom, who was somewhat darker after the rain, perked up and marched on a brown dachshund. Tom and the dachshund circled in one spot, or rather Tom circled while the dackel turned abruptly in one piece every now and then, until Dreyer whistled. He walked slowly, looking right and left, trying to find the newly built cinema that Willy had mentioned the night before. He found himself in a district he had seldom visited although it was not far from his house. He turned into a park to give the dog more exercise and then cut across a piece of wasteland adjoining an unfamiliar boulevard. A little farther he crossed a square and saw at the corner of the next street a tall house bared of most of its scaffolding: its first story was ornamented with a huge picture, advertising the film to be shown on the opening night, July 15, based on Goldemar's play *King, Queen, Knave* which had been such a hit several years ago. The display consisted of three gigantic transparent-looking playing cards resembling stained-glass windows which would probably be very effective when lit up at night: the King wore a maroon dressing gown, the Knave a red turtleneck sweater, and the Queen a black bathing suit. 'Must not forget to order those rooms tomorrow,' reflected Dreyer, and another important note that the faithful Miss Reich would write over her signature: Dr Eier must leave the city and to his great regret cannot continue to pay for the flat where you persist in receiving other idiots, or something along those lines.

He was about to turn back when Tom gave a short muffled

bark and Franz came out of a little café wiping his mouth with his knuckles.

'Well, well, well, fancy running into you,' exclaimed Dreyer. 'Starting the day with a schnapps, eh?'

'My landlord has stopped serving me breakfast,' said Franz. What a horrible encounter. Side by side they walked, eyed by luminous puddles.

They almost never had occasion to be alone together, and Dreyer now realized that they had absolutely nothing to talk about. It was an odd feeling. He tried to clarify it for himself. He saw Franz practically every other evening at his house but always in Martha's presence; Franz fitted naturally into those usual surroundings, occupying a place long since set aside for him, and Dreyer never spoke to him in any but a joking casual way seeking no information, and expressing no feeling, accepting Franz on trust amid the rest of the familiar objects and people, and interrupting with irrelevant remarks the silly and dull narratives that Franz vaguely directed at Martha. Dreyer was well aware of his own secret shyness, of his inability to have a frank, serious, heart-to-heart talk with a person whom ruthless chance confronted him with. Now he felt both apprehension and an urge to laugh at the silence that was being wedged between him and Franz. He had not the least idea what to do about it. Ask him where he was going? He cleared his throat and gave Franz a sidelong glance. Franz looked at the ground as he walked.

'Where are you going?' asked Dreyer.

'I live near here,' said Franz with an indefinite gesture. Dreyer was looking at him not unkindly. Let him look, thought Franz. Everything in life is senseless, and this walk is senseless too.

'Fine, fine,' said Dreyer. 'I think I've never been here. I cut through a wilderness of kitchen gardens, and then suddenly there were half-built houses all around me. By the way, you know what – why don't you show me your apartment?'

Franz nodded. Silence. Presently he pointed to the right and both involuntarily quickened their step in order to accomplish at least one not wholly aimless act – a right turn. Tom, too, looked ennuied. He was not overfond of Franz.

'How stupid,' thought Dreyer. 'I must find something to tell him. We are not following a hearse.' He wondered if he should not tell him about the electric mannequins. It might interest a young man. The subject in fact was so entertaining that he had to make quite an effort not to gush about it at home. Lately the

Inventor had asked him not to visit the workshop, saying he wanted to prepare a surprise, and then the other day, looking very smug, he invited Dreyer to come. The sculptor who looked like a scientist and the professor who looked like an artist also seemed extremely pleased with themselves. Two young men from the store, Moritz and Max, could hardly hide their giggles. Pulling at a cord, the Inventor drew open a black curtain, also an innovation, and a pale dignified gentleman in dinner jacket, with a carnation in his buttonhole, walked out of the side door at the left, crossed the room at a lifelike though somcwhat somnambulic gait, and left by the side door at the right. Behind the scenes he was seized by Moritz and Max, who changed his clothes while a youth in white, with a racket under his arm, wandered across the room in his turn and was immediately followed by somnambule number one, now wearing a grey suit with an elegant tie and carrying a briefcase. He dropped it absentmindedly before leaving the stage but Moritz retrieved it and followed him to the exit. Meanwhile the youth reappeared, now sporting a cherry-red blazer, and after him the older man, soberly clad in a raincoat, ambled along in his melancholy and mysterious dream.

Dreyer found the show absolutely entrancing: not only did those grandly trousered legs and properly shod feet move with a stylized grace that no mechanical toy had ever achieved before, but the two faces were fashioned with exquisite care in the same wax-like substance as the hands. And when vulgar Max humourously impersonated the younger automannequin by stalking and prancing in his wake on the delightful youth's final appearance, none could doubt which of the two personages had more human charm, though one Inventor was so much more experienced than the other. Presently the mature gentleman came by for the last time, and at this point his creator had devised matters in such a way as to have the re-tuxedoed one (minus the carnation mislaid in some avatar) stop in mid-stage, jiggle his feet a little as if demonstrating a dance step, and then continue toward the exit with his arm crooked as if escorting an invisible lady. 'Next time,' said the Inventor, 'a woman will be added. Beauty is easy to render because beauty is based on the rendering of beauty, but we are still working on her hips, we want her to roll them, and that is difficult.'

But could one describe all this to Franz? Told in a jocular tone it would be of no interest, and if made serious, Franz might not believe it since Dreyer had pulled his leg too frequently in the past. All at once a saving thought flashed through his mind. Franz did not know yet that he was being invited to the seaside and of course should be told the good news; and simultaneously Dreyer recalled the end of the anecdote that had eluded him on the eve. First, though, he told him about the trip, saving the anecdote for the last. Franz mumbled that he was very grateful. Dreyer explained to him what to buy for the trip, charging everything to Uncle, *selbstverständlich!* Franz, reviving a little, thanked him again more eloquently.

'Are you thinking of marriage?' asked Dreyer (Franz made the gesture of a clown's stooge when presented with a conundrum). 'Because I might find you a very amorous bride.'

Franz grinned. 'I'm too poor,' he replied. 'Perhaps if I got a raise.'

'That's an idea,' said Dreyer.

'We are almost there,' said Franz, and almost fell over Tom, who had stopped.

Dreyer decided he would wait to tell his story – which was really an extremely funny one – until they were in Franz's room: certain vehement gestures and extravagant attitudes had to accompany the story. This was a fatal postponement. He never told it. They were now in front of the house where another good anecdote was in the process of what botanically minded folklorists call 'exfoliating.' Tom stopped again, looking up and then back. 'March-march,' said Dreyer, and with his knee pushed the intelligent hound.

'I live there,' said Franz pointing at the fifth floor.

'Well, let's go in by all means,' said Dreyer, and held the door open for Tom, who shot upstairs with a whimper of excitement.

'Good Lord, I must get him some other quarters. No nephew of mine should live in a slum,' reflected Dreyer, as he climbed the stairs whose meagre carpeting disappeared at an elevation well below timberline. While they climbed Martha had time to finish darning a last hole. She was sitting on the dear decrepit couch leaning over her work, her lips puckering and moving in a happy domestic pout. The landlord had said that Franz would be back in a moment. He had popped out to eat a bigger breakfast than a sick old woman could prepare. Martha got up to return the socks to their drawer. She was already wearing the emblematic slippers and had laid out the little rubber basin coquettishly covered with a clean towel. She stopped in a half-bent attitude holding her breath. 'He's here,' she thought and gave a blissful sigh. Then a strange patter of nonhuman footfalls came along the corridor; a horribly familiar bark rang out. 'Quiet, Tom, behave yourself,' said Dreyer's cheerful voice. 'Third door on your right,' said Franz's voice. Martha made for the door in order to turn the key in the lock. The key was on the other side. 'Here?' asked Dreyer, and the handle moved. She braced her whole body against the door, holding the handle with her strong hand. The key was heard to turn this way and that. Tom was ardently sniffing under the door. The handle attempted to jerk again. There were now two men against her. She slipped and lost a slipper, which had happened already in another life. 'What's the matter?' said Dreyer's voice. 'Your door doesn't open.' Her efficient lover was helping to press on the door. 'Two idiots,' thought Martha coldly, and started to slide again. She heaved with her shoulder and forced it shut. Franz was muttering: 'I don't understand it at all. Maybe it's some joke of my landlord's.' Tom was barking his head off. He shall be destroyed tomorrow. Dreyer was chuckling and advising Franz to call the police. 'Let's kick it in,' he said. Martha felt she could not hold the door any longer. Suddenly there was silence, and in the silence a squeaky querulous voice uttered the magic anti-sesame: 'Your girl is in there.'

Dreyer turned. An old man in a dressing gown, clutching a kettle, was shaking his shaggy grey head at the young imbecile who had covered his face with his hands. Tom was sniffing at the old man. Dreyer burst out laughing and, dragging the dog by the collar, started to walk away. Franz accompanied him to the hallway, and tripped over a pail. 'Aha, that's what you're up to,' said Dreyer. He winked, nudged Franz in the solar plexus, and went out. Tom looked back – and then followed his master. Franz, wooden-faced and a bit unsteady on his feet, returned along the corridor and opened the now unresisting door. Rosy, dishevelled, panting, as though after a fight, Martha was looking for her slippers.

Impetuously she embraced Franz. Beaming and laughing, she kissed him on the lips, on the nose, on his spectacles, then sat him down beside her on the bed, gave him a drink of water, he rocked limply, and dropped his head in her lap; she stroked his hair and softly, soothingly, explained to him the only, the liquid, the resplendent solution.

She was home before her husband, and when he arrived, and Tom trotted up to her, she gave the dog a withering derisive look.

'Listen,' said Dreyer, 'our little Franz – no, just imagine—' he spluttered and shook his head for a long time until he finally told her. The image of his sombre and awkward nephew fondling a big, hefty sweetheart was unspeakably comic. He recalled Franz hopping on one foot in soiled underpants and his mirth increased. 'I think you're simply envious,' said Martha, and he tried to hug her.

The very next time Franz came to supper his clever uncle began poking fun at him. Martha kicked her husband under the table. 'My dear Franz,' said Dreyer, moving out of her shoe's range, 'perhaps you don't feel like going away to a distant shore, perhaps you are perfectly happy in town. You can speak frankly. After all I was young myself.'

Or else he would turn to Martha and casually observe: 'You know, I've hired a private detective. His job is to see that my clerks lead an ascetic life, do not drink, do not gamble, and especially do not—' Here he pressed his fingers to his lips as if he had said too much, and glanced at his victim. 'Of course I'm joking,' he continued in mock confusion, and added in a thin artificial voice, as if changing the subject: 'What lovely weather we're having.'

Only a few days remained before the scheduled departure. Martha was so happy, so calm, that nothing could now affect her very deeply: her husband's witticisms would soon end as would everything else – his cigar, his eau de cologne, his shadow with the shadow of a book on the white terrace. One thing only – the fact that the director of the Seaview Hotel had had the impudence to take advantage of the vacational influx and demand a colossal price for the rooms – only this could still perturb her. It was certainly a pity that Dreyer's removal would be so expensive – especially now, when they had to save every penny because before you knew it he could in those last few days lose, she said, his entire fortune. Some grounds for such apprehension did exist. But at the same time she experienced a certain odd satisfaction at the thought that now, at the very moment when he was to die under her supervision, Dreyer seemed to have exhausted the brilliant business imagination, the gift of daring enterprise, thanks to which he had prepared a fortune to leave to his not ungrateful widow.

She did not know that paradoxically, at that period of decline and indolence, Dreyer had quietly started on the very expensive affair of the automannequins. Question: Were they not too glamorous, too extravagant, too original and luxurious, for the needs of a stodgy bourgeois store in Berlin? On the other hand, he did not doubt one minute that the invention would fetch a spectacular price if one could dazzle and enchant the prospective buyer. Mr Ritter, an American businessman who had the knack of making fancy stuff work for him, was soon to arrive. I'll sell it, reflected Dreyer. Wouldn't mind selling the whole store as well.

Secretly he realized that he was a businessman by accident and that *his* fantasies were not saleable. His father had wanted to be an actor, had been a make-up man in a travelling circus, had tried to design theatrical scenery, wonderful velvet costumes, and had ended as a moderately successful tailor. In his boyhood Kurt had wanted to be an artist – any kind of artist – but instead had spent many dull years working in his father's shop. The greatest artistic satisfaction he ever derived was from his commercial ventures during the inflation. But he knew quite well that he would appreciate even more other arts, other inventions. What prevented him from seeing the world? He had the means – but there was some fatal veil between him and every dream that beckoned to him. He was a bachelor with a beautiful marble wife, a passionate hobbyist without anything to collect, an explorer not knowing on what mountain to die, a voracious reader of unmemorable books, a happy and healthy failure. Instead of arts and adventures, he meanly contented himself with a suburban villa, with a humdrum vacation at a Baltic resort – and even that thrilled him as the smell of a cheap circus used to intoxicate his gentle bumbling father.

That little trip to Pomerania Bay was in fact proving to be quite a boon for everybody concerned, including the god of chance (Cazelty or Sluch, or whatever his real name was), once you imagined that god in the role of a novelist or a playwright, as Goldemar had in his most famous work. Martha was getting ready for the seaside with systematic and blissful zest. Lying on Franz's breast, sprawling all over him, strong and heavy, and a little sticky from the heat, she whispered into his mouth and ear that his torments would be soon allayed. She purchased – not at her husband's store – oh, no – various festive fripperies, a black bathing suit, a beachrobe zigzagged with blue and green, flannel slacks, a new camera, and a lot of bright clothes, which, she chided herself with a smile, was reckless since she would be so soon in mourning. Dreyer depended on the emporium for a tremendous beach ball and a new type of water wings.

She wrote to her sister Hilda, who had tentatively suggested they all spend summer together, that this year plans were uncertain, they might go for a few days to the seaside, or again they might not, she would write if they did and found they wanted to stay longer. She permitted Frieda to remain in the attic but forbade her to receive visitors there. She told the gardener that hysterical Tom had bitten her, that she did not wish to upset her husband, but that she wanted the beast to be put quickly to sleep as soon as they left for Gravitz. The gardener seemed about to demur, but she pushed a fifty-mark note into his honest, caterpillar-stained claw, and the old soldier shrugged his consent.

On the eve of their departure she inspected all the rooms of the villa, furniture, dishes, pictures, whispering to herself and to them that in a very short time she would return, she would return free and happy. That day Franz showed her a letter from his mother. The woman wrote that Emmy would be getting married in a year. 'In a year,' smiled Martha, 'in a year, my darling, another wedding will be taking place too. Come on, cheer up, stop picking your navel. Everything is fine.'

They were meeting for the last time in the shabby room which already had an apprehensive unnatural look as happens when a furnished room parts with its tenant forever. Martha had already taken the red slippers home with her and hidden them in a trunk but she did not quite know what to do with the doilies, the two pretty cushions, and the dainty implementa so full of memories. With a heavy heart she advised Franz to wrap it all up and mail it to his sister as a thoughtful wedding present. The little room was aware it was being talked about and was assuming a more and more strained expression. The lewd bidders were appraising the big-nippled bronze-bangled slave girl for the last time. The pattern on the wallpaper – bouquets of blood-brown flowers in a regular succession of repeated variations – arrived at the door from three directions but then there was no further place to go, and they could not leave the room, just as human thoughts, admirably coordinated though they may be, cannot escape the confines of their private circle of hell. Two suitcases stood in a corner, one brand-new in brown leatherette, with its pretty little key still attached to the grip, a sweetheart's gift; the other, a black fibrous affair, bought a year ago at a market stall, and still quite usable except that one lock would sometimes fly open without provocation. All that had been brought into this room, or had accumulated there in the course of ten months, disappeared in those two suitcases which were to depart on the morrow – forever.

That last night Franz did not go out for supper. He closed the empty chest-of-drawers, looked around, opened the window, and seated himself with his feet on the ledge. He must somehow get through this night. The best thing was not to move, not to think, to sit and listen to the far-off automobile horns, to gaze at the blue ink of the sky, at a distant balcony where a lamp glowed under its orange shade, and two happy, innocent, carefree people were playing chess, bent over the bright oasis of the happy table. That third of a man's consciousness, the imaginable future, had ceased to exist for Franz except as a dark cage full of monstrous tomorrows huddled up in an amorphous heap. What had struck Martha as the first realistic, logical solution of all their problems had all but dealt the last blow to his sanity. It would be as she had said – or would it? A flutter of panic brushed his heart. Maybe it was not yet too late. . . . Maybe he should write to his mother, or to his sister and her fiancé to come and take him away. Last Sunday fate had almost saved him, it might save him again, yes – send a telegram home, come down with typhus, or perhaps lean forward a little and slip into the ever-ready embrace of greedy gravity. But the flutter passed. It would be as she had said.

Barefoot, coatless, he sat there a long time hugging his knees without moving, without changing the position of his thighs, even though a knob on the ledge hurt him and a humming mosquito was preparing to strike at his temple. It was by now quite dark in the doomed room, but there was nobody to turn on the light and there would never be anybody if he fell off the sill. On the distant balcony the chess game had long since ended. One by one, or by twos and even threes, all the windows had grown dark. Presently he felt stiff and cold, and slowly clambered back into the room and went to bed. Sometime after midnight the landlord passed noiselessly along the corridor. He checked if there was a slit of light under Franz's door, listened with bent head, and went back to his room. He knew perfectly well that there was no Franz behind the door, that he had created Franz with a few deft dabs of his facile fancy. Yet the jest had to be brought to some natural conclusion. It would be silly to have a figment of one's imagination using up expensive electricity or trying to open a jugular vein with a razor. Besides, old Enricht was getting bored with this particular creature of his. It was time to dispose of him, and replace him with a new one. One sweep of his thought arranged the matter: let this be the fictitious lodger's last night; let him go tomorrow morning – leaving the usual insolent mess as they all do. He postulated, therefore, that tomorrow was the first of the month, that the lodger himself wished to leave – that, in fact, he had paid what he owed. Everything now was in order. Thus, having invented the necessary conclusion, old Enricht, alias Pharsin, dragged up in retrospect and added to it in a lump that which in the past must have led up to this conclusion. For he knew perfectly well – had known for the last eight years at least – that the whole world was but a trick of his, and that all those people – eight former lodgers, doctors, policemen, garbage collectors, Franz, Franz's lady friend, the noisy gentleman with the noisy dog, and even his own, Pharsin's, wife, a quiet little old lady in a lace cap, and he himself, or rather his inner roommate, an elder companion, so to speak, who had been a teacher of mathematics eight years ago, owed their existence to the power of his imagination and suggestion and the dexterity of his hands. In fact, he himself could at any moment turn into a mousetrap, a mouse, an old couch, a slave girl led away by the highest bidder. Such magicians should be made emperors.

The waking hour struck. With a scream, shielding his head with his arms, Franz leapt off the bed and rushed to the door; there he stopped, trembling, looking around myopically, already aware that nothing special had happened, that it was seven a.m. on a hazy, tender, melting morning with its hullabaloo of sparrows and an express train that was to leave in an hour and a half.

He had slept in his day shirt and had sweated profusely. His clean linen was already packed and anyway it was not worth the trouble of changing. The washstand was bare except for the thin relic of what had been a beige cake of violet-scented soap. He spent a long time scraping up with his fingernail a hair that was stuck to the soap; the hair would assume a different curve but refuse to come off. Dry soap collected under his fingernails. He started to wash his face. That single hair now stuck to his cheek, then to his neck, then tickled his lip. The day before he had packed the landlord's towel. He paused pondering – and dried himself with a corner of the bed sheet. There was no point in shaving. His hairbrush was packed but he had a pocket comb. His scalp felt scaly and itched. He buttoned up his wrinkled shirt. Never mind. Nothing mattered. Trying to ignore loathsome contacts, he attached his soft collar, which immediately grasped him around the neck like a cold compress. A broken fingernail caught in the silk of his tie. His second-best trousers, which had lain where they had been shed, at the foot of the bed, had gathered some nameless fluff. The clothes brush was packed. The ultimate disaster occurred while he was putting on his shoes: a shoelace broke. He had to suck the tip and ease it into its hole with the result that two short ends were diabolically difficult to make into a knot. Not only animals, but so-called inanimate objects, feared and hated Franz.

At last he was ready. He put on his wristwatch and pocketed the alarm clock. Yes, it was time to leave for the station. He donned his raincoat and hat, responded with a shudder to his reflection in the mirror, picked up the suitcases, and, bumping against the doorjamb as if he were a clumsy passenger in a speeding train, went out into the corridor. The remnants of his physical self that he left behind were a little dirty water at the bottom of the wash basin and a full chamber pot in the middle of the room.

He stopped in the passage, stunned by an unpleasant thought: good manners bade him take leave of old Enricht. He put down the suitcases and knocked hurriedly at the landlord's bedroom door. No answer. He pushed the door and stepped in. The old woman whose face he had never seen sat with her back to him in her usual place. 'I'm leaving; I want to say good-bye,' he said, advancing toward the armchair. There was no old woman at all – only a grey wig stuck on a stick and a knitted shawl. He knocked the whole dusty contraption to the floor. Old Enricht came out from behind a screen. He was stark naked and had a paper fan in his hand. 'You no longer exist, Franz Bubendorf,' he said dryly, indicating the door with his fan.

Franz bowed and went out without a word. On the stairs he felt dizzy. Setting down his load on a step, he stood clutching the banister. Then he bent over it as over a ship's side and was noisily and hideously sick. Weeping, he collected his valises, re-clicked the reluctant lock. As he proceeded downstairs, he kept meeting various traces of his misadventure. At last the house opened, let him out, and closed again.

12

The main thing of course was the sea: greyish blue, with a blurred horizon, immediately above which a series of cloudlets glided single-file as if along a straight grove, all alike, all in profile. Next came the curve of the bathing beach with its army of striped booth-like shelters, clustering especially densely at the root of the pier which stretched far out amid a flock of rowboats for hire. If one looked from the Seaview Hotel, the best at Gravitz, one could catch now and then one of the booths suddenly leaning forward and crawling over to a new location, like a red-and-white scarab. On the land side of the beach ran a stone promenade, bordered by locust trees on whose black trunks, after the rain, snails would come to life and stick out of their round shells a pair of sensitive yellow little horns that made no less sensitive Franz's flesh creep. Still farther inland came in a row the facades of lesser hotels, pensions, souvenir shops. The balcony of the Dreyers acted the hotel's name. Franz's room sulkily faced a town street parallel to the promenade. Beyond that stretched the second-class hotels, then another parallel lane with the third-class accommodations. The further from the sea the cheaper they grew as if the sea were a stage and they, rows of seats. Their names attempted in one way or another to suggest the sea's presence. Some of them did it with matter-of-fact pride, others preferred metaphors and symbols. Here and there occurred feminine names such as 'Aphrodite' to which no boarding house could really live up. There was one villa that either in irony or owing to a topographical error called itself Helvetia. As the distance from the beach increased, the names grew more and more poetical. Then abruptly they gave up and became Central Hotel, Post Hotel, and the inevitable Continental. Hardly anybody hired any of the poor boats near the pier, and no wonder. Dreyer, a wretched sailor, could not imagine how he or any other tourist would care to go out rowing on that desolate expanse of water, when there were so many other things to do at the seaside. For instance? Well, sunbathing; but the sun was a little cruel to the russet of his skin. Sitting around in cafés was not unpleasant although it could be overdone too. There was the Blue Terrace café where the pastry, he thought, was so good. The other day as they were having ice chocolate there, Martha counted at least three foreigners among the crowd. One, judging by his newspaper, was a Dane. The other two were a less easily determinable pair: the girl was trying in vain to attract the attention of the café cat, a small black animal sitting on a chair and licking one hind paw rigidly raised like a shouldered club. Her companion, a suntanned fellow, smoked and smiled. What language were they speaking? Polish, Esthonian? Leaning near them against the wall was some kind of net: a bag of pale-bluish gauze on a ring fixed to a rod of light metal.

'Shrimp catchers,' said Martha. 'I want shrimps for dinner tonight.' (She clicked her front teeth.)

'No,' said Franz. 'That's not a fisherman's net. That's for catching mosquitoes.'

'Butterflies,' said Dreyer, lifting an index finger.

'Who wants to catch butterflies?' remarked Martha.

'Oh, it must be good sport,' said Dreyer. 'In fact, I think to have a passion for something is the greatest happiness on earth.'

'Finish your chocolate,' said Martha.

'Yes,' said Dreyer. 'I think it's fascinating, the secrets you find in most ordinary people. That reminds me: Piffke – yes, yes, fat pink Piffke – collects beetles and is a famous expert on them.'

'Let's go,' said Martha. 'Those arrogant foreigners are staring at you.'

'Let's go for a good ramble,' suggested Dreyer.

'Why don't we hire a boat?' said Martha for a change.

'Count me out,' said Dreyer.

'Anyway, let's go somewhere else,' said Martha.

As she passed the cat's chair, she tilted it and said 'Shoo,' and the cat, magically four-legged again, slipped off the seat and vanished.

Dreyer strolled off alone, leaving his wife and nephew on another terrace. This was the second or third tour he was making of the local display windows. Immemorial souvenirs. Picture postcards. The most frequent object of their derision was human obesity and its necessary opposite, Herr and Frau Matchshin of Hungerburg. A monstrous bottom in bathing tights was being pinched by a red crab (resurrected from the boiled), but the nipped lady beamed, thinking it was the hand of an admirer. A red dome above the water was the belly of a fat man floating on his back. There was a 'Kiss at Sunset,' emblemized by a pair of huge pygal-shaped impressions left on the sand. Skinny, spindle-legged husbands in shorts accompanied pumpkin-bosomed wives. Dreyer was touched by the many photographs going back to the preceding century: the same beach, the same sea, but women in broad-shouldered blouses and men in straw hats. And to think that those over-dressed kiddies were now businessmen, officials, dead soldiers, engravers, engravers' widows.

A sea breeze made the awnings clack. Little bags of pink muslin were cramed with seashells – or was it hard candy? A barometer in the image of a gents' and ladies' lavatory with different sexes emerging according to differences in the weather engaged for a while his awed attention. A second-rate store of men's clothes advertised a liquidation sale. Local seascapists depicted storm-tossed ships, foam-spattered rocks, and the reflection of a yellow moon in an indigo sea. And for no particular reason Dreyer suddenly felt very sad.

Weaving his way among the ramparts of sand that surrounded each bather's ephemeral domain, hurrying to nowhere in order to prove by a great show of haste how much his merchandise was in demand, an itinerant photographer, ignored by the lazy crowd, walked with his camera, yelling into the wind: 'The artist is coming! The divinely favoured, *der gottbegnadete* artist is coming!'

On the threshold of a shop that sold only Oriental wares – silks, vases, idols (who needed all that at the seaside?) – stood an ordinary untanned little man who followed with his dark eyes the promenaders as he waited in vain for a customer. Whom did he resemble? Yes, poor old Sarah's sick husband.

In the café where he presently joined our two farcical schemers, Martha was brought the wrong pastry and flew into a rage; for a long time she called to the overworked waiter, a mere boy, while the pastry (a splendid cream-oozing éclair) lay on its plate, lonely, despised, unwanted.

Less than a week had passed, and several times already that tender melancholy had come over Dreyer. True, he had experienced it before ('the melting heart of an egotist,' Erica had once called it, adding: 'You can hurt people or humiliate them, you are touched not by the blind man but by his dog'); but of late the melancholy had become less tender, or the tenderness more demanding. Perhaps it was the sun that had softened him up or maybe he was growing old, losing maybe something, and coming to resemble in some obscure way the pictureman whose services no one wanted and whose cry the children mocked.

When he went to bed that night he could not go to sleep – an unusual occurrence. On the previous day the sun, under the pretense of a caress, had so mutilated his back that he yearned for a spell of dull weather. They had been playing plop-catch, standing in the water up to their hips, Martha, Franz, two other young men, one of them a dancing instructor, the other a college student, the son of a Leipzig furrier. The dancing instructor had knocked Franz's blue glasses off with the ball, and the glasses had nearly drowned. Afterwards Franz and Martha had swum far out. He had stood and watched from the beach, cursing his lack of buoyancy. He borrowed a telescope from a kind ten-year-old stranger and for quite a while had kept an envious round eye on the two dark heads bobbing side by side in their blue safe round world. As soon as his back healed, he thought, he would start to take lessons in the hotel pool. Ouch, really burns! Impossible to find a painless position. Wooing sleep, he lay with closed eyes and saw the circular moat they had been digging to make their beach booth stand more cozily; he saw the tensed hairy leg of Franz digging nearby; then, the impossibly bright page of the verse anthology he had tried to read as he lay in the sun. Oh, how it burns! Martha had promised it would get well tomorrow, definitely, would never hurt again. Yes, of course, the skin would grow stronger. Skin or no skin, I must win that bet tomorrow. Silly bet. Women can measure distances in centimeters, up skirts and down sleeves, but not leagues of water or miles of sand, or the upright glare of a door ajar. He turned over to the wall and in order to put himself asleep (not realizing how drowsy he was already despite the upright glare now between his shoulders) he began to repeat in his mind their sunset walk to Rockpoint. She liked bets and boats. She had maintained that a rowing-boat would make it faster there than a man on foot – even a man whose back burned in each of the four positions. He re-assumed the initial one, facing her door, and started to walk westward again but this time alone – she was in the other bedroom, and had not yet put out her light. If one walked westward with the slit of the sun in one's eyes along the bay after leaving the populated part of the beach, one found that the sandy strip between the heath on your left and the sea on your right gradually narrowed until your progress was stopped by an agony of jumbled rocks. I think I shall turn . . . good God. . . .

If instead of following the concave brink of the bay one takes a concentric path slightly inland as I am doing now, Rockpoint is reachable, I think, in twenty minutes or less, let us rearrange our left arm . . . how much more comfortable a limbless sleeper would be . . . and here is that path leading west from the poor back of the hotel. I traverse a hamlet and continue through a beech grove for a couple of kilometers. How quiet, how soft. . . . He stopped to rest on a bed in the grove but then gave a start and again saw the vertical line of burning pain.

He continued his wager walk. Oh, he must hurry. Or was his pedometer slow? Or was that aspirin working at last? He emerged from the woods into heather, and presently the path, turning right, with a change of pillow, joined the coastline again at the spur called Rockpoint. Here one could stop and wait for the absurd little boat with Martha rowing like mad and enjoy the view. He enjoyed the view. He heard himself emitting a hippopotamian snore and regained consciousness. Rockpoint was a lonely little promontory, but she would come to one's bed if one won the bet. On one's right. . . . He rolled onto his right side and stopped hearing his heart. That's better. Aspirin comes from *sperare, speculum, spiegel.* Now he could see the sweep of the beach parallel to the trail one had followed, and followed, and followed. That shimmer over there, beyond a tiny rocky island, three kilometers east as the acrobat flies, was our stretch of the Gravitz beach with the sugar lumps of hotels. The little black boat with Martha in black evening dress, her eardrops blazing, had to skirt of course that little black island on the outside but otherwise geometrically speaking the seaway was shorter, the string of the bow, the sting of the bay, though even so, even a weary walker. . . .

When finally her husband's snore found a permanent rhythm, Martha got up, closed the door, and went back to her uncomfortable bed – it was much too soft and too far from the window which was open: beyond, there rose a steady soft incessant noise as if the black garden were a bath being run. Alas, it was not the sounding sea but the rain. Never mind, rain or no rain. Let him take an umbrella.

She put out the light, but it was no use trying to sleep. She stepped with Franz into the fatal bark, and he rowed her to the promontory. The process that had put her husband to sleep kept her awake. The rustle of the rain mingled with the buzz in her ears. Two hours passed – it was a much longer journey than anybody could have expected. She picked up her watch from the bed table and pondered its phosphorescent information. The sun was still in Siberia.

At half past seven Franz stirred. He had been told to get up at exactly half past seven. It was exactly half past seven. A baker in the encyclopedia who had poisoned an entire parish told the prison barber who was shaving his neck that never in his life had he slept so well. Franz had slept nine hours. His own contribution to the murder was up to now an accurate calculation of the distance to Rockpoint by land and by sea. The victim had to be there a few minutes before the boat arrived. He would be dead tired and grateful to be ferried back.

Franz opened his window, which faced south with no sea to view, but at least it revealed a small balcony one story lower on which on three consecutive afternoons at the siesta hour he had watched the spread-eagled barmaid sunning herself on a towel. The floor of the balcony was darkly damp. It might dry in time for her siesta if the sun came out before noon. 'By this evening it will all be over,' he reflected mechanically and was unable to imagine either that evening or the following day, as one is unable to imagine eternity.

Gritting his teeth he pulled on his clammy bathing trunks. The pockets of his robe were full of sand. He softly closed the door behind him and set out along the long white corridors. There was sand also in the toes of his canvas shoes, producing there a blunt blind sensation. His uncle and aunt were already sitting on their balcony having coffee. It was a sunless day, with a white sky, a grey sea, and a cheerless breeze. Aunt Martha poured Franz some coffee. She was also wearing her robe over a bathing suit. Green designs ran across the fluffy dark blue. She held back the broad sleeve with her free hand as she passed the cup to Franz.

Dreyer in blazer and flannel pants was reading the resort's guest list, occasionally pronouncing aloud a funny name. He had intended to wear a delicate pale-lemon Chinese tie that had cost fifty marks but Martha said it looked like rain and the tie would be ruined. So he had put on another, an old lavender one. In such trifles Martha usually was right. Dreyer drank two cups of coffee and enjoyed a roll with delicious transparent honey trickling over the edges. Martha drank three cups and did not eat anything. Franz had half a cup and ate nothing either. The wind swept across the balcony.

'Professor Klister of Swister,' read Dreyer. 'Sorry. Lister of Swistok.'

'If you're finished, let's go,' said Martha.

'Blavdak Vinomori,' read Dreyer triumphantly.

'Let's go,' said Martha, wrapping her robe around her and trying to keep her teeth from chattering. 'Before it starts raining again.'

'It's so early, my love,' he drawled, casting a furtive glance at the plate of rolls. 'Why does nobody at home ever give butter that curly shape?'

'Let's go,' repeated Martha, rising. Franz got up also. Dreyer looked at his golden watch.

'I'll beat you anyway,' he said gleefully. 'You two go on ahead. I'll give you fifteen minutes. I could spare even more.'

'Fine,' said Martha.

'We'll see who wins,' said Dreyer.

'We'll see,' said Martha.

'Your oars or my calves,' said Dreyer.

'Let me through, I can't get out,' she exclaimed sharply, pushing with her knee and still fumbling at her robe.

Dreyer moved his chair, she passed.

'My back is much better,' he said, 'but Franz is seasick or something.'

Franz, without looking at him, shook his head. With sunglasses over his usual spectacles and his bright red robe he looked like Blavdak Vinomori should look.

'Don't get drowned, Blavdak,' said Dreyer and began his second roll.

The glass door closed. Chewing, and sucking his honey-smeared fingers, Dreyer considered with disapproval the big pale sea. A bit of beach was visible from the balcony, with its striped shelter boxes untidily scattered and slightly askew. He did not envy the hardy bathers. The spot where one rented boats was a little farther to the west, near the pier, and could not be seen from the balcony. An old man dressed like an opera captain let them. How chilly, soggy, and uninteresting everything was without the sun. Never mind. It would be a brisk bracing walk. As in the old days, the very old days, Martha had agreed to play with him a little and had not refused at the last minute because of the bad weather as he had secretly feared.

He looked again at his watch. Yesterday and the day before his office had called precisely at this time. Today, more than likely, Sarah would telephone again. He would call her back later. It was not worth waiting.

He wiped his lips firmly, brushed the crumbs off his lap, and went to the bathroom. That cold shower had been agony but now he felt fine. He paused before the mirror and ran his little silver brush right and left over his English moustache. His German nose was peeling. Not very attractive. A knock at the door.

The office had managed to catch him. Dreyer, beating his

pocket, hurried to the telephone. The talk was brief. He wavered – should he take an umbrella – decided he would not and went out by the back entrance.

The two young fellows whom they had met yesterday were sitting sideways on a bench playing chess. Both held their legs crossed. White had his hand ensconced between the knee of the left leg and the calf of the other leg and dangled his right foot slightly. Black's arms were folded on his breast. Their gaze left the board as they greeted Dreyer. He stopped for a moment and gaily warned White that Black's knight was planning to attack White's king and queen with a forked check. Martha, who loved bets but thought them undignified, had asked him not to tell anybody about their little rendezvous at Rockpoint, so he said nothing about it and went on his way. 'Old idiot,' muttered Black, whose position was desperate.

Dreyer followed a boulevard of sorts, then a path, then walked through the hamlet where he observed that the bus to Swistok was leaving the post office and looked at his watch. It would catch the express to Berlin. As he turned right to rejoin the coastline, he glimpsed the sea and saw the speck of a boat in the blurry distance. He thought he distinguished two bright bathrobes but was not sure, and, quickening his step almost to a trot, entered the beechwood.

Franz rowed in silence, now grimly lowering his face, then in a sweep of despair turning it skyward. Martha sat at the helm. Before renting the boat, she had gone in the water for a minute, thinking it would warm her up. That had been a mistake. The sun that had made a half-promise had not kept it. The cold wet suit now stuck to her chest, hips, and sides. She was too excited and happy to pay much attention to such trifles. A delightfully compliant mist veiled the receding beach. The boat started to round the little rocky island where seagulls were the only witnesses. The oarlocks creaked ponderously.

'You don't want to ask anything, you remember everything, darling?'

Leaning forward on the back stroke, Franz nodded. And again stared at the empty sky as he pushed the resilient water.

'. . . when I say, only when I say – remember?'

Another grim nod.

'Let us go over it quickly – all right? You remain in the bow—'

The oarlocks creaked, an inquisitive gull circled over them, a wave lifted the boat to inspect it. Franz bowed in answer. He tried not to look at his insane aunt but whether he stared at the damp bottom of the boat along which lay a second pair of oars or followed the happy seagull with his eyes, he nevertheless perceived Martha with his entire being and saw, even without looking, her rubber cap, her broad-jawed dreadful face, her shaven shins, her heavy coronation robes. And he knew exactly how it would all be, how Martha would cry out the password, how both rowers would stand up to change places . . . the boat would rock . . . not easy to get past each other . . . careful . . . one more step . . . nearer . . . now!

'. . . remember – just one big push, with your whole body,' said Martha, and he slowly bent forward again.

'You must send him flying out, toppling in, face forward, and then you row like hell.'

Now a chill breeze was penetrating her body with dampness and yet the elation persisted. She gazed intently at the in-curved shore, at its fringe of forest, at the mauve stretch of heather, searching for the place, near a pointed rock, where they were to land. She saw it. She pulled taut the left rope of the rudder.

Franz, as he swung backwards with a soundless moan, heard Martha laugh hoarsely, cough, clear her throat, cough and laugh again. A sizeable wave took possession of the boat. He stopped rowing for a moment. The sweat trickled down his temples in spite of the cold. Martha rose and fell with the wave's motion, shivering, aged beyond belief, her grey face shining like rubber.

She was watching a tiny dark figure that had suddenly appeared on the deserted strip of jutting land.

'Quicker,' she said, trembling and plucking at the icy-cold clinging bathing suit as if it were a sheet, and she dying. 'Oh, please! He's waiting.'

Franz laid down the oars, slowly took off both pairs of glasses, slowly wiped the lenses of both on the flap of his robe.

'I told you to hurry!' she shouted. 'You don't need those silly sunglasses. Franz, do you hear?'

He put the sunglasses into the pocket of his robe. He raised the other pair skyward. He looked through the lenses at the clouds; then he slowly put them on and took up the oars again.

The dark little figure became more distinct and acquired a face like a grain of maize. Martha was moving her torso back and forth, perhaps repeating Franz's movements, perhaps trying to speed up the boat.

Now the blue jacket and grey pants were distinguishable. He stood with his feet planted apart and his arms akimbo.

'This is the critical moment,' said Martha, already speaking in a whisper. 'He will never get into a boat if he does not now. Try to look more cheerful.'

She was twisting the end of the rudder ropes in her hands. The shore was drawing near.

Dreyer stood looking at them and smiling. In his palm he held a flat gold watch. He had arrived eight minutes ahead of them, eight whole minutes. The boat was called 'Lindy.' Cute.

'Welcome,' he said, putting the watch back in his pocket.

'You must have run all the way,' said Martha, breathing heavily and glancing around.

'Nothing of the sort. Took it easy. Even stopped to rest along the way.'

She continued her survey. Sand, rocks, and further on, heathery slopes and woods. Not a soul, not a dog ever came here.

'Get into the boat,' she said.

Lapping little waves jolted the boat ever so slightly. Franz was listlessly fussing with the second pair of oars.

Dreyer said: 'Oh, I'll return the same way. It's wonderful in the woods. I made friends with a squirrel. We'll meet at the Siren Café.'

'Get in,' she repeated sharply. 'You can row a little. You're getting fat. Look how tired Franz is. I can't row alone.'

'Really, my love, I don't feel like it at all. I hate rowing, and my back smarts again.'

'All right,' she said, 'it was part of the bet and if you don't get in at once, I'm not playing, the bet is cancelled.'

Martha was slapping her palm with the rudder rope. He rolled up his eyes, sighed and, trying not to wet his feet, started awkwardly, cautiously, to get into the boat. 'Illogical and unfair,' he said, and fell down heavily in the middle seat.

The second pair of oars were in the locks. Dreyer took off his blazer. The boat moved off.

A sense of blissful peace now descended on Martha. The plan had worked, the dream had come true. A deserted beach, a deserted sea, and fog. Just to be safe they should go out some distance north of the shore. An odd, cool, not unpleasant emptiness was in her chest and head as if the breeze had blown right through her, cleaning her inwardly, removing all the trash. And through that cool vibration she heard his carefree voice.

'You keep getting tangled up in my oars, Franz – that's no

way to row. You have never rowed in your life, I suspect. Of course, I can understand that your thoughts are far away. . . . There again. You must pay a little more attention to what I'm trying to do. Together, together! She hasn't forgotten you. I hope you left her your address. One, two. I'm positive there'll be a letter for you today saying she's with child. Rhythm! Rhythm!'

Franz watched his firm stout neck, the yellow strands of hair thinning on pink suede, the white shirt now growing taut on his back, then ballooning. But he saw it all as if through a dream.

'Ah, children, it was glorious in the woods,' the voice was saying. 'The beeches, the gloom, the bindweed. Keep in rhythm!'

Martha, through half-closed eyes, was looking with interest at this face which she was seeing for the last time. Beside her lay his blazer; it contained the golden timepiece, the silver moustache brush, and a plump wallet. She was glad these things would not be lost. A little bonus. Somehow, she did not realize at that moment that the jacket with its contents would have to be thrown in the water too. This rather complicated question arose only later when the main matter had already been settled. Now her thoughts were circling slowly, almost languidly. The anticipation of hard-won happiness was ravishing.

'I must admit I was wrong in thinking this would irritate my back. You promised, darling, it would be all right today, and sure enough it's much better. Remember, I've won the bet. And I can row a hundred times better than that rascal behind me. My shirt keeps rubbing the itchy spots, and that feels good. I think I shall take off my tie.'

They were now sufficiently far from the shore. It was drizzling. A number of white spectators had found their seats on their black island. The tie joined the blazer. The wavelets broke and foamed around the boat.

'Actually, it's my last day,' said Dreyer, energetically rowing.

That tragic pronouncement left Franz unmoved; there was already nothing in the world that could shock him. Martha, however, gave her husband a curious glance. Premonitions, eh?

'I have to leave for the city early tomorrow,' he explained. 'I just had a call.'

The rain was growing stronger. Martha glanced around, then looked at Franz. They could begin.

'Listen, Kurt,' she said quietly, 'I feel like rowing a bit. You take Franz's place, and Franz will steer.'

'No, wait, my love,' said Dreyer, trying to do as Franz was

doing – to flatten his oars over the water, swallow-like on the backstroke. 'I'm just getting warmed up. Franz and I have got our rhythm synchronized. His form is improving. Sorry, my love – I think I splashed you.'

'I'm cold,' said Martha. 'Please get up and let me row.'

'Five more minutes,' said Dreyer, trying again to feather his oars, and again failing.

Martha shrugged. The sensation of power was ecstatic; she was willing to prolong that sensation.

'Eight more strokes,' she said with a smile. 'The years of our marriage. I'll count.'

'Come on, don't spoil it. We'll let you row soon. After all, I'm leaving tomorrow.'

He felt hurt that she was not interested to know why he had to go. She must think it was just a routine trip, some ordinary office business.

'An amusing surprise,' he said casually.

She was moving her lips with singular concentration.

'Tomorrow,' he said, 'I'm making a hundred thousand dollars at one stroke.'

Martha, who had got to the end of her count, raised her head.

'I'm selling an extraordinary patent. That's the kind of business we are doing.'

Franz suddenly laid down his oars and began wiping his glasses. For some reason he thought Dreyer was talking to him and as he wiped the sweat and the rain away, he nodded and cleared his throat. Actually he had reached a stage at which human speech, unless representing a command, was meaningless.

'You didn't think I was so smart, eh?' said Dreyer, who had also stopped rowing. 'At one stroke – just think!'

'I suppose this is one of your jokes,' she said, frowning.

'Word of honour,' he said plaintively. 'I'm the sole owner of a miraculous invention, and I'm going to sell it to Mr Ritter, whom you know.'

'What is it – some kind of trouser press?'

He shook his head.

'Something to do with sports, with tennis?'

'It's a big glorious secret,' he said, 'and you're a goose not to believe me.'

She turned away, biting her chapped underlip, and stared for a long time at the inky horizon, where a grey fringe of rain hung against a narrow light-coloured band of sky.

'You're sure it's a hundred thousand dollars? Is that definite?'

It was not, but he nodded, and pulled at the oars, hearing that the rower behind him had resumed his work.

'Can't you tell me a little more?' she asked, still looking away. 'You're sure it won't drag on? You'll have that money in a few days?'

'Why yes, I hope so. And I'll come back here and we'll go rowing again. And Franz will teach me to swim.'

'It can't be; you're deceiving me,' she cried.

Dreyer started to laugh, not understanding why she chose not to believe him.

'I shall return with a great bag of gold,' he said. 'Like a medieval merchant from Bagdad on a donkey. Oh, I'm pretty certain I'll clinch that deal tomorrow.'

The rain would stop one moment and the next start pouring again, as if practising. Dreyer, noticing how far out they had gone, began turning the boat with his right oar; Franz mechanically backed water with his left. Martha sat lost in thought, now consulting the filling of a back tooth with her tongue, now running it over her lips. Presently Dreyer offered to let her row. She gave a silent shake of her head.

The rain now came down in earnest, and Dreyer felt its soothing coolness through the raw silk of his shirt. He tingled with vigour, this was great fun, with every stroke he rowed better. The shore appeared through the mist; one could make out the flags and the striped shelters; the long pier was beginning slowly and carefully to take aim at the moving target of their boat.

'So you'll be back Saturday, not later than Saturday?' asked Martha.

Franz could see, through Dreyer's soaked shirt, flesh-coloured patches which showed now here, now there, a geography of hideous pink, depending on which country adhered to the skin in the process of rowing.

'Saturday or Sunday,' Dreyer said zestfully and, as the surf adopted him, caught a crab.

The rain lashed down. Martha's robe enveloped her in heavy humidity that made her ribs ache. What could she care about neuralgia, bronchitis, irregular heart beat? She was entirely immersed in the question – was she doing the right thing or not. Yes, she was. Yes, the sun would again shine. They would go boating again, now that he had discovered this new sport. Every now and then she would glance past her husband at Franz. He must be perplexed and disappointed, poor pet. He is tired. His poor mouth is open. My baby! Never mind, we'll soon be back, and you'll rest, and I'll bring you some brandy, and we'll lock the door.

'Lindy' was returned intact. Bending their heads under the fierce downpour, our three holidayers walked across soggy dark sand and then up slippery steps to the desolate promenade. When they finally reached their apartment, Martha was unpleasantly surprised to find her door open. The two maids she disliked most, one a thief, the other a slut, were busy, too busy, making her room, which she had told them to do always *punkt* at ten, and now it was almost noon. But a strange apathy weighed upon her. She said nothing, and went to wait in Dreyer's bedroom. There she pulled off her heavy robe and sank into an armchair, feeling too tired to peel off her bathing suit and get a towel from the bathroom. Anyway, her husband was in the bathroom; she saw him through the open door. Naked, full of ruddy life, various parts of his anatomy leaping, he was giving himself a robust rub-down, and helling every time he touched his red-blotched shoulders. One of the girls knocked to say Madam's room was ready, and Martha had to make a great effort in order to undertake the long journey into the next room.

She washed and dressed – with infinite intervals of languor. A turtleneck thick red sweater which Franz had lent her on the esplanade the night before – or was it two nights? – looked a little too masculine but it was the warmest thing she could find. However, it hardly muffled the fits of shivering that kept tormenting her body, while her mind was enjoying such peace, such euphoria. Of course, she had done the right thing. Moreover, the dress rehearsal had gone perfectly. Everything was under control.

'Everything is under control,' said Dreyer through the door. 'I hope you are as hungry as I am. We'll have lunch in the grill in ten minutes. I'll be waiting for you in the reading room.'

All she could envisage was a cup of black coffee, and a little brandy. When her husband had gone, she stepped across the corridor and knocked at Franz's door. It was unlocked, the room was empty. His robe sprawled on the floor, and there were other untidy details, but she did not have the strength to do anything about it. She found him in a corner of the lounge. The barmaid, a skinny artificial blonde, was bothering him with vulgar small talk.

Meanwhile the rain did not cease. The needle that marked on a roll the violet graph of atmospheric pressure acquired a sacred significance. People on the promenade approached it as they would a crystal ball. Its competitor in the gallery, a conservative barometer, also refused to be propitiated either by prayer or knuckleknock. Someone had forgotten a little red pail on the beach and it was already filled to the brim with rain water. The photographers moped; the restaurateurs rejoiced. One could find all the same faces now in one café, now in another. Toward evening the rain thinned, and then stopped. Dreyer held his breath as he made carom shots. The word spread that the needle had risen one millimetre. 'Fine weather tomorrow,' said a prophet, expressively striking his palm with his fist. Red at night, sailor's delight. Despite the cool air, many dined on public verandas. The evening mail arrived: a major event. On the promenade the after-dinner shuffling of many feet began under the lights, bemisted by the damp. There was dancing at the *kursaal*.

In the afternoon, she had lain down under a quilt and two blankets; but the chill endured. For supper she could eat only a pickle and a couple of pale cooked cherries. Now, in the Tanz Salon, she felt a stranger to the icy noise around. The black petals of her vaporous dress did not seem right, as if they would come apart at any moment. The tight touch of silk on her calves and the strip of garter along her bare thigh were infernal contacts. A coloured snowstorm of confetti left its flakes sticking to her bare back, and at the same time, limbs and spine did not belong to her. A pain, of another musical tone than intercostal neuralgia or that strange ache which a great cardiologist had told her came from a 'shadow behind the heart,' entered into excruciating concords with the orchestra. The dance rhythm did not lull or delight her as it usually did, but, instead, traced an angular line, the graph of her fever, along the surface of her skin. With every movement of her head, a compact pain rolled like a bowling ball from temple to temple. At one of the best tables around the hall, she had for a right-hand neighbour the dance instructor, a famous young man who flitted all summer from resort to resort like a velvet butterfly; on her left was Schwarz, the dark-eyed student, son of a Leipzig millionaire. The slipper under the table had apparently been kicked off by her. She heard Martha Dreyer ask questions, supply answers, comment on the horror of the thundering hall. The fizzy little stars of champagne pricked an unfamiliar tongue, without warming her blood or quenching her thirst. With an invisible hand she took Martha by the left wrist and felt her pulse. It was not there, however, but somewhere behind her ear or in the neck, or in the grinning instruments of the band, or in Franz and Dreyer, sitting opposite her. All around, growing from the hands of the dancers, glossy blue, red, green balloons bobbed on long strings and each contained the entire ballroom, and the chandeliers, and the tables, and herself. The tight embrace of the foxtrot engendered no heat in her body. She noticed that Martha was dancing also, holding high a green world. Her partner in full erection against her leg was declaring his love in panting sentences from some lewd book. Again the stars of champagne crept upwards, and the balloons resumed their bobbing, and again most of Martha's leg was in Weiss's crotch, and he moaned as his cheek touched hers, and his fingers explored her naked back.

She was sitting again at the table. Red, blue, green spots were swimming in Franz's glasses. Dreyer was guffawing vulgarly slapping the table with his palm and leaning back. She extended her foot beneath the table and pressed. Franz gave a start, stood up, and bowed. She placed her hand on his dear bony shoulder. How happy they had been in the rhythm of that earlier novel in those first chapters, under the picture of the dancing slave girl between the whirling dervishes. For one delicious moment the music pierced her private fog, reached her, enveloped her. Everything was fine again, for this was he, Franz, his shy hands, his breath, the soft fuzz on the back of his neck, under her fingernails, and those precious, adorable motions that *she* had taught him.

'Closer, closer,' she murmured. 'Make me feel warm.'

'I'm tired,' he murmured back. 'I'm tired to death. Please don't do what you are doing, please.'

The music reared its trumpets and then collapsed. Franz followed her back to the table. People around her were clapping. The dancing instructor slipped past her with a bright-yellow girl. Walnut-brown Mr Vinomori, the iris brimming meaningfully in the white of his eyes, was bowing to her, enticing. She saw Martha Dreyer nestle up to him and begin a tango.

Uncle and nephew remained sitting alone. Dreyer was beating time with his finger, watching the dancers, waiting for the recurrent return of his wife's green earrings, and, with a kind of awe, listening to the strong voice of a girl singer. Stocky and joyless, she bawled out, straining her throat and prancing in time to the music: 'Montevideo, Montevideo is not the right place for *meinen Leo.*' She was jostled by the dancers; endlessly she repeated the ear-splitting refrain; a fat man in tuxedo, her owner, hissed at her, telling her to choose some other song because nobody was enjoying it; Dreyer had heard this *Montevideo* both yesterday and the day before, and he was again filled with a bizarre melancholy, and felt embarrassed for the poor dumpy girl when her voice cracked on a note and she recovered the tune with a brave smile. Franz sat beside him, shoulder to shoulder, and seemed also to be watching the dancers. He was a little drunk and his muscles ached from that morning rowing. He felt like letting his forehead fall onto the table to remain thus forever, between a full ashtray and an empty bottle. A reptile, a supple dragon was tormenting him elaborately and hideously, turning him inside out – and there was no end to that torment. A human being, and after all he was a human being, was not supposed to go on enduring such oppression.

It was at that moment that Franz regained consciousness like an insufficiently drugged patient on the operating table. As he came to, he knew he was being cut open, and he would have howled horribly if he were not in an invented ballroom. He looked around, toying with the string of a balloon tied to a bottle. He saw, reflected in a rococo mirror, the meek back of Dreyer's head nodding in time to the music.

Franz looked away; his gaze became entangled amid the legs of the dancers and attached itself desperately to a gleaming blue dress. The foreign girl in the blue dress danced with a remarkably handsome man in an old-fashioned dinner jacket. Franz had long since noticed this couple; they had appeared to him in fleeting glimpses, like a recurrent dream image or a subtle leitmotiv – now at the beach, now in a café, now on the promenade. Sometimes the man carried a butterfly net. The girl had a delicately painted mouth and tender grey-blue eyes, and her fiancée or husband, slender, elegantly balding, contemptuous of everything on earth but her, was looking at her with pride; and Franz felt envious of that unusual pair, so envious that his oppression, one is sorry to say, grew even more bitter, and the music stopped. They walked past him. They were speaking loudly. They were speaking a totally incomprehensible language.

'Your aunt dances like a goddess,' said the student, sitting down beside him.

'I'm very tired,' remarked Franz irrelevantly. 'I rowed a lot today. Rowing is a very healthy sport'

Meanwhile Dreyer was saying with an ingratiating wink: 'Am I also permitted to invite you for a dance? If I promise not to tread on your feet?'

'Get me out of here,' said Martha. 'I'm not feeling well.'

13

Barely awake and still blinking, his yellow pyjamas unbuttoned on his pink stomach, Dreyer went out on the balcony. The wet foliage scintillated blindingly. The sea was milky-bluish, sparked with silver. On the adjacent balcony his wife's bathing suit was drying. He returned to his darkish bedroom, in a hurry to dress and leave for Berlin. At eight o'clock there was a bus that took forty minutes to reach Swistok and its railway; a taxi would bring him there in less than half an hour to catch an earlier train. He tried not to sing under the shower so as not to disturb neighbours. He had an enjoyable shave on the balcony in front of an absolutely stable and unbreakable new type of mirror screwed onto the balustrade. Diving back into the penumbra, he briskly dressed.

Very softly he opened the door into the adjacent bedroom. From the bed came Martha's rapid voice: 'We're going to a tombola in a gondola. Please hurry.'

She often talked in her sleep babbling about Franz, Frieda, Oriental gymnastics.

As he slapped his sides to check if he had distributed everything among the proper pockets, Dreyer laughed and said: 'Good-by, my love. I'm leaving the city.'

She muttered something in a waking voice, then said distinctly: 'Give me some water.'

'I'm in a hurry,' he said. 'You get it yourself. Okay? Time for you to go swimming with Franz. Heavenly morning.'

He bent over the dark bed, kissed her hair and walked through his own bedroom into the long corridor leading to the lift.

He had his coffee on the Kurhaus terrace. He had two rolls with butter and honey. He consulted his watch and ate a third. On the beach one could see the bright robes of early swimmers and the sea was growing more and more luminous. He lit a cigarette and popped into the taxi that the concierge had called.

The sea was left behind. By that time a few more bathers were dotting the flashing green-blue. From every balcony came the delicate tinkle of breakfast. Automatically tucking a hateful ball under his arm, Franz marched down the corridor and knocked at Martha's door. Silence. The door was locked. He knocked at Dreyer's door, entered and found his uncle's room in disorder. He concluded, correctly, that Dreyer had already left for Berlin. A terrible day was in store. The door into Martha's room was ajar. It was dark there. Let her sleep. This was good. He started to tiptoe away but from the darkness came Martha's voice: 'Why don't you give me that water?' she said with listless insistence.

Franz located a decanter and a glass and moved toward the bed. Martha slowly raised herself, freed a bare arm, and drank avidly. He put the decanter back on the dresser and was about to resume his stealthy retreat.

'Franz, come here,' she called in that same toneless voice.

He sat down on the edge of her bed, grimly expecting she would command him to fulfil a duty that he had managed to evade since they came here.

'I think I am very ill,' she said pensively, not raising her head from the pillow.

'Let me ring for your coffee,' said Franz. 'It's sunny today and here it's so dark.'

She began to speak again. 'He's used up all the aspirin. Go to the pharmacy and get me some. And tell them to take that oar away – it keeps hurting me.'

'Oar? That's your hot-water bottle. What's the matter with you?'

'Please, Franz. I can't speak. And I'm cold. I need lots of blankets.'

He brought one from Dryer's room, and clumsily, carelessly, fuming at a woman's whim, covered her with it.

'I don't know where the pharmacy is,' he said.

Martha asked: 'You brought it? What have you brought?'

He shrugged and went out.

He found the pharmacy without difficulty. Besides the aspirin tablets he bought a tube of shaving cream and a postcard with a view of the bay. The package had safely arrived but Emmy wondered in her last letter if he was quite right in the head and he thought he'd send her a few words of protest and reassurance. As he walked back to the hotel along the sunny promenade, he stopped to look down at the beach. He had separated the aspirin container from the shaving cream which he now put into his pocket. A sudden breeze took possession of the paper baglet which had contained both. At that moment the puzzling foreign couple overtook him. They were both in beach robes and walked rapidly, rapidly conversing in their mysterious tongue. He thought that they glanced at him and fell silent for an instant. After passing him they began talking again; he had the impression they were discussing him, and even pronouncing his name. It embarrassed, it incensed him, that this damned happy foreigner hastening to the beach with his tanned, pale-haired, lovely companion, knew absolutely everything about his predicament and perhaps pitied, not without some derision, an honest young man who had been seduced and appropriated by an older woman who, despite her fine dresses and face lotions, resembled a large white toad. And generally speaking, tourists at these swanky resorts are always inquisitive, mocking, cruel people. He felt the shame of his hairy nudity barely concealed by the charlatan robe. He cursed the breeze and the sea and, clutching the container with the tablets, entered the lobby of his hotel. The flimsy paper he had lost fluttered along the promenade, settled, fluttered again, and slithered past the happy couple; then it was wafted toward a bench in an embrasure of the balustrade, where an old man sitting in the sun meditatively pierced it with the point of his cane. What happened to it next is not known. Those hurrying to the beach did not follow its fate. Wooden steps led down to the sand. One was anxious to reach the sea's slow shining folds. The white sand sung underfoot. Among a hundred similarly striped shelters it was easy to recognize one's own – and not only by the number it bore: those rentable objects grow accustomed to their chance owner remarkably fast, becoming part of his life simply and trustfully. Three or four shelters away was the Dreyers' niche; now it stood empty – neither Dreyer, nor his wife, nor his nephew was there. A huge rampart of sand surrounded it. A little boy in red trunks was climbing all over that rampart, and the sand trickled down, sparkling, and presently a whole chunk of it crumbled. Mrs Dreyer would not have liked to see strange children ruining her fortress. Within its confines and around them the impatient elements had already had time to scramble the prints of bare feet. None could distinguish now Dreyer's robust imprint from Franz's narrow sole. A while later Schwarz and Weiss came over, saw with surprise that nobody was there yet. 'Fascinating, adorable woman,' one of them said, and the other looked across the beach at the promenade, at the hotels beyond it, and replied: 'Oh, I'm sure they'll be down in a few minutes. Let's go for a swim and come back later.' The shelter and its moat remained deserted. The little boy had run back to his sister who had brought a blue pailful of toy water and after magic manipulations and pattings was carefully shaking out of the pail an impeccably formed cone of chocolate sand. A white butterfly went by, battling the breeze. Flags flapped. The photographer's shout approached. Bathers entering the shallow water moved their legs like skiers without their poles.

And in the meantime a cluster of these seaside images – gleams on the green folding wave – were travelling south at fifty miles an hour comfortably collected in Dreyer's mind, and the further he travelled from the sea in the Berlin express, the more insistently they demanded attention. The foretaste of the affairs awaiting him in the city grew a little insipid at the thought that at the very moment he was being transformed again into a businessman with a businessman's schemes and fancies, and that there, by the sea, on the white sand of true reality, he was leaving freedom behind. And the closer he came to the metropolis, the more attractive seemed to him that shimmering *plage* that one could see like a mirage from Rockpoint.

At home, the gardener informed him of Tom's death: the dog, he thought, had been hit by a truck, it was found unconscious and had died, he said, in his arms. Dreyer gave him fifty marks for his sympathy, reflecting sadly that nobody besides that rather coarse old soldier had really loved the poor beast. At the office he learned that Mr Ritter would meet him not in the lobby of the Adlerhof but at the bar of the Royal. Before going there, he rang up Isolda at her mother's at Spandau and pleaded abjectly for a brief date later in the evening, but Isolda said she was busy, and suggested he call her again tomorrow or the day after tomorrow and take her to the premiere of the film, *King, Queen, Knave,* and then one would see.

His American guest, a pleasant, cultured person with steel-grey hair and a triple chin, asked about Martha, whom he had met a couple of years before, and Dreyer was disappointed to discover that all the English learned since the day of that pleasant party was not sufficient to cope with the nasal prounuciation of Mr Ritter – whereupon the latter courteously switched to an old-fashioned brand of German. Another disappointment awaited Dreyer at the 'laboratory.' Instead of the three automannequins promised him, only two were available for the show – the initial elderly gentleman, wearing a replica of Dreyer's blue blazer, and a stiff-looking, bronze-wigged lady in a green dress with high cheekbones and a masculine chin.

'You might have thrown in a little more bosom,' observed Dreyer reproachfully.

'Scandinavian type,' said the Inventor.

'Scandinavian type,' said Dreyer. 'Female impersonator, rather.'

'An amalgam, if you like. We ran into some trouble, a rib failed to function properly. After all, I need more time than God did, Mr Director. But I'm sure you'll love the way her hips work.'

'Another thing,' said Dreyer. 'I don't much care for the old chap's necktie. You must have got it in Croatia or Liechtenstein. Anyway it is not one of those my store provided. In fact, I remember the one he had on last time; it was a beautiful light blue like yours.'

Moritz and Max tittered.

'I confess,' said the Inventor calmly, 'to have borrowed it for this important occasion.' He started to worry the front stud of the tall collar under his rustling beard, but before it could spring, Dreyer had already swished off his own pearl-grey tie and remained with an open shirt collar for the rest of his known existence.

Mr Ritter was dozing in an armchair in the 'theatre.' Dreyer coughed loudly. His guest woke up rubbing his eyes like a child. The show started.

Gyrating her angular hips, the woman passed across the stage more like a streetwalker than a sleepwalker. She was followed by the drunken viveur. Presently she jerked by again in a mink coat, reeled, recovered, completed her agonizing stretch, and the sound of a massive thud came from the wings. Her would-be client did not appear. There was a long pause.

'That meal you bought me was certainly something,' said Mr Ritter. 'I'll have my revanche when madame and you visit me in Miami next spring. I have a Spanish chef who worked for years in a French restaurant in London so you do really get quite a cosmopolitan menu.'

This time the woman drifted past on slow roller skates, in a black evening dress, her legs rigid, her profile like that of a skull, her décolleté revealing a tricot smudged by the hasty hands of her maker. His two accomplices failed to catch her behind the scenes where her brief career ended in an ominous clatter. There was another pause. Dreyer wondered what aberration of the mind had ever made him accept, let alone admire, those tipsy dummies. He hoped the end of the show had come but Mr Ritter and he had not yet seen the best number.

White-gloved, in evening dress, one hand raised to his top hat, the old chap entered, looking refreshed and gay. He stopped in front of the spectators and started to remove his hat in a complicated, much too complicated, salute. Something crunched.

'*Halt*,' howled the Inventor with great presence of mind and darted toward the mechanical maniac. 'Too late!' The hat was doffed with a flourish but the arm came off too.

A photographer's black curtain was mercifully drawn.

'*How have you liked*?' asked Dreyer in English.

'Fascinating,' said Mr Ritter and started to leave. 'You'll hear from me in a couple of days. I have to decide, you see, which of two projects to finance.'

'Is the other similar?'

'Oh, no. Oh, goodness, no. The other has to do with running water in luxury hotels. Water made to produce recognizable tunes. The music of water in a literal sense. An orchestra of faucets. Wash your hands in a barcarolla, bathe in *Lohengrin*, rinse your silver in Debussy.'

'Or drown in a Bach,' punned Dreyer.

He spent the rest of the evening at home, trying to read an English play called *Candida*, and every now and then lapsing into lazy thought. The automannequins had given all they could give. Alas, they had been pushed too far. Bluebeard had squandered his hypnotic force, and now they had lost all significance, all life and charm. He was grateful to them, in a vague sort of way, for the magical task they had performed, the excitement, the expectations. But they only disgusted him now.

He worked through another scene, dutifully leafing through his dictionary at every stumble. He would ring up Isolda tomorrow. He would hire a pretty English girl to teach him the language of Shaw and Galsworthy. He would simply resell the invention to Bluebeard. Ah, brilliant idea! For a token sum of ten dollars.

How quiet the house was. No Tom, no Martha. She was not a good loser, poor girl. All at once he understood what subtle extra was added to the lifeless silence: all the clocks had stopped in the house.

A little after eleven he rose from his comfortable seat and was about to go up to the bedroom when the telephone placed a cold hand on his shoulder.

He was now speeding in a hired limousine driven by a broad-shouldered chauffeur through an infinite nocturnal expanse of woods and field, and northern towns, their names garbled by the impatient darkness – Nauesack, Wusterbeck, Pritzburg, Nebukow. Their weak lights fumbled at him in passing, the car shook and swayed, he had been promised they would make it in five hours, but they did not, and a grey morning was already abustle with bicycles weaving among crawling trucks when he reached Swistok, from which it was twenty miles to Gravitz.

The desk clerk, a dark-haired young man with hollow cheeks and big glasses, informed him that one of their guests happened to be Professor Lister of international fame; he had visited Madame last night, and was with her now.

As Dreyer strode toward his apartment, the doctor, a tall bald old man in a monastic-looking dressing gown with a brown satchel under his arm, came out of Martha's room. 'It is unheard-of,' he growled at Dreyer without bothering to shake hands with him. 'A woman has pneumonia with a temperature of 106 and nobody bothers. Her husband leaves her in that state and goes for a trip. Her nephew is a nincompoop. If a maid had not alerted me last night you would be still carousing in Berlin.'

'So the situation is serious,' said Dreyer.

'Serious? The respiratory count is fifty. The heart behaves fantastically. It is not a normal organ for a women of twenty-nine.'

'Thirty-four,' said Dreyer. 'There is a mistake in her passport.'

'Or thirty-four. Anyway, she should be transported at once to the Swistok clinic where I can have her treated adequately.'

'Yes, at once,' said Dreyer.

The old man nodded crossly and swept away. One of the maids Martha disliked, the one who had stolen at least three handkerchiefs in as many days, was now dressed as a nurse (she had worked in winter at the clinic).

Plain brown or the heather tweed? Franz on the terrace of a café was in the middle of a nervous yawn when the doctor bellowed past, heading for a quick swim before going to Swistok. Plain brown. Gruff Lister could not help being touched by the young fellow's dejection and shouted to him from the promenade: 'Your uncle is here.'

Franz went up to Dreyer's room and stood listening to the

moaning and muttering in the adjacent room. Would fate allow her to divulge their secrets? He knocked very lightly on the door. Dreyer came out of the sickroom, and he likewise was touched by Franz's distraught appearance. Presently from the balcony they saw the ambulance enter the drive.

Over the waves, small angular waves, that rose and fell in time to her breathing, Martha floated in a white boat, and at the oars sat Dreyer and Franz. Franz smiled at her over Dreyer's bent head, and she saw her gay parasol reflected in the happy gleam of his glasses. Franz was wearing one of the long nightshirts that had belonged to his father, and continued to smile at her expectantly as the boat dipped and creaked as if on springs. And Martha said: 'It's time. We can begin.' Dreyer stood up, Franz stood up also, and both reeled, laughing heartily, locked in an involuntary embrace. Franz's long shirt rippled in the wind, and now he was standing alone, still laughing and swaying, and out of the water a hand protruded. 'Take the oar, hit him,' cried Martha, choking with laughter. Franz, standing firmly on the blue glass of the water, raised the oar, and the hand disappeared. They were now alone in the boat, which was no longer a boat but a café with one large marble table, and Franz was sitting opposite her, and his odd attire had ceased to matter. They were drinking beer (how thirsty she was). Franz shared her unsteady glass while Dreyer kept slapping the table with his wallet to summon the waiter. 'Now,' she said, and Franz said something in Dreyer's ear, and Dreyer got up, laughing, and they both went away. While Martha waited her chair rose and fell, it was a floating café. Franz came back alone carry-her late husband's blue jacket over his arm; he nodded to her significantly and tossed it on the empty chair. Martha wanted to kiss Franz but the table separated them and the marble edge bit into her chest. Coffee was brought – three pots, three cups – and it took her some time to realize there was one portion too many. The coffee was too hot, so she decided that since a drizzle had set in, it was best to wait for the rain to dilute the coffee, but the rain was hot too and Franz kept urging her to go home, pointing at their villa across the road. 'Let's begin,' she said. All three got up, and Dreyer, pale and sweaty, started to pull on his blue jacket. That perturbed her. It was dishonest, it was illegal. She gestured in mute indignation. Franz understood and, talking to him firmly, began leading away Dreyer, who staggered as he fumbled for the armhole of his blazer. Franz returned alone but no sooner had he sat down than Dreyer appeared from another direction, furtively making his way back, and his face was now utterly ghastly and inadmissible. With a sidelong glance at her he shook his head and seated himself without a word at the oars of the bed. Martha was overcome by such impatience that as soon as the bed began to move she screamed. The new boat rode through long corridors. She wanted to stand up but an oar blocked her way. Franz rowed steadily. Something kept telling her that not all had been properly done. She remembered – the jacket! The blue jacket lay at the bottom of the boat, its arms looked empty but the back was not flat enough, in fact it bulged, it humped suspiciously, and now the two sleeves were swelling. She saw the thing trying to rise on all fours, and grabbed it, and Franz and she swung it back and forth and hurled it out of the boat. But it would not sink. It slithered from wave to wave as if alive. She nudged it with an oar; it clutched at the oar, trying to clamber aboard. Franz reminded her that it still contained the watch, and the coat, now a blue mackintosh because of the water, slowly sank, limply moving its exhausted sleeves. They watched it disappear. Now the job was done, and an enormous, turbulent joy engulfed her. Now it was easy to breathe, that drink they had given her was a wonderful poison, Benedictine and bile, and her husband was already dressed, saying: 'Hurry up, I'm taking you to a ball,' but Franz had mislaid her jewels.

Before leaving with her for the hospital, Dreyer told Franz to hold the fort, they would be back in a few days. There was probably not much difference basically between Martha's delirium and her wretched lover's state of mind. Once, on the eve of a school examination, when he desperately needed a passing mark in order not to repeat a whole class year, a clever sly boy said to him there was a trick that always worked if you knew how to apply it. With the utmost clarity, with all the forces of your mind bunched up in an iron fist, you had to visualize not what you wanted, not the passing mark, not her death, not freedom, but the other possibility, failure, the absence of your name from the list of those who had passed, and a healthy, ravenous, implacable Martha returning to her merry seaside inferno to make him carry out the scheme they had postponed. But according to the boy's advice, that did not suffice: the really hard part of the trick was ignoring success utterly and naturally as if the very thought of it did not exist in one's mind. Franz could not recall if he had achieved that feat in the case of the examination (which eventually he did pass) but he knew that he was incapable of managing it now. No matter how distinctly he imagined the three of them sitting again on the terrace of the Marmora tavern, and renewing the wager, and again getting Dreyer into the boat, he would notice out of the corner of his eye that the boat had floated away without them and that Dreyer was telephoning from the hospital to say she was dead.

Going to the other extreme, he allowed himself the dangerous luxury of imagining the freedom, the ecstasy of freedom awaiting him. Then, after that awful voluphy of thought, he tried other ways of tricking fate. He counted the boats for hire and added their sum to that of the number of people in the open-air café on the beach, telling himself that odd would mean death. The number was odd but now he wondered if somebody had not left or come while he counted.

The day before he had resolved to take advantage of solitude and make a purchase that Dreyer might have ridiculed with his usual wit, and Martha thought frivolous at such a critical time in their lives. It was his old dream of fashionable plus-fours. He had spent a couple of hours in several shops. He had practically bought a pair but then had said he'd think it over, and decide which he wanted, the brown or the purplish tweed. He now returned to that shop and tried on the plain brown pair and it turned out to be a little too wide in the waist. He said he would take it if they could make the adjustment before closing time. This they promised. He also bought two pairs of brown woollen stockings. Then he went for a swim, and after that had three or four brandies at the bar, vainly waiting for the attractive blonde to get get rid of two elderly men flirting with her, ponderously and obscenely. Suddenly it occurred to him that his choosing the more conservative tint meant his having envisaged death rather than life which those confetti-like specks in the tweed might suggest. But when he returned to the tailor's the plus-fours were ready, and he did not have the courage to change his order.

Next morning Franz, wearing the new plus-fours and a turtleneck sweater, was looking at the rain over his second cup of after-lunch coffee when the desk clerk – who resembled him according to Uncle Clown – brought him two messages. Dreyer had telephoned that madame wanted her emerald earrings – and Franz immediately realized that if madame contemplated going to a dance, no death was expected. The clerk explained that Mr Director Dreyer wanted his nephew to get those jewels from his aunt's dresser and drive in a taxi to Swistok without delay. She had evidently recovered from her slight cold so swiftly that the doctor allowed her to go out that very night. Franz reflected bitterly that, of all the contingencies he had attempted to forestall, this was the only one he had not imagined specifically. The other message was a telegram that had been read over the telephone and transcribed thus by the multilingual desk: WISCH TU CLYNCH DEEL MUSS HAVE THAT DRUNK STOP HUNDRED OAKEY RITTER. It made no sense, but who cared. Cursing Lister, the miracle worker, he rode up in the lift with the pseudo-Franz, and a stout locksmith, hoarse-voiced and reeking of beer. The key was in Martha's handbag which had gone with her to Swistok. The locksmith started working on the lock of the dresser. He wiped his nose and went down on one knee, then on both. The false Franz and the more or less real one stood side by side, staring at his dirty soles.

The drawer was fully extricated. Franz opened a black jewel box and showed the emeralds to the gloomy clerk.

Half an hour later he arrived at the hospital – a new white building in a pine grove on the outskirts of the town. The taximan demanded a tip and slammed the door angrily when Franz shook his head. A remarkably cheerful nurse had another message for him. His uncle, she said with a happy smile, was expecting him at the inn – about a mile down the highway. Franz walked the distance with his left hand pressed to his left side where the jewel box bulged. They chafed slightly between the thighs. As he approached the inn, he saw Martha come out of it briskly and consult the sky, one finger on the trigger of her umbrella. She gave Franz a quick look and went the way he had come. She was younger than Martha, and the mouth was different, but the eyes and the walk were Martha's. That meant a gay reunion in a Swistok inn. Uncle, nephew, and two aunts.

He found Dreyer in the hall of the inn. He was inspecting an ornamental pewter and kept looking at it even when Franz was already thrusting the black box and the telegram into the vicinity of his person. Dreyer thrust both in his pocket without opening either, and replaced the pewter on its hook.

He turned toward Franz, who saw only then that it was not Dreyer but a demented stranger in a rumpled open shirt, with swollen eyes and a tawny-stubbled trembling jaw.

'It's too late,' he said, 'too late to put on for the dance, but still not too late to wear—'

He pulled Franz by the sleeve with such force that Franz almost lost his balance, but Dreyer only wanted to lead him to the desk.

'Take him up,' he said to the innkeeper's widow. And then, turning to Franz: 'We'll have to stay here till tomorrow. The worst formalities begin afterwards. Go to your room now. Hilda has just come from Hamburg. She will fetch you in a couple of hours.'

'Is it—' began an amazed Franz, 'is it—?'

'Is it all over?' asked the new sobbing Dreyer. 'Oh, it is over! Now go.'

Franz attempted to catch his benefactor's hand and shake it in token of ardent condolence but Dreyer dreadfully mistook the adumbrated gesture for the rudiment of an embrace, and wet bristles came into brief contact with Franz's glowing cheek.

Her last words had been (in a sweet remote voice he had never heard before): 'Darling, where did you put my emerald slippers – no, I mean earrings? I want them. We shall all dance, we shall all die.' And then – with her good old familiar sharpness: 'Frieda, why is the dog here again? He was killed. He can't be here any more.'

And the fools say second sight does not exist.

Franz followed the old woman upstairs. She led him into a darkened room. Quickly she threw back the shutters, quickly she opened the lower stage of the bed table to see if the nightpot was there. Quickly she left.

Franz marched to the open window. Dreyer crossed the road and sat down on a bench under a tree. Franz closed the window. He was now alone. A woman in the next room, a miserable tramp whom a commercial traveller had jilted, heard through the thin wall what sounded like several revellers all talking together, and roaring with laughter, and interrupting one another, and roaring again in a frenzy of young mirth.

GLORY

I

Funny as it may seem, Martin's grandfather Edelweiss was a Swiss – a robust Swiss with a fluffy moustache, who in the 1860s had been tutor to the children of a St Petersburg landowner named Indrikov, and had married his youngest daughter. Martin assumed at first that the velvety white Alpine flower, that pet of herbariums, had been named in honour of his grandfather. Even later he could not fully relinquish this notion. He remembered his grandfather distinctly, but only in one form and position: a corpulent old man, dressed completely in white, fair-whiskered, wearing a Panama hat and a piqué waistcoat rich in breloques (the most amusing of which was a dagger the size of a fingernail), sitting on a bench in front of the house in a linden's mobile shade. It was on this very bench that his grandfather had died, holding in the palm of his hand his beloved gold watch, whose lid was like a little golden mirror. Apoplexy overtook him during this timely gesture and, according to family legend, the hands stopped at the same moment as his heart.

For many years after, Grandfather Edelweiss was preserved in a massive leather album; in his day photographs were made tastefully, with elaborate deliberation. The operation was no joking matter; the patient had to be immobilized for a long time, and permission to smile had yet to come – with the advent of the snapshot. The complexity of heliography accounted for the weightiness and solidity of Grandfather's manly poses in those somewhat pale but very good-quality pictures: Grandfather as a youth with a freshly killed woodcock at his feet; Grandfather astride the mare Daisy; Grandfather on a striped veranda seat, with a black dachshund that had refused to sit still, and had come out with three tails in the photograph. Only in 1918 did Grandfather Edelweiss disappear altogether, for the album went up in flames, as did the table where the album lay, and, in fact, the whole country house, which the peasant chaps from the nearby village foolishly burned to the ground as it stood, instead of realizing a profit from the furnishings.

Martin's father was a dermatologist, and a famous one. Like Grandfather, he too was very white-skinned and stout, enjoyed fishing for gobies in his spare time, and possessed a magnificent collection of daggers and sabers, as well as long, strange pistols, on account of which the users of more modern weapons nearly sent him before the firing squad. In the beginning of 1918 he grew bloated and short of breath, and died around March 10 in unclear circumstances. His wife Sofia and their son were living at the time near Yalta: the town kept trying on now one regime, now another, and could not make up its finicky mind.

She was a rosy, freckled, youthful woman, with pale hair in a big bun, high eyebrows that were thickish toward the bridge of her nose and nearly imperceptible toward her temples, and little slits (once made for now absent earrings) in the elongated lobes of her delicate ears. Only recently, in their Northern country place, she still used to play a powerful, agile game of tennis on the garden court, which had been in existence since the eighties. In the autumn she would spend a lot of time riding a black Enfield bicycle along the avenues of their park, across noisily rustling carpets of dry leaves. Or else she would set out on foot along the resilient shoulder of the highway and cover the long way, dear to her since childhood, from Olkhovo to Voskresensk, raising and lowering the end of her expensive coral-knobbed cane like a seasoned walker. In St Petersburg she was known as an Anglomaniac, and relished this fame – she would discuss eloquently such topics as Boy Scouts or Kipling, and found a quite special delight in frequent visits to Drew's English Shop where, still on the stairs, before a large poster (a woman thickly lathering a boy's head) you were greeted by a wonderful smell of soap and lavender, with something more mixed in, something that suggested collapsible rubber tubs, soccer balls, and round, heavy, tightly swaddled Christmas puddings. It follows that Martin's first books were in English: his mother loathed the Russian magazine for children *Zadushevnoe Slovo* (The Heartfelt Word), and inspired in him such aversion for Madame Charski's young heroines with dusky complexions and titles that even much later Martin was wary of any book written by a woman, sensing even in the best of such books an unconscious urge on the part of a middle-aged and perhaps chubby lady to dress up in a pretty name and curl up on the sofa like a pussy cat. Sofia detested diminutives, kept a strict check on herself so as not to use them, and was annoyed if her husband said 'Sonny's got the coughikins again – let's check his *temperaturka*': Russian children's literature swarmed with cute lisping words, when not committing the sin of moralizing.

If Martin's grandfather's family name bloomed in the mountains, the magical origin of his grandmother's maiden name was a far cry from the various Volkovs (Wolfs), Kunitsyns (Martens) or Belkins (Squirrelsons), and belonged to the fauna of Russian fable. Once upon a time there prowled marvelous beasts in our country. But Sofia found Russian fairy tales clumsy, cruel, and squalid, Russian folksongs inane, and Russian riddles idiotic. She had little faith in Pushkin's famous nanny, and said that the poet himself had invented her, together with her fairy tales, knitting needles, and heartache. Thus in early childhood Martin failed to become familiar with something that subsequently, through the prismatic wave of memory, might have added an extra enchantment to his life. However, he had no lack of enchantments, and no cause to regret that it was not the Russian knight-errant Ruslan but Ruslan's occidental brother that had awakened his imagination in childhood. But then what does it matter whence comes the gentle nudge that jars the soul into motion and sets it rolling, doomed never again to stop?

2

On the bright wall above the narrow crib, with its lateral meshes of white cord and the small icon at its head (lacquered saint's brown face framed in foil, crimson underside plush somewhat eaten by moths or by Martin himself), hung a watercolour depicting a dense forest with a winding path disappearing into its depths. Now in one of the English books that his mother used to read to him (how slowly and mysteriously she would pronounce the words and how wide she would open her eyes when she reached the end of a page, covering it with her small, lightly freckled hand as she asked, 'And what do you think happened next?') there was a story about just such a picture with a path in the woods, right above the bed of a little boy, who, one fine night, just as he was, nightshirt and all, went from his bed into the picture, onto the path that disappeared into the woods. His mother, thought Martin anxiously, might notice the resemblance between the watercolour on the wall and the illustration in the book; she would then become alarmed and, according to his calculations, avert the nocturnal journey by removing the picture. Therefore every time he prayed in bed before going to sleep (first came a short prayer in English: 'Gentle Jesus meek and mild, listen to a little child,' and then 'Our Father' in the sibilant, and sibylline, Slavonic version), pattering rapidly and trying to get his knees up on the pillow – which his mother considered inadmissible on ascetic grounds – Martin prayed God that she would not notice that tempting path right over his head. When, as a youth, he recalled the past, he would wonder if one night he had not actually hopped from bed to picture, and if this had not been the beginning of the journey, full of joy and anguish, into which his whole life had turned. He seemed to remember the chilly touch of the ground, the green twilight of the forest, the bends of the trail (which the hump of a great root crossed here and there), the tree trunks flashing by as he ran past them barefoot, and the strange dark air, teeming with fabulous possibilities.

Grandmother Edelweiss, née Indrikov, worked diligently at watercolours in her youth, and, as she mixed the blue paint with the yellow on her porcelain palette, she could hardly foresee that in this nascent greenery her grandson would one day wander. The thrill which Martin discovered and which, in various manifestations and blendings, accompanied him throughout his life from that moment on, proved to be precisely the feeling that his mother hoped to develop in him, even though she herself would have been hard put to find a name for it; she just knew that every evening she must feed Martin what she had once been fed by her late governess, old, wise Mrs Brook, whose son had collected orchids in Borneo, had flown over the Sahara in a balloon, and had died in a Turkish bath when the boiler burst. She would read, and Martin would listen, kneeling on a chair with his elbows propped on the lamplit round table, and it was very hard to stop and lead him to bed, since he would always beg her to read some more. Sometimes she would carry him upstairs to the nursery on her back – this was called 'logging.' At bedtime he would be given an English biscuit from a blue-papered tin box. The top ones were of wonderful kinds, coated with sugar; next came ginger and coconut cookies; and on the sad night when he reached the bottom layer he would have to reconcile himself to a third-rate variety, plain and insipid.

Nothing was wasted on Martin – neither the crunchy English cookies, nor the adventures of King Arthur's knights. What a rapturous moment that was when a youth – perchance a nephew of Sir Tristram's? – donned for the first time piece by piece his shiny, convex plate armour and rode off to his first single combat! There were also those distant, circular islands at which a damsel gazed from the shore, her garments streaming in the wind and a hooded falcon perched on her wrist. And Sinbad with his red kerchief and the gold ring in his ear; and the sea serpent, its green tire-shaped segments jutting out of the water all the way to the horizon. And the child finding the spot where the end of the rainbow met the ground. And, like an echo of all this, an image somehow related to it, there was the magnificent model of a brown-paneled sleeping car in the window of the *Société des Wagons-Lits et des Grands Express Européens* on the Nevsky Avenue, where one was walked on a dull frosty day with slight spinners of snow, and had to wear black knit snow pants over one's stockings and shorts.

3

His mother's love for Martin was so jealous, so violent, and so intense that it seemed to make the heart hoarse. When her marriage broke up and she began living separately with Martin, he would go on Sundays to visit his father at their former apartment, where he would potter for a long time with pistols and daggers, while his father read the paper impassively, and answered every now and then, without looking up, 'Yes, loaded,' or 'Yes, poisoned.' On these occasions Sofia could hardly bear to stay at home, tormented by the ridiculous thought that her indolent husband might try something after all, and keep his son with him. Martin, on the other hand, was very affectionate and polite with his father, so as to mitigate the punishment as much as possible; since he believed that his father had been banished for a misdemeanor committed one summer evening, at their country house, when he had done something to the piano that made it emit an absolutely staggering sound, as if someone had stepped on its tail, and the day after had left for St Petersburg and never returned. This happened in the very same year when the grand duke of Austria was assassinated in a seraglio. Martin imagined that seraglio and its divan very distinctly, with the grand duke, in a plumed hat, defending himself with his sword against half-a-dozen black-cloaked conspirators, and was disappointed when his error became evident. The blow on the piano keys occurred in his absence: he was in the adjoining room, brushing his teeth with thick, foamy, sweet-tasting toothpaste, rendered especially attractive by the inscription in English: 'We could not improve the paste, so we improved the tube.' Indeed, the aperture formed a transverse slit, so that the paste, as it was squeezed out, slid onto the brush not like a worm but like a ribbon.

That last discussion with her husband Sofia recalled in its entirety, complete in every detail and shading, on the day the news of his death reached her in Yalta. Her husband had been sitting near a little wicker table, examining the tips of his short, outspread fingers, and she had been telling him that they could not go on like that any longer, that they had long since become strangers, that she was willing to take her son and leave, even tomorrow. Her husband smiled lazily and answered in a quiet, slightly husky voice that she was right, alas, and said he would leave himself, and find a separate apartment in town. His quiet voice, his placid obesity, and, most of all, the file with which he continually mangled his soft nails drove her out of her wits, and the calm with which they both discussed their separation seemed to her monstrous, even though violent language and tears would of course have been more awful still. Presently he got up, and, still fiddling with the nail file, began pacing back and forth across the room, speaking with a gentle smile about the minor household details of their forthcoming separate existence (and here a town carriage played an absurd role). Then, suddenly and without any reason, as he passed the open piano, he brought his closed fist down on the keyboard with all his might, and it was as if a discordant howl had burst in through a momentarily opened door. After this he resumed the interrupted sentence in the same quiet voice, and the next time he passed the piano he carefully closed the lid.

The death of his father, whom he did not love much, shocked Martin for the very reason that he did not love him as he should; and besides, he could not rid himself of the thought that his father had died in disgrace. It was then that Martin understood for the first time that human life flowed in zigzags, that now the first bend had been passed, and that his life had turned at the instant his mother summoned him from the cypress avenue to the terrace and said in a strange voice, 'I have received a letter from Zilanov,' then continuing in English, 'I want you to be brave, very brave – it is about your father – he is no more.' Martin turned pale and smiled a bewildered smile. Then he roamed for a long time in Vorontsov Park, repeating now and then an infantine nickname he had once bestowed on his father, and trying to imagine – and imagining with a certain warm, dreamy cogency – that his father was beside him, in front, behind, under that cedar over there, there on that sloping lawn, nearby, far off, everywhere.

It was hot, even though a rainstorm had raged a short time before. Blowflies buzzed around the glossy medlar shrubs. An ill-tempered black swan floated in the pool, moving from side to side its bill which was so crimson that it seemed painted. Petals had fallen from the almond trees, and stood out pale on the dark earth of the damp path, like almonds in gingerbread. Not far from some enormous cedars of Lebanon grew a lone birch tree, with that particular slant to its foliage that only a birch has (as if a girl had let her hair down on one side to be combed, and stood still). A zebra-striped swallowtail glided past, its tails extended and joined. The sparkling air, the shadows of the cypresses (old trees, with a rusty cast, their small cones half-hidden under their cloaks); the black glass of the pool, where concentric circles spread around the swan; the radiant blue into which serrated Mount Petri rose wearing a broad belt of karakul-like pine – everything was permeated with agonizing bliss, and it seemed to Martin that somehow his father played a part in the distribution of shadow and shine.

'If you were twenty instead of fifteen,' said his mother that evening, 'if you had already finished high school, and if I were no longer alive, then, of course, you could . . . I suppose it would be your duty to—' She paused in mid-sentence, thinking of the White Army and seeing with her mind's eye the South Russian prairie and Cossack-capped horsemen, among whom she tried to recognize Martin from afar. But thank God, he stood next to her, in an open-necked shirt, his hair close-cropped, his skin sun-browned, with untanned little lines radiating from the corners of his eyes. 'While, on the other hand, if we return to St Petersburg—' she went on in a questioning tone, and at some anonymous station a shell exploded, and the locomotive reared up. 'All this will probably end one day,' she added after a pause. 'In the meantime we must think up something.'

'I'm going for a swim,' put in Martin, with a conciliatory intonation. 'The whole gang is there – Nicky, Lida.'

'Yes, go, by all means,' said Sofia. 'After all, the revolution will end some day, and it will be strange remembering it. Our stay in the Crimea has done wonders for your health. And you will somehow finish your schooling at the Yalta Gymnasium. Look, isn't that cliff beautifully lit up over there?'

That night neither mother nor son could sleep, and both thought about death. Sofia tried to think in an undertone, that is, without sobbing or sighing (the door to her son's room was ajar). She recalled again, punctiliously and in detail, everything that had led up to her separation from Edelweiss. Going over every instant, she saw clearly that in this circumstance and in that she could not have acted otherwise. But still a mistake lurked hidden somewhere; still, if they had not parted, he would not have died like that, alone in an empty room, suffocating, helpless, perhaps recalling their last year of happiness (and very comparative happiness at that), and their last trip abroad, to Biarritz, the excursion to Croix-de-Mouguère, and the little galleries of Bayonne. She firmly believed in a certain power that bore the same resemblance to God as the house of a man one has never seen, his belongings, his greenhouse and beehives, his distant voice, heard by chance in an open field, bear to their owner. It would have embarrassed her to call that power 'God,' just as there are Peters and Ivans who cannot pronounce 'Pete' or 'Vanya" without a sensation of falsity, while there are others who, in reporting a long conversation to you, will pronounce their own names or, still worse, nicknames, with gusto twenty times or so. This power had no connection with the Church, and neither absolved nor chastised any sins. It was just that she sometimes felt ashamed in the presence of a tree, of a cloud, of a dog, or of the air itself that bore an ill word just as religiously as a kind one. And now Sofia, as she thought about her unpleasant, unloved husband and about his death, even though she repeated the words of prayers natural to her ever since childhood, actually strained her whole being so that – fortified by two or three happy memories, through the mist, through great extensions of space, through all that would always remain incomprehensible – she might give her husband a kiss on the forehead.

She never discussed things of that kind openly with Martin, but she always had the feeling that everything else they talked about created for Martin, through her voice and her love, the same sense of divinity as lived within her. Lying in the next room and feigning to snore so his mother would not think he was awake, Martin also recalled harrowing things, also tried to comprehend his father's death and to catch a wisp of posthumous tenderness in the dark of the room. He thought about his father with the full force of his soul, and even made certain experiments: if, right now, a board in the floor creaks or there is a knock of some kind, that means he hears me and responds. Martin felt afraid, waiting for the knock. The closeness of the night air oppressed him; he could hear the surf boom; mosquitoes emitted their high-pitched whine. Or else, with absolute clarity, he would suddenly see his father's round face, his pince-nez, the fair crop of his brush cut, the fleshy button of a wart near his nostril, and the shiny ring formed of two little gold serpents around the knot of his tie. Then, when at last he fell asleep, he found himself sitting in a classroom with his homework not done, while Lida kept idly scratching her shin as she told him that Georgians did not eat ice cream: *'Gruziny ne edyat morozhenogo.'*

4

He did not inform either Lida or her brother of his father's death since he doubted that he could utter the news naturally, while it would have been indecorous to tell it with feeling. From early childhood his mother had taught him that to discuss in public a profound emotional experience – which, in the open air, immediately evanesces and fades, and oddly, becomes similar to an analogous experience of one's interlocutor – was not only vulgar, but also a sin against sentiment. She detested the ribbons of funeral wreaths with silver inscriptions such as 'To a Young Hero,' or 'To Our Unforgettable Darling Daughter,' and disapproved of sedate but mawkish people who, when they lost a dear one, find it possible to shed tears in public while, in another moment, on a day of good luck, even though bursting with joy, they would never allow themselves to break out laughing in a passing stranger's face. Once, when Martin was about eight, he had attempted to shear the hair off a shaggy little dog, and had inadvertently cut its ear. Embarrassed for some reason to explain that he simply had intended to snip off the excess tufts, before painting it to look like a tiger, Martin met his mother's indignation with stoic silence. She ordered him to lower his pants and lie down prone. He did so in complete silence, and in complete silence she whipped him with a riding switch of tawny bullgut. Then he pulled up his pants, and she helped him button them to his little undervest, as he had begun doing it askew. He then went out, and only there, in the park, let himself go, wailing his heart out, the tears mixed with bilberries. Meanwhile his mother was weeping in her bedroom, and in the evening she was barely able to hold back new tears as a very cheerful and plump Martin sat in the tub, nudging along a celluloid swan, and presently stood up to let his back be lathered, and she saw the vivid pink stripes on his tender buttocks. Such chastisement took place only once, nor did Sofia ever lift her hand threatening to slap him for this or that petty misdemeanor as French and German mothers do.

Martin, who had learned early to control his tears and conceal his emotions, astonished his schoolteachers with his insensitivity. Meanwhile, he soon discovered in himself a trait that he felt compelled to conceal with particular tenacity, and at sixteen, in the Crimea, this was the cause of a certain amount of torment. Martin noticed that on occasion he was so afraid of seeming unmanly, to become known as a coward, that he involuntarily reacted in just the way a coward would – the blood left his face, his legs trembled, and his heart pounded tightly in his chest. Admitting to himself that he was not possessed of genuine, innate *sang-froid*, he nevertheless firmly resolved to behave always as a fearless man would in his place. At the same time vanity and self-esteem were highly developed in him. Lida's brother Kolya, though of the same age as Martin, was skinny and short. Martin felt that he could pin him without much trouble. And yet the possibility of a chance defeat made him so nervous, and he imagined it with such hideous clarity, that never once did he try to start a wrestling match with that coeval; however, he would willingly accept a challenge from Ivanov, a twenty-year-old cavalry officer, with muscles like round rocks (killed six months later in the battle of Melitopol), who would rough him up mercilessly and, after an exhausting tussle, at last press him, red and grinning, to the grass. There also was that night, that warm Crimean night, with the blue-black of cypresses, brought out by the chalky white of ghostly Tartar walls in the moonlight, when, on his way home from Adreiz, where Lida's family lived, a human shape abruptly appeared at a turn of the flinty path that led to the highway, and a deep voice asked, 'Who goes there?' Martin noted with chagrin that his heart missed a beat. 'Aha, must be Dedman the Tartar,' added the voice, and a man's face advanced menacingly through the torn black web of shadows.

'No,' said Martin. 'Please let me pass.'

'And I say you are Dedman-Akhmet,' insisted the other, quietly but even more grimly, and, in a gleam of moonlight, Martin noticed that he was holding a large revolver in his hand. 'All right – stand against the wall,' said the man, his tone no longer threatening, but conciliatory and matter-of-fact. Shadow again engulfed the pale hand and dark weapon, but a glistening speck remained where it had been. Martin was faced with two alternatives. The first was to insist on an explanation; the second, to dodge into the darkness and run. 'I think you've mistaken me for someone else,' he said awkwardly and gave his name.

'Against the wall, against the wall,' shouted the man in a treble.

'There isn't any wall right here,' said Martin.

'I'll wait until there is,' enigmatically observed the man and, with a crunch of pebbles, either squatted or sat down – it was impossible to tell in the dark. Martin remained standing where he was, feeling a kind of faint itch in the whole left part of his chest, where the now invisible barrel must be pointing.

'One move and I'll kill you,' murmured the man, and added something unintelligible. Martin stood for a while, and then for a while longer, trying painfully to think what a daredevil, unarmed, would do in his place; he could think of nothing, and suddenly asked:

'Would you like a cigarette? I have some.'

He did not know how this had escaped, and immediately felt ashamed, especially since the offer remained without reply. Then Martin decided that the only means of redeeming his shameful words was to go straight at the man, to knock him down if necessary, but to pass. He thought of the picnic planned for tomorrow, of Lida's legs, evenly coated with a lacquer-smooth reddish-gold tan, and imagined that perhaps he was making preparations of some kind for their meeting – and here Martin caught himself feeling a strange hostility toward his father, for which he reproached himself for a long time. The sea's woosh could be heard, with regularly spaced booms; loud crickets engaged in clockwork competitive chirring; and here was this imbecile in the dark. Martin, as he now realized, was protecting his heart with his hand; calling himself a coward one last time, he moved forward abruptly. Nothing happened. He stumbled over the man's leg, but the latter did not remove it: he was sitting hunched over, head bowed, snoring softly, and giving off a thick, rich reek of wine.

After getting home safely, and enjoying a good night's sleep,

Martin, as he stood next morning on the wisteria-entwined balcony, regretted that he had not disarmed the inert reveler: it would have been nice enigmatically displaying the confiscated revolver. He remained cross with himself because, in his opinion, he had not quite risen to the occasion upon encountering long-awaited danger. How many times, on the highroad of his dreams, wearing a half-mask and jack boots, he had stopped either a stagecoach, or a bulky berlin, or a horseman, and then distributed the merchants' ducats to the poor! During his term as captain of a pirate corvette he had stood with his back to the mainmast, singlehandedly fighting off the onrush of the mutinous crew. He had been sent into the depths of Africa to search for a lost explorer, and when at last he found him – in the wildwood of a nameless region – he went up to him with a polite bow, flaunting his self-control. He would escape from hard-labour camps across tropical swamplands; walk toward the pole past astonished, erect penguins; astride a lathery steed, with bared saber, he would be the first to burst into insurgent Moscow. And now Martin would catch himself embellishing in retrospect the inept and rather insipid nocturnal incident, which bore no more resemblance to the real life he lived in his fantasies than an incoherent dream does to full, authentic reality. And as sometimes, when recounting a dream, we smooth over, round off, embellish here and there, so as to raise it at least to the level of plausible, realistic absurdity, in exactly the same way Martin, when rehearsing the account of his night-time encounter (which he did not, however, intend to make public), made the stranger more sober, his revolver more functional, and his own words wittier.

5

The next day, while passing a soccer ball back and forth with Kolya or searching with Lida, on the shingly beach, for seaside curios (a round pebble with a coloured belt, a little horseshoe, grainy and red-brown with rust; pale-green sea-polished fragments of bottle glass that reminded him of his early childhood and Biarritz), Martin wondered at the night's adventure, doubted that it had really happened, and promoted it more and more decisively into that realm where all that he selected from the world for the use of his soul would take root and begin living a marvellous, independent existence. A wave would swell, boil with foam, and topple rotundly, spreading and running up on the shingle. Then, unable to hold fast, it would slip back to the grumbling of awakened pebbles; and hardly had it receded when a new one, with the same round, joyful splash, would come toppling and stretching out in a transparent stratum to the limit set for it. Kolya was throwing a piece of board he had found for Lady, the fox terrier, to retrieve and she would lift both front paws together and bounce across the water before tensely proceeding to swim. The next wave that came would catch her up and sweep her powerfully back to deposit her in perfect safety on the shore. Then she would drop on the shingle before her the stick wrested from the sea and shake herself violently. While the two boys were bathing in the buff, Lida, who took her dip with her mother and Sofia much earlier in the morning, would retire toward some rocks which she called Ayvazovskian in honour of that painter's seascapes. Kolya swam with a tumbling motion, Tartar-style, while Martin prided himself on his swift and correct crawl, which he had learned from an English house-tutor during his last summer in the North. However, neither of the boys would swim very far out, and in this connection one of Martin's sweetest and creepiest daydreams was of a desolate, stormy sea, after a shipwreck, and himself alone in the dark, holding above water a Creole girl with whom he had danced the tango on deck the evening before. After a swim, it was wonderfully pleasant to stretch out naked on the hot stones and, with head tipped back, look at the cypresses, thrust like black daggers deep into the sky. Kolya, a Yalta doctor's son who had lived all his life in the Crimea, accepted these cypresses, and the ecstatic sky, and the marvellously blue sea with its dazzling metallic scales, as something normal and routine, and it was difficult to draw him into Martin's favourite games, and transform him into the Creole's husband, by chance cast up onto the same uninhabited island.

In the evening they would climb along narrow corridors of cypresses to Adreiz. The large, ridiculous villa, with its many stairways, passages, and galleries (so amusingly constructed that sometimes you simply could not tell on what level you were, or having gone up a few steep steps you suddenly found yourself not on the expected mezzanine floor but on the garden terrace), was already shining through with yellow kerosene light, and the sound of voices and the clink of crockery came from the main veranda. Lida would go over to the adult camp. Kolya would gorge himself and immediately go off to bed. Martin sat in the dark on the bottom steps and, consuming cherries out of his hand, hearkened to the gay, brightly lit voices, to Ivanov's guffaws, Lida's cozy patter, and an argument between her father and the painter Danilevski, a garrulous stutterer. In general the guests were numerous: giggly girls in bright kerchiefs, officers from Yalta, and panicky elderly neighbours, who had taken *en masse* to the hills during an incursion of the Reds the previous winter. It was never clear who had brought whom and who was friends with whom, but the hospitality of Lida's mother, an inconspicuous woman who wore a gorget and spectacles, knew no bounds. Thus one day appeared Arkady Zaryanski, a lanky, deathly pale man who had some connection or other with the theatre – one of those absurd people who tour battlefronts giving poetry recitals with musical accompaniment, arrange performances on the eve of a town's devastation, run off to buy epaulets and never manage to run far enough, returning instead, puffing happily, with a miraculously obtained top hat for the last act of *A Dream of Love*. He was balding and had a fine, dynamic profile, but *en face* he turned out to be less handsome: bags swelled beneath the mud-coloured eyes, and one incisor was missing. As for his personality, he was a gentle, kind, sensitive man, and, when they all would go out for a walk at night, he would sing in a velvety baritone the *romance* beginning:

> Do you recall our sitting on the seashore,
> The sunset's glow with scarlet striped the sky,

or tell an Armenian joke in the darkness, and in the darkness someone would laugh. On meeting him for the first time, Martin, with amazement and even with a certain horror, recognized in him the drunk who had invited him to stand against the wall and be shot, but apparently Zaryanski remembered nothing, so that Dedman's identity remained unclear. Zaryanski was an outstanding drinker, and got violent when in his cups, but the revolver, which reappeared one day – during a picnic on the mountain plateau above Yalta, on a night steeped in moonlight, cricket-chirr, and muscatel wine – turned out to have an empty cylinder: for a long time Zaryanski went on shouting, threatening, and mumbling, talking of some fatal love of his; they covered him with a military greatcoat, and he went to sleep. Lida sat close to the campfire with her chin propped on her hands, and with shiny, dancing eyes, reddish brown from the flames, watched the escaping sparks. Presently Martin stood up, stretched his legs, ascended a dark turfy slope, and walked to the edge of the precipice. Right under his feet he saw a broad black abyss, and beyond it the sea, which seemed to be raised and brought closer, with a full moon's wake, the 'Turkish Trail' spreading in the middle and narrowing as it approached the horizon. To the left, in the murky, mysterious distance, shimmered the diamond lights of Yalta. And when Martin would turn, he saw the flaming, restless nest of the fire a short distance away, and the silhouettes of people around it, and someone's hand adding a branch. The crickets kept crepitating; from time to time there came a sweet whiff of burning juniper; and above the black alpestrine steppe, above the silken sea, the enormous, all-engulfing sky, dove-grey with stars, made one's head spin, and suddenly Martin again experienced a feeling he had known on more than one occasion as a child: an unbearable intensification of all his senses, a magical and demanding impulse, the presence of something for which alone it was worth living.

6

That moon's scintillating wake enticed one in the same ways as had the forest path in the nursery picture, and the clustered lights of Yalta amid the extensive blackness of unknown composition and properties reminded him too of a childhood impression: aged nine, wearing only his nightshirt, with chilled heels, he knelt at a sleeping-car window; the Sud Express hurtled across the French countryside. Sofia, having put her son to bed, had joined her husband in the dining car; the maid was sound asleep in the upper berth. It was dark in the narrow compartment; only the blue fabric of the night lamp's flexible shade let some light through; its tassel swayed, and panels creaked softly. Having wriggled out from under the sheet, he had crawled along the blanket to the window and raised the leathern curtain – for this he had to undo a button, after which the curtain slid smoothly up. He shivered with cold, and his knees ached, but he could not tear himself away from the window, beyond which the oblique hillsides of night rushed past. It was then that he suddenly saw what he now remembered on the Crimean plateau – a handful of lights in the distance, in a fold of darkness between two black hills: the lights would hide and reappear, and then they came twinkling from a completely different direction, and abruptly vanished, as if somebody had covered them with a black kerchief. Soon the train braked and stopped in darkness. Strangely disembodied noises became audible within the car: monotonous speech, coughing; then his mother's voice passed down the corridor; and, deducing that his parents were returning from the dining car and might look in on the way to the adjacent compartment, Martin slipped quickly back into bed. A little later the train began to move, but then stopped for good, emitting a long, softly sibilant sigh of relief, and simultaneously pale stripes of light passed slowly across the dark compartment. Martin once again crawled over to the window: he saw a lighted station platform; a man passed trundling an iron baggage cart with a muffled clatter, and on the cart was a crate with the mysterious inscription 'FRAGILE.' Several midges and one large moth circled around a gas lantern; shadowy people shuffled along the platform conversing about unknown things as they went; then there was a jangle of buffers and the train glided off. Lamps passed and disappeared; a small structure, brightly lit inside and housing a row of levers, appeared and also passed. The train rocked gently as it switched tracks, everything grew dark beyond the window, and once again there was only the rushing night. And again, out of nowhere, no longer between two hills but somehow much closer and more tangible, the familiar lights spilled forth, and the engine emitted a long, plaintive whistle as if it, too, was sorry to leave them behind. Then came a sharp bang, and an oncoming train shot past – and vanished as if it had never existed. The undulating black night resumed its smooth course and the elusive lights gradually thinned into nothingness.

When they had finally disappeared Martin fastened the window shade and lay down. He awoke very early. The train's motion seemed smoother and more relaxed, as if it had become accustomed to the rapid pace. When he unfastened the shade he felt a momentary dizziness, for the ground was running past in the opposite direction, and the early ash-pale light of the clear sky was unexpected too, and absolutely new to him were the terraced, olive-covered slopes.

From the station they went to Biarritz in a hired landau along a dusty road bordered by dusty brambles, and since Martin saw blackberries for the first time in his life, and the station was for some reason called 'The Negress,' he was full of questions. Today, at the age of sixteen, he kept comparing the Crimean sea with the ocean in Biarritz: yes, the Biscay waves were higher, and the breakers more violent, and the fat Basque *baigneur* in his perennially wet bathing suit ('That's a killing profession,' his father used to say) would take Martin by the hand and lead him into shallow water; then they would both turn their backs to the surf and a huge, roaring wave would rush upon them from behind, drowning and overturning the entire world. On the first, mirrorlike strip of beach a swarthy-faced woman with grey wisps of hair on her chin would meet those who had finished bathing and throw a fluffy beach towel over one's shoulders. Further on, in a cabin that smelled of tar, an attendant would help you yank off the clammy and clingy bathing suit and would bring a tub of hot, almost boiling water, where you had to immerse your feet. Then, when Martin and his parents had dressed, they would sit on the beach – Mother, with her big white hat, under a frilly white umbrella; Father also under an umbrella, but a cream-coloured masculine one; and Martin, in striped jersey and sunbrowned straw hat with 'HMS *Indomitable*' on the ribbon around its crown. His pants rolled all the way up, he would build a sand castle surrounded by moats. A waffle man, wearing a beret, would come by and turn with a grinding noise the handle of the red tin cask that contained his wares, and those large, curved chunks of waffle, mixed with flying sand and sea salt, remained among the most vivid memories of that period. Behind the beach, on the stone promenade, inundated by the waves on stormy days, a pert, well-rouged, far from young flower woman would insert a carnation in the buttonhole of Father's white jacket, while Father kindly and comically observed the procedure of insertion, thrusting out his lower lip and pressing the folds of his chin against the lapel.

It was a shame, at the end of September, to leave the happy seaside and the white villa with its gnarled fig tree that refused to yield even one ripe fruit. On the way home they stopped in Berlin, where boys on roller skates, and even an occasional adult with a briefcase under his arm, would clatter by along the asphalt of streets. And then there were marvellous toy shops (locomotives, tunnels, viaducts), and tennis courts in the outskirts of the city, on the Kurfürstendamm, and the starry-night ceiling of the Wintergarten, and a trip to the pine woods of Charlottenburg on a cool, clear day, in a white electric cab.

At the frontier where one had to change trains Martin realized that he had forgotten in his compartment the penholder with the tiny glass lens, in which, when held up to your eye, a mother-of-pearl and blue landscape would flash into being; but during supper at the station (hazel hen with lingonberry sauce) the sleeping-car attendant brought it, and Father gave him a ruble. Snow and frost met one on the Russian side of the border, a whole mountain of logs swelled up on the tender, the crimson Russian locomotive was equipped with a fan-shaped snowplow, and abundant white steam flowed, curling, from the huge smokestack. The Nord-Express, russified at Verzhbolovo, retained the brown facings of its cars, but now became more sedate, wide-flanked, thoroughly heated, and, instead of gathering full speed right away, took a long time to gain momentum after a stop. It was pleasant to perch on one of the flap seats in the blue-carpeted corridor, and the fat lantern-jawed attendant, in his chocolate-coloured uniform, stroked Martin on the head in passing. White fields stretched outside; here and there leafless sallows stuck up out of the snow. By a crossing gate stood a woman in felt boots, holding a green flag; a peasant, who had jumped down from his sledge, shielded with his mittens the eyes of his backing nag. And at night he saw something wonderful: past the black, mirrory window flew thousands of sparks – arrow-like flourishes of a fire-tipped pen.

7

From that year on Martin developed a passion for trains, travels, distant lights, the heartrending wails of locomotives in the dark of night, and the waxworks vividness of local stations flashing by, with people never to be seen again. The slow heaving off, the grating of the rudder chain, the internal tremor of the Canadian freighter on which he and his mother left Crimea in April 1919, the stormy sea and the driving rain were not as conducive to viatic excitement as an express train, and only very gradually did Martin get penetrated with this new enchantment. A dishevelled raincoated young woman with a black and white scarf around her neck strolled about the deck, blowing at the hair that tickled her face, accompanied by her pale husband until the sea got the better of him, and in her figure, in her flying scarf, Martin fully recognized the travel thrill that captivated him at the sight of the checkered cap and suede gloves his father would put on in a railroad compartment, or the crocodile satchel worn with its strap over her shoulder by that little French girl with whom it was such fun to roam along a fast train's long corridor, inserted into the fleeting landscape. This young woman was the only one that looked an exemplary sailor, very much unlike the rest of the passengers whom the captain of this rashly chartered vessel, finding no cargo in crazed Crimea, had agreed to take on board so as not to make the return journey empty. Despite the abundant luggage – lumpy, hastily gathered, fastened with rope instead of straps – all these people somehow gave the impression of travelling light, of sailing as if by chance the formula of distant journeys could not accommodate their bewilderment and melancholy. They were fleeing before a mortal danger but for some reason Martin was little disturbed by the fact that this was so, that the ashen-faced profiteer over there with a load of precious stones in a belt next to his skin, had he stayed ashore, would have been killed on the spot by the first Red Army fellow to be tempted by his diamond innards. And Martin followed the Russian shore with an almost indifferent gaze as it receded in the rainy mist, so restrainedly, so simply, without a single sight that might have hinted at the supernatural length of the separation. Only when everything had vanished in the fog did he avidly recall, in a flash, Adreiz, and the cypresses, and the cheerful house, whose denizens would reply to the astonished questions of restless neighbours, 'Flee? But where would we live if not in the Crimea?' And his recollection of Lida was coloured differently than their former, actual relationship: he remembered how once, when she was complaining about a mosquito bite and was scratching the place, grown red through the tan, on her calf, he wanted to show her how you were supposed to cut a cross on the swelling with your fingernail, and she had slapped him on the hand for no reason at all. He also remembered the farewell visit, when neither of them knew what to talk about, and kept mentioning Kolya, who had gone shopping in Yalta, and what a relief it was when he finally arrived. Lida's elongated, delicate face, about which there was something doelike, now haunted Martin quite obsessively. As he lay on a couch beneath a ticking clock in the cabin of the captain, with whom he had become great friends, or shared, in reverent silence, the watch of the first mate, a pockmarked Canadian who spoke rarely – and when he did, pronounced English as if masticating it – but who had sent a mysterious chill through Martin's heart once when he informed him that old salts never sit down even when they go into retirement, that grandchildren sit while their grandfathers walk ('the sea remains in one's legs'); as he grew accustomed to all this nautical novelty, to the tang of oil and the ship's rolling, to the diverse and strange varieties of bread, one of which tasted like the Russian Eucharistic *prosfora*, Martin kept trying to convince himself that he had gone voyaging out of grief, that he was mourning an ill-starred love, but that no one, seeing his tranquil, already windburned face, could have suspected his anguish. Mysterious, wonderful people cropped up: there was the person who had chartered the ship, a sullen puritan from Nova Scotia, whose raincoat hung in the captain's toilet (which was in a state of hopeless disrepair), pendulating right over the seat. There was the second mate, by the name of Patkin, a Jew originally from Odessa, who, despite his American speech, could still perceive the blurry outlines of Russian words. And among the seamen there was a certain Silvio, a Spanish-American, who always walked barefoot and carried a dagger. One day the captain appeared with an injured hand, saying at first that the cat had scratched him, but later out of friendship confiding to Martin that he had gashed it on Silvio's teeth when he hit him for drunkenness on board. Thus was Martin initiated into seamen's life. The complex architectural structure of the ship, all those steps, mazy passages, swinging doors, soon yielded their secrets to him, and it became difficult to find a still unfamiliar corner. Meanwhile the lady with the striped scarf seemed to share Martin's curiosity, flitting past in the most unexpected places, always with wind-blown hair, always gazing into the distance; already by the second day her husband was laid up, moping, collarless, on the oilcloth'd bench in the saloon, while on another bench lay Sofia, with a slice of lemon between her lips. Now and then Martin, too, felt a sucking void in the pit of his stomach and a kind of general unsteadiness, while the lady was indefatigable, and Martin had already picked her as the one to save in case of disaster. But in spite of the turbulent sea the ship safely reached the harbour of Constantinople one cold, milkily gloomy dawn, and suddenly a wet Turk appeared on deck, and Patkin, who felt the quarantine should be reciprocal, yelled 'I'll "sunk" you!' at him (*ye tebya utonu*), and even threatened him with a pistol. Next day they moved on into the Sea of Marmara, and the Bosporus left no impression at all in Martin's memory except for three or four minarets that looked like factory chimneys in the mist, and the voice of the lady in the raincoat, who talked to herself out loud as she gazed at the gloomy coast; Martin, straining to overhear, seemed to distinguish the adjective 'amethyst' (*ametistovïy*), but decided he was mistaken.

8

After Constantinople the sky cleared, though the sea remained '*ochen* (very) choppy,' as Patkin expressed it. Sofia ventured on deck, but promptly returned to the saloon, saying that there was nothing more hateful in the world than this servile sinking and rising of all one's insides in rhythm with the rising and sinking of the ship's prow. The lady's husband moaned, inquired of God when this would end, and hurriedly, with trembling hands, grabbed for the basin. Martin, whom his reclining mother was holding by the hand, felt that unless he left at once, he would throw up too. At that moment the lady came in with a flick of her scarf, and addressed a compassionate question to her husband. Her husband, without speaking or opening his eyes, made a Russian slicing gesture with his hand across his Adam's apple (meaning: I'm being slaughtered), whereupon she asked the same question of Sofia, who responded with a martyred smile. 'You don't look too happy either,' said the lady, with a severe glance at Martin. Then she staggered, tossed the end of her scarf over her shoulder, and went out. Martin followed her, and the fresh wind in his face and the sight of the bright-blue, white-capped sea made him feel better. She was sitting on some coiled ropes, writing in a small morocco notebook. The other day one of the passengers had said about her 'not bad, that broad,' and Martin turned angrily but could not identify the rascal among several despondent, middle-aged men with turned-up collars. Now, as he looked at her red lips, which she kept licking as her pencil whipped across the page, he was embarrassed, did not know what to talk about, and felt a salty taste on his lips. She wrote on and seemed not to notice him. And yet Martin's nice round face, his seventeen years, a certain trim solidity of build and movement, often present in Russians, but for some reason classified as 'something British' – the whole appearance of Martin in his belted blue overcoat had made a certain impression on the lady.

She was twenty-five, her name was Alla, and she wrote poetry: three things, one would think, that were bound to make a woman fascinating. Her favourite poets were two fashionable mediocrities, Paul Géraldy and Victor Gofman; and her own poems, so sonorous, so spicy, always addressed the man in the polite form ('you,' not 'thou') and were asparkle with rubies as red as blood. One of them had recently enjoyed great success in St Petersburg society. It began thus:

> On purple silks, beneath an Empire pall,
> You vampirized me and caressed me all,
> And we tomorrow die, burned to the end;
> Our lovely bodies with the sand will blend.

The ladies would copy it from each other, learn it by heart and recite it, and one naval cadet even set it to music. Married at eighteen, she remained faithful to her husband for more than two years, but the world all around was saturated with the rubineous fumes of sin; clean-shaven, persistent males would schedule their own suicides at seven Thursday evening, midnight Christmas Eve, or three in the morning under her windows; the dates got jumbled, and it was hard to keep all of those assignations. A Grand Duc languished because of her; Rasputin pestered her for a month with telephone calls. And sometimes she said that her life was but the light smoke of an amber-perfumed Régie cigarette.

Martin did not understand any of this at all. Her poetry left him somewhat perplexed. When he said that Constantinople was anything but amethyst-coloured, Alla objected that he was devoid of poetic imagination, and, on their arrival in Athens, gave him Pierre Louys's *Chansons de Bilitis* in the cheap edition illustrated with the naked forms of adolescents, from which she would read to him, meaningfully pronouncing the French, in the early evening on the Acropolis, the most appropriate place, one might say. What he found particularly appealing about her speech was the ripply way she pronounced the letter 'r,' as if there were not just one letter, but a whole gallery, accompanied, as if that were not enough, by its reflection in water. And instead of those French corybantics, guitar-filled Petersburgan white nights, or libertine sonnets of five dactylic stanzas, he managed to find in this girl with the hard-to-assimilate name something quite, quite different. The acquaintance that had imperceptibly begun on shipboard continued in Greece, at the seaside, in one of the white hotels of Phaleron. Sofia and her son ended up in a nasty, tiny room; its only window gave on a dusty courtyard where, at dawn, with various agonizing preparatives, with a preliminary flapping of wings and other sounds, a young cock commenced his series of hoarse, cheerful cries. Martin slept on a hard blue couch; Sofia's bed was narrow and unsteady with a lumpy mattress. The only representative of the insect kingdom in the room was a solitary flea, which, in recompense, was very crafty, voracious, and absolutely uncatchable. Alla, who had had the good fortune to get an excellent room with twin beds, offered to have Sofia sleep with her, sending her husband over to Martin in exchange. After saying, several times in a row, 'I wouldn't think of it, I wouldn't think of it,' Sofia willingly accepted, and the transfer took place that very same day. Chernosvitov was big, lanky, and sullen, and filled the little room with his presence. Apparently his blood immediately poisoned the flea, as it did not reappear. His toilet implements – a small mirror bisected by a crack, eau-de-cologne, a shaving brush that he always forgot to rinse and that would stand the whole day, all stuck together by gelid lather, on windowledge, table, or chair – depressed Martin, and the encroachment was especially hard to bear at bedtime, when he was obliged to clear his couch of the man's various neckties and mesh undershirts. While undressing, Chernosvitov would scratch himself listlessly between gaping yawns; then he would place an enormous, naked foot on the edge of the chair and, thrusting his hand into his hair, freeze in this uncomfortable attitude, until he slowly came once more into motion, wound his watch, got into bed, and then, for a long time and with many grunts and groans, kneaded the mattress with his body. Some time later, in the dark, his voice would always pronounce the same sentence: 'One special request, my boy: don't foul the air.' While shaving in the morning, he would invariably say, 'Pimplekill face cream. Indispensable at your age.' As he dressed, choosing, whenever possible, socks that guaranteed decorum by having holes at the big toe rather than above the heel, he would exclaim (quoting a popular bard), 'Ah, yes, in our day we were young coursers too,' and whistle softly through his teeth. This was all very monotonous and unfunny. Martin would smile politely.

Yet his awareness of a certain risk afforded some consolation. Any night, in a treacherous dream, he might distinctly pronounce a full-voweled name, and any night the exasperated husband might steal up with a sharpened razor. Chernosvitov, of course, used only a safety razor; he treated this little instrument just as sloppily as his brush, and the ashtray always contained a rusty blade with a fringe of petrified foam dotted with black hairs. His sullenness and his insipid sayings seemed to Martin proof of a deep-seated but restrained jealousy. Going as he did to Athens on business for the whole day, he could not help suspecting that his wife was passing the time alone with the good-humoured, calm, yet worldly-wise young fellow that Martin fancied himself.

9

It was very hot and very dusty. The cafés served one a tiny cup of sweet black goo to accompany a huge glass of ice-cold water. On the beach fences, posters with the name of a Russian soprano were growing tattered. The electric train that ran to Athens filled the idle blue day with a soft rumble, whereupon everything grew quiet again. The sleepy little houses of Athens reminded one of a Bavarian townlet. The tawny mountains in the distance were wonderful. Pale poppies quivered in the wind among bits of broken marble on the Acropolis. Right in the middle of the street, haphazardly, began the tracks on which stood the cars of resort-bound trains. Oranges were ripening in the gardens. There might be a vacant lot with a superb growth of columns – one of them fallen and fractured in three places. All of this crumbling, yellow marble was gradually being turned over to nature's curatorship. Martin's hotel, destined to remain new for its allotted span, would share the same fate.

As he stood on the seashore with Alla, he told himself with an ecstatic chill that he was in a lovely remote land; and what a condiment that was to being in love, what bliss to stand in the wind next to a laughing woman with wind-blown hair, whose bright skirt would now be worried, now pressed against her knees by the same breeze that had once filled Ulysses' sails. One day, while they strolled across the uneven sand, she stumbled, Martin caught her, she glanced over her shoulder at the sole of her shoe, raised high, heel-upward, then stumbled again; that settled it, and he pressed his mouth against her half-open lips.

During this lengthy, rather clumsy embrace they both nearly lost their balance. She freed herself and, laughing, declared he kissed too wetly and ought to take some lessons. Martin was aware of a humiliating trembling in his legs, and of the pounding of his heart. He was furious with himself for this agitation, which reminded him of the moment after a fight at school when his classmates exclaimed: 'Look how pale he is!' However, this first kiss of his life – shut-eyed and deep, with a kind of quivering point inside whose exact origin he did not immediately understand – was so wonderful, so generously fulfilled his forefeeling, that his dissatisfaction with himself was soon dispelled. The windy wild day passed in passionate repetitions and improvements, and that evening Martin felt as tired as if he had been toting logs. And when Alla, accompanied by her husband, entered the dining room, where he and his mother were already peeling their oranges, and sat down at the next table (nimbly undoing the miter of her napkin, dropping it in her lap with a slight upward flight of her hands, then moving closer to the table together with her chair) a slow flush invaded Martin's face, and for a long time he lacked the courage to meet her gaze, but when at last he did, he failed to find an answering embarrassment in her look.

Martin's avid, unbridled imagination would have been incompatible with chastity. Fantasies known as 'impure' had plagued him for the last two or three years, and he made no particular effort to resist them. At first they existed separately from the actual infatuations of his early boyhood. One memorable winter night in St Petersburg, after he had taken part in some home theatricals and was still made up, with charcoaled eyebrows, and dressed in a white Russian blouse, he shut himself in a closet with a coeval girl cousin, also made up and with a kerchief at eyebrow level, and as he squeezed her moist little hands, Martin had keenly sensed the romantic nature of his behaviour, but had not been excited by it. Mayne Reid's hero Maurice Gerald, having stopped his steed side-by-side with that of Louise Pointdexter, put his arm around the blonde Creole's limber waist, and here the author exclaimed in a personal aside: 'What can compare with such a kiss?' Things like that provided a far greater erotic thrill. What fired him as a rule was the remote, the forbidden, the vague – anything sufficiently indistinct to make his fantasy work at establishing details – whether a portrait of Lady Hamilton or a popeyed schoolmate's whisperings about 'houses of evil repute.' Now the mist had thinned, visibility had improved. He was too engrossed in those sensations to give due attention to Alla's actual pronouncements: 'I shall remain for you a glamorous dream,' 'I am insanely voluptuous,' 'You will never forget me, as one forgets "an old novel read long ago" (know that song?),' 'And you must never, never talk about me to your future mistresses.'

As for Sofia she was pleased and displeased at the same time. When some acquaintance would coyly report, 'We were out strolling today and we saw him, yes, we did – with the poetess on his arm – lost his head completely, that boy of yours,' Sofia replied that this was all quite natural at his age. Martin's early revelation of manly passions made her proud, yet she could not ignore the fact that even though Alla was a sweet, affable young lady, she was perhaps a little too 'fast,' as the English say, and, while excusing her son's folly, Sofia did not excuse Alla's attractive vulgarity. Fortunately their stay in Greece was coming to an end: within a few days Sofia expected from Henry Edelweiss (her husband's cousin) in Switzerland a reply to a very frank letter, written with great difficulty, about her husband's death and the exhaustion of their means. Henry used to visit them in Russia, was good friends with her and her husband, was fond of his nephew, and always enjoyed the reputation of an honest and generous man. 'Do you remember, Martin, when was the last time that Uncle Henry came to see us? In any case it was *before*, wasn't it?' That '*before*,' always lacking an object, meant before the quarrel, before the separation from her husband, and Martin also would say 'before' or 'after' without further qualification. 'I think it was after,' he answered, recalling how Uncle Henry had arrived at their dacha, had had a long private interview with his mother, and emerged red-eyed, as he was particularly lachrymose, and even cried at the movies. 'Yes, of course – how stupid of me,' Sofia said quickly, suddenly reconstructing his visit, the discussion they had about her husband, Henry's exhortations that they make up. 'And you remember him well, don't you? Every time he came he brought you something.'

'The last time it was a room-to-room telephone,' said Martin, making a face: installing the telephone was boring, and when somebody finally did install it, running it from the nursery to his mother's room, it never worked well, then broke down altogether, and was abandoned, along with other previous gifts from Uncle, such as *The Swiss Family Robinson*, for instance, which was extremely dull after the real *Robinson Crusoe*, or the little tin freight cars, which had provoked secret tears of disappointment, for Martin liked only passenger trains.

'Why are you grimacing?' asked Sofia.

He explained, and she said with a laugh. 'That's true, that's true,' and stopped to think for a moment about Martin's childhood, about irretrievable, ineffable things, and there was a heartrending charm about this reverie: how quickly everything passes! . . . Just think – has begun to shave, has clean nails, that smart lilac necktie, that woman. 'That woman is very sweet, of course,' said Sofia, 'but don't you think she's just a little too lively? You shouldn't get carried away like this. Tell me – no, I prefer not to ask you anything. Only they say she was a terrible flirt in St Petersburg. And don't tell me you really like her poetry? That female demonism? She has such an affected way of reciting verse. Is it true you've reached the point of – I don't know, of holding hands, or something like that?'

Martin smiled enigmatically.

'I'm sure there's nothing between you,' Sofia said slyly, considering with love the twinkling, equally sly eyes of her son. 'I'm certain there is nothing. You aren't old enough yet.'

Martin laughed, she pulled him close, and planted a juicy, greedy kiss on his cheek. All this was taking place at a garden table on the terrace before the hotel, early in the morning. The day promised to be lovely; the cloudless sky still had a hazy cast, as a sheet of gauze paper sometimes covers an exceptionally vivid frontispiece in an expensive edition of fairy tales. Martin carefully removed this translucent sheet, and there, down the white steps, swinging her low hips ever so slightly, wearing a bright-blue skirt across which an orderly ripple ran back and forth as, stepping down with calculated unhurriedness, first one foot and then the other extended the tip of its polished shoe, rhythmically balancing her brocaded handbag and already smiling, her hair parted on one side, came a limpid-eyed, slender-necked woman with large black earrings that also swung in rhythm with her descent. Martin went to meet her, kissed her hand, stepped back, and she, laughing and trilling her 'r's,' greeted Sofia, who sat in a wicker armchair smoking a thick English cigarette, her first after morning coffee.

'You were sleeping so prettily, Alla, that I didn't want to wake you,' said Sofia, her long, enamelled cigarette holder held at a distance and glancing out of the corner of her eye at Martin, who now sat on the balustrade, swinging his legs. Bubbling over with excitement Alla began recounting the dreams she had seen last night, marvellous marble dreams with priests of ancient Greece, whose capacity to appear in dreams Sofia strongly doubted. And the freshly watered gravel glistened moistly.

Martin's curiosity grew. The rambles on the beach, and the kisses that anyone could spy on began to seem too lengthy a foreword; at the same time his desire for the main text was mixed with anxiety: Martin failed to imagine certain details, and his inexperience alarmed him. The unforgettable day on which Alla said that she was not made of wood, that he must not caress her like that, and that after lunch, when her husband was safely away in the city, and Sofia was enjoying her siesta, she would slip into Martin's room to show him somebody's poems – that day was the very same one that opened with the conversation about Uncle Henry and the room-to-room telephone. When, later in Switzerland, Uncle Henry gave Martin a black statuette (a soccer player dribbling the ball) for his birthday, Martin could not understand why, at the very instant his uncle placed that useless object on the table, he pictured with astounding clarity a distant, tender morning in Greece with Alla descending the white stairs. Right after dinner he had gone to his room and begun to wait. Chernosvitov's shaving brush he hid behind the mirror: somehow its presence encumbered him. From the courtyard came the clang of water pails, the splashing of water, and the sound of guttural speech. The yellow window curtain swelled mellowly, and a spot of sunlight changed its shape on the floor. Instead of circles the flies described parallelograms and trapezoids around the shaft of the ceiling lamp, settling every now and then on the brass. He took off his jacket and collar, lay down supine on the couch, and communed with the thump of his heart. When he heard her light footfalls and the knock on his door, something seemed to snap in the pit of his stomach. 'Look, I've brought a whole batch,' said Alla in a conniving whisper, but at the moment Martin could not care less about verse. 'What a wild boy, goodness, what a wild boy,' she kept whispering as she helped him discreetly. Martin hurried, pursued rapture, overtook it, and she covered his mouth with her hand, saying under her breath 'Sh, sh – the people next door . . .'

'This, at least, is a little object that will stay with you always,' said Uncle Henry in a clear voice, and leaned back, openly admiring the statuette. 'At eighteen a person must already think about decorating his future study and, since you're fond of English games—'

'It's beautiful,' said Martin, not wishing to hurt his uncle, and ran his fingers over the motionless ball at the tip of the player's boot.

Around the wooden chalet grew dense firs; fog hid the mountains. Hot, tawny Greece was indeed left far behind. But how vibrant the emotion of that proud, festive day: I have a mistress! What a conspiratorial air the blue couch had had later that evening! At bedtime Chernosvitov as usual scratched his shoulder blades, assumed weary attitudes, then creaked in the dark, requested that winds should not go free, and at last snored, whistling through his nose, while Martin thought, ah, if only he knew. . . . And then, one day, when by all rights her husband ought to have been in the city, and in his and Martin's room Alla was rearranging her dress (having already 'taken a peek into paradise,' as she put it), while Martin sweaty and dishevelled, was searching for a cufflink dropped in that same paradise, suddenly, with a powerful nudge at the door, Chernosvitov came in and said, 'So that's where you are, my dear. I forgot, of course, to take Spiridonov's letter with me. Fine muddle that would have been.'

Alla ran her hand over her wrinkled skirt and asked with a frown, 'Has he signed yet?'

'That old bastard Bernstein keeps dawdling,' said Chernosvitov, digging in a suitcase. 'If they want to delay payment, they can damn well get out of the mess by themselves, the swine.'

'Don't forget the postponement, that's the main thing,' said Alla. 'Well, have you found it?'

'Damn his mother to mucking hell,' muttered Chernosvitov, rummaging through some envelopes. 'It's got to be here. It can't have got lost after all.'

'If it is lost, then the whole thing has fallen through,' she said with displeasure.

'Dawdling, dawdling,' muttered Chernosvitov. 'That's no way to do business. It's enough to drive you nuts. I'll be very glad if Spiridonov refuses.'

'Now, don't you get upset like that, it'll turn up,' said Alla, but she, too, was visibly disturbed.

'Here it is, thank heavens!' cried Chernosvitov, and scanned the paper he had found, while his jaw hung loose with concentration.

'Don't forget to mention the postponement,' Alla reminded him.

'Righto,' said Chernosvitov and hurried out of the room.

This business conversation left Martin somewhat perplexed.

Neither husband nor wife had pretended: they had really quite forgotten that he was present, absorbed as they were by their problems. Alla, however, immediately resumed her previous mood, joked about the inefficiency of Greek door locks that opened all by themselves, and shrugged off Martin's alarmed question, 'Oh, don't worry, he didn't notice anything.' That night Martin could not get to sleep for a long time, and, with the same perplexity, kept listening to the complacent snoring. When, three days later, he sailed with his mother for Marseilles, the Chernosvitovs came to see them off at Piraeus; they stood on the pier, arm in arm, and Alla was smiling and waving a mimosa branch. The day before, though, she had shed a tear or two.

10

Upon her, upon that frontispiece, which, after the removal of the gauze paper, had proved to be a little coarse, a little too gaudy, Martin replaced the haze and through it the colours reassumed their mysterious charm.

Then, on the big transatlantic liner, where everything was clean, polished, and spacious, which had a store selling toilet articles, a picture gallery, and a barber shop, and whose passengers danced the two-step and the fox-trot at night on the deck, he thought with rapt nostalgia about that amiable woman, with the touchingly hollow chest and the clear eyes, and about the way her fragile frame crunched in his embrace, causing her to say softly, 'Ouch, you'll break me.' Meanwhile Africa drew close, the purple strip of Sicily passed by on the northern horizon, then the ship glided between Corsica and Sardinia, and all these patterns of torrid land that existed somewhere around, somewhere near, but passed by unseen, captivated Martin with their disembodied presence. During the night journey from Marseilles to Switzerland he thought he recognized his beloved lights among the hills, and, even though it was no longer a *train de luxe* but a plain express, jolty, dark, grimy with coal dust, the magic was strong as ever: those lights, those wails in the night. From Lausanne they drove by car to the chalet situated about a thousand meters higher in the mountains and Martin, who was sitting beside the chauffeur, every now and then would look back smiling at his mother and uncle, who both wore large motoring goggles and both held their hands in their laps clasped the same way. Henry Edelweiss had remained a bachelor, wore a bushy moustache, and certain intonations of his, and his way of fiddling with a toothpick or a nail file, reminded Martin of his father. On greeting Sofia at the Lausanne station Uncle Henry broke into tears, covering his face with his hand, but later, in the restaurant, he calmed down and, in his somewhat pompous French, began talking about Russia and his trips there in the past. 'How fortunate,' he said to Sofia, 'how very fortunate that your parents did not live to see that terrible revolution. I remember perfectly the old princess, with her white hair. How fond she was of poor, poor Serge,' and, at the recollection of his cousin, azure tears again welled in Henry's eyes.

'Yes, my mother was fond of him, it's true,' said Sofia, 'but then she was fond of everybody and everything. But tell me, how do you find Martin,' she hastily continued, trying to take Henry's mind off melancholy subjects, which, in his soft-moustached mouth, took on a shade of unbearable sentimentality.

'Yes, yes, he looks like him,' nodded Henry. 'The same forehead, the same fine—'

'But hasn't he grown up?' quickly interrupted Sofia. 'And you know, he has already been in love, passionately—'

Uncle Henry passed on to political matters. 'That revolution,' he asked rhetorically, 'how long can it last? Yes, nobody knows. Poor, beautiful Russia is perishing. Perhaps the firm hand of a dictator will put an end to the excesses. But many beautiful things – your lands, your devastated lands, your country mansion, burned down by the rascally mob – to all that you can bid adieu.'

'How much does a pair of skis cost here?' asked Martin.

'I don't know,' replied Uncle Henry with a sigh. 'I have never indulged in that English sport. By the way, you speak French with a British accent. That is bad. We'll have to change all that.'

'He's forgotten a lot,' Sofia interceded for her son. 'The last few years Mlle Planche no longer gave him lessons.'

'Dead,' said Uncle Henry with feeling. 'One more death.'

'No, no,' smiled Sofia. 'Whatever gave you that idea? She married a Finn and is living peacefully in Vyborg.'

'In any case this is all very sad,' said Uncle Henry. 'I wanted so much for Serge to come here with you one day. But one never obtains what one longs for, and God alone knows what is to come. If you have assuaged your hunger and are sure you don't want anything more, we can start.'

The road was brightly sunlit and had many turns; a wall of rock with thorny bushes blooming in its cracks rose on the right, while on the left there was a precipice and a valley where water in crescents of foam ran down over ledges; then came dark conifers clustering in close ranks now on one side, now on the other; mountains loomed all around, imperceptibly changing position; they were greenish with streaks of snow; greyer ones looked out from behind their shoulders, and far beyond there were giants of an opaque violet whiteness, and these never moved, and the sky above them seemed faded in comparison with the bright-blue patches between the tops of the black firs under which the car passed. Suddenly, with a sensation still new to him, Martin remembered the dense fir fringe of their park in Russia as seen through a lozenge of blue glass on the veranda. And when, stretching his slightly vibrating legs and feeling a transparent humming in his head, he got out of the car, he was struck by the fresh rough smell of earth and melting snow, and by the rustic beauty of his uncle's house. It stood by itself half a kilometer from the nearest hamlet, and the top balcony offered one of those marvellous views that are even frightening in their airy perfection. The same Russian vernal blue sky looked into the window of the neat little WC, with its odour of wood and resin. All around, in the garden with its bare, black platbands and white apple bloom, and in the fir forest right behind the orchard, and on the dirt road leading to the village, there was a cool, happy silence, a silence that *knew* something, and Martin felt a little dizzy, perhaps from this silence, perhaps from the smells, or perhaps from the newfound blissful immobility after the three-hour drive.

In this chalet Martin lived until late fall. It was presumed that he would enter the University of Geneva that very winter; however, after a lively exchange of letters with friends in England, Sofia sent him to Cambridge. Uncle Henry did not immediately reconcile himself to this: he disliked the English, whom he considered a cold, perfidious nation. On the other hand the thought of the expenses the famous university required not only did not sadden him, but, on the contrary, was tempting. Fond as he was of economizing on trifles, clenching a penny in his left hand, he willingly wrote large checks with the right, especially when the expense was an honourable one. Sometimes, rather touchingly, he would feign eccentric pigheadedness, slapping the table with his palm, puffing out his moustache, and shouting, 'If I do it, I do it because it gives me pleasure!' With a sigh Sofia would slip the bracelet watch from Geneva on her wrist, while moist-eyed Henry would dig in his pocket for a voluminous handkerchief, trumpet once, twice, and then smooth his moustache to the right and to the left.

With the onset of summer the cross-marked sheep were herded higher into the mountains. A babbling metallic tinkling, of unknown origin and from an unknown direction, would gradually become audible. Floating nearer, it enveloped the listener, giving him an odd tickling sensation in the mouth. Then, in a cloud of dust, came flowing a grey, curly, tightly packed mass of sheep rubbing against each other, and the moist, hollow tinkle of the bells, which delighted all of one's senses, mounted, swelled so mysteriously that the dust itself seemed to be ringing as it billowed above the moving backs of the sheep. From time to time one of them would get separated from the rest and trot past, whereupon a shaggy dog would drive it back into the flock; and behind, gently treading, walked the shepherd. Then the tintinnabulation would change timbre, and once more grow hollowed and softer, but for a long time it would hang in the air together with the dust. 'Nice, nice!' murmured Martin to himself, hearing the tinkle out to the end, and continued on his favourite walk, which began with a country lane and forest trails. The fir grove abruptly thinned out, lush green meadows appeared, and the stony path sloped down between hawthorn hedges. Occasionally a cow with wet pink nose would stop on its way up in front of him, twitch its tail and with a lurch of the head move on. Behind the cow came a spry little old woman with a stick, who glanced malevolently at Martin. Further down, surrounded by poplars and maples, stood a large white hotel, whose owner was a distant relative of Henry Edelweiss.

In the course of that summer Martin grew still sturdier, his shoulders broadened, and his voice acquired an even, deep tone. At the same time he was in a state of inner confusion, and feelings he did not quite understand were evoked by such things as the country coolness of the rooms, so keenly perceptible after the outdoor heat; a fat bumblebee knocking against the ceiling with a chagrined droning; the paws of the fir trees against the blue of the sky; or the firm brown bolete found at the edge of the forest. The imminent journey to England excited and gladdened him. His memory of Alla Chernosvitov had reached its ultimate perfection, and he would say to himself that he had not sufficiently appreciated the happy days in Greece. The thirst she had quenched, only to intensify it, so tormented him during that alpine summer that at night he could not go to sleep for a long time, imagining, among numerous adventures, all the girls awaiting him in the dawning cities, and occasionally he would repeat aloud some feminine name – Isabella, Nina, Margarita – a name still cold and untenanted, a vacant, echoing house, whose mistress was slow to take up residence; and he would try to guess which of these names would suddenly come alive, becoming so alive and familiar that he would never again be able to pronounce it as mysteriously as now.

In the mornings, Marie, the niece of the old chambermaid, would come to help with the household chores. She was seventeen, very quiet and comely with cheeks of a dark-pink hue and yellow pigtails tightly wound about her head. Sometimes, while Martin would be in the garden, she would throw open an upstairs window, shake out her dustcloth, and remain motionless, gazing, perhaps, at the bright clouds, at their oval shadows gliding along the mountain slopes, then pass the back of her hand across her temple, and slowly turn away. Martin would go up to the bedrooms, determine from the drafts where the cleaning was going on, and would find Marie kneeling in meditation amidst the gloss of wet floorboards; he would see her from behind, with her black wool stockings and her green polka-dot dress. She never looked at Martin, except once – and what an event that was! – when, passing by with an empty pail, she smiled uncertainly, tenderly – not at him, though, but at the chicks. He resolutely vowed to start a conversation with her, and to give her a furtive hug. Once, however, after she had left, Sofia sniffed the air, made a face, and hurriedly opened all the windows, and Martin was filled with dismay and aversion toward Marie, and only very gradually, in the course of her subsequent appearances in the distance – framed in a casement, or glimpsed through the foliage near the well – he began again to succumb to that enchantment; only now he was afraid to come closer. Thus something happy and languorous lured him from afar, but was not addressed to him. Once, when he had scrambled far up the mountainside he squatted on a big round-browed rock, and below a herd passed along the winding trail, with a melodious, melancholy jingling and, behind it, a gay, ragged shepherd and a smiling girl who was knitting a stocking as she walked. They went by without a glance at Martin, as if he were incorporeal, and he watched them for a long time. Without breaking step, the man put his arm around his companion's shoulders, and from her nape you could tell that she kept knitting on and on as they walked into another valley. Or else, bare-armed young ladies in white frocks, yelling and chasing off the horseflies with their rackets, would appear by the tennis court in front of the hotel, but, as soon as they started playing, how clumsy and helpless they became, particularly since Martin himself was an excellent player, beating to shreds any young Argentine from the hotel: at an early age he had assimilated the concord essential for the enjoyment of all the properties of the sphere, a coordination of all the elements participating in the stroke dealt to the white ball, so that the momentum begun with an arching swing still continues after the loud twang of taut strings, passing as it does through the muscles of the arm all the way to the shoulder, as if closing the smooth circle out of which, just as smoothly, the next one is born. One hot August day Bob Kitson, a professional from Nice, turned up at the court, and invited Martin to play. Martin felt that familiar, stupid tremor, the vengeance of too vivid an imagination. Nevertheless he started well, now volleying at the net, now driving powerfully from the baseline to the furthest corner. Spectators gathered around the court, and this pleased him. His face was aflame, he felt a maddening thirst. Serving, crashing down on the ball, and transforming at once the incline of his body into a dash netward, Martin was about to win the set. But the professional, a lanky, coolheaded youth with glasses, whose game until then had resembled a lazy stroll, suddenly came awake and with five lightning shots evened the score. Martin began to feel weary and worried. He had the sun in his eyes. His shirt kept coming out from under his belt. If his opponent took this point that *was* the end of it. Kitson hit a lob from an uncomfortable corner position, and Martin, retreating in a kind of cakewalk, got ready to smash the ball. As he brought down his racket he had a fleeting vision of defeat and the malicious rejoicing of his habitual partners. Alas, the ball plumped limply into the net. 'Bad luck,' said Kitson jauntily, and Martin grinned back, heroically controlling his disappointment.

11

On the way home he mentally replayed every shot, transforming defeat into victory, and then shaking his head: how very, very hard it was to capture happiness! Brooks burbled, concealed among the foilage; blue butterflies fluttered up from damp spots on the road; birds bustled in the bushes: everything was depressingly sunny and carefree. That evening after dinner they sat as usual in the drawing room; the door to the piazza was wide open, and, since there had been a power failure, candles burned in the chandeliers. From time to time their flame would slant, and black shadows reach out from under the armchairs. Martin picked his nose as he read a small volume of Maupassant with old-fashioned illustrations: moustachioed Bel Ami, in a stand-up collar, was shown undressing with a lady's maid's skill a coy, broad-hipped woman. Uncle Henry had laid down his newspaper and, arms akimbo, considered the cards that Sofia was laying out on a green-baize table. The warm, black night pressed in through window and door. Suddenly Martin raised his head and hearkened as if there were a vague beckoning in this harmony of night and candle flame. 'The last time this patience came out was in Russia,' said Sofia. 'In general it comes out very seldom.' Spreading her fingers she collected the cards scattered about the table and began shuffling them anew. Uncle Henry sighed.

Tired of reading, Martin stretched and went out on the terrace. It was very dark out, and the air smelled of dampness and night-blooming flowers. A star fell: as so often annoyingly happens, it fell not quite in his field of vision, but off to the side, so that his eye caught only the twinge of a soundless change in the sky. The outlines of the mountains were indistinct, and here and there, in the folds of the darkness, dots of light scintillated in twos and threes. 'Travel,' said Martin softly, and he repeated this word for a long time, until he had squeezed all meaning out of it, upon which he set aside the long, silky skin it had shed – and next moment the word had returned to life. 'Star. Mist. Velvet. Travelvet,' he would articulate carefully and marvel every time how tenuously the sense endures in the sound. In what a remote spot this young man had arrived, what far lands he had already seen, and what was he doing here, at night, in the mountains, and why was everything in the world so strange, so thrillful? 'Thrillful,' Martin repeated aloud, and liked the word. Another star went tumbling. He fixed his eyes on the sky as, once upon a time, when they were driving home in the victoria from a neighbour's estate along a dark forest road, a very small Martin, rocking on the brink of slumber, would throw back his head and watch the heavenly river, between the amassments of trees, along which he was floating. Where again in his life, he wondered, would he gaze – as then, as now – at the night sky? on what pier, at what station, in what town square? A feeling of opulent solitude, which he often had experienced amid crowds – the delight he took in saying to himself: Not one of these people, going about their business, knows who I am, where I am from, what I am thinking about right now – this feeling was indispensable to complete happiness, and Martin, in a breathless trance, imagined how, completely alone, in a strange city – say, London – he would roam at night along unfamiliar streets. He saw the black hansom cabs splashing through the fog, a policeman in a shiny black cape, lights on the Thames, and other images out of English novels. He had left his luggage at the station and was walking past innumerable illuminated English shops, excitedly looking for Isabel, Nina, Margaret – someone whose name he could give to that night. And she – who would she think *he* was? An artist, a sailor, a gentleman burglar? She would not accept his money, she would be tender, and in the morning she would not want to let him go. How foggy the streets were, though, and how crowded, and how difficult the search! And although there was much that looked different, and the hansoms were mostly extinct, he nevertheless recognized certain things when, one autumn evening, he walked baggageless out of Victoria Station; he recognized the dark, greasy air, the bobby's wet oilskin cape, the reflections, the swashy sounds. At the station he had taken an excellent shower in a cheerful, clean cubicle, dried himself with a warm, fluffy towel brought by a ruddy-cheeked attendant, put on clean linen and his best suit, and checked both his bags, and now he was proud that he had managed so sensibly. He hardly felt fatigued by his journey; there was only buoyant excitement. Huge buses fiercely, heavily splattered the pools on the asphalt. Lighted advertisements went running up dark-red façades and dissipating again. He would pass girls; he would turn to look; but the prettier the face, the harder it was to take the plunge. Inviting cafés such as in Athens or Lausanne did not exist here, and in the pub where he drank a glass of beer he found only men, inflamed, morose, with red veins on the whites of their prominent eyes. Little by little a vague sense of irritation overcame him: surely, the Russian family with which, by epistolary agreement, he was to stay for a week, was right then waiting for him, worrying. Should he quietly take a taxi and forget about that imaginary night? But his lack of faith in it struck him as shameful – how intensely he had longed for it that morning at dawn, looking out of the train window at the plains, the cold pink sky, the black silhouette of a windmill. 'Cowardliness and betrayal,' Martin said softly. He noticed that he was walking along the same street for the second time, recognizing it by a shop window filled with pearl necklaces. He stopped and made a cursory check of his long-standing aversion for pearls: oysters' hemorrhoids with a sickly sheen. A girl under an umbrella stopped beside him. Martin glanced out of the corner of his eye: slender figure, black suit, glittering hat pin. She turned her face toward him, smiled, and, pursing her lips, made a small 'oo' sound. In her eyes Martin saw the sparkling lights, the play of reflected colours, the shimmer of rain, and hoarsely muttered 'Good evening.'

As soon as they were in the dark of the taxicab he embraced her, frenzied by the feel of her supple slenderness. She covered her face with her hands, giggling. Later, in the hotel room, when he awkwardly extracted his billfold, she said, 'No, no. If you want, take me tomorrow to a fancy restaurant.' She asked where he came from, whether he was French, and at his behest started guessing: Belgian? Danish? Dutch? She did not believe him when he said he was Russian. Later he hinted that he lived by gambling on ocean liners, told her of his travels, embellishing a bit here, adding something there, and, as he described a Naples he had never seen, he gazed lovingly at her bare, childish shoulders and blond bob, and felt completely happy. Early next morning, as he slept, she dressed quickly and left, stealing ten pounds from his billfold. 'Morning after the orgy,' thought Martin with a smile, slapping shut the billfold, which he had picked up from the floor. He doused himself from the pitcher, splashing water all over the place, and kept smiling as he thought of the blissful night. It was something of a pity that she had left so foolishly, that he would never meet her again. Her name was Bess. When he went out of the hotel and started walking the spacious morning streets, he felt like jumping and singing with joy and, to give release to his spirits, climbed a ladder leaning against a lamppost, and as a result had a long and comical argument with an elderly passer-by, who from below gestured threateningly with his cane.

12

A second scolding came from Olga Zilanov. The day before that lady had waited for him late into the night and, since she assumed for some reason that he was younger and more helpless than he actually turned out to be, she grew increasingly worried. He explained that on the previous day he had misplaced the address, had found it too late in a seldom-visited pocket, and had spent the night at a hotel near the station. Mrs Zilanov wanted to know why he had not telephoned, and which hotel. Martin invented a good, uncommon name, Good-Night Hotel, explaining that he had looked for her number in the book but had not found it. 'Shame on you,' said Mrs Zilanov crossly, and suddenly smiled a marvellous, beautiful smile that completely transfigured her flabby, melancholy face. Martin remembered that smile from St Petersburg days, and, as he had been a child then, and as women usually smile when addressing strange children, his memory had retained a radiant-faced image of Mrs Zilanov, and he had at first been perplexed to find her so old and gloomy.

Her husband, who had been a well-known public figure in Russia, happened to be out of town, and Martin was lodged in his study. The study and the dining room were on the first floor, the parlour on the second, and the bedrooms on the third. The whole quiet, residential street consisted of such narrow houses, indistinguishable from each other, with an identical, vertical configuration of rooms inside. A dash of colour was contributed by a plump red letter-pillar at the corner. Behind the right row of houses were gardens where rhododendrons bloomed in the summer, and behind the left row a small park containing tall elms and a grass tennis court was growing yellow and bare of leaves.

Zilanov's elder daughter Nelly had recently married a Russian army officer who had arrived in England after captivity in Germany. Sonia, the younger daughter, was about to finish a London preparatory school to which she had transferred from the Stoyunin Gymnasium in St Petersburg. There was also Mrs Zilanov's sister Elena and her daughter Irina, a poor hideous half-witted creature.

The week he spent in that house, while getting used to England, seemed rather tiresome to him. The whole livelong day he was among strangers, and could not take one step alone. Sonia needled him, making fun of his wardrobe – shirts with starched cuffs and stiffish fronts, his favourite bright-purple socks, his orange-yellow knobby-capped shoes, bought in Athens. 'These are American,' said Martin with a studied calm.

'The Americans make them specially to sell to Negroes and Russians,' glibly replied Sonia. Furthermore, it turned out that Martin had not brought a dressing gown with him, and when, in the mornings, he would go to the bathroom proudly wrapped in his bedclothes, Sonia would say that this reminded her of her cousins and their chums at the Lyceum school who, when visiting the Zilanovs' country house, slept naked, walked around in the morning draped in bedsheets, and relieved themselves in the garden. In the end Martin made so many purchases in London that ten pounds was not enough, and he had to write to his uncle, which was particularly unpleasant because of the hazy explanations necessitated by the disappearance of the other ten pounds. Yes, it was a hard, unfortunate week. Even his English accent, on which Martin quietly prided himself, proved to be an occasion for derisive corrections on Sonia's part. Thus Martin quite unexpectedly found himself classified as ignorant, adolescent, and a mamma's boy. He felt this was unfair, that he had had infinitely more experiences and adventures than a sixteen-year-old maiden. It was therefore with a certain malicious glee that he drubbed some young men of hers at tennis, and on his last night had a chance to show he could dance an impeccable two-step (which he had learned back in Mediterranean days) to Hawaiian wails from the phonograph.

At Cambridge he felt still more foreign. Upon talking to his English fellow students he noted with wonder his unmistakably Russian essence. From his semi-English childhood he retained only such things as had been relegated by native Englishmen of his age, who had read the same books as children, in the dimness of the past properly allotted to nursery things, while Martin's life at a certain point had made an abrupt turn and taken a different course, and for this very reason his childhood surroundings and habits had assumed a certain fairy-tale flavour, and a book he had been fond of in those days was now more enchanting and vivid in his memory than the same book in the memory of his English coevals. He remembered various expressions that ten years ago had been current among English schoolboys, but now were considered either vulgar or ridiculously old-fashioned. Plum pudding, blazing with a blue flame, was served in St

Petersburg not only at Christmas, as in England, but any day of the year, and, in the opinion of many people, the Edelweiss chef made a better one than could be bought in a store. Petersburgers played soccer on hard ground, not on turf, and the penalty kick was called 'pendel,' a term unknown in England. No longer would Martin dare wear the colours of the striped jersey bought once, long ago, at Drew's, the English shop on the Nevski, for they corresponded to the athletic uniform of a public school he had never attended. In truth, all this English-ness, really of a rather haphazard nature, was filtered through his motherland's quiddity and suffused with peculiar Russian tints.

13

The splendid autumn he had just seen in Switzerland somehow kept lingering in the background of his first Cambridge impressions. In the mornings a delicate haze would enshroud the Alps. A broken cluster of rowan berries lay in the middle of the road, whose ruts were filmed with micalike ice. Despite the absence of wind the bright-yellow birch leafage thinned out with every passing day, and the turquoise sky gazed through it with pensive gaiety. The luxuriant ferns grew reddish; iridescent shreds of spiderweb, which Uncle Henry called 'the Virgin's hair,' floated about. Martin would look up, thinking that he heard the remote blare of migrating cranes, but no cranes were to be seen. He used to wander around a great deal, as if searching for something; he rode the dilapidated bicycle belonging to one of the menials along the rustling paths, while his mother, seated on a bench beneath a maple, pensively pierced the damp crimson leaves on the brown ground with the point of her walking stick. Such wild, varied beauty did not exist in England, where nature had a tame greenhouse quality, and an unimaginative autumn faded away in geometrical gardens under a drizzly sky. But the pinkish-grey walls, the rectangular lawns, frosted with pale silver on the rare sunny mornings, the narrow river, the stone bridge whose arch formed a full circle with its perfect reflection, all had a beauty of their own.

Neither the foul weather nor the icy chill of the bedroom, where tradition forbade heating, could alter the meditative *joie de vivre* characteristic of Martin. He grew sincerely fond of his little living room, with its comfortable, fireplace, its dusty pianola, innocuous lithographs on the walls, low wicker armchairs, and the cheap china bric-a-brac on the shelves. When, late at night, the sacred flame of the fireplace threatened to die, he would scrape the embers together, pile some wood chips on them, heap on a mountain of coal, fan the fire with the asthmatic bellows, and make the chimney draw by spreading an ample sheet of the *Times* across the mouth of the hearth. The taut sheet would grow warm and transparent, and the lines of print, mingling with the lines showing through from the reverse side, looked like the bizarre lettering of some mumbo-jumbo language. Then, as the hum and tumult of the fire increased, a fox-red, darkening spot would appear on the paper and suddenly burst through. The whole sheet, now aflame, would be instantly sucked in and sent flying up. And a belated passer-by, a gowned don, could observe, through the gloom of the gothic night, a fiery-haired witch emerge from the chimney into the starry sky. Next day Martin would pay a fine.

Being of lively and sociable temperament Martin did not remain alone for long. Fairly soon he made friends with his downstairs neighbour Darwin, as well as with various men at the soccer field, the club, and the dining hall. He noticed that everyone felt it his duty to discuss Russia with him and to learn what he thought about the Revolution, intervention, Lenin and Trotsky; while some, who had visited Russia, praised Russian hospitality and asked if he happened to know a Mr Ivanov in Moscow. Such talk nauseated Martin; casually taking a volume of Pushkin from his desk he would read aloud 'Autumn' in Archibald Moon's translation:

> O dismal period, visual enchantment!
> Sweet is to me thy farewell loveliness!
> I love the sumptuous withering of nature,
> The woods arrayed in gold and purple dress.

This caused some astonishment, and only Darwin, a large, sleepy-looking Englishman in a canary-yellow jumper, who sprawled in an armchair, making wheezing sounds with his pipe and gazing up at the ceiling, would nod approvingly.

This Darwin, who often dropped in after dinner, elucidated certain strict, primordial rules in full detail for Martin's edification: a student must not walk outdoors in hat and overcoat, no matter how cold it was; one did not shake hands or wish a good morning, but greeted an acquaintance one happened to meet, even if it were Atom Thompson himself, with a grin and a breezy interjection. It was bad form to go out on the river in an ordinary rowboat: for this purpose there were punts and canoes. One should never repeat the old college witticisms, of which freshmen become immediately enarmored. 'Remember, though,' Darwin added wisely, 'that even in observing these traditions you mustn't overdo, for sometimes, to shock the snobs, it's a good thing to go out in a bowler hat and with an umbrella under your arm.' Martin got the impression that Darwin had already been at the university a long time, several years, and he felt sorry for him as he did for any homebody. Darwin amazed him by his sleepiness, the sluggishness of his movements, a certain comfortableness about his whole being. Trying to stir his envy, Martin impetuously told him about his wanderings, unconsciously throwing in some of what he had invented for Bess's benefit, and barely noticing how the fiction had consolidated. True, these exaggerations were innocent enough: the two or three picnics on the Crimean plateau turned into a habitual roaming of the steppes with a stick and knapsack; Alla Chernosvitov became a mysterious companion on yacht cruises, his walks with her a prolonged sojourn on one of the Greek islands, and the purplish outline of Sicily actual gardens and villas. Darwin would nod approvingly as he gazed at the ceiling. His eyes were pale bluish, vacant, and expressionless; the soles that he always exhibited, fond as he was of semireclining poses with his feet lodged in some high, comfortable position, were equipped with a complicated system of rubber strips. Everything about him, from those solidly shod feet to his bony nose, was high-quality, large, and imperturbable.

14

About three times a month Martin was summoned by his 'tutor,' that is the professor in charge of keeping an eye on lecture attendance, visiting the sick student, giving permission for trips to London, and making reprimands when one was fined (for getting home after midnight or not wearing the academic gown in the evening). He was a wizened, pigeon-toed, keen-eyed little old man, a Latinist, a translator of Horace, and a great oyster fancier. 'Your English is improving,' he once said to Martin. 'That's good. Have you got to know many people?'

'Oh, yes,' answered Martin.

'Are you friends with Darwin, for instance?'

'Oh, yes,' Martin repeated.

'I'm glad. He's a splendid specimen. Three years in the trenches, France and Mesopotamia, the Victoria Cross, and not a scratch, either morally or physically. Literary success might have gone to his head, but that didn't happen either.'

Besides the facts that Darwin had interrupted his college studies at eighteen to enlist and had recently published a collection of short stories which connoisseurs were raving about, Martin learned that he was a boxing Blue, that he had spent his childhood in Madeira and Hawaii, and that his father was a famous admiral. Martin's own meager experience seemed insignificant, pathetic, and he felt ashamed about certain yarns he had spun. When Darwin slouched into his room that evening, the situation seemed both humorous and embarrassing to Martin. Little by little he began to fish for information about Mesopotamia and the short stories, and Darwin kept giving facetious answers, saying that the best book he had ever written was a little manual for students entitled 'A Complete Description of Sixty-seven Ways of Getting inside Trinity College after Closing of the Gates, with a Detailed Plan of its Walls and Railings, First and Last Edition, Verified many Times by the Author, who has never been Caught.' But Martin insisted on what was interesting and important to him: the collection of short stories connoisseurs were raving about. At last Darwin said, 'All right, I'll give you a copy. Let's go to my digs.'

He had furnished his digs himself according to his taste. There were supernaturally comfortable leather armchairs, in which the body would melt as it sank into a yielding abyss, and on the mantelpiece stood a large photograph depicting a bitch lying in complete mollitude on her side and the plump behinds of her six sucklings in a row. Martin had already seen numerous students' rooms: there were those like his, pleasant, but not pampered by the lodger, containing extraneous objects belonging to the landlord; there was the athlete's room with silver trophies on a shelf and a broken oar on the wall; there was the den littered with books and dusted with cigarette ash; finally, there was one of the nastiest abodes you could discover – nearly bare, with bright-yellow wallpaper, a room where there was only one picture, but that one a Cézanne (charcoal doodle vaguely resembling the female form), and where a fourteenth-century bishop of coloured wood stood proffering the stump of his forearm. The most cordial digs of all were Darwin's, especially if you looked carefully and browsed a bit: what a gem, for example, that sea of newspaper issues Darwin had edited in the trenches! The paper was cheerful, jaunty, full of funny jingles; heaven only knows how and where the type was set; and it used chance clichés to beautify blanks – corset advertisements found in the ruins of some printing plant.

'Here,' said Darwin, producing a book, 'take it.'

The book proved to be remarkable. The pieces were not really short stories – no, they were rather more like tractates, twenty tractates of equal length. The first was called 'Corkscrews,' and contained a thousand interesting things about corkscrews, their history, beauty, and virtues. Another was on parrots, a third on playing cards, a fourth on infernal machines, a fifth on reflections in water. And there was one on trains, and in it Martin found everything he loved: the telegraph poles, cutting short the wires' upward sweep, the dining car with those bottles of Vichy or Evian that seemed to scan through the window the trees flying past; and those crazy-eyed waiters, and that minuscule kitchen, where swaying and sweating a white-capped man cook could be seen crumbing a fish.

If Martin had ever thought of becoming a writer and been tormented by a writer's covetousness (so akin to the fear of death), by that constant state of anxiety compelling one to fix indelibly this or that evanescent trifle, perhaps these dissertations on minutiae that were deeply familiar to him might have aroused in him a pang of envy and the desire to write of the same things still better. Instead, such warm goodwill toward Darwin overwhelmed him that his eyes even began to tickle. And next morning when, on the way to his lecture, he overtook his friend at the corner, he said with perfect decorum and not looking him in the face that he had liked the book, and silently walked beside him, falling in with Darwin's indolent but swingy step.

The lecture halls were scattered about the whole town. If one lecture immediately followed another but was given in a different hall, you had to hop on your bicycle, or else scuttle along back alleys and cross the echoing stone of courts. Limpid chimes called back and forth from tower to tower; the din of motors, the crepitation of wheels, and the tinkle of bicycle bells filled the narrow streets. During the lecture the glittering swarm of bicycles clustered at the gates, awaiting their owners. The black-gowned lecturer would mount the platform and with a thump put his tasseled square cap on the lectern.

15

When he entered the university it took Martin a long time to decide on a field of study. There were so many, and all were fascinating. He procrastinated on their outskirts, finding everywhere the same magical spring of vital elixir. He was excited by the viaduct suspended over an alpine precipice, by steel come to life, by the divine exactitude of calculation. He understood that impressionable archeologist who, after having cleared the path to as yet unknown tombs and treasures, knocked on the door before entering, and, once inside, fainted with emotion. Beauty dwells in the light and stillness of laboratories: like an expert diver gliding through the water with open eyes, the biologist gazes with relaxed eyelids into the microscope's depths, and his neck and forehead slowly begin to flush, and, tearing himself away from the eyepiece, he says, 'That settles everything.' Human thought, flying on the trapezes of the star-filled universe, with mathematics stretched beneath, was like an acrobat working with a net but suddenly noticing that in reality there is no net, and Martin envied those who attained that vertigo and, with a new calculation, overcame their fear. Predicting an element or creating a theory, discovering a mountain chain or naming a new animal, were all equally enticing. In the study of history Martin liked what he could imagine clearly, and therefore he was fond of Carlyle. With his poor memory for dates and scorn for generalizations, he avidly sought out what was live and human, what belonged to that class of astonishing details which well may satiate coming generations as they watch old, drizzly films of our day. He vividly visualized the shivering white day, the simplicity of the black guillotine, and the clumsy tussle on the scaffold, where the executioners roughly handle a bare-shouldered fat man while, in the crowd, a good-natured *citoyen* raises by the elbows a *citoyenne* whose curiosity exceeds her stature.

There were other vaguer fields, such as the mists of law, government, economics. What scared him away from them was that the scintilla he sought in everything was too deeply buried there. Undecided what to undertake, what to select, Martin gradually rejected all that might take a too exclusive hold over him. Still to be considered was literature. Here, too, Martin found intimations of bliss; how thrilling was that humdrum exchange about weather and sport between Horace and Maecenas, or the grief of old Lear, uttering the mannered names of his daughters' whippets that barked at him! Just as, in the Russian version of the New Testament, Martin enjoyed coming across 'green grass' or 'indigo chiton,' in literature he sought not the general sense, but the unexpected, sunlit clearings, where you can stretch until your joints crunch, and remain entranced. He read a very great deal, but it was mostly rereading; and he did have occasional accidents in the course of literary conversation. For example, he once confused Plutarch with Petrarch, and once called Calderón a Scottish poet.

Not every writer was able to stir him. He remained unmoved when, on his uncle's advice, he read Lamartine, or when his uncle himself declaimed '*Le Lac*' with a sob in his voice, shaking his head and adding with helpless emotion, '*Comme c'est beau.*' The prospect of studying wordy, watery works and their influence on other wordy, watery works did not attract him. At this rate he probably never would have made a choice if some mysterious voice had not kept whispering that he was not free to choose, that there was one thing he *must* study. During the sumptuous Swiss autumn he felt for the first time that he was, after all, an exile, doomed to live far from home. That word 'exile' had a delicious sound: Martin considered the blackness of the coniferous night, sensed a Byronic pallor on his cheeks, and saw himself in a cloak. This cloak he donned at Cambridge, albeit it was only a lightweight academic gown, of a bluish fabric, semitransparent when held up to the light, with many pleats on the shoulders and with winglike half-sleeves that were worn thrown back. The bliss of spiritual solitude and the excitement of travel took on a new significance. It was as if Martin had found the right key to all the vague, tender, and fierce feelings that besieged him.

At that time the chair of Russian literature and history was occupied by the distinguished scholar Archibald Moon. He had lived fairly long in Russia, and had been everywhere, met everyone, seen everything there. Now, pale and dark-haired, with a pince-nez on his thin nose, he could be observed riding by, sitting perfectly upright, on a bicycle with high handlebars; or, at dinner in the renowned hall with oaken tables and huge stained-glass windows, he would jerk his head from side to side like a bird, and crumble bread extremely fast between his long fingers. They said the only thing this Englishman loved in the world was Russia. Many people could not understand why he had not remained there. Moon's reply to questions of that kind would invariably be: 'Ask Robertson' (the orientalist) 'why he did not stay in Babylon.' The perfectly reasonable objection would be raised that Babylon no longer existed. Moon would nod with a sly, silent smile. He saw in the Bolshevist insurrection a certain clear-cut finality. While he willingly allowed that, by-and-by, after the primitive phases, some civilization might develop in the 'Soviet Union,' he nevertheless maintained that Russia was concluded and unrepeatable, that you could embrace it like a splendid amphora and put it behind glass. The clay kitchen pot now being baked there had nothing in common with it. The civil war seemed absurd to him: one side fighting for the ghost of the past, the other for the ghost of the future, and meanwhile Archibald Moon quietly had stolen Russia and locked it up in his study. He admired this finality. It was coloured by the blue of waters and the transparent porphyry of Pushkin's poetry. For nearly two years now he had been working on an English-language history of Russia, and he hoped to squeeze it all into one plump volume. An obvious motto ('A thing of beauty is a joy forever'), ultrathin paper, a soft Morocco binding. The task was a difficult one: to find a harmony between erudition and tight picturesque prose, to give a perfect image of one orbicular millennium.

16

Archibald Moon amazed and captivated Martin. His slow Russian speech, from which it had taken him years of patience to weed out the last vestige of English velarity, was smooth, simple, and expressive. His knowledge was distinguished by freshness, precision, and depth. He would read aloud from Russian poets whose very names Martin did not know. Holding down the page with long, slightly trembling fingers, Archibald Moon poured out iambic tetrameters. The room was in penumbra, and the lamplight picked out only the page and Moon's face, with a pale gloss on the cheekbones, fine creases on the forehead, and translucent pink ears. When he had finished he would compress his thin lips, take off his pince-nez as carefully as if it were a dragonfly, and clean the lenses with chamois cloth. Martin sat on the edge of his armchair with his square black cap on his knees.

'For Heaven's sake take off your gown and put that cap away somewhere,' Moon would say with a pained frown. 'Don't tell me you enjoy fussing with that tassel. Away, away with it.'

He would push a glass cigarette box with the college blazon on its silver lid toward Martin, or, from a cabinet in the wall, produce a bottle of whisky, a soda siphon and two glasses.

'By the way, do you know what a grape-transporting cart is called there?' he asked with a toss of his head, and, having ascertained that Martin did not, went on with gusto: '*Mozhara, mozhara,* sir,' and it was not clear which gave him greater pleasure: that he knew the Crimea better than did Martin, or that he could pronounce the word 'sir' according to its Russian pronunciation which rhymes it with 'air.' He joyfully informed Martin that the Russian '*huligan*' came from the name of a gang of Irish robbers, and that Golodai Island was named not after '*golod*' (hunger) but for an Englishman named Holliday who built a factory there. Once, when, speaking of some ignorant journalist (whom Moon had wrathfully taken to task in *The Times*), Martin said that the journalist had not replied because he probably *sdreyfil* (had funked), Moon raised his eyebrows, consulted a dictionary, and asked Martin if by chance he had ever lived in the Volga region. On another occasion, when Martin used the colloquialism *ugrobil* ('bumped off'), Moon grew angry and shouted that such a word did not and could not exist in Russian. 'I've heard it, everybody knows it,' Martin said meekly, and was sustained by Sonia, who was sitting on the couch next to Mrs Zilanov and watching not without curiosity Martin playing the host.

'Russian wordbuilding, the birth of neologisms,' said Moon, suddenly turning to the smiling Darwin, 'ended together with Russia, that is, two years ago. Everything subsequent is *blatnaya muzïka* (thieves' lingo).'

'I don't understand Russian, please translate,' replied Darwin.

'Yes, we keep drifting into it,' said Mrs Zilanov. 'That's not nice. English, please, everybody.' Meanwhile Martin lifted a metal dome from above the muffins and crumpets (which a waiter had brought from the college canteen), checked whether they had sent the right thing, and moved the platter closer to the flaming hearth. In addition to Darwin and Moon he had invited a Russion student whom everyone called simply by his first name, Vadim, and now Martin did not know whether to wait for him or go ahead with tea. This was the first time that mother and daughter Zilanov had come to visit him, and he was in constant fear of derision from Sonia. She wore a navy-blue suit and sturdy little brown shoes, with long tongues that passed beneath the laces and then folded back on top, covering them and ending in leathern lappets. Her bobbed black, somewhat coarse-looking hair fell in an even fringe over her forehead. The dimples of her pale cheeks went singularly well with her dull-dark, slightly slanting eyes. That morning, when Martin had met her and Mrs Zilanov at the station, and afterward, when he was showing them the ancient courts, the fountains, the avenues of gigantic, bare trees, out of which flew cawing the heavy and awkward crows, Sonia had looked moody and cross, and said she was cold. As she gazed over a stone parapet at the ripply Cam, at its mat-green banks and at the grey towers beyond, she suddenly narrowed her eyes and inquired of Martin if he were planning to join General Yudenich's anti-Bolshevist forces in the North. Martin answered with surprise that he was not.

'And what's that pinkish house over there?'

'That's the library building,' Martin explained. A few minutes later, as he walked under an arcade beside Sonia and her mother, he said enigmatically, 'One side is fighting for the ghost of the past and the other for the ghost of the future.'

'Yes, exactly,' Mrs Zilanov chimed in. 'This contrast keeps me from really appreciating Cambridge. I'm bothered by the fact that alongside all these marvellous old buildings there are so many cars, bicycles, sporting-goods stores, footballs—'

'They used to play football in Shakespeare's time too,' said Sonia. 'What bothers *me*,' she added, 'is the platitudes some people spout.'

'Sonia, behave yourself, please,' said her mother.

'Oh, I didn't mean you,' said Sonia with a sigh. They walked on in silence.

'I think it's beginning to drizzle-drozzle,' said Martin, stretching out his palm.

'Why not say "Jupiter Pluvius" or "Lord Rainsford"?' observed Sonia sarcastically, and changed step to match her mother's. Later, at lunch in the town's best restaurant, she cheered up. The 'simian name' of Martin's friend amused her, and she liked Darwin's dialogue with the unbelievably cozy old waiter.

'What are you studying?' her mother asked politely.

'I? Nothing,' replied Darwin raising his head. 'I just thought this fish had one more bone than it was supposed to.'

'No, no, I meant your studies, the lectures you attend.'

'Sorry, I misunderstood you,' said Darwin, 'but your question catches me unawares all the same. Somehow my memory does not stretch from one lecture to the next. Only this morning I asked myself what the deuce was I reading. Mnemonics? Hardly.'

After lunch they had another walk, but a much pleasanter one, for, in the first place, the sun came out, and, in the second, Darwin took them all to a gallery where, according to him, there was an ancient, remarkably alert echo: stamp your foot, and it would bounce off a distant wall like a rubber ball. Darwin stamped, but no echo turned up, and he said some American must have bought it for his house in Massachusetts. Then they strolled over to Martin's room, and soon Archibald Moon arrived, and Sonia asked Darwin softly why the professor's nose was powdered. Moon started to speak in his mellow Russian, flaunting rare and rich proverbs. The girl's conduct, thought Martin, was decidedly reprehensible. She would sit with stone-like countenance, or laugh for no reason at all as her eyes met Darwin's. The latter sat with crossed legs, tamping the tobacco in his pipe.

'I wonder why Vadim hasn't shown up yet,' said Martin uneasily, and touched the teapot's full cheek.

'Oh, go ahead and pour,' said Sonia, whereupon Martin busied himself with the teacups. They all grew silent, watching him. Moon smoked a tan-tinted cigarette belonging to the kind referred to as Russian in England.

'Does your mother write to you often?' asked Mrs Zilanov.

'Every week,' answered Martin.

'She must miss you,' said Mrs Zilanov, and blew on her tea.

'Well, I don't see the national lemon,' Moon subtly observed, in Russian again. Darwin, lowering his voice, asked Sonia to translate. Moon gave him a sidelong glance and switched to English; deliberately and maliciously imitating the average Cambridge manner, he said that there had been some rain, but that now it had cleared, and most likely would not rain any more; he mentioned boat races; he gave a detailed version of the well-known joke about the student, the closet, and the girl cousin. Darwin kept smoking and murmuring, 'Very good, sir, very good. That's your authentic, sober Briton at moments of leisure.'

17

A pounding of feet came from the stairs, the door flew open, and Vadim appeared. Simultaneously his bicycle, which he had left in the lane with one pedal lowered and propped against the edge of the sidewalk, tumbled with a jingling noise, which easily reached the low second story. Vadim's small hands had bitten nails, and were red from holding the handlebars in the cold. His face, suffused with an extraordinarily delicate and uniform rosiness, bore an expression of dazed confusion, which he tried to conceal by panting as if he were out of breath and making sniffling sounds with his nose which was habitually humid inside. He had on wrinkled pale-grey flannel trousers, an excellently tailored brown jacket, and an old pair of pumps that he wore at all times and in all kinds of weather. Still sniffling and smiling a bewildered smile, he said hello to everybody and sat down beside Darwin, whom he liked very much and for some reason called '*Mamka*' (wet-nurse). Vadim had one inevitable jingle, with a limerick arrangement of Russian rhymes: *Priyátno zret', kogdá bol'shóy medvéd' vedyót pod rúchku málen'kuyu súchku, chtob eyó poét'* (What fun to stare when a great big bear walks home arm in arm with a tiny bitch to lay her there). His rapid, staccato manner of speaking was accompanied by all kinds of hissing, trumpeting, and squeaking sounds like the speech of a child short both of ideas and words but incapable of keeping still. When embarrassed he would grow even more disjointed and absurd, and would seem like a cross between a shy, tongue-tied adult and a whimsical infant. Otherwise, he was a nice, chummy, attractive fellow, always ready for a laugh and capable of subtle perception (once, at a much later date, out for a row on the river with Martin one spring evening, when a chance breath of air brought a vague odour of myrtle from Heaven knows where, Vadim said 'Smells like the Crimea,' which was perfectly true). He was a great hit with English people. His college tutor, a fat, asthmatic old man, specialist in molusks, pronounced his name with gutteral tenderness and treated his perfect idleness with perfect indulgence. One dark night Martin and Darwin helped Vadim take the sign off a tobacco shop, and that sign had graced his room ever since. Vadim also procured a police helmet, by means of a simple but ingenious trick: for half-a-crown that he flashed in the moonlight he asked a goodnatured bobby to help him climb over a wall, and, once on top, he leaned down and snatched the helmet off the man's head. He was also the instigator in the episode of the fiery chariot: it happened during the Guy Fawkes Day celebration; the entire city was spewing fireworks, a bonfire burned in the square, and Vadim and his pals harnessed themselves to an old landau acquired for a couple of pounds, filled it with straw and set it on fire. Dragging this landau they sped through the streets, nearly burning down the town hall. On top of everything he was a master of foul language – one of those who become attached to a ditty and repeat it endlessly and are fond of comfortable mother-oriented oaths, caressive physiological terms, and fragments of obscene poetry attributed to Lermontov. His education was undistinguished, his English very droll and endearing but barely intelligible. He had a passion for the navy, for minelayers, for the beauty of dreadnoughts in battle array. He could play for hours with toy soldiers, firing peas from a silver cannon. His quips, his pumps, his shyness and mischievousness, his delicate profile, with its outline of golden bloom – all this, combined with the splendour of his princely title, had an irresistible, heady effect on Archibald Moon, somewhat like the champagne and salted almonds which he relished formerly, a lone, pale Englishman in a bemisted pince-nez, listening to Moscow gypsies. At present, however, Moon sat by the fire with a cup in his hand, munching a muffin and listening to Mrs Zilanov, who was telling him about the Russian newspaper her husband planned to start in Paris. Martin, meanwhile, reflected with alarm that it had been a mistake to invite Vadim, who sat silent, embarrassed by Sonia, and furtively kept shooting raisins, borrowed from the cake, at Darwin. Sonia had grown silent too, and sat gazing pensively at the pianola. With an easy swing Darwin walked over to the fireplace, knocked the ashes out of his pipe, and, turning his back to the flames, began warming himself. 'Mamka,' Vadim mouthed softly and chuckled.

Mrs Zilanov kept speaking excitedly of matters that did not interest Moon in the slightest. It grew dark outside, and somewhere far off newsboys were shouting 'pie-pa, pie-pa!'

18

It was time for the Zilanovs to catch the train back to London. Archibald Moon said good-bye at the very first corner and, with a tender smile for Vadim (who behind his back usually referred to him by an indecent noun supplemented by 'on rollers'), glided away, holding himself very erect. For a while Vadim rode slowly right next to the sidewalk, with one hand on the shoulder of Darwin, who walked alongside; then he said a quick but fussy good-bye and sped off, making a sound with his lips like a broken klaxon. They reached the station, and Darwin brought platform tickets for himself and Martin. Sonia was tired, irritated, and kept slitting her eyes.

'Well, thank you for the hospitality, for the nice party,' said Mrs Zilanov. 'Give my regards to your mother when you write to her.'

But Martin did not transmit the regards: such things are seldom transmitted. As a rule, he had trouble writing letters: how to tell, for example, about that rather muddled, somehow unsuccessful and unpleasant day? He scribbled ten lines or so, recounted the anecdote about the student, the closet, and the cousin, assured his mother that he was in perfect health, ate regularly, and wore an undershirt (which was not true). Suddenly, in his mind, he saw the mailman walking across the snow; the snow crunched slightly, and blue footprints remained on it. He described it thus: 'My letter will be brought by the mailman. It is raining here.' He thought it over and crossed out the mailman, leaving only the rain. He wrote out the address in a large and careful hand remembering for the tenth time as he did so what a fellow student had once said to him: 'Judging by your last name I thought you were American.' He regretted that he always remembered about working this into his letter only after it had been sealed; and he was too lazy to reopen it. He inadvertently made a blot in a corner of the envelope. He squinted at it for a long time, and finally made it into a black cat seen from the back. Mrs Edelweiss preserved this envelope along with his letters. She would gather them into a batch at the end of each semester and tie them crosswise with a ribbon. Several years later she had occasion to reread them. The first-semester letters were relatively abundant. Here was Martin's arrival in Cambridge; here was the first mention of Darwin, of Vadim, of Archibald Moon; here was a letter dated November ninth, his nameday: 'This is the day,' wrote Martin, 'when the goose sets foot on the ice, and the fox changes his lair'; and here was a letter with the crossed-out but distinctly legible line. 'My letter will be brought by the mailman.' Mrs Edelweiss recalled with piercing clarity how she used to walk with Henry along the scintillating road between fir trees weighted down by lumps of snow, and suddenly there was the rich tinkling of multiple bells, the postal sleigh, the letter, and she hastened to take off her gloves in order to open the envelope. She recalled how, during that period, and for almost a year after, she was terribly afraid that without telling her anything, Martin might join the Northern White Army. She found some consolation in the knowledge that there, at Cambridge, a veritable angel exerted a pacifying influence on her son – excellent, sensible Archibald Moon. Yet Martin might still slip away. Her mind was completely at ease only when Martin was with her in Switzerland, on vacation. Years later, when she reread those letters with such anguish, they seemed, despite their tangibility, of a more ghostly nature than the intervals between them. Her memory packed the intervals with Martin's living presence – Christmas, Easter, summer. Thus, for a period of three years, until Martin finished college, her life was like a series of windows. She remembered them well, those windows. There was the first winter holiday, and the skis Henry had bought him on her advice, and Martin putting them on. 'I must be brave,' Mrs Edelweiss softly said to herself. 'After all, miracles do happen. One must only have faith and wait. If Henry appears once more with that black armband, I shall simply leave him.' And she smiled through the tears that streamed down her face, as with trembling hands she continued unwrapping the letters.

That first Christmas homecoming, which remained so vividly impressed in his mother's memory, was also a festive occasion for Martin. He had a queer sensation of having returned to Russia, so white was everything, but, being ashamed of his own sensitivity, he did not share it with his mother, thus depriving her in the future of yet another poignant recollection. His uncle's gift pleased him; for an instant there materialized a snow-covered slope in a St Petersburg suburb – although, of course, in those distant days the toes of Russian felt boots used to be inserted in the plain loops of light children's skis, which, moreover, had a string (for the skier to hold on) attached to their upturned tips. Not so the new ones – real, substantial skis of flexible ash, and the boots, too, were real ski boots. Bending one knee, Martin adjusted the heel cable and bent back the stiff lever of the side throw. It's ice-cold metal stung his fingers. When he had put on the other ski as well, he picked up his mittens from the snow, straightened up, stamped his feet once or twice to see if everything was secure, and swung forward.

Yes, he found himself back in Russia. Here were the splendid 'rugs' of snow spreading in the Pushkin poem which Archibald Moon recited so sonorously, reveling in the scuds of its iambic tetrameter. Above the burdened firs the blue sky shone clear and bright. The cluster of snow dislodged by a jay, flying from perch to perch, would dissipate in midair. Martin passed through the woods into the clearing from which, the previous summer, he used to descend to the local Majestic. He could see it far below, with a straight column of rose-coloured smoke coming out of a chimney. What was it about that hotel that lured him so strongly, why must he again hasten there, when in the summer all he had found there had been a bevy of raucous, angular English flappers? But there was no doubt that it beckoned to him: the reflected sunlight in its windows flashed a silent sign of invitation. Martin was even frightened by such enigmatic intrusion, such abstruse insistence. He had seen that signal before, displayed by some detail of the landscape. There he must go down: it would be wrong to ignore such blandishments. The firm surface began whistling delightfully under his skis as Martin sped down the slope faster and faster. And how many times afterwards, sleeping in his chilly Cambridge room, he dream-sped like that and suddenly, in a stunning explosion of snow, fell and awakened. Everything was as usual. He could hear the clock ticking in the adjacent parlour. A mouse was rolling a lump of sugar on the floor. Footfalls passed on the sidewalk and faded away. He would turn over in bed and instantly fall asleep again; in the morning, still drowsy, he heard other sounds from the parlour: Mrs Newman fussing about, moving things, putting coals on the fire, tearing paper, scratching a match – and presently she departed, and the silence was gradually and delectably filled with the morning hum of the ignited hearth.

'Nothing special there after all,' reflected Martin, and reached toward the night table for cigarettes. 'Mostly middleaged blokes in sweaters. Good example of how metaphysics can fool you. Ah, it's Saturday today – off to London. How come Darwin keeps getting letters from Sonia? I'll have to worm it out of him. Good idea to cut Grzhezinsky's lecture. Here comes the hag to wake me.'

Mrs Newman brought his tea. She was elderly, red-haired, and had foxy little eyes. 'Last night, sir, you went out without your gown,' she remarked phlegmatically. 'I'll have to inform your tutor.' She drew open the curtains, gave a brief but exact report on the weather, and was gone.

Martin put on his bathrobe, descended the creaky staircase, and knocked on Darwin's door. Darwin, already shaven and washed, was eating scrambled eggs and bacon; Marshall, a fat textbook on political economy, lay open near his plate.

'Got another letter today?' sternly inquired Martin.

'From my tailor,' said Darwin chewing juicily.

'Sonia's handwriting isn't too good,' remarked Martin.

'It's rotten,' agreed Darwin, gulping some coffee. Martin walked around behind him, placed both hands around Darwin's neck, and started squeezing.

'The bacon went down anyway,' said Darwin in a smugly strained voice.

19

That evening they were both off for London. Darwin spent the night in one of those charming two-room flats provided by clubs for bachelors – and Darwin's club was one of the smartest and staidest in London, with overstuffed armchairs, glossy magazines, and thick silent rugs. Martin ended up this time in one of the upstairs bedrooms at the Zilanovs', Nelly being in Reval, and her husband marching on St Petersburg. When Martin arrived, nobody was at home but Mihail Platonovich Zilanov himself, busy writing in his study. A sturdy, thickset man, with Tartar features and the same dark lusterless eyes as Sonia, he invariably wore cylindrical detachable cuffs and a starched shirt; the shirt front bulged, imparting a dovelike quality to his chest. He was one of those Russians who, upon awaking, first of all pull on trousers with dangling suspenders; who wash only face, nape, and hands in the morning, but wash them most thoroughly, and who regard their weekly bath as an event not devoid of a certain risk. He had done a goodly amount of travelling around in his time, was intensely active in liberal politics, conceived life as a succession of congresses in various cities, had miraculously escaped a Soviet death, and always carried a bulging briefcase. And when someone said meditatively, 'What shall I do with these books – it's raining,' he would wordlessly, instantly, and extremely skillfully swaddle the books in a sheet of newspaper, rummage in his briefcase, produce some string and, in a flash, tie it crosswise around the neat package, a process which the luckless acquaintance, shifting from foot to foot, watched with apprehensive *attendrissement*. 'There you are, sir,' Zilanov would say and, after a hasty good-bye, was off to Riga, Belgrade, or Paris. He always travelled light, with three clean handkerchiefs in his briefcase, and would sit in the railway carriage completely blind to picturesque spots (which the fast train traversed in its trusting efforts to please), immersed in a brochure and making occasional notes in the margin. While marvelling at his inattention to landscapes, comforts, and cleanliness, Martin nevertheless admired Zilanov for that plodding dryish courage of his, and every time he saw him could not help recalling that this seemingly unathletic and unfashionable man, who probably played only billiards and perhaps bowls, had escaped from the Bolshevists by crawling through a drainpipe, and had once fought a duel with the Octobrist Tuchkov.

'Welcome,' said Zilanov extending a swarthy hand. 'Sit down.' Martin sat down. Zilanov again contemplated the half-filled sheet of paper upon his desk, picked up his pen, imparted to it a hovering flicker directly above the paper before transforming the flicker into the rapid glide of writing, then simultaneously gave the pen its freedom and said, 'They should be back any moment now.'

Martin reached for a newspaper lying on a nearby table. It turned out to be a Russian émigré one, published in Paris.

'How's school?' asked Zilanov, without raising his eyes from the evenly running pen.

'Pretty good,' said Martin, putting down the paper. 'How long have they been out?' Zilanov did not answer: the pen was going at full tilt. A few minutes later, though, he spoke again, still not looking at Martin. 'Idling away your time, I imagine. Only thing colleges care about here is *le sport.*'

Martin grinned. Zilanov rapidly thumped a blotter all over the lines he had written and said, 'Your mother keeps asking me for additional information, but I don't know anything more. I wrote her in the Crimea at the time, telling her everything I knew.' Martin cleared his throat.

'*Shto vi* (what's that)?' asked Zilanov, who had picked up that bit of bad Russian in Moscow.

'Nothing,' replied Martin.

'I'm referring to your father's death, of course,' said Zilanov, glancing with dull eyes at Martin. 'If you remember, it was I who notified you at the time.'

'Yes, yes, I know,' said Martin, nodding hurriedly. He always felt embarrassed when strangers – even with the best intentions – spoke to him about his father.

'Our last meeting is as clear in my mind as if it had happened today,' Zilanov went on. 'We chanced to meet on the street. I was already in hiding then. At first I did not want to go up to him. But Sergey Robertovich looked so appallingly sick. I remember, he was very concerned about what was happening to you and your mother in the Crimea. And a couple of days later I went to see him, and there they were carrying out the coffin.'

Martin kept nodding, searching agonizingly for a way to change the subject. Zilanov was telling him all this for the third time, and, on the whole, the narrative was a rather pale one. Zilanov turned over the sheet. His pen quivered and started again. To kill time Martin again reached for the newspaper, but just then the front-door lock clicked and from the entrance hall came the sound of voices, of shuffling feet, and Irina's awful cackling laugh.

20

Martin went out to greet them, and, as generally happened when he encountered Sonia, he instantly had the sensation that he stood in relief against a dark background. The same thing had happened on her last visit to Cambridge (she had come with her father, who had tormented him with questions about the age of various colleges and the number of books in the Library, while she and Darwin kept quietly laughing about something or other), and it came upon him again now, that strange torpor. His light-blue necktie, the sharp points of his soft collar, his double-breasted suit, all seemed to be in order, and yet Martin had the impression, under Sonia's impenetrable gaze, that he was dressed shabbily, that his hair was badly brushed, that he had shoulders like a furniture mover's, and that the roundness of his face was the shape of stupidity. No less repulsive were his big knuckles, which had reddened and grown swollen of late, what with his goalkeeping and his boxing lessons. The solid sense of contentment somehow related to the strength in his shoulders, the coolness of sleekly shaven cheeks, the reliability of a recently filled tooth, all of it vanished instantly in Sonia's presence. And what appeared particularly silly to him was the way his eyebrows petered out: they were thick only at their starting point and then, templeward, took on a look of surprised sparseness.

Supper was served. Mrs Pavlov, a pudgy and dour lady who resembled her sister (but smiled even more seldom than she), kept a habitual and discreet eye on Irina, seeing to it that her daughter ate decorously, without leaning on the table too much and without licking her knife. Zilanov arrived a moment later, rapidly and energetically inserted a corner of his napkin under his collar and, half-rising in his chair, snatched from clear across the table a roll which he immediately sliced and buttered. His wife was reading a letter from Reval, and, as she read, saying to Martin, 'Help yourself.' On his left Irina fidgeted, scratched her armpit, and uttered sounds of endearment addressed to her cold mutton. On his right sat Sonia, and the way she had of taking salt with the tip of her knife, her short black hair with its harsh gloss, and the dimple on her pale cheek ineffably irritated him. After supper there came a telephone call from Darwin, who suggested they go dancing. Sonia played coy for a while, then agreed. Martin went to change and was already pulling on his silk socks, when Sonia told him through the door that she was tired and would not go after all. Half an hour later Darwin arrived, very gay, very big and elegant, his top hat cocked, with tickets to a very expensive ball in his pocket. Martin told him that Sonia had wilted and gone to bed, whereupon Darwin drank a cup of tepid tea, gave an almost natural yawn, and said that in this world everything was for the best. Martin knew that he had travelled to London for the sole purpose of seeing Sonia, and when Darwin, in his unneeded top hat and opera cloak, went off whistling down the empty dark street, Martin felt very hurt for him. He softly closed the front door and went upstairs to his bedroom. Sonia slipped out into the passage to meet him, wearing a kimono and looking very short in heelless bedroom slippers.

'Is he gone?' she asked.

'Really rotten of you,' Martin commented under his breath without stopping.

'You could have stopped him,' she said after him, adding quickly, 'I know what – I'll go down and ring him up and go dancing, that's what I'll do.'

Without answering, Martin slammed his door, angrily brushed his teeth, yanked open his bed as if he wanted to throw somebody out of it, and, dispatching the light with a murderous twist of his fingers, pulled the covers over his head. But a few minutes later the thickness of the blanket did not prevent him from hearing Sonia's steps hurrying up the passage and her door shutting – was it possible that she had actually been downstairs and telephoned? He listened attentively, and, after a new period of silence, there were her footsteps again, only now they had a different, lighter, almost ethereal sound. Martin could not restrain himself. He stepped out into the corridor and caught sight of Sonia hopping downstairs in a flamingo-coloured frock, a fluffy fan in one hand and something bright encircling her black hair. She had left her door open and the light on. In her room there remained a cloudlet of powder, like the smoke following a shot; a stocking, killed outright, lay under a chair; and the motley innards of the wardrobe had spilled onto the carpet.

Instead of being glad for his friend, Martin felt very hurt. All was still, except for the heavy snores that came from the master bedroom. 'God damn her,' he muttered, and for a while debated with himself whether he too should join them at the ball – after all, there were three tickets. He saw himself dashing up the sumptuous stairs, wearing his pumps with flat bows, his dinner jacket and silk shirt with the frilled front (as sported by the dandies that year). The flame of music shot from the open doors. The resilient, tender caress of a girl's soft leg, which keeps giving way and yet pressing against you, the fragrant hair by your very lips, a cheek that leaves its powder on your silk lapel – all these immemorial and tender banalities stirred Martin deeply. He enjoyed dancing with a fair stranger, enjoyed the vacuous, chaste talk, through which you listen closely to that bewitching, vague something going on inside you and inside her, which will last a couple of bars more and then, finding no resolution, will vanish forever and be utterly forgotten. But while the bond of bodies is still unbroken, the outlines of a potential love affair begin to form, and the rough draft already comprises everything: the sudden silence between two people in some dimly lit room; the man carefully placing with trembling fingers on the edge of an ashtray the just-lit but impedient cigarette; the woman's eyes slowly closing as in a filmed scene; and the rapt darkness, and in it a point of light, a glossy limousine travelling fast through the rainy night, and suddenly, a white terrace and the dazzling ripple of the sea, and Martin softly saying to the girl he has carried off, 'Your name – what's your name?' Leafy shadows play on her luminous dress. She gets up, she goes away. The rapacious croupier rakes in Martin's last chips, and he has nothing left but to thrust his hands into the empty pockets of his dinner jacket and descend slowly into the casino garden and, then, sign on as a longshoreman – and there she is again, aboard someone else's yacht, sparkling, laughing, flinging coins into the water.

'Funny thing,' said Darwin one night, as he and Martin came out of a small Cambridge cinema, 'it's all unquestionably poor, vulgar, and rather implausible, and yet there is something exciting about all that flying foam, the *femme fatale* on the yacht, the ruined and ragged he-man swallowing his tears.'

'It's nice to travel,' said Martin. 'I'd like to travel a lot.'

This fragment of conversation, surviving by chance from one April night, came back to Martin when, at the beginning of summer vacation, already in Switzerland, he received a letter from Darwin in Tenerife. Tenerife – God, what a lovely, emerald word! It was morning. Marie, with disastrously deteriorated looks and an oddly bloated appearance, was kneeling in a corner, wringing out a floor rag into a pail. Large white clouds glided above the mountains, catching on the peaks, and from time to time some smoky filaments would descend the slopes, on which the light changed continuously with the ebb and flow of the sun. Martin went out into the garden, where Uncle Henry, wearing a monstrous straw hat, was talking with the village curé. When the curé, a small man with glasses, which he kept adjusting with the thumb and little finger of his left hand, made a low bow and, with a rustle of his black cassock, walked off by the shiny white wall and climbed into his cabriolet hitched to a fat, pinkish-white horse all speckled with mustard, Martin said, 'It's wonderful here, and I adore this region, but, perhaps, just for a few weeks, I would like to take a trip somewhere – the Canary Islands, for instance.'

'What folly, what folly,' answered Uncle Henry with fright, and his moustache bristled slightly. 'Your mother, who waited for you so anxiously, who is so happy that you are staying with her until October – and suddenly you leave . . .'

'We could all go together,' said Martin.

'*Quelle folie,*' Uncle Henry repeated. 'Later, when you finish your studies, I'll have no objection. I have always believed that a young man should see the world. Remember that your mother is only now recovering from the shocks she suffered. No, no, no.'

Martin shrugged and, with his hands in the pockets of his shorts, wandered off along the trail that led to the waterfall. He knew his mother was waiting for him there by the larch-shaded grotto: that was the agreement. She would go out walking very early and, not wanting to wake Martin, would leave him a note: 'By the grotto at ten' or 'Near the spring on the road to Ste. Claire.' However, even though he knew she was waiting, Martin suddenly changed direction, left the trail and started upward across the heather.

21

The slope became steeper and steeper, the sun was scorching, flies kept trying to get at his lips and eyes. Upon reaching a circular birch grove, he rested, smoked a cigarette, pulled up his sports stockings tighter, and resumed the ascent, munching on a birch leaf. The heather was crunchy and slippery. Now and then he caught his foot in the low thornbushes. At the top of the incline gleamed an amassment of rocks, between which ran a crevice. It fanned out toward him, and was filled with fine debris that came into motion as soon as he stepped upon it. This way could not serve to reach the peak, so Martin began to climb straight up the face of the rocks. Occasionally some root or moss patch at which he clutched detached itself from the stone, and feverishly he would seek a support with his foot, or else it was his foothold that gave, and he would be left hanging by his hands and have to pull himself painfully up. The peak was almost within reach when he suddenly slipped and started to slither down, clutching at shrublets of rough flowers; he lost his grip, felt a burning pain as his knee scraped against the rock, attempted to embrace the steepness that was gliding up and past him – and abruptly salvation bumped against his soles.

He found himself on a cornice; to the right it narrowed and merged with the cliff, but to the left it could be seen going on for a few yards before turning a corner – what then happened to it remained unknown. His ledge recalled the stage setting of nightmares. He stood, pressing closely to the rock against which he had bruised his chest on the way down, and dared not unglue himself from it. With an effort glancing over his shoulder, he saw under his heels a prodigious precipice, a sun-illumined abyss with, in its depths, several outdistanced firs running in panic after the descending forest, ivory white hotel. 'So that's what its message was,' thought Martin with a superstitious shiver. 'I'll fall, I'll perish, that's what it's watching for. That – that—' It was equally terrifying to look down the precipice or up the vertical cliff above him. A width of bookshelf underfoot and a knobby spot in the rock wall to which his fingers clung was all that Martin retained of the solid world to which he was used.

He experienced faintness, dizziness, sickening fear, yet at the same time he observed himself from the outside, noting with odd lucidity his open-collared flannel shirt, his clumsy clinging position on the ledge, the thistle ball that had attached itself to his stocking and the entirely black butterfly that fluttered by with enviable casualness like a quiet little devil and began to rise along the rock face; and though there was no one around to make showing off worth while, Martin began to whistle; then he vowed to himself that he would pay no attention to the invitation of the abyss and began to displace his feet slowly, as he moved to the left. Ah, if only one could see what the cornice did after it turned that corner! The rock wall seemed to push against his breast, crowding him toward the precipice, whose impatient breath he felt on his back. His nails dug into the stone, the stone was hot, the tufts of flowers were of an intense blue, a lizard traced a quick incomplete figure eight and froze again, flies tickled his face. Every now and then he had to stop, and he heard himself complaining to himself – I cannot any more, I cannot – and when he caught himself doing that, he began to produce with his lips a rudimentary tune, a fox-trot or the 'Marseillaise,' then moistened his lips and, again complaining, resumed his sidewise progress. There remained only a yard or so to the turn when something began to spill from under his shoe sole; he could not help turning his head, and in the sunny void the white spot of the hotel started to rotate slowly. Martin closed his eyes and stopped short, but then he controlled his nausea and began to move again. At the turn he said rapidly 'Please, I beg you, please,' and his request was immediately granted: beyond the turn the shelf widened, became a platform, and beyond was the already familiar scree and the heather-covered slope.

Then he caught his breath. His entire body ached and vibrated. His nails had become dark red as if he had been picking strawberries; the knee he had barked was smarting. The danger that he had just experienced seemed to him far more real than the one into which he had blundered in the Crimea. Now he felt proud of himself but this pride suddenly lost all its flavour when Martin asked himself if he could again perform, this time deliberately, what he had performed accidentally. In a few days he gave in, climbed again up the heather-grown steeps, but when he reached the platform from where the cornice started, he could not make himself step on it. This angered him, he tried to incite himself, he taunted his own cowardice, imagined Darwin looking at him with a mocking smile – stood there for a while, then shrugged and turned back, doing his best to ignore the ruffian who was raging within him. Again and again, to the very end of vacation, that rowdy made irruptions and would riot so offensively that finally Martin decided not to walk up that mountain any more to avoid being tormented by the sight of the narrow shelf which he dared not tread.

In October he returned to England in a stinging mood of self-depreciation. Straight from the station he went to see the Zilanovs. The housemaid who opened the door was new, and this was unpleasant, making it seem he had come to a strange house. Sonia, dressed all in black, stood in the middle of the living room smoothing her temples, then proffered her hand, in a straight sharp gesture as was her wont. With amazement Martin realized that not once during the summer had he thought of her, not once had he written, but that nonetheless it would have been worth while to travel a long way, if only for the sake of that embarrassment that he now felt as he looked at her pale sullen face. 'You probably have not heard of our grief,' said Sonia and in an oddly cross tone related that the week before, on the same day, they had received information that Nelly had died in childbirth in Brindisi, and her husband had been killed in the Crimea. 'Ah, then he left Yudenich to join Wrangel,' said Martin lamely, and with exceptional clarity visualized that husband of Nelly's whom he had seen but once, and Nelly herself who at the time had seemed to him dull and insipid, and now had gone and died in Brindisi. 'Mother is in a terrible state,' said Sonia leafing through a book that lay abandoned on the sofa. 'And father's been traveling in secret to God knows what places, possibly as far as Kiev,' she added after a while and separating several pages with a thumb allowed them to mill rapidly. Martin seated himself in an armchair rubbing his hands. Sonia slapped the book closed and said raising her face: 'Darwin has been perfect, simply perfect. He was a tremendous help to us. So touching, and not one wrong word. Are you staying for the night?' 'Actually,' said Martin, 'I could go up to Cambridge tonight. It would surely bother you to put me up, and so forth.' 'No, what nonsense,' said Sonia and sighed. The sound of the dinner gong reached them from downstairs, and this clashed with the atmosphere of mourning that pervaded the house. Martin went to wash his hands. As he entered the lavatory he collided with Zilanov who did not make it a custom to lock the door. He glanced at Martin out of lusterless eyes while unhurriedly buttoning his fly. 'Accept my deepest sympathy,' muttered Martin and stupidly clicked his heels. Zilanov lowered his lids in sign of gratitude and shook hands with Martin. The fact that all this occurred on the threshold of the lavatory underlined the absurdity of the handclasp and the ready-made words. Zilanov slowly walked off, his thighs twitching as if he were shaking down something between them. Martin's nose, as its owner noticed in the mirror, was wrinkled in anguish. 'After all I *did* have to say something,' he muttered through his teeth.

Dinner proceeded in silence if one discounted the old-fashioned slurp with which Zilanov ate his soup. Irina and her mother were at an out-of-town sanitarium, and Mrs Zilanov did not come down, so that they dined just the three of them. The telephone rang, and Zilanov marched to his study chewing on the way. 'I know you don't like mutton,' Sonia said softly, and Martin silently smiled a slightly muted smile. 'Iogolevich will drop in,' said Zilanov resuming his place at the table. 'He has just returned from St Petersburg. Pass me the mustard. He says he crossed the border wrapped in a shroud.' 'Less conspicuous on snow,' said Martin a moment later to keep up the conversation, but no conversation ensued.

22

Aleksandr Naumovich Iogolevich turned out to be a fat bearded man in a knit grey waistcoat and shabby black suit, with dandruff on his shoulders. The side-ears of his black prunella boots stuck out, and the ankle ties of his underpants glimmered through his sagging socks. The way he completely ignored inanimate objects (such as the arm support of the chair which he mechanically kept tapping with his hand, or the thick book on which he sat down by mistake, then took out from under him without a smile, and put aside without glancing at it) pointed to a secret affinity with Zilanov. Nodding his large frizzly head, he only responded with a short clucking of his tongue to the news of his friend's bereavement; then quickly passing the palm of his hand down his coarsely fashioned face, without any preliminaries, launched into his story. It was obvious that the only thing that filled his consciousness, the only thing that preoccupied and affected him, was Russia's woe, and with trepidation Martin pictured to himself what would happen were he to interrupt Iogolevich's stormy tense speech by telling the anecdote about the student and his girl cousin. Sonia sat at a distance, propping her elbows on her knees, and her face on her palms. Zilanov listened, one finger stretched along his nose, occasionally removing the finger to say: 'Excuse me, Aleksandr Naumovich, but, for instance, when you mention ' and Iogolevich would stop for an instant, blink, then resume his tale, with a constant remarkable motion of his rough, ceaselessly changing features – his shaggy brows, the nostrils of his pear-shaped nose, the folds of his bearded cheeks – nor did his hands with black hair on the phalanges rest for one second: they lifted something, tossed it upward, seized it again, strewed it in every direction, and all the while, hotly, in a rolling delivery, he spoke of executions, of famine, of St Petersburg turned into a desert, of the regime's malice, stupidity and vulgarity. He left after midnight and suddenly turning around on the threshold asked how much *kaloshi* (rubbers) cost in London. After the door had closed, Zilanov remained standing, lost in thought, then went upstairs to his wife. The doorbell rang three minutes later: Iogolevich had come back; it turned out that he did not know the way to the tube station. Martin offered to take him there and while striding at Iogolevich's side cast about in distress for a subject of conversation. 'Remind your father,' said Iogolevich abruptly, 'I quite forgot to tell him that Maksimov is impatient to receive the article on his impressions from visiting the Southern Volunteer Army. He will know what it's about. Just tell him. Maksimov has written to your father before.' 'Certainly,' answered Martin; was about to add something but checked himself.

He slowly returned to the house, imagining now Iogolevich crossing the border wrapped in a white sheet, then Zilanov with his briefcase at some demolished railroad station under the starry Ukrainian sky. All was silent in the house when he went up the stairs. He kept yawning while he undressed. He felt an odd, vague anguish. The lamp on the bedside table burned bright, the wide bed looked white and soft, his dressing gown of lustrous blue silk had been taken out of his bag by the maid and was slung invitingly over the armchair. He noticed with a shock of vexation that he had forgotten to bring up from the living room a book he had set his heart on there, and had been looking forward to reading in bed. He pulled on his dressing gown and walked down to the second floor. The book was a dilapidated volume of Chekhov's stories. He found it – for some reason it was lying on the floor – and returned to his bedroom. But the heartache did not dissipate, although Martin was one of those people for whom a good book before sleep is something to look forward to all day. Such a person, upon happening to recall, amidst routine occupations, that on his bedside table a book is waiting for him, in perfect safety, feels a surge of inexpressible happiness. Martin began to read, choosing the story he knew, loved, could read through one hundred times in a row: 'The Lady with the Little Dog.' Ah, how nicely she lost that lorgnette in the crowd on the pier in Yalta! And here, without any apparent reason, he realized what it was that disturbed him so. Only a year before, in this room, Nelly had slept, and now she was dead.

'What nonsense,' muttered Martin, and tried to resume his reading, but this proved impossible. He recalled those nights of long ago when he waited for the ghost of his father to make a scratching sound in a corner. Martin's heart started to beat fast; the bed became hot and uncomfortable. He imagined how he himself would be dying some day, and felt as if the ceiling were coming down on him slowly and inexorably. Something began to drum rapidly in the darker part of the room, and his heart missed a beat. But it was merely water that had been spilled on the washstand and was now dripping onto the linoleum. Yet how strange: if ghosts exist, then all is well for it proves that souls *can* move after death – why then is it so frightening? 'How shall I be dying myself?' thought Martin and began to pass mentally in review several varieties of death. He saw himself placed against a wall, standing there with as much air in his lungs as he could inhale, waiting for the volly of rifle shots and recollecting with wild despair this present minute, this bright room, the soft night, unconcern, safety. Then there were illnesses, dreadful illnesses rending one's entrails. Or it might be a railway accident. Or, simply, the serene slowing down of old age, death in one's sleep. Or else, a dark wood and pursuit. 'Nonsense,' thought Martin. 'I have plenty of time in reserve. Besides, every year represents a whole epoch. Why worry? Yet perhaps Nelly is here, and is seeing me now? Perhaps – now, this instant – she will give me a sign?' He looked at his watch, it was close to two. The tension was becoming unbearable. That silence seemed to be waiting: the distant hoot of an automobile horn would have been rapture. The level of silence kept rising, and all at once poured over the brim: someone on tiptoe was coming barefoot along the passage.

'Are you asleep?' came the whispered question through the door, and for an instant a constriction in his throat prevented Martin from replying. She slipped in, she softly shifted from tiptoe to heel. She wore yellow pajamas, her black hair was rumpled. Thus she remained standing for a moment or two blinking through matted lashes. Martin, sitting up in bed, grinned foolishly. 'Sleep is utterly out of the question,' said Sonia in an odd voice. 'I'm jumpy. I'm scared. And on top of it, those horrors he talked about!' 'Why are you barefoot, Sonia? Want my slippers?' She shook her head, pouting pensively, then tossed her hair and cast a vague glance at Martin's bed. '*Allez hop*,' said Martin, tapping the blanket at the foot of the bed. She climbed onto the bed, first kneeled upon it, then moved about slowly, and finally curled up on the blanket in the corner formed by footboard and wall. Martin pulled out the pillow from under his head to pace it behind her back. '*Spasibo* (thanks),' she said quite soundlessly: the outline of the word could only be guessed from the movement of her plump pale lips. 'Are you comfortable?' asked Martin nervously, pulling up his knees so as not to be in her way, but presently he bent forward again, and taking his dressing gown from the adjacent chair, covered her bare feet with it. 'Give me a cigarette,' she asked after a minute of silence. A waft of delicate warmth emanated from her; a thin chainlet of gold surrounded her adorable neck. She inhaled, slitting her eyes, and handed the cigarette to Martin. 'Too strong,' she said sadly. 'What did you do this summer?' inquired Martin struggling to subdue a dark something that was quite mad and unthinkable and that even induced a febrile chill. 'Nothing in particular. We went to Brighton.' She sighed and added 'I flew in a hydroplane.' 'And I very nearly got killed,' said Martin. 'Yes, yes, very nearly. High up in the mountains. Rock climbing. Lost my hold. Saved by a miracle.' Sonia smiled dimly and said 'You know, Martin, she always maintained that the most important thing in life was always to do one's duty and think of nothing else. It's a very deep thought, isn't it?' 'Yes, possibly,' Martin replied, shoving the unfinished cigarette into the ashtray with an uncertain hand. 'Possibly. But sometimes a bit boring.' 'Oh, no, not at all— You don't understand, she didn't mean work or job, but a kind of – well, the kind of thing which has an inner importance.' She paused, and Martin saw her shiver in her light little pyjamas. 'You are cold,' he said. 'Yes, I think I am. And *that* was the duty to be performed, but some – I, for instance – do not have any such thing inside.' 'Sonia,' said Martin, 'maybe you'd like—?' He turned back a corner of the blanket, and she rose to a kneeling position and moved slowly in his direction. 'And it seems to me,' she continued as she crawled under the bedclothes, which Martin, hearing nothing of what she was saying, awkwardly pulled over her and himself, 'It seems to me that lots of people do not know this, and because they don't—' With a deep intake of breath Martin embraced her and attached his lips to her cheek. Sonia seized him by the wrist, and forthwith rolled out of the bed. 'Good God,' she said, 'Good God!' Her dark eyes glistened with tears, and within an instant her whole face was wet, with bright long streaks creeping down her cheeks. 'Oh please, please don't – I merely – oh I don't know, oh Sonia—' Martin kept muttering, not daring to touch her, losing his head at the thought that she might start screaming and arouse the entire household. 'How couldn't you see,' she said plaintively, 'how couldn't you see that this was the way I used to come to Nelly, and we talked and talked till dawn.' She turned away and left the room crying. Martin sat in a chaos of bedclothes with a helplessly ingratiating expression on his face. She closed the door behind her, but reopened it, and introduced her head: 'Idiot,' she said in a perfectly calm, businesslike manner, whereupon the patter of her bare feet receded along the passage.

For some time Martin kept staring at the white door. Then he put out the light and attempted to sleep. This appeared to be hopeless. He reflected that at daybreak he must dress, get packed, and noiselessly leave the house to go straight to the station; unfortunately he fell asleep amidst those meditations and woke up only at a quarter past nine. 'Maybe it was all a dream?' he said to himself with some hope, but at once shook his head and with a pang of excruciating shame wondered how he would meet Sonia again after this. He had on unfortunate morning: when he rushed in to take his bath, there, at the washstand was Zilanov, his short legs in black trousers set wide apart, his torso in a thick flannel undershirt bent forward, dousing his face over the basin, rubbing cheeks and forehead until the skin squeaked, snorting under the spouting faucet, pressing each nostril in turn, fiercely relieving his nose, and expectorating. 'Come in, come in, I'm through,' he exclaimed and, blinded by water, dripping, and holding his arms in the semblance of short wings, he dashed to his bedroom where he preferred to keep his towel.

Then, a little later, as Martin was on his way downstairs to the dining room to drink his cup of hemlock, he ran into Mrs Zilanov: her face, livid and swollen, looked awful, and he felt dreadfully embarrassed, not daring to utter stock words of compassion, but not knowing any others. In acknowlegement of his silence she put her arms about him, kissed him on the forehead – and, with a hopeless wave of her hand, walked away, to the bottom of the corridor, where her husband mentioned to her something about a passport with a totally unexpected tender break in his voice of which he had seemed wholly incapable. Sonia met Martin in the dining room, and the first thing she said to him was, 'I forgive you, because you are Swiss, and "cretin" is a Swiss word, jot that down.' Martin had planned to explain that he had had no wicked intentions, which on the whole was the truth, that all he had wanted to do was to lie close to her and keep kissing her cheek – but Sonia looked so cross and cheerless in her black dress that he thought it best to say nothing. 'Papa is leaving today for Brindisi,' she said, 'thank goodness they did give him a visa at last.' She contemplated with disapproval the poorly contained greed with which Martin, who always felt ravenous in the morning, was devouring his fried eggs. Martin told himself there was no point in hanging around, the day promised to be topsy-turvy, the seeing-off ritual and all the rest. 'Darwin has telephoned,' added Sonia.

23

Darwin made his appearance with comedy precision – immediately in the wake of Sonia's remark, as if he had been waiting in the wings. The seaside sun had given him a roast-beef complexion and he wore a marvellous pale-grey suit. Sonia's greeting struck Martin as a little too languorous. Martin himself was gasped, hit on the shoulder, hit in the ribs, and asked repeatedly why he had not phoned. Indeed, the usually indolent Darwin displayed that day unprecedented energy. At Liverpool Street station he took a stranger's trunk from the porter to carry it balanced on his nape. In the Pullman, midway between London and Cambridge, after a glance at his wristwatch, he called the conductor, handed him a banknote, and solemnly pulled the emergency cord. The train groaned agonizingly and came to a stop, while Darwin smugly explained to everybody at large that he was born exactly twenty-four years ago. A day later, one of the livelier newspapers had a note about it conspicuously headlined: 'YOUNG AUTHOR STOPS TRAIN ON BIRTHDAY.' Meanwhile Darwin had been summoned by his tutor whom he was now trying to hypnotize with a detailed report on the leech commerce, what were the better sorts and how they were bred.

The same damp greeted Martin in his bedroom; there was the same interchime of towers, and in the same old way Vadim would tumble in with a sample of the same rhymed Russian alphabet consisting of couplets, the first verse containing a didactic item of general interest ('Armenians like to fish and hunt' or 'Balloons are never made of brick') and the second, equally didactic, beginning with the same letter, but quite unrelated to the first line and considerably more improper.

Archibald Moon, however, although in a sense the same, seemed to be different: Martin could not manage to recapture the old enchantment. Moon told him that during the summer he had completed as many as sixteen new pages of his History of Russia, fully sixteen pages; he explained that he was able to accomplish so much because he devoted to work every hour of the long summer day, and as he said it he made with his fingers a gesture representing the ripple and plasticity of every phrase that he had nursed to life; in the gesture Martin seemed to discern something extremely depraved, and to listen to Moon's rich speech was like chewing thick elastic Turkish Delight powdered with confectioner's sugar. For the first time Martin felt personally offended by Moon's treating Russia as an inanimate article of luxury. When he confided this to Darwin, Darwin laughed and nodded, and said that Moon was like that because of his addiction to uranism. This called for closer attention, and after one occasion when Moon without any excuse stroked Martin's hair with trembling fingers, Martin stopped dropping in, and would noiselessly climb out of his window and down a rainpipe into the lane whenever there came that yearnful, lonesome knock on the door of his room. He nevertheless continued to attend Moon's lectures, but now in studying Russian literature he endeavoured to efface from his hearing Moon's intonations, which kept pursuing him, especially in the rhythm of verse. He ended by switching to another teacher, grand old Professor Stephens, whose interpretation of Pushkin and Tolstoy was as honest as it was ponderous, and who spoke Russian in gasps and barks with the frequent addition of Serbian and Polish. Still it took time to shake off Archibald Moon for good. He would recall with involuntary admiration the artistry of Moon's discourse, but the moment after would perceive as a vivid reality the picture of Moon carrying away to his rooms a sarcophagus with Russia's mummy. In the end Martin did get entirely rid of Moon, while appropriating this and that element, but converting it into his own property, and then, at last, the voices of the Russian muses began to sound in complete purity. Moon would occasionally be seen in the street in the company of a beautiful chubby youth with abundant blond hair who impersonated girls in the university productions of Shakespeare's plays, whereat Moon would melt with tender emotion in an orchestra seat, and together with other amateurs try to shush Darwin, who, sprawling in feigned rapture, exploded with clownish applause at the wrong moments.

But Martin had some unsettled accounts with Darwin, too. It happened sometimes that Darwin went to London alone, and Martin spent Saturday night, till daybreak, till a total exhaustion of coal, sitting in the sepulchral draft of the fireplace and persistently, savagely, as if pressing upon an aching tooth, imagining Sonia and Darwin in a dark automobile. Once, when unable to stand it any longer, he set off for London, to attend a dance to which he had not been invited, and paced the halls under the impression that he looked very pale and stern, but then happened to catch in a mirror the reflection of his pink round face with a bump on the forehead – the result of his diving for the ball under rushing feet the day before. Presently, they arrived: Sonia costumed as a gypsy girl, seemingly having forgotten that not quite four months had elapsed since her sister's death; and Darwin dressed as an Englishman out of a Continental novel: a large-checked suit, a tropical helmet with a bandana to protect the nape from the Pompeiian sun, a Baedeker under his arm, and carotty sidewhiskers. There was music, there was *serpentin,* there was a snowstorm of confetti, and for one intoxicating moment Martin felt he was taking part in a subtle drama of masks. The music stopped. Ignoring Darwin's obvious desire to be alone with Sonia, Martin climbed into the same taxicab with them. In a chance beam of light that penetrated the dark car he thought he noticed Darwin and Sonia holding hands and tried wretchedly to convince himself that it had only been a trick of shimmer and shadow. Even more depressing were the occasions when Sonia came to Cambridge: Martin felt unwanted, imagined they kept trying to shed him. His second summer in Switzerland was marked by his beating one of the best Swiss tennis players – but what did Sonia care about his triumphs in tennis, boxing, or soccer? Sometimes Martin visualized in a picturesque daydream how he would return to Sonia from fighting in the Crimea, and the word 'cavalry' thundered by, the wind whistled, clods of black mud flew in one's face – attack, attack! – tac-a-tac of the horseshoes, anapaest of the gallop. But it was too late now, fighting in the Crimea had ceased long ago, long gone was the day Nelly's husband riding full speed at an enemy machine gun came nearer and nearer to it until he inadvertently swept across the invisible line into a region still tingling with echoes of earthly life, but where there are neither machine guns nor cavalry attacks. 'Always remiss, always remiss,' grumbled Martin at himself gloomily, and with the piercing sense that something had been missed forever, kept again and again imagining the ribbon of St George, the light wound in the left shoulder (it had to be the left), and Sonia coming to meet him at Victoria Station. He was irritated by his mother's tender smile, by the words she could not withhold: 'Now you see it was all for nothing, and you would have perished for nothing. Nelly's husband – that's a different matter, he was a real professional soldier, such people cannot exist without a war, and he died the way he wanted to die. But those thousands of youngsters mowed down—' However, in the presence of foreigners, she would hotly insist on the necessity of continued military action – especially now that all was over, and there was nothing there that could lure her son. In later years, when she remembered her relief and her calm, Mrs Edelweiss groaned aloud – oh yes, she could have preserved him, should not have so easily dismissed her forebodings, been more observant, been always on the lookout – and who knows? it might have been better had he really joined the White Army, been wounded, caught the typhus, and, at this price, got rid once for all of the attraction that danger has for young boys. But why harbor such thoughts, why give in to despair? More courage, more faith. People do get lost, and then come back. A rumour may circulate that someone has been seized at the border and shot as a spy, yet, all at once, there he is, alive, with his familiar laugh and deep voice, right there, in the entry hall. And if Henry again—

24

Not only his mother's fleeting smile of content had irritated Martin that second summer; there was something else besides, something far more unpleasant. Life at the chalet seemed to him strangely changed, as if moving on tiptoe, with bated breath. It was odd to hear Uncle Henry call Mrs Edelweiss not 'Sophie,' as before, but '*chère amie*'; and she, too, addressed him now and then as 'my dear.' A new softness, an increased welling of sentiment, showed in him; his voice had grown lower, his movements gentler; one's praise for the soup or the joint was now enough to veil his eyes with moisture. The cult around Martin's father's memory had acquired a tinge of unbearable mysticism; Mrs Edelweiss was more than ever conscious of her guilt before her late husband, while Uncle Henry seemed to be tracing for her a difficult but sure road of expiation when remarking how happy Serge's spirit must be to see her in his cousin's house; once he even produced a nail file and with agreeable melancholy began to pass it back and forth over his nails, but at this Mrs Edelweiss could not contain herself and emitted a hollow laugh, which unexpectedly became a fit of hysterics. In his haste to help, Martin opened the kitchen faucet so briskly that the water splashed his white flannels.

Not infrequently did he observe his mother as she walked in

the garden leaning wearily on Henry's arm, or as she fetched for Henry a bedtime cup of fragrant linden tea. It was all depressing, embarrassing, and strange. Just before his departure for Cambridge she obviously wanted to break the news to him, but she found it as embarrassing as he; she faltered and only said that she perhaps would soon write to him of an important event; and indeed, that winter, Martin received a letter, not from her but from his uncle, who on six pages informed him in a flowing hand in bombastic tear-jerking language that he was marrying Martin's mother – a very modest ceremony at the village church – and only upon reaching the postscriptum Martin realized that the wedding had already taken place and mentally thanked his mother for having scheduled this grim celebration to coincide with his absence. At the same time he kept asking himself how he would face her again, what they would talk about, and would he manage to forgive her the betrayal. For no matter how you approached it, it was, beyond any doubt, a betrayal of his father's memory. Furthermore, he was plagued by the thought that for stepfather he had Uncle Henry of the fluffy whiskers and limited wits. When Martin arrived for Christmas, his mother could not stop hugging him and weeping, as if forgetting, to oblige Uncle Henry, her usual restraint; and there was simply nowhere to hide from the soft emotion in his stepfather's kindly eyes and from the solemnity of that little cough of his.

In general, during his last university year, Martin was made aware again and again of the presence of some malevolent force obstinately trying to convince him that life was not at all the easy happy thing he had imagined. Sonia's existence, the constant gratuitous attention it extorted from his soul, her visits that only tormented him, the derisive tone of the banter that had become established between them, all of it was extremely exhausting. That unrequited love did not prevent him, however, from running after every pretty girl, and tingling with bliss when, for instance, Rose, the goddess of the tearoom, consented to go with him for a motorcar drive. In that shop, much frequented by students, you could buy pastry of every imaginable colour: bright-red with speckles of cream that made them look like deadly amanitas; purplish-blue, like violet-scented soap; and glossy-black, Negroid, with a white soul. One went on devouring cake after cake till one's innards got glued together, in the ever-present hope of at last discovering something really good. With a dusky flush on her velvety cheeks and a liquid gaze, clad in a black dress with a soubrette's little apron, Rose tripped rapidly back and forth through the room nimbly evading collision with the other waitress navigating also at full speed. Martin immediately noticed Rose's thick-fingered red hand not in the least embellished by the tiny star of a cheap ring, and decided wisely never again to look at her hands but to concentrate on her long eyelashes which she lowered so beautifully while writing out a check. One day, while drinking rich sweet chocolate, he passed her a note, and that same evening walked with her in the rain. On Saturday he hired the usual ramshackle limousine and spent the night with her at an ancient inn, some fifty kilometers from Cambridge. He felt somewhat taken aback, though flattered, when she said it was her first affair; she made love stormily, clumsily, rustically, and Martin who had expected to find in her a frivolous and experienced siren, felt so disconcerted that he turned to Darwin for advice. 'You'll get kicked out of the university,' calmly said Darwin. 'Nonsense,' retorted Martin frowning. Yet when, three weeks later, Rose, as she put down a cup of chocolate before him, informed him in a quick whisper that she was pregnant, it seemed as if that meteorite which ordinarily lands somewhere in the Gobi desert had fallen straight upon him.

'Congratulations,' said Darwin; after which, not without artistry, he began to delineate the fate of a sinful girl with a babe in her belly. 'And *you* will be sent down. That's a fact.' 'No one will know, I shall straighten out everything,' stammered Martin. 'It's hopeless,' said Darwin.

Martin suddenly lost his temper and walked out banging the door. He ran out into the lane, and nearly crashed under the impact of a large pillow that his friend had skillfully aimed at his head from the second-floor window. When Martin reached the corner and glanced back, he saw Darwin come out, pick up the pillow, shake it, and return to the house. 'Cruel brute,' muttered Martin and went straight to the tearoom. It was crowded. Bright-eyed, dusky Rose flitted from table to table, tripped along with a tray, or, tenderly moistening her pencil with the tip of her tongue, wrote out a check. He also wrote some lines on a leaf from his agenda, namely 'I want you to marry me. Martin Edelweiss.' He thrust the leaflet into her hideous hand; then he left, spent a couple of hours roaming about the town, returned home, lay down on the sofa, and remained lying until nightfall.

25

At nightfall Darwin dropped in, magnificently flung off his gown, sat down by the fire, and immediately began livening up the coals with the poker. Martin lay in silence, full of self-pity, again and again imagining himself coming out of the church with Rose, who was wearing white kid gloves, pulled on with difficulty. 'Sonia is coming alone tomorrow,' said Darwin unconcernedly. 'Her mother's got the flu, a bad case of flu.' Martin said nothing, but visualized with a stab of excitement tomorrow's soccer match. 'How are you going to play, though?' said Darwin. 'That, of course, is the question.' Martin remained silent. 'Badly, probably,' Darwin resumed. 'Goalkeeping needs presence of mind, and you're in one hell of a state. You know, I just had a chat with that woman.'

Silence. The tower chimes rang across the town.

'A poetic nature, inclined to fantasy,' Darwin went on a minute later. 'She's no more pregnant than, for instance, I am. Want to bet a fiver that I can twist this poker into a monogram?' (Martin lay like a dead man.) 'I interpret your silence as assent. Let's see.'

He grunted once, twice. 'No, can't do it today. The money's yours. I paid exactly five pounds for your stupid declaration. We're even, and everything's in order.'

Martin was silent, only his heart had begun beating violently.

'But,' said Darwin, 'just remember, if you ever set foot in that bad and expensive pastry shop again, you'll get kicked out of the university. That lass can be impregnated by a mere handshake, don't forget that.'

Darwin got up and stretched. 'You're not very talkative, chum. I must confess that you and your hetaera have somehow marred tomorrow for me – I mean the morrow one has in one's mind.'

He went out, quietly closing the door behind him, and Martin had three simultaneous thoughts: that he was terribly hungry, that you couldn't find another friend like that, and that tomorrow this friend would propose. At that moment he joyously and ardently wished that Sonia would accept, but the moment passed, and next morning, when he and Darwin met Sonia at the station, he felt the old familiar, dreary jealousy (his only, rather pathetic advantage over Darwin was his recent, wine-toasted transition to the intimate second-person singular, the

Russian '*ty*,' with Sonia in England that form had died out with the bowmen; nonetheless Darwin had also drunk *auf Brunderschaft* with her, and had addressed her all evening with the archaic 'thou').

'Hello, flower,' she said casually to Martin, alluding to his botanical last name; then, at once turning away, she began telling Darwin things that might have interested Martin too.

'What's so attractive about her, after all?' he thought for the thousandth time. 'All right, she has those dimples, that pale complexion – that's not enough. Here eyes are so-so, gypsyesque, and her teeth are uneven. And her lips are so thick, so glossy – if one could just stop them, shut them up with a kiss. And she thinks she looks English in that blue suit and those low-heeled shoes. Don't you people see she's just a short little thing?' Who these 'people' were Martin did not know; and they would have had a difficult time passing judgment, for, as soon as Martin achieved an attitude of indifference toward Sonia, he would suddenly notice what a graceful back she had, how she tilted her head – and her slanted eyes ran across him with a swift chill, and the undercurrent of mirth in her speech bathed the base of each phrase, until, abruptly, her laughter burst into the open; and she would stress her words with a shake of her tightly furled umbrella, which she held not by its handle but by its body of silk. And, ambling despondently, now behind them, now alongside, on the cobbled pavement (it was impossible for three people to walk abreast on the sidewalk because of the resilient cushion of air surrounding Darwin's massive form, and because of Sonia's short, weaving steps) Martin reflected that, adding up all the random hours he had spent with her, here and in London, the total would be no more than a month and a half of constant companionship – and to think that he had first met her more than two years ago, and that now the third, and last, Cambridge winter was already on the wane, yet he really could not tell what sort of person she was, and whether or not she was in love with Darwin, and how she would react if Darwin were to tell her about yesterday's experience, and whether she had spoken to anyone about that night, that miserable, yet by now oddly ravishing and not in the least shameful night when, shivering, barefoot, in her skimpy yellow pyjamas, she had been borne ashore by a wave of silence and gently deposited on his blanket.

They reached their destination. Sonia washed her hands in Darwin's bedroom. She took out her puff, blew on it, and powdered her face. The luncheon table was laid for five. Vadim had of course been invited, but Archibald Moon had long since disappeared from their circle of friends, and it was even a little strange to recall that he had once been considered a desirable guest. The fifth member of the party was a slender, snub-nosed, blond youth, not handsome but nicely built and somewhat eccentrically dressed. He had the fine, elongated hands with which popular novelists endow artistic individuals, yet he was neither poet nor painter, and the graceful, delicate fluttery something about him, along with his knowledge of French and Italian and slightly un-British but very elegant manners, was attributed at Cambridge to his father's Florentine origin. Teddy, kindly, ethereal Teddy, belonged to the Roman Church, liked climbing and skiing in the Alps, was a good oarsman, played the old royal game of court tennis, and, while he knew how to be very tender with women, carried chastity to a ridiculous extreme (a year later, however, he announced a certain change in a note to Martin from Paris: 'Yesterday,' he wrote, 'I got myself a wench, quite clean, and all that.' Underneath the studied vulgarity there was something sorrowful and nervous about that statement. Martin recalled his sudden fits of melancholy and self-castigation, his love for Leopardi and for snow, and how he had furiously smashed a perfectly innocent Etruscan vase upon receiving an insufficiently brilliant grade in an examination).

'What fun to stare when a great big bear' – and Sonia echoed Vadim, who had long since become chummy with her (but prudently omitted the punch line after 'tiny bitch') – '*vedyot za ruchku malen'kuyu suchku,*' while Teddy, who did not understand Russian, cocked his head to inquire, 'What does "*malenxus*" mean?'

Whereupon everybody laughed, and no one would explain, and he began addressing Sonia thus, 'Have some more peas, *malenxus*.'

'Jittery, jittery?' Vadim asked Martin.

'Don't be silly,' replied Martin. 'I didn't sleep well last night and that means muffing today. They have three international-class players, and we have only two.'

'Can't stand soccer,' declared Teddy. Darwin upheld him. Both were Etonians, and Eton had its own special ball game in place of soccer.

26

Martin was in fact jittery, and considerably so. He kept goal for Trinity; his team, after a keen struggle, had reached the finals, and that day was to meet St John's for the Cambridge University championship. Martin was proud that he, a foreigner, had made the first team, and, for his brilliant play, had qualified for the title of College Blue entitling him to wear a splendid light-blue blazer. He would now recollect with pleasant amazement his childhood days in Russia when, curled up in a soft hollow of the nursery night, and having abandoned himself to reveries that would imperceptibly bear him off into sleep, he would see himself as a crack footballer. It was enough for him to close his eyes and picture a soccer field or, say, the long, brown, diaphragm-joined cars of an express that he was driving himself, and his mind would gradually catch the rhythm, grow blissfully serene, be cleansed, as it were, and, sleek and oiled, slip into oblivion. Instead of a train, going full tilt (gliding through bright-yellow birch forests, then above foreign cities, across bridges that spanned streets, and on, southward, through tunnels which had their own sudden daybreak, and along the shore of a dazzling sea), it might be an airplane, a race car, a bobsleigh, taking a sharp turn in a whirl of flying snow, or else simply a forest path along which you run and run. As he reminisced, Martin noted a certain peculiarity about his life: the property that his reveries had of crystallizing and mutating into reality, as previously they had mutated into sleep. This seemed to him a guarantee that the new series of reveries he had recently evolved – about an illegal, clandestine expedition – would also grow solid and be filled with life, as his dreams about soccer matches had grown solid and incarnate, those dreams in which he used to luxuriate so lengthily, so artfully, when, afraid to reach the delicious essence too quickly, he would dwell in detail on the pregame preparations – pulling on the stockings with the coloured tops, putting on the black shorts, tying the laces of the robust boots.

He grunted and unbent. It was warm changing near his fireplace, and this helped in a way to dilute the tremor of his excitement. The celestial blazer buttoned snugly over the white V-necked sweater. How worn were his goalkeeper's gloves! There; he was ready. His clothes lay all around where he had discarded them. He gathered everything up and carried it into the bedroom. Compared with the warmth of the woollen sweater his bare-kneed legs felt wonderfully cool in their roomy, light shorts. 'Whew!' he said as he entered Darwin's room, 'you can't say I didn't change fast.'

'Let's go,' said Sonia, getting up from the sofa.

Teddy gave her a beseeching look. 'I beg a thousand pardons,' he implored, 'but, believe me, I can't come with you, I am expected elsewhere.'

He left. Vadim also left, promising to cycle over to the playing fields later.

'Maybe it really isn't so interesting after all,' said Sonia, addressing Darwin. 'Perhaps we might as well not go?'

'No, no, we'll go by all means,' said Darwin with a smile, giving Martin a squeeze on the shoulder. As the three of them set out along the street, Martin noticed that Sonia never looked at him once, and yet this was the first time he had appeared before her in soccer array.

'Let's walk a little faster,' he said, 'or else we may be late.'

'No great harm in that,' said Sonia, stopping in front of a shop window.

'All right, I'll go on ahead,' said Martin and, thumping firmly with the rubber cleats on his boots, took a short cut through an alley and strode off toward the pitch.

Quite a lot of spectators had turned out, owing partly to the fine day, with its pale-blue wintry sky and brisk air. Martin went on into the pavilion, where the other players had already gathered. Armstrong, the team captain, a lanky fellow with a clipped moustache, smiled shyly as he told Martin for the hundredth time that he ought to wear knee guards. A moment later all eleven players trotted single-file out of the pavilion, and Martin felt a beloved blend of impressions: the sharp smell of the damp turf, its resilience underfoot, thousands of people in the stands, the black bare spot in front of the goal, and the thud of the ball kicked around by the other team. The referee brought out and placed within the white circle of the field's hub a brand-new light-yellow ball. The players got into position and the whistle blew. At that instant Martin's nervousness vanished and, calmly leaning against the left upright, he glanced around in search of Darwin and Sonia. The action was taking place at the opposite end of the pitch, and he could revel in the cold air, in the mat green of the turf, in the chatter of the people standing just behind the goal net, and the glory of feeling that his boyhood dream had come true, that the red-haired chap over there, the St John's captain, who was receiving and passing the ball with such exquisite accuracy, had recently played against Scotland, and that there was somebody in the crowd for whom it was worth making a special effort. In childhood years sleep would overtake him just in those opening minutes of the game, for Martin would get so engrossed in the details of the preface that he never got to the main part of the text. Thus he would protract the delight, postponing to another, less sleepy night the game itself, bright and swift, with the pounding of feet getting closer and now he could hear the panting of the attacks as the redhead broke loose – and there he came, his shock of hair bobbing, and then his fabled toe drove the ball whistling just above the ground toward the corner of the goal, but the custodian with a full-length dive succeeded in stopping that bolt, and now the ball was already in his hands and, eluding the nearest opponents, Martin sent it, with all the force of his thigh and calf, in a resounding punt that curved over the field to the roar of the stands.

During the short half-time interval the players sprawled on the ground, sucking on lemons, and when the teams changed goals, Martin, from his new position, tried again to make out Sonia and Darwin in the crowd. There was not much time for gawking, though, for the play immediately grew heated, and he constantly had to crouch on the alert. Several times, all doubled over, he caught cannonballs; several times he fisted high shots away; and thus he kept his goal virgin to the end of the game, smiling with joy when, a second before the final whistle, the opposing goalie fumbled the slippery ball, whereupon Armstrong promptly tapped it into the net.

Everything was over, the spectators flooded the field, and still he was unable to spot Sonia and Darwin. Somewhere beyond the grandstand, among the departing crowds, he noticed Vadim on his bike, weaving cautiously and tooting with his lips. 'They decamped quite a while ago,' he said in answer to Martin's question, 'right after half-time, and, you know—' here followed some quip about Darwin which Martin, however, did not hear to the end, as at that moment Philpott, one of his teammates, squeezed by on a chugging red motorcycle and offered him a lift. Martin got on behind and Philpott accelerated. 'Might as well not have managed to turn that last one over the bar,' thought Martin, wrinkling his face against the motley wind. He felt depressed and bitter, and when he had dismounted at the corner of his lane and was walking home, he ruminated with revulsion over the preceding day and Rose's craftiness, and felt even more hurt. 'They must be having tea somewhere,' he muttered, but just in case looked into Darwin's room. Sonia was reclining on the couch, and at the moment he entered, her hand went up in a clutching flick, trying to catch a clothes moth as it flew past.

'And Darwin?' asked Martin.

'Alive. Went out for some pastries,' she answered, malevolently following with her eyes the uncaught, whitish speck.

'Shame you didn't stay to the end,' said Martin, sinking into the abyss of an armchair. 'We won. One to nothing.'

'You ought to wash up,' she remarked. 'Just look at your knees. They're a sight! And you've tracked something black in here.'

'All right. Just let me recover my breath.' He breathed deeply several times and got up with a tired grunt.

'Wait a minute,' said Sonia. 'You've got to hear this, you'll die laughing. He just offered me his hand and heart. Of course, I knew it would happen – kept ripening and finally burst.' She stretched and glanced darkly at Martin, whose eyebrows had gone up. 'Intelligent expression you have,' she said, and, looking away, she continued, 'I simply don't understand what he expected. Very nice chap, etcetera, but a log, a log of real English oak. I'd die of boredom in a week. There it is, flying around again, that moth.'

Martin cleared his throat and said, 'I don't believe you. I know you said yes.'

'You're crazy!' shouted Sonia, sitting up and slapping the couch with both hands. 'How can you imagine such a thing?'

'Darwin is intelligent, perceptive, anything but a log,' Martin said in a strained voice.

She gave the couch another blow. 'But he isn't a real person – can't you see that, you idiot? This is getting downright insulting. He's not a person, but a dummy. Nothing inside except heaps of humour. That's just fine for going to a dance, but, in the long run, humour can get pretty exasperating.'

'He's a writer, connoisseurs, are raving about his stories,' murmured Martin with an effort, and decided that now he had done his duty, had tried enough to convince her, and that there was a limit to noble behaviour.

'Exactly, exactly – for connoisseurs only! Very charming, very well written, but so superficial, so comfortable, so—'

Here Martin felt the rush of a radiant torrent that had burst through the locks, he remembered the tricky cross he had collected so nicely, remembered that the Rose business was settled, that there was a banquet at the club that evening, that he was healthy and strong, that tomorrow, the day after tomorrow, and for many, many days more life would go on, replete with all kinds of happiness. All this overwhelmed him in one dizzy instant, and he merrily seized Sonia in his arms together with the cushion she had clutched at, and started kissing her moist teeth, her eyes, her cold nose, and she struggled, and kicked, and her black, violet-scented hair kept getting in his mouth; at last, laughing loudly, he dropped her on the sofa. Here the door was pushed open. At first a foot appeared, then, laden with goodies, Darwin entered. He tried to close the door with his foot but dropped a paper sack out of which tumbled meringues.

'Martin's been throwing cushions,' said Sonia in a plaintive, breathless voice. 'One to nothing is not so grand after all, why behave like a madman?'

27

Next day both Martin and Darwin had an armpit temperature of 100.5° Fahr., aches and pains, sore throats, and a singing in the ears: all the symptoms of flu. Pleasant as it might be to think that the agent of contagion had probably been Sonia, both of them felt rotten, and Darwin, who steadfastly refused to stay in bed, looked, in his colourful dressing gown, like a heavyweight boxer, all red and dishevelled after a long fight. Vadim, heroically disdaining contagion, brought medicines, while Martin, who had thrown a laprobe and his winter coat (neither of which did much to allay his chills) on top of his blanket, lay in bed with a scowl on his face, and, in every pattern, in every relationship between chance objects, sports, or shadows, saw human profiles – snoutish mugs, Bourbon noses, Negroid pouts: one wonders why fever specializes so assiduously in drawing rather vulgar caricatures. He would doze off, and immediately be dancing the fox-trot with a skeleton, which, as it danced, began coming unscrewed and losing bones, and he had to snatch them up and hold them in place, at least until the end of that dance; or else he had to take an outrageous examination, quite different from the one Martin had really to take a few months later, in May. In the dream test he was offered monstrous problems with large iron X's wrapped in cotton wool, while in the real one, in a spacious hall intersected by a dusty sunbeam, philology students had to knock off three compositions in one hour, and Martin, glancing now and then at the wall clock, wrote in his large, round hand about Ivan the Terrible's Gangmen, about Baratynski, about Peter the First's reforms, about Loris-Melikov.

His life at Cambridge was nearing its end, and something of a radiant apotheosis attended the final days; while awaiting examination results you could bask all afternoon in the sun, lying on cushions as you floated languidly down the Cam under the majestic auspices of the pink chestnut trees. That spring Sonia moved with her family to Berlin, where Zilanov had begun editing a Russian-language weekly, and now Martin, supine under the softly progressing branches, recalled his last trip to London. Darwin had not wanted to come; he indolently asked to have regards transmitted to Sonia, wiggled his fingers in the air, and plunged back in his book. When Martin arrived, the Zilanovs' house was in that dreary state of havoc that is so hateful to elderly, homey dogs – fat dachshunds, for instance. The maid and a tousled-haired youth with a cigarette behind his ear were carrying a trunk downstairs. A tearful Irina sat alone in the living room, biting her nails and thinking impenetrable thoughts. Some glass object fell and broke in one of the bedrooms, and the phone in the study rang in immediate response but nobody paid any attention to it. In the dining room a plate, covered by another, meekly waited, but what food it contained remained a mystery. Zilanov arrived from somewhere, wearing a black overcoat despite the warm weather, and sat down to write as coolly as if it were an ordinary day. A confirmed nomad, he evidently did not care in the least that in an hour it would be time to leave for the station, and that a crate of books, still to be nailed shut, stood in a corner; he just sat and wrote, in a current of air that stirred shreds of excelsior and the sheets of old newspapers. Sonia was standing in the middle of her room, her hands pressed to her temples, her moody gaze shuttling between a large package and a suitcase that was already full. Martin sat on the low windowledge smoking. Several times either her mother or her aunt came in, looked for something, failed to find it, and went out. 'Are you glad to be going to Berlin?' Martin gloomily asked, considering his cigarette, with its excrescence of ash that resembled lichened fir foliage with an ominous sunset showing through.

'I don't care,' said Sonia, gauging mentally whether the suitcase would shut.

'Sonia,' said Martin a minute later.

'What? What is it?' she muttered, coming out of her trance, and suddenly began fussing fast, planning to take the suitcase by surprise, with a sudden onslaught.

'Sonia,' said Martin, 'is it really true—' Her aunt came in, looked into a corner, and, replying negatively to somebody in the corridor, went out hurriedly without closing the door.

'Can it really be true,' said Martin, 'that we'll never see each other again?'

'That's for God to decide,' said Sonia absently.

'Sonia,' Martin began again. She glanced at him with a grimace (or was it a smile?).

'You know,' she said, 'he sent back all my letters, all the photos, everything. Funny chap. He could have kept those letters. I spent half an hour ripping them up and flushing them down, and now the toilet's clogged.'

'You didn't behave well with him,' grimly said Martin. 'You can't build up a person's hopes and then turn him down.'

'You keep out,' cried Sonia with a little squeal in her voice. 'Hopes of what? How dare you talk about hopes? What vulgarity, what filth! And, in general, why don't you stop pestering me? Try to sit on this bag instead,' she added, one tone lower in pitch. Martin sat down on the lid and pressed hard.

'Won't shut,' he said hoarsely. 'And I don't know why you have to fly into a rage like that. I just wanted to say—'

At that point something clicked reluctantly and, without giving the suitcase time to collect itself, Sonia turned the little key in its lock. 'Everything's fine now,' she said. 'Come over here, Martin. Let's have a heart-to-heart talk.'

Zilanov peeked into the room. 'Where's Mother?' he asked. 'Didn't I say to leave my desk alone? Now the ashtray has disappeared, it had two stamps in it.'

When he was gone, Martin took Sonia's hand in both of his, squeezed it between his palms, and heaved a melancholy sigh.

'You're a very sweet boy after all,' said Sonia. 'We'll write to each other, and maybe some time you'll come to Berlin, or perhaps some day we'll meet in Russia – won't that be fun?'

Martin kept shaking his head and felt the tears welling. Sonia snatched her hand away. 'Oh well, if you want to sulk,' she said crossly, 'do by all means, to your heart's content.'

'Ah, Sonia,' he uttered sorrowfully.

'Just exactly what is it you want from me?' she asked, narrowing her eyes. 'Please tell me, what is it you want from me?' Martin turned his head away and shrugged.

'Listen,' she said, 'it's time to go down, time to leave, and your moping only exasperates me. For goodness' sake, why can't we keep everything nice and simple?'

'You'll get married in Berlin,' Martin mumbled hopelessly. As in a farce the maid dashed in and took the suitcase. Mrs Zilanov, already hatted, appeared behind her.

'Time to go, time to go,' she said. 'You took everything in here? Didn't forget anything? This is dreadful,' she addressed Martin. 'We had planned on a leisurely departure tomorrow.'

She vanished, but for a while her voice in the passage went on explaining to somebody about her husband's urgent business, and Martin felt so piercingly, so ineffably saddened by all this commotion and disorder that he actually yearned to bundle Sonia off, to get rid of her as quickly as possible, and return to Cambridge and its lazy sunshine.

Sonia smiled, took him by the shoulder, and kissed him on the bridge of his nose. 'I don't know – maybe,' she whispered, and, quickly wriggling out of Martin's violent embrace, raised a warning finger. '*Tout beau*, doggy,' she said, and then made big eyes, for at that moment, from downstairs, came the sound of awful, impossible, house-shaking sobs. 'Come on, come on,' hurried Sonia. 'I can't understand why the poor child is so unhappy about moving away. Cut it out, damn it – let me go!'

At the bottom of the stairs Irina was tossing, howling, clutching at the banister. Her mother kept coaxing her softly, 'Ira, Irochka,' while Zilanov, using an oft-tested expedient, took out his handkerchief, quickly made a long-eared, fat knot, pulled the handkerchief over his hand, and manoeuvered in such a way as to make a little fellow in nightshirt and cap cozily getting into bed.

At the station she burst into tears again, only more quietly and hopelessly. Martin slipped her a box of candy that had actually been intended for Sonia. Zilanov had no sooner taken his seat than he opened a newspaper. Mrs Zilanov and Mrs Pavlov were counting suitcases with their eyes. With a clatter the doors began closing; the train moved. Sonia thrust her head out, leaning her elbows on the lowered window, and for a few instants Martin walked alongside the car; then he fell behind, and an already much diminished Sonia blew him a kiss, and Martin stumbled against some box on the platform.

'Well, there they go,' he sighed, and felt a certain relief. He made his way to the other station, bought the new issue of a humour magazine with a puppet, all nose, chin, and hump, on the cover, and, when he had extracted the last joke out of it, fixed his gaze on the gentle fields that were sliding past. 'My darling, my darling,' he repeated several times, and, gazing through a hot tear at the green scenery, he imagined how, after many adventures, he would arrive in Berlin, look up Sonia, and like Othello, begin to tell a story of hairbreadth escapes, of most disastrous chances. 'No, it can't go on like this,' he said, rubbing his eyelid with a finger and tensing his upper lip. 'No, no. Less talk and more action.' Closing his eyes, and wedging himself comfortably into the corner, he started preparing for a dangerous expedition, studying an imaginary map. No one knew what he planned to do, Darwin alone might be informed – good-bye, good luck, the northbound train moves, and amidst these preparations he fell asleep, as he once used to fall asleep while putting on football apparel in his reveries. It was dark when he arrived in Cambridge. Darwin was still reading the same book, and yawned like a lion when Martin came in. And here Martin yielded to a little mischievous temptation, which he was subsequently to pay for. Counterfeiting a pensive smile, he stared at nothing, and Darwin, having unhurriedly completed his yawn, gave him a curious look.

'I am the happiest man in the world,' said Martin in a low voice full of feeling. 'Oh, if I could only tell you everything.'

In a sense, this was no lie, for when he had dozed off on the train, he had dreamt a dream grown out of something that Sonia had said. In the dream she pressed his head to her smooth shoulder and bent over him, tickling him with her lips, murmuring warm muffled words of tenderness, and now it was hard to separate fancy from fact.

'Well, I'm very happy for you,' said Darwin. A sudden embarrassment overcame Martin, and, whistling to himself, he went off to bed. A week later he received a postcard with a view of the Brandenburg Gate crossed by Sonia's spidery handwriting, which he spent a long time deciphering, trying in vain to read a hidden meaning into trivial words.

And now, gliding down the river beneath low-hanging boughs in bloom, Martin went back over his last meeting with her in

London, analyzing it, testing it with different acids: a pleasant, but not very fruitful labour. It was a hot day; the sun penetrated his closed eyelids with a languorous strawberry crimson; he could hear the restrained splash of water and the gentle far-off music of floating phonographs. Presently he opened his eyes and, in a flood of sunlight, there was Darwin reclining on the cushions opposite, dressed as he in white flannel pants and open-necked shirt. The pole propelling their punt was wielded by Vadim. His cracked pumps glistened with drops of water and there was an intent expression on his sharp-featured face – he was fond of navigation, and now performed a sacred rite, as it were, skillfully, rhythmically manipulating the pole, pulling it out of the water with a methodical change of hold and bearing down on it anew. The punt glided between flowery banks; the transparent green water reflected now chestnut trees, now brambles in milk-white bloom; occasionally a petal would fall, and you could see its reflection hurrying up to meet it out of the watery depths, and then both would converge. Lazily, soundlessly – if one discounted the cooing of phonographs – other punts, or now and then a canoe, glided past. Martin noticed ahead an open bright-coloured parasol which rotated this way and that, but nothing was visible of the girl twirling it except a hand, incongruously clad in a white glove. Her punt was manned by a young chap with glasses, poling very inexpertly, so that the boat followed a weaving course, and Vadim seethed with contempt, and did not know on which side to pass. At the very first bend it headed inexorably for the bank, the convex parasol showed in profile, and Martin recognized Rose.

'Look, how amusing,' he said, and Darwin, without moving the fat arms upon which his nape rested, turned his eyes in the direction of Martin's gaze.

'You shall not say hello to her,' he observed calmly.

Martin smiled, 'Oh yes, I certainly will.'

'If you do,' drawled Darwin, 'I'll knock your head off.'

There was a strange look in his eyes, and Martin felt uneasy; but for the very reason that Darwin's threat did not sound jocular and frightened him, Martin shouted as he floated past the punt entangled in the riverside shrubbery, 'Hello, hello, Rose!' And she smiled silently, her eyes sparkling and her parasol spinning, and in his exertions the bespectacled chap dropped his pole with a splash, and next moment they were concealed by the bend, and Martin again lay back and contemplated the sky.

After they had glided in silence for some minutes, Darwin

greeted somebody in his turn. 'John!' he roared, 'paddle over here!'

John grinned and started backing water. This black-browed, crew-cut portly young man was a gifted mathematician who had recently won a prize for one of his papers. He sat low in his pirogue (Vadim's nomenclature), moving a shiny paddle close to the boat's side.

'I say, John,' announced Darwin, 'I've been challenged to a fight here, and I want you as second. We'll choose a quiet spot and land.'

'Righto,' answered John, without showing the least surprise, and, as he paddled alongside, began a lengthy account about a student who had recently acquired a seaplane, and promptly crashed it during an attempt to take off from the narrow Cam. Martin reclined on his cushions, motionless. Here it was, the familiar tremor and weakness in the legs. Maybe Darwin was joking after all. What did he have to get so furious about?

Vadim, immersed in the mystique of navigation, had apparently heard nothing. Three or four bends later Darwin asked him to head for shore. Evening was already drawing near. The river was deserted at that point. Vadim aimed the punt at a little green tongue of land that projected from beneath a leafy canopy. They thumped gently to a stop.

28

Darwin jumped ashore first and helped Vadim moor the boat. Martin stretched, got up unhurriedly, and also debarked.

'Began reading Chekhov yesterday,' John said to him, wriggling his eyebrows. 'Very grateful to you for the advice. Appealing, humane writer.'

'Oh, he certainly is,' said Martin, and quickly thought to himself, 'Is there really going to be a fight?'

'There,' said Darwin, drawing near. 'If we go through these bushes we'll come out in a meadow, and we'll be out of sight of the river.'

Only here did Vadim understand what was about to take place. 'Mamka will kill you,' he said to Martin in Russian.

'Nonsense,' replied Martin. 'I'm just as good a boxer as he is.'

'Forget about boxing,' Vadim whispered feverishly. 'Give him a good kick right away!' and he specified exactly where. He was rooting for Martin solely out of patriotism.

The little meadow, ringed by hazel trees, proved velvet-smooth. Darwin rolled up his sleeves, but, on second thought, rolled them back down and took off his shirt, exposing a massive pink torso with a muscular gloss at the shoulders and a path of golden hairs down the middle of his broad chest. He tightened his belt, and suddenly broke into a smile. It's all a joke, thought Martin joyously, but, just to be safe, he too removed his shirt. His skin was of a creamier shade, with numerous little birth-marks, common among Russians. Next to Darwin he seemed sparer, even though solidly built and broad-shouldered. He pulled his cross over his head, gathered the chain in his palm, and thrust this handful of trickling gold in his pocket. The evening sun flooded his back with warmth.

'How do you want it, with breathers?' asked John, sprawling comfortably on the grass. Darwin glanced questioningly at Martin, who stood with spread legs and folded arms.

'Makes no difference to me,' remarked Martin, while through his mind rushed the thought: 'No, it's the real thing – how ghastly—'

Vadim slouched around restlessly with his hands in his pockets, sniffling, smirking uneasily, and then sat down cross-legged beside John.

John took out his watch. 'Anyway, they oughtn't to have more than five minutes in all – agreed, Vadim?'

Vadim nodded in confusion.

'Well, you can begin,' said John.

Fists clenched, legs flexed, the two started dancing around one another. Martin still could not imagine himself hitting Darwin in the face, in that large, clean-shaven face with the soft wrinkles around the mouth; however, when Darwin's left shot out and caught Martin on the jaw, everything changed: all anxiety vanished, he felt relaxed and radiant inside, and the ringing in his head, from the jolt it had received, sang of Sonia, over whom, in a sense, they were fighting this duel. Dodging another lunge, he punched Darwin's gentle face, ducked under Darwin's retaliating right, attempted an uppercut, and received himself such a black, star-spangled blow in the eye that he staggered and only just managed to evade the most vicious of half-a-dozen swipes. He crouched, he feinted, and jabbed Darwin in the mouth so nicely that his knuckles felt the hardness of teeth through the wetness of lips, but at once was punished himself in the belly by running into what seemed the protruding end of an iron girder. They bounced away from each other and resumed circling. Darwin had a red trickle at the corner of his mouth. He spat twice and the fight went on. John pensively puffing on his pipe, juxtaposed in his mind Darwin's experience and Martin's speed and decided that if he were to choose between these two heavyweights in the ring, he would be inclined to bet on the elder. Martin's left eye was already closed and swollen, and both combatants were glossy with sweat and smeared with blood. In the meantime Vadim had got all worked up, and was shouting excitedly in Russian; John shushed him. Bang! on the ear. Martin lost his balance, and, as he was tumbling, Darwin managed to hit him a second time, whereupon Martin sat down heavily on a pebbly patch, hurting his coccyx, but instantly sprang up and returned to the fray. Despite the buzzing pain in his head, and the crimson fog in his eyes, Martin felt sure he was inflicting more injury on Darwin than Darwin on him, but John, a lover of pugilism, already saw clearly that Darwin was only now getting into his stride, and that in a few moments the younger of the two would be down for good. But Martin miraculously withstood a series of resonant hooks and even managed to slam the other again on the mouth. He was panting now, and not thinking too clearly, and what he saw before him was no longer called Darwin, and in fact had no human name at all, but had become simply a pink, slippery, rapidly moving mass that must be punched with every last bit of strength. He succeeded in planting yet another very solid and satisfying blow somewhere – he did not see where – but immediately a multitude of fists pummeled him at length from all sides, wherever he turned; he stubbornly searched for a breach in this whirlwind, found one, hammered at a continuum of squelchy pulp, suddenly felt that his own head was flying off, slipped, and remained hanging on Darwin in a humid clinch.

'Time!' came John's voice from remote space, and the fighters separated. Martin collapsed on the grass, and Darwin, his bloodied mouth forming a grin, plumped down beside him, tenderly put his arm around Martin's shoulders, and both froze motionless, inclining their heads and breathing heavily.

'You ought to wash up,' said John, while Vadim approached cautiously and started examining their bruised faces.

'Can you stand?' Darwin asked solicitously. Martin nodded and, leaning on him, straightened up. They trudged toward the river, arms across each other's shoulders. John patted them on their clammy bare backs; Vadim went on ahead to look for a secluded cove. There, Darwin helped Martin give face and frame a good wash, then Martin did the same for him, and both kept asking each other in low, solicitous tones where it hurt and if the water did not sting.

29

Dusk was deepening, the nightingales had begun bubbling, the dim meadows and the dark shrubs breathed dampness. The river mists engulfed John and his black canoe. Vadim, once again propelling the punt, a white, ghostlike figure in the gloom, wordlessly and with a somnambulically smooth motion immersed his spectral pole. Martin and Darwin lay side by side on the cushions, limp, languid, swollen, staring with their three good eyes at the sky, across which a dark branch passed every now and then. And that sky, and the branch, and the barely plashing water, and the figure of Vadim, mysteriously ennobled by his love of navigation, and the coloured lights of the paper lanterns on the bows of passing punts, and the thought that in a few days Cambridge would end, that perhaps the three of them were gliding for the last time along the narrow, misty river – all this merged in Martin's mind into something wondrous and spellbinding, and the leaden pain in his head and the ache in his shoulders struck him as having an exalted, romantic quality, for thus wounded Tristram had floated alone with his harp.

One last bend, and there was the shore. The shore on which Martin landed was very fair, very bright, and full of variety. He knew, though, that for example Uncle Henry remained firmly convinced that these three years of aquatics in Cambridge had gone to waste, because Martin had indulged in a philological cruise, and not even a very distant one, instead of learning a useful profession. But Martin in all honesty did not understand why it was worse to be an expert in Russian letters than a transportation engineer or a merchant. Actually, Uncle Henry's menagerie – and everybody has one – housed, among other creatures, a little black beast, and that *bête noire* was to him the twentieth century. Now this amazed Martin, since in his opinion one could not even imagine a better century than the one in which he lived. No other epoch had had such brilliance, such daring, such projects. Everything that had glimmered in previous ages – the passion for exploration of unknown lands, the audacious experiments, the glorious exploits of disinterested curiosity, the scientists who went blind or were blown to bits, the heroic conspiracies, the struggle of one against many – now emerged with unprecedented force. The cool suicide of a man after his having lost millions on the stock market struck Martin's imagination as much as, for instance, the death of a Roman general falling on his sword. An automobile advertisement, brightly beckoning in a wild, picturesque gorge from an absolutely inaccessible spot on an alpine cliff thrilled him to tears. The complaisant and affectionate nature of very complicated and very simple machines, like the tractor or the linotype, for example, induced him to reflect that the good in mankind was so contagious that it infected metal. When, at an amazing height in the blue sky above the city, a mosquito-sized airplane emitted fluffy, milk-white letters a hundred times as big as it, repeating in divine dimensions the flourish of a firm's name, Martin was filled with a sense of marvel and awe. But Uncle Henry, as if throwing tidbits to his black beastie, spoke with horror and revulsion about the twilight of Europe, about postwar fatigue, about our practical age, about the invasion of inanimate machines; in his imagination there existed some diabolical connection between the fox-trot and skyscrapers on one side and women's fashions and cocktails on the other. Furthermore, Uncle Henry had the impression he lived in an age of terrible haste, and it was particularly funny when he chatted about this haste, on a summer day, at the edge of a mountain road, with the local priest, while the clouds sailed serenely and the abbé's old, pink horse, shaking off flies with a tinkle, blinking its white eyelashes, would lower its head in a movement full of ineffable charm and munch succulently on the roadside grass, with its skin twitching or a hoof shifting now and then, and, if the talk about the mad haste of our days, about the almighty dollar, about the Argentines who seduced all the girls of Switzerland, dragged on too long, and the last tender stalk among coarser ones had been eaten at a given spot, it would move ahead a little, accompanied by the creak of the gig's high wheels. And Martin could not take his eyes off the gentle equine lips and the blades of grass caught in the bit.

'Here, this young man, for example,' Uncle Henry would say,

indicating Martin with his walking stick, 'he has finished college, one of the most expensive colleges in the world, and you ask him what he has learned, what he is prepared for. I absolutely don't know what he is going to do next. In my time young men became doctors, soldiers, notaries, while he is probably dreaming of being an aviator or a gigolo.'

Martin had no idea what exactly he served as an example of, but the abbé apparently understood Uncle Henry's paradoxes and smiled commiseratingly. Sometimes Martin was so irritated by talk of this kind that he was ready to say something rude to his uncle – who was also, alas, his stepfather – but would stop in time, for he had noticed the look that appeared on his mother's face whenever Henry waxed eloquent at dinner. That look contained a faint trace of friendly raillery, and a certain sadness, and a mute appeal to forgive the crank, and yet something else inexpressible but very wise. Martin would keep still, mentally answering Uncle Henry like this, for example: 'It's not true that I devoted my time to trifles at Cambridge. It's not true that I did not learn anything. Columbus, before trying to take hold of his east ear across his west shoulder, travelled to Iceland incognito to gather certain information, knowing that the sailors there were a canny and far-ranging breed. I, too, plan to explore a distant land.'

30

His mother did not pester him with the tedious talk of which Uncle Henry was so fond; she did not inquire what occupation he would choose, feeling as she did that all this would somehow work out by itself. She was satisfied with the happiness at hand – of his being with her now, healthy, broad-shouldered, tanned; of his slamming away at tennis, speaking in a bass voice, shaving daily, and making young, bright-eyed Madame Guichart, a local merchant's wife, blush as red as a poppy. Sometimes she wondered when Russia would at last snap out of the evil dream, when the striped pole of the frontier gate would rise and everyone return and resume his former place, and, goodness, how the trees have grown, how the house has shrunk, what sorrow and joy, what a smell of earth! In the mornings she would wait for the postman just as avidly as during her son's years at Cambridge, and now, when a letter came for Martin (and it was not often), in an office envelope, addressed in a spidery hand and bearing a Berlin postmark, she felt the keenest joy and, snatching the letter, hurried to his room. Martin still lay in bed, very tousled, sucking on a cigarette with his hand at his chin. He saw in the mirror the sun-bright wound of the opening door, and that special expression on his mother's pink, freckled face: by the fold of her lips, tightly compressed but ready to spread into a smile, he could tell there was a letter.

'Nothing for you today,' Mrs Edelweiss would lightly say, holding one hand behind her back, but her son's impatient fingers were already reaching out, and, beaming, she would press the envelope to her chest, and both would laugh. Then, not wishing to spoil his enjoyment, she would go to the window, lean out on its sill, cupping her face in her hands, and gaze with a feeling of complete happiness at the mountains, and in particular at one distant, rosy peak that was visible only from this window. Martin, who had consumed the letter in one gulp, pretended to be considerably happier than he actually was, so that his mother imagined those letters from the little Zilanov girl to be full of tenderness, and would probably have felt sadly hurt if she ever got to read them. She remembered the Zilanov girl with strange clarity: a black-haired, pale little thing who was always sick with an inflamed throat or convalescing after one, her neck either bandaged or yellow from iodine. She remembered how she had once taken ten-year-old Martin to a Christmas party at the Zilanovs' St Petersburg flat, and little Sonia was wearing a lacy white dress with a broad silk sash around the hips. As for Martin, he did not remember this at all; there had been many Christmas parties, and they merged in his memory. Only one thing remained very vivid, for it had recurred every time: his mother saying it was time to go home, and thrusting her fingers inside the collar of his sailor suit from behind to see if he was not too sweaty after all the running, while he, with a huge gold-papered cracker, kept trying to wrench himself free, but his mother's grip was tenacious, and presently his overpants (which reached nearly to his armpits) were being pulled on, and on went his overshoes and fur coat, with its tight-closing hook at the throat and the hideously tickly Caucasian hood, and next minute there was the streetlamps' frosty rainbow running across the window of the close carriage. It thrilled Martin to note that the expression of his mother's eyes was the same now as then, that now, too, she touched his neck when he came home after tennis, and that she brought Sonia's letter with the same tenderness as she had once brought, in its long cardboard box, an air rifle ordered from England.

The rifle had turned out to be not quite as he had expected, not matching exactly its foredream, just as now the letters from Sonia were not the kind he would have liked. She wrote, as it were, in abrupt jerks, without a single mystery-breathing phrase, and he had to be content with such remarks as 'I often recall good old Cambridge,' or 'Best of everything, my dear little flower, give me your paw to shake.' She told him that she had an office job – typing and shorthand – that they were having a very difficult time with Irina – constant hysterics – that her father had not got anywhere with his Russian-language newspaper and was now setting up a publishing business – books by *émigré* writers – that there was never a penny in the house – which was rather sad – that they had many friends – which was lots of fun – that the streetcars in Berlin were green, and that Berliners played tennis in braces and starched collars. Martin's endurance lasted all through summer, fall, and winter; then, in mid-April 1923, on his twenty-first birthday, he announced to Uncle Henry that he was leaving for Berlin. The latter looked dour, and said with displeasure, 'To me, *mon ami*, that seems devoid of all sense. You will always have time to see Europe. In point of fact, I was going to take you and your mother to Italy next autumn. But you can't go on loafing forever. In short, I was going to suggest that you try your youthful powers in Geneva.' (Martin knew full well what was meant: several times already this dismal subject had crept stealthily forth; it concerned some commercial firm or other belonging to the Petit brothers, with whom Uncle Henry had business relations.) 'That you try *tes jeunes forces*,' Uncle Henry repeated. 'In this cruel age, in this very practical age, a young man must learn to earn his bread and elbow his way through life. You have a solid knowledge of the English language. Foreign correspondence in the world of affairs is a most interesting thing. As for Berlin— Your German has not much improved, has it? I can't see what you are going to do there.'

'Suppose I do nothing,' Martin said gloomily.

Uncle Henry looked at him with surprise. 'That's a bizarre answer. I don't know what your father would have thought of an answer like that. I think he would be as astonished as I am that a young man full of sap and health despises all work. Please understand,' he hastily added, noticing that Martin had reddened unpleasantly, 'I am not being stingy – *je ne suis pas mesquin*. I am rich enough, thank God, to provide for you – I make a duty and a joy of it – but it would be folly not to take a job. Europe is passing through an unbelievable crisis, and a man can lose a fortune in the twinkling of an eye. That's the way it is, and you can't do a thing about it.'

'I don't need your money,' Martin said softly and rudely. Uncle Henry pretended not to hear, but tears welled in his eyes.

'Don't you have any ambition at all? Don't you ever think about making a career? We Edelweisses always knew how to work. Your grandfather began as a poor tutor – teaching French *à des princes russes*. When he proposed to your grandmother her parents threw him out of the house. And back he comes a year later, the director of an export company, and then, obviously, all obstacles were swept away.'

'I don't need your money,' repeated Martin, even more softly. 'And as for Grandfather, that's nothing but a silly family legend, and you know it.'

'What's the matter with him, what's the matter with him?' Uncle Henry muttered in fright. 'What right do you have to offend me like this? What wrong have I done you? I, who have always—'

'The short of the matter is that I'm going to Berlin,' Martin interrupted, and left the room, trembling.

31

That evening there was a reconciliation, embraces, noseblowing, emotional throat-clearing – but Martin stood his ground. His mother, who sensed his longing to see Sonia, proved to be an ally, and smiled bravely as he got into the car.

Hardly had the house disappeared from view when Martin changed places with the chauffeur. Holding the wheel delicately, almost tenderly, as if it were something alive and precious, and watching the powerful car gobble up the road, he experienced nearly the same sensation as when, in childhood, seated on the floor with his feet resting on the piano pedals, he would hold the stool with its round, revolving seat between his legs and handle it like a steering wheel, taking splendid curves at full speed, pushing the pedal again and again (which made the piano hum), and slitting his eyes against the imaginary wind. Then, in the German express, where, between the corridor windows, hung small maps of regions the train did not pass through, Martin relished the journey, eating chocolate, smoking, poking his cigarette butt under the metal lid of the ashtray, filled with the remains of cigar. It was night by the time he neared Berlin. Looking from the train onto the wet lighted streets he relived his childhood impression of Berlin, whose fortunate inhabitants could enjoy daily, if they wished, the sight of trains with fabulous destinations, gliding across a black bridge over a humdrum thoroughfare; in this respect Berlin differed from St Petersburg, where railroad operations were concealed like a secret rite. A week later, though, when his eyes had got used to the city, Martin was already powerless to reconstruct that perspective from which its features had seemed familiar. It was as when you meet someone you have not seen for years: first you recognize his figure and voice; then you look more closely, and there, before your eyes, the transformation imperceptibly wrought by time is run through in quick display. Features alter, likeness deteriorates, and you have before you a stranger, looking smug after having devoured his own young and fragile double, whom it will henceforth be hard to picture, unless chance comes to the rescue. When Martin deliberately visited in Berlin that intersection, that square, which he had seen as a child, there was nothing that gave him the least shiver of excitement, but on the other hand, a chance whiff of coal or automobile exhaust, a certain special pale hue of the sky seen through a lace curtain, or the shudder of the windowpanes awakened by a passing truck, instantly brought back the essence of city, hotel, and drab morning, part of an image that Berlin had once impressed upon him. The toy shops on the once elegant Friedrichstrasse had thinned out and lost their sparkle, and the locomotives in their windows looked smaller and shabbier. The pavement of this street had been torn up, and shirt-sleeved workmen were drilling, and digging deep smoky holes, so that you had to pick your way over planking, and sometimes even across loose sand. In the Panopticon of Waxworks in the Unter den Linden the man in a shroud, energetically climbing out of his grave, and the Iron Maiden, that instrument of strong and hard torture, had lost their ghoulish charm. Martin went to the Kurfürstendamn to look for that enormous roller-skating rink that he remembered so well, with its rumble of wheels, instructors in red uniforms, band shell, slightly salty mocha cake served in the encircling boxes, and the *pas de patineurs* that he used to dance to any kind of music, flexing now his right, now his left skate-shod leg (and what a spill he took once!), only to find a dozen years had been enough to abolish it completely. The Kurfürstendamm itself had changed too, maturing growing longer, and somewhere – perhaps beneath a new building – lay the grave of a twenty-court tennis establishment, where Martin had been a couple of times with his mother, who would accompany her underhand service with a bright-voiced 'Play!' and whose skirt would rustle as she ran. Now, without even leaving the city limits, he could reach the Grunewald, where the Zilanovs lived, to learn from Sonia that it was pointless to go to Wertheim's for his shopping, and that it was by no means obligatory to visit the Wintergarten, under whose fabulous star-dusted black ceiling tight-corseted Prussian officers sat at lighted tables in the boxes, while on stage twelve bare-legged girls sang with brassy voices and undulated with linked arms from right to left and back again, kicking up twelve white legs, and little Martin had uttered a soft exclamation of surprise upon recognizing in them the demure, pretty English misses who, like him, went skating daily at the wooden rink.

But perhaps the most unexpected thing about this new, much expanded, postwar Berlin, so peaceful, rustic and bumbling, compared to the compact and elegant city of Martin's childhood, was the free-mannered, loud-voiced Russian that chattered everywhere, in the trams, in the shops, on street corners, on the balconies of apartment houses. Some ten years before, in one of his prophetic daydreams (and any person with a lot of imagination has prophetic daydreams occasionally – such is the statistics of daydreams), Martin, a schoolboy in the secure St Petersburg of 1913, imagined himself in years to come as an exile, and felt tears rising when, on the strange dim railway platform of his reverie, he unexpectedly encountered – whom? – a compatriot, sitting on a trunk, on a night of shiverings and delays, and what a marvellous talk they had! For the roles of these fellow exiles he simply chose Russians he had noticed during that earlier trip abroad: a family in Biarritz, complete with governess, tutor, clean-shaven valet, and brown dachshund; a fascinating fair-haired lady at the Kaiserhof in Berlin; or, in the corridor of the Nord-Express, an old gentleman in a black skullcap, whom Martin's father had identified, in a whisper, as 'the writer Boborykin.' Then, having selected for them appropriate costumes and speeches, he would dispatch them to meetings with himself in the remotest parts of the world. Today, in 1923, that chance fantasy (the consequence of Heaven knows what children's book) found full incarnation, marked even by some overplaying. When the fat, heavily made-up Russian lady in the tram hung with blatant dejection from her strap, and volleyed over her shoulder some resounding Russian to her companion, an old man with a grey moustache, 'Astounding, really astounding, how not one of these ill-bred foreigners offers his seat,' Martin jumped up and, with a radiant smile, repeating what he had rehearsed in his boyhood fantasies, exclaimed, '*Pozhaluysta!*' and, instantly growing pale from the experienced thrill, clutched the strap in his turn. The peaceable Germans whom the lady had called ill-bred were all tired, hungry working people, and the grey sandwiches they chewed in the streetcar, even if they did irritate Russians, were indispensable. For real dinners were expensive that year of monstrous inflation, and, when Martin changed a dollar note in the tram, instead of investing that dollar in real estate, the conductor's hands would shake with amazement and joy. Martin earned his American *valuta* in a special way, which made him very proud. True, the labour was arduous. Ever since May, when he had stumbled upon that job (thanks to Kindermann, a charming Russian-German, who for a couple of years already had been teaching tennis to whatever wealthy clients turned up), and until mid-October, when he left to spend the winter with his mother, and then again in the spring of 1924, Martin worked almost daily from early morning to sunset, holding five balls in his left hand (Kindermann managed to hold six) and sending them one by one across the net with an identical smooth stroke of his racket, while the tense, middle-aged pupil (male or female) on the other side of the net swung diligently and as often as not did not hit anything. At first Martin would get so tired, his right shoulder would ache and his feet burn so badly, that as soon as he had earned his five or six dollars he would go to bed. His hair grew lighter and his skin darker from the sun, so that he seemed a negative of himself. His landlady, a major's widow from whom he concealed his profession so as to seem more mysterious, supposed that the poor fellow – like many cultured people, alas – was obliged to work as a labourer, lugging rocks, for instance (hence the suntan), and was embarrassed about it, as would be any refined person. In the evening, with genteel sighs, she would treat him to sausage that her daughter sent from their Pomeranian estate. The lady was six feet tall, with a ruddy complexion, used cologne on Sundays and kept a parrot and a tortoise in her room. She considered Martin an ideal roomer: he was seldom at home, did not receive guests, and never used the bath (the latter was amply replaced by the shower at the tennis club and the lake in Grunewald). This bath was plastered with the landlady's hair on the inside, anonymous rags dried on a clothesline overhead, and an old, dusty, rusted bicycle leaned against the opposite wall. Moreover, it was no easy task getting there: one had to follow a long, dark corridor, with an extraordinary number of corners and piled full of all sorts of junk. Martin's room, on the other hand, was not bad at all, and had its amusing side. It contained such objects of luxury as an upright piano, locked tight from time immemorial, and a massive, complicated barometer that had stopped working a couple of years before the war, while on the green wall above the couch, like a constant benevolent reminder, the same naked old chap armed with a trident rose out of his Böcklinian waves as he did – although in a plainer frame – on the wall of the Zilanovs' parlour.

32

The first time Martin visited them and saw their cheap, dingy flat, consisting of four rooms and a kitchen, where a strange Sonia with a different hairdo sat on the table, swinging her legs in their darned-up stockings, sniffling, and peeling potatoes, Martin realized that he could expect nothing but sorrows from Sonia, and that his Berlin trip was pointless. Everything about her was unfamiliar: the bronze-coloured sweater, the exposed ears, the stuffy voice – she was in the throes of a bad cold, and the skin was red around her nostils; she would stop peeling to blow her nose, give a dejected grunt, and slice off a new spiral of brown skin with her knife. For supper they had buckwheat groats with margarine instead of butter. Irina came to table holding a kitten from which she was inseparable and greeted Martin with a joyous and dreadful laugh. Both mothers had aged during the past year and had grown to resemble each other even more. Only Zilanov was still his old self, and cut into the bread as mightily as ever.

'I hear' – crunch, creak – 'that Gruzinov is in Lausanne. Did you' – creak – 'happen to run into him? Great friend of mine and a remarkably strong-willed, determined person.'

Martin had not the faintest notion who Gruzinov was but did not ask any questions for fear of committing a blunder. After dinner Sonia washed the plates and he dried them, breaking one.

'It's an impossible situation,' she exclaimed, and elucidated, 'I mean not our finances but my nose, I can't breathe through it. The financial situation is also pretty bad for that matter.'

Then she accompanied him downstairs to unlock the front door; at the press of a button there was a cute click and the staircase lights flashed on, and Martin kept clearing his throat and could not manage a single word of the many he had prepared. Evenings of a quite different nature followed – a multitude of guests, dancing to records, dancing in a nearby café, the murk of the corner cinema. New people materialized around Martin on all sides, nebulae gave birth to worlds. Definite labels and features were found for the Russian substance scattered about Berlin, for all those elements of expatriation which so excited Martin, be it merely a snatch of routine conversation amid the shoving sidewalk crowd, a chameleon word (such as that russified plural with its wandering accent: *dóllary, dollár*y, *dollará*), or a squabbling couple's recitative, caught in passing ('And I'm telling you—' for female voice; 'Oh, have it your way—' for male voice); or, on a summer night, a man with his head thrown back clapping his hands under a lighted window and shouting a resonant name and patronymic that made the whole street vibrate and caused a taxi to emit a nervous squeal and shy to one side after nearly running over the vociferous visitor, who had by now backed to the centre of the asphalt, the better to see if the person he needed would appear like Punch in the window. Through the Zilanovs Martin met people among whom he at first felt ignorant and alien. In a certain sense he experienced all over again what had embarrassed him when he first saw the Zilanovs in London. And now, when at the apartment of Stepan Bubnov the talk rolled on in great waves, full of allusions to modern authors, and knowledgeable Sonia cast at Martin a sidelong glance of ironic compassion, Martin blushed, faltered, was about to launch his own frail little contribution on the billows of other people's speeches, but feared it would capsize immediately, and so kept still. In compensation, shamed by the backwardness of his erudition, he devoted every hour of rain to reading, and very soon became familiar with that special smell, the smell of prison libraries, which emanated from Soviet literature.

33

The writer Bubnov (who used to point out with satisfaction how many distinguished Russian literary names of the twentieth century began with the letter B) was a bearish, balding man of thirty, with a huge forehead, deep-set eyes, and a square chin. He smoked a pipe, sucking in his cheeks deeply with every puff, wore an old black bow tie, and considered Martin a fop and a foreigner. As to Martin, he was much taken with Bubnov's energetic, rotund delivery and with his quite justified fame. Bubnov, whose writing career had begun in exile, had already had three excellent novels brought out by a Russian *émigré* publisher in Berlin, and was now writing a fourth. Its hero was Christopher Columbus, or, to be more exact, a Muscovite scrivener who, after many escapades, had miraculously ended up as a sailor on one of Columbus's caravels. Bubnov knew no language other than Russian, so that when he had to go to the State Library for his research and Martin happened to be free, he willingly took him along. Martin's command of German being mediocre, he was glad when a text chanced to be in French, English, or, better still, Italian. True, he knew that language even less than German, but he particularly prized his scant knowledge, remembering how he used to read Dante with melancholy Teddy's assistance. Bubnov's flat was frequented by the *émigré* literary set – fictionists, journalists, pimply young poets; in Bubnov's opinion these were all people of middling talent, and he reigned over them justly, hearing out, with his hand over his eyes, yet another poem about nostalgia for the homeland or recollections of St Petersburg (with the Bronze Horseman inevitably present) and then saying, as he unscreened his beetling brows and kneaded his chin, 'Yes, that's good.' Then, focusing his pale-hazel eyes on some fixed point, he would repeat 'Good' with a less convinced intonation; and, once again changing the direction of his gaze, he would say, 'Not bad,' and then, 'Only, you know, you make Petersburg a little too portable.' And thus, gradually lowering his evaluation, he would reach the point where he muttered in hollow tones, with a sigh, 'That stuff is all wrong, all unnecessary,' and dejectedly shake his head; upon which, abruptly, with vivid enthusiasm he would thunder out a poem by Pushkin. Once, when a young poet took offense and objected, 'That's by Pushkin, and this is by me,' Bubnov thought for a moment and replied, 'Still, yours is worse.'

Then again, there would be occasions when some newcomer brought a really fine piece, whereupon Bubnov – especially if the piece were in prose – would grow strangely glum and remain out of sorts for several days. Bubnov's friendship with Martin, who never wrote anything (except letters to his mother and for this was dubbed by a wit 'our Madame de Sévigné'), remained sincere and free of misgivings. There was even a night when, relaxed and transparent after his third mug of Pilsener, Bubnov began talking dreamily (and this brought back a campfire in the Crimean mountains) about a girl whose soul was a song, whose dark eyes sang, whose skin was pale like precious porcelain. Then, with a fierce look, he added, 'Yes, that's trite, that's nauseous, ugh! Despise me if you like, I may lack all talent, but I'm in love with her. Her name is like a church dome, like the swish of doves' wings. I see radiant light in her name, that special light, the "kana-inum" of the ancient Khadir sages. A light from there, from the East. Ah, that's a great mystery, an awesome mystery—' Lowering his voice to a demented whisper, he added, 'A woman's charm is a terrible thing – you understand me, terrible. And her poor little slippers are worn down at the heel, yes, worn down—'

Martin felt uncomfortable and nodded in silence. In Bubnov's company he always had a strange feeling, as if it were all a dream, and somehow he did not have complete faith either in him or in the Khadir elders. Sonia's other acquaintances, for example jolly, bright Kallistratov, a former officer now in the 'automobile transport business,' or the pleasant, fair-skinned and buxom Veretennikov girl, who played the guitar and sang 'There's a Volgan high cliff' in a rich contralto, or young Iogolevich, an intelligent, viperish, taciturn youth in horn-rimmed glasses who had read Proust and Joyce, were far less complicated than Bubnov. Mixed in with these friends of Sonia's were the elderly acquaintances of her parents, all respectable, politically active, pure-hearted people, fully deserving a future obituary of a hundred limpid lines. But when, one July day, old Iogolevich heavily fell prone on the sidewalk, dead of heart failure, and the *émigré* papers carried a great deal of stuff about the 'irreplaceable loss' and the 'true toiler,' and Mihail Platonovich Zilanov, improperly hatless, with his briefcase under his arm, walked in the vanguard of the funeral procession among the roses and the black marble of Jewish graves, Martin had the impression that the obituary writer's words 'he burned with love for Russia' or 'he always held high his pen' somehow debased the deceased inasmuch as those same words would have been equally applicable both to Zilanov and to the venerable necrologist himself. Most of all Martin felt sorry for the originality of the deceased, who was truly irreplaceable – his gestures, his beard, his sculpturesque wrinkles, the sudden shy smile, the jacket button that hung by a thread, and his way of licking a stamp with his entire tongue before sticking it on the envelope and banging it with his fist. In a certain sense this was all of greater value than the social merits for which there existed such easy little clichés, and with an odd shift of thought Martin swore to himself that he himself would never join a political party or attend a meeting, that he would never be the personage who is 'given the floor' or who 'adjourns the proceedings,' while revelling in the joys of civic virtue. And often Martin would marvel at his inability to mention his long-treasured secret plans to Zilanov or to Zilanov's friends or to any of those industrious, upstanding Russians, so full of disinterested love for their country.

34

But Sonia, ah, Sonia— From his night-time thoughts about the glorious and dark expedition, from his literary chats with Bubnov, from his daily labours at the tennis club, he would return to her again and again and hold a match over the gas stove for her, whereupon, with a loud gush, the blue flame would extend all its claws. To talk to her of love was useless, but once, while walking her home from the café, where they had imbibed Swedish punch through straws to the wail of a Rumanian violin, he was overwhelmed with such soft passion, because of the warm night and because in every doorway there stood a motionless couple, so infectious was their gaiety and whispering, and sudden silences, and the crepuscular undulation of lilacs in villa gardens, and the fantastic shadows with which the light of a streetlamp animated the scaffolding of a house in the process of renovation, that he forgot his usual reserve, his usual fear that Sonia would make fun of him, and, by some miracle, began to speak – of what? – of Horace. Yes, Horace had lived in Rome, and Rome, despite a good number of marble edifices, looked like a sprawling village, and there you could see people chasing after a mad dog, and hogs splashing in the mud with their black piglets, and construction was going on all over the place: carpenters hammered away; a wagon carrying Ligurian marble or an enormous pine would clatter past. But toward evening the racket would cease, just as Berlin grew silent at twilight, after which came the rattle of iron chains from shops being shut for the night, quite like the rattling of the Berlin shops' shutters at closing time, and Horace strolled off to the Field of Mars, debile but paunchy, with a bald head and big ears, clad in a sloppy toga, and listen to the tender whispers under the porticoes, to the enchanting laughter in dark nooks.

'You're such a dear,' Sonia said all at once, 'that I have to kiss you – wait, let's go over there.'

Near a park gate, under the overflow of dark foliage, Martin pulled Sonia to him, and, so as not to lose the least part of that moment, he did not close his eyes as he slowly kissed her cool, soft lips, watching the while a reflection of pale light on her cheek, and the quivering of her lowered eyelids: they rose for an instant, revealing a moist, blind glistening, and shut again; little shivers shook her, her lips parted under his, but breaking the spell her hand pushed his face aside, and her teeth were chattering, and in a half-whisper she implored him to stop.

'And what if I'm in love with somebody else?' asked Sonia with unexpected vivacity when they were once again strolling along the street.

'That would be awful,' said Martin. He sensed there had been a moment when he could have taken a firm hold of Sonia, but now she had flipped away again.

'Remove your arm,' she remarked, 'I can't walk like that – you behave like a Sunday shop clerk,' and his last hope, the blissful sensation of her warm upper arm under the palm of his hand, vanished also.

'At least he has talent,' she said, 'and you, you're nothing, just a travelling playboy.'

'Talent? Whom are you talking about?'

She did not answer and kept silent all the way home. She did, however, kiss him again on the doorstep, throwing her bare arm around his neck, and her expression was serious and her gaze downcast as she locked the door from the inside. He watched through the door pane: there she goes, up the stairs, caressing the banister, and now the stair bend conceals her – and that is her light going out.

'She did the same to Darwin,' thought Martin, and he felt a tremendous urge to see his old friend; Darwin, however, was far away in America, on an assignment for a London newspaper. Next day all trace of romance had vanished, as if it had never been, and Sonia went with friends to the country, to Peacock Island, for a swim and a picnic, and Martin didn't even know about it. That evening, a minute before closing time, he had bought a large crimson-ribboned plush dog and was approaching her house with the thing under his arm when he met the whole returning party on the street; Sonia had Kallistratov's jacket over her shoulders, and between him and her there flashed repeatedly a chance jest, whose meaning nobody bothered to explain to Martin.

He wrote her a letter, and stayed away for several days. She replied a week or so later with a colour postcard showing a pretty boy bending over the back of a green bench on which sat a pretty girl, admiring a bouquet of roses, with a German rhyme in gilt letters at the bottom: 'Let a true heart leave unsaid what is told by roses red.' On the reverse Sonia had scribbled: 'Aren't they sweet? That's real courtship for you. Look, I need your assistance, three strings have snapped on my racket.' And not a word about the letter! However, during one of his next visits she said, 'I think it's ridiculous that you can't skip a day or two now and then. Surely, Kindermann will replace you.'

'He has his own lessons,' replied Martin hesitantly, but he did speak to Kindermann, and so, one marvellous, impeccably cloudless morning, Martin and Sonia were off for the lacustrine, reedy, piny outskirts of the city, and Martin heroically kept his promise not to make 'marmalade' eyes, as she put it, and did not attempt to kiss her. Something they discussed that day happened to lead to a series of quite special exchanges between them. With the intent of striking Sonia's imagination, Martin vaguely alluded to his having joined a secret group of anti-Bolshevist conspirators that organized reconnaissance operations. It was perfectly true that such a group did exist; in fact, a common friend of theirs, one Lieutenant Melkikh, had twice crossed the border on dangerous missions; it was also true that Martin kept looking for an opportunity to make friends with him (once he had even invited him to dinner) and always regretted that while in Switzerland he had not met the mysterious Gruzinov, whom Zilanov had mentioned, and who, according to information Martin had gathered, emerged as a man of great adventures, a terrorist, a very special spy, and the mastermind of recent peasant revolts against the Soviet rule.

'It never occurred to me,' said Sonia, 'that you thought about things like that. Only, you know, if you really have joined that organization, it's very naive to start blabbing about it right away.'

'Oh, I was only joking,' said Martin, and slit his eyes enigmatically so as to make Sonia believe he had deliberately turned it into a joke. She, however, did not catch that nuance; stretched out on the dry, needle-strewn ground, beneath the pines whose trunks the sun blotched with colour, she put her bare arms behind her head, exposing her lovely armpits which she had recently started to shave and which were now shaded as if with a pencil, and said it was a strange thing, but she too had often thought about it – about there being a land where ordinary mortals were not admitted.

'What shall we call that land?' asked Martin, suddenly recollecting his games with Lida on the Crimean fairy-tale shore.

'Some northern name,' answered Sonia. 'Look at that squirrel.' The squirrel, playing hide-and-seek, jerkily climbed a tree trunk and vanished amidst the foliage.

'Zoorland, for example,' said Martin. 'A Norman mariner mentions it.'

'Yes, of course – Zoorland,' Sonia concurred, and he grinned broadly, somewhat astounded by her unexpectedly revealed capacity for daydreaming.

'May I remove an ant?' he asked parenthetically.

'Depends where.'

'Stocking.'

'Scram chum' (addressing the ant). She brushed it off and continued, as if reciting, 'Winters are cold there, and monster icicles hang from the eaves, a whole system of them, like organ pipes. Then they melt and everything gets very watery, and there are sootlike specks on the thawing snow. Oh, I can tell you everything about it. For instance, they've just passed a law that all inhabitants must shave their heads, so that now the most important, most influential people are the barbers.'

'Equality of heads,' said Martin.

'Yes. And of course the bald ones are best off. And you know—'

'Bubnov would have a grand time there,' Martin interjected facetiously.

For some reason Sonia took offense and dried up. Yet from that day on she occasionally condescended to play Zoorland with him, and Martin was tormented by the thought that she might be making sophisticated fun of him and that any moment she might cause him to take a false step, prodding him toward the boundary beyond which phantasmata become tasteless – and the dreamwalker is jolted into seeing the roof edge from which he is dangling, his own hiked-up nightshirt, the crowd looking up from the sidewalk, the firemen's helmets. But even if this was a form of derision on Sonia's part, no matter, no matter, he enjoyed the opportunity to let himself go in her presence. They studied Zoorlandian customs and laws. The region was rocky and windy, and the wind was recognized as a positive force since by championing equality in not tolerating towers and tall trees, it only subserved the public aspirations of atmospheric strata that kept diligent watch over the uniformity of the temperature. And, naturally, pure arts, pure science were outlawed, lest the honest dunces be hurt to see the scholar's brooding brow and offensively thick books. Shaven-headed, wearing brown cassocks, the happy Zoorlanders warmed themselves by bonfires as the strings of burning violins snapped with loud reports, and discussed plans to level the land by blowing up mountains that stuck up too presumptuously. Sometimes during the general conversation – at table, for instance – Sonia would suddenly turn to him and quickly whisper, 'Have you heard, there's a new law forbidding caterpillars to pupate,' or 'I forgot to tell you, Savior-and-Mauler' (the sobriquet of one of the chieftains) 'has ordered physicians to stop casting around and to treat all illnesses in exactly the same way.'

35

When he returned for the winter to Switzerland, Martin looked forward to an entertaining correspondence, but Sonia made no mention of Zoorland in her infrequent letters. In one of them, however, she asked him to give her father's regards to Gruzinov.

It turned out that Gruzinov was staying at the Majestic, the hotel that had had such an odd attraction for Martin. But when he skied down to it, he found that Gruzinov had left and would be away for some time. He transmitted Zilanov's regards to Gruzinov's wife, a young-looking, brightly dressed lady in her forties, with blue-black hair and a cautious smile that attempted to conceal protruding front teeth always smeared with lipstick. Martin had never seen such exquisite hands as hers. They were small and soft, and adorned with glowing rings. But though everybody considered her attractive, and admired her grace and melodious, caressive voice, Martin's senses remained unstirred; in fact it irked him to think that, maybe, she was trying to charm him. His suspicions were unfounded. Mrs Gruzinov was as indifferent to him as to the tall big-nosed Englishman with grey bristly hair on his narrow head and a striped scarf around his neck who took her sleigh-riding.

'My husband won't be back before July,' she said, and began questioning Martin about the Zilanovs. 'Yes, yes. I do pity her mother' (Martin had mentioned Irina). 'You know, don't you, how it all started?' Martin knew. During the civil war, in Southern Russia, Irina, then a quiet, plump, normal though melancholy girl of fourteen, was on a train with her mother: they had had to be content with a bench in a freight car crammed with all sorts of riffraff, and during the long journey two rowdies, ignoring the protests of some of their pals, palpated, pinched, and tickled the child, saying monstrous obscenities to her. Mrs Pavlov, wearing the smile of helpless horror, and doing her best to protect her, kept repeating, 'Never mind, Irochka, never mind – oh please leave the child alone, you should be ashamed of yourselves – never mind, Irochka—' then, on the next train, nearer to Moscow, with similar cries and mutterings, she again cradled her daughter's head when other roughs, deserters or the like, ejected her corpulent husband by squeezing him through the window with the train going full speed. Yes, he was very fat, and he laughed hysterically, having got stuck halfway through, but finally, with a unanimous heave-ho they succeeded, he disappeared from sight, and there only remained the blind snow driving past the empty window. Miraculously he rejoined his family at some little railway station buried in snow; and, miraculously, too, Irina survived a severe typhoid infection; but she lost the power of speech, and it was only a year later in London that she learned to produce mooing sounds with different intonations and to pronounce 'ma-ma' with tolerable clarity.

Martin, who somehow had never paid much attention to Irina, having soon become used to her mental deficiency, now experienced a strange shock as Mrs Gruzinov added, 'That's how they have in their home a permanent living symbol.' The night of Zoorland seemed to him even darker, its wild-wood deeper, and Martin already knew that nothing and nobody could prevent him from penetrating, as a free pilgrim, into those woods, where plump children are tortured in the dark, and a smell of burning and of putrefaction permeates the air. When he returned in the spring to Berlin and to Sonia, he could have almost believed (so crowded with adventures had been his winter-night fantasies) that he had already concluded that solitary and courageous expedition, and now was going to talk and talk about his adventures. As he entered her room, he said (being anxious to express it before the familiar frustrating effect of her lusterless eyes had reasserted itself): 'Like this, like this, I shall return some day, and then, ah, then—' 'There'll never be anything,' she exclaimed in the tones of Pushkin's Naïna ('Hero, I still do not love thee!'). She was even paler than usual, her office work was very fatiguing; at home she wore an old black velvet dress with a narrow leather belt around the hips and backless slippers with frayed pompons. Often after supper she would put on her raincoat and leave, and Martin, after strolling aimlessly from room to room for a time, would leave too and walk slowly to the streetcar stop, hands deep in trouser pockets; at the opposite end of Berlin he would whistle tenderly under the window of a cabaret dancer whom he had met at the tennis club. She flitted out onto the balcony, froze for an instant at its parapet, disappeared, flitted out again and tossed him the house key wrapped in paper. In her bedroom Martin drank green crème de menthe and kissed her naked golden-brown back, and, tossing her head, she would tightly contract her shoulder blades. He liked to watch her as she rapidly paced the room setting close together her muscular suntanned legs and furiously reviling always the same theatrical agent; he liked her bizarre little face with its orange-tinted incarnadine, unnaturally thin eyebrows, and smoothly brushed-back hair; and he vainly tried not to think of Sonia. One night in May he emitted his soft whistle with a special trill, but instead of his mistress, an elderly man in braces came out onto the balcony and Martin sighed and walked away. He went back by tram to the Zilanovs' street and started to walk back and forth between two lamps. Sonia returned past midnight, alone, and while she rummaged in her handbag in search of her keys, Martin approached and asked timidly where she had been. 'Won't you ever leave me alone?' cried Sonia and without waiting for an answer turned her key with a double crunch, and the heavy door swung open, stopped for a moment, banged shut. Then came a time when Martin began to imagine that not only Sonia, but all their common acquaintances, were avoiding him, that he was unwanted, that no one cared for him. He dropped in on Bubnov, and the latter stared at him in an odd way, excused himself, and continued to write. At last – feeling that after a little more of this he would turn into Sonia's shadow and to the end of his life continue to haunt Berlin's sidewalks, wasting on a futile passion the important and solemn thing that was ripening in him – Martin decided to have done with Berlin in order to think over in purifying solitude the plan of the expedition. In mid-May 1924, with the ticket for Strasbourg already in his wallet, he went to take leave of Sonia, and, of course, did not find her at home. Amidst the twilight of the room, all in white, sat Irina, seeming to float in the dusk like a ghostly turtle. She did not take her eyes off him. He wrote on an envelope, 'Polar night decreed in Zoorland,' put it on the pillow in Sonia's room, got into the waiting taxicab, and, wearing neither overcoat nor hat, with only one bag, left for the station.

36

As soon as the train began to move, Martin revived, regained his gaiety, began to enjoy the excitement of travelling – something that he considered to be a kind of indispensable training. When he transferred to a French train going south by way of Lyon, it seemed to him that he was definitely free of Sonia's nebulous spells. Beyond Lyon, the southern night gradually spread overhead; the pale rectangles of the reflected coach windows sped along the black bank; in the dirty, insufferably stuffy second-class compartment, Martin's only companion was a middle-aged Frenchman. The man discarded his coat and in one downward run of his fingers undid all the buttons of his waistcoat; pulled off his cuffs as if screwing off his wrists, and carefully placed the two starched cylinders in the baggage net. He perched on the edge of the seat and swaying – the train was going fast – with lifted chin, he unfastened his collar and tie; and since the tie was of the ready-made variety that unhooked in the back, one again had the impression that here was a man taking himself apart and about to remove his head. The front skin of his neck was as flabby as a turkey's; he moved his head right and left with relief, then bent over and, grunting, changed from boots to bedroom slippers. With his shirt opened on his curly chest he now looked like a hearty enough fellow who had had one too many: for those fellow travellers in a night coach, with their shiny pale faces and glazed eyes, always appear to be drunk with the carriage's swaying and heat. From a hamper he produced a bottle of red wine and a large orange; first he took a swallow from the bottle, smacked his lips, forcefully pressed home the squeaking cork, then began to strip the orange with his thumb after biting open the skin on its pate. At this moment his eyes met those of Martin who had just put down his Tauchnitz on his knee in preparation for a yawn, and the Frenchman spoke. 'We're already in Provence,' he said jovially, one shaggy eyebrow pointing toward the window, in whose mirror-black glass his dim double was peeling an orange too.

'*Oui, on sent le sud,*' answered Martin.

'You an Englishman?' queried the other tearing in two his peeled grey-tufted orange.

'Correct,' answered Martin. 'How did you guess?'

The Frenchman, chewing juicily, shrugged one shoulder: 'It was not very hard,' he said, swallowed, and, after a look of inspection, pointed a hairy finger at the Tauchnitz. Martin smiled indulgently. 'And I'm from Lyon,' the Frenchman continued. 'I'm in the wine business. I have to travel a lot but I like to be moving about. One gets to see new places, new people – the world, *quoi*. I have a wife and a small daughter,' he added, wiping with a bit of newspaper the tips of his spread-out fingers. Then, contemplating Martin again, his battered bag and wrinkled trousers, and concluding that a British *milord* would hardly be travelling second class, he observed with an anticipatory nod: 'You're a traveller?' Martin understood that this was a mere abbreviation for 'commercial traveller.'

'Yes, I am indeed a traveller,' he answered, diligently imitating a British accent, 'but in a wider sense of the word. I am travelling very far.'

'But you are in the commerce?'

Martin shook his head.

'Then you're doing it for pleasure?'

'If you like,' said Martin.

The Frenchman ruminated in silence; presently he asked, 'At the moment, you're going to Marseilles, aren't you?'

'Yes, probably to Marseilles. Not all my preparations are completed, yet.'

The Frenchman nodded but was visibly puzzled.

'In such cases,' Martin went on, 'preparations must be made with the greatest care. I spent close to a year in Berlin where I had hoped to obtain some essential information, and you can't imagine—'

'My nephew is an engineer,' the Frenchman hopefully interposed.

'Oh no, I am not concerned with technology, that was not why I visited Germany. But, as I was saying: You can't imagine how difficult it is to ferret out that sort of information. The fact is I'm planning to explore a certain remote, almost inaccessible region. It has been reached by a few adventurers, but how to find them, how to make them talk? What do I have? Only a map,' and Martin pointed to his valise, which indeed contained, besides his silk shirts and collapsible tub, a map on a scale of a vershok to a verst, acquired in Berlin at the former Military Headquarters. There followed a silence. The train clattered and swayed.

'I always affirm,' the Frenchman said, 'that our colonies have a great future. Naturally, yours do too, and you have so many of them. One of my friends spent ten years in the tropics and he says he would gladly go back. He told me once how he saw monkeys using a fallen tree trunk to cross a river, each holding the tail of the one in front – it was devilishly *drôle* – holding tails! holding tails!'

'Colonies are something else again,' said Martin. 'I'm not planning to go to our colonies. My trail will take me through perilous places, and – who knows – I may not be able to return.'

'Is that a scientific expedition or something?' asked the Frenchman squashing a yawn with his back teeth.

'Partly. But – how shall I put it? – science, knowledge – all that is not the main point. The main point, the main purpose is— No, I really don't know how to explain.'

'I know, I know,' said the Frenchman wearily. 'You, *les Anglais,* are fond of wagers, of records' (his '*records*' sounded like a drowsy growl). 'Who wants a bare rock in the sky? Or –

good Lord, how sleepy one gets on a train! – or icebergs or whatever one calls them – or, indeed, the North Pole? Or those marshes where one perishes from malaria?'

'Yes, you may have put your finger on it. And yet even that, even *le sport,* is not all. There are besides – how shall I say? – glory, love, tenderness for the soil, a thousand rather mysterious feelings.'

The Frenchman gaped and then, moving forward, lightly slapped Martin on the knee. 'One is mocking me, eh?' he commented good-naturedly. 'Oh no, not at all!' 'Come,' he said leaning back in his corner. 'You are too young to roam the Saharas. With your permission, I'll now put out the light and take a nap.'

37

Darkness. Almost at once the Frenchman began to snore. 'Yes, he did believe I was English. *Ong sahng le soude.* Like this I shall travel north, exactly like this, in a coach that one cannot stop – and after that, after that—' He began to follow a forest path, the path unwound, kept unwinding, but sleep did not come to meet him. Martin opened his eyes. Good idea to lower the window. A mild night flooded his face and straining his eyes Martin leaned out, but invisible dust flew into his eyes, speed blinded him; he drew back his head. A cough resounded in the darkened compartment. 'No, no. Be so kind,' said a cross voice. 'I have no desire to sleep under the stars. Close it, close it.' 'Close it yourself,' said Martin. He stepped out into the lighted corridor and walked past the compartments where one could guess the jumbled presence of slumbering, helpless, half-undressed bodies, wheezes and sighs, mouths opened fish-fashion, a sinking head jerked up again, a soft foot right next to a stranger's nose. Making his way from one vestibule to another across the grind of connecting plates, Martin passed through two third-class coaches. The sliding doors of some of the compartments stood open; in one of them grey-blue soldiers were noisily playing cards. Further on, in the corridor of a sleeping car, Martin stopped at a half-lowered window, and recalled, with exceptional clarity, his childhood journey through Southern France: that *strapontin* seat by the window, that cloth loop which permitted him to drive the train, that lovely melody in three languages – especially: *pericoloso*. He reflected what a strange, strange life had fallen to his lot, it seemed as if he had never left a fast train, had merely wandered from car to car – and one was occupied by young Englishmen, among whom was Darwin in the act of solemly taking hold of the emergency cord; in the other were Alla and her husband; or else the Crimean crowd; or snoring Uncle Henry; or the Zilanovs, her father with his eternal newspaper, and Sonia, her velvet-dark eyes staring through the window. 'And then I'll continue on foot, on foot,' muttered Martin excitedly – a forest, a winding path – what huge trees! Here, in this sleeping car, his childhood must have travelled, must have shivered, as it undid the button of the leathern blind; and if one followed the blue corridor a little farther, one would get to the dining car where his parents had supper, and there would be on the table the same mock-up of a chocolate bar in a violet wrapping, and over the door a helical ventilator would shimmer in a garden of ads. At that moment, in response to his recollections, Martin saw through the window what he had seen as a child – a necklace of lights, far away, among dark hills. Someone seemed to pour them from one hand into the other, and pocket them. While he looked, the train began to slow down, and Martin told himself that if it stopped, he would get off and go in search of those lights. A station platform drifted into sight, then the moonlight disk of a clock, and the train came to a halt exhaling a sigh. Martin dashed back to his coach, twice burst into the snoring dark of a wrong compartment, found the right one, snapped on the light, and the Frenchman half-rose from his seat rubbing his eyes with his fists. Martin jerked down his valise, and snatched up his Tauchnitz. In his haste he failed to notice that the train had begun to move again, and therefore very nearly fell when he jumped down onto the gliding platform. A long row of windows passed by, and were gone. Nothing remained except empty rails with the glitter of coal dust between them.

Still panting, Martin traversed the platform. A porter who was pushing a luggage cart with a big box labelled '*Fragile*' said to him gaily, with the metallic accent peculiar to Provence: 'You woke up at the right moment, Monsieur.' 'Tell me,' Martin inquired, 'what's in that box?' The porter looked at it as if he had only just noticed its presence, and read out the address: 'Museum of Natural Science.' 'Ah yes, a collection of insects, no doubt,' said Martin, and walked toward the little group of tables at the entrance of the dimly lit buffet.

The air was velvety and warm; around a milky white arc light swirled pale midges and one ample dark moth with hoary margins. A six-foot poster adorned the wall: it was an attempt on the part of the War Department to picture for the benefit of young men the allurements of military service: in the foreground, a valiant French soldier; in the back, a date palm, a dromedary, and a burnoosed Arab; and in the corner, two opulent forms in charshafs.

The platform was deserted. A little way down stood some cages with sleeping hens. On the farther side of the rails one could make out a tangle of black bushes. The air smelled of coal, juniper, and urine. A dusky old woman looked out of the *buvette*, and Martin asked for an *apéritif* whose delightful name he had seen advertised. A workman in blue sat down at the next table and fell asleep with his head on his arm.

'There is something I would like to know,' said Martin to the woman. 'Just before the train stopped, I saw lights in the distance.' 'Where? Was it there?' she asked pointing in the direction from which the train had arrived. Martin nodded. 'That could only have been Molignac,' she said. 'Yes, Molignac. A small village.' Martin paid and walked with his bag toward the exit. A dark square, plane trees, a row of ghostly houses and a narrow street. He had already turned into it when he realized he had forgotten to look at the station sign, and now did not know the name of the town where he chanced to be. It thrilled him pleasantly. Who knows – perhaps, by some caprice of space, he was already beyond the Zoorland border, in the uncertain night, and presently would be challenged.

38

When he woke up next morning, Martin could not at once reconstruct the previous day; and the reason why he woke up was that flies were tickling his face. A remarkably soft bed; an ascetic washstand, and, beside it, a toilet utensil in the shape of a violin; hot blue light was breathing through a chink in the window curtain. It was a long time since he had had such a good night of sleep, a long time since he had been so hungry. He drew the curtain aside and saw before him a dazzling white wall. Further off to the left there were shops with striped awnings, a piebald dog sat on the pavement scratching behind its ear with its hind paw, and a streamlet of glittering water ran along the curb.

The sound of the bell button he pressed resounded through the entire two-story inn and, stomping boldly, there arrived a bright-eyed dirty maid. He ordered a lot of bread, a lot of butter, a lot of coffee, and when she had brought it all, asked her how he could get to Molignac. She proved to be talkative and inquisitive. Martin mentioned casually that he was German, had been sent here by a museum to collect insects; at this she glanced pensively at the wall where there were some suspicious looking reddish-brown spots. Gradually it transpired that in a month, and maybe even before, a bus line would be established between the town and Molignac. 'It means, one has to walk?' asked Martin. 'Fifteen kilometers,' exclaimed the maid with horror. 'What an idea! And in this heat!'

He left his things at the inn and, having bought a map of the region at the tobacconist's whose sign was a tricolour pipe protruding over the door, started to stride down the sunny side of the street, and immediately noticed that his open shirt collar and absence of headgear were attracting general attention. The town seemed drawn in bright chalks and was sharply divided into light and shadow; it boasted numerous pastry shops. Presently the crowded houses dropped away, and the paved road between its double row of huge plane trees with flesh-coloured patterns on their green trunks went flowing past vineyards. The rare people he met, such as stone breakers, schoolchildren, and country wives in black straw hats, ate him up with their eyes. It occurred to Martin to try out something that might prove useful in the future. He proceeded to advance with the utmost stealth, crossing ditches and hiding behind brambles whenever he glimpsed in the distance a cart drawn by a donkey in black blinders or a dusty ramshackle motor van. After a couple of kilometers he abandoned the road altogether and began to work his way parallel to it along the hillside where he was screened by the oak scrub, the glossy myrtles, the nettle trees. The sun blazed fiercely, cicadas trilled, the hot spicy smells made him dizzy and for a minute he lay in the shade wiping his sticky neck with his handkerchief. A glance at the map showed him that at the fifth kilometer the road made a loop, and that to rejoin it one might cut across yonder hill, all yellow with flowering broom. When he came down on the other side, the white snake of the road did reappear, and as he walked on parallel to it through the fragrant undergrowth, he rejoiced at his capacity to find his bearings.

Suddenly he heard the cool sound of running water. No better music could exist in the world! A brook quivered on flat stones in a tunnel formed by the foliage. Martin got down on his knees, quenched his thirst, and heaved a deep sigh. He lit a cigarette. In the brilliant air the match burned with an invisible flame and from its sulphur a sweetish taste spread to his tongue. Thus, sitting on a rock and listening to the brook's gurgling, Martin enjoyed his fill of viatic freedom from all concerns: he was a wanderer, alone and lost in a marvellous world, completely indifferent toward him, in which butterflies danced, lizards darted, and leaves glistened – the same way as they glisten in a Russian or African wood.

It was long past midday when Martin reached Molignac. So this was where they sparkled at night, the lights which had beckoned to him ever since his childhood! Silence, a burning heat. Through the knotty streamlets of water that ran by the narrow sidewalk shone its varicoloured bed made of broken crockery. On the cobblestones timid, dreadfully emaciated white dogs were napping. In the middle of a small square stood a monument: a female personage, with wings, raising a banner.

First of all Martin visited the post office, a cool, darkish and drowsy place. There he wrote his mother a postcard, to the accompaniment of the piercing complaint of a housefly, one of whose legs had got stuck in the glue of the treacle-coloured flypaper affixed to a windowledge. That postcard was the first of a new little batch of letters which Mrs Edelweiss stored in her chest of drawers: the penultimate batch.

39

He told the woman who ran the only Molignac inn that he was Swiss (which was confirmed by his passport) and gave her to understand that he had long been roving the world, working at odd jobs here and there. The same information he conveyed to her brother, a farmer, purple with wine and sanguineness, by whom, in consequence of the rover's complete destitution, he was hired as day labourer. It was thus the third time in a couple of days that Martin changed his nationality, testing the credulity of strangers and learning to live incognito. The fact of his having been born in a remote northern land had long since acquired a shade of enchanting mystery. A carefree visitor from a distant shore, he strolled through the bazaars of the infidels, and everything was entertaining and colourful, but no matter where he might go, nothing could weaken in him the wonderful sense of being different and elect. Such words, such notions and images, as those that Russia had engendered did not exist in other countries, and it often happened that he would lapse into incoherence, or start to laugh nervously when vainly trying to explain to a foreigner the various meanings of some special term, say, *poshlost'*. He felt flattered by the infatuation of the English with Chekhov, by that of the Germans with Dostoevski. Once, in Cambridge, he discovered in a sixty-year-old issue of the local review a poem coolly signed: A. Jameson. It began:

I walk along the road alone.
My stony path spreads far,
Still is the night and cold the stone,
And star talks unto star.

and was a shameless paraphrase of Lermontov's greatest lyrical poem. A strange pensiveness would pervade him when, at times, from the depths of a Berlin courtyard would rise the sound of a hurdy-gurdy which was not aware that the tune it had borrowed had once touched the hearts of sentimental drunks in Russian taverns. Music! Martin regretted that an inner sentinel forbade to his vocal cords the sounds that lived in his ears. Still, when his fellow workers, young Italians, sang loudly, among the branches of Provence cherry trees, Martin would start his own song – hoarsely, boldly, and phenomenally out of tune – and that song would echo the nights when at picnics in the Crimea the baritone Zaryanski, drowned out by the choir, sang about the 'seven-stringed companion,' or the 'little goblet.'

Far below him the lucerne rippled in the wind, from above the glowing blue pressed upon him, silver-veined leaves rustled close to his cheek, and the oilcloth-lined basket suspended from a bough gradually acquired weight as it got filled with the glossy-black fruit Martin pulled off by its taut stems. After the cherries had been harvested came sun-steeped apricots, and precious peaches which had to be tenderly cradled in one's palm lest they get bruised. There also were other kinds of labour. Naked to the waist, his back already the hue of terra cotta, Martin, to humour the young maize, loosened and heaped up the soil, grubbed out with the sharp corner of his hoe the wily and stubborn speargrass, or for hours on end stood bending over the shoots of infant trees, apple and pear, clicking his pruning shears. He especially enjoyed conducting the water from the reservoir in the yard to the nurseries, where the mattocked furrows joined with one another and with the hollows dug around the stems. As the water spread all over the young plantation, it picked its way like a live thing; here it would stop, there run on, extending bright tentacles, and Martin, grimacing occasionally from the stings of tiny thistleheads, sloshed up to his ankles in fat purple mud, driving in forcefully an iron shield for a barrier or, on the contrary, helping a streamlet to break through; the hollowed earth would fill with bubbling brown water and, feeling in it with a spade, he mercifully softened the soil, until something gave delightfully, and the percolating water sank away, washing the roots. He felt happy he knew how to satisfy a plant's thirst, happy that chance had helped him to find work that could serve to try out both his shrewdness and his endurance. Together with the other labourers he lodged in a shed, drank, as they did, one and a half liters of wine a day, and found satisfaction in looking like them – except for the little blond beard that he had quietly let grow.

In the evening, before turning in, he would walk over to the cork woods beyond the farm, and smoke and muse. Overhead the nightingales whistled in short rich phrases, from the pond came the rubbery croaking of frogs. The air was tender and dullish, not quite twilight yet, but no longer day, and the terraced olives and the mythographic hills in the distance, and that pine standing separate on a rock – the whole landscape was reliefless and a little swoony under an evenly fading sky which oppressed and lulled one, and made one long for the vivifying stars to appear. Night fell, lights trembled on the silhouetted hills, the windows of the farmhouse lit up; and when far, far away, in the unknown gloom, a tiny rattling train would pass by broken into small fiery segments, and vanish, Martin told himself with deep satisfaction that from there, from that train, the farm and Molignac looked like a handful of jewels. He was glad to have heeded the call of those lights, to have uncovered their lovely quiet essence. One Sunday night, in Molignac, he noticed a small white house, at the foot of steep vineyards; a crooked old post said: 'FOR SALE.' And, indeed, would it not be better to dismiss the perilous, daredevil project, to renounce the desire to peer into the merciless Zoorland night, and to get settled with a young wife right here, on this wedge of fertile soil waiting for an industrious master? Yes, he had to decide: time was running out, the dark autumn night he had marked for slipping across the border was nearing, and he now felt rested, refreshed, sure of being able to get away with any kind of impersonation, of never losing his presence of mind, of adjusting whenever and wherever it might be to the kind of life that circumstances demanded.

Testing fate, he wrote to Sonia. The answer came quickly and after reading it, Martin sighed with relief. 'Stop tormenting me,' wrote Sonia. 'Enough, for Christ's sake. I will never marry you. Moreover, I loathe vineyards, the heat, snakes, and, especially, garlic. Cross me out, do me that favour, darling.'

The same day he left for town on the brand-new bus, shaved off his beard, fetched his valise from the inn, and walked over to the station. There, at the same table, his head on his arm, slept the same workman. The lamps were being lit, bats skimmered by, the greenish sky was fading. *Proshchay, proshchay* (adieu, adieu) sounded in Martin's ears with the refrain of a Russian song as he looked at the tousled junipers on the other side of the already vibrating rails, at the signal lights, at the black outline of a man pushing the black outline of a luggage cart.

The night express pounded into the station; a minute later it started again and Martin experienced a momentary urge to jump out and return to the happy, fairy-tale farm. But the station had already ceased to exist. He stood looking through the window, waiting for the appearance of his beloved lights, to bid them good-bye. Here they came, far away, spilled jewels in the blackness, unbelievably lovely – 'Tell me,' Martin asked the conductor, 'Those lights there – that's Molignac, isn't it?' 'What lights?' the man asked glancing at the window, but at this moment everything was shut out by the sudden rise of a dark bank. 'In any case, it's not Molignac,' said the conductor. 'Molignac can't be seen from the railroad.'

At the kiosk of the Lausanne station Martin bought the Sunday issue of a Russian *émigré* paper published in Berlin. He could hardly believe his eyes when he found in the lower half of the second page a feuilleton entitled: 'ZOORLAND.' It was signed 'S. Bubnov,' and turned out to be a short story in that author's admirable style 'with a touch of the fantastic,' as critics like to put it. In it Martin recognized with disgust and embarrassment (as if he were witnessing some dreadfully obscene act) much of what he and Sonia used to think up – now oddly illumined by the imagination of an intruder. 'How treacherous she is, after all,' Martin reflected and in a surge of acute and hopeless jealousy recalled having once observed Bubnov and her walking arm in arm down a dark street; and how he had tried to believe what she told him on the following day – that she had gone to the movies with the Veretennikov girl.

It was drizzling, and only the lower half of the mountains could be made out, when, wedged among hampers and corpulent females, he reached by public charabanc the village situated at ten minutes' walk from his uncle's villa. Mrs Edelweiss knew that her son was about to arrive. For three days she had been expecting a wire, and had looked forward to the excitement of driving down to the station to meet him. She was in the living room doing some embroidery when there came from the garden her son's deep young voice and the soft husky laughter which was typical of his demeanour when he came back after a long separation. He was walking beside flushed Marie, who was trying to relieve him of his valise while he shifted it from one hand to the other and back again as he walked. His face was copper-dark, the colour of his eyes seemed to have paled by contrast, and he smelled wonderfully of stale tobacco, wet woollen jacket, and train. 'You've come for a long, long time now,' she kept repeating in a happy barking voice. 'Generally speaking, yes,' Martin answered sedately. 'I'll just have to go to Berlin on business in about a fortnight, then I'll return.' 'Oh, forget about business, it can wait!' she cried – and Uncle Henry, who, had been resting in his room after lunch, woke up, listened, quickly put on his shoes, and came down.

'The prodigal son,' he said entering. 'Delighted to see you again.' Martin touched his cheek with his own, and both simultaneously kissed the void, as was their wont on such occasions. 'I hope – for some time?' the uncle asked, without taking his eyes off Martin; still staring, he groped for the back of a chair and sat down with knees apart. 'Generally speaking, yes,' answered Martin while he devoured some ham. 'I'll just have to go to Berlin in about a fortnight, but I'll return.' 'You won't,' said Mrs Edelweiss laughing, 'I know you. Come, tell us how it all was. Can it be that you actually plowed, and made hay, and milked the cows?' 'Milking is fun,' said Martin and spreading two fingers showed how one does it (milking was precisely the one thing he never did at Molignac – that was the job of his namesake, Martin Roc – and it was not clear why he began his story with a spurious detail when there was so much else, authentic, to tell).

Next morning, as Martin glanced at the mountains, he thought again, to the same sobbing tune, 'Adieu, adieu,' but at once scolded himself for unworthy faintheartedness. At that moment his mother came in with a letter, and from the threshold said cheerfully, before her son would have time to assume mistakenly that it was from Sonia, 'I think it's Darwin's hand. I forgot to give it to you last night.' After reading the very first lines Martin began to chuckle quietly. Darwin wrote that he was about to marry a splendid English girl he had met at a hotel in Niagara Falls; that he was travelling around a great deal; and that in a week's time he would be in Berlin. 'Do invite him here,' Mrs Edelweiss said quickly. 'What could be simpler?' 'No, no, I tell you I have to go to Berlin. It all fits in perfectly.'

'Martin,' she began but hesitated and stopped. 'What's the matter?' he asked gaily. 'How is it working out? – Oh, you know what I mean – Maybe you're already engaged?' Martin slit his eyes, laughed, but did not answer. 'I shall be very fond of her,' whispered Mrs Edelweiss piously. 'Let's go for a walk. Such glorious weather,' said Martin, pretending to be deliberately changing the subject. 'You go,' she replied. 'Like a fool, I invited, precisely today, the old Drouet couple. They would die of a heart attack if one tried to phone them.'

In the garden Uncle Henry was adjusting a ladder against the trunk of an apple tree; then, with the greatest care, he climbed up to the third rung. By the draw well, arms akimbo, stood Marie looking away, forgetful of the pail which overran with gleaming water. She had gained much weight these last years, but at that instant, with the sun playing on her dress, on her neck, left uncovered by her twisted, tightly bunched-up braids, she reminded him of his fleeting infatuation. She suddenly turned her face toward him. It was a fat and expressionless face.

40

As he walked with springy steps through the mountainside fir forest whose blackness was broken from place to place by the radiance of a slender birch tree, he anticipated with rapture a similar sun-pierced thicket on a far Northern plain with spider-webs spread on the sunbeams, and with damp hollows choked with willow herb, and, beyond, the luminous open spaces, the empty autumnal fields, and the squat little white church on a hillock tending as it were the isbas that looked on the point of wandering away; and, encircling the hillock, there would be the bright bend of a river brimming with enmeshed reflections. He was almost surprised when he glimpsed an alpine slope through the conifers.

This reminded him that before he left he had an account with his conscience to settle. Unhurriedly, purposefully, he ascended the slope and reached the broken grey rocks. He climbed up the stony steepness and found himself on the same little platform from which the familiar cornice started to round the sheer cliff. Without hesitation, obeying an inner command that could not be disregarded, he began to sidle along the narrow shelf. When it tapered to an end he looked down over his shoulder and saw, under his very heels, the sunny precipice and at the bottom of it the porcelain hotel. 'There,' said Martin to the little white thing, 'lump it!' and fighting dizziness, began to move the way he had come. He stopped again, however, and, checking his self-control, attempted to extract his cigarette case from his hip pocket and light up. There came a moment when without holding onto the cliff he merely leant his chest against it, and felt the abyss behind him strain and pull at his calves and shoulders. He did not light that cigarette only because he dropped the matchbox. The absolute noiselessness of its fall was awesome, and when he resumed his progress along the cornice the feeling persisted that the matchbox was still plunging through space. Upon safely reaching the platform, Martin grunted with joy, and in the same purposeful way, with a stern sense of duty fulfilled, climbed down scree and heather, found the right path and descended toward the Majestic – to see what it would have to say. By the tennis court in the garden Mrs Gruzinov sat on a bench next to a white-trousered man. Martin hoped she would not notice him. He was loath to dissipate so soon the treasure he had brought down from the mountain-top. 'Hello, Martin,' she cried, and Martin grinned and went up to her. 'Yurochka, this is the son of Dr Edelweiss,' said Mrs Gruzinov to her companion. The latter half-rose and without removing his straw hat drew back his elbow, took good aim, and shooting his palm out, vigorously shook hands with Martin. 'Gruzinov,' he said softly, as if imparting a secret.

'Have you come for long, Martin?' asked Mrs Gruzinov with a smile, and hastened to lower her downy upper lip over her front teeth tinted with pink.

'Generally speaking, yes. I must take a quick business trip to Berlin, and then I shall be back.'

'Martin Sergeevich?' Gruzinov inquired, and after Martin had answered in the affirmative, dropped his eyes and once more repeated to himself Martin's patronymic.

'Well, you certainly have—?' said Mrs Gruzinov, and her beautiful hands outlined the shape of a vase in the air.

'No wonder,' Martin replied, 'I worked on a farm in the south of France. Life is so peaceful there that one cannot help gaining weight.'

Gruzinov pressed his finger and thumb to the corners of his mouth, a gesture which leant a somewhat peasant-woman expression to his substantial-looking, clean-featured face with a complexion so creamy as to suggest making toffee out of his cheeks.

'I've got it,' he said. 'The person's name is Kruglov, he married a Turkish woman.' ('Come, sit down,' interjected Mrs Gruzinov, and in two moves of her soft, generously perfumed body she made room for Martin.) 'He happens to have a small zamindary in the south of France,' Gruzinov explained, 'and I believe he makes a living by supplying the city with jasmin. Have you also been staying in the odorofacient region?' Martin told him the name of the nearest town. 'That's it,' chimed in Gruzinov. 'That's not far from where he dwells. Or maybe it isn't. Are you attending the university in Berlin?'

'No, I finished Cambridge.'

'Very interesting,' said Gruzinov weightily. 'They still have some Roman aqueducts there,' he continued turning to his wife. 'Imagine, my dear, those Romans, so far from home, establishing themselves in a foreign land, and doing it, mind you, really well, comfortably, in patrician style.'

Martin had not met with any particular aqueducts in Cambridge, yet he found it necessary to nod. In the presence of remarkable people, people with an extraordinary past, he always felt a pleasant excitement, and now was trying to settle how to derive the most from this new acquaintance. It turned out, however, that Yuri Gruzinov was not one to be easily put into that euphoric state of mind in which a man scrambles out of his own self, as out of a burrow, and sun-bathes in the buff. Yuri Gruzinov refused to scramble out. He was perfectly benevolent, and at the same time impenetrable; was ready to converse on any subject – natural phenomena or human affairs – but there would always be something about his talk that suddenly compelled his interlocutor to wonder if his leg was not being atrociously pulled by that appetizingly smooth, compact, dapper gentleman, whose icy eyes seemed somehow to be absent from the conversation. In the past, when Martin heard people tell of Gruzinov's passion for danger, of his illegal crossings of the most perilous border in the world and of the mysterious rebellions he was said to spark in Zoorland, Martin imagined him as a man of powerful, aquiline aspect. But now, watching Gruzinov separate with a little plop the two parts of his spectacle case and hook on reading glasses of the plain, granny sort that might have suited the nose of an elderly carpenter with a yardstick folded in his blouse pocket – Martin realized that Gruzinov could not have looked different. His simplicity grading into a certain flaccidity of demeanour, the old-fashioned stylishness of his clothes (that striped flannel waistcoat for instance), his obscure jokes, his circumstantiality – all this formed a solid cocoon which Martin could not manage to tear. However, the fact of having met him almost on the eve of attempting a secret exploit struck Martin as a portent of its success. And Martin had been doubly lucky: for had he returned to Switzerland but one month later, Gruzinov would not have been there: he would already have been in Bessarabia.

41

The walks they took: to the Waterfall to Ste Claire; to the Grotto where once a hermit had lived. And back. September 1924 was especially fair. There might be a wet fog in the morning but by noon the world would delicately scintillate in the sun, the tree trunks would be glossed, blue puddles would shine on the road, and the sun-warmed mountains would be discarding their misty raiment. Mrs Edelweiss walked in front with Mrs Gruzinov; Gruzinov and Martin followed. Gruzinov strode along with pleasure, leaning firmly on his homemade stick and resenting it if anyone stopped to admire the view: he maintained that views destroyed the rhythm of the ramble. It happened once that a sheepdog dashed out of a farmyard and stood, growling, in their path. Mrs Gruzinov said 'I'm scared' and hid behind her husband's back, and Martin took his mother's cane out of her hand, while she tried to pacify the dog by emitting in its direction sounds used in Russia to urge on the horses. Alone Gruzinov did the right thing: he pretended to pick up a stone from the road, and the dog at once jumped away. A trifle, of course, but Martin cherished that kind of trifle. On another occasion, thinking that Martin had trouble walking without a stick up a very steep path, Gruzinov produced a jackknife from his pocket, selected a suitable sapling, and, wielding the knife with great precision, skilfully and silently manufactured a walking stick for him. It was smooth and white, still living, still cool to the touch. Another trifle, but somehow that stick seemed to smell of Russia. Mrs Edelweiss found Gruzinov delightful and once more told her husband at lunch that he simply must make friends with the man, that Gruzinov had become a legendary figure among *émigrés*.

'No doubt, no doubt,' Uncle Henry replied pouring vinegar over his salad, 'but he is an adventurer, and does not quite belong to our set. But, of course, invite him if you want.'

Martin regretted that he would not hear Gruzinov engage Uncle Henry in a conversation about the despotism of machines and the materialism of our age. After lunch Martin followed Uncle Henry into his study and said, 'I am leaving on Tuesday for Berlin. May I have a word with you?' 'What makes you gad about like that?' asked Uncle Henry with displeasure, and added, rolling his eyes and shaking his head, 'Your mother will be extremely upset – you know it yourself.' 'I am obliged to go,' Martin continued. 'I have a matter to settle.' 'An affair of the heart?' Uncle Henry was curious to know. Martin shook his head without smiling. 'What then?' muttered Uncle Henry examining the tip of a toothpick he had been using for some time to conduct excavations. 'Well, it's about money,' said Martin firmly enough. 'I want to ask you for a loan. You know that I earn well in the summer. I shall repay you then.' 'How much?' asked Uncle Henry, his face assuming a pleased expression, and moisture filming his eyes. He loved to show Martin his generosity. 'Five hundred francs.' Uncle Henry's eyebrows rose. 'Ah, a gambling debt, isn't it?' 'If you are disinclined—' began Martin looking with hatred at the way Uncle Henry sucked his toothpick. Uncle Henry took fright immediately. 'I have a rule,' he said in a conciliatory tone of voice. 'One should never expect frankness from a young man. I was young myself, and I know how rash a youth can be. It is only natural. But games of chance should be— Wait, wait, where are you going? I'll give you, I'll give you what you want, only too happy. And as to repaying—' 'Exactly five hundred then,' said Martin. 'And I shall be leaving on Tuesday.'

The door opened slightly. 'May I come in?' asked Mrs Edelweiss in a thin voice. 'What kind of secrets are you having together?' she continued a little archly, shifting her gaze from son to husband. 'Why can't I be told?' 'It's still the same subject – those Brothers Petit,' answered Martin. 'By the way, he is leaving on Tuesday,' said Uncle Henry and put the toothpick in his waistcoat pocket. 'What, so soon?' she said plaintively. 'Yes, so soon, so soon, so soon,' her son replied with unwonted irritation, and walked out of the room. 'He'll go crazy without a job,' observed Uncle Henry, commenting on the noise of the slammed door.

42

When Martin entered the hotel garden whose sight bored him now, he found Gruzinov by the tennis court, on which a rather lively game was in progress between two young men. 'Look at them – skipping like two goats,' Gruzinov said. 'We used to have a blacksmith in Kostroma who was marvellous at tag-bat, he could belt a ball over the belfry or beyond the river – just like that. If we had him here, he would beat these lads hollow.' 'Tennis rules are different,' Martin remarked. 'He would have given it to them – rules or no rules,' Gruzinov retorted calmly. A silence. The knock of tennis balls. Martin slitted his eyes. 'The blond one has a rather classy drive.' 'You're a funny boy,' said Gruzinov and patted him on the shoulder. At that moment his wife appeared, gracefully swinging her hips. She noticed two English girls whom she knew and proceeded to navigate in their direction. 'Yuri Timofeich,' Martin said, 'I would like to consult you about something highly important and confidential.' 'Be glad to oblige. I'm as mute as a grave.' Martin looked around and hesitated. 'Let's go to my room,' suggested Gruzinov.

The hotel room was cluttered with objects, darkish, and imbued with Mrs Gruzinov's perfume. Gruzinov threw open the window – for one instant he resembled a large dark bird spread against a golden background, then sunlight invaded the floor in one stride, stopping short at the door which Martin had noiselessly closed behind him. 'The room is a mess, I'm afraid, hope you don't mind,' said Gruzinov with a sidelong glance at the double bed disarranged by the midday siesta. 'Take that armchair, my friend. These little apples are sweet as sugar. Help yourself.' 'Actually, I wanted to talk to you about the following matter: I have a pal who plans to cross illegally from Latvia to Russia—' 'Take this one, with the blush,' interposed Gruzinov. 'I keep thinking,' continued Martin, 'can he make it or not. Let us suppose he has thoroughly studied a topographic map, but that is not sufficient, there are sure to be frontier guards, intelligence agents, spies, all over. I wanted to ask you – well – for some pointers.' Gruzinov, his elbow propped on the table, was eating an apple, turning it around, taking a crunching bite out of it, now here now there, then turning it again to select a new point of attack. 'And why should your pal want to go roaming there?' he inquired with a rapid glance at Martin. 'I don't know, he keeps it a secret. I believe he wants to visit some relatives in Ostrov or Pskov.' 'What kind of passport?' asked Gruzinov. 'Foreign passport, he is a foreign citizen, Lithuanian or something.' 'Then what's the matter – do they refuse to give him a visa?' 'That I don't know. I believe he does not *want* to have any visa, he means to do it his own way. Or maybe, indeed, they do not give him permission to enter.' Gruzinov finished his apple and said, 'I keep looking for that special taste which our "antonovka" apples have. Sometimes I think: there, I've found it, but then I smack it more carefully, and no, the tang is not the same. Visas are a complicated business, generally speaking. Did I ever tell you how my brother-in-law outsmarted the American quota?' 'I thought you might want to give some kind of advice,' said Martin lamely. 'An odd thought! Surely your pal knows it all better.' 'And yet I'm a little worried about him,' Martin said softly. He reflected with sadness that the conversation was turning out to be very different from what he had imagined, and that Gruzinov would never tell him how he had crossed the border so many times. 'And no wonder you do worry,' said Gruzinov, 'especially if he is a novice. However, one can always find a guide there.' 'Oh no, that would be dangerous!' exclaimed Martin, 'One might run into a traitor.' 'Naturally, one has to be cautious,' Gruzinov agreed, rubbing one eye and studying Martin through fat pale fingers. 'And, of course,' he added in a dullish voice, 'it's very important to know the locality.'

Here Martin quickly produced a rolled-up map. He knew it by heart, had often amused himself by copying it from memory – but for the moment he had to conceal his knowledge. 'You see, I have even provided myself with a chart,' he said breezily. 'For some reason it seems to me that Nick will cross here, for instance, or else here.' 'Ah, so his name is Nicolas,' said Gruzinov. 'I'll note it, I'll note it. This is a fine map. Wait a bit' – (the spectacle case was produced, the glasses gleamed). 'Let's see, what scale is this? Oh, good. Here's Carnagore, here's Torturovka, right on the border. I had a chum – also Nick by a strange coincidence – who once waded across this river here and went that way there; and another time he started from here and then all the way through the wood – it's a very dense wood, called Rogozhin, and then, if one turns northeast—'

Gruzinov's speech became lively and he talked faster and faster, prodding the map with the point of a safety pin which he had unbent, and in one minute he had traced half-a-dozen itineraries, and continued to spill out the names of villages, and to conjure up invisible footpaths; and the more animatedly he spoke, the clearer Martin could see that Gruzinov was making fun of him. From the garden two feminine voices called Gruzinov's name with the first syllable accented instead of the second. He looked out. The two English girls wanted him to come and have ice cream (he was popular with young ladies, for whose benefit he assumed the character of an easygoing simpleton), 'How they like to bother me,' Gruzinov said, 'I never eat ice cream, anyway.' It seemed to Martin for an instant that sometimes somewhere the same words had been spoken (as in Blok's play *Incognita*), and that then as now he was perplexed by something, was trying to explain something. 'Now here's my advice,' said Gruzinov, dexterously rolling up the map and handing it back to Martin. 'Tell Nicky to stay at home and find something constructive to do. A nice fellow, I'm sure, and it would be a pity if he lost his way.' 'He knows everything better than I do,' replied Martin vengefully.

They went down into the garden. Martin forced himself to keep smiling and felt hatred for Gruzinov, his cold eyes, his smooth impenetrable forehead. One thing, howeved, gladdened him: the talk had taken place, was now in the past; true, he had been treated like a schoolboy – never mind, to hell with Gruzzy, Martin's conscience was now clear, he could now pack his things and leave in peace.

43

On the day of departure he woke up very early as he used to on Christmas morn in his childhood. Observing an English custom, his mother would have stolen into the nursery in the middle of the night to hang a stocking stuffed with presents at the foot of his bed. For the sake of complete credibility she would put on a cotton-wool beard and her husband's bashlyk. If Martin had happened not to be sleeping, he would have seen St Nicholas with his own eyes. Then, in the morning, with lamps switched on and glowing a dull yellow under the gloomy gaze of the wintry St Petersburg dawn (that brown sky over the dark house across the street, those façades, those cornices traced in white by the snow), Martin would palpate his mother's long crackling stocking tightly packed to its top with little parcels that could be distinguished through its silk; with bated breath he would thrust in his hand and begin pulling out and unwrapping tiny toy animals, and diminutive *bonbonnières* which represented only an introduction to the full-size present – an engine with carriages and tin rails (of which huge eights could be constructed) waiting for him in the drawing room. Today also a train was waiting for him; it would be leaving Lausanne toward evening to reach Berlin next morning by nine. Mrs Edelweiss felt quite sure that the only purpose of his trip was to see the Zilanov girl; she had noticed that no letters arrived for him from Berlin and was tormented by the thought that perhaps the Zilanov girl did not love Martin enough and would make a bad wife for him. She did her best to make his departure as cheerful as possible, concealing under a somewhat feverish animation her anxiety and sorrow. Uncle Henry, who suffered from a swollen cheek, remained morose and untalkative throughout dinner. Martin looked at the pepper caster Uncle Henry was reaching for, and it struck him that this was the last time he would see it. The pepper caster was in the shape of a fat manikin with perforations in his bald silver head. Quickly Martin transferred his gaze to his mother, taking in her slender pale-freckled hands, her delicate profile and the slightly raised eyebrow (as if she were amazed by the sight of the rich ragout), and again he told himself that this was the last time he would see those freckles, that eyebrow, that dish. Simultaneously all the furniture in the room, and the rainy view in the window, and the clock with its wooden dial over the sideboard, and the enlarged photographs of bewhiskered frock-coated worthies in their black frames, everything in short seemed to break into tragic speech demanding attention before the impending separation. 'May I accompany you to Lausanne?' asked his mother. 'Oh, I know you don't care to be seen off,' she hastened to add as she saw Martin wrinkle his nose, 'but I would not go just for the sake of seeing you off, I would merely like to go for a ride, and besides I have to buy a few things.' Martin sighed. 'All right. I shan't go if you do not want me to,' said Mrs Edelweiss with exceptional gaiety. 'I stay behind when I'm not invited. But you are to wear your warm overcoat, on this I insist.'

Mother and son always spoke Russian between themselves, and this constantly irritated Uncle Henry, who knew only one word, *nichevo,* in which for some reason he perceived a symbol of Slav fatalism. That day he felt depressed, besides being bothered by the pain in his jaw, and now he sharply pushed back his chair, swept off the crumbs from his stomach with his napkin, and sucking on his tooth retired to his study. 'How old he is,' thought Martin watching his grey nape. 'Or is it the light – such gloomy weather.'

'Well, it's almost time for you to get ready,' remarked Mrs Edelweiss. 'The car has probably been brought up.' She looked out of the window. 'Yes, it has. Look, how amusing – nothing to be seen in the fog over there, as if there were no mountains at all. Amusing, isn't it?' 'I think I forgot my razor,' said Martin.

He went up to his room, packed his razor and slippers, and had trouble clicking shut the locks of his bag. In Riga or Rezhitsa he would buy plain coarse things – a cap, a short sheepskin coat, boots. Perhaps, a pistol? *'Proshchay, proshchay'* in rapid tempo sang out the bookcase crowned with the black figurine of a football player, which by some occult association of memories always made him think of Alla Chernosvitov.

In the roomy entrance hall downstairs stood Mrs Edelweiss, her hands thrust into the pockets of her raincoat, and hummed as was her wont in moments of stress. 'Hadn't you better stay at home?' she said as Martin came down. 'Really, *why* go away?' From the door on the right, with the antelope's head over it, came Uncle Henry, and looking at Martin from under his brows he asked, 'Are you sure you have enough money?' 'Quite enough,' answered Martin, 'thank you.' 'Good-bye,' said Uncle Henry. 'I am taking leave of you here because I avoid going out today. Had someone else ever had such a toothache, he would long ago have been in the madhouse.'

'Let's go,' said Mrs Edelweiss. 'I'm afraid you'll miss your train.'

Rain, wind. His mother's hair immediately became disarranged, and she kept smoothing it over her ears. 'Wait,' she said, just before reaching the garden wicket, at a spot near two firs between the trunks of which a hammock was hung in summer. 'Wait, I want to kiss you,' Martin put down his valise. 'Give her my greetings,' she whispered with a meaningful smile, and Martin nodded. Oh, to get going! This is unbearable.

The chauffeur obligingly opened the wicket for them. The car glistened with moisture, the rain made a tinkling sound against it. 'And please do write, if only once a week,' she said, and stepped back, and waved her hand smiling, and slushing along in the mud the black car vanished beyond the fir avenue.

44

The night journey, in a Schnellzug sleeping car of a dark dirty-plum colour, seemed to have no end: there were moments when Martin sank into sleep, then woke up with a start, then again found himself clattering down amusement-park slopes and again swung up, and caught through the dull knock of the wheels the snores of the lower-bunk passenger, a rhythmic wheeze that sounded like part of the train's motion.

Long before arrival, while everybody in the carriage was still asleep, Martin descended from his elevation, and taking sponge, soap, towel, shaving kit and collapsible tub proceeded to the lavatory. First of all he spread over its sickening floor layered sheets of a London *Times* he had bought in Lausanne; next he unfolded upon them his rather wobbly-rimmed but still serviceable rubber tub; he took off his pyjamas and proceeded to coat with soap lather his muscular sun-tanned body. There was not much space, the car rocked violently, he was conscious of the transparent proximity of the racing rails, and of the danger of coming inadvertently in contact with filthy fixtures; but Martin could not manage without his morning bath (in the sea, in a pond, in a shower, or in this tub), which represented, he thought, a kind of heroic defence: a defence against the obstinate attack of the earth advancing by means of a film of insidious dust, as if it could not wait to take possession of a man before his time. No matter how poorly Martin might have slept, after bathing he would be permeated with a beneficent vigour. At such times the thought of death, the thought that sometime, maybe soon (who could know?), he would be compelled to surrender and go through what billions and trillions of humans had gone through before him – this thought of an inevitable death accessible to everyone troubled him but slightly. It gained strength only toward evening, and with the coming of night would sometimes swell to monstrous dimensions. The custom of performing executions at dawn seemed charitable to Martin: may the Lord permit it to happen in the morning when a man has control over himself – clears his throat, smiles, then stands straight, spreading his arms.

When he stepped out onto the platform of the Anhalter station, he inhaled with pleasure the cold, smoky morning air. Far away, in the direction from which the train had arrived, one could see through the opening of the iron-and-glass arch a pale-blue sky and a gleam of rails, and in comparison to this luminosity all was drab under the station vault. He walked past the dusky cars; past the huge hissing and sweating engine, and having surrendered his ticket into the human hand of a control booth, descended the steps to the street. Out of attachment to the images of his childhood, he had decided to select as the starting point of his journey the Friedrich station, where, one remote day, his parents and he, after staying at the nearby Continental, had caught the Nord-Express. His valise was quite heavy, but Martin was in such an excited and restless state that he decided to walk. However, by the time he reached Potsdamerstrasse he began to feel ravenous, and upon estimating the remaining distance to the Friedrich Bahnhof, wisely took the bus. From the very start of that unusual day all his senses were on edge – it seemed to him that he was committing to memory the faces of all the passers-by, and that he absorbed with particular keenness colours, smells, and sounds. The automobile honkings that on rainy nights used to torture his hearing by their swinish moist tones now sounded somehow extramundane, melodious and doleful. As he sat in the bus he heard a ripple of Muscovite speech near him. It came from a couple, of Soviet rather than *émigré* aspect, and their two round-eyed little boys. The elder had settled close to the window, the younger kept pressing against his brother. 'A restaurant,' the bigger one said ecstatically. 'Look, a restaurant!' said the smaller one, pressing. 'I can see for myself,' snapped his brother. 'It's a restaurant,' said the smaller one with conviction. 'Shut up, idiot,' said his brother. 'It's not the Linden yet, is it?' the mother asked worriedly. 'It's still the Post Dammer,' said the father with authority. 'We've already passed the Post Dammer,' cried the boys, and there ensued a short argument. 'What an archway, that's class for you,' exulted the elder boy stabbing at the window with his finger. 'Don't yell like that,' remarked the father. 'What's that?' 'I said don't yell.' The boy looked hurt. 'In the first place I spoke softly, and did not yell at all.' 'Archway,' uttered the smaller boy with awe. The whole family became absorbed in the contemplation of the Brandenburg Gate. 'Historical site,' the bigger boy said. 'An ancient arch, yes,' confirmed the father. 'How shall we wriggle through?' the bigger boy wondered, fearing for the sides of the bus, 'it's a squeeze!' 'We did wriggle through,' the smaller boy whispered with relief. 'And now this is the Unter,' cried the mother, 'time to get off.' 'The Unter is such a long, long street,' said the bigger boy, 'I saw it on the map.' 'This is President Street,' said the smaller boy dreamily. 'Shut up, idiot! It's the Unter Linden.' Then, in chorus, 'Unter is long, long, long,' and a male solo voice, 'It's an endless journey.'

Here Martin got off. His childhood, he thought with strange anguish, his childish excitement had been similar, and yet utterly different. The juxtaposition lasted one instant: it sang by and subsided.

After checking his bag and buying a ticket for the evening train to Riga, he seated himself in the resonant station café where he was brought a regular sunburst of fried eggs. In the latest issue of an *émigré* weekly that he read as he ate he found a vicious review of Bubnov's latest book *Caravella*. Having appeased his hunger, he lit a cigarette and looked around. A young girl at the nearest table sat writing, and wiping her tears. She looked at him for an instant with dim wet eyes, pressing her pencil against her lips, and, having found the word she sought, scribbled again, holding her pencil the way children do: almost at the tip, with forefinger tensely bent. Black coat opened at neck, shabby rabbit-fur collar, amber beads, tender white neck, handkerchief crumpled in fist. He paid for his meal and, planning to follow her, began waiting for her to get up. But when she had finished writing, she leaned her elbows on the table and continued to sit there, looking up, with parted lips. She remained sitting for a long time while somewhere beyond the windowpanes trains were leaving, and Martin, who had to get to the Latvian consulate before closing time, decided to give her just five minutes more, and go. The five minutes passed. 'All I would do would be to ask her to meet me for a drink in the afternoon – only that,' he pleaded mentally, imagining at the same time how he would allude to a distant perilous journey and how she would weep. Another minute passed. 'All right, forget it,' said Martin, and, throwing his raincoat over his shoulder in the English manner, made for the exit.

45

The taxi sped with a susurrous sound; he admired the Tiergarten crowding around him, the lovely warm tints of its autumn foliage: 'O dismal period, visual enchantment—' Flowerless but still sumptuous chestnut trees looked at their own reflection in the canal. As he drove over the bridge Martin recognized Hercules' stone lion and noted that the recently repaired part of its tail still remained too white and would probably take a long time to acquire the seasoned tinge of the rest of the group – how much? ten, fifteen years? Why is it so difficult to imagine oneself at forty?

The basement floor of the Latvian consulate was alive with people. 'Knock-knock' went the rubber stamp. Within a few minutes the Swiss citizen Edelweiss had come out of there and walked over to a nearby gloomy mansion where he obtained the inexpensive Lithuanian transit visa.

Now he could seek out Darwin. His hotel faced the Zoological Gardens. 'Not in,' said the clerk. 'No, I don't know when he'll be back.'

'How tiresome,' thought Martin returning to the street. 'I should have given him a definite date – not merely "one of these days." A blunder. How tiresome!' He looked at his watch. Half past eleven. His passport was in order, his ticket was in his pocket. The day which had announced itself as crammed with activity all at once turned out to be empty. What next? Visit the zoo? Write mother a letter? No, that would come later.

But while he was meditating, muffled work went on in the depths of his consciousness. He resisted it, tried to ignore it, for he had firmly decided after the rejection of his desperate proposal never to see Sonia again. Alas – the air of Berlin was saturated with memories of her. Over there, at the zoo, they had stared together at the golden-red Chinese pheasant, at the fabulous nostrils of the hippopotamus, at the yellow dog dingo that could jump so high. 'She is at her office now,' reflected Martin, 'and I do have to call on the Zilanovs.'

The Kurfürstendamm began to drift by. Automobiles passed the streetcar, the streetcar passed the bicycles; then came the bridge, the smoke from the trains that ran far below, thousands of rails, the mysterious blue sky. Then a turn, and he was amidst the autumnal loveliness of Grunewald.

Surprisingly, it was Sonia who let him in. She wore a black jumper, looked slightly dishevelled, her slanted eyes appeared sleepy, there seemed to be unfamiliar dimples in her pale cheeks. 'Whom do I see,' she drawled making a very low bow, her arms dangling in front of her. 'Welcome, welcome,' she said unbending, and one black strand of hair fell in an arc on her temple. She threw it back with a flick of her index finger. 'Come this way,' she said and started walking along the passage slap-slapping softly with her bedroom slippers. 'I was afraid you might be at the office,' said Martin, trying not to look at the adorable back of her neck. 'Headache,' she said without turning and emitted a little grunt as she picked up in passing a mopping rag which she threw onto a trunk in the corridor. They entered the drawing room. 'Sit down and tell me all,' she said, dropping asprawl in an armchair, but at once she got up and sat down again with one leg under her.

The drawing room was its old self: the dark Böcklin on the wall, the worn plush of the furniture, some kind of indestructible pale-leaved plant in a pot, and that depressing chandelier in the shape of a tailed swimmer with the bosom and head of a Bavarian girl and deer horns growing out of all parts of her.

'Actually, I arrived only today,' said Martin lighting a cigarette. 'I intend to work here. That is, not here actually but in the neighbourhood. It is a factory and, as a matter of fact, I shall work there as a simple workman.' 'Not really?' murmured Sonia and added, noticing his ash and questing gaze, 'Never mind, shed it on the floor.' 'Now there is this amusing circumstance,' Martin continued. 'You see, actually I don't want Mother to know that I'm a factory hand. So please, if she happens to write to your mother – sometimes, you know, she likes to find out if I'm all right in a roundabout way – well, then, do you see, she should be told, please, that I often come to see you. In reality, of course, I shall visit you very, very seldom, there will be no time for that.'

'You've lost your good looks,' said Sonia meditatively. 'And there's something coarse about your face – maybe it's the tan.'

'I've wandered all over southern France,' Martin said huskily, 'worked on farms, lived like a bum, and, on Sundays, got dressed up and went to Monte Carlo for a bit of good time. Fascinating thing, roulette! And you, what have you been doing? Is everybody all right?'

'The ancestors are all right,' said Sonia with a sigh, 'but Irina has become quite unmanageable. What a cross to bear! And the financial situation is as gloomy as ever. Father says we must move to Paris. Have you been in Paris?'

'Yes, for one day,' replied Martin negligently (that one day spent in Paris, many years ago, on the way from Biarritz to Berlin, children with hoops in the Tuileries Gardens, toy sailboats on the pond, an old man feeding the sparrows, the silvery filigree of the tower, Napoleon's tomb where the columns resembled wreathed *sucre d'orge*). 'Yes, just in passing. Incidentally, have you heard the latest news – Darwin is here.'

Sonia smiled and blinked several times. 'Oh, do bring him! You absolutely must, it would be such fun.'

'I have not seen him yet. He is here on business for *The Morning News*. They sent him on a trip to America. But the main thing is this: He has a fiancée back in England, and he is getting married in the spring.'

'How marvellous!' said Sonia softly. 'Everything according to pattern. I can imagine her so well: tall, eyes like saucers, and her mother just like her, only leaner and ruddier. Poor Darwin!'

'Nonsense, I'm sure she's very pretty and intelligent.'

'Well, what else can you tell me,' asked Sonia after a silence. Martin shrugged. How rash of him to have used up all at once his entire stock of conversational topics. It seemed weirdly absurd to him that there was Sonia sitting in front of him, and he dared not say anything of importance, dared not allude to her last letter, dared not ask if she was going to marry Bubnov – dared not say or do anything. He tried to see himself sitting there, in this same room, after his return: would he then, too, blurt out everything at once? And would Sonia lightly scratch her shin through the silk, as she did now, looking past him at things unknown to him? It occurred to him that he might have come at the wrong moment, that she might be expecting someone else, that she felt ill at ease with him. But he could not bring himself to leave, as he also could not think of anything amusing to say, and Sonia seemed to be deliberately trying to provoke him with her silence. In another moment he would lose control and spill it all – his expedition, and his love, and that innermost, mysterious something, which bound together the expedition, the love, and Pushkin's ode to autumn.

The entrance door slammed, steps were heard, Zilanov entered the drawing room: 'Ah,' he said, 'delighted. How is your mother?' A little later Mrs Zilanov came in through another door and asked the same question. 'Won't you have lunch with us?' she said. They moved to the dining room. Irina, upon seeing Martin, froze still, then suddenly rushed over to him and started kissing him with wet lips. 'Ira, Irochka,' her mother kept repeating with a helpless smile. Dark meatballs were heaped on a large serving dish. Zilanov unfolded his napkin and stuck one corner behind his collar.

During the meal Martin showed Irina how to cross the second and third fingers so that you could touch a single small pellet of bread and feel two. For a long time she was unable to adjust her fingers properly, but when at last, with Martin's assistance, the pellet divided into two under her touch, Irina cooed with rapture. Just as a monkey seeing its reflection in a fragment of mirror looks to see if there is not another monkey underneath, so she, too, kept bending her head to check if there were not two crumbs under her fingers after all. When lunch was over and Sonia showed Martin to the telephone which was beyond the bend of a passage lined with boxes and trunks, Irina rushed after them with a moan fearing that Martin might be leaving for good. After convincing herself that this was not so, she returned to the dining room to crawl under the table there in search of her bread pellet that had rolled out of sight. 'I want to call Darwin,' said Martin. 'I must look up the number of his hotel.' Sonia's face lit up, as she said, spluttering with excitement, 'Oh, let me, I'll do it, I'll talk to him, it will be fantastic. Come, I'll completely mystify him.' 'No, don't,' replied Martin, 'what's the use?' 'Then I'll only connect you. No harm in that, is there? What was the number?' She leaned over the telephone book he had opened, and he felt the warmth of her hair. On her cheek, just below the eye, was a little stray lash. Repeating the number rapidly in an undertone so as not to forget it, she seated herself on a trunk and picked up the receiver. 'You're only connecting us, mind you,' Martin remarked sternly. With painstaking clarity Sonia gave the number and waited, with shifting eyes, her heels tapping softly against the side of the trunk. Then she smiled, cuddling the receiver still closer to her ear, and Martin stretched out his hand, but Sonia pushed it aside with her shoulder and hunched over while asking for Darwin in a bright tone of voice. 'Give it me,' said Martin, 'this is not fair.' But Sonia gathered herself together even tighter. 'I'll cut you off,' threatened Martin. She made a sharp movement to protect the lever, and at the same moment her eyebrows went up. 'No, nothing, thank you,' she said and hung up. 'Not at home,' she told Martin, looking at him from below. 'You may rest assured, my dear, I shall not call him again. And you you've remained the same boor that you were.' She slithered down from the trunk, groped, found her lost slipper with her toe, and went back to the dining room. The table was being cleared, Irina's mother was talking to her but she kept turning away. 'Shall I find you here later?' asked Zilanov. 'Well, I don't know. As a matter of fact, I should be going now.' 'I'll say goodbye to you just in case,' said Zilanov and retired to his room to work.

'Do not forget us,' said the two ladies simultaneously and each touched the other's black sleeve, with a smile that acknowledged the superstition. Martin bowed. Irina made a dash for him and clutched the lapels of his jacket with both hands. He felt embarrassed, tried cautiously to unclasp her fingers; but she held tight, and when Mrs Pavlov took hold of her shoulders from behind the poor creature broke out into loud sobs. Martin could hardly conceal his revulsion as he observed the dreadful expression of her face, the red rash on her forehead. With a sharp, if not rough movement, he tore loose from her hold. She was led away, her chesty howl retreated, and subsided at last. 'The same worries all the time,' said Sonia as she accompanied Martin to the hallway. Martin put on his raincoat – the raincoat was a complicated affair, and it took him some time to arrange the belt properly. 'Drop in sometime in the evening,' said Sonia as she watched his operation, her hands deep in the front pockets of her jumper. Gloomily Martin shook his head. 'We'll get together and dance,' Sonia said and with her legs close together, she shifted first her toes, then her heels, then again toes and again heels, in a slight sideways motion. 'Well,' said Martin slapping his pockets. 'I don't think I had any parcels.' 'Remember?' asked Sonia and began to whistle softly the tune of a London fox-trot. Martin cleared his throat. 'I don't like your hat,' she remarked. 'They don't wear them like that any more.' '*Proshchay*,' said Martin, and skillfully grabbing Sonia pushed his lips against her bared teeth, her cheek, the tender part behind her ear, then let her go (she backed away and almost fell), and quickly left, involuntarily slamming the door.

46

He noticed that he was grinning and out of breath, and that his heart was beating fast. 'Well, that's that,' he said to himself, and began walking away with bold strides as if he were in a hurry. But there was no place to go. Darwin's absence confused his plans. As he went along the Kurfürstendamm, he kept noting with vague sadness Berlin's familiar features: the austere church at the crossroads, so lonely amidst pagan cinemas; the Tauentzienstrasse, where pedestrians inexplicably avoid the median boulevard, preferring to progress in a tight flow close to the display windows. The blind man, who sold sight and light, kept thrusting a box of matches into eternal darkness; there were stalls with heather and asters, stalls with bananas and apples; a person in a brown overcoat stood on the seat of an old convertible, holding out fanwise tablets of a nameless chocolate whose exquisite quality he eloquently decribed to a small crowd of loafers. Martin turned into a side street and entered a Russian bookshop where *émigré* and Soviet works lay next to foreign magazines. A corpulent gentleman with the face of a polite reptile spread on the counter what he called *novinki*, 'novelties.'

Martin found nothing to his liking and bought a copy of *Punch*. What next? That meal at the Zilanovs' had been decidedly scant. He directed his steps toward the Pir Goroy where he used to eat a year ago. From there he rang up Darwin's hotel. Darwin had not yet returned. '*Zwanzig pfennig, pozhaluysta,*' said the thickly powdered lady behind the counter. '*Merci.*'

The proprietor was the painter Danilevski, whom Martin had known at Adreiz, a short man wearing a stiff collar, with a rosy infantile face and a blond wart under one eye. He came up to Martin's table and asked shyly, 'Bo-borshch all right?' (like many stammerers he was strangely attracted to sounds that were the hardest to master). 'Yes, indeed,' answered Martin, and as always felt heartrending tenderness as he visualized Danilevski against the backdrop of the Crimean night.

The latter sat down and watched with approval Martin consuming his soup. 'Did I tell you that according to certain information they've be-be-been living all these years at Adreiz – remarkable!'

(Can it be that they were never disturbed in their manor? reflected Martin. Can it be that everything has remained the same – those little pears, for example, drying on the veranda roof?)

'Mohicans,' murmured Danilevski pensively.

The room was emptyish. Small divans, a stove with a zigzag pipe, newspapers on wooden holders.

'All this will be improved. I might paint the walls with -bah! bah! -babas, if only it were not so sad. Bo-bright dresses, but livid faces with eyes like horses. At least, that's the way it comes out in my sketches. Or else one could do clouds and below – and below – the fringe of a forest. We shall enlarge the premises, I asked a carpenter to come yesterday, but he never turned up.'

'Many customers?'

'Usually, yes. This is not the right time for dinner, so do not draw conclusions. The literary burrow-burrow brotherhood is well represented. Rakitin, for instance, the journalist, you know, the one that sports spats . . . And a few days ago, boo, a few days ago, boo, Sergey Bubnov, right here, smashed dishes, he's drinking heavily, disappointment in love, engagement babaroken.'

Danilevski sighed, his fingers drumming on the table; then he slowly got up and went into the kitchen. He reappeared as Martin was taking his hat from the rack. 'There'll be shashlik tomorrow,' said Danilevski. 'We'll be expecting you.' Martin experienced a fleeting desire to say something very kind to that dear melancholy man with such a euphonious stutter; but what could one say?

47

He crossed the paved court with its noseless statue in the middle of a lawn on which grew a few thujas, pushed open a familiar door, walked up the stairs that reeked of cabbage and cats, and rang the bell. One of the lodgers, a young German, came out and said Bubnov was ill, but knocked in passing on the latter's door, and the writer's great voice, now hoarse and ill-humoured, was heard to holler '*Herein!*'

Bubnov was sitting on the bed, clad in black trousers and an open shirt, his face was swollen and unshaven, his eyelids inflamed. Sheets of paper were strewn over the bed, the floor, and the table, on which stood a glass of turbid tea. It turned out that Bubnov was putting the finishing touches to a short story and at the same time attempting to compose in German an impressive letter to the gentleman of the Finanzamt who were demanding he pay his taxes. He was not drunk but neither could one call him sober. His thirst had passed, but everything in him had been twisted out of shape and shaken loose by the hurricane; his thoughts wandered about looking for their old dwellings and finding only ruins. He showed no surprise at the appearance of Martin, whom he had not seen since spring, and at once started to upbraid a certain critic as if Martin were responsible for that critic's review. 'They're baiting me,' Bubnov kept repeating fiercely, and his face with the deep orbits looked rather ghastly. He had a tendency to assume that all disparaging reviews of his books were inspired by extraneous considerations, by envy, personal dislike, or the desire to avenge an offense. And listening to his disjointed survey of literary intrigue Martin found it amazing that anyone could take so much to heart another man's opinion, and he fought the temptation to tell Bubnov that his novella *Zorrland* was a failure, a pseudoartistic and worthless piece. But when Bubnov abruptly abandoned that topic and began to talk about his having been jilted, Martin cursed the wrongheaded curiosity that had brought him here. 'I will not name her, thou must not ask me,' said Bubnov who could switch to the Russian emotional second person singular with an actor's ease. 'Yet remember, I shall not be the last to perish because of her. God, how I loved her! How happy I was! It was the kind of tremendous feeling that makes one hear the thunder of angel wings. But she got frightened of my heavenly heights—'

Martin stayed on a little, felt a welling of intolerable heartache, and got up in silence. Sobbing, Bubnov accompanied him to the door. A few days later (when he was already in Latvia), Martin discovered in an *émigré* newspaper another of Bubnov's 'novellas,' fresh from the oven. This time it was excellent, and in it the protagonist, a young German, wore the tie Martin had on that day, pale grey with pink stripes (the treasured relic of a Cambridge club), which Bubnov, though seemingly engrossed in his grief, had appropriated as would a deft thief who wipes his tears with one hand while removing a man's watch with the other.

Stopping at a stationer's Martin bought half-a-dozen postcards and replenished his fountain pen; then he proceeded to Darwin's hotel where he resolved to wait to the very last moment of remaining time and go straight from there to the station. The late afternoon sky was a sunless cheerless blank. The sound of automobile horns now seemed muffled by the mist. An open van passed by drawn by a pair of scrawny horses; upon it enough furniture was heaped to furnish a house: a couch, a chest of drawers, a gilt-framed seascape, and a lot of other melancholy chattels. A woman in mourning crossed the damp-dappled asphalt; she was pushing a pram, and in it sat a blue-eyed attentive infant; on reaching the sidewalk she pushed down the handle forcing the pram to rear. A poodle ran past in pursuit of a black whippet; the latter stopped and looked back in fear, raising one bent front paw and quivering. 'What's the matter, for goodness' sake,' thought Martin. 'What's all this to me? I know I'm going to return. I must return.' He entered the vestibule of the hotel. Darwin still had not come back.

He found a comfortable armchair upholstered in leather, unscrewed the cap of his pen and began to write his mother. Space on the postcard was limited, his handwriting was larger, so he did not manage to say much. 'Everything is all right,' he wrote, strongly pressing down on the pen. 'I stopped at the same old place, address your letters there. I hope Uncle's toothache is better. Have not yet seen Darwin. The Zilanovs send greetings. Shall not write for a week as I have absolutely nothing to say.

Many kisses.' He reread all this twice and unaccountably felt sick at heart and a chill ran down his back. 'No nonsense, please,' Martin told himself, and, again pressing hard, wrote the Major's widow asking her to hold his mail for him. After posting the cards he returned to his chair, leaned back in it, and began to wait, glancing now and then at the clock. A quarter of an hour passed, then twenty minutes, then twenty-five. Two mulatto girls with unusually thin legs went up the stairs. All of a sudden he heard behind his back the powerful breathing he at once recognized. He jumped up, and Darwin, with throaty ejaculations, slapped him on the shoulder. 'You scoundrel,' mumbled Martin happily, 'you scoundrel, I've been looking for you since morning.'

48

Darwin had gained some weight, his hair looked thinner, he had grown a well-trimmed little moustache. Somehow both he and Martin felt embarrassed and could not find a subject of conversation; they kept poking each other, grinning and rumbling. 'What are you going to drink,' Darwin asked when they had entered his small but smart hotel room, 'whisky and soda? A cocktail? Or simply some tea?' 'No matter, no matter, anything you like,' answered Martin, taking up from the table a large photograph in an expensive frame. 'She,' said Darwin. Portrait of a young woman with a diadem. Those brows meeting above the bridge of the nose, those light eyes, that long graceful neck – everything about her looked very definitive and domineering. 'Her name's Evelyn, she sings rather well, I'm sure you'll become very good friends with her.' Darwin took the portrait and gave it a dreamy look before returning it to its place. 'Well,' he asked dropping onto the couch and immediately stretching out his legs, 'what's new? I see you still wear the C.C.C. tie.'

A waiter brought the cocktails. Without pleasure Martin took a sip of gin-laced vermouth and recounted in a couple of sentences how he had spent the last two years. It surprised him that as soon as he fell silent, Darwin began to talk about himself, circumstantially and self-complacently – something that never used to happen before. How strange it was to hear from those indolent, chaste lips a tale of success, of earnings, of splendid hopes for the future! It also transpired that now he no longer composed those charming trifles about leeches or sunsets, but wrote articles on political and financial subjects, and was particularly interested in the sepulchral-sounding 'moratoria,' whatever they were. When Martin, taking advantage of a sudden pause, reminded Darwin of the burning chariot, of Rose, of their fight, Darwin said indifferently 'Yes, those were the times,' and to his horror Martin realized that Darwin's recollections had died, or were absent, and the only thing that remained was a discoloured signboard.

'And what is Prince Vadim doing?' asked Darwin stifling a yawn.

'Vadim is in Brussels. Has a job there. And the Zilanovs are here. I often see Sonia. She still has not married.'

Darwin emitted a huge puff of smoke. 'Give her my greetings,' he said. 'But what about you? Pity you're sort of drifting. I'll introduce you to some important people tomorrow, I'm sure you'll like journalism.'

Martin coughed. Time had come to discuss the main matter, the matter he had so much wished to discuss with Darwin.

'Thanks,' he said, 'but that's impossible, I'll be leaving Berlin in an hour's time.'

Darwin raised himself slightly: 'Not really? Where are you going?'

'You'll see in a minute. I'm now going to tell you something no one else knows. For several years – yes, several years – but that's not essential—'

He faltered. Darwin sighed, and said, 'I've guessed everything. I'll act as best man.'

'Stop it, please. This is serious. I've been trying all day to get to you for the special purpose of talking it over. The fact is I'm planning to cross illegally into Russia from Latvia, just for twenty-four hours, yes, and then walk back again. Now here's where you come in: I'll give you four postcards, you'll send them to my mother, one every week – every Thursday let's say. I expect to be back within a shorter time, but I can't foretell how long it will take me to investigate things, to select the exact itinerary, and so forth. Of course I've already collected a lot of crucial information from a certain person. But I may get stuck, may not be able to wriggle out immediately. You understand, my mother must not know anything about it, must receive my postcards from Berlin regularly. I gave her my old address, it is all quite simple.'

Silence.

'Yes, of course, it is all quite simple,' said Darwin.

Silence again.

'Only I do not quite see what's the purpose of it.'

'Give it a little thought, and you will.'

'Some plot against the good old Soviets? Want to see someone? Deliver a secret message, rig up something? I confess that as a boy I rather fancied those gloomy bearded chaps who threw bombs at the troika of the ruthless governor.'

Morosely, Martin shook his head.

'And if you merely want to visit the land of your fathers – although your father was half-Swiss, wasn't he? – still, if you want to see it so badly, would it not be simpler to obtain a regular Soviet visa and cross the border by train? Don't want to? Perhaps, after the assassination in that Swiss café, you think you won't be given a visa? All right, I'll get you a British passport.'

'What you're imagining is all wrong,' said Martin, 'I expected you'd understand everything at once.'

Darwin folded an arm under his head. He could not make up his mind whether or not Martin was pulling his leg, and if not, what really prompted him to embark on that preposterous undertaking. For a while he puffed on his pipe, then said:

'If, finally, what you are after is just pure risk, there's no need to travel so far. Let us invent something unusual, something that can be executed right now, right here, without overstepping the windowsill. And then let's have a bite and go to a music hall.'

Martin remained silent, and his face looked sad.

'This is absurd,' reflected Darwin, 'absurd and rather peculiar. Stayed quietly in Cambridge while they had their civil war, and now craves a bullet in the head for spying. Is he trying to mystify me? What an idiotic conversation.'

Martin gave a start, looked at his watch, and got up.

'Look here, stop playing the fool,' said Darwin, smoke pouring profusely from his pipe. 'After all, this is scarcely polite. We have not seen each other since Cambridge. Either tell me all, intelligibly, or admit that you were joking, and we'll talk of other things.'

'I've told you all,' said Martin. 'All. And now I must go.'

He put on his raincoat, picked up his hat from the floor. Darwin, who lay calmly on the couch, yawned and turned his face to the wall. 'So long,' said Martin but Darwin did not respond. 'So long,' Martin repeated. 'Nonsense, it can't be true,' thought Darwin. He yawned again, and closed his eyes. 'He won't leave,' thought Darwin and sleepily pulled up one leg. For some time there endured an amusing silence. At last Darwin laughed softly and turned his head. But there was nobody in the room. It seemed impossible that Martin could have left so noiselessly. Perhaps he was hiding behind the furniture. Darwin remained lying a few minutes longer, then glanced warily around the already dimming room, put down his legs and straightened up. 'Enough of it, now. Come out,' he said as he heard a slight rustle from the baggage recess between the wardrobe and the door. Nobody came out. Darwin went over and glanced into the recess. Nobody. Only a sheet of wrapping paper left over from some purchase. Darwin turned on the light, stood frowning, then opened the door leading into the passage. The passage was long, well lighted, and empty. The evening breeze tried to shut the window. 'To hell with him,' said Darwin – and was lost in thought again. But suddenly he shook himself up and very deliberately started to change for dinner.

He felt uneasy, a feeling he seldom experienced lately. Not only had Martin's arrival excited him as a tender echo of their university days, but it had been in itself extraordinary, everything about Martin had been extraordinary – the roughish tan, the breathless voice, the bizarre dark utterances, and that new haughty look in his eyes. However, Darwin had recently had such a well-balanced kind of life, his heart had been beating so regularly (even when he proposed), his mind had so firmly concluded that after the troubles and thrills of youth he had now reached a smoothly paved road, that he could now hardly fail to subdue the disturbing impression made by Martin, and force himself to believe that the silly jester would reappear this very night. He had already donned his dinner jacket and was examining his powerful figure and large Roman-nosed face in the wardrobe glass, when the telephone rang on the night table. Either because the connection was bad or because he did not remember Martin's telephone tone, he identified it with difficulty: 'Reminding you of my request,' said the blurred deep voice. 'You'll get the batch within a few days, you'll send them off one by one. My train is about to leave. What? I said: my train— Yes, yes, train—'

The voice vanished. Darwin resoundingly put down the receiver and for a while kept scratching his cheek. Then he walked to the lift and rode down. There he asked for the timetable. Yes, correct. What the devil—

That night he did not go anywhere. He kept waiting for something, some sort of further development. When he sat down to write a letter to his fiancée he found nothing to write about. Several days passed. On Wednesday he received a fat envelope from Riga and found inside four picture postcards with Berlin views addressed to Mrs Edelweiss in Switzerland. On one of them, inserted in the Russian text, Darwin discovered a sentence in English 'I often go to music halls with Darwin.' It gave him an eerie shock. On Thursday morning, with the dreadful feeling that he was taking part in some evil affair, he gingerly inserted the card with the earliest date into the blue mailbox next to the hotel entrance. A week passed; he posted the second card. After that he could not stand it any longer and travelled to Riga, where he visited the British consul, the Swiss consul, the General Registry, the police, but obtained no information whatever. Martin seemed to have dissolved in the air. Darwin returned to Berlin and reluctantly mailed the third postcard. On Friday, a huge man, obviously a foreigner, called at Zilanov's new publishing house (Russian calendars and political pamphlets); upon taking a closer look, Zilanov recognized in him the young Englishman who had courted his daughter in London. Speaking German (which Zilanov understood somewhat better than English) Darwin calmly related his conversation with Martin. 'But wait,' said Zilanov. 'There is something not logical here. He said to my daughter he would work in a factory near Berlin. You are sure he went away? What a strange history!' At first I thought he was joking,' said Darwin, 'but now I don't know what to think. If he has really—' 'What a crazy fellow,' exclaimed Zilanov. 'Who would have supposed! The young man produced an effect of good sense, of solidity. It's simply hard to believe, you know, looks like some kind of provocation. *Gut.* The first thing to do is to find if my daughter knows anything about this. Let's go to my quarters.'

When Sonia saw her father coming in with Darwin and noticed the odd, solemn expression of their faces, she thought for one hundredth part of an instant that Darwin had come to make, this time officially, an offer of marriage (such momentary nightmares are known to occur). 'Hello, hello, Sonia,' cried out Darwin with very artificial offhandedness. Zilanov, fixing his dull dark eyes on his daughter and 'preparing her,' begged her not to be frightened, and told her practically the whole story right there, in the hallway. Sonia turned white as a sheet and sank down on one of the vestibule chairs. 'But that's awful,' she said softly. After a little pause, she slapped her knees and repeated in a still smaller voice: 'That's awful.' 'Did he tell you anything? Do you have any information?' Zilanov kept asking her in Russian and German. Darwin stood rubbing his cheek, trying not to look at Sonia. He felt the most appalling thing a man of his race and set can feel: the urge to break into tears. 'Of course, I know all about it,' said Sonia in a thin crescendo. Mrs Zilanov appeared in the background, and her husband signalled to her not to disturb them. 'Just what do you know? Come, out with it,' said Zilanov, and touched Sonia on the shoulder. She suddenly doubled over and began to sob loudly, burying her face in her hands. Then she unbent, emitted a great gasp as if she were choking, swallowed, and began to scream between sobs, 'They'll kill him, oh God, they'll kill him.' 'Control yourself,' said Zilanov. 'Don't scream. I demand that you explain quietly and clearly what it was that he told you. Olya' (addressing his wife), 'take this gentleman somewhere— Yes, to the drawing room, *ach*, never mind the electrician. Sonia, stop screaming! You'll frighten Irina. Stop, I demand it.'

He spent a long time comforting and questioning her. Darwin sat gravely in the drawing room. An electrician was also there, busy mending a socket and plug, looking up and down again as the light went on and off.

'The child is obviously right in demanding that immediate measures be taken,' said Zilanov when he and Darwin had regained the street. 'But what can one do? Besides, I don't think there is as much romance of adventure here as seems to her She tends to see things that way. Very high-strung nature. I simply refuse to believe that a young man, pretty much removed from Russian political problems and more of a foreign cut I'd say, could prove capable of – well, of a high deed, if you like. Naturally, I shall get in touch with certain people, and I may have to go to Latvia, but the matter is fairly hopeless, if he has really tried to steal across the border. By the way, it is so strange, but I was the one, yes, I, who years ago informed Frau Edelweiss of the death of her first husband.'

A few more days passed. The only point to become clear was that one had to be patient and wait. Not Zilanov, but Darwin went to Switzerland to inform Mrs Edelweiss. In Lausanne everything looked grey, a fine rain was falling. Higher up in the mountains there was an odour of damp snow, and water dripped from the trees because of the sudden thaw that had followed the first frosts. The car he had hired brought him quickly to the village, skidded on a curve and overturned in the ditch. The only damage was the chauffeur's bruised arm. Darwin scrambled out, shook the wet snow off his overcoat and asked a villager how far it was to Henry Edelweiss's place. He was shown the shortest way – a footpath through a fir forest. Once out of the woods, he crossed a dirt road, went up an avenue, and saw the ornate greenish-brown house. The rubber soles of his sturdy shoes left patterned impressions on the dark soil in front of the wicket. These footprints slowly filled with muddy water, and a little later the wicket he had not closed properly creaked in a gust of damp wind and violently swung open. Then a titmouse alighted on it, uttered a *tsi-tsi-tsi* and an *incha-incha,* and flew over to the branch of a fir. Everything was very wet and dim. An hour elapsed. Darwin emerged from the brown depths of the melancholy garden, closed the wicket behind him (it promptly opened again), and started back along the path through the woods. There he paused to light his pipe. His ample camelhair coat was unbuttoned, the ends of his striped scarf dangled at his chest. It was quiet in the woods, all one could hear was a faint gurgle: water was running somewhere under the wet grey snow. Darwin listened and for no perceptible reason shook his head. His pipe, which had gone out, emitted a helpless sucking sound. He said something under his breath, rubbed his cheek pensively, and walked on. The air was dingy, here and there tree roots traversed the trail, black fir needles now and then brushed against his shoulder, the dark path passed between the tree trunks in picturesque and mysterious windings.